I0819848

Collected Works of E F Benson

By

E F Benson

Cover Photograph: cliff1066™

ISBN: 978-1-78139-290-4

Contents

ACROSS THE STREAM

COLLECTED STORIES

PAYING GUESTS

MRS AMES

SPOOK STORIES

ACROSS THE STREAM

INTRODUCTION

There is a very large class of persons alive to-day who believe that not only is communication with the dead possible, but that they themselves have had actual experience of it. Many of these are eminent in scientific research, and on any other subject the world in general would accept their evidence.

There is possibly a larger class of persons who hold that all such communications, if genuine, come not from the dead but from the devil. This is the taught opinion of the Roman Catholic Church.

A third class, far more numerous than both of these, is sure that any one who holds either of these beliefs is a dupe of conjurers, or the victim of his own disordered brain. This type of robust intellect has, during the last ten decades, affirmed that hypnotism, aviation in machines heavier than air, telepathy, wireless telegraphy, and other non-proved phenomena, are superstitious and unscientific balderdash. In an earlier century it was equally certain that the earth did not go round the sun. It is, happily, never disconcerted by the frequency with which the superstitions and impossibilities of one generation become the science of the next.

The first part of this book may be accepted by the first of these three classes, the second by the second, and none of it by the third. Its aim is to state rather than solve the subject with which it deals, and to suggest that the dead and the devil alike may be able to communicate with the living.

E. F. BENSON.

BOOK I

CHAPTER I

Certain scenes, certain pictures of his very early years of childhood, stood out for Archie like clear sunlit peaks above the dim clouds that shrouded the time when the power of memory was only beginning to germinate. He had no doubt (and was probably right about it) as to which the earliest of those was: it was the face of his nurse Blessington, leaning over his crib. She held a candle in her hand which a little dazzled him, but the sight of her face, tender and anxious, and divinely reassuring, was the point of that memory. He had been asleep, and had awoke with a start, and, finding himself alone in the midst of the immense desolation of the dark that pressed on him like an invader from all sides, he had lifted up his voice and yelled. Then, as by a conjuring-trick, Blessington had appeared with her comforting presence that quite robbed the dark of its terrors. It must still have been early in the night, for she had not yet gone to bed, and had on above her smooth grey hair her cap with its adorable blue ribands in it. At her throat was the brooch made of the same stuff as the shining shillings with which a year or two later she bought the buns and sponge-cakes for tea. He remembered no more than that; he knew nothing of what she had said: the whole of that memory consisted in the fact of the secure comfort and relief which her face brought. It was just a vignette of memory, the earliest of all; there was nothing whatever before it, and nothing for some time after.

Gradually the horizon widened; scenes and situations in which Archie was still a detached observer, as if looking through a telescope, made themselves visible. He remembered gazing through the bars of the high nursery fire-guard at the joyful glow of the fuel. At the corner of the grate (he remembered this with extreme distinctness), there was a black coal, the edge of which was soft and bubbly. A thin streamer of smoke blew out of it, and from time to time this smoke caught light and flared very satisfactorily. But all that, the joyfulness and the satisfaction, was external to him; it was the coals and the streams of burning gas that were in themselves joyful and satisfactory. That must have been in the winter, and it was in the same winter perhaps that he came home with Blessington and two other children—girls, and larger than himself—whom he grew to believe were his sisters, through a wood of fir-trees between the trunks of which shone a round red ball that resembled the coals in the nursery-grate. He knew—perhaps Blessington, perhaps a sister, perhaps his mother had told him—that it was Christmas Eve, and he saw that when Blessington spoke to him she steamed delightfully at the mouth, as if there had been a hot bath just inside her lips. At her suggestion he found he could do it, too, and his sisters also; whereafter they played hot-baths all the way home. But of the Christmas Day that followed he had no recollection whatever.

His observation became a little less detached; he began to form in his mind an explorer's map of the places where these phenomena occurred, to be dimly aware that he was taking some sort of part in them, and was not a mere spectator, and one summer evening he definitely knew that the day-nursery and the night-nursery and the room beyond where his sisters slept were all part of the red-brick house which he and others inhabited, just as, according to Blessington, the rabbit which he had seen pop into its hole in the wood beyond the lawn, had a home within it. He had already had his bath, on a patch of sunlight that lay across the nursery-floor, and escaping, slippery as a trout, from Blessington's towelling hands, had run with a squeal of delight across to the window. Outside was the lawn, which hitherto he had thought of as a thing apart, a picture by itself, and beyond was the wood where the rabbit had a house. On the lawn was his mother, playing croquet with his two sisters, and of a sudden it flashed upon him that the wood and the rabbit, the lawn and the croquet-players, the night-nursery, Blessington, the shine of the sun low in the west, and his own wet self were all in some queer manner part of the same thing, and made up that to which he and Blessington went back when, at the limit of their walk, she said it was time to go home.

"Oh, there's mummy," he cried. "Mummy!" And he danced naked at the window.

Blessington caught him in the towel again.

"Well, I never!" she said. "That's not the way for a young gentleman to behave. There, let me dry you, dear, and put your night-shirt on, and you shall say good-night to your mamma out of the window."

This was duly done, and it struck Archie as a very novel and delightful discovery that he could say good-night to his mother when she was on the croquet-lawn and he up in the night-nursery. It shed a new light on existence generally, and coloured with a new interest the few drowsy moments which intervened between his being put into bed and falling asleep. Blessington still moved quietly about the room, emptying his bath, and putting his clothes tidy, and he just remembered her kissing him when she had finished. He was already too suffused with drowsiness to make any response, and he slid softly out over the tides of sleep.

That night he became acquainted with a new sort of experience, something hitherto quite foreign to him. Once again he woke in the night and found himself surrounded by the vast dark, save where, in a corner of the nursery, there burned the shaded night-light. But now there was no sense of terror; he did not want to call for Blessington, but lay open-eyed and absorbed in the amazing thing that was happening. The night-nursery (where he knew he was), and he with it, were expanding and extending, till they comprised the lawn and the wood beyond the lawn, and all else that he had ever known. His sisters and his mother and father were all there, though he could not see them; Blessington was there, and Graves the butler, and Walter and William, the two footmen. He could not see them, any more than he could see the moon and the sun, which were there also, but they were there as part of an unusual presence that filled the place. He could not see that unusual presence either, but it was tremendously real and filled him not in the least with awe, but with the feeling with which Blessington's face and his mother's face inspired him... And the next thing that he was aware of was the rattle of the blind, and Blessington's voice saying, "Eh, what a time of morning to have slept to. I know a sleepy-head!"

He recounted this remarkable experience to Blessington at breakfast, who was quite sure that it was all a dream; a nice dream, but a dream.

"Wasn't a dream," said Archie firmly.

"And where did Mr. Contradiction go?" asked Blessington.

Archie knew where Mr. Contradiction went, for Mr. Contradiction lived in a very dull corner of the nursery with his face to the wall for five minutes.

"Well, it didn't seem like a dream," he said. "May I get down?"

"Yes, and say your grace."

"Thank God for my good dinner," said Archie, who was not attending.

"Say it again, dear," said Blessington; "and think."

"I meant breakfast," said Archie. "Amen."

The discovery of the connection, made last night, between himself in the night-nursery and his mother on the lawn, which proved that the lawn and the house were part of the same thing, produced further results that day. Instead of memory consisting of different and severed pictures, it began to flow into one coherent whole. He knew, of course, already that at the end of the nursery passage was a wooden wicket-gate, and that outside that was the long gallery that skirted round three sides of the hall, while on the fourth ran a broad staircase each step of which had to be surmounted and descended either by a series of jumps, or, if the feet were tired, by the extension of one foot on to the next stair where it was joined by the other; but he began now to put these isolated facts together, and form them into the conception of a house. When the staircase was negotiated you found yourself in a large oak-floored hall, where you were not allowed to slide on purpose, though both Blessington and his mother had the sense to distinguish between deliberate and unintentional slidings. There were bright rugs spread here and there over the hall, forming islands in a glassy sea. Archie knew it was not made of glass really, but he chose to think that it was, for it had the qualities of a looking-glass in that it reflected his own bare-legged form above it, and the slipperiness of glass as exhibited in the window-panes of the nursery, and he chose also to think that it was to the hall-floor that the hymn alluded which was sung last Sunday morning in a dazzling and populous place to which his mother had taken him. The people who sang loudest were two rows of boys dressed in crinkly white night-shirts, in company with some grown-up men who were attired in the same curious manner. But none of them went to bed, and at a pause in the proceedings Archie had suddenly asked his mother, in a piercing voice, why they didn't go to bed. Evidently that had puzzled her too, for she had no reply to give him except "Hush, darling!" which wasn't an answer at all. Then another man had begun talking all by himself. He had a quantity of hair on his chin which wagged in so delightful a manner when he spoke that Archie watched him entranced for a little, and then, afraid that his mother was missing this lovely sight, said:

"O mummy, *isn't* that a funny man?"

Upon which Blessington, magically communicated with, appeared by his side and whispered that they were going for a walk, and towed him down the aisle, still rapturously looking back at the funny man. Archie had thought it all very entertaining, but he was told afterwards by his father that he had disgraced himself and should not go to church again for many Sundays to come.

Archie was frightened of his father, and always went warily by the door of the room at the dark corner of the hall where this tremendous person lived. There were other dangers about that corner, for on the floor were two tiger-skins which looked as if the animal in question had, with the exception of its head, been squashed out flat, like as when he and Blessington sometimes put a flower they had gathered on their walks between two sheets of blotting-paper, and piled books on the top, so that it ceased to be a flower, and became the map of a flower. Archie wished the tigers' heads had been pressed in the same way; as it was, they were disconcertingly solid and life-like, with long teeth and snarling mouths and glaring eyes. He had always made Blessington come right up to his father's door with him when he went in to say good-night, so that she should pilot him safely past the tigers on his entry and escort him by them again on his return. But one night his father had come out with him, and, finding Blessington waiting there, had divined, as by some awful black magic, why the nurse was waiting, and had decreed that Archie should in future make his way across the danger zone unattended. But, next evening, the trembling Archie, hurrying away in the dusk, had fallen down on the glassy sea between the awful Scylla and Charybdis, and, convinced that his last hour had come, when these two cruel heads beheld him prostrate on the floor, had cried himself to sleep from terror of that awful ending. But next day his mother, who understood about things in general better than anybody, had caused the tigers to make friends with him, and in token of their amity they had each of them presented him with a whisker-hair. That assured their friendship, and they wished it to be understood that their snarlings and glarings were directed, not at Archie, but at Archie's enemies. This naturally changed their whole aspect, and Archie, after he had wished his father good-night, kissed the hairy heads that had once been so terrifying, and thanked them for successfully keeping his enemies from molesting him.

But though now the presence of the tigers, ceasing to be a terror by night, had become a protection to Archie, their corner of the hall still constituted a danger zone to be gone by swiftly and silently, lest a raised voice or an incautious noise should cause him to be called from within the closed door of his father's room. There were risks in that room; you never quite knew whether you were not going to be blamed for doing something which you had no idea was blame-worthy. One day Archie had found a lovely wax match with a blue head to it on the floor, and had put it in his pocket, where he fingered it delightedly, for he knew it to be the sort which flamed when you rubbed it against your boot or the bricks of the house, as he had seen his father do. But then, when a little later he had come to sit on his father's knee and be shown pictures in a book of natural history, it was detected that his small fingers smelled of phosphorus, and when the reason was disdiscovered, he was told by his father that he had stolen that match. To Archie's mind there was something inexplicably unfair and unjust about this; he knew quite well that the match was not his, but he had no idea that it was stealing if you appropriated something that was dropped on the floor. A thing dropped on the floor was nobody's, and anybody, so he supposed, might take it. It had been quite another affair when he had taken eight lumps of sugar out of the basin on the tea-table in the drawing-room and hidden them in his domino-box. He had been perfectly well aware that he was stealing them, and had no sense of injustice when his mother had promptly and soundly smacked him for it. But he intensely resented being told by his father that he had stolen (even though he was not smacked) when he had not the least idea that a match dropped on the floor was a stealable article at all, and he felt it far more bitter to be unjustly blamed than justly punished.

"But I didn't know it was stealing, daddy," said he.

"But didn't you know it wasn't yours?"

"Yes."

"And didn't you know that to take what isn't yours is stealing?"

Archie couldn't explain, but he was still quite sure he had not been stealing...

His father's room then, at least when that potentate was in it, was a place where extreme caution was necessary, and, however cautious you were (he had not felt guilty of the smallest temerity in picking up that match), you could never be quite sure that Fate, like some great concealed cat, would not pounce upon you from the most unexpected quarter. But, considered in itself, the room had a tremendous attraction for him. There was a delicious smell about it, subtly compounded of the leather backs of books and the aroma of tobacco, which to Archie's dawning perception had something virile and masculine about it. He could understand the manliness of the place, it answered to something that was shared by him, and not shared by his mother or Blessington or his sisters, and belonged to a man. The furniture and the appurtenances of the room conveyed the same message; they were strong and solid, without frillings or frippery, and had a decisive air and a purpose about them which somehow concerned that mysterious difference between boys and girls and between men and women. His mother's sitting-room, it is true, seemed to Archie a fairy-palace of loveliness, with its spindle-legged tables, its lace-edged curtains, its soft, silky cushions, its china, its glittering silver toys on a particular black lacquer table, its nameless feminine fragrance. But this room, with its solid leather chairs, which held small limbs as in a tender male embrace, its gun-case in the corner, its whip-rack, its few solid, sober pictures which hung above the book-shelves, struck a different and more intimate and more intelligible note. Archie felt that he knew what it was all about... it was about a man, to which *genus* he himself belonged. This particular specimen, his father, might be unjust to him, and severe to him, but in some secret inexplicable manner Archie understood him, though fearing him, better than he understood either his mother or Blessington, both of whom he loved. His two sisters, in the same way, had a quality of enigma about them.

These floating impressions, the untranslatable instincts of early childhood, began to thicken, when Archie was getting on for six years old, into thoughts capable of being solidified into language. He could not have solidified them himself, but if any one capable of presenting them to him in actual words had asked him, "Is it this you mean?" he would have assented. And his solidified thoughts would have taken the following mould:

There was something odd about females, and it was a mystery into which he did not at all want to enquire. They wore skirts, which perhaps concealed some abnormality, which would be fearful to contemplate. They had soft faces and soft bodies; when his mother took him on her knee—she already said that he was getting too big a boy to sit on her knee, which to Archie sounded very grand and delightful—she was soft to his shoulder, and her cheek was soft to his. But when he sat on his father's knee he felt a hard, firm substance behind him, and the contrast was similar to the contrast between his mother's soft cushions and his father's leather-clad chairs. And his father had a hard, bristly cheek on which to receive Archie's good-night kiss. Judged by the standards of pleasure and luxury, it was not nearly as nice as his mother's, but it gave him, however great need there was for caution, a sense of identity with himself. He was of that species... And this conception of abnormality in women was strongly confirmed when, one morning, he went as usual to his mother's bedroom to see her before she went down to breakfast. She had been late in getting up that day, and, not finding her in her bedroom, Archie's attention had been arrested by hearing sounds from her bathroom next door, and very naturally had turned the handle in order to enter. But a voice from inside had said:

"Is that you, darling? Wait just a minute."

"But I want to come in now," said Archie. "I'm coming in."

"Archie, I shall be very angry if you come in before I give you leave," said the voice. Then there were rustlings. "Come in now."

And there was his mother standing by her bath, which smelt deliciously fragrant, in a lovely blue bath-towel dressing-gown.

"Good-morning, darling," said she. "But you must never come into a lady's bathroom unless she gives you leave."

"Why not?" said Archie. "You come to see me in my bath without my saying 'Yes.'"

She gave that delicious bubble of laughter that reminded Archie of the sound of cool lemonade being poured out of the bottle.

"I shan't when you're as old as me," she said. "I shall always ask your leave. And probably you won't give it me."

"Why not? It's only me," said Archie.

"You'll know when you're older," said she.

CHAPTER I

Archie rather despised that argument: it seemed to apply to so many situations in life. But he had already formed the very excellent habit of crediting his mother with the gift of common sense, for was it not she who had discovered that the snarl of the tiger-heads was a snarl not at Archie, but at his enemies? But on this occasion it merely confirmed his conviction that women were somehow deformed. They wore skirts instead of breeches, and though, judging by his younger sister, they were normal up to about the level of the knee, it seemed likely that their legs extended no farther, but that they became like peg-tops, swelling out in one round piece till their bodies were reached. What confirmed this impression was that they seemed to run from their knees instead of striding with a swung leg. Blessington always ran like that: her feet twinkled in ridiculously short steps, and after a moment or two she said:

"Eh, I can't run any more. I've got a bone in my leg."

"And haven't I?" asked Archie.

"No, dear: you're just made of gristle and quicksilver," said Blessington, with a sudden lyrical spasm as she looked at the shining face of her most beloved.

"What's quicksilver?" asked Archie. "And why haven't I got a bone in my leg? O-o-oh!" and a sudden thought struck him. "Have women got bones in their legs and not boys? Is that why they can't run properly? Mummy can't run, nor can you; but William can, damn him."

"Master Archie!" said Blessington in her most severe voice.

"What for?" asked Archie.

"You must never say that, Master Archie," said Blessington, who only called him Master Archie on impressive occasions. "You must never say what you said after 'William can.'"

"But daddy said it to William this morning," said Archie.

Blessington still wore the iron mask on her face. It was lucky for her that Archie did not know how puzzled she was as to the correct answer.

"Your papa says what he thinks fit," she said, "and that is right for him. But young gentlemen never say it."

"How old shall I have to be—" began Archie.

"And look at your shoe-lace all untied," said Blessington with extreme promptitude. "Do it up at once, or you'll be treading on it. And then it will be time for you to go in, and you can write your letter to Miss Marjorie before your dinner."

Miss Marjorie was the elder of Archie's two sisters. She was ten years older than he, and at the present time was staying with her grandmother, whom Archie strongly suspected of being either a witch or a man. She was large and rustling, and had a bass voice and a small moustache and a small husband, who was an earl, to whom, when he came to stay with Archie's father, who appeared to be his son, every one paid a great deal of unnecessary attention. Both of them, Archie's father, and Archie's father's father, were lords, and Archie distinctly thought he ought to be a lord too, considering that both his father and his grandfather were. Blessington had hinted that he would be a lord too, some day, if he were good, but when pressed she couldn't say when. In fact, there was a ridiculous reticence about the whole matter, for when he had asked his mother, in the presence of his grandfather, when he was going to be a lord, his grandfather, quite inexplicably, had giggled with laughter, and said:

"I've got one foot in the grave already, Archie, and you want me to have both."

That was a very cryptic remark, and when Archie asked William the footman what grandpapa Tintagel had meant, William had said that he couldn't say, sir. On which Archie, looking hastily round, and feeling sure that Blessington was not present, had repeated "Damn you, William," as daddy said.

Then William, after endeavouring not to show two rows of jolly white teeth, had said:

"You must never say that to me, Master Archie."

In fact, there was clearly a league. Blessington and William, who didn't love each other, as Archie had ascertained by direct questions to each, were at one over the question of him not saying that. Under the stress of independent evidence, Archie decided not to say it any more, without further experiments as to the effect "it" would have on his mother. If William and Blessington were both agreed about it, it had clearly better not be done, any more than it was wise to walk about among the flowers of the big, herbaceous border. The gardener and the gardener's boy and his mother were all of one mind about that, and the gardener's boy had threatened to turn the hose on to him if he caught him at it. The gardener's boy was quite grown up, and so for Archie he had a weight of authority that befitted his years.

It was a lovely, disconnected life. There were all sorts of delightful and highly coloured strands that contributed to it, and others of a more sombre hue, and others again quite secret, which concerned Archie alone, and of which he never spoke to anybody. Of the delightful and highly coloured strands there were many. Waking in the morning, and knowing that there was going to be another day was one of them, and perhaps that was the most delightful of all except when, rarely, it was clouded with some trouble of the evening before, as when Archie had broken a window in his father's study in the laudable attempt to kill a wasp with a fire-shovel, and had been told by Blessington that his father wished to see him the moment he was dressed in the morning. But usually the wakings were ecstatic; and often he used to return to consciousness in those summer months long before Blessington came in to call him. The window was always open—all the windows in the night-nursery were opened as soon as he got into bed—and the blinds were up, and on the ceiling was the most delicious green light, for the early sun shone through the branches of the beeches outside, and painted Archie's ceiling with a pale, milky green which was adorable to contemplate. He would pull up his night-shirt, and with his bare arms clasp his bare knees, and, lying on his back, rather unsteadily anchored, would roll backwards and forwards looking at the green light, and rehearsing all the delightful probabilities of the day. Sometimes his mother had promised him that he should go out fishing on the lake when his lessons were done, and this implied the wonderful experience of seeing Walter or William come out on to the lawn, and pour out of a tin gardening can a mixture of mustard and water. When the footman did that it was certain that in a short time the grass would be covered with worms, which William put in a tin box lined with moss. Then Archie and William, sometimes with a sister, whose presence, Archie thought, was not wholly desirable, since she impeded the free flow of talk between him and William, would go down to the lake, and William, who could do everything, put worms on hooks (they did not seem to mind, for they said no word of protest), and sculled across to the sluice above which was deep water, where the fish fed, and away from the reeds, where the line got entangled, so that it was impossible to know whether you were engaged with a fish or a vegetable. The fishing-rod came out of his father's study—that was another delightful male attribute about the room—and when Archie went in to ask for it, William came too, not in his livery, but in ordinary clothes, and his father said, "Take good care of Master Archie, William. Good sport, Archie." Sometimes again, if he was not busy, Lord Davidstow came out with Archie instead of William. That was somehow an honour, but Archie did not like it so much.

Once there was a great happening. William produced a curious object that looked like the bowl of a spoon with hooks set all round it. He said there were going to be no worms this time, and, instead of drifting about, he rowed up and down, while Archie, with his rod over the stern, saw the spoon flashing through the water. Then a great shadow came over it, and Archie felt the rod bend in his hands. He was so excited that he stepped on to the seat of the boat, in order to see better, and promptly fell overboard.

He was not the least frightened, and rather enjoyed the splash and the sense of soda-water round him. With both hands he held on to the fishing-rod, which seemed an absolutely essential thing to do, and sank down, down in the deep water, seeing it green and yellow above his head. And then instantly he knew he was going to be drowned, and a feeling precisely identical to that which he had experienced one night when he woke, of a universal presence round about him, took complete possession of him. Then, even before he was conscious of the least sense of choking or discomfort, but was still only aware of coolness and depth and greenness, a great dark splaying object came right down upon him from above, and he found himself tucked underneath a human arm, coatless and in shirt-sleeves which he took to be William's. But still Archie did not let go of the fishing-rod, and mistakenly trying to speak, bidding William take care of it, his mouth and apparently his whole interior filled with water, and drowning suddenly seemed to be a disagreeable process. Next moment, however, his head emerged from the water again, and William caught hold of the boat.

"Let go the rod, Master Archie," said he, "and catch hold of the boat."

"But there's a fish on it," spluttered Archie.

"Do as I tell you, sir," said William quite crossly.

Archie had been told that, when he went out in the boat with William, he had to do precisely as William told him. He was not, it is true, in the boat at the moment, but the injunction probably applied. So he let go of the rod, and the moment afterwards found himself violently propelled over the side of the boat, and tumbled all abroad on the floor of it. They were but a dozen yards from land, and William having once got Archie into the boat, grabbed hold of the rod with his spare hand, and swam, shoving the boat in front of him.

"Oh, well done, William. Oh, William, I love you," screamed Archie when, having righted himself, he observed this brilliant manoeuvre. "Is the fish there still?"

William scrambled up the bank, still holding the rod.

"Run indoors at once, Master Archie," he said. "Don't wait a moment."

"But William, is the fish—" began Archie.

"Do as I tell you, sir," said William again. "I'll bring the fish for you, if I get him."

Archie ran with backward glances across the lawn, where he was met by Blessington who had observed the accident out of the window, and, before he could explain half the thrilling things that had happened, was undressed and rubbed down and put between blankets. And then, after a few minutes, in came William, having also changed his clothes, with a great pike, and his father followed and shook hands with William, and his mother did the same, saying things that made William blush and stand first on one foot and then on the other, murmuring: "It was nothing at all, my lady," and Archie asked if he and William might go out again that afternoon, and catch another pike. Then in came his younger sister, Jeannie, who was only two years his senior. She appeared to be on the point of crying, and she flung her arms round Archie's neck in an uncomfortable sort of way, and Archie told her she was messing him. After that, in reaction from those thrilling affairs, he felt suddenly tired, and, being encouraged to go to sleep, nestled down in the blankets and woke up to find that there was his fish stuffed for dinner, and for himself and William an era of unexampled popularity.

Archie did not understand at the time why he had suddenly blossomed into such favouritism, unless it was for having clung tight to his father's fishing-rod but he enjoyed it immensely. It was pleasant, too, not long afterwards, to be given a gold watch by his father, to present to William, with a gold chain provided by his mother. And William permitted him to put the gold watch into one waistcoat pocket, and the end of the gold chain into the other, and his father and mother and Jeannie all shook hands with William again (every one seemed to be spending their time in shaking hands with William). So Archie, since William was his friend more than anybody else's, kissed him, in order to mark the difference between himself and other people with regard to him. He was surprised to find that William had got a soft cheek like his mother's, and supposed that men's faces grew hard as they grew older. He instantly mentioned this surprising fact, and William appeared rather glad to leave the room. But in all Archie's life no event ever occurred which approached the splendour and public magnificence of this whole experience.

Every day the world widened, and, lying looking at the green light on the ceiling in the cool still mornings of that summer which seemed to last for years and years, Archie found himself not only speculating on what fresh joys the day would bring, but joining together in his mind the happenings that at the time seemed disconnected, but which proved to be part of a continuous thread of existence. Just as the nursery passage, and the steep stairs, and his father's room, and the lawn, and the lake passed from being isolated phenomena into pieces of a whole, so things that happened proved to be the experiences of the person who was known to others as Archie Morris, and to Archie as himself. Sometimes he so tingled with vigour when he woke that, contrary to orders, he stepped out of bed and leaned out of the window, to look at the bright dewy world, with one ear alert to hear Blessington's foot along the passage, in order to leap back into bed again, for now he had the night-nursery to himself, and Blessington slept next door. At that hour the lawn would be covered with a shimmering grey mantle, pearl-coloured, and here and there a few diamonds had got in by mistake which shone with just the brilliance of his mother's necklace. Perhaps these were the bed-clothes of the lawn, and when day came, they were covered over by the green bed-spread like that which lay on his own bed. The lake away to the right had different bed-clothes, thicker ones, but of the same colour. No doubt they were thicker because the lake was colder, for on some mornings he could not see through them at all. To the left, out of the window, rose the wood where the rabbits lived; sometimes one of them, an early riser like Archie, would have found a gap in the netting and was out on the lawn nibbling the grass. The gardener did not approve of that, for the lawn, it appeared, belonged to the people who lived in Archie's house, and not to the folk in the wood, and this was a trespass on the part of the rabbits, for which thc punishment, rather a severe one, was death by shooting. This had added a new terror to the notice in another wood where he and Blessington sometimes walked, which announced that trespassers would be prosecuted. Blessington was foolhardy enough to disregard that notice altogether, saying that it was his daddy's notice, and didn't apply to them; but for some time Archie never chose that walk for fear that Blessington might be wrong about it, and that they would meet somebody in the wood who would instantly shoot them both for trespassing. But in childish fashion he kept those terrors to himself, sooner than enquire about them, till one day they actually did meet in that wood a man with a gun. Then in a sudden wild terror Archie clung to Blessington, crying out, "Oh, ask him not to shoot us this time!"

"Eh, darling," said Blessington. "Who's going to shoot us? It's only one of your daddy's keepers."

"No, but he will shoot us," screamed Archie. "We're trespassers, and he'll shoot us like the rabbits."

Matters being thereupon explained, and Archie convinced that he and Blessington were not going to be shot for trespassing, he found that he could make up for himself an entrancing story of how Master Rabbit and his nurse (who were good) never trespassed on the lawn, and that the rabbits he saw there corresponded to Grandmamma Tintagel, and so he did not care whether they were shot or not.

These stories which he told himself in the early morning, looking out on to the lawn, or lying curled up on his back in bed, looking at the green ceiling, were not vague, dream-like imaginings, but were endowed with a vividness that made Blessington's entry with his bath and his clothes seem less real than they. It became impossible indeed for him to disentangle reality (as judged by people like his father and the gardener) from imagination. He told himself so strongly that there was Grandmamma Tintagel sitting on the lawn, trespassing and nibbling grass for her breakfast, that her presence there, or her absence when there was no trespassing rabbit, became things as vivid as his subsequent dressing and breakfast. Had he been definitely asked if he believed it was Grandmamma Tintagel, he would have said "No"; but in his imaginative life, so hard for a child to dissociate from his real life, there was no question as to her identity. It happened also that at this time his mother was reading to him the realest of all books, namely, *Alice in Wonderland*. No imaginative boy of five could possibly doubt the actual existence of the White Rabbit in that convincing history, and Archie would not have been surprised if, one morning, there had proved to be a white rabbit sitting by the fence, who looked at his watch and put on his gloves. Yet he never spoke of this possibility even to Blessington or William; it did not belong to the sphere of things about which it was reasonable to converse to grown-up people, simply because they were stupid about certain matters and would not understand him. The fact that Grandmamma Tintagel sometimes sat on the lawn in the early morning was among the topics which he kept quite completely to himself.

There were other such topics. Sometimes, when he lay in bed, waiting for Blessington to call him, and did not choose to get up and look out of the window, it was because these other secret affairs engaged him. If he lay still, and stared at the green-hued ceiling, curious waves of shadow appeared to pass over it, and it seemed like that sunny floor of water that had closed above his head on the morning when he fell out of the boat. There was he lying in bed deep below some surface of liquid light that cut him off from the outer world, and he wondered if in a moment a splayed starfish of arms and legs which turned out to be William would dive down for him, and bring him up among the common things again. But William never made this impressive entry through the ceiling, and if he stared long enough, Archie only seemed to himself to slip down and down, gently and rapturously, through deep water, and another world, the world of hidden things that dwelt below the surface, came slowly into existence, like as when, on mounting a slope, fresh valleys and hillsides arise and unfurl themselves. Only, in this case, you had to go down somewhere inside yourself to become aware of them. And something, some inner consciousness, recognized and hailed them. It was not that he was getting sleepy, and sinking into the waters of dreams; rather the experience was the result of a more vivid life and awakened perceptions. But he never got further than that, and during the day he was far too busy with the affairs of normal life to trouble about those perceptions that dawned on him on still quiet mornings when he lay a-bed and stared at the ceiling with its flickering green lights and moving shadows.

CHAPTER II

Archie's birthday was in November, and for a day or two before that tremendous annual event there was always a certain atmosphere of mystery abroad, which he was conscious of at odd minutes. He met Marjorie on the morning of the day before he would be six, walking down the nursery passage with a parcel in her hand, the contents of which she would not divulge. That afternoon, too, his mother drove into the neighbouring town in the motor, and would not take him with her, on the excuse that she had some shopping to do, though it was the commonest thing in the world for her to take him with her when she went shopping. This year he vaguely connected these odd happenings with his birthday, as he did also the fact that a week ago Blessington had brought a total stranger into the nursery, who had very politely asked him to take off his coat. The stranger had then knelt down on the floor in front of him, and had produced a tape, with which he proceeded to measure Archie all over, from his hip to his knee and his knee to his ankle, and round his waist, and round his chest, and all along his arms, making notes of those things in a book. Blessington had told him that Mr. Johnson wanted to see how much he had grown, which was certainly a very gratifying attention, especially since Archie had grown a good deal, and was extremely proud of the fact. Mr. Johnson congratulated him too, and said that he himself hadn't grown as much as that for many a year, and tried to account for his visit on general grounds of interest in Archie. But in spite of that Archie connected this call with his birthday, though he did not arrive at the deduction that it meant clothes.

His mother came up to tea in the nursery on her return from her mysterious drive, and said that she had just caught sight of the fairy Abracadabra as she drove down the High Street; she had not known that Abracadabra was in the neighbourhood. She asked Archie if Abracadabra had called while she was out, and Archie, after a moment's pause, said that he hadn't seen her… but in that pause something of the glory faded out of the bright trailing clouds. When he was asked that directly he did not feel sure whether he believed in Abracadabra in the same way in which he believed in Blessington or Jeannie. So short a time ago—last summer only—Alice in Wonderland and the identity of Grandmamma Tintagel had been so much realler than the paltry happenings that took place in the light of common day. Now, quite suddenly and unexpectedly, at the mere question as to whether he had seen Abracadabra they all began to fade; indeed, it was more than fading: it was as if they passed out of sight behind a corner.

Archie had been told that he must never, if he could help it, hurt people's feelings. The particular occasion when that had been brought home to him was when his sister Jeannie had to wear a rather delightful sort of band round her front teeth, which showed a tendency to grow crooked. She was shy about it and hoped nobody saw it, and when Archie called the attention of the public to it, she turned very red. He had not had the least intention of embarrassing her, for he thought the band rather nice himself, and would have liked to have had one had his teeth been sufficiently advanced for such a decoration. But on this occasion he saw instantly and clearly that he must not hurt his mother's feelings by expressing scepticism about Abracadabra. Perhaps his mother still believed in her herself (though there were difficulties about supposing that, seeing that if Abracadabra was not Abracadabra she was certainly his mother); but, in any case, she thought Archie believed in Abracadabra, which made quite sufficient reason for his appearing to do so. If Abracadabra was an invention designed to awe, delight, and mystify him, the most elementary obligation of not embarrassing other people enjoined on him that he must be awed, delighted, and mystified. Perhaps by next year something would have happened to Abracadabra, for nowadays she only made her appearance on his birthday, whereas he could remember when she paid Jeannie also a birthday visit. But this year she had not come on Jeannie's birthday, and the various members of the family had given her birthday presents themselves, which did not happen when Abracadabra came, for she was the chief dispenser of offerings.

So Archie replied that Abracadabra had not been during his mother's absence, and, in order to spare his mother the mortification of knowing that he had doubts about that benevolent fairy, laid himself out to ask intelligent questions.

"Why didn't you speak to her, mummy?" he said, "when you saw her in the High Street?"

"Because she was in a hurry; she went by like a flash of lightning, in her pearl chariot."

"Was there any thunder?" asked he.

"Yes, just one clap; but that might have been the wheels of the chariot. What do you think she'll bring you?"

Archie was holding his mother's hand, and slipping her rings up and down her fingers. As he held it, he suddenly became aware what one of these presents would be.

"A clock-work train," he said quickly.

He knew more than that about the clock-work train. He felt perfectly certain that it was in his mother's bedroom at this moment, reposing in the big cupboard where she kept her dresses.

"Do you want a clock-work train?" she asked.

"Yes, mummy, frightfully," said he, feeling that he was playing a part, for he knew his mother knew that he wanted a clock-work train.

"What else?"

CHAPTER II

"Oh, thousands of things. Particularly a pen that writes without your dipping it in the ink."

"Well, if I were you I should write down all the things you want, and leave the paper lying on your counterpane when you go to sleep."

"What'll that do?" asked Archie.

"It's the fairy-post. Instead of putting letters into boxes to be posted when you want them to reach the fairies, you have always to put them on your bed. Mind you address it to Her Fairy Majesty the Empress Abracadabra. Then, when the fairies come round to collect the post, they will find it there, and take it to Abracadabra. And perhaps if she comes to-morrow—let me see, it must be a year since she was here—she will bring a few things for your birthday. I can't tell; but I think that is the best chance of getting them."

Certainly this seemed a very pleasant sort of plan; Archie had never heard of it before, and the extremely matter-of-fact tone in which his mother spoke lit again a dawning hope in his mind that perhaps it was all true. Why shouldn't be a fairy Abracadabra, and a fairy-post, just as there had been, and now was no longer, a glassy sea between the rugs in the hall, and snarling tigers to keep off his enemies? If you believed a thing enough, it became real, with a few trifling exceptions—as, for instance, when, on one of the days last summer, a day crammed full of the most delightful events, Archie had found himself firmly believing that that particular day was never coming to an end. True, it had come to an end, but that perhaps was because he hadn't believed strongly enough... There was a lovely story which his mother had read him about a man called Joshua, who wanted a day to remain until he had killed all his enemies, and sure enough the sun stood still until he had accomplished that emphatic task. He never doubted that, because it came out of the Bible, and in the spirit of Joshua he set himself now to believe in Abracadabra and the fairy-post. And, with that in his mind, he kept his eyes firmly away from the cupboard where his mother kept her dresses that evening, when her maid opened it, lest he should see there the parcel which he felt secretly convinced was there, and contained the clock-work train which his mother had bought, and which Abracadabra would to-morrow assuredly bring out of the basket of pure gold with which she habitually travelled.

Archie put the letter for the fairy-post on his bed, and determined to keep awake so that he should see the fairy postman come for it. It was a very cold night, and a big fire burned in his grate, so that, though the windows as usual were all open, there was a clear, brisk warmth about the room and a frosty and soapy smell, for his bright brown hair had been washed that night—this was a special evening bath-night, for by now baths had been promoted to the morning—and stuck up all over his head in a novel and independent manner. Blessington had dried it by the fire for him with hot towels, and a very extraordinary thing had happened, for when she brushed it afterwards it gave forth little cracklings, which she told him was electricity which was the thing that made the lamps burn. She had allowed him to take a brush to bed with him, and make more cracklings for five minutes until she returned to put his light out, and Archie made a wonderful story to himself as he looked at the fire, that he would get an electric lamp and paste it to his head, so that he should be able to read by the light of his hair. All at once this seemed so feasible, so easy of belief that he pictured to himself everybody walking about the house in the evening lit by themselves... And then William came round the corner (he did not know what corner), carrying an electric pike for a birthday present to himself, and when Blessington stole in five minutes afterwards, Archie's brush had slipped from his fingers and his breath came evenly between his parted lips. There was a gap in his front teeth because a tooth had come out only to-day, embedded in a piece of toffy he was eating, which had made Archie squeal with laughter, for here was a new substance called tooth-toffee... And Blessington softly lifted his arm and laid it under the bedclothes without awaking him, and looked at him a moment with her old face beaming with love, and put down on his chair out of sight at the bottom of his bed the new sailor-suit, and took away the note to her Fairy Majesty the Empress Abracadabra.

* * * * *

Archie woke next morning and instantly remembered that he had attained the magnificent age of six. Six had long seemed to him one of the most delightful ages to be. Eighteen was another, mainly because William was eighteen, but six was the best of all, for at eighteen you must inevitably feel that you have lived your life, and that there is nothing much left to live for; for the rest would be but a slow descent into the vale of years. But to-day he was six, and it was his birthday, and... and there was no sign of the letter he had written to Abracadabra on his counterpane. But it might have slipped on to the floor, and not have been taken away by fairies after all. Or it might have slipped over the bottom of the bed; and Archie got up to see. No: there was no note there, but on the chair at the foot of his bed was a suit of sailor-clothes...

Archie gave a gasp: certainly their presence there constituted a possibility that they were for him; but he hardly dared let himself contemplate so dazzling a prospect, for fear it should be whisked out of sight. Yet who could they be for, if not for him? They couldn't be Blessington's, for she was a female, and wore mystery-cloaking skirts. Sailor-suits were boys' clothes: Harry Travers, the son of a neighbouring squire, aged eight, had a sailor-suit—it was the thing that Archie most envied about that young man. Harry had taken the coat and trousers off one day in the summer when the two boys were playing in the copse by the lower end of the lake, and had let Archie put them on for three minutes. That had been a thrilling adventure; it implied undressing out of doors, which was a very unusual thing to do, and he loved the feeling of the rough serge down his bare calves. He had, of course, offered Harry the privilege of putting on his knickerbockers and jacket, if he could get into them without splitting them, but Harry, from that Pisgah-summit of eight years, had no desire to go back to the childish things of the land of bondage, but had danced about bare-legged while Archie enjoyed his three minutes in these voluminous and grown-up lendings. And now perhaps for him, too, not for three minutes only, but for every day… and he took a leap back into bed again as Blessington's tread sounded on the boards outside.

Archie pretended to be asleep, for he wanted to be awakened by Blessington and hear his birthday greetings. He loved the return of consciousness in the morning—when he had not already been awake, and speculating about Grandmamma Tintagel on the lawn—to find Blessington, with her hand on his shoulder, gently stirring him, and her face close to his, whispering to him, "Eh, it's time to get up." So this morning, not for the first time, he simulated sleep in order to recapture that lovely sense of being awakened by love. (You must understand that he did not put it to himself like that, for Archie, just at the age of six, was not a mature and self-conscious prig, but he wanted to know what Blessington's greeting to him would be, when she thought she woke him up on the morning of his sixth birthday.)

From the narrow chink of his eyelids not quite closed, he could see some of her movements. She took the exciting suit of sailor-clothes from the bottom of his bed, and laid it on the chair where she always put his clothes with a flannel shirt of a quite unusual shape, and his socks on top. Already Archie had heart-burnings at the knowledge of his knowledge of the sailor-suit. Blessington meant it to be a surprise to him, and a surprise he determined it should be. In the interval there was another surprise: how would Blessington wake him? She would be sure to rise to the immense importance of the occasion. She moved quietly about; she shut the windows, and brought in his bath. And then she came close up to his bed. He felt her hand stealing underneath the bedclothes to his shoulder and she shook it gently—"Eh, Master Six," she said.

Oh, she had done exactly the right thing! She had divined Archie, as he had divined himself, knowing himself. That was just the only thing to think about this morning. He ceased to imagine: Blessington, out of her simplicity of love, had given the real birthday greeting.

He rolled a little sideways, and there was her face close to his, and her hand still underneath his bed-clothes. He put up both of his hands and caught it.

"Many happy returns," said Blessington. "Wake up, my darling: it's your birthday. Happy returns," she repeated.

Archie released her hand and flung his arm round her neck.

"Oh, Blessington, isn't it fun?" he said. "What did you do when you were six?"

"I got up directly," said Blessington, kissing him, "and had my bath and put my clothes on. Now, will you do the same, for I'm going downstairs for ten minutes, and then I shall be back."

"All right," said Archie.

She went out, and Archie again, as with the question of Abracadabra last night, felt he must make it a surprise that there were sailor-clothes on his chair. It was quite likely that he would not be supposed to notice them at once, and so he stripped off his night-shirt, and took his bath in the prescribed manner. He had to lie down on the floor first of all, and wave his legs about; then he had to stand upright, still with no clothes on, and put his hands each side of his waist, and wave his body about eight times in each direction. Then he was allowed to pour out the hot water into his bath, in order to encourage himself, but before he stepped into that delicious steamy warmth he had to bend down eight times with a long frosty expulsion of breath, and stand up eight times with a great draught of cold air in his lungs. All this had been explained to him by a stranger—not Mr. Johnson—who, a year ago, had come into his nursery and had been very much interested in his anatomy. Archie understood that this was a doctor, though he didn't give him any medicine, but had merely showed him how to do these things, after first putting a sort of plug on Archie's chest which communicated with two other plugs that the stranger put in his ears. Then Archie had to say "ninety-nine" several times, which seemed to be a sort of game, though it didn't lead any further (the doctor, for instance, didn't say "a hundred"), and then he had to promise to practise those contortions every morning.

All this was done, and Archie fled from the cold of the morning to his bath. The water was of that divinest temperature so that when he stopped still it was lovely, but when he moved he almost screamed with the rapturous heat of it. It cooled a little as he sat in it, and, still remembering that he was six, he poured a sponge-full down his spine. That over, he might wash his face and his neck, and well behind his ears with soap. Up till a few months ago Blessington had always superintended the bath, and done these things for him; but now he did them for himself as agent, with Blessington as inspector-general in the background, who might always make the strictest scrutiny into the place behind the ears and the toe-nails to see that the effects of the bath were perfectly satisfactory. If not, Blessington superintended again for the next three mornings; so Archie was very careful, since it was so much grander to wash oneself than to be washed by anybody else.

Then came the most exciting part of the bath, for close at the side of it was a big tin full of the coldest possible water. He had then to stand up in his bath, and, after washing his face in the cold water, to put cold water everywhere within reach of him on one arm and then the other, on a chest, on a stomach, on one leg and on another right down to the foot, and finally (a vocal piece) to squeeze a full sponge down his back. Archie squealed at this, and flew for a towel.

He flung himself into his new clothes and was already half-dressed when Blessington returned.

"Oh, Blessington," he said, "look at me, and they're just as easy to manage as the old ones, and may I go to see Harry after breakfast and show him?"

"Master Harry will be here for tea," said Blessington.

"Yes, but I want him to know sooner than that. Did they come just ordinarily, like other clothes? Or are they a birthday present?"

"Well, I should say they were a birthday present," said Blessington.

"Who from?" demanded Archie.

And then suddenly he guessed.

"Oh, Blessington," he said. "I like them better than anything!" he said.

"Well, dear, and I wish you health to wear them and strength to tear them," she said. "Eh, but how you're disarranging my cap!"

CHAPTER II

Archie promptly handselled his clothes by spilling egg on the coat, and bread-and-butter upside down on the trousers, and, when the time came for him to make his public entry into the world, was seized with a sudden fit of shyness at the thought of anybody seeing him. The housemaid would stare, and William would laugh, and Marjorie would pretend not to know him, and for the moment of leaving the day-nursery (which from this morning was to be known as Archie's sitting-room) he would almost have wished himself back in his knickerbockers. But the remembered rough touch of the serge on his legs provided encouragement, and soon the new glories burst upon a sympathetic and not a mocking world. They were at breakfast downstairs, and Archie, though he had already had his, was bidden by his father to have a cup of coffee, which he poured out himself at the side-table, and to drink it slowly, and at the bottom of it, among the melted sugar, there came to his astonished eyes the gleam of silver, and there was a new half-crown with his father's happy returns. Thereafter came a hurried visit to Harry, a motor drive with his mother and Jeannie, Archie sitting on the box-seat and permitted to blow the bugle practically as often as he wanted, and the return to dinner, to find that the two things he liked best, namely boiled rabbit and spotted dog pudding, formed that memorable repast.

Up till now he had received only two birthday presents, the clothes and the half-crown, and he could not help feeling that a visit from Abracadabra was more than likely, since no one else had made the slightest allusion to clock-work trains or pens that wrote without being dipped. But in the afternoon, as he returned home from his walk with Blessington and Jeannie in the early dusk, he received an impression which was to be more inextricably connected with his sixth birthday than even the sailor suit. They were within a few yards of the front-door when there ran out of the bushes Cyrus, the great blue Persian cat. He held something in his mouth, which Archie saw to be a bird. There he stood for a moment with the gleaming eyes of the successful hunter, and twitching tail, and then trotted in front of them towards the porch. Simultaneously Jeannie called out:

"Oh, Blessington, Cyrus has caught a thrush. We must get it from him; it may be still alive."

Till then Archie had only thought about the cleverness of Cyrus in catching a bird, which was clearly a very remarkable feat, since Cyrus could only run and climb, and a bird could fly. But, as Jeannie spoke, he suddenly thought of himself in the jaws of a tiger, of the clutch of the long white teeth, of the fear, and the helplessness; and a queer tremor made him catch his breath, as there smote upon him an emotion that had never yet been awakened by the passage of his sunny days. Pity took hold of him for the bright-eyed bird. It suffered; his imagination told him that, and never yet had the fact of suffering come home to him.

They hemmed Cyrus in, and Blessington took the thrush out of his mouth, while Cyrus growled and struck at her with his paws, and then, greatly incensed, bounded out into the garden again, so as not to lose the chance, at this cat-hour of dusk, of a further stalk and capture. They carried the bird into the hall, where they looked at it, but it lay quite still in Blessington's hand, with its helpless little claws relaxed, and with its eyes fast glazing in death. Its beak was open, and on its speckled breast were two oozing drops of blood, that stained the feathers.

"Eh, poor thing, it's dead," said Blessington.

Archie felt all the desolation of an unavailing pity.

"No, it can't be dead, Blessington," he said. "It'll get all right, won't it?" and his lip quivered.

"No, dear, it's quite dead," said Blessington; "but if you like we'll bury it. There'll be just time before tea. Shall I run upstairs and get a box to bury it in?"

Without doubt this was a consoling and attractive proposal, and while Blessington went to get a suitable coffin, Archie held the "small slain body" in reverent hands. It was warm and soft and still; by now the bright eyes had grown quite dull, and the blood on the speckled breast was beginning to coagulate, and once again, even with the novel prospect of a bird-funeral in front of him, Archie's heart melted in pity.

"Why did Cyrus kill it, Jeannie?" he said. "The thrush hadn't done any harm."

"Cats do kill birds," said Jeannie. "Same as birds kill worms, or you and William kill worms when you go out fishing."

"Yes, but worms aren't birds," said Archie. "Worms aren't nice; they don't fly and sing. It's an awful shame."

Blessington returned with a suitable cardboard box which had held chocolates, and into this fragrant coffin the little limp body was inserted. This certainly distracted Archie from his new-found emotion.

"Oh, that will be nice for it," he said. "It will smell the chocolate."

"It can't; it's dead," said hopeless Jeannie.

But Blessington understood better.

"Yes, dear, the chocolate will be nice for it," she said, "and then we'll cover it up with leaves and put the lid on."

"Oh, and may it have a cris—a crisantepum?" said Archie. "May I pick one?"

"Yes, just one."

Archie laid this above the bird's head, and the lid was put on.

"Oh, and let's have a procession to the tool-shed to get a trowel," said Jeannie.

"Yes!" squealed Archie, now thoroughly immersed in the fascinating ritual. "And I'll carry the coffin and go first, and you and Blessington shall walk behind and sing."

"Well, we must be quick," said Blessington.

"No, not quick," said Jeannie. "It's a funeral. What shall we sing?"

"Oh, anything. 'The Walrus and the Carpenter.' That's sad, because the oysters were dead."

So, to the moving strains, the procession headed across the lawn, and found a trowel in the tool-shed, and excavated a grave underneath the laurestinus. The coffin was once more opened to see that the thrush was quite comfortable, and then deposited in its sepulchre, and the earth filled in above it. But Archie felt that the ceremony was still incomplete.

"Ought we to say a prayer, Jeannie?" he said.

CHAPTER II

"No, it's only a thrush."

Archie considered a moment.

"I don't care," he said. "I shall all the same."

He took off his sailor cap and knelt down, closing his eyes.

"God bless the poor thrush," he said. "Good-night, thrush. I can't think of anything more. Amen. Say Amen, Jeannie."

"Amen," said Jeannie.

"And do get up from that damp earth, dear," said Blessington. "And let's see who can run the fastest back to the house."

Blessington ran the least fast, and Archie tripped over a croquet-hoop, and so Jeannie won, and very nearly began telling her mother about it all before Archie arrived. But, though breathless, he shrilly chipped in.

"And then I picked a crisantepum, and we had a procession across the lawn, and made a lovely grave by the tool-house, and I said prayers, though Jeannie told me you didn't have prayers for thrushes. Mummy, when I grow up, may I be a clergyman?"

"Why, dear?"

"Don't they have lots of funerals?"

"Pooh; that's the undertaker," said Jeannie. "Besides, I did say Amen, Archie."

"I know. But mummy, why did Cyrus kill the thrush? Why did he want to hurt it and kill it? That was the part I didn't like, and I expect the thrush hated it. Wasn't it cruel of him? But if he kills another, may we have another funeral?"

He stood still a moment, cudgelling his small brain in order to grasp exactly what he felt.

"The poor thrush!" he said. "I wish Cyrus hadn't killed it. But, if it's got to be dead, I like funerals."

* * * * *

Tea, on such solemn occasions as birthday feasts, took place for Archie, not in the nursery, but in the drawing-room, as better providing the proper pomp. He appreciated that, and secretly was pleased that Harry Travers should be ushered by William into the drawing-room, and have the door held open for him, and be announced as Mr. Travers. With that streak of snobbishness common to almost all small boys Archie thought it rather jolly, without swaggering at all, to be able to greet his friend in the midst of these glories, so that he could see their splendour for himself. In other ways, he would have perhaps preferred the nursery, and certainly would have done so when the moment came for him to cut his birthday-cake, for the sugar on the side of it cracked and exploded, as such confectionery will do, when Archie hewed his way down that white perpendicular cliff, and (a number of fragments falling on the floor), he had to stand quite still, knife in hand, till William got a housemaid's brush and scoop and removed the debris, for fear it should be trodden into the carpet.

Marjorie had not appeared at tea at all, and when this sumptuous affair was over, Jeannie and Harry and Archie gathered round Lady Davidstow on the hearthrug with a box of chocolates planted at a fair and equal distance between them, and she told them the most delicious story about a boy whose mother had lost his birthdays, so that year after year went by without his having a birthday at all. The lights had been put out, and only the magic of leaping fire-light guided their hands to the chocolate-box, and every moment the phantasy of the story got more and more interwoven with the reality of the chocolates. Eventually, while the birthday-less boy's mother was clearing out the big cupboard underneath the stairs, she came across all his birthdays put away in a purple box with a gold lock on it.

"Was it the cupboard underneath the stairs in the hall here?" asked Archie, for questions were permitted.

"Yes. There they all were: eight birthdays in all, so he had one every day for more than a week. My dears! What's that?"

It certainly was very startling. A noise like a mixture between the Chinese gong and the bell for the servants' dinner broke in upon the quiet, with the most appalling clamour. Archie swallowed a chocolate whole, and Harry, with great prudence, took two more in a damp hand to sustain him in these rather alarming occurrences.

"It sounds as if it was in the hall," said Lady Davidstow. "Harry, will you open the door and see what it is?"

"Yes, I'll go," he said firmly. "But—but shan't Archie come too?"

The noise ceased as suddenly as it had begun, and with a pleasing sense of terror the two boys went to the drawing-room door and opened it.

"But it's quite dark," said Archie. "Oh, mummy, what *is* happening?"

"I can't think. I only know one person who makes a noise the least like that."

"Oh, is it Abracadabra?" asked Archie excitedly, finding that his scepticism of the day before had vanished like smoke. It had occurred to him that Abracadabra was his mother, but here was his mother telling them stories.

"Well, the only time I ever heard her sneeze it was just like that," said Lady Davidstow.

Archie came running back, shrieking with laughter.

"And what does she do when she blows her nose?" he asked.

The words were hardly out of his mouth when a piercing trumpet-blast sounded, and his mother got up.

"She did it then," she whispered. "What had we better do? Shall we go into the hall? She would like us to be there to meet her, perhaps, if she's coming."

She went to the door, followed by the children, and they all looked out into the black hall. The wood-fire in the hearth there had died down to a mere smoulder of red, which sent its illumination hardly farther than the stone fender-curb.

"But there's something there," said Lady Davidstow in an awe-struck whisper. "There's something sitting in the chair."

"Oh, mummy," said Archie, coming close to her. "I don't think I like it."

"I'm sure there's nothing to be frightened at, Archie," said she. "Which of us shall go and see what it is?"

CHAPTER II

There was no volunteer for this hazardous job, for now, with eyes more accustomed to the faint light, they could all see that it was not Something there, but Somebody. The outlines of a head, of a body, of legs all clothed in black, could be seen, and Somebody sat there perfectly still...

Then all of a sudden the gong and the bell and the trumpet broke out into a clamour fit to wake the dead, the great chandelier in the hall flared into light, and the black figure sprang up, throwing its darkness behind it, and there, glittering with silks and gems and gold and the flowers of fairyland, stood Abracadabra. She had on a huge poke-bonnet which cast a shadow over her face, and left it terrifyingly vague. Her bonnet was trimmed with sunflowers and lilies of the valley, and round the edge of it went a row of diamonds which were quite as big as the drops in a glass chandelier. Another necklace of the same brilliance went round her throat and rested on a crimson satin bodice covered with gold. From her shoulders sprang spangled wings, and from below her skirt, with its garlands of roses, were silver shoes with diamond buckles. In her hand she carried a blue wand hung with bells, and by her side was a clothes-basket (such was its shape) made of gold.

She stamped her foot with rage.

"Here's a nice welcome, Lady Davidstow," she said in a thin, cracked voice. "I sneezed to show I was coming, and, when I got through the keyhole, I found the hall dark, and no one to receive me. How dare you?"

Lady Davidstow advanced with faltering steps and fell on her knees.

"Oh, your majesty, forgive me," she said.

"Why should I forgive you?" squeaked the infuriated fairy. "Why shouldn't I take you away in my basket and put you in the Tower of Toads?"

Archie gasped. He would have given much for a touch of yesterday's scepticism, but he couldn't find an atom of it. The thought of his mother being whisked off to the Tower of Toads was insupportable.

"Oh, please don't," he said.

"And who is that?" asked Abracadabra.

Archie almost wished he hadn't spoken, and took hold of Jeannie on one side and Harry on the other.

"It's me; it's Archie," he said.

"And you don't want me to take your ridiculous mother away?" she asked.

"No, please don't," said Archie.

"Very well, as it's your birthday, I won't. Instead I'll make her extra lady-in-waiting on my peacock-staircase, and mistress of my tortoise-shell robes."

"Oh, mummy, that will be lovely for you," said Archie, remembering that his mother was something of the kind to somebody already.

Then there came the giving of presents, with the surprises that occurred during such processes. Archie was told to advance and put his hand in the left far corner of the golden basket, and, as he prepared to do so, Abracadabra sneezed so loudly that he fled back to the bottom stair of the staircase where they had been all commanded to sit. There was a tennis racquet for Harry, but the lights all went out when he had just reached the clothes-basket, and Abracadabra blew her nose so preposterously that his ear sang with it afterwards. There was a great parcel for Lady Davidstow, as big as a football, which was found to contain, when all the paper was stripped off, nothing more than a single acid drop, in order to teach the mistress of the tortoise-shell robes better manners when her mistress came to pay a visit, and Blessington, summoned from the nursery, was presented with a new cap. But the bulk of the gifts, as was proper, was for Archie, a clock-work train, and a pen that needed no dipping, and a fishing-rod, and a second suit of sailor-clothes. And then the light went out again, and Abracadabra began sneezing and blowing her nose with such deafening violence that the screen which stood just behind her rocked with the concussion, and the children, at the suggestion of the mistress of the tortoise-shell robes, groped their way back into the drawing-room with their presents, and shut the door till Abracadabra was better. And when, from the cessation of these awful noises, they conjectured she might be better, and ventured out into the hall again, that audience-chamber was just as usual, and Archie's father came out of his room, looking vexed, and asking what that beastly noise was about. But when he heard it was Abracadabra, who had gone away again, he was greatly upset and said that it wasn't a beastly noise at all, but the loveliest music he had ever heard.

Then came bed-time, and Archie, still excited, said his prayers with a special impromptu clause for Abracadabra, and another for the thrush, which he suddenly remembered again, and then lay staring at the fire with his hands clasped round his knees, as his custom was. Certainly Abracadabra had been wonderfully real to-day, and certainly she was not his mother. Then he recollected that Marjorie had not appeared at all, and wondered if Marjorie perhaps was Abracadabra, or if the thrush was Abracadabra, of Cyrus… And his hands relaxed their hold on his knees, and when Blessington came in he did not know that she kissed him and tucked the bed-clothes up under his chin.

CHAPTER III

Archie did not often come into contact with Miss Schwarz, his sisters' governess; she was not a person to be lightly encountered. Sometimes, if Blessington was busy, he and Jeannie went out for their walk with his eldest sister and Miss Schwarz, and on these occasions Miss Schwarz and Marjorie would talk together in an unknown guttural tongue, very ugly to hear, which Archie vaguely understood was German, and the sort of thing that everybody spoke in the country to which Miss Schwarz went for her holiday at Midsummer and Christmas. That uncouth jargon, full of such noises as you made when you cleared your throat, was quite unintelligible, and it seemed odd that Marjorie should converse in it when she could speak ordinary English; but it somehow seemed to suit Miss Schwarz, who had a sallow face, prominent teeth, and cold grey eyes. Otherwise he did not often meet her, for she led an odd secret existence in his sisters' school-room, breakfasting and having lunch downstairs in the dining-room, but eating her evening meal all by herself in the school-room. She had a black, unrustling dress for the day, and a black rustling dress for the evening, and a necklace of onyx beads which she used to finger with her dry thin hands, which reminded Archie of the claws of a bird. His mother had told him that, after Christmas, he would do his lessons with Miss Schwarz, and this prospect rather terrified him. He supposed that Miss Schwarz would probably teach him in the guttural language that Jeannie was beginning to understand too, and he had moments of secret terror when he pictured Miss Schwarz, enraged at his not comprehending her, striking at him with those claw-like hands.

He was coming upstairs one evening, rather later than usual, for his father had been showing him the contents of a cabinet of butterflies, and Archie, enraptured with the gorgeous, brilliant creatures, had begged to be allowed to wait till the gong rang for dinner. On his way upstairs he remembered that he had lent Jeannie the pen that wrote without being dipped, with which to write her German exercise. She had gone to bed early that night with a bad cold, and Archie, recognizing the impossibility of going to sleep without the precious pen in his possession again, ran along the passage to the school-room, where he was likely to find it. This might entail a momentary encounter with Miss Schwarz, but the recovery of the pen was essential, and he entered.

Miss Schwarz had finished her dinner, and was sitting by the fire on which steamed a kettle. She held a big glass in her hand, and was pouring something into it from a bottle. There was a high colour in her usually sallow face, and as she saw Archie she made one of those guttural exclamations.

"What do you want?" she said, and though she spoke English, Archie noticed that she spoke it in the same thick, guttural manner as German.

Archie froze with terror. This was quite a new Miss Schwarz, a gleaming, eager Miss Schwarz.

"Oh, I lent Jeannie my pen," he stammered. "I came to look for it, but it doesn't matter."

"Nonsense! That is not why!" said Miss Schwarz angrily. Then she suddenly seemed to take hold of herself. "*Ach*, that sweet little pen. You will find it on the table, my dear. Luke, and find it. And then say good-night to poor Miss Schwarz. *Ach*, I am so ill this evening. Such a heartburn, and I was just about to take the medicine vat makes it better. Do not tell any one, dear Archie, that poor Miss Schwarz is ill. I wish to troble nobody. Poor Miss Schwarz naiver geeve troble if she can 'elp. *Ach*, you have your pen! Good-night, my deear."

Archie fled down the passage to the nursery with terror giving wings to his heels. This Miss Schwarz angry one moment, and affectionate and effusive the next, was a new and a more awful person than the one he was acquainted with, and he felt sure she must be very ill indeed. It would be a terrible affair if Miss Schwarz was found dead in her bed, in spite of her medicine, just because he had not told anybody that she was ill, and so a doctor had not been fetched. There would be a burden on his conscience for ever if he did not tell somebody. He burst into the nursery with a wild look behind him, to make sure that Miss Schwarz was not following him in her evening rustling dress.

"Oh Blessington," he cried, "Miss Schwarz is ill; do go and see what is the matter. I went to the school-room for my pen, and she was sitting by the fire, all red, and angry, and then polite, mixing her medicine."

Blessington got up from her rocking-chair.

"Eh, I'll go and see," she said.

"Don't tell her I told you," said Archie.

"Nay, of course I won't. Now you begin your undressing, and I'll be back very soon."

Excited and frightened and yet hugely interested, Archie stood at the door of his room listening. Suddenly he heard the sound of Miss Schwarz's voice raised almost to a scream. Then there came the crash of a glass, and the ringing of a bell, while still Miss Schwarz's voice gabbled on, shrill and guttural. Trembling, and yet unable to resist the call of his curiosity, he stole to the corner of the nursery passage, and saw William come upstairs and go along to the school-room. Then Blessington came out, and, instead of coming back to the nursery, she went downstairs, and presently his father came up again with her. He, too, went along the school-room passage, and suddenly, as if a tap had been turned off, the shrill voice ceased. Once, for a moment, it broke out again, and as suddenly stopped, and then came the very odd sight of Miss Schwarz being led along the landing to her room by his father and Blessington. Blessington and Miss Schwarz entered together, his father went downstairs after a moment's conversation with William, and presently William came along the landing towards the nursery.

"Oh, William, what's happened?" said Archie. "Is Miss Schwarz very ill?"

"Well, she ain't very well," said William. "Lumme!"

"What does that mean?" asked Archie.

"It don't mean anything particular, Master Archie."

"Will Miss Schwarz be better in the morning?" asked Archie.

"Lord, yes. They're always better in the morning, though they don't feel so. Now Blessington won't be back yet awhile, so I'm to look after you, and see you safe to bed."

Suddenly the thought of lying helpless in bed, with no Blessington next door, and the possibility of Miss Schwarz guessing that Archie had told of her illness, filled him with awful apprehension. She might come screaming down the passage, with her claw-like hands starving for Archie's face.

"Oh, William, don't leave me till Blessington comes back," he entreated.

"No, sir, of course I won't. There, let me undo your shoes for you. You've got the laces in a knot."

"And she won't hurt Blessington either?" asked Archie.

"Bless you, no sir," said William. "And there's your night-shirt. Now jump into bed, and I'll open the windows."

William put out the light, and Archie, with a delicious sense of security seeing him seated by the fire, dozed off. Once, just before he got fairly to sleep, an awful vision of Miss Schwarz's red face came across the field of his closed eyelids, and he started up. But in a moment William was by him.

"It's all right, sir," he said. "I'm on the look out."

* * * * *

There was a decided air of mystery concerning Miss Schwarz next morning. She was better, but she remained unseen, and nobody would answer any questions about her. But in the afternoon Archie met Walter and the odd man carrying her luggage downstairs, and he gleaned the information that she was going away, and again, later in the day, Archie saw a housemaid coming out of her bedroom with a basket full of her medicine-bottles, and he drew the conclusion that she must have been ill a long time without anybody knowing. Not a syllable of news could he obtain from anybody, and, as the image of Miss Schwarz faded now that her dark, ill-omened presence was withdrawn, there was left in Archie's mind no more than a general sense of some connection between screaming voices, red faces, indistinct utterance, and the drinking of yellow medicine out of a large glass, instead of the usual small one.

There was a pleasant holiday sense for a few days after the departure of Miss Schwarz, for Marjorie took Jeannie's and Archie's lessons, which made a perfect festival of learning; but immediately almost came the ominous news that a new governess was coming next day. Archie believed that Miss Schwarz was a typical specimen of the genus governess, who were all probably in league together, and that some colleague of Miss Schwarz's, bent on avenging her, would render his own security a very precarious matter. It was, indeed, some consolation to know that Miss Bampton was a personal friend of his mother's and was not a "regular" governess at all but was just going to stay at Lacebury and teach lessons; yet Archie wondered, when he went downstairs on the morning after her arrival, whether he would not detect, under the guise of his mother's friend, some secret agent of Miss Schwarz.

Jeannie had lately been promoted to have breakfast with the rest of the family, and as Archie opened the door he heard a burst of laughter. There was Miss Schwarz's secret agent sitting next his father, and she it must have been who had made them all laugh, for she was not laughing herself, and Archie already knew that a joke was laughed at most by the people who hadn't made it. She was a little roundabout person, with blue eyes and a short nose and pincenez, and she got up as he entered.

"And is this Archie?" she said. "Why, I always thought of Archie as a baby. And here's an able-bodied seaman! How are you, Archie?"

Archie stared a moment. He reviewed his suspicion about governesses in general, but certainly if this plump, genial female was a secret colleague of Miss Schwarz her disguise was of the most ingenious kind. But it was as well to be careful.

"I'm quite well, thank you," he said, and, perceiving that a kiss had been intended, presented a sideways cheek. Miss Bampton made a sucking sound against it, and sat down again.

"Well, as I was saying," she went on, "the only plan of teaching is the co-operative principle. There are such heaps of jolly things to learn, that if the girls and I have a meeting, as I suggested, after breakfast, I'm sure we can find plenty of subjects between us. So I summon the meeting for a quarter past ten in the school-room."

Archie suddenly felt he was being left out. A meeting to discuss what you were going to learn sounded most promising in the way of lessons. He ran round to his mother's side.

"Oh, mummy, may I go to the meeting?" he said.

"You must ask Miss Bampton," said she.

Archie stifled his sense of distrust, for he wanted tremendously to go to a meeting where you settled what you were going to learn. He hated lessons, in the ordinary acceptation of that term, with their tiresome copy-books, in which he had to write the same moral maxim all down the page, and the stupid exercise—called French lesson—in which he had to address himself to a cat, and say in French "of a cat," "to a cat," "with the female cat," "with the male cat," and a thing called geography, which was a brown book with lists of countries and capital towns in it. But co-operative lessons, though he had no idea what co-operation meant, sounded far more attractive.

"May I come to the meeting, Miss Bampton?" he said.

"Yes, my dear, of course," said Miss Bampton, "if your mother will let you."

CHAPTER III

Thereupon there dawned for Archie a great light. Hitherto his lessons had been conducted by his mother, with occasional tuition from his father, and they had always made the impression that they were tasks, not difficult in themselves, but dull. He had learned the various modes of access in French to male and female cats, he had grasped the fact that Rome and not Berlin was the capital of Italy, and Paris not Vienna the capital of France. But these pieces of information were mere disconnected formulae, lessons, in other words, which had to be learned, and which, if imperfectly learned, caused him to be called lazy or inattentive. In the same way, the fact that he had to write in a laborious round hand all down the page "To be good is to be happy" meant nothing more than the necessity of filling the page without a plethora of blots or erasures. But from the date of this exciting meeting on co-operative learning, a whole new horizon dawned on him. It was settled at once that he was to do his lessons with Miss Bampton, and from that moment they ceased to be lessons at all. Instead of the lists of countries and capitals to be learned by heart, there was provided a jig-saw puzzle of the map of Europe, and Italy became a leg and foot, perpetually kicking Sicily, and Rome the button through which Italy's bootlace passed. And, instead of the dreary copy-book maxims heading each page, Miss Bampton, in a hand quite as perfect as Mr. Darnell's, wrote the most stimulating sentiments on the top of each blank leaf. "He would not sit down, so we bit him" was one, and Archie, with the tip of his tongue at the corner of his mouth, an attitude which is almost indispensable to round-hand orthography, was filled with delightful conjectures as to who the person was who would not sit down, and who were those tigerish people who bit him in consequence. And then Miss Bampton had the most delightful plans of where lessons might be done. One day, when it was snowing hard, she conceived the brilliant plan of doing lessons in the motor in the garage, which gave the most extraordinary stimulus to the proceedings, for early English history was the lesson that morning, and so she and Archie and Jeannie were royal Anglo-Saxons, specially invited to come in their coach to the coronation of William the Conqueror (1066), and it would never do if, at the Coronation banquet afterwards, he asked them questions about their ancestors and they didn't know. Another day, when the sun shone frostily, and the lawn was covered with hoar-frost they wrapped themselves up in furs, and worked at geography, as Laplanders, in the summer-house. Marjorie was too old to need such spurs to industry, but Miss Bampton had enticing schemes for her also, giving her verse translations of Heine and Goethe, and encouraging her to see how near she got to the original when she translated them back into their native tongue.

The Christmas holidays, looked forward to with such eager expectation in the baleful reign of Miss Schwarz, drew near; but now, instead of counting the hours till the moment when Miss Schwarz, safe in the motor, would blow claw-fingered kisses to them, the children got up a Round Robin (or rather, a triangular Robin, which Marjorie translated into German), begging Miss Bampton to stop with them for the holidays. For she was as admirable in play-time as she was over their lessons: she told them enchanting stories on their walks, and painted for them in real smelly oil-paints the most lovely snow-scenes, pine-woods laden with whiteness, and cottages with red blinds lit from within. Never had any one such a repertory of games to be played in the long dark hours between tea and bed-time, and it was during one of these that Archie made a curious discovery.

The game in question was "Animal, Vegetable, or Mineral?" One of them thought of anything in heaven or earth or in the waters under the earth, and the rest, by questions answered only by "Yes" or "No," had to arrive at it. On this occasion Miss Bampton had thought: it was known to be Animal and not in the house.

Archie was sitting on the floor in the school-room leaning against Miss Bampton's knee. He had been staring at the coals, holding Miss Bampton's hand in his, when suddenly there came over him precisely the same sensation that he remembered feeling one night, years ago, when he woke and imagined himself and the night-nursery expanding and extending till they embraced all that existed. That sensation throbbed and thrilled through him now, and he said:

"Oh, Miss Bampton, how easy! Why, it's the longest tail-feather of the thrush that Cyrus killed."

"Oh, Archie, don't guess," said Jeannie. "It's no use just guessing."

"But it is!" said Archie. "I'm not guessing. I know. Isn't it, Miss Bampton?"

It certainly was, and so, by the rules of the game, since it had been guessed in under five minutes, Miss Bampton had to think again. But now Archie tried in vain to recapture the mood that made Miss Bampton's mind so transparently clear to him. He knew what that mood felt like, that falling away of the limitations of consciousness, that expansion and extension of himself; but he could not feel it; it would not come by effort on his part; it came, he must suppose, as it chose, like a sneeze…

As Christmas drew near another amazing talent of Miss Bampton's showed itself. Marjorie had been up to London one day, to combine the pains of the dentist with the pleasure of a play, and came back with a comforted tooth and the strong desire to act. Instantly Miss Bampton rose to the occasion.

"Let's get up a play to act to your father and mother on New Year's night," she said.

"Oh, it would be fun," said Marjorie. "But what play could we act?"

"I'll write you one," said Miss Bampton. And write it she did, with a speed and a lavishness of plot that would have astonished more deliberate dramatists. There was a villain, a usurper king (Miss Bampton); there was a fairy (Marjorie); there was the rightful and youthful king (Archie); who lived (Act I) in painful squalor in a dungeon, attended only by the jailer's daughter (Jeannie) who knew his identity and loved him, whether he was in a dungeon or on a throne. Luckily, he loved her too, anywhere, and they were kind to a beggar-woman, who turned out to be the fairy, and did the rest. Miss Bampton was consigned to the lowest dungeon, and everybody else lived happily ever afterwards.

Then came the question of dresses, and Marjorie rather thoughtlessly exclaimed:

CHAPTER III

"I'm sure mother will let me have her Abracadabra clothes for the fairy. Oh—I forgot," she added, remembering that Archie was present.

There was an attempt (feeble, so Archie thought it) on the part of Miss Bampton to explain this away. She said that Abracadabra kept a suit of birthday clothes in every house she visited. Archie received the information quite politely, said, "Oh, I see," and remained wholly incredulous. His faith in the Abracadabra myth had tottered before; this was the blow that finally and completely compassed its ruin, and it disappeared in the limbo of discredited imaginings, like the glassy sea between the rugs in the hall, and the snarl of the tigers at his enemies. Never again would the combined crash of the servant's dinner-bell and the Chinese gong make him wonder at the magnificence of Abracadabra's sneezings, and when the play arrived at the stage of dress-rehearsal it was no shock to see Marjorie in Abracadabra's poke-bonnet and bediamonded bodice.

But it must not be supposed that, with the disappearance of those childish illusions, the world became in any way duller or less highly coloured to Archie; it grew, on the contrary, more and more fairy-like. The outburst of spring that year filled him with an ecstasy that could best be expressed by running fast and jumping in the air with shouts of joy. The unfolding of gummy buds on the horse-chestnut by the lake filled him with a rapture all the keener because he could not comprehend it; presently, the sight of pale green five-fingered leaves, weak as new-dropped lambs, made him race round and round Blessington till she got giddy. There was a smell of damp earth in the air, of young varnished grass-blades pushing up among the discoloured and faded foliage of the lawn, and, for the hard bright skies or the sullen clouds of winter, a new and tender blue was poured over the heavens, and clouds white as washed fleeces pursued one another aloft, even as their shadows bowled over the earth beneath. Birds began to sing again, and sparrows, chattering in the ivy, pulled straws and twigs about, practising for the nest-building time which would soon be upon them. A purplish mist hung over the birch-trees, and soon it changed to a mist of green as the buds expanded. Violets hidden behind their leaves bedecked the lane-sides, and one morning the first primrose appeared. Last year, no doubt, and in all preceding springs the same things had happened; but now for the first time they were significant, and penetrated further than the mere field of vision. They filled Archie with an unreasoning joy.

Anything in the shape of natural history received strong encouragement from Lord Davidstow, as well as anything (Archie did not fully grasp this) that tended to keep him out of doors when his short lessons were done, and he and Jeannie started this year a series of joint collections. Certain rules had to be observed: flowers that they picked must be duly pressed and mounted on sheets of cartridge paper, and their names must be ascertained. One bird's egg might be taken in the absence of the mother-bird from any nest which contained four, and must be blown and put in its labelled cell in the egg-cabinet; but when three specimens of any sort had been collected, no more must be acquired. That, perhaps, was the collection Archie liked best, though the joys of the aquarium ran it close. The aquarium was a big bread-bowl lined at the bottom with spa and crystals, and in it lived caddis-worms and water-snails and a dace—probably weak in the head, for he had allowed himself to be caught in the landing-net without the least effort to get out of the way. He had an inordinate passion for small bread-pills, in pursuit of which he was so violently active that he often hit his nose against the side of the aquarium so hard that you could positively hear the stunning blow. When satiated he would still continue to rush after bread-pills, but, after holding them in his mouth a moment, he would expel them again with such force that he resembled some submarine discharging torpedoes.

Then there was the butterfly and moth collection, which was of short duration, and was abandoned on account of a terrible happening. The insects were emptied into the killing-bottle, and when dead transfixed with a pin, and set. But one morning Archie, examining the setting-board to see if they were stiff and ready to be transferred into the cork-lined boxes, found, to his horror, that, so far from being stiff, two butterflies, a tortoiseshell and a brimstone, were alive still, with waving antennae and twitching bodies. That dreadful incident poisoned the joy of that collection; he felt himself guiltier of a worse outrage than Cyrus, and all Blessington's well-meant consolations that insects hardly felt anything at all would not induce him to run the risk of committing further atrocities. For a day and a night the two had writhed under their crucifixion, and that day the caterpillars were released from their breeding-cage (even including that piece of preciousness, the caterpillar of the convolvulus hawk with a horn on his tail), and the killing-bottle was relegated to the attic.

The Sunday church-goings for which an intermission had been ordained in consequence of Archie's infant remarks about the amusingness of the man with the wagging beard, had long ago been resumed again, and this year he had a sudden attack of spurious and sentimental religion that caused his mother some little anxiety. He developed a dreadful conscience, and came to her with a serious face and confessed trivial wrong-doings. (This phase, she comforted herself to think, occurred in the autumn of this year, at a time when there was nothing much to be done in the way of collecting.) One morning Archie came to her with a crime that sorely oppressed him. Nearly two years ago, somebody had sent her a painted Easter egg, an ostrich's egg, adorned with gilt designs of a cross and a crown and some rays, which Archie had been forbidden to touch.

"I touched it," he said. "I wetted my finger and rubbed it on the crown, and some of it came off."

"Well, dear, of course you shouldn't have done it, if I had told you not to," she said. "But don't bother about it any more. What made you come and tell me so long after?"

Archie grew more solemn still.

"I was leaning out of the nursery-window," he said, "and I heard Charles singing 'A few more years shall roll.' So I came and told you before I 'was asleep within the tomb.'"

His mother laughed, quite as if she was amused.

"We'll hope there'll be more than a few years before that, darling," she said.

"And shall I be forgiven now I've told you?" asked Archie.

"Yes, of course. Don't think anything more about it."

Archie would have preferred a more sentimental treatment of his offence, and rather wished his mother bore a stronger resemblance to Mrs. Montgomery, in the *Wide, Wide World*, whose edifying tears fell so fast and frequently, and after this he tended to keep his misdeeds more to himself and repent of them in secret. Simultaneously also the copy of the *Wide, Wide World*, which he had discovered in a passage book-case, mysteriously vanished, and no one appeared to have the slightest idea where it had gone. So, unable to stuff himself further with that brand of mawkishness, the desire that his mother should be more like Mrs. Montgomery faded somewhat, and there seemed but little pleasure in repentance at all, if your confessions were received in so unsentimental a manner, and it was no fun really keeping them to oneself. But for some weeks Sunday morning service in church (he had expressed a wish to go to evening church as well, but his mother had told him that once was as much as was good for him) became the emotional centre of his life, though his religion was strangely mixed up with a far more mundane attraction. There was a particular choir-boy there with blue eyes, pink cheeks, and a crop of yellow curls who sang solos, and thrilled Archie with a secret and perfectly sexless emotion. Only last Sunday he had sung "Oh, for the wings of a dove," and religion and childish adoration together had brought Archie to the verge of tears. He longed to be good, to live, until a few more years should roll (for he felt that he was going to die young), a noble and beautiful life; he longed also to fly away and be at rest with the choir-boy. He made up pathetic scenes in which he should be lying on his death-bed, with his weeping family round him, and the choir-boy would sing to him as he died, and they would smile at each other. When this vision proved almost too painful for contemplation he would console himself by picturing an alternative scheme, in which there were to be no death-beds at all, but instead he would get into the church choir, and sit next the choir-boy, and they would sing duets together before a rapt congregation. But, adorable though his idol was, he did not really want to know him, or even find out who he was. The idol existed for him in some remote sphere, becoming incarnate just for an hour on Sunday morning, a golden-haired surpliced voice, that suggested the vanished thrills of the *Wide, Wide World*. He pronounced certain words rather oddly, and had a slight lisp which Archie tried to copy, until one day his father told him never to say "Yeth" again, or he should write out "Yes" a hundred times.

Then came the most exciting discovery: this vocal angel proved to be the son of the head-keeper, and it was therefore perfectly easy to make his acquaintance. The notion of meeting him face to face, of exchanging a "good-morning" with him was almost overpowering, and yet Archie instinctively shrank from bringing the idol into contact with actual life. He began to choose for his walk the rather dank and gloomy path that led past the keeper's cottage, and yet, when that abode where the idol lived came within sight, Archie, with beating heart would avert his eyes, for fear he should see him. Then one day, as they got opposite the gate, a small boy in corduroy knickerbockers with a rather greasy scarf round his neck and a snuffling nose came out, and touched his cap. There could be no doubt about his identity, and Archie suffered the first real disillusionment of his life. The fading of Abracadabra was nothing to this: that had been a gradual disillusionment, whereas this was sudden as a lightning-stroke. He was a shattered idol, and from that moment Archie could hardly recall what it had been about, or recapture the faintest sense of the emotion which had filled him before that encounter in the wood which caused it to reel and totter and fall prone from its unsubstantial pedestal. This blow, on the top of the robust reception of his confession, did much to restore Archie to the ways of normal boyhood, and it was really rather a relief to his mother, when his expanding experimenting nature took a very different turn, and he became for a time obstreperously naughty. She thought, quite rightly, that this evinced a greater vigour. That it undoubtedly did, and the imagination contained in some of Archie's exploits rivalled the more visionary power that constructed death-bed scenes for himself and the idealization (cruelly shattered) of the choir-boy.

One very dreary November afternoon, shortly after his seventh birthday, he was sitting alone in his mother's room. All day the sullen heavens had poured their oblique deluge on the earth, and sheets of water were being flung against the windows by the cold south-easterly gale. Archie was suffering from a slight cold, and had not been out of doors for a couple of days, and this unusual detention in the house had caused him to be very cross, and also had dammed up within him a store of energy which could not disperse itself innocuously in violent movement. Jeannie had gone for a motor-drive with his mother, Marjorie and Miss Bampton were closely engaged over their rotten German, and Archie that morning had been stingingly rebuked by his father for sliding down the banisters in the hall, a mode of progress strictly forbidden. Blessington had not been less stinging, for an hour ago Archie had been extremely rude to her, and, with a dignity that he both respected and resented, she had said, "Then I've nothing more to say to you, Master Archie, till you've remembered your manners again." And had thereupon continued her sewing.

Archie knew he had been rude, but his sense of that was not yet strong enough to enable him to apologize, though of sufficient energy to make him feel woebegone and neglected. He had been allowed by his mother to sit in her room that afternoon, when she went out with Jeannie, and to investigate what was known as her "work-box," which contained her "treasures." In earlier days these had been a source of deep delight: there was a minute china elephant with a silk palanquin on his back; there was a porcupine's quill, there was a set of dolls' tea-things, a pink umbrella, the ferrule of which was a pencil, a chain of amber. Once these had held magic for Archie: they were "mummy's treasures," and could only be seen on wet afternoons or in hours of toothache. But to-day they appeared to him perfectly rubbishy; not a gleam of glamour remained; they were as dull as the leaden skies of this interminable afternoon.

CHAPTER III

Archie lay in the window-seat, and wondered that his sailor-trousers only a year ago had given him so complete a sense of happiness. He rubbed one leg against the other, trying to recollect how it was that that rough serge against his bare calf felt so manly. He tried to interest himself in *Alice in Wonderland*, and marvelled that he could have cared about an adventure with a pack of cards. He longed to throw the book at the foolish Dresden shepherdess that stood on the mantelpiece. He supposed there would be trouble if he did, that his mother would be vexed, but trouble was better than this nothing-at-all. Probably it would rain again to-morrow, and he would have another day indoors, and the thought of Nothing Happening either to-day or to-morrow seemed the same as the thought of nothing happening for ever and ever.

There was a bright fire in the hearth and beyond the steel fender a thick hearthrug of long white sheep's wool. Suddenly Archie remembered the odour that diffused itself when, one day, a fragment of hot coal flew out of the fire, and lodged in this same hearthrug. There was a fatty, burning smell, most curious, and simultaneously the wild, irresistible desire of doing something positively wicked enthralled him. Instantly he knew what he was going to do, and with set, determined face, he took the fire-shovel in one hand and the tongs in the other, and heaped the shovel high with burning coals. He emptied them on the hearthrug.

The smoke of singeing, burning wool arose, and he took several more lumps of glowing coal from the fire-place and deposited them on the rug. Then a panic seized him, and he tried to stamp the conflagration out. But he only stamped the glowing coals more firmly in, and, though amazed at his audacity, he did not really want to extinguish it. He wanted something to happen. Quite deliberately, though with cheeks burning with excitement, he walked out of the room, leaving the door open, and simultaneously heard the crunch of the gravel under the wheels of his mother's returning motor. He did not wish to see her, and went straight to the night-nursery (now his exclusive bedroom) and locked himself in. But he was not in the least sorry for what he had done: if anything he wished he had put more coals there. Nor was he frightened at the thought of possible consequences. Merely, he did not care what happened, so long as something happened. That, he reflected, it was pretty certain to do. But he made no plans.

Before very long he heard some one turning the handle of his door, and he kept quite still. Then his father's voice said:

"Are you there, Archie?" And still he said nothing.

The voice grew louder and the handle rattled.

"Archie, open your door immediately," said his father.

Not in the least knowing why, Archie proceeded to do so. He still felt absolutely defiant and desperate, but for some instinctive reason he obeyed.

Enormous and terrible, his father stood before him.

"Did you put those coals on your mother's hearthrug?" asked Lord Davidstow.

"No," said Archie.

"Then how did you know they were there?" asked his father.

Archie had something of the joy of the desperate adventurer.

"Because I put them there," he said.

"Then you have lied to me as well."

"Yes," said Archie.

Lord Davidstow pointed to the door.

"Go downstairs at once," he said, "and wait in my study."

Archie obeyed, still not knowing why. At the top of the stairs was standing his mother, who took a step forward towards him.

"Archie, my darling—" she began.

"Leave the boy to me," said his father, who was following him. Archie marched downstairs, still without a tremor. It occurred to him that his father was going to kill him, as Cyrus killed the thrush. There was a whispered conversation between his mother and father and he heard his mother say, "No, don't, don't," and he felt sure that this referred to his being killed. But he was quite certain that, whatever happened, he was not going to say he was sorry.

He went into his father's study and shut the door. On the table he noticed that there was standing one of Miss Schwarz's medicine-bottles, and a syphon beside it, and wondered whether Miss Schwarz had come back. But there was no other sign of her.

In another moment his father entered.

"Now, you thoroughly deserve a good whipping, Archie," he said. "You might have burned the house down, and if you were a poor boy you'd have been put into prison for this. But your mother has been pleading for you, and, if you'll say you are sorry, and beg her pardon for burning her hearthrug, I'll let you off just this time."

Well, he was not going to be killed, but he was going to be whipped. Archie felt his heart beating small and fast with apprehension; but he was not sorry, and did not intend to say he was.

"Well?" said his father.

"I'm not sorry," said Archie.

"I'll give you one more chance," said his father, moving towards a cupboard above one of the bookcases.

"I'm not sorry," said Archie again.

His father opened the cupboard.

"Lock the door," he said.

But, before he could lock it, it was opened from without, and his mother entered. His father had already a cane in his hand, and he turned round as she came in. She looked at him and then at Miss Schwarz's medicine-bottle on the table.

"Go away, Marion," he said. "I'm going to give the boy a lesson."

She pointed at the bottle.

"You had better learn yours first," she said.

"Never mind that. Archie says he's not sorry. It is my duty to teach him."

Suddenly Archie felt tremendously interested. He had no idea what all this was about, or what his father's lesson was, but he felt he was in the presence of some drama apart from his own. It was with a sense of the interruption of this that he saw his mother turn to him.

"Archie, my dear," she said. "You have vexed and grieved me very much. Supposing I had felt wicked and had burned you stylograph pen, shouldn't I be sorry for having injured you? And aren't you sorry for having burned my hearthrug? What had I done to deserve that? Hadn't I given you leave to sit in my room, and look at my treasures? Why did you hurt me?"

Immediately the whole affair wore a different aspect. Instead of anger and justice, there was the sound of love. His heart melted, and he ran to her.

"Oh mummy, I didn't mean to vex you," he cried. "I didn't think of that. You hadn't done anything beastly to me."

He burst into tears.

"Oh, mummy, forgive me," he said. "I don't mind being whipped, at least not much; but I'm sorry; I beg your pardon. Please stop my allowance till I've paid for it."

"Yes, dear, it's only right that you should pay some of it. You shall have no more allowance for three weeks. Now go straight upstairs, and go to bed till I come to you and tell you that you may get up. And Blessington tells me you have been rude to her. Go and beg her pardon first."

* * * * *

The effect of this episode on Archie's mind was that his mother understood, and his father didn't. The prospect of a whipping had not made him falter in his resolve not to say he was sorry, so long as he wasn't sorry, but the moment his mother had put his misdeeds in a sensible light he saw them sensibly, and would not have minded being whipped if by that drastic method he could have borne witness to the reality of his sorrow. But only three days later he received six smart cuts with that horrible cane for climbing on to the unparapetted roof of the house out of his bedroom window, which he had been expressly forbidden to do. But then there was no question of being sorry or not—as a matter of fact he was not—summary justice was executed for mere disobedience, and, before doing the same thing again, he added up the pleasure of going on the roof, and balanced it against the pain inflicted on the tight seat of his sailor-trousers as he bent over a chair, and found it wanting.

It was during this same month which saw his seven completed years that he did a very strange and unintelligible thing, though he suffered it rather than committed it. He did it, that is to say, quite involuntarily, and did not know he was doing it till it was done. This was the manner of it.

Miss Bampton had set him one of her delightful exercises in handwriting in his copy-book. "Never brush your teeth with the housemaid's broom" she had written in her beautiful copper-plate hand at the top of the page, and Archie was sitting with his tongue out copying this remarkable maxim, and amusing himself with conjectures as to what other strange habits such people as were likely to brush their teeth with the housemaid's broom might be supposed to have—perhaps they would lace their boots with the tongs, or write their letters with a poker... He had got about half-way down the page when suddenly there came over him that sensation with which he was beginning to become familiar, that feeling of extension and expansion within himself, that falling away of the limitations of consciousness which opened some new interior world to him.

His pen paused, and then in the wrist of his right hand and in the fingers that still held his pen he felt a curious imperative kind of twitching, and knew that they wanted to write of their own volition, as it were, though it was not his copy that they were concerned with. Under this sensation of absolute compulsion, he took a sheet of paper that lay at his elbow, and let his pen rest on it, watching with the intensest curiosity what it would do. He had no idea what would happen, but he felt that something had to be written. For a couple of minutes perhaps his pen traced random lines on the paper, moving from left to right with a much greater speed than it was wont to go, and the letters began to form themselves with a rapidity and certainty unknown to his careful, halting calligraphy, and in firm upright characters. He saw his own name traced on the paper followed by a sentence, and then his pen (still apparently obedient to some unknown impulse from his fingers) gave a great dash and stopped altogether. And this is what he read:

"Archie, do let me talk to you sometimes.

"MARTIN."

The queer sensation had ceased altogether, and Archie stared blankly at the words that he knew his hand had written. But what they meant, he had no notion, nor did he know who Martin was. The whole thing was quite unintelligible to him, both the impulse that made him write, and that which he had written.

Miss Bampton had left the room on some errand, when she had set Archie his copy, and came back at this moment expecting to find the copy finished. She looked over his shoulder to see how he was getting on.

"My dear, haven't you got further than that?" she said. "I thought you would have finished it by this time."

She saw the other piece of paper half-concealed by Archie's left hand.

"Why, you've been writing something else," she said. "That's why you haven't got on further. Let me look."

"Please not," said Archie. "It's private."

Miss Bampton remembered that, a week ago, Archie had been seized with a strong desire for literary composition, and had composed a very remarkable short story, which may be given in full.

"CHAPTER I

"There was once a merderer with yellow eyes, and his wife said to him,

"'If you merder me you will be hung.'

"And he was hung on Tuesday next.

"FINIS."

When Archie had brought this yarn to her she had laughed so uncontrollably that he was hurt. So, in the hope of finding another such (though Archie had no business to write stories in lesson-time) she said:

CHAPTER III

"My dear, do show me; I won't laugh."

Archie hesitated; he felt shy about disclosing this sentence he had written, but, on the other hand, Miss Bampton, who appeared to know everything, might help him towards the interpretation.

"Well, it's not a story," he said. "It's just this. I wrote it without knowing. Oh, Miss Bampton, what does it mean, and who is Martin?"

If it was Archie who hesitated before, it was Miss Bampton who hesitated now. Suddenly she had a clever thought.

"My dear, you've been thinking about the Martins that built in the sandpit last spring," she said. "Don't you remember how you and Jeannie made up a story about them?"

This was true enough, but it failed to satisfy Archie. Also he had a notion that Miss Bampton had made a call on her ingenuity in offering this explanation.

"But isn't there any other Martin?" he asked.

"None that you ever knew, Archie," she said. "I think it's one of those in the sandpit. Now get on with your copy, and we'll walk there before your dinner."

The incident passed into the medley of impressions that were crowding so quickly into the storehouse of Archie's consciousness, but it did not lie there quite unconnected with others. He laid it on the same shelf, so to speak, as that which held the memory of his waking vision one night in remote days, and held also the fact of his knowing what Miss Bampton had thought of in the guessing game. But those were among the secret things of which he spoke to nobody. One more impression for secret pondering, though of different sort from those, he had lately added to his store, and that was when a whipping seemed imminent, and he saw one of Miss Schwarz's medicine-bottles standing on his father's table.

CHAPTER IV

Lady Davidstow and Miss Bampton were sitting together that night in Lady Davidstow's bedroom. She had sent her maid away, saying that she would not want her again that night, and now she held in her hand the sheet of paper covered with lines of meaningless scribbles, with the one intelligible sentence at the end, which Archie had written that day when he should have been doing his copy. In the other hand she held a letter written in ink that was now rather faded, and she was comparing the two. She looked at them for some time in silence, then turned to Miss Bampton.

"Yes, you are quite right, Cathie," she said. "What Archie wrote might actually be in Martin's handwriting. Look for yourself: there's the last letter he ever wrote to me."

Miss Bampton took the two papers from her.

"There's absolutely no difference," she said. "The moment I saw what Archie had written, I thought of Martin's handwriting. And then it was signed 'Martin.' Are you sure he has never heard of him? Not that that would account for the handwriting."

Lady Davidstow shook her head.

"I think it's impossible," she said. "Jeannie assured me she had never spoken to him about Martin, nor has Blessington. He may have heard his name. He probably has heard his name mentioned. I remember mentioning it in Archie's hearing the other day, but he didn't pay the slightest attention. And he can't possibly recollect him even in the vaguest way. It is five years now since Martin died, and Archie was then only just two, and for six months before that Martin was with me at Grives."

Cathie Bampton laid down the two papers.

"I can't think why you never told Archie about him," she said.

Lady Davidstow's great grey eyes grew dim.

"Ah, my dear, if you were Martin's mother and Archie's mother you would know," she said. "If you had seen your eldest son die of consumption and your second son threatened with it, you would understand how natural it was not to tell Archie yet of the brother he had never consciously seen. Jack agreed with me, too. I have long been prepared for Archie asking questions, which certainly I would answer truthfully, and let the knowledge come to him quietly by degrees. I may have done wrong; I don't know. But I think I did right. I couldn't begin saying to

Archie, 'You had a brother, but he died.' More would have come out; that he died of consumption; that for fear of that Archie lives so much in the open air."

"But, my dear, how will Archie begin to know unless you tell him?"

"Oh, in many ways. There is Martin's picture, for instance, in my room. Archie may ask who it is. Or, when he hears Martin's name mentioned, he will ask some time who Martin was. Indeed, I have often thought it odd that he hasn't. Only the other day Jack was talking to me about it, suggesting that it was time that Archie knew. Indeed, he rather urged me to tell him. And now, all of a sudden, we find Archie writing in Martin's handwriting, and signing with Martin's name."

"Shall you tell Lord Davidstow?" asked Miss Bampton.

"No, I certainly shall not. Jack hates all that approaches the neighbourhood of anything that might be called occult or spiritualistic. He says 'Pshaw,' as you know, if even hypnotism is mentioned. I did tell him about Archie's intuition in that guessing game, and, as you again know, he asked you not to play it any more, though at the same time he insisted that it was a mere guess on Archie's part."

Cathie was silent a moment.

"And those scribbles of Archie's?" she asked. "Do they not make it more difficult for you to tell him about Martin now? A sensitive boy like that might get it into his head that his dead brother was writing to him."

"Certainly I don't want Archie to think that," said his mother. "No, I shall put off telling him now."

"And if he asks?" said Miss Bampton.

"I have an idea that he won't ask."

She got up and moved about the room for a moment in silence.

"My dear, all children have got a secret life of their own," she said, "and, oh, how their mothers want to be admitted! But every young thing has a walled-up place in his heart, to which he admits nobody, and, if you ask to be admitted, not only is the door shut, but locked. We all had our secret places, and I make a guess that this bit of paper—by the way, mind you put it back in the school-room where Archie left it—lives in Archie's secret place. How I long to get in, the darling! But all I can do is to wait outside, and take what he gives me. Archie doesn't tell me everything, why should he? He didn't tell me what it was that made him put the burning coals out of the fire on to my hearthrug."

"Probably he didn't know."

"Something inside him knew, or else he wouldn't have done it. All we do is accountable for by what is inside us. Impulses come from within."

"But they are suggested by what is without," said Miss Bampton.

"Yes; that's the box on which the match is struck, but the fire is in the match. All you can do for a child, even your own child, is to suggest, and hope he'll take your suggestions."

Miss Bampton got up.

"It's late; I must go," she said. "But I want to ask you one thing. Do you believe in the possibility of Martin's having made a communication to Archie?"

"Yes; I think I do. That's why this affair has upset me so. The idea is so strange and new, that I'm frightened about it, though why I should be so I can't tell. With my whole heart I believe that my darling is living somewhere in an existence as individual as ever, and even more vivid, because the weakness and the illness and the weariness are past. So why should I be frightened at the thought that he could communicate with Archie? Ah, my dear, if only he would communicate with me! Or with Jack! Poor Jack, how he would scout the idea! How shocked he would be! I suppose that's part of my secret garden which I keep from Jack!"

She held her friend a moment after kissing her.

"Jack never really got over Martin's death," she said. "He couldn't bring himself into line with it. It was then that it became a settled habit with him to try to forget… Just lately he has been very bad. There, good-night, my dear; I can't talk about it."

* * * * *

The whole incident affected Archie far less than it affected either his mother or his governess, and next day when he found his scribbled paper lying where he had left it the day before, it excited no further curiosity in his mind. He put the thought of it away on his shelf of secret things which had nothing to do with his ordinary normal life. In certain moods, which, after all only lasted for a moment or two, the things that shelf contained became far more real to him than any other of his experiences; but for weeks and months at a time its contents remained out of his reach, and if he shared them, as his mother had said, with nobody else, he had no share in them himself except at these odd, queer moments. So when, next day, he came across this curious sentence again, caught by him, as by some process of wireless telegraphy, he felt but little interest in it, though he sat for a couple of minutes with his pen held idly in his hand, just to see if anything else happened. But there was no sensation that ever so faintly resembled the twitching and yearning of his hand to write he knew not what, and he crumpled the paper up, and put it into the fire. Somewhere below the threshold of his conscious self lay the perceptions that were concerned with it, those perceptions that guessed what Miss Bampton had thought of, that somehow swam up to the surface, as he used to lie in bed of a morning, and sink into the depths that lay below the green-tinted ceiling of his room; and, while they lay dormant, it was as if they never existed.

But now for some weeks there had been no light whatever on his ceiling, and morning after morning he awoke with no sense of exhilaration at all in the coming of another day, but with a drowsy depression lying thick upon him, as he heard the rustle of the endless rain in the shrubs outside, and languidly went through those exercises that used to invigorate him but now only tired him. All through the month the damp chilly weather persisted, and day after day the same lowering heavens obscured the sun; never in this bright Sussex upland had there been so continuous a succession of rain-streaked hours. The wonder of seeing the lake slowly rising till it engulfed the lower end of the lawn, and made an island of the summer-house failed to stir him, and there was no magic in the unique experience of punting across the lawn to it. Then, one morning early in December, the deluge was stayed, once more the sun slid up a cloudless sky, and the whole nature of the world was changed.

Archie had again been indoors for a couple of days, with a return of the cold that really was responsible for the burning of his mother's hearthrug, and once more the ecstasy of living possessed him. As consolation for his imprisonment, he and Jeannie were both given a holiday, and, breakfast over, they scampered out, and once more saw their shadows racing in front of them. The game was to tread on somebody else's shadow. Blessington's shadow did not count because anybody could tread on that; but it required real agility to tread on Jeannie's, for it had the nippiest way of dodging before your foot could really descend on it. So they ran in circles round Blessington, and Marco, the collie, ran in circles round them; and though it counted two to tread on Marco's shadow (you must not hold Marco and then stamp on his shadow), no one had got nearer than a doubtful claim to have trod on his tail.

Quite suddenly Archie stopped; he had an odd, warm sensation in his mouth that required investigation. Two days ago Jeannie's nose had bled, which Archie thought rather grand. There had been rather a fuss about it: she was laid down on the floor, and Miss Bampton put the door-key down her back, and eventually some ice was brought, and it was all quite important. But now it was not his nose that was bleeding, but his mouth.

"Oh, I say, I'm bleeding in my mouth," he said. "That's just as good as Jeannie's nose."

Even while he spoke he felt rather giddy, and instantly Blessington's arm was round him.

"Eh, my dear," she said. "That'll never do. You lean against me, and we'll go home very quietly. You mustn't chase any more shadders this morning."

As a matter of fact, Archie did not want to. He felt a rather enjoyable lightness in his head, but he felt weak also, and disinclined to run.

"Oh, here it is again," he said, and once more, now with a sensation of choking, he coughed up blood.

He saw Blessington's tender, anxious face above him, exactly as it had appeared in the earliest of all his memories, and, as then, felt absolutely comfortable in the thought that she was there. Her arm was close round his neck now, and with her other hand she made a sign to Jeannie.

"Run straight back home, dear," she said, "and tell your mamma to come out here at once, and bring William. Master Archie and I are going to sit down quietly till she comes."

Archie rather enjoyed all this. He was completely in Blessington's hands, and utterly content to be so. Then Blessington did a very odd thing.

"Well, I'm so hot with seeing you and Miss Jeannie running about," she said, "that I'm going to sit down, and wait for a bit. And you'll wait with me, dear, won't you? There! Put your head on my knee and lie down. I know you're hot with running about."

As by a conjuring trick, Archie knew that Blessington's cloak with its collar of rabbit's fur was tucked round him. It was rather odd to be lying with his head on Blessington's knee out of doors in the winter, but he had no desire to question the propriety of all this, for it fitted in so well with his main desire, which was to stop still. A couple of minutes ago he had been running about at top-speed; now he had no wish except to do as he was told, to put himself into responsible hands. It was all rather dreamlike; his mother and William were coming here soon, but that seemed quite natural. And it was still rather grand to bleed at the mouth. Then came a gentle singing in his ears, a pleasant sense of complete indolence, that never quite passed into unconsciousness, and presently it was just as natural to find himself in William's arms. Out of a half-opened eye he saw William was in livery, for the blue and white stripes of his low waistcoat were close to him, and his cheek rested on William's shirt-front. And then he saw that there was a bright red stain there which certainly was not part of William's ordinary livery.

"Oh, William, I've messed you," he said. "I am sorry."

"That's all right, Master Archie," said William. "It wasn't a new shirt this morning."

Some dim reminiscence about something William had told him concerning beer-money and washing came into his head. William had beer-money or washing; he could not remember which.

"I shall pay for it anyhow," he said.

Still feeling rather dizzy, he had the impression of his own room with Blessington and his mother near him. Apparently he had been laid on the floor, for his bed looked tall beside him. Then he was not on the floor any more, but in his bed, and whether it was at once or later, he never knew, but presently there was in the room the stranger who once had made him play the pointless game of saying "ninety-nine!" Here he was again with a plug against Archie's chest, and two other plugs in his own ears. Archie remembered him quite distinctly: he was a doctor who didn't give any medicine.

"Shall I say 'ninety-nine'?" he asked.

"No, just think 'ninety-nine,' and don't talk. If you think 'ninety-nine' it will do just as well."

Archie had no desire to do anything beyond what he was told to do. He thought "ninety-nine," and the stranger smiled very kindly at him.

"That's capital," he said. "Now just go on thinking 'ninety-nine'..." and whether he floated out of the window, or vanished like the Cheshire cat, or walked away in the ordinary manner, Archie was quite unaware.

Then he was hungry, and, behold, there was Blessington with boiled rabbit, and he was sleepy and hungry again, and again sleepy. Sometimes his mother was there, and sometimes his father, who looked rather odd, and sometimes William brought coals, though the housemaid usually did that; and there was Blessington again, who washed his face, and then, uncovering him limb by limb, washed these also. Archie could not understand why he acquiesced in this odd state of things, or why he did not ask to get up and run about and play the shadow-game again. But merely he was quite content to lie still, and he hoped that when Jeannie came and talked to him she would not suggest the resumption of the game that had been so ecstatic but had been interrupted so suddenly. And Miss Bampton came in, and read to him something she had been writing. He noticed that she read from printed pages, not like the pages of an ordinary book, but long strips. It appeared that it was a story she had written which had got printed, and he asked whether his story about "the merderer" would ever get printed. They all came in, and talked gently and melted away again.

Then arrived a memorable morning when, instead of being gently awakened by Blessington, he awoke entirely of his own accord, and felt strong and cross. Cross he certainly proved to be, for when the morning washing began, which hitherto had been a pleasant and luxurious performance, he found that Blessington could do nothing right. She put soap into his eyes, she tickled his feet and scratched his shoulder with her disgusting flannel. Archie made firm complaints against each of these outrages, of a sort that would usually lead to rebuke on Blessington's part. Indeed, he had not been nearly so rude on the occasion when he had been told to apologize to her.

But now she merely beamed at each disagreeable remark, and, instead of scolding him, she made a most cryptic answer.

"Eh, my darling," she said. "Thank God you feel like blaming me again."

"What *do* you mean, Blessington?" said Archie angrily. "Oh, do take care of my little toe. You've nearly pulled it off once already."

"Well then, I'll kiss it," said Blessington. And did.

Archie looked at her.

"Why are you crying?" he asked, wriggling his foot away from her. He did not want it to be kissed.

"Crying? I'm just laughing," said Blessington. And that was true; she was laughing. But she was crying also.

An idea struck Archie which had not occurred to him before.

"Am I ill, Blessington?" he asked. "Am I going to die?"

At that there was no question of what Blessington was doing. Her laughing quite ceased, and she gave a great sob.

"No, my darling, you're not going to die," she said. "Get that out of your silly head. You're not..."

And then she broke down altogether, and hid her face in the towel with which she had been washing Archie's left foot. He saw her shoulders shaking; he knew that, for some reason, she could not speak. But she was crying, and was not cross with him for being cross. It behoved a man to administer consolation.

"Oh, don't cry, Blessington," he said. "What is there to cry about? Unless it's because I'm so cross."

"I don't mind your crossness," she said. "You let me finish wiping your foot. And then I'll go down and tell your mamma—"

"Oh, don't say I was cross," said Archie. "I'm sorry I was cross."

"Nay, I'll just tell her how much better you feel this morning. And I shouldn't wonder if there was a great treat coming, something you'll like ever so much."

"Is it another train?" asked Archie.

"Bless the boy!" said she. "How you think about trains!"

* * * * *

Archie ate his breakfast, and passed an entrancing morning. Everybody seemed desirous of congratulating him, as if he had done something particularly meritorious, as on the occasion of his not getting drowned when he jumped out of the boat after the pike. He held a sort of levee, the most remarkable incident of which was the appearance of Miss Bampton with a piece of white chalk, with which she drew on the green drugget by his bed, so that he could easily see it, a great map of England and Central Europe. There was the South of England, with London written large, and here was Lacebury also conspicuously marked. Then there was the English Channel with France below it, and Paris in the middle, and away to the right, some distance below, the Lake of Geneva. Then, still explaining, she made marks like caterpillars which were mountains, and said that now the mountains were covered with snow, even down to the tails of the caterpillars and below was the Lake of Geneva, quite blue. All the roads were covered with snow up by the caterpillars' tails, and there were no wheels on the carriages, but they slid over the frozen snow instead. There was skating up there, for they made lakes which were covered with ice. They just put water into flat places, and there was your lake, and it instantly froze. It never rained there, but if it wanted to do anything, it just snowed. Usually it didn't want to do anything, and there was the sun and the snow, and wouldn't it be jolly to go there?

This presented itself to Archie's mind as a purely abstract proposition. Of course it would be jolly to go to a place where you saw the real mountains and had a glimpse of the real Lake of Geneva, and slid instead of walking; but what next? Did any one ever go there?

Apparently. Right at the tail of the caterpillar was a place called Grives. There it was, written down: the railway only went as far as Bex, and there the sledges began. And always the sun shone, so that you sat out of doors with the snow all round you, and felt perfectly warm.

Suddenly Archie could stand it no longer. It was like talking to a starving man about roast beef. There was roast beef somewhere in the world, and he wanted it so badly. In the same way something inside Archie starved for sun and snow and thin air.

"Oh, shut up, Miss Bampton," he said. "I want it so frightfully."

His mother was sitting on the edge of his bed watching the map of Europe.

"Archie, we're going to Grives in a few days," she said. "You and Blessington and Jeannie and I."

* * * * *

It was memorable moment when the boat rose up and then curtsied to the big seas that were jostling each other up the Channel. Archie's only knowledge of the sea was culled from a single visit to Brighton two years ago, and the sea to him then appeared but one among an assembly of unusual bright objects: nigger-minstrels and tin buckets and piers and penny-in-the-slot machines. But on this bright winter day he hailed a new and glorious creature, when he saw the steep white-capped waves, grey in the bulk but lit with lovely green where they grew thin, come streaming up to the ship's side and fall away again in puffs of white smoke and squirts of high-flung foam. Warmly wrapped up in his new fur-coat, he sat on deck sheltered from the weather and watched with ecstatic wonder the rollicking, untamed creatures that sent the boat now over on one side, now on the other, and threw it up and caught it again within their firm, liquid embrace. Behind it lay a wake of white foam, like a long string still tying them to dazzling chalk cliffs and the wave-smothered pier, and overhead the masts, thrumming to the wind, struck right and left across a wide arc of the sky, and their shadows sped across the deck. These swervings and upliftings and descents of the ship as she whacked her way across the shifting mountains produced in him no physical discomfort, but only the sense that a new and glorious being had come into his life.

All too soon, even as the jig-saw puzzle of the map of Europe had warned him by the narrowness of the straits, the shores of France began to rear themselves up above the wave-moulded horizon, and presently another pier received them, and men spoke a strange tongue (probably French, though it might have been Hebrew) and made novel gestures, and wore blouses, and boots that turned up at the toes more than was usual in England. There were no platforms: you had to climb the sheer carriage side from ground-level, and the engines were altogether different, and the movement of the train was other than that he was accustomed to. Then, sure enough, they came after nightfall to a great town, and drove across it, keeping firmly to the wrong side of the road, though, as everybody else did the same, there were not so many collisions as might have been expected. Then came the novelty of eating dinner in a restaurant perched up in another station, from the windows of which you could romantically observe train after train sliding out into the winter night. Before long Archie's train did the same, and then came the glorious experience of undressing in a train, while it was going at full speed. There was never so remarkable a bedroom, all gold and looking-glass and stamped leather, and instead of his bed and Blessington's being put on the floor, one, which Archie begged to have, was put above the other. Close by him in the roof of the carriage was the electric light which, when you turned a small handle the requisite distance, dwindled to a mere speck. At some timeless hour he woke up, and found a very polite stranger in his bedroom, to whom Blessington explained that they had neither spirits nor lace nor tobacco in their luggage. And the total stranger then apparently guessed that he had been misinformed, for he went away again without another word.

The clever train found its way without any mistake through the darkness of the long winter's night, for next morning it was skimming along by the edge of a lake so large that no wonder it appeared on the jig-saw map of Europe. The lake at home, once an almost boundless sheet of water, was no more than a wayside puddle to this; the hills at home were no more than the tunnelled earth of moles compared with those slopes on which the rows of pines looked smaller than the edging of a table-cloth against the blue. Blue? Archie thought he had never known what blue was till now, not what sunshine was until he saw the dazzle of it on those sparkling slopes. And they, so his mother told him, were not mountains at all: they were only hills; but soon he should see what mountains meant. As they passed through the glittering towns that stood on the edge of the lake, he could see the sleighs sliding over the streets with jingle of bells crisply sounding in the alert air. Other smaller sleighs were drawn by pleased, smiling dogs. There was never such a morning of discoveries. The only drawback was that, though it ought only to have been ten o'clock, the Swiss chose that it should be eleven, and thus an hour of this immortal day was lost; but his mother told him that the French had taken care of it, and would give it back to them when they returned.

All this was romantic enough, but the romance grew more deep-hued yet when, in the early afternoon, Archie was packed into a sleigh and the journey up through the pine-woods began. White-capped and white-cloaked stood the red-trunked trees, and now and then, with a falling puff of snow, a laden branch, free of its burden, sprang upwards again. Then the pines were tired of climbing, and the sleigh left them and came out on to a plateau high above the valley. And could that have been sunshine down there? For the valley seemed choked with grey fog, and here above was real sunshine and air that refreshed you as with wine. The hills that had appeared so gigantic had sunk below them, but behind them rose the spears and precipices, remote and blue, of the real mountains, and, as they went upwards, these soared ever above them, and presently the blue on them was tinged with apricot and rose in the glow of the declining sun. And the driver cracked his whip, and the horses jingled their bells in response, and, pointing with it to a row of toy houses still far above them, he grinned at Archie and said "Grives."

The rose of sunset had faded and the snows were turned to ivory-crystal beneath the full moon when they entered the long, lit village street, with its old carved wooden houses, deep-balconied towards the south, and the modern hotels now just opening again for the winter season. These, too, they left behind them, and again mounting a steep slope, came to where, round a sudden corner, stood the big chalet which Archie's mother had taken.

"And here we are," she said.

Archie sat staring. Somehow he felt he knew the house; perhaps it was a house he had dreamed of. There were pines to right and left of it, just as there were in this picture of a house that existed somewhere in his mind; it had the same broad balconies, where you could lie all day in the sun, and look over the village roofs below and across the valley from which all afternoon they had climbed. He felt he knew it inside too: there would be rooms with wooden walls, and china stoves—where had he heard of china stoves?—and the smell of pine-wood haunting all the house. It was extraordinarily interesting…

CHAPTER IV

A big, genial woman had turned up the electric light outside the door when she heard the crack of the driver's whip, and stood bareheaded, ready to welcome them. Archie felt that he knew something about her too.

"Ah, *miladi*," she said to his mother in very crisp good English, yet with a funny precision, as if she had learned it as a lesson, "I give you welcome back to Grives. And how is my dear Madame Blessington?"

Archie thought his mother interrupted these greetings rather suddenly.

"How are you madame Seiler?" she said. "And here is my daughter Jeannie and Archie"—and she added something in an undertone, which sounded like the language Miss Schwarz used to talk.

Madame Seiler whisked round with renewed cordiality.

"And such lovely weather you have come to," she said. "The sun all day and the frost all night. But we keep out the frost and let the sun in."

They passed into the entrance-hall, aromatic and warm, heated by a big china stove that roared pleasantly, and instantly, without any reason, there came into Archie's mind the remembrance of the words his hand had scribbled one morning with the signature "Martin." It came out of the darkness like a light seen distantly at night; it flashed like a signal and vanished again. But for one second it had been there, remote, but visible and luminous.

Lady Davidstow, for some obscure and grown-up reason, thought good at supper that night to explain incidentally that she had written to Madame Seiler that Blessington was coming, and that was how she had known Blessington's name. Archie had a very strong and wholesome confidence in his mother, but he knew that grown-up people sometimes made statements which have got (by the rules) to be accepted, but which do not always convince. Blessington's saying that she could not run any more because she had a bone in her leg was an instance of this class of statement, as also was the occasion when his mother spoke, a year ago, about Abracadabra's sneezings. This mode of accounting for Madame Seiler's knowing Blessington's name came under the same head: as far as it went it might be true, and though it did not particularly interest him whether it was true, so to speak, all the way, he felt that there was something mildly mysterious about it. And, having made this unconvincing statement, his mother at once passed on to more interesting topics.

It was a blow, when Blessington called him next morning, to be told that he was tired with the journey and must stop in bed for breakfast. That was a perfectly unfounded statement, but, like those others, had grumblingly to be accepted, though Archie knew quite well that he had never felt less tired.

"You mayn't feel it, dear," said Blessington, "but you are."

"I should think I ought to know best," said Archie.

"No, I know best," said Blessington firmly. "And your mamma says so, too."

Archie began to wonder they were not right. He did not feel tired, as he had told Blessington, but something inside him said that it did not want to run about, or even skate, but it was very well pleased that his body, well wrapped up, should sit up in bed, and bask in the sun which blazed in through the opened French window communicating with the big balcony outside his room. Then, after breakfast, there came in his mother with a big jovial man, whose name was Dr. Dobie.

"I never saw such a lazy fellow," exclaimed this rather attractive person. "Fancy not being up yet!"

"They wouldn't let me," said Archie.

"Well, as soon as I've had a look at you, up you shall get," said the doctor. "But I can't wait till you're dressed. Now, undo your coat a minute."

Once again the instrument with plugs was produced, and the ninety-nine game played.

"That's capital," said the doctor, "and now in a minute I'll have done with you. Just put that into your mouth with the end under your tongue. There, like that."

This was a very short process, and Dr. Dobie got up.

"Now, my plan for you is this," he said. "You shall dress and lie out in the sun on your balcony. And, after you've had dinner, you shall go for a sleigh drive, and walk a little on your way back. Then balcony again, till it's dark."

"But mayn't I skate?" asked Archie, who didn't really want to.

"No, not just yet. We'll have you skating before long, but not at present. The more you do as you're told, the sooner you'll skate."

During the next week, but so gradually that at no moment was it a discovery, it dawned on Archie that he was ill, and that his illness dated from the time when his mouth bled. The knowledge did not in the least depress him, because with it came the absolute certainty in his own mind that he was going to get quite well again. For the most part he did not feel ill, though there was often an uncomfortable period towards evening when he felt sometimes hot and sometimes cold, and one moment would want another coat on, and soon would have liked to throw off all the clothes he had. These odd feelings were accompanied by a sort of extra vividness in his perceptions: he felt tingling and alert, and the lights seemed brighter than their wont. But when this had been more marked than usual in the evening, he always felt very tired next day, and more than once he did not get up at all but had his bed pulled out on to the balcony. Then, as the weeks passed on, there was less of this, and before long he was allowed to tie his toboggan to the back of the sleigh, and be towed up-hill through the pine-wood that climbed the slopes behind the village. That was a delightful experience; on each side stood the snowy trees frosted like a Christmas cake, now almost meeting above the narrow track, and then standing away from it again, so that the deluge of sun poured down as into a pool, while from in front came the jingle of the horse's bells, and from below him the squeak of his runners. Then they came out again on to the ski-ing slopes, where visitors to Grives played the entrancing game of seeing, apparently, who could fall down most often in the most complicated manner. Where the slope was steepest there was erected a sort of platform, so that the runner, flying down the slope above, was shot into the air, touching ground again yards below. Or, on other mornings, when things went well, and there had been no hot-and-cold period the evening before, he tobogganed down the slope below the house to the edge of the skating-rink and sat there in the snow, with everything round frozen hard, yet feeling perfectly warm, so potent were the beams of this ineffable sun through the thin, dry air. Jeannie was learning to skate and progressed, in wobbling half-circles, and shrilly announced that this and no other was the outside edge. Or four of the experts in a railed-off and hallowed place at the end of the huge rink would put down an orange, and proceed to weave a mystic dance in obedience to the shouted orders of one of them. At one moment all four would be swiftly converging on a back-edge to their orange, and, just at the moment when a complicated collision seemed imminent, would somehow change their direction, and, lo, all four were sailing outwards and forwards again in big, sweeping curves. Then there were the hoarse, angry cries of the curlers to listen to, and the pleasant sight of the stone sliding swiftly down the ice and butting, with a hollow chunk, into any other that stood in its way. And then a slow sliding stone would come down, and people swept violently in front of it to encourage it not to lie down and die, which for the most part it did. But always too soon, his mother or Blessington would come to tell him that it was time to go home again and he would tie his toboggan to the back of the sleigh, and be pulled up-hill to the house. That was a tiresome moment, and Archie found himself wondering, with a pang of jealousy, why, when so many were hale and hearty round him, it should be just he who was obliged to go and lie down on the roofed balcony, instead of skating or curling. But even when he had set-backs, and had to lie all day on the balcony, he never faltered in his belief that he was going to get well.

Here then, in brief, were the outward aspects of Archie's life at Grives, new and attractive and full of sun and dry, powdery snow. He took no active part in the activities, and was but an observer, but all the time there were inward aspects of his life, which no one shared with him, and which no one ever observed. He was always on the alert, even on those mornings of tiredness after he had had a rise of temperature the evening before, for the development of a certain thing, the existence of which came to him only in hints and whispers. But the thing itself was always there, though he had no control over its manifestations. He could no more bring it into the exterior life of the senses, he could no more see or hear it or produce any evidence of it, as he willed, than he could make the sun pierce and scatter the clouds, which for a whole week in January alternately rained and snowed on to Grives. All he could do was to wait for it, and he waited in a perpetual serene excitement. It came always when he was alone: he got to think of solitude, in this present stage, as an essential for its manifestation. And, as the weeks went on, he associated it more and more with the balcony on which he lay for the greater part of the day. It, the thing he waited for, and was completely silent about even when he had intimate good-night talks with his mother, was no other than "Martin" (whoever Martin might be) whose presence had come into his mind with such unexpected vividness when first he saw the chalet. Never was the idea of "Martin" absent from his mind: it might lurk concealed behind the excitement of trailing after the sleigh, or of watching the skaters on the ice, but at all times it was ready to enfilade him. And, among all the diversions of the snow and the ice and the sun, he had an inward eye turned towards this inscrutable "Martin"—no winged nester in the sand-cliffs, but somebody, somebody…

Lessons in a mild way had begun again before this wretched rainy and snowy week, and Miss Bampton sent out from home the most entrancing and topical copies. "Hot outside-edge for lunch," was one, in allusion to the news of Jeannie's skating; "Cold inside-edge for dinner" was another. Whatever the weather was, Archie was out of doors all day, and Jeannie, during lesson-time, used to sit out on his balcony and do her more advanced tasks, which, with his, were taken in to Lady Davidstow for correction. More often his mother used to sit on the balcony, too, but during this damp, abominable week she suffered from a heavy cold, and the lessons were brought to her by Jeannie. And on this particular morning, Jeannie had finished her French translation first, and so went in to her mother to have it corrected, leaving Archie to finish the last three lines of his copy.

Ever since his first entry into the house, there had been for him nothing more than the perception of Martin's presence. With the patience of a child who wants something, a thing only equalled by the patience of a cat watching a mouse-hole, he had never taken his inward eye off this. He was always ready for it. As Jeannie went in with her completed French lesson, he laid down his pen, and looked for a moment at the streaming icicles on the eaves of his shelter, and listened with a sense of depression to the drip of the melted water that formed grey pits in the whiteness of the snow below. Because there was a thaw, the air felt colder than when there were twenty degrees of frost, and the blanket on his couch was studded with condensed moisture. "It is warmer," thought Archie to himself, "so it ought to *be* warmer. But it's colder."

At this moment he felt a sudden thrill in his right wrist, and thought that a melted drop had fallen on it. But he saw there was no drop there, and wondered at this sensation of touch. Then he saw his fingers begin to twitch, and instantly recognized the sensation he had felt once before. He swept his incomplete copy off his pad of blotting-paper, and took his pen up again. Surely he could write on his blotting-paper.

At first the meaningless scribbles appeared, made more grotesque and senseless by the running of the ink. There was a pencil on the table by him, and he took that up instead of the pen, while his hand twitched and jerked to be at its task again. The day before he had pinched his finger in the hinge of a slamming window, and he saw the moon-shaped blot of blood below the nail quivering as his fingers starved to hold an instrument of writing again. Then his hand settled down, like a hovering bird on to a bough, as he picked up the pencil.

For a little while the scribbles went on: then, watching the marks on the blotting-paper just as an excited spectator watches the action of a play, he saw words coming. His brain did not know what they were till they appeared on the paper.

"Archie, Archie," said the pencil, "I want to talk to you. I can't always, but sometimes I can. Dear Archie, try to be ready when I get through. Lovely to talk to you. Can't to mother."

CHAPTER IV

An incontrollable excitement seized the boy. "Oh, who is it?" he said aloud. "Is it Martin?"

He felt the twitching die away in his fingers, and presently he was left sitting there, his copy on the floor and the scrawl on the blotting-paper. But he had, somewhere inside him, a sense of extraordinary satisfaction. Something or somebody had "got through," whatever that meant. The words in pencil on his blotting-paper had "got through." And he turned it over hastily, and picked up the unfinished copy, as the door-handle into his room rattled, and Jeannie came out on to the balcony again with her corrected French exercise.

Several days of this chilly dripping weather, with the *foehn* wind from the south went by, and when that ceased, and the wind veered to the north, blowing high over Grives, and raising feathers of snowdust on the peaks to the north, while the sheltered valley basked in calm and sunlight again, there were eventful days of carting the snow from the rinks before any further development took place in Archie's secret life. This carting of the snow was splendid fun, for, when a hand-sleigh of it was piled high, Archie would squat on the front of it (thereby adding considerably to the weight) and in a shrill voice direct the men who pushed it to right or left, in order to reach the steep bank down which they discharged their burden. When they were come to the edge of it, some large, strong man lifted Archie off his perch, and waited with him, while the sleigh was pushed to the very brink, and its burden overturned in a jolly lumpy avalanche that poured down the built-up bank of the rink. Then Archie mounted his throne again and was pulled back to where the men with spades loaded up again... When the sleigh seemed to be sufficiently full he called out "Stop," and made the return journey to the side of the rink. This was all tremendously grand, and he had an idea that the clearing of the rink could never have taken place without him. Certainly his sleigh worked much faster than any other, for, in his honour, those who pushed always ran to discharge their burden at top speed, instead of going slowly like the others.

"Oh, that was a pace," he would say as somebody lifted him off. "Look, mummy, they're going to turn it over."

The rink then was clear again (thanks to Archie's great exertions) before his secret life made any step forward. But one afternoon, when he had been watching the skating from his balcony, something further occurred. He was alone, for his mother had gone down with Jeannie to the rink, and Blessington had gone shopping, and there was a bell by him, by means of which he could summon Madame Seiler if he wanted anything. But he had no thoughts of summoning Madame Seiler; he was extremely content to lie in the sun, and watch the rink sometimes, and sometimes to read a fascinating book called *The Rose and the Ring*, which his mother had given him. There were absurd pictures of Prince Bulbo, an enormously fat young gentleman, whom Archie did not wish to resemble, but was rather afraid of resembling, since Dr. Dobie at his last visit had told him he was getting fat...

It was all very peaceful and happy, and he had lost interest in Jeannie's falls and even in Prince Bulbo's executions, and was staring placidly at a very bright spot of glistening snow which caught the sun at the edge of the rink, when lines of shadow began to pass over the field of his vision, exactly as they used to pass over the green-lit ceiling of his night-nursery at home. This was interesting: he did not feel in the least sleepy, but very wide awake, and was conscious of sinking down through this lovely luminous air, with the bright spot of light getting every moment higher above him, when he suddenly heard his name called.

"Archie, Archie," said the voice, which was close to him, and wonderfully friendly. And at the same moment he felt on the back of his hand the touch of another hand that was smooth and young and somehow familiar, though he had never felt it before.

He tried not to disturb the impression. There was some sort of spell on him, light as a gossamer-web, which the slightest movement, physical or mental, on his part, might break.

"Yes, I'm Archie," he said.

But, the moment he spoke, he knew that he had spoken somehow in the wrong way. Another part of him, not his lips and their voluntary movements, should have answered. He ought to have thought the answer with that part of him that saw the lines of shadow passing across the bright steel surface of the rink below, that felt himself sinking down and down beneath the bright spot opposite... He could not have explained, but he knew it was so, and instantly there was he back on his balcony again with *The Rose and the Ring* in his hand, and Jeannie on the rink. Madame Seiler clattering dishes in the kitchen, and himself all alone, lying in the sunshine. He knew that something inside him had been tremendously happy when his name was called and his hand touched in that intimate manner, and, now that the touch and the voice were gone, he felt something akin to what he felt when he was feverish, and Blessington had said "good-night" and left him. But then, he always knew that Blessington had only gone into the next room, and could be summoned. And he could not summon him who had called "Archie" to him. He had not the least doubt that it was Martin who had called, that it was Martin's hand that had been laid on his. But who was this dear person called "Martin," and where was Martin? Secure in the knowledge that it was Martin who had come to him, and touched him and called to him, he put down his book, and shut his eyes so that his feeling of being alone should be intensified.

"Martin," he whispered. "Oh, Martin!"

He lay there tense and excited, sure that Martin would come again. Then in a dim, child-like manner, not formulating anything to himself, but only feeling his way, he knew he had called wrong. He must call differently, if he hoped to have any reply, call from inside. But, the more earnestly he attempted to "call from inside," the further he got away from that "inside" mood, which he knew, but could not recapture.

"Oh, what rot!" he said at length, and picked up *The Rose and the Ring* again to ascertain whether Bulbo was really going to be executed on this second occasion when he piled his table on his bed and his chair on his table, and his hat-box on his chair, and peeped out of the window from his horrid cell, to see whether it was eight o'clock yet...

Every day, in this return of frost and sunshine, Archie felt stronger, and soon the desire to skate took firm hold of him. Oddly enough, the pleasant Dr. Dobie began to agree with him, and within a day or two of the time when Archie's desire to skate became a pressing need, Dr. Dobie sanctioned it, and Archie had a humiliating hour or two. He had seen Jeannie lean outwards, and announce the outside edge, he had seen Jeannie lean a little inwards and proclaim the inside edge and round she went in curves that Archie could not but envy. He had only got to lean outwards and inwards like that, and surely he was master of his curves. But he found that his curves were master of him, and tumbled him down instead, or would have done so if a kind Swiss on skates had not always been on hand to prevent any disaster of this kind. But then Jeannie had learned, so it seemed to Archie, by falling down, and he resented the hand that saved him from falling.

"Do let me fall down," he said. "I can't learn unless I fall down."

"Better not fall down, sir," said this amiable young man. "I hold you; you learn best so."

"But Jeannie didn't," said Archie.

"No; but she is a girl," whispered his Swiss.

"Oh, ought girls to fall down and not boys?" asked Archie, rather interested in this new difference between the sexes.

* * * * *

Archie was allowed, by the end of January, to skate for half an hour before lunch with his Swiss hovering over him like a friendly eagle, to have lunch with Jeannie seated side by side on a toboggan at the edge of the rink, and skate for half an hour again afterwards at the end of which time a second eagle appeared in the person of Blessington or his mother, and carried him off to the sleigh. Right on through half February lasted the golden frosty weather; then came a great snowfall, and with that the frost broke. The snow degenerated into rain, the wind veered again into the slack south, and the roofs dripped and the trees tossed their white burdens from them. But, as the snow melted, wonderful things happened in the earth at the summons of the suns of spring, for gentians pushed their lengthening stems up through the thinning crust, and put forth their star-like flowers, deep as the blue of night and brilliant as the blue of day. The call of the spring, though yet the snow-wreaths lingered, pierced through them, and the listening grasses and bulbs pricked up their little green ears above the soil. Wonderful as last spring had been, the first that Archie had ever consciously noticed, this Alpine Primavera was twice as magical, for winter was caught in her very arms, and warmed to life again. Morning by morning the pine-woods steamed like the hot flank of a horse, and when the mists cleared nature's great colour-box had been busy again with fresh greens, and more vivid reds on the tree-trunks, and weak, pale snowdrops and mountain crocuses shone like silver and gold in the sheltered hollows. A more tender blue took the place of the crystallized skies of winter, and for the barren, brilliant light of the January sun was exchanged a fruitful and caressing luminousness that flooded the world instead of merely looking down upon it. Soon from the lower slopes the snow was quite vanished, and instead of the tinkle of sleigh-bells there came from the pastures the deeper note from the bells of feeding cattle, which all winter long had been penned up in chalets, eating the dry cakes of last year's harvest of grass.

Archie had been lying in his balcony one morning writing an account of these things to Miss Bampton. His mother had gone back to England to take Jeannie home, but would be back at the end of the week, and in the absence of an instructor Archie's task was to write a long letter daily to somebody at home. This he enjoyed doing, for the search for words in which to express himself had begun to interest him, and he had just written: "If you listen very hard, you can almost hear the grass and the flowers fizzing. Is it the sap? It's like fizzing anyhow. That's what I mean."

As he paused at the end of his third page, he felt something in his hand that also reminded him of fizzing. There was that queer thrill and twitching in his fingers, which he recognized at once, and words, not searched for by him, but coming from some other source, began to trace themselves on the blank fourth page. To-day there were no preliminary scrawls, the firm, upright handwriting was coherent from the first.

"Archie, I've got through again," it wrote. "Isn't it fun? If you want a test ("Test?" thought Archie, "what's that?") you'll find a circle cut on the bark of the pine opposite the front-door. Dig in the earth just below it. There's a box and some things in it. I hid them."

A wave of conscious excitement came over the boy, and instantly his hand stopped writing.

"Oh, bother; it's stopped," he said to himself. "I wish I hadn't interrupted it."

But he had interrupted it, and, since he could not get back into that particular quiescence which, he had begun to see, always accompanied these manifestations, he could at least do what the writing suggested, and, slipping off his couch, he tip-toed downstairs in order not to let Blessington hear his exit.

There were two pine-trees, either of which might have been described as opposite the front-door, and he searched in vain round the first of these for any sign of the circle cut on the bark. Then, coming to the other, he at once saw, with a sudden beating of his heart, a rough circle cut in the bark just opposite his eyes. A grey ring of lichen had grown into it, making it so conspicuous that he wondered he had never noticed it before. Next moment he was down on his knees, grubbing up the loose earth directly below it, with the eager, absolute certainty of success. The earth came away very easily, and his hole was not yet a foot deep when he saw something white and shining at the bottom of it, and presently he drew out a small, round tin box, like that which stood on the table in his father's study, and held tobacco. He hastily filled the earth into his excavation again, and, undetected, tip-toed back to his balcony.

CHAPTER IV

For a while the lid resisted his efforts to open it, but soon he got it loose and looked inside. On the top lay a folded piece of paper; below there was a stick of chocolate in lead paper, a pencil, a match-box, and a photograph of a boy about nine years old whom Archie instantly knew to be like himself. Then he opened the piece of folded paper, and saw words written on it in a hand he knew quite well:

"This is Martin Morris's," was the inscription, "and belongs to him alone, and not anybody else at all ever."

Archie read this, looked at the photograph again, and a flood of light poured in on his mind. It was no wonder that he had felt that Martin was friendly and affectionate, that Martin wanted to talk to him, that Martin told him of the *cache* he had made, for to whom should he tell it but to his brother?

Yes: Martin was here, for Martin had written to him, had called him... And then, in a moment, more light flashed on him. Certainly Martin was alive, but he was not alive in the sense that his mother was alive or Blessington. In that sense Martin was dead. There was nothing in the least shocking or terrifying in the discovery, and it burst upon him as the sense of spring had done. It was just a natural thing, wonderfully beautiful, to find out for certain, as he felt he had found out, that there was close to him, always perhaps, and certainly at times, this presence of the brother whom he had never seen, but who in some way, not more inexplicable than the appearance of the blue gentians pricking up through the snow, could occasionally speak to him, calling him by name, or using his hand to write with.

A few days afterwards Lady Davidstow arrived back from England, and on the first evening of her return, after dusk had fallen, Archie was sitting on the floor against her knee in front of the one open fire-place in the house, where pine-logs fizzed and smouldered and burst into flame, and glowed into a core of heat. Sometimes, for that pleasant hour before bed-time, she read to him, but to-night there had been no reading, for she had been telling him of the week she had passed at home. They had moved up to London while she was there, and London was miry and foggy and cold.

"Altogether disgusting, dear," she said. "You don't want to go there, do you?"

"Not an atom," said Archie firmly. "I like this place better than any I have ever been in."

"I'm so glad, Archie. I was afraid you would dislike it after the frost went."

Archie was staring dreamily at the fire, and suddenly he knew that Martin was here, and he looked quickly round wondering if, by any new and lovely miracle, he should see the boy whose face was now familiar to him from the photograph. But there was nothing visible; only the firelight leaped on the wooden walls.

"What is it, Archie?" asked his mother.

Suddenly Archie felt that he could preserve his secret no longer. As on the day in church when he wanted his mother to share with him the pleasure of that glorious comedian, the man with the wagging beard, so now he wanted her to share with him the secret joy of Martin's presence.

"Mummy, I want to tell you about Martin," he said. "You know whom I mean: Martin, my brother."

"Archie, who has been telling you about Martin?" she asked.

Archie laughed.

"Why, Martin, of course. It's too lovely. Once he called me out loud, and he writes for me. He's written for me three times, once at home and twice here. I knew he was particularly here, the moment we got here. And last time he told me about what he had hidden under the pine-tree, and I found it. Don't you want to see it? I hid it away in the paper in my portmanteau. Oh, and what is a test? He said it was a test."

"A test? A test is a proof."

Archie laughed again.

"That makes sense," he said. "Now shall I show you the test? I kept it all together with what he wrote to me about it first."

He came back in a moment with his precious possession.

"Look, that's what he wrote on the paper of my letter to Miss Bampton," he said. "He said there was a circle cut on the pine-tree, and I found it, and I dug as he told me, and found this. Look! Isn't it lovely, and that's Martin's photograph, isn't it?"

It was impossible to question the validity of this evidence, and, indeed, Lady Davidstow had no desire to do so. For herself, she believed implicitly in the fact of life everlasting, without which the whole creation of God, with its pains and its agonies and its yearning and its love, becomes the cruellest of all sorry jests concocted by the omnipotent power of a mind infinitely brutal and cynical, who tortures the puppets He has created with unutterable anguish, or ravishes their souls with a joy as meaningless as dreams. Well she remembered Martin's cutting the circle on the pine-tree, but what its significance was he had never told her. But now, five years after his death, he had told it, she could not doubt, to the brother who had no normal remembrance of him. There they were, the little pathetic tokens of his childish secrecy, a pencil, a piece of chocolate, a photograph, and, above all, the well-formed, upright handwriting identical with that of the message traced on the last page of Archie's unsent letter. How it happened, what was the strange mechanism that fashioned by material means this mysterious communication between the living and the dead she had no idea, but of its having happened she had no doubt.

She turned these relics over, she kissed the handwriting so long buried, and tears of tender amazement rose in her eyes.

"Oh Archie, my darling," she said. "You lucky boy!"

"Aren't I?" said Archie. "But does Martin never write to you?"

"No, dear; I suppose he cannot."

"And why is he so particularly here?" demanded Archie.

She paused a moment.

"He died here," she said.

"In this house?" asked he. "Which room?"

CHAPTER IV

"Blessington's."
Archie gave a great sigh.
"Oh, mummy, do let me have that room instead of mine!" he said.

BOOK II

CHAPTER V

Archie was precariously perched on the side of his little Una-rigged, red-sailed boat, looking with dancing blue eyes at the rocky coast all smothered in billows and sunlit spray some quarter of a mile ahead, and wondering if he would be able to make the harbour of Silorno on this tack. He wondered also what was the best thing to do if he could not. There seemed to be two alternatives, the one to beat out to sea again and come in on another tack, the other to run before the wind to the head of the bay, away to the right, where he knew there was a sandy beach, tumble himself out as best he might, and, he was afraid, see his beloved *Amphitrite* being pounded to bits by the rollers; for, with all his optimism, he could not picture himself hauling her up out of harm's way. But even this seemed preferable to the other alternative, for to beat out again in such a sea seemed really a challenge to the elements to swamp him, in which case he was like to lose the *Amphitrite* and his own life as well.

The wind was blowing with all the violence of a summer Italian gale straight down the bay from the open sea. A high wall of rock against which the breakers smashed themselves, and would smash anything else that rode them, was in front of him; then came the narrow opening into Silorno harbour for which he was making, after which the rocks, on the top of which ran the road to Santa Margharita, continued right up to the head of the bay. It had been rough when he started to sail there, in order to get some cigarettes, which now were stowed away in his coat which he had wrapped round them and placed where it would receive as small a share as possible of the spray that from time to time fell in a solid sheet into the boat. That seemed almost the most important thing of all, to keep the cigarettes dry, for it would be too futile to have taken all this trouble, and so greatly have ventured himself and his *Amphitrite*, if at the end the cigarettes should prove to be a mash of tobacco and salt water, for they were only in a cardboard box. And next in importance came the need of demonstrating to his mother and Harry and Helena and Jessie that he had been perfectly wise and prudent in sailing across to Santa Margharita, in spite of their land-lubber fears, in a freshening gale and a lumpy sea, in order to get these Egyptian cigarettes instead of the despised Italian brand. He made no doubt that the whole party of them were at this moment watching him through glasses from the terraced garden of the Castello that sat perched at the top of the steep, olive-clothed hill in front of him, and he spared a second to wave a hand in their direction in case they were there. But he did it in a rather hurried manner, for he wanted that hand to be ready to loosen the sheet in case any more wind was on its way to him, and the other hand must retain its hold on the tiller.

Archie was clad in a jersey stained and whitened with salt-water, and the rest of his attire consisted of grey flannel trousers. His coat was defending to its last dry stitch the trophy of cigarettes; his shoes he had put under his coat, for it was just as well to keep them dry, while, if by any chance he had to swim, they would be of no use to him either dry or wet. The sleeves of his jersey rolled up nearly to his shoulder, disclosed slim, strong arms, incredibly browned with a month of sea-bathing, and his sockless feet were of the same fine tan of constant exposure. His hair, thick and dripping from the spray, had for the present lost its tawny curliness, and he had to throw back his head from time to time, in order to keep it out of his eyes. And in his mind there was the same wildness of out-of-doors rapture that characterized the youth of his supple body: he could have laughed with pleasure at the mere fact of this doubtful battle between himself and the wind-maddened sea. But all the time in some secret chamber of his brain there sat, so to speak, a steadfast and keen observer, who was making notes with all his might, and pushing them down into the cool caves of memory, to be brought forth (in case Archie came safely to land) from their cold storage, and fitted with words which should reproduce the exultation of wind and sun and sea. And in a chamber more secret yet, a chamber not in his brain but in his heart, sat the knowledge that among the others his second cousin, Helena Vautier, in particular was surely looking at him from the terraced garden high above the cliff. She should see (and, for that matter, so should her sister Jessie) how to handle a boat. She had been strong in her dissuasion of his starting at all, and that, if Archie was quite honest with himself, was one of the principal reasons why he had insisted on doing so. She had mentioned casually the other day that there was nothing in the world she liked better than the careless "go-to-the-deuce" attitude towards danger which to her represented manliness, and Archie had been only too delighted to give her this vigorous exhibition of it. But it tremendously pleased him that, on his announcement of his intention to go across the bay, she should have so strenuously dissuaded him. To his mind that conveyed the impression that she liked him as much as she liked exhibitions of manliness.

He was already opposite the opening into the harbour and still several hundred yards distant, and for the time all the attention of the observer who some day was going to put this experience into words, and of the other observer who knew that Helena was watching him, was diverted to the job that engaged his more superficial self. But that part of him, intent and eager though it was on the hazard that lay before it, sang and shouted with glee at the fact that he was alone out here on the sea. For this very sane and healthy personage, Archie Morris, might almost be described as an aqua-maniac, so intense was his passion for that gladdest and most glorious creature of God. He did not want to be a sailor, for a sailor inhabited an impregnable fort which, though surrounded by sea, was still impenetrably removed from it, and defied it by means of colossal cylinders and pounding pistons and steel sides. Best of all was to be swimming in the sea, but not far removed from that was to coax and wheedle the sea through the medium of a big sail and a tiny boat: being alone with the sea, as with all lovers, was necessary to the full realization of passion. A river was a fair substitute for the sea or a lake; but there had to be a quantity of water. He loved to dive, and open his eyes under water, so as to see the sun shining through it. That was a very early passion, dating from the time when he had stepped out of a boat in his anxiety about a pike that was on the end of his line...

Then, for a moment, all other considerations were subordinated to keen physical activity. The wind was sweeping him across the mouth of the harbour, and he had either to put about at once to avoid being taken onto the rocks at its northern end, or, risking being swamped, put his helm even harder a-port, and tighten his sheet. With his habit of swift decision, he determined to go for it, and, throwing his leg across the tiller, he pulled on his sheet with both hands. The spray from the waves that broke themselves on the rocks fell solid and drenched him, but next moment, with but a yard or two to spare, he skimmed by them into the broadening harbour. There the promontory on which the Castello stood came between him and the wind, his sail flapped idly, and in dead calm he picked up his sculls to row the *Amphitrite* to her anchorage. But, before he took them up, he laughed aloud.

"Gosh, what sport!" he said.

* * * * *

The anchorage of the *Amphitrite* lay in a bay not far from the entrance to the harbour, screened by the steep-climbing olive groves belonging to this Castello of Silorno which Archie's mother had taken for the months of May and June: Silorno itself, that incredibly picturesque huddle of pink and yellow walls, of campaniles, and lacemakers, who, with bright coloured kerchiefs over their comely heads, plied their wooden bobbins all day in the shade of its narrow streets, rose, roof over roof, at the head of the harbour. A big cobbled piazza sloped down to the quay wall where sailors chatted and dozed in the shadow all day, putting to sea for their night-fishing by the light of flares about the time of sunset. The village was impenetrable to wheeled traffic, for the road along the bay came to an end at its outskirts, and thereafter became a narrow cobbled track, built in steps where the steepness of its streets demanded. Round the town rose an amphitheatre of hills broken only by the low saddle, where the final promontory on which the Castello stood swam out seawards in three wooded humps of hills. And, sitting here, you could observe on days like these the breakers crashing on the reefs to the right, where the seas rolled in from the open Mediterranean, while the land-locked harbour, into which Archie had just brought his boat, lay smooth as a mirror at your feet towards the left. Straight in front ran the ascending path that passed below the Castello to the head of the promontory, where enlightened Italian enterprise was building an execrable and totally useless lighthouse to supplant the little Madonna chapel that had stood there for centuries.

Archie took down his sail, anchored the *Amphitrite*, and punted himself across in a small boat to the landing-stage at the foot of the hill on which the Castello stood. Here the trees stood untroubled by the gale that poured high over them from the south, though on the other side of the harbour the wind roared in the olives, and turned their green to the grey of the underleaf, and the great surges beat and burst on the rocks he had narrowly avoided. But here that tumultuous stir was unfelt, and the resinous smell of pines and the clean odour of the eucalyptus-trees hung in the warm and sheltered air. Out of that denser shade he passed into the belt of olives that grew higher on the slope, mixed with angled and contorted fig-trees, where the fruit was already beginning to swell and ripen. Above rose the great grey bastion of the retaining fortress wall, tufted with stone-crop and valerian that was rooted in the crevices, and above that again was spread the umbrella of the stone-pine that grew at the corner of the garden. The path he followed wound round the base of this wall and passed below its easterly side, where he came into the blast of the warm south wind again that swept along the face of the Castello, and made the cypresses bend and buckle like fishing-rods which feel the jerk and pull of some hooked giant of the waters. The hillside here plunged very precipitously downwards to the bay three hundred feet below, wrinkled with waves, and feathered with foam, and, lover of the sea though he was, he felt content to observe that tumult of windy water. Not a sail was visible right across to the farther shore of the gulf, and to-night there would be no illumination of the fishing-boats that in calm weather rode out there, twinkling and populous as a town. But he stood looking at the sea a moment before he turned into the narrow stone passage that led to the gate of the house, as a man may look with love on his horse that, unruly and obstreperous, has yet carried him so gallantly.

A girl came up the cobbled way from the town just as he turned in. She had on a very simple linen dress that the wind blew close to her body, and a flapping linen sunbonnet, tied below her chin, to prevent the wind capturing it. She was tall and slight, moved easily, as with a boyish carelessness; a very pleasant face, also boyish and quite plain, peered from under her flapping bonnet. Her hands were noticeable: they were large but extremely well shaped, and the fingers showed both perception and efficiency. It may be remarked that Archie had never noticed her hands at all.

"Hullo, Jess," said he. "I'm just back. Lord, I've had such a ripping afternoon. And the cigarettes are quite dry. Where have you been?"

"Just down into Silorno. Cousin Marion wanted a telegram sent about their sleeping-berths to-morrow."

Archie frowned. He had noticed that Jessie was often sent on errands. People who can absolutely be relied on usually are.

"I should have thought my mother might have sent Pasqualino," he observed.

The girl laughed.

"Oh, she wanted to, but I said I would go instead. You see, Cousin Marion and Helena were getting in what might be called rather a state about you. I tried to infect them with my own calm, but they wouldn't catch it. So I thought a little walk would be pleasant."

"Oh, was Helena frightened?" asked Archie rather greedily.

"Yes. So was Cousin Marion. I wasn't."

CHAPTER V

"Then you were beastly unsympathetic. I had an awful shave getting into the harbour," remarked Archie.

"But you knew what you were about, and I didn't, nor did Helena. So I preferred to have confidence in you and go for a walk, rather than observe you in what looked remarkably like danger."

Archie had walked up from the landing-stage with his shoes and his coat under his arm. The coat was too wet to put on, so he dusted his feet with it, and resumed his shoes.

"Oh, a ripping afternoon," he said again.

The sound of the clanging gate into the Castello was heard out in the garden, and as they walked up the dim stone-flagged passage that led out into it, another girl came running in. She, like her sister, was tall and slight, but there the resemblance altogether ended. A delicate, small-featured face, entirely feminine, gleamed below yellow hair; her eyes, set rather wide apart, giving her an adorably childish look, opened very widely below their dark eyelashes. Beside her, Jessie looked somewhat like a well-bred plough-boy.

"Oh, Archie!" she cried. "How horribly rash of you! Your mother and I have had a terrible half-hour."

"I bring you cigarettes to soothe your disordered nerves," said Archie sententiously. "I am happy to say that they are dry, though I am not."

Jessie had walked on, with that pleasant expression on her face that might or might not be a smile, and the two were left alone for a moment.

"As if I cared about the cigarettes," she said.

"You did this morning. But you weren't really anxious, were you?"

"Indeed I was. You were naughty to sail back in this gale. Do be good now and change your clothes at once. I will bring you some fresh tea into the garden. Cousin Marion and I have had tea. We drank cup after cup to fortify ourselves, and looked over the wall at your boat between each sip. Then we trembled and had another sip. Before you got past that horrid rock, we had drained the teapot and broken our chairs with our tremblings."

The strict veracity of this entertaining summary did not of course concern Archie; it was sufficient that it had Helena's light and picturesque touch. It made a tableau that caused him to smile to himself as he changed his shirt, that was now stiffening with salt, and put on a pair of socks over his tanned feet. All this he did hurriedly, for it was the last evening, so he told himself, that they would all be together, by which he really meant that it was the last evening on which Helena would be here, since to-morrow, at break of dawn, she and his mother would start for England, leaving Jessie, Harry Travers, and himself to follow after another fortnight. When, a week before, that scheme had been suggested, it seemed to Archie the most admirable of plans, since, though his mother and Helena would be gone, he would secure another fortnight of intercourse with his beloved sea instead of inhabiting that smoky cave known as London. But since then Helena had begun to dawn on him, though as yet it would be an exaggeration to say that he was in love with her. But she was dawning, her light illuminated the sky above the horizon, and, if the plan was to be suggested again to him in his present attitude of attracted expectancy, it is probable that he would have voted for London and Helena, rather than an extension of his days at the Castello.

The scheme had originally been Helena's, and, like all her plans, had been exceedingly well thought out, before it was produced in the guise of an impulse, prompted by kindliness and thought for others. It was, when edited as an impulse, of the simplest and most considerate sort. The hot weather did not really suit Cousin Marion, so why should not Cousin Marion go back to England with herself, Helena, as travelling companion? Of course Silorno was the most delicious place, and she would be ever so sorry to go, but certainly Cousin Marion felt the heat, and, though she was far too unselfish to suggest breaking up the party, she would be glad to go northwards earlier than the end of June, when her two months' tenancy expired.

Helena had produced this plan to Archie one morning as they sat after breakfast under the stone-pine.

"But my mother would not in the least mind going home alone, if she preferred to go before the end of June," he said.

Helena shook her head.

"Oh, I know she would say she didn't mind," she said, "or she would stop on in spite of her headaches sooner than break up the party—"

"Has she been having headaches?" asked Archie.

"Yes, but you mustn't know that. She told me not to tell any one," said Helena, with complete self-possession. "Promise, Archie."

"All right."

Helena felt quite safe now.

"So she must go back sooner than at the end of June," she continued, "and clearly I am the right person to go with her, for she hates travelling alone."

"Oh, we'll all go then," said Archie.

"It isn't the least necessary. Jessie or I must go with her, for she certainly wouldn't hear of your going, and Jessie is enjoying this so much that I couldn't bear that she should have her days here cut short. So it's for me to go."

"That's awfully good of you," said he, only as yet half convinced.

"It isn't the least. It's a necessity, though you are so kind as to make a virtue of it. And then there's this as well. Cousin Marion would never consent to go, if she thought it was for her sake that I was going with her. So you must go to her, and say you think that it's me whom the heat doesn't suit, and you will see if she doesn't say at once that she will go back with me. And the real reason for her going will be our secret, just yours and mine."

Archie looked at her for a moment in silence, and the silence was one of unspoken admiration. Somehow this kindly thoughtful plan kindled his appreciation of her beauty: her beauty took on a tenderer and more touching look. Before now, it had vaguely occurred to him that, of the two sisters, it was Jessie who most gave up her own way to serve the ways of others; but this secret of Helena's made him feel that he had done her an injustice.

CHAPTER V

"But I don't want you to give up your time here if you enjoy it," he said.

"Ah, don't make me tell a fib, and say that I don't enjoy it," she said. "I will if you press me. I'll say it bores me frightfully, sooner than give up my plan."

"Well, I think it's wonderfully kind of you," he said. "Now I'm to tell my mother that you are feeling the heat, and see what she says. Is that it?"

"Yes, just that," said Helena.

Archie had strolled indoors to put this plan to the test, and before he returned a quarter of an hour later with his mother Helena had approved of her own ingenuity very warmly. She had, if her scheme succeeded, secured for herself an additional fortnight of the London season, for she and Jessie were, for the present, going to make their home with their cousins and she was already satisfied that her unselfishness had made a considerable impression on Archie. This was the most important thing: hitherto she felt she had failed to make her mark, so to speak. He was on excellent friendly terms with her, just as he was with Jessie, but she wanted (or at any rate wished for) something more than that. It was not that she wanted him to flirt with her; she had much more serious ends in view. She wanted (and here was her perspicacity) to dazzle his eyes by means of touching his heart, for she guessed, with clear-sighted vision, that he was the kind of young man who, if he did not mean everything, would mean nothing, and she believed that she could not entangle his affection by mere superficial appeals. And, indeed, she was not a flirt herself; she was poor, and clever, and attractive, and she proposed to use her cleverness and attraction in the legitimate pursuit of securing a husband who was not poor. That Archie was now Lord Davidstow, and at his father's death would be Lord Tintagel, was in his favour, and to make an impression on him, and then to go self-sacrificingly away, seemed to her a very promising manoeuvre. She was not in the least afraid of leaving Jessie with him, for, with her habitual adroitness, she had conveyed to her sister, by little sighs, glances, and words that seemed to escape from her lips unawares, what her design (yet without making it appear a design) on Archie was. She had but allowed her feelings, all unconsciously, to betray themselves, as when she said "Darling, wouldn't it be lovely to be Archie's sister, instead of only cousin?" That put it quite plainly enough, and she felt sure that Jessie understood. And, in addition to this impregnable safeguard of Jessie's loyalty, she was satisfied that Jessie's friendliness with Archie was of the most unsentimental character. Indeed, to speak of her sense of security with regard to Jessie would be a labouring of the point: she was so secure that her security scarcely struck her, any more than the security of a house consciously strikes its inhabitant.

* * * * *

The week that had passed between the acceptance of her plan and this, the last night of her stay at Silorno, confirmed the soundness of her strategy. Archie's frank friendliness towards herself had undergone a subtle change, while his relations with her sister remained precisely on the same calm tableland of comradeship. But below his comradeship with herself, like the sun glowing faintly through a mist without heat at present, but with penetration of light, she knew that there was growing an emotional brightness. It was with light and with a nameless quickening that his eye dwelt on her, and now as they sat in the deep dusk of the garden, illumined only by the stars that twinkled like minute golden oranges in the boughs of the stone-pine, she knew that he was looking at the pale wraith of her face, which was all the starlight left her with, in a manner that was not yet a week old. It was so dark, here in the deep shade, that she saw nothing of his sun-tanned face beyond a featureless oval, but when, from time to time, he drew on his cigarette, it leaped into distinctness. There was emotion there, or, at any rate, the stuff from which emotion is made; there was need, not yet wholly conscious of itself, but waiting, like buried treasure, to be released.

And on her side, also, something was astir behind her calculated plan. She felt sorry, until the wisdom of her project laid its calming hand upon her again, that she was being so unselfish as to accompany Cousin Marion back to town. It would have been extraordinarily pleasant to sit here many times more with Archie, and both watch and take part in the growth of the situation of which the seed had been deliberately planted by herself. It was but a weak little spike as yet, but undeniably there was the potentiality of growth in it.

Suddenly his face leapt into light, as he struck a match, and the gain of a fortnight's London season seemed to her insignificant. And the success of her plan, the wisdom of which she still endorsed, was but a frigid triumph, for she felt to a degree yet unknown to her his personal charm.

"Oh, Archie, I wish I wasn't going away," she said. "It has been a nice time. I wish—no, I suppose that's selfish of me."

"I want to know what is selfish of you," said he.

"Do you? Well, as it's our last evening you shall. I wish I thought you would miss me more."

He moved just a shade closer to her.

"Oh, I shall miss you quite enough," he said.

She laughed.

"I don't think you will," she said. "You'll have your bathing and your boating and your writing. I expect you will have a very jolly time."

He seemed to think over this.

"Yes, I shall have all those things," he said. "And I like them. Why shouldn't I? But—no, like you, I won't say that."

"But I did," she remarked.

"Well, I will too. I shall miss you much more than I should have missed you if you had gone away a week ago."

She, too, hesitated a moment. Then very coolly she replied:

"Thank you very much."

There was calculation in that: she had thought over her polite, chilly manner swiftly but carefully. And she had calculated rightly. He chucked away the cigarette he had only just lit.

"Helena, have I offended you?" he asked. "Why do you speak like that?"

Again she traversed a second's swift thought.

CHAPTER V

"Of course you haven't offended me," she said lightly. "You'll have to try harder than that if you want to offend me. My dear, do try again. Try to make me feel hurt."

Archie was a little excited. There was some small intimate contest going on, that affected him physically, with secret delight, just as he was affected in his limbs by some cross-current to the direction of his swimming, or in his brain by the tussle for the word he wanted when he was writing. He was sparring with something dear to him.

"Try to hurt me," she said softly.

"Very well," said he. "I'm glad you're going away to-morrow. Will that do?"

She laughed again.

"It would do excellently well if you meant it," she said. "But you don't mean it."

"You're very hard to please," said he.

"Not in the least. If you want to please me, say that you'll be very glad to see me again in a few weeks."

"I certainly shall, but I shan't say it. You know it quite well enough without my assurance."

She leaned forward a little.

"But say it all the same, Archie," she said. "Say it quite out loud."

Archie threw back his head and shouted at the stone-pine.

"I shall be very glad to see you again in—what was it?—in a few weeks," he cried.

"Ah, that is nice of you. No, I'm not sure that it's nice, because you've brought Jessie and Mr. Harry out into the garden."

That seemed to be the case, for undeniably the two moved out into the bright square of light cast from the lit passage within. Archie got up swiftly and suddenly, with a bubble of laughter.

"Oh, let's be like the garden scene in *Faust*," he whispered. "Don't you know, when the two couples wander about? Ah, they've seen us: they don't do that in well-conducted opera."

This was true enough, for immediately Helena's name was called by her sister. She gave a little sigh.

"Yes, darling," she said.

"Cousin Marion thinks it's time you went to bed," said Jessie. "And is Archie there too? She wants to see him."

Archie and Helena exchanged a quick glance in the darkness. They knew it, rather than saw it: Helena, at any rate, was quite certain of it.

"I must go in then," he said. "Your fault for making me shout."

Helena recollected a revue that she and Archie had seen together.

"The woman pays," she said in a histrionic falsetto, and without further word ran into the house, feeling very well satisfied with herself. She was sure that she had made herself a little enigmatical to him, had roused his curiosity. Decidedly he wanted to know more…

* * * * *

Archie always slept in a hammock slung between the stone-pine and the acacia in the garden, for though that year which he had spent at Grives, with which our history of his childhood closed, seemed to have eradicated the deadly seeds, he was still recommended to pass as much of his time as possible out of doors. The fourteen years that had elapsed since then had given him six feet of robust height, and there seemed now but little danger of the hereditary foe again beleaguering him. He had spent five years at Eton, and now had just finished his course at Cambridge, where he had contrived to combine classics and rowing in a thoroughly satisfactory manner, distinguishing himself in each. Even as he seemed to have outgrown his physical weakness, so too he had outgrown, to all appearance, those strange abnormal experiences which had been his in childhood, his power of automatic writing and the inexplicable communications from his dead brother. Certainly since his fourteenth year there had been no more of them; it was as if they had belonged entirely to the years when he trailed the clouds of glory that hang about childhood. But even now, in the normal vigour of his young manhood, they did not seem to him to be in the least unreal; indeed, they were to him, in spite of their fantastic and unusual nature, the most substantial treasures in his store-house of memory. The difference was that now they were sealed up: some key had been turned on them in his interior life, and they were inaccessible to him. But never for a moment did he doubt that they were there: out of reach they might be, but he still possessed them, and, though he made no effort to unlock the door, he believed that the key to them was neither lost nor broken, but, rusted, maybe, with unuse, still existed within him. Some day, he felt sure, the impulse would come to him, either from without or within, to search for it, and he knew precisely where, with every prospect of finding, he would look for it. For he still had the power of letting himself lapse into that trance-condition in which he sank into a depth of sunlit waters, and in that mysterious abyss he knew he could find the key to the sealed treasures. It was long since he had penetrated there, but he knew his way.

* * * * *

To-night, as he lay in his hammock, he felt no wish or inclination to sleep, but lay with eyes open looking into the sombre dark of the pine above his head, where the stars twinkled at the edge of the needles of the foliage. The gale that had raged that afternoon had blown itself out: not a breath of breeze sighed in the pine, and of the fierceness of those uproarious hours there was nothing left but the ever-diminishing thunder of the waves three hundred feet below. From horizon to zenith the sky was bare and kirtled with stars, and to the east over the hills across the bay, the dove-colour that precedes the rising of the moon was soaking through the heavens. A faint odour from the thicket of tobacco-plants that grew at the foot of his hammock were spreading through the air, ineffably fragrant, and the dew brought with it the smell of damp and fruitful earth.

CHAPTER V

Archie lay quite still, content to rest without sleep; he was sure that he would go to sleep soon, imperceptibly to himself, and he waited quite tranquilly for the soft tide to engulf him, letting his memory hover now and then over his adventures of the afternoon, but always bringing it back to the half-hour he had sat with Helena, close to where he now lay. He had, as sleep approached, the vague sense of sinking into some quiet depth; but his mind was too tranquilly disposed to do more than register this impression, and then, quite suddenly, without the transition state of drowsiness, he went fast asleep. He had noticed just before that the moon had risen.

He slept long and dreamlessly, and then began to dream with extraordinary vividness. He dreamed that he had not gone to sleep at all, but still lay in his hammock, in the shade of the pine, while the garden outside was full of the white blaze of the moonlight and ebony clear-cut shadows. The thunder of the surf had quite died away, the tobacco-plants still gave out their odour, and the stars, a little quenched by the moon, had faded in the boughs of the pine. And then he perceived (but with no sense of strangeness) that there was something new in the garden, for, close to the door into the house, was standing a white marble statue. This brought his legs over the side of his hammock, and he got up to go and look at it, and then remembered, so he thought, all about it. It was the statue of Helena, which she had told him was a gift from her to him, and it did not seem at all unnatural that it should have been brought out and put in the garden. But, as he had not seen it yet, he walked now across to it, and found an admirable and lovely figure. It was clad in a long Greek chiton, low at the throat and reaching nearly to her feet, which were sandalled. One hand was advanced to him with a beckoning gesture; the other, with its exquisite arm bare to the shoulder, hung by her side. The statue was life-size, for, as it stood on its low marble plinth, the face was just on a level with his. Exquisite in its fidelity and its beauty was that small head on its slender neck, and it endorsed the message of her beckoning hand. The lips, uncurled in a half-smile, mysteriously invited him; the body, too, was a little inclined forward towards him; next moment, surely, she would step down from her pedestal, and, like Galatea, shake off the semblance of stone, and declare herself his.

Standing there, entranced and strangely excited, Archie drank in the amazing loveliness of the figure. White and flawless, without speck or stain, the snow of the Parian quarries gleamed in the moonlight. And then he saw that, just where the neck flowed, with the strength and tenderness of a river, into the shoulders, there was a small dark spot, and, taking a step nearer, he put out his hand to flick it away. But it did not come away: it was as if some little excrescence had stuck to the marble, and, making a second attempt, he felt that it was soft, and that it grew a little longer. It moved, too; it wriggled like the head of a worm, and then, with a faint feeling of disgust, he saw that it was indeed the head of a worm protruding from the marble, just as a worm comes up through earth. Even as he looked, there came another such speck near the mouth; this also grew and wriggled, then came another on the arm which was put forward to welcome him.

Archie stood there, transfixed no longer by admiration and wonder, but by an ever-growing sense of horror. Everywhere, from face and hair and hand, and from the folds of the lovely Greek drapery there started out those loathsome reptiles. Some nightmare of catalepsy invaded him; he could not move, he could not call out, he could not turn away his eyes, but he had to watch until where lately this masterpiece of lovely limbs had stood, there was a column, as high as himself, of wriggling corruption, bred apparently from within. Then, horror adding itself to horror, this portent of decay began to move slowly towards him.

Still he could not move, but at last, when it was not more than a foot or two from him, he found his voice, and could scream for help. He could just hear himself shouting, but no help came. Already he could feel the touch of those horrible things, and with a supreme effort he managed to move his head away from that myriad loathsome touch, and lo! he was seated upright in his hammock, and the moon was low in the west, and over the eastern hills was the light that preceded day. His face streamed with the agony of the nightmare.

He sat still a little while, drinking in reassurance from the miracle of the tranquil dawn, and wondering at the suddenness with which he had gone to sleep, so that his disquieting dream had seemed the uninterrupted continuation of his consciousness. And, as his fright faded, there faded also the memory of what his dream had been: there had been something about a statue, something about worms, something connected with Helena. Even as he thought about it, it continued to recede from him, and before he dozed off again, the whole thing had slipped out of his memory, and when, an hour later, he got up to accompany the travellers on their early start, as far as the station, there was nothing whatever left of it. He knew only that he had awoke in a state of inexplicable terror, arising from some dream which had vanished from his memory like a mist at dawn.

The three left behind adjusted themselves, as friends can do, to their narrowed circle, and moved sensibly closer to each other. They all had their tasks to sweeten the enjoyment of their leisure, for to Jessie fell the Martha-cares of the house, which she transacted by the aid of an Italian dictionary with the cook Assunta; to Harry Travers, now a junior don at Cambridge, the preparation of a course of history lectures next term; to Archie the incessant practice in the endless and elusive art of writing prose. The love of expressing what he loved in words was no less than a passion with him, and it is almost needless to add that the sea was his inspiring theme. He certainly had the prime essential of devotion both to his subject and to the technique of his art, and these little essays, called *Idylls of the Sea*, promised, if ever he could persuade himself to finish them, to be a really exquisite piece of work. They were the simplest sketches of fishers and ships and the like, but to satisfy him, the sea had to sound in every line of them, even as it sounded in the ears of those about whom he wrote. Just now he was trying to recapture all that had made the ecstasy to him of that risky voyage homewards across the bay a few days before, and to fire his words with that thrill which he never quite despaired of communicating.

CHAPTER V

As a rule, their day arranged itself very regularly: early breakfast was succeeded by a couple of hours of task, and a couple more were spent in bathing, no affair of hurried undressing, of chilly immersion and a huddling on of clothes, but of long baskings on the shore, and a mile-long ploughing, for Archie at least, out into the bay or along the coast and round beyond the furthest promontory. Much though he liked the companionship of the others, he was never sorry when first Jessie, and then Harry turned shorewards again, for the companionship of the sea was closest to him when he was alone. He would burrow his way through it on the sidestroke, buried in the foam of his progress, and, when exhausted and breathless, turn on to his back to be cradled and rocked by it, secure in its enveloping presence, even as in the days of childhood he would lie happy and serene in the knowledge that Blessington was close by him. Or he would dive deep and see through "the fallen day" the dazzle of the sun of the surface far above him, and then swim up again, and, after the greenness and the paleness below, find a red and glowing firmament. But best of all was it to swim out very far from land, and then just exist with arms and legs spread wide, encompassed and surrounded by mere sea. He did not want to think about anything at all, or to belabour his brain with strivings to cast into words the sea-sense; that would come afterwards, when with gnawed pencil and erased sentences he sat in the garden; but he only opened himself out to it, and drank it in through eye and ear and skin and widespread limbs... And all this, even when physically he most realized this sea-sense, was but a symbol, and the more vivid the physical consciousness of the sea became, the dimmer it also became in the light of what it stood for. For even as the sea, eternally incorruptible, received into itself, without stain, all that the putrefying land with its ordure and sewers poured into it, so round human life, with its sores and its decay, there lay an immense and eternal incorruption, which purified all life as it passed into it, and turned it into something pellucid and immortal. Dying would be like that, dying was no more than being poured into this jubilant ocean, and becoming part of its clean, exuberant life...

But Archie had no intention of dying just yet, and indeed these metaphysical speculations only reached him like the sound of chimes blown across the water, while far clearer was Harry's voice, calling from the beach, "Archie, it's after twelve"; and thereupon Archie would turn on his chest and swim back to land, with a frill of foam encircling his sunburnt throat and a wake of bubbles following the strokes of his strong legs. Thereafter he would cast himself onto the beach with a straw hat tipped over his eyes, and his sun-tanned legs and arms spread star-fish fashion, and lie there drinking in the sun, while Harry and Jessie reviled him for causing lunch, for which they hungered, to be again half an hour behind the scheduled time. And Archie, lighting a cigarette, turned on his elbow and called them greedy hogs for thinking about lunch, when it was possible to lie in the sun, and swim in the sea. Then, as likely as not, he would himself be aware of a celestial appetite, and step into a pair of flannel trousers and a sea-stained shirt, and in turn revile their tardiness in climbing the olived terraces that lay between them and the Castello.

They lunched in the garden, in a strip of shade outside the house, and thereafter, without any pretence at all about the matter, Harry and Jessie went to their rooms for an honest Italian siesta, with no excuse of lying on beds and reading, but with the avowed object of lying on beds and sleeping. But this two hours' swimming and basking and communion with the sea, instead of making Archie sleepy, gave him his most productive hours of work, and wide-eyed and eager he would sit with jotted notes and scribbling-paper round him, read over the last few pages of his current story, and correct and erase and rewrite with an unquenchable optimism. There would be moments of despair, moments of wrestling with a recalcitrant sentence, when he walked about in the blaze of the sun, and bit his pencil till his teeth cracked through into the lead, moments of triumph when the impalpable sensation he wished to record seemed to surrender itself to the embrace of verbs and adjectives. Up till tea-time, when the others shuffled (or so he termed it) out of the house after their slumbers, he tasted the glories and the travail of creation, or, it might be, the pangs of fruitless labour; but he knew, at any rate, the joys of ecstatic mental activity.

On one such day, some weeks after his mother and Helena had gone back to England, he felt himself fit to burst with all that he had stored within him, ready for expression. As they drank their coffee he had employed himself in sharpening a couple of pencils (for the work of transcription into ink came later in the day), so as not to interrupt, by any physical intrusion, the flow of all he knew was ready to be crystallized into words. Sometimes the least distraction broke some kind of thread when he was in communication with the sea... It may be added that no one was ever less pompous about his aspirations.

To-day Harry observed the sharpening of the pencils, and commented.

"So a masterpiece is signalled, Archie," he said.

Archie blew the lead-dust from his finger.

"Quite right, old boy," he said. "Lord! I'm full of great thoughts. Do go to bed, and then I'll begin."

Jessie joined in.

"Archie, do let me hold your pencils for you," she said, "like Dora in *David Copperfield*. I shall feel as if I was doing something."

Archie laughed.

"You would be," he remarked. "You would be making an uncommon nuisance of yourself."

"You are polite."

"No, I'm not, I'm rude. I'm being rude on purpose. I want you to be offended and go away. I want Harry to go away too. I want you both to lie on your beds and snore like hogs."

"I was thinking of getting a book and reading out here," said Jessie. "I feel it's unsociable to leave you alone."

"When you've finished being funny," remarked Archie, "you may go to bed. You may get down at once. Say your grace and get down. You, too, Master Harry. Oh, Harry, do you remember how you used to come to tea in the nursery and Blessington made us behave properly till tea was over?"

"Then did you behave improperly?" asked Jessie.

"I don't think we did really. Once we went into the shrubbery and changed clothes. At least I put on yours, but you couldn't put on mine because they were too small. That's what Browning calls 'Time's Revenges.' I couldn't put on yours now, could I? The Italian authorities would prosecute me for indecency. Lord! what a little fellow you are, Harry! Time for a little fellow to go to bed. Oh, don't rag; I never said you weren't strong. Yes, Jessie, you're strong too, and it's like a girl to pull my hair. Ah, do shut up."

Archie had reasonable cause for complaint. Jessie had suddenly come behind him, and taken a great handful of touzled hair into her grasp, so that Archie's head was held immovable, while Harry tickled his ribs. You can do nothing with your arms if your head is held quite still. Presently the wicked ceased from troubling, and Archie was left alone. But after Jessie had gone to her room she stood still a moment before making herself comfortable for her nap, and then she laid across her nose and mouth the outspread hand that had grasped Archie's hair. In her fingers there remained some faint odour of warm sea-salt, and, as by a separate memory of their own, there remained in them the sense of their closing over that brown, bright, springy handful.

CHAPTER VI

Archie thought no more either of his tickled ribs or his outraged hair when his friends had definitely removed themselves, and with a sigh of delight he took up a sharpened pencil and a block of scribbling paper. He had grasped something, he thought, this morning, that must instantly be committed to words, before he even read over his last page or two, for his hand starved and itched to be writing. There was an odd trembling in his fingers, and his conscious brain was full of what he wanted to say. But when he put his pencil on to the block, and concentrated his mind on that liquid message of the sea that had reached him to-day, he found that his hand had nothing to write. His brain was full of what he wanted to write, but his hand disowned the controlling impulse. Again and once again he cast the thought in his brain into reasonable language, but there his hand still stayed, as if some signal was against it. Simply it would not proceed.

Archie had known similar obstacles before, though they had never been so strong as this. Probably the thought was not yet clarified enough, and for that the usual remedy was a stroll about the garden, a look at the sea from the parapetted wall. He tried this, returning again with a conviction that now he would be able to give words to the impression that was so strong in his conscious brain, and, as he took up his pencil again, again his hand seemed to be yearning to write. There was that coral-lipped anemone at the edge of the water, there was a shoal of little fishes which, as they turned, became a sheet of dazzling silver, ... all that was ready for the hand that twitched in expectancy. But again his hand would have nothing to say to that: the brain-signal showed itself to an uncomprehending instrument.

Suddenly, and with distaste, Archie perceived what was happening, and, divorcing from his mind the message that his brain was tingling to convey, he let his mere hand, untroubled by a fighting consciousness, do what it chose. It was no longer in his own control: something, somebody else possessed it. But it was with conscious reluctance that he resigned this mechanism to the controlling agent who was not himself. He watched with absolute detachment the words that came on his paper in a firm, upright handwriting quite unlike his own.

"Archie, you have had a warning," his hand wrote. "Now you must manage for yourself. I shall watch, but I mayn't do more. You have got to do your best and your highest. That's the root of probation. But I am always your most loving brother. When you were a child I could reach you... (Then followed some meaningless scribbles). But it's Martin."

CHAPTER VI

The pencil gave a great dash across the paper, and instantly Archie knew that his hand had returned to its normal allegiance. At once the sea-thoughts that had occupied him seethed and roared in his brain, and his hand was straining to put them down. He tore off the involuntary message from his block, and, laying it aside, plunged with all the force of his conscious self into this ecstasy of conveying, with black marks on white paper, all that had obsessed him this morning as he swam out to sea, and lay between sun and water, the happiest of earthly animals, and the nearest to the key of the symbol. Then, after a half-hour of pure interpretation, that was finished too, and he lay back in his chair and picked up the Martin-message again. It seemed a nonsensical affair when he so regarded it. What was his warning, after all? What did that mean? He had had no warning of any sort. But it was strange that, after all those years of silence, Martin should come to guide him again, though at the self-same time he told him not to look for further guidance.

Archie put the paper with its well-remembered, upright handwriting back on the table again, lay back in his long chair, drowsy, and fatigued after his spell of fiery writing. Almost at once sleep began to invade him; the outline of the stone-pine, etched against the sky, grew blurred as his eyelids fluttered and closed. And then, without pause or transition, he saw a white statue standing close to him, on the neck of which there wriggled the tail of a worm, protruding from the fair white surface, and instantly his forgotten dream leaped into his mind, with a pang of horror. That was what his dream had been: there had been a statue standing just there, white in the moonlight, and even as he worshipped and adored it with love and boundless admiration, those foul symbols of decay had wreathed about it. Next moment he plucked himself from his dozing, and there was no statue there at all, but the far more comfortable figure of Jessie, standing in its place, with laughter in her eye.

"Oh, that's what you do, Archie," she said, "when you pretend to come out into the garden to work, and despise Harry and me for sleeping."

Archie jumped up from his chair and brandished in her face the pages of his consciously written manuscript. The leaf on which the message from Martin was written still lay apart from those on the table.

"I may have closed my eyes for one second," he said. "But I've written all that since lunch. Oh, it's got the sea in it, Jessie; I really believe there's the sea there. I'll read it you this evening, if you'll apologize for saying that I go to sleep instead of writing."

She picked up the other leaf.

"Yes, I apologize," she said, "though you were asleep when I came out. But I want to hear what you've written, so I apologize for having thought so. And there's this other page as well."

Archie took it from her.

"That doesn't belong," he said. "That—"

He paused a moment.

"Do you remember what I told you about the messages I used to have from Martin when I was a child?" he asked.

Jessie nodded.

"Yes; and they have ceased altogether for years, haven't they?" she said quickly.

"Until to-day. Just now, half an hour ago, I had another. But I can't make anything out of it. He tells me that I've had a warning. I don't know what it means."

Jessie felt all the habitual contempt of the thoroughly normal and healthy mind for anything akin to psychical experiences. All ghosts, in her view, were to be classed under the headings of rats or lobster-salad; all such things as table-tappings and the doings of mediums under the heading of trickery. But, knowing what she did of Archie's childish experiences, she could not put them down as trickery, and so was unable exactly to despise them as fraudulent. For that very reason she rather feared them; they made her feel uncomfortable.

She glanced at the paper he held out to her, but without taking it.

"Oh, Archie I distrust all that," she said. "I was really very glad when you told me that for all these years you had had no communication from him. Please don't have any more."

He laughed. They had talked about this before.

"But you don't understand," he said. "It has nothing to do with my wanting or not; it just comes. This afternoon I couldn't help writing any more than—than one can help sneezing."

"You can if you rub your nose the wrong way," said Jessie flippantly.

"No amount of rubbing my nose either the right way or the wrong way would have the slightest effect," said Archie. "The thing is imperative: if Martin wants me to write, I must write. But he says here that he's not going to guide me; I must look after myself. I'm sorry for that."

"I'm not," said Jessie quickly. "There's something strange and uncanny about it. I'm not sure that I think it's right even."

She paused a moment.

"Archie, do you really believe that it is the spirit of Martin that makes you write?" she said. "Are you sure—"

He interrupted her.

"I know what you mean," he said. "It's what the Roman Catholics teach, that any communication of the sort, given that it is genuine, and not some mere mediumistic trick, is not less than converse with some evil being impersonating, masquerading as the spirit from whom the communication apparently comes. Do you mean that?"

Jessie frowned, fingering the edge of the table.

"Yes, I suppose I do," she said. "I think the whole thing is dangerous; I don't think it's a thing to meddle with."

"But I don't meddle with it," said Archie. "It meddles with me. Besides, did you ever hear of such an unwarranted assumption? Mightn't I almost as well say that a letter which reaches me from my mother doesn't really come from her, but from some evil creature impersonating her? It seems simpler to suppose that it comes from her, that her signature is genuine, just as I believe Martin's to be. Do you really think that when I was a poor little consumptive chap at Grives I was really possessed by an evil spirit? Isn't that rather too horrible an imagining? A nice state the next world must be in, if that sort of thing is allowed! I don't for a moment think it is. Can you reconcile with the idea of supreme Love governing and creating all life, the notion that there, behind the scenes, there are evil and awful beings who can get leave to communicate with a child, as I was, pretending to be the spirit of the brother I never knew? Does it sound likely?"

Jessie paused a moment again. She hated the subject, she hated the idea of Archie's being concerned in these dim avenues to the unseen. She had, for herself, a perfectly unreasoning and childlike faith that there was this world, and the next world, and that God reigned supreme over both. But somehow it offended this instinctive attitude that the next world, and those who had gone there, should be mixed up with this world. They were not dead; she did not think they had ceased to exist; but they had done with this world, and it was something like a profanity to meddle with them. But then Archie had not meddled, as he most truly said: they seemed to have meddled with him. Their meddling had stopped altogether for a dozen years, and here on this half-sheet of paper was the evidence that something of the sort had begun again.

"I thought you had dropped all interest in it," she said. "I thought it was all finished, like a childish fairy-story, like the Abracadabra legend Cousin Marion told me about. Oh, there's tea; shall we have tea?"

Pasqualino had spread their table underneath the stone-pine, and she hailed this as a possible dismissal of the whole affair. She did not want to talk any more about it, and, if below her silence there should lurk a fear, she preferred to cover it up, not examine it. Archie got up.

"Certainly let us have tea," he said. "Perhaps your mind will be clearer after tea. I'm not going to quit the question, Jessie. The historian is at his histories, and we shall be alone, you and I, and I want to talk it out. Something has happened, you see, this afternoon. Martin—or somebody—has written again. You were quite right to imagine that for me the whole thing was finished, had become an Abracadabra-myth as you said. As far as normal life goes, I thought it had too. But I always knew that it might come back. And it has come back without my asking for it, though it—he—says he's going to leave me alone. But, after all, he says, 'You've got to do your best and your highest.' Now I ask you, as a reasonable female, does that look like a message from a devil? No, it's Martin all right, bless him. But let's have tea."

They moved across into the shadow of the pine, where the table sparkled with the specks of stray sunshine that filtered through the boughs. And Jessie, sane and normal, held on to those evidences of the kindly ordinary human life, as an anchor to prevent her drifting out into perilous seas. But to Archie no seas were perilous: they might engulf his body and drown him, and, as it seemed to him, they might engulf his spirit, but they were not perilous in his view. They were just the sea, the great encompassing presence...

"Archie, you are so odd," she said, knowing that he meant to have the subject talked out, and that his will dominated hers, "You spend the day bathing and sailing and writing; you eat and you sleep, and then suddenly you spring a surprise upon me, and show me a letter you have had from Martin. Which is you, the surprise or the Archie that I know?"

Archie's mouth was extraordinarily full of rusk and cherry-jam. He politely disposed of them before replying.

"But they're both me," he said. "Of course we have all two existences."

"Dual personality?" she asked.

"Dual fiddlesticks. What I mean is that in everybody there is the conscious self and the subconscious self, but they do not make a dual personality, but one personality. Most people—you, for instance, or Harry, or my mother—transact everything through the conscious personality. For all practical purposes your subconscious self doesn't exist. But in some, and I'm one of them—the subconscious self is accessible. I can reach it if I want. I can make it act. It is the essential life which we all of us contain, and, as such, it is that part of ourselves with which the essential life of those who have quitted this unessential life can communicate. Martin doesn't communicate with that part of me which directs and controls my conversation with you. He speaks to my subconscious self, and, by some rather unusual arrangement, my subconscious life can speak to my conscious life and convey what he says to my hand, or, as once happened, when at Grives I heard him call me, to my ear. I am a medium in fact, though that would usually suggest something charlatanish. I can bring my subconscious life to the surface; sometimes, as when Martin speaks to it, it comes to the surface of its own accord, with strong compulsion over my conscious self."

He paused a moment.

"It's all very odd," he said. "Until this afternoon, my subconscious self had lain quite quiet for years. Now suddenly it asserts itself and produces that page of writing, because Martin talked to it, and told it to make my hand write. What other explanation is there, unless indeed you imagine that I have merely perpetrated a silly hoax? But I swear to you that something outside myself made me write. Baldly stated, it was Martin who spoke to my subconscious self, and my subconscious self said to my conscious self, 'Take a pencil and write.' I know that is so."

Once again Jessie had to anchor herself against this current running out to sea. There was Archie sitting opposite her, large and brown and hungry, talking of things which were altogether fantastic, unless they were dangerous. And somehow, they were not either fantastic or dangerous to him; they were as ordinary as the cherry-jam which he was so profusely eating. She had suddenly come on a great undiscovered tract of country, dubious and full of dangers.

"I dislike it all," she said. "I'm too ordinary, I suppose, my—my subconscious self doesn't act, you would say. But what proof is there that there is such a thing as the subconscious self? Why should I suppose that there is anything of the sort? I have no reason to suppose it. It is all nonsense."

Archie laughed.

"My dear Jessie," he said, "you are arguing not with me but with yourself. You have an uneasy conviction that I am right."

"Not a bit," she said. "I want a proof."

Archie rubbed his hand over his head.

"I wonder how I can give it you most easily," he said. "Of course there are lots of ways, though it is quite a long time since I have practised any of them."

He thought for a moment.

"Well, here's one," he said. "The subconscious self—to talk more nonsense, as you say—is practically unlimited by the material laws of the world. It is a sort of X-ray, a sort of wireless… I can set my subconscious self to work, and I will, to prove its existence to you."

His voice sank a little, and Jessie saw that his eyes were fixed on a bright speck of sunlight that gleamed on the table-cloth. A sudden ridiculous terror seized her.

"Don't, Archie," she said. "It's such nonsense."

"It isn't nonsense," said he quietly, "and you mustn't be such a baby. There's nothing to be frightened at."

As he spoke he took his eyes off the bright speck at which he had been staring, and looked at her with his blue, dancing glance.

"What are you going to do?" she said.

"Whatever you like. Let me look at that bright spot there, while you sit quiet, for two minutes, and I'll tell you anything you choose. Think of something, anything will do, and I'll tell you what you're thinking about."

"Oh, just thought-reading," said she.

"*Just* thought-reading! But what is thought-reading? If you can remember what you thought about when you went up to your bedroom to sleep after lunch to-day, for instance, I'll tell you that. Or, there is Harry writing his history lecture for next term at this moment. I'll tell you the words he is writing. At least I think I shall be able to. But I'm out of practice. I have not cultivated the particular mood for years. But I had it when I was a child, and I expect I can get back into it."

Jessie felt an extreme curiosity about this. She had, even as Archie had said, an uneasy conviction that he was right, and for her peace of mind she longed to have that conviction shattered. In her reasonable self she did not believe that Archie could possibly tell her what Harry was writing, but behind that reasonable self sat something unreasonable which wanted to be convinced that this was all nonsense.

"But you won't have a fit or anything, will you?" she asked.

"No. Pour boiling tea over me if I do, and I shall come to myself."

"But what are you going to do?"

"I'm going to look at something bright. That spot of sun on the table-cloth will do. Then I shall just submerge, like a submarine, and tell you what Harry is writing at this moment, if that is the test you select. What fun it all is! I haven't done it, as I said, for ever so long. Oh, take a bit of paper, and write down what I say. I don't suppose I shall be able to remember it."

Again his voice sank, as he fixed his eyes on the bright spot he had indicated, and Jessie, watching him, pencil and paper in hand, saw an extraordinary change come over his face. For a few seconds it got troubled, and his eyes stared painfully, while his breath came quickly in and out of his nostrils. Then he grew quite quiet again, his mouth smiled, and he spoke very slowly as if the words were dictated by a writer.

"It is hopeless to try to comprehend in the whole," he said, "the splendour of that unique age. We can only think of it in fragments. One afternoon there was a new play by Sophocles; another day Pericles made the funeral oration for the fallen; on another the great Propylaea to the Acropolis were finished, Socrates talked in the market-place, or supped with Alcibiades. In the space of a few years all those things happened, and as yet more than twenty centuries have failed to grasp their full significance. And in this, my last lecture to you—"

Archie rubbed his eyes and sat up.

"He has finished for the present," he said.

There was a stir in the room just above them, where they sat in the garden, and Harry looked out.

"Any tea left?" he said.

Archie looked up.

"Hullo, Harry," he said. "I thought you were going to finish your lecture and not appear till dinner."

"I was, but I think I'll finish it up to-morrow."

"Bring it down and read us as far as you've got," said Archie. "Jessie won't mind."

"All right. It got a little purplish at the end, and that's why I stopped. I hate purples."

He moved away from the window, and Archie spoke to Jessie. "Did I say anything?" he asked.

"Yes; I've got it all down."

Archie jumped up.

"Now you'll see," he said. "You won't sauce me again in—in the wicious pride of your youth, as Mr. Venus remarked. I'm sure I got through that time."

* * * * *

It was the knowledge that he had indeed "got through" that Jessie took up to bed with her that night. Word for word Harry had read out at the end of his lecture precisely the sentences that Archie, in that queer dreamy state, had dictated to her, just before Harry had looked out of the window and asked if there was any tea left. There was no room for doubt: even as Archie had said, some piece of his mind had been able to divine exactly what Harry was writing at that moment. In his conscious state he could not know what that was, but according to his own account certain people, of whom he was one, were able to direct not only their conscious selves but also the subconscious self that lay below. It, so he asserted, was practically unfettered by material laws: it could perceive what was happening at a distance, at a spot invisible to it, and it could penetrate as by some X-ray process into other minds. For its free action (in his case at any rate) the conscious self had to be obliterated; by looking at that bright spot on the table-cloth he had been able to put it to sleep, to hypnotize it, thus allowing the subconscious self to pass the portals where normally the conscious self kept guard, and to do its errand.

So far there was nothing to disquiet her or make her uncomfortable. It was, as she had said, "just thought-reading," an example of a purely natural law, which, however dimly understood, was fully admitted by scientific investigators. No one, except the most hide-bound of pedants, questioned the existence of the subconscious self, and, if here was an example of an abnormal development of it, still there was nothing to fight shy of. She had asked for a proof of its powers, and undeniably she had got it…

But Archie had gone far beyond that in his exposition of the powers of the subconscious self, and it was this which caused her a very vivid disquiet. Through the subconscious self, in those who had the gift of releasing it, of allowing its activities, could come, so he believed, communications from the individual consciousnesses which had passed out of the material world. Even as the subconscious self could get into touch with the thoughts of living people (as she had seen for herself that afternoon), so also could it get into touch with the thoughts of the dead. It was thus, so Archie announced, that when he was a mere child, and knew nothing whatever of conscious and subconscious selves, Martin, the brother whom he had never heard of, used his hand to write with, as if it was his own, and with it wrote in the handwriting which had been his. Jessie fully believed in the survival of personality; to her the so-called dead had but passed on to a further and higher plane of existence; but there was to her something inexplicably repugnant in the notion that they could come back, and speak or write to those who still lived on this plane of existence.

Jessie lingered late by her window, overlooking the bay, trying to disentangle and lay bare the roots of her repugnance. It was late; below in the garden she could perceive the grey lines of Archie's hammock swung between the acacia and the pine, and Archie lying there like a chrysalis. He was just like that, she thought; most of the world were only caterpillars, eating their way through the allotted span of their years, but Archie was a stage more advanced than anybody she had ever known. This world and the next were one to him, not by any spiritual insight, but from that instinctive conviction that there was really no difference between the living and the so-called dead. It was not by any enlightenment, through any stress of prayer and aspiration that he had arrived at that. He had been gifted with it as a child; he was a medium, who by some special gift could talk to a brother, who had died long years ago, with just the same naturalness as he talked to her. If he died to-night, he would find nothing strange about it: he would but burst his chrysalis, hang for a moment, weak and fluttering, and then expand his wings. But to most people death was an awful affair. They were caterpillars; they had to learn the intermediate stage, which he was already familiar with. And yet the fact that he was a stage more advanced coupled with it a sort of helplessness for him. There he lay in his cocoon; any evil thing might attack him…

Jessie shook herself, mind and body; she was being fantastic in her fears and her misgivings, and with set purpose she forced herself to drink in, be penetrated by the assured serenity of the material world that lay spread before her. Above wheeled the stars in the silent sky, and on the silent sea shone the constellations from the fishing-boats. The trees stood motionless in the holy summer-hushed night beneath, while, though all seemed to sleep, the great renewing forces of the world were ripening the olives and enriching the twisted buds that would flower in fresh harvest of azure on the Morning Glory when the sun warmed them. There was nothing to disturb her; she could let her soul lie open to the night and think out the cause for her disquietude.

She hated the idea of commerce between the living and the dead; there was the root of it. The strangeness of the idea made it seem unnatural. Yet where, if she examined it more closely, was the unnaturalness? Why should not loving souls, who had passed that tiny rivulet called Death into the fuller life beyond, be allowed to call from the other side to those they loved? Was there not something exquisite, something supremely tender in the thought that Martin, who had been but little more than a child when he died in that Swiss chalet, should tell Archie about the cache he had made under the pine-tree? It was a childish communication, it brought no message of consolation or encouragement; but it was just what Martin, had he been alive on this side of Death, might have told Archie. Besides, who knew that he did not give that as a test, as a proof of his identity, for surely nothing could have been devised so convincing? And if God willed that the dead should be able, under certain circumstances, to speak from the sunlit beyond to those who still moved among material shadows, who was she, Jessie, to question so wonderful an ordinance? And if he could speak like that to a young and innocent child, why should he not continue to speak to his brother when he grew up?

She looked elsewhere for the grounds of her repugnance, and for a moment thought she had found them. For she had once been to a seance, at the house of a professional medium, and that afternoon still was vivid and degrading in her memory. They had all sat round a table in a darkened room while the medium went into trance, and instantly ridiculous knockings and melodies from a musical-box began to resound in the gloom. These were supposed to be played by spirits called Durward and Felisy, who, for some absolutely unconjecturable reason, liked spending the afternoon in these puerile idiocies. Meantime, the medium breathed heavily, which was the only evidence that he was in trance at all, and after a while said, "Here's the dear Cardinal," in a husky voice, and his niece, who sat next him, informed the circle that this was Cardinal Newman, who, like Durward and Felisy, could find nothing better to do on the other side than attend these awful sittings, for he always came when you paid your guinea to the medium and sat in the dark. To encourage him they lifted up their voices, at the suggestion of the medium's niece, and sang "Lead, kindly Light," which gratified him so much that he joined in singing the second verse and sang his own hymn to the tune given in *Hymns Ancient and Modern*. Then, when the hymn was over, he made some moral reflections and blessed them in Latin. Then there came materializations; the head and shoulders of Durward appeared in the middle of the table. He was dressed in white, and had a large black beard, and round his ear the wire with which the beard was attached to his face was clearly visible. During this the circle was warned to keep their hands touching all round the table, for, if any one made a break, the consequences to the medium might be very serious, since the spirit had built itself up from material derived from the medium and the "electric fluid" contributed by the sitters. So, if the electric fluid was withdrawn the material would not be able to get back into the medium, who would completely collapse and possibly die, though whether Durward would thereupon again become a visible and permanent dweller on this planet was not explained. By this time Jessie had been so convinced of the wicked and profane fraudulence of all these proceedings that she furtively withdrew one of her hands, and thus cut off the electric fluid altogether. But Durward didn't mind a bit, but continued to tell them about the joys of Paradise, which, according to his account, must have been like the Crystal Palace erected in the middle of the Botanical Gardens. And when he had regaled them enough he withdrew in the direction where the medium sat, took off his beard, and became Felisy with a veil and an alto voice. Surely all this was enough to make one despair and contemn the whole idea of intercourse with spirits...

But Jessie suddenly became aware of a basic illogicality in her position. It was not intercourse with spirits she despised, but those despicable swindlers who, with the aid of false beards and musical-boxes, pretended that they could materialize and cause communication with spirits. She did not deride the memory of that afternoon because the spirits of Cardinal Newman and Durward and Felisy had moved among them, but because they hadn't. It was no use accounting for her repugnance towards genuine intercourse with spirits by her repugnance towards quacks and charlatans. The whole history of spiritualism teemed with these undesirable gentry and these faked phenomena, but they had no more connection with Archie and his communications from his brother than had a forged bank-note with the credit of the Bank of England. She found she did believe that the knowledge, say, of the cache beneath the pine-tree came to Archie from other than normal human sources. It was known to no living being in the world, so far as she could tell, and if she looked for an explanation she must search for it in the supposition that the knowledge came to him from a living intelligence beyond the veil. She intensely disliked being forced to that conclusion, and now she knew why. It was for the reason she had suggested to him this afternoon.

These things came from those regions, those conditions of existence into which people passed when they died. But in those regions there existed not only the souls of the dead who lived in an environment and under conditions at which we could not ever so faintly conjecture, but other spirits, some good, some evil. Every good impulse that came into the hearts of men, came from over there; so, too, did every evil impulse that would blight, if it could, the garden of God. And who knew whether the man who by that strange faculty which Archie possessed of opening the doors of his subliminal self, through which, as he averred, these messages came, might not open them to other and evil things? If possession by an evil spirit was a psychical possibility (and certainly it was not more fantastically strange than such phenomena as Archie could produce) would it not be thus, and in no other way, that the evil possession would enter? Yet in childhood Archie had, in ignorance and in white defencelessness, opened more than once the door of his soul, and no harm surely had come to him. Was she being unreasonable, full of fear where no fear was, twittering with groundless and superstitious fancies?

There was yet another side to the question. If the spirits of the dead could indeed return, and speak of what they knew, was it not worth while running some risk on the chance of the wonders they might tell of the existence which now was theirs? Whatever else might be of interest in human life, supreme over all was any hint or fragment of information about the timeless and everlasting day that lay beyond the dawnings and settings of the sun. Nay, more: if to any one was given this wonderful gift by means of which voices could reach him from beyond the veil, was it not his duty to use this endowment for the enlightenment and consolation of those who mourned and who sat in darkness? God would never have bestowed so spiritual a gift on any, if He did not mean it to be used. The Christian Faith taught that the dead were alive in a wider sense than ever they had been on earth; why then should it be forbidden, to those who had this amazing gift, to speak with them, to learn about their life? The Roman Church had fulminated its anathemas on Galileo, a thing scarcely credible to a more enlightened age; it was more than possible that its pronouncements against this intercourse with the dead was but one instance the more of a similar cowardice and narrowness. Who could doubt that a man of science three hundred years ago would have been burned as a dabbler in diabolism and witchcraft, if he had exhibited a manifestation of wireless telegraphy or an X-ray photograph? But nowadays there was not a living being who did not rank such as the discoveries of a natural law. The sorcery of one age was the science of the next.

Jessie propounded this to herself, and her reason could not find a flaw in it. But something that sat behind her reason—superstition it might be, or instinct, or spiritual perception—refused to accept the conclusion. Like a child afraid of the dark, it trembled and hung back, and no amount of logical assurance from its nurse, no amount of demonstration that the room when dark contained only the familiar things which the light made manifest, could reassure it. It didn't like the dark; nothing could persuade it that danger did not lurk in blackness…

Well, it was no use going over all the ground again, she knew it thoroughly now. Reason made no headway against instinct, or instinct against reason, and she swept the matter from her mind, and tried to calm a certain intimate agitation that trembled there, by letting her eyes pour into her soul the superb serenity of the Italian night. The moon had risen and spread across the bay a silver path to the edge of the world, and in the sky the wheeling innumerable worlds kept sentinel over the earth. Never had she looked on a stillness more peaceful and more steadfast. Not a breeze stirred in the cypresses, but in the thickets of ilex below the Love that moved the sun and the other stars thrilled in the hearts of innumerable nightingales. That Love permeated everywhere; the world was soaked in its peace...

And just then, over the hills to the north, there flickered a flash of lightning from some storm very far away. Long afterwards, and scarcely audible, came a muffled murmur of thunder.

* * * * *

Jessie came downstairs next morning before either of the two young men were astir, and indeed, on going into the garden, she found Archie still serenely slumbering in his hammock in spite of the sun that filtered through the pine-tree on to his brown face and curly head. But perhaps some intangible shaft from her pierced down into the gulfs of sleep, for immediately he sat up, flushed with slumber like a child, but fresh and bright-eyed from his night in the open air.

"Hullo, Jess," he said. "You down already? I suppose I'd better get up. Is it shocking for a young lady to see a young gentleman's bare feet and his pyjamas? If so, you must shut your eyes. Now you're going to see them. Don't scream."

"I shall," said Jessie. "You always wear patent leather boots and a fur-coat when we bathe."

"Yes, that is so. But bear it for once. Lord, what a morning!"

He threw off his blanket and dangled his legs over the side of the hammock, and instantly lit a cigarette.

"Archie, why do you smoke before breakfast?" she asked.

"Because it makes me feel so jolly dizzy. Ah, you can't guess how good a cigarette tastes when you have had nothing but your tongue and your teeth in your mouth for eight or nine hours. Hullo! Here's the post. English papers? Who cares for what happens in England? No letters for me, two for Harry, and one for you. Good-bye; I shan't wash much because I shall bathe all the morning."

Jessie's letter proved to be from Helena, and its contents instantly absorbed her whole attention. Colonel Vautier, her father and Lady Tintagel's first cousin, had gone out to Egypt over some government irrigation work, and, instead of coming back in June, would be detained out there till September. In consequence, Lady Tintagel hoped that the two girls would live with her instead of going back to their father's house till his return. Helena's comment on this was enthusiastic, and also very characteristic.

"Darling Jessie," she said, after the statement of this proposal, "I do hope you'll say 'yes.' Cousin Marion encloses a note for you, so you'll see how much she wants us to, and Uncle Jack—I've begun to call him Uncle Jack, though he isn't an uncle at all—gave quite a pleased sort of grunt when it was mentioned, which means that he approves. So don't be independent, and say you would sooner go back to Oakland Crescent, because I've simply set my heart on stopping here. It's horrible at home in the summer with the sun blazing into those little tiny rooms and the smell of greens flooding the house. And it really would be a kindness to Cousin Marion; she says so herself, as you'll find when you read her note. And besides, there's another reason which I know you can guess. In fact, I think it's our duty to come, and when duty takes the form of anything so pleasant as this, there really is not the slightest reason for neglecting it. And, as I'm the youngest, I feel that you should do as I want. Besides, it's the greatest fun here. There are no end of dances and parties and dinners, and there are horses to ride and motor-cars. I'm having the loveliest tune, so it will be very selfish of you if you want to go home. But I know you will say 'yes.'"

A charming enclosure from Lady Tintagel accompanied this:

"I so much hope that you and Helena will stop with us. You must think of it as a great kindness to me, for it will be the utmost comfort to me, now that both my girls are married, to have you two with me for the rest of the season. I spoke to Archie about it while we were at Silorno, so ask him whether he approves or not. I hope all goes well with you. Is Archie quite black yet from bathing? Send me a line as soon as you have thought it over. Helena is having the greatest success in town; every one thinks her charming, and admires her enormously."

Jessie read this over as she waited for Archie to rejoin her at breakfast. There was every reason for accepting so cordial an invitation, and it would give pleasure to Helena, to Cousin Marion, and apparently also to Archie. She knew she would have to consent: there was no cause that could be spoken about which she could possibly adduce for refusing. A week ago that cause did not exist, but now she wondered how she could bear to see Helena and Archie in the close companionship which this would imply, and watch his feeling for her expanding from the bud into the flower. If she had thought that Helena loved him it would all be different. But she felt certain that Helena did not. There, for her, was the poignancy of it...

In a manner that she could not explain, Jessie knew that she knew the tokens by which love betrays its existence. She, barely yet twenty-two, had somewhere stored in her soul the language of love, which it speaks even when it thinks it is dumb—talking in its sleep, it may be. She had seen in the last week of Helena's sojourn here that Archie talked to her like that. "There was neither speech nor language": he said nothing of which the words betrayed his dawning passion, but his love spoke in his silence, even as the rosy clouds high above the earth herald the dawn. It was her own knowledge that enlightened her: she too knew the silent language, and knew that Archie conversed in it, though no word came, when he talked to Helena. Something kindled behind his eye, some secret alertness possessed him... But there was the defencelessness and the blindness of love, for when Helena answered him she but pretended to talk the same tongue, and Jessie, knowing it, knew that she spoke a mere paltry gibberish. It sounded the same, or it looked the same; but it was nonsense, it was not authentic. Yet Archie never talked in the secret tongue to Jessie; and, in consequence, she had never answered him in it. To-day it seemed her native tongue when she talked to him, and all she said must needs be translated out of that into the language of those who were friends, dear friends, but no more than friends.

All this was instantaneous: she seemed to read it between the lines of Helena's letter. She recalled, too, between the lines, the tokens that she knew. Archie would look at Harry, as they sat at dinner, then at his mother, then at her, in order that in due time he might look at Helena. And when he spoke to any of them they never got more than one ear and an inattentive mind from him. The other ear and the attention were always with Helena. Helena knew that quite well: no woman or girl could fail to know it, and, by way of response, she had made this Scythian retreat to England. No doubt that was clever of her, but in Jessie's opinion clever people are found out even sooner than stupid ones. The only inexplicable folk are the wise, and wisdom has very little to do with cleverness. Wisdom is perhaps the cleverness of the soul, that looks down with pity on the manoeuvres of the mind.

Archie made his absurd entry. He had a dressing-gown on, perhaps some sort of abbreviated bathing-dress, and canvas-shoes.

"I didn't dress," he said, "for where's the use of dressing if you are going to undress again almost immediately?"

"Aren't you going to work this morning?" asked Jessie.

"No. This one day, as Mr. Wordsworth said, we'll give to idleness. I'm going to bathe all the morning instead of half the morning. I want a holiday. I think I'm overworked. What's happening in that foolish England, if you've read the papers?"

"I haven't," said she.

Suddenly his face changed; he began to talk the secret language, which Jessie understood and Helena counterfeited.

"And what other news?" he asked. "You had a letter from somebody."

Jessie pretended not to understand what she knew so well.

"Yes, I did have a letter," she said, determined that Archie should be more direct than this.

"From Helena or mother?" he said carelessly. "I haven't heard from either of them, except that telegram to say they had got home safely."

He was talking the secret language still; the very carelessness of his tone betrayed it.

"I heard from them both," she said. "The letter was from Helena, and there was an enclosure from Cousin Marion."

Archie said nothing in answer to this, but it seemed to the girl that his silence was just as eloquent in the language without words. Eventually he remarked that Harry was very late, and Jessie knew that he had beaten her. He always did, just because he had nothing, with regard to her, at stake.

"Archie, I want to talk to you about what they have written to me," she said.

"Talk away," said Archie. "I say, what good little fishes!"

Jessie was not proposing to yield like that. If he, in the code of the secret language, professed an indifference to what he was longing to hear, she would be indifferent too.

To Archie's intense irritation she continued to talk about little fishes, in a tone of great interest, till Harry's entrance. She agreed they were very good; probably they were fresh sardines caught last night by the fishers. Or were they… and she could not remember the Italian name of the other little fish which were so like sardines.

Archie's serene brow clouded, and he but grunted a greeting to Harry. And next moment her heart smote her. She knew how easily Archie could put the sun out for her without meaning to do it, but she had, out of a sort of piqued femininity, intentionally done the same for him. She felt as if she had spoiled a child's pleasure. He was so like a child, but lovers were made of child-stuff. He got up almost immediately, and, full of a tender penitence, she followed him.

One behind the other they went out into the garden, where Archie, in a superb unconsciousness of her presence, became instantly absorbed in the despised English papers.

"Archie!" she said.

He rustled with his paper.

"Oh, er—what?" he answered.

"I wanted to talk to you about Helena's letter," she said, "only you would talk about sardines. Put that paper down; I can't talk through the paper."

She noticed that he kept his finger on a paragraph, and she would have betted her last shilling that he had no idea what that paragraph was about. And, though a moment before she had been penitent, now she stiffened herself and determined that he should meet her more gracefully than that.

"I'm sorry; I'm interrupting you," she said. "I'll tell you some other time."

Archie suddenly threw the paper into the air.

"Oh, aren't we behaving like idiots?" he said. "At heart I am, and so are you really. But I'll confess: I'm just longing to know what Helena writes about. But aren't you an idiot, too? I shall like it enormously if you say you are."

"I am an idiot, too," said the girl. "And Cousin Marion wants Helena and me to live with her till father comes home. She told me to ask you if you approved."

He leaned forward to her.

"Ah, do, Jessie," he said. "I hope you will. I can't see why you shouldn't. Can you?"

She looked straight into the eager blue eyes that were so close to hers. For her there was a wealth of frankness and friendliness, but the light in them was not for her, and she knew it.

"Helena wants to," she said.

"Does that mean that you don't?" he asked. "I'm sorry if that is so."

She got up.

"No, it doesn't mean that a bit," she said. "It's delightful of you and Cousin Marion to want us. Of course we'll come."

Archie rose too.

"That's perfectly ripping of you," he said. "We shall be a jolly party, we four."

Quite suddenly a pause fell, very awkwardly, very constrainedly.

CHAPTER VI

"You see, my father doesn't appear much," he said at length. "That's what I meant. He is very often in the country, and—well, we don't see him much."

Archie soon took himself off to the sea, armed with paper and pencils, for, with four hours in front of him, there would be much basking to be done between his bathes. Already another of those sea-sketches was beginning to take shape in his mind, and he found that there was no hour so fruitful in inspiration as when, after a swim, he returned to this empty, sandy beach, and lay spread out to the sun to be dried and browned and made eager for another dip. So, to-day, after the first swim, he lay for a while on his back with his arms across his face to shield his eyes from the glare, and opened his brain, so to speak, to let the sea-thoughts invade it. They came swarming in at his invitation, and presently he turned over and propped himself on his elbow and began to catch them and pin them to his paper. The rim of the sea, with its weed-fringed rocks, its diaper of moving light in the shallow water, the shoals of little fishes, almost invisible one moment, the next, as they turned, becoming a shield of silver flakes, were all ready to be hammered into sentences; and yet the hammer paused...

Somehow at the back of his mind was a topic that inhibited his hand, or would not allow the connection between hand and brain to be made, and he thought he knew what this was, for only this morning he had heard that Helena was to be an inmate of their house in London. Yet it did not seem to be that which was preventing him, and he wondered whether it was the thought of his father and his habitual intoxication, which was always like a black background at home, and which just for a moment had popped out into his conversation with Jessie, that hindered him. But that again did not seem a sufficient cause for his inability to start the mechanism which translated thought into language.

And then he became aware that his fingers itched and ached to write with a compelling force which he knew well. And yet only yesterday Martin had said that he should not come to him again. But the quality of the force seemed unmistakable, and presently he yielded to that which he really had not the power to resist and wrote as his hand bade him write.

There were but a few sentences scribbled, and then his pencil, as usually happened when the message was complete, gave a dash. He had no notion what he had written, and when it was finished he read it through.

"Archie, I have come through this once more," it said, "to repeat that you have been warned. But I can't get through again.—MARTIN."

So here again was this inexplicable mention of a warning, and Archie's conscious mind was blank with regard to any such warning. But the repetition of it did not long occupy him, for immediately he found that the inhibition between his brain and his hand was gone, and sentence after sentence of his sea-sketch flowed through his fingers. By degrees, but not till a couple of his pages were full, did the inspiration exhaust itself, and then he lay back on the sand again full of the ecstasy that always accompanies the completion of a piece of work that has been done as the creator meant to do it. Bad or good, it has fulfilled his intention.

His brain brooded over that for a little, and then slipped back to the incident that had preceded it. He could make nothing at all of it, and, determining to dismiss it from his mind, and speak of it to nobody, he tore up the sheet that contained the message, buried the fragments in the sand, and lay back again roasting himself in the sun. Soon that delectable warmth would increase on his bare limbs, till they cried out for the cool embraces of the sea again, and he would fling himself into it. But just for a little longer he would stew and stupefy himself in the sun and with half-closed eyes watch the vibration of the hot air over the beach and listen to the hiss of the ripples. Except for them the morning was extremely quiet, the sun poured down over his outspread limbs, the sea waited for him. And, as he lay there and dozed, the memory of his evil dream went across his brain like a flash, and vanished again.

* * * * *

Already the Italian days were beginning to draw to their sunny end; they were numbered and could be easily counted. Both Archie and Jessie counted them when they woke in the morning, and in the evening both said to themselves, "Another day gone." But their reflections on this diminishing tale and the colour of their emotions were absolutely opposed, for while they both intensely enjoyed these Italian hours, Jessie counted them with the grudging sense of a school-boy who enumerates the remaining days of his holiday; but to Archie they were the days of term-time which still (though enjoyable) must be got through before the holidays began. Never before had he contemplated a stay in town with eagerness; but now, as he thought of her who would be living with them, he had never been so expectantly enamoured of London.

At the close of their last day the divine serenity of June weather was troubled, and, as evening drew on, the clouds, which for a few hours past had been weaving wisps and streamers over the sky, grew to a thick curtain that stretched from horizon to horizon. It was of opaque grey, but here and there in it were lines and patches of much darker texture, as if it had been rent, and had been darned again with a blacker thread. Instead of the coolness which succeeded sunset, the heat, clear no longer, but impure like the air of a closed room, got ever sultrier, and, for the refreshment of the evening breeze from the sea, there was exchanged a stifling stagnation. All life had gone out of the atmosphere: it was as if some immense Othello was smothering the world. The air was heavy and charged with electricity, but as yet no remote winking of lightning nor rumble of thunder showed that there was relief coming.

They had dined out in the garden, where the candles burned unwaveringly in the stillness, and afterwards had strolled to the far angle of the supporting wall of the fortress, where, if anywhere, they might find some hint of movement in this intolerable calm. But no breath visited them even there, and the very bamboos that grew at the corner of the garden-bed were as motionless as if they had been made of lead.

Archie mopped his streaming forehead.

CHAPTER VI

"If it interests anybody," he remarked, "I may say that I am going to die. I can't bear it any longer. I think I shall die in about half an hour."

Jessie fanned herself. That did not do a particle of good, it only seemed to make her hotter, as when you stir the water in a hot bath. But she tried to interest herself in Archie's approaching decease.

"And are we to take your corpse back to England to-morrow?" she asked.

"Just as you like. I shall have no more use for it. Lord, and I haven't finished packing yet. Fancy having to pack in this heat."

"You needn't, surely, if you're going to die."

"I must. My immortal manuscript would be lost in the general confusion caused by my death. Or shall I go to bed? It can't be hotter in my hammock than here. Yes, I shall get into my pyjamas, go to bed, and do my packing in the morning."

He trailed off into the house, and presently appeared again attired for bed and strolled across to them.

"Well, I'll *wish* you a good-night," he said, "but I very much doubt whether you'll get it. You needn't do the same to me, for I know I shan't, and your wishes would be hollow."

He moved away again towards the stone-pine where his hammock was hung, a pale tall ghost of a figure against the blackness.

Then, quite suddenly, some panic impulse seized Jessie, the result perhaps of her overstrung nerves and the overcharged atmosphere, and she sprang up, not knowing why.

"Wait a moment, Archie," she cried. "Don't go—something is going to happen."

Even as she spoke the whole world seemed enveloped in fire, and the core of the fire, a white-hot line, plunged downwards into the stone-pine, which was rent from top to bottom. Absolute blackness filled with the deafening roar of the thunder and deluging rain succeeded, and they rushed towards the shelter of the house.

For a moment they all three stood there recovering their balance from that tremendous crash and convulsion. Then Archie, with his soaked silk clinging close to his shoulders and legs, turned to Jessie.

"I wonder why you called out to me," he said. "What made you do it? You saved my life, I expect."

Jessie laughed; little as she was given to hysteria that laugh was half-way towards uncontrollable tears.

"Why, I didn't want you to die in half an hour," she said lightly.

* * * * *

But she remembered that moment when it came for her to save Archie's life indeed. Some inexplicable signal from love had flashed upon her that night, and should flash upon her again.

CHAPTER VII

Helena was having breakfast by the open window of her bedroom in her cousin's house. It was not yet nine in the morning, and, though she had been dancing till three o'clock, she had already had her bath, and was feeling as fresh as if she had had eight instead of hardly more than four hours in bed. Outside the square was still empty of passengers, and the pale primrose-coloured sunshine of a London June shone on a wet roadway and rain-refreshed trees, for a shower had fallen not long ago, and through the open window there came in the delicious smell of damp earth. But she gave little heed to that or to the breakfast she was eating with so admirable an appetite, for her brain, cool and alert in this early hour, was very busy over her own concerns. Soon she would have to go down to Cousin Marion and see if she could be of any use to her, for it was quite worth while doing jobs for Cousin Marion, as she always paid kindnesses back with a royal generosity. And she must get some flowers to give a welcoming air to Archie's room, who with Jessie was expected back to-day. That also would not be a waste of the time she might have spent more directly on herself. She would get some for Jessie, too, for she had the character of unselfish thoughtfulness to keep up. It would be unnecessary to pay for them, for she could get them at the shop where Cousin Marion dealed.

Helena had enjoyed the most entrancing fortnight, during which time she had occasionally thought of Silorno, and had oftener talked of it to Cousin Marion, for she had that valuable social gift of appearing to talk with keen attention of one thing while she was thinking about something quite different. She could easily interject "Dear Archie, it will be nice to have him back," or "Darling Jessie wrote me such a delicious letter: she is enjoying herself!" and if Cousin Marion expressed a wish to see the letter, it was equally easy to say that she had torn it up. Meantime her brain would be busy with recollections of the day before, as they bore on her plans for the day to come. They might go off on to tangents for brief spaces, but her well-ordered and singly-purposed mind was never long in recalling them to their main topic.

Helena had made something of a sensation during these last weeks. She was not beautiful, but she was quite enchantingly pretty, and her mind had the qualities which might rightly be supposed to underlie that delicious face and inform those slim, graceful limbs. Nothing seemed to mar her good-nature and her superb gift of enjoying herself. It was worth while being agreeable to everybody, and if her lot happened for an hour or two a day to be cast with elderly bores, she was indefatigable in her attention to them at the time, and in telling their friends afterwards how immensely she had enjoyed talking to them. It paid to do that sort of thing, provided that it was done with a gaiety that made it appear genuine and spontaneous: if your appreciation came bubbling out of you, no one suspected you of design, and she seemed the most designless, delicious girl in London, for it is next to impossible to see through an object that dazzles you. To crown all these gifts, she had the intensest power of enjoying herself, and there is not another key that unlocks so many doors. In this whirl and mill-race of entertainment which characterized the last gay summer that London would see for long, there was no time to make friends, but only to take the scalps of enthusiastic acquaintances. That perhaps was lucky for her.

But Helena, as she finished her breakfast, recalled her mind from these shining experiences, except in so far as they bore on the theme that insistently occupied her. There was no doubt, especially after that quiet talk in the paved garden outside the ball-room last night, that Bertie Harlow was dazzled, according to plan. Heaven only knew when he had last been to a ball, for he was close on forty (Helena had naturally looked him up in a Peerage, since she liked to know about her friends), and she felt pretty certain that he had danced with no one but her. You could perhaps hardly call his share of the performance dancing; he had "stepped a measure," and twice trodden on her toe; but, after all, it did not matter whether your husband danced or not, since naturally, when those relations had been arrived at, he would not dance with you. Many women no doubt, when they were married, would think it an advantage that their husbands did not dance, since then they would not dance with anybody else. But it was not in Helena's nature prospectively to grudge him such amusements, should he desire them, when once she had got him. But she had to get him first, and to do that she had to keep him dazzled. He must not get accustomed to her.

Helena had a very strong belief in the desirability of simplifying life. This did not in the least imply that she thought there was anything attractive in the simple life: her simplification amounted to this, that she formulated exactly what she wanted, and then without deflection of aim did the very best with her efficient armoury of weapons to get it; while the second clause in the simplification of life was to find out what irritated or bored you, and with all your power eliminate it from your existence. If you could not get what you wanted without getting something that bored you, it was merely necessary to ascertain how the balance between these conflicting interests lay. As practically applied to the case in hand, she was aware that Lord Harlow bored her, though not badly, and that his nose irritated her. That she would almost certainly get used to, while on the other side of the scale were quantities of things she liked. She liked immense wealth, position, and the liberty she would undoubtedly enjoy if she married this amiable man, whom so many had tried to capture. That in itself was an incentive to her pride, and, without being a snob, she saw no objection to being a Marchioness.

But here the simplification ended, and a complication intruded itself. It was not so long ago that she had sat under the stone-pine with Archie, and seen his face glow in the darkness as he drew on his cigarette. In point of attractiveness there was naturally no comparison between her cousin and this amiable middle-aged man; but, owing to the impossibility of even the most limited polyandry, it was clearly no use to think of marrying them both, and all that was left was to choose between them, supposing, as she most sincerely did, that it was, or soon would be, for her to choose. Certainly she was not in love with Archie, if she took as an example of that the ridiculous symptoms exhibited by Daisy Hollinger, who by some strange freak was in love with Lord Harlow. Helena had behaved very wisely over that, for she had instantly seen the advantage of becoming great friends, in her sense of the word, with poor Daisy, who poured out to her a farrago of amorous imbecility, and Helena was sure that she was not in love with Archie like that. Anything so insane seemed incomprehensible to her (and was).

But Archie was a dear—she had quite wished he would kiss her that night, of course in a cousinly fashion, which she would have scorned to be offended with, whereas she did not in the least look forward to the moment when Lord Harlow would kiss her. Apart from that, the simplification of life came in again, and against Archie there were certain items which it would be imprudent to disregard. His father was a drunkard, and Archie himself had been consumptive as a child. Consumption ran in families, for Archie's brother had died of it; and so perhaps did drunkenness, though she did Archie the justice of trying and failing to remember that she had ever seen him drink wine at all. These were serious objections in a husband.

There was another, perhaps not less serious. She knew from Cousin Marion that Uncle Jack had lately lost a great deal of money; there was even the question of shutting up or letting the London house next winter. Of course, if she married Archie, they could not spend the winter down at Lacebury, or live with poor Uncle Jack; but London, as wife of an impoverished son, would be very different from London as the wife of a very wealthy man who, so to speak, was nobody's son. Finally, there were certain stories that Cousin Marion had told her about queer messages and communications that had come to Archie, while he was still a child, from his dead brother. That seemed to Helena's practical mind pure nonsense, and yet she had been pleased to hear that, since he was but young in his teens, these rather uncomfortable phenomena had ceased. She felt that she did not believe in them; but, though they had no real existence, she disliked the thought of them. And, though it was so long since there had been any repetition of them, they might (though they were all nonsense) crop up again. She had no belief in ghosts, but she would not willingly have slept in a haunted room. The dead were dead, whereas she was very much alive.

Well, it was time to dress and go down to Cousin Marion. This long, frank meditation (for she was always frank with herself, which perhaps was the reason that she had so little of that commodity to spare for other people) had helped considerably to clear her mind and provoke simplification. And, like a good housewife who will permit no waste of what can possibly be used, she thought she would have a very useful function for Archie to perform when he arrived that evening.

She found Lady Tintagel busy with her morning's post. There was a quantity of invitations, most of which, owing to press of others, had to be declined, and Helena having marked each of those with an "Accept" or "Refuse," laid them aside to answer. There was one, where the Russian dancers were to perform, which she very much regretted having to say "no" to, since that evening was already filled, and wondered if by any contrivance it would be possible to manage it. A glance at Lady Tintagel's engagement book showed her that the prohibiting acceptance was for a dinner and concert at Lady Awcock's, where all that was stately and Victorian spent evenings of unparalleled dreariness. Helena had already produced the most favourable impression on Lady Awcock by listening to her practically endless dissertations on political society forty years ago, and she thought she could manage it.

"And shall I enter all the invitation you accept in your engagement-book, Cousin Marion?" she asked.

"Yes, my dear, will you? That's really all I have for you this morning. What will you do with yourself?"

Helena gathered up cards and engagement-book.

"I think I shall stop at home," she said. "You often do want something more, you know, and I hate not being here to do it for you."

"Nothing of the sort. There's the motor for you if you want to go and see anybody."

Helena considered.

"Oh, I should like to do one thing," she said. "It won't take long. May I get some flowers for Archie's room and Jessie's? Flowers do look so cool and refreshing when you've been a day and a night in the train."

"Of course you may. It was nice of you to think of that. But then you do think of rather nice things for other people."

"Oh, shut up, Cousin Marion," laughed the girl.

* * * * *

Helena retired to the table in the window with her materials and proceeded to execute a very neat and simple piece of work. The entries in Lady Tintagel's engagement-book were only made in pencil, and she erased the inconvenient Lady Awcock's name from the evening some fortnight ahead and wrote in its place that of the giver of the Russian party, to whom instead of a refusal she sent a line, in her cousin's name, of grateful acceptance. Then she wrote a charming little letter of penitence to Lady Awcock, abasing herself and at the same time pitying herself. She had done the stupidest thing; for she had accepted Lady Awcock's invitation on an evening when they were already engaged. The letter proceeded: "I can't tell you how disappointed I am, dear Lady Awcock, for I was so looking forward to another talk with you, and to hear more of those interesting things you told me; but perhaps, if I have not disgusted you beyond forgiveness, you would ask me again some day. And would you be wonderfully kind and not tell Lady

Tintagel what a stupid thing I have done, for she lets me keep her engagement-book for her, and if she knew, I am afraid she would never trust me again."

This last touch thoroughly pleased Helena; it was confiding and childlike. For the rest she relied on Cousin Marion not happening to remember that they had once accepted an invitation to Lady Awcock's, and, even if she did have some impression of it, her engagement-book, with no such entry appearing in it, would show her that her memory had played her false. But probably Cousin Marion would remember nothing whatever about it; indeed, in the multiplicity of engagement, it seemed to Helena that the risk she ran was negligible.

Helena found time to go to Victoria to meet the travellers that afternoon, and to reflect, as she waited for the boat-train to come in, that she in her cool pink blouse and her skirt of Poiret stuff would certainly present a very refreshing contrast to poor Jessie in dishevelled and dusty travelling-clothes. She did not in the least want Jessie to look bedraggled except in so far as she herself would gain by the contrast, for she was good-natured enough not to want any one to be at a disadvantage as long as that did not add to her own advantage. Jessie was a dreadfully bad sailor, too; but it was quite enough that she should have travelled for a night and a day, without hoping that she had had a bad crossing. Helena merely wanted to appear fresh and brilliant herself. At length the train came in, and, though she quite distinctly saw Archie step out, she continued searching for him with her eyes in the crowd, until he made his way up to her.

"Ah, my dear," she said, "how lovely to see you! And don't be cross with me for coming to meet you if it bores you to be met at the station. But I did want to welcome you. And where's Jessie? There she is! Jessie darling, what fun!"

Archie did not look as if he was at all bored to be met at the station.

"That's perfectly ripping of you," he said. "I am glad you came. We've been baked and boiled all the way from Silorno. And the crossing! I thought it was always calm in the summer."

"Archie, don't allude to it," said Jessie.

Helena took her sister's arm.

"Darling Jessie, I am so sorry," she said. "Archie's a wretch for mentioning it. Now you go straight to the motor and sit there quietly. Archie and I will see to your luggage."

If Archie, as is probable, drew the contrast he was intended to draw between the sisters, Helena on her side drew another between him and Lord Harlow. There he stood, looking eagerly at her as they waited the emergence of their trunks, face and neck and hands so tanned by the sun that every one else looked ill and anaemic by him. He was tall and lithe and slender, with the quick movements of some wild animal, and in his brown face his blue eyes shone like transparent turquoises. He seemed an incarnation of sun and sea and wholesome virility, and, as the thought of the rather heavy Kalmuck face of Lord Harlow, and staid aspect suitable to his forty years, she almost wondered whether, in her estimate made this morning, she had allowed enough for personal charm. But there had been other factors as well, and who knew whether below this engaging exterior there were not planted the seeds of tragic outcome? But it was certainly pleasant to reflect that his exuberance of young manhood would, she made no doubt, be all hers if she made up her mind to want it. In any case, was there another girl in London who had so attractive a second string to her bow?

Archie had, on the appearance of one of their pieces of luggage, insinuated himself into the crowd and Helena was left outside, when a sight odd to see at a station attracted her attention. Beyond, the platform lay empty, and out of some porter's shed there, there bounded a big tabby cat with a mouse in its mouth. Its tail switched, its eyes gleamed with the joy of the successful hunter; but it did not prepare to eat the mouse immediately. It trotted a little farther off, lay down, and, depositing its prey, dabbed at it softly with velvet paws and sheathed claws. It even let it run a few inches away from it, and then gently shepherded it back again. Once it let it seem to escape altogether, gave it a start of at least a couple of yards, while it watched it with quivering shoulders, and then playfully bounded in the air, and reminded it that it was not its own master. Then there came a dismal little squeak as from a slate-pencil; the poor mouse's troubles were over, and a pleased cat blinked in the sun and licked its lips.

Helena followed this gruesome little drama with an interest that surprised and even rather shocked her. She was altogether on the side of the cat; the cat, according to its lights, was not being cruel, it was merely doing the natural thing with a mouse. It happened to like teasing its prey, letting it think that it had escaped, sheathing the claws that had caught it, and playing with it. There was nothing horrible about it: the cat was doing as nature intended it to do. She was rather sorry for the mouse, but that is what came of being a mouse... And there was Archie, triumphant, with a porter and his rescued luggage. Archie had a way with officials: he smiled at them in a confident, friendly way, and they always did what he wanted and never searched his traps.

* * * * *

There was a dance somewhere that night, but Helena, letting the fact be reluctantly dragged out of her that there was such a thing, only said how nice it would be to go to bed early.

"Are you tired, dear?" asked Lady Tintagel.

Helena made a little deprecating face, the face of the prettiest little martyr in the cause of truth ever beheld.

"No, I can't exactly say I am," she said. "I think—I think I was speaking on behalf of Archie and Jessie."

"But I'm not tired either," said he. "Let's go to somebody's dance. I can't dance an atom, but Helena shall teach me. There's nothing like practice in public. What dance is it, by the way?"

"Oh, that's all right," said she. "It's your Uncle and Aunt Toby. But, Archie, I'm sure you're tired."

"But I'm not, I tell you. It's whether you want to go."

Lady Tintagel struck in.

"If you all go on being so unselfish," she said, "you will never settle anything. Try to be selfish for one moment Helena; it won't hurt. Do you want to go?"

"Enormously," said she, with a sign of resignation.

"And you, Archie?"

"Dying for it. Let's call a taxi."

"And you, Jessie?"

"I should hate it," said Jessie very confidently.

The matter, of course, was settled on those lines, and Helena was duly credited with having wanted to go enormously, but with having done her utmost to efface herself for the sake of others. This was precisely the end she had in view all along, and now, having had the dance, so to speak, forced on her, she was quite free to enjoy herself. She had produced precisely the impression she wanted on Archie and his mother, and, though it was likely that Jessie, with her long familiarity with such manoeuvres, was not equally unenlightened, she knew, by corresponding familiarity, Jessie's loyalty. She gave a little butterfly kiss to Cousin Marion, and a murmur of delighted thanks, and went to her sister to finish up this very complete little picture.

"Darling Jessie," she said, "go to bed soon and sleep well. I shall tiptoe in, in the morning, and, if you're still asleep, I shall tell them not to wake you till you ring. May I do that, Cousin Marion?"

Jessie understood all this perfectly well, and her mouth had that curve in it that might or might not be a smile.

"Good-night," she said. "Have a nice dance, and teach Archie well."

To speak of luck is often nothing more than another mode of expressing the success that usually attends foresight; chance favours the wise calculation. Helena last night had dropped the most casual hint to Lord Harlow that she was probably going to this dance to-night, but she was satisfied that he had been attending, and was not unprepared to see him there. Even if she had not been able to come, she suspected that he would do so, and her absence would have been delightfully explained to him afterwards. But there he was, not dancing, but standing about near the door of the ball-room, and quite obviously interested in arrivals. Undoubtedly he saw the brilliant entry of herself and Archie, but she contrived to put a few of the crowd between herself and him as she passed near him, and for the present gave him no more than a glance and a smile, a downdropt eye, and then one glance again, and passed with Archie into the ball-room. There an ordinary old-fashioned waltz was in progress, and not one of those anaemic strollings about which were becoming popular, and she slid off with her radiant partner on to a floor not overfull. She had a moment's misgiving when she remembered that Archie had said he couldn't dance, for it would vex her to appear in the clutch of a bungler; but, after all, Archie could hardly be awkward if he tried. Immediately all her fears vanished, for they had hardly gone up the short side of the room before she knew that if any one was the bungler it was she. She might have guessed, from seeing him walk and move, that he could dance; what she could not have guessed was that anybody could dance like this. They floated, they glided; it was the floor surely that moved under them; it was the wind of that swinging, voluptuous tune that wafted them on as in some clear eddy of sunlit water.

"But, my dear, you said you couldn't dance," she exclaimed.

"Oh, this sort of thing," said he. "I meant the steppings and crawlings of the new style."

Helena was too content to talk; her whole being glowed with the satisfaction of this flowing movement. The floor got ever emptier: lines of expectant fox-trotters and bunny-huggers stood round the wall, but none of them objected to watching for a little longer the entrancing couple who now had the floor almost to themselves. Couple after couple dropped off and stood looking, and to Helena's gleaming eyes they passed in streaks of black and white and many-coloured hues as she and Archie moved ever more freely and largely over the untenanted space. She could just see the faces of friends as she passed, and knew that Lord Harlow had come in and was standing by the door. There was no question of luck in that; he was but doing what she knew he was obliged to do. Then the web of sound that poured out of the gallery grew more brightly coloured as it quickened to its close, and still Archie and she moved without effort as if they were part of it and of each other. And then the whole fabric of that divine dream of melody and motion was shattered, for the dance was over.

Archie had not spoken either since he intimated that he had alluded to steppings and crawlings, and now he paused for a moment in the middle of the room, breathing just a little quickly and bewildered as with some dazzling light. Ever since he had put his arm round the girl and taken her hand in his, he had had that sense of sinking into sunlit waters, where he arrived at his true and naked self. Now he had swum up again, and he was clothed in black coat and white shirt, and Helena was standing a step apart from him, and every one else at the edge of the room was very far away. Instantly a mingling of wild consternation and triumph seized him.

"Oh, Helena, were we doing that all by ourselves?" he said. "How frightful! Let's get out of it. But wasn't it divine? May we do it again soon? Or will they have nothing but crawlings?"

It appeared that crawlings were to be the next item, and Archie noticed that in the crowd that now came about them again a particular man had his eye on them, and was unmistakably burrowing towards them.

"Yes, Archie; of course we will," said the girl. "Go and see your aunt, and ask if we may have another waltz ever so soon. Oh, here's Lord Harlow; I want to introduce you."

This was done, and Lord Harlow turned to Helena again.

"I feel as if I had been present at some Bacchic festival," he said in a very precise voice. "But you should have vine-leaves in your hair, and er—your partner a tunic and a thyrsus. I feel myself as prosaic as a Bradshaw. But may I be your Bradshaw?"

Helena looked from one to the other; if she had had a tail she would certainly have been switching it.

"Ah, do," she said. "A Bradshaw is quite indispensable. Archie, go and get a thyrsus—will a poker do, Lord Harlow?—and persuade Mrs. Morris to have another waltz before long."

Now that the sheer animal exhilaration of that adorable waltz, which quite precluded talking, was over, it seemed perfectly suitable, as she plodded along the weary way of the fox-trot, to talk again, and in answer to Lord Harlow, who had not caught Archie's name, she said:

"Yes, Lord Davidstow. Surely I told you about him" (she knew that she had purposely not done so). "He is Lady Tintagel's son, with whom I am staying."

Lord Harlow quietly assimilated this as he turned slowly round.

"And does he do other things as well as he dances?" he asked.

"I think he does," said she, "though I never really thought about it. When people are such dears as Archie, one doesn't consider what they do. They just are."

"He certainly is. He appears very much alive."

"Yes, he's madly alive."

She gave him a swift glance, and, guessing she had gone far enough on that tack, she put about.

"I think it's possible to be too much alive," she said. "It's like a hot-water bottle that is too hot: it burns you. But you can't help being carried off your feet by it—I don't mean the hot-water bottle."

He paused a moment for the purpose of phrasing.

"I must weight you with a Bradshaw," he said. "That will keep you to earth. We can't spare you."

Helena laughed.

"You say things *too* neatly," she said. "What a delicious notion! What have you done all day?"

"I have waited for this evening."

"And I hope it doesn't disappoint you now that it has come," she said.

"It is up to my highest expectations just now," said he.

Suddenly it flashed into Helena's mind that this was the temperature of his wooing. He was engaged in that now: those neat and proper sentences, turned as on a lathe, were the expression of it, they and the mild pleased glances that he gave her; and yet, discreet and veiled as it all was, she divined that, according to his nature and his years, it was love that inspired it. She found it quite easy to adjust herself to that level, and if his kiss (when the time came for that) was of the same respectful and finished quality, she could deal with that too. But she wondered how Archie would make love… It was necessary to fox-trot a little longer, and, while trotting, trot also conversationally, and with intention she let herself press a little more against his arm.

"Oh, I am glad of that," she said lightly. "It is such a dreadful pity when people are disappointed. But I think I would sooner anticipate something nice and fail to get it, than not anticipate at all. Can you imagine not looking forward to the delicious things you want?"

"Do you want very much?" he asked.

"Yes, everything. And I want it not only for myself but for everybody."

She made the mental note that he was very shy, for he had nothing in response to this, except that his shirt creaked. But that suited her very well; she did not want him to follow this up, just yet.

Meantime the sedate marchings and retreats and occasional revolution of the fox-trot went decorously on. The room was very full, and, when there was nowhere to march to, they stopped where they were and marked time and rocked a little to and fro. Then perhaps a narrow lane opened in front of them, and they waddled down it, brushing shoulders against the hedges. She had seen Archie go to Mrs. Morris, after which he had appeared for a moment in the gallery where the band was, and now he was back again, standing near the door and watching her. She gave him little glances from time to time, elevated her eyebrows as if in deprecation of this unexhilarating performance, or smiled at him, guessing that he had arranged for another waltz.

At last the end came, the fox-trotters ceased to clutch each other, and walked away with about as much Terpsichorean fervour as they had been dancing with. Dull though the last twenty minutes had been from that standpoint, Helena felt quite satisfied with it, while motion—or perhaps emotion—had made her partner hot; he gently wiped his forehead with a very fine cambric handkerchief.

"Perfectly delicious," he said. "I should have liked that to go on for ever. And how long shall I have to wait before it begins again?"

Archie had sidled through the crowd up to them.

"Helena, we're going to have another waltz at once," he cried. "Don't let us waste any of it."

She laid her hand on his arm.

"We?" she said. "Are you quite certain?"

"May I say 'we' also?" asked Lord Harlow.

She turned towards him, but her hand still rested on Archie, and he felt the slight pressure from her fingertips.

"Oh, I was only teasing my cousin," she said. "I had promised him another waltz. But, later, may I borrow my Bradshaw again?"

The band struck up, setting her a-tingle for the repetition of what had gone before.

"Oh, Archie, come on," she cried. "*Au revoir*, Bradshaw."

Alert for movement, with the heady tune of the waltz already mounting into them like wine, they stepped off on to the floor. It was like stepping on to some moving platform; it and the tune, without any conscious effort of their own, seemed to carry them away. But Archie had one question to ask before he abandoned himself.

"Bradshaw?" he said. "I thought you told me his name was Harlow."

She gave a little bubble of laughter.

"Oh, that was only a joke," she said. "He told me that you and I were like a Bacchic festival, and he felt as prosy as a Bradshaw in consequence."

"But what does it matter to him what we are like?" asked he.

"Well, it was a compliment; he meant it nicely," said she. "Don't let us talk; it rather spoils it."

* * * * *

Helena reviewed those manoeuvres when she got home that night, and she congratulated herself on the neatness and efficiency of her dispositions. She felt sure that she had stirred up a livelier ferment in Lord Harlow, and had also managed to inspire him with a vague distrust and jealousy of her intimacy with Archie. She suspected that he was a little sluggish in his emotions, and this would serve admirably as a stimulant. She quite realized that she had not yet brought him up to the point of proposing to her, for his inured bachelor habits would want a good deal of breaking; but it was clear to her that she had made a crack in them, and that the judicious use of Archie might be profitably used to widen that crack. Under the influence merely of her charms, he might hold together for a long time yet, and she wanted him, if she could have it entirely her own way, to propose to her about the end of the season. The effect of Archie constantly with her would be cumulative: it was not a wedge that would cause him to fly into splinters forthwith; it would just widen the crack, prevent it closing again, and then widen it a little more.

And meanwhile it was extremely pleasant always to have this wedge in her hand, to hammer from time to time, as it suited her main plan, and at others to stroke and play with. She was not in love with Archie, but it made her purr to see that he was certainly falling in love with her, to dab him with sheathed claws, to wish that he had those material advantages which had made her choose the elder man. It clearly served her purpose to use him, and the using of him gave her pleasure. But the pleasure was secondary—it was the assistance he gave her in breaking up Lord Harlow that was of primary importance.

* * * * *

Archie brought all his gaiety and charm to bear on his love-making. Falling in love did not appear to him, at this stage, anything but the most exhilarating, almost hilarious experience. The flirtation that Helena seemed to be having with Lord Harlow amused him enormously; not for a moment did he believe that Helena meant anything. Lord Harlow was not the only man on whom Helena exercised the perfectly legitimate attraction of her extreme prettiness and her enthusiastic child-like enjoyment.

"Oh, every one is so kind and so awfully nice," she said to him one day as they returned from an early morning ride. "I love them all by the handful."

"Including the Bradshaw?" asked he.

"Yes, certainly including the Bradshaw. Don't you like him? He likes you so much."

Archie considered this.

"I don't know if I like him or not," he said. "I don't think I ever thought about it. He doesn't matter. But you matter awfully to him. Did you know that you are the most outrageous flirt, Helena?"

"Archie, how horrid of you!" said she. "Just because I like people, and to a certain extent they like me. Why should I be cross and unpleasant to people, as if it was wicked to like them?"

"Well, if you'll give me long odds I will bet you that the Bradshaw asks you to—to be his 'ABC' before the end of the season," said Archie.

"My dear, what nonsense!" said she, with a sudden thrill of pleasure. "What can have put that into your head?"

"I can see it. That's the way a man like the Bradshaw looks at a girl when his—his affections are engaged. He looks as if a very dear aunt was dead. He has *amour triste*."

That certainly hit off a type of gaze to which Helena felt that she had been subjected, and she laughed.

"Well, I'll give you five to one in half-crowns," she said.

"Don't. Some day I shall have twelve and sixpence."

They turned and cantered back along the soft track. The dew of night had not yet vanished from the grass, and the geometric looking plane-leaves, the rhododendrons, and the flower-beds were still varnished with moisture, and, early though it was, riders and foot-passengers were plentiful. Probably the day would be hot, for the heat haze, purplish-brown in the distance, was beginning to form in the air, softly veiling the further view. Presently they dropped again into a walking-pace, and Helena, whose mind had been busy on Archie's description of a certain sort of love-lorn look, spoke of a subject suggested by it.

"How do you think Jessie is?" she asked.

"That's exactly what my mother asked me last night," said he. "She's rather silent and preoccupied, isn't she?"

"That struck me," said the girl. "I thought perhaps she wasn't very well, but she told me there was nothing the matter. Darling Jessie is so reserved. She never tells me anything. Certainly she looks well: do you think she has anything on her mind?"

"I don't see what she could have. But it's odd that it has struck all of us."

Helena sighed and shook her head with a pretty, unreproachful air.

"I sometimes wish that Jessie would make more of a friend of me," she said. "I try so hard to get close to her, but all the time I feel she is keeping me at arm's length. It would be lovely to have a sister who would admit me to her own, own self. But I always have to tap, so to speak, at Jessie's door, and she so often says she won't open it."

"Was she always like that?" asked Archie, seeing that Helena's eyes were dim and bright.

"Yes, but lately I think it has been worse. I wish Jessie would let me in. However, I am always waiting, and I think Jessie knows that. It is no use pressing for confidence, is it? One can only wait."

This picture, so simply and pathetically conveyed by Helena of herself waiting, a little dim-eyed, for Jessie to admit her, was very convincing, and Archie wondered at the contrast between the two sisters, the one so childlike in her confidence that all the world was her friend, the other holding herself rather detached, rather aloof, without that welcoming charm of manner that surely was the expression of an adorable mind. It was not wholly the light of his dawning love that in-invested the sketch with such tender colouring, for there was a great finish and consistency in Helena's presentation of herself which might have deceived the most neutral and heart-whole of observers.

Such was the first impression: then suddenly some instinct that lay below the surface surged up in rebellion against it, and washed the tender colouring out. It told him that the impression was a false one, that Jessie, so far from being callous and self-centred, as was the suggestion conveyed by Helena's words, was of faithful and golden heart. And then, looking idly over the crowd that was growing thick on the broad gravel walk, he suddenly caught sight of Jessie herself looking at them. She was some little distance behind the rails that separated the ride from the path, and she instantly looked away, spoke to a girl who was with her, and strolled on. But Archie felt quite sure that she had seen them.

He turned to Helena.

"Surely that is Jessie," he said to her, pointing with his whip.

Helena had seen her also, and she smiled rather sadly, rather wistfully.

"Yes," she said. "But she doesn't want us, Archie."

And at that the instinct which had spoken to him so emphatically a moment before sank out of hearing again, and the colour returned to Helena's deft little sketch.

CHAPTER VIII

It was four o'clock on an afternoon of mid-July, and the westering sun had begun to blaze into the drawing-room windows of Colonel Vautier's house in Oakland Crescent. It was pleasant enough there in the winter, for the room, being small, was easily heated; but in the summer, with even greater ease it grew oven-like, and Helena, sitting by the open window for the sake of any air that might possibly wander into the dusty crescent, was obliged to pull down the blinds. She had tried sitting in her father's study, but that had an infection of stray cigar-smoke about it which she did not want to catch, and the dining-room and her own bedroom, since they faced the same way as the drawing-room, presented no counter-attractions. So, reluctantly, she was compelled to sit here, while Jessie, with a book in her hand, sat at the other end of the room. Jessie had a slight attack of hay-fever, and from time to time indulged in a fit of sneezing. It seemed to Helena that she was being very inconsiderate: it was always possible to stifle a sneeze. But Jessie never thought about other people. Helena, by way of waiting patiently at Jessie's door (according to the tender image she had fashioned for Archie's benefit) had just expressed this opinion slightly veiled, and she was pleased to see that at this moment Jessie left the room. A sound of sneezing from outside indicated that at last her sister had grasped how exceedingly unpleasant her hay-fever was for other people. Then there came the sound of ascending steps, and she guessed that Jessie had gone to her bedroom. The floors were wretchedly thin and ill-constructed; you could, from any room in the house, hear movements from any other room, especially since Colonel Vautier and Jessie had such solid, resounding steps when they went anywhere.

Left to herself, Helena cleared her decks, and enumerated her cause of complaint against Providence, who ought to have been so kind to an innocent, loving little soul. In the first place, her father had finished his irrigation business in Egypt unexpectedly soon, and instead of arriving in London not before September, had come two months earlier than the most pessimistic daughter could have expected. The news of his approaching arrival had provoked a perfect conspiracy against Helena's comfort and her plans, for every one, including Cousin Marion, who had been so insistent on the girls' staying with her till he got home, had taken it for granted that they would at once rejoin him. Surely it would have been sufficient for Jessie to go (and she did Jessie the justice of allowing that she was perfectly ready to do so), leaving Helena to help Cousin Marion in the answering of her letters in the morning for some half-hour, in the entertaining of her numerous guests, and in accompanying her to any of those pleasant gaieties which swarmed about that desirable house. But instead, Cousin Marion had been quite unaware, to all appearance, of the hints Helena had subtly suggested, and Archie had been equally uncomprehending. When she had said, "This house seems so much more like my home than any other," he had certainly glowed with pleasure, but had not thought it was meant to have any application with regard to her going back to Oakland Crescent. No one had taken her hints; it had occurred to nobody how suitable it was that Jessie should go to look after her father, and Helena remain to look after her cousin. But since her hints were not taken, Helena, like the excellent tactician she was, had retreated in preference to standing her ground and suffering defeat. She had to retreat, and she retreated with exactly the proper mixture of regret at leaving Grosvenor Square and of joy at her father's premature return. And when his taxi cab drew up palpitating at the door, it was she who ran down the three concrete steps from the front-door and across the awful little dusty yard called the front garden, with its cinder path that circulated round one laurel-bush, and flung herself into his arms, and helped the parlour-maid to carry in his bag, while Jessie waited in the narrow entrance that reeked of the ascending fumes of dinner, for the parlour-maid, as usual, had left open the door at the head of the kitchen stairs.

There was a grudge against Providence even deeper than this unnecessary transplanting of herself to Oakland Crescent, when she might so comfortably have flourished in Grosvenor Square, Archie had dined with them two nights ago, before taking her on to a dance, and in the interval that followed dinner, when her father and Archie remained downstairs, she had a painful scene with Jessie. Jessie, according to Helena's public version, had misunderstood her in the cruellest manner, but she knew that her real complaint here was not that her sister had cruelly misunderstood her, but had, in fact, cruelly understood her, which was more intolerable than any misunderstanding could have been. She could have borne a misunderstanding very patiently, but to be understood was of the nature of an exposure, of a kind scarcely decent, and impossible to forget.

It had begun so stupidly, so innocuously. She had but left a few orchids on her dressing-table, and Jessie, who naturally was not going to the dance, but was remaining at home to keep her father company, most kindly offered to get them for her. She came down again so ominously silent that Helena had asked her what the trouble was, and it appeared that Jessie had seen on the dressing-table the card of Lord Harlow with a safety-pin attached to it.

"Yes, darling, why not?" Helena had said. "He sent me those lovely orchids—thank you so much for getting them. He is going to be there to-night, and as he sent expressly for them from Harlow, naturally I shall wear them. It would be rude not to, don't you think?"

Jessie did not reply, and Helena repeated her question. For answer, Jessie had said in that soft rich voice which was the only thing that Helena envied her:

"You revolt me."

CHAPTER VIII

Helena became quite cool and collected. She might represent herself as being tearful and pathetic at the thought of Jessie's unkindness, but that attitude was useless with Jessie alone, and she never adopted it.

"Oh! May I ask why I revolt you?" she asked.

"Certainly, although you know already. Archie is in love with you."

Helena adopted the phrases of affection. She did so simply to irritate her sister.

"Darling, how delicious you are!" she said. "But mayn't I wear a flower from Tom, Dick, or Harry for that reason? I don't grant the reason for a moment; but, even if I did, what then? Besides, Archie hasn't given me any flowers, and one must have flowers at a dance."

But Jessie refused to be irritated. Helena's speech seemed to have exactly the opposite effect on her: she became gentle and apologetic.

"I'm sorry I said that you revolted me," she said. "It was thoughtless and stupid. But, O Helena, you are so thoughtless too. Do forgive me for questioning you, but—but are you intending to marry Lord Harlow if he asks you? If so, do make it clear to Archie, before things get worse, that you have no thought of him. You like him, don't you? You might save his suffering."

This was the understanding, not the misunderstanding, that was so cruel. But Helena was quite capable of being cruel too. She smelled her orchids, and pinned them into her gown. Simultaneously she heard feet on the stairs, and Archie's resonant laugh. She got up.

"I might almost think you were jealous of Archie's affection for me, darling," she said, in her most suave tones.

Before the door opened she saw Jessie's face flame with colour, and laughed to herself at the defencelessness of love. Next moment Archie launched himself into the room.

"Hullo! What fine orchids!" he said. "Who sent you them, Helena? I bet you the Bradshaw did. What a thing it is to have opulent admirers! I wish I had got some."

But since that evening, now nearly a week ago, Jessie had not spoken to Helena except when mere manners in the presence of other people required it. That was a tiresome, uncomfortable situation. In a big house it would not have mattered much, for they could easily have sat in different rooms; but here it made an awkwardness in the narrow existence. But Helena had the consolation of knowing that she had not merely knocked at Jessie's door, but had battered it in. The secret chamber stood open to her, and the shrine in it was revealed before unpitying eyes.

Here, then, were two grievances against the world, that might have taxed the patience of Job, and certainly super-taxed the patience of Helena. On the top of these, Ossa on Pelion, was perched an anxiety that had begun seriously to trouble her, for already it was the middle of July and Lord Harlow had as yet said nothing which suggested that he was going to propose to her. She knew that she charmed and captivated him, who had never looked seriously at a girl twice (nor at poor Daisy once); but he was undeniably a long time making up his mind, and Helena, though accustomed to repose the greatest confidence in herself, did not feel sure that she would prove equal to defeating the long-standing habit of celibacy. Even the continuous use of Archie in the capacity of a wedge seemed to make no impression, and she was beginning to be desperately afraid that the wedge would turn in her hand, and ask her to marry him before Lord Harlow succumbed. This would be a very awkward situation; most inauspicious developments might follow, for it would be tragic if she accepted Archie, and Lord Harlow proposed immediately afterwards, while, if she refused Archie, it would be a crown of tragedy if Lord Harlow did not propose at all. She had determined, in fact, if Archie proposed first, to ask him to wait for his answer.

A little breeze was stirring now, and Helena pulled up the blind to let it and the sun enter together, rather than endure this stifling stagnancy any longer, and gazed with the profoundest disgust at the mean outlook. The house stood in the centre of a small curve of three-storied buildings; in front was its little square of cindery walk with the one laurel in the middle, and a row of iron palings with a gate that would not shut which separated it from the road. On the other side of that was a small demilune of a garden, which gave the place the title of Crescent, and beyond that a straight row of houses all exactly alike. A milkman was going his rounds with alto cries, and slovenly cooks and parlour-maids came out of area gates with milk-jugs in their hands. A lean and mournful cat, with dirty, dishevelled fur, as unlike as possible to the sleek, smart mouser she had seen at the station, sat on a gate-post, blinking in the sun, and every now and then uttering a faint protest against existence generally. Helena could have found it in her heart to mew in answer.

The hot afternoon wore itself away, and presently the parlour-maid came in to lay a table for tea. This entailed a great many comings-in and a great many goings-out, and she usually left the door open, so that there oozed its way up the stairs a mixed smell of cigars and incipient cooking. The cigar smell came from the little back room adjoining the dining-room where Colonel Vautier, with tropical habits, spent the hour after tiffin (it seemed that he could not say "lunch") in dozings and smokings. Meantime the parlour-maid came in and out, now with a large brass tea-tray, to place on the table, now with plates and cups and saucers to put on it. She breathed strongly through her nose, and wore a white apron with white braces over her sloping shoulders.

From outside, during these trying moments, there came the sound of a motor-horn, and immediately afterwards the soft crunch of gravel below a motor's wheels. From where she sat, Helena could look out of the window, and from her torpid discontent she leaped with a bound into a state of alert expectancy. She hazarded, so to speak, all the small change she had in her pocket. For a moment she put her slim fingers in front of her eyes and thought intensely. Then she spoke to the parlour-maid.

"Take a tray of tea to Colonel Vautier in his study," she said, "and say that I have got a headache and told you to bring his tea to him there. Tell Miss Jessie"—Helena paused a moment—"tell her that a friend of mine has come to see me, and that I want to talk to him privately here. That's all: now open the door, and say that I am in."

Helena rushed to the looking-glass above the fire-place, and disarranged her hair a little. She took a book at random out of the shelves, and sat down with it. She heard a little stir in the hall below, and had a moment of agony in thinking that her father's door had opened. Then the stairs creaked under ascending footsteps, and her visitor was announced.

"Who?" she said, as the parlour-maid spoke his name, and then he entered.

She rose from her chair, with a smile that was almost incredulous.

"But how lovely of you!" she said. "I am delighted. What a business you must have had to find your way to our dear little slum."

Her hopes rose high: he looked like a man who had made up his mind. He was clearly nervous, but it was the nervousness of a man who has definitely sat down in the dentist's chair, and has resolved to get rid of that aching. He sat down in the chair Helena indicated, and looked round the room. It really was rather pretty. Helena had the knack of projecting her graceful self into any room she much used. Archie had sent a hamper of roses only this morning.

"Slum?" he said. "I should like to live in this slum."

Helena looked at him gravely.

"Well, there is a spare room," she said, "which we can let you. You won't mind a gurgling cistern next door, will you? But wasn't it lovely? Daddy came home a whole month earlier than I had expected, so I flew back here to be with him. Cousin Marion wanted me to stop with her, and let Jessie come back. It was sweet of her to want me, but how could I remain when Daddy was here? Tea?"

She gave him his cup, and continued her careful prattle.

"So of course I flew here," she said. "Sometimes I rather wish that a fairy-prince would descend, and pick up the house, and put it somewhere where there weren't quite so many barrel-organs; but one gets accustomed to everything. I think Daddy and Jessie must be out. They planned going out together, I know, and I haven't seen either of them since lunch. They are such dears! They are so much to each other! Sometimes I should get a little bit jealous of each of them, if I allowed myself to. Ah! do have one of those little cakes. They are made in the house; you probably smelled them as you came upstairs. How lucky I asked the cook to make some to-day. Sometimes she is cross, and won't; but to-day she was kind. Did she have a brain-wave, do you think, and know that you were coming?"

He ate one of the little cakes which really came from the pastry-cook's just round the corner, and while his mouth was full, Helena proceeded with her talented conversation. She was working at full horse-power, she wanted to dazzle without intermission.

"I daresay all the people who were so friendly will find their way here in time," she said, "but will you pity me, just in a superficial way, sometimes during August? Darling daddy has so much to do at the Colonial Office, or the Irrigation Office, or whatever it is, that he will have to be here all August."

"But he won't keep you in London?" asked he.

Helena laughed.

"Certainly he won't, for I shall keep myself," she said. "I shall try to persuade Jessie to go down to Lacebury with Cousin Marion, and I think I shall succeed. And where will you be? Up in Scotland, I suppose."

He put down the end of the cigarette which Helena had given him. He was less likely, if he was smoking, to smell the faint odour of cigar that had mounted the stairs. But, as a matter of fact, he would not have noticed the smell of burned feathers just then.

He turned to her quickly.

"I shall be—wherever you will permit me to be," he said. "But, wherever that is, mayn't we be together? I want never to be away from you any more. I want nothing else in the world but that."

Helena raised dewy eyes to him.

"Do you mean…?" she began. "Do you mean…?"

"Yes. And I want your answer."

"That is, 'yes,' too," she said.

She had an almost irresistible desire to burst into peals of laughter, but it was not so difficult to transform that into an aspect of radiant happiness. He kissed her, and she could feel his hands laid on her shoulders, trembling. And, out of sheer gratitude, she found herself able to respond quite passably, for the innate respectability of passion touched her. He had paid her the sincerest compliment that a man can pay a girl, in expressing his desire to have her always with him, to be the father of her children, to renounce such freedom as had been his, and to take in exchange for it a devoted slavery. And, since it was exactly that which she had set her purpose to accomplish, it was no wonder that she was content.

But, as soon as he had left her, without translating into the sphere of practical arrangements the when and how of their mutual pledge, Helena, after one tip-toe dance round the drawing-room, sat down again and was instantly immersed in those considerations. He would have liked to dine with them that night, but Archie was coming, and so, before he called again next morning, it was necessary to indulge in careful thought so as to produce a spontaneous suggestion next day. On her face she wore the happiness of child-like smiles, and throughout her meditations that never faded. Occasionally it was as if the sun was withdrawn behind some fleece of a summer cloud, but, if there had been a machine for the registration of her internal sunshine, there would scarcely have been a break in the record of serene hours.

Archie occupied her first; she was sorry for Archie, because the blow that this would be to him glanced back on to her. She had long ago made up her mind not to marry him if she could succeed in the quest now accomplished, but she regretted that now she would never see his eyes glow as he blurted out—she knew he would blurt it out, and probably kiss her with that light, rough eagerness which was so characteristic of him—the tale of his love. Not so many weeks ago, at Silorno, she had determined to marry him, but that was before the wider horizon opened to her. If he had proposed to her then she would certainly have accepted him, but she felt, though so much finer a future had now dawned on her, a sort of grudge against him for not having done so. That made the thought of telling him not unpleasant to her; there was an excitement in the thought of seeing his blank face—would it be blank? She thought so—when he heard her news. Perhaps the sight of how much it hurt him would hurt her also, but that pain would somehow enfold a rapture, for it would be clear how much he wanted her. But why had he not kissed her, when they sat on that last evening in the dark garden at Silorno? All might have been different then. Never till this afternoon had a man kissed her, and that kiss had struck her as being a little prim and proper. Archie would not and could not have been prim, he would have been quick and impulsive; there would have been something romantic about it, for with him she could have supplied that gleam of romance herself.

There had been fleecy clouds during this part of her meditation, and they gathered again, ever so light, as she thought of Cousin Marion and Jessie. Everybody was so clever nowadays, and she was afraid that Cousin Marion had seen that Archie was in love with her, even as Jessie had done. It would be tiresome if they behaved censoriously about it, and replied frigidly to congratulations, and made cold faces at the wedding. But she thought she could get round Cousin Marion, who, from experience, she knew was very easily convinced, but Jessie was more clear-sighted… And then, with a sense of refreshment, she remembered how Jessie had betrayed herself not so many days ago. Thereat the sun came out quite serenely again, and remained out when she thought of her father. He loved shooting, and Helena determined that he should enjoy quantities of shooting. He loved all sorts of the nice things that money made so easily procurable, comfort and good cigars and riding and bathrooms attached to bedrooms. Certainly there should be a delicious room for him in all her houses; she would name it "daddy's room." The filial sentimentality of this quite overcame her, and she murmured "darling daddy," and felt just as if she had sacrificed herself for him and made this marriage in order to secure him a comfortable old age. Bertie and he would get on excellently together: they could talk about tiger-shooting, and temples, and exotic affairs—for Bertie was a great traveller, and, if he wanted to travel again, she had no intention of being an apron-stringing wife. Marriage became a sacrilege rather than a sacrament if it was an affair of watch-dogs on the leash, ready to follow up trails. And again she softly applauded the nobility of her sentiments.

There was a faint stir and rattle of crockery in the room below, which implied that the parlour-maid was removing her father's tea. Helena knew all the noises of the house, down to the gurgling sound of tooth-cleaning that came from her father's bedroom, which showed that he was nearly dressed, and now, correctly interpreting the chink of plate and tea-cup, she was certain of finding him in his study with his after-tea cigar. Very likely Jessie had gone there too; for she often took the evening paper in to her father and read him the news, and Helena hoped that this was the case to-day. She could let Jessie know the event of the afternoon with less embarrassment if there was somebody else present. She could tell her father about it much more easily than she could tell Jessie alone. She would sit close to him, and whisper and hide her head… her sense of drama would make it all quite simple.

She fastened one of the cream-coloured roses that Archie had brought her into the front of her dress and went down to her father's room. It was a stale little apartment, dry and brown and smoked like a kippered herring, furnished chiefly with books and files and decorated with the produce of oriental bazaars, spears and shells and things suggestive of mummies. He was in a big basket chair close to the window, and in the window-seat, as she had hoped, sat Jessie, with the evening paper.

Helena had not forgotten that she had sent a message to him that she had a headache, and to Jessie that a friend had come to see her with a wish for a private conversation. She made these little plans quickly perhaps but always coolly, and remembered them afterwards. Sometimes a little delicate adjustment was necessary, but she seldom got caught out…

"Darling daddy," she said, "may I pay you a little visit? Or are you and Jessie engrossed in something I shan't understand?"

"No, come in, dear," said he. "How's the headache?"

She hovered for a moment like some bright bird, and then perched herself on the arm of his chair, between him and her sister.

"It's quite gone, ever so many thanks," she said. "I think I must have had a little snooze just before tea, which took it away. And then, as I told Jessie, somebody came here especially to have a little talk to me. Daddy, how delicious your cigar smells!"

"And who was you visitor?" he asked.

"Lord Harlow," said she very softly, and paused.

Jessie had put down her paper, and Helena could feel that she was listening in tense expectation. She did not look round, but firmly laid her hand on Jessie's clasping it. The other she tucked into her father's arm, and leaned her head against his shoulder.

"Daddy, I had a long talk to him," she said, "and he is coming here again tomorrow morning. At least, he did the talking, and I only spoke when he had said what he had come to say. Oh, my dear, I am so happy, so awfully, awfully happy."

Helena felt that she had done that quite beautifully. If she had thought about it for ever so long, she could not have improved on it. A few boisterous ejaculations from her father followed, and, finding that Jessie had disengaged her hand, she completed the circle round her father's arm. Then presently she rose, with smiling and suffused face, just kissed him, and left the room.

"Well, I'm sure that's the best bit of news I've heard for a long time," he said. "Certainly he is a good deal older than she, but there's no harm in that. I was twenty years older than your mother, Jessie. And what do you think of it all?"

"I think Helena will be very happy," said Jessie.

"So do I, and I'm sure she deserves to be. If she's as kind and loving to her husband as she has been to her father, we shan't hear any complaints. Dear me! What a bit of news!"

He was silent a moment.

"How we old folk get out of touch with young people!" he said. "If I had been told to guess who it was who would ask Helena to be his wife, I should have said it was Archie. Didn't you think that Archie was very fond of her?"

Mixed with Jessie's misery for Archie's sake, and with her bitter contempt for her sister, was a pity for Helena, as deep as the sea, that she could be what she was. She could wear the roses Archie had sent her, and not be burned alive by them…

"I never thought that Helena really cared for him," she said quietly.

"No? Well, you were more clear-sighted than I. But I fancy Marion thought so too. He's dining with us to-night, isn't he? Or will Helena put him off? And are we to say anything to him about it?"

"I expect Helena will tell us what she wishes," said Jessie.

He laughed.

"No doubt she will. She—what's the phrase?—she pulls the strings in this piece, doesn't she? Bless me, it's after six o'clock. We might go across the bridge and have a stroll in Battersea Park. I expect Helena will like to be left alone. Yes; what is it?"

The parlour-maid had come in, with the request that Colonel Vautier would go to see Helena for a minute now, or some time before dinner. Accordingly he went upstairs, in high good humour, stumbling on the carpet-rods.

"Oh, daddy, how sweet of you to come to me at once!" she said. "Archie's dining here to-night, and I think I will tell him my news myself. He's such a dear; it would hurt him to hear it from anybody else."

Colonel Vautier felt that he had perhaps not been so wrong after all.

"Yes, my dear, that is kind and thoughtful of you," he said.

"So I'll tell him as soon as he gets here," said she. "Will you and Jessie be very kind and let me have two minutes with him?"

Helena's eyes wandered away a minute, and returned rather dewy to her father's face.

"Perhaps you would tell Jessie for me," she said.

She opened her eyes very wide, in a sort of childlike bewilderment.

"I wonder why Jessie is so cold to me," she said. "I must have vexed her somehow without meaning it. I feel sad about it. She did not say one word when I told you and her my news; she did not kiss me…"

"Jessie is never very demonstrative," said her father, intending to speak to Jessie about this.

"No; perhaps that's all. Thank you ever so much, daddy."

She watched them going out together, and thought what a pity it was that some people were so frank as to say that others revolted them, even though they apologized afterwards. It never paid to be coarse and rude like that…

Helena, according to her plan, was in the drawing-room among his roses when Archie arrived.

"It was delicious of you to send them," she said. "And I've got—something for you."

"Hurrah!" said Archie. "What is it?"

She had put a half sovereign and a half-crown on the corner of the mantel-piece, and handed it to him.

"A tip?" he said.

"No; a bet. I am poor but honest."

He looked at the money.

"Twelve and six?" he said. "When did you bet me twelve-and-six?"

Helena came a step closer to him. Even in the middle of London there was something of sea-wind and open spaces about Archie.

"Oh, you stupid boy!" she said. "How many half-crowns is that?"

Suddenly Archie remembered the wager he had made with her one morning in the Park, that Lord Harlow would propose to her before the end of the season. He pocketed the money with a shout of laughter.

"Ha! I knew I should win," he said, "but it wasn't nice of me to laugh. I take back the laugh. Poor old Bradshaw! Did he mind much?"

Helena looked at him, still standing close to him, smiling and in silence. She really found him most attractive at that moment, and she wondered with how changed a face he would presently look at her.

"Yes, he proposed to me this afternoon," she said, still smiling, and still looking at him.

"Well, poor old Bradshaw!" said Archie once more. But he did not say it with quite the same confidence.

She laid her hand, that soft hand with sheathed claws, on his arm.

"Archie, aren't you going to wish me happiness?" she asked.

The lines of his laughter still lingered on his handsome mouth, but now they were merely stamped there and meant nothing.

"Wish you happiness?" he rapped out in a hard snappish voice.

"Yes; isn't it usual between friends?"

"Do you mean you've accepted him?" he asked.

"Yes, my dear. Haven't I told you?"

"Is it a joke?" he asked. "Shall I laugh?"

Helena moved a little away from him, and rang the bell. Archie looked so strange. She had expected something far more moving and dramatic than this wooden immobility.

"Tell Colonel Vautier and Miss Jessie that Lord Davidstow has come," she said to the parlour-maid.

Archie said nothing till the door had closed again. He felt that he was made of wood, that everything was made of wood, he and Helena and the roses he had sent, and the Persian rug on which he stood. And when he spoke, it was as if a machine in his mouth said the words which had nothing whatever to do with him.

"I congratulate you," he said. "I hope you will be very happy."

Colonel Vautier entered; he had been to the cellar to get out a bottle of champagne in which to drink the health of Helena and the man she had chosen.

"Good evening, my dear Archie," he said. "I know Helena has told you her news."

Archie shook hands, and then his eyes went back to Helena again. She had never looked more entrancingly pretty, but she was made of wood. And then Jessie came in; they were all there, and dinner was ready, and down they went. In this wooden world, everything went on in precisely the same way as it had done when people were made of flesh and blood. Some cunning mechanical contrivance enabled them to talk and smile and eat: food tasted the same and so did the champagne in which presently they drank Helena's health. It was the same prickly, bubbly stuff, with a little sting in it, that he so seldom drank. But it unfroze the surface of the stricture that bound him, as when the first stir of a thawing wind moistens the surface of ice. He began to feel again, to be conscious that somewhere within him was a deep well of the waters of pain. But anything was better than that cataleptic insensibility, which was like being unconscious, and, all the time, knowing that he was unconscious.

They were not going out that night, and after dinner they sat down to a rubber of bridge, in which as usual Helena took Archie as a partner, because she always insisted that she could form some idea of the principles on which he played, whereas the other two but wandered in a starless and Cimmerian gloom when mated with him. But Helena claimed that her spiritual affinity with Archie enabled her to perceive that, when he declared hearts, he wished her to understand that he hadn't got any, and that she would do well to declare something different. "Bridge, properly understood," Archie had enunciated once, "is a form of poker: you must bewilder and terrify your adversary. And then the fun begins, and you get fined." What added to the hilarity was the concentrated seriousness which Jessie and her partner brought to bear on the game, and the miser's greed and avaricious eye with which Jessie was popularly supposed to see her score mounting. All these jokes, these squibs of light-hearted nonsense, were there to-night, but there was nothing behind them. It was as if they were spoken from habit; a frigid rehearsal of some pithless drama was going on; they were tinsel flowers stuck into arid and seedless ground, and sprang no longer from the warm earth.

The sense of wooden unreality soon began to close in again on Archie, with that utter absence of feeling which was so far more terrible than any feeling could be, that soulless insensitiveness as of a live consciousness that knew it was dead, and he rose from the table after Helena had delivered him from the consequence of some outrageous declaration, and went across to a side-table where were placed syphons and spirits. But now, instead of pouring himself out a glass of soda-water, he half filled his tumbler with whisky, and but added a cream of bubble on the top of it. Immediately almost his sense of touch with life returned; there stole back into himself and the figures of Colonel Vautier and Jessie the perception of their several identities, and into Helena the love with which he had endowed her. But that, and all that it implied, was better than feeling nothing at all. He knew, too, that when Jessie spoke to him, or looked at him, her voice and her eyes held for him a supreme and infinite sympathy. He could not reach it, but he knew it was there. Perhaps when he got used to those new conditions of nightmare existence, he could make it accessible, get into touch with it. At present he scarcely wanted it; he wanted nothing so long as this perception of life still ran in his brain, except Helena. He thought that she rather pitied him too, but it was not her pity he wanted, for it was she who had brought her pity on himself.

They played two or three rubbers; Jessie's miserly greed was assuaged by precisely the sum that Archie had won from Helena, and Colonel Vautier, after seeing him out, went back to his study to indulge himself in the cigar which was not permitted in the drawing-room, and the two sisters were left there. Helena's brain had long been busy, beneath the habitual jests of their game, over her future relations with Jessie, and she had come to the conclusion that the sooner they talked the matter out the better. She found that it affected her comfort to be practically not on speaking terms with her sister, and, since she had no shrinking from what might be a painful interview for others, she had made up her mind to ascertain exactly how Jessie meant to behave to her in the few weeks for which they would be in close daily and hourly contact, for Lord Harlow had expressed his mind very clearly about an early date for their wedding, and Helena entirely agreed with him.

Jessie, on her part, could scarcely manage to think about her sister at all. With Archie in front of her all evening she had barely been conscious of anything but his bitter and miserable disillusionment, his awakening from the dream that had become so real to him. She was still seated at the card-table, and with that need for trivial employment which so often accompanies emotional crises, she was building a house with the cards they had been using, devoting apparently her whole faculties to its breathless construction. The strong, beautiful hands which Archie had never noticed hovered over it, alighting with their building materials, putting each card delicately and firmly in place, and her grave face watched the ascending stories, as if Babylon the Great was rising again for the marvel of mankind. Then Helena sat down by her, and, leaning her arm on the table, caused a vibration that demolished Babylon from garret to cellar.

"Oh, Jessie, I'm so sorry," she said, and she was; the fall of an ingenious card-house was the sort of thing that provoked her pity.

Jessie swept the cards together and seemed about to get up.

"It doesn't matter," she said. "It is bed-time, isn't it?"

Helena put her head wistfully on one side.

"Aren't you being horribly unkind to me?" she said. She did not suppose it was much use playing on the pathetic stop, that made, as a general rule, so insincere a bleating in her sister's ears, but it was worth trying.

"I don't think there is any use in talking, Helena," she said. "If I am unkind, if I can't bear what you have done, it is because I simply can't help it."

CHAPTER VIII

Helena fingered the debris of the card-house with those more delicate fingers that could caress and claw so exquisitely. Essentially, she cared not one atom what Jessie thought of her, but she wanted not to be uncomfortable for the next few weeks.

"Ah, that is it?" she added. "You are satisfied to hate and detest me because you can't help it. That seems to you a final and unanswerable excuse. But nobody else may do anything because she can't help it."

"But you could have helped what you have done," said Jessie. "You made Archie think you cared for him. You let him fall in love with you on that assumption."

"He let himself fall in love with me," said Helena. "That was not my fault. Besides..."

She was silent a moment, weaving delicate spider-threads in her mind. She really wanted to propitiate Jessie just now, otherwise she would certainly have reminded her that she, anyhow, had allowed herself to fall in love with Archie, though she would not say that that was Archie's fault. It would have been amusing to suggest that, but it did not seem to tend towards reconciliation. She bent her graceful head a little lower over the fallen card-house. It had collapsed with tragic suddenness, even as Archie had collapsed.

"Besides," she went on, "it was open to Archie to propose to me. He did not. We were several weeks together at Silorno. And then I came to London and met Bertie. Was it my fault that I fell in love with him? I think you are horribly unkind to me."

Jessie came a step nearer.

"Are you in love with him?" she asked. "If you tell me you are in love with him..."

"Do you think I should marry him if I was not?" asked Helena, looking the picture of limpid, childlike innocence.

Jessie made no reply. She could not say that she believed Helena was in love with him, though she was assuredly going to marry him. She could not tell a lie of that essential kind; merely the words would not come.

"If I have wronged you in any way, Helena," she said at length, "I am most sincerely sorry for it. I ask your forgiveness unconditionally."

Helena rose, wreathed in tender smiles and liquid eyes.

"Darling, you have my forgiveness with all my heart," she said. "And may I ask you one thing? Will you try to feel a little more kindly towards me? If you only knew how your unkindness hurts me."

* * * * *

But Jessie, lying awake that night, striving, with all the sincerity that permeated her from skin to marrow, to make the effort that Helena had asked of her, made no headway at all. She utterly distrusted and disbelieved her. And somewhere, lying beneath the darkness of the windless night, was Archie, for whose happiness she would have given her heart's last blood. But all of it would not help him one atom while he, in the perverse dispensations of destiny, wanted only what he could not get, Helena's love. He could not get it because it did not exist. She did not love; the faculty had been denied her.

* * * * *

Suddenly she felt frightened about Archie. He had sunk somewhere out of reach this evening; a lid had shut down on him. Once or twice it had seemed to lift for a moment, and she remembered what made it lift.

BOOK III

CHAPTER IX

Late one afternoon about a week after, Archie was sitting with his old nurse, Blessington, in the room that had once been his day-nursery. He had left London the day after Helena had so honourably paid him the five half-crowns he had won from her, and since then he had been living here alone with his father. This evening, his mother and Jessie were coming down from town, his mother to remain here till she went up to London again for Helena's wedding which had been fixed for the end of the first week in August, while Jessie was but coming for a long week-end. Helena remained in town, where she was very busy shopping, and unpacking the lovely presents which Lord Harlow sent or brought to her, morning, noon, and night. They were really delightful presents, and the material of them was large precious stones, exquisitely set.

Archie had long made it a habit, when he was at home, to pay a visit to his old nurse before he went to dress for dinner. She had become housekeeper after the fledging of the family, and now, half-way through the decade of her seventies, did little more, when Archie was away, than sit white-haired and stately with her sewing or her knitting, and feel that she was very busy. But when Archie came home she would burst into violent activities, and constitute herself his nurse again, to whom he was always "Master Archie," and quite a little boy still. It mattered not one rap to her that he had his own valet, none other indeed than William, who in days gone by had fished him out of the lake, and received a gold watch and chain for the rescue, for Blessington was always in and out of his room, taking coats and trousers away to have buttons more securely adjusted, and loading her work-basket with piles of his socks and underclothing in which her eyes, still needle-sharp for all her seventy-five years, had detected holes that required darning. This habit of hers sometimes drove William nearly mad, for Blessington would take away all Archie's washing when it came back from the laundry, in order to inspect it thoroughly, and when his distracted valet wanted clean clothes, and applied to her for them, she would often entirely forget that she had taken them, and firmly deny the appropriation. Then William would craftily manage to get her to open her cupboard door, and lo, there was all Archie's clean linen. And Blessington would exclaim, "Eh, I must have taken it, and it went out of my head." Or she would abstract his sponge from the bathroom in order to put a stitch into it, and Archie, sitting in his bath, would find nothing to wash himself with. But Blessington was a sacred and a beloved institution, and as long as she was happy (which she most undoubtedly was when Archie was there to look after and inconvenience) no one minded these magpie-annexations of portable property.

* * * * *

Of all hours in the day Blessington loved best this evening visit of Archie's, when he sat among the tokens of his childhood, the play-table which now scarcely reached up to his knees, the little arm-chair, with its bar of wood strung through the arms so as to imprison and guard the sitter, the box of oak-bricks with which he used to build houses of amazing architecture, the depleted regiments of lead-soldiers which still stood on the mantel-shelf. Her great delight was to recall to him the days of his childhood, his naughtiness, the scrapes he got into, the whole patchwork of memories that retained still such lively and beloved colouring. And for him, too, during this last week, there had been in these talks a way of escape from this nightmare of his present experience; it was he himself, after all, who had put the coals on his mother's hearthrug, had fished for pike with William, had attended, in rapturous trepidation, the advents of Abracadabra. These days seemed much further off from him than they did from her, for a bitter impassable water lay between them and him, while for her they had only receded a little further into the placid and sunny distance of her days. But, when he talked them over with her, he could recapture a dreamlike illusion of getting back into a life of which the most alarming feature was the presence of his father. Over everything else there hung enchantment.

He was sitting now in Blessington's rocking-chair, having tried without success to squeeze himself into the imprisoning seat of his childhood, and she was recalling the awful episode of the burnt rug.

"Eh, whatever possessed you to go and do it," she said, "I can't understand to this day, Master Archie. I'm speaking of when you set fire to your mamma's rug."

"Tell me about that," said Archie.

"Well, it was on an afternoon when you had a cold, and your mamma had allowed you to sit in her room while she went out driving. And what must you do but empty all the fire from the hearth on to her rug. You nearly got a whipping for that from your papa!"

Archie remembered that moment quite well, and how he had stood in his father's study, frightened but defiant, and refusing to say he was sorry when he was not. Then his mother had come in and had pointed to a bottle on the table, and told his father that he ought to learn his lesson first before he gave Archie one… That had puzzled him at the time, though it was clear enough now. His father still had that lesson to learn, and Archie, during this last week, had begun to understand a little why his father had not yet learned it, if learning it implied the giving up of all that battles stood for.

He recalled himself with a jerk: he wanted to get back into the enchanted land which Blessington's reminiscences outlined for him.

"Yes, that hearthrug," he said. "That was a bad business, wasn't it, Blessington? What do you think put it into my head to empty the fire on to it?"

"Bless the boy, I don't know," said Blessington. "It was just mischief."

"Yes, but what's mischief?" asked Archie.

Blessington was a simple and direct theologian.

"Well, I shouldn't wonder if it's doing what Sapum wants you to do," said she, Sapum being her equivalent for the arch-enemy.

"I shouldn't wonder either," said Archie. "But it's rather beastly of Sapum to take possession of a very small boy with a bad cold in the head."

"Eh, he takes possession of us all, if we let him," observed Blessington. "But that was the naughtiest thing you ever did, dear. I wouldn't lay it up to you now."

"Was I good as a rule?" asked he.

"Yes, Master Archie, for a boy you were," said Blessington. "Boys are more trouble than girls, as is natural and proper."

"But doesn't Sapum enter into girls, too?" asked he, with another thought in his mind.

"Yes, to be sure, but not so violent-like. And when after that you were took ill, and we all went out to—eh, what's the name of that place in Switzerland—I must say you were wonderfully good. It was as if some angel took possession of you, not one of Sapum's flibertigibbits. You were no trouble at all; and see how quick you got well."

Archie rocked himself backwards and forwards for a minute in silence.

"I wish I could remember Martin," he said at length. "Tell me something about Martin."

"Eh, dear lamb!" said she. "Couldn't he be naughty too, when the fit took him! But then he got ill, and many's the time when I've longed for him to be naughty again, and he hadn't the spirit for it. He didn't want to die, and right up to the end he thought he'd get better. You papa never loved any one like he loved him, and nobody could help loving him. He was like a April morning, dear—sunshine one minute and squalls the next. And there was months, Master Archie, when we thought you would follow him."

Blessington grew a little tearful, with the sweet, easy tears of old-age over this, and Archie changed the subject.

"And Abracadabra, now?" he asked. "What evenings those birthdays evenings were, weren't they? I wish Abracadabra came still, bringing all we wanted. What would you choose, Blessington?"

Blessington beamed again.

"Eh, I know what I'd choose," she said. "I'd choose a nice young lady to come here, and you and she take a fancy to each other, dear. That's what I'd choose. Isn't there some nice young lady, Master Archie?"

Archie stopped his rocking for a moment, and a bitter word was on the end of his tongue. Then he smiled back at his nurse's radiant face.

"I'm going to marry you, Blessington," he said, "when you're old enough. Don't you go flirting with anybody else now."

Blessington gave a little cackle of soft, toothless laughter.

"Well, I never," she said. "Who ever heard such a thing?"

"Well, you've heard of it now," said he. "Blessington, I believe there's somebody else after you. I say, did you ever have any lovers once upon a time?"

Blessington looked solemn again.

"Well, there was your papa's game-keeper once," she said, "who made a silly of himself, as if I'd got nothing better to do than go and marry him. I didn't suffer any of his nonsense… And there's the sound of the motor. That'll be your mamma and Miss Jessie coming. There's a nice young lady now!"

"Do you like her better than Miss Helena?" asked Archie.

Blessington nodded her head very emphatically.

"Not that I say she isn't a nice young lady, too," she said mysteriously.

"What's the matter with her then?" asked Archie.

Blessington looked the incarnation of discretion.

"I say nothing," she said. "But there's some as are artful, and some as are not. Now, my dear, you must go and see your mamma, or she'll be wondering where you are."

"I'm with my young woman," said Archie.

"There! Get along with you," said Blessington. "Eh, Master Archie, I love a talk over old times with you."

* * * * *

Archie went reluctantly away to greet his mother and Jessie, for these talks with Blessington had become to him a sort of oasis in this weary wilderness of scorching sand through which he had to travel all day and for many hours of the night. She was the comforter of the troubles of his earliest childhood; it was she who had always been by him if some nightmare snatched him from sleep, or if the dark developed terrors, and that habit of calling on her for aid, established among the mists of dawning consciousness he found still alive as an instinct, when there came on him now the maturer woes of love and manhood. Throughout his school life and his three years at Cambridge, he had never quite let go of Blessington's hand, which had been the first to direct and sustain his tottering attempts at locomotion. Now, too, she was the only member of his immediate circle who did not know of his trouble, and it was an unutterable relief to feel that he was not being pitied and sympathized with by somebody. For, though there is nothing in the world better than sympathy and pity, no sufferer smarting from a recent wound wants to live exclusively in such surroundings. Pity and sympathy, though they heal, yet touch the wound, and he never got over the impression when he was with his mother, for instance, that his wound was being dressed… Jessie did not force that on him so much, yet with her he was always being reminded of the fact that she was Helena's sister. But with Blessington he could go back into the sunlight of the past: talk with her, and another occupation, temporary, he told himself, to tide him over those days, enabled him to get away to some extent, from himself.

He met his mother in the hall, and instantly those anxious eyes of love, which, for all his affection for her, he found irritating, were on him. She was at his wound again, taking off the bandages, seeing how it was getting on…

"And how are you, darling?" she said, looking at him with the tenderness that got on his nerves.

Archie kissed her.

"I am quite well, thanks," he said. "I have just been having a talk with Blessington."

"My dear, how she would like that!" said Lady Tintagel with eager cordiality. "That was thoughtful of you."

Archie jerked himself away from her: though his mother said nothing direct, he felt that pity filled her mind. He was in its presence, and longed to get away from it. All the time another distinct piece of his mind wanted to hear about Helena. But he could not ask any question about her.

"How are you, Archie?" said Jessie quietly.

Archie's exasperation suddenly flared up.

"I have just told my mother I am very well," he said. "I am still very well, thank you."

Jessie laughed; she managed better than Lady Tintagel.

"In that case, come and have a game of golf-croquet with me," she said. "There's time before we need dress, isn't there? I do want some air so badly after town."

Archie glanced at the clock; he usually went to his father's study about this time, when they celebrated the approaching advent of dinner with a cocktail or two. That was the beginning of the tolerable part of the day: there was plenty of wine at dinner, and afterwards a succession of whiskies and sodas, and to be alive became quite a bearable condition again. On that first evening when Helena had told him her news and paid her half-crowns he had found that alcohol broke down his sense of being stunned, of being made of wood. Now he drank for another reason: by drink he got rid of the misery of normal consciousness and emerged into some sort of life again. It stimulated his brain, he could by its means escape for a little from that one perpetual thought of Helena that went round in his head like a stick in a backwater, and get into the current again. Sometimes he would go to his room, taking a whisky and soda with him, and wrestle with the sea-sketches he had so enthusiastically worked at at Silorno. By degrees the liquid in his glass ebbed, and his pile of cigarette-ends mounted, and he would go back for fresh supplies. But, while these hours lasted, he lived, and what to-morrow should bring he did not in the least care. He could escape for a few hours now, and that was sufficient. Also, when he went to bed, he could sleep heavily and dreamlessly.

There was still time for a game with Jessie, before going in to his father; Jessie would take longer to dress for dinner than he, and there would be a few minutes to spare after she went upstairs. But, even as they were strolling across the lawn to get the croquet-balls from their box, she a little ahead of him as he nursed a match for his cigarette, he looked up, and there in front of him might have been Helena. The two were of the same height and build, they moved like each other. It was Jessie, of course, but just for a second, while his match burned up in the hollow of his hand, it was not she at all…

He threw the match away.

"Get the balls out, will you?" he said. "I've left my cigarette-case in my father's room."

He ran back to the house, and went in through the garden door of his father's study. Lord Tintagel was sitting in the big leather arm-chair, with his feet up on another, and a glass beside him.

"Just come for a cocktail, father," said Archie. "Hullo, they're not here yet. It doesn't matter; I'll take a glass of whisky and soda."

"By all means; take what you like," said the other drowsily. "You mother's come, hasn't she?"

"Yes, mother and Jessie," said Archie, pouring himself out some whisky. The soda-water was nearly exhausted, but the dregs of it gurgled pleasantly over the spirit. He drank it in a couple of gulps.

"What are you going to do now?" asked his father.

"Only have a game with Jessie."

"All right. Call in here when it's time to go up and dress. There'll be a cocktail for you then. Infernal lazy fellows the servants are not to bring them in earlier. Chuck me over the evening paper, will you?"

The evening remission from deadness and dullness and misery had begun for Archie. He played his game with Jessie, drank his cocktail, and by the end of dinner had risen to such naturalness of good spirits again, that his mother commended herself for the wisdom of her plan that he should leave London and seek a change of mind in a change of scene. He had done some writing since he had been here; he seemed pleased with the way it was going, and she talked hopefully to Jessie when they held a rather protracted sitting in the drawing-room before the two men joined them. Perhaps they had both overrated the strength of Archie's attachment: certainly to-night he did not appear like a boy who had so lately suffered an overwhelming disappointment in his affections.

"And Blessington says he has been just as delightful and affectionate to her as usual," said Lady Tintagel. "He goes and talks to her every evening as he always did. I think you must have been wrong, dear Jessie, when you thought he was so mortally hurt."

Jessie did not reply at once: she felt sure that she, with the insight of that love which is more comprehending than any mother's love, was somehow right about that point. It was not the mere lapse of a week that had restored Archie. Besides, Blessington did not know about his troubles. She could easily conjecture what a relief he might find in that. She knew that she would feel the same in his place; she could understand how much easier it was to behave normally with those who did not know than with those who did. Yet Archie's father knew, and all through dinner she had seen how friendly and intimate the two had become. Archie used to be constrained and awkward with his father, while his father used to be rather contemptuous of him. But this evening there had been none of that on either side, and now they lingered together a long time over their talk and their cigarettes. It was as if some bond of sympathy was springing up between them. But she shrank from admitting the explanation to herself: it might be that a man, who had been so bitterly disappointed about a girl, found something in another man that suited his mood. Women would remind him of a woman...

There was a shout of laughter in the hall outside, and Archie came in, followed by his father. He did not communicate the grounds for his merriment, but, looking a little flushed, very handsome, and very content, sat down on the sofa by his mother.

"Well, mother darling?" he said.

Instantly her love yearned forth to him.

"My dear, it is good to hear you laugh," she said. "What have you and your father been talking about?"

The sense of being watched, the love that irritated did not trouble Archie now. The sunny hours would stretch unclouded until he fell into bed. He laughed again, looking across to his father.

"I say, father," he said, "shall I tell her, or would she think it not quite...?"

"Just as you like," said Lord Tintagel.

The door into the garden, already ajar, swung gently open, admitting a breath of cool night-air into the room. It stirred in Jessie's hair as it passed her, and moved across to Archie, making the flowers in a vase near him vibrate. And for just that moment some impulse from the untainted tranquillity stirred in his soul, and his overheated, stimulated brain drank it thirstily in. His own laughter, and the subject of his laughter, the whole contents of the last hour or two, seemed stale and stuffy. The air of them was thick with the fumes of wine, with the fancies and images that it evoked, smoke-wreaths that hung heavy in the atmosphere, swirling and turning like dancers and melting into other shapes. But for that moment when the night-air came in from the crystal-clear dusk outside, that liquid tabernacle of sapphire in the holy night, where stars sang together and nightingales burned, the hot fumes dispersed, and he drew in long, tranquillizing breaths. This physical impression had, too, its psychical counterpart, for even as the air that stirred in Jessie's hair brought a coolness and a refreshment to him, so from the girl herself there seemed to stream into it a current of something wholesome and human and unfevered, unvexed by desire, and untouched by bitterness...

"It's rather hot in here," he said. "Will you come for a stroll, Jessie?"

They went out together... The heavens were full of stars, and a slip of a moon was near to its setting. Over the beds below the windows there hovered the fainter fragrance of sleeping flowers that stood with hanging heads and leaves that glimmered with the falling dew. Beyond lay the dimmed mirror of the lake, and beside it rose the dark mass of the wood in which the nightingales were singing. The scene seemed prepared for some human love-duet, when lovers fancy that nature is arranging her most sensuous effects for their benefit, though in reality she is but pursuing the path ordained for her by the wheeling seasons, and predicted by barometers and apparatus that is concerned only with heat and movements of the moon. And, of lovers, there was one of each pair absent, as the two walked quietly towards the wood of the nightingales; for Jessie there was no eager mate, and for Archie none… Two hungry souls, both longing, both unsatisfied, went forth on that twilit pilgrimage. Spring still stirred in them, and there burned above them the everlasting choir of the stars. But that helped in no way: had they been lovers, an autumn squall or a winter snow-storm would have served their purpose just as well.

Archie chattered for a little while, comparing the moon to a clipped finger-nail, the dimmed mirror of the lake to a frozen rink in Switzerland, with all the hollowness of superficial talk, when the tongue speaks from habit, which is as lightly rooted as the seed on stony ground. Heart-whole, he had often chattered like that, and Jessie had sunned herself and responded to those silly things; but now she knew, as well as he, that the babble was no more than blown sea-foam. It made her heart ache that he should talk it to her, for, though she made no claim on his love, it was miserable that he could not recognize how true a friend it was who was by his side in this song-haunted darkness. She knew—none better—that he had no love to give her, but her love that was so disciplined to go hungry without crying out, starved for a word from him that should fly the flag of friendship, noblest of all ensigns that are not of royal emblazonment.

They had come to the edge of the lake, and a moor-hen steered its water-logged flight across the surface. And then Archie's foolish chatter died, and he was silent as he watched the rayed ripple of water. The wash died away in the reeds, and chuckled on the bank, and at last he spoke.

"Why did Helena treat me like that?" he said. "It wasn't fair on me. Why did she encourage me? She might so easily have shown me that she didn't care. She knew: don't tell me she didn't know! Do answer me. Didn't she know? All the time that we were in town together she knew. And she let me go on. She was waiting to see if she could catch the Bradshaw. If she couldn't, perhaps she would have taken me. Was it so? You ought to know: you're her sister."

His voice had risen from the first reproach of his speech to a fury of indignation.

"Did she love me or didn't she?" he cried. "Do tell me if you know."

His passion had found combustible material in her: she flamed with it.

"Helena doesn't love anybody," she said. "Oh, Archie, poor Helena!"

"Poor Helena!" said he. "Why 'poor'? Surely it's far more comfortable to love nobody. Oh, don't remind me of that stupid rot about it being better to have loved and lost. Anyhow, a worse thing is to have loved and not found. That's what has happened to me, and she made me think I had found. She meant to make me think that. Damned well she succeeded, too. And, if you're right about her not loving anybody, do you mean that she doesn't love the Bradshaw?"

Archie had closed a grip on her arm: now she shook his hand off, though loving to have it there.

"I can't answer you that," she said. "And I oughtn't to have said that Helena loves nobody. I withdraw that entirely."

"The saying of it, you mean," said he. "You don't withdraw your belief in it."

"I don't know the truth of it. What I said was only my opinion, and I withdraw it. I oughtn't to have said it."

"But you keep your opinion?" asked he.

"You shouldn't ask me that. I have withdrawn what I said. Please accept that."

In this high noon of stars she could see his face very clearly. It was not angry any longer: it was just empty, as if there was no one there behind the eyes and the mouth. It was a face empty, swept, and garnished, ready for any occupant who might take possession. The sweet, clean water of his nature must have run out on to desert sands; the cistern of the body into which it had so swiftly and boyishly bubbled all these years was empty. Just for one second that impression lasted, inscrutably frightening her, with some nightmare touch.

"Archie," she cried, "are *you* there? Is it you?" She heard a dreary little laugh for answer.

"Oh, I suppose so," he said. "I answer to my name, don't I?"

She longed, with a force of passion quite new to her, to be able to reach him in some way, to let her love be coined into the commoner metal of friendship, if only that could get to him, and give him the sense that he had something in his pocket worth having, even though it was not gold. She would have gleefully melted all her love into a currency that could have enriched him, for he did not want her love, and she had no other use for it except to help him in some way. And, as if to answer her yearning, he took her arm again, not angrily now, but with the quiet pressure of a man with a sympathetic friend.

"You're a good pal, Jessie," he said. "I'm awfully grateful to you. You won't play me false with your friendship, will you?"

"No, my dear," said she, stumbling a little on the words. "I'm—I'm not like that. The more you count on me the better I shall be pleased. I'm stupid at saying things, but, oh Archie, if a friend is any use to you, you've got one. And let me say, just once, how sorry I am for all this miserable business."

"Thanks, Jessie," said he.

They had turned back towards the house, and Jessie, unconscious of anything else except Archie, saw that they were already half across the lawn that lay dripping with dew. Her thin satin shoes were soaked, and the hem of her dress trailed on the grass. But she regarded that no more than she would have regarded it had she been walking in the dark with her lover.

Then Archie spoke again—there was no more emotion in his voice than if he had been speaking through a telephone.

"Do keep on trying to be friends with me, Jessie," he said. "I'm nothing at all just now; I'm dead, but will you watch by the corpse? It likes to know you are there. There's no complaint if you go away, but when sometimes you have nothing to do, you might just sit with it."

"Archie, dear, don't talk such nonsense," she said.

"I daresay it is nonsense, but it seems to me sense. I don't feel as if I was anybody… I can imagine what a house feels like that has been happily lived in for years, when the family goes away, and leaves it empty. There's a board up 'To let, unfurnished,' and the windows get dirty, and the knocker and door-handle, which were so well rubbed and polished, get dull. There used to be curtains in the windows, and in the evening passers-by in the street could see chinks of light from within, and perhaps hear sounds of laughter. But now there are no curtains, and the pictures have gone from the walls, leaving oblong marks where they used to hang. And the spirit of the house stares mournfully out, thinking of the days when there was laughter and love within its walls. Haven't you ever seen a house like that? They're common enough."

She pressed the hand that lay loose in the crook of her elbow.

"Oh, Archie, you give me such a heartache," she said.

"Well, I won't again. But if you think me wanting in affection to mother, or you, or anybody, just remember that I'm an empty house for the present. I daresay somebody will take me again."

Jessie felt that this was a truer Archie than he who had stopped so long in the dining-room and come in afterwards with a shout of laughter over something that he would not recount. But by now their stroll had taken them close to the long grey front of the house, and for the present Archie had no more to say, and was evidently meaning to go indoors again. Upstairs all was dark, but below, the five windows of the drawing-room, uncurtained and open, cast oblongs of light on to the gravel, and next to them the two windows of Lord Tintagel's study were lit. Even as they stepped from the grass on to the walk, and their footsteps became audible again, his figure, silhouetted against the light, appeared there, and the window-sash rattled as he opened it wider.

"Is that you, Archie?" he called. "Come in and see me before you go upstairs."

"All right, father," said he, "we're just coming in."

Jessie heard a fresh vigour in his quickened voice, and in the light from the windows she could see that his face was alert again. And it was with a sense of certainty that she guessed what had given him this sudden animation. Perhaps it was only the knowledge of his father's habits that informed her, perhaps it was a brain-wave passing from him to her that told her that inside his father's room were the things for which he craved, the cool hiss of bubbling water on to the ice that swam in the spirits…

"You're not going to sit up long, are you?" she said.

"Oh, I don't know. My father and I often have a talk in the evening. And sometimes I do some writing before I go to bed. It's quite a good time for writing when every one has gone to bed and the house is quiet."

"You always used to say at Silorno that you wrote best in the morning."

"Yes, but that was at Silorno, where I could lie on the beach, and go for a swim at intervals. Lord! What jolly days they were! It's a pity they are all dead."

They went through the French window into the drawing-room, and found that Lady Tintagel had already gone upstairs. Archie stood by Jessie, shifting from one foot to the other, in evident impatience at her lingering.

"Well, you'll be wanting to go to bed," he said. "I daresay you'll go in and have a talk with my mother. And, do you know, my father's waiting for me; I think I'll join him. I shall soon come upstairs, I expect. I feel rather like writing to-night."

"I'm glad you're going on with that," she said. "That's something left, isn't it? The house isn't quite empty, Archie."

He laughed.

"No, I can trace my name in the dust on the window-panes," he said. "But I'll go to my father. Good-night, Jessie."

* * * * *

Lord Tintagel, rather unusually, was deep in the evening paper when Archie entered. Archie noticed, with some surprise, that his glass still stood untouched on the tray.

"Rather nasty news," he said, not looking up. "Give me my drink, Archie, there's a good fellow. Plenty of ice and not much soda."

"And what's the news?" asked Archie.

"Well, it looks as if there might really be trouble brewing. Servia has appealed to Russia against the Austrian ultimatum. I wonder if Germany can really be at the bottom of it all. And the city takes a gloomy view of it. All Russian securities are heavily down."

"Does that affect you?" asked Archie, bringing him his drink.

"Yes, I've got a big account open in them. I wonder if I had better sell. Of course there won't be war; we're always having these scares, and they always come to nothing. But if dealers are anxious, prices may fall a good bit yet, and I should find it difficult to pay my differences."

Archie poured himself out his first tumbler. He held it in his hand a moment, not tasting it, now that he had got it. Delay, when the delay was voluntary, would but add deliciousness to the moment when his mouth and throat would feel that cold sting…

"I don't understand," he said, watching the bubbles stream up from the sides and bottom of his glass.

His father threw down the paper.

"It's as simple as heads and tails," he said. "I've bought a quantity of Russian mining shares, without paying for them, in the hope that they will go up. If they do, I shall sell at the higher price and pocket the difference. But if they go down I shall have to pay the difference at the next account. If the shares are each worth L8 now, and at the next account are only standing at L6, I shall have to pay L2 on each share. If I like, I can telegraph to my broker to sell now, while they're at L8. I shall have a loss because I bought them at L9, but I shall no longer be running any risks. But it's thirsty work talking. Just fill my glass again."

"But then, if the scare dies down again, I suppose your shares will go up," said Archie.

His father laughed.

"Sound business head you've got, Archie," he said. "You've got the hang of it; it's just heads and tails. Never you speculate: it's a rotten business. I've got into the habit now, but I recommend you not to take to it. It's easy enough to take to it, but it's the devil to break it. Same with other things. Make a habit of virtue, and you'll never go to the deuce."

He watched Archie a moment, who with head thrown back, and young, strong throat throbbing as he swallowed, was reaping the rewards of his delay in drinking. And when, with brightened eyes, he put his glass down, he stood there like some modern incarnation of Dionysus, his face pure Greek from the low-growing brown curls to the straight nose and the short round chin. With a cloak over his shoulders in exchange for his dress-clothes, with sandals for his patent leather shoes, and a wine-cup for his tall glass, he might have stepped straight from some temple-frieze, and his father wondered how any girl in her senses could have chosen the precise, pedantic man whom she was soon going to marry, when Archie was but waiting, as she must have known, for his moment. He, poor fellow, was often a very dreary and dispirited boy all day; but in the evening he came to himself again, and was what he used to be. And yet, though it seemed to Lord Tintagel a cruel thing to wish to deprive him of the few hours of the joy of living that were his during the day, he was smitten, with the easy and vague remorse of a man only half-sober, to see the effect that alcohol had on Archie, who, all his life till now, had scarcely tasted it. But he remembered when he himself had been at that stage; he remembered also his father giving him just such a warning as he now proposed to give Archie. He wished he had taken notice of it, and he hoped that Archie would.

That evening, thirty years ago, he recalled now with extreme distinctness. The scene had taken place in this very room, and his father, already half-tipsy, as his habit was, had warned him of the dangers of drink, and he remembered how laughable and grotesque such a warning had seemed coming from lips that had lost all precision of utterance. But he told himself that he was not going to commit any such absurdity: he was perfectly sober, indeed it seemed very likely that it had never entered Archie's head to think of him as a drunkard. Sometimes he stumbled a little going upstairs at night, sometimes he had an impression that his pronunciation was not quite distinct; but he never became incapable, as he could remember his father becoming, and being carried off to bed by two perspiring footmen.

He put down his second glass without tasting it.

"There's something I want to speak to you about, Archie," he said, "and you mustn't be vexed with me, because I'm only doing what I believe to be my duty. You won't be vexed, will you?"

Archie looked at him in surprise.

"No, I don't suppose I shall, father," he said. "What is it?"

His father got up and stood by his chair quite steadily, for he leaned back against the high chimney-piece.

"Well, I want to you be careful about that stuff," he said, pointing to the bottle. "That's one of the habits I was speaking about, which they say is so easy to keep clear of, but so hard to break. You drink rather freely, you know, whereas a few months ago you never touched wine or spirits. It's an awful snare—you may get badly entangled in it before you know you are caught at all."

Archie kept his lucid eyes fixed on his father's, and not a tremor of his beautiful mouth betrayed his inward laughter, his derisive merriment at this solemn adjuration delivered by a man who spoke very carefully for fear of his words all running into each other like the impress of ink on blotting-paper. It really was ludicrously funny, and the immortal Mr. Stiggins came into his mind.

"I hope you don't think a whisky and soda after dinner is dangerous, father," he said. "You usually have one yourself, you know."

He moved across to the table as he spoke, and handed his father the drink he had mixed for him but a few moments before. Lord Tintagel, quite missing the irony of the act, began sipping it as he talked.

"No, of course not, my dear boy," he said. "I'm not a faddist who thinks there's a microbe of delirium tremens in every glass of wine. But—though you may never have heard it—your grandfather was a man who habitually took too much, and it's strange how that sort of failing runs in families."

Archie's mouth broadened into a smile.

"Skipping a generation now and then," he said gravely.

His father turned sharply on him.

"Eh? What?" he asked.

He looked hard at Archie for a moment—as hard, that is, as his rather wandering power of focus allowed him—and suddenly beheld himself with Archie's eyes, even as, thirty years ago, he had beheld his father when he spoke to him on precisely the same theme. He put down his glass, and a wave of shame as he saw himself as Archie saw him, went over him.

"I know: this doesn't come very well from me, Archie," he said. "It's ridiculous, isn't it? But I meant well."

He looked at the boy with a pathetic, deprecating glance.

"If I make an effort, will you make one, too?" he asked. "I've gone far along that road, and I should be sorry to see you following me. I should indeed. Just now I know you're unhappy, and a bottle of wine makes things more tolerable, doesn't it?"

Archie, in his empty, exasperated heart felt a sort of pity for his father, which was based on scorn. Something inside Lord Tintagel was probably serious and sincere, and yet it was what he had drunk that stimulated his scruples for Archie. He was in a mellow, kindly, moralizing stage in his cups that Archie had often noticed before. Certainly he himself did not want to become like that, but he felt that he was not within measurable distance of the need of making any resolution on the subject, so far was he from needing the exercise of his will. Just at present, even as his father had said, he was unhappy, and his unhappiness melted in the sunshine of drink. He did not care for it in itself; he but took it, so he told himself, like medicine because his mind was ailing.

"Well, let us talk about it to-morrow," he said. "We'll make some rule, shall we, father? And don't imagine for a moment that I am vexed with you. But I shall go upstairs now, I think. I've got some writing I want to do."

He hesitated a moment.

"I'll just take a night-cap with me," he said. "Good-night, father."

"Good-night, my dear boy; God bless you! We'll have a talk to-morrow."

Archie took the glass he had filled out into the hall, and waited there a moment, and the pity faded from his mind, leaving only contempt. It was just the maudlin mood that had prompted his father to be so ridiculous, and talk about resolutions. Certainly resolutions would do him no harm, and the keeping of them would undoubtedly do him good, for, instead of the firm, masterful man whom Archie had known as the rather prodigious denizen of that formidable room, there sat there now a weak, entangled creature. Archie could hardly believe that, in years not so long past, he had been afraid of his father: now his whole force, that dominating, intangible quality, had vanished. Occasionally he still flew into fits of anger that alarmed nobody, but that was all that was left of his power.

Archie sat for a few minutes on the hall-table, instead of going upstairs, for he meant, with a certain object in view, to go back to his father's room, on some trivial errand, and, as he waited, the big clock ticked him back into boyhood. There was the fire-place by which Abracadabra sat on the last of her appearances; there the screen behind which, as he had subsequently ascertained, William had hidden with a trumpet and the servants' dinner-bell, there the side-door into the gardens through which, pleasingly excited, he had hurried with the box for coffin of the dead bird which the cat had killed... A hundred memories crowded about him, and not one, save where Blessington was concerned, held any romance or tenderness for him. They were as meaningless as pictures taken out from the empty house and leaning against the railings in the street: in the house itself, his bitter, lonely spirit, there was nothing left but the places where once they hung.

He went back to his father's room, crossing the hall with light foot, and turning the handle of the door with swiftness and silence. There was his father by the table, filling his glass again. It was just that which Archie wished to verify.

"I only came back for a book," he said. "Good-night again."

CHAPTER X

Archie went straight up to his room: his brimming glass was difficult to carry quite steadily, and he reduced its contents half-way upstairs. William had orders always to put whisky and soda in his room in case he wanted to sit up and write; but sometimes William forgot, or, at any rate, did not obey, and Archie wondered if the man did it on purpose, with perhaps the same excellent intentions as those which flowered so decorously in his father's mind. But to-night all was as it should be, and, as it was very hot, Archie undressed and put on his pyjamas before settling down to work. Writing, the absorbing joy of creation, the delicate etching of sentences that bit into the plate, still possessed him when he had taken the requisite evening dose.

But to-night, though he had got his material ready, his hand could not accomplish the fashioning of it, and he got up and walked with bare feet, once or twice up and down the room, wondering why he could not link up his thoughts to his power of expression. He was nearly at the end of one of those sea-stories, which he had begun at Silorno, and he knew exactly what he meant to say. The brain-centre that dictated was charged, and sufficiently stimulated, and yet he could get nothing on to paper that was worth putting there, though he was ready to write, and wanted to write.

He had not drunk too much and made himself fuddled; he had not drunk too little, and left the bitter weeds of daily consciousness uncovered, like rocks at low tide.

He sat and thought, wrote and impatiently erased again, and at last put down his pen. Perhaps even this, the only living interest that just now existed for him, was being taken from him also, and was following down the channel which had emptied itself into Helena. She had taken from him everything else that meant life: it would be like her consistency to take that also, and leave him nude and empty. It was not that she wanted the gift which she—in his vague, excited thought—seemed to be robbing him of; it was only that she and the memory of how she had treated him was a vampire to his blood. She had sucked him empty, drained him dry of happiness, of joy of life, of human interests. More than that, his love, the best thing which he had to give her, and for which she had no use, she now seemed to have treated with some devilish alchemy, so that it turned bitter; hate, like some oozy scum, rose from the depths of it, and covered its crystal with poisonous growth.

CHAPTER X

This would never do; the rocks at low tide had become uncovered, and, while he slipped and stumbled among them, bruising himself at every step with the thought of Helena, he could never get that abstraction and detachment which he knew were the necessary conditions of his writing. And all power of achieving that seemed taken from him; he felt himself an impotent atom, unable to order the workings of his own brain, defenceless against any thoughts that might assault him.

The house was perfectly quiet; the stillness of the midsummer night had flowed into its open windows and drowned it deep in that profound tranquillity that was yet tense with the energy of the spinning world and the far-flung orbits of the myriad stars. The moon had long since sunk, but the galaxy of uncounted worlds flared on their courses, driven onwards by the inexhaustible eternity of creative forces that ran through the stars, even as it ran through the humblest herb that put forth its unnoticed blossom on the wayside. But Archie, in this bitter stagnation that paralysed him, seemed to himself to have no part in life: all that current of energy that bubbled through the world, with its impulses of good and evil, love and hate, seemed to have been cut off from him. He neither loved nor hated any more. There was the nightmare of this death in life: at any price, and under whatever inspiration, he longed to be in the current again. Tonight even drink had failed him.

He had walked across to the window, and came back to his chair at the table where was spread the sheet of paper covered with the scrawlings and erasures which were all the last two hours had to show. And at this precise moment, as he looked at them in a dull despair, and idea flashed across the blank field of his brain. Perhaps there might still be some spark of life, of individuality latent without him, which he could reach by that surrender of his conscious self which had been familiar to him in his childhood. There, just in front of him, below his shaded lamp, lay his cigarette-case, with one bright point of light on it, and, lying back in his chair with half-closed eyes he gazed at this in order to produce that hypnotic condition in which the subconscious self comes to the surface.

Almost at once the mysterious spell began to act. Across the field of his vision there began to pass waves of light and shadow, moving upwards with a regular motion, while through them like a buoy moored in a rough sea there remained steadfast that bright speck on his cigarette-case, now for a moment submerged in a wave of shadow, but appearing again. Upwards and upwards moved the waves, and then it seemed that it was they which were stationary, while he himself was sinking down through them, as through crystal-clear waters, looking up at the sunny surface which rose ever higher and more remote above him. As he sank into this dim, delicious world, the sensation of being alive again and in touch with living intelligences grew momently more vivid. It was the very seat and hearth of life that in him before had been cold and numbed; now, though surface perceptions were gradually withdrawn, his essential being tingled with the rapture of returning vitality.

Once or twice during this descent his ears, through which there poured the roar of rushing waters, had been startled as by some surface perception of the sound of loud rappings somewhere in the room; but they had not disturbed his steadfast gaze at the point of light; and once again he had heard a voice faintly familiar near him that said "I am coming." But he was far too intent on his progress to let the interruption break in upon it, and indeed those sounds seemed to be less an interruption than a confirmation to his surface-senses of what was happening to him... And then he knew, as he sank down to rest at last on the bottom of that unsounded sea, who it was who was filling him with the sense of life again, for, echoing not only in his ears, but somewhere in his soul, he heard the same voice, which he now clearly recognized, and which had spoken to him years ago at Grives, say, "Archie, I am here."

* * * * *

Archie was conscious on two separate planes of consciousness. All round him and high above him were the gleams and aqueous shadows of the subconscious world, but here and there those seemed to be pierced, and through them, as through rents of mist, he had glimpses of the material plane. He could see, for instance, part of the sheet of paper in front of him, and he could see the far corner of his table. And by it, very faint and unfocusable, part of it in the mists of the subconscious world, part in the harder outlines of reality, there was standing the figure of a young man. How it was dressed he could not see, or did not care to notice, but when for a moment the mist cleared off its face, he recognized the strong likeness to himself, even as he had recognized the likeness to himself in the photograph which he had found in the cache. But here was no photograph: instead, mysteriously translated into outlines and features visible to mortal eyes, was the semblance of Martin himself. It wavered and flickered, like the blown flame of a candle, but it was there, standing at the corner of his table. And, as it spoke, he saw the mouth move and the throat throb.

"I have managed to come back, Archie," he said, "because you were in such trouble, and because you didn't understand the warning you had. Do you understand now?"

The whole explanation flashed on him.

"The dream?" he said. "The white statue of Helena and the worms?"

"Surely. It was odd you didn't understand. You only loved the white statue. You loathed what came out of it, just as you loathe what has come out of the white statue since."

Archie leaned forward, peering into the mist that at this moment quite enveloped the figure.

"But I love her, too, Martin," he cried. "I long for her."

Out of the mist came the unseen voice:

"You long for what she looks like," it said. "You hate what she is."

"That may be. But the whole thing makes me utterly miserable."

Table and figure, the white paper and the tray with syphon and whisky became suddenly visible.

CHAPTER X

"You must learn not to be miserable," said that compassionate mouth. "Be very patient, Archie. You think you are stumbling through absolute darkness, but in reality, you are flooded with light. I can't see the darkness which you feel is so impenetrable: I only see you walking towards the ineffable radiance, always moving towards it. Occupy yourself, and try to grow indifferent to that part of Helena which you hate. Cling to love always. Just cling to love. Never hate; some time you may get to love what you hated."

The voice sank lower.

"The power is failing," it said. "I am losing touch with you."

"Oh, don't go," said Archie. "Martin, stop with me. Talk to me. I want to say so much to you."

He reached out his hand, and for a moment, out of the sunlit mists that had gathered again he felt, perfectly clearly, the touch of fingers that pressed his. But they died away into nothing as he clasped them, and the voice faded to the faintest whisper.

"I will come again, dear Archie," it said. "It is easiest at night."

* * * * *

The lines of shadow and light that undulated before his eyes grew thinner and more transparent, and he could see the drawn-back window-curtains and the black square of the night through them. The bright point at which he had been looking withdrew on to the surface of his cigarette-case, and slowly the whole room emerged into its normal appearance. Archie became suddenly conscious of a profound physical fatigue, and, leaving all thought and reflection till to-morrow, put out his light and stepped into bed. But instead of the empty desolation that had made a wilderness round him, waters of healing had broken out in his soul, and the desert blossomed…

Archie slept that night the clean out-door sleep which he had been used to at Silorno, and woke next morning, not with the crapulous drowsiness that now usually accompanied his wakings, but with the alert refreshment that slumber in the open air gave him. He sprang into full possession of his faculties and complete memory of what he had experienced the night before. He was quite aware that any scientific interpreter (science being best defined as the habit of denying what passes the limits of materialistic explanation) would have said that, tired with the effort to write, he had fallen asleep over his table and dreamed. But he knew better than that: the experience with its audible and visible phenomena, was not a dream, nor did it ever so faintly resemble one. A dream at best was a fantastic unreality; what he had experienced at his writing-table last night was based upon the firm foundations of reality itself. It was no hash-up of his own conscious or subconscious reflections, no extract distilled from his own mind. It came from without and entered into him, and, unlike most of the communications that purported to reach the minds of sensitives from the world that lay beyond the perception of their normal senses, there was guidance and help in it. Often, if not invariably, these messages from beyond were trivial and nugatory; it was a just criticism to say that the senders of them did not appear possessed of much worth the trouble of sending. But Martin's visit had not been concerned with trifles like that: he had sympathized, as a brother might, with Archie's trouble; he had explained, so that Archie could no longer doubt, the manner of the warning he had received before but not understood; he had spoken of Archie as being wrapped, according to his own sensations, in impenetrable darkness, though, to one who looked from beyond, he was ever moving towards the ineffable radiance. It was the same discarnate intelligence that, when he was a child, had conveyed to him the knowledge of that cache under the pine-tree, which was unknown to any living being (as men count living) and that could not have been conveyed to him through any telepathic channel except one that had its source and spring not in this world. And now, from the same source, had come this message from one who saw through the gross darkness of Archie's emptiness and bitter heart, and had promised to be with him again. Archie had no doubt whatever, as he got up with an alertness that had not been his for weeks, of the genuineness of the communication. It linked on with Martin's previous visits, and the glimpses he had received of the materialized form of his visitor confirmed exactly the recognition, years before, of the photograph he had found in the cache which Martin had told him of. And the Power in whose hands were all things had compassionated his trouble and had allowed, in pity for his need, the gateless barrier to be again unbarred, and a spirit, individual and recognized, to pass to and fro between him and the realms of the light invisible.

It was just when his soul despaired that this happened; when he felt himself denuded of all that he had loved, empty, and cast out from life itself. Just in that hour had Martin been permitted to come back to him…

He found his mother and Jessie at breakfast when he went down; his father, as usual, had not appeared, and again, as last night when he came out of the dining-room after a prolonged sitting, he felt kindly and affectionate. But this was not from the sottish satisfaction of wine: the light came from that subtle window in his soul, from which once more the shutters had been thrown back. The moment Jessie saw him she felt the quality of that change; he was like the Archie of Silorno again.

"Good morning, mother darling," he said, kissing her. "Good morning, Jessie. How bright and early we all are! And has everybody slept as serenely as I?"

"You didn't sleep very long, Archie, did you?" asked the girl, whose room was next his. "I heard you hammering at something after I had gone to bed, and I awoke once and heard you talking to somebody."

Archie, at the side-table helping himself to sausage, paused a moment. He made up his mind that for the present, anyhow, he preferred that Jessie should not know about the return of Martin. Perhaps he would tell her quietly when alone…

"Hammering?" he said. "Yes, there was a despatch-case, and I couldn't find the key. So I whacked it open. About talking—yes, I was writing last night, and I believe I read it aloud to myself before I went to bed. I never know what a thing is like unless I read it aloud."

"Oh, do read it aloud to me," said the girl.

"When it's in order: it wasn't quite in order when I read it over. But I was sleepy and went to bed."

Jessie said no more, but for some reason this account left her unsatisfied. The hammering had not sounded quite like the forcing of the lock of a despatch-case; it had been like sharp blows on wood, and for a moment she had thought that Archie was tapping loudly on the door that separated their rooms. It had stopped, and began again a little later. As for the talking, it had sounded precisely like two voices; one undeniably Archie's, the other low and indistinct.

Archie changed the subject the moment he had given this explanation, and made some very surprising observations.

"Helena is married on the 10th of August, isn't she?" he asked. "I must get her a wedding present. And I shall come to her wedding. That will convey my good wishes in the usual manner, won't it? I want to assure her of them."

Both of the women looked at him in the intensest surprise. To Lady Tintagel he had never mentioned Helena's name since the day she had accepted Lord Harlow, while to Jessie, only last night, he had loaded her with the bitterest reproaches, and had spoken of the abject despair and emptiness which had come upon him in consequence of what she had done. And he looked at each of them in turn with that vivid, brilliant glance which had been so characteristic of him.

"Yes, I make a public recantation," he said. "It suddenly dawned on me last night that I have been behaving just about as stupidly as a man can behave. I've said nothing to you, mother, but Jessie knows. I want her to try to forget what, for instance, I said to her last night. I can do better than that, and at any rate I propose to try. All the time that I haven't been mad with resentment I've been dead. Well, I hereupon announce the resurrection of Archibald. That's all I've got to say on the subject."

* * * * *

At that moment, swift as an arrow's flight, and certain as an intuition, there came to Jessie the odd idea that it was not Archie who was speaking at all. It might be his lips and tongue that fashioned the audible syllables, but it was not he in the sense that it had been he down by the lake last night. Savage and bitter as he had been there, he was authentic; now, all that he said, despite the absolute naturalness of his manner, seemed to ring false. She could not account for this impression in the least. It was not the suddenness of the change in his attitude, though that surprised her: it was some remoter quality, which her brain could not analyse. Something more intimate to herself than her brain had perceived it, and mere thought, mere reason, were blind to it.

Archie did not accompany his mother and Jessie to church that morning, but waited for Lord Tintagel's appearance, and the discussion of the good resolutions which were to be so beneficial to each of them. He sat in his father's study, and, having to wait some time before he made a shaky and disastrous entrance, thought over, in connection with the events of last night, what he himself had said that morning at breakfast. That surely was the gist of Martin's message to him: he must try to grow indifferent to that part of Helena which he hated; he must learn not to be miserable, to grasp the fact that the darkness in which he seemed to walk appeared to Martin no darkness at all, but a flood of light from the ineffable radiance. It was in the glow of that revelation that he had spoken at breakfast, trusting in the truth of it, and yet, as he sat now, waiting for his father, he knew he did not feel the truth of it. But, in obedience to Martin, that was how he had to behave. He must behave like that—this was what Martin meant—until he felt the soul within him grow up, like some cellar-sown plant, into the light. Hopefully and bravely had he announced his intention, but now, when in cooler mood he scrutinized it, he began to feel how tremendous was the task set him, how firmly rooted was that passionate resentment which must be alchemized into love. It had been true—Martin saw that so well—that it was the white statue, the fair form he had loved, and loved still with no less ardour than before. That, it seemed, according to his interpretation, Archie must keep: it was the other that must be transformed. But it would have been an easier task, he thought, to let his love slide into indifference, then raise his hate to the same level. But that was not the King's road, the Royal Banners did not flame along such mean-souled ways as these. He must cling to such love for Helena as he had, and transform the hate. But, first and foremost, cling to the love…

It was thus that he stated to himself the message that Martin seemed to have brought him last night, and, stated thus, it was a spiritual aspiration of high endeavour, and it did not occur to him how, stated ever so little differently, and yet following the lines of the communication, it assumed a diabolical aspect. The love which he had for Helena was a carnal love, that sprang from desire for her enchanting prettiness; that love he was to cling to, not sacrifice an iota of it. The hate that he felt for her, arising from her falseness, her encouragement of him for just so long as she was uncertain whether she could capture a man who was nothing to her, but whose position and wealth she coveted, Archie was to transform into indifference; he was to get over it. But, though it was hate, it had a spiritual quality, for it was hatred of what was mean and base, whereas his love for her had no spiritual quality: it was no more than lust, and to that under the name of love he was to cling… Here, then, was another interpretation of the words he had heard last night, and, according to it, it would have been fitter to attribute the message to some intelligence far other than the innocent soul of the brother who had so mysteriously communicated with him in childlike ways. But that interpretation (and here was the subtlety of it) never entered Archie's head at all. A message of apparent consolation and hope had come to him when he was feeling the full blast of his bitterness, the wind that blew from the empty desert of his heart and his stagnant brain. He had called for help from the everlasting and unseen Cosmos that encompasses the little blind half-world of material existence, and from it, somewhere from it, a light had shone into his dark soul, no mere flicker, or so it seemed this morning, like that spurious sunshine which he and his father basked in together, but rays from a more potent luminary.

Till now Archie, with the ordinary impulse of a disappointed man, had tried to banish from his mind (with certain exterior aids) the picture of the face and the form that he loved. But now he not only need not, but he must not, do that any longer: he had to cling to love. And while he waited for his father he kept recalling certain poignant moments in the growth of Helena's bewitchment of him. One was the night when they sat together for the last time in the dark garden at Silorno, and he wondered whether the suggestion of a cousinly kiss would disturb her. What had kept him back was the knowledge that it would not be quite a cousinly kiss on his part... Then there was the moment when he had caught sight of her on the platform at Charing Cross: she had come to meet his train on his arrival from abroad... Best of all, perhaps, for there his passion had most been fed with the fuel of her touch, had been the dance at his aunt's that same night, when the rhythm of the waltz and the melodious command of the music had welded their two young bodies into one. It was not "he and she" who had danced: it was just one perfect and complete individual. Here, on this quiet Sunday morning, the thought of that made him tingle and throb. It was that sort of memory which Martin told him he must keep alive... It was his resentment, his anger, that must die, not that. Helena had chosen somebody else, but he must long for her still.

Lord Tintagel appeared, unusually white and shaky, and, as lunch-time was approaching, he rang for the apparatus of cocktails.

"I sat up late last night, Archie," he said, "bothering myself over those Russian shares. It's really of you and your mother I am thinking. It won't be long before all the mines in Russia will matter nothing to me, for a few feet of earth will be all I shall require. But, before I went to bed, I came to the conclusion that I was wrong to worry. I think the scare will soon pass, and the shares recover. Indeed, I think the wisest thing would be not to sell, and cut my loss, but to buy more, at the lower price. I shall telegraph to my broker to-morrow. But I got into no end of a perplexity about it, and I feel all to bits this morning."

He mixed himself a cocktail with a shaking hand, and shuffled back to his chair.

"Help yourself, Archie," he said. "Let me see, we were going to have a talk about something this morning. What was it? That worry about my Russians has put everything out of my head."

Once again, as last night, it struck Archie as immensely comical that this white-faced, shaky man, who was his father, should be pulling himself together with a strong cocktail in order to discuss the virtues of temperance, and make the necessary resolutions whereby to acquire them. He felt neither pity nor sympathy with him, nor yet disgust; it was only the humour of the situation, the farcical absurdity of it, that appealed to him.

"We were going to make good resolutions not to drink quite so much," he said.

Lord Tintagel finished his cocktail and put the glass down.

"To be sure; that was it," he said. "It's time we took ourselves in hand. Your grandfather gave me a warning, and I wish to God I had taken it. But we'll help each other—eh, Archie? That will make it easier for both of us."

"I don't care a toss whether I take alcohol or not," said Archie. "As you remarked last night, father, I hardly touched it till a month ago."

Lord Tintagel laughed.

"But you've shown remarkable aptitude for it since," he said. "You found no difficulty at all in getting the hang of the thing."

Faintly, like a lost echo, there entered into Archie's mind the inherent horror of such an interview between father and son. But it was drowned by the inward laughter with which the scene inspired him, and his spirit, whatever it was that watched the play, looked on as from some curtained box, where, unseen, it could giggle at unseemliness, at some uncensored farce. Last night the same thing had amused him, but then he was in that contented oblivion of his troubles which alcohol lent him, whereas now it was morning and the time when he was least likely to take any but the most bitter and savage view of a situation. But all morning he had been possessed by the sunny lightness of heart with which Martin's communication of last night had inspired him. He must be patient, disperse and blow away by the great winds of love the hatred and intolerance that had been obscuring his soul. And surely it was not only for Helena that he must feel that nobler impulse: all that touched his daily life must be treated with the same manly tenderness. Nothing must shock him, nothing must irritate him, for such emotions were narrow and limited, incompatible with the oceanic quality of love. All this seemed directly inspired by Martin, who had brought him the first ray of true illumination. And yet, while he sunned himself in the light, there was something that apparently belonged to his bitter, his disappointed self that cried out for recognition, insisting that these dreams of love and tolerance were of a fibre infinitely coarser than its own rebellious attitude. It strove and cried, and the smooth edification of Martin's voice silenced it again.

The suggested compact between father and son soon framed itself into a treaty. There was to be nothing faddish or unreasonable about it: wine should circulate in its accustomed manner at dinner; but here, once and for all, was the end of trays brought to Lord Tintagel's study. A glass or two of claret should be allowed at lunch, but the cocktails and the whiskies in the evening were to be closed from henceforth. And the arrangement entered into appeared to be of a quality that sacrificed the desire of each for the sake of the other, or so at least it passed in their minds. Archie stifled the snigger of his inward laughter, and thought how clear was his duty to save his father, even at this late day, from falling wholly into the pit he had digged, while to his father the compact represented itself as an effort to save Archie from the path he had begun to tread. But, even as they agreed on their abstemious proceedings, there occurred to the minds of both of them a vague, luminous thought, like the flash of summer lightning far away which might move nearer…

Once again Archie was seized with the ironic mockery that all the time had quaked like a quick-sand below his seriousness.

"I haven't had my cocktail yet, father." he said. "I'll drink success to our scheme. You've had yours, you know. Our plan dates from now, when I've had mine. After that—no more."

His father's eyes followed him as he mixed the gin and vermouth.

"Well, upon my word, Archie," he said, "you ought to ask me to have a drink with you."

Archie somehow clung to the fact that his father had had a cocktail and that he had not.

"Have another by all means," he said, "and I'll have two. But do be fair, father."

And once again the horrible sordidness of these proceedings struck, as it seemed, his worse self, that part of himself that had all those weeks been uninspired by Martin. Martin was all love and tolerance: he gave no directions on such infinitesimal subjects as cocktails or whiskies. He, outside the material plane, was concerned only with the motive, the spiritual aspiration, with love and all its ineffable indulgences.

* * * * *

Jessie was leaving for town early next morning, and once again, as twenty-four hours ago, she and Archie strolled out after dinner into the dusk. But to-night, his father and he had followed the two ladies almost immediately into the drawing-room, and the two younger folk had left their elders playing a game of piquet together. That was quite unlike the usual procedure after dinner, for Lord Tintagel generally dozed for a little in his chair, and then retired to his study. But to-night he showed no inclination either to doze or to go away, and it was by his suggestion that the card-table had been brought out. He seemed to Jessie rather restless and irritable, and had said that it was impossible to play cards with chattering going on. That had been the immediate cause of her stroll with Archie. The remark had been addressed very pointedly to Archie and also very rudely. But Archie, checking his hot word in reply, almost without an effort, had apologized for the distraction, quietly and sufficiently.

"Awfully sorry, father," he had said. "I didn't mean to disturb you. Come out for a stroll, Jessie."

So there they were in the dusk again, and again Archie took Jessie's arm.

"Father's rather jumpy to-night," he said. "But I think he wanted to get rid of us: he may wish to talk to my mother. So it was best to leave them, wasn't it?"

Jessie's heart swelled. She knew from last night all that Archie was suffering, but the whole day he had been like this—gentle, considerate, infinitely sensitive to others, incapable of taking offence.

"Yes, much best," she said. "You know, Archie, you do behave nicely."

He knew what she meant. He knew how easy it would have been to make some provocative rejoinder to his father. But simply, he had not wanted to. Martin, and Martin's counsel, was still like sunlight within him.

"Oh, bosh," he said. "The gentle answer is so much easier than any other. I should have had to pump up indignation. But he was rather rude, wasn't he? Isn't it lucky that one doesn't feel like that?"

Archie drew in a long breath of the vigorous night-air. To himself it seemed that he drew in a long breath of the inspiration that had come to him last night.

"Jessie, I'm going to save father," he said. "We had an awfully nice talk this morning, and it was so pathetic. He has been a heavy drinker for years, you know. His father was so before him. So one mustn't think it is his fault, any more than it was my fault that I had consumption when I was little. It isn't a vice, it's a disease. Well, I've made a compact with him. I found that he had got it into his head—God knows how—that I—I know you'll laugh—was beginning to take to that beastly muck too. So I saw my opportunity. He's fond of me, you know; he really is, and it had seriously occurred to him that I was getting the habit. So I took advantage of that. I said I wouldn't have any more whiskies and cocktails if he wouldn't. We made a bargain about it. Without swagger, it was rather a good piece of work, don't you think?"

Jessie knew exactly what she honestly felt, and what she honestly felt she could not possibly say. For though it was a good bargain on Archie's part, the virtue of it would affect not only Lord Tintagel, but Archie himself. But the knowledge of this added to the sincerity of her reply.

"Oh, Archie," she said, "that was brilliant of you. Do you—do you think your father will keep to it?"

"He can't help it," said Archie triumphantly. "I'm going to be down here, except when I go up to town for Helena's wedding, and I'm always in and out of his room. I should know if he doesn't keep to it."

He paused, thinking out further checks on his father.

"There's William, too," he said. "William's devoted to me, simply, as far as I can tell, because he saved my life when I was a tiny kid. If I ask William to tell me whether my father gets drinks through him quietly when I'm not there, I'm sure he will let me know. How would that be?"

Jessie had an uncomfortable moment. The idea of getting a servant to report to Archie on his father's proceedings was as repugnant to her as, she thought, it must be to Archie. Possibly his main motive, that of taking care of his father, was so dominant in him that he did not pause to consider the legitimacy of any means. But, somehow, it was very unlike Archie to have conceived so backstairs an idea.

"Oh, I wouldn't quite do that," she said. "You wouldn't either, Archie."

"I don't see why not. The cure is more important than the means."

Jessie suddenly felt a sort of bewilderment. It could scarcely have been Archie who said that, according to her knowledge of Archie.

"But surely that's impossible," she said. "What would you feel if you found your father had been setting William to spy and report on you?"

Archie's voice suddenly rose.

"Oh, what nonsense!" he said. "You speak as if I was going to break my bargain with my father. I never heard such nonsense."

Once again the sense of bewilderment came over Jessie. That wasn't like Archie…

"I don't imply anything of the kind," she said. "But I do feel that it's impossible for you to get William to have an eye on your father, and report to you. And I'm almost certain that you really agree with me."

CHAPTER X

Archie considered this, and then laughed.

"I suppose I do," he said. "But the ardour of the newly born missionary was hot within me. Are missionaries born or made, by the way? Anyhow, I'm a missionary now. Nobody could have guessed that I was going to be a missionary."

Their stroll to-night was only up and down the broad gravel walk in front of the windows. It was very hot and all the drawing-room windows were open, so also were those of Lord Tintagel's study and the windowed door that led into the garden. As they passed this Archie saw a footman bring in a tray on which were set the usual evening liquids, and he guessed that his father had forgotten or had omitted to say that the syphon and some ice was all that would be needed. He thought for a moment, intently and swiftly.

"Jessie, they've brought in that beastly whisky again," he said. "I must tell them to take it away: my father mustn't see it. Just go down opposite the drawing-room windows, will you, and make sure my father is still playing cards, while I take the bottle away. Make me a sign."

Archie waited outside till this was given, and then went into his father's room. The man had gone away, and he took up the whisky-bottle with the intention of putting it back in the dining-room. But, even as his fingers closed on it, without warning, his desire for drink swooped down on him like the coming of a summer storm. He half filled a glass with the spirit, poured soda-water on the top and gulped it down. That was what he wanted, and then, with a swift cunning, he rinsed out the glass with soda-water, drank that also, and, filling it half up again with water, put it on the table by the chair where he usually sat. Then there was the bottle to dispose of, and he went out into the hall to take it to the dining-room. But, even as he crossed the foot of the stairs, another notion irresistibly possessed him, and up he went three steps at a time, and concealed it behind some clothes in his chest of drawers. He had discovered an excellent reason for doing that, for, if he left it in the dining-room, his father might find it there. It was much safer in his room. Then, tingling and content, and feeling that Martin would approve (indeed it seemed that he had prompted) this missionary enterprise, he rejoined Jessie again, his eyes sparkling, his mouth gay and quivering.

"I've done it," he said. "I thought at first of taking the bottle to the dining-room, but my father might have found it there."

"What did you do with it?" asked Jessie.

Archie took no time to consider.

"I rang the bell and told James to take it away again to the pantry," he said.

"That was clever of you, Archie."

"I know that. They're still playing cards, aren't they? Let's have one more turn, then. Jessie, I wish you weren't going away to-morrow."

"I must. I promised my father to get back. And Helena wants me."

"Oh well, that settles it," said Archie. "Helena must have all she wants. That is part of Helena, isn't it?"

For a moment Jessie thought that he was speaking with the bitterest irony, but immediately afterwards she withdrew that, for it struck her that Archie was, in some inexplicable way, perfectly sincere: there was the unmistakable ring of truth in his voice; he meant what he said. And, as if to endorse that, he went on:

"We all do what Helena wants: you, I, the Bradshaw, all of us. She wants to be loved, isn't that it? and to want to be loved is a royal command; all proper people must obey. I have been a rebel you know, and,—oh Jessie, how awfully ashamed I am! I let myself hate Helena; I encouraged myself to hate her. But I've returned to my allegiance, thank God."

She turned an enquiring face to him.

"Archie, dear," she said, "I am so thankful that you are so changed. You're utterly different from what you have been. Last night you were bitter and terrible: you made my heart ache. But all to-day you've been absolutely your old self again. And it's so immense and so sudden. Can't you tell me at all what caused it? I should love to know, if you feel like telling me."

He took her arm again.

"I'll tell you one thing," he said. "You did me a lot of good last night when you made me realize your friendship. That helped; I do believe that helped."

Jessie could not quite accept this, though it warmed her heart that Archie thought of that.

"But you always knew my friendship," she said.

"I know I did. But I appreciated it most when I felt absolutely empty. There's something more than that, though..."

He paused.

"Ah, do tell me," said Jessie.

He could not make up his mind on the instant, for he knew Jessie's repugnance to the whole idea of those supernatural communications. But he felt warm and alert and expansive; besides, her friendship, which he truly valued, yearned for his confidence, which is the meat and drink of friendship. Sometimes it was necessary to deceive your friends; it had been necessary for him to deceive her about the disposal of the whisky-bottle; but, though she might not approve, he could at least tell her what had made sunshine all day for him, and what was making it now.

"It's this," he said. "Martin came to me last night. I talked to him; I saw him. It has put me right: he has made me see things quite differently. He told me to be patient, to cling to love always, to let my hate be turned into love. I can't express to you at all what a difference that made to me. I felt he knew; he could see, as he said, that the darkness in which I thought I walked was not darkness at all. I know you have no sympathy with his coming to me: it seems to you either nonsense or something very dangerous. But I know you have sympathy with the result of it."

Suddenly his explanation of the voices she had heard last night occurred to him.

"When you told me this morning that you had heard talking in my room," he said, "I did not mean to tell you about Martin, and so I invented something—oh yes, that I had been reading aloud what I had written, to account for it. It wasn't true, but I had to tell some fib. And did you really hear conversation going on? That's awfully interesting."

"I thought I did," said she. "And there was knocking or hammering. Did you invent something about that too?"

"Oh yes," said Archie. "But I don't really know what the knocking was. As I was going off into trance, I heard loud knocking of some sort, but I didn't let it disturb the oncoming of the trance. It deepened, and then Martin came, and I talked with him and saw him."

"Oh Archie, how do you know it was he?" she cried, wildly enough, hardly knowing what she meant, but speaking from the dictate of some nightmare that screamed and struggled in her mind.

"Why, of course it was he," said Archie. "I recognized him, superficially, that is to say, from my knowledge of my own face, just as I recognized the photograph in the cache at Grives from its likeness to me. But I know it was he in some far more essential and inward manner. It *was* Martin."

"Will he come again?" asked the girl.

"I hope so, many times. Indeed, he promised to. I needed him, he got permission to come to me in my need. Is he not ministering to it? Haven't you seen the immense change in me?"

Undeniably she had seen that, and for a moment a little pang of human disappointment came over her.

"I'm afraid, then, the knowledge of my friendship hasn't had much to do with it," she said.

"Jessie, don't think I undervalue that," said Archie, speaking quite frankly and sincerely. "I thank you for it tremendously; I love to know it is there. I may count on it always, mayn't I?"

They still stood a moment under the star-swarming sky, sundered by the night from all other presences.

"I needn't assure you of that," she said. "And, Archie, I may be utterly wrong in what I feel about Martin's communications to you. Who knows what conditions exist for the souls of those we have loved, and whom we neither of us believe have died with the decay of the perishable body? But, my dear, do be careful. If in some miraculous way you have been given access which is denied to almost all mankind, do use it only in truth and love and reverence."

"You're frightened about it," said Archie.

"I know I am. If Martin can come to you, why should not other spirits? Other spirits, intelligences terrible and devilish, might deceive you into thinking that they were he. You remember at Silorno he said he couldn't come again."

"I know; but I wasn't in sore need then," said he.

They had again come opposite Lord Tintagel's study, and, even as they passed, Archie saw him with his finger on the bell. Instantly he guessed that he was ringing to know why the whisky had not been brought. The footman would come and say that he had brought it…

Archie felt an exhilarated acuteness of brain: the situation had only to be put before him for him to see the answer to it. In his presence, remembering the contract of the morning, his father could not ask for the whisky.

"Come in and say good-night to my father, Jess," he said.

They entered together and immediately afterwards the footman came in from the hall-door. Lord Tintagel looked at him, then back at Archie, who was watching.

"It's nothing, James," he said. "I rang for something, but it doesn't matter."

The man left the room and immediately afterwards Jessie said good-night and went also. Archie turned to his father with a broad, kindly smile.

"Father, I believe I'm a great thought-reader," he said. "I believe I can tell you what you rang for."

His father's grim face relaxed.

"You young devil," he said.

Archie laughed.

"I've guessed right, then," he said. "You surely don't want to drink success to our contract again."

"But I don't know why James didn't bring the whisky as usual," said he. "I—I forgot to tell him not to."

"But I didn't," said Archie.

"I see. Well, a bargain's a bargain. Only now there doesn't seem to be any particular reason for not going to bed."

Archie yawned rather elaborately, and went to the table where, earlier in the evening, he had put down his glass half filled with soda. He drank it, sniffing to see if there was any taint of spirit about it. But he had rinsed it thoroughly.

"I came in during my stroll with Jessie and took some soda," he said. "Not a bad drink, but I think it makes one sleepy. I shall go to bed, too."

* * * * *

Jessie left early next morning, expecting to be gone before anybody else made an appearance. But, just as she got into the motor, Archie, rosy and suffused with sleep, like a child that has lain still and grown all night, came flying downstairs in dressing-gown and pyjamas.

"Had to come down and say good-bye, Jessie," he said. "Do come back; come down for next Sunday, and we'll go up together for Helena's wedding. Promise!"

Jessie looked at that "morning face" which glowed with the exuberance of boyish health and happiness. She herself had slept very badly, dozing for a little and then being awakened by the sound of talking next door, and of peremptory resounding tappings. And here was Archie, radiant and fresh and revitalized, and her love glowed at the thought that he wanted her, even though it was but friendship that he sought and friendship that he had to offer.

"Yes, Archie, I should love to come," she said.

"That's ripping. I say, shall I drive with you to the station just as I am? Why shouldn't I? Pyjamas and dressing-gown are perfectly decent if William will fetch me my slippers, which I seem to have forgotten, unless he lends me his boots."

CHAPTER X

"Your bath's ready, my lord," said William with a broad grin.
"Well, perhaps I'll have it then. Good-bye, Jess. Come early on Saturday."

CHAPTER XI

Archie was lying on the turf in front of the enclosed bathing-place where the stream debouched into the lake. There was a good stretch of deep water free from weeds, and for the last half-hour he had been swimming and diving in it. Now, with hair drying back into its crisp curls under the hot sun, he lay on the short warm turf, with his chin supported on his hands, in an ecstasy of animal content. At this edge of the water the bank was made firm and solid with wooden boarding that went down into deep water, but across the estuary of the stream, broadening out into the lake, the shallow margin was fringed with bulrushes and loosestrife. A strip of low-lying meadow land behind was pink with campion and ragged-robin and starred with meadow-sweet, the scent of which mingled with the undefinable cool smell of running water. A bed of gravel made the bottom of the stream, and through the sunlit water the pebbles gleamed like topazes through some liquid veil.

Never before had Archie been so permeated with the sense of the amazing loveliness of the world, and of the ineffable joy of living and of being part of it. He had wrestled with the swiftness of the stream as it narrowed, had clung to rocks and tree-roots below the surface, letting the current comb over and around and almost through him, then, letting go of his anchorage, had been floated down into the lake again with arms and legs outspread, and now, lying close-pressed to the turf with wet chest and dripping shoulders, he seemed to be part of the triumph of the summer, and of the immortal youth of the world. Surely there was no further heaven than this possible, namely, to be young and to desire and to have desire gratified, and whet the appetite for more. There was no clearer duty in the day than to be bathed in the bliss of life, to suck out the last drop of sweetness from the world which had been created for the joy of men and the glory of God. There was no such thing as evil; evil was but the label attached by the sour-minded to the impulses and acts for which they had not sufficient vitality… And it was Martin who had taught him all this.

Archie had come back home this morning after a day and a couple of nights in town. He had bought Helena her wedding present, he had taken his completed manuscript to his publishers, he had dined and danced and supped, and filled the hours of day and night with the extravagant excesses in which up till now he had never indulged. Some innate fastidiousness or morality had led him to look on the looser pleasures of youth with disdain or disgust; now he smiled indulgently at himself for his narrow priggishness. How utterly wrong he had been to think that such things stained or soiled a boy; they had but caused him to realize himself and intensified existence for him. They were the exercise of the faculties and possibilities with which God had endowed him, and which were not meant to rust in disuse. It was right for him "richly to enjoy," as Martin had said: it was a crime against love and life to starve on a meatless diet… Above all, he had seen Helena again, had confessed and recanted the bitterness he had felt towards her, and she had forgiven him, and welcomed him back "with blessings on the falling out, that all the more endears," as the prim little poem said.

Archie laughed quietly to himself and said aloud:

"When we fall out with those we love, And kiss again with tears."

"But there weren't many tears," he added.

He understood Helena now. She wanted, so sensibly, to make herself quite comfortable for this journey through life. If Marquises with millions desired her to go shares with them, naturally she consented. But to do that was not the least the same as taking vows and going into a nunnery. It was the nunnery that she was coming out of. Of course, just for the present Archie understood he would not see her, for she and the Bradshaw were going a yachting tour in the Norwegian fjords. But they would be back again before the end of September. So much and no more had her voice told him, but her eyes said much more intimate things, though naturally she did not express them, and when he asked if he might kiss her (that cousinly kiss which she had wanted at Silorno) her lips agreed with what her eyes said. She had never been so adorably pretty, and she had never been so demurely clever. She had said nothing which a girl who was to become another man's wife in a few days should not say, and yet Archie felt that he understood perfectly all the things she did not say. Most brilliant perhaps of all was her warning, "I shall tell the Bradshaw that I allowed you to kiss me," she cried. "But I'm not frightened: he is such a dear."

Gone, then, were all Archie's troubles and bitternesses on this point. He had love to cling to, and he scarcely felt jealous of the Bradshaw. For, if things had been the other way about, and Helena had been engaged to him, would she have allowed the Bradshaw to kiss her? He knew very well that she would not.

Archie turned over on to his back, and lay with arms and legs spread out to the sun, warming himself as with the memory of that expedition to London. But he had not in the least wished to postpone his return, since the joy of life lay so largely in its contrasts, and after thirty-six hours of that fiery furnace there had come a temporary satiety, and he wanted to lie and sleep like a gorged tiger. Soon he would awake and be hungry again, but it was part of the joy of life to be satisfied and doze, and stretch out tranquil limbs. And, lying there, his ribs began to twitch again into laughter as he thought of the contract he had made with his father last Sunday. Archie had entered into it, with the view of encouraging and helping his father to rid himself of the chain that was riveted so closely round him, and he was delighted to do it, if his father derived support for his abstinence in the thought that he was helping Archie. But Archie need not abstain, so long as his father thought he was doing so, and only just now he had filled with water and sunk in the weeds several empty bottles that he had brought out in his towels from his bedroom. He knew perfectly well that he was in no danger of becoming a slave to the habit, it had served him as medicine to mitigate his misery with regard to Helena, and, now that that was quite removed, it helped him to get into communication with Martin. Of that he felt convinced. Once or twice he had tried to do so without drinking, and had failed; but alcohol seemed to drug the surface-consciousness and clear the way of access, and it was for that he used it now. It was more that it cleared the access than that it drugged him, for he found that it produced not the least effect in the way of making his head hazy or his movements wavering: it only seemed to sweep clean those mysterious channels through which communication came. The power of communicating he could not possibly give up: all happiness and joy of life sprang from it; therefore he could not possibly give up that which facilitated it. But he performed the purpose of the contract by keeping his indulgences secret from his father, and once again Archie's ribs, with their smoothly swelling muscles under his brown skin, throbbed with amusement as he pictured his father's heroic struggle with himself. Occasionally Archie had doubts whether that struggle was quite consistently successful, for once or twice Lord Tintagel had shown signs of evening content and serenity, followed by morning shakiness, which indicated that he had made some temporary armistice. Archie thought that perhaps he would lay some trap for his father, or make some quiet detective investigations to satisfy himself on this point. But beyond doubt his father was putting up quite a good fight on behalf of a non-existent cause. His will was to abstain, and, if occasionally he failed, it was unchristian to judge failure hardly. Besides, Archie only conjectured that sometimes his father's resolution was unequal to the strain imposed on it; he did not know.

* * * * *

All this week Archie's sense of comradeship and brotherliness with Martin had marvellously increased. There was nothing priggish or puritanical about Martin, nor anything namby-pamby that suggested wings and halos and hymns. He was intensely human, and sympathized completely with the fact of Archie's being a glorious young animal, bursting with exuberant health. That seemed quite clear, for when this morning, sometime about four o'clock, Archie had gently let himself into the house in Grosvenor Square a little ashamed and weary, and went up to his bedroom, he became instantly aware that Martin was waiting for him. There was no need for him to light his electric lamps, for dawn was already breaking, and, drawing his curtains apart, he threw off his clothes, so as to let the delicious chill of morning refresh his skin, and sat down for a moment in front of his dressing-table and looked fixedly at a bright point of light on the bevel of his looking-glass. Almost immediately the waves of light and shadow began to pass before his eyes, and the room was full of vivid, peremptory tappings. Then he was aware that there appeared in the reflected image of himself a strange luminous focus over his left breast and a little wisp of mist, like a puff of escaping steam, began to come from it. This grew and collected in wavering masses of weaving lines, formless at first, but then arranging themselves into definite shapes, and he saw, with a thrill of excitement and wonder, that out of them there was being built up the image of Martin, which had issued out of himself. Soon it was complete, and Archie in the glass beheld Martin's face leaning lovingly over his shoulder, and Martin's arm bare like his own, and, warm and solid to the touch, was thrown round his neck.

"Archie, I've been with you all night," he said. "I love to see you and feel you realize yourself. Throw yourself into life: live to the uttermost, and have no thought for the morrow. There is nothing in the world but love and joy. Cling to them, press close to them, lose yourself in them..."

Martin's smile was compassionate no longer: it was a sunbeam of radiant happiness, and that happiness, so it seemed to Archie, had its source in sympathy with and love for him.

"Don't ever think you are yielding to base impulses," he went on, "provided only you are happy. Happiness is the seal and witness of what is right for you: it is the mark of God's approval. Evil is always painful and repugnant; that is the seal and witness of it. The fruit of the spirit is love, joy, peace; and aren't you more at peace, more full of joy now that you have resolved to put hate out of your heart? Isn't it sweeter to kiss Helena than to curse her?"

* * * * *

Suddenly, like the stroke of a black wing, there passed through Archie an impulse of sheer abhorrence. All that Martin said sounded divinely comforting and uplifting, but did there not lurk in it the whole gospel of Satanism? And, as that thought crossed his mind, he saw an expression of the tenderest reproach dim for a moment the brightness of his brother's eyes, and the mouth drooped.

"But you are tired now," said he, "and your trust in me is a little weakened. Sleep well: it is dawn already."

The apparition faded, or rather it appeared to be withdrawn again into himself, and, emerging from the light trance, Archie was conscious only of an overpowering but delicious fatigue, the fatigue of utter satisfaction. He had had a glorious thirty-six hours, and, as Martin said, he was tired. And Martin approved.

He slept the deep, recuperative sleep of youth for four or five hours, and awoke hungry and eager, and clear-eyed. He left town immediately after breakfast, motored himself down home with William holding on to the side of the car as he slowed round corners and came straight out to his beloved bathing-place. It was bliss to be alive.

* * * * *

He had not seen Jessie during his short raid on London, for really there had not been a moment to spare; besides, Jessie was coming down next day for the week-end. But she knew he had been in town, for Helena said she had seen him, and, with her usual acuteness, had told her sister that Archie was deliciously his old self again, and that they were the greatest friends. That, to Jessie's very sensible judgment and to the intuition her love gave her, was the most inexplicable of developments. Only a week ago there was no reproach bitter enough for Archie's opinion on Helena's conduct to him, no angry taunt of misery sufficient for her vilification. And then, in a moment, the whole of that bitterness had been dried up, the Marah had been sweetened. More than that, the normal joy of life had returned in full flood to him, and the cause of all this was, in his account, the fact that the spirit of Martin had shown him the true light. That Archie possessed that mysterious, and, in her view, dangerous gift of mediumistic perception she did not doubt, for there was no questioning those weird manifestations of occult power which she knew had occurred in his childhood, and she felt now that she ought only to stand in an awed wonder and thankfulness that this supernormal perception of his had, in a moment, worked in him what could be called no less than a miracle. But, though she ought to feel that, she knew that she felt nothing of the kind, and, as she travelled down next day to Lacebury, she set herself to analyse the causes of her mistrust.

They were simple enough. First of all, there was her rooted antipathy to the whole notion of spirit-communication. Instinctively it shocked her and seemed opposed to all religious faith. Beyond that, there were but a couple of the most insignificant matters that appeared to her possibly connected with her mistrust, the one that Archie had made a false, swift invention to account for the noises she had heard coming from his room, the other that he had proposed to get William to spy on his father with a view to ascertaining whether he was keeping his part of their bargain. She knew they were both tiny incidents, but the spirit that prompted them was in both cases utterly unlike Archie. She could not imagine Archie making such an invention or such a suggestion, from what she knew of him, it was outside him to do so. And if it was the influence—to call it no more than that—of Martin which prompted these things, if it was the same direction as that which had taken away all his bitterness towards Helena, what sort of influence was that? Finally, could it be right that the boy whom Helena had so cruelly led on only to disappoint should, on the eve of her marriage, suddenly become close friends with her again? There certainly he obeyed the precept of that which had spoken with him, and had promised to communicate again, and she could not but think it a dangerous, if not a diabolical counsel. But she tried to reserve her judgment; in a few minutes now she would see Archie again, and could note what change for good or ill this week had brought. Very likely she had been disquieting herself in vain, making wounds out of pin-pricks and mountains out of mole-hills.

Archie had come to meet her, and, as the train slowed down into the station, she saw him out of the carriage window. But he did not see her, for his eyes were intent on a very horrible sight. There were two tipsy women violently quarrelling, and, just as the train got in, they flew at each other, scratching and striking. The encounter lasted not more than a few seconds, for a couple of porters ran in and separated them, but Jessie had seen Archie's face alight with glee and amusement. As they were separated he frowned and shrugged his shoulders, and seemed to remonstrate with the man who had stopped their fighting. At that instant he saw her get out of her compartment, and ran to meet her, his face quite changed. But the moment before it had not been Archie's face at all: it had been the face of some beautiful and devilish creature, alert with evil excitement.

"Hullo, Jessie, there you are," he said. "It's ripping to see you. Look at those two viragos there; they flew at each other like wild beasts. It was a horrible sight."

He turned a sideways eye on her, cunning and watchful, which utterly belied the frankness of his speech, and her heart sank, and a vague, nameless terror seized her, as once again she found herself thinking that this was not Archie, who so gaily took her bag for her, and ever and again looked back to where a small crowd had collected round the two women. They had a few minutes to wait, while her luggage was brought out, and once more he sauntered back into the station, leaving her in the car. From outside she could hear hoarse screams, and, long after her trunk had been put into the car, she watched the door for Archie's exit. First one and then the other of the women were brought out to be taken to the police-station, and at last he emerged.

"Sorry to keep you waiting, Jessie," he said. "But my mother wanted some magazine from the bookstall. Now, if you aren't nervous, we'll make up for lost time."

The road lay straight and empty before them, opening out like torn linen as they raced along it. Some way ahead there were a couple of cottages by the road-side, and, as they came near them, there wandered out into the road an old and lame collie. Instantly Archie's face changed into a mask of impatient malignancy.

"Archie, take care," said Jessie, "there's a dog on the road."

"Well, that's the dog's look-out," said he. "What right has a mangy brute like that to stop us?"

He made no attempt whatever to slow down, but just at the last moment he caused the car to swerve violently, and they missed the dog by a hair's-breadth. And he turned on her a face from which all impatience and anger had vanished, and from it looked out Archie's soul in agonized struggle.

"I couldn't, I couldn't!" he said. "I didn't touch it, Jessie: it's all right."

"I thought you must run over it," said she. "Why didn't you slow down, Archie?"

That glimpse of the agonized soul utterly vanished again.

"People have got no business to keep a decrepit old beast like that," he said. "I expect the kindest thing I could do would be to turn round and put it out of its misery. Never mind. I'll do it some other day."

Jessie clung to her glimpse of the other Archie.

"No, you won't," she said. "You'll risk your life and mine, too, not to hurt it."

He laughed.

"One can't tell what one will do," he said. "I hated and loathed that dog, but I couldn't run over it, when it came to. Hope I didn't give you an awful shaking, Jessie."

After lunch Archie proposed a campaign against a certain great pike which he had seen, and, while he went to his room to change his clothes, Jessie paid a visit to Blessington. The old lady was delighted to see her, and dusted a perfectly speckless chair for her.

"And it's jolly for you, isn't it, Blessington, having Archie here so long?" said Jessie.

Blessington made no answer for a moment.

"I make no complaints," she said, "and I daresay Master Archie is very busy."

"Why, what do you mean?" asked the girl.

Blessington's wrinkled old face began to work, and she looked piteously at Jessie.

"It's a week since Master Archie set foot in my room," she said. "Why does he never come to see me now, Miss Jessie? And when I meet him about the house, he's never got a word to give me. Me, who has looked after him and loved him since he was born."

At this moment Archie's step was heard outside, and he came in.

"Oh, Blessington, I wish you wouldn't go meddling with my things," he said roughly. "William tells me you took some flannels of mine away to mend or put a button on. Where are they?"

Blessington got up without a word and went to her cupboard.

"Here they are, my lord," she said. "I have mended them."

"Well, please don't carry my clothes away again. Come on, Jessie. I'll be ready in a moment."

Blessington's hands came together with a trembling movement as Archie twitched the flannel coat away from her. But he did not even look at her, and went out of her room, banging the door.

Blessington sat down again, and began to cry quietly. "There now, you see, Miss Jessie," she said. "And that's my own Master Archie."

For a minute or so Jessie sat with her, trying vainly to comfort her, and shocked beyond expression at Archie's brutal callousness to his old nurse. And then the door opened again, and Archie looked in. Once again all his anger and impatience had died out of his face, his real soul looked from his eyes as from a prison-house, and his voice shook as he spoke.

"Go away, please, Jessie, and leave me with Blessington for a minute," he said.

And then he came across the room to her, and knelt down by her, and took her withered old hand in his, and stroked it and kissed it. So much Jessie saw before she closed the door behind her.

"Blessington, my old darling," said Archie, "I can't think why I have been so beastly to you. It wasn't me, that's all I can tell you. I always love you. Can you forgive me?"

Blessington's loyal devotion rose triumphant.

"Eh, I know how busy you've been, Master Archie," she said, "and I know what a thoughtless body I am with your things. But I'd like you to be angry with me fifty times, if you'll only come back to me at the end. There pray-a-don't kiss my hand, dear. It isn't right for you to do that."

CHAPTER XI

"Where's your darling face then?" said Archie. "If you don't give me a kiss this minute, I shall know you've been flirting with father's keeper again."

Blessington gave a little squeal of laughter.

"Eh, and him dead this twenty years," she said. "And you know, my dear, that whatever you did, and asked me to give you a kiss afterwards, give it you I would, because nothing you could do would stop my loving you."

Blessington's love, Helena's love... which was real? Two things so utterly different could not both be love. And for him, too, which love was real, his love for Blessington, all ashed over save for the little spark that somehow lived below the cold cinders, or his love for Helena that blazed and scintillated? Suddenly the thought of that glowed within him, and it seemed dreadful to kiss this withered cheek. And yet the dim old eyes had never wavered in their loyalty and love for his worthless, corrupted self.

"And shall we have a talk this evening again before dinner?" he asked.

"Eh, that would be nice if you're not too busy," said she.

"All right, then. But I must run along now: Jessie's waiting."

"That'll never do to keep her waiting," said Blessington. "And if you're going on the lake, Master Archie, pray be careful and don't fall in."

* * * * *

Lady Tintagel with Jessie and Archie were going up to town on Monday to attend Helena's wedding the day after, and all through the hours of that week-end there was piling up ever higher and more menacingly the storm that so soon was to burst upon Europe in tempest of shot and shell. Before they left on Monday afternoon war was already declared between Russia and Germany, between Germany and France, the territory of Belgium was violated by the barbarian hordes who issued from the Central Empires, and Belgium had appealed to England to uphold the treaty which Germany had torn up to light the fires or war. But, as in so many English homes in these days, the inevitable still seemed the incredible, and, though from time to time they discussed the situation, life went on its normal course. Indeed, there was nothing else to be done: whether England was going to war or not, dinner-time came round as usual...

Of them all, it was on Lord Tintagel that the suspense and anxiety beat most strongly, and that because the panic on the Stock Exchanges of Europe threatened him with losses that might bring him within reach of ruin. But Lady Tintagel still clung to a baseless hope, less substantial than a mirage in the desert, that diplomacy would still avert disaster, Archie went about the customary diversions of life with more than usual enjoyment and absorption, while for Jessie there loomed in the immediate foreground a dread and a horror, which, though it concerned not warring millions, but just one individual, engrossed her entire soul.

It was as if she saw him whom she loved with all the strength of her deep and loyal heart in danger of drowning, not in material waters that could but kill the body and set free the soul, but in some awful flooding evil which threatened to submerge and swallow the very source and spiritual life of him. And, all the time, he swam and splashed about in those waters, below which lay hell itself, with the same joyful gaiety as he used to churn his way out to sea at Silorno. As by some hideous irony, the love of deep waters far from shore that all his life had possessed him, so that his physical self was at the zenith of its capacity for enjoyment when the profound gulfs were below him, and the land far off, so now evil, essential and primeval evil, had beckoned his soul out over unplumbed depths that seemed to him bright with celestial sunshine. Not yet was he doomed to sink there, though she guessed, as in a nightmare, in what deadly peril he stood, for now and again some inkling of that which menaced him reached his true self, and he turned back with shuddering and contrition from some evil prompting. All the time this betrayed itself to Jessie in things that might so reasonably have been called mere trifles. An impatient, impetuous boy, as Archie undoubtedly was, might so naturally have lost his temper with a decrepit old dog which strayed on to the path of his flying car, and made him say that it would be the kindest thing to run over it. That same boy might so naturally have felt an unedifying curiosity in two drunken women fighting together, or have reasonably been annoyed when, in a hurry to change his clothes, he found that his old nurse had taken them away. Indeed, it was the strength of his own reaction against such impulses that showed how alien he knew them to be to his real self. But her own feeling about them was the final test, for she knew it was based on the infallible intuition of her love for him. It was impossible that that should be mistaken, and it told her that it was not Archie at all who had committed these acts, which might be trifling in themselves, but, like wisps of cloud in the sky, showed which way the great winds were blowing. And on the top of these was something which Jessie could not conceive of as being a trifle, namely, Archie's complete reconciliation with her sister. She could not believe that it was a noble impulse which prompted that, and extinguished his bitter resentment against her as easily as a candle is blown out. He was right to be bitter against her, and the love, with which he seemed inspired again, was not love at all. But he believed that this desire was love, and according to his account it was the spirit of Martin which had taught him that and opened his blinded eyes. It was Martin, then, who possessed him. And that, to Jessie, was the most incredible of all. It was not, and it could not be, Martin.

She sat by her open window that Sunday night, wishing that she could think that some madness had fallen upon her, which caused her to conceive such inconceivable things. Archie's laugh still sounded in her ears, gay and boyish, as she had heard it but two minutes before she came up to bed. And she shuddered at the cause of it. Once again, she and Archie had strolled out after dinner, and, on passing the windows of his father's study, their steps noiseless on the grass, Archie had laid his hand on her arm with a gesture to command silence, and had tiptoed with her across the gravel to his father's windows. Lord Tintagel was inside, and, even as they looked, he took a bottle out of which he had been pouring something, and locked it up in a cupboard.

Archie turned a face beaming with merriment on her.

"Come in," he whispered, "to say good-night. Leave it all to me. It will be huge fun."

CHAPTER XI

He waited a moment, and began talking loudly to her on some indifferent subject for a few seconds. The he said:

"Come and say good-night to my father, Jessie," and they entered together.

Lord Tintagel was seated in his chair by this time: there was just one empty glass on the tray, with a syphon, and no sign of a second one. Archie began walking up and down the room, his eyes looking swiftly and stealthily in every direction.

"Jessie and I have just come in to say good-night," he said. "We're all going up to town to-morrow. Won't you really come, father?"

"I've already said I won't," said Lord Tintagel sharply.

Archie suddenly saw what he had been looking for.

"Hullo, here's a funny thing," he said. "Here's a glass on the floor."

He picked it up, smelled it, and burst into a peal of laughter.

"Father, it's too bad of you!" he said. "There have I been keeping our bargain, while you—"

He broke off, laughing again.

"No, I'll confess," he said, "because I'm so pleased at having found you out. I've been having some quiet drinks up in my bedroom while you've been doing the same down here. What did you do with your bottles? I put mine in the lake. I say, that is funny, isn't it? But it's rather unsociable. Let's follow Germany's example, and call our treaty waste paper."

And Archie had laughed over that miserable sordid exposure, just as light-heartedly as he had laughed over the jolly innocent humours at Silorno, and, sick at heart, Jessie had left the two together with the bottle which there was no need to conceal any more.

She sat long at her window in a miserable state of horror and fear and agitation, now trying to persuade herself that she was taking these things too heavily—Helena had always told her she took things heavily—now letting her fears issue in terrible cohort and looking them in the face. It was her powerlessness to help that most tortured her, her fate of having to stand and watch while Archie pushed out ever farther, with delight and joy, on to the perilous seas. But now there was to her a reality about it all which she had never wholly felt before. Often she had told herself that she was imagining perils, but to-night, in the darkness and the quiet, she felt herself face to face with the grim, deadly facts. Spiritual and ghostly enemies were about, and next moment she had slid on to her knees. No words came: she tried just to open her heart to that light that surely shone through the evil that swarmed about her. Something, ever so faint, glimmered there, and presently she rose again with her soul fixed on that little spark shining within her. In any case, she must make every effort to help, instead of succumbing to her sense of powerlessness.

At that moment she heard light, swift footsteps on the stairs, and instantly her mind was made up, and she came out into the broad passage just as Archie was opposite her door. His face was eager and alert; there was no trace of intoxication there.

"Hullo, Jessie," he said, smiling. "Not gone to bed yet?"

She had to be wise: mere helpless prayer would avail nothing if she did not exert herself and make use of her wits and her love.

"No: I didn't feel sleepy," she said. "You don't look sleepy either. Are you going to bed?"

"No, not yet," said Archie.

Jessie came a step closer to him.

"Oh, Archie, are you going to talk to Martin?" she asked. "Mayn't I come? I should so love to, for I know all that Martin means to you. You know I did hear him talking to you before. It would be lovely if I could hear you talking together, so that I knew what he said."

Archie looked at her.

"Well, I don't know why not," he said. "But you must promise not to interrupt. Perhaps you'll neither hear nor see anything. But I don't see why you shouldn't try. It's just a seance. Come along, Jessie."

He led the way into his bedroom, and shut the door.

"I shall really rather like you to be here," he said. "I'm glad you suggested it. For now and then I go into very deep trance, and then I can't remember what exactly has happened. I only know that there has been round me an atmosphere—to call it that—in which I glow and expand. Sometimes I rather think I struggle and groan: you mustn't mind that. It's only the protest of my material earthly self. Come on: let's begin. I long for Martin to come."

Jessie felt her dread and horror of the occult surge up in her, and it required all her resolution to remain here. But the call of her love was imperative: if she was to be permitted to help Archie at all, she must learn what it was that possessed him, and find means to combat it. She had to know first what it was, penetrate, so far as her love had power, into the source of it, diagnose it, if she was to help in curing.

"What are you going to do?" she said.

"It's very simple; you'll soon see. Sit down, Jessie."

He went to the window and drew aside the curtains. He put on the table in front of where he was to sit the silver top of some toilet-bottle, and then went to the door and turned out all the electric lights at the switch-board. The moonlight outside, without shining directly into the room, made the objects in it clearly though duskily visible, and Jessie, where she sat with her back to the light, could see Archie's face and outline, when her eyes got accustomed to the dimness, quite distinctly. He sat close to her at the end of the writing-table, and just in front of him glimmered the stopper from the toilet-bottle.

"Now I'm going to look at that till I go off into trance," he said. "Watch what happens very closely, for I may go into deep trance, and promise me not to move till I come round again. I daresay you will neither hear nor see anything, but I don't know."

For some few minutes, as far as the girl could judge, they sat in silence. Once or twice Archie shifted his position slightly, and she heard his shirt-front creak a little as he breathed quietly and normally. Outside a little wind stirred, and the tassel of the blind tapped against the sill.

Then there came a change: his breathing grew louder, as if he panted for air, and now and again he moaned, and she saw his head drop forward. This moaning sound was horrible to hear, and, but for her promise, and the insistent urging of her love, she must have got up and roused him. His breath whistled between his lips as he took it in, and his face seemed to be shining with some dew of anguish, and his arms twisted and writhed as if struggling against some overmastering force. Then suddenly all sign of struggle ceased, he sat bent forward, but perfectly still, and from the table in front of him came three loud, peremptory raps, as of splitting wood. From the dusk of the room came others which she could not localize.

Archie raised his head, and, instead of leaning over the table, sank back in his chair, his arms hanging limp by his side. He began to whisper to himself, and soon Jessie caught the words.

"Martin, are you here?" he kept repeating. "Martin, are you here? Martin, Martin?"

There was more light in the room now. It came from a pale greyish efflorescence of illumination, globular in shape, that lay apparently over his left breast. It made its immediate neighbourhood quite bright: she could see the stud in his shirt with absolute distinctness. Out of it there came a little wisp of mist that floated up like a stream of smoke above his shoulders. In the air there, independently of this, there was forming another mist-like substance, and the stream that came away from Archie seemed to join this. It began to take shape: it spread upwards and downwards into the semblance of a column, its edges losing themselves in the dark. Lines began to be interwoven within it: it was as if something was forming inside it, like a chicken in an egg. It lost its vagueness of outline, plaiting and weaving itself together: there appeared an arm bare to the shoulder; above that she could see a neck, and slowly above the neck there grew a smiling, splendid face. There seemed to be a grey robe cast about the body, from which the bare arm protruded, but much of this was vague.

Jessie felt as if some awful paralysis of terror lay over her spirit. The whole room, cool and fresh with the night-air passing through the open window, reeked, to her spiritual sense, with evil and unnameable corruption. Over her conscious superficial self, the mechanism that directed her limbs and worked in her brain, she had complete control: for Archie's sake she was learning about this hellish visitor who came to him. But within, her soul cried out in a horror of uttermost darkness. Then her will took hold of that too: whatever God permitted must be faced for the sake of love.

Just then Archie spoke in an odd muffled voice.

"I'm going very deep," he said. "But, Martin, you've made me so happy all day. You've hardly left me at all. You're getting to be part of me, aren't you? Let's talk about Helena. I say, she is a devil, isn't she?"

Jessie had not known that anything could be so horrible as the smiling face that the apparition bent on him.

"But you've ceased hating her," it said. "You love her, don't you? Always cling to love!"

"I know, I adore her. I believe she loves me too." He laughed and licked his lips and his voice sank, so that Jessie could catch no word of what he said. But he spoke for a long time, laughing occasionally, and making horrible little movements with his arms as if he clasped something. Now and then he would perhaps ask a question, for in the same inaudible manner the apparition answered him, laughing sometimes in response. Once or twice in that devilish colloquy she caught a word or two of hideous and carnal import, and her sickened love nearly withered within her. But because love is immortal, and cannot perish though all the blasts of hell rage against it, it still stood firm, though scorched and beaten upon. If she let it die, she felt that she would be no better than that visible incarnation of evil that smiled and bent over Archie.

Presently that devilish whispering ceased, and she saw that the apparition was beginning to lose its clearness of outline. Slowly it began to disintegrate into the weavings of mist out of which it came, and Archie said, "Good-bye, Martin, but not for long." Some of these streamers seemed to disperse in the air, others, like an eddying water-spout, seemed to draw back into that focus of light which lay over Archie's breast. Then that too began to fade, and in the stillness and quiet she again heard the creaking of his shirt as he lay back in his chair with closed eyes. Then the struggles and moanings, the writhings of his arms began again, and again subsided, and he lay quite still. Outside the night-wind stirred and dropped.

Then Archie spoke in a tired, husky voice.

"Hullo, Jessie," he said, "it's all over. By Jove, it was ripping. But I went awfully deep. I can remember nothing after Martin came. What did he say?"

Jessie got up.

"I heard hardly anything," she said. "He spoke in whispers, and so did you."

"Did you see him?" asked Archie.

"Yes, quite clearly. But I think I'll go to bed now. You look very tired."

He had got up and turned on the electric light, and stood by the door rubbing his eyes.

"Yes, I am tired," he said, "but I'm divinely happy. Tell me to-morrow whatever you can remember. Good-night, Jess. You are a good sort."

He detained her hand for a moment.

"We're cousins, Jess," he said, "and you're an awfully good friend. Won't you give me a kiss?"

For one second she shrank from him in nameless horror. The next she put it all from her, for her shrinking, no angel of the Lord, but a weak, cowardly impulse, stood full in the path of love, and while it was there she could not reach Archie.

"Why, of course," she said, kissing him. "Good-night, Archie; sleep well."

She went to her room, and turned on all the lights. She felt as if she had been assisting at some unclean orgy, she felt tainted and defiled by the very presence of that white evil thing that had stood close to her, and whispered and laughed with Archie. As yet she had but looked on it; what lay in front of her was to grapple with it and tear it out of the tabernacle which it had begun to inhabit. As far as she could understand the situation, it was not wholly in possession as yet, for part of it, when it materialized, seemed to form itself in the air, and part only to ooze out of its victim. Through what adventures and combats her way should take her she could form no conception, but what she had gained to-night, which was worth a hundred times the sickness and horror of her soul, was the certain knowledge that some spirit of discarnate evil was making its home in her beloved. It had usurped the guise of Martin, it masqueraded as Martin, Archie thought it was Martin. She remembered how, just a week ago, he had told her that he was like an empty house, denuded of the spirit that dwelt there, a living corpse by which he asked her to sit sometimes. At the time that had seemed to her just the figure by which he expressed the desolation of his heart; now it revealed itself as a true and literal statement. And there had begun to enter into him, as tenant of the uninhabited rooms, the horror that she had seen.

Jessie fell on her knees by her bedside, and opened her heart to the Infinite Love. It was through Its aid alone that she would be able to accomplish the rescue for which she was willing to give her life and soul.

CHAPTER XII

Archie was walking back to the house in Grosvenor Square from Oakland Crescent, on the afternoon of Helena's wedding. Owing to the acute suspense of the European situation, the plans of the newly married couple had been changed, and, instead of setting off at once in the yacht for a month in the Norwegian fjords, they had gone to a house of Lord Harlow's in Surrey to await developments in the crisis or some kind of settlement. It was still uncertain whether England would be drawn into the war, though opinion generally regarded that as inevitable, and in this case no doubt Lord Harlow, an ex-Guardsman, would rejoin his regiment. Archie's mother, after the departure of the bridal couple, had also left town for Lacebury, taking with her Jessie and Colonel Vautier for a few days' visit; but Archie had decided to stop another night in London.

There had been the usual crowds and chatterings and excitement, the front pew kept for a princess, the signing of names in the vestry, the red carpets and wedding-marches, and the whole ceremony had filled Archie with the greatest amusement. But the subsequent proceedings had not amused him so much, and Helena's departure, looking prettier than ever, with her husband, had annoyed and exasperated him. He did not like to think of them together, and, though only a couple of nights ago he and Martin had found good cause for whispers and laughter over this, it was not so diverting when it actually occurred as it had promised to be. Part of that midnight seance which he could not at first remember had found its way into his conscious mind, and he knew that had been talked about, and had ascertained, with considerable relief, that Jessie had not been able to hear it. But now there was a savage bitterness in his mind about it; Helena seemed to have played him false again. She ought to have refused to marry the Bradshaw at the last moment, and it was an ineffectual balm to know she did not care for him. Perhaps, as Jessie had once said (though withdrawing it afterwards), she cared for nobody, but now Archie believed that she cared for him. It maddened him to think that she was the Bradshaw's "ABC," and in those circumstances he had judged it better to remain in town for the night, and distract his mind and soothe his longings with the amusement and aids to forgetfulness which London was so ready to offer to a young man who was looking for adventures.

But London proved disappointing: it did not seem to be thinking of its amusements at all. Archie called to see a friend who last week had shown himself an eager and admirable companion, but, found him to-day disinclined for another night of similar diversion, for he could neither think nor talk about anything else than the imminence of war. Archie felt himself quite incapable of taking any active interest in that; it weighted nothing in the balance compared with the stern duty of seeking enjoyment and forgetting about Helena. What if England did go to war with Germany? Certainly he hoped she would not; she had made no more than a friendly understanding with her Allies—indeed they were not even Allies, they were but well-disposed nations—but, even if she did, what then? There was an English fleet, was there not, which cost an immense amount of money to render invincible; but it was invincible. Why, then, should he bother about it, since he was not a sailor? It was further supposed that Germany had an invincible army; and there you were! And if England had no army at all to speak of, it was quite clear she could no more fight Germany on land than Germany could fight her by sea. So what on earth prevented a little dinner at a restaurant and an hour at a music-hall and a little supper somewhere and anything that turned up? Something always turned up, and was usually amusing for an hour or two. But his friend thought otherwise, and kept diving out into the street to get some fresh edition of an evening paper hot from the press and crammed with fresh inventions, and Archie left this insane patriot in disgust at his excitement over so detached an affair as a European war. He tried a second friend with no better success; there was a certain excuse for him, as he was a subaltern in the Guards. But for the first friend there was none, as he was only in an office in the city.

There were still four or five hours to get through before it would be reasonable to think about dinner, after which, even if he started alone, the hours would take care of themselves very pleasantly; but he had to fill the interval somehow. There were some proofs of his book waiting for him at home, and, hoping to get interested in this first-born public child of his brain, he sat down with a view to correcting them. But he found himself reading the pages as if there was nothing intelligible printed on them. True, if he forced himself to attend, he could see that grammatical sentences succeeded each other; but they conveyed no further impression. There was a lot about the sea, but why on earth had he taken the trouble to write it? He could remember writing it; he could call up an image of himself sitting in the garden at Silorno, eagerly writing, conscientiously erasing, walking up and down in the attempt to frame a phrase that should exactly reproduce some mood of his mind. But what had inspired those strivings and despairs and exultations?

Here was the record of them, and it seemed now to be about nothing. "The rain in the night had washed the white soil into the rim of the sea, and it was clouded like absinthe." He could well remember the search for, and the finding of that particular simile. He and Harry had been into Genoa a week before, and, out of curiosity, had ordered absinthe at a cafe. The drink, *qua* drink, was mildly unpleasant, resembling aniseed, but it had been worth while having it, merely to have got that perfectly fitting simile. The effect, too, had been rather remarkable; it produced a sort of heady lightness and sense of well-being; colours seemed strangely vivid and intensified, and…

Archie got up from his meaningless proofs. It was absinthe that would help him to fill up those dull hours till dinner-time, and he remembered having seen in some little French restaurant in Soho the stuff he wanted. Very likely you could get it anywhere, but he wanted it from that particular place, for there had come in one evening, when he dined there, a most melancholy-looking person who had ordered it and sat and sipped. Somehow the man's face had made an impression on him, so unhappy was it. He remembered also his face half an hour afterwards, when he began his dinner, and no serener, more contented countenance could have been imagined... So he must have his absinthe from that restaurant; clearly they had a very good brand of it there.

As he drove out alone that evening to dine, he heard the newsvendors shouting out the English ultimatum to Germany, and saw the placards in the streets. The shouting sounded wonderfully musical, and below the roar of the street traffic was a muffled harmony as of pealing bells. The drab colours of London were shot with prismatic hues; never had the streets appeared so beautiful. There was even beauty in the fact of the outbreak of war, for England was going to war for the sake of liberty, which was a fine, a noble adventure. And how lovely the English girls and boys were, who crowded the pavements! They were like beds of exquisite flowers. For himself, he was going back to dine at the French restaurant in Soho, for that would be in the nature of supporting our new Allies. Afterwards there were the streets and the music-halls, and all the mysteries of the short summer night. Then dawn would break, rose-coloured dawn, with her finger on her lips, and sweet, silent mouth, a little ashamed of her sister, night, but sympathetic at heart. Dawn was always a little prudish, a little Quakerish.

* * * * *

The days of a divine August went by, and the line of German invasion swept forward like a tide that knows no ebb over all Belgium and North-East France. The British Expeditionary Force started, and was swept back like the flotsam on the seashore. The call came for the raising of an army, and east and west, north and south, the recruiting offices were like choked waterways, and still the flood of men, in whose hearts the fact of England had awoke, poured in. Hospitals were gorged with the returning wounded; women by the hundred and by the thousand volunteered as nurses, and went to hospitals to be trained. The whole of comfortable England, intent hitherto on its sports, its leisure, its general superiority to the rest of the world, suddenly became aware that an immense and vital danger threatened it. A chorus of objurgation arose from the brazen-throated press, each organ striving to shout the loudest, at the unpreparedness of the country, and much valuable energy was spent in headlines and recriminations. There was a shortage of guns, a shortage of ammunition, a shortage of everything which constitutes the sinews of war. The only thing of which there was not a shortage was of those who threw aside all other considerations, such as income and secure living and life itself, and gave themselves to assist, in what manner they could, the cause for which England had gone to war.

CHAPTER XII

To Archie this all seemed a very hysterical and uncomfortable attack of nerves. In several ways it affected him personally, for William, than whom there was no more reliable servant, was among the first to leave his well-paid situation and present himself at a recruiting office. Archie hated that: there would be the nuisance of getting a new servant, who did not know where precisely he ought to put Archie's tooth-powder, and how to arrange his clothes. William had announced the fact too, in the suddenest of manners; he brought it out as he brought in Archie's morning tea.

"And if you can spare me at once, my lord," he said, "I had better go on Saturday."

Archie felt peculiarly devilish that morning; it rained, and the absinthe that should have arrived last night had not come.

"I think it's very inconsiderate of you, William," he said. "But I suppose you expect to get on well, and draw higher pay than you get here. So I shall have to raise your wages. All right; I'll give you a pound a month more, and don't let me hear any more about it."

He knew perfectly well that this was not William's reason, but it amused him to suggest it. He wanted to see how William would take it. The fact that he knew that the man was devoted to him made the point.

William busied himself with razors and tooth-brushes, replying nothing.

"Can't you hear what I say?" asked Archie, pouring himself out his tea.

William faced round.

"Yes, Master Archie," he said. "I heard. But I knew you didn't mean that. You know how I've served you and worked for you all these years. You would scorn to think that of me, I should say."

Archie had noticed the "Master Archie" instead of "my lord"; both William and Blessington often forgot that he was "my lord," and it always used to please him that to the sense of love he was still a young boy. And, in spite of his irritation and peevish morning temper, it touched some part of him that still loved below the corruption that was spreading over him like some jungle-growing lichen. But he had to force his way through that to reply.

"You must do as you think right, William," he said.

William had finished the arrangements of his dressing, and stood for a moment by his bedside with Archie's evening clothes bundled on to his arm.

"Yes, Master Archie," he said. "And you'll be joining up too before long, won't you? I should dearly love to be your soldier-servant, sir, if you could manage it."

All Archie's ill-humour returned at that unfortunate suggestion.

"Perhaps you had better not be impertinent," he said. "That'll do."

William's face fell.

"I had no thought of impertinence, my lord," he said. "I only thought—"

"I told you that would do," said Archie.

* * * * *

Three days afterwards William left. He came to say good-bye to Archie, who did not look up from the paper he was reading. Archie was suffering inconvenience from his departure, and this was the best way of making William feel it. But when the door had shut again, and William was gone, he felt a sudden horror of the thing that seemed to be himself, and he ran out, and called William back. All these days he had not had a word or kindly gesture for him…

"Good-bye, William," he said. "I wish you all good luck. I've treated you like a beast these last days, and I'm awfully sorry. You're the best fellow a man could have, and you must try to forget the horrid way I've behaved."

William stood with his hand in Archie's for a moment.

"You're always my Master Archie, sir," he said.

* * * * *

Well, there was an end of William: before he had got back to his paper again Archie wondered what had possessed him to throw a kind word to a dog like that, who had left him at three days' notice to join this ridiculous military conspiracy. William did not care how much he inconvenienced Archie, who had always treated him more like a subordinate friend than a servant. He had helped William in a hundred ways: had given him old clothes, had constantly asked after his mother, had left his letters about for William to read if he chose. It seemed rank treachery…

Others were treacherous too; his mother, for instance, was immediately going up to town, to take charge of the house in Grosvenor Square, which was to be turned into a hospital for wounded officers. She was to become a sort of housekeeper, so Archie figured it, and merely superintend domestic arrangements. She would have nothing to do with the nursing and the surgery, which had a certain fascination… He could picture a sort of pleasure in seeing a man's leg cut off, or in standing by while doctors pulled bandages off festering wounds. To feel well and strong while others were suffering had an intelligible interest: to witness decay and corruption and pain was a point that appealed to him now. But Lady Tintagel was going to do nothing of the sort: she was just going to be a housekeeper. It was very selfish of her; Archie would certainly want, from time to time, to go up to town and spend a night or two there, and now he would have to go to a hotel or a club, instead of profiting by the spacious privacy of his father's house. Charity begins at home; and his mother had started charity on most extraneous lines. Jessie had followed this lead, "the lead of so-called trumps," as Archie framed a private phrase. She would start by being not even a housekeeper, but a sort of kitchen-maid at the same hospital. She had an insane desire to work, to do something that cost her something, instead of engaging a kitchen-maid, and paying her wages to go to some hospital or other. There was a craze for "personal service," instead of getting other people to do work for you, if you felt work had to be done. People wanted to "do their bit," to employ an odious expression which was beginning to obtain currency. The nation was going to be mobilized; hand and heart had to serve some vague national idea. Occasionally, as on the night when war was declared, Archie saw an aesthetic beauty in the notion of upholding rights and liberties; but he had not then reckoned with the fact that personal inconvenience might result from that quixotic revolution. Quixotism was fine in theory, but it was a dream, not to be encouraged in waking hours, when far more important and realizable commodities, like whisky and absinthe, engaged the true attention.

But, whoever else was treacherous, his father at least was loyal, and showed no sign of becoming a butler or a footman, to correspond with his wife and Jessie. Occasionally some grave report concerning the German advance through Belgium used to reach his brain, and he would walk up and down his room in the evening with a martial tread, and a glance at a sword that hung above his writing-table, and wish he was younger and able to "have a go" at those invading locusts. But invariably this mood, which was always short, was succeeded by another, not bellicose but domestic.

"This damned war is going to break up home-life in England," he would say, "and I've no doubt that was what the Germans aimed at. And they're succeeding too. Look at this house: there's you mother going to leave us, and there's Helena's husband expecting every day to be sent to France, and there's Jessie leaving her father to wash up dishes. What's going to become of our English homes if that goes on?—for, mark you, they are the root of our national life. It's digging up the trees' roots to break up English homes. You and I, Archie, are the only ones who are staunch to our homes. Pass me that bottle, will you?"

"May I help myself on the way?" said Archie.

"Yes, of course, my dear boy. I say, it was a funny state of things when you and I used to have our evening drinks alone, instead of enjoying them and chatting over them together. Your man, William, too, he's gone and enlisted, hasn't he? The old bulwarks of England are going fast: the homes are being broken up, and the very servants come and go as they choose. An establishment was an establishment in the old days: it all stood and fell together, if you see what I mean. But I wish I was young enough to have a go at the Boches."

"I'm thinking of going," Archie would say, merely in order to enjoy his father's reply.

"Well, in my opinion, you'll be doing a very wrong thing, then," said Lord Tintagel. "I hope you won't seriously think of that. I tell you your duty is here, with your poor old father. When I'm gone you may do what you please, and I daresay you won't have very long to wait. But, while I'm here, I hope you'll remember that they say in church 'Honour thy father and thy mother.' You can't go behind the commandments, or the psalms, whichever it is."

But these sessions in Lord Tintagel's room of an evening, with the liquid in the decanter sinking steadily like a well in time of drought, were becoming rather tedious to Archie. Since his discovery of absinthe they had even become rather gross, and he congratulated himself on having seen the sordidness of mere swilling. That sort of thing was only fit for coarse, rough tastes; it seemed to him to lack all delicacy and aesthetic value, and he often left his father, who congratulated him on his abstemiousness after no more than a friendly glass of good fellowship, and went upstairs to his room to enjoy subtler and more refined sensations. Indeed, his chief interest in that half-hour or so in his father's room was derived from the sight of his father's heavy potations, the struggle of his maundering thoughts to emerge into language, much as a tilted half-moon struggles to pierce the flying clouds on some tempestuous night. The sight of his father's deterioration and gradual wreck somehow fascinated him; there was decay and corruption there, and those no longer aroused in him that horror with which in dream he had observed the emergence of the writhing worms from the white statue of Helena. Such things were no longer disgusting and repulsive: they claimed kinship with something in his soul that was very potent. Once Martin had alluded to that vision as a warning, and he had not taken that warning, in consequence of which he had passed an utterly miserable month after Helena's rejection of him. Now values had altogether changed: decay no longer revolted him. But, with a hypocrisy that had become characteristic of him, he told himself that the sight of his father's nightly intoxication was a lesson to himself. He must observe that degrading spectacle, and learn from it what the result of too much whisky was. And then he retired to his bedroom to think it over as he sipped the clouded aroma of his absinthe.

Jessie came down for another week-end before she took her kitchen-maid situation, and brought the news that a fresh draft of Lord Harlow's regiment was ordered to the front, and that he would leave for France within the next day or two.

Archie felt a wild desire to laugh, to skip, to show his intense appreciation of these tidings. But he remembered that Jessie was not his confidante to that extent, and checked his exuberant inclination.

"Poor Helena!" he said, with an accent of great sincerity. "She must be broken-hearted. Why, they've only been married a fortnight, if as much."

It was excellently said, and Jessie felt she would have shown herself an infidel, with regard to the general decency of the human race, if she had not accepted those words with the sincerity with which they surely must have been uttered. She resolutely put away from her all those misgivings that had assailed her when first she knew of Archie's changed attitude towards her sister.

"You have been a brick about Helena," she said. "I want to tell you that. Your forgiveness of the way she treated you seems to me beyond all praise."

"Oh, nonsense," said he lightly. "Besides, it was so dreadfully uncomfortable being always angry and miserable. Martin showed me that. But about Helena: how is she bearing it?"

It was now Jessie's turn to be obliged to cloak her meaning.

"Very calmly and bravely," she said.

"She would," said Archie enthusiastically. "One always felt there was a steel will behind all Helena's gentleness. What will she do, do you think? Would she perhaps like to come down here? There isn't much to offer her, but then London in August doesn't offer much either."

Suddenly all Jessie's mistrust stirred and erected itself. She could not believe that this scheme, which would throw Helena and Archie completely together, could be made with the apparent innocence with which it was put forward. How was it possible that Archie, who so few weeks ago was in such depths of misery and bitterness, could honourably suggest so dangerous a plan? It could not be Archie who suggested it: it came from that smiling white presence which she had seen in his room not many nights ago. And it was just that which she could not say to him.

"It's nice of you to think of that," she said.

"Not a bit: it would be nice for me, not nice of me. And besides," he added, with an amazing cynicism, "it would be my way of 'doing my bit,' which everybody is talking about, if I could make things cheerfuller for pretty women like poor Helena, whose husband has gone out to fight."

The moment he had said it he was sorry. But for the moment he had forgotten he was speaking to Jessie: the sentence had come out of his mouth as if he was but talking to himself. Also it introduced the suggestion of his own forbearance to enlist.

There was a rather awkward silence, and he felt irritated with Jessie for not changing the subject which he had so incautiously brought forward. But that was like her. She had no tact in such matters, refusing to be insincere, when insincerity was so simple a matter. His irritation grew on him, and at the same time he wanted to know what Jessie thought of his remaining inertly here, while all his contemporaries were enlisting. Why he wanted to know he did not define: the motive perhaps belonged to the time when Jessie had been so good a friend, and perhaps he knew that she was so still.

"Or do you think that I ought to behave like William, and serve my country?" he asked.

Jessie sat with eyes downcast for a moment. Then she raised them and looked him in the face, with all her affection and sincerity alight in them.

"Do you really want to know what I think, Archie?" she asked.

"Certainly I do."

"Well, I can't understand your not doing it," she said. "At the same time, I think it is a matter about which you must decide for yourself."

The sincerity of his manner equalled hers. He never spoke with more apparent frankness.

"Shall I tell you why I don't?" he said. "It's this. Do you remember one night our finding that my father was breaking the contract he made with me about drinking? Do you remember how sordid and horrible the discovery was?"

Jessie remembered quite well how Archie had laughed at it.

"I remember the evening," she said.

"Well, we've renewed our contract," said he, "and I'm the only person in the world who can keep my father to it. If I left him he would drink himself to death. Where, then, do you think my duty lies, Jessie? Isn't it clearly for me to save my father? Can there be a more obvious duty than that? Do you think I have a very delightful life down here, all alone with him? Wouldn't it be vastly easier for me to join my friends and go out alongside of them? I know my conduct lays me open to misconception, but I must be thick-skinned over that. But I hope you won't misjudge me. Besides, my father has said that he forbids me to go. Of course I could leave him; he doesn't lock me up. But I can't see how I should be right in leaving him. I'm the one anchor he has left."

He paused a moment, thinking over, with that stupendous swiftness of brain that was the result of Martin's inspiration, all he had said, and remembered his light cynicism with regard to his "bit."

"I know I rather shocked you just now," he said, "when I spoke of its being 'my bit' to console pretty women whose husbands had gone out. But sometimes one has to be flippant to conceal one's real thoughts on a serious subject, for I did not foresee then that we should talk it out. So there's the end of that jest."

So that had been a jest, not to be taken seriously. But it was a grimmer affair for Jessie not to be able to take seriously Archie's seriousness. For a moment the frankness of his manner had convinced her, but very soon her conviction collapsed like a house of cards as he went on speaking. The horribleness of the discovery of his father's drinking, for instance, when what she remembered was Archie's laughter! If he could say that, what credence could possibly be placed in the picture he had drawn of himself as his father's last hope? Or what in the image of himself as one who must silently bear cruel misconception? She could believe none of it...

Yet it was not the Archie whom she loved with all the sweetness and strength of her nature who spoke, but the Thing that was possessing him and filling his soul from the reservoir of some immense abyss of pure evil. She felt sure she did not misjudge him; true and infinitely tragic was her comprehension.

"It is entirely for you to decide, Archie," she said. "I think I fully appreciate the worth of your reasons."

Indeed, she knew not what else to say, though the bitter doubleness of her words cut her to the heart. But, if she could help Archie at all, she must at all costs retain such confidence as he gave her, must not give him the chance of quarrelling with her.

To her great relief, he seemed to accept the literal value of her words, and took her arm. And this time she felt in her soul that there was sincerity in his speech.

"You are a good friend, Jessie," he said. "Don't give me up, will you?"

"I couldn't," she said quietly.

* * * * *

They were strolling together by the edge of the lake in the hour of sunset, and Jessie, though sick at heart and tortured by the weight of her forebodings, and the tempest of fire and blood which had burst on Europe, yet tried to open her heart to the sweet spell of the tranquil evening. Somewhere behind the cloud of evil which had so suddenly taken shape in that host of barbarians who already had overrun Belgium, and which, no less, was invading the spirit of the boy she loved with the uttermost fibre of her being, there shone the eternal serenity of Omnipotent Mercy. But He dealt through human means; it was through those who had left love and home and ease behind them to perish in France that that torrent would be stayed, and through her, though in ways she could not conjecture, would come the delivery of her beloved. And in the rose-flecked sky, the leafy towers of the elms, the bosom of the lake, that Power also dwelt, no less than in the hearts that yearned for its presence and its manifestation. As in a glass darkly she beheld its reflection, which nothing could ever shatter. Of that she must never lose sight, nor cease to keep her inward eye fixed on the gleam, which some day would signal to her.

About a week later Archie was spending a delectable morning at the bathing-place. Never had there been so superb an imitation of Italian weather in England as this year, and day after day went by in unclouded brightness and strong, fresh heat. In those delightful conditions it had been perfectly easy for him to take his mind completely away from the war, and the misconceptions which he was possibly suffering under. He gave every morning but the briefest glance to the paper, for there was a tiresome uniformity about the news, and a monotonous regularity about the daily map, which marked the progress of the German line across North-East France. He gave hardly more thought to Helena, who seemed to think it more appropriate to stay in London with her father, just for the present, but had written the most characteristic of letters, saying how sweet Archie's sympathy was to her, and how acute her anxiety concerning her husband. Certainly at the moment this was the right attitude to take, and Archie really did not much care whether she was here with him or not, for he had found his way into the Paradise that forms the portico of the palace where the absinthe-drinker dwells, and not yet had he penetrated into the halls of Hell that lie beyond.

His pleasure in the fact of being alive, in the colours of morning and evening, in the touch of cool waters, in the whispering of wind among the firs, were quickened to an inconceivable degree; it was impossible to want anything except the privilege of enjoying this amazing thrill of existence. And with it there had returned to him the need of expressing himself in writing; a new aspect of the world had been revealed to him, and without struggle, but with an even-flowing pen he set himself to record it, in veiled phrases and descriptions through which, as in chinks of light seen at the edges of drawn blinds, there came hints and suggestions of the fresh world that had dawned on him. Where before it was the clear stainlessness of the sea, the purifying breath of great winds that had been his theme, now instead the satyr crouched in the bushes, the snake lay coiled in the heather. It was from the slime and mud and from among blind crawling things that the water-lily sprang, and where before the enchantment of life moved him, he felt now only the call of putrefaction and decay. The lethal side of the created world had become exquisite in his eyes, and the beauty of it was derived from its everlasting corruption, not from the eternal upspringing of life. Lust, not love, was the force that kept it young, and renewed it so that the harvest of its decay should never ceased to be reaped. His mind had become a mirror that distorted into grotesque and evil shapes every image of beauty that was reflected in it, and rejoiced in them; it seemed to him that all nature, as well as all human motive, was based upon this exquisite secret that he had discovered. But it would never do to state it with what he considered the bald realism of those ludicrous sea-pieces he had written at Silorno; he must wrap his message up in a sort of mystic subtlety so that only those who had implanted in them the true instinct should be able to fill their souls with the perfume of his flowers. Others might guess and wonder and be puzzled, and perhaps see so far as to put down his book with disgust that was still half incredulous; but only the initiated would be able to grasp wholly the message that lurked in his hints and allusions. His style, underneath this new inspiration, had developed into an instrument of marvellous beauty, and often, when he had written a page or two, he would read it out aloud to himself, in wonder at that exquisite diction, and all the time he felt that he was reading aloud to Martin, and that Martin had dictated to him.

He was employed thus on this particular morning down at the bathing-place. He had already had a long swim, and, without dressing, lay down on the short turf and got out his writing-pad, when his new servant, who had taken William's place, came down with a telegram for him. He was a very good-looking boy, quick in movement and swift to smile, and already Archie wondered how he could have regretted the departure of plain middle-aged William. Only last evening Archie, idly glancing through a field-glass, had seen the boy far off in the meadow beyond the lake in company with an extremely pretty housemaid whom he had often noticed about the passages. The two had sat there some time talking, and then Archie saw the boy look quickly round, and kiss her. He liked that immensely; that was the way youth should behave. He almost hoped that it was Thomas who had taken from his table one of those new ten-shilling notes that he had missed. He mustn't do it too often, for that would be a bore; but Archie liked to think the boy had taken it, and perhaps converted it into a decoration for the pretty housemaid. Anyhow, Thomas, with his handsome face and his kissings in the meadow, and his possible pilferings, was an attractive boy, and clearly developing along the right lines.

The boy hesitated a moment, seeing Archie dripping and naked.

"I beg your pardon, my lord," he said, "but there came a telegram for you, and I thought I had better bring it down."

"Certainly, but why beg my pardon?" said Archie. "Don't be prudish. I daresay you've got arms and legs as well as me, haven't you?"

Thomas grinned with that odd shy look that Archie had noticed before.

"Yes, my lord," he said.

"Then what is there to be ashamed of?"

Archie opened the telegram and read it, and suddenly bit his lip to prevent his laughing.

"Is there an answer, my lord?" asked the boy. "I brought a form down in case."

"Well done. Yes, there is an answer."

Archie hesitated a moment before directing the form to Helena. Then he wrote:

"Deepest sympathy with the terrible news. Command me in all ways. Your devoted Archie."

"Send that at once, will you?" he said.

CHAPTER XII

When the boy had gone Archie read the telegram again, which was from Jessie, and told him that Lord Harlow had been killed at the front. Then he smothered his face in his bent elbow, and lay shaking with laughter.

CHAPTER XIII

On a September morning, some fortnight later, Archie was waiting in the drawing-room at Oakland Crescent for Helena's entry. He had seen her twice since her husband's death, and it struck him now that she always kept him waiting when she asked him to come and see her, and ascribed to that the very probable motive that she expected thereby to increase his eagerness for her coming. Certainly he wanted her to come, because he was much interested and amused in the conventional little comedy she was playing, and he looked forward to the third act, on which the curtain would presently ring up. In the interval he sat very serenely smiling to himself, and tickling the end of his nose with three white feathers that he had received in the street to-day. That always diverted him extremely; a rude young woman would come up (she was invariably square and plain, and had a knobby face like a chest of drawers) and say, "Aren't you ashamed not to be serving your country? You're a coward, you are," and then she would give him a white feather. He had quite a collection of them now; there were nine already which he carefully kept in his stud-box, and these three all in one day were a splendid haul.

He had, to occupy his mind very pleasantly, the remembrance of his previous interviews with Helena, which formed the two existing acts of the comedy. In the first she had come in, looking deliciously pretty in her deep mourning, and, with her head a little on one side, had held out both her hands to him. They had stood with hands clasped for quite a long time, and then Archie kissed her because he was rather tired of holding her hands, and because he enjoyed kissing anything so pretty. That had caused a break, and they sat down side by side, and Helena made some queer movements in her throat, which seemed to Archie to be designed to convey the impression that she was repressing her emotion. But they did not quite fulfil their design; they looked rather as if they were due to the desire to pump up rather than keep down. Then Helena gave a long sigh.

"Oh, Archie," she said, "I am utterly broken-hearted. It was so sudden, so terribly sudden. I shall never get over it. Think! We had been married only a fortnight, and next day I got a letter from him, after I knew he was dead. Such a sweet little letter, so cheerful and so loving."

Archie expected something of this sort: its conventionality, its utter insincerity, amused him enormously. And, wanting more of it, he said just the proper sort of thing to encourage her to give it him.

CHAPTER XIII

"Oh, my dear," he said, "but how you will love and cherish that letter! I don't suppose you were once out of his thoughts all the time he was in France."

She shook her head.

"I am sure of it," she said. "Ah, what a privilege to have been loved as I was loved by such a noble, manly heart. I must always think of that, mustn't I?"

Archie took her hand again. The touch of those soft, cool fingers gave him pleasure; so, too, did the answering pressure of them.

"Yes, indeed," he said. "And you must remember, too, that it's better to have loved and lost than never to have loved at all."

She repeated the quotation in a dreamy meditative voice.

"Yes, that is so true: it does me good to think of that," she said. "And I mustn't think of him as dead really. He is just as living as ever he was. He was so fond of you too. We often spoke of you. And his quaint, quiet humour!..."

That was the general note of the first act: it had been short, for the conversation suitable to it was necessarily limited. The second showed a great advance in scope and variety of topics. Also the *tempo* was quite changed: instead of its being *largo*, it was at least *andante con moto*.

This time, after again keeping him waiting, she had entered with a smile.

"What a comfort you are, Archie!" she said. "I have been looking forward to seeing you again. Somehow you understand me, which nobody else does. I feel all the time that neither darling Jessie, whenever I see her, which isn't often, for she is so busy, nor daddy quite understand me. I mean to be brave, and not lose courage, not lose gaiety even, and I think—I think that they both misjudge me. They expect me to be utterly broken. So I was at first, as you know so well, but I tried to take to heart what you said, and force myself not to despair. I feel I oughtn't to do that: I must take the burden of life up again with a smile."

Her hand lay open on her knee; as she said this, she turned it over towards him, making an invitation that seemed unconscious. He slipped his long brown fingers into that rosy palm. She was astonishingly like a girl he met a night or two ago.

"I must get over this awful feeling of loneliness," she said, "and you are helping me so deliciously to do so. Daddy is busy all day; I scarcely see him. Jessie is busy also. I think she enjoys washing up knives and forks and plates for soldiers, though of course that doesn't make it any less sweet of her to do it. But, anyhow, she hasn't got much time for me. I wish—no, I suppose it's wrong to wish that."

"Well, confess, then," said Archie, smiling at her.

"Yes, dear father-confessor, though I ought to say boy-confessor, for you look so young! Well, I'll confess to you. I—I'm sure you won't be shocked with me. I wish Jessie cared for me a little more. She is my sister, after all. But I daresay it's my fault. I haven't got the key to her heart. And, with Jessie and daddy so full of other affairs, I do feel lonely. But when you are here I don't. I don't know what I should have done without you, Archie. I think I might have killed myself."

This was glorious. Archie gave a splendid shudder.

"Don't talk like that," he said, in a tone of affectionate command. "You don't know how it hurts."

"Ah, I'm sorry. It was selfish of me. Do you forgive me?"

"You know I do," said he.

She had brought into the room with her a long envelope, and rather absently she took out from it an enclosure of papers.

"I got this to-day from the lawyers," she said. "It's about my darling's will, I think. I wonder if you would help me to understand it, I am so stupid at figures."

She slid a little closer to him, leaning her hand on his shoulder and looking over him as he read. The document required, as a matter of fact, very little exercise of intelligence. The house in Surrey where they had spent the week of the honeymoon was hers; and so was a very decent income of L15,000 a year, left to her without any condition whatever for her life; it was hers absolutely. The disposition of the rest of his fortune depended on whether she had a child. The details of that were not given: his lawyer only informed her what was hers.

She hid her face on the hand that rested on Archie's shoulder.

"Oh, Archie, I can never go back to that house," she said, "at least not for a long time. It would be tearing open the old wound again."

"Yes, I understand that," said he, with another pressure of his fingers. And, thinking of the L15,000 a year without conditions, he had a wild temptation to console her further by quoting—

"Let us grieve not, only find
Strength in what remains behind."

But he refrained: though, apparently, there was no limit to Helena's insincerity, there might be some in her acceptance of the insincerity of others.

"Oh, you do understand me so well," she said. "And, Archie, I want to ask a horribly selfish thing of you, but I can't help it. I am all alone now, except for you. You won't go out to the war, will you? I don't think I could bear it if you did."

It was quite easy for him to promise that, but an allusion to the misconception he might incur made his acquiescence sound difficult and noble.

Since then, up to the day when he was now expecting her entry for the third act, he had thought over the whole situation with the imaginative vision which absinthe inspired. He had not the slightest doubt in his mind that Helena, according to her capacity for loving, was in love with him, and that she thought he was still in love with her. But, when he considered it all, he found he had no longer the slightest intention of marrying her, even though she had L15,000 a year for life without conditions attached. Plenty of money was no doubt a preventive of discomfort in this life, and he felt it was fine of him not to be attracted by so ignoble a bait. But no amount of money would really compensate for the inseparable companionship of Helena, with her foolishness, her apparent inability to understand that her insincerities, so far from being convincing and beautiful, were no more than the most puerile and transparent counterfeits. Certainly she aroused the ardour of his senses, but how long would that last? And, even while it lasted, how could it compare with his ardour for his absinthe-coloured dreams, and the ecstasy of his communion with the spirit that had made its home in him? She would interrupt all that; and, as a companion, she could not compare with his father. She would always be wanting to be caressed and made much of and admired and taken care of. It would soon become most horribly tedious.

There was a further reason against marrying her, which was as potent as any. He would forfeit his revenge on her, if he did that. Once, dim ages ago, it seemed, and on another plane of existence, he had loved her, and she, knowing it, had fed his devotion with smiles and glances, and at the end had chosen him whose body now decayed in some graveyard of North France, already probably desecrated by the on-swarming Germans. Now it was Archie's turn; already, he was sure, she expected to marry him, and she would learn that he had not the least intention of doing so. That delightful situation might easily be arrived at in the third act for which he was waiting now.

This time she came with flowers in her hand, and presently, as they sat side by side on the sofa talking, she put one into his button-hole. Instantly he interrupted himself in what he was saying and kissed it.

She gave him that long glance which he had once thought meant so much. It had not meant much then, from her point of view, but it meant a good deal more now. But to Archie it had passed from being a gleam of wonder to a farthing dip.

"Oh, you foolish boy!" she said.

He almost thought he heard Martin laugh.

"I don't see anything foolish about it," he said. "At least, if it's foolish, I've always been foolish."

Her lips moved, though not to speak: they just gathered themselves together, and a little tremor went down the arm that rested against his. He was perfectly certain of both those signals, and next moment he had folded her to him, and she lay less than unresisting in his arms.

Then she gently thrust him from her.

"Ah, how wrong of me," she said, "and yet perhaps it's not wrong. The dear Bradshaw would always want me to be happy. Perhaps he even thought of this when he left me so free. For this time, Archie, I shan't come to you empty-handed. But, of course, we mustn't think of all that for many months yet."

Archie, flushed and merry-eyed, looked at her with boyish surprise.

"Think of what?" he said.

"Ah, you force me to say it, do you? Of our marriage."

He was adorable in her eyes just then; she could hardly realize that so few months ago she had definitely put him from her. His warm, smooth face, his crisp, curling hair, the youthful roughness and ardour of his embrace, inflamed and ravished her.

He looked at her still inquiringly a moment, then threw back his head and laughed.

"Oh, you're delicious!" he said. "But marriage? What do you mean? A cousinly kiss, a little sympathy, a few dear little surrenders of each of us to the other: that's all I intended. Well, I must be off. Good-bye!"

Next moment, still choking with laughter, he was downstairs and out into the street. He could not resist looking up at the window, and waving a gay hand towards it. Something within him, that seemed the very essence of his being, shout-shouted and sang with glee.

* * * * *

The house in Grosvenor Square, where his mother had become housekeeper and Jessie kitchen-maid, had at present in it only a few wounded officers from France, and during these two or three days in town Archie could still occupy his own bedroom, while his servant slept in the dressing-room adjoining. He was out very late that night, for the completeness of his revenge on Helena ran like a feeding fire through his veins, and both nourished and burned him.

Dawn had already broken when he let himself in, and went very quietly upstairs, not intending to go to bed till he had had an interview with Martin. All night he had felt as if Martin was bursting to come forth again; he was already intensely present, even though Archie had not yet sunk his conscious self and opened the door of mystic communication. That controlling spirit foamed and simmered within him; he could all but break open the door himself, and project himself without invitation. He was still just confined, but only just; it seemed that at any minute he might assert himself. But Archie, with the gourmand instinct that delays an actual fulfilment, teasing itself, while it knows the fulfilment is assured, lingered over his undressing, and planned to make himself cool and comfortable in his pyjamas, before he abandoned the fortress of his normal self. He brushed his teeth, he sponged face and neck with cold water, he arranged his chair in the window, and put on the table by his bed the moonstone stud on which he would focus his eyes, and stretched himself long and luxuriously till he heard his shoulder joints crack. Martin seemed in a great hurry to come to-night, but Martin must just wait till he was ready. And then, all of a sudden, he heard a tremendous noise of rapping. He knew that Martin had come, and an awful terror seized his soul, for Martin had come without being called.

At that precise moment his servant next door started up, wide awake, with some loud sound in his ears that seemed to come from Archie's bedroom. He tapped at his door, but, getting no answer, went in. He found Archie lying on the floor, curled up together, like some twisted root of a tree, foaming at the mouth. He ran downstairs to get help, and brought up one of the nurses who was on duty. She instantly telephoned for a doctor, and woke Lady Tintagel.

* * * * *

All that day Archie lay in this strange seizure, apparently quite unconscious. Sometimes a paroxysm would take hold of him, and he lay with staring eyes and teeth that ground against each other, and limbs that curled into fantastic shapes. In the intervals he remained still, stiff and rigid, his eyes for the most part shut, breathing quickly, as if he had been running. Then once again the panic and the agony would grip him, and with eyes wide with terror and foaming mouth he struggled and fought against the Thing that mastered him. But each paroxysm left him weaker, and it was clear that he would not be able to stand many more of these attacks. Yet no one could wish them prolonged; it would but be merciful if the end came soon, and spared him further suffering.

Towards sunset that day Jessie was sitting by him, with orders to call the nurse next door if he showed signs of the restlessness which preceded the return of a seizure. She knew that, humanly speaking, he was dying, but her faith never faltered that he might still be saved, and that through her and her love salvation might come to him. Medical science was of no avail; it could not combat the spiritual foe that had taken him prisoner. That rescue had to be made through spiritual means, and the two-edged sword by which alone his captor could be vanquished was the bright-shining weapon of love and prayer. It was in her hand now, as she watched and waited.

He lay quite still, breathing quickly and with a shallow inspiration, but there were no signs of the restlessness for which she had to look out. But presently she observed that his eyes were no longer closed, but were open and looking steadily at the brass knob at the foot of his bed on which a sunbeam, entering through a chink at the side of the drawn window-blind made a focus of light. And, all at once, she guessed that he was looking at this with purpose, and her soul, sword in hand, crouched ready to spring. Then from the bed came Archie's voice.

"Martin," it said.

There was a dead silence, and she saw forming in the air a little in front of him a nucleus of mist. It gathered volume from a little jet as of steam that appeared to come from Archie himself. Thicker and thicker it grew; strange lines began to interlace themselves within it, and these took form. The dimness of its outline grew firm and distinct, the shape stood detached and clear, and, bending over Archie with a smile triumphant and cruel, stood the semblance she had seen once before at midnight in Archie's room. He was no longer looking at the knob at the foot of his bed, but with eyes wide open and blank with some nameless terror he gazed at the apparition.

Jessie rose and stood opposite it on the other side of his bed. Her two-edged sword was drawn now, and its bright blade gleamed in the darkness of the evil that flooded the room. And then it seemed that that incarnation of it that stood beside Archie's bed was aware, for it turned and looked her full in the face, bringing to bear on her the utmost of its hellish potency.

For one moment against that awful assault her soul cried out in panic. It had not dreamed that from all the crimes with which the world had withered and bled there could be distilled a tincture so poisonous. And then her love rallied her scattered courage, and she stood firm again. Nothing in the world but love and prayer could prevail, but nothing, if once she could fully realize that, could prevail against them. In her hand, as in the hand of all who are foes to evil, was the irresistible weapon, could she but use its power to the full…

She stood, as she knew, in the face of the deadliest peril by which any living thing, into which the breath of God has passed, can be confronted. There is no soul so strong that evil can cease to be a menace for it, and here, facing her, was the power that had already perverted all that Archie held of goodness and humanity. There it stood, one victim already its helpless prisoner, and it lusted for more. And the wordless struggle, as old as evil itself, began.

She would not give ground. Her soul laid itself open, and let the light invisible shine on it. In this struggle there were no strivings or wrestlings; she had but to stay quiet, and in just that achievement of quietness the struggle lay. Once for a moment all Hell swirled and exulted round her, for her love for Archie let itself contemplate the human and material aspect of him; the next she put all that away from her, and again stood with his soul, so to speak, in her uplifted hands, offering it to God. In the very storm-centre of this evil which shrieked and raged round her, there must be, and there was, a space where the peace that passeth understanding dwelt in serene calm. The storm might shift and envelope her again in its bellowings, but again and yet again she had to regain the centre where no blast of it could penetrate.

How long this lasted she could not tell. Her body was quite conscious of its ordinary perceptions; the blind tapped on the window, and there came from outside the stir of distant traffic. But she did not take her gaze from those awful eyes that sometimes smiled, sometimes blazed with hate. Steadily and firmly she looked at them and through them, for behind them, as behind the cloud, was the sunlight of God.

And then there came a change. It seemed that the power she fought was weakening. Its eyes shifted; they no longer looked undeviatingly at her, but glanced round for a moment, as if they looked for some way of escape. They would come back to her again with fresh assault of smiles or hate, but each time they seemed less potent. More than once they left her face altogether for a while, and were directed on Archie, as if seeking the refuge there that they knew; but, with a wordless command that they were forced to obey, she summoned them back to her again, making the spirit that directed them turn the strength of its fury on her. She gave it no rest, fixing it on herself by the strength of love and prayer.

The eyes began to grow dim; the outline of the form began to waver. The interlacing lines out of which it was woven began to unravel again, and it grew shapeless. But it was not being absorbed into Archie; there were no streams of mist between him and it, as when it had first taken substance. Already through it she could see the wall behind it, and it grew ever fainter and thinner…

There was nothing left of it now, and for the first time since the struggle began, she looked at Archie. He was lying quite still with eyes closed again. And then she saw that by her side was standing another presence. It was identical in form and shape with that which had vanished, and it bent on Archie so amazing a look of love that her soul, spent and sick with struggle, felt itself uplifted and refreshed again. And for one moment it looked at her, and it was as if Archie himself was looking at her. And then it was there no longer. She hardly knew whether her physical eyes had seen it externally, or whether it had been some spirit-vision conveyed to them from within.

CHAPTER XIII

There came a sound from next door, and the nurse, who was there ready to be summoned, entered.

"Has he been quite quiet?" she asked, and, without waiting for an answer, she went to the bed. She looked at Archie a moment, then felt his elbows and knees, finding them pliant again instead of being stiff and rigid, and listened to his quiet breathing.

"But there has come an extraordinary change," she said. "The seizure has passed, and yet he's alive."

She beamed at Jessie.

"Well, you are a good nurse," she said. "But I think I'll just fetch the doctor."

She went out of the room, and Archie, who had lain quite motionless with closed eyes, suddenly stirred and looked at the girl.

"Why, Jessie," he said.

She came close to the bed.

"Yes?"

"What's happened?" said he. "I've had some awful nightmare. And then you broke it up. Hasn't Martin been here too?"

"Yes, Archie, I think so," she said.

He lay in silence a moment.

"Have you saved me again, Jessie?" he said. "You did once before at—at Silorno, when the lightning struck the pine."

She could find no answer for him; not a word could she speak.

He held out his hand to her.

"Jessie!..." he said.

THE BLOTTING BOOK

CHAPTER I

Mrs. Assheton's house in Sussex Square, Brighton, was appointed with that finish of smooth stateliness which robs stateliness of its formality, and conceals the amount of trouble and personal attention which has, originally in any case, been spent on the production of the smoothness. Everything moved with the regularity of the solar system, and, superior to that wild rush of heavy bodies through infinite ether, there was never the slightest fear of comets streaking their unconjectured way across the sky, or meteorites falling on unsuspicious picnicers. In Mrs. Assheton's house, supreme over climatic conditions, nobody ever felt that rooms were either too hot or too cold, a pleasantly fresh yet comfortably warm atmosphere pervaded the place, meals were always punctual and her admirable Scotch cook never served up a dish which, whether plain or ornate, was not, in its way, perfectly prepared. A couple of deft and noiseless parlour-maids attended to and anticipated the wants of her guests, from the moment they entered her hospitable doors till when, on their leaving them, their coats were held for them in the most convenient possible manner for the easy insertion of the human arm, and the tails of their dinner-coats cunningly and unerringly tweaked from behind. In every way in fact the house was an example of perfect comfort; the softest carpets overlaid the floors, or, where the polished wood was left bare, the parquetry shone with a moonlike radiance; the newest and most entertaining books (ready cut) stood on the well-ordered shelves in the sitting-room to beguile the leisure of the studiously minded; the billiard table was always speckless of dust, no tip was ever missing from any cue, and the cigarette boxes and match-stands were always kept replenished. In the dining-room the silver was resplendent, until the moment when before dessert the cloth was withdrawn, and showed a rosewood table that might have served for a mirror to Narcissus.

Mrs. Assheton, until her only surviving son Morris had come to live with her some three months ago on the completion of his four years at Cambridge, had been alone, but even when she was alone this ceremony of drawing the cloth and putting on the dessert and wine had never been omitted, though since she never took either, it might seem to be a wasted piece of routine on the part of the two noiseless parlourmaids. But she did not in the least consider it so, for just as she always dressed for dinner herself with the same care and finish, whether she was going to dine alone or whether, as tonight, a guest or two was dining with her, as an offering, so to speak, on the altar of her own self-respect, so also she required self-respect and the formality that indicated it on the part of those who ministered at her table, and enjoyed such excellent wages. This pretty old-fashioned custom had always been the rule in her own home, and her husband had always had it practised during his life. And since then—his death had occurred some twenty years ago—nothing that she knew of had happened to make it less proper or desirable. Kind of heart and warm of soul though she was, she saw no reason for letting these excellent qualities cover any slackness or breach of observance in the social form of life to which she had been accustomed. There was no cause, because one was kind and wise, to eat with badly cleaned silver, unless the parlour-maid whose office it was to clean it was unwell. In such a case, if the extra work entailed by her illness would throw too much on the shoulders of the other servants, Mrs. Assheton would willingly clean the silver herself, rather than that it should appear dull and tarnished. Her formalism, such as it was, was perfectly simple and sincere. She would, without any very poignant regret or sense of martyrdom, had her very comfortable income been cut down to a tenth of what it was, have gone to live in a four-roomed cottage with one servant. But she would have left that four-roomed cottage at once for even humbler surroundings had she found that her straitened circumstances did not permit her to keep it as speckless and *soignée* as was her present house in Sussex Square.

This achievement of having lived for nearly sixty years so decorously may perhaps be a somewhat finer performance than it sounds, but Mrs. Assheton brought as her contribution to life in general a far finer offering than that, for though she did not propose to change her ways and manner of life herself, she was notoriously sympathetic with the changed life of the younger generation, and in consequence had the confidence of young folk generally. At this moment she was enjoying the fruits of her liberal attitude in the volubility of her son Morris, who sat at the end of the table opposite to her. His volubility was at present concerned with his motor-car, in which he had arrived that afternoon.

"Darling mother," he was saying, "I really was frightened as to whether you would mind. I couldn't help remembering how you received Mr. Taynton's proposal that you should go for a drive in his car. Don't you remember, Mr. Taynton? Mother's nose *did* go in the air. It's no use denying it. So I thought, perhaps, that she wouldn't like my having one. But I wanted it so dreadfully, and so I bought it without telling her, and drove down in it to-day, which is my birthday, so that she couldn't be too severe."

Mr. Taynton, while Morris was speaking, had picked up the nutcrackers the boy had been using, and was gravely exploding the shells of the nuts he had helped himself to. So Morris cracked the next one with a loud bang between his white even teeth.

"Dear Morris," said his mother, "how foolish of you. Give Mr. Morris another nutcracker," she added to the parlour-maid.

"What's foolish?" asked he, cracking another.

"Oh Morris, your teeth," she said. "Do wait a moment. Yes, that's right. And how can you say that my nose went in the air? I'm sure Mr. Taynton will agree with me that that is really libellous. And as for your being afraid to tell me you had bought a motor-car yourself, why, that is sillier than cracking nuts with your teeth."

Mr. Taynton laughed a comfortable middle-aged laugh.

"Don't put the responsibility on me, Mrs. Assheton," he said. "As long as Morris's bank doesn't tell us that his account is overdrawn, he can do what he pleases. But if we are told that, then down comes the cartloads of bricks."

"Oh, you are a brick all right, Mr. Taynton," said the boy. "I could stand a cartload of you."

Mr. Taynton, like his laugh, was comfortable and middle-aged. Solicitors are supposed to be sharp-faced and fox-like, but his face was well-furnished and comely, and his rather bald head beamed with benevolence and dinner.

"My dear boy," he said, "and it is your birthday—I cannot honour either you or this wonderful port more properly than by drinking your health in it."

He began and finished his glass to the health he had so neatly proposed, and Morris laughed.

"Thank you very much," he said. "Mother, do send the port round. What an inhospitable woman!"

Mrs. Assheton rose.

"I will leave you to be more hospitable than me, then, dear," she said.

"Shall we go, Madge? Indeed, I am afraid you must, if you are to catch the train to Falmer."

Madge Templeton got up with her hostess, and the two men rose too. She had been sitting next Morris, and the boy looked at her eagerly.

"It's too bad, your having to go," he said. "But do you think I may come over to-morrow, in the afternoon some time, and see you and Lady Templeton?"

Madge paused a moment.

"I am so sorry," she said, "but we shall be away all day. We shan't be back till quite late."

"Oh, what a bore," said he, "and I leave again on Friday. Do let me come and see you off then."

But Mrs. Assheton interposed.

"No, dear," she said, "I am going to have five minutes' talk with Madge before she goes and we don't want you. Look after Mr. Taynton. I know he wants to talk to you and I want to talk to Madge."

Mr. Taynton, when the door had closed behind the ladies, sat down again with a rather obvious air of proposing to enjoy himself. It was quite true that he had a few pleasant things to say to Morris, it is also true that he immensely appreciated the wonderful port which glowed, ruby-like, in the nearly full decanter that lay to his hand. And, above all, he, with his busy life, occupied for the most part in innumerable small affairs, revelled in the sense of leisure and serene smoothness which permeated Mrs. Assheton's house. He was still a year or two short of sixty, and but for his very bald and shining head would have seemed younger, so fresh was he in complexion, so active, despite a certain reassuring corpulency, was he in his movements. But when he dined quietly like this, at Mrs. Assheton's, he would willingly have sacrificed the next five years of his life if he could have been assured on really reliable authority—the authority for instance of the Recording Angel—that in five years time he would be able to sit quiet and not work any more. He wanted very much to be able to take a passive instead of an active interest in life, and this a few hundreds of pounds a year in addition to his savings would enable him to do. He saw, in fact, the goal arrived at which he would be able to sit still and wait with serenity and calmness for the event which would certainly relieve him of all further material anxieties. His very active life, the activities of which were so largely benevolent, had at the expiration of fifty-eight years a little tired him. He coveted the leisure which was so nearly his.

Morris lit a cigarette for himself, having previously passed the wine to Mr. Taynton.

"I hate port," he said, "but my mother tells me this is all right. It was laid down the year I was born by the way. You don't mind my smoking do you?"

This, to tell the truth, seemed almost sacrilegious to Mr. Taynton, for the idea that tobacco, especially the frivolous cigarette, should burn in a room where such port was being drunk was sheer crime against human and divine laws. But he could scarcely indicate to his host that he should not smoke in his own dining-room.

"No, my dear Morris," he said, "but really you almost shock me, when you prefer tobacco to this nectar, I assure you nectar. And the car, now, tell me more about the car."

Morris laughed.

"I'm so deeply thankful I haven't overdrawn," he said. "Oh, the car's a clipper. We came down from Haywards Heath the most gorgeous pace. I saw one policeman trying to take my number, but we raised such a dust, I don't think he can have been able to see it. It's such rot only going twenty miles an hour with a clear straight road ahead."

Mr. Taynton sighed, gently and not unhappily.

"Yes, yes, my dear boy, I so sympathise with you," he said. "Speed and violence is the proper attitude of youth, just as strength with a more measured pace is the proper gait for older folk. And that, I fancy is just what Mrs. Assheton felt. She would feel it to be as unnatural in you to care to drive with her in her very comfortable victoria as she would feel it to be unnatural in herself to wish to go in your lightning speed motor. And that reminds me. As your trustee—"

Coffee was brought in at this moment, carried, not by one of the discreet parlour-maids, but by a young man-servant. Mr. Taynton, with the port still by him, refused it, but looked rather curiously at the servant. Morris however mixed himself a cup in which cream, sugar, and coffee were about equally mingled.

"A new servant of your mother's?" he asked, when the man had left the room.

"Oh no. It's my man, Martin. Awfully handy chap. Cleans silver, boots and the motor. Drives it, too, when I'll let him, which isn't very often. Chauffeurs are such rotters, aren't they? Regular chauffeurs I mean. They always make out that something is wrong with the car, just as dentists always find some hole in your teeth, if you go to them."

Mr. Taynton did not reply to these critical generalities but went back to what he had been saying when the entry of coffee interrupted him.

"As your mother said," he remarked, "I wanted to have a few words with you. You are twenty-two, are you not, to-day? Well, when I was young we considered anyone of twenty-two a boy still, but now I think young fellows grow up more quickly, and at twenty-two, you are a man nowadays, and I think it is time for you, since my trusteeship for you may end any day now, to take a rather more active interest in the state of your finances than you have hitherto done. I want you in fact, my dear fellow, to listen to me for five minutes while I state your position to you."

Morris indicated the port again, and Mr. Taynton refilled his glass.

"I have had twenty years of stewardship for you," he went on, "and before my stewardship comes to an end, which it will do anyhow in three years from now, and may come to an end any day—"

"Why, how is that?" asked Morris.

"If you marry, my dear boy. By the terms of your father's will, your marriage, provided it takes place with your mother's consent, and after your twenty-second birthday, puts you in complete control and possession of your fortune. Otherwise, as of course you know, you come of age, legally speaking, on your twenty-fifth birthday."

Morris lit another cigarette rather impatiently.

"Yes, I knew I was a minor till I was twenty-five," he said, "and I suppose I have known that if I married after the age of twenty-two, I became a major, or whatever you call it. But what then? Do let us go and play billiards, I'll give you twenty-five in a hundred, because I've been playing a lot lately, and I'll bet half a crown."

Mr. Taynton's fist gently tapped the table.

"Done," he said, "and we will play in five minutes. But I have something to say to you first. Your mother, as you know, enjoys the income of the bulk of your father's property for her lifetime. Outside that, he left this much smaller capital of which, as also of her money, my partner and I are trustees. The sum he left you was thirty thousand pounds. It is now rather over forty thousand pounds, since we have changed the investments from time to time, and always, I am glad to say, with satisfactory results. The value of her property has gone up also in a corresponding degree. That, however, does not concern you. But since you are now twenty-two, and your marriage would put the whole of this smaller sum into your hands, would it not be well for you to look through our books, to see for yourself the account we render of our stewardship?"

Morris laughed.

"But for what reason?" he asked. "You tell me that my portion has increased in value by ten thousand pounds. I am delighted to hear it. And I thank you very much. And as for—"

He broke off short, and Mr. Taynton let a perceptible pause follow before he interrupted.

"As for the possibility of your marrying?" he suggested.

Morris gave him a quick, eager, glance.

"Yes, I think there is that possibility," he said. "I hope—I hope it is not far distant."

"My dear boy—" said the lawyer.

"Ah, not a word. I don't know—"

Morris pushed his chair back quickly, and stood up—his tall slim figure outlined against the sober red of the dining-room wall. A plume of black hair had escaped from his well-brushed head and hung over his forehead, and his sun-tanned vivid face looked extraordinarily handsome. His mother's clear-cut energetic features were there, with the glow and buoyancy of youth kindling them. Violent vitality was his also; his was the hot blood that could do any deed when the life-instinct commanded it. He looked like one of those who could give their body to be burned in the pursuit of an idea, or could as easily steal, or kill, provided only the deed was vitally done in the heat of his blood. Violence was clearly his mode of life: the motor had to go sixty miles an hour; he might be one of those who bathed in the Serpentine in mid-winter; he would clearly dance all night, and ride all day, and go on till he dropped in the pursuit of what he cared for. Mr. Taynton, looking at him as he stood smiling there, in his splendid health and vigour felt all this. He felt, too, that if Morris intended to be married to-morrow morning, matrimony would probably take place.

But Morris's pause, after he pushed his chair back and stood up, was only momentary.

"Good God, yes; I'm in love," he said. "And she probably thinks me a stupid barbarian, who likes only to drive golfballs and motorcars. She—oh, it's hopeless. She would have let me come over to see them to-morrow otherwise."

He paused again.

"And now I've given the whole show away," he said.

Mr. Taynton made a comfortable sort of noise. It was compounded of laughter, sympathy, and comprehension.

"You gave it away long ago, my dear Morris," he said.

"You had guessed?" asked Morris, sitting down again with the same quickness and violence of movement, and putting both his elbows on the table.

"No, my dear boy, you had told me, as you have told everybody, without mentioning it. And I most heartily congratulate you. I never saw a more delightful girl. Professionally also, I feel bound to add that it seems to me a most proper alliance—heirs should always marry heiresses. It"—Mr. Taynton drank off the rest of his port—"it keeps properties together."

Hot blood again dictated to Morris: it seemed dreadful to him that any thought of money or of property could be mentioned in the same breath as that which he longed for. He rose again as abruptly and violently as he had sat down.

CHAPTER I

"Well, let's play billiards," he said. "I—I don't think you understand a bit. You can't, in fact."

Mr. Taynton stroked the tablecloth for a moment with a plump white forefinger.

"Crabbed age and youth," he remarked. "But crabbed age makes an appeal to youth, if youth will kindly call to mind what crabbed age referred to some five minutes ago. In other words, will you, or will you not, Morris, spend a very dry three hours at my office, looking into the account of my stewardship? There was thirty thousand pounds, and there now is—or should we say 'are'—forty. It will take you not less than two hours, and not more than three. But since my stewardship may come to an end, as I said, any day, I should, not for my own sake, but for yours, wish you to see what we have done for you, and—I own this would be a certain private gratification to me—to learn that you thought that the trust your dear father reposed in us was not misplaced."

There was something about these simple words which touched Morris. For the moment he became almost businesslike. Mr. Taynton had been, as he knew, a friend of his father's, and, as he had said, he had been steward of his own affairs for twenty years. But that reflection banished the businesslike view.

"Oh, but two hours is a fearful time," he said. "You have told me the facts, and they entirely satisfy me. And I want to be out all day to-morrow, as I am only here till the day after. But I shall be down again next week. Let us go into it all then. Not that there is the slightest use in going into anything. And when, Mr. Taynton, I become steward of my own affairs, you may be quite certain that I shall beg you to continue looking after them. Why you gained me ten thousand pounds in these twenty years—I wonder what there would have been to my credit now if I had looked after things myself. But since we are on the subject I should like just this once to assure you of my great gratitude to you, for all you have done. And I ask you, if you will, to look after my affairs in the future with the same completeness as you have always done. My father's will does not prevent that, does it?"

Mr. Taynton looked at the young fellow with affection.

"Dear Morris," he said gaily, "we lawyers and solicitors are always supposed to be sharks, but personally I am not such a shark as that. Are you aware that I am paid £200 a year for my stewardship, which you are entitled to assume for yourself on your marriage, though of course its continuance in my hands is not forbidden in your father's will? You are quite competent to look after your affairs yourself; it is ridiculous for you to continue to pay me this sum. But I thank you from the bottom of my heart for your confidence in me."

A very close observer might have seen that behind Mr. Taynton's kind gay eyes there was sitting a personality, so to speak, that, as his mouth framed these words, was watching Morris rather narrowly and anxiously. But the moment Morris spoke this silent secret watcher popped back again out of sight.

"Well then I ask you as a personal favour," said he, "to continue being my steward. Why, it's good business for me, isn't it? In twenty years you make me ten thousand pounds, and I only pay you £200 a year for it. Please be kind, Mr.

Taynton, and continue making me rich. Oh, I'm a jolly hard-headed chap really; I know that it is to my advantage."

Mr. Taynton considered this a moment, playing with his wine glass. Then he looked up quickly.

"Yes, Morris, I will with pleasure do as you ask me," he said.

"Right oh. Thanks awfully. Do come and play billiards."

Morris was in amazing luck that night, and if, as he said, he had been playing a lot lately, the advantage of his practice was seen chiefly in the hideous certainty of his flukes, and the game (though he received twenty-five) left Mr. Taynton half a crown the poorer. Then the winner whirled his guest upstairs again to talk to his mother while he himself went round to the stables to assure himself of the well-being of the beloved motor. Martin had already valeted it, after its run, and was just locking up when Morris arrived.

Morris gave his orders for next day after a quite unnecessary examination into the internal economy of the beloved, and was just going back to the house, when he paused, remembering something.

"Oh Martin," he said, "while I am here, I want you to help in the house, you know at dinner and so on, just as you did to-night. And when there are guests of mine here I want you to look after them. For instance, when Mr. Taynton goes tonight you will be there to give him his hat and coat. You'll have rather a lot to do, I'm afraid."

Morris finished his cigarette and went back to the drawing-room where Mr. Taynton was already engaged in the staid excitements of backgammon with his mother. That game over, Morris took his place, and before long the lawyer rose to go.

"Now I absolutely refuse to let you interrupt your game," he said. "I have found my way out of this house often enough, I should think. Good night, Mrs. Assheton. Good night Morris; don't break your neck my dear boy, in trying to break records."

Morris hardly attended to this, for the game was critical. He just rang the bell, said good night, and had thrown again before the door had closed behind Mr. Taynton. Below, in answer to the bell, was standing his servant.

Mr. Taynton looked at him again with some attention, and then glanced round to see if the discreet parlour-maids were about.

"So you are called Martin now," he observed gently.

"Yes, sir."

"I recognised you at once."

There was a short pause.

"Are you going to tell Mr. Morris, sir?" he asked.

"That I had to dismiss you two years ago for theft?" said Mr. Taynton quietly. "No, not if you behave yourself."

Mr. Taynton looked at him again kindly and sighed.

"No, let bygones be bygones," he said. "You will find your secret is safe enough. And, Martin, I hope you have really turned over a new leaf, and are living honestly now. That is so, my lad? Thank God; thank God. My umbrella? Thanks. Good night. No cab: I will walk."

CHAPTER II

Mr. Taynton lived in a square, comfortable house in Montpellier Road, and thus, when he left Mrs. Assheton's there was some two miles of pavement and sea front between him and home. But the night was of wonderful beauty, a night of mid June, warm enough to make the most cautious secure of chill, and at the same time just made crisp with a little breeze that blew or rather whispered landward from over the full-tide of the sleeping sea. High up in the heavens swung a glorious moon, which cast its path of white enchanted light over the ripples, and seemed to draw the heart even as it drew the eyes heavenward. Mr. Taynton certainly, as he stepped out beneath the stars, with the sea lying below him, felt, in his delicate and sensitive nature, the charm of the hour, and being a good if not a brisk walker, he determined to go home on foot. And he stepped westward very contentedly.

The evening, it would appear, had much pleased him—for it was long before his smile of retrospective pleasure faded from his pleasant mobile face. Morris's trust and confidence in him had been extraordinarily pleasant to him: and modest and unassuming as he was, he could not help a secret gratification at the thought. What a handsome fellow Morris was too, how gay, how attractive! He had his father's dark colouring, and tall figure, but much of his mother's grace and charm had gone to the modelling of that thin sensitive mouth and the long oval of his face. Yet there was more of the father there, the father's intense, almost violent, vitality was somehow more characteristic of the essential Morris than face or feature.

What a happy thing it was too—here the smile of pleasure illuminated Mr. Taynton's face again—that the boy whom he had dismissed two years before for some petty pilfering in his own house, should have turned out such a promising lad and should have found his way to so pleasant a berth as that of factotum to Morris. Kindly and charitable all through and ever eager to draw out the good in everybody and forgive the bad, Mr. Taynton had often occasion to deplore the hardness and uncharity of a world which remembers youthful errors and hangs them, like a mill-stone, round the neck of the offender, and it warmed his heart and kindled his smile to think of one case at any rate where a youthful misdemeanour was lived down and forgotten. At the time he remembered being in doubt whether he should not give the offender up to justice, for the pilfering, petty though it had been, had been somewhat persistent, but he had taken the more merciful course, and merely dismissed the boy. He had been in two minds about it before, wondering whether it would not be better to let Martin have a sharp lesson, but to-night he was thankful that he had not done so. The mercy he had shown had come back to bless him also; he felt a glow of thankfulness that the subject of his clemency had turned out so well. Punishment often hardens the criminal, was one of his settled convictions. But Morris—again his thoughts went back to Morris, who was already standing on the verge of manhood, on the verge, too, he made no doubt of married life and its joys and responsibilities. Mr. Taynton was himself a bachelor, and the thought gave him not a moment of jealousy, but a moment of void that ached a little at the thought of the common human bliss which he had himself missed. How charming, too, was the girl Madge Templeton, whom he had met, not for the first time, that evening. He himself had guessed how things stood between the two before Morris had confided in him, and it pleased him that his intuition was confirmed. What a pity, however, that the two were not going to meet next day, that she was out with her mother and would not get back till late. It would have been a cooling thought in the hot office hours of to-morrow to picture them sitting together in the garden at Falmer, or under one of the cool deep-foliaged oaks in the park.

Then suddenly his face changed, the smile faded, but came back next instant and broadened with a laugh. And the man who laughs when he is by himself may certainly be supposed to have strong cause for amusement.

Mr. Taynton had come by this time to the West Pier, and a hundred yards farther would bring him to Montpellier Road. But it was yet early, as he saw (so bright was the moonlight) when he consulted his watch, and he retraced his steps some fifty yards, and eventually rang at the door of a big house of flats facing the sea, where his partner, who for the most part, looked after the London branch of their business, had his *pied-à-terre*. For the firm of Taynton and Mills was one of those respectable and solid businesses that, beginning in the country, had eventually been extended to town, and so far from its having its headquarters in town and its branch in Brighton, had its headquarters here and its branch in the metropolis. Mr. Godfrey Mills, so he learned at the door had dined alone, and was in, and without further delay Mr. Taynton was carried aloft in the gaudy bird-cage of the lift, feeling sure that his partner would see him.

The flat into which he was ushered with a smile of welcome from the man who opened the door was furnished with a sort of gross opulence that never failed to jar on Mr. Taynton's exquisite taste and cultivated mind. Pictures, chairs, sofas, the patterns of the carpet, and the heavy gilding of the cornices were all sensuous, a sort of frangipanni to the eye. The apparent contrast, however, between these things and their owner, was as great as that between Mr. Taynton and his partner, for Mr. Godfrey Mills was a thin, spare, dark little man, brisk in movement, with a look in his eye that betokened a watchfulness and vigilance of the most alert order. But useful as such a gift undoubtedly is, it was given to Mr. Godfrey Mills perhaps a shade too obviously. It would be unlikely that the stupidest or shallowest person would give himself away when talking to him, for it was so clear that he was always on the watch for admission or information that might be useful to him. He had, however, the charm that a very active and vivid mind always possesses, and though small and slight, he was a figure that would be noticed anywhere, so keen and wide-awake was his face. Beside him Mr. Taynton looked like a benevolent country clergyman, more distinguished for amiable qualities of the heart, than intellectual qualities of the head. Yet those—there were not many of them—who in dealings with the latter had tried to conduct their business on these assumptions, had invariably found it necessary to reconsider their first impression of him. His partner, however, was always conscious of a little impatience in talking to him; Taynton, he would have allowed, did not lack fine business qualities, but he was a little wanting in quickness.

Mills's welcome of him was abrupt.

"Pleased to see you," he said. "Cigar, drink? Sit down, won't you? What is it?"

"I dropped in for a chat on my way home," said Mr. Taynton. "I have been dining with Mrs. Assheton. A most pleasant evening. What a fine delicate face she has."

Mills bit off the end of a cigar.

"I take it that you did not come in merely to discuss the delicacy of Mrs. Assheton's face," he said.

"No, no, dear fellow; you are right to recall me. I too take it—I take it that you have found time to go over to Falmer yesterday. How did you find Sir Richard?"

"I found him well. I had a long talk with him."

"And you managed to convey something of those very painful facts which you felt it was your duty to bring to his notice?" asked Mr. Taynton.

Godfrey Mills laughed.

"I say, Taynton, is it really worth while keeping it up like this?" he asked. "It really saves so much trouble to talk straight, as I propose to do. I saw him, as I said, and I really managed remarkably well. I had these admissions wrung from me, I assure you it is no less than that, under promise of the most absolute secrecy. I told him young Assheton was leading an idle, extravagant, and dissipated life. I said I had seen him three nights ago in Piccadilly, not quite sober, in company with the class of person to whom one does not refer in polite society. Will that do?"

"Ah, I can easily imagine how painful you must have found—" began Taynton.

But his partner interrupted.

"It was rather painful; you have spoken a true word in jest. I felt a brute, I tell you. But, as I pointed out to you, something of the sort was necessary."

Mr. Taynton suddenly dropped his slightly clerical manner.

"You have done excellently, my dear friend," he said. "And as you pointed out to me, it was indeed necessary to do something of the sort. I think by now, your revelations have already begun to take effect. Yes, I think I will take a little brandy and soda. Thank you very much."

He got up with greater briskness than he had hitherto shown.

CHAPTER II

"And you are none too soon," he said. "Morris, poor Morris, such a handsome fellow, confided to me this evening that he was in love with Miss Templeton. He is very much in earnest."

"And why do you think my interview has met with some success?" asked Mills.

"Well, it is only a conjecture, but when Morris asked if he might call any time to-morrow, Miss Templeton (who was also dining with Mrs. Assheton) said that she and her mother would be out all day and not get home till late. It does not strike me as being too fanciful to see in that some little trace perhaps of your handiwork."

"Yes, that looks like me," said Mills shortly.

Mr. Taynton took a meditative sip at his brandy and soda.

"My evening also has not been altogether wasted," he said. "I played what for me was a bold stroke, for as you know, my dear fellow, I prefer to leave to your nimble and penetrating mind things that want dash and boldness. But to-night, yes, I was warmed with that wonderful port and was bold."

"What did you do?" asked Mills.

"Well, I asked, I almost implored dear Morris to give me two or three hours to-morrow and go through all the books, and satisfy himself everything is in order, and his investments well looked after. I told him also that the original £30,000 of his had, owing to judicious management, become £40,000. You see, that is unfortunately a thing past praying for. It is so indubitably clear from the earlier ledgers—"

"But the port must indeed have warmed you," said Mills quickly. "Why, it was madness! What if he had consented?"

Mr. Taynton smiled.

"Ah, well, I in my slow synthetic manner had made up my mind that it was really quite impossible that he should consent to go into the books and vouchers. To begin with, he has a new motor car, and every hour spent away from that car just now is to his mind an hour wasted. Also, I know him well. I knew that he would never consent to spend several hours over ledgers. Finally, even if he had, though I knew from what I know of him not that he would not but that he *could* not, I could have—I could have managed something. You see, he knows nothing whatever about business or investments."

Mills shook his head.

"But it was dangerous, anyhow," he said, "and I don't understand what object could be served by it. It was running a risk with no profit in view."

Then for the first time the inherent strength of the quietness of the one man as opposed to the obvious quickness and comprehension of the other came into play.

"I think that I disagree with you there, my dear fellow," said Mr. Taynton slowly, "though when I have told you all, I shall be of course, as always, delighted to recognise the superiority of your judgment, should you disagree with me, and convince me of the correctness of your view. It has happened, I know, a hundred times before that you with your quick intuitive perceptions have been right."

But his partner interrupted him. He quite agreed with the sentiment, but he wanted to learn without even the delay caused by these complimentary remarks, the upshot of Taynton's rash proposal to Morris.

"What did young Assheton say?" he asked.

"Well, my dear fellow," said Taynton, "though I have really no doubt that in principle I did a rash thing, in actual practice my step was justified, because Morris absolutely refused to look at the books. Of course I know the young fellow well: it argues no perspicuity on my part to have foreseen that. And, I am glad to say, something in my way of putting it, some sincerity of manner I suppose, gave rise to a fresh mark of confidence in us on his part."

Mr. Taynton cleared his throat; his quietness and complete absence of hurry was so to speak, rapidly overhauling the quick, nimble mind of the other.

"He asked me in fact to continue being steward of his affairs in any event. Should he marry to-morrow I feel no doubt that he would not spend a couple of minutes over his financial affairs, unless, *unless*, as you foresaw might happen, he had need of a large lump sum. In that case, my dear Mills, you and I would—would find it impossible to live elsewhere than in the Argentine Republic, were we so fortunate as to get there. But, as far as this goes I only say that the step of mine which you felt to be dangerous has turned out most auspiciously. He begged me, in fact, to continue even after he came of age, acting for him at my present rate of remuneration."

Mr. Mills was listening to this with some attention. Here he laughed dryly.

"That is capital, then," he said. "You were right and I was wrong. God, Taynton, it's your manner you know, there's something of the country parson about you that is wonderfully convincing. You seem sincere without being sanctimonious. Why, if I was to ask young Assheton to look into his affairs for himself, he would instantly think there was something wrong, and that I was trying bluff. But when you do the same thing, that simple and perfectly correct explanation never occurs to him."

"No, dear Morris trusts me very completely," said Taynton. "But, then, if I may continue my little review of the situation, as it now stands, you and your talk with Sir Richard have vastly decreased the danger of his marrying. For, to be frank, I should not feel at all secure if that happened. Miss Templeton is an heiress herself, and Morris might easily take it into his head to spend ten or fifteen thousand pounds in building a house or buying an estate, and though I think I have guarded against his requiring an account of our stewardship, I can't prevent his wishing to draw a large sum of money. But your brilliant manoeuvre may, we hope, effectually put a stop to the danger of his marrying Miss Templeton, and since I am convinced he is in love with her, why"—Mr. Taynton put his plump finger-tips together and raised his kind eyes to the ceiling—"why, the chance of his wanting to marry anybody else is postponed anyhow, till, till he has got over this unfortunate attachment. In fact, my dear fellow, there is no longer anything immediate to fear, and I feel sure that before many weeks are up, the misfortunes and ill luck which for the last two years have dogged us with such incredible persistency will be repaired."

Mills said nothing for the moment but splashed himself out a liberal allowance of brandy into his glass, and mixed it with a somewhat more carefully measured ration of soda. He was essentially a sober man, but that was partly due to the fact that his head was as impervious to alcohol as teak is to water, and it was his habit to indulge in two, and those rather stiff, brandies and sodas of an evening. He found that they assisted and clarified thought.

"I wish to heaven you hadn't found it necessary to let young Assheton know that his £30,000 had increased to £40,000," he said. "That's £10,000 more to get back."

"Ah, it was just that which gave him, so he thought, such good cause for reposing complete confidence in me," remarked Mr. Taynton. "But as you say, it is £10,000 more to get back, and I should not have told him, were not certain ledgers of earlier years so extremely, extremely unmistakable on the subject."

"But if he is not going to look at ledgers at all—" began Mills.

"Ah, the concealment of that sort of thing is one of the risks which it is not worth while to take," said the other, dropping for a moment the deferential attitude.

Mills was silent again. Then:

"Have you bought that option in Boston Coppers," he asked.

"Yes; I bought to-day."

Mills glanced at the clock as Mr. Taynton rose to go.

"Still only a quarter to twelve," he said. "If you have time, you might give me a detailed statement. I hardly know what you have done. It won't take a couple of minutes."

Mr. Taynton glanced at the clock likewise, and then put down his hat again.

"I can just spare the time," he said, "but I must get home by twelve; I have unfortunately come out without my latchkey, and I do not like keeping the servants up."

He pressed his fingers over his eyes a moment and then spoke.

* * * * *

Ten minutes later he was in the bird-cage of the lift again, and by twelve he had been admitted into his own house, apologising most amiably to his servant for having kept him up. There were a few letters for him and he opened and read those, then lit his bed-candle and went upstairs, but instead of undressing, sat for a full quarter of an hour in his armchair thinking. Then he spoke softly to himself.

"I think dear Mills means mischief in some way," he said. "But really for the moment it puzzles me to know what. However, I shall see tomorrow. Ah, I wonder if I guess!"

Then he went to bed, but contrary to custom did not get to sleep for a long time. But when he did there was a smile on his lips; a patient contented smile.

CHAPTER III

Mr. Taynton's statement to his partner, which had taken him so few minutes to give, was of course concerned only with the latest financial operation which he had just embarked in, but for the sake of the reader it will be necessary to go a little further back, and give quite shortly the main features of the situation in which he and his partner found themselves placed.

Briefly then, just two years ago, at the time peace was declared in South Africa, the two partners of Taynton and Mills had sold out £30,000 of Morris Assheton's securities, which owing to their excellent management was then worth £40,000, and seeing a quite unrivalled opportunity of making their fortunes, had become heavy purchasers of South African mines, for they reasoned that with peace once declared it was absolutely certain that prices would go up. But, as is sometimes the way with absolute certainties, the opposite had happened and they had gone down. They cut their loss, however, and proceeded to buy American rails. In six months they had entirely repaired the damage, and seeing further unrivalled opportunities from time to time, in buying motorcar shares, in running a theatre and other schemes, had managed a month ago to lose all that was left of the £30,000. Being, therefore, already so deeply committed, it was mere prudence, the mere instinct of self-preservation that had led them to sell out the remaining £10,000, and to-day Mr. Taynton had bought an option in Boston Copper with it. The manner of an option is as follows:

Boston Copper to-day was quoted at £5 10S 6d, and by paying a premium of twelve shillings and sixpence per share, they were entitled to buy Boston Copper shares any time within the next three months at a price of £6 3s. Supposing therefore (as Mr. Taynton on very good authority had supposed) that Boston Copper, a rapidly improving company, rose a couple of points within the next three months, and so stood at £7 10S 6d; he had the right of exercising his option and buying them at £6 3S thus making £1 7S 6d per share. But a higher rise than this was confidently expected, and Taynton, though not really of an over sanguine disposition, certainly hoped to make good the greater part if not all of their somewhat large defalcations. He had bought an option of 20,000 shares, the option of which cost (or would cost at the end of those months) rather over £10,000. In other words, the moment that the shares rose to a price higher than £6 3s, all further appreciation was pure gain. If they did not rise so high, he would of course not exercise the option, and sacrifice the money.

CHAPTER III

That was certainly a very unpleasant thing to contemplate, but it had been more unpleasant when, so far as he knew, Morris was on the verge of matrimony, and would then step into the management of his own affairs. But bad though it all was, the situation had certainly been immensely ameliorated this evening, since on the one hand his partner had, it was not unreasonable to hope, said to Madge's father things about Morris that made his marriage with Madge exceedingly unlikely, while on the other hand, even if it happened, his affairs, according to his own wish, would remain in Mr. Taynton's hands with the same completeness as heretofore. It would, of course, be necessary to pay him his income, and though this would be a great strain on the finances of the two partners, it was manageable. Besides (Mr. Taynton sincerely hoped that this would not be necessary) the money which was Mrs. Assheton's for her lifetime was in his hands also, so if the worst came to the worst—

Now the composition and nature of the extraordinary animal called man is so unexpected and unlikely that any analysis of Mr. Taynton's character may seem almost grotesque. It is a fact nevertheless that his was a nature capable of great things, it is also a fact that he had long ago been deeply and bitterly contrite for the original dishonesty of using the money of his client. But by aid of those strange perversities of nature, he had by this time honestly and sincerely got to regard all their subsequent employments of it merely as efforts on his part to make right an original wrong. He wanted to repair his fault, and it seemed to him that to commit it again was the only means at his disposal for doing so. A strain, too, of Puritan piety was bound up in the constitution of his soul, and in private life he exercised high morality, and was also kind and charitable. He belonged to guilds and societies that had as their object the improvement and moral advancement of young men. He was a liberal patron of educational schemes, he sang a fervent and fruity tenor in the choir of St. Agnes, he was a regular communicant, his nature looked toward good, and turned its eyes away from evil. To do him justice he was not a hypocrite, though, if all about him were known, and a plebiscite taken, it is probable that he would be unanimously condemned. Yet the universal opinion would be wrong: he was no hypocrite, but only had the bump of self-preservation enormously developed. He had cheated and swindled, but he was genuinely opposed to cheating and swindling. He was cheating and swindling now, in buying the option of Boston Copper. But he did not know that: he wanted to repair the original wrong, to hand back to Morris his fortune unimpaired, and also to save himself. But of these two wants, the second, it must be confessed, was infinitely the stronger. To save himself there was perhaps nothing that he would stick at. However, it was his constant wish and prayer that he might not be led into temptation. He knew well what his particular temptation was, namely this instinct of self-preservation, and constantly thought and meditated about it. He knew that he was hardly himself when the stress of it came on him; it was like a possession.

Mills, though an excellent partner and a man of most industrious habits, had, so Mr. Taynton would have admitted, one little weak spot. He never was at the office till rather late in the morning. True, when he came, he soon made up for lost time, for he was possessed, as we have seen, of a notable quickness and agility of mind, but sometimes Taynton found that he was himself forced to be idle till Mills turned up, if his signature or what not was required for papers before work could be further proceeded with. This, in fact, was the case next morning, and from half past eleven Mr. Taynton had to sit idly in his office, as far as the work of the firm was concerned until his partner arrived. It was a little tiresome that this should happen to-day, because there was nothing else that need detain him, except those deeds for the execution of which his partner's signature was necessary, and he could, if only Mills had been punctual, have gone out to Rottingdean before lunch, and inspected the Church school there in the erection of which he had taken so energetic an interest. Timmins, however, the gray-haired old head clerk, was in the office with him, and Mr. Taynton always liked a chat with Timmins.

"And the grandson just come home, has he Mr. Timmins?" he was saying. "I must come and see him. Why he'll be six years old, won't he, by now?"

"Yes, sir, turned six."

"Dear me, how time goes on! The morning is going on, too, and still Mr. Mills isn't here."

He took a quill pen and drew a half sheet of paper toward him, poised his pen a moment and then wrote quickly.

"What a pity I can't sign for him," he said, passing his paper over to the clerk. "Look at that; now even you, Timmins, though you have seen Mr. Mills's handwriting ten thousand times, would be ready to swear that the signature was his, would you not?"

Timmins looked scrutinisingly at it.

"Well, I'm sure, sir! What a forger you would have made!" he said admiringly. "I would have sworn that was Mr. Mills's own hand of write. It's wonderful, sir."

Mr. Taynton sighed, and took the paper again.

"Yes, it is like, isn't it?" he said, "and it's so easy to do. Luckily forgers don't know the way to forge properly."

"And what might that be, sir?" asked Timmins.

"Why, to throw yourself mentally into the nature of the man whose handwriting you wish to forge. Of course one has to know the handwriting thoroughly well, but if one does that one just has to visualise it, and then, as I said, project oneself into the other, not laboriously copy the handwriting. Let's try another. Ah, who is that letter from? Mrs. Assheton isn't it. Let me look at the signature just once again."

Mr. Taynton closed his eyes a moment after looking at it. Then he took his quill, and wrote quickly.

"You would swear to that, too, would you not, Timmins?" he asked.

"Why, God bless me yes, sir," said he. "Swear to it on the book."

The door opened and as Godfrey Mills came in, Mr. Taynton tweaked the paper out of Timmins's hand, and tore it up. It might perhaps seem strange to dear Mills that his partner had been forging his signature, though only in jest.

CHAPTER III

"'Fraid I'm rather late," said Mills.

"Not at all, my dear fellow," said Taynton without the slightest touch of ill-humour. "How are you? There's very little to do; I want your signature to this and this, and your careful perusal of that. Mrs. Assheton's letter? No, that only concerns me; I have dealt with it."

A quarter of an hour was sufficient, and at the end Timmins carried the papers away leaving the two partners together. Then, as soon as the door closed, Mills spoke.

"I've been thinking over our conversation of last night," he said, "and there are some points I don't think you have quite appreciated, which I should like to put before you."

Something inside Mr. Taynton's brain, the same watcher perhaps who looked at Morris so closely the evening before, said to him. "He is going to try it on." But it was not the watcher but his normal self that answered. He beamed gently on his partner.

"My dear fellow, I might have been sure that your quick mind would have seen new aspects, new combinations," he said.

Mills leaned forward over the table.

"Yes, I have seen new aspects, to adopt your words," he said, "and I will put them before you. These financial operations, shall we call them, have been going on for two years now, have they not? You began by losing a large sum in South Africans—"

"We began," corrected Mr. Taynton, gently. He was looking at the other quite calmly; his face expressed no surprise at all; if there was anything in his expression beyond that of quiet kindness, it was perhaps pity.

"I said 'you,'" said Mills in a hectoring tone, "and I will soon explain why. You lost a large sum in South Africans, but won it back again in Americans. You then again, and again contrary to my advice, embarked in perfect wild-cat affairs, which ended in our—I say 'our' here—getting severely scratched and mauled. Altogether you have frittered away £30,000, and have placed the remaining ten in a venture which to my mind is as wild as all the rest of your unfortunate ventures. These speculations have, almost without exception, been choices of your own, not mine. That was *one* of the reasons why I said 'you,' not 'we.'"

He paused a moment.

"Another reason is," he said, "because without any exception the transactions have taken place on your advice and in your name, not in mine."

That was a sufficiently meaning statement, but Mills did not wish his partner to be under any misapprehension as to what he implied.

"In other words," he said, "I can deny absolutely all knowledge of the whole of those operations."

Mr. Taynton gave a sudden start, as if the significance of this had only this moment dawned on him, as if he had not understood the first statement. Then he seemed to collect himself.

"You can hardly do that," he said, "as I hold letters of yours which imply such knowledge."

Mills smiled rather evilly.

"Ah, it is not worth while bluffing," he said. "I have never written such a letter to you. You know it. Is it likely I should?"

Mr. Taynton apparently had no reply to this. But he had a question to ask.

"Why are you taking up this hostile and threatening attitude?"

"I have not meant to be hostile, and I have certainly not threatened," replied Mills. "I have put before you, quite dispassionately I hope, certain facts. Indeed I should say it was you who had threatened in the matter of those letters, which, unhappily, have never existed at all. I will proceed.

"Now what has been my part in this affair? I have observed you lost money in speculations of which I disapproved, but you always knew best. I have advanced money to you before now to tide over embarrassments that would otherwise have been disastrous. By the exercise of diplomacy—or lying—yesterday, I averted a very grave danger. I point out to you also that there is nothing to implicate me in these—these fraudulent employments of a client's money. So I ask, where I come in? What do I get by it?"

Mr. Taynton's hands were trembling as he fumbled at some papers on his desk.

"You know quite well that we are to share all profits?" he said.

"Yes, but at present there have not been any. I have been, to put it plainly, pulling you out of holes. And I think—I think my trouble ought to be remunerated. I sincerely hope you will take that view also. Or shall I remind you again that there is nothing in the world to connect me with these, well, frauds?"

Mr. Taynton got up from his chair, strolled across to the window where he drew down the blind a little, so as to shut out the splash of sunlight that fell on his table.

"You have been betting again, I suppose," he asked quietly.

"Yes, and have been unfortunate. Pray do not trouble to tell me again how foolish it is to gamble like that. You may be right. I have no doubt you are right. But I think one has as much right to gamble with one's own money as to do so with the money of other people."

This apparently seemed unanswerable; anyhow Mr. Taynton made no reply. Then, having excluded the splash of sunlight he sat down again.

"You have not threatened, you tell me," he said, "but you have pointed out to me that there is no evidence that you have had a hand in certain transactions. You say that I know you have helped me in these transactions; you say you require remuneration for your services. Does not that, I ask, imply a threat? Does it not mean that you are blackmailing me? Else why should you bring these facts—I do not dispute them—to my notice? Supposing I refuse you remuneration?"

Mills had noted the signs of agitation and anxiety. He felt that he was on safe ground. The blackmailer lives entirely on the want of courage in his victims.

CHAPTER III

"You will not, I hope, refuse me remuneration," he said. "I have not threatened you yet, because I feel sure you will be wise. I might, of course, subsequently threaten you."

Again there was silence. Mr. Taynton had picked up a quill pen, the same with which he had been writing before, for the nib was not yet dry.

"The law is rather severe on blackmailers," he remarked.

"It is. Are you going to bring an action against me for blackmail? Will not that imply the re-opening of—of certain ledgers, which we agreed last night had better remain shut?"

Again there was silence. There was a completeness in this reasoning which rendered comment superfluous.

"How much do you want?" asked Mr. Taynton.

Mills was not so foolish as to "breathe a sigh of relief." But he noted with satisfaction that there was no sign of fight in his adversary and partner.

"I want two thousand pounds," he said, "at once."

"That is a large sum."

"It is. If it were a small sum I should not trouble you."

Mr. Taynton again got up and strayed aimlessly about the room.

"I can't give it you to-day," he said. "I shall have to sell out some stock."

"I am not unreasonable about a reasonable delay," said Mills.

"You are going to town this afternoon?"

"Yes, I must. There is a good deal of work to be done. It will take me all to-morrow."

"And you will be back the day after to-morrow?"

"Yes, I shall be back here that night, that is to say, I shall not get away from town till the afternoon. I should like your definite answer then, if it is not inconvenient. I could come and see you that night, the day after to-morrow—if you wished."

Mr. Taynton thought over this with his habitual deliberation.

"You will readily understand that all friendly relations between us are quite over," he said. "You have done a cruel and wicked thing, but I don't see how I can resist it. I should like, however, to have a little further talk about it, for which I have not time now."

Mills rose.

"By all means," he said. "I do not suppose I shall be back here till nine in the evening. I have had no exercise lately, and I think very likely I shall get out of the train at Falmer, and walk over the downs."

Mr. Taynton's habitual courtesy came to his aid. He would have been polite to a thief or a murderer, if he met him socially.

"Those cool airs of the downs are very invigorating." he said. "I will not expect you therefore till half past nine that night. I shall dine at home, and be alone."

"Thanks. I must be going. I shall only just catch my train to town."

Mills nodded a curt gesture of farewell, and left the room, and when he had gone Mr. Taynton sat down again in the chair by the table, and remained there some half hour. He knew well the soundness of his partner's reasoning; all he had said was fatally and abominably true. There was no way out of it. Yet to pay money to a blackmailer was, to the legal mind, a confession of guilt. Innocent people, unless they were abject fools, did not pay blackmail. They prosecuted the blackmailer. Yet here, too, Mills's simple reasoning held good. He could not prosecute the blackmailer, since he was not in the fortunate position of being innocent. But if you paid a blackmailer once, you were for ever in his power. Having once yielded, it was necessary to yield again. He must get some assurance that no further levy would take place. He must satisfy himself that he would be quit of all future danger from this quarter. Yet from whence was such assurance to come? He might have it a hundred times over in Godfrey Mills's handwriting, but he could never produce that as evidence, since again the charge of fraudulent employment of clients' money would be in the air. No doubt, of course, the blackmailer would be sentenced, but the cause of blackmail would necessarily be public. No, there was no way out.

Two thousand pounds, though! Frugally and simply as he lived, that was to him a dreadful sum, and represented the savings of at least eighteen months. This meant that there was for him another eighteen months of work, just when he hoped to see his retirement coming close to him. Mills demanded that he should work an extra year and a half, and out of those few years that in all human probability still remained to him in this pleasant world. Yet there was no way out!

Half an hour's meditation convinced him of this, and, as was his sensible plan, when a thing was inevitable, he never either fought against it nor wasted energy in regretting it. And he went slowly out of the office into which he had come so briskly an hour or two before. But his face expressed no sign of disquieting emotion; he nodded kindly to Timmins, and endorsed his desire to be allowed to come and see the grandson. If anything was on his mind, or if he was revolving some policy for the future, it did not seem to touch or sour that kindly, pleasant face.

CHAPTER IV

Mr. Taynton did not let these very unpleasant occurrences interfere with the usual and beneficent course of his life, but faced the crisis with that true bravery that not only meets a thing without flinching, but meets it with the higher courage of cheerfulness, serenity and ordinary behaviour. He spent the rest of the day in fact in his usual manner, enjoying his bathe before lunch, his hour of the paper and the quiet cigar afterward, his stroll over the springy turf of the downs, and he enjoyed also the couple of hours of work that brought him to dinner time. Then afterward he spent his evening, as was his weekly custom, at the club for young men which he had founded, where instead of being exposed to the evening lures of the sea-front and the public house, they could spend (on payment of a really nominal subscription) a quieter and more innocent hour over chess, bagatelle and the illustrated papers, or if more energetically disposed, in the airy gymnasium adjoining the reading-room, where they could indulge in friendly rivalry with boxing gloves or single-stick, or feed the appetites of their growing muscles with dumb-bells and elastic contrivances. Mr. Taynton had spent a couple of hours there, losing a game of chess to one youthful adversary, but getting back his laurels over bagatelle, and before he left, had arranged for a geological expedition to visit, on the Whitsuntide bank holiday next week, the curious raised beach which protruded so remarkably from the range of chalk downs some ten miles away.

On returning home, it is true he had deviated a little from his usual habits, for instead of devoting the half-hour before bed-time to the leisurely perusal of the evening paper, he had merely given it one glance, observing that copper was strong and that Boston Copper in particular had risen half a point, and had then sat till bed-time doing nothing whatever, a habit to which he was not generally addicted.

He was seated in his office next morning and was in fact on the point of leaving for his bathe, for this hot genial June was marching on its sunny way uninterrupted by winds or rain, when Mr. Timmins, after discreetly tapping, entered, and closed the door behind him.

"Mr. Morris Assheton, sir, to see you," he said. "I said I would find out if you were disengaged, and could hardly restrain him from coming in with me. The young gentleman seems very excited and agitated. Hardly himself, sir."

"Indeed, show him in," said Mr. Taynton.

A moment afterward the door burst open and banged to again behind Morris. High colour flamed in his face, his black eyes sparkled with vivid dangerous light, and he had no salutation for his old friend.

"I've come on a very unpleasant business," he said, his voice not in control.

Mr. Taynton got up. He had only had one moment of preparation and he thought, at any rate, that he knew for certain what this unpleasant business must be. Evidently Mills had given him away. For what reason he had done so he could not guess; after his experience of yesterday it might have been from pure devilry, or again he might have feared that in desperation, Taynton would take that extreme step of prosecuting him for blackmail. But, for that moment Taynton believed that Morris's agitation must be caused by this, and it says much for the iron of his nerve that he did not betray himself by a tremor.

"My dear Morris," he said, "I must ask you to pull yourself together. You are out of your own control. Sit down, please, and be silent for a minute. Then tell me calmly what is the matter."

Morris sat down as he was told, but the calmness was not conspicuous.

"Calm?" he said. "Would you be calm in my circumstances, do you think?"

"You have not yet told me what they are," said Mr. Taynton.

"I've just seen Madge Templeton," he said. "I met her privately by appointment. And she told me—she told me—"

Master of himself though he was, Mr. Taynton had one moment of physical giddiness, so complete and sudden was the revulsion and reaction that took place in his brain. A moment before he had known, he thought, for certain that his own utter ruin was imminent. Now he knew that it was not that, and though he had made one wrong conjecture as to what the unpleasant business was, he did not think that his second guess was far astray.

"Take your time, Morris," he said. "And, my dear boy, try to calm yourself. You say I should not be calm in your circumstances. Perhaps I should not, but I should make an effort. Tell me everything slowly, omitting nothing."

This speech, combined with the authoritative personality of Mr. Taynton, had an extraordinary effect on Morris. He sat quiet a moment or two, then spoke.

"Yes, you are quite right," he said, "and after all I have only conjecture to go on yet, and I have been behaving as if it was proved truth. God! if it is proved to be true, though, I'll expose him, I'll—I'll horsewhip him, I'll murder him!"

Mr. Taynton slapped the table with his open hand.

"Now, Morris, none of these wild words," he said. "I will not listen to you for a moment, if you do not control yourself."

Once again, and this time more permanently the man's authority asserted itself. Morris again sat silent for a time, then spoke evenly and quietly.

"Two nights ago you were dining with us," he said, "and Madge was there. Do you remember my asking her if I might come to see them, and she said she and her mother would be out all day?"

"Yes; I remember perfectly," said Mr. Taynton.

CHAPTER IV

"Well, yesterday afternoon I was motoring by the park, and I saw Madge sitting on the lawn. I stopped the motor and watched. She sat there for nearly an hour, and then Sir Richard came out of the house and they walked up and down the lawn together."

"Ah, you must have been mistaken," said Mr. Taynton. "I know the spot you mean on the road, where you can see the lawn, but it's half a mile off. It must have been some friend of hers perhaps staying in the house."

Morris shook his head.

"I was not mistaken," he said. "For yesterday evening I got a note from her, saying she had posted it secretly, but that she must see me, though she was forbidden to do so, or to hold any communication with me."

"Forbidden?" ejaculated Mr. Taynton.

"Yes, forbidden. Well, this morning I went to the place she named, outside on the downs beyond the park gate and saw her. Somebody has been telling vile lies about me to her father. I think I know who it is."

Mr. Taynton held up his hand.

"Stop," he said, "let us have your conjecture afterward. Tell me first not what you guess, but what happened. Arrange it all in your mind, tell it me as connectedly as you can."

Morris paused a moment.

"Well, I met Madge as I told you, and this was her story. Three days ago she and her father and mother were at lunch, and they had been talking in the most friendly way about me, and it was arranged to ask me to spend all yesterday with them. Madge, as you know, the next night was dining with us, and it was agreed that she should ask me verbally. After lunch she and her father went out riding, and when they returned they found that your partner Mills, had come to call. He stayed for tea, and after tea had a talk alone with Sir Richard, while she and her mother sat out on the lawn. Soon after he had gone, Sir Richard sent for Lady Templeton, and it was nearly dressing-time when she left him again. She noticed at dinner that both her father and mother seemed very grave, and when Madge went up to bed, her mother said that perhaps they had better not ask me over, as there was some thought of their being away all day. Also if I suggested coming over, when Madge dined with us, she was to give that excuse. That was all she was told for the time being."

Morris paused again.

"You are telling this very clearly and well, my dear boy," said the lawyer, very gravely and kindly.

"It is so simple," said he with a biting emphasis. "Then next morning after breakfast her father sent for her. He told her that they had learned certain things about me which made them think it better not to see any more of me. What they were, she was not told, but, I was not, it appeared, the sort of person with whom they chose to associate. Now, before God, those things that they were told, whatever they were, were lies. I lead a straight and sober life."

Mr. Taynton was attending very closely.

"Thank God, Madge did not believe a word of it," said Morris, his face suddenly flushing, "and like a brick, and a true friend she wrote at once to me, as I said, in order to tell me all this. We talked over, too, who it could have been who had said these vile things to her father. There was only one person who could. She had ridden with her father till tea-time. Then came your partner. Sir Richard saw nobody else; nobody else called that afternoon; no post came in."

Mr. Taynton had sprung up and was walking up and down the room in great agitation.

"I can't believe that," he said. "There must be some other explanation. Godfrey Mills say those things about you! It is incredible. My dear boy, until it is proved, you really must not let yourself believe that to be possible. You can't believe such wickedness against a man, one, too, whom I have known and trusted for years, on no evidence. There is no direct evidence yet. Let us leave that alone for the moment. What are you going to do now?"

"I came here to see him," said Morris. "But I am told he is away. So I thought it better to tell you."

"Yes, quite right. And what else?"

"I have written to Sir Richard, demanding, in common justice, that he should see me, should tell me what he has heard against me, and who told him. I don't think he will refuse. I don't see how he can refuse. I have asked him to see me tomorrow afternoon."

Mr. Taynton mentally examined this in all its bearings. Apparently it satisfied him.

"You have acted wisely and providently," he said. "But I want to beg you, until you have definite information, to forbear from thinking that my dear Mills could conceivably have been the originator of these scandalous tales, tales which I know from my knowledge of you are impossible to be true. From what I know of him, however, it is impossible he could have said such things. I cannot believe him capable of a mean or deceitful action, and that he should be guilty of such unfathomable iniquity is simply out of the question. You must assume him innocent till his guilt is proved."

"But who else could it have been?" cried Morris, his voice rising again.

"It could not have been he," said Taynton firmly.

There was a long silence; then Morris rose.

"There is one thing more," he said, "which is the most important of all. This foul scandal about me, of course, I know will be cleared up, and I shall be competent to deal with the offender. But—but Madge and I said other things to each other. I told her what I told you, that I loved her. And she loves me."

The sternness, the trouble, the anxiety all melted from Mr. Taynton's face.

"Ah, my dear fellow, my dear fellow," he said with outstretched hands. "Thank you for telling me. I am delighted, overjoyed, and indeed, as you say, that is far more important than anything else. My dear Morris, and is not your mother charmed?"

Morris shook his head.

CHAPTER IV

"I have not told her yet, and I shall not till this is cleared up. It is her birthday the day after to-morrow; perhaps I shall be able to tell her then."

He rose.

"I must go," he said. "And I will do all I can to keep my mind off accusing him, until I know. But when I think of it, I see red."

Mr. Taynton patted his shoulder affectionately.

"I should have thought that you had got something to think about, which would make it easy for you to prevent your thoughts straying elsewhere," he said.

"I shall need all the distractions I can get," said Morris rather grimly.

* * * * *

Morris walked quickly back along the sea front toward Sussex Square, and remembered as he went that he had not yet bought any gift for his mother on her birthday. There was something, too, which she had casually said a day or two ago that she wanted, what was it? Ah, yes, a new blotting-book for her writing-table in the drawing-room. The shop she habitually dealt at for such things, a branch of Asprey's, was only a few yards farther on, and he turned in to make inquiries as to whether she had ordered it. It appeared that she had been in that very morning, but the parcel had not been sent yet. So Morris, taking the responsibility on himself, counterordered the plain red morocco book she had chosen, and chose another, with fine silver scrollwork at the corners. He ordered, too, that a silver lettered inscription should be put on it. "H.A. from M.A." with the date, two days ahead, "June 24th, 1905." This he gave instructions should be sent to the house on the morning of June 24th, the day after to-morrow. He wished it to be sent so as to arrive with the early post on that morning.

* * * * *

The promise which Morris had made his old friend not to let his thoughts dwell on suspicion and conjecture as yet uncertain of foundation was one of those promises which are made in absolute good faith, but which in their very nature cannot be kept. The thought of the hideous treachery, the gratuitous falsehood, of which, in his mind, he felt convinced Godfrey Mills had been guilty was like blood soaking through a bandage. All that he could do was to continue putting on fresh bandages—that was all of his promise that he was able to fulfil, and in spite of the bandages the blood stained and soaked its way through. In the afternoon he took out the motor, but his joy in it for the time was dead, and it was only because in the sense of pace and swift movement he hoped to find a narcotic to thought, that he went out at all. But there was no narcotic there, nor even in the thought of this huge joy of love that had dawned on him was there forgetfulness for all else, joy and sorrow and love, were for the present separated from him by these hideous and libellous things that had been said about him. Until they were removed, until they passed into non-existence again, nothing had any significance for him. Everything was coloured with them; bitterness as of blood tinged everything. Hours, too, must pass before they could be removed; this long midsummer day had to draw to its end, night had to pass; the hour of early dawn, the long morning had to be numbered with the past before he could even learn who was responsible for this poisoned tale.

And when he learned, or rather when his conjecture was confirmed as to who it was (for his supposition was conjecture in the sense that it only wanted the actual seal of reality on it) what should he do next? Or rather what must he do next? He felt that when he knew absolutely for certain who had said this about him, a force of indignation and hatred, which at present he kept chained up, must infallibly break its chain, and become merely a wild beast let loose. He felt he would be no longer responsible for what he did, something had to happen; something more than mere apology or retraction of words. To lie and slander like that was a crime, an insult against human and divine justice. It would be nothing for the criminal to say he was sorry; he had to be punished. A man who did that was not fit to live; he was a man no longer, he was a biting, poisonous reptile, who for the sake of the community must be expunged. Yet human justice which hanged people for violent crimes committed under great provocation, dealt more lightly with this far more devilish thing, a crime committed coldly and calculatingly, that had planned not the mere death of his body, but the disgrace and death of his character. Godfrey Mills—he checked the word and added to himself "if it was he"—had morally tried to kill him.

Morris, after his interview that morning with Mr. Taynton, had lunched alone in Sussex Square, his mother having gone that day up to London for two nights. His plan had been to go up with her, but he had excused himself on the plea of business with his trustees, and she had gone alone. Directly after lunch he had taken the motor out, and had whirled along the coast road, past Rottingdean through Newhaven and Seaford, and ten miles farther until the suburbs of Eastbourne had begun. There he turned, his thoughts still running a mill-race in his head, and retracing his road had by now come back to within a mile of Brighton again. The sun gilded the smooth channel, the winds were still, the hot midsummer afternoon lay heavy on the land. Then he stopped the motor and got out, telling Martin to wait there.

He walked over the strip of velvety down grass to the edge of the white cliffs, and there sat down. The sea below him whispered and crawled, above the sun was the sole tenant of the sky, and east and west the down was empty of passengers. He, like his soul, was alone, and alone he had to think these things out.

Yes, this liar and slanderer, whoever he was, had tried to kill him. The attempt had been well-planned too, for the chances had been a thousand to one in favour of the murderer. But the one chance had turned up, Madge had loved him, and she had been brave, setting at defiance the order of her father, and had seen him secretly, and told him all the circumstances of this attack on him. But supposing she had been just a shade less brave, supposing her filial obedience had weighed an ounce heavier? Then he would never have known anything about it. The result would simply have been, as it was meant to be, that the Templetons were out when he called. There would have been a change of subject in their rooms when his name was mentioned, other people would have vaguely gathered that Mr.

Morris Assheton's name was not productive of animated conversation; their gatherings would have spread further, while he himself, ignorant of all cause, would have encountered cold shoulders.

Morris's hands clutched at the short down grass, tearing it up and scattering it. He was helpless, too, unless he took the law into his own hands. It would do no good, young as he was, he knew that, to bring any action for defamation of character, since the world only says, if a man justifies himself by the only legal means in his power, "There must have been something in it, since it was said!" No legal remedy, no fines or even imprisonment, far less apology and retraction satisfied justice. There were only two courses open: one to regard the slander as a splash of mud thrown by some vile thing that sat in the gutter, and simply ignore it; the other to do something himself, to strike, to hit, with his bodily hands, whatever the result of his violence was.

He felt his shoulder-muscles rise and brace themselves at the thought, all the strength and violence of his young manhood, with its firm sinews and supple joints, told him that it was his willing and active servant and would do his pleasure. He wanted to smash the jaw bone that had formed these lies, and he wanted the world to know he had done so. Yet that was not enough, he wanted to throttle the throat from which the words had come; the man ought to be killed; it was right to kill him just as it was right to kill a poisonous snake that somehow disguised itself as a man, and was received into the houses of men.

Indeed, should Morris be told, as he felt sure he would be, who his slanderer and defamer was, that gentleman would be wise to keep out of his way with him in such a mood. There was danger and death abroad on this calm hot summer afternoon.

CHAPTER V

It was about four o'clock on the afternoon of the following day, and Mr. Taynton was prolonging his hour of quietude after lunch, and encroaching thereby into the time he daily dedicated to exercise. It was but seldom that he broke into the routine of habits so long formed, and indeed the most violent rain or snow of winter, the most cutting easterly blasts of March, never, unless he had some definite bodily ailment, kept him indoors or deprived him of his brisk health-giving trudge over the downs or along the sea front. But occasionally when the weather was unusually hot, he granted himself the indulgence of sitting still instead of walking, and certainly to-day the least lenient judge might say that there were strong extenuating circumstances in his favour. For the heat of the past week had been piling itself up, like the heaped waters of flood and this afternoon was intense in its heat, its stillness and sultriness. It had been sunless all day, and all day the blanket of clouds that beset the sky had been gathering themselves into blacker and more ill-omened density. There would certainly be a thunderstorm before morning, and the approach of it made Mr. Taynton feel that he really had not the energy to walk. By and by perhaps he might be tempted to go in quest of coolness along the sea front, or perhaps later in the evening he might, as he sometimes did, take a carriage up on to the downs, and come gently home to a late supper. He would have time for that to-day, for according to arrangement his partner was to drop in about half past nine that evening. If he got back at nine, supposing he went at all, he would have time to have some food before receiving him.

He sat in a pleasant parquetted room looking out into the small square garden at the back of his house in Montpellier Road. Big awnings stretched from the window over the broad gravel path outside, and in spite of the excessive heat the room was full of dim coolness. There was but little furniture in it, and it presented the strongest possible contrast to the appointments of his partner's flat with its heavy decorations, its somewhat gross luxury. A few water-colours hung on the white walls, a few Persian rugs strewed the floor, a big bookcase with china on the top filled one end of the room, his writing-table, a half dozen of Chippendale chairs, and the chintz-covered sofa where he now lay practically completed the inventory of the room. Three or four bronzes, a Narcissus, a fifteenth-century Italian St. Francis, and a couple of Greek reproductions stood on the chimney-piece, but the whole room breathed an atmosphere of aesthetic asceticism.

Since lunch Mr. Taynton had glanced at the paper, and also looked up the trains from Lewes in order to assure himself that he need not expect his partner till half past nine, and since then, though his hands and his eyes had been idle, his mind had been very busy. Yet for all its business, he had not arrived at much. Morris, Godfrey Mills, and himself; he had placed these three figures in all sorts of positions in his mind, and yet every combination of them was somehow terrible and menacing. Try as he would he could not construct a peaceful or secure arrangement of them. In whatever way he grouped them there was danger.

The kitchen passage ran out at right angles to the room in which he sat, and formed one side of the garden. The windows in it were high up, so that it did not overlook the flowerbeds, and on this torrid afternoon they were all fully open. Suddenly from just inside came the fierce clanging peal of a bell, which made him start from his recumbent position. It was the front-door bell, as he knew, and as it continued ringing as if a maniac's grip was on the handle, he heard the steps of his servant running along the stone floor of the passage to see what imperative summons this was. Then, as the front door was opened, the bell ceased as suddenly as it had begun, and the moment afterward he heard Morris's voice shrill and commanding.

"But he has got to see me," he cried, "What's the use of you going to ask if he will?"

Mr. Taynton went to the door of his room which opened into the hall.

"Come in, Morris," he said.

Though it had been Morris's hand which had raised so uncontrolled a clamour, and his voice that just now had been so uncontrolled, there was no sign, when the door of Mr. Taynton's room had closed behind them, that there was any excitement of any sort raging within him. He sat down at once in a chair opposite the window, and Mr. Taynton saw that in spite of the heat of the day and the violence of that storm which he knew was yelling and screaming through his brain, his face was absolutely white. He sat with his hands on the arms of the Chippendale chair, and they too were quite still.

"I have seen Sir Richard," said he, "and I came back at once to see you. He has told me everything. Godfrey Mills has been lying about me and slandering me."

Mr. Taynton sat down heavily on the sofa.

"No, no; don't say it, don't say it," he murmured. "It can't be true, I can't believe it."

"But it is true, and you have got to believe it. He suggested that you should go and talk it over with him. I will drive you up in the car, if you wish—"

Mr. Taynton waved his hand with a negative gesture.

"No, no, not at once," he cried. "I must think it over. I must get used to this dreadful, this appalling shock. I am utterly distraught."

Morris turned to him, and across his face for one moment there shot, swift as a lightning-flash, a quiver of rage so rabid that he looked scarcely human, but like some Greek presentment of the Furies or Revenge. Never, so thought his old friend, had he seen such glorious youthful beauty so instinct and inspired with hate. It was the demoniacal force of that which lent such splendour to it. But it passed in a second, and Morris still very pale, very quiet spoke to him.

"Where is he?" he asked. "I must see him at once. It won't keep."

Then he sprang up, his rage again mastering him.

"What shall I do it with?" he said. "What shall I do it with?"

For the moment Mr. Taynton forgot himself and his anxieties.

"Morris, you don't know what you are saying," he cried. "Thank God nobody but me heard you say that!"

Morris seemed not to be attending.

"Where is he?" he said again, "are you concealing him here? I have already been to your office, and he wasn't there, and to his flat, and he wasn't there."

"Thank God," ejaculated the lawyer.

"By all means if you like. But I've got to see him, you know. Where is he?"

"He is away in town," said Mr. Taynton, "but he will be back to-night. Now attend. Of course you must see him, I quite understand that. But you mustn't see him alone, while you are like this."

"No, I don't want to," said Morris. "I should like other people to see what I've got to—to say to him—that, that partner of yours."

"He has from this moment ceased to be my partner," said Mr. Taynton brokenly. "I could never again sign what he has signed, or work with him, or—or—except once—see him again. He is coming here by appointment at half-past nine. Suppose that we all meet here. We have both got to see him."

Morris nodded and went toward the door. A sudden spasm of anxiety seemed to seize Mr. Taynton.

"What are you going to do now?" he asked.

"I don't know. Drive to Falmer Park perhaps, and tell Sir Richard you cannot see him immediately. Will you see him to-morrow?"

"Yes, I will call to-morrow morning. Morris, promise me you will do nothing rash, nothing that will bring sorrow on all those who love you."

"I shall bring a little sorrow on a man who hates me," said he.

He went out, and Mr. Taynton sat down again, his mouth compressed into hard lines, his forehead heavily frowning. He could not permanently prevent Morris from meeting Godfrey Mills, besides, it was his right to do so, yet how fraught with awful risks to himself that meeting would be! Morris might easily make a violent, even a murderous, assault on the man, but Mills was an expert boxer and wrestler, science would probably get the upper hand of blind rage. But how deadly a weapon Mills had in store against himself; he would certainly tell Morris that if one partner had slandered him the other, whom he so trusted and revered, had robbed him; he would say, too, that Taynton had been cognizant of, and had approved, his slanders. There was no end to the ruin that would certainly be brought about his head if they met. Mills's train, too, would have left London by now; there was no chance of stopping him. Then there was another danger he had not foreseen, and it was too late to stop that now. Morris was going again to Falmer Park, had indeed started, and that afternoon Godfrey Mills would get out of the train, as he had planned, at the station just below, and walk back over the downs to Brighton. What if they met there, alone?

CHAPTER V

For an hour perhaps Mr. Taynton delved at these problems, and at the end even it did not seem as if he had solved them satisfactorily, for when he went out of his house, as he did at the end of this time to get a little breeze if such was obtainable, his face was still shadowed and overclouded. Overclouded too was the sky, and as he stepped out into the street from his garden-room the hot air struck him like a buffet; and in his troubled and apprehensive mood it felt as if some hot hand warned him by a blow not to venture out of his house. But the house, somehow, in the last hour had become terrible to him, any movement or action, even on a day like this, when only madmen and the English go abroad, was better than the nervous waiting in his darkened room. Dreadful forces, forces of ruin and murder and disgrace, were abroad in the world of men; the menace of the low black clouds and stifling heat was more bearable. He wanted to get away from his house, which was permeated and soaked in association with the other two actors, who in company with himself, had surely some tragedy for which the curtain was already rung up. Some dreadful scene was already prepared for them; the setting and stage were ready, the prompter, and who was he? was in the box ready to tell them the next line if any of them faltered. The prompter, surely he was destiny, fate, the irresistible course of events, with which no man can struggle, any more than the actor can struggle with or alter the lines that are set down for him. He may mumble them, he may act dispiritedly and tamely, but he has undertaken a certain part; he has to go through with it.

Though it was a populous hour of the day, there were but few people abroad when Mr. Taynton came out to the sea front; a few cabs stood by the railings that bounded the broad asphalt path which faced the sea, but the drivers of these, despairing of fares, were for the most part dozing on the boxes, or with a more set purpose were frankly slumbering in the interior. The dismal little wooden shelters that punctuated the parade were deserted, the pier stretched an untenanted length of boards over the still, lead-coloured sea, and it seemed as if nature herself was waiting for some elemental catastrophe.

And though the afternoon was of such hideous and sultry heat, Mr. Taynton, though he walked somewhat more briskly than his wont, was conscious of no genial heat that produced perspiration, and the natural reaction and cooling of the skin. Some internal excitement and fever of the brain cut off all external things; the loneliness, the want of correspondence that fever brings between external and internal conditions, was on him. At one moment, in spite of the heat, he shivered, at another he felt that an apoplexy must strike him.

For some half hour he walked to and fro along the sea-wall, between the blackness of the sky and the lead-coloured water, and then his thoughts turned to the downs above this stricken place, where, even in the sultriest days some breath of wind was always moving. Just opposite him, on the other side of the road, was the street that led steeply upward to the station. He went up it.

* * * * *

It was about half-past seven o'clock that evening that the storm burst. A few huge drops of rain fell on the hot pavements, then the rain ceased again, and the big splashes dried, as if the stones had been blotting paper that sucked the moisture in. Then without other warning a streamer of fire split the steeple of St. Agnes's Church, just opposite Mr. Taynton's house, and the crash of thunder answered it more quickly than his servant had run to open the door to Morris's furious ringing of the bell. At that the sluices of heaven were opened, and heaven's artillery thundered its salvoes to the flare of the reckless storm. In the next half-hour a dozen houses in Brighton were struck, while the choked gutters overflowing on to the streets made ravines and waterways down the roadways. Then the thunder and lightning ceased, but the rain still poured down relentlessly and windlessly, a flood of perpendicular water.

Mr. Taynton had gone out without umbrella, and when he let himself in by his latch-key at his own house-door about half-past eight, it was no wonder that he wrung out his coat and trousers so that he should not soak his Persian rugs. But from him, as from the charged skies, some tension had passed; this tempest which had so cooled the air and restored the equilibrium of its forces had smoothed the frowning creases of his brow, and when the servant hurried up at the sound of the banged front-door, he found his master soaked indeed, but serene.

"Yes, I got caught by the storm, Williams," he said, "and I am drenched. The lightning was terrific, was it not? I will just change, and have a little supper; some cold meat, anything that there is. Yes, you might take my coat at once."

He divested himself of this.

"And I expect Mr. Morris this evening," he said. "He will probably have dined, but if not I am sure Mrs. Otter will toss up a hot dish for him. Oh, yes, and Mr. Mills will be here at half-past nine, or even sooner, as I cannot think he will have walked from Falmer as he intended. But whenever he comes, I will see him. He has not been here already?"

"No, sir," said Williams, "Will you have a hot bath, sir?"

"No, I will just change. How battered the poor garden will look tomorrow after this deluge."

* * * * *

Mr. Taynton changed his wet clothes and half an hour afterwards he sat down to his simple and excellent supper. Mrs. Otter had provided an admirable vegetable soup for him, and some cold lamb with asparagus and endive salad. A macedoine of strawberries followed and a scoop of cheese. Simple as his fare was, it just suited Mr. Taynton's tastes, and he was indulging himself with the rather rare luxury of a third glass of port when Williams entered again.

"Mr. Assheton," he said, and held the door open.

Morris came in; he was dressed in evening clothes with a dinner jacket, and gave no salutation to his host.

"He's not come yet?" he asked.

But his host sprang up.

"Dear boy," he said, "what a relief it is to see you. Ever since you left this afternoon I have had you on my mind. You will have a glass of port?"

Morris laughed, a curious jangling laugh.

"Oh yes, to drink his health," he said.

He sat down with a jerk, and leaned his elbows on the table.

"He'll want a lot of health to carry him through this, won't he?" he asked.

He drank his glass of port like water, and Mr. Taynton instantly filled it up again for him.

"Ah, I remember you don't like port," he said. "What else can I offer you?"

"Oh, this will do very well," said Morris. "I am so thirsty."

"You have dined?" asked his host quietly.

"No; I don't think I did. I wasn't hungry."

The Cromwellian clock chimed a remnant half hour.

"Half-past," said Morris, filling his glass again. "You expect him then, don't you?"

"Mills is not always very punctual," said Mr. Taynton.

For the next quarter of an hour the two sat with hardly the interchange of a word. From outside came the swift steady hiss of the rain on to the shrubs in the garden, and again the clock chimed. Morris who at first had sat very quiet had begun to fidget and stir in his chair; occasionally when he happened to notice it, he drank off the port with which Mr. Taynton hospitably kept his glass supplied. Sometimes he relit a cigarette only to let it go out again. But when the clock struck he got up.

"I wonder what has happened," he said. "Can he have missed his train? What time ought he to have got in?"

"He was to have got to Falmer," said Mr. Taynton with a little emphasis on the last word, "at a quarter to seven. He spoke of walking from there."

Morris looked at him with a furtive sidelong glance.

"Why, I—I might have met him there," he said. "I went up there again after I left you to tell Sir Richard you would call to-morrow."

"You saw nothing of him?" asked the lawyer.

"No, of course not. Otherwise—There was scarcely a soul on the road; the storm was coming up. But he would go by the downs, would he not?"

"The path over the downs doesn't branch off for a quarter of a mile below Falmer station," said Mr. Taynton.

The minutes ticked on till ten. Then Morris went to the door.

"I shall go round to his rooms to see if he is there," he said.

"There is no need," said his host, "I will telephone."

The instrument hung in a corner of the room, and with very little delay, Mills's servant was rung up. His master had not yet returned, but he had said that he should very likely be late.

"And he made an appointment with you for half-past nine?" asked Morris again.

"Yes. I cannot think what has happened to detain him."

Morris went quickly to the door again.

"I believe it is all a trick," he said, "and you don't want me to meet him. I believe he is in his rooms the whole time. I shall go and see."

Before Mr. Taynton could stop him he had opened the front-door and banged it behind him, and was off hatless and coatless through the pouring perpendicular rain.

Mr. Taynton ran to the door, as if to stop him, but Morris was already halfway down the street, and he went upstairs to the drawing-room. Morris was altogether unlike himself; this discovery of Mills's treachery seemed to have changed his nature. Violent and quick he always was, but to-night he was suspicious, he seemed to distrust Mr. Taynton himself. And, a thing which his host had never known him do before, he had drunk in that half hour when they sat waiting, close on a bottle of port.

The evening paper lay ready cut for him in its accustomed place, but for some five minutes Mr. Taynton did not appear to notice it, though evening papers, on the money-market page, might contain news so frightfully momentous to him. But something, this strangeness in Morris, no doubt, and his general anxiety and suspense as to how this dreadful knot could unravel itself, preoccupied him now, and even when he did take up the paper and turn to the reports of Stock Exchange dealings, he was conscious of no more than a sort of subaqueous thrill of satisfaction. For Boston Copper had gone up nearly a point since the closing price of last night.

It was not many minutes, however before Morris returned with matted and streaming hair and drenched clothes.

"He has not come back," he said. "I went to his rooms and satisfied myself of that, though I think they thought I was mad. I searched them you understand; I insisted. I shall go round there again first thing to-morrow morning, and if he is not there, I shall go up to find him in town. I can't wait; I simply can't wait."

Mr. Taynton looked at him gravely, then nodded.

"No, I guess how you are feeling," he said, "I cannot understand what has happened to Mills; I hope nothing is wrong. And now, my dear boy, let me implore you to go straight home, get off your wet things and go to bed. You will pay heavily for your excitement, if you are not careful."

"I'll get it out of him." said Morris.

CHAPTER VI

Morris, as Mr. Taynton had advised, though not because he advised it, had gone straight home to the house in Sussex Square. He had stripped off his dripping clothes, and then, since this was the line of least resistance he had gone to bed. He did not feel tired, and he longed with that aching longing of the son for the mother, that Mrs. Assheton had been here, so that he could just be in her presence and if he found himself unable to speak and tell her all the hideous happenings of those last days, let her presence bring a sort of healing to his tortured mind. But though he was conscious of no tiredness, he was tired to the point of exhaustion, and he had hardly got into bed, when he fell fast asleep. Outside, hushing him to rest, there sounded the sibilant rain, and from the sea below ripples broke gently and rhythmically on the pebbly beach. Nature, too, it seemed, was exhausted by that convulsion of the elements that had turned the evening into a clamorous hell of fire and riot, and now from very weariness she was weeping herself asleep.

It was not yet eleven when Morris had got home, and he slept dreamlessly with that recuperative sleep of youth for some six hours. Then, as within the secret economy of the brain the refreshment of slumber repaired the exhaustion of the day before, he began to dream with strange lurid distinctness, a sort of resurrection dream of which the events of the two days before supplied the bones and skeleton outline. As in all very vivid and dreadful dreams the whole vision was connected and coherent, there were no ludicrous and inconsequent interludes, none of those breakings of one thread and hurried seizures of another, which though one is dreaming very distinctly, supply some vague mental comfort, since even to the sleeper they are reminders that his experiences are not solid but mere phantasies woven by imperfect consciousness and incomplete control of thought. It was not thus that Morris dreamed; his dream was of the solid and sober texture of life.

He was driving in his motor, he thought, down the road from the house at Falmer Park, which through the gate of a disused lodge joins the main road, that leads from Falmer Station to Brighton. He had just heard from Sir Richard's own lips who it was who had slandered and blackened him, but, in his dream, he was conscious of no anger. The case had been referred to some higher power, some august court of supreme authority, which would certainly use its own instruments for its own vengeance. He felt he was concerned in the affair no longer; he was but a spectator of what would be. And, in obedience to some inward dictation, he drove his motor on to the grass behind the lodge, so that it was concealed from the road outside, and walked along the inside of the park-palings, which ran parallel with it.

The afternoon, it seemed, was very dark, though the atmosphere was extraordinarily clear, and after walking along the springy grass inside the railings for some three hundred yards, where was the southeastern corner of the park enclosure, he stopped at the angle and standing on tip-toe peered over them, for they were nearly six feet high, and looked into the road below. It ran straight as a billiard-cue just here, and was visible for a long distance, but at the corner, just outside the palings, the footpath over the downs to Brighton left the road, and struck upward. On the other side of the road ran the railway, and in this clear dark air, Morris could see with great distinctness Falmer Station some four hundred yards away, along a stretch of the line on the other side of it.

As he looked he saw a puff of steam rise against the woods beyond the station, and before long a train, going Brightonward, clashed into the station. Only one passenger got out, and he came out of the station into the road. He was quite recognisable even at this distance. In his dream Morris felt that he expected to see him get out of the train, and walk along the road; the whole thing seemed preordained. But he ceased tiptoeing to look over the paling; he could hear the passenger's steps when he came nearer.

He thought he waited quietly, squatting down on the mossy grass behind the paling. Something in his hands seemed angry, for his fingers kept tearing up the short turf, and the juice of the severed stems was red like blood. Then in the gathering darkness he heard the tip-tap of footsteps on the highway. But it never occurred to him that this passenger would continue on the highroad; he was certainly going over the downs to Brighton.

The air was quite windless, but at this moment Morris heard the boughs of the oak-tree immediately above him stir and shake, and looking up he saw Mr. Taynton sitting in a fork of the tree. That, too, was perfectly natural; Mr. Taynton was Mills's partner; he was there as a sort of umpire. He held a glass of port wine in one hand, and was sipping it in a leisurely manner, and when Morris looked up at him, he smiled at him, but put his finger to his lips, as if recommending silence. And as the steps on the road outside sounded close he turned a meaning glance in the direction of the road. From where he sat high in the tree, it was plain to Morris that he must command the sight of the road, and was, in his friendly manner, directing operations.

Suddenly the sound of the steps ceased, and Morris wondered for the moment whether Mills had stopped. But looking up again, he saw Mr. Taynton's head twisted round to the right, still looking over the palings. But Morris found at once that the footsteps were noiseless, not because the walker had paused, but because they were inaudible on the grass. He had left the road, as the dreamer felt certain he would, and was going over the downs to Brighton. At that Morris got up, and still inside the park railings, followed in the direction he had gone. Then for the first time in his dream, he felt angry, and the anger grew to rage, and the rage to quivering madness. Next moment he had vaulted the fence, and sprang upon the walker from behind. He dealt him blows with some hard instrument, belabouring his head, while with his left hand he throttled his throat so that he could not scream. Only a few were necessary, for he knew that each blow went home, since all the savage youthful strength of shoulder and loose elbow directed them. Then he withdrew his left hand from the throttled throat of the victim who had ceased to struggle, and like a log he fell back on to the grass, and Morris for the first time looked on his face. It was not Mills at all; it was Mr. Taynton.

* * * * *

The terror plucked him from his sleep; for a moment he wrestled and struggled to raise his head from the pillow and loosen the clutch of the night-hag who had suddenly seized him, and with choking throat and streaming brow he sat up in bed. Even then his dream was more real to him than the sight of his own familiar room, more real than the touch of sheet and blanket or the dew of anguish which his own hand wiped from his forehead and throat. Yet, what was his dream? Was it merely some subconscious stringing together of suggestions and desires and events vivified in sleep to a coherent story (all but that recognition of Mr. Taynton, which was nightmare pure and simple), or *had it happened*?

With waking, anyhow, the public life, the life that concerned other living folk as well as himself, became predominant again. He had certainly seen Sir Richard the day before, and Sir Richard had given him the name of the man who had slandered him. He had gone to meet that man, but he had not kept his appointment, nor had he come back to his flat in Brighton. So to-day he, Morris, was going to call there once more, and if he did not find him, was going to drive up to London, and seek him there.

But he had been effectually plucked from further sleep, sleep had been strangled, and he got out of bed and went to the window. Nature, in any case, had swept her trouble away, and the pure sweet morning was beginning to dawn in lines of yellow and fleeces of rosy cloud on the eastern horizon.

All that riot and hurly-burly of thunder, the bull's eye flashing of lightning, the perpendicular rain were things of the past, and this morning a sky of pale limpid blue, flecked only by the thinnest clouds, stretched from horizon to horizon. Below the mirror of the sea seemed as deep and as placid as the sky above it, and the inimitable freshness of the dawn spoke of a world rejuvenated and renewed.

It was, by his watch, scarcely five; in an hour it would be reasonable to call at Mills's flat, and see if he had come by the midnight train. If not his motor could be round by soon after six, and he would be in town by eight, before Mills, if he had slept there, would be thinking of starting for Brighton. He was sure to catch him.

Morris had drawn up the blind, and through the open window came the cool breath of the morning ruffling his hair, and blowing his nightshirt close to his skin, and just for that moment, so exquisite was this feeling of renewal and cleanness in the hour of dawn, he thought with a sort of incredulous wonder of the red murderous hate which had possessed him the evening before. He seemed to have been literally beside himself with anger and his words, his thoughts, his actions had been controlled by a force and a possession which was outside himself. Also the dreadful reality of his dream still a little unnerved him, and though he was himself now and awake, he felt that he had been no less himself when he throttled the throat of that abhorred figure that walked up the noiseless path over the downs to Brighton, and with vehement and savage blows clubbed it down. And then the shock of finding it was his old friend whom he had done to death! That, it is true, was nightmare pure and simple, but all the rest was clad in sober, convincing garb of events that had really taken place. He could not at once separate his dream from reality, for indeed what had he done yesterday after he had learned who his traducer had been? He scarcely knew; all events and facts seemed colourless compared to the rage and mad lust for vengeance which had occupied his entire consciousness.

Thus, as he dressed, the thoughts and the rage of yesterday began to stir and move in his mind again. His hate and his desire that justice should be done, that satisfaction should be granted him, was still in his heart. But now they were not wild and flashing flames; they burned with a hard, cold, even light. They were already part of himself, integral pieces and features of his soul. And the calm beauty and peace of the morning ceased to touch him, he had a stern piece of business to put through before he could think of anything else.

* * * * *

It was not yet six when he arrived at the house in which was Mills's flat. A few housemaids were about, but the lift was not yet working, and he ran upstairs and rang at the bell. It was answered almost immediately, for Mills's servant supposed it must be his master arriving at this early hour, since no one else would come then, and he opened the door, half dressed, with coat and trousers only put over his night things.

"Is Mr. Mills back yet?" asked Morris.

"No, sir."

Morris turned to go, but then stopped, his mind still half-suspicious that he had been warned by his partner, and was lying *perdu*.

"I'll give you another ten shillings," he said, "if you'll let me come in and satisfy myself."

The man hesitated.

"A sovereign," said Morris.

* * * * *

He went back to Sussex Square after this, roused Martin, ordering him to bring the motor round at once, and drank a cup of tea, for he would breakfast in town. His mother he expected would be back during the morning, and at the thought of her he remembered that this was June 24th, her birthday, and that his present to her would be arriving by the early post. He gave orders, therefore, that a packet for him from Asprey's was not to be unpacked, but given to her on her arrival with her letters. A quarter of an hour later he was off, leaving Martin behind, since there were various businesses in the town which he wanted him to attend to.

CHAPTER VI

Mr. Taynton, though an earlier riser than his partner, considered that half past nine was soon enough to begin the day, and punctually at that time he came downstairs to read, as his custom was, a few collects and some short piece of the Bible to his servants, before having his breakfast. That little ceremony over he walked for a few minutes in his garden while Williams brought in his toast and tea-urn, and observed that though the flowers would no doubt be all the better for the liberal watering of the day before, it was idle to deny that the rain had not considerably damaged them. But his attention was turned from these things to Williams who told him that breakfast was ready, and also brought him a telegram. It was from Morris, and had been sent off from the Sloane Square office an hour before.

"Mills is not in town; they say he left yesterday afternoon. Please inform me if you know whether this is so, or if you are keeping him from me. Am delayed by break-down. Shall be back about five.—Morris, Bachelors' Club."

Mr. Taynton read this through twice, as is the habit of most people with telegrams, and sent, of course, the reply that all he knew was that his partner intended to come back last night, since he had made an appointment with him. Should he arrive during the day he would telegraph. He himself was keeping nothing from Morris, and had not had any correspondence or communication with his partner since he had left Brighton for town three days before.

The telegram was a long one, but Mr. Taynton still sat with poised pen. Then he added, "Pray do nothing violent, I implore you." And he signed it.

* * * * *

He sat rather unusually long over his breakfast this morning, though he ate but little, and from the cheerful smiling aspect of his face it would seem that his thoughts were pleasant to him. He was certainly glad that Morris had not yet come across Mills, for he trusted that the lapse of a day or two would speedily calm down the lad's perfectly justifiable indignation. Besides, he was in love, and his suit had prospered; surely there were pleasanter things than revenge to occupy him. Then his face grew grave a moment as he thought of Morris's mad, murderous outburst of the evening before, but that gravity was shortlived, and he turned with a sense of pleasant expectation to see recorded again the activity and strength of Boston Coppers. But the reality was far beyond his expectations; copper had been strong all day, and in the street afterward there had been renewed buying from quarters which were usually well informed. Bostons had been much in request, and after hours they had had a further spurt, closing at £7 10S. Already in these three days he had cleared his option, and at present prices the shares showed a profit of a point. Mills would have to acknowledge that his perspicacity had been at fault, when he distrusted this last purchase.

He left his house at about half-past ten, and again immured himself in the bird-cage lift that carried him up to his partner's flat, where he inquired if he had yet returned. Learning he had not, he asked to be given pen and paper, to write a note for him, which was to be given to him on his arrival.

"Dear Mills,

"Mr. Morris Assheton has learned that you have made grave accusations about him to Sir Richard Templeton, Bart. That you have done so appears to be beyond doubt, and it of course rests with you to substantiate them. I cannot of course at present believe that you could have done so without conclusive evidence; on the other hand I cannot believe that Mr. Assheton is of the character which you have given him.

"I therefore refrain, as far as I am able, from drawing any conclusion till the matter is cleared up.

"I may add that he deeply resents your conduct; his anger and indignation were terrible to see.

"Sincerely yours,

"Edward Taynton. Godfrey Mills, Esq."

Mr. Taynton read this through, and glanced round, as if to see whether the servants had left the room. Then he sat with closed eyes for a moment, and took an envelope, and swiftly addressed it. He smudged it, however, in blotting it, and so crumpled it up, threw it into the waste-paper basket. He then addressed a second one, and into this he inserted his letter, and got up.

The servant was waiting in the little hall outside.

"Please give this to Mr. Mills when he arrives," he said. "You expected him last night, did you not?"

Mr. Taynton found on arrival at his office that, in his partner's absence, there was a somewhat heavy day of work before him, and foresaw that he would be occupied all afternoon and indeed probably up to dinner time. But he was able to get out for an hour at half-past twelve, at which time, if the weather was hot, he generally indulged in a swim. But today there was a certain chill in the air after yesterday's storm, and instead of taking his dip, he walked along the sea front toward Sussex Square. For in his warm-hearted way, seeing that Morris was, as he had said, to tell his mother today about his happy and thoroughly suitable love affair, Mr. Taynton proposed to give a little *partie carrée* on the earliest possible evening, at which the two young lovers, Mrs. Assheton, and himself would form the table. He would learn from her what was the earliest night on which she and Morris were disengaged, and then write to that delightful girl whose affections dear Morris had captured.

But at the corner of the square, just as he was turning into it, there bowled swiftly out a victoria drawn by two horses; he recognised the equipage, he recognised also Mrs. Assheton who was sitting in it. Her head, however, was turned the other way, and Mr. Taynton's hand, already half-way up to his hat was spared the trouble of journeying farther.

But he went on to the house, since his invitation could be easily conveyed by a note which he would scribble there, and was admitted by Martin. Mrs. Assheton, however, was out, a fact which he learned with regret, but, if he might write a note to her, his walk would not be wasted. Accordingly he was shown up into the drawing-room, where on the writing-table was laid an open blotting-book. Even in so small a detail as a blotting-book the careful appointment of the house was evident, for the blotting-paper was absolutely clean and white, a virgin field.

Mr. Taynton took up a quill pen, thought over for a moment the wording of his note and then wrote rapidly. A single side of notepaper was sufficient; he blotted it on the pad, and read it through. But something in it, it must be supposed, did not satisfy him, for he crumpled it up. Ah, at last and for the first time there was a flaw in the appointment of the house, for there was no wastepaper basket by the table. At any rate one must suppose that Mr. Taynton did not see it, for he put his rejected sheet into his pocket.

He took another sheet of paper, selecting from the various stationery that stood in the case a plain piece, rejecting that which was marked with the address of the house, wrote his own address at the head, and proceeded for the second time to write his note of invitation.

But first he changed the quill for his own stylograph, and wrote with that. This was soon written, and by the time he had read it through it was dry, and did not require to be blotted. He placed it in a plain envelope, directed it, and with it in his hand left the room, and went briskly downstairs.

Martin was standing in the hall.

"I want this given to Mrs. Assheton when she comes in, Martin," he said.

He looked round, as he had done once before when speaking to the boy.

"I left it at the door," he said with quiet emphasis. "Can you remember that? I left it. And I hope, Martin, that you have made a fresh start, and that I need never be obliged to tell anybody what I know about you. You will remember my instructions? I left this at the door. Thank you. My hat? Yes, and my stick."

Mr. Taynton went straight back to his office, and though this morning there had seemed to him to be a good deal of work to be got through, he found that much of it could be delegated to his clerks. So before leaving to go to his lunch, he called in Mr. Timmins.

"Mr. Mills not been here all morning?" he asked. "No? Well, Timmins, there is this packet which I want him to look at, if he comes in before I am back. I shall be here again by five, as there is an hour's work for me to do before evening. Yes, that is all, thanks. Please tell Mr. Mills I shall come back, as I said. How pleasant this freshness is after the rain. The 'clear shining after rain.' Wonderful words! Yes, Mr. Timmins, you will find the verse in the second book of Samuel and the twenty-third chapter."

CHAPTER VII

Mr. Taynton made but a short meal of lunch, and ate but sparingly, for he meant to take a good walk this afternoon, and it was not yet two o'clock when he came out of his house again, stick in hand. It was a large heavy stick that he carried, a veritable club, one that it would be easy to recognise amid a host of others, even as he had recognised it that morning in the rather populous umbrella stand in the hall of Mrs. Assheton's house. He had, it may be remembered, more office work to get through before evening, so he prepared to walk out as far as the limits of the time at his disposal would admit and take the train back. And since there could be nothing more pleasurable in the way of walking than locomotion over the springy grass of the downs, he took, as he had done a hundred times before, the road that led to Falmer. A hundred yards out of Brighton there was a stile by the roadside; from there a footpath, if it could be dignified by the name of path at all, led over the hills to a corner of Falmer Park. From there three or four hundred yards of highway would bring him to the station. He would be in good time to catch the 4.30 train back, and would thus be at his office again for an hour's work at five.

His walk was solitary and uneventful, but, to one of so delicate and sensitive a mind, full of tiny but memorable sights and sounds. Up on these high lands there was a considerable breeze, and Mr. Taynton paused for a minute or two beside a windmill that stood alone, in the expanse of down, watching, with a sort of boyish wonder, the huge flails swing down and aspire again in the circles of their tireless toil. A little farther on was a grass-grown tumulus of Saxon times, and his mind was distracted from the present to those early days when the unknown dead was committed to this wind-swept tomb. Forests of pine no doubt then grew around his resting place, it was beneath the gloom and murmur of their sable foliage that this dead chief was entrusted to the keeping of the kindly earth. He passed, too, over the lines of a Roman camp; once this sunny empty down re-echoed to the clang of arms, the voices of the living were mingled with the cries and groans of the dying, for without doubt this stronghold of Roman arms was not won, standing, as it did, on the top-most commanding slope of the hills, without slaughter. Yet to-day the peaceful clumps of cistus and the trembling harebell blossomed on the battlefield.

From this point the ground declined swiftly to the main road. Straight in front of him were the palings of Falmer Park, and the tenantless down with its long smooth curves, was broken up into sudden hillocks and depressions. Dells and dingles, some green with bracken, others half full of water lay to right and left of the path, which, as it approached the corner of the park, was more strongly marked than when it lay over the big open spaces. It was somewhat slippery, too, after the torrent of yesterday, and Mr. Taynton's stick saved him more than once from slipping. But before he got down to the point where the corner of the park abutted on the main road, he had leaned on it too heavily, and for all its seeming strength, it had broken in the middle. The two pieces were but luggage to him and just as he came to the road, he threw them away into a wooded hollow that adjoined the path. The stick had broken straight across; it was no use to think of having it mended.

* * * * *

He was out of the wind here, and since there was still some ten minutes to spare, he sat down on the grassy edge of the road to smoke a cigarette. The woods of the park basked in the fresh sunshine; three hundred yards away was Falmer Station, and beyond that the line was visible for a mile as it ran up the straight valley. Indeed he need hardly move till he saw the steam of his train on the limit of the horizon. That would be ample warning that it was time to go.

Then from far away, he heard the throbbing of a motor, which grew suddenly louder as it turned the corner of the road by the station. It seemed to him to be going very fast, and the huge cloud of dust behind it endorsed his impression. But almost immediately after passing this corner it began to slow down, and the cloud of dust behind it died away.

At the edge of the road where Mr. Taynton sat, there were standing several thick bushes. He moved a little away from the road, and took up his seat again behind one of them. The car came very slowly on, and stopped just opposite him. On his right lay the hollow where he had thrown the useless halves of his stick, on his left was the corner of the Falmer Park railings. He had recognised the driver of the car, who was alone.

Morris got out when he had stopped the car, and then spoke aloud, though to himself.

"Yes, there's the corner," he said, "there's the path over the downs. There—"

Mr. Taynton got up and came toward him.

"My dear fellow," he said, "I have walked out from Brighton on this divine afternoon, and was going to take the train back. But will you give me the pleasure of driving back with you instead?"

Morris looked at him a moment as if he hardly thought he was real.

"Why, of course," he said.

Mr. Taynton was all beams and smiles.

"And you have seen Mills?" he asked. "You have been convinced that he was innocent of the terrible suspicion? Morris, my dear boy, what is the matter?"

Morris had looked at him for a moment with incredulous eyes. Then he had sat down and covered his face with his hands.

"It's nothing," he said at length. "I felt rather faint. I shall be better in a minute. Of course I'll drive you back."

He sat huddled up with hidden face for a moment or two. Mr. Taynton said nothing, but only looked at him. Then the boy sat up.

"I'm all right," he said, "it was just a dream I had last night. No, I have not seen Mills; they tell me he left yesterday afternoon for Brighton. Shall we go?"

For some little distance they went in silence; then it seemed that Morris made an effort and spoke.

"Really, I got what they call 'quite a turn' just now," he said. "I had a curiously vivid dream last night about that corner, and you suddenly appeared in my dream quite unexpectedly, as you did just now."

"And what was this dream?" asked Mr. Taynton, turning up his coat collar, for the wind of their movement blew rather shrilly on to his neck.

"Oh, nothing particular," said Morris carelessly, "the vividness was concerned with your appearance; that was what startled me."

Then he fell back into the train of thought that had occupied him all the way down from London.

"I believe I was half-mad with rage last night," he said at length, "but this afternoon, I think I am beginning to be sane again. It's true Mills tried to injure me, but he didn't succeed. And as you said last night I have too deep and intense a cause of happiness to give my thoughts and energies to anything so futile as hatred or the desire for revenge. He is punished already. The fact of his having tried to injure me like that was his punishment. Anyhow, I am sick and tired of my anger."

The lawyer did not speak for a moment, and when he did his voice was trembling.

"God bless you, my dear boy," he said gently.

Morris devoted himself for some little time to the guiding of the car.

"And I want you also to leave it all alone," he said after a while. "I don't want you to dissolve your partnership with him, or whatever you call it. I suppose he will guess that you know all about it, so perhaps it would be best if you told him straight out that you do. And then you can, well, make a few well-chosen remarks you know, and drop the whole damned subject forever."

Mr. Taynton seemed much moved.

"I will try," he said, "since you ask it. But Morris, you are more generous than I am."

Morris laughed, his usual boyish high spirits and simplicity were reasserting themselves again.

"Oh, that's all rot," he said. "It's only because it's so fearfully tiring to go on being angry. But I can't help wondering what has happened to the fellow. They told me at his flat in town that he went off with his luggage yesterday afternoon, and gave orders that all letters were to be sent to his Brighton address. You don't think there's anything wrong, do you?"

"My dear fellow, what could be wrong?" asked Mr. Taynton. "He had some business to do at Lewes on his way down, and I make no doubt he slept there, probably forgetting all about his appointment with me. I would wager you that we shall find he is in Brighton when we get in."

"I'll take that," said Morris. "Half a crown."

"No, no, my usual shilling, my usual shilling," laughed the other.

* * * * *

Morris set Mr. Taynton down at his office, and by way of settling their wager at once, waited at the door, while the other went upstairs to see if his partner was there. He had not, however, appeared there that day, and Mr. Taynton sent a clerk down to Morris, to ask him to come up, and they would ring up Mr. Mills's flat on the telephone.

This was done, and before many seconds had elapsed they were in communication. His valet was there, still waiting for his master's return, for he had not yet come back. It appeared that he was getting rather anxious, for Mr. Taynton reassured him.

"There is not the slightest cause for any anxiety," were his concluding words. "I feel convinced he has merely been detained. Thanks, that's all. Please let me know as soon as he returns."

He drew a shilling from his pocket, and handed it to Morris. But his face, in spite of his reassuring words, was a little troubled. You would have said that though he might not yet be anxious, he saw that there was some possibility of his being so, before very long. Yet he spoke gaily enough.

"And I made so sure I should win," he said. "I shall put it down to unexpected losses, not connected with business; eh, Mr. Timmins? Or shall it be charity? It would never do to put down 'Betting losses.'"

But this was plainly a little forced, and Morris waited till Mr. Timmins had gone out.

"And you really meant that?" he asked. "You are really not anxious?"

"No, I am not anxious," he said, "but—but I shall be glad when he comes back. Is that inconsistent? I think perhaps it is. Well, let us say then that I am just a shade anxious. But I may add that I feel sure my anxiety is quite unnecessary. That defines it for you."

Morris went straight home from here, and found that his mother had just returned from her afternoon drive. She had found the blotting book waiting for her when she came back that morning, and was delighted with the gift and the loving remembering thought that inspired it.

"But you shouldn't spend your money on me, my darling," she said to Morris, "though I just love the impulse that made you."

"Oh, very well," said Morris, kissing her, "let's have the initials changed about then, and let it be M.A. from H.A."

Then his voice grew grave.

"Mother dear, I've got another birthday present for you. I think—I think you will like it."

She saw at once that he was speaking of no tangible material gift.

"Yes, dear?" she said.

"Madge and me," said Morris. "Just that."

And Mrs. Assheton did like this second present, and though it made her cry a little, her tears were the sweetest that can be shed.

* * * * *

Mother and son dined alone together, and since Morris had determined to forget, to put out of his mind the hideous injury that Mills had attempted to do him, he judged it to be more consistent with this resolve to tell his mother nothing about it, since to mention it to another, even to her, implied that he was not doing his best to bury what he determined should be dead to him. As usual, they played backgammon together, and it was not till Mrs. Assheton rose to go to bed that she remembered Mr. Taynton's note, asking her and Morris to dine with him on their earliest unoccupied day. This, as is the way in the country, happened to be the next evening, and since the last post had already gone out, she asked Morris if Martin might take the note round for her tonight, since it ought to have been answered before.

That, of course, was easily done, and Morris told his servant to call also at the house where Mr. Mills's flat was situated, and ask the porter if he had come home. The note dispatched his mother went to bed, and Morris went down to the billiard room to practise spot-strokes, a form of hazard at which he was singularly inefficient, and wait for news. Little as he knew Mills, and little cause as he had for liking him, he too, like Mr. Taynton, felt vaguely anxious and perturbed, since "disappearances" are necessarily hedged about with mystery and wondering. His own anger and hatred, too, like mists drawn up and dispersed by the sun of love that had dawned on him, had altogether vanished; the attempt against him had, as it turned out, been so futile, and he genuinely wished to have some assurance of the safety of the man, the thought of whom had so blackened his soul only twenty-four hours ago.

His errands took Martin the best part of an hour, and he returned with two notes, one for Mrs. Assheton, the other for Morris. He had been also to the flat and inquired, but there was no news of the missing man.

Morris opened his note, which was from Mr. Taynton.

"Dear Morris,

"I am delighted that your mother and you can dine to-morrow, and I am telegraphing first thing in the morning to see if Miss Madge will make our fourth. I feel sure that when she knows what my little party is, she will come.

"I have been twice round to see if my partner has returned, and find no news of him. It is idle to deny that I am getting anxious, as I cannot conceive what has happened. Should he not be back by tomorrow morning, I shall put the matter into the hands of the police. I trust that my anxieties are unfounded, but the matter is beginning to look strange.

"Affectionately yours,

"Edward Taynton."

There is nothing so infectious as anxiety, and it can be conveyed by look or word or letter, and requires no period of incubation. And Morris began to be really anxious also, with a vague disquietude at the sense of there being something wrong.

CHAPTER VIII

Mr. Taynton, according to the intention he had expressed, sent round early next morning (the day of the week being Saturday) to his partner's flat, and finding that he was not there, and that no word of any kind had been received from him, went, as he felt himself now bound to do, to the police office, stated what had brought him there, and gave them all information which it was in his power to give.

It was brief enough; his partner had gone up to town on Tuesday last, and, had he followed his plans should have returned to Brighton by Thursday evening, since he had made an appointment to come to Mr. Taynton's house at nine thirty that night. It had been ascertained too, by—Mr. Taynton hesitated a moment—by Mr. Morris Assheton in London, that he had left his flat in St. James's Court on Thursday afternoon, to go, presumably, to catch the train back to Brighton. He had also left orders that all letters should be forwarded to him at his Brighton address.

Superintendent Figgis, to whom Mr. Taynton made his statement, was in manner slow, stout, and bored, and looked in every way utterly unfitted to find clues to the least mysterious occurrences, unearth crime or run down the criminal. He seemed quite incapable of running down anything, and Mr. Taynton had to repeat everything he said in order to be sure that Mr. Figgis got his notes, which he made in a large round hand, with laborious distinctness, correctly written. Having finished them the Superintendent stared at them mournfully for a little while, and asked Mr. Taynton if he had anything more to add.

"I think that is all," said the lawyer. "Ah, one moment. Mr. Mills expressed to me the intention of perhaps getting out at Falmer and walking over the downs to Brighton. But Thursday was the evening on which we had that terrible thunderstorm. I should think it very unlikely that he would have left the train."

Superintendent Figgis appeared to be trying to recollect something.

"Was there a thunderstorm on Thursday?" he asked.

"The most severe I ever remember," said Mr. Taynton.

"It had slipped my memory," said this incompetent agent of justice.

But a little thought enabled him to ask a question that bore on the case.

"He travelled then by Lewes and not by the direct route?"

"Presumably. He had a season ticket via Lewes, since our business often took him there. Had he intended to travel by Hayward's Heath," said Mr. Taynton rather laboriously, as if explaining something to a child, "he could not have intended to get out at Falmer."

Mr. Figgis had to think over this, which he did with his mouth open.

"Seeing that the Hayward's Heath line does not pass Falmer," he suggested.

Mr. Taynton drew a sheet of paper toward him and kindly made a rough sketch-map of railway lines.

"And his season ticket went by the Lewes line," he explained.

Superintendent Figgis appeared to understand this after a while. Then he sighed heavily, and changed the subject with rather disconcerting abruptness.

"From my notes I understand that Mr. Morris Assheton ascertained that the missing individual had left his flat in London on Thursday afternoon," he said.

"Yes, Mr. Assheton is a client of ours, and he wished to see my partner on a business matter. In fact, when Mr. Mills was found not to have returned on Thursday evening, he went up to London next day to see him, since we both supposed he had been detained there."

Mr. Figgis looked once more mournfully at his notes, altered a palpably mistaken "Wednesday" into Thursday, and got up.

"The matter shall be gone into," he said.

*　*　*　*　*

Mr. Taynton went straight from here to his office, and for a couple of hours devoted himself to the business of his firm, giving it his whole attention and working perhaps with more speed than it was usually his to command. Saturday of course was a half-holiday, and it was naturally his desire to get cleared off everything that would otherwise interrupt the well-earned repose and security from business affairs which was to him the proper atmosphere of the seventh, or as he called it, the first day. This interview with the accredited representative of the law also had removed a certain weight from his mind. He had placed the matter of his partner's disappearance in official hands, he had done all he could do to clear up his absence, and, in case—but here he pulled himself up; it was at present most premature even to look at the possibility of crime having been committed.

Mr. Taynton was in no way a vain man, nor was it his habit ever to review his own conduct, with the object of contrasting it favourably with what others might have done under the circumstances. Yet he could not help being aware that others less kindly than he would have shrugged sarcastic shoulders and said, "probably another blackmailing errand has detained him." For, indeed, Mills had painted himself in very ugly colours in his last interview with him; that horrid hint of blackmail, which still, so to speak, held good, had cast a new light on him. But now Taynton was conscious of no grudge against him; he did not say, "he can look after himself." He was anxious about his continued absence, and had taken the extreme step of calling in the aid of the police, the national guardian of personal safety.

He got away from his office about half-past twelve and in preparation for the little dinner festival of this evening, for Miss Templeton had sent her joyful telegraphic acceptance, went to several shops to order some few little delicacies to grace his plain bachelor table. An ice-pudding, for instance, was outside the orbit, so he feared of his plain though excellent cook, and two little dishes of chocolates and sweets, since he was at the confectioner's, would be appropriate to the taste of his lady guests. Again a floral decoration of the table was indicated, and since the storm of Thursday, there was nothing in his garden worthy of the occasion; thus a visit to the florist's resulted in an order for smilax and roses.

* * * * *

He got home, however, at his usual luncheon hour to find a telegram waiting for him on the Heppelwhite table in the hall. There had been a continued buying of copper shares, and the feature was a sensational rise in Bostons, which during the morning had gone up a clear point.

Mr. Taynton had no need to make calculations; he knew, as a man knows the multiplication table of two, what every fraction of a rise in Bostons meant to him, and this, provided only he had time to sell at once, meant the complete recovery of the losses he had suffered. With those active markets it was still easily possible though it was Saturday, to effect his sale, since there was sure to be long continued business in the Street and he had but to be able to exercise his option at that price, to be quit of that dreadful incubus of anxiety which for the last two years had been a millstone round his neck that had grown mushroom like. The telephone to town, of course, was far the quickest mode of communication, and having given his order he waited ten minutes till the tube babbled and croaked to him again.

There is a saying that things are "too good to be true," but when Mr. Taynton sat down to his lunch that day, he felt that the converse of the proverb was the correcter epigram. Things could be so good that they must be true, and here, still ringing in his ears was one of them—Morris—it was thus he phrased it to himself—was "paid off," or, in more business-like language, the fortune of which Mr. Taynton was trustee was intact again, and, like a tit-bit for a good child, there was an additional five or six hundred pounds for him who had managed the trust so well. Mr. Taynton could not help feeling somehow that he deserved it; he had increased Morris's fortune since he had charge of it by £10,000. And what a lesson, too, he had had, so gently and painlessly taught him! No one knew better than he how grievously wrong he had got, in gambling with trust money. Yet now it had come right: he had repaired the original wrong; on Monday he would reinvest this capital in those holdings which he had sold, and Morris's £40,000 (so largely the result of careful and judicious investment) would certainly stand the scrutiny of any who could possibly have any cause to examine his ledgers. Indeed there would be nothing to see. Two years ago Mr. Morris Assheton's fortune was invested in certain railway debentures and Government stock. It would in a few days' time be invested there again, precisely as it had been. Mr. Taynton had not been dealing in gilt-edged securities lately, and could not absolutely trust his memory, but he rather thought that the repurchase could be made at a somewhat smaller sum than had been realised by their various sales dating from two years ago. In that case there was a little more *sub rosa* reward for this well-inspired justice, weighed but featherwise against the overwhelming relief of the knowledge he could make wrong things right again, repair his, yes, his scoundrelism.

How futile, too, now, was Mills's threatened blackmail! Mills might, if he chose, proclaim on any convenient housetop, that his partner had gambled with Morris's £40,000 that according to the ledgers was invested in certain railway debentures and other gilt-edged securities. In a few days, any scrutiny might be made of the securities lodged at the County Bank, and assuredly among them would be found those debentures, those gilt-edged securities exactly as they appeared in the ledgers. Yet Mr. Taynton, so kindly is the nature of happiness, contemplated no revengeful step on his partner; he searched his heart and found that no trace of rancour against poor Mills was hoarded there.

Whether happiness makes us good, is a question not yet decided, but it is quite certain that happiness makes us forget that we have been bad, and it seemed to Mr. Taynton, as he sat in his cool dining-room, and ate his lunch with a more vivid appetite than had been his for many months, it seemed that the man who had gambled with his client's money was no longer himself; it was a perfectly different person who had done that. It was a different man, too, who, so few days ago had connived at and applauded the sorry trick which Mills had tried to play on Morris, when (so futilely, it is true) he had slandered him to Sir Richard. Now he felt that he—this man that to-day sat here—was incapable of such meannesses. And, thank God, it was never too late; from to-day he would lead the honourable, upright existence which the world (apart from his partner) had always credited him with leading.

He basked in the full sunshine of these happy and comfortable thoughts, and even as the sun of midsummer lingered long on the sea and hills, so for hours this inward sunshine warmed and cheered him. Nor was it till he saw by his watch that he must return from the long pleasant ramble on which he had started as soon as lunch was over, that a cloud filmy and thin at first began to come across the face of the sun. Once and again those genial beams dispersed it, but soon it seemed as if the vapours were getting the upper hand. A thought, in fact, had crossed Mr. Taynton's mind that quite distinctly dimmed his happiness. But a little reflection told him that a very simple step on his part would put that right again, and he walked home rather more quickly than he had set out, since he had this little bit of business to do before dinner.

He went—this was only natural—to the house where Mr. Mills's flat was situated, and inquired of the porter whether his partner had yet returned. But the same answer as before was given him, and saying that he had need of a document that Mills had taken home with him three days before he went up in the lift, and rang the bell of the flat. But it was not his servant who opened it, but sad Superintendent Figgis.

For some reason this was rather a shock to Mr. Taynton; to expect one face and see another is always (though ever so slightly) upsetting, but he instantly recovered himself and explained his errand.

"My partner took home with him on Tuesday a paper, which is concerned with my business," he said. "Would you kindly let me look round for it?"

Mr. Figgis weighed this request.

"Nothing must be removed from the rooms," he said, "till we have finished our search."

"Search for what?" asked Mr. Taynton.

"Any possible clue as to the reason of Mr. Mills's disappearance. But in ten minutes we shall have done, if you care to wait."

"I don't want to remove anything." said the lawyer. "I merely want to consult—"

At the moment another man in plain clothes came out of the sitting-room. He carried in his hand two or three letters, and a few scraps of crumpled paper. There was an envelope or two among them.

"We have finished, sir," he said to the Superintendent.

Mr. Figgis turned to the lawyer, who was looking rather fixedly at what the other man had in his hand.

"My document may be among those," he said.

Mr. Figgis handed them to him. There were two envelopes, both addressed to the missing man, one bearing his name only, some small torn-up scrap of paper, and three or four private letters.

"Is it among these?" he asked.

Mr. Taynton turned them over.

"No," he said, "it was—it was a large, yes, a large blue paper, official looking."

"No such thing in the flat, sir," said the second man.

"Very annoying," said the lawyer.

An idea seemed slowly to strike Mr. Figgis.

"He may have taken it to London with him," he said. "But will you not look round?"

Mr. Taynton did so. He also looked in the waste-paper basket, but it was empty.

So he went back to make ready to receive his guests, for the little party. But it had got dark; this "document" whatever it was, appeared to trouble him. The simple step he had contemplated had not led him in quite the right direction.

The Superintendent with his colleague went back into the sitting-room on the lawyer's departure, and Mr. Figgis took from his pocket most of his notes.

"I went to the station, Wilkinson," he said, "and in the lost luggage office I found Mr. Mills's bag. It had arrived on Thursday evening. But it seems pretty certain that its owner did not arrive with it."

"Looks as if he did get out at Falmer," said Wilkinson.

Figgis took a long time to consider this.

"It is possible," he said. "It is also possible that he put his luggage into the train in London, and subsequently missed the train himself."

CHAPTER VIII

Then together they went through the papers that might conceivably help them. There was a torn-up letter found in his bedroom fireplace, and the crumpled up envelope that belonged to it. They patiently pieced this together, but found nothing of value. The other letters referred only to his engagements in London, none of which were later than Thursday morning. There remained one crumpled up envelope (also from the paperbasket) but no letter that in any way corresponded with it. It was addressed in a rather sprawling, eager, boyish hand.

"No letter of any sort to correspond?" asked Figgis for the second time.

"No."

"I think for the present we will keep it," said he.

* * * * *

The little party at Mr. Taynton's was gay to the point of foolishness, and of them all none was more light-hearted than the host. Morris had asked him in an undertone, on arrival, whether any more had been heard, and learning there was still no news, had dismissed the subject altogether. The sunshine of the day, too, had come back to the lawyer; his usual cheerful serenity was touched with a sort of sympathetic boisterousness, at the huge spirits of the young couple and it was to be recorded that after dinner they played musical chairs and blind-man's buff, with infinite laughter. Never was an elderly solicitor so spontaneously gay; indeed before long it was he who reinfected the others with merriment. But as always, after abandonment to laughter a little reaction followed, and when they went upstairs from his sitting-room where they had been so uproarious, so that it might be made tidy again before Sunday, and sat in the drawing-room overlooking the street, there did come this little reaction. But it was already eleven, and soon Mrs. Assheton rose to go.

The night was hot, and Morris was sitting to cool himself by the open window, leaning his head out to catch the breeze. The street was very empty and quiet, and his motor, in which as a great concession, his mother had consented to be carried, on the promise of his going slow, had already come for them. Then down at the seaward end of the street he heard street-cries, as if some sudden news had come in that sent the vendors of the evening papers out to reap a second harvest that night. He could not, however, catch what it was, and they all went downstairs together.

Madge was going home with them, for she was stopping over the Sunday with Mrs. Assheton, and the two ladies had already got into the car, while Morris was still standing on the pavement with his host.

Then suddenly a newsboy, with a sheaf of papers still hot from the press, came running from the corner of the street just above them, and as he ran he shouted out the news which was already making little groups of people collect and gather in the streets.

Mr. Taynton turned quickly as the words became audible, seized a paper from the boy, giving him the first coin that he found, and ran back into the hall of his house, Morris with him, to beneath the electric light that burned there. The shrill voice of the boy still shouting the news of murder got gradually less loud as he went further down the street.

They read the short paragraph together, and then looked at each other with mute horror in their eyes.

CHAPTER IX

The inquest was held at Falmer on the Monday following, when the body was formally identified by Mr. Taynton and Mills's servant, and they both had to give evidence as regards what they knew of the movements of the deceased. This, as a matter of fact, Mr. Taynton had already given to Figgis, and in his examination now he repeated with absolute exactitude what he had said before including again the fact that Morris had gone up to town on Friday morning to try to find him there. On this occasion, however, a few further questions were put to him, eliciting the fact that the business on which Morris wanted to see him was known to Mr. Taynton but could not be by him repeated since it dealt with confidential transactions between the firm of solicitors and their client. The business was, yes, of the nature of a dispute, but Mr. Taynton regarded it as certain that some amicable arrangement would have been come to, had the interview taken place. As it had not, however, since Morris had not found him at his flat in town, he could not speak for certain on this subject. The dispute concerned an action of his partner's, made independently of him. Had he been consulted he would have strongly disapproved of it.

The body, as was made public now, had been discovered by accident, though, as has been seen, the probability of Mills having got out at Falmer had been arrived at by the police, and Figgis immediately after his interview with Mr. Taynton on the Saturday evening had started for Falmer to make inquiries there, and had arrived there within a few minutes of the discovery of the body. A carpenter of that village had strolled out about eight o'clock that night with his two children while supper was being got ready, and had gone a piece of the way up the path over the downs, which left the road at the corner of Falmer Park. The children were running and playing about, hiding and seeking each other in the bracken-filled hollows, and among the trees, when one of them screamed suddenly, and a moment afterward they both came running to their father, saying that they had come upon a man in one of these copses, lying on his face and they were frightened. He had gone to see what this terrifying person was, and had found the body. He went straight back to the village without touching anything, for it was clear both from what he saw and from the crowd of buzzing flies that the man was dead, and gave information to the police. Then within a few minutes from that, Mr. Figgis had arrived from Brighton, to find that it was superfluous to look any further or inquire any more concerning the whereabouts of the missing man. All that was mortal of him was here, the head covered with a cloth, and bits of the fresh summer growth of fern and frond sticking to his clothing.

After the identification of the body came evidence medical and otherwise that seemed to show beyond doubt the time and manner of his death and the possible motive of the murderer. The base of the skull was smashed in, evidently by some violent blow dealt from behind with a blunt heavy instrument of some sort, and death had probably been instantaneous. In one of the pockets was a first edition of an evening paper published in London on Thursday last, which fixed the earliest possible time at which the murder had been committed, while in the opinion of the doctor who examined the body late on Saturday night, the man had been dead not less than forty-eight hours. In spite of the very heavy rain which had fallen on Thursday night, there were traces of a pool of blood about midway between the clump of bracken where the body was found, and the path over the downs leading from Falmer to Brighton. This, taken in conjunction with the information already given by Mr. Taynton, made it practically certain that the deceased had left London on the Thursday as he had intended to do, and had got out of the train at Falmer, also according to his expressed intention, to walk to Brighton. It would again have been most improbable that he would have started on his walk had the storm already begun. But the train by which his bag was conveyed to Brighton arrived at Falmer at half-past six, the storm did not burst till an hour afterward. Finally, with regard to possible motive, the murdered man's watch was missing; his pockets also were empty of coin.

This concluded the evidence, and the verdict was brought in without the jury leaving the court, and "wilful murder by person or persons unknown" was recorded.

* * * * *

Mr. Taynton, as was indeed to be expected, had been much affected during the giving of his evidence, and when the inquest was over, he returned to Brighton feeling terribly upset by this sudden tragedy, which had crashed without warning into his life. It had been so swift and terrible; without sign or preparation this man, whom he had known so long, had been hurled from life and all its vigour into death. And how utterly now Mr. Taynton forgave him for that base attack that he had made on him, so few days ago; how utterly, too, he felt sure Morris had forgiven him for what was perhaps even harder to forgive. And if they could forgive trespasses like these, they who were of human passion and resentments, surely the reader of all hearts would forgive. That moment of agony short though it might have been in actual duration, when the murderous weapon split through the bone and scattered the brain, surely brought punishment and therefore atonement for the frailties of a life-time.

Mr. Taynton, on his arrival back at Brighton that afternoon, devoted a couple of solitary hours to such thoughts as these, and others to which this tragedy naturally gave rise and then with a supreme effort of will he determined to think no more on the subject. It was inevitable that his mind should again and again perhaps for weeks and months to come fall back on these dreadful events, but his will was set on not permitting himself to dwell on them. So, though it was already late in the afternoon, he set forth again from his house about tea-time, to spend a couple of hours at the office. He had sent word to Mr. Timmins that he would probably come in, and begin to get through the arrears caused by his unavoidable absence that morning, and he found his head clerk waiting for him. A few words were of course appropriate, and they were admirably chosen.

"You have seen the result of the inquest, no doubt, Mr. Timmins," he said, "and yet one hardly knows whether one wishes the murderer to be brought to justice. What good does that do, now our friend is dead? So mean and petty a motive too; just for a watch and a few sovereigns. It was money bought at a terrible price, was it not? Poor soul, poor soul; yes, I say that of the murderer. Well, well, we must turn our faces forward, Mr. Timmins; it is no use dwelling on the dreadful irremediable past. The morning's post? Is that it?"

Mr. Timmins ventured sympathy.

"You look terribly worn out, sir," he said. "Wouldn't it be wiser to leave it till to-morrow? A good night's rest, you know, sir, if you'll excuse my mentioning it."

"No, no, Mr. Timmins, we must get to work again, we must get to work."

Nature, inspired by the spirit and instinct of life, is wonderfully recuperative. Whether earthquake or famine, fire or pestilence has blotted out a thousand lives, those who are left, like ants when their house is disturbed, waste but little time after the damage has been done in vain lamentations, but, slaves to the force of life, begin almost instantly to rebuild and reconstruct. And what is true of the community is true also of the individual, and thus in three days from this dreadful morning of the inquest, Mr. Taynton, after attending the funeral of the murdered man, was very actively employed, since the branch of the firm in London, deprived of its head, required supervision from him. Others also, who had been brought near to the tragedy, were occupied again, and of these Morris in particular was a fair example of the spirit of the Life-force. His effort, no doubt, was in a way easier than that made by Mr. Taynton, for to be twenty-two years old and in love should be occupation sufficient. But he, too, had his bad hours, when the past rose phantom-like about him, and he recalled that evening when his rage had driven him nearly mad with passion against his traducer. And by an awful coincidence, his madness had been contemporaneous with the slanderer's death. He must, in fact, have been within a few hundred yards of the place at the time the murder was committed, for he had gone back to Falmer Park that day, with the message that Mr. Taynton would call on the morrow, and had left the place not half an hour before the breaking of the storm. He had driven by the corner of the Park, where the path over the downs left the main road and within a few hundred yards of him at that moment, had been, dead or alive, the man who had so vilely slandered him. Supposing—it might so easily have happened—they had met on the road. What would he have done? Would he have been able to pass him and not wreaked his rage on him? He hardly dared to think of that. But, life and love were his, and that which might have been was soon dreamlike in comparison of these. Indeed, that dreadful dream which he had had the night after the murder had been committed was no less real than it. The past was all of this texture, and mist like, it was evaporated in the beams of the day that was his.

Now Brighton is a populous place, and a sunny one, and many people lounge there in the sun all day. But for the next three or four days a few of these loungers lounged somewhat systematically. One lounged in Sussex Square, another lounged in Montpellier Road, one or two others who apparently enjoyed this fresh air but did not care about the town itself, usually went to the station after breakfast, and spent the day in rambling agreeably about the downs. They also frequented the pleasant little village of Falmer, gossiping freely with its rural inhabitants. Often footmen or gardeners from the Park came down to the village, and acquaintances were easily ripened in the ale-house. Otherwise there was not much incident in the village; sometimes a motor drove by, and one, after an illegally fast progress along the road, very often turned in at the park gates. But no prosecution followed; it was clear they were not agents of the police. Mr. Figgis, also, frequently came out from Brighton, and went strolling about too, very slowly and sadly. He often wandered in the little copses that bordered the path over the downs to Brighton, especially near the place where it joined the main road a few hundred yards below Falmer station. Then came a morning when neither he nor any of the other chance visitors to Falmer were seen there any more. But the evening before Mr. Figgis carried back with him to the train a long thin package wrapped in brown paper. But on the morning when these strangers were seen no more at Falmer, it appeared that they had not entirely left the neighbourhood, for instead of one only being in the neighbourhood of Sussex Square, there were three of them there.

Morris had ordered the motor to be round that morning at eleven, and it had been at the door some few minutes before he appeared. Martin had driven it round from the stables, but he was in a suit of tweed; it seemed that he was not going with it. Then the front door opened, and Morris appeared as usual in a violent hurry. One of the strangers was on the pavement close to the house door, looking with interest at the car. But his interest in the car ceased when the boy appeared. And from the railings of the square garden opposite another stranger crossed the road, and from the left behind the car came a third.

"Mr. Morris Assheton?" said the first.

"Well, what then?" asked Morris.

The two others moved a little nearer.

"I arrest you in the King's name," said the first.

Morris was putting on a light coat as he came across the pavement. One arm was in, the other out. He stopped dead; and the bright colour of his face slowly faded, leaving a sort of ashen gray behind. His mouth suddenly went dry, and it was only at the third attempt to speak that words came.

"What for?" he said.

"For the murder of Godfrey Mills," said the man. "Here is the warrant. I warn you that all you say—"

CHAPTER IX

Morris, whose lithe athletic frame had gone slack for the moment, stiffened himself up again.

"I am not going to say anything," he said. "Martin, drive to Mr. Taynton's at once, and tell him that I am arrested."

The other two now had closed round him.

"Oh, I'm not going to bolt," he said. "Please tell me where you are going to take me."

"Police Court in Branksome Street," said the first.

"Tell Mr. Taynton I am there," said Morris to his man.

There was a cab at the corner of the square, and in answer to an almost imperceptible nod from one of the men, it moved up to the house. The square was otherwise nearly empty, and Morris looked round as the cab drew nearer. Upstairs in the house he had just left, was his mother who was coming out to Falmer this evening to dine; above illimitable blue stretched from horizon to horizon, behind was the free fresh sea. Birds chirped in the bushes and lilac was in flower. Everything had its liberty.

Then a new instinct seized him, and though a moment before he had given his word that he was not meditating escape, liberty called to him. Everything else was free. He rushed forward, striking right and left with his arms, then tripped on the edge of the paving stones and fell. He was instantly seized, and next moment was in the cab, and fetters of steel, though he could not remember their having been placed there, were on his wrists.

CHAPTER X

It was a fortnight later, a hot July morning, and an unusual animation reigned in the staid and leisurely streets of Lewes. For the Assizes opened that day, and it was known that the first case to be tried was the murder of which all Brighton and a large part of England had been talking so much since Morris Assheton had been committed for trial. At the hearing in the police-court there was not very much evidence brought forward, but there had been sufficient to make it necessary that he should stand his trial. It was known, for instance, that he had some very serious reason for anger and resentment against his victim; those who had seen him that day remembered him as being utterly unlike himself; he was known to have been at Falmer Park that afternoon about six, and to have driven home along the Falmer Road in his car an hour or so later. And in a copse close by to where the body of the murdered man was found had been discovered a thick bludgeon of a stick, broken it would seem by some violent act, into two halves. On the top half was rudely cut with a pen-knife M. ASSHE ... What was puzzling, however, was the apparent motive of robbery about the crime; it will be remembered that the victim's watch was missing, and that no money was found on him.

But since Morris had been brought up for committal at the police-court it was believed that a quantity more evidence of a peculiarly incriminating kind had turned up. Yet in spite of this, so it was rumoured, the prisoner apparently did more than bear up; it was said that he was quite cheerful, quite confident that his innocence would be established. Others said that he was merely callous and utterly without any moral sense. Much sympathy of course was felt for his mother, and even more for the family of the Templetons and the daughter to whom it was said that Morris was actually engaged. And, as much as anyone it was Mr. Taynton who was the recipient of the respectful pity of the British public. Though no relation he had all his life been a father to Morris, and while Miss Madge Templeton was young and had the spring and elasticity of youth, so that, though all this was indeed terrible enough, she might be expected to get over it, Mr. Taynton was advanced in years and it seemed that he was utterly broken by the shock. He had not been in Brighton on the day on which Morris was brought before the police-court magistrates, and the news had reached him in London after his young friend had been committed. It was said he had fainted straight off, and there had been much difficulty in bringing him round. But since then he had worked day and night on behalf of the accused. But certain fresh evidence which had turned up a day or two before the Assizes seemed to have taken the heart out of him. He had felt confident that the watch would have been found, and the thief traced. But something new that had turned up had utterly staggered him. He could only cling to one hope, and that was that he knew the evidence about the stick must break down, for it was he who had thrown the fragments into the bushes, a fact which would come to light in his own evidence. But at the most, all he could hope for was, that though it seemed as if the poor lad must be condemned, the jury, on account of his youth, and the provocation he had received, of which Mr. Taynton would certainly make the most when called upon to bear witness on this point, or owing to some weakness in the terrible chain of evidence that had been woven, would recommend him to mercy.

The awful formalities at the opening of the case were gone through. The judge took his seat, and laid on the bench in front of him a small parcel wrapped up in tissue paper; the jury was sworn in, and the prisoner asked if he objected to the inclusion of any of those among the men who were going to decide whether he was worthy of life or guilty of death, and the packed court, composed about equally of men and women, most of whom would have shuddered to see a dog beaten, or a tired hare made to go an extra mile, settled themselves in their places with a rustle of satisfaction at the thought of seeing a man brought before them in the shame of suspected murder, and promised themselves an interesting and thrilling couple of days in observing the gallows march nearer him, and in watching his mental agony. They who would, and perhaps did, subscribe to benevolent institutions for the relief of suffering among the lower animals, would willingly have paid a far higher rate to observe the suffering of a man. He was so interesting; he was so young and good-looking; what a depraved monster he must be. And that little package in tissue paper which the judge brought in and laid on the bench! The black cap, was it not? That showed what the judge thought about it all. How thrilling!

Counsel for the Crown, opened the case, and in a speech grimly devoid of all emotional appeal, laid before the court the facts he was prepared to prove, on which they would base their verdict.

The prisoner, a young man of birth and breeding, had strong grounds for revenge on the murdered man. The prosecution, however, was not concerned in defending what the murdered man had done, but in establishing the guilt of the man who had murdered him. Godfrey Mills, had, as could be proved by witnesses, slandered the prisoner in an abominable manner, and the prosecution were not intending for a moment to attempt to establish the truth of his slander. But this slander they put forward as a motive that gave rise to a murderous impulse on the part of the prisoner. The jury would hear from one of the witnesses, an old friend of the prisoner's, and a man who had been a sort of father to him, that a few hours only before the murder was committed the prisoner had uttered certain words which admitted only of one interpretation, namely that murder was in his mind. That the provocation was great was not denied; it was certain however, that the provocation was sufficient.

Counsel then sketched the actual circumstances of the crime, as far as they could be constructed from what evidence there was. This evidence was purely circumstantial, but of a sort which left no reasonable doubt that the murder had been committed by the prisoner in the manner suggested. Mr. Godfrey Mills had gone to London on the Tuesday of the fatal week, intending to return on the Thursday. On the Wednesday the prisoner became cognisant of the fact that Mr. Godfrey Mills had—he would not argue over it—wantonly slandered him to Sir Richard Templeton, a marriage with the daughter of whom was projected in the prisoner's mind, which there was reason to suppose, might have taken place. Should the jury not be satisfied on that point, witnesses would be called, including the young lady herself, but unless the counsel for the defence challenged their statement, namely that this slander had been spoken which contributed, so it was argued, a motive for the crime it would be unnecessary to intrude on the poignant and private grief of persons so situated, and to insist on a scene which must prove to be so heart-rendingly painful.

(There was a slight movement of demur in the humane and crowded court at this; it was just these heart-rendingly painful things which were so thrilling.)

It was most important, continued counsel for the prosecution that the jury should fix these dates accurately in their minds. Tuesday was June 21st; it was on that day the murdered man had gone to London, designing to return on June 23d, Thursday. The prisoner had learned on Wednesday (June 22d) that aspersions had been made, false aspersions, on his character, and it was on Thursday that he learned for certain from the lips of the man to whom they had been made, who was the author of them. The author was Mr. Godfrey Mills. He had thereupon motored back from Falmer Park, and informed Mr. Taynton of this, and had left again for Falmer an hour later to make an appointment for Mr. Taynton to see Sir Richard. He knew, too, this would be proved, that Mr. Godfrey Mills proposed to return from London that afternoon, to get out at Falmer station and walk back to Brighton. It was certain from the finding of the body that Mr. Mills had travelled from London, as he intended, and that he had got out at this station. It was certain also that at that hour the prisoner, burning for vengeance, and knowing the movements of Mr. Mills, was in the vicinity of Falmer.

To proceed, it was certain also that the prisoner in a very strange wild state had arrived at Mr. Taynton's house about nine that evening, knowing that Mr. Mills was expected there at about 9.30. Granted that he had committed the murder, this proceeding was dictated by the most elementary instinct of self-preservation. It was also in accordance with that that he had gone round in the pelting rain late that night to see if the missing man had returned to his flat, and that he had gone to London next morning to seek him there. He had not, of course, found him, and he returned to Brighton that afternoon. In connection with this return, another painful passage lay before them, for it would be shown by one of the witnesses that again on the Friday afternoon the prisoner had visited the scene of the crime. Mr. Taynton, in fact, still unsuspicious of anything being wrong had walked over the Downs that afternoon from Brighton to Falmer, and had sat down in view of the station where he proposed to catch a train back to Brighton, and had seen the prisoner stop his motor-car close to the corner where the body had been found, and behave in a manner inexplicable except on the theory that he knew where the body lay. Subsequently to the finding of the body, which had occurred on Saturday evening, there had been discovered in a coppice adjoining a heavy bludgeon-like stick broken in two. The top of it, which would be produced, bore the inscription M. ASSHE…

Mr. Taynton was present in court, and was sitting on the bench to the right of the judge who had long been a personal friend of his. Hitherto his face had been hidden in his hands, as this terribly logical tale went on. But here he raised it, and smiled, a wan smile enough, at Morris. The latter did not seem to notice the action. Counsel for the prosecution continued.

All this, he said, had been brought forward at the trial before the police-court magistrates, and he thought the jury would agree that it was more than sufficient to commit the prisoner to trial. At that trial, too, they had heard, the whole world had heard, of the mystery of the missing watch, and the missing money. No money, at least, had been found on the body; it was reasonable to refer to it as "missing." But here again, the motive of self-preservation came in; the whole thing had been carefully planned; the prisoner, counsel suggested, had, just as he had gone up to town to find Mr. Mills the day after the murder was committed, striven to put justice off the scent in making it appear that the motive for the crime, had been robbery. With well-calculated cunning he had taken the watch and what coins there were, from the pockets of his victim. That at any rate was the theory suggested by the prosecution.

The speech was admirably delivered, and its virtue was its extreme impassiveness; it seemed quite impersonal, the mere automatic action of justice, not revengeful, not seeking for death, but merely stating the case as it might be stated by some planet or remote fixed star. Then there was a short pause, while the prosecutor for the Crown laid down his notes. And the same slow, clear, impassive voice went on.

"But since the committal of the prisoner to stand his trial at these assizes," he said, "more evidence of an utterly unexpected, but to us convincing kind has been discovered. Here it is." And he held up a sheet of blotting paper, and a crumpled envelope.

"A letter has been blotted on this sheet," he said, "and by holding it up to the light and looking through it, one can, of course, read what was written. But before I read it, I will tell you from where this sheet was taken. It was taken from a blotting book in the drawing-room of Mrs. Assheton's house in Sussex Square. An expert in handwriting will soon tell the gentlemen of the jury in whose hand he without doubt considers it to be written. After the committal of the prisoner to trial, search was of course made in this house, for further evidence. This evidence was almost immediately discovered. After that no further search was made."

The judge looked up from his notes.

"By whom was this discovery made?" he asked.

"By Superintendent Figgis and Sergeant Wilkinson, my lord. They will give their evidence."

He waited till the judge had entered this.

"I will read the letter," he said, "from the negative, so to speak, of the blotting paper."

"June 21st.

"TO GODFREY MILLS, ESQ.

"You damned brute, I will settle you. I hear you are coming back to Brighton to-morrow, and are getting out at Falmer. All right; I shall be there, and we shall have a talk.

"MORRIS ASSHETON."

A sort of purr went round the court; the kind humane ladies and gentlemen who had fought for seats found this to their taste. The noose tightened.

"I have here also an envelope," said the prosecutor, "which was found by Mr. Figgis and Mr. Wilkinson in the waste-paper basket in the sitting-room of the deceased. According to the expert in handwriting, whose evidence you will hear, it is undoubtedly addressed by the same hand that wrote the letter I have just read you. And, in his opinion, the handwriting is that of the prisoner. No letter was found in the deceased man's room corresponding to this envelope, but the jury will observe that what I have called the negative of the letter on the blotting-paper was dated June 21st, the day that the prisoner suspected the slander that had been levelled at him. The suggestion is that the deceased opened this before leaving for London, and took the letter with him. And the hand, that for the purposes of misleading justice, robbed him of his watch and his money, also destroyed the letter which was then on his person, and which was an incriminating document. But this sheet of blotting paper is as valuable as the letter itself. It proves the letter to have been written."

* * * * *

Morris had been given a seat in the dock, and on each side of him there stood a prison-warder. But in the awed hush that followed, for the vultures and carrion crows who crowded the court were finding themselves quite beautifully thrilled, he wrote a few words on a slip of paper and handed it to a warder to give to his counsel. And his counsel nodded to him.

The opening speech for the Crown had lasted something over two hours, and a couple of witnesses only were called before the interval for lunch. But most of the human ghouls had brought sandwiches with them, and the court was packed with the same people when Morris was brought up again after the interval, and the judge, breathing sherry, took his seat. The court had become terribly hot, but the public were too humane to mind that. A criminal was being chased toward the gallows, and they followed his progress there with breathless interest. Step by step all that was laid down in the opening speech for the prosecution was inexorably proved, all, that is to say, except the affair of the stick. But from what a certain witness (Mr. Taynton) swore to, it was clear that this piece of circumstantial evidence, which indeed was of the greatest importance since the Crown's case was that the murder had been committed with that bludgeon of a stick, completely broke down. Whoever had done the murder, he had not done it with that stick, since Mr. Taynton deposed to having been at Mrs. Assheton's house on the Friday, the day after the murder had been committed, and to having taken the stick away by mistake, believing it to be his. And the counsel for the defence only asked one question on this point, which question closed the proceedings for the day. It was:

"You have a similar stick then?"

And Mr. Taynton replied in the affirmative.

The court then rose.

* * * * *

On the whole the day had been most satisfactory to the ghouls and vultures and it seemed probable that they would have equally exciting and plentiful fare next day. But in the opinion of many Morris's counsel was disappointing. He did not cross-examine witnesses at all sensationally, and drag out dreadful secrets (which had nothing to do with the case) about their private lives, in order to show that they seldom if ever spoke the truth. Indeed, witness after witness was allowed to escape without any cross-examination at all; there was no attempt made to prove that the carpenter who had found the body had been himself tried for murder, or that his children were illegitimate. Yet gradually, as the afternoon went on, a sort of impression began to make its way, that there was something coming which no one suspected.

The next morning those impressions were realised when the adjourned cross-examination of Mr. Taynton was resumed. The counsel for the defence made an immediate attack on the theories of the prosecution, and it told. For the prosecution had suggested that Morris's presence at the scene of the murder the day after was suspicious, as if he had come back uneasily and of an unquiet conscience. If that was so, Mr. Taynton's presence there, who had been the witness who proved the presence of the other, was suspicious also. What had he come there for? In order to throw the broken pieces of Morris's stick into the bushes? These inferences were of course but suggested in the questions counsel asked Mr. Taynton in the further cross-examination of this morning, and perhaps no one in court saw what the suggestion was for a moment or two, so subtly and covertly was it conveyed. Then it appeared to strike all minds together, and a subdued rustle went round the court, followed the moment after by an even intenser silence.

Then followed a series of interrogations, which at first seemed wholly irrelevant, for they appeared to bear only on the business relations between the prisoner and the witness. Then suddenly like the dim light at the end of a tunnel, where shines the pervading illuminating sunlight, a little ray dawned.

"You have had control of the prisoner's private fortune since 1886?"

"Yes."

"In the year 1896 he had £8,000 or thereabouts in London and North-Western Debentures, £6,000 in Consols, £7,000 in Government bonds of South Australia?"

"I have no doubt those figures are correct."

"A fortnight ago you bought £8,000 of London and North-Western Debentures, £6,000 in Consols, £7,000 in Government bonds of South Australia?"

Mr. Taynton opened his lips to speak, but no sound came from them.

"Please answer the question."

If there had been a dead hush before, succeeding the rustle that had followed the suggestions about the stick, a silence far more palpable now descended. There was no doubt as to what the suggestion was now.

The counsel for the prosecution broke in.

"I submit that these questions are irrelevant, my lord," he said.

"I shall subsequently show, my lord, that they are not."

"The witness must answer the question," said the judge. "I see that there is a possible relevancy."

The question was answered.

"Thank you, that is all," said the counsel for the defence, and Mr. Taynton left the witness box.

It was then, for the first time since the trial began, that Morris looked at this witness. All through he had been perfectly calm and collected, a circumstance which the spectators put down to the callousness with which they kindly credited him, and now for the first time, as Mr. Taynton's eyes and his met, an emotion crossed the prisoner's face. He looked sorry.

CHAPTER XI

For the rest of the morning the examination of witnesses for the prosecution went on, for there were a very large number of them, but when the court rose for lunch, the counsel for the prosecution intimated that this was his last. But again, hardly any but those engaged officially, the judge, the counsel, the prisoner, the warder, left the court. Mr. Taynton, however, went home, for he had his seat on the bench, and he could escape for an hour from this very hot and oppressive atmosphere. But he did not go to his Lewes office, or to any hotel to get his lunch. He went to the station, where after waiting some quarter of an hour, he took the train to Brighton. The train ran through Falmer and from his window he could see where the Park palings made an angle close to the road; it was from there that the path over the Downs, where he had so often walked, passed to Brighton.

Again the judge took his seat, still carrying the little parcel wrapped up in tissue paper.

There was no need for the usher to call silence, for the silence was granted without being asked for.

The counsel for the defence called the first witness; he also unwrapped a flat parcel which he had brought into court with him, and handed it to the witness.

"That was supplied by your firm?"

"Yes sir."

"Who ordered it?"

"Mr. Assheton."

"Mr. Morris Assheton, that is. Did he order it from you, you yourself?"

"Yes, sir."

"Did he give any specific instructions about it?"

"Yes, sir."

"What were they?"

"That the blotting book which Mrs. Assheton had already ordered was to be countermanded, and that this was to be sent in its stead on June 24th."

"You mean not after June 24th?"

"No, sir; the instructions were that it was not to be sent before June 24th."

"Why was that?"

"I could not say, sir. Those were the instructions."

"And it was sent on June 24th."

"Yes, sir. It was entered in our book."

The book in question was produced and handed to the jury and the judge.

"That is all, Mrs. Assheton."

She stepped into the box, and smiled at Morris. There was no murmur of sympathy, no rustling; the whole thing was too tense.

"You returned home on June 24th last, from a visit to town?"

"Yes."

"At what time?"

"I could not say to the minute. But about eleven in the morning."

"You found letters waiting for you?"

"Yes."

"Anything else?"

"A parcel."

"What did it contain?"

"A blotting-book. It was a present from my son on my birthday."

"Is this the blotting-book?"

"Yes."

"What did you do with it?"

"I opened it and placed it on my writing table in the drawing-room."

"Thank you; that is all."

There was no cross-examination of this witness, and after the pause, the counsel for the defence spoke again.

"Superintendent Figgis."

"You searched the house of Mrs. Assheton in Sussex Square?"

"Yes, sir."

"What did you take from it?"

"A leaf from a blotting-book, sir."

"Was it that leaf which has been already produced in court, bearing the impress of a letter dated June 21st?"

"Yes, sir."

"Where was the blotting-book?"

"On the writing-table in the drawing-room, sir."

"You did not examine the blotting-book in any way?"

"No, sir."

Counsel opened the book and fitted the torn out leaf into its place.

"We have here the impress of a letter dated June 21st, written in a new blotting-book that did not arrive at Mrs. Assheton's house from the shop till June 24th. It threatens—threatens a man who was murdered, supposedly by the prisoner, on June 23d. Yet this threatening letter was not written till June 24th, after he had killed him."

Quiet and unemotional as had been the address for the Crown, these few remarks were even quieter. Then the examination continued.

"You searched also the flat occupied by the deceased, and you found there this envelope, supposedly in the handwriting of the prisoner, which has been produced by the prosecution?"

"Yes, sir."

"This is it?"

"Yes, sir."

"Thank you. That is all."

Again there was no cross-examination, and the superintendent left the witness box.

Then the counsel for the defence took up two blank envelopes in addition to the one already produced and supposedly addressed in the handwriting of the prisoner.

"This blue envelope," he said, "is from the stationery in Mrs. Assheton's house. This other envelope, white, is from the flat of the deceased. It corresponds in every way with the envelope which was supposed to be addressed in the prisoner's hand, found at the flat in question. The inference is that the prisoner blotted the letter dated June 21st on a blotting pad which did not arrive in Mrs. Assheton's house till June 24th, went to the deceased's flat and put it an envelope there."

These were handed to the jury for examination.

"Ernest Smedley," said counsel.

Mills's servant stepped into the box, and was sworn.

"Between, let us say June 21st and June 24th, did the prisoner call at Mr. Mills's flat?"

"Yes, sir, twice."

"When?"

"Once on the evening of June 23d, and once very early next morning."

"Did he go in?"

"Yes, sir, he came in on both occasions."

"What for?"

"To satisfy himself that Mr. Mills had not come back."

"Did he write anything?"

"No, sir."

"How do you know that?"

"I went with him from room to room, and should have seen if he had done so."

"Did anybody else enter the flat during those days?"

"Yes, sir."

"Who?"

"Mr. Taynton."

The whole court seemed to give a great sigh; then it was quiet again. The judge put down the pen with which he had been taking notes, and like the rest of the persons present he only listened.

"When did Mr. Taynton come into the flat?"

"About mid-day or a little later on Friday."

"June 24th?"

"Yes, sir."

"Please tell the jury what he did?"

The counsel for the prosecution stood up.

"I object to that question," he said.

The judge nodded at him; then looked at the witness again. The examination went on.

"You need not answer that question. I put it to save time, merely. Did Mr. Taynton go into the deceased's sitting-room?"

"Yes, sir."

"Did he write anything there?"

"Yes, sir."

"Was he alone there?"

"Yes, sir."

"Thank you."

Again the examining counsel paused, and again no question was asked by the prosecution.

"Charles Martin," said the counsel for defence.

"You are a servant of the prisoner's?"

"Yes, sir."

"You were in his service during this week of June, of which Friday was June 24th?"

"Yes, sir."

"Describe the events—No. Did the prisoner go up to town, or elsewhere on that day, driving his motorcar, but leaving you in Brighton?"

"Yes, sir."

"Mrs. Assheton came back that morning?"

"Yes, sir."

"Did anyone call that morning? If so, who?"

"Mr. Taynton called."

"Did he go to the drawing-room?"

"Yes, sir."

"Did he write anything there?"

"Yes, sir; he wrote a note to Mrs. Assheton, which he gave me when he went out."

"You were not in the drawing-room, when he wrote it?"

"No, sir."

"Did he say anything to you when he left the house?"

"Yes, sir,"

"What did he say?"

The question was not challenged now.

"He told me to say that he had left the note at the door."

"But he had not done so?"

"No, sir; he wrote it in the drawing-room."

"Thank you. That is all."

But this witness was not allowed to pass as the others had done. The counsel for the prosecution got up.

"You told Mrs. Assheton that it had been left at the door?"

"Yes, sir."

CHAPTER XI

"You knew that was untrue?"

"Yes, sir."

"For what reason did you say it, then?"

Martin hesitated; he looked down, then he looked up again, and was still silent.

"Answer the question."

His eyes met those of the prisoner. Morris smiled at him, and nodded.

"Mr. Taynton told me to say that," he said, "I had once been in Mr. Taynton's service. He dismissed me. I—"

The judge interposed looking at the cross-examining counsel.

"Do you press your question?" he asked. "I do not forbid you to ask it, but I ask you whether the case for the prosecution of the—the prisoner is furthered by your insisting on this question. We have all heard, the jury and I alike, what the last three or four witnesses have said, and you have allowed that—quite properly, in my opinion—to go unchallenged. I do not myself see that there is anything to be gained by the prosecution by pressing the question. I ask you to consider this point. If you think conscientiously, that the evidence, the trend of which we all know now, is to be shaken, you are right to do your best to try to shake it. If not, I wish you to consider whether you should press the question. What the result of your pressing it will be, I have no idea, but it is certainly clear to us all now, that there was a threat implied in Mr. Taynton's words. Personally I do not wish to know what that threat was, nor do I see how the knowledge of it would affect your case in my eyes, or in the eyes of the jury."

There was a moment's pause.

"No, my lord, I do not press it."

Then a clear young voice broke the silence.

"Thanks, Martin," it said.

It came from the dock.

The judge looked across to the dock for a moment, with a sudden irresistible impulse of kindliness for the prisoner whom he was judging.

"Charles Martin," he said, "you have given your evidence, and speaking for myself, I believe it to be entirely trustworthy. I wish to say that your character is perfectly clear. No aspersion whatever has been made on it, except that you said a note had been delivered at the door, though you knew it to have been not so delivered. You made that statement through fear of a certain individual; you were frightened into telling a lie. No one inquires into the sources of your fear."

But in the general stillness, there was one part of the court that was not still, but the judge made no command of silence there, for in the jury-box there was whispering and consultation. It went on for some three minutes. Then the foreman of the jury stood up.

"The jury have heard sufficient of this case, my lord," he said, "and they are agreed on their verdict."

* * * * *

For a moment the buzzing whispers went about the court again, shrilling high, but instantaneously they died down, and the same tense silence prevailed. But from the back of the court there was a stir, and the judge seeing what it was that caused it waited, while Mrs. Assheton moved from her place, and made her way to the front of the dock in which Morris sat. She had been in the witness-box that day, and everyone knew her, and all made way for her, moving as the blades of corn move when the wind stirs them, for her right was recognised and unquestioned. But the dock was high above her, and a barrister who sat below instantly vacated his seat, she got up and stood on it. All eyes were fixed on her, and none saw that at this moment a telegram was handed to the judge which he opened and read.

Then he turned to the foreman of the jury.

"What verdict, do you find?" he asked.

"Not guilty."

Mrs. Assheton had already grasped Morris's hands in hers, and just as the words were spoken she kissed him.

* * * * *

Then a shout arose which bade fair to lift the roof off, and neither judge nor ushers of the court made any attempt to quiet it, and if it was only for the sensation of seeing the gallows march nearer the prisoner that these folk had come together, yet there was no mistaking the genuineness of their congratulations now. Morris's whole behaviour too, had been so gallant and brave; innocent though he knew himself to be, yet it required a very high courage to listen to the damning accumulation of evidence against him, and if there is one thing that the ordinary man appreciates more than sensation, it is pluck. Then, but not for a long time, the uproar subsided, and the silence descended again. Then the judge spoke.

"Mr. Assheton," he said, "for I no longer can call you prisoner, the jury have of course found you not guilty of the terrible crime of which you were accused, and I need not say that I entirely agree with their verdict. Throughout the trial you have had my sympathy and my admiration for your gallant bearing." Then at a sign from the judge his mother and he were let out by the private door below the bench.

After they had gone silence was restored. Everyone knew that there must be more to come. The prisoner was found not guilty; the murder was still unavenged.

Then once more the judge spoke.

"I wish to make public recognition," he said, "of the fairness and ability with which the case was conducted on both sides. The prosecution, as it was their duty to do, forged the chain of evidence against Mr. Assheton as strongly as they were able, and pieced together incriminating circumstances against him with a skill that at first seemed conclusive of his guilt. The first thing that occurred to make a weak link in their chain was the acknowledgment of a certain witness that the stick with which the murder was supposed to have been committed was not left on the spot by the accused, but by himself. Why he admitted that we can only conjecture, but my conjecture is that it was an act of repentance and contrition on his part. When it came to that point he could not let the evidence which he had himself supplied tell against him on whom it was clearly his object to father the crime. You will remember also that certain circumstances pointed to robbery being the motive of the crime. That I think was the first idea, so to speak of the real criminal. Then, we must suppose, he saw himself safer, if he forged against another certain evidence which we have heard."

The judge paused for a moment, and then went on with evident emotion.

"This case will never be reopened again," he said, "for a reason that I will subsequently tell the court; we have seen the last of this tragedy, and retribution and punishment are in the hands of a higher and supreme tribunal. This witness, Mr. Edward Taynton—has been for years a friend of mine, and the sympathy which I felt for him at the opening of the case, when a young man, to whom I still believe him to have been attached, was on his trial, is changed to a deeper pity. During the afternoon you have heard certain evidence, from which you no doubt as well as I infer that the fact of this murder having been committed was known to the man who wrote a letter and blotted it on the sheet which has been before the court. That man also, as it was clear to us an hour ago, directed a certain envelope which you have also seen. I may add that Mr. Taynton had, as I knew, an extraordinary knack of imitating handwritings; I have seen him write a signature that I could have sworn was mine. But he has used that gift for tragic purposes.

"I have just received a telegram. He left this court before the luncheon interval, and went to his house in Brighton. Arrived there, as I have just learned, he poisoned himself. And may God have mercy on his soul."

Again he paused.

"The case therefore is closed," he said, "and the court will rise for the day. You will please go out in silence."

COLLECTED STORIES

How Fear Departed from the Long Gallery

Church-Peveril is a house so beset and frequented by spectres, both visible and audible, that none of the family which it shelters under its acre and a half of green copper roofs takes psychical phenomena with any seriousness. For to the Peverils the appearance of a ghost is a matter of hardly greater significance than is the appearance of the post to those who live in more ordinary houses. It arrives, that is to say, practically every day, it knocks (or makes other noises), it is observed coming up the drive (or in other places). I myself, when staying there, have seen the present Mrs. Peveril, who is rather short-sighted, peer into the dusk, while we were taking our coffee on the terrace after dinner, and say to her daughter:

"My dear, was not that the Blue Lady who has just gone into the shrubbery. I hope she won't frighten Flo. Whistle for Flo, dear."

(Flo, it may be remarked, is the youngest and most precious of many dachshunds.)

Blanche Peveril gave a cursory whistle, and crunched the sugar left unmelted at the bottom of her coffee-cup between her very white teeth.

"Oh, darling, Flo isn't so silly as to mind," she said. "Poor blue Aunt Barbara is such a bore!"

"Whenever I meet her she always looks as if she wanted to speak to me, but when I say, 'What is it, Aunt Barbara?' she never utters, but only points somewhere towards the house, which is so vague. I believe there was something she wanted to confess about two hundred years ago, but she has forgotten what it is."

Here Flo gave two or three short pleased barks, and came out of the shrubbery wagging her tail, and capering round what appeared to me to be a perfectly empty space on the lawn.

"There! Flo has made friends with her," said Mrs. Peveril. "I wonder why she -- in that very stupid shade of blue."

From this it may be gathered that even with regard to psychical phenomena there is some truth in the proverb that speaks of familiarity. But the Peverils do not exactly treat their ghosts with contempt, since most of that delightful family never despised anybody except such people as avowedly did not care for hunting or shooting, or golf or skating. And as all of their ghosts are of their family, it seems reasonable to suppose that they all, even the poor Blue Lady, excelled at one time in field-sports. So far, then, they harbour no such unkindness or contempt, but only pity. Of one Peveril, indeed, who broke his neck in vainly attempting to ride up the main staircase on a thoroughbred mare after some monstrous and violent deed in the back-garden, they are very fond, and Blanche comes downstairs in the morning with an eye unusually bright when she can announce that Master Anthony was "very loud" last night. He (apart from the fact of his having been so foul a ruffian) was a tremendous fellow across country, and they like these indications of the continuance of his superb vitality. In fact, it is supposed to be a compliment, when you go to stay at Church-Peveril, to be assigned a bedroom which is frequented by defunct members of the family. It means that you are worthy to look on the august and villainous dead, and you will find yourself shown into some vaulted or tapestried chamber, without benefit of electric light, and are told that great-great-grandmamma Bridget occasionally has vague business by the fireplace, but it is better not to talk to her, and that you will hear Master Anthony "awfully well" if he attempts the front staircase any time before morning. There you are left for your night's repose, and, having quakingly undressed, begin reluctantly to put out your candles. It is draughty in these great chambers, and the solemn tapestry swings and bellows and subsides, and the firelight dances on the forms of huntsmen and warriors and stern pursuits. Then you climb into your bed, a bed so huge that you feel as if the desert of Sahara was spread for you, and pray, like the mariners who sailed with St. Paul, for day. And, all the time, you are aware that Freddy and Harry and Blanche and possibly even Mrs. Peveril are quite capable of dressing up and making disquieting tappings outside your door, so that when you open it some inconjecturable horror fronts you. For myself, I stick steadily to the assertion that I have an obscure valvular disease of the heart, and so sleep undisturbed in the new wing of the house where Aunt Barbara, and great-great-grandmamma Bridget and Master Anthony never penetrate. I forget the details of great-great-grandmamma Bridget, but she certainly cut the throat of some distant relation before she disembowelled herself with the axe that had been used at Agincourt. Before that she had led a very sultry life, crammed with amazing incident.

But there is one ghost at Church-Peveril at which the family never laugh, in which they feel no friendly and amused interest, and of which they only speak just as much as is necessary for the safety of their guests. More properly it should be described as two ghosts, for the "haunt" in question is that of two very young children, who were twins. These, not without reason, the family take very seriously indeed. The story of them, as told me by Mrs. Peveril, is as follows:

In the year 1602, the same being the last of Queen Elizabeth's reign, a certain Dick Peveril was greatly in favour at Court. He was brother to Master Joseph Peveril, then owner of the family house and lands, who two years previously, at the respectable age of seventy-four, became father of twin boys, first-born of his progeny. It is known that the royal and ancient virgin had said to handsome Dick, who was nearly forty years his brother's junior, "'Tis pity that you are not master of Church-Peveril," and these words probably suggested to him a sinister design. Be that as it may, handsome Dick, who very adequately sustained the family reputation for wickedness, set off to ride down to Yorkshire, and found that, very conveniently, his brother Joseph had just been seized with an apoplexy, which appeared to be the result of a continued spell of hot weather combined with the necessity of quenching his thirst with an augmented amount of sack, and had actually died while handsome Dick, with God knows what thoughts in his mind, was journeying northwards. Thus it came about that he arrived at Church-Peveril just in time for his brother's funeral. It was with great propriety that he attended the obsequies, and returned to spend a sympathetic day or two of mourning with his widowed sister-in-law, who was but a faint-hearted dame, little fit to be mated with such hawks as these. On the second night of his stay, he did that which the Peverils regret to this day. He entered the room where the twins slept with their nurse, and quietly strangled the latter as she slept. Then he took the twins and put them into the fire which warms the long gallery. The weather, which up to the day of Joseph's death had been so hot, had changed suddenly to bitter cold, and the fire was heaped high with burning logs and was exultant with flame. In the core of this conflagration he struck out a cremation-chamber, and into that he threw the two children, stamping them down with his riding-boots. They could just walk, but they could not walk out of that ardent place. It is said that he laughed as he added more logs. Thus he became master of Church-Peveril.

The crime was never brought home to him, but he lived no longer than a year in the enjoyment of his blood-stained inheritance. When he lay a-dying he made his confession to the priest who attended him, but his spirit struggled forth from its fleshly coil before Absolution could be given him. On that very night there began in Church-Peveril the haunting which to this day is but seldom spoken of by the family, and then only in low tones and with serious mien. For only an hour or two after handsome Dick's death, one of the servants passing the door of the long gallery heard from within peals of the loud laughter so jovial and yet so sinister which he had thought would never be heard in the house again. In a moment of that cold courage which is so nearly akin to mortal terror he opened the door and entered, expecting to see he knew not what manifestation of him who lay dead in the room below. Instead he saw two little white-robed figures toddling towards him hand in hand across the moon-lit floor.

The watchers in the room below ran upstairs startled by the crash of his fallen body, and found him lying in the grip of some dread convulsion. Just before morning he regained consciousness and told his tale. Then pointing with trembling and ash-grey finger towards the door, he screamed aloud, and so fell back dead.

During the next fifty years this strange and terrible legend of the twin-babies became fixed and consolidated. Their appearance, luckily for those who inhabit the house, was exceedingly rare, and during these years they seem to have been seen four or five times only. On each occasion they appeared at night, between sunset and sunrise, always in the same long gallery, and always as two toddling children scarcely able to walk. And on each occasion the luckless individual who saw them died either speedily or terribly, or with both speed and terror, after the accursed vision had appeared to him. Sometimes he might live for a few months:

he was lucky if he died, as did the servant who first saw them, in a few hours. Vastly more awful was the fate of a certain Mrs.

Canning, who had the ill-luck to see them in the middle of the next century, or to be quite accurate, in the year 1760. By this time the hours and the place of their appearance were well known, and, as up till a year ago, visitors were warned not to go between sunset and sunrise into the long gallery.

But Mrs. Canning, a brilliantly clever and beautiful woman, admirer also and friend of the notorious sceptic M. Voltaire, wilfully went and sat night after night, in spite of all protestations, in the haunted place. For four evenings she saw nothing, but on the fifth she had her will, for the door in the middle of the gallery opened, and there came toddling towards her the ill-omened innocent little pair. It seemed that even then she was not frightened, but she thought it good, poor wretch, to mock at them, telling them it was time for them to get back into the fire. They gave no word in answer, but turned away from her crying and sobbing. Immediately after they disappeared from her vision and she rustled downstairs to where the family and guests in the house were waiting for her, with the triumphant announcement that she has seen them both, and must needs write to M. Voltaire, saying that she had spoken to spirits made manifest. It would make him laugh. But when some months later the whole news reached him he did not laugh at all.

Mrs. Canning was one of the great beauties of her day, and in the year 1760 she was at the height and zenith of her blossoming. The chief beauty, if it is possible to single out one point where all was so exquisite, lay in the dazzling colour and incomparable brilliance of her complexion. She was now just thirty years of age, but, in spite of the excesses of her life, retained the snow and roses of girlhood, and she courted the bright light of day which other women shunned, for it but showed to great advantage the splendour of her skin. In consequence she was very considerably dismayed one morning, about a fortnight after her strange experience in the long gallery, to observe on her left cheek, an inch or two below her turquoise-coloured eyes, a little greyish patch of skin, about as big as a threepenny piece. It was in vain that she applied her accustomed washes and unguents: vain, too, were the arts of her fardeuse and of her medical adviser. For a week she kept herself secluded, martyring herself with solitude and unaccustomed physics, and for result at the end of the week she had no amelioration to comfort herself with: instead this woeful grey patch had doubled itself in size. Thereafter the nameless disease, whatever it was, developed in new and terrible ways. From the centre of the discoloured place there sprouted forth little lichen-like tendrils of greenish-grey, and another patch appeared on her lower lip. This, too, soon vegetated, and one morning, on opening her eyes to the horror of a new day, she found that her vision was strangely blurred. She sprang to her looking-glass, and what she saw caused her to shriek aloud with horror. From under her upper eye-lid a fresh growth had sprung up, mushroom-like, in the night, and its filaments extended downwards, screening the pupil of her eye. Soon after, her tongue and throat were attacked: the air passages became obstructed, and death by suffocation was merciful after such suffering.

More terrible yet was the case of a certain Colonel Blantyre who fired at the children with his revolver. What he went through is not to be recorded here.

It is this haunting, then, that the Peverils take quite seriously, and every guest on his arrival in the house is told that the long gallery must not be entered after nightfall on any pretext whatever. By day, however, it is a delightful room and intrinsically merits description, apart from the fact that the due understanding of its geography is necessary for the account that here follows. It is full eighty feet in length, and is lit by a row of six tall windows looking over the gardens at the back of the house. A door communicates with the landing at the top of the main staircase, and about half-way down the gallery in the wall facing the windows is another door communicating with the back staircase and servants' quarters, and thus the gallery forms a constant place of passage for them in going to the rooms on the first landing. It was through this door that the baby-figures came when they appeared to Mrs. Canning, and on several other occasions they have been known to make their entry here, for the room out of which handsome Dick took them lies just beyond at the top of the back stairs. Further on again in the gallery is the fireplace into which he thrust them, and at the far end a large bow-window looks straight down the avenue. Above this fireplace there hangs with grim significance a portrait of handsome Dick, in the insolent beauty of early manhood, attributed to Holbein, and a dozen other portraits of great merit face the windows. During the day this is the most frequented sitting-room in the house, for its other visitors never appear there then, nor does it then ever resound with the harsh jovial laugh of handsome Dick, which sometimes, after dark has fallen, is heard by passers-by on the landing outside. But Blanche does not grow bright-eyed when she hears it: she shuts her ears and hastens to put a greater distance between her and the sound of that atrocious mirth.

But during the day the long gallery is frequented by many occupants, and much laughter in no wise sinister or saturnine resounds there. When summer lies hot over the land, those occupants lounge in the deep window seats, and when winter spreads his icy fingers and blows shrilly between his frozen palms, congregate round the fireplace at the far end, and perch, in companies of cheerful chatterers, upon sofa and chair, and chair-back and floor. Often have I sat there on long August evenings up till dressing-time, but never have I been there when anyone has seemed disposed to linger over-late without hearing the warning: "It is close on sunset: shall we go?" Later on in the shorter autumn days they often have tea laid there, and sometimes it has happened that, even while merriment was most uproarious, Mrs. Peveril has suddenly looked out of the window and said, "My dears, it is getting so late: let us finish our nonsense downstairs in the hall." And then for a moment a curious hush always falls on loquacious family and guests alike, and as if some bad news had just been known, we all make our silent way out of the place.

But the spirits of the Peverils (of the living ones, that is to say) are the most mercurial imaginable, and the blight which the thought of handsome Dick and his doings casts over them passes away again with amazing rapidity.

A typical party, large, young, and peculiarly cheerful, was staying at Church-Peveril shortly after Christmas last year, and as usual on December 31, Mrs. Peveril was giving her annual New Year's Eve ball. The house was quite full, and she had commandeered as well the greater part of the Peveril Arms to provide sleeping-quarters for the overflow from the house. For some days past a black and windless frost had stopped all hunting, but it is an ill windlessness that blows no good (if so mixed a metaphor may be forgiven), and the lake below the house had for the last day or two been covered with an adequate and admirable sheet of ice. Everyone in the house had been occupied all the morning of that day in performing swift and violent manoeuvres on the elusive surface, and as soon as lunch was over we all, with one exception, hurried out again. This one exception was Madge Dalrymple, who had had the misfortune to fall rather badly earlier in the day, but hoped, by resting her injured knee, instead of joining the skaters again, to be able to dance that evening. The hope, it is true, was the most sanguine sort, for she could but hobble ignobly back to the house, but with the breezy optimism which characterises the Peverils (she is Blanche's first cousin), she remarked that it would be but tepid enjoyment that she could, in her present state, derive from further skating, and thus she sacrificed little, but might gain much.

Accordingly, after a rapid cup of coffee which was served in the long gallery, we left Madge comfortably reclined on the big sofa at right-angles to the fireplace, with an attractive book to beguile the tedium till tea. Being of the family, she knew all about handsome Dick and the babies, and the fate of Mrs. Canning and Colonel Blantyre, but as we went out I heard Blanche say to her, "Don't run it too fine, dear," and Madge had replied, "No; I'll go away well before sunset." And so we left her alone in the long gallery.

Madge read her attractive book for some minutes, but failing to get absorbed in it, put it down and limped across to the window. Though it was still but little after two, it was but a dim and uncertain light that entered, for the crystalline brightness of the morning had given place to a veiled obscurity produced by flocks of thick clouds which were coming sluggishly up from the north-east. Already the whole sky was overcast with them, and occasionally a few snow-flakes fluttered waveringly down past the long windows. From the darkness and bitter cold of the afternoon, it seemed to her that there was like to be a heavy snowfall before long, and these outward signs were echoed inwardly in her by that muffled drowsiness of the brain, which to those who are sensitive to the pressures and lightness of weather portends storm. Madge was peculiarly the prey of such external influences: to her a brisk morning gave an ineffable brightness and briskness of spirit, and correspondingly the approach of heavy weather produced a somnolence in sensation that both drowsed and depressed her.

It was in such mood as this that she limped back again to the sofa beside the log-fire. The whole house was comfortably heated by water-pipes, and though the fire of logs and peat, an adorable mixture, had been allowed to burn low, the room was very warm. Idly she watched the dwindling flames, not opening her book again, but lying on the sofa with face towards the fireplace, intending drowsily and not immediately to go to her own room and spend the hours, until the return of the skaters made gaiety in the house again, in writing one or two neglected letters. Still drowsily she began thinking over what she had to communicate: one letter several days overdue should go to her mother, who was immensely interested in the psychical affairs of the family. She would tell her how Master Anthony had been prodigiously active on the staircase a night or two ago, and how the Blue Lady, regardless of the severity of the weather, had been seen by Mrs. Peveril that morning, strolling about. It was rather interesting: the Blue Lady had gone down the laurel walk and had been seen by her to enter the stables, where, at the moment, Freddy Peveril was inspecting the frost-bound hunters. Identically then, a sudden panic had spread through the stables, and the horses had whinnied and kicked, and shied, and sweated. Of the fatal twins nothing had been seen for many years past, but, as her mother knew, the Peverils never used the long gallery after dark.

Then for a moment she sat up, remembering that she was in the long gallery now. But it was still but a little after half-past two, and if she went to her room in half an hour, she would have ample time to write this and another letter before tea. Till then she would read her book. But she found she had left it on the window-sill, and it seemed scarcely worth while to get it. She felt exceedingly drowsy.

The sofa where she lay had been lately recovered, in a greyish green shade of velvet, somewhat the colour of lichen. It was of very thick soft texture, and she luxuriously stretched her arms out, one on each side of her body, and pressed her fingers into the nap. How horrible that story of Mrs. Canning was: the growth on her face was of the colour of lichen. And then without further transition or blurring of thought Madge fell asleep.

She dreamed. She dreamed that she awoke and found herself exactly where she had gone to sleep, and in exactly the same attitude. The flames from the logs had burned up again, and leaped on the walls, fitfully illuminating the picture of handsome Dick above the fireplace. In her dream she knew exactly what she had done to-day, and for what reason she was lying here now instead of being out with the rest of the skaters. She remembered also (still dreaming), that she was going to write a letter or two before tea, and prepared to get up in order to go to her room. As she half-rose she caught sight of her own arms lying out on each side of her on the grey velvet sofa.

But she could not see where her hands ended, and where the grey velvet began: her fingers seemed to have melted into the stuff. She could see her wrists quite clearly, and a blue vein on the backs of her hands, and here and there a knuckle. Then, in her dream, she remembered the last thought which had been in her mind before she fell asleep, namely the growth of the lichen-coloured vegetation on the face and the eyes and the throat of Mrs. Canning. At that thought the strangling terror of real nightmare began: she knew that she was being transformed into this grey stuff, and she was absolutely unable to move. Soon the grey would spread up her arms, and over her feet; when they came in from skating they would find here nothing but a huge misshapen cushion of lichen-coloured velvet, and that would be she. The horror grew more acute, and then by a violent effort she shook herself free of the clutches of this very evil dream, and she awoke.

For a minute or two she lay there, conscious only of the tremendous relief at finding herself awake. She felt again with her fingers the pleasant touch of the velvet, and drew them backwards and forwards, assuring herself that she was not, as her dream had suggested, melting into greyness and softness. But she was still, in spite of the violence of her awakening, very sleepy, and lay there till, looking down, she was aware that she could not see her hands at all. It was very nearly dark.

At that moment a sudden flicker of flame came from the dying fire, and a flare of burning gas from the peat flooded the room. The portrait of handsome Dick looked evilly down on her, and her hands were visible again. And then a panic worse than the panic of her dreams seized her.

Daylight had altogether faded, and she knew that she was alone in the dark in the terrible gallery.

This panic was of the nature of nightmare, for she felt unable to move for terror. But it was worse than nightmare because she knew she was awake. And then the full cause of this frozen fear dawned on her; she knew with the certainty of absolute conviction that she was about to see the twin-babies.

She felt a sudden moisture break out on her face, and within her mouth her tongue and throat went suddenly dry, and she felt her tongue grate along the inner surface of her teeth. All power of movement had slipped from her limbs, leaving them dead and inert, and she stared with wide eyes into the blackness. The spurt of flame from the peat had burned itself out again, and darkness encompassed her.

Then on the wall opposite her, facing the windows, there grew a faint light of dusky crimson.

For a moment she thought it but heralded the approach of the awful vision, then hope revived in her heart, and she remembered that thick clouds had overcast the sky before she went to sleep, and guessed that this light came from the sun not yet quite sunk and set. This sudden revival of hope gave her the necessary stimulus, and she sprang off the sofa where she lay. She looked out of the window and saw the dull glow on the horizon. But before she could take a step forward it was obscured again. A tiny sparkle of light came from the hearth which did no more than illuminate the tiles of the fireplace, and snow falling heavily tapped at the window panes. There was neither light nor sound except these.

But the courage that had come to her, giving her the power of movement, had not quite deserted her, and she began feeling her way down the gallery. And then she found that she was lost. She stumbled against a chair, and, recovering herself, stumbled against another. Then a table barred her way, and, turning swiftly aside, she found herself up against the back of a sofa.

Once more she turned and saw the dim gleam of the firelight on the side opposite to that on which she expected it. In her blind gropings she must have reversed her direction. But which way was she to go now. She seemed blocked in by furniture. And all the time insistent and imminent was the fact that the two innocent terrible ghosts were about to appear to her.

Then she began to pray. "Lighten our darkness, O Lord," she said to herself. But she could not remember how the prayer continued, and she had sore need of it. There was something about the perils of the night. All this time she felt about her with groping, fluttering hands. The fire-glimmer which should have been on her left was on her right again; therefore she must turn herself round again. "Lighten our darkness," she whispered, and then aloud she repeated, "Lighten our darkness."

She stumbled up against a screen, and could not remember the existence of any such screen.

Hastily she felt beside it with blind hands, and touched something soft and velvety. Was it the sofa on which she had lain? If so, where was the head of it. It had a head and a back and feet--it was like a person, all covered with grey lichen. Then she lost her head completely. All that remained to her was to pray; she was lost, lost in this awful place, where no one came in the dark except the babies that cried. And she heard her voice rising from whisper to speech, and speech to scream. She shrieked out the holy words, she yelled them as if blaspheming as she groped among tables and chairs and the pleasant things of ordinary life which had become so terrible.

Then came a sudden and an awful answer to her screamed prayer. Once more a pocket of inflammable gas in the peat on the hearth was reached by the smouldering embers, and the room started into light. She saw the evil eyes of handsome Dick, she saw the little ghostly snow-flakes falling thickly outside. And she saw where she was, just opposite the door through which the terrible twins made their entrance. Then the flame went out again, and left her in blackness once more. But she had gained something, for she had her geography now. The centre of the room was bare of furniture, and one swift dart would take her to the door of the landing above the main staircase and into safety. In that gleam she had been able to see the handle of the door, bright-brassed, luminous like a star. She would go straight for it; it was but a matter of a few seconds now.

She took a long breath, partly of relief, partly to satisfy the demands of her galloping heart.

But the breath was only half-taken when she was stricken once more into the immobility of nightmare.

There came a little whisper, it was no more than that, from the door opposite which she stood, and through which the twin-babies entered. It was not quite dark outside it, for she could see that the door was opening. And there stood in the opening two little white figures, side by side. They came towards her slowly, shufflingly. She could not see face or form at all distinctly, but the two little white figures were advancing. She knew them to be the ghosts of terror, innocent of the awful doom they were bound to bring, even as she was innocent. With the inconceivable rapidity of thought, she made up her mind what to do. She had not hurt them or laughed at them, and they, they were but babies when the wicked and bloody deed had sent them to their burning death. Surely the spirits of these children would not be inaccessible to the cry of one who was of the same blood as they, who had committed no fault that merited the doom they brought. If she entreated them they might have mercy, they might forebear to bring the curse on her, they might allow her to pass out of the place without blight, without the sentence of death, or the shadow of things worse than death upon her.

It was but for the space of a moment that she hesitated, then she sank down on to her knees, and stretched out her hands towards them.

"Oh, my dears," she said, "I only fell asleep. I have done no more wrong than that--"

She paused a moment, and her tender girl's heart thought no more of herself, but only of them, those little innocent spirits on whom so awful a doom was laid, that they should bring death where other children bring laughter, and doom for delight. But all those who had seen them before had dreaded and feared them, or had mocked at them.

Then, as the enlightenment of pity dawned on her, her fear fell from her like the wrinkled sheath that holds the sweet folded buds of Spring.

"Dears, I am so sorry for you," she said. "It is not your fault that you must bring me what you must bring, but I am not afraid any longer. I am only sorry for you. God bless you, you poor darlings."

She raised her head and looked at them. Though it was so dark, she could now see their faces, though all was dim and wavering, like the light of pale flames shaken by a draught. But the faces were not miserable or fierce--they smiled at her with shy little baby smiles. And as she looked they grew faint, fading slowly away like wreaths of vapour in frosty air.

Madge did not at once move when they had vanished, for instead of fear there was wrapped round her a wonderful sense of peace, so happy and serene that she would not willingly stir, and so perhaps disturb it. But before long she got up, and feeling her way, but without any sense of nightmare pressing her on, or frenzy of fear to spur her, she went out of the long gallery, to find Blanche just coming upstairs whistling and swinging her skates.

"How's the leg, dear," she asked. "You're not limping any more."

Till that moment Madge had not thought of it.

"I think it must be all right," she said; "I had forgotten it, anyhow. Blanche, dear, you won't be frightened for me, will you, but--but I have seen the twins."

For a moment Blanche's face whitened with terror.

"What?" she said in a whisper.

"Yes, I saw them just now. But they were kind, they smiled at me, and I was so sorry for them. And somehow I am sure I have nothing to fear."

It seems that Madge was right, for nothing has come to touch her. Something, her attitude to them, we must suppose, her pity, her sympathy, touched and dissolved and annihilated the curse.

Indeed, I was at Church-Peveril only last week, arriving there after dark. Just as I passed the gallery door, Blanche came out.

"Ah, there you are," she said: "I've just been seeing the twins. They looked too sweet and stopped nearly ten minutes. Let us have tea at once."

At Abdul Ali's Grave

Luxor, as most of those who have been there will allow, is a place of notable charm, and boasts many attractions for the traveller, chief among which he will reckon an excellent hotel containing a billiard-room, a garden fit for the gods to sit in, any quantity of visitors, at least a weekly dance on board a tourist steamer, quail shooting, a climate as of Avilion, and a number of stupendously ancient monuments for those archeologically inclined. But to certain others, few indeed in number, but almost fanatically convinced of their own orthodoxy, the charm of Luxor, like some sleeping beauty, only wakes when these things cease, when the hotel has grown empty and the billiard-marker "has gone for a long rest" to Cairo, when the decimated quail and the decimating tourist have fled northwards, and the Theban plain, Dana to a tropical sun, is a gridiron across which no man would willingly make a journey by day, not even if Queen Hatasoo herself should signify that she would give him audience on the terraces of Deir-el-Bahari.

A suspicion however that the fanatic few were right, for in other respects they were men of estimable opinions, induced me to examine their convictions for myself, and thus it came about that two years ago, certain days toward the beginning of June saw me still there, a confirmed convert.

Much tobacco and the length of summer days had assisted us to the analysis of the charm of which summer in the south is possessed, and Weston--one of the earliest of the elect--and myself had discussed it at some length, and though we reserved as the principal ingredient a nameless something which baffled the chemist, and must be felt to be understood, we were easily able to detect certain other drugs of sight and sound, which we were agreed contributed to the whole. A few of them are here sub joined.

The waking in the warm darkness just before dawn to find that the desire for stopping in bed fails with the awakening.

The silent start across the Nile in the still air with our horses, who, like us, stand and sniff at the incredible sweetness of the coming morning without apparently finding it less wonderful in repetition.

The moment infinitesimal in duration but infinite in sensation, just before the sun rises, when the grey shrouded river is struck suddenly out of darkness, and becomes a sheet of green bronze.

The rose flush, rapid as a change of colour in some chemical combination, which shoots across the sky from east to west, followed immediately by the sunlight which catches the peaks of the western hills, and flows down like some luminous liquid.

The stir and whisper which goes through the world: a breeze springs up; a lark soars, and sings; the boatman shouts "Yallah, Yallah"; the horses toss their heads.

The subsequent ride.

The subsequent breakfast on our return.

The subsequent absence of anything to do.

At sunset the ride into the desert thick with the scent of warm barren sand, which smells like nothing else in the world, for it smells of nothing at all.

The blaze of the tropical night.

Camel's milk.

Converse with the fellahin, who are the most charming and least accountable people on the face of the earth except when tourists are about, and when in consequence there is no thought but backsheesh.

Lastly, and with this we are concerned, the possibility of odd experiences.

The beginning of the things which make this tale occurred four days ago, when Abdul Mi, the oldest man in the village, died suddenly, full of days and riches. Both, some thought, had probably been somewhat exaggerated, but his relations affirmed without variation that he had as many years as he had English pounds, and that each was a hundred. The apt roundness of these numbers was incontestable, the thing was too neat not to be true, and before he had been dead for twenty-four hours it was a matter of orthodoxy. But with regard to his relations, that which turned their bereavement, which must soon have occurred, into a source of blank dismay instead of pious resignation, was that not one of these English pounds, not even their less satisfactory equivalent in notes, which, out of the tourist season, are looked upon at Luxor as a not very dependable variety of Philosopher's stone, though certainly capable of producing gold under favourable circumstances, could be found. Abdul Au with his hundred years was dead, his century of sovereigns--they might as well have been an annuity--were dead with him, and his son Mohamed, who had previously enjoyed a sort of brevet rank in anticipation of the event, was considered to be throwing far more dust in the air than the genuine affection even of a chief mourner wholly justified.

Abdul, it is to be feared, was not a man of stereotyped respectability; though full of years and riches, he enjoyed no great reputation for honour. He drank wine whenever he could get it, he ate food during the days of Ramadan, scornful of the fact, when his appetite desired it, he was supposed to have the evil eye, and in his last moments he was attended by the notorious Achmet, who is well known here to be practised in Black Magic, and has been suspected of the much meaner crime of robbing the bodies of those lately dead. For in Egypt, while to despoil the bodies of ancient kings and priests is a privilege for which advanced and learned societies vie with each other, to rob the corpses of your contemporaries is considered the deed of a dog.

Mohamed, who soon exchanged the throwing of dust in the air for the more natural mode of expressing chagrin, which is to gnaw the nails, told us in confidence that he suspected Achmet of having ascertained the secret of where his father's money was, but it appeared that Achmet had as blank a face as anybody when his patient, who was striving to make some communication to him, went out into the great silence, and the suspicion that he knew where the money was gave way, in the minds, of those who were competent to form an estimate of his character, to a but dubious regret that he had just failed to learn that very important fact.

So Abdul died and was buried, and we all went to the funeral feast, at which we ate more roast meat than one naturally cares about at five in the afternoon on a June day, in consequence of which Weston and I, not requiring dinner, stopped at home after our return from the ride into the desert, and talked to Mohamed, Abdul's son, and Hussein, Abdul's youngest grandson, a boy of about twenty, who is also our valet, cook and housemaid, and they together woefully narrated of the money that had been and was not, and told us scandalous tales about Achmet concerning his weakness for cemeteries. They drank coffee and smoked, for though Hussein was our servant, we had been that day the guests of his father, and shortly after they had gone, up came Machmout.

Machmout, who says he thinks he is twelve, but does not know for certain, is kitchen-maid, groom and gardener, and has to an extraordinary degree some occult power resembling clairvoyance. Weston, who is a member of the Society for Psychical Research, and the tragedy of whose life has been the detection of the fraudulent medium Mrs. Blunt, says that it is all thought-reading, and has made notes of many of Machmout's performances, which may subsequently turn out to be of interest. Thought-reading, however, does not seem to me to fully explain the experience which followed Abdul's funeral, and with Machmout I have to put it down to White Magic, which should be a very inclusive term, or to Pure Coincidence, which is even more inclusive, and will cover all the inexplicable phenomena of the world, taken singly. Machmout's method of unloosing the forces of White Magic is simple, being the ink-mirror known by name to many, and it is as follows.

A little black ink is poured into the palm of Machmout's hand, or, as ink has been at a premium lately owing to the last post-boat from Cairo which contained stationery for us having stuck on a sand-bank, a small piece of black American cloth about an inch in diameter is found to be a perfect substitute. Upon this he gazes. After five or ten minutes his shrewd monkey-like expression is struck from his face, his eyes, wide open, remain fixed on the cloth, a complete rigidity sets in over his muscles, and he tells us of the curious things he sees. In whatever position he is, in that position he remains without the deflection of a hair's breadth until the ink is washed off or the cloth removed. Then he looks up and says "Khahás," which means, "It is finished."

We only engaged Machmout's services as second general domestic a fortnight ago, but the first evening he was with us he came upstairs when he had finished his work, and said, "I will show you White Magic; give me ink," and proceeded to describe the front hall of our house in London, saying that there were two horses at the door, and that a man and woman soon came out, gave the horses each a piece of bread and mounted. The thing was so probable that by the next mail I wrote asking my mother to write down exactly what she was doing and where at half-past five (English time) on the evening of June 12. At the corresponding time in Egypt Machmout was describing speaking to us of a "sitt" (lady) having tea in a room which he described with some minuteness, and I am waiting anxiously for her letter. The explanation which Weston gives us of all these phenomena is that a certain picture of people I know is present in my mind, though I may not be aware of it,--present to my subliminal self, I think, he says,--and that I give an unspoken suggestion to the hypnotised Machmout. My explanation is that there isn't any explanation, for no suggestion on my part would make my brother go out and ride at the moment when Machmout says he is so doing (if indeed we find that Machmout's visions are chronologically correct). Consequently I prefer the open mind and am prepared to believe anything. Weston, however, does not speak quite so calmly or scientifically about Machmout's last performance, and since it took place he has almost entirely ceased to urge me to become a member of the Society for Psychical Research, in order that I may no longer be hidebound by vain superstitions.

Machmout will not exercise these powers if his own folk are present, for he says that when he is in this state, if a man who knew Black Magic was in the room, or knew that he was practising White Magic, he could get the spirit who presides over the Black Magic to kill the spirit of White Magic, for the Black Magic is the more potent, and the two are foes. And as the spirit of White Magic is on occasions a powerful friend--he had before now befriended Machmout in a manner which I consider incredible--Machmout is very desirous that he should abide long with him. But Englishmen it appears do not know the Black Magic, so with us he is safe. The spirit of Black Magic, to speak to whom it is death, Machmout saw once "between heaven and earth, and night and day," so he phrases it, on the Karnak road. He may be known, he told us, by the fact that he is of paler skin than his people, that he has two long teeth, one in each corner of his mouth, and that his eyes, which are white all over, are as big as the eyes of a horse.

Machmout squatted himself comfortably in the corner, and I gave him the piece of black American cloth. As some minutes must elapse before he gets into the hypnotic state in which the visions begin, I strolled out on to the balcony for coolness. It was the hottest night we had yet had, and though the sun had set three hours, the thermometer still registered close on 100°.

Above, the sky seemed veiled with grey, where it should have been dark velvety blue, and a fitful puffing wind from the south threatened three days of the sandy intolerable khamseen. A little way up the street to the left was a small café in front of which were glowing and waning little glowworm specks of light from the water pipes of Arabs sitting out there in the dark. From inside came the click of brass castanets in the hands of some dancing-girl, sounding sharp and precise against the wailing bagpipe music of the strings and pipes which accompany these movements which Arabs love and Europeans think so unpleasing. Eastwards the sky was paler and luminous, for the moon was imminently rising, and even as I looked the red rim of the enormous disc cut the line of the desert, and on the instant, with a curious aptness, one of the Arabs outside the café broke out into that wonderful chant--"I cannot sleep for longing for thee, O full moon. Far is thy throne over Mecca, slip down, O beloved, to me."

Immediately afterwards I heard the piping monotone of Machmout's voice begin, and in a moment or two I went inside.

We have found that the experiments gave the quickest result by contact, a fact which confirmed Weston in his explanation of them by thought transference of some elaborate kind, which I confess I cannot understand. He was writing at a table in the window when I came in, but looked up.

"Take his hand," he said; "at present he is quite incoherent."

"Do you explain that?" I asked.

"It is closely analogous, so Myers thinks, to talking in sleep. He has been saying something about a tomb. Do make a suggestion, and see if he gives it right. He is remarkably sensitive, and he responds quicker to you than to me. Probably Abdul's funeral suggested the tomb!"

A sudden thought struck me.

"Hush!" I said, "I want to listen."

Machmout's head was thrown a little back, and he held the hand in which was the piece of cloth rather above his face. As usual he was talking very slowly, and in a high staccato voice, absolutely unlike his usual tones.

"On one side of the grave," he pipes, "is a tamarisk tree, and the green beetles make fantasia about it. On the other side is a mud wall. There are many other graves about, but they are all asleep. This is the grave, because it is awake, and it moist and not sandy."

"I thought so," said Weston. "It is Abdul's grave he is talking about."

"There is a red moon sitting on the desert," continued Machmout, "and it is now. There is the puffing of khamseen, and much dust coming. The moon is red with dust, and because it is low."

"Still sensitive to external conditions," said Weston. "That is rather curious. Pinch him, will you?"

I pinched Machmout; he did not pay the slightest attention.

"In the last house of the street, and in the doorway stands a man. Ah! ah!" cried the boy, suddenly, "it is the Black Magic he knows. Don't let him come. He is going out of the house," he shrieked, "he is coming--no, he is going the other way towards the moon and the grave. He has the Black Magic with him, which can raise the dead, and he has a murdering knife, and a spade. I cannot see his face, for the Black Magic is between it and my eyes."

Weston had got up, and, like me, was hanging on Machmout's words.

"We will go there," he said. "Here is an opportunity of testing it. Listen a moment."

"He is walking, walking, walking," piped Machmout, "still walking to the moon and the grave. The moon sits no longer on the desert, but has sprung up a little way."

I pointed out of the window.

"That at any rate is true," I said.

Weston took the cloth out of Machmout's hand, and the piping ceased. In a moment he stretched himself, and rubbed his eyes.

"Khalás," he said.

"Yes, it is Khalás."

"Did I tell you of the sitt in England?" he asked.

"Yes, oh, yes," I answered; "thank you, little Machmout. The White Magic was very good to-night. Get you to bed."

Machmout trotted obediently out of the room, and Weston closed the door after him.

"We must be quick," he said. "It is worth while going and giving the thing a chance, though I wish he had seen something less gruesome. The odd thing is that he was not at the funeral, and yet he describes the grave accurately. What do you make of it?"

"I make that the White Magic has shown Machmout that somebody with Black Magic is going to Abdul's grave, perhaps to rob it," I answered resolutely.

"What are we to do when we get there?" asked Weston.

"See the Black Magic at work. Personally I am in a blue funk. So are you."

"There is no such thing as Black Magic," said Weston. "Ah, I have it. Give me that orange."

Weston rapidly skinned it, and cut from the rind two circles as big as a five shilling piece, and two long, white fangs of skin. The first he fixed in his eyes, the two latter in the corners of his mouth.

"The Spirit of Black Magic?" I asked.

"The same."

He took up a long black burnous and wrapped it round him. Even in the bright lamp light, the spirit of Black Magic was a sufficiently terrific personage.

"I don't believe in Black Magic," he said, "but others do. If it is necessary to put a stop to--to anything that is going on, we will hoist the man on his own petard. Come along. Whom do you suspect it is--I mean, of course, who was the person you were thinking of when your thoughts were transferred to Machmout."

"What Machmout said," I answered, "suggested Achmet to me."

Weston indulged in a laugh of scientific incredulity, and we set off.

The moon, as the boy had told us, was just clear of the horizon, and as it rose higher, its colour at first red and sombre, like the blaze of some distant conflagration, paled to a tawny yellow. The hot wind from the south, blowing no longer fitfully but with a steadily increasing violence, was thick with sand, and of an incredibly scorching heat, and the tops of the palm trees in the garden of the deserted hotel on the right were lashing themselves to and fro with a harsh rattle of dry leaves. The cemetery lay on the outskirts of the village, and, as long as our way lay between the mud walls of the huddling street, the wind came to us only as the heat from behind closed furnace doors. Every now and then with a whisper and whistle rising into a great buffeting flap, a sudden whirlwind of dust would scour some twenty yards along the road, and then break like a shore-quenched wave against one or other of the mud walls or throw itself heavily against a house and fall in a shower of sand. But once free of obstructions we were opposed to the full heat and blast of the wind which blew full in our teeth. It was the first summer khamseen of the year, and for the moment I wished I had gone north with the tourist and the quail and the billiard marker, for khamseen fetches the marrow out of the bones, and turns the body to blotting paper.

We passed no one in the street, and the only sound we heard, except the wind, was the howling of moonstruck dogs.

The cemetery is surrounded by a tall mud-built wall, and sheltering for a few moments under this we discussed our movements. The row of tamarisks close to which the tomb lay went down the centre of the graveyard, and by skirting the wall outside and climbing softly over where they approached it, the fury of the wind might help us to get near the grave without being seen, if anyone happened to be there. We had just decided on this, and were moving on to put the scheme into execution, when the wind dropped for a moment, and in the silence we could hear the chump of the spade being driven into the earth, and what gave me a sudden thrill of intimate horror, the cry of the carrion-feeding hawk from the dusky sky just overhead.

Two minutes later we were creeping up in the shade of the tamarisks, to where Abdul had been buried. The great green beetles which live on the trees were flying about blindly, and once or twice one dashed into my face with a whirr of mail-clad wings. When we were within some twenty yards of the grave we stopped for a moment, and, looking cautiously out from our shelter of tamarisks, saw the figure of a man already waist deep in the earth, digging out the newly turned grave. Weston, who was standing behind me, had adjusted the characteristics of the spirit of Black Magic so as to be ready for emergencies, and turning round suddenly, and finding myself unawares face to face with that realistic impersonation, though my nerves are not precariously strong, I could have found it within me to shriek aloud. But that unsympathetic man of iron only shook with suppressed laughter, and, holding the eyes in his hand, motioned me forward again without speaking to where the trees grew thicker. There we stood not a dozen yards away from the grave.

We waited, I suppose, for some ten minutes, while the man, whom we saw to be Achmet, toiled on at his impious task. He was entirely naked, and his brown skin glistened with the dews of exertion in the moonlight. At times he chattered in a cold uncanny manner to himself, and once or twice he stopped for breath. Then he began scraping the earth away with his hands, and soon afterwards searched in his clothes, which were lying near, for a piece of rope, with which he stepped into the grave, and in a moment reappeared again with both ends in his hands. Then, standing astride the grave, he pulled strongly, and one end of the coffin appeared above the ground. He chipped a piece of the lid away to make sure that he had the right end, and then, setting it upright, wrenched off the top with his knife, and there faced us, leaning against the coffin lid, the small shrivelled figure of the dead Abdul, swathed like a baby in white.

I was just about to motion the spirit of Black Magic to make his appearance, when Machmout's words came into my head: "He had with him the Black Magic which can raise the dead," and sudden overwhelming curiosity, which froze disgust and horror into chill unfeeling things, came over me.

"Wait," I whispered to Weston, "he will use the Black Magic."

Again the wind dropped for a moment, and again, in the silence that came with it, I heard the chiding of the hawk overhead, this time nearer, and thought I heard more birds than one.

Achmet meantime had taken the covering from off the face, and had undone the swathing band, which at the moment after death is bound round the chin to close the jaw, and in Arab burial is always left there, and from where we stood I could see that the jaw dropped when the bandage was untied, as if, though the wind blew towards us with a ghastly scent of mortality on it, the muscles were not even now set, though the man had been dead sixty hours. But still a rank and burning curiosity to see what this unclean ghoul would do next stifled all other feelings in my mind. He seemed not to notice, or, at any rate, to disregard that mouth gaping awry, and moved about nimbly in the moonlight.

He took from a pocket of his clothes, which were lying near, two small black objects, which now are safely embedded in the mud at the bottom of the Nile, and rubbed them briskly together.

By degrees they grew luminous with a sickly yellow pallor of light, and from his hands went up a wavy, phosphorescent flame. One of these cubes he placed in the open mouth of the corpse, the other in his own, and, taking the dead man closely in his arms as though he would indeed dance with death, he breathed long breaths from his mouth into that dead cavern which was pressed to his. Suddenly he started back with a quick-drawn breath of wonder and perhaps of horror, and stood for a space as if irresolute, for the cube which the dead man held instead of lying loosely in the jaw was pressed tight between clenched teeth. After a moment of irresolution he stepped back quickly to his clothes again, and took up from near them the knife with which he had stripped off the coffin lid, and holding this in one hand behind his back, with the other he took out the cube from the dead man's mouth, though with a visible exhibition of force, and spoke.

"Abdul," he said, "I am your friend, and I swear I will give your money to Mohamed, if you will tell me where it is."

Certain I am that the lips of the dead moved, and the eyelids fluttered for a moment like the wings of a wounded bird, but at that sight the horror so grew on me that I was physically incapable of stifling the cry that rose to my lips, and Achmet turned round. Next moment the complete Spirit of Black Magic glided out of the shade of the trees, and stood before him. The wretched man stood for a moment without stirring, then, turning with shaking knees to flee, he stepped back and fell into the grave he had just opened.

Weston turned on me angrily, dropping the eyes and the teeth of the Afrit.

"You spoiled it all," he cried. "It would perhaps have been the most interesting..." and his eye lighted on the dead Abdul, who peered open-eyed from the coffin, then swayed, tottered, and fell forward, face downwards on the ground close to him. For one moment he lay there, and then the body rolled slowly on to its back without visible cause of movement, and lay staring into the sky. The face was covered with dust, but with the dust was mingled fresh blood. A nail had caught the cloth that wound him, underneath which, as usual, were the clothes in which he had died, for the Arabs do not wash their dead, and it had torn a great rent through them all, leaving the right shoulder bare.

Weston strove to speak once, but failed. Then:

"I will go and inform the police," he said, "if you will stop here, and see that Achmet does not get out."

But this I altogether refused to do, and, after covering the body with the coffin to protect it from the hawks, we secured Achmet's arms with the rope he had already used that night, and took him off to Luxor.

Next morning Mohamed came to see us.

"I thought Achmet knew where the money was," he said exultantly.

"Where was it?"

"In a little purse tied round the shoulder. The dog had already begun stripping it. See"--and he brought it out of his pocket--"it is all there in those English notes, five pounds each, and there are twenty of them."

Our conclusion was slightly different, for even Weston will allow that Achmet hoped to learn from dead lips the secret of the treasure, and then to kill the man anew and bury him. But that is pure conjecture.

The only other point of interest lies in the two black cubes which we picked up, and found to be graven with curious characters. These I put one evening into Machmout's hand, when he was exhibiting to us his curious powers of "thought transference." The effect was that he screamed aloud, crying out that the Black Magic had come, and though I did not feel certain about that, I thought they would be safer in mid-Nile. Weston grumbled a little, and said that he had wanted to take them to the British Museum, but that I feel sure was an afterthought.

Mrs. Amworth

The village of Maxley, where, last summer and autumn, these strange events took place, lies on a heathery and pine-clad upland of Sussex. In all England you could not find a sweeter and saner situation. Should the wind blow from the south, it comes laden with the spices of the sea; to the east high downs protect it from the inclemencies of March; and from the west and north the breezes which reach it travel over miles of aromatic forest and heather. The village itself is insignificant enough in point of population, but rich in amenities and beauty. Half-way down the single street, with its broad road and spacious areas of grass on each side, stands the little Norman Church and the antique graveyard long disused: for the rest there are a dozen small, sedate Georgian houses, red-bricked and long-windowed, each with a square of flower-garden in front, and an ampler strip behind; a score of shops, and a couple of score of thatched cottages belonging to labourers on neighbouring estates, complete the entire cluster of its peaceful habitations. The general peace, however, is sadly broken on Saturdays and Sundays, for we lie on one of the main roads between London and Brighton and our quiet street becomes a race-course for flying motor-cars and bicycles.

A notice just outside the village begging them to go slowly only seems to encourage them to accelerate their speed, for the road lies open and straight, and there is really no reason why they should do otherwise. By way of protest, therefore, the ladies of Maxley cover their noses and mouths with their handkerchiefs as they see a motor-car approaching, though, as the street is asphalted, they need not really take these precautions against dust. But late on Sunday night the horde of scorchers has passed, and we settle down again to five days of cheerful and leisurely seclusion. Railway strikes which agitate the country so much leave us undisturbed because most of the inhabitants of Maxley never leave it at all.

I am the fortunate possessor of one of these small Georgian houses, and consider myself no less fortunate in having so interesting and stimulating a neighbour as Francis Urcombe, who, the most confirmed of Maxleyites, has not slept away from his house, which stands just opposite to mine in the village street, for nearly two years, at which date, though still in middle life, he resigned his Physiological Professorship at Cambridge University and devoted himself to the study of those occult and curious phenomena which seem equally to concern the physical and the psychical sides of human nature. Indeed his retirement was not unconnected with his passion for the strange uncharted places that lie on the confines and borders of science, the existence of which is so stoutly denied by the more materialistic minds, for he advocated that all medical students should be obliged to pass some sort of examination in mesmerism, and that one of the tripos papers should be designed to test their knowledge in such subjects as appearances at time of death, haunted houses, vampirism, automatic writing, and possession.

"Of course they wouldn't listen to me," ran his account of the matter, "for there is nothing that these seats of learning are so frightened of as knowledge, and the road to knowledge lies in the study of things like these. The functions of the human frame are, broadly speaking, known.

"They are a country, anyhow, that has been charted and mapped out. But outside that lie huge tracts of undiscovered country, which certainly exist, and the real pioneers of knowledge are those who, at the cost of being derided as credulous and superstitious, want to push on into those misty and probably perilous places. I felt that I could be of more use by setting out without compass or knapsack into the mists than by sitting in a cage like a canary and chirping about what was known. Besides, teaching is very bad for a man who knows himself only to be a learner: you only need to be a self-conceited ass to teach."

Here, then, in Francis Urcombe, was a delightful neighbour to one who, like myself, has an uneasy and burning curiosity about what he called the "misty and perilous places"; and this last spring we had a further and most welcome addition to our pleasant little community, in the person of Mrs. Amworth, widow of an Indian civil servant. Her husband had been a judge in the North-West Provinces, and after his death at Peshawar she came back to England, and after a year in London found herself starving for the ampler air and sunshine of the country to take the place of the fogs and griminess of town. She had, too, a special reason for settling in Maxley, since her ancestors up till a hundred years ago had long been native to the place, and in the old churchyard, now disused, are many gravestones bearing her maiden name of Chaston. Big and energetic, her vigorous and genial personality speedily woke Maxley up to a higher degree of sociality than it had ever known. Most of us were bachelors or spinsters or elderly folk not much inclined to exert ourselves in the expense and effort of hospitality, and hitherto the gaiety of a small tea-party, with bridge afterwards and goloshes (when it was wet) to trip home in again for a solitary dinner, was about the climax of our festivities. But Mrs. Amworth showed us a more gregarious way, and set an example of luncheon-parties and little dinners, which we began to follow. On other nights when no such hospitality was on foot, a lone man like myself found it pleasant to know that a call on the telephone to Mrs. Amworth's house not a hundred yards off, and an inquiry as to whether I might come over after dinner for a game of piquet before bed-time, would probably evoke a response of welcome. There she would be, with a comrade-like eagerness for companionship, and there was a glass of port and a cup of coffee and a cigarette and a game of piquet. She played the piano, too, in a free and exuberant manner, and had a charming voice and sang to her own accompaniment; and as the days grew long and the light lingered late, we played our game in her garden, which in the course of a few months she had turned from being a nursery for slugs and snails into a glowing patch of luxuriant blossoming.

She was always cheery and jolly; she was interested in everything, and in music, in gardening, in games of all sorts was a competent performer. Everybody (with one exception) liked her, everybody felt her to bring with her the tonic of a sunny day. That one exception was Francis Urcombe; he, though he confessed he did not like her, acknowledged that he was vastly interested in her. This always seemed strange to me, for pleasant and jovial as she was, I could see nothing in her that could call forth conjecture or intrigued surmise, so healthy and unmysterious a figure did she present. But of the genuineness of Urcombe's interest there could be no doubt; one could see him watching and scrutinising her. In matter of age, she frankly volunteered the information that she was forty-five; but her briskness, her activity, her unravaged skin, her coal-black hair, made it difficult to believe that she was not adopting an unusual device, and adding ten years on to her age instead of subtracting them.

Often, also, as our quite unsentimental friendship ripened, Mrs. Amworth would ring me up and propose her advent. If I was busy writing, I was to give her, so we definitely bargained, a frank negative, and in answer I could hear her jolly laugh and her wishes for a successful evening of work. Sometimes, before her proposal arrived, Urcombe would already have stepped across from his house opposite for a smoke and a chat, and he, hearing who my intending visitor was, always urged me to beg her to come. She and I should play our piquet, said he, and he would look on, if we did not object, and learn something of the game. But I doubt whether he paid much attention to it, for nothing could be clearer than that, under that penthouse of forehead and thick eyebrows, his attention was fixed not on the cards, but on one of the players. But he seemed to enjoy an hour spent thus, and often, until one particular evening in July, he would watch her with the air of a man who has some deep problem in front of him. She, enthusiastically keen about our game, seemed not to notice his scrutiny. Then came that evening, when, as I see in the light of subsequent events, began the first twitching of the veil that hid the secret horror from my eyes. I did not know it then, though I noticed that thereafter, if she rang up to propose coming round, she always asked not only if I was at leisure, but whether Mr. Urcombe was with me. If so, she said, she would not spoil the chat of two old bachelors, and laughingly wished me good night.

Urcombe, on this occasion, had been with me for some half-hour before Mrs. Amworth's appearance, and had been talking to me about the medieval beliefs concerning vampirism, one of those borderland subjects which he declared had not been sufficiently studied before it had been consigned by the medical profession to the dust-heap of exploded superstitions. There he sat, grim and eager, tracing, with that pellucid clearness which had made him in his Cambridge days so admirable a lecturer, the history of those mysterious visitations. In them all there were the same general features: one of those ghoulish spirits took up its abode in a living man or woman, conferring supernatural powers of bat-like flight and glutting itself with nocturnal blood-feasts.

When its host died it continued to dwell in the corpse, which remained undecayed. By day it rested, by night it left the grave and went on its awful errands. No European country in the Middle Ages seemed to have escaped them; earlier yet, parallels were to be found, in Roman and Greek and in Jewish history.

"It's a large order to set all that evidence aside as being moonshine," he said. "Hundreds of totally independent witnesses in many ages have testified to the occurrence of these phenomena, and there's no explanation known to me which covers all the facts. And if you feel inclined to say 'Why, then, if these are facts, do we not come across them now?' there are two answers I can make you. One is that there were diseases known in the Middle Ages, such as the black death; which were certainly existent then and which have become extinct since, but for that reason we do not assert that such diseases never existed. Just as the black death visited England and decimated the population of Norfolk, so here in this very district about three hundred years ago there was certainly an outbreak of vampirism, and Maxley was the centre of it. My second answer is even more convincing, for I tell you that vampirism is by no means extinct now. An outbreak of it certainly occurred in India a year or two ago."

At that moment I heard my knocker plied in the cheerful and peremptory manner in which Mrs. Amworth is accustomed to announce her arrival, and I went to the door to open it.

"Come in at once," I said, "and save me from having my blood curdled. Mr. Urcombe has been trying to alarm me."

Instantly her vital, voluminous presence seemed to fill the room.

"Ah, but how lovely!" she said. "I delight in having my blood curdled. Go on with your ghost-story, Mr. Urcombe. I adore ghost-stories."

I saw that, as his habit was, he was intently observing her.

"It wasn't a ghost-story exactly," said he. "I was only telling our host how vampirism was not extinct yet. I was saying that there was an outbreak of it in India only a few years ago."

There was a more than perceptible pause, and I saw that, if Urcombe was observing her, she on her side was observing him with fixed eye and parted mouth. Then her jolly laugh invaded that rather tense silence.

"Oh, what a shame!" she said. "You're not going to curdle my blood at all. Where did you pick up such a tale, Mr. Urcombe? I have lived for years in India and never heard a rumour of such a thing. Some story-teller in the bazaars must have invented it: they are famous at that."

I could see that Urcombe was on the point of saying something further, but checked himself.

"Ah! very likely that was it," he said.

But something had disturbed our usual peaceful sociability that night, and something had damped Mrs. Amworth's usual high spirits. She had no gusto for her piquet, and left after a couple of games. Urcombe had been silent too, indeed he hardly spoke again till she departed.

"That was unfortunate," he said, "for the outbreak of--of a very mysterious disease, let us call it, took place at Peshawar, where she and her husband were. And--"

"Well?" I asked.

"He was one of the victims of it," said he. "Naturally I had quite forgotten that when I spoke."

The summer was unreasonably hot and rainless, and Maxley suffered much from drought, and also from a plague of big black night-flying gnats, the bite of which was very irritating and virulent. They came sailing in of an evening, settling on one's skin so quietly that one perceived nothing till the sharp stab announced that one had been bitten. They did not bite the hands or face, but chose always the neck and throat for their feeding-ground, and most of us, as the poison spread, assumed a temporary goitre. Then about the middle of August appeared the first of those mysterious cases of illness which our local doctor attributed to the long-continued heat coupled with the bite of these venomous insects. The patient was a boy of sixteen or seventeen, the son of Mrs. Amworth's gardener, and the symptoms were an anaemic pallor and a languid prostration, accompanied by great drowsiness and an abnormal appetite. He had, too, on his throat two small punctures where, so Dr. Ross conjectured, one of these great gnats had bitten him. But the odd thing was that there was no swelling or inflammation round the place where he had been bitten.

The heat at this time had begun to abate, but the cooler weather failed to restore him, and the boy, in spite of the quantity of good food which he so ravenously swallowed, wasted away to a skin-clad skeleton.

I met Dr. Ross in the street one afternoon about this time, and in answer to my inquiries about his patient he said that he was afraid the boy was dying. The case, he confessed, completely puzzled him: some obscure form of pernicious anaemia was all he could suggest. But he wondered whether Mr. Urcombe would consent to see the boy, on the chance of his being able to throw some new light on the case, and since Urcombe was dining with me that night, I proposed to Dr. Ross to join us. He could not do this, but said he would look in later. When he came, Urcombe at once consented to put his skill at the other's disposal, and together they went off at once. Being thus shorn of my sociable evening, I telephoned to Mrs. Amworth to know if I might inflict myself on her for an hour. Her answer was a welcoming affirmative, and between piquet and music the hour lengthened itself into two. She spoke of the boy who was lying so desperately and mysteriously ill, and told me that she had often been to see him, taking him nourishing and delicate food. But to-day--and her kind eyes moistened as she spoke she was afraid she had paid her last visit. Knowing the antipathy between her and Urcombe, I did not tell her that he had been called into consultation; and when I returned home she accompanied me to my door, for the sake of a breath of night air, and in order to borrow a magazine which contained an article on gardening which she wished to read.

"Ah, this delicious night air," she said, luxuriously sniffing in the coolness. "Night air and gardening are the great tonics. There is nothing so stimulating as bare contact with rich mother earth. You are never so fresh as when you have been grubbing in the soil--black hands, black nails, and boots covered with mud." She gave her great jovial laugh. "I'm a glutton for air and earth," she said. "Positively I look forward to death, for then I shall be buried and have the kind earth all round me. No leaden caskets for me--I have given explicit directions. But what shall I do about air? Well, I suppose one can't have everything. The magazine? A thousand thanks, I will faithfully return it. Good night: garden and keep your windows open, and you won't have anaemia."

"I always sleep with my windows open," said I.

I went straight up to my bedroom, of which one of the windows looks out over the street, and as I undressed I thought I heard voices talking outside not far away. But I paid no particular attention, put out my lights, and falling asleep plunged into the depths of a most horrible dream, distortedly suggested no doubt, by my last words with Mrs. Amworth. I dreamed that I woke, and found that both my bedroom windows were shut. Half-suffocating I dreamed that I sprang out of bed, and went across to open them. The blind over the first was drawn down, and pulling it up I saw, with the indescribable horror of incipient nightmare, Mrs. Amworth's face suspended close to the pane in the darkness outside, nodding and smiling at me. Pulling down the blind again to keep that terror out, I rushed to the second window on the other side of the room, and there again was Mrs. Amworth's face. Then the panic came upon me in full blast; here was I suffocating in the airless room, and whichever window I opened Mrs. Amworth's face would float in, like those noiseless black gnats that bit before one was aware. The nightmare rose to screaming point, and with strangled yells I awoke to find my room cool and quiet with both windows open and blinds up and a half-moon high in its course, casting an oblong of tranquil light on the floor. But even when I was awake the horror persisted, and I lay tossing and turning.

I must have slept long before the nightmare seized me, for now it was nearly day, and soon in the east the drowsy eyelids of morning began to lift.

I was scarcely downstairs next morning--for after the dawn I slept late--when Urcombe rang up to know if he might see me immediately. He came in, grim and preoccupied, and I noticed that he was pulling on a pipe that was not even filled.

"I want your help," he said, "and so I must tell you first of all what happened last night. I went round with the little doctor to see his patient, and found him just alive, but scarcely more. I instantly diagnosed in my own mind what this anaemia, unaccountable by any other explanation, meant. The boy is the prey of a vampire."

He put his empty pipe on the breakfast-table, by which I had just sat down, and folded his arms, looking at me steadily from under his overhanging brows.

"Now about last night," he said. "I insisted that he should be moved from his father's cottage into my house. As we were carrying him on a stretcher, whom should we meet but Mrs. Amworth? She expressed shocked surprise that we were moving him. Now why do you think she did that?"

With a start of horror, as I remembered my dream that night before, I felt an idea come into my mind so preposterous and unthinkable that I instantly turned it out again.

"I haven't the smallest idea," I said.

"Then listen, while I tell you about what happened later. I put out all light in the room where the boy lay, and watched. One window was a little open, for I had forgotten to close it, and about midnight I heard something outside, trying apparently to push it farther open. I guessed who it was--yes, it was full twenty feet from the ground--and I peeped round the corner of the blind."

"Just outside was the face of Mrs. Amworth and her hand was on the frame of the window. Very softly I crept close, and then banged the window down, and I think I just caught the tip of one of her fingers."

"But it's impossible," I cried. "How could she be floating in the air like that? And what had she come for? Don't tell me such--"

Once more, with closer grip, the remembrance of my nightmare seized me.

"I am telling you what I saw," said he. "And all night long, until it was nearly day, she was fluttering outside, like some terrible bat, trying to gain admittance. Now put together various things I have told you."

He began checking them off on his fingers.

"Number one," he said: "there was an outbreak of disease similar to that which this boy is suffering from at Peshawar, and her husband died of it. Number two: Mrs. Amworth protested against my moving the boy to my house. Number three: she, or the demon that inhabits her body, a creature powerful and deadly, tries to gain admittance. And add this, too: in medieval times there was an epidemic of vampirism here at Maxley. The vampire, so the accounts run, was found to be Elizabeth Chaston...I see you remember Mrs. Amworth's maiden name. Finally, the boy is stronger this morning. He would certainly not have been alive if he had been visited again."

"And what do you make of it?"

There was a long silence, during which I found this incredible horror assuming the hues of reality.

"I have something to add," I said, "which may or may not bear on it. You say that the--the spectre went away shortly before dawn."

"Yes."

I told him of my dream, and he smiled grimly.

"Yes, you did well to awake," he said. "That warning came from your subconscious self, which never wholly slumbers, and cried out to you of deadly danger. For two reasons, then, you must help me: one to save others, the second to save yourself."

"What do you want me to do?" I asked.

"I want you first of all to help me in watching this boy, and ensuring that she does not come near him. Eventually I want you to help me in tracking the thing down, in exposing and destroying it. It is not human: it is an incarnate fiend. What steps we shall have to take I don't yet know."

It was now eleven of the forenoon, and presently I went across to his house for a twelve-hour vigil while he slept, to come on duty again that night, so that for the next twenty-four hours either Urcombe or myself was always in the room where the boy, now getting stronger every hour, was lying. The day following was Saturday and a morning of brilliant, pellucid weather, and already when I went across to his house to resume my duty the stream of motors down to Brighton had begun. Simultaneously I saw Urcombe with a cheerful face, which boded good news of his patient, coming out of his house, and Mrs. Amworth, with a gesture of salutation to me and a basket in her hand, walking up the broad strip of grass which bordered the road. There we all three met. I noticed (and saw that Urcombe noticed it too) that one finger of her left hand was bandaged.

"Good morning to you both," said she. "And I hear your patient is doing well, Mr. Urcombe. I have come to bring him a bowl of jelly, and to sit with him for an hour. He and I are great friends. I am overjoyed at his recovery."

Urcombe paused a moment, as if making up his mind, and then shot out a pointing finger at her.

"I forbid that," he said. "You shall not sit with him or see him. And you know the reason as well as I do."

I have never seen so horrible a change pass over a human face as that which now blanched hers to the colour of a grey mist. She put up her hand as if to shield herself from that pointing finger, which drew the sign of the cross in the air, and shrank back cowering on to the road.

There was a wild hoot from a horn, a grinding of brakes, a shout--too late--from a passing car, and one long scream suddenly cut short. Her body rebounded from the roadway after the first wheel had gone over it, and the second followed. It lay there, quivering and twitching, and was still.

She was buried three days afterwards in the cemetery outside Maxley, in accordance with the wishes she had told me that she had devised about her interment, and the shock which her sudden and awful death had caused to the little community began by degrees to pass off. To two people only, Urcombe and myself, the horror of it was mitigated from the first by the nature of the relief that her death brought; but, naturally enough, we kept our own counsel, and no hint of what greater horror had been thus averted was ever let slip. But, oddly enough, so it seemed to me, he was still not satisfied about something in connection with her, and would give no answer to my questions on the subject. Then as the days of a tranquil mellow September and the October that followed began to drop away like the leaves of the yellowing trees, his uneasiness relaxed. But before the entry of November the seeming tranquillity broke into hurricane.

I had been dining one night at the far end of the village, and about eleven o'clock was walking home again. The moon was of an unusual brilliance, rendering all that it shone on as distinct as in some etching. I had just come opposite the house which Mrs. Amworth had occupied, where there was a board up telling that it was to let, when I heard the click of her front gate, and next moment I saw, with a sudden chill and quaking of my very spirit, that she stood there. Her profile, vividly illuminated, was turned to me, and I could not be mistaken in my identification of her. She appeared not to see me (indeed the shadow of the yew hedge in front of her garden enveloped me in its blackness) and she went swiftly across the road, and entered the gate of the house directly opposite. There I lost sight of her completely.

My breath was coming in short pants as if I had been running--and now indeed I ran, with fearful backward glances, along the hundred yards that separated me from my house and Urcombe's. It was to his that my flying steps took me, and next minute I was within.

"What have you come to tell me?" he asked. "Or shall I guess?"

"You can't guess," said I.

"No; it's no guess. She has come back and you have seen her. Tell me about it."

I gave him my story.

"That's Major Pearsall's house," he said. "Come back with me there at once."

"But what can we do?" I asked.

"I've no idea. That's what we have got to find out."

A minute later, we were opposite the house. When I had passed it before, it was all dark; now lights gleamed from a couple of windows upstairs. Even as we faced it, the front door opened, and next moment Major Pearsall emerged from the gate. He saw us and stopped.

"I'm on my way to Dr. Ross," he said quickly, "My wife has been taken suddenly ill. She had been in bed an hour when I came upstairs, and I found her white as a ghost and utterly exhausted. She had been to sleep, it seemed--but you will excuse me."

"One moment, Major," said Urcombe. "Was there any mark on her throat?"

"How did you guess that?" said he. "There was: one of those beastly gnats must have bitten her twice there. She was streaming with blood."

"And there's someone with her?" asked Urcombe.

"Yes, I roused her maid."

He went off, and Urcombe turned to me. "I know now what we have to do," he said. "Change your clothes, and I'll join you at your house."

"What is it?" I asked.

"I'll tell you on our way. We're going to the cemetery."

He carried a pick, a shovel, and a screw-driver when he rejoined me, and wore round his shoulders a long coil of rope. As we walked, he gave me the outlines of the ghastly hour that lay before us.

"What I have to tell you," he said, "will seem to you now too fantastic for credence, but before dawn we shall see whether it outstrips reality. By a most fortunate happening, you saw the spectre, the astral body, whatever you choose to call it, of Mrs. Amworth, going on its grisly business, and therefore, beyond doubt, the vampire spirit which abode in her during life animates her again in death. That is not exceptional--indeed, all these weeks since her death I have been expecting it. If I am right, we shall find her body undecayed and untouched by corruption."

"But she has been dead nearly two months," said I.

"If she had been dead two years it would still be so, if the vampire has possession of her. So remember: whatever you see done, it will be done not to her, who in the natural course would now be feeding the grasses above her grave, but to a spirit of untold evil and malignancy, which gives a phantom life to her body."

"But what shall I see done?" said I.

"I will tell you. We know that now, at this moment, the vampire clad in her mortal semblance is out; dining out. But it must get back before dawn, and it will pass into the material form that lies in her grave. We must wait for that, and then with your help I shall dig up her body. If I am right, you will look on her as she was in life, with the full vigour of the dreadful nutriment she has received pulsing in her veins. And then, when dawn has come, and the vampire cannot leave the lair of her body, I shall strike her with this"--and he pointed to his pick--"through the heart, and she, who comes to life again only with the animation the fiend gives her, she and her hellish partner will be dead indeed. Then we must bury her again, delivered at last."

We had come to the cemetery, and in the brightness of the moonshine there was no difficulty in identifying her grave. It lay some twenty yards from the small chapel, in the porch of which, obscured by shadow, we concealed ourselves. From there we had a clear and open sight of the grave, and now we must wait till its infernal visitor returned home. The night was warm and windless, yet even if a freezing wind had been raging I think I should have felt nothing of it, so intense was my preoccupation as to what the night and dawn would bring. There was a bell in the turret of the chapel, that struck the quarters of the hour, and it amazed me to find how swiftly the chimes succeeded one another.

The moon had long set, but a twilight of stars shone in a clear sky, when five o'clock of the morning sounded from the turret. A few minutes more passed, and then I felt Urcombe's hand softly nudging me; and looking out in the direction of his pointing finger, I saw that the form of a woman, tall and large in build, was approaching from the right. Noiselessly, with a motion more of gliding and floating than walking, she moved across the cemetery to the grave which was the centre of our observation. She moved round it as if to be certain of its identity, and for a moment stood directly facing us. In the greyness to which now my eyes had grown accustomed, I could easily see her face, and recognise its features.

She drew her hand across her mouth as if wiping it, and broke into a chuckle of such laughter as made my hair stir on my head. Then she leaped on to the grave, holding her hands high above her head, and inch by inch disappeared into the earth. Urcombe's hand was laid on my arm, in an injunction to keep still, but now he removed it.

"Come," he said.

With pick and shovel and rope we went to the grave. The earth was light and sandy, and soon after six struck, we had delved down to the coffin lid. With his pick he loosened the earth round it, and, adjusting the rope through the handles by which it had been lowered, we tried to raise it.

This was a long and laborious business, and the light had begun to herald day in the east before we had it out, and lying by the side of the grave. With his screw-driver he loosed the fastenings of the lid, and slid it aside, and standing there we looked on the face of Mrs. Amworth. The eyes, once closed in death, were open, the cheeks were flushed with colour, the red, full-lipped mouth seemed to smile.

"One blow and it is all over," he said. "You need not look."

Even as he spoke he took up the pick again, and, laying the point of it on her left breast, measured his distance. And though I knew what was coming I could not look away...

He grasped the pick in both hands, raised it an inch or two for the taking of his aim, and then with full force brought it down on her breast. A fountain of blood, though she had been dead so long, spouted high in the air, falling with the thud of a heavy splash over the shroud, and simultaneously from those red lips came one long, appalling cry, swelling up like some hooting siren, and dying away again. With that, instantaneous as a lightning flash, came the touch of corruption on her face, the colour of it faded to ash, the plump cheeks fell in, the mouth dropped.

"Thank God, that's over," said he, and without pause slipped the coffin lid back into its place.

Day was coming fast now, and, working like men possessed, we lowered the coffin into its place again, and shovelled the earth over it...The birds were busy with their earliest pipings as we went back to Maxley.

Between the Lights

The day had been one unceasing fall of snow from sunrise until the gradual withdrawal of the vague white light outside indicated that the sun had set again. But as usual at this hospitable and delightful house of Everard Chandler where I often spent Christmas, and was spending it now, there had been no lack of entertainment, and the hours had passed with a rapidity that had surprised us. A short billiard tournament had filled up the time between breakfast and lunch, with Badminton and the morning papers for those who were temporarily not engaged, while afterwards, the interval till tea-time had been occupied by the majority of the party in a huge game of hide-and-seek all over the house, barring the billiard-room, which was sanctuary for any who desired peace. But few had done that; the enchantment of Christmas, I must suppose, had, like some spell, made children of us again, and it was with palsied terror and trembling misgivings that we had tiptoed up and down the dim passages, from any corner of which some wild screaming form might dart out on us. Then, wearied with exercise and emotion, we had assembled again for tea in the hall, a room of shadows and panels on which the light from the wide open fireplace, where there burned a divine mixture of peat and logs, flickered and grew bright again on the walls. Then, as was proper, ghost-stories, for the narration of which the electric light was put out, so that the listeners might conjecture anything they pleased to be lurking in the corners, succeeded, and we vied with each other in blood, bones, skeletons, armour and shrieks. I had, just given my contribution, and was reflecting with some complacency that probably the worst was now known, when Everard, who had not yet administered to the horror of his guests, spoke. He was sitting opposite me in the full blaze of the fire, looking, after the illness he had gone through during the autumn, still rather pale and delicate. All the same he had been among the boldest and best in the exploration of dark places that afternoon, and the look on his face now rather startled me.

"No, I don't mind that sort of thing," he said. "The paraphernalia of ghosts has become somehow rather hackneyed, and when I hear of screams and skeletons I feel I am on familiar ground, and can at least hide my head under the bed-clothes."

"Ah, but the bed-clothes were twitched away by my skeleton," said I, in self-defence.

"I know, but I don't even mind that. Why, there are seven, eight skeletons in this room now, covered with blood and skin and other horrors. No, the nightmares of one's childhood were the really frightening things, because they were vague. There was the true atmosphere of horror about them because one didn't know what one feared. Now if one could recapture that--"

Mrs. Chandler got quickly out of her seat.

"Oh, Everard," she said, "surely you don't wish to recapture it again. I should have thought once was enough."

This was enchanting. A chorus of invitation asked him to proceed: the real true ghost-story first-hand, which was what seemed to be indicated, was too precious a thing to lose.

Everard laughed. "No, dear, I don't want to recapture it again at all," he said to his wife.

Then to us: "But really the--well, the nightmare perhaps, to which I was referring, is of the vaguest and most unsatisfactory kind. It has no apparatus about it at all. You will probably all say that it was nothing, and wonder why I was frightened. But I was; it frightened me out of my wits. And I only just saw something, without being able to swear what it was, and heard something which might have been a falling stone."

"Anyhow, tell us about the falling stone," said I.

There was a stir of movement about the circle round the fire, and the movement was not of purely physical order. It was as if--this is only what I personally felt--it was as if the childish gaiety of the hours we had passed that day was suddenly withdrawn; we had jested on certain subjects, we had played hide-and-seek with all the power of earnestness that was in us. But now--so it seemed to me--there was going to be real hide-and-seek, real terrors were going to lurk in dark corners, or if not real terrors, terrors so convincing as to assume the garb of reality, were going to pounce on us. And Mrs. Chandler's exclamation as she sat down again, "Oh, Everard, won't it excite you?" tended in any case to excite us. The room still remained in dubious darkness except for the sudden lights disclosed on the walls by the leaping flames on the hearth, and there was wide field for conjecture as to what might lurk in the dim corners. Everard, moreover, who had been sitting in bright light before, was banished by the extinction of some flaming log into the shadows. A voice alone spoke to us, as he sat back in his low chair, a voice rather slow but very distinct.

"Last year," he said, "on the twenty-fourth of December, we were down here, as usual, Amy and I, for Christmas. Several of you who are here now were here then. Three or four of you at least."

I was one of these, but like the others kept silence, for the identification, so it seemed to me, was not asked for. And he went on again without a pause.

"Those of you who were here then," he said, "and are here now, will remember how very warm it was this day year. You will remember, too, that we played croquet that day on the lawn. It was perhaps a little cold for croquet, and we played it rather in order to be able to say--with sound evidence to back the statement--that we had done so."

Then he turned and addressed the whole little circle.

"We played ties of half-games," he said, "just as we have played billiards to-day, and it was certainly as warm on the lawn then as it was in the billiard-room this morning directly after breakfast, while to-day I should not wonder if there was three feet of snow outside. More, probably; listen."

A sudden draught fluted in the chimney, and the fire flared up as the current of air caught it.

The wind also drove the snow against the windows, and as he said, "Listen," we heard a soft scurry of the falling flakes against the panes, like the soft tread of many little people who stepped lightly, but with the persistence of multitudes who were flocking to some rendezvous. Hundreds of little feet seemed to be gathering outside; only the glass kept them out. And of the eight skeletons present four or five, anyhow, turned and looked at the windows. These were small-paned, with leaden bars. On the leaden bars little heaps of snow had accumulated, but there was nothing else to be seen.

"Yes, last Christmas Eve was very warm and sunny," went on Everard. "We had had no frost that autumn, and a temerarious dahlia was still in flower. I have always thought that it must have been mad."

He paused a moment.

"And I wonder if I were not mad too," he added.

No one interrupted him; there was something arresting, I must suppose, in what he was saying; it chimed in anyhow with the hide-and-seek, with the suggestions of the lonely snow.

Mrs. Chandler had sat down again, but I heard her stir in her chair. But never was there a gay party so reduced as we had been in the last five minutes. Instead of laughing at ourselves for playing silly games, we were all taking a serious game seriously.

"Anyhow, I was sitting out," he said to me, "while you and my wife played your half-game of croquet. Then it struck me that it was not so warm as I had supposed, because quite suddenly I shivered. And shivering I looked up. But I did not see you and her playing croquet at all. I saw something which had no relation to you and her--at least I hope not."

Now the angler lands his fish, the stalker kills his stag, and the speaker holds his audience.

And as the fish is gaffed, and as the stag is shot, so were we held. There was no getting away till he had finished with us.

"You all know the croquet lawn," he said, "and how it is bounded all round by a flower border with a brick wall behind it, through which, you will remember, there is only one gate.

"Well, I looked up and saw that the lawn--I could for one moment see it was still a lawn--was shrinking, and the walls closing in upon it. As they closed in too, they grew higher, and simultaneously the light began to fade and be sucked from the sky, till it grew quite dark overhead and only a glimmer of light came in through the gate.

"There was, as I told you, a dahlia in flower that day, and as this dreadful darkness and bewilderment came over me, I remember that my eyes sought it in a kind of despair, holding on, as it were, to any familiar object. But it was no longer a dahlia, and for the red of its petals I saw only the red of some feeble firelight. And at that moment the hallucination was complete. I was no longer sitting on the lawn watching croquet, but I was in a low-roofed room, something like a cattle-shed, but round. Close above my head, though I was sitting down, ran rafters from wall to wall. It was nearly dark, but a little light came in from the door opposite to me, which seemed to lead into a passage that communicated with the exterior of the place. Little, however, of the wholesome air came into this dreadful den; the atmosphere was oppressive and foul beyond all telling, it was as if for years it had been the place of some human menagerie, and for those years had been uncleaned and unsweetened by the winds of heaven. Yet that oppressiveness was nothing to the awful horror of the place from the view of the spirit. Some dreadful atmosphere of crime and abomination dwelt heavy in it, its denizens, whoever they were, were scarce human, so it seemed to me, and though men and women, were akin more to the beasts of the field. And in addition there was present to me some sense of the weight of years; I had been taken and thrust down into some epoch of dim antiquity."

He paused a moment, and the fire on the hearth leaped up for a second and then died down again. But in that gleam I saw that all faces were turned to Everard, and that all wore some look of dreadful expectancy. Certainly I felt it myself, and waited in a sort of shrinking horror for what was coming.

"As I told you," he continued, "where there had been that unseasonable dahlia, there now burned a dim firelight, and my eyes were drawn there. Shapes were gathered round it; what they were I could not at first see. Then perhaps my eyes got more accustomed to the dusk, or the fire burned better, for I perceived that they were of human form, but very small, for when one rose with a horrible chattering, to his feet, his head was still some inches off the low roof. He was dressed in a sort of shirt that came to his knees, but his arms were bare and covered with hair.

"Then the gesticulation and chattering increased, and I knew that they were talking about me, for they kept pointing in my direction. At that my horror suddenly deepened, for I became aware that I was powerless and could not move hand or foot; a helpless, nightmare impotence had possession of me. I could not lift a finger or turn my head. And in the paralysis of that fear I tried to scream, but not a sound could I utter.

"All this I suppose took place with the instantaneousness of a dream, for at once, and without transition, the whole thing had vanished, and I was back on the lawn again, while the stroke for which my wife was aiming was still unplayed. But my face was dripping with perspiration, and I was trembling all over.

"Now you may all say that I had fallen asleep, and had a sudden nightmare. That may be so; but I was conscious of no sense of sleepiness before, and I was conscious of none afterwards. It was as if someone had held a book before me, whisked the pages open for a second and closed them again."

Somebody, I don't know who, got up from his chair with a sudden movement that made me start, and turned on the electric light. I do not mind confessing that I was rather glad of this.

Everard laughed.

"Really I feel like Hamlet in the play-scene," he said, "and as if there was a guilty uncle present. Shall I go on?"

I don't think anyone replied, and he went on.

"Well, let us say for the moment that it was not a dream exactly, but a hallucination.

"Whichever it was, in any case it haunted me; for months, I think, it was never quite out of my mind, but lingered somewhere in the dusk of consciousness, sometimes sleeping quietly, so to speak, but sometimes stirring in its sleep. It was no good my telling myself that I was disquieting myself in vain, for it was as if something had actually entered into my very soul, as if some seed of horror had been planted there. And as the weeks went on the seed began to sprout, so that I could no longer even tell myself that that vision had been a moment's disorderment only. I can't say that it actually affected my health. I did not, as far as I know, sleep or eat insufficiently, but morning after morning I used to wake, not gradually and through pleasant dozings into full consciousness, but with absolute suddenness, and find myself plunged in an abyss of despair.

"Often too, eating or drinking, I used to pause and wonder if it was worth while.

"Eventually, I told two people about my trouble, hoping that perhaps the mere communication would help matters, hoping also, but very distantly, that though I could not believe at present that digestion or the obscurities of the nervous system were at fault, a doctor by some simple dose might convince me of it. In other words I told my wife, who laughed at me, and my doctor, who laughed also, and assured me that my health was quite unnecessarily robust.

"At the same time he suggested that change of air and scene does wonders for the delusions that exist merely in the imagination. He also told me, in answer to a direct question, that he would stake his reputation on the certainty that I was not going mad.

"Well, we went up to London as usual for the season, and though nothing whatever occurred to remind me in any way of that single moment on Christmas Eve, the reminding was seen to all right, the moment itself took care of that, for instead of fading as is the way of sleeping or waking dreams, it grew every day more vivid, and ate, so to speak, like some corrosive acid into my mind, etching itself there. And to London succeeded Scotland.

"I took last year for the first time a small forest up in Sutherland, called Glen Callan, very remote and wild, but affording excellent stalking. It was not far from the sea, and the gillies used always to warn me to carry a compass on the hill, because sea-mists were liable to come up with frightful rapidity, and there was always a danger of being caught by one, and of having perhaps to wait hours till it cleared again. This at first I always used to do, but, as everyone knows, any precaution that one takes which continues to be unjustified gets gradually relaxed, and at the end of a few weeks, since the weather had been uniformly clear, it was natural that, as often as not, my compass remained at home.

"One day the stalk took me on to a part of my ground that I had seldom been on before, a very high table-land on the limit of my forest, which went down very steeply on one side to a loch that lay below it, and on the other, by gentler gradations, to the river that came from the loch, six miles below which stood the lodge. The wind had necessitated our climbing up--or so my stalker had insisted--not by the easier way, but up the crags from the loch. I had argued the point with him for it seemed to me that it was impossible that the deer could get our scent if we went by the more natural path, but he still held to his opinion; and therefore, since after all this was his part of the job, I yielded. A dreadful climb we had of it, over big boulders with deep holes in between, masked by clumps of heather, so that a wary eye and a prodding stick were necessary for each step if one wished to avoid broken bones. Adders also literally swarmed in the heather; we must have seen a dozen at least on our way up, and adders are a beast for which I have no manner of use. But a couple of hours saw us to the top, only to find that the stalker had been utterly at fault, and that the deer must quite infallibly have got wind of us, if they had remained in the place where we last saw them. That, when we could spy the ground again, we saw had happened; in any case they had gone. The man insisted the wind had changed, a palpably stupid excuse, and I wondered at that moment what other reason he had--for reason I felt sure there must be--for not wishing to take what would clearly now have been a better route. But this piece of bad management did not spoil our luck, for within an hour we had spied more deer, and about two o'clock I got a shot, killing a heavy stag. Then sitting on the heather I ate lunch, and enjoyed a well-earned bask and smoke in the sun. The pony meantime had been saddled with the stag, and was plodding homewards.

"The morning had been extraordinarily warm, with a little wind blowing off the sea, which lay a few miles off sparkling beneath a blue haze, and all morning in spite of our abominable climb I had had an extreme sense of peace, so much so that several times I had probed my mind, so to speak, to find if the horror still lingered there. But I could scarcely get any response from it.

"Never since Christmas had I been so free of fear, and it was with a great sense of repose, both physical and spiritual, that I lay looking up into the blue sky, watching my smoke-whorls curl slowly away into nothingness. But I was not allowed to take my ease long, for Sandy came and begged that I would move. The weather had changed, he said, the wind had shifted again, and he wanted me to be off this high ground and on the path again as soon as possible, because it looked to him as if a sea-mist would presently come up."

"'And yon's a bad place to get down in the mist,' he added, nodding towards the crags we had come up.

"I looked at the man in amazement, for to our right lay a gentle slope down on to the river, and there was now no possible reason for again tackling those hideous rocks up which we had climbed this morning. More than ever I was sure he had some secret reason for not wishing to go the obvious way. But about one thing he was certainly right, the mist was coming up from the sea, and I felt in my pocket for the compass, and found I had forgotten to bring it.

"Then there followed a curious scene which lost us time that we could really ill afford to waste, I insisting on going down by the way that common sense directed, he imploring me to take his word for it that the crags were the better way. Eventually, I marched off to the easier descent, and told him not to argue any more but follow. What annoyed me about him was that he would only give the most senseless reasons for preferring the crags. There were mossy places, he said, on the way I wished to go, a thing patently false, since the summer had been one spell of unbroken weather; or it was longer, also obviously untrue; or there were so many vipers about.

"But seeing that none of these arguments produced any effect, at last he desisted, and came after me in silence.

"We were not yet half down when the mist was upon us, shooting up from the valley like the broken water of a wave, and in three minutes we were enveloped in a cloud of fog so thick that we could barely see a dozen yards in front of us. It was therefore another cause for self-congratulation that we were not now, as we should otherwise have been, precariously clambering on the face of those crags up which we had come with such difficulty in the morning, and as I rather prided myself on my powers of generalship in the matter of direction, I continued leading, feeling sure that before long we should strike the track by the river. More than all, the absolute freedom from fear elated me; since Christmas I had not known the instinctive joy of that; I felt like a schoolboy home for the holidays. But the mist grew thicker and thicker, and whether it was that real rain-clouds had formed above it, or that it was of an extraordinary density itself, I got wetter in the next hour than I have ever been before or since. The wet seemed to penetrate the skin, and chill the very bones. And still there was no sign of the track for which I was making.

"Behind me, muttering to himself, followed the stalker, but his arguments and protestations were dumb, and it seemed as if he kept close to me, as if afraid.

"Now there are many unpleasant companions in this world; I would not, for instance, care to be on the hill with a drunkard or a maniac, but worse than either, I think, is a frightened man, because his trouble is infectious, and, insensibly. I began to be afraid of being frightened too.

"From that it is but a short step to fear. Other perplexities too beset us. At one time we seemed to be walking on flat ground, at another I felt sure we were climbing again, whereas all the time we ought to have been descending, unless we had missed the way very badly indeed. Also, for the month was October, it was beginning to get dark, and it was with a sense of relief that I remembered that the full moon would rise soon after sunset. But it had grown very much colder, and soon, instead of rain, we found we were walking through a steady fall of snow.

"Things were pretty bad, but then for the moment they seemed to mend, for, far away to the left, I suddenly heard the brawling of the river. It should, it is true, have been straight in front of me and we were perhaps a mile out of our way, but this was better than the blind wandering of the last hour, and turning to the left, I walked towards it. But before I had gone a hundred yards, I heard a sudden choked cry behind me, and just saw Sandy's form flying as if in terror of pursuit, into the mists. I called to him, but got no reply, and heard only the spurned stones of his running.

"What had frightened him I had no idea, but certainly with his disappearance, the infection of his fear disappeared also, and I went on, I may almost say, with gaiety. On the moment, however, I saw a sudden well-defined blackness in front of me, and before I knew what I was doing I was half stumbling, half walking up a very steep grass slope.

"During the last few minutes the wind had got up, and the driving snow was peculiarly uncomfortable, but there had been a certain consolation in thinking that the wind would soon disperse these mists, and I had nothing more than a moonlight walk home. But as I paused on this slope, I became aware of two things, one, that the blackness in front of me was very close, the other that, whatever it was, it sheltered me from the snow. So I climbed on a dozen yards into its friendly shelter, for it seemed to me to be friendly.

"A wall some twelve feet high crowned the slope, and exactly where I struck it there was a hole in it, or door rather, through which a little light appeared. Wondering at this I pushed on, bending down, for the passage was very low, and in a dozen yards came out on the other side.

"Just as I did this the sky suddenly grew lighter, the wind, I suppose, having dispersed the mists, and the moon, though not yet visible through the flying skirts of cloud, made sufficient illumination.

"I was in a circular enclosure, and above me there projected from the walls some four feet from the ground, broken stones which must have been intended to support a floor. Then simultaneously two things occurred.

"The whole of my nine months' terror came back to me, for I saw that the vision in the garden was fulfilled, and at the same moment I saw stealing towards me a little figure as of a man, but only about three foot six in height. That my eyes told me; my ears told me that he stumbled on a stone; my nostrils told me that the air I breathed was of an overpowering foulness, and my soul told me that it was sick unto death. I think I tried to scream, but could not; I know I tried to move and could not. And it crept closer.

"Then I suppose the terror which held me spellbound so spurred me that I must move, for next moment I heard a cry break from my lips, and was stumbling through the passage. I made one leap of it down the grass slope, and ran as I hope never to have to run again. What direction I took I did not pause to consider, so long as I put distance between me and that place. Luck, however, favoured me, and before long I struck the track by the river, and an hour afterwards reached the lodge.

"Next day I developed a chill, and as you know pneumonia laid me on my back for six weeks.

"Well, that is my story, and there are many explanations. You may say that I fell asleep on the lawn, and was reminded of that by finding myself, under discouraging circumstances, in an old Picts' castle, where a sheep or a goat that, like myself, had taken shelter from the storm, was moving about. Yes, there are hundreds of ways in which you may explain it. But the coincidence was an odd one, and those who believe in second sight might find an instance of their hobby in it."

"And that is all?" I asked.

"Yes, it was nearly too much for me. I think the dressing-bell has sounded."

The House with the Brick-Kiln

The hamlet of Trevor Major lies very lonely and sequestered in a hollow below the north side of the south downs that stretch westward from Lewes, and run parallel with the coast. It is a hamlet of some three or four dozen inconsiderable houses and cottages much girt about with trees, but the big Norman church and the manor house which stands a little outside the village are evidence of a more conspicuous past. This latter, except for a tenancy of rather less than three weeks, now four years ago, has stood unoccupied since the summer of 1896, and though it could be taken at a rent almost comically small, it is highly improbable that either of its last tenants, even if times were very bad, would think of passing a night in it again. For myself--I was one of the tenants--I would far prefer living in a workhouse to inhabiting those low-pitched oak-panelled rooms, and I would sooner look from my garret windows on to the squalor and grime of Whitechapel than from the diamond-shaped and leaded panes of the Manor of Trevor Major on to the boskage of its cool thickets, and the glimmering of its clear chalk streams where the quick trout glance among the waving water-weeds and over the chalk and gravel of its sliding rapids.

It was the news of these trout that led Jack Singleton and myself to take the house for the month between mid-May and mid-June, but as I have already mentioned a short three weeks was all the time we passed there, and we had more than a week of our tenancy yet unexpired when we left the place, though on the very last afternoon we enjoyed the finest dry-fly fishing that has ever fallen to my lot. Singleton had originally seen the advertisement of the house in a Sussex paper, with the statement that there was good dry-fly fishing belonging to it, but it was with but faint hopes of the reality of the dry-fly fishing that we went down to look at the place, since we had before this so often inspected depopulated ditches which were offered to the unwary under high-sounding titles. Yet after a half-hour's stroll by the stream, we went straight back to the agent, and before nightfall had taken it for a month with option of renewal.

We arrived accordingly from town at about five o'clock on a cloudless afternoon in May, and through the mists of horror that now stand between me and the remembrance of what occurred later, I cannot forget the exquisite loveliness of the impression then conveyed. The garden, it is true, appeared to have been for years untended; weeds half-choked the gravel paths, and the flower-beds were a congestion of mingled wild and cultivated vegetations. It was set in a wall of mellowed brick, in which snap-dragon and stone-crop had found an anchorage to their liking, and beyond that there stood sentinel a ring of ancient pines in which the breeze made music as of a distant sea. Outside that the ground sloped slightly downwards in a bank covered with a jungle of wild-rose to the stream that ran round three sides of the garden, and then followed a meandering course through the two big fields which lay towards the village. Over all this we had fishing-rights; above, the same rights extended for another quarter of a mile to the arched bridge over which there crossed the road which led to the house. In this field above the house on the fourth side, where the ground had been embanked to carry the road, stood a brick-kiln in a ruinous state. A shallow pit, long overgrown with tall grasses and wild field-flowers, showed where the clay had been digged.

The house itself was long and narrow; entering, you passed direct into a square panelled hall, on the left of which was the dining-room which communicated with the passage leading to the kitchen and offices. On the right of the hall were two excellent sitting-rooms looking out, the one on to the gravel in front of the house, the other on to the garden. From the first of these you could see, through the gap in the pines by which the road approached the house, the brick-kiln of which I have already spoken. An oak staircase went up from the hall, and round it ran a gallery on to which the three principal bedrooms opened. These were commensurate with the dining-room and the two sitting-rooms below. From this gallery there led a long narrow passage shut off from the rest of the house by a red-baize door, which led to a couple more guest-rooms and the servants' quarters.

Jack Singleton and I share the same flat in town, and we had sent down in the morning Franklyn and his wife, two old and valued servants, to get things ready at Trevor Major, and procure help from the village to look after the house, and Mrs. Franklyn, with her stout comfortable face all wreathed in smiles, opened the door to us. She had had some previous experience of the "comfortable quarters" which go with fishing, and had come down prepared for the worst, but found it all of the best. The kitchen-boiler was not furred; hot and cold water was laid on in the most convenient fashion, and could be obtained from taps that neither stuck nor leaked. Her husband, it appeared, had gone into the village to buy a few necessaries, and she brought up tea for us, and then went upstairs to the two rooms over the dining-room and bigger sitting-room, which we had chosen for our bedrooms, to unpack. The doors of these were exactly opposite one another to right and left of the gallery, and Jack, who chose the bedroom above the sitting-room, had thus a smaller room, above the second sitting-room, unoccupied, next his and opening out from it.

We had a couple of hours' fishing before dinner, each of us catching three or four brace of trout, and came back in the dusk to the house. Franklyn had returned from the village from his errand, reported that he had got a woman to come in to do housework in the mornings, and mentioned that our arrival had seemed to arouse a good deal of interest. The reason for this was obscure; he could only tell us that he was questioned a dozen times as to whether we really intended to live in the house, and his assurance that we did produced silence and a shaking of heads. But the country-folk of Sussex are notable for their silence and chronic attitude of disapproval, and we put this down to local idiosyncrasy.

The evening was exquisitely warm, and after dinner we pulled out a couple of basket-chairs on to the gravel by the front door, and sat for an hour or so, while the night deepened in throbs of gathering darkness. The moon was not risen and the ring of pines cut off much of the pale starlight, so that when we went in, allured by the shining of the lamp in the sitting-room, it was curiously dark for a clear night in May. And at that moment of stepping from the darkness into the cheerfulness of the lighted house, I had a sudden sensation, to which, during the next fortnight, I became almost accustomed, of there being something unseen and unheard and dreadful near me. In spite of the warmth, I felt myself shiver, and concluded instantly that I had sat out-of-doors long enough, and without mentioning it to Jack, followed him into the smaller sitting-room in which we had scarcely yet set foot. It, like the hall, was oak-panelled, and in the panels hung some half-dozen of water-colour sketches, which we examined, idly at first, and then with growing interest, for they were executed with extraordinary finish and delicacy, and each represented some aspect of the house or garden. Here you looked up the gap in the fir-trees into a crimson sunset; here the garden, trim and carefully tended, dozed beneath some languid summer noon; here an angry wreath of storm-cloud brooded over the meadow where the trout-stream ran grey and leaden below a threatening sky, while another, the most careful and arresting of all, was a study of the brick-kiln. In this, alone of them all, was there a human figure; a man, dressed in grey, peered into the open door from which issued a fierce red glow. The figure was painted with miniature-like elaboration; the face was in profile, and represented a youngish man, clean-shaven, with a long aquiline nose and singularly square chin. The sketch was long and narrow in shape, and the chimney of the kiln appeared against a dark sky. From it there issued a thin stream of grey smoke.

Jack looked at this with attention.

"What a horrible picture!" he said, "and how beautifully painted! I feel as if it meant something, as if it was a representation of something that happened, not a mere sketch. By Jove!--"

He broke off suddenly and went in turn to each of the other pictures.

"That's a queer thing," he said. "See if you notice what I mean."

With the brick-kiln rather vividly impressed on my mind, it was not difficult to see what he had noticed. In each of the pictures appeared the brick-kiln, chimney and all, now seen faintly between trees, now in full view, and in each the chimney was smoking.

"And the odd part is that from the garden side, you can't really see the kiln at all," observed Jack, "it's hidden by the house, and yet the artist F. A., as I see by his signature, puts it in just the same."

"What do you make of that?" I asked.

"Nothing. I suppose he had a fancy for brick-kilns. Let's have a game of picquet."

A fortnight of our three weeks passed without incident, except that again and again the curious feeling of something dreadful being close at hand was present in my mind. In a way, as I said, I got used to it, but on the other hand the feeling itself seemed to gain in poignancy. Once just at the end of the fortnight I mentioned it to Jack.

"Odd you should speak of it," he said, "because I've felt the same. When do you feel it? Do you feel it now, for instance?"

We were again sitting out after dinner, and as he spoke I felt it with far greater intensity than ever before. And at the same moment the house-door which had been closed, though probably not latched, swung gently open, letting out a shaft of light from the hall, and as gently swung to again, as if something had stealthily entered.

"Yes," I said. "I felt it then. I only feel it in the evening. It was rather bad that time."

Jack was silent a moment.

"Funny thing the door opening and shutting like that," he said. "Let's go indoors."

We got up and I remember seeing at that moment that the windows of my bedroom were lit; Mrs. Franklyn probably was making things ready for the night. Simultaneously, as we crossed the gravel, there came from just inside the house the sound of a hurried footstep on the stairs, and entering we found Mrs. Franklyn in the hall, looking rather white and startled.

"Anything wrong?" I asked.

She took two or three quick breaths before she answered:

"No, sir," she said, "at least nothing that I can give an account of. I was tidying up in your room, and I thought you came in. But there was nobody, and it gave me a turn. I left my candle there; I must go up for it."

I waited in the hall a moment, while she again ascended the stairs, and passed along the gallery to my room. At the door, which I could see was open, she paused, not entering.

"What is the matter?" I asked from below.

"I left the candle alight," she said, "and it's gone out." Jack laughed.

"And you left the door and window open," said he.

"Yes, sir, but not a breath of wind is stirring," said Mrs. Franklyn, rather faintly.

This was true, and yet a few moments ago the heavy hall-door had swung open and back again. Jack ran upstairs.

"We'll brave the dark together, Mrs. Franklyn," he said.

He went into my room, and I heard the sound of a match struck. Then through the open door came the light of the rekindled candle and simultaneously I heard a bell ring in the servants' quarters. In a moment came steps, and Franklyn appeared.

"What bell was that?" I asked.

"Mr. Jack's bedroom, sir," he said.

I felt there was a marked atmosphere of nerves about for which there was really no adequate cause. All that had happened of a disturbing nature was that Mrs. Franklyn had thought I had come into my bedroom, and had been startled by finding I had not. She had then left the candle in a draught, and it had been blown out. As for a bell ringing, that, even if it had happened, was a very innocuous proceeding.

"Mouse on a wire," I said. "Mr. Jack is in my room this moment lighting Mrs. Franklyn's candle for her."

Jack came down at this juncture, and we went into the sitting-room. But Franklyn apparently was not satisfied, for we heard him in the room above us, which was Jack's bedroom, moving about with his slow and rather ponderous tread. Then his steps seemed to pass into the bedroom adjoining and we heard no more.

I remember feeling hugely sleepy that night, and went to bed earlier than usual, to pass rather a broken night with stretches of dreamless sleep interspersed with startled awakenings, in which I passed very suddenly into complete consciousness. Sometimes the house was absolutely still, and the only sound to be heard was the sighing of the night breeze outside in the pines, but sometimes the place seemed full of muffled movements and once I could have sworn that the handle of my door turned. That required verification, and I lit my candle, but found that my ears must have played me false. Yet even as I stood there, I thought I heard steps just outside, and with a considerable qualm, I must confess, I opened the door and looked out. But the gallery was quite empty, and the house quite still. Then from Jack's room opposite I heard a sound that was somehow comforting, the snorts of the snorer, and I went back to bed and slept again, and when next I woke, morning was already breaking in red lines on the horizon, and the sense of trouble that had been with me ever since last evening had gone.

Heavy rain set in after lunch next day, and as I had arrears of letter-writing to do, and the water was soon both muddy and rising, I came home alone about five, leaving Jack still sanguine by the stream, and worked for a couple of hours sitting at a writing-table in the room overlooking the gravel at the front of the house, where hung the water-colours. By seven I had finished, and just as I got up to light candles, since it was already dusk, I saw, as I thought, Jack's figure emerge from the bushes that bordered the path to the stream, on to the space in front of the house. Then instantaneously and with a sudden queer sinking of the heart quite unaccountable, I saw that it was not Jack at all, but a stranger. He was only some six yards from the window, and after pausing there a moment he came close up to the window, so that his face nearly touched the glass, looking intently at me. In the light from the freshly-kindled candles I could distinguish his features with great clearness, but though, as far as I knew, I had never seen him before, there was something familiar about both his face and figure. He appeared to smile at me, but the smile was one of inscrutable evil and malevolence, and immediately he walked on, straight towards the house door opposite him, and out of sight of the sitting-room window.

Now, little though I liked the look of the man, he was, as I have said, familiar to my eye, and I went out into the hall, since he was clearly coming to the front door, to open it to him and learn his business. So without waiting for him to ring, I opened it, feeling sure I should find him on the step. Instead, I looked out into the empty gravel-sweep, the heavy-falling rain, the thick dusk.

And even as I looked, I felt something that I could not see push by me through the half-opened door and pass into the house. Then the stairs creaked, and a moment after a bell rang.

Franklyn is the quickest man to answer a bell I have ever seen, and next instant he passed me going upstairs. He tapped at Jack's door, entered and then came down again.

"Mr. Jack still out, sir?" he asked.

"Yes. His bell ringing again?"

"Yes, sir," said Franklyn, quite imperturbably.

I went back into the sitting-room, and soon Franklyn brought a lamp. He put it on the table above which hung the careful and curious picture of the brick-kiln, and then with a sudden horror I saw why the stranger on the gravel outside had been so familiar to me. In all respects he resembled the figure that peered into the kiln; it was more than a resemblance, it was an identity.

And what had happened to this man who had inscrutably and evilly smiled at me? And what had pushed in through the half-closed door?

At that moment I saw the face of Fear; my mouth went dry, and I heard my heart leaping and cracking in my throat. That face was only turned on me for a moment, and then away again, but I knew it to be the genuine thing; not apprehension, not foreboding, not a feeling of being startled, but Fear, cold Fear. And then though nothing had occurred to assuage the Fear, it passed, and a certain sort of reason usurped--for so I must say--its place. I had certainly seen somebody on the gravel outside the house; I had supposed he was going to the front door. I had opened it, and found he had not come to the front door. Or--and once again the terror resurged--had the invisible pushing thing been that which I had seen outside? And if so, what was it? And how came it that the face and figure of the man I had seen were the same as those which were so scrupulously painted in the picture of the brick-kiln?

I set myself to argue down the Fear for which there was no more foundation than this, this and the repetition of the ringing bell, and my belief is that I did so. I told myself, till I believed it, that a man--a human man--had been walking across the gravel outside, and that he had not come to the front door but had gone, as he might easily have done, up the drive into the high-road.

I told myself that it was mere fancy that was the cause of the belief that Something had pushed in by me, and as for the ringing of the bell, I said to myself, as was true, that this had happened before. And I must ask the reader to believe also that I argued these things away, and looked no longer on the face of Fear itself. I was not comfortable, but I fell short of being terrified.

I sat down again by the window looking on to the gravel in front of the house, and finding another letter that asked, though it did not demand, an answer, proceeded to occupy myself with it. Straight in front led the drive through the gap in the pines, and passed through the field where lay the brick-kiln. In a pause of page-turning I looked up and saw something unusual about it; at the same moment an unusual smell came to my nostril. What I saw was smoke coming out of the chimney of the kiln, what I smelt was the odour of roasting meat. The wind--such as there was--set from the kiln to the house. But as far as I knew the smell of roast meat probably came from the kitchen where dinner, so I supposed, was cooking. I had to tell myself this: I wanted reassurance, lest the face of Fear should look whitely on me again.

Then there came a crisp step on the gravel, a rattle at the front door, and Jack came in.

"Good sport," he said, "you gave up too soon."

And he went straight to the table above which hung the picture of the man at the brick-kiln, and looked at it. Then there was silence; and eventually I spoke, for I wanted to know one thing.

"Seen anybody?" I asked.

"Yes. Why do you ask?"

"Because I have also; the man in that picture."

Jack came and sat down near me.

"It's a ghost, you know," he said. "He came down to the river about dusk and stood near me for an hour. At first I thought he was real--was real, and I warned him that he had better stand further off if he didn't want to be hooked. And then it struck me he wasn't real, and I cast, well, right through him, and about seven he walked up towards the house."

"Were you frightened?"

"No. It was so tremendously interesting. So you saw him here too. Whereabouts?"

"Just outside. I think he is in the house now."

Jack looked round.

"Did you see him come in?" he asked.

"No, but I felt him. There's another queer thing too; the chimney of the brick-kiln is smoking."

Jack looked out of the window. It was nearly dark, but the wreathing smoke could just be seen.

"So it is," he said, "fat, greasy smoke. I think I'll go up and see what's on. Come too?"

"I think not," I said.

"Are you frightened? It isn't worth while. Besides, it is so tremendously interesting."

Jack came back from his little expedition still interested. He had found nothing stirring at the kiln, but though it was then nearly dark the interior was faintly luminous, and against the black of the sky he could see a wisp of thick white smoke floating northwards. But for the rest of the evening we neither heard nor saw anything of abnormal import, and the next day ran a course of undisturbed hours. Then suddenly a hellish activity was manifested.

That night, while I was undressing for bed, I heard a bell ring furiously, and I thought I heard a shout also. I guessed where the ring came from, since Franklyn and his wife had long ago gone to bed, and went straight to Jack's room. But as I tapped at the door I heard his voice from inside calling loud to me. "Take care," it said, "he's close to the door."

A sudden qualm of blank fear took hold of me, but mastering it as best I could, I opened the door to enter, and once again something pushed softly by me, though I saw nothing.

Jack was standing by his bed, half-un-- I saw him wipe his forehead with the back of his hand.

"He's been here again," he said. "I was standing just here, a minute ago, when I found him close by me. He came out of the inner room, I think. Did you see what he had in his hand?"

"I saw nothing."

"It was a knife; a great long carving knife. Do you mind my sleeping on the sofa in your room to-night? I got an awful turn then. There was another thing too. All round the edge of his clothes, at his collar and at his wrists, there were little flames playing, little white licking flames." But next day, again, we neither heard nor saw anything, nor that night did the sense of that dreadful presence in the house come to us. And then came the last day. We had been out till it was dark, and as I said, had a wonderful day among the fish. On reaching home we sat together in the sitting-room, when suddenly from overhead came a tread of feet, a violent pealing of the bell, and the moment after yell after yell as of someone in mortal agony. The thought occurred to both of us that this might be Mrs. Franklyn in terror of some fearful sight, and together we rushed up and sprang into Jack's bedroom.

The doorway into the room beyond was open, and just inside it we saw the man bending over some dark huddled object. Though the room was dark we could see him perfectly, for a light stale and impure seemed to come from him. He had again a long knife in his hand, and as we entered he was wiping it on the mass that lay at his feet. Then he took it up, and we saw what it was, a woman with head nearly severed. But it was not Mrs. Franklyn.

And then the whole thing vanished, and we were standing looking into a dark and empty room. We went downstairs without a word, and it was not till we were both in the sitting-room below that Jack spoke.

"And he takes her to the brick-kiln," he said rather unsteadily.

"I say, have you had enough of this house? I have. There is hell in it."

About a week later Jack put into my hand a guide-book to Sussex open at the description of Trevor Major, and I read:

"Just outside the village stands the picturesque manor house, once the home of the artist and notorious murderer, Francis Adam. It was here he killed his wife, in a fit, it is believed, of groundless jealousy, cutting her throat and disposing of her remains by burning them in a brick-kiln."

"Certain charred fragments found six months afterwards led to his arrest and execution."

So I prefer to leave the house with the brick-kiln and the pictures signed F. A. to others.

The Man Who Went Too Far

The little village of St. Faith's nestles in a hollow of wooded till up on the north bank of the river Fawn in the country of Hampshire, huddling close round its grey Norman church as if for spiritual protection against the fays and fairies, the trolls and "little people," who might be supposed still to linger in the vast empty spaces of the New Forest, and to come after dusk and do their doubtful businesses. Once outside the hamlet you may walk in any direction (so long as you avoid the high road which leads to Brockenhurst) for the length of a summer afternoon without seeing sign of human habitation, or possibly even catching sight of another human being.

Shaggy wild ponies may stop their feeding for a moment as you pass, the white scuts of rabbits will vanish into their burrows, a brown viper perhaps will glide from your path into a clump of heather, and unseen birds will chuckle in the bushes, but it may easily happen that for a long day you will see nothing human. But you will not feel in the least lonely; in summer, at any rate, the sunlight will be gay with butterflies, and the air thick with all those woodland sounds which like instruments in an orchestra combine to play the great symphony of the yearly festival of June.

Winds whisper in the birches, and sigh among the firs; bees are busy with their redolent labour among the heather, a myriad birds chirp in the green temples of the forest trees, and the voice of the river prattling over stony places, bubbling into pools, chuckling and gulping round corners, gives you the sense that many presences and companions are near at hand.

Yet, oddly enough, though one would have thought that these benign and cheerful influences of wholesome air and spaciousness of forest were very healthful comrades for a man, in so far as Nature can really influence this wonderful human genus which has in these centuries learned to defy her most violent storms in its well-established houses, to bridle her torrents and make them light its streets, to tunnel her mountains and plough her seas, the inhabitants of St. Faith's will not willingly venture into the forest after dark. For in spite of the silence and loneliness of the hooded night it seems that a man is not sure in what company he may suddenly find himself, and though it is difficult to get from these villagers any very clear story of occult appearances, the feeling is widespread. One story indeed I have heard with some definiteness, the tale of a monstrous goat that has been seen to skip with hellish glee about the woods and shady places, and this perhaps is connected with the story which I have here attempted to piece together.

It too is well-known to them; for all remember the young artist who died here not long ago, a young man, or so he struck the beholder, of great personal beauty, with something about him that made men's faces to smile and brighten when they looked on him. His ghost they will tell you "walks" constantly by the stream and through the woods which he loved so, and in especial it haunts a certain house, the last of the village, where he lived, and its garden in which he was done to death. For my part I am inclined to think that the terror of the forest dates chiefly from that day.

So, such as the story is, I have set it forth in connected form. It is based partly on the accounts of the villagers, but mainly on that of Darcy, a friend of mine and a friend of the man with whom these events were chiefly concerned.

The day had been one of untarnished midsummer splendour, and as the sun drew near to its setting, the glory of the evening grew every moment more crystalline, more miraculous.

Westward from St. Faith's the beechwood which stretched for some miles toward the heathery upland beyond already cast its veil of clear shadow over the red roofs of the village, but the spire of the grey church, over-topping all, still pointed a flaming orange finger into the sky. The river Fawn, which runs below, lay in sheets of sky-reflected blue, and wound its dreamy devious course round the edge of this wood, where a rough two-planked bridge crossed from the bottom of the garden of the last house in the village, and communicated by means of a little wicker gate with the wood itself. Then once out of the shadow of the wood the stream lay in flaming pools of the molten crimson of the sunset, and lost itself in the haze of woodland distances.

This house at the end of the village stood outside the shadow, and the lawn which sloped down to the river was still flecked with sunlight. Garden-beds of dazzling colour lined its gravel walks, and down the middle of it ran a brick pergola, half-hidden in clusters of rambler-rose and purple with starry clematis. At the bottom end of it, between two of its pillars, was slung a hammock containing a shirtsleeved figure.

The house itself lay somewhat remote from the rest of the village, and a footpath leading across two fields, now tall and fragrant with hay, was its only communication with the high road.

It was low-built, only two stories in height, and like the garden, its walls were a mass of flowering roses. A narrow stone terrace ran along the garden front, over which was stretched an awning, and on the terrace a young silent-footed manservant was busied with the laying of the table for dinner. He was neat-handed and quick with his job, and having finished it he went back into the house, and reappeared again with a large rough bath-towel on his arm. With this he went to the hammock in the pergola.

"Nearly eight, sir," he said.

"Has Mr. Darcy come yet?" asked a voice from the hammock.

"No, sir."

"If I'm not back when he comes, tell him that I'm just having a bathe before dinner."

The servant went back to the house, and after a moment or two Frank Halton struggled to a sitting posture, and slipped out on to the grass. He was of medium height and rather slender in build, but the supple ease and grace of his movements gave the impression of great physical strength: even his descent from the hammock was not an awkward performance. His face and hands were of very dark complexion, either from constant exposure to wind and sun, or, as his black hair and dark eyes tended to show, from some strain of southern blood. His head was small, his face of an exquisite beauty of modelling, while the smoothness of its contour would have led you to believe that he was a beardless lad still in his teens. But something, some look which living and experience alone can give, seemed to contradict that, and finding yourself completely puzzled as to his age, you would next moment probably cease to think about that, and only look at this glorious specimen of young manhood with wondering satisfaction.

He was dressed as became the season and the heat, and wore only a shirt open at the neck, and a pair of flannel trousers. His head, covered very thickly with a somewhat rebellious crop of short curly hair, was bare as he strolled across the lawn to the bathing-place that lay below. Then for a moment there was silence, then the sound of splashed and divided waters, and presently after, a great shout of ecstatic joy, as he swam up-stream with the foamed water standing in a frill round his neck. Then after some five minutes of limb-stretching struggle with the flood, he turned over on his back, and with arms thrown wide, floated down-stream, ripple-cradled and inert. His eyes were shut, and between half-parted lips he talked gently to himself.

"I am one with it," he said to himself, "the river and I, I and the river. The coolness and splash of it is I, and the water-herbs that wave in it are I also. And my strength and my limbs are not mine but the river's. It is all one, all one, dear Fawn." A quarter of an hour later he appeared again at the bottom of the lawn, dressed as before, his wet hair already drying into its crisp short curls again. There he paused a moment, looking back at the stream with the smile with which men look on the face of a friend, then turned towards the house. Simultaneously his servant came to the door leading on to the terrace, followed by a man who appeared to be some half-way through the fourth decade of his years. Frank and he saw each other across the bushes and garden-beds, and each quickening his step, they met suddenly face to face round an angle of the garden walk, in the fragrance of syringa.

"My dear Darcy," cried Frank, "I am charmed to see you." But the other stared at him in amazement.

"Frank!" he exclaimed.

"Yes, that is my name," he said, laughing; "what is the matter?" Darcy took his hand.

"What have you done to yourself?" he asked.

"You are a boy again."

"Ah, I have a lot to tell you," said Frank.

"Lots that you will hardly believe, but I shall convince you--"

He broke off suddenly, and held up his hand.

"Hush, there is my nightingale," he said.

The smile of recognition and welcome with which he had greeted his friend faded from his face, and a look of rapt wonder took its place, as of a lover listening to the voice of his beloved.

His mouth parted slightly, showing the white line of teeth, and his eyes looked out and out till they seemed to Darcy to be focussed on things beyond the vision of man. Then something perhaps startled the bird, for the song ceased.

"Yes, lots to tell you," he said. "Really I am delighted to see you. But you look rather white and pulled down; no wonder after that fever. And there is to be no nonsense about this visit. It is June now, you stop here till you are fit to begin work again. Two months at least."

"Ah, I can't trespass quite to that extent."

Frank took his arm and walked him down the grass.

"Trespass? Who talks of trespass? I shall tell you quite openly when I am tired of you, but you know when we had the studio together, we used not to bore each other. However, it is ill talking of going away on the moment of your arrival. Just a stroll to the river, and then it will be dinner-time."

Darcy took out his cigarette case, and offered it to the other.

Frank laughed.

"No, not for me. Dear me, I suppose I used to smoke once. How very odd!"

"Given it up?"

"I don't know. I suppose I must have. Anyhow I don't do it now. I would as soon think of eating meat."

"Another victim on the smoking altar of vegetarianism?"

"Victim?" asked Frank. "Do I strike you as such?"

He paused on the margin of the stream and whistled softly. Next moment a moor-hen made its splashing flight across the river, and ran up the bank. Frank took it very gently in his hands and stroked its head, as the creature lay against his shirt.

"And is the house among the reeds still secure?" he half-crooned to it. "And is the missus quite well, and are the neighbours flourishing? There, dear, home with you," and he flung it into the air.

"That bird's very tame," said Darcy, slightly bewildered.

"It is rather," said Frank, following its flight.

During dinner Frank chiefly occupied himself in bringing himself up-to-date in the movements and achievements of this old friend whom he had not seen for six years. Those six years, it now appeared, had been full of incident and success for Darcy; he had made a name for himself as a portrait painter which bade fair to outlast the vogue of a couple of seasons, and his leisure time had been brief. Then some four months previously he had been through a severe attack of typhoid, the result of which as concerns this story was that he had come down to this sequestered place to recruit.

"Yes, you've got on," said Frank at the end. "I always knew you would. A.R.A. with more in prospect. Money? You roll in it, I suppose, and, O Darcy, how much happiness have you had all these years? That is the only imperishable possession. And how much have you learned? Oh, I don't mean in Art. Even I could have done well in that."

Darcy laughed.

"Done well? My dear fellow, all I have learned in these six years you knew, so to speak, in your cradle. Your old pictures fetch huge prices. Do you never paint now?"

Frank shook his head.

"No, I'm too busy," he said.

"Doing what? Please tell me. That is what everyone is for ever asking me."

"Doing? I suppose you would say I do nothing."

Darcy glanced up at the brilliant young face opposite him.

"It seems to suit you, that way of being busy," he said. "Now, it's your turn. Do you read? Do you study? I remember you saying that it would do us all--all us artists, I mean--a great deal of good if we would study any one human face carefully for a year, without recording a line."

"Have you been doing that?"

Frank shook his head again.

"I mean exactly what I say," he said. "I have been doing nothing. And I have never been so occupied. Look at me; have I not done something to myself to begin with?"

"You are two years younger than I," said Darcy, "at least you used to be. You therefore are thirty-five. But had I never seen you before I should say you were just twenty. But was it worth while to spend six years of greatly-occupied life in order to look twenty? Seems rather like a woman of fashion."

Frank laughed boisterously.

"First time I've ever been compared to that particular bird of prey," he said. "No, that has not been my occupation--in fact I am only very rarely conscious that one effect of my occupation has been that. Of course, it must have been if one comes to think of it. It is not very important."

"Quite true my body has become young. But that is very little; I have become young."

Darcy pushed back his chair and sat sideways to the table looking at the other.

"Has that been your occupation then?" he asked.

"Yes, that anyhow is one aspect of it. Think what youth means! It is the capacity for growth, mind, body, spirit, all grow, all get stronger, all have a fuller, firmer life every day. That is something, considering that every day that passes after the ordinary man reaches the full-blown flower of his strength, weakens his hold on life. A man reaches his prime, and remains, we say, in his prime for ten years, or perhaps twenty. But after his primest prime is reached, he slowly, insensibly weakens. These are the signs of age in you, in your body, in your art probably, in your mind. You are less electric than you were. But I, when I reach my prime--I am nearing it--ah, you shall see." The stars had begun to appear in the blue velvet of the sky, and to the east the horizon seen above the black silhouette of the village was growing dove-coloured with the approach of moon-rise.

White moths hovered dimly over the garden-beds, and the footsteps of night tip-toed through the bushes. Suddenly Frank rose.

"Ah, it is the supreme moment," he said softly. "Now more than at any other time the current of life, the eternal imperishable current runs so close to me that I am almost enveloped in it. Be silent a minute."

He advanced to the edge of the terrace and looked out, standing stretched with arms outspread. Darcy heard him draw a long breath into his lungs, and after many seconds expel it again. Six or eight times he did this, then turned back into the lamplight.

"It will sound to you quite mad, I expect," he said, "but if you want to hear the soberest truth I have ever spoken and shall ever speak, I will tell you about myself. But come into the garden if it is not damp for you. I have never told anyone yet, but I shall like to tell you. It is long, in fact, since I have even tried to classify what I have learned."

They wandered into the fragrant dimness of the pergola, and sat down. Then Frank began:

"Years ago, do you remember," he said, "we used often to talk about the decay of joy in the world. Many impulses, we settled, had contributed to this decay, some of which were good in themselves, others that were quite completely bad. Among the good things, I put what we may call certain Christian virtues, renunciation, resignation, sympathy with suffering, and the desire to relieve sufferers, but out of those things spring very bad ones, useless renunciation, asceticism for its own sake, mortification of the flesh with nothing to follow, no corresponding gain that is, and that awful and terrible disease which devastated England some centuries ago, and from which by heredity of spirit we suffer now, Puritanism. That was a dreadful plague, the brutes held and taught that joy and laughter and merriment were evil: it was a doctrine the most profane and wicked. Why, what is the commonest crime one sees? A sullen face. That is the truth of the matter. Now all my life I have believed that we are intended to be happy, that joy is of all gifts the most divine. And when I left London, abandoned my career, such as it was, I did so because I intended to devote my life to the cultivation of joy, and, by continuous and unsparing effort to be happy. Among people, and in constant intercourse with others, I did not find it possible; there were too many distractions in towns and work-rooms, and also too much suffering. So I took one step backwards or forwards, as you may choose to put it, and went straight to Nature, to trees, birds, animals, to all those things which quite clearly pursue one aim only, which blindly follow the great native instinct to be happy without any care at all for morality, or human law or divine law. I wanted, you understand, to get all joy first-hand and unadulterated, and I think it scarcely exists among men; it is obsolete."

Darcy turned in his chair.

"Ah, but what makes birds and animals happy?" he asked. "Food, food and mating."

Frank laughed gently in the stillness.

"Do not think I became a sensualist," he said. "I did not make that mistake. For the sensualist carries his miseries pick-a-back, and round his feet is wound the shroud that shall soon enwrap him. I may be mad, it is true, but I am not so stupid anyhow as to have tried that. No, what is it that makes puppies play with their own tails, that sends cats on their prowling ecstatic errands at night?"

He paused a moment.

"So I went to Nature," he said. "I sat down here in this New Forest, sat down fair and square, and looked. That was my first difficulty, to sit here quiet without being bored, to wait without being impatient, to be receptive and very alert, though for a long time nothing particular happened. The change in fact was slow in those early stages."

"Nothing happened?" asked Darcy, rather impatiently, with the sturdy revolt against any new idea which to the English mind is synonymous with nonsense. "Why, what in the world should happen?"

Now Frank as he had known him was the most generous but most quick-tempered of mortal men; in other words his anger would flare to a prodigious beacon, under almost no provocation, only to be quenched again under a gust of no less impulsive kindliness. Thus the moment Darcy had spoken, an apology for his hasty question was half-way up his tongue. But there was no need for it to have travelled even so far, for Frank laughed again with kindly, genuine mirth.

"Oh, how I should have resented that a few years ago," he said. "Thank goodness that resentment is one of the things I have got rid of. I certainly wish that you should believe my story--in fact, you are going to--but that you at this moment should imply that you do not does not concern me."

"Ah, your solitary sojournings have made you inhuman," said Darcy, still very English.

"No, human," said Frank. "Rather more human, at least rather less of an ape."

"Well, that was my first quest," he continued, after a moment, "the deliberate and unswerving pursuit of joy, and my method, the eager contemplation of Nature. As far as motive went, I daresay it was purely selfish, but as far as effect goes, it seems to me about the best thing one can do for one's follow-creatures, for happiness is more infectious than small-pox. So, as I said, I sat down and waited; I looked at happy things, zealously avoided the sight of anything unhappy, and by degrees a little trickle of the happiness of this blissful world began to filter into me. The trickle grew more abundant, and now, my dear fellow, if I could for a moment divert from me into you one half of the torrent of joy that pours through me day and night, you would throw the world, art, everything aside, and just live, exist. When a man's body dies, it passes into trees and flowers. Well, that is what I have been trying to do with my soul before death."

The servant had brought into the pergola a table with syphons and spirits, and had set a lamp upon it. As Frank spoke he leaned forward towards the other, and Darcy for all his matter-of-fact common sense could have sworn that his companion's face shone, was luminous in itself. His dark brown eyes glowed from within, the unconscious smile of a child irradiated and transformed his face. Darcy felt suddenly excited, exhilarated.

"Go on," he said. "Go on. I can feel you are somehow telling me sober truth. I daresay you are mad; but I don't see that matters."

Frank laughed again.

"Mad?" he said. "Yes, certainly, if you wish. But I prefer to call it sane. However, nothing matters less than what anybody chooses to call things. God never labels his gifts; He just puts them into our hands; just as he put animals in the garden of Eden, for Adam to name if he felt disposed.

"So by the continual observance and study of things that were happy," continued he, "I got happiness, I got joy. But seeking it, as I did, from Nature, I got much more which I did not seek, but stumbled upon originally by accident. It is difficult to explain, but I will try.

"About three years ago I was sitting one morning in a place I will show you tomorrow. It is down by the river brink, very green, dappled with shade and sun, and the river passes there through some little clumps of reeds. Well, as I sat there, doing nothing, but just looking and listening, I heard the sound quite distinctly of some flute-like instrument playing a strange unending melody. I thought at first it was some musical yokel on the highway and did not pay much attention. But before long the strangeness and indescribable beauty of the tune struck me.

"It never repeated itself, but it never came to an end, phrase after phrase ran its sweet course, it worked gradually and inevitably up to a climax, and having attained it, it went on; another climax was reached and another and another. Then with a sudden gasp of wonder I localised where it came from. It came from the reeds and from the sky and from the trees. It was everywhere, it was the sound of life. It was, my dear Darcy, as the Greeks would have said, it was Pan playing on his pipes, the voice of Nature. It was the life-melody, the world-melody."

Darcy was far too interested to interrupt, though there was a question he would have liked to ask, and Frank went on:

"Well, for the moment I was terrified, terrified with the impotent horror of nightmare, and I stopped my ears and just ran from the place and got back to the house panting, trembling, literally in a panic. Unknowingly, for at that time I only pursued joy, I had begun, since I drew my joy from Nature, to get in touch with Nature. Nature, force, God, call it what you will, had drawn across my face a little gossamer web of essential life. I saw that when I emerged from my terror, and I went very humbly back to where I had heard the Pan-pipes. But it was nearly six months before I heard them again."

"Why was that?" asked Darcy.

"Surely because I had revolted, rebelled, and worst of all been frightened. For I believe that just as there is nothing in the world which so injures one's body as fear, so there is nothing that so much shuts up the soul. I was afraid, you see, of the one thing in the world which has real existence. No wonder its manifestation was withdrawn."

"And after six months?"

"After six months one blessed morning I heard the piping again. I wasn't afraid that time."

"And since then it has grown louder, it has become more constant. I now hear it often, and I can put myself into such an attitude towards Nature that the pipes will almost certainly sound. And never yet have they played the same tune, it is always something new, something fuller, richer, more complete than before."

"What do you mean by 'such an attitude towards Nature'?" asked Darcy.

"I can't explain that; but by translating it into a bodily attitude it is this."

Frank sat up for a moment quite straight in his chair, then slowly sunk back with arms outspread and head drooped.

"That;" he said, "an effortless attitude, but open, resting, receptive. It is just that which you must do with your soul."

Then he sat up again.

"One word more," he said, "and I will bore you no further. Nor unless you ask me questions shall I talk about it again. You will find me, in fact, quite sane in my mode of life. Birds and beasts you will see behaving somewhat intimately to me, like that moor-hen, but that is all. I will walk with you, ride with you, play golf with you, and talk with you on any subject you like. But I wanted you on the threshold to know what has happened to me. And one thing more will happen."

He paused again, and a slight look of fear crossed his eyes.

"There will be a final revelation," he said, "a complete and blinding stroke which will throw open to me, once and for all, the full knowledge, the full realisation and comprehension that I am one, just as you are, with life. In reality there is no 'me,' no 'you,' no 'it.' Everything is part of the one and only thing which is life. I know that that is so, but the realisation of it is not yet mine.

"But it will be, and on that day, so I take it, I shall see Pan. It may mean death, the death of my body, that is, but I don't care. It may mean immortal, eternal life lived here and now and for ever.

"Then having gained that, ah, my dear Darcy, I shall preach such a gospel of joy, showing myself as the living proof of the truth, that Puritanism, the dismal religion of sour faces, shall vanish like a breath of smoke, and be dispersed and disappear in the sunlit air. But first the full knowledge must be mine."

Darcy watched his face narrowly.

"You are afraid of that moment," he said. Frank smiled at him.

"Quite true; you are quick to have seen that. But when it comes I hope I shall not be afraid."

For some little time there was silence; then Darcy rose. "You have bewitched me, you extraordinary boy," he said. "You have been telling me a fairy-story, and I find myself saying, 'Promise me it is true.'"

"I promise you that," said the other.

"And I know I shan't sleep," added Darcy.

Frank looked at him with a sort of mild wonder as if he scarcely understood.

"Well, what does that matter?" he said.

"I assure you it does. I am wretched unless I sleep."

"Of course I can make you sleep if I want," said Frank in a rather bored voice.

"Well, do."

"Very good: go to bed. I'll come upstairs in ten minutes."

Frank busied himself for a little after the other had gone, moving the table back under the awning of the verandah and quenching the lamp. Then he went with his quick silent tread upstairs and into Darcy's room. The latter was already in bed, but very wide-eyed and wakeful, and Frank with an amused smile of indulgence, as for a fretful child, sat down on the edge of the bed.

"Look at me," he said, and Darcy looked.

"The birds are sleeping in the brake," said Frank softly, "and the winds are asleep. The sea sleeps, and the tides are but the heaving of its breast. The stars swing slow, rocked in the great cradle of the Heavens, and--"

He stopped suddenly, gently blew out Darcy's candle, and left him sleeping.

Morning brought to Darcy a flood of hard common sense, as clear and crisp as the sunshine that filled his room. Slowly as he woke he gathered together the broken threads of the memories of the evening which had ended, so he told himself, in a trick of common hypnotism. That accounted for it all; the whole strange talk he had had was under a spell of suggestion from the extraordinary vivid boy who had once been a man; all his own excitement, his acceptance of the incredible had been merely the effect of a stronger, more potent will imposed on his own. How strong that will was, he guessed from his own instantaneous obedience to Frank's suggestion of sleep. And armed with impenetrable common sense he came down to breakfast. Frank had already begun, and was consuming a large plateful of porridge and milk with the most prosaic and healthy appetite.

"Slept well?" he asked.

"Yes, of course. Where did you learn hypnotism?"

"By the side of the river."

"You talked an amazing quantity of nonsense last night," remarked Darcy, in a voice prickly with reason.

"Rather. I felt quite giddy. Look, I remembered to order a dreadful daily paper for you. You can read about money markets or politics or cricket matches." Darcy looked at him closely. In the morning light Frank looked even fresher, younger, more vital than he had done the night before, and the sight of him somehow dinted Darcy's armour of common sense.

"You are the most extraordinary fellow I ever saw," he said. "I want to ask you some more questions."

"Ask away," said Frank.

For the next day or two Darcy plied his friend with many questions, objections and criticisms on the theory of life, and gradually got out of him a coherent and complete account of his experience. In brief, then, Frank believed that "by lying naked," as he put it, to the force which controls the passage of the stars, the breaking of a wave, the budding of a tree, the love of a youth and maiden, he had succeeded in a way hitherto undreamed of in possessing himself of the essential principle of life. Day by day, so he thought, he was getting nearer to, and in closer union with, the great power itself which caused all life to be, the spirit of nature, of force, or the spirit of God. For himself, he confessed to what others would call paganism; it was sufficient for him that there existed a principle of life. He did not worship it, he did not pray to it, he did not praise it. Some of it existed in all human beings, just as it existed in trees and animals; to realise and make living to himself the fact that it was all one, was his sole aim and object.

Here perhaps Darcy would put in a word of warning.

"Take care," he said. "To see Pan meant death, did it not."

Frank's eyebrows would rise at this.

"What does that matter?" he said. "True, the Greeks were always right, and they said so, but there is another possibility. For the nearer I get to it, the more living, the more vital and young I become."

"What then do you expect the final revelation will do for you?"

"I have told you," said he. "It will make me immortal."

But it was not so much from speech and argument that Darcy grew to grasp his friend's conception, as from the ordinary conduct of his life. They were passing, for instance, one morning down the village street, when an old woman, very bent and decrepit, but with an extraordinary cheerfulness of face, hobbled out from her cottage. Frank instantly stopped when he saw her.

"You old darling! How goes it all?" he said.

But she did not answer, her dim old eyes were riveted on his face; she seemed to drink in like a thirsty creature the beautiful radiance which shone there. Suddenly she put her two withered old hands on his shoulders.

"You're just the sunshine itself," she said, and he kissed her and passed on.

But scarcely a hundred yards further a strange contradiction of such tenderness occurred. A child running along the path towards them fell on its face and set up a dismal cry of fright and pain. A look of horror came into Frank's eyes, and, putting his fingers in his ears, he fled at full speed down the street, and did not pause till he was out of hearing. Darcy, having ascertained that the child was not really hurt, followed him in bewilderment.

"Are you without pity then?" he asked. Frank shook his head impatiently.

"Can't you see?" he asked. "Can't you understand that that sort of thing, pain, anger, anything unlovely, throws me back, retards the coming of the great hour! Perhaps when it comes I shall be able to piece that side of life on to the other, on to the true religion of joy. At present I can't."

"But the old woman. Was she not ugly?"

Frank's radiance gradually returned.

"Ah, no. She was like me. She longed for joy, and knew it when she saw it, the old darling."

Another question suggested itself.

"Then what about Christianity?" asked Darcy.

"I can't accept it. I can't believe in any creed of which the central doctrine is that God who is Joy should have had to suffer. Perhaps it was so; in some inscrutable way I believe it may have been so, but I don't understand how it was possible. So I leave it alone; my affair is joy."

They had come to the weir above the village, and the thunder of riotous cool water was heavy in the air. Trees dipped into the translucent stream with slender trailing branches, and the meadow where they stood was starred with midsummer blossomings. Larks shot up carolling into the crystal dome of blue, and a thousand voices of June sang round them. Frank, bare-headed as was his wont, with his coat slung over his arm and his shirt sleeves rolled up above the elbow, stood there like some beautiful wild animal with eyes half-shut and mouth half-open, drinking in the scented warmth of the air. Then suddenly he flung himself face downwards on the grass at the edge of the stream, burying his face in the daisies and cowslips, and lay stretched there in wide-armed ecstasy, with his long fingers pressing and stroking the dewy herbs of the field. Never before had Darcy seen him thus fully possessed by his idea; his caressing fingers, his half-buried face pressed close to the grass, even the clothed lines of his figure were instinct with a vitality that somehow was different from that of other men. And some faint glow from it reached Darcy, some thrill, some vibration from that charged recumbent body passed to him, and for a moment he understood as he had not understood before, despite his persistent questions and the candid answers they received, how real, and how realised by Frank, his idea was.

Then suddenly the muscles in Frank's neck became stiff and alert, and he half-raised his head.

"The Pan-pipes, the Pan-pipes," he whispered. "Close, oh, so close."

Very slowly, as if a sudden movement might interrupt the melody, he raised himself and leaned on the elbow of his bent arm. His eyes opened wider, the lower lids drooped as if he focussed his eyes on something very far away, and the smile on his face broadened and quivered like sunlight on still water, till the exultance of its happiness was scarcely human. So he remained motionless and rapt for some minutes, then the look of listening died from his face, and he bowed his head, satisfied.

"Ah, that was good," he said. "How is it possible you did not hear? Oh, you poor fellow! Did you really hear nothing?"

A week of this outdoor and stimulating life did wonders in restoring to Darcy the vigour and health which his weeks of fever had filched from him, and as his normal activity and higher pressure of vitality returned, he seemed to himself to fall even more under the spell which the miracle of Frank's youth cast over him. Twenty times a day he found himself saying to himself suddenly at the end of some ten minutes silent resistance to the absurdity of Frank's idea: "But it isn't possible; it can't be possible," and from the fact of his having to assure himself so frequently of this, he knew that he was struggling and arguing with a conclusion which already had taken root in his mind. For in any case a visible living miracle confronted him, since it was equally impossible that this youth, this boy, trembling on the verge of manhood, was thirty-five.

Yet such was the fact.

July was ushered in by a couple of days of blustering and fretful rain, and Darcy, unwilling to risk a chill, kept to the house. But to Frank this weeping change of weather seemed to have no bearing on the behaviour of man, and he spent his days exactly as he did under the suns of June, lying in his hammock, stretched on the dripping grass, or making huge rambling excursions into the forest, the birds hopping from tree to tree after him, to return in the evening, drenched and soaked, but with the same unquenchable flame of joy burning within him.

"Catch cold?" he would ask; "I've forgotten how to do it, I think I suppose it makes one's body more sensible always to sleep out-of-doors. People who live indoors always remind me of something peeled and skinless."

"Do you mean to say you slept out-of-doors last night in that deluge?" asked Darcy. "And where, may I ask?"

Frank thought a moment.

"I slept in the hammock till nearly dawn," he said. "For I remember the light blinked in the east when I awoke. Then I went--where did I go--oh, yes, to the meadow where the Pan-pipes sounded so close a week ago. You were with me, do you remember? But I always have a rug if it is wet."

And he went whistling upstairs.

Somehow that little touch, his obvious effort to recall where he had slept, brought strangely home to Darcy the wonderful romance of which he was the still half-incredulous beholder. Sleep till close on dawn in a hammock, then the tramp--or probably scamper--underneath the windy and weeping heavens to the remote and lonely meadow by the weir! The picture of other such nights rose before him; Frank sleeping perhaps by the bathing-place under the filtered twilight of the stars, or the white blaze of moon-shine, a stir and awakening at some dead hour, perhaps a space of silent wide-eyed thought, and then awandering through the hushed woods to some other dormitory, alone with his happiness, alone with the joy and the life that suffused and enveloped him, without other thought or desire or aim except the hourly and never-ceasing communion with the joy of nature.

They were in the middle of dinner that night, talking on indifferent subjects, when Darcy suddenly broke off in the middle of a sentence.

"I've got it," he said. "At last I've got it."

"Congratulate you," said Frank. "But what?"

"The radical unsoundness of your idea. It is this: 'All Nature from highest to lowest is full, crammed full of suffering; every living organism in Nature preys on another, yet in your aim to get close to, to be one with Nature, you leave suffering altogether out; you run away from it, you refuse to recognise it. And you are waiting, you say, for the final revelation."

Frank's brow clouded slightly.

"Well," he asked, rather wearily.

"Cannot you guess then when the final revelation will be? In joy you are supreme, I grant you that; I did not know a man could be so master of it. You have learned perhaps practically all that Nature can teach. And if, as you think, the final revelation is coming to you, it will be the revelation of horror, suffering, death, pain in all its hideous forms. Suffering does exist: you hate it and fear it."

Frank held up his hand.

"Stop; let me think," he said.

There was silence for a long minute.

"That never struck me," he said at length. "It is possible that what you suggest is true. Does the sight of Pan mean that, do you think? Is it that Nature, take it altogether, suffers horribly, suffers to a hideous inconceivable extent? Shall I be shown all the suffering?" He got up and came round to where Darcy sat.

"If it is so, so be it," he said. "Because, my dear fellow, I am near, so splendidly near to the final revelation. To-day the pipes have sounded almost without pause. I have even heard the rustle in the bushes, I believe, of Pan's coming. I have seen, yes, I saw to-day, the bushes pushed aside as if by a hand, and piece of a face, not human, peered through. But I was not frightened, at least I did not run away this time."

He took a turn up to the window and back again.

"Yes, there is suffering all through," he said, "and I have left it all out of my search. Perhaps, as you say, the revelation will be that. And in that case, it will be good-bye. I have gone on one line. I shall have gone too far along one road, without having explored the other. But I can't go back now. I wouldn't if I could; not a step would I retrace! In any case, whatever the revelation is, it will be God. I'm sure of that."

The rainy weather soon passed, and with the return of the sun Darcy again joined Frank in long rambling days. It grew extraordinarily hotter, and with the fresh bursting of life, after the rain, Frank's vitality seemed to blaze higher and higher. Then, as is the habit of the English weather, one evening clouds began to bank themselves up in the west, the sun went down in a glare of coppery thunder-rack, and the whole earth broiling under an unspeakable oppression and sultriness paused and panted for the storm. After sunset the remote fires of lightning began to wink and flicker on the horizon, but when bed-time came the storm seemed to have moved no nearer, though a very low unceasing noise of thunder was audible. Weary and oppressed by the stress of the day, Darcy fell at once into a heavy uncomforting sleep.

He woke suddenly into full consciousness, with the din of some appalling explosion of thunder in his ears, and sat up in bed with racing heart. Then for a moment, as he recovered himself from the panic-land which lies between sleeping and waking, there was silence, except for the steady hissing of rain on the shrubs outside his window. But suddenly that silence was shattered and shredded into fragments by a scream from somewhere close at hand outside in the black garden, a scream of supreme and despairing terror. Again and once again it shrilled up, and then a babble of awful words was interjected. A quivering sobbing voice that he knew said:

"My God, oh, my God; oh, Christ!"

And then followed a little mocking, bleating laugh. Then was silence again; only the rain hissed on the shrubs.

All this was but the affair of a moment, and without pause either to put on clothes or light a candle, Darcy was already fumbling at his door-handle. Even as he opened it he met a terror-stricken face outside, that of the man-servant who carried a light.

"Did you hear?" he asked.

The man's face was bleached to a dull shining whiteness. "Yes, sir," he said. "It was the master's voice."

Together they hurried down the stairs and through the dining-room where an orderly table for breakfast had already been laid, and out on to the terrace. The rain for the moment had been utterly stayed, as if the tap of the heavens had been turned off, and under the lowering black sky, not quite dark, since the moon rode somewhere serene behind the conglomerated thunder-clouds, Darcy stumbled into the garden, followed by the servant with the candle. The monstrous leaping shadow of himself was cast before him on the lawn; lost and wandering odours of rose and lily and damp earth were thick about him, but more pungent was some sharp and acrid smell that suddenly reminded him of a certain chalet in which he had once taken refuge in the Alps. In the blackness of the hazy light from the sky, and the vague tossing of the candle behind him, he saw that the hammock in which Frank so often lay was tenanted. A gleam of white shirt was there, as if a man were sitting up in it, but across that there was an obscure dark shadow, and as he approached the acrid odour grew more intense.

He was now only some few yards away, when suddenly the black shadow seemed to jump into the air, then came down with tappings of hard hoofs on the brick path that ran down the pergola, and with frolicsome skippings galloped off into the bushes. When that was gone Darcy could see quite clearly that a shirted figure sat up in the hammock. For one moment, from sheer terror of the unseen, he hung on his step, and the servant joining him they walked together to the hammock.

It was Frank. He was in shirt and trousers only, and he sat up with braced arms. For one half-second he stared at them, his face a mask of horrible contorted terror. His upper lip was drawn back so that the gums of the teeth appeared, and his eyes were focussed not on the two who approached him, but on something quite close to him; his nostrils were widely expanded, as if he panted for breath, and terror incarnate and repulsion and deathly anguish ruled dreadful lines on his smooth cheeks and forehead. Then even as they looked the body sank backwards, and the ropes of the hammock wheezed and strained.

Darcy lifted him out and carried him indoors. Once he thought there was a faint convulsive stir of the limbs that lay with so dead a weight in his arms, but when they got inside, there was no trace of life. But the look of supreme terror and agony of fear had gone from his face, a boy tired with play but still smiling in his sleep was the burden he laid on the floor. His eyes had closed, and the beautiful mouth lay in smiling curves, even as when a few mornings ago, in the meadow by the weir, it had quivered to the music of the unheard melody of Pan's pipes. Then they looked further.

Frank had come back from his bathe before dinner that night in his usual costume of shirt and trousers only. He had not dressed, and during dinner, so Darcy remembered, he had rolled up the sleeves of his shirt to above the elbow. Later, as they sat and talked after dinner on the close sultriness of the evening, he had unbuttoned the front of his shirt to let what little breath of wind there was play on his skin. The sleeves were rolled up now, the front of the shirt was unbuttoned, and on his arms and on the brown skin of his chest were strange discolorations which grew momently more clear and defined, till they saw that the marks were pointed prints, as if caused by the hoofs of some monstrous goat that had leaped and stamped upon him.

The Bus-Conductor

My friend, Hugh Grainger, and I had just returned from a two days' visit in the country, where we had been staying in a house of sinister repute which was supposed to be haunted by ghosts of a peculiarly fearsome and truculent sort. The house itself was all that such a house should be, Jacobean and oak-panelled, with long dark passages and high vaulted rooms. It stood, also, very remote, and was encompassed by a wood of sombre pines that muttered and whispered in the dark, and all the time that we were there a southwesterly gale with torrents of scolding rain had prevailed, so that by day and night weird voices moaned and fluted in the chimneys, a company of uneasy spirits held colloquy among the trees, and sudden tattoos and tappings beckoned from the window-panes. But in spite of these surroundings, which were sufficient in themselves, one would almost say, to spontaneously generate occult phenomena, nothing of any description had occurred. I am bound to add, also, that my own state of mind was peculiarly well adapted to receive or even to invent the sights and sounds we had gone to seek, for I was, I confess, during the whole time that we were there, in a state of abject apprehension, and lay awake both nights through hours of terrified unrest, afraid of the dark, yet more afraid of what a lighted candle might show me.

Hugh Grainger, on the evening after our return to town, had dined with me, and after dinner our conversation, as was natural, soon came back to these entrancing topics.

"But why you go ghost-seeking I cannot imagine," he said, "because your teeth were chattering and your eyes starting out of your head all the time you were there, from sheer fright."

"Or do you like being frightened?"

Hugh, though generally intelligent, is dense in certain ways; this is one of them.

"Why, of course, I like being frightened," I said. "I want to be made to creep and creep and creep. Fear is the most absorbing and luxurious of emotions. One forgets all else if one is afraid."

"Well, the fact that neither of us saw anything," he said, "confirms what I have always believed."

"And what have you always believed?"

"That these phenomena are purely objective, not subjective, and that one's state of mind has nothing to do with the perception that perceives them, nor have circumstances or surroundings anything to do with them either. Look at Osburton.

It has had the reputation of being a haunted house for years, and it certainly has all the accessories of one. Look at yourself, too, with all your nerves on edge, afraid to look round or light a candle for fear of seeing something! Surely there was the right man in the right place then, if ghosts are subjective."

He got up and lit a cigarette, and looking at him--Hugh is about six feet high, and as broad as he is long--I felt a retort on my lips, for I could not help my mind going back to a certain period in his life, when, from some cause which, as far as I knew, he had never told anybody, he had become a mere quivering mass of disordered nerves. Oddly enough, at the same moment and for the first time, he began to speak of it himself.

"You may reply that it was not worth my while to go either," he said, "because I was so clearly the wrong man in the wrong place. But I wasn't. You for all your apprehensions and expectancy have never seen a ghost. But I have, though I am the last person in the world you would have thought likely to do so, and, though my nerves are steady enough again now, it knocked me all to bits."

He sat down again in his chair.

"No doubt you remember my going to bits," he said, "and since I believe that I am sound again now, I should rather like to tell you about it. But before I couldn't; I couldn't speak of it at all to anybody. Yet there ought to have been nothing frightening about it; what I saw was certainly a most useful and friendly ghost. But it came from the shaded side of things; it looked suddenly out of the night and the mystery with which life is surrounded.

"I want first to tell you quite shortly my theory about ghost-seeing," he continued, "and I can explain it best by a simile, an image. Imagine then that you and I and everybody in the world are like people whose eye is directly opposite a little tiny hole in a sheet of cardboard which is continually shifting and revolving and moving about. Back to back with that sheet of cardboard is another, which also, by laws of its own, is in perpetual but independent motion. In it too there is another hole, and when, fortuitously it would seem, these two holes, the one through which we are always looking, and the other in the spiritual plane, come opposite one another, we see through, and then only do the sights and sounds of the spiritual world become visible or audible to us. With most people these holes never come opposite each other during their life. But at the hour of death they do, and then they remain stationary. That, I fancy, is how we 'pass over.'

"Now, in some natures, these holes are comparatively large, and are constantly coming into opposition. Clairvoyants, mediums are like that. But, as far as I knew, I had no clairvoyant or mediumistic powers at all. I therefore am the sort of person who long ago made up his mind that he never would see a ghost. It was, so to speak, an incalculable chance that my minute spy-hole should come into opposition with the other. But it did: and it knocked me out of time."

I had heard some such theory before, and though Hugh put it rather picturesquely, there was nothing in the least convincing or practical about it. It might be so, or again it might not.

"I hope your ghost was more original than your theory," said I, in order to bring him to the point.

"Yes, I think it was. You shall judge."

I put on more coal and poked up the fire. Hugh has got, so I have always considered, a great talent for telling stories, and that sense of drama which is so necessary for the narrator. Indeed, before now, I have suggested to him that he should take this up as a profession, sit by the fountain in Piccadilly Circus, when times are, as usual, bad, and tell stories to the passers-by in the street, Arabian fashion, for reward. The most part of mankind, I am aware, do not like long stories, but to the few, among whom I number myself, who really like to listen to lengthy accounts of experiences, Hugh is an ideal narrator. I do not care for his theories, or for his similes, but when it comes to facts, to things that happened, I like him to be lengthy.

"Go on, please, and slowly," I said. "Brevity may be the soul of wit, but it is the ruin of story-telling. I want to hear when and where and how it all was, and what you had for lunch and where you had dined and what--Hugh began:

"It was the 24th of June, just eighteen months ago," he said. "I had let my flat, you may remember, and came up from the country to stay with you for a week. We had dined alone here--"

I could not help interrupting.

"Did you see the ghost here?" I asked. "In this square little box of a house in a modern street?"

"I was in the house when I saw it." I hugged myself in silence.

"We had dined alone here in Graeme Street," he said, "and after dinner I went out to some party, and you stopped at home. At dinner your man did not wait, and when I asked where he was, you told me he was ill, and, I thought, changed the subject rather abruptly.

"You gave me your latch-key when I went out, and on coming back, I found you had gone to bed. There were, however, several letters for me, which required answers. I wrote them there and then, and posted them at the pillar-box opposite. So I suppose it was rather late when I went upstairs.

"You had put me in the front room, on the third floor, overlooking the street, a room which I thought you generally occupied yourself. It was a very hot night, and though there had been a moon when I started to my party, on my return the whole sky was cloud-covered, and it both looked and felt as if we might have a thunderstorm before morning. I was feeling very sleepy and heavy, and it was not till after I had got into bed that I noticed by the shadows of the window-frames on the blind that only one of the windows was open. But it did not seem worth while to get out of bed in order to open it, though I felt rather airless and uncomfortable, and I went to sleep.

"What time it was when I awoke I do not know, but it was certainly not yet dawn, and I never remember being conscious of such an extraordinary stillness as prevailed. There was no sound either of foot-passengers or wheeled traffic; the music of life appeared to be absolutely mute. But now, instead of being sleepy and heavy, I felt, though I must have slept an hour or two at most, since it was not yet dawn, perfectly fresh and wide-awake, and the effort which had seemed not worth making before, that of getting out of bed and opening the other window, was quite easy now and I pulled up the blind, threw it wide open, and leaned out, for somehow I parched and pined for air. Even outside the oppression was very noticeable, and though, as you know, I am not easily given to feel the mental effects of climate, I was aware of an awful creepiness coming over me. I tried to analyse it away, but without success; the past day had been pleasant, I looked forward to another pleasant day to-morrow, and yet I was full of some nameless apprehension. I felt, too, dreadfully lonely in this stillness before the dawn.

"Then I heard suddenly and not very far away the sound of some approaching vehicle; I could distinguish the tread of two horses walking at a slow foot's pace. They were, though not yet visible, coming up the street, and yet this indication of life did not abate that dreadful sense of loneliness which I have spoken of. Also in some dim unformulated way that which was coming seemed to me to have something to do with the cause of my oppression.

"Then the vehicle came into sight. At first I could not distinguish what it was. Then I saw that the horses were black and had long tails, and that what they dragged was made of glass, but had a black frame. It was a hearse. Empty.

"It was moving up this side of the street. It stopped at your door.

"Then the obvious solution struck me. You had said at dinner that your man was ill, and you were, I thought, unwilling to speak more about his illness. No doubt, so I imagined now, he was dead, and for some reason, perhaps because you did not want me to know anything about it, you were having the body removed at night. This, I must tell you, passed through my mind quite instantaneously, and it did not occur to me how unlikely it really was, before the next thing happened.

"I was still leaning out of the window, and I remember also wondering, yet only momentarily, how odd it was that I saw things--or rather the one thing I was looking at--so very distinctly. Of course, there was a moon behind the clouds, but it was curious how every detail of the hearse and the horses was visible. There was only one man, the driver, with it, and the street was otherwise absolutely empty. It was at him I was looking now. I could see every detail of his clothes, but from where I was, so high above him, I could not see his face. He had on grey trousers, brown boots, a black coat buttoned all the way up, and a straw hat. Over his shoulder there was a strap, which seemed to support some sort of little bag. He looked exactly like--well, from my description what did he look exactly like?"

"Why--a bus-conductor," I said instantly.

"So I thought, and even while I was thinking this, he looked up at me. He had a rather long thin face, and on his left cheek there was a mole with a growth of dark hair on it. All this was as distinct as if it had been noonday, and as if I was within a yard of him. But--so instantaneous was all that takes so long in the telling--I had not time to think it strange that the driver of a hearse should be so unfunereally dressed.

"Then he touched his hat to me, and jerked his thumb over his shoulder.

"'Just room for one inside, sir,' he said.

"There was something so odious, so coarse, so unfeeling about this that I instantly drew my head in, pulled the blind down again, and then, for what reason I do not know, turned on the electric light in order to see what time it was. The hands of my watch pointed to half-past eleven.

"It was then for the first time, I think, that a doubt crossed my mind as to the nature of what I had just seen. But I put out the light again, got into bed, and began to think. We had dined; I had gone to a party, I had come back and written letters, had gone to bed and had slept. So how could it be half-past eleven?...Or--what half-past eleven was it?

"Then another easy solution struck me; my watch must have stopped. But it had not; I could hear it ticking.

"There was stillness and silence again. I expected every moment to hear muffled footsteps on the stairs, footsteps moving slowly and smally under the weight of a heavy burden, but from inside the house there was no sound whatever. Outside, too, there was the same dead silence, while the hearse waited at the door. And the minutes ticked on and ticked on, and at length I began to see a difference in the light in the room, and knew that the dawn was beginning to break outside. But how had it happened, then, that if the corpse was to be removed at night it had not gone, and that the hearse still waited, when morning was already coming?

"Presently I got out of bed again, and with the sense of strong physical shrinking I went to the window and pulled back the blind. The dawn was coming fast; the whole street was lit by that silver hueless light of morning. But there was no hearse there.

"Once again I looked at my watch. It was just a quarter-past four. But I would swear that not half an hour had passed since it had told me that it was half-past eleven.

"Then a curious double sense, as if I was living in the present and at the same moment had been living in some other time, came over me. It was dawn on June 25th, and the street, as natural, was empty. But a little while ago the driver of a hearse had spoken to me, and it was half-past eleven. What was that driver, to what plane did he belong? And again what half-past eleven was it that I had seen recorded on the dial of my watch?

"And then I told myself that the whole thing had been a dream. But if you ask me whether I believed what I told myself, I must confess that I did not.

"Your man did not appear at breakfast next morning, nor did I see him again before I left that afternoon. I think if I had, I should have told you about all this, but it was still possible, you see, that what I had seen was a real hearse, driven by a real driver, for all the ghastly gaiety of the face that had looked up to mine, and the levity of his pointing hand. I might possibly have fallen asleep soon after seeing him, and slumbered through the removal of the body and the departure of the hearse. So I did not speak of it to you.

There was something wonderfully straight-forward and prosaic in all this; here were no Jacobean houses oak-panelled and surrounded by weeping pine-trees, and somehow the very absence of suitable surroundings made the story more impressive. But for a moment a doubt assailed me.

"Don't tell me it was all a dream," I said.

"I don't know whether it was or not. I can only say that I believe myself to have been wide awake. In any case the rest of the story is--odd.

"I went out of town again that afternoon," he continued, "and I may say that I don't think that even for a moment did I get the haunting sense of what I had seen or dreamed that night out of my mind. It was present to me always as some vision unfulfilled. It was as if some clock had struck the four quarters, and I was still waiting to hear what the hour would be.

"Exactly a month afterwards I was in London again, but only for the day. I arrived at Victoria about eleven, and took the underground to Sloane Square in order to see if you were in town and would give me lunch. It was a baking hot morning, and I intended to take a bus from the King's Road as far as Graeme Street. There was one standing at the corner just as I came out of the station, but I saw that the top was full, and the inside appeared to be full also. Just as I came up to it the conductor, who, I suppose, had been inside, collecting fares or what not, came out on to the step within a few feet of me. He wore grey trousers, brown boots, a black coat buttoned, a straw hat, and over his shoulder was a strap on which hung his little machine for punching tickets. I saw his face, too; it was the face of the driver of the hearse, with a mole on the left cheek. Then he spoke to me, jerking his thumb over his shoulder.

"'Just room for one inside, sir,' he said.

"At that a sort of panic-terror took possession of me, and I knew I gesticulated wildly with my arms, and cried, 'No, no!' But at that moment I was living not in the hour that was then passing, but in that hour which had passed a month ago, when I leaned from the window of your bedroom here just before the dawn broke. At this moment too I knew that my spy-hole had been opposite the spy-hole into the spiritual world. What I had seen there had some significance, now being fulfilled, beyond the significance of the trivial happenings of to-day and to-morrow. The Powers of which we know so little were visibly working before me. And I stood there on the pavement shaking and trembling.

"I was opposite the post-office at the corner, and just as the bus started my eye fell on the clock in the window there. I need not tell you what the time was.

"Perhaps I need not tell you the rest, for you probably conjecture it, since you will not have forgotten what happened at the corner of Sloane Square at the end of July, the summer before last. The bus pulled out from the pavement into the street in order to get round a van that was standing in front of it. At the moment there came down the King's Road a big motor going at a hideously dangerous pace. It crashed full into the bus, burrowing into it as a gimlet burrows into a board."

He paused.

"And that's my story," he said.

Caterpillars

I saw a month or two ago in an Italian paper that the Villa Cascana, in which I once stayed, had been pulled down, and that a manufactory of some sort was in process of erection on its site.

There is therefore no longer any reason for refraining from writing of those things which I myself saw (or imagined I saw) in a certain room and on a certain landing of the villa in question, nor from mentioning the circumstances which followed, which may or may not (according to the opinion of the reader) throw some light on or be somehow connected with this experience.

The Villa Cascana was in all ways but one a perfectly delightful house, yet, if it were standing now, nothing in the world--I use the phrase in its literal sense--would induce me to set foot in it again, for I believe it to have been haunted in a very terrible and practical manner.

Most ghosts, when all is said and done, do not do much harm; they may perhaps terrify, but the person whom they visit usually gets over their visitation. They may on the other hand be entirely friendly and beneficent. But the appearances in the Villa Cascana were not beneficent, and had they made their "visit" in a very slightly different manner, I do not suppose I should have got over it any more than Arthur Inglis did.

The house stood on an ilex-clad hill not far from Sestri di Levante on the Italian Riviera, looking out over the iridescent blues of that enchanted sea, while behind it rose the pale green chestnut woods that climb up the hillsides till they give place to the pines that, black in contrast with them, crown the slopes. All round it the garden in the luxuriance of mid-spring bloomed and was fragrant, and the scent of magnolia and rose, borne on the salt freshness of the winds from the sea, flowed like a stream through the cool vaulted rooms.

On the ground floor a broad pillared loggia ran round three sides of the house, the top of which formed a balcony for certain rooms of the first floor. The main staircase, broad and of grey marble steps, led up from the hall to the landing outside these rooms, which were three in number, namely, two big sitting-rooms and a bedroom arranged en suite. The latter was unoccupied, the sitting-rooms were in use. From these the main staircase was continued to the second floor, where were situated certain bedrooms, one of which I occupied, while from the other side of the first-floor landing some half-dozen steps led to another suite of rooms, where, at the time I am speaking of, Arthur Inglis, the artist, had his bedroom and studio. Thus the landing outside my bedroom at the top of the house commanded both the landing of the first floor and also the steps that led to Inglis' rooms. Jim Stanley and his wife, finally (whose guest I was), occupied rooms in another wing of the house, where also were the servants' quarters.

I arrived just in time for lunch on a brilliant noon of mid-May. The garden was shouting with colour and fragrance, and not less delightful after my broiling walk up from the marina, should have been the coming from the reverberating heat and blaze of the day into the marble coolness of the villa. Only (the reader has my bare word for this, and nothing more), the moment I set foot in the house I felt that something was wrong. This feeling, I may say, was quite vague, though very strong, and I remember that when I saw letters waiting for me on the table in the hall I felt certain that the explanation was here: I was convinced that there was bad news of some sort for me. Yet when I opened them I found no such explanation of my premonition: my correspondents all reeked of prosperity. Yet this clear miscarriage of a presentiment did not dissipate my uneasiness. In that cool fragrant house there was something wrong.

I am at pains to mention this because to the general view it may explain that though I am as a rule so excellent a sleeper that the extinction of my light on getting into bed is apparently contemporaneous with being called on the following morning, I slept very badly on my first night in the Villa Cascana. It may also explain the fact that when I did sleep (if it was indeed in sleep that I saw what I thought I saw) I dreamed in a very vivid and original manner, original, that is to say, in the sense that something that, as far as I knew, had never previously entered into my consciousness, usurped it then. But since, in addition to this evil premonition, certain words and events occurring during the rest of the day might have suggested something of what I thought happened that night, it will be well to relate them.

After lunch, then, I went round the house with Mrs. Stanley, and during our tour she referred, it is true, to the unoccupied bedroom on the first floor, which opened out of the room where we had lunched.

"We left that unoccupied," she said, "because Jim and I have a charming bedroom and dressing-room, as you saw, in the wing, and if we used it ourselves we should have to turn the dining-room into a dressing-room and have our meals downstairs. As it is, however, we have our little flat there, Arthur Inglis has his little flat in the other passage; and I remembered (aren't I extraordinary?) that you once said that the higher up you were in a house the better you were pleased. So I put you at the top of the house, instead of giving you that room."

It is true, that a doubt, vague as my uneasy premonition, crossed my mind at this. I did not see why Mrs. Stanley should have explained all this, if there had not been more to explain. I allow, therefore, that the thought that there was something to explain about the unoccupied bedroom was momentarily present to my mind.

The second thing that may have borne on my dream was this.

At dinner the conversation turned for a moment on ghosts. Inglis, with the certainty of conviction, expressed his belief that anybody who could possibly believe in the existence of supernatural phenomena was unworthy of the name of an ass.

The subject instantly dropped. As far as I can recollect, nothing else occurred or was said that could bear on what follows.

We all went to bed rather early, and personally I yawned my way upstairs, feeling hideously sleepy. My room was rather hot, and I threw all the windows wide, and from without poured in the white light of the moon, and the love-song of many nightingales. I undressed quickly, and got into bed, but though I had felt so sleepy before, I now felt extremely wide-awake. But I was quite content to be awake: I did not toss or turn, I felt perfectly happy listening to the song and seeing the light. Then, it is possible, I may have gone to sleep, and what follows may have been a dream. I thought, anyhow, that after a time the nightingales ceased singing and the moon sank. I thought also that if, for some unexplained reason, I was going to lie awake all night, I might as well read, and I remembered that I had left a book in which I was interested in the dining-room on the first floor. So I got out of bed, lit a candle, and went downstairs. I went into the room, saw on a side-table the book I had come to look for, and then, simultaneously, saw that the door into the unoccupied bedroom was open. A curious grey light, not of dawn nor of moonshine, came out of it, and I looked in. The bed stood just opposite the door, a big four-poster, hung with tapestry at the head. Then I saw that the greyish light of the bedroom came from the bed, or rather from what was on the bed. For it was covered with great caterpillars, a foot or more in length, which crawled over it. They were faintly luminous, and it was the light from them that showed me the room. Instead of the sucker-feet of ordinary caterpillars they had rows of pincers like crabs, and they moved by grasping what they lay on with their pincers, and then sliding their bodies forward. In colour these dreadful insects were yellowish-grey, and they were covered with irregular lumps and swellings. There must have been hundreds of them, for they formed a sort of writhing, crawling pyramid on the bed. Occasionally one fell off on to the floor, with a soft fleshy thud, and though the floor was of hard concrete, it yielded to the pincerfeet as if it had been putty, and, crawling back, the caterpillar would mount on to the bed again, to re-join its fearful companions. They appeared to have no faces, so to speak, but at one end of them there was a mouth that opened sideways in respiration.

Then, as I looked, it seemed to me as if they all suddenly became conscious of my presence.

All the mouths, at any rate, were turned in my direction, and next moment they began dropping off the bed with those soft fleshy thuds on to the floor, and wriggling towards me. For one second a paralysis as of a dream was on me, but the next I was running upstairs again to my room, and I remember feeling the cold of the marble steps on my bare feet. I rushed into my bedroom, and slammed the door behind me, and then--I was certainly wide-awake now--I found myself standing by my bed with the sweat of terror pouring from me. The noise of the banged door still rang in my ears. But, as would have been more usual, if this had been mere nightmare, the terror that had been mine when I saw those foul beasts crawling about the bed or dropping softly on to the floor did not cease then. Awake, now, if dreaming before, I did not at all recover from the horror of dream:

it did not seem to me that I had dreamed. And until dawn, I sat or stood, not daring to lie down, thinking that every rustle or movement that I heard was the approach of the caterpillars. To them and the claws that bit into the cement the wood of the door was child's play: steel would not keep them out.

But with the sweet and noble return of day the horror vanished: the whisper of wind became benignant again: the nameless fear, whatever it was, was smoothed out and terrified me no longer. Dawn broke, hueless at first; then it grew dove-coloured, then the flaming pageant of light spread over the sky.

The admirable rule of the house was that everybody had breakfast where and when he pleased, and in consequence it was not till lunch-time that I met any of the other members of our party, since I had breakfast on my balcony, and wrote letters and other things till lunch. In fact, I got down to that meal rather late, after the other three had begun. Between my knife and fork there was a small pill-box of cardboard, and as I sat down Inglis spoke.

"Do look at that," he said, "since you are interested in natural history. I found it crawling on my counterpane last night, and I don't know what it is."

I think that before I opened the pill-box I expected something of the sort which I found in it.

Inside it, anyhow, was a small caterpillar, greyish-yellow in colour, with curious bumps and excrescences on its rings. It was extremely active, and hurried round the box, this way and that.

Its feet were unlike the feet of any caterpillar I ever saw: they were like the pincers of a crab. I looked, and shut the lid down again.

"No, I don't know it," I said, "but it looks rather unwholesome. What are you going to do with it?"

"Oh, I shall keep it," said Inglis. "It has begun to spin: I want to see what sort of a moth it turns into."

I opened the box again, and saw that these hurrying movements were indeed the beginning of the spinning of the web of its cocoon. Then Inglis spoke again.

"It has got funny feet, too," he said. "They are like crabs' pincers. What's the Latin for crab?"

"Oh, yes, Cancer. So in case it is unique, let's christen it: 'Cancer Inglisensis.'" Then something happened in my brain, some momentary piecing together of all that I had seen or dreamed. Something in his words seemed to me to throw light on it all, and my own intense horror at the experience of the night before linked itself on to what he had just said. In effect, I took the box and threw it, caterpillar and all, out of the window. There was a gravel path just outside, and beyond it, a fountain playing into a basin. The box fell on to the middle of this.

Inglis laughed.

"So the students of the occult don't like solid facts," he said. "My poor caterpillar!"

The talk went off again at once on to other subjects, and I have only given in detail, as they happened, these trivialities in order to be sure myself that I have recorded everything that could have borne on occult subjects or on the subject of caterpillars. But at the moment when I threw the pill-box into the fountain, I lost my head: my only excuse is that, as is probably plain, the tenant of it was, in miniature, exactly what I had seen crowded on to the bed in the unoccupied room. And though this translation of those phantoms into flesh and blood--or whatever it is that caterpillars are made of--ought perhaps to have relieved the horror of the night, as a matter of fact it did nothing of the kind. It only made the crawling pyramid that covered the bed in the unoccupied room more hideously real.

After lunch we spent a lazy hour or two strolling about the garden or sitting in the loggia, and it must have been about four o'clock when Stanley and I started off to bathe, down the path that led by the fountain into which I had thrown the pill-box. The water was shallow and clear, and at the bottom of it I saw its white remains. The water had disintegrated the cardboard, and it had become no more than a few strips and shreds of sodden paper. The centre of the fountain was a marble Italian Cupid which squirted the water out of a wine-skin held under its arm. And crawling up its leg was the caterpillar. Strange and scarcely credible as it seemed, it must have survived the falling-to-bits of its prison, and made its way to shore, and there it was, out of arm's reach, weaving and waving this way and that as it evolved its cocoon.

Then, as I looked at it, it seemed to me again that, like the caterpillar I had seen last night, it saw me, and breaking out of the threads that surrounded it, it crawled down the marble leg of the Cupid and began swimming like a snake across the water of the fountain towards me. It came with extraordinary speed (the fact of a caterpillar being able to swim was new to me), and in another moment was crawling up the marble lip of the basin. Just then Inglis joined us.

"Why, if it isn't old 'Cancer Inglisensis' again," he said, catching sight of the beast. "What a tearing hurry it is in!"

We were standing side by side on the path, and when the caterpillar had advanced to within about a yard of us, it stopped, and began waving again as if in doubt as to the direction in which it should go. Then it appeared to make up its mind, and crawled on to Inglis' shoe.

"It likes me best," he said, "but I don't really know that I like it. And as it won't drown I think perhaps--"

He shook it off his shoe on to the gravel path and trod on it.

All afternoon the air got heavier and heavier with the Sirocco that was without doubt coming up from the south, and that night again I went up to bed feeling very sleepy; but below my drowsiness, so to speak, there was the consciousness, stronger than before, that there was something wrong in the house, that something dangerous was close at hand. But I fell asleep at once, and--how long after I do not know--either woke or dreamed I awoke, feeling that I must get up at once, or I should be too late. Then (dreaming or awake) I lay and fought this fear, telling myself that I was but the prey of my own nerves disordered by Sirocco or what not, and at the same time quite clearly knowing in another part of my mind, so to speak, that every moment's delay added to the danger. At last this second feeling became irresistible, and I put on coat and trousers and went out of my room on to the landing. And then I saw that I had already delayed too long, and that I was now too late.

The whole of the landing of the first floor below was invisible under the swarm of caterpillars that crawled there. The folding doors into the sitting-room from which opened the bedroom where I had seen them last night were shut, but they were squeezing through the cracks of it and dropping one by one through the keyhole, elongating themselves into mere string as they passed, and growing fat and lumpy again on emerging. Some, as if exploring, were nosing about the steps into the passage at the end of which were Inglis' rooms, others were crawling on the lowest steps of the staircase that led up to where I stood. The landing, however, was completely covered with them: I was cut off. And of the frozen horror that seized me when I saw that I can give no idea in words.

Then at last a general movement began to take place, and they grew thicker on the steps that led to Inglis' room. Gradually, like some hideous tide of flesh, they advanced along the passage, and I saw the foremost, visible by the pale grey luminousness that came from them, reach his door. Again and again I tried to shout and warn him, in terror all the time that they would turn at the sound of my voice and mount my stair instead, but for all my efforts I felt that no sound came from my throat. They crawled along the hinge-crack of his door, passing through as they had done before, and still I stood there, making impotent efforts to shout to him, to bid him escape while there was time.

At last the passage was completely empty: they had all gone, and at that moment I was conscious for the first time of the cold of the marble landing on which I stood barefooted. The dawn was just beginning to break in the Eastern sky.

Six months after I met Mrs. Stanley in a country house in England. We talked on many subjects and at last she said:

"I don't think I have seen you since I got that dreadful news about Arthur Inglis a month ago."

"I haven't heard," said I.

"No? He has got cancer. They don't even advise an operation, for there is no hope of a cure: he is riddled with it, the doctors say."

Now during all these six months I do not think a day had passed on which I had not had in my mind the dreams (or whatever you like to call them) which I had seen in the Villa Cascana.

"It is awful, is it not?" she continued, "and I feel I can't help feeling, that he may have--"

"Caught it at the villa?" I asked.

She looked at me in blank surprise.

"Why did you say that?" she asked. "How did you know?"

Then she told me. In the unoccupied bedroom a year before there had been a fatal case of cancer. She had, of course, taken the best advice and had been told that the utmost dictates of prudence would be obeyed so long as she did not put anybody to sleep in the room, which had also been thoroughly disinfected and newly white-washed and painted. But--

And the Dead Spake

There is not in all London a quieter spot, or one, apparently, more withdrawn from the heat and bustle of life than Newsome Terrace. It is a cul-de-sac, for at the upper end the roadway between its two lines of square, compact little residences is brought to an end by a high brick wall, while at the lower end, the only access to it is through Newsome Square, that small discreet oblong of Georgian houses, a relic of the time when Kensington was a suburban village sundered from the metropolis by a stretch of pastures stretching to the river. Both square and terrace are most inconveniently situated for those whose ideal environment includes a rank of taxicabs immediately opposite their door, a spate of 'buses roaring down the street, and a procession of underground trains, accessible by a station a few yards away, shaking and rattling the cutlery and silver on their dining tables. In consequence Newsome Terrace had come, two years ago, to be inhabited by leisurely and retired folk or by those who wished to pursue their work in quiet and tranquillity. Children with hoops and scooters are phenomena rarely encountered in the Terrace and dogs are equally uncommon.

In front of each of the couple of dozen houses of which the Terrace is composed lies a little square of railinged garden, in which you may often see the middle-aged or elderly mistress of the residence horticulturally employed. By five o'clock of a winter's evening the pavements will generally be empty of all passengers except the policeman, who with felted step, at intervals throughout the night, peers with his bull's-eye into these small front gardens, and never finds anything more suspicious there than an early crocus or an aconite. For by the time it is dark the inhabitants of the Terrace have got themselves home, where behind drawn curtains and bolted shutters they will pass a domestic and uninterrupted evening. No funeral (up to the time I speak of) had I ever seen leave the Terrace, no marriage party had strewed its pavements with confetti, and perambulators were unknown. It and its inhabitants seemed to be quietly mellowing like bottles of sound wine. No doubt there was stored within them the sunshine and summer of youth long past, and now, dozing in a cool place, they waited for the turn of the key in the cellar door, and the entry of one who would draw them forth and see what they were worth.

Yet, after the time of which I shall now speak, I have never passed down its pavement without wondering whether each house, so seemingly-tranquil, is not, like some dynamo, softly and smoothly bringing into being vast and terrible forces, such as those I once saw at work in the last house at the upper end of the

Terrace, the quietest, you would have said, of all the row. Had you observed it with continuous scrutiny, for all the length of a summer day, it is quite possible that you might have only seen issue from it in the morning an elderly woman whom you would have rightly conjectured to be the housekeeper, with her basket for marketing on her arm, who returned an hour later. Except for her the entire day might often pass without there being either ingress or egress from the door. Occasionally a middle-aged man, lean and wiry, came swiftly down the pavement, but his exit was by no means a daily occurrence, and indeed when he did emerge, he broke the almost universal usage of the Terrace, for his appearances took place, when such there were, between nine and ten in the evening. At that hour sometimes he would come round to my house in Newsome Square to see if I was at home and inclined for a talk a little later on. For the sake of air and exercise he would then have an hour's tramp through the lit and noisy streets, and return about ten, still pale and unflushed, for one of those talks which grew to have an absorbing fascination for me. More rarely through the telephone I proposed that I should drop in on him: this I did not often do, since I found that if he did not come out himself, it implied that he was busy with some investigation, and though he made me welcome, I could easily see that he burned for my departure, so that he might get busy with his batteries and pieces of tissue, hot on the track of discoveries that never yet had presented themselves to the mind of man as coming within the horizon of possibility.

My last sentence may have led the reader to guess that I am indeed speaking of none other than that recluse and mysterious physicist Sir James Horton, with whose death a hundred half-hewn avenues into the dark forest from which life comes must wait completion till another pioneer as bold as he takes up the axe which hitherto none but himself has been able to wield.

Probably there was never a man to whom humanity owed more, and of whom humanity knew less. He seemed utterly independent of the race to whom (though indeed with no service of love) he devoted himself: for years he lived aloof and apart in his house at the end of the Terrace.

Men and women were to him like fossils to the geologist, things to be tapped and hammered and dissected and studied with a view not only to the reconstruction of past ages, but to construction in the future. It is known, for instance, that he made an artificial being formed of the tissue, still living, of animals lately killed, with the brain of an ape and the heart of a bullock, and a sheep's thyroid, and so forth. Of that I can give no first-hand account; Horton, it is true, told me something about it, and in his will directed that certain memoranda on the subject should on his death be sent to me. But on the bulky envelope there is the direction, "Not to be opened till January, 1925." He spoke with some reserve and, so I think, with slight horror at the strange things which had happened on the completion of this creature. It evidently made him uncomfortable to talk about it, and for that reason I fancy he put what was then a rather remote date to the day when his record should reach my eye. Finally, in these preliminaries, for the last five years before the war, he had scarcely entered, for the sake of companionship, any house other than his own and mine. Ours was a friendship dating from school-days, which he had never suffered to drop entirely, but I doubt if in those years he spoke except on matters of business to half a dozen other people. He had already retired from surgical practice in which his skill was unapproached, and most completely now did he avoid the slightest intercourse with his colleagues, whom he regarded as ignorant pedants without courage or the rudiments of knowledge. Now and then he would write an epoch-making little monograph, which he flung to them like a bone to a starving dog, but for the most part, utterly absorbed in his own investigations, he left them to grope along unaided. He frankly told me that he enjoyed talking to me about such subjects, since I was utterly unacquainted with them. It clarified his mind to be obliged to put his theories and guesses and confirmations with such simplicity that anyone could understand them.

I well remember his coming in to see me on the evening of the 4th of August, 1914.

"So the war has broken out," he said, "and the streets are impassable with excited crowds."

"Odd, isn't it? Just as if each of us already was not a far more murderous battlefield than any which can be conceived between warring nations."

"How's that?" said I.

"Let me try to put it plainly, though it isn't that I want to talk about. Your blood is one eternal battlefield. It is full of armies eternally marching and countermarching. As long as the armies friendly to you are in a superior position, you remain in good health; if a detachment of microbes that, if suffered to establish themselves, would give you a cold in the head, entrench themselves in your mucous membrane, the commander-in-chief sends a regiment down and drives them out. He doesn't give his orders from your brain, mind you--those aren't his headquarters, for your brain knows nothing about the landing of the enemy till they have made good their position and given you a cold."

He paused a moment.

"There isn't one headquarters inside you," he said, "there are many. For instance, I killed a frog this morning; at least most people would say I killed it. But had I killed it, though its head lay in one place and its severed body in another? Not a bit: I had only killed a piece of it. For I opened the body afterwards and took out the heart, which I put in a sterilised chamber of suitable temperature, so that it wouldn't get cold or be infected by any microbe. That was about twelve o'clock to-day. And when I came out just now, the heart was beating still. It was alive, in fact."

"That's full of suggestions, you know. Come and see it."

The Terrace had been stirred into volcanic activity by the news of war: the vendor of some late edition had penetrated into its quietude, and there were half a dozen parlour-maids fluttering about like black and white moths. But once inside Horton's door isolation as of an Arctic night seemed to close round me. He had forgotten his latch-key, but his housekeeper, then newly come to him, who became so regular and familiar a figure in the Terrace, must have heard his step, for before he rang the bell she had opened the door, and stood with his forgotten latch-key in her hand.

"Thanks, Mrs. Gabriel," said he, and without a sound the door shut behind us. Both her name and face, as reproduced in some illustrated daily paper, seemed familiar, rather terribly familiar, but before I had time to grope for the association, Horton supplied it.

"Tried for the murder of her husband six months ago," he said. "Odd case. The point is that she is the one and perfect housekeeper. I once had four servants, and everything was all mucky, as we used to say at school. Now I live in amazing comfort and propriety with one. She does everything. She is cook, valet, housemaid, butler, and won't have anyone to help her. No doubt she killed her husband, but she planned it so well that she could not be convicted. She told me quite frankly who she was when I engaged her."

Of course I remembered the whole trial vividly now. Her husband, a morose, quarrelsome fellow, tipsy as often as sober, had, according to the defence cut his own throat while shaving; according to the prosecution, she had done that for him. There was the usual discrepancy of evidence as to whether the wound could have been self-inflicted, and the prosecution tried to prove that the face had been lathered after his throat had been cut. So singular an exhibition of forethought and nerve had hurt rather than helped their case, and after prolonged deliberation on the part of the jury, she had been acquitted. Yet not less singular was Horton's selection of a probable murderess, however efficient, as housekeeper.

He anticipated this reflection.

"Apart from the wonderful comfort of having a perfectly appointed and absolutely silent house," he said, "I regard Mrs. Gabriel as a sort of insurance against my being murdered. If you had been tried for your life, you would take very especial care not to find yourself in suspicious proximity to a murdered body again: no more deaths in your house, if you could help it. Come through to my laboratory, and look at my little instance of life after death."

Certainly it was amazing to see that little piece of tissue still pulsating with what must be called life; it contracted and expanded faintly indeed but perceptibly, though for nine hours now it had been severed from the rest of the organisation. All by itself it went on living, and if the heart could go on living with nothing, you would say, to feed and stimulate its energy, there must also, so reasoned Horton, reside in all the other vital organs of the body other independent focuses of life.

"Of course a severed organ like that," he said, "will run down quicker than if it had the co-operation of the others, and presently I shall apply a gentle electric stimulus to it. If I can keep that glass bowl under which it beats at the temperature of a frog's body, in sterilised air, I don't see why it should not go on living. Food--of course there's the question of feeding it. Do you see what that opens up in the way of surgery? Imagine a shop with glass cases containing healthy organs taken from the dead. Say a man dies of pneumonia. He should, as soon as ever the breath is out of his body, be dissected, and though they would, of course, destroy his lungs, as they will he full of pneumococci, his liver and digestive organs are probably healthy. Take them out, keep them in a sterilised atmosphere with the temperature at 98.4, and sell the liver, let us say, to another poor devil who has cancer there. Fit him with a new healthy liver, eh?"

"And insert the brain of someone who has died of heart disease into the skull of a congenital idiot?" I asked.

"Yes, perhaps; but the brain's tiresomely complicated in its connections and the joining up of the nerves, you know. Surgery will have to learn a lot before it fits new brains in. And the brain has got such a lot of functions. All thinking, all inventing seem to belong to it, though, as you have seen, the heart can get on quite well without it. But there are other functions of the brain I want to study first. I've been trying some experiments already."

He made some little readjustment to the flame of the spirit lamp which kept at the right temperature the water that surrounded the sterilised receptacle in which the frog's heart was beating.

"Start with the more simple and mechanical uses of the brain," he said. "Primarily it is a sort of record office, a diary. Say that I rap your knuckles with that ruler. What happens? The nerves there send a message to the brain, of course, saying--how can I put it most simply--saying, 'Somebody is hurting me.' And the eye sends another, saying 'I perceive a ruler hitting my knuckles,' and the ear sends another, saying 'I hear the rap of it.' But leaving all that alone, what else happens? Why, the brain records it. It makes a note of your knuckles having been hit."

He had been moving about the room as he spoke, taking off his coat and waistcoat and putting on in their place a thin black dressing-gown, and by now he was seated in his favourite attitude cross-legged on the hearth-rug, looking like some magician or perhaps the afrit which a magician of black arts had caused to appear. He was thinking intently now, passing through his fingers his string of amber beads, and talking more to himself than to me.

"And how does it make that note?" he went on. "Why, in the manner in which phonograph records are made. There are millions of minute dots, depressions, pockmarks on your brain which certainly record what you remember, what you have enjoyed or disliked, or done or said."

"The surface of the brain anyhow is large enough to furnish writing-paper for the record of all these things, of all your memories. If the impression of an experience has not been acute, the dot is not sharply impressed, and the record fades: in other words, you come to forget it. But if it has been vividly impressed, the record is never obliterated. Mrs. Gabriel, for instance, won't lose the impression of how she lathered her husband's face after she had cut his throat. That's to say, if she did it.

"Now do you see what I'm driving at? Of course you do. There is stored within a man's head the complete record of all the memorable things he has done and said: there are all his thoughts there, and all his speeches, and, most well-marked of all, his habitual thoughts and the things he has often said; for habit, there is reason to believe, wears a sort of rut in the brain, so that the life principle, whatever it is, as it gropes and steals about the brain, is continually stumbling into it. There's your record, your gramophone plate all ready. What we want, and what I'm trying to arrive at, is a needle which, as it traces its minute way over these dots, will come across words or sentences which the dead have uttered, and will reproduce them. My word, what Judgment Books! What a resurrection!"

Here in this withdrawn situation no remotest echo of the excitement which was seething through the streets penetrated; through the open window there came in only the tide of the midnight silence. But from somewhere closer at hand, through the wall surely of the laboratory, there came a low, somewhat persistent murmur.

"Perhaps our needle--unhappily not yet invented--as it passed over the record of speech in the brain, might induce even facial expression," he said. "Enjoyment or horror might even pass over dead features. There might be gestures and movements even, as the words were reproduced in our gramophone of the dead. Some people when they want to think intensely walk about: some, there's an instance of it audible now, talk to themselves aloud."

He held up his finger for silence.

"Yes, that's Mrs. Gabriel," he said. "She talks to herself by the hour together. She's always done that, she tells me. I shouldn't wonder if she has plenty to talk about."

It was that night when, first of all, the notion of intense activity going on below the placid house-fronts of the Terrace occurred to me. None looked more quiet than this, and yet there was seething here a volcanic activity and intensity of living, both in the man who sat cross-legged on the floor and behind that voice just audible through the partition wall. But I thought of that no more, for Horton began speaking of the brain-gramophone again...Were it possible to trace those infinitesimal dots and pock-marks in the brain by some needle exquisitely fine, it might follow that by the aid of some such contrivance as translated the pock-marks on a gramophone record into sound, some audible rendering of speech might be recovered from the brain of a dead man. It was necessary, so he pointed out to me, that this strange gramophone record should be new; it must be that of one lately dead, for corruption and decay would soon obliterate these infinitesimal markings. He was not of opinion that unspoken thought could be thus recovered: the utmost he hoped for from his pioneering work was to be able to recapture actual speech, especially when such speech had habitually dwelt on one subject, and thus had worn a rut on that part of the brain known the speech-centre.

"Let me get, for instance," he said, "the brain of a railway porter, newly dead, who has been accustomed for years to call out the name of a station, and I do not despair of hearing his voice through my gramophone trumpet. Or again, given that Mrs. Gabriel, in all her interminable conversations with herself, talks about one subject, I might, in similar circumstances, recapture what she had been constantly saying. Of course my instrument must be of a power and delicacy still unknown, one of which the needle can trace the minutest irregularities of surface, and of which the trumpet must be of immense magnifying power, able to translate the smallest whisper into a shout. But just as a microscope will show you the details of an object invisible to the eye, so there are instruments which act in the same way on sound. Here, for instance, is one of remarkable magnifying power. Try it if you like."

He took me over to a table on which was standing an electric battery connected with a round steel globe, out of the side of which sprang a gramophone trumpet of curious construction. He adjusted the battery, and directed me to click my fingers quite gently opposite an aperture in the globe, and the noise, ordinarily scarcely audible, resounded through the room like a thunderclap.

"Something of that sort might permit us to hear the record on a brain," he said. After this night my visits to Horton became far more common than they had hitherto been.

Having once admitted me into the region of his strange explorations, he seemed to welcome me there. Partly, as he had said, it clarified his own thought to put it into simple language, partly, as he subsequently admitted, he was beginning to penetrate into such lonely fields of knowledge by paths so utterly untrodden, that even he, the most aloof and independent of mankind, wanted some human presence near him. Despite his utter indifference to the issues of the war--for, in his regard, issues far more crucial demanded his energies--he offered himself as surgeon to a London hospital for operations on the brain, and his services, naturally, were welcomed, for none brought knowledge or skill like his to such work. Occupied all day, he performed miracles of healing, with bold and dexterous excisions which none but he would have dared to attempt. He would operate, often successfully, for lesions that seemed certainly fatal, and all the time he was learning. He refused to accept any salary; he only asked, in cases where he had removed pieces of brain matter, to take these away, in order by further examination and dissection, to add to the knowledge and manipulative skill which he devoted to the wounded. He wrapped these morsels in sterilised lint, and took them back to the Terrace in a box, electrically heated to maintain the normal temperature of a man's blood. His fragment might then, so he reasoned, keep some sort of independent life of its own, even as the severed heart of a frog had continued to beat for hours without connection with the rest of the body. Then for half the night he would continue to work on these sundered pieces of tissue scarcely dead, which his operations during the day had given him. Simultaneously, he was busy over the needle that must be of such infinite delicacy.

One evening, fatigued with a long day's work, I had just heard with a certain tremor of uneasy anticipation the whistles of warning which heralded an air-raid, when my telephone bell rang. My servants, according to custom, had already betaken themselves to the cellar, and I went to see what the summons was, determined in any case not to go out into the streets. I recognised Horton's voice. "I want you at once," he said.

"But the warning whistles have gone," said I. "And I don't like showers of shrapnel."

"Oh, never mind that," said he. "You must come. I'm so excited that I distrust the evidence of my own ears. I want a witness. Just come."

He did not pause for my reply, for I heard the click of his receiver going back into its place.

Clearly he assumed that I was coming, and that I suppose had the effect of suggestion on my mind. I told myself that I would not go, but in a couple of minutes his certainty that I was coming, coupled with the prospect of being interested in something else than air-raids, made me fidget in my chair and eventually go to the street door and look out. The moon was brilliantly bright, the square quite empty, and far away the coughings of very distant guns. Next moment, almost against my will, I was running down the deserted pavements of Newsome Terrace. My ring at his bell was answered by Horton, before Mrs. Gabriel could come to the door, and he positively dragged me in.

"I shan't tell you a word of what I am doing," he said. "I want you to tell me what you hear. Come into the laboratory."

The remote guns were silent again as I sat myself, as directed, in a chair close to the gramophone trumpet, but suddenly through the wall I heard the familiar mutter of Mrs. Gabriel's voice. Horton, already busy with his battery, sprang to his feet.

"That won't do," he said. "I want absolute silence."

He went out of the room, and I heard him calling to her. While he was gone I observed more closely what was on the table. Battery, round steel globe, and gramophone trumpet were there, and some sort of a needle on a spiral steel spring linked up with the battery and the glass vessel, in which I had seen the frog's heart beat. In it now there lay a fragment of grey matter.

Horton came back in a minute or two, and stood in the middle of the room listening.

"That's better," he said. "Now I want you to listen at the mouth of the trumpet. I'll answer any questions afterwards."

With my ear turned to the trumpet, I could see nothing of what he was doing, and I listened till the silence became a rustling in my ears. Then suddenly that rustling ceased, for it was overscored by a whisper which undoubtedly came from the aperture on which my aural attention was fixed. It was no more than the faintest murmur, and though no words were audible, it had the timbre of a human voice.

"Well, do you hear anything?" asked Horton.

"Yes, something very faint, scarcely audible."

"Describe it," said he.

"Somebody whispering."

"I'll try a fresh place," said he.

The silence descended again; the mutter of the distant guns was still mute, and some slight creaking from my shirt front, as I breathed, alone broke it. And then the whispering from the gramophone trumpet began again, this time much louder than it had been before--it was as if the speaker (still whispering) had advanced a dozen yards--but still blurred and indistinct.

More unmistakable, too, was it that the whisper was that of a human voice, and every now and then, whether fancifully or not, I thought I caught a word or two. For a moment it was silent altogether, and then with a sudden inkling of what I was listening to I heard something begin to sing. Though the words were still inaudible there was melody, and the tune was "Tipperary."

From that convolvulus-shaped trumpet there came two bars of it.

"And what do you hear now?" cried Horton with a crack of exultation in his voice. "Singing, singing! That's the tune they all sang. Fine music that from a dead man. Encore! you say? Yes, wait a second, and he'll sing it again for you. Confound it, I can't get on to the place. Ah! I've got it: listen again."

Surely that was the strangest manner of song ever yet heard on the earth, this melody from the brain of the dead. Horror and fascination strove within me, and I suppose the first for the moment prevailed, for with a shudder I jumped up.

"Stop it!" I said. "It's terrible."

His face, thin and eager, gleamed in the strong ray of the lamp which he had placed close to him. His hand was on the metal rod from which depended the spiral spring and the needle, which just rested on that fragment of grey stuff which I had seen in the glass vessel.

"Yes, I'm going to stop it now," he said, "or the germs will be getting at my gramophone record, or the record will get cold. See, I spray it with carbolic vapour, I put it back into its nice warm bed. It will sing to us again. But terrible? What do you mean by terrible?"

Indeed, when he asked that I scarcely knew myself what I meant. I had been witness to a new marvel of science as wonderful perhaps as any that had ever astounded the beholder, and my nerves--these childish whimperers--had cried out at the darkness and the profundity.

But the horror diminished, the fascination increased as he quite shortly told me the history of this phenomenon. He had attended that day and operated upon a young soldier in whose brain was embedded a piece of shrapnel. The boy was in extremis, but Horton had hoped for the possibility of saving him. To extract the shrapnel was the only chance, and this involved the cutting away of a piece of brain known as the speech-centre, and taking from it what was embedded there. But the hope was not realised, and two hours later the boy died. It was to this fragment of brain that, when Horton returned home, he had applied the needle of his gramophone, and had obtained the faint whisperings which had caused him to ring me up, so that he might have a witness of this wonder. Witness I had been, not to these whisperings alone, but to the fragment of singing.

"And this is but the first step on the new road," said he. "Who knows where it may lead, or to what new temple of knowledge it may not be the avenue? Well, it is late: I shall do no more to-night."

"What about the raid, by the way?"

To my amazement I saw that the time was verging on midnight. Two hours had elapsed since he let me in at his door; they had passed like a couple of minutes. Next morning some neighbours spoke of the prolonged firing that had gone on, of which I had been wholly unconscious.

Week after week Horton worked on this new road of research, perfecting the sensitiveness and subtlety of the needle, and, by vastly increasing the power of his batteries, enlarging the magnifying power of his trumpet. Many and many an evening during the next year did I listen to voices that were dumb in death, and the sounds which had been blurred and unintelligible mutterings in the earlier experiments, developed, as the delicacy of his mechanical devices increased, into coherence and clear articulation. It was no longer necessary to Impose silence on Mrs. Gabriel when the gramophone was at work, or now the voice we listened to had risen to the pitch of ordinary human utterance, while as for the faithfulness and individuality of these records, striking testimony was given more than once by some living friend of the dead, who, without knowing what he was about to hear, recognised the tones of the speaker. More than once also, Mrs. Gabriel, bringing in syphons and whisky, provided us with three glasses, for she had heard, so she told us, three different voices in talk. But for the present no fresh phenomenon occurred; Horton was but perfecting the mechanism of his previous discovery and, rather grudging the time, was scribbling at a monograph, which presently he would toss to his colleagues, concerning the results he had already obtained. And then, even while Horton was on the threshold of new wonders, which he had already foreseen and spoken of as theoretically possible, there came an evening of marvel and of swift catastrophe.

I had dined with him that day, Mrs. Gabriel deftly serving the meal that she had so daintily prepared, and towards the end, as she was clearing the table for our dessert, she stumbled, I supposed, on a loose edge of carpet, quickly recovering herself. But instantly Horton checked some half-finished sentence, and turned to her.

"You're all right, Mrs. Gabriel?" he asked quickly.

"Yes, sir, thank you," said she, and went on with her serving.

"As I was saying," began Horton again, but his attention clearly wandered, and without concluding his narrative, he relapsed into silence, till Mrs. Gabriel had given us our coffee and left the room.

"I'm sadly afraid my domestic felicity may be disturbed," he said. "Mrs. Gabriel had an epileptic fit yesterday, and she confessed when she recovered that she had been subject to them when a child, and since then had occasionally experienced them."

"Dangerous, then?" I asked.

"In themselves not in the least," said he. "If she was sitting in her chair or lying in bed when one occurred, there would be nothing to trouble about. But if one occurred while she was cooking my dinner or beginning to come downstairs, she might fall into the fire or tumble down the whole flight. We'll hope no such deplorable calamity will happen. Now, if you've finished your coffee, let us go into the laboratory. Not that I've got anything very interesting in the way of new records. But I've introduced a second battery with a very strong induction coil into my apparatus. I find that if I link it up with my record, given that the record is a--a fresh one, it stimulates certain nerve centres. It's odd, isn't it, that the same forces which so encourage the dead to live would certainly encourage the living to die, if a man received the full current. One has to be careful in handling it. Yes, and what then? you ask."

The night was very hot, and he threw the windows wide before he settled himself cross-legged on the floor.

"I'll answer your question for you," he said, "though I believe we've talked of it before.

"Supposing I had not a fragment of brain-tissue only, but a whole head, let us say, or best of all, a complete corpse, I think I could expect to produce more than mere speech through the gramophone. The dead lips themselves perhaps might utter--God! what's that?"

From close outside, at the bottom of the stairs leading from the dining room which we had just quitted to the laboratory where we now sat, there came a crash of glass followed by the fall as of something heavy which bumped from step to step, and was finally flung on the threshold against the door with the sound as of knuckles rapping at it, and demanding admittance. Horton sprang up and threw the door open, and there lay, half inside the room and half on the landing outside, the body of Mrs. Gabriel. Round her were splinters of broken bottles and glasses, and from a cut in her forehead, as she lay ghastly with face upturned, the blood trickled into her thick grey hair.

Horton was on his knees beside her, dabbing his handkerchief on her forehead.

"Ah! that's not serious," he said; "there's neither vein nor artery cut. I'll just bind that up first."

He tore his handkerchief into strips which he tied together, and made a dexterous bandage covering the lower part of her forehead, but leaving her eyes unobscured. They stared with a fixed meaningless steadiness, and he scrutinised them closely.

"But there's worse yet," he said. "There's been some severe blow on the head. Help me to carry her into the laboratory. Get round to her feet and lift underneath the knees when I am ready. There! Now put your arm right under her and carry her."

Her head swung limply back as he lifted her shoulders, and he propped it up against his knee, where it mutely nodded and bowed, as his leg moved, as if in silent assent to what we were doing, and the mouth, at the extremity of which there had gathered a little lather, lolled open. He still supported her shoulders as I fetched a cushion on which to place her head, and presently she was lying close to the low table on which stood the gramophone of the dead. Then with light deft fingers he passed his hands over her skull, pausing as he came to the spot just above and behind her right ear. Twice and again his fingers groped and lightly pressed, while with shut eyes and concentrated attention he interpreted what his trained touch revealed.

"Her skull is broken to fragments just here," he said. "In the middle there is a piece completely severed from the rest, and the edges of the cracked pieces must be pressing on her brain."

Her right arm was lying palm upwards on the floor, and with one hand he felt her wrist with fingertips.

"Not a sign of ...," he said. "She's dead in the ordinary sense of the word. But life persists in an extraordinary manner, you may remember. She can't be wholly dead: no one is wholly dead in a moment, unless every organ is blown to bits. But she soon will be dead, if we don't relieve the pressure on the brain. That's the first thing to be done. While I'm busy at that, shut the window, will you, and make up the fire. In this sort of case the vital heat, whatever that is, leaves the body very quickly. Make the room as hot as you can--fetch an oil-stove, and turn on the electric radiator, and stoke up a roaring fire. The hotter the room is the more slowly will the heat of life leave her."

Already he had opened his cabinet of surgical instruments, and taken out of it two drawers full of bright steel which he laid on the floor beside her. I heard the grating chink of scissors severing her long grey hair, and as I busied myself with laying and lighting the fire in the hearth, and kindling the oil-stove, which I found, by Horton's directions, in the pantry, I saw that his lancet was busy on the exposed skin. He had placed some vaporising spray, heated by a spirit lamp close to her head, and as he worked its fizzing nozzle filled the air with some clean and aromatic odour. Now and then he threw out an order.

"Bring me that electric lamp on the long cord," he said. "I haven't got enough light. Don't look at what I'm doing if you're squeamish, for if it makes you feel faint, I shan't be able to attend to you."

I suppose that violent interest in what he was doing overcame any qualm that I might have had, for I looked quite unflinching over his shoulder as I moved the lamp about till it was in such a place that it threw its beam directly into a dark hole at the edge of which depended a flap of skin. Into this he put his forceps, and as he withdrew them they grasped a piece of blood-stained bone.

"That's better," he said, "and the room's warming up well. But there's no sign of pulse yet.

"Go on stoking, will you, till the thermometer on the wall there registers a hundred degrees."

When next, on my journey from the coal-cellar, I looked, two more pieces of bone lay beside the one I had seen extracted, and presently referring to the thermometer, I saw, that between the oil-stove and the roaring fire and the electric radiator, I had raised the room to the temperature he wanted. Soon, peering fixedly at the seat of his operation, he felt for her pulse again.

"Not a sign of returning vitality," he said, "and I've done all I can. There's nothing more possible that can be devised to restore her."

As he spoke the zeal of the unrivalled surgeon relaxed, and with a sigh and a shrug he rose to his feet and mopped his face. Then suddenly the fire and eagerness blazed there again. "The gramophone!" he said. "The speech centre is close to where I've been working, and it is quite uninjured. Good heavens, what a wonderful opportunity. She served me well living, and she shall serve me dead. And I can stimulate the motor nerve-centre, too, with the second battery. We may see a new wonder tonight."

Some qualm of horror shook me.

"No, don't!" I said. "It's terrible: she's just dead. I shall go if you do."

"But I've got exactly all the conditions I have long been wanting," said he. "And I simply can't spare you. You must be witness: I must have a witness. Why, man, there's not a surgeon or a physiologist in the kingdom who would not give an eye or an ear to be in your place now.

"She's dead. I pledge you my honour on that, and it's grand to be dead if you can help the living."

Once again, in a far fiercer struggle, horror and the intensest curiosity strove together in me.

"Be quick, then," said I.

"Ha! That's right," exclaimed Horton. "Help me to lift her on to the table by the gramophone. The cushion too; I can get at the place more easily with her head a little raised."

He turned on the battery and with the movable light close beside him, brilliantly illuminating what he sought, he inserted the needle of the gramophone into the jagged aperture in her skull.

For a few minutes, as he groped and explored there, there was silence, and then quite suddenly Mrs. Gabriel's voice, clear and unmistakable and of the normal loudness of human speech, issued from the trumpet. "Yes, I always said that I'd be even with him," came the articulated syllables. "He used to knock me about, he did, when he came home drunk, and often I was black and blue with bruises.

"But I'll give him a redness for the black and blue."

The record grew blurred; instead of articulate words there came from it a gobbling noise. By degrees that cleared, and we were listening to some dreadful suppressed sort of laughter, hideous to hear. On and on it went.

"I've got into some sort of rut," said Horton. "She must have laughed a lot to herself."

For a long time we got nothing more except the repetition of the words we had already heard and the sound of that suppressed laughter. Then Horton drew towards him the second battery.

"I'll try a stimulation of the motor nerve-centres," he said. "Watch her face."

He propped the gramophone needle in position, and inserted into the fractured skull the two poles of the second battery, moving them about there very carefully. And as I watched her face, I saw with a freezing horror that her lips were beginning to move.

"Her mouth's moving," I cried. "She can't be dead."

He peered into her face.

"Nonsense," he said. "That's only the stimulus from the current. She's been dead half an hour. Ah! what's coming now?"

The lips lengthened into a smile, the lower jaw dropped, and from her mouth came the laughter we had heard just now through the gramophone. And then the dead mouth spoke, with a mumble of unintelligible words, a bubbling torrent of incoherent syllables.

"I'll turn the full current on," he said.

The head jerked and raised itself, the lips struggled for utterance, and suddenly she spoke swiftly and distinctly.

"Just when he'd got his razor out," she said, "I came up behind him, and put my hand over his face, and bent his neck back over his chair with all my strength. And I picked up his razor and with one slit--ha, ha, that was the way to pay him out. And I didn't lose my head, but I lathered his chin well, and put the razor in his hand, and left him there, and went downstairs and cooked his dinner for him, and then an hour afterwards, as he didn't come down, up I went to see what kept him. It was a nasty cut in his neck that had kept him--"

Horton suddenly withdrew the two poles of the battery from her head, and even in the middle of her word the mouth ceased working, and lay rigid and open.

"By God!" he said. "There's a tale for dead lips to tell. But we'll get more yet."

Exactly what happened then I never knew. It appeared to me that as he still leaned over the table with the two poles of the battery in his hand, his foot slipped, and he fell forward across it.

There came a sharp crack, and a flash of blue dazzling light, and there he lay face downwards, with arms that just stirred and quivered. With his fall the two poles that must momentarily have come into contact with his hand were jerked away again, and I lifted him and laid him on the floor. But his lips as well as those of the dead woman had spoken for the last time.

The Dust-Cloud

The big French windows were open on to the lawn, and, dinner being over, two or three of the party who were staying for the week at the end of August with the Combe-Martins had strolled out on to the terrace to look at the sea, over which the moon, large and low, was just rising and tracing a path of pale gold from horizon to shore, while others, less lunar of inclination, had gone in search of bridge or billiards. Coffee had come round immediately after dessert, and the end of dinner, according to the delectable custom of the house, was as informal as the end of breakfast.

Every one, that is to say, remained or went away, smoked, drank port or abstained, according to his personal tastes. Thus, on this particular evening it so happened that Harry Combe-Martin and I were very soon left alone in the dining-room, because we were talking unmitigated motor "shop," and the rest of the party (small wonder) were bored with it, and had left us. The shop was home-shop, so to speak, for it was almost entirely concerned with the manifold perfections of the new six-cylinder Napier which my host in a moment of extravagance, which he did not in the least regret, had just purchased; in which, too, he proposed to take me over to lunch at a friend's house near Hunstanton on the following day. He observed with legitimate pride that an early start would not be necessary, as the distance was only eighty miles and there were no police traps.

"Queer things these big motors are," he said, relapsing into generalities as we rose to go.

"Often I can scarcely believe that my new car is merely a machine. It seems to me to possess an independent life of its own. It is really much more like a thoroughbred with a wonderfully fine mouth."

"And the moods of a thoroughbred?" I asked.

"No; it's got an excellent temper, I'm glad to say. It doesn't mind being checked, or even stopped, when it's going its best. Some of these big cars can't stand that. They get sulky--I assure you it is literally true--if they are checked too often."

He paused on his way to ring the bell. "Guy Elphinstone's car, for instance," he said: "it was a bad-tempered brute, a violent, vicious beast of a car."

"What make?" I asked.

"Twenty-five horse-power Amédée. They are a fretful strain of car; too thin, not enough bone--and bone is very good for the nerves. The brute liked running over a chicken or a rabbit, though perhaps it was less the car's ill-temper than

Guy's, poor chap. Well, he paid for it--he paid to the uttermost farthing. Did you know him?"

"No; but surely I have heard the name. Ah, yes, he ran over a child, did he not?"

"Yes," said Harry, "and then smashed up against his own park gates."

"Killed, wasn't he?"

"Oh, yes, killed instantly, and the car just a heap of splinters. There's an old story about it, I'm told, in the village: rather in your line."

"Ghosts?" I asked.

"Yes, the ghost of his motor-car. Seems almost too up-to-date, doesn't it?"

"And what's the story?" I demanded.

"Why, just this. His place was outside the village of Bircham, ten miles out from Norwich; and there's a long straight bit of road there--that's where he ran over the child--and a couple of hundred yards further on, a rather awkward turn into the park gates. Well, a month or two ago, soon after the accident, one old gaffer in the village swore he had seen a motor there coming full tilt along the road, but without a sound, and it disappeared at the lodge gates of the park, which were shut. Soon after another said he had heard a motor whirl by him at the same place, followed by a hideous scream, but he saw nothing."

"The scream is rather horrible," said I.

"Ah, I see what you mean! I only thought of his syren. Guy had a syren on his exhaust, same as I have. His had a dreadful frightened sort of wail, and always made me feel creepy."

"And is that all the story?" I asked: "that one old man thought he saw a noiseless motor, and another thought he heard an invisible one?"

Harry flicked the ash off his cigarette into the grate. "Oh dear no!" he said. "Half a dozen of them have seen something or heard something. It is quite a heavily authenticated yarn."

"Yes, and talked over and edited in the public-house," I said.

"Well, not a man of them will go there after dark. Also the lodge-keeper gave notice a week or two after the accident. He said he was always hearing a motor stop and hoot outside the lodge, and he was kept running out at all hours of the night to see what it was."

"And what was it?"

"It wasn't anything. Simply nothing there. He thought it rather uncanny, anyhow, and threw up a good post. Besides, his wife was always hearing a child scream, and while her man toddled out to the gate she would go and see whether the kids were all right. And the kids themselves--"

"Ah, what of them?" I asked.

"They kept coming to their mother, asking who the little girl was who walked up and down the road and would not speak to them or play with them."

"It's a many-sided story," I said. "All the witnesses seem to have heard and seen different things."

"Yes, that is just what to my mind makes the yarn so good," he said. "Personally I don't take much stock in spooks at all. But given that there are such things as spooks, and given that the death of the child and the death of Guy have caused spooks to play about there, it seems to me a very good point that different people should be aware of different phenomena. One hears the car, another sees it, one hears the child scream, another sees the child. How does that strike you?"

This, I am bound to say, was a new view to me, and the more I thought of it the more reasonable it appeared. For the vast majority of mankind have all those occult senses by which is perceived the spiritual world (which, I hold, is thick and populous around us), sealed up, as it were; in other words, the majority of mankind never hear or see a ghost at all. Is it not, then, very probable that of the remainder--those, in fact, to whom occult experiences have happened or can happen--few should have every sense unsealed, but that some should have the unsealed ear, others the unsealed eye--that some should be clairaudient, others clairvoyant?

"Yes, it strikes me as reasonable," I said. "Can't you take me over there?"

"Certainly! If you will stop till Friday I'll take you over on Thursday. The others all go that day, so that we can get there after dark."

I shook my head. "I can't stop till Friday, I'm afraid," I said. "I must leave on Thursday. But how about to-morrow? Can't we take it on the way to or from Hunstanton?"

"No; it's thirty miles out of our way. Besides, to be at Bircham after dark means that we shouldn't get back here till midnight. And as host to my guests--"

"Ah! things are only heard and seen after dark, are they?" I asked. "That makes it so much less interesting. It is like a séance where all lights are put out."

"Well, the accident happened at night," he said. "I don't know the rules, but that may have some bearing on it, I should think."

I had one question more in the back of my mind, but I did not like to ask it. At least, I wanted information on this subject without appearing to ask for it.

"Neither do I know the rules of motors," I said; "and I don't understand you when you say that Guy Elphinstone's machine was an irritable, cross-grained brute, that liked running over chickens and rabbits. But I think you subsequently said that the irritability may have been the irritability of its owner. Did he mind being checked?"

"It made him blind-mad if it happened often," said Harry. "I shall never forget a drive I had with him once: there were hay-carts and perambulators every hundred yards. It was perfectly ghastly; it was like being with a madman. And when we got inside his gate, his dog came running out to meet him. He did not go an inch out of his course: it was worse than that--he went for it, just grinding his teeth with rage. I never drove with him again."

He stopped a moment, guessing what might be in my mind. "I say, you mustn't think--you mustn't think--" he began.

"No, of course not," said I.

Harry Combe-Martin's house stood close to the weather-eaten, sandy cliffs of the Suffolk shore, which are being incessantly gnawed away by the hunger of the insatiable sea. Fathoms deep below it, and now any hundred yards out, lies what was once the second port in England; but now of the ancient town of Dunwich, and of its seven great churches, nothing remains but one, and that ruinous and already half destroyed by the falling cliff and the encroachments of the sea. Foot by foot, it too is disappearing, and of the graveyard which surrounded it more than half is gone, so that from the face of the sandy cliff on which it stands there stick out like straws in glass, as Dante says, the bones of those who were once committed there to the kindly and stable earth.

Whether it was the remembrance of this rather grim spectacle as I had seen it that afternoon, or whether Harry's story had caused some trouble in my brain, or whether it was merely that the keen bracing air of this place, to one who had just come from the sleepy languor of the Norfolk Broads, kept me sleepless, I do not know; but, anyhow, the moment I put out my light that night and got into bed, I felt that all the footlights and gas-jets in the internal theatre of my mind sprang into flame, and that I was very vividly and alertly awake. It was in vain that I counted a hundred forwards and a hundred backwards, that I pictured to myself a flock of visionary sheep coming singly through a gap in an imaginary hedge, and tried to number their monotonous and uniform countenances, that I played noughts and crosses with myself, that I marked out scores of double lawn-tennis courts,--for with each repetition of these supposedly soporific exercises I only became more intensely wakeful. It was not in remote hope of sleep that I continued to repeat these weary performances long after their inefficacy was proved to the hilt, but because I was strangely unwilling in this timeless hour of the night to think about those protruding relics of humanity; also I quite distinctly did not desire to think about that subject with regard to which I had, a few hours ago, promised Harry that I would not make it the subject of reflection. For these reasons I continued during the black hours to practise these narcotic exercises of the mind, knowing well that if I paused on the tedious treadmill my thoughts, like some released spring, would fly back to rather gruesome subjects. I kept my mind, in fact, talking loud to itself, so that it should not hear what other voices were saying.

Then by degrees these absurd mental occupations became impossible; my mind simply refused to occupy itself with them any longer; and next moment I was thinking intently and eagerly, not about the bones protruding from the gnawed section of sandcliff, but about the subject I had said I would not dwell upon. And like a flash it came upon me why Harry had bidden me not think about it. Surely in order that I should not come to the same conclusion as he had come to.

Now the whole question of "haunt"--haunted spots, haunted houses, and so forth--has always seemed to me to be utterly unsolved, and to be neither proved nor disproved to a satisfactory degree. From the earliest times, certainly from the earliest known Egyptian records, there has been a belief that the scene of a crime is often revisited, sometimes by the spirit of him who has committed it--seeking rest, we must suppose, and finding none; sometimes, and more inexplicably, by the spirit of his victim, crying perhaps, like the blood of Abel, for vengeance.

And though the stories of these village gossips in the alehouse about noiseless visions and invisible noises were all as yet unsifted and unreliable, yet I could not help wondering if they (such as they were) pointed to something authentic and to be classed under this head of appearances. But more striking than the yarns of the gaffers seemed to me the questions of the lodge-keeper's children. How should children have imagined the figure of a child that would not speak to them or play with them? Perhaps it was a real child, a sulky child. Yes--perhaps. But perhaps not. Then after this preliminary skirmish I found myself settling down to the question that I had said I would not think about; in other words, the possible origin of these phenomena interested me more than the phenomena themselves. For what exactly had Guy Elphinstone, that savage driver, done? Had or had not the death of the child been entirely an accident, a thing (given he drove a motor at all) outside his own control? Or had he, irritated beyond endurance at the checks and delays of the day, not pulled up when it was just possible he might have, but had run over the child as he would have run over a rabbit or a hen, or even his own dog? And what, in any case, poor wretched brute, must have been his thoughts in that terrible instant that intervened between the child's death and his own, when a moment later he smashed into the closed gates of his own lodge? Was remorse his--bitter, despairing contrition? That could hardly have been so; or else surely, knowing only for certain that he had knocked a child down, he would have stopped; he would have done his best, whatever that might be, to repair the irreparable harm. But he had not stopped: he had gone on, it seemed, at full speed, for on the collision the car had been smashed into matchwood and steel shavings. Again, with double force, had this dreadful thing been a complete accident, he would have stopped. So then--most terrible question of all--had he, after making murder, rushed on to what proved to be his own death, filled with some hellish glee at what he had done? Indeed, as in the church-yard on the cliff, bones of the buried stuck starkly out into the night.

The pale tired light of earliest morning had turned the window-blinds into glimmering squares before I slept; and when I woke, the servant who called me was already rattling them briskly up on their rollers, and letting the calm serenity of the August day stream into the room. Through the open windows poured in sunlight and sea-wind, the scent of flowers and the song of birds; and each and all were wonderfully reassuring, banishing the hooded forms that had haunted the night, and I thought of the disquietude of the dark hours as a traveller may think of the billows and tempests of the ocean over which he has safely journeyed, unable, now that they belong to the limbo of the past, to recall his qualms and tossings with any vivid uneasiness. Not without a feeling of relief, too, did I dwell on the knowledge that I was definitely not going to visit this equivocal spot. Our drive to-day, as Harry had said, would not take us within thirty miles of it, and tomorrow I but went to the station and away. Though a thorough-paced seeker after truth might, no doubt, have regretted that the laws of time and space did not permit him to visit Bircham after the sinister dark had fallen, and test whether for him there was visible or audible truth in the tales of the village gossips, I was conscious of no such regret. Bircham and its fables had given me a very bad night, and I was perfectly aware that I did not in the least want to go near it, though yesterday I had quite truthfully said I should like to do so. In this brightness, too, of sun and sea-wind I felt none of the malaise at my waking moments which a sleepless night usually gives me; I felt particularly well, particularly pleased to be alive, and also, as I have said, particularly content not to be going to Bircham. I was quite satisfied to leave my curiosity unsatisfied.

The motor came round about eleven, and we started at once, Harry and Mrs. Morrison, a cousin of his, sitting behind in the big back seat, large enough to hold a comfortable three, and I on the left of the driver, in a sort of trance--I am not ashamed to confess it--of expectancy and delight. For this was in the early days of motors, when there was still the sense of romance and adventure round them. I did not want to drive, any more than Harry wanted to; for driving, so I hold, is too absorbing; it takes the attention in too firm a grip: the mania of the true motorist is not consciously enjoyed. For the passion for motors is a taste--I had almost said a gift--as distinct and as keenly individual as the passion for music or mathematics. Those who use motors most (merely as a means of getting rapidly from one place to another) are often entirely without it, while those whom adverse circumstances (over which they have no control) compel to use them least may have it to a supreme degree. To those who have it, analysis of their passion is perhaps superfluous; to those who have it not, explanation is almost unintelligible. Pace, however, and the control of pace, and above all the sensuous consciousness of pace, is at the root of it; and pleasure in pace is common to most people, whether it be in the form of a galloping horse, or the pace of the skate hissing over smooth ice, or the pace of a free-wheel bicycle humming down-hill, or, more impersonally, the pace of the smashed ball at lawn-tennis, the driven ball at golf, or the low boundary hit at cricket. But the sensuous consciousness of pace, as I have said, is needful: one might experience it seated in front of the engine of an express train, though not in a wadded, shut-windowed carriage, where the wind of movement is not felt. Then add to this rapture of the rush through riven air the knowledge that huge relentless force is controlled by a little lever, and directed by a little wheel on which the hands of the driver seem to lie so negligently. A great untamed devil has there his bridle, and he answers to it, as Harry had said, like a horse with a fine mouth. He has hunger and thirst, too, unslakeable, and greedily he laps of his soup of petrol which turns to fire in his mouth; electricity, the force that rends clouds asunder, and causes towers to totter, is the spoon with which he feeds himself; and as he eats he races onward, and the road opens like torn linen in front of him. Yet how obedient, how amenable is he!--for with a touch on his snaffle his speed is redoubled, or melts into thin air, so that before you know you have touched the rein he has exchanged his swallow-flight for a mere saunter through the lanes. But he ever loves to run; and knowing this, you will bid him lift up his voice and tell those who are in his path that he is coming, so that he will not need the touch that checks. Hoarse and jovial is his voice, hooting to the wayfarer; and if his hooting be not heard he has a great guttural falsetto scream that leaps from octave to octave, and echoes from the hedges that are passing in blurred lines of hanging green. And, as you go, the romantic isolation of divers in deep seas is yours; masked and hooded companions may be near you also, in their driving-dress for this plunge through the swift tides of air; but you, like them, are alone and isolated, conscious only of the ripped riband of road, the two great lantern-eyes of the wonderful monster that look through drooped eyelids by day, but gleam with fire by night, the two ear-laps of splash-boards, and the long lean bonnet in front which is the skull and brain-case of that swift untiring energy that feeds on fire, and whirls its two tons of weight up hill and down dale, as if some new law as ever-lasting as gravity, and like gravity making it go ever swifter, was its sole control.

For the first hour the essence of these joys, any description of which compared to the real thing is but as a stagnant pond compared to the bright rushing of a mountain stream, was mine. A straight switchback road lay in front of us, and the monster plunged silently down hill, and said below his breath, "Ha-ha--ha-ha--ha-ha," as, without diminution of speed, he breasted the opposing slope. In my control were his great vocal cords (for in those days hooter and syren were on the driver's left, and lay convenient to the hand of him who occupied the box-seat), and it rejoiced me to let him hoot at a pony-cart, three hundred yards ahead, with a hand on his falsetto scream if his ordinary tones of conversation were unheard or disregarded. Then came a road crossing ours at right angles, and the dear monster seemed to say, "Yes, yes,--see how obedient and careful I am. I stroll with my hands in my pockets." Then again a puppy from a farmhouse staggered warlike into the road, and the monster said, "Poor little chap! get home to your mother, or I'll talk to you in earnest." The poor little chap did not take the hint, so the monster slackened speed and just said "Whoof!" Then it chuckled to itself as the puppy scuttled into the hedge, seriously alarmed; and next moment our self-made wind screeched and whistled round us again.

Napoleon, I believe, said that the power of an army lay in its feet: that is true also of the monster. There was a loud bang, and in thirty seconds we were at a standstill. The monster's off fore-foot troubled it, and the chauffeur said, "Yes, sir--burst."

So the burst boot was taken off and a new one put on, a boot that had never been on foot before. The foot in question was held up on a jack during this operation, and the new boot laced up with a pump. This took exactly twenty-five minutes. Then the monster got his spoon going again, and said, "Let me run: oh, let me run!"

And for fifteen miles on a straight and empty road it ran. I timed the miles, but shall not produce their chronology for the benefit of a forsworn constabulary.

But there were no more dithyrambics that morning. We should have reached Hunstanton in time for lunch. Instead, we waited to repair our fourth puncture at

1.45 p.m., twenty-five miles short of our destination. This fourth puncture was caused by a spicule of flint three-quarters of an inch long--sharp, it is true, but weighing perhaps two pennyweights, while we weighed two tons. It seemed an impertinence. So we lunched at a wayside inn, and during lunch the pundits held a consultation, of which the upshot was this:

We had no more boots for our monster, for his off fore-foot had burst once, and punctured once (thus necessitating two socks and one boot). Similarly, but more so, his off hind-foot had burst twice (thus necessitating two boots and two socks). Now, there was no certain shoemaker's shop at Hunstanton, as far as we knew, but there was a regular universal store at King's Lynn, which was about equidistant.

And, so said the chauffeur, there was something wrong with the monster's spoon (ignition), and he didn't rightly know what, and therefore it seemed the prudent part not to go to Hunstanton (lunch, a thing of the preterite, having been the object), but to the well-supplied King's Lynn.

And we all breathed a pious hope that we might get there.

Whizz: hoot: purr! The last boot held, the spoon went busily to the monster's mouth, and we just flowed into King's Lynn. The return journey, so I vaguely gathered, would be made by other roads; but personally, intoxicated with air and movement, I neither asked nor desired to know what those roads would be. This one small but rather salient fact is necessary to record here, that as we waited at King's Lynn, and as we buzzed homewards afterwards, no thought of Bircham entered my head at all. The subsequent hallucination, if hallucination it was, was not, as far as I know, self-suggested. That we had gone out of our way for the sake of the garage, I knew, and that was all. Harry also told me that he did not know where our road would take us.

The rest that follows is the baldest possible narrative of what actually occurred. But it seems to me, a humble student of the occult, to be curious.

While we waited we had tea in an hotel looking on to a big empty square of houses, and after tea we waited a very long time for our monster to pick us up. Then the telephone from the garage inquired for "the gentleman on the motor," and since Harry had strolled out to get a local evening paper with news of the last Test Match, I applied ear and mouth to that elusive instrument. What I heard was not encouraging: the ignition had gone very wrong indeed, and "perhaps" in an hour we should be able to start. It was then about half-past six, and we were just seventy-eight miles from Dunwich.

Harry came back soon after this, and I told him what the message from the garage had been.

What he said was this: "Then we shan't get back till long after dinner. We might just as well have camped out to see your ghost."

As I have already said, no notion of Bircham was in my mind, and I mention this as evidence that, even if it had been, Harry's remark would have implied that we were not going through Bircham.

The hour lengthened itself into an hour and a half. Then the monster, quite well again, came hooting round the corner, and we got in.

"Whack her up, Jack," said Harry to the chauffeur. "The roads will be empty. You had better light up at once."

The monster, with its eyes agleam, was whacked up, and never in my life have I been carried so cautiously and yet so swiftly. Jack never took a risk or the possibility of a risk, but when the road was clear and open he let the monster run just as fast as it was able. Its eyes made day of the road fifty yards ahead, and the romance of night was fairyland round us. Hares started from the roadside, and raced in front of us for a hundred yards, then just wheeled in time to avoid the ear-flaps of the great triumphant brute that carried us. Moths flitted across, struck sometimes by the lenses of its eyes, and the miles peeled over our shoulders. When it occurred we were going top-speed.

And this was It--quite unsensational, but to us quite inexplicable unless my midnight imaginings happened to be true.

As I have said, I was in command of the hooter and of the syren. We were flying along on a straight down-grade, as fast as ever we could go, for the engines were working, though the decline was considerable. Then quite suddenly I saw in front of us a thick cloud of dust, and knew instinctively and on the instant, without thought or reasoning, what that must mean.

Evidently something going very fast (or else so large a cloud could not have been raised) was in front of us, and going in the same direction as ourselves. Had it been something on the road coming to meet us, we should of course have seen the vehicle first and run into the dust-cloud afterwards. Had it, again, been something of low speed--a horse and dog-cart, for instance--no such dust could have been raised. But, as it was, I knew at once that there was a motor travelling swiftly just ahead of us, also that it was not going as fast as we were, or we should have run into its dust much more gradually. But we went into it as into a suddenly lowered curtain.

Then I shouted to Jack. "Slow down, and put on the brake," I shrieked. "There's something just ahead of us." As I spoke I wrought a wild concerto on the hooter, and with my right hand groped for the syren, but did not find it. Simultaneously I heard a wild, frightened shriek, just as if I had sounded the syren myself. Jack had felt for it too, and our hands fingered each other. Then we entered the dust-cloud.

We slowed down with extraordinary rapidity, and still peering ahead we went dead-slow through it. I had not put on my goggles after leaving King's Lynn, and the dust stung and smarted in my eyes. It was not, therefore, a belt of fog, but real road-dust. And at the moment we crept through it I felt Harry's hands on my shoulder.

"There's something just ahead," he said. "Look! don't you see the tail light?"

As a matter of fact, I did not; and, still going very slow, we came out of that dust-cloud. The broad empty road stretched in front of us; a hedge was on each side, and there was no turning either to right or left. Only, on the right, was a lodge, and gates which were closed. The lodge had no lights in any window.

Then we came to a standstill; the air was dead-calm, not a leaf in the hedgerow trees was moving, not a grain of dust was lifted from the road. But behind, the dust-cloud still hung in the air, and stopped dead-short at the closed lodge-gates. We had moved very slowly for the last hundred yards: it was difficult to suppose that it was of our making. Then Jack spoke, with a curious crack in his voice.

"It must have been a motor, sir," he said. "But where is it?"

I had no reply to this, and from behind another voice, Harry's voice, spoke. For the moment I did not recognise it, for it was strained and faltering.

"Did you open the syren?" he asked. "It didn't sound like our syren. It sounded like, like--"

"I didn't open the syren," said I.

Then we went on again. Soon we came to scattered lights in houses by the wayside.

"What's this place?" I asked Jack.

"Bircham, sir," said he.

The Cat

Many people will doubtless, remember that exhibition at the Royal Academy, not so many seasons ago which came to be known as Alingham's year, when Dick Alingham vaulted, with one bound, as it were, out of the crowd of strugglers and seated himself with admirably certain poise on the very topmost pinnacle of contemporary fame. He exhibited three portraits, each a masterpiece, which killed every picture within range. But since that year nobody cared anything for pictures whether in or out of range except those three, it did not signify so greatly. The phenomenon of his appearance was as sudden as that of the meteor, coming from nowhere and sliding large and luminous across the remote and star-sown sky, as inexplicable as the bursting of a spring on some dust-ridden rocky hillside. Some fairy godmother, one might conjecture, had bethought herself of her forgotten godson, and with a wave of her wand bestowed on him this transcendent gift. But, as the Irish say, she held her wand in her left hand, for her gift had another side to it. Or perhaps, again, Jim Merwick is right, and the theory he propounds in his monograph, "On certain obscure lesions of the nerve centres," says the final word on the subject.

Dick Alingham himself, as was indeed natural, was delighted with his fairy godmother or his obscure lesion (whichever was responsible), and (the monograph spoken of above was written after Dick's death) confessed frankly to his friend Merwick, who was still struggling through the crowd of rising young medical practitioners, that it was all quite as inexplicable to himself as it was to anyone else.

"All I know about it," he said, "is that last autumn I went through two months of mental depression so hideous that I thought again and again that I must go off my head. For hours daily, I sat here, waiting for something to crack, which as far as I am concerned would end everything.

"Yes, there was a cause; you know it."

He paused a moment and poured into his glass a fairly liberal allowance of whisky, filled it half up from a syphon, and lit a cigarette. The cause, indeed, had no need to be enlarged on, for Merwick quite well remembered how the girl Dick had been engaged to threw him over with an abruptness that was almost superb, when a more eligible suitor made his appearance. The latter was certainly very eligible indeed with his good looks, his title, and his million of money, and Lady Madingley--ex-future Mrs. Alingham--was perfectly content with what she had done.

She was one of those blonde, lithe, silken girls, who, happily for the peace of men's minds, are rather rare, and who remind one of some humanised yet celestial and bestial cat.

"I needn't speak of the cause," Dick continued, "but, as I say, for those two months I soberly thought that the only end to it would be madness. Then one evening when I was sitting here alone--I was always sitting alone--something did snap in my head. I know I wondered, without caring at all, whether this was the madness which I had been expecting, or whether (which would be preferable) some more fatal breakage had happened. And even while I wondered, I was aware that I was not depressed or unhappy any longer."

He paused for so long in a smiling retrospect that Merwick indicated to him that he had a listener.

"Well?" he said.

"It was well indeed. I haven't been unhappy since. I have been riotously happy instead. Some divine doctor, I suppose, just wiped off that stain on my brain that hurt so. Heavens, how it hurt! Have a drink, by the way?"

"No, thanks," said Merwick. "But what has all this got to do with your painting?"

"Why, everything. For I had hardly realised the fact that I was happy again, when I was aware that everything looked different. The colours of all I saw were twice as vivid as they had been, shape and outline were intensified too. The whole visible world had been dusty and blurred before, and seen in a half-light. But now the lights were turned up, and there was a new heaven and a new earth. And in the same flash, I knew that I could paint things as I saw them. Which," he concluded, "I have done."

There was something rather sublime about this, and Merwick laughed.

"I wish something would snap in my brain, if it kindles the perceptions in that way," said he, "but it is just possible that the snapping of things in one's brain does not always produce just that effect."

"That is possible. Also, as I gather, things don't snap unless you have gone through some such hideous period as I have been through. And I tell you frankly that I wouldn't go through that again even to ensure a snap that would make me see things like Titian."

"What did the snapping feel like?" asked Merwick.

Dick considered a moment.

"Do you know when a parcel comes, tied up with string, and you can't find a knife," he said, "and therefore you burn the string through, holding it taut? Well, it was like that: quite painless, only something got weaker and weaker, and then parted, softly without effort. Not very lucid, I'm afraid, but it was just like that. It had been burning a couple of months, you see."

He turned away and hunted among the letters and papers which littered his writing-table till he found an envelope with a coronet on it. He chuckled to himself as he took it up.

"Commend me to Lady Madingley," he said, "for a brazen impudence in comparison with which brass is softer than putty. She wrote to me yesterday, asking me if I would finish the portrait I had begun of her last year, and let her have it at my own price.

"Then I think you have had a lucky escape," remarked Merwick. "I suppose you didn't even answer her."

"Oh, yes, I did: why not? I said the price would be two thousand pounds, and I was ready to go on at once. She has agreed, and sent me a cheque for a thousand this evening."

Merwick stared at him in blank astonishment. "Are you mad?" he asked.

"I hope not, though one can never be sure about little points like that. Even doctors like you don't know exactly what constitutes madness."

Merwick got up.

"But is it possible that you don't see what a terrible risk you run?" he asked. "To see her again, to be with her like that, having to look at her--I saw her this afternoon, by the way, hardly human--may not that so easily revive again all that you felt before? It is too dangerous: much too dangerous."

Dick shook his head.

"There is not the slightest risk," he said; "everything within me is utterly and absolutely indifferent to her. I don't even hate her: if I hated her there might be a possibility of my again loving her. As it is, the thought of her does not arouse in me any emotion of any kind. And really such stupendous calmness deserves to be rewarded. I respect colossal things like that."

He finished his whisky as he spoke, and instantly poured himself out another glass.

"That's the fourth," said his friend.

"Is it? I never count. It shows a sordid attention to uninteresting detail. Funnily enough, too, alcohol does not have the smallest effect on me now."

"Why drink then?"

"Because if I give it up this entrancing vividness of colour and clarity of outline is a little diminished.

"Can't be good for you," said the doctor.

Dick laughed.

"My dear fellow, look at me carefully," he said, "and then if you can conscientiously declare that I show any signs of indulging in stimulants, I'll give them up altogether."

Certainly it would have been hard to find a point in which Dick did not present the appearance of perfect health. He had paused, and stood still a moment, his glass in one hand, the whisky-bottle in the other, black against the front of his shirt, and not a tremor of unsteadiness was there. His face of wholesome sunburnt hue was neither puffy nor emaciated, but firm of flesh and of a wonderful clearness of skin. Clear too was his eye, with eyelids neither baggy nor puckered; he looked indeed a model of condition, hard and fit, as if he was in training for some athletic event. Lithe and active too was his figure, his movements were quick and precise, and even Merwick, with his doctor's eye trained to detect any symptom, however slight, in which the drinker must betray himself, was bound to confess that no such was here present. His appearance contradicted it authoritatively, so also did his manner; he met the eye of the man he was talking to without sideway glances; he showed no signs, however small, of any disorder of the nerves. Yet Dick was altogether an abnormal fellow; the history he had just been recounting was abnormal, those weeks of depression, followed by the sudden snap in his brain which had apparently removed, as a wet cloth removes a stain, all the memory of his love and of the cruel bitterness that resulted from it. Abnormal too was his sudden leap into high artistic achievement from a past of very mediocre performance. Why should there then not be a similar abnormality here?

"Yes, I confess you show no sign of taking excessive stimulant," said Merwick, "but if I attended you professionally--ah, I'm not touting--I should make you give up all stimulant, and go to bed for a month."

"Why in the name of goodness?" asked Dick.

"Because, theoretically, it must be the best thing you could do. You had a shock, how severe, the misery of those weeks of depression tells you. Well, common sense says, 'Go slow after a shock; recoup.' Instead of which you go very fast indeed and produce. I grant it seems to suit you; you also became suddenly capable of feats which--oh, it's sheer nonsense, man."

"What's sheer nonsense?"

"You are. Professionally, I detest you, because you appear to be an exception to a theory that I am sure must be right. Therefore I have got to explain you away, and at present I can't."

"What's the theory?" asked Dick.

"Well, the treatment of shock first of all. And secondly, that in order to do good work, one ought to eat and drink very little and sleep a lot. How long do you sleep, by the way?"

Dick considered.

"Oh, I go to bed about three usually," he said; "I suppose I sleep for about four hours."

"And live on whisky, and eat like a Strasburg goose, and are prepared to run a race to-morrow."

"Go away, or at least I will. Perhaps you'll break down, though. That would satisfy me.

"But even if you don't, it still remains quite interesting."

Merwick found it more than quite interesting in fact, and when he got home that night he searched in his shelves for a certain dusky volume in which he turned up a chapter called "Shock." The book was a treatise on obscure diseases and abnormal conditions of the nervous system. He had often read it before, for in his profession he was a special student of the rare and curious. And the following paragraph which had interested him much before, interested him more than ever this evening.

"The nervous system also can act in a way that must always even to the most advanced student be totally unexpected. Cases are known, and well-authenticated ones, when a paralytic person has jumped out of bed on the cry of 'Fire.' Cases too are known when a great shock, which produces depression so profound as to amount to lethargy, is followed by abnormal activity, and the calling into use of powers which were previously unknown to exist, or at any rate existed in a quite ordinary degree. Such a hyper-sensitised state, especially since the desire for sleep or rest is very often much diminished, demands much stimulant in the way of food and alcohol. It would appear also that the patient suffering from this rare form of the after-consequences of shock has sooner or later some sudden and complete break-down. It is impossible, however, to conjecture what form this will take. The digestion, however, may become suddenly atrophied, delirium tremens may, without warning, supervene, or he may go completely off his head..."

But the weeks passed on, the July suns made London reel in a haze of heat, and yet Alingham remained busy, brilliant, and altogether exceptional. Merwick, unknown to him, was watching him closely, and at present was completely puzzled. He held Dick to his word that if he could detect the slightest sign of over-indulgence in stimulant, he would cut it off altogether, but he could see absolutely none. Lady Madingley meantime had given him several sittings, and in this connection again Merwick was utterly mistaken in the view he had expressed to Dick as to the risks he ran. For, strangely enough, the two had become great friends. Yet Dick was quite right, all emotion with regard to her on his part was dead, it might have been a piece of still-life that he was painting, instead of a woman he had wildly worshipped.

One morning in mid-July she had been sitting to him in his studio, and contrary to custom he had been rather silent, biting the ends of his brushes, frowning at his canvas, frowning too at her.

Suddenly he gave a little impatient exclamation.

"It's so like you," he said, "but it just isn't you. There's a lot of difference! I can't help making you look as if you were listening to a hymn, one of those in four sharps, don't you know, written by an organist, probably after eating muffins. And that's not characteristic of you!"

She laughed.

"You must be rather ingenious to put all that in," she said.

"I am."

"Where do I show it all?"

Dick sighed.

"Oh, in your eyes of course," he said. "You show everything by your eyes, you know. It is entirely characteristic of you. You are a throw-back; don't you remember we settled that ever so long ago, to the brute creation, who likewise show everything by their eyes."

"Oh-h. I should have thought that dogs growled at you, and cats scratched."

"Those are practical measures, but short of that you and animals use their eyes only, whereas people use their mouths and foreheads and other things. A pleased dog, an expectant dog, a hungry dog, a jealous dog, a disappointed dog--one gathers all that from a dog's eyes. Their mouths are comparatively immobile, and a cat's is even more so.

"You have often told me that I belong to the genus cat," said Lady Madingley, with complete composure.

"By Jove, yes," said he. "Perhaps looking at the eyes of a cat would help me to see what I miss. Many thanks for the hint."

He put down his palette and went to a side table on which stood bottles and ice and syphons.

"No drink of any kind on this Sahara of a morning?" he asked.

"No, thanks. Now when will you give me the final sitting? You said you only wanted one more."

Dick helped himself.

"Well, I go down to the country with this," he said, "to put in the background I told you of.

"With luck it will take me three days' hard painting, without luck a week or more. Oh, my mouth waters at the thought of the background. So shall we say to-morrow week?"

Lady Madingley made a note of this in a minute gold and jewelled memorandum book.

"And I am to be prepared to see cat's eyes painted there instead of my own when I see it next?" she asked, passing by the canvas.

Dick laughed.

"Oh, you will hardly notice the difference," he said. "How odd it is that I always have detested cats so--they make me feel actually faint, although you always reminded me of a cat."

"You must ask your friend Mr. Merwick about these metaphysical mysteries," said she.

The background to the picture was at present only indicated by a few vague splashes close to the side of the head of brilliant purple and brilliant green, and the artist's mouth might well water at the thought of the few days painting that lay before him. For behind the figure in the long panel-shaped canvas was to be painted a green trellis, over which, almost hiding the woodwork, there was to sprawl a great purple clematis in full flaunting glory of varnished leaf and starry flower.

At the top would be just a strip of pale summer sky, at her feet just a strip of grey-green grass, but all the rest of the background, greatly daring, would be this diaper of green and purple. For the purpose of putting this in, he was going down to a small cottage of his near Godalming, where he had built in the garden a sort of outdoor studio, an erection betwixt a room and a mere shelter, with the side to the north entirely open, and flanked by this green trellis which was now one immense constellation of purple stars. Framed in this, he well knew how the strange pale beauty of his sitter would glow on the canvas, how she would start out of the background, she and her huge grey hat, and shining grey dress, and yellow hair and ivory white skin and pale eyes, now blue, now grey, now green. This was indeed a thing to look forward to, for there is probably no such unadulterated rapture known to men as creation, and it was small wonder that Dick's mood, as he travelled down to Godalming, was buoyant and effervescent. For he was going, so to speak, to realise his creation: every purple star of clematis, every green leaf and piece of trellis-work that he put in, would cause what he had painted to live and shine, just as it is the layers of dusk that fall over the sky at evening which make the stars to sparkle there, jewel-like.

His scheme was assured, he had hung his constellation--the figure of Lady Madingley--in the sky: and now he had to surround it with the green and purple night, so that it might shine.

His garden was but a circumscribed plot, but walls of old brick circumscribed it, and he had dealt with the space at his command with a certain originality. At no time had his grass plot (you could scarcely call it "lawn") been spacious; now the outdoor studio, twenty-five feet by thirty, took up the greater part of it. He had a solid wooden wall on one side and two trellis walls to the south and east, which creepers were beginning to clothe and which were faced internally by hangings of Syrian and Oriental work. Here in the summer he passed the greater part of the day, painting or idling, and living an outdoor existence. The floor, which had once been grass, which had withered completely under the roof, was covered with Persian rugs; a writing-table and a dining-table were there, a bookcase full of familiar friends and a half-dozen of basket chairs. One corner, too, was frankly given up to the affairs of the garden, and a mowing machine, a hose for watering, shears, and spade stood there. For like many excitable persons, Dick found that in gardening, that incessant process of plannings and designings to suit the likings of plants, and make them gorgeous in colour and high of growth, there was a wonderful calm haven of refuge for the brain that had been tossing on emotional seas. Plants, too, were receptive, so responsive to kindness; thought given to them was never thought wasted, and to come back now after a month's absence in London was to be assured of fresh surprise and pleasure in each foot of garden-bed. And here, with how regal a generosity was the purple clematis to repay him for the care lavished on it. Every flower would show its practical gratitude by standing model for the background of his picture.

The evening was very warm, warm not with any sultry premonition of thunder, but with the clear, clean heat of summer, and he dined alone in his shelter, with the after-flames of the sunset for his lamp. These slowly faded into a sky of velvet blue, but he lingered long over his coffee, looking northwards across the garden towards the row of trees that screened him from the house beyond. These were acacias, most graceful and feminine of all green things that grow, summer-plumaged now, yet still fresh of leaf. Below them ran a little raised terrace of turf and nearer the beds of the beloved garden; clumps of sweet-peas made an inimitable fragrance, and the rose-beds were pink with Baroness Rothschild and La France, and copper-coloured with Beauté inconstante, and the Richardson rose. Then, nearer at hand, was the green trellis foaming with purple.

He was sitting there, hardly looking, but unconsciously drinking in this great festival of colour, when his eye was arrested by a dark slinking form that appeared among the roses, and suddenly turned two shining luminous orbs on him. At this he started up, but his movement caused no perturbation in the animal, which continued with back arched for stroking, and poker-like tail, to advance towards him, purring. As it came closer Dick felt that shuddering faintness, which often affected him in the presence of cats, come over him, and he stamped and clapped his hands. At this it turned tail quickly: a sort of dark shadow streaked the garden-wall for a moment, and it vanished. But its appearance had spoiled for him the sweet spell of the evening, and he went indoors.

The next morning was pellucid summer: a faint north wind blew, and a sun worthy to illumine the isles of Greece flooded the sky. Dick's dreamless and (for him) long sleep had banished from his mind that rather disquieting incident of the cat, and he set up his canvas facing the trellis-work and purple clematis with a huge sense of imminent ecstasy. Also the garden, which at present he had only seen in the magic of sunset, was gloriously rewarding, and glowed with colour, and though life--this was present to his mind for the first time for months--in the shape of Lady Madingley had not been very propitious, yet a man, he argued to himself, must be a very poor hand at living if, with a passion for plants and a passion for art, he cannot fashion a life that shall be full of content. So breakfast being finished, and his model ready and glowing with beauty, he quickly sketched in the broad lines of flowers and foliage and began to paint.

Purple and green, green and purple: was there ever such a feast for the eye? Gourmet-like and greedy as well, he was utterly absorbed in it. He was right too: as soon as he put on the first brush of colour he knew he was right. It was just those divine and violent colours which would cause his figure to step out from the picture, it was just that pale strip of sky above which would focus her again, it was just that strip of grey-green grass below her feet that would prevent her, so it seemed, from actually leaving the canvas. And with swift eager sweeps of the brush which never paused and never hurried, he lost himself in his work.

He stopped at length with a sense of breathlessness, feeling too as if he had been suddenly called back from some immense distance off. He must have been working some three hours, for his man was already laying the table for lunch, yet it seemed to him that the morning had gone by in one flash. The progress he had made was extraordinary, and he looked long at his picture.

Then his eye wandered from the brightness of the canvas to the brightness of the garden-beds.

There, just in front of the bed of sweet-peas, not two yards from him, stood a very large grey cat, watching him.

Now the presence of a cat was a thing that usually produced in Dick a feeling of deadly faintness, yet, at this moment, as he looked at the cat and the cat at him, he was conscious of no such feeling, and put down the absence of it, in so far as he consciously thought about it, to the fact that he was in the open air, not in the atmosphere of a closed room. Yet, last night out here, the cat had made him feel faint. But he hardly gave a thought to this, for what filled his mind was that he saw in the rather friendly interested look of the beast that expression in the eye which had so baffled him in his portrait of Lady Madingley. So, slowly, and without any sudden movement that might startle the cat, he reached out his hand for the palette he had just put down, and in a corner of the canvas not yet painted over, recorded in half a dozen swift intuitive touches, what he wanted. Even in the broad sunlight where the animal stood, its eyes looked as if they were internally smouldering as well as being lit from without: it was just so that Lady Madingley looked. He would have to lay colour very thinly over white...

For five minutes or so he painted them with quiet eager strokes, drawing the colour thinly over the background of white, and then looked long at that sketch of the eye to see if he had got what he wanted. Then he looked back at the cat which had stood so charmingly for him. But there was no cat there. That, however, since he detested them, and this one had served his purpose, was no matter for regret, and he merely wondered a little at the suddenness of its disappearance. But the legacy it had left on the canvas could not vanish thus, it was his own, a possession, an achievement. Truly this was to be a portrait which would altogether outdistance all he had ever done before. A woman, real, alive, wearing her soul in her eyes, should stand there, and summer riot round her.

An extraordinary clearness of vision was his all day, and towards sunset an empty whisky-bottle.

But this evening he was conscious for the first time of two feelings, one physical, one mental, altogether strange to him: the first an impression that he had drunk as much as was good for him, the second a sort of echo in his mind of those tortures he had undergone in the autumn, when he had been tossed aside by the girl, to whom he had given his soul, like a soiled glove.

Neither was at all acutely felt, but both were present to him.

The evening altogether belied the brilliance of the day, and about six o'clock thick clouds had driven up over the sky, and the clear heat of summer had given place to a heat no less intense, but full of the menace of storm. A few big hot drops, too, of rain warned him further, and he pulled his easel into shelter, and gave orders that he would dine indoors. As was usual with him when he was at work, he shunned the distracting influence of any companionship, and he dined alone. Dinner finished, he went into his sitting-room prepared to enjoy his solitary evening. His servant had brought him in the tray, and till he went to bed he would be undisturbed. Outside the storm was moving nearer, the reverberation of the thunder, though not yet close, kept up a continual growl: any moment it might move up and burst above in riot of fire and sound.

Dick read a book for a while, but his thoughts wandered. The poignancy of his trouble last autumn, which he thought had passed away from him for ever, grew suddenly and strangely more acute, also his head was heavy, perhaps with the storm, but possibly with what he had drunk. So, intending to go to bed and sleep off his disquietude, he closed his book, and went across to the window to close that also. But, half-way towards it, he stopped. There on the sofa below it sat a large grey cat with yellow gleaming eyes. In its mouth it held a young thrush, still alive.

Then horror woke in him: his feeling of sick-faintness was there, and he loathed and was terrified at this dreadful feline glee in the torture of its prey, a glee so great that it preferred the postponement of its meal to a shortening of the other. More than all, the resemblance of the eyes of this cat to those of his portrait suddenly struck him as something hellish. For one moment this all held him bound, as if with paralysis, the next his physical shuddering could be withstood no longer, and he threw the glass he carried at the cat, missing it. For one second the animal paused there glaring at him with an intense and dreadful hostility, then it made one spring of it out of the open window. Dick shut it with a bang that startled himself, and then searched on the sofa and the floor for the bird which he thought the cat had dropped. Once or twice he thought he heard it feebly fluttering, but this must have been an illusion, for he could not find it.

All this was rather shaky business, so before going to bed he steadied himself, as his unspoken phrase ran, with a final drink. Outside the thunder had ceased, but the rain beat hissing on to the grass. Then another sound mingled with it the mewing of a cat, not the long-drawn screeches and cries that are usual, but the plaintive calls of the beast that wants to be admitted into its own home. The blind was down, but after a while he could not resist peeping out. There on the window-sill was seated the large grey cat. Though it was raining heavily its fur seemed dry, for it was standing stiffly away from its body. But when it saw him it spat at him, scratching angrily at the glass, and vanished.

Lady Madingley...heavens, how he had loved her! And, infernally as she had treated him, how passionately he wanted her now! Was all his trouble, then, to begin over again? Had that nightmare dawned anew on him? It was the cat's fault: the eyes of the cat had done it. Yet just now all his desire was blurred by this dullness of brain that was as unaccountable as the re-awakening of his desire. For months now he had drunk far more than he had drunk to-day, yet evening had seen him clear-headed, acute, master of himself, and revelling in the liberty that had come to him, and in the cool joy of creative vision. But to-night he stumbled and groped across the room.

The neutral-coloured light of dawn awoke him, and he got up at once, feeling still very drowsy, but in answer to some silent imperative call. The storm had altogether passed away, and a jewel of a morning star hung in a pale heaven. His room looked strangely unfamiliar to him, his own sensations were unfamiliar, there was a vagueness about things, a barrier between him and the world. One desire alone possessed him, to finish the portrait. All else, so he felt, he left to chance, or whatever laws regulate the world, those laws which choose that a certain thrush shall be caught by a certain cat, and choose one scapegoat out of a thousand, and let the rest go free.

Two hours later his servant called him, and found him gone from his room. So as the morning was so fair, he went out to lay breakfast in the shelter. The portrait was there, it had been dragged back into position by the clematis, but it was covered with strange scratches, as if the claws of some enraged animal or the nails perhaps of a man had furiously attacked it. Dick Alingham was there, too, lying very still in front of the disfigured canvas. Claws, also, or nails had attacked him, his throat was horribly mangled by them. But his hands were covered with paint, the nails of his fingers too were choked with it.

The Gardener

Two friends of mine, Hugh Grainger and his wife, had taken for a month of Christmas holiday the house in which we were to witness such strange manifestations, and when I received an invitation from them to spend a fortnight there I returned them an enthusiastic affirmative. Well already did I know that pleasant heathery country-side, and most intimate was my acquaintance with the subtle hazards of its most charming golf-links. Golf, I was given to understand, was to occupy the solid day for Hugh and me, so that Margaret should never be obliged to set her hand to the implements with which the game, so detestable to her, was conducted...

I arrived there while yet the daylight lingered, and as my hosts were out, I took a ramble round the place. The house and garden stood on a plateau facing south; below it were a couple of acres of pasture that sloped down to a vagrant stream crossed by a foot-bridge, by the side of which stood a thatched cottage with a vegetable patch surrounding it. A path ran close past this across the pasture from a wicket-gate in the garden, conducted you over the foot-bridge, and, so my remembered sense of geography told me, must constitute a short cut to the links that lay not half a mile beyond. The cottage itself was clearly on the land of the little estate, and I at once supposed it to be the gardener's house. What went against so obvious and simple a theory was that it appeared to be untenanted. No wreath of smoke, though the evening was chilly, curled from its chimneys, and, coming closer, I fancied it had that air of "waiting" about it which we so often conjure into unused habitations. There it stood, with no sign of life whatever about it, though ready, as its apparently perfect state of repair seemed to warrant, for fresh tenants to put the breath of life into it again. Its little garden, too, though the palings were neat and newly painted, told the same tale; the beds were untended and unweeded, and in the flower-border by the front door was a row of chrysanthemums, which had withered on their stems. But all this was but the impression of a moment, and I did not pause as I passed it, but crossed the foot-bridge and went on up the heathery slope that lay beyond. My geography was not at fault, for presently I saw the club-house just in front of me. Hugh no doubt would be just about coming in from his afternoon round, and so we would walk back together. On reaching the club-house, however, the steward told me that not five minutes before Mrs. Grainger had called in her car for her husband, and I therefore retraced my steps by the path along which I had already come. But I made a detour, as a golfer will, to walk up the fairway of the seventeenth and eighteenth holes just for the pleasure of recognition, and looked respectfully at the yawning sandpit which so inexorably guards the eighteenth green, wondering in what circumstances I should visit it next, whether with a step complacent and superior, knowing that my ball reposed safely on the green beyond, or with the heavy footfall of one who knows that laborious delving lies before him.

The light of the winter evening had faded fast, and when I crossed the foot-bridge on my return the dusk had gathered. To my right, just beside the path, lay the cottage, the whitewashed walls of which gleamed whitely in the gloaming; and as I turned my glance back from it to the rather narrow plank which bridged the stream I thought I caught out of the tail of my eye some light from one of its windows, which thus disproved my theory that it was untenanted. But when I looked directly at it again I saw that I was mistaken: some reflection in the glass of the red lines of sunset in the west must have deceived me, for in the inclement twilight it looked more desolate than ever. Yet I lingered by the wicket gate in its low palings, for though all exterior evidence bore witness to its emptiness, some inexplicable feeling assured me, quite irrationally, that this was not so, and that there was somebody there. Certainly there was nobody visible, but, so this absurd idea informed me, he might be at the back of the cottage concealed from me by the intervening structure, and, still oddly, still unreasonably, it became a matter of importance to my mind to ascertain whether this was so or not, so clearly had my perceptions told me that the place was empty, and so firmly had some conviction assured me that it was tenanted. To cover my inquisitiveness, in case there was someone there, I could inquire whether this path was a short cut to the house at which I was staying, and, rather rebelling at what I was doing, I went through the small garden, and rapped at the door. There was no answer, and, after waiting for a response to a second summons, and having tried the door and found it locked, I made the circuit of the house. Of course there was no one there, and I told myself that I was just like a man who looks under his bed for a burglar and would be beyond measure astonished if he found one.

My hosts were at the house when I arrived, and we spent a cheerful two hours before dinner in such desultory and eager conversation as is proper between friends who have not met for some time. Between Hugh Grainger and his wife it is always impossible to light on a subject which does not vividly interest one or other of them, and golf, politics, the needs of Russia, cooking, ghosts, the possible victory over Mount Everest, and the income tax were among the topics which we passionately discussed. With all these plates spinning, it was easy to whip up any one of them, and the subject of spooks generally was lighted upon again and again.

"Margaret is on the high road to madness," remarked Hugh on one of these occasions, "for she has begun using planchette. If you use planchette for six months, I am told, most careful doctors will conscientiously certify you as insane. She's got five months more before she goes to Bedlam."

"Does it work?" I asked.

"Yes, it says most interesting things," said Margaret. "It says things that never entered my head. We'll try it to-night."

"Oh, not to-night," said Hugh. "Let's have an evening off."

Margaret disregarded this.

"It's no use asking planchette questions," she went on, "because there is in your mind some sort of answer to them. If I ask whether it will be fine to-morrow, for instance, it is probably I--though indeed I don't mean to push--who makes the pencil say 'yes.'"

"And then it usually rains," remarked Hugh.

"Not always: don't interrupt. The interesting thing is to let the pencil write what it chooses."

"Very often it only makes loops and curves--though they may mean something--and every now and then a word comes, of the significance of which I have no idea whatever, so I clearly couldn't have suggested it. Yesterday evening, for instance, it wrote 'gardener' over and over again. Now what did that mean? The gardener here is a Methodist with a chin-beard. Could it have meant him? Oh, it's time to dress. Please don't be late, my cook is so sensitive about soup."

We rose, and some connection of ideas about "gardener" linked itself up in my mind.

"By the way, what's that cottage in the field by the foot-bridge?" I asked. "Is that the gardener's cottage?"

"It used to be," said Hugh. "But the chin-beard doesn't live there: in fact nobody lives there."

"It's empty. If I was owner here, I should put the chin-beard into it, and take the rent off his wages. Some people have no idea of economy. Why did you ask?"

I saw Margaret was looking at me rather attentively.

"Curiosity," I said. "Idle curiosity."

"I don't believe it was," said she.

"But it was," I said. "It was idle curiosity to know whether the house was inhabited. As I passed it, going down to the club-house, I felt sure it was empty, but coming back I felt so sure that there was someone there that I rapped at the door, and indeed walked round it."

Hugh had preceded us upstairs, as she lingered a little.

"And there was no one there?" she asked. "It's odd: I had just the same feeling as you about it."

"That explains planchette writing 'gardener' over and over again," said I. "You had the gardener's cottage on your mind."

"How ingenious!" said Margaret. "Hurry up and dress."

A gleam of strong moonlight between my drawn curtains when I went up to bed that night led me to look out. My room faced the garden and the fields which I had traversed that afternoon, and all was vividly illuminated by the full moon. The thatched cottage with its white walls close by the stream was very distinct, and once more, I suppose, the reflection of the light on the glass of one of its windows made it appear that the room was lit within. It struck me as odd that twice that day this illusion should have been presented to me, but now a yet odder thing happened.

Even as I looked the light was extinguished.

The morning did not at all bear out the fine promise of the clear night, for when I woke the wind was squealing, and sheets of rain from the south-west were dashed against my panes. Golf was wholly out of the question, and, though the violence of the storm abated a little in the afternoon, the rain dripped with a steady sullenness. But I wearied of indoors, and, since the two others entirely refused to set foot outside, I went forth mackintoshed to get a breath of air. By way of an object in my tramp, I took the road to the links in preference to the muddy short cut through the fields, with the intention of engaging a couple of caddies for Hugh and myself next morning, and lingered awhile over illustrated papers in the smoking-room. I must have read for longer than I knew, for a sudden beam of sunset light suddenly illuminated my page, and looking up, I saw that the rain had ceased, and that evening was fast coming on. So instead of taking the long detour by the road again, I set forth homewards by the path across the fields. That gleam of sunset was the last of the day, and once again, just as twenty-four hours ago, I crossed the foot-bridge in the gloaming. Till that moment, as far as I was aware, I had not thought at all about the cottage there, but now in a flash the light I had seen there last night, suddenly extinguished, recalled itself to my mind, and at the same moment I felt that invincible conviction that the cottage was tenanted. Simultaneously in these swift processes of thought I looked towards it, and saw standing by the door the figure of a man. In the dusk I could distinguish nothing of his face, if indeed it was turned to me, and only got the impression of a tallish fellow, thickly built. He opened the door, from which there came a dim light as of a lamp, entered, and shut it after him.

So then my conviction was right. Yet I had been distinctly told that the cottage was empty: who, then, was he that entered as if returning home? Once more, this time with a certain qualm of fear, I rapped on the door, intending to put some trivial question; and rapped again, this time more drastically, so that there could be no question that my summons was unheard. But still I got no reply, and finally I tried the handle of the door. It was locked. Then, with difficulty mastering an increasing terror, I made the circuit of the cottage, peering into each unshuttered window. All was dark within, though but two minutes ago I had seen the gleam of light escape from the opened door.

Just because some chain of conjecture was beginning to form itself in my mind, I made no allusion to this odd adventure, and after dinner Margaret, amid protests from Hugh, got out the planchette which had persisted in writing "gardener." My surmise was, of course, utterly fantastic, but I wanted to convey no suggestion of any sort to Margaret...For a long time the pencil skated over her paper making loops and curves and peaks like a temperature chart, and she had begun to yawn and weary over her experiment before any coherent word emerged. And then, in the oddest way, her head nodded forward and she seemed to have fallen asleep.

Hugh looked up from his book and spoke in a whisper to me.

"She fell asleep the other night over it," he said.

Margaret's eyes were closed, and she breathed the long, quiet breaths of slumber, and then her hand began to move with a curious firmness. Right across the big sheet of paper went a level line of writing, and at the end her hand stopped with a jerk, and she woke.

She looked at the paper.

"Hullo," she said. "Ah, one of you has been playing a trick on me!"

We assured her that this was not so, and she read what she had written.

"Gardener, gardener," it ran. "I am the gardener. I want to come in. I can't find her here."

"O Lord, that gardener again!" said Hugh.

Looking up from the paper, I saw Margaret's eyes fixed on mine, and even before she spoke I knew what her thought was.

"Did you come home by the empty cottage?" she asked.

"Yes: why?"

"Still empty?" she said in a low voice. "Or--or anything else?"

I did not want to tell her just what I had seen--or what, at any rate, I thought I had seen. If there was going to be anything odd, anything worth observation, it was far better that our respective impressions should not fortify each other.

"I tapped again, and there was no answer," I said.

Presently there was a move to bed: Margaret initiated it, and after she had gone upstairs Hugh and I went to the front door to interrogate the weather. Once more the moon shone in a clear sky, and we strolled out along the flagged path that fronted the house. Suddenly Hugh turned quickly and pointed to the angle of the house.

"Who on earth is that?" he said. "Look! There! He has gone round the corner."

I had but the glimpse of a tallish man of heavy build.

"Didn't you see him?" asked Hugh. "I'll just go round the house, and find him; I don't want anyone prowling round us at night. Wait here, will you, and if he comes round the other corner ask him what his business is."

Hugh had left me, in our stroll, close by the front door which was open, and there I waited until he should have made his circuit. He had hardly disappeared when I heard, quite distinctly, a rather quick but heavy footfall coming along the paved walk towards me from the opposite direction. But there was absolutely no one to be seen who made this sound of rapid walking.

Closer and closer to me came the steps of the invisible one, and then with a shudder of horror I felt somebody unseen push by me as I stood on the threshold. That shudder was not merely of the spirit, for the touch of him was that of ice on my hand. I tried to seize this impalpable intruder, but he slipped from me, and next moment I heard his steps on the parquet of the floor inside. Some door within opened and shut, and I heard no more of him. Next moment Hugh came running round the corner of the house from which the sound of steps had approached.

"But where is he?" he asked. "He was not twenty yards in front of me--a big, tall fellow."

"I saw nobody," I said. "I heard his step along the walk, but there was nothing to be seen."

"And then?" asked Hugh.

"Whatever it was seemed to brush by me, and go into the house," said I.

There had certainly been no sound of steps on the bare oak stairs, and we searched room after room through the ground floor of the house. The dining-room door and that of the smoking-room were locked, that into the drawing-room was open, and the only other door which could have furnished the impression of an opening and a shutting was that into the kitchen and servants' quarters. Here again our quest was fruitless; through pantry and scullery and boot-room and servants' hall we searched, but all was empty and quiet. Finally we came to the kitchen, which too was empty. But by the fire there was set a rocking-chair, and this was oscillating to and fro as if someone, lately sitting there, had just quitted it. There it stood gently rocking, and this seemed to convey the sense of a presence, invisible now, more than even the sight of him who surely had been sitting there could have done. I remember wanting to steady it and stop it, and yet my hand refused to go forth to it.

What we had seen, and in especial what we had not seen, would have been sufficient to furnish most people with a broken night, and assuredly I was not among the strong-minded exceptions. Long I lay wide-eyed and open-eared, and when at last I dozed I was plucked from the border-land of sleep by the sound, muffled but unmistakable, of someone moving about the house. It occurred to me that the steps might be those of Hugh conducting a lonely exploration, but even while I wondered a tap came at the door of communication between our rooms, and, in answer to my response, it appeared that he had come to see whether it was I thus uneasily wandering. Even as we spoke the step passed my door, and the stairs leading to the floor above creaked to its ascent. Next moment it sounded directly above our heads in some attics in the roof.

"Those are not the servants' bedrooms," said Hugh. "No one sleeps there. Let us look once more: it must be somebody."

With lit candles we made our stealthy way upstairs, and just when we were at the top of the flight, Hugh, a step ahead of me, uttered a sharp exclamation.

"But something is passing by me!" he said, and he clutched at the empty air. Even as he spoke, I experienced the same sensation, and the moment afterwards the stairs below us creaked again, as the unseen passed down.

All night long that sound of steps moved about the passages, as if someone was searching the house, and as I lay and listened that message which had come through the pencil of the planchette to Margaret's fingers occurred to me. "I want to come in. I cannot find her here."...

Indeed someone had come in, and was sedulous in his search. He was the gardener, it would seem. But what gardener was this invisible seeker, and for whom did he seek?

Even as when some bodily pain ceases it is difficult to recall with any vividness what the pain was like, so next morning, as I dressed, I found myself vainly trying to recapture the horror of the spirit which had accompanied these nocturnal adventures. I remembered that something within me had sickened as I watched the movements of the rocking-chair the night before and as I heard the steps along the paved way outside, and by that invisible pressure against me knew that someone had entered the house. But now in the sane and tranquil morning, and all day under the serene winter sun, I could not realise what it had been. The presence, like the bodily pain, had to be there for the realisation of it, and all day it was absent. Hugh felt the same; he was even disposed to be humorous on the subject.

"Well, he's had a good look," he said, "whoever he is, and whomever he was looking for. By the way, not a word to Margaret, please. She heard nothing of these perambulations, nor of the entry of--of whatever it was. Not gardener, anyhow: who ever heard of a gardener spending his time walking about the house? If there were steps all over the potato-patch, I might have been with you."

Margaret had arranged to drive over to have tea with some friends of hers that afternoon, and in consequence Hugh and I refreshed ourselves at the club-house after our game, and it was already dusk when for the third day in succession I passed homewards by the whitewashed cottage. But to-night I had no sense of it being subtly occupied; it stood mournfully desolate, as is the way of untenanted houses, and no light nor semblance of such gleamed from its windows.

Hugh, to whom I had told the odd impressions I had received there, gave them a reception as flippant as that which he had accorded to the memories of the night, and he was still being humorous about them when we came to the door of the house.

"A psychic disturbance, old boy," he said. "Like a cold in the head. Hullo, the door's locked."

He rang and rapped, and from inside came the noise of a turned key and withdrawn bolts.

"What's the door locked for?" he asked his servant who opened it.

The man shifted from one foot to the other.

"The bell rang half an hour ago, sir," he said, "and when I came to answer it there was a man standing outside, and--"

"Well?" asked Hugh.

"I didn't like the looks of him, sir," he said, "and I asked him his business. He didn't say anything, and then he must have gone pretty smartly away, for I never saw him go."

"Where did he seem to go?" asked Hugh, glancing at me.

"I can't rightly say, sir. He didn't seem to go at all. Something seemed to brush by me."

"That'll do," said Hugh rather sharply.

Margaret had not come in from her visit, but when soon after the crunch of the motor wheels was heard Hugh reiterated his wish that nothing should be said to her about the impression which now, apparently, a third person shared with us. She came in with a flush of excitement on her face.

"Never laugh at my planchette again," she said. "I've heard the most extraordinary story from Maud Ashfield--horrible, but so frightfully interesting."

"Out with it," said Hugh.

"Well, there was a gardener here," she said. "He used to live at that little cottage by the foot-bridge, and when the family were up in London he and his wife used to be caretakers and live here."

Hugh's glance and mine met: then he turned away.

I knew, as certainly as if I was in his mind, that his thoughts were identical with my own.

"He married a wife much younger than himself," continued Margaret, "and gradually he became frightfully jealous of her. And one day in a fit of passion he strangled her with his own hands. A little while after someone came to the cottage, and found him sobbing over her, trying to restore her. They went for the police, but before they came he had cut his own throat. Isn't it all horrible? But surely it's rather curious that the planchette said 'Gardener. I am the gardener. I want to come in. I can't find her here.' You see I knew nothing about it. I shall do planchette again to-night. Oh dear me, the post goes in half an hour, and I have a whole budget to send. But respect my planchette for the future, Hughie."

We talked the situation out when she had gone, but Hugh, unwillingly convinced and yet unwilling to admit that something more than coincidence lay behind that "planchette nonsense," still insisted that Margaret should be told nothing of what we had heard and seen in the house last night, and of the strange visitor who again this evening, so we must conclude, had made his entry.

"She'll be frightened," he said, "and she'll begin imagining things. As for the planchette, as likely as not it will do nothing but scribble and make loops. What's that? Yes: come in!"

There had come from somewhere in the room one sharp, peremptory rap. I did not think it came from the door, but Hugh, when no response replied to his words of admittance, jumped up and opened it. He took a few steps into the hall outside, and returned.

"Didn't you hear it?" he asked.

"Certainly. No one there?"

"Not a soul."

Hugh came back to the fireplace and rather irritably threw a cigarette which he had just lit into the fender.

"That was rather a nasty jar," he observed; "and if you ask me whether I feel comfortable, I can tell you I never felt less comfortable in my life. I'm frightened, if you want to know, and I believe you are too."

I hadn't the smallest intention of denying this, and he went on.

"We've got to keep a hand on ourselves," he said. "There's nothing so infectious as fear, and Margaret mustn't catch it from us. But there's something more than our fear, you know."

"Something has got into the house and we're up against it. I never believed in such things before."

"Let's face it for a minute. What is it anyhow?"

"If you want to know what I think it is," said I, "I believe it to be the spirit of the man who strangled his wife and then cut his throat. But I don't see how it can hurt us. We're afraid of our own fear really."

"But we're up against it," said Hugh. "And what will it do? Good Lord, if I only knew what it would do I shouldn't mind. It's the not knowing...Well, it's time to dress."

Margaret was in her highest spirits at dinner. Knowing nothing of the manifestations of that presence which had taken place in the last twenty-four hours, she thought it absorbingly interesting that her planchette should have "guessed" (so ran her phrase) about the gardener, and from that topic she flitted to an equally interesting form of patience for three which her friend had showed her, promising to initiate us into it after dinner. This she did, and, not knowing that we both above all things wanted to keep planchette at a distance, she was delighted with the success of her game. But suddenly she observed that the evening was burning rapidly away, and swept the cards together at the conclusion of a hand.

"Now just half an hour of planchette," she said.

"Oh, mayn't we play one more hand?" asked Hugh. "It's the best game I've seen for years."

"Planchette will be dismally slow after this."

"Darling, if the gardener will only communicate again, it won't be slow," said she.

"But it is such drivel," said Hugh.

"How rude you are! Read your book, then."

Margaret had already got out her machine and a sheet of paper, when Hugh rose.

"Please don't do it to-night, Margaret," he said.

"But why? You needn't attend."

"Well, I ask you not to, anyhow," said he.

Margaret looked at him closely.

"Hughie, you've got something on your mind," she said. "Out with it. I believe you're nervous. You think there is something queer about. What is it?"

I could see Hugh hesitating as to whether to tell her or not, and I gathered that he chose the chance of her planchette inanely scribbling.

"Go on, then," he said.

Margaret hesitated: she clearly did not want to vex Hugh, but his insistence must have seemed to her most unreasonable.

"Well, just ten minutes," she said, "and I promise not to think of gardeners."

She had hardly laid her hand on the board when her head fell forward, and the machine began moving. I was sitting close to her, and as it rolled steadily along the paper the writing became visible.

"I have come in," it ran, "but still I can't find her. Are you hiding her? I will search the room where you are."

What else was written but still concealed underneath the planchette I did not know, for at that moment a current of icy air swept round the room, and at the door, this time unmistakably, came a loud, peremptory knock. Hugh sprang to his feet.

"Margaret, wake up," he said, "something is coming!"

The door opened, and there moved in the figure of a man. He stood just within the door, his head bent forward, and he turned it from side to side, peering, it would seem, with eyes staring and infinitely sad, into every corner of the room.

"Margaret, Margaret," cried Hugh again.

But Margaret's eyes were open too; they were fixed on this dreadful visitor.

"Be quiet, Hughie," she said below her breath, rising as she spoke. The ghost was now looking directly at her. Once the lips above the thick, rust-coloured beard moved, but no sound came forth, the mouth only moved and slavered. He raised his head, and, horror upon horror, I saw that one side of his neck was laid open in a red, glistening gash...

For how long that pause continued, when we all three stood stiff and frozen in some deadly inhibition to move or speak, I have no idea: I suppose that at the utmost it was a dozen seconds.

Then the spectre turned, and went out as it had come. We heard his steps pass along the parqueted floor; there was the sound of bolts withdrawn from the front door, and with a crash that shook the house it slammed to.

"It's all over," said Margaret. "God have mercy on him!"

Now the reader may put precisely what construction he pleases on this visitation from the dead.

He need not, indeed, consider it to have been a visitation from the dead at all, but say that there had been impressed on the scene, where this murder and suicide happened, some sort of emotional record, which in certain circumstances could translate itself into images visible and invisible. Waves of ether, or what not, may conceivably retain the impress of such scenes; they may be held, so to speak, in solution, ready to be precipitated. Or he may hold that the spirit of the dead man indeed made itself manifest, revisiting in some sort of spiritual penance and remorse the place where his crime was committed. Naturally, no materialist will entertain such an explanation for an instant, but then there is no one so obstinately unreasonable as the materialist. Beyond doubt a dreadful deed was done there, and Margaret's last utterance is not inapplicable.

The China Bowl

I had long been on the look-out for one of the small houses at the south end of that delectable oblong called Barrett's Square, but for many months there was never revealed to me that which I so much I desired to see--namely, a notice-board advertising that one of these charming little abodes was to be let.

At length, however, in the autumn of the current year, in one of my constant passages through the square, I saw what my eye had so long starved for, and within ten minutes I was in the office of the agent in whose hands the disposal of No. 29 had been placed.

A communicative clerk informed me that the present lessee, Sir Arthur Bassenthwaite, was anxious to get rid of the remainder of his lease as soon as possible, for the house had painful associations for him, owing to the death of his wife, which had taken place there not long before.

He was a wealthy man, so I was informed, Lady Bassenthwaite having been a considerable heiress, and was willing to take what is professionally known as a ridiculously low price, in order to get the house off his hand without delay. An order 'to view' was thereupon given me, and a single visit next morning was sufficient to show that this was precisely what I had been looking for.

Why Sir Arthur should be so suddenly anxious to get rid of it, at a price which certainly was extremely moderate, was no concern of mine, provided the drains were in good order, and within a week the necessary business connected with the transference of the lease was arranged. The house was in excellent repair, and less than a month from the time I had first seen the notice-board up, I was ecstatically established there.

I had not been in the house more than a week or two when, one afternoon, I was told that Sir Arthur had called, and would like to see me if I was disengaged. He was shown up, and I found myself in the presence of one of the most charming men I have ever had the good fortune to meet.

The motive of his call, it appeared, was of the politest nature, for he wished to be assured that I found the house comfortable and that it suited me. He intimated that it would be a pleasure to him to see round, and together we went over the whole house, with the exception of one room.

This was the front bedroom on the third floor, the largest of the two spare rooms, and at the door, as I grasped the handle, he stopped me.

'You will excuse me,' he said, 'for not coming in here. The room, I may tell you, has the most painful associations for me.'

This was sufficiently explicit; I made no doubt that it was in this room that his wife had died.

It was a lovely October afternoon, and, having made the tour of the house, we went out into the little garden with its tiled walk that lay at the back, and was one of the most attractive features of the place. Low brick walls enclosed it, separating it on each side from my neighbours, and at the bottom from the pedestrian thoroughfare that ran past the back of the row of houses.

Sir Arthur lingered here some little while, lost, I suppose, in regretful memories of the days when perhaps he and his companion planned and executed the decoration of the little plot.

Indeed, he hinted as much when, shortly after, he took his leave.

'There is so much here,' he said, 'that is very intimately bound up with me. I thank you a thousand times for letting me see the little garden again.' And once more, as he turned to go into the house, his eyes looked steadfastly and wistfully down the bright borders.

The regulations about the lighting of houses in London had some little while previously demanded a more drastic dusk, and a night or two later, as I returned home after dinner through the impenetrable obscurity of the streets, I was horrified to find a bright light streaming cheerfully from the upper windows in my house, with no blinds to obscure it.

It came from the front bedroom on the third floor, and, letting myself in, I proceeded hurriedly upstairs to quench this forbidden glow. But when I entered, I found the room in darkness, and, on turning up the lights myself, I saw that the blinds were drawn down, so that even if it had been lit, I could not have seen from outside the illumination which had made me hasten upstairs.

An explanation easily occurred to me: no doubt the light I had seen did not come from my house, but from windows of a house adjoining. I had only given one glance at it, and with this demonstration that I had been mistaken, I gave no further conscious thought to the matter. But subconsciously I felt that I knew that I had made no mistake: I had not in that hurried glance confused the windows of the house next door with my own; it was this room that had been lit.

I had moved into the house, as I have said, with extraordinary expedition, and for the next day or two I was somewhat busily engaged, after my day's work was over, in sorting out and largely destroying accumulations of old books and papers, which I had not had time to go through before my move. Among them I came across an illustrated magazine which I had kept for some forgotten reason, and turning over the pages to try to ascertain why I had preserved it, I suddenly came across a picture of my own back-garden. The title at the top of the page showed me that the article in question was an interview with Lady Bassenthwaite, and her portrait and that of her husband made a frontispiece to it.

The coincidence was a curious one, for here I read about the house which I now occupied, and saw what it had been like in the reign of its late owners. But I did not spend long over it, and added the magazine to the pile of papers destined for destruction. This grew steadily, and when I had finished turning out the cupboard which I had resolved to empty before going to bed, I found it was already an hour or more past midnight.

I had been so engrossed in my work that I had let the fire go out, and myself get hungry, and went into the dining-room, which opened into the little back-garden, to see if the fire still smouldered there, and a biscuit could be found in the cupboard. In both respects I was in luck, and whilst eating and warming myself, I suddenly thought I heard a step on the tiled walk in the garden outside.

I quickly went to the window and drew aside the thick curtain, letting all the light in the room pour out into the garden, and there, beyond doubt, was a man bending over one of the beds.

Startled by this illumination, he rose, and without looking round, ran to the end of the little yard and, with surprising agility, vaulted on to the top of the wall and disappeared.

But at the last second, as he sat silhouetted there, I saw his face in the shaded light of a gas-lamp outside, and, to my indescribable astonishment, I recognized Sir Arthur Bassenthwaite. The glimpse was instantaneous, but I was sure I was not mistaken, any more than I had been mistaken about the light which came from the bedroom that looked out on to the square.

But whatever tender associations Sir Arthur had with the garden that had once been his, it was not seemly that he should adopt such means of indulging them. Moreover, where Sir Arthur might so easily come, there, too, might others whose intentions were less concerned with sentiment than with burglary.

In any case, I did not choose that my garden should have such easy access from outside, and next morning I ordered a pretty stiff barrier of iron spikes to be erected along the outer wall. If Sir Arthur wished to muse in the garden, I should be delighted to give him permission, as, indeed, he must have known from the cordiality which I was sure I showed him when he called, but this method of his seemed to me irregular. And I observed next evening, without any regret at all, that my order had been promptly executed. At the same time I felt an invincible curiosity to know for certain if it was merely for the sake of a solitary midnight vigil that he had come.

I was expecting the arrival of my friend Hugh Grainger the next week, to stay a night or two with me, and since the front spare room, which I proposed to give him, had not at present been slept in, I gave orders that a bed should be made up there the next night for me, so that I could test with my own vile body whether a guest would be comfortable there.

This can only be proved by personal experience. Though there may be a table apparently convenient to the head of the bed, though the dressing-table may apparently be properly disposed, though it seem as if the lighting was rightly placed for reading in bed, and for the quenching of it afterwards without disturbance, yet practice and not theory is the only method of settling such questions, and next night accordingly I both dressed for dinner in this front spare room, and went to bed there.

Everything seemed to work smoothly; the room itself had a pleasant and restful air about it, and the bed exceedingly comfortable, I fell asleep almost as soon as I had put out the electric light, which I had found adequate for reading small print. To the best of my knowledge, neither the thought of the last occupant of the room nor of the light that I believed I had seen burning there one night entered my head at all.

I fell asleep, as I say, at once, but instantly that theatre of the brain, on the boards of which dreams are transacted, was brightly illuminated for me, and the curtain went up on one of those appalling nightmare-pieces which we can only vaguely remember afterwards.

There was the sense of flight--clogged, impotent flight from before some hideous spiritual force--the sense of powerlessness to keep away from the terror that gained on me, the strangling desire to scream, and soon the blessed dawning consciousness that it was but with a dream that I wrestled.

I began to know that I was lying in bed, and that my terrors were imaginary, but the trouble was not over yet, for with all my efforts I could not raise my head from the pillow nor open my eyes.

Then, as I drew nearer to the boundaries of waking, I became aware that even when the spell of my dream was altogether broken I should not be free. For through my eyelids, which I knew had closed in a darkened room, there now streamed in a vivid light, and remembering for the first time what I had seen from the square outside, I knew that when I opened them they would look out on to a lit room, peopled with who knew what phantoms of the dead or living.

I lay there for a few moments after I had recovered complete consciousness, with eyes still closed, and felt the trickle of sweat on my forehead. That horror I knew was not wholly due to the self-coined nightmare of my brain; it was the horror of expectancy more than of retrospect.

And then curiosity, sheer stark curiosity, to know what was happening on the other side of the curtain of my eyelids prevailed, and I sat and looked.

In the armchair just opposite the foot of my bed sat Lady Bassenthwaite, whose picture I had seen in the illustrated magazine. It simply was she; there could be no doubt whatever about it.

She was dressed in a bedgown, and in her hand was a small fluted china bowl with a cover and a saucer. As I looked she took the cover off, and began to feed herself with a spoon. She took some half-dozen mouthfuls, and then replaced the cover again. As she did this she turned full face towards where I lay, looking straight at me, and already the shadow of death was fallen on her.

Then she rose feebly, wearily, and took a step towards the bed. As she did this, the light in the room, from whatever source it came, suddenly faded, and I found myself looking out into impenetrable darkness.

My curiosity for the present was more than satisfied, and in a couple of minutes I had transferred myself to the room below.

Hugh Grainger, the ruling passion of whose life is crime and ghosts, arrived next day, and I poured into an eager ear the whole history of the events here narrated.

'Of course, I'll sleep in the room,' he said at the conclusion. 'Put another bed in it, can't you, and sleep there, too. A couple of simultaneous witnesses of the same phenomena are ten times more valuable than one. Or do you funk?' he added as a kind afterthought.

'I funk, but I will,' I said.

'And are you sure it wasn't all part of your dream?' he asked.

'Absolutely positive.'

Hugh's eye glowed with pleasure.

'I funk, too,' he said. 'I funk horribly. But that's part of the allurement. It's so difficult to get frightened nowadays. All but a few things are explained and accounted for. What one fears is the unknown. No one knows yet what ghosts are, or why they appear, or to whom.

He took a turn up and down the room.

'And what do you make of Sir Arthur creeping into your garden at night?' he asked. 'Is there any possible connection?'

'Not as far as I can see. What connection could there be?'

'It isn't very obvious certainly. I really don't know why I asked. And you liked him?'

'Immensely. But not enough to let him get over my garden wall at midnight,' said I.

Hugh laughed.

'That would certainly imply a considerable degree of confidence and affection,' he said.

I had caused another bed to be moved into Hugh's room, and that night, after he had put out the light, we talked awhile and then relapsed into silence. It was cold, and I watched the fire on the hearth die down from flame into glowing coal, and from glow into clinkering ash, while nothing disturbed the peaceful atmosphere of the quiet room. Then it seemed to me as if something broke in, and instead of lying tranquilly awake, I found a certain horror of expectancy, some note of nightmare begin to hum through my waking consciousness. I heard Hugh toss and turn and turn again, and at length he spoke.

'I say, I'm feeling fairly beastly,' he said, 'and yet there's nothing to see or hear.'

'Same with me,' said I.

'Do you mind if I turn up the light a minute, and have a look round?' he asked.

'Not a bit.'

He fumbled at the switch, the room leapt into light, and he sat up in bed frowning. Everything was quite as usual, the bookcase, the chairs, on one of which he had thrown his clothes; there was nothing that differentiated this room from hundreds of others where the occupants lay quietly sleeping.

'It's queer,' he said, and switched off the light again.

There is nothing harder than to measure time in the dark, but I do not think it was long that I lay there with the sense of nightmare growing momentarily on me before he spoke again in an odd, cracked voice.

'It's coming,' he said.

Almost as soon as he spoke I saw that the thick darkness of the room was sensibly thinning.

The blackness was less complete, though I could hardly say that light began to enter. Then by degrees I saw the shape of chairs, the lines of the fireplace, the end of Hugh's bed begin to outline themselves, and as I watched the darkness vanished altogether, as if a lamp had been turned up.

And in the chair at the foot of Hugh's bed sat Lady Bassenthwaite, and again putting aside the cover of her dish, she sipped the contents of the bowl, and at the end rose feebly, wearily, as in mortal sickness. She looked at Hugh, and turning, she looked at me, and through the shadow of death that lay over her face, I thought that in her eyes was a demand, or at least a statement of her case. They were not angry, they did not cry for justice, but the calm inexorable gaze of justice that must be done was there...Then the light faded and died out.

I heard a rustle from the other bed and the springs creaked.

'Good Lord,' said Hugh, 'where's the light?'

His fingers fumbled and found it, and I saw that he was already out of bed, with streaming forehead and chattering teeth.

'I know now,' he said. 'I half guessed before. Come downstairs.'

Downstairs we went, and he turned up all the passage lights as we passed. He led the way into the dining room, picking up the poker and the shovel as he went by the fireplace, and he threw open the door into the garden. I switched up the light, which threw a bright square of illumination over the garden.

'Where did you see Sir Arthur?' he said. 'Where? Exactly where?'

Still not guessing what he sought, I pointed out to him the spot, and loosening the earth with the poker, he dug into the bed. Once again he plunged the poker down, and as he removed the earth I heard the shovel grate on something hard. And then I guessed.

Already Hugh was at work with his fingers in the earth, and slowly and carefully he drew out fragments of a broken china cover. Then, delving again, he raised from the hole a fluted china bowl. And I knew I had seen it before, once and twice.

We carried this indoors and cleaned the earth from it. All over the bottom of the bowl was a layer of some thick porridge-like substance, and a portion of this I sent next day to a chemist, asking him for his analysis of it. The basis of it proved to be oatmeal, and in it was mixed a considerable quantity of arsenic.

Hugh and I were together in my little sitting room close to the front door, where on the table stood the china bowl with the fragments of its cover and saucer, when this report was brought to us, and we read it together. The afternoon was very dark and we stood close to the window to decipher the minute handwriting, when there passed the figure of Sir Arthur Bassenthwaite. He saw me, waved his hand, and a moment afterwards the front door bell rang.

'Let him come in,' said Hugh. 'Let him see that on the table.'

Next moment my servant entered, and asked if the caller might see me.

'Let him see it,' repeated Hugh. 'The chances are that we shall know if he sees it unexpectedly.'

There was a moment's pause while in the hall, I suppose, Sir Arthur was taking off his coat.

Outside, some few doors off, a traction engine, which had passed a minute before, stopped, and began slowly coming backwards again, crunching the newly-laid stones. Sir Arthur entered.

'I ventured to call,' he began, and then his glance fell on the bowl. In one second the very aspect of humanity was stripped from his face. His mouth drooped open, his eyes grew monstrous and protruding, and what had been the pleasant, neat-featured face of a man was a mask of terror, a gargoyle, a nightmare countenance. Even before the door that had been open to admit him was closed, he had turned and gone with a crouching, stumbling run from the room, and I heard him at the latch of the front door.

Whether what followed was design or accident, I shall never know, for from the window I saw him fall forward, almost as if he threw himself there, straight in front of the broad crunching wheels of the traction engine, and before the driver could stop, or even think of stopping, the iron roller had gone over his head.

Gavon's Eve

It is only the largest kind of ordnance map that records the existence of the village of Gavon, in the shire of Sutherland, and it is perhaps surprising that any map on whatever scale should mark so small and huddled a group of huts, set on a bare, bleak headland between moor and sea, and, so one would have thought, of no import at all to any who did not happen to live there. But the river Gavon, on the right bank of which stand this half-dozen of chimneyless and wind-swept habitations, is a geographical fact of far greater interest to outsiders, for the salmon there are heavy fish, the mouth of the river is clear of nets, and all the way up to Gavon Loch, some six miles inland, the coffee-coloured water lies in pool after deep pool, which verge, if the river is in order and the angler moderately sanguine, on a fishing probability amounting almost to a certainty. In any case, during the first fortnight of September last I had no blank day on those delectable waters, and up till the 15th of that month there was no day on which some one at the lodge in which I was stopping did not land a fish out of the famous Picts' pool. But after the 15th that pool was not fished again. The reason why is here set forward.

The river at this point, after some hundred yards of rapid, makes a sudden turn round a rocky angle, and plunges madly into the pool itself. Very deep water lies at the head of it, but deeper still further down on the east side, where a portion of the stream flicks back again in a swift dark backwater towards the top of the pool again. It is fishable only from the western bank, for to the east, above this backwater, a great wall of black and basaltic rock, heaved up no doubt by some fault in strata, rises sheer from the river to the height of some sixty feet. It is in fact nearly precipitous on both sides, heavily serrated at the top, and of so curious a thinness, that at about the middle of it where a fissure breaks its topmost edge, and some twenty feet from the top, there exists a long hole, a sort of lancet window, one would say, right through the rock, so that a slit of daylight can be seen through it. Since, therefore, no one would care to cast his line standing perched on that razor-edged eminence, the pool must needs be fished from the western bank. A decent fly, however, will cover it all.

It is on the western bank that there stand the remains of that which gave its title to the pool, namely, the ruins of a Pict castle, built out of rough and scarcely hewn masonry, unmortared but on a certain large and impressive scale, and in a very well-preserved condition considering its extreme antiquity. It is circular in shape and measures some twenty yards of diameter in its internal span. A staircase of large blocks with a rise of at least a foot leads up to the main gate, and opposite this on the side towards the river is another smaller postern through which down a rather hazardously steep slope a scrambling path, where progress demands both caution and activity, conducts to the head of the pool which lies immediately beneath it. A gate-chamber still roofed over exists in the solid wall: inside there are foundation indications of three rooms, and in the centre of all a very deep hole, probably a well. Finally, just outside the postern leading to the river is a small artificially levelled platform, some twenty feet across, as if made to support some super-incumbent edifice. Certain stone slabs and blocks are dispersed over it.

Brora, the post-town of Gavon, lies some six miles to the south-west, and from it a track over the moor leads to the rapids immediately above the Picts' pool, across which by somewhat extravagant striding from boulder to boulder a man can pass dry-foot when the river is low, and make his way up a steep path to the north of the basaltic rock, and so to the village. But this transit demands a steady head, and at the best is a somewhat giddy passage. Otherwise the road between it and Brora lies in a long detour higher up the moor, passing by the gates of Gavon Lodge, where I was stopping. For some vague and ill-defined reason the pool itself and the Picts' Castle had an uneasy reputation on the countryside, and several times trudging back from a day's fishing I have known my gillie take a longish circuit, though heavy with fish, rather than make this short cut in the dusk by the castle. On the first occasion when Sandy, a strapping yellow-bearded viking of twenty-five, did this he gave as a reason that the ground round about the castle was "mossy," though as a God-fearing man he must have known he lied. But on another occasion he was more frank, and said that the Picts' pool was "no canny" after sunset. I am now inclined to agree with him, though, when he lied about it, I think it was because as a God-fearing man he feared the devil also.

It was on the evening of September 14 that I was walking back with my host, Hugh Graham, from the forest beyond the lodge. It had been a day unseasonably hot for the time of year, and the hills were blanketed with soft, furry clouds. Sandy, the gillie of whom I have spoken, was behind with the ponies, and, idly enough, I told Hugh about his strange distaste for the Picts' pool after sunset. He listened, frowning a little.

"That's curious," he said. "I know there is some dim local superstition about the place, but last year certainly Sandy used to laugh at it. I remember asking him what ailed the place, and he said he thought nothing about the rubbish folk talked. But this year you say he avoids it."

"On several occasions with me he has done so."

Hugh smoked a while in silence, striding noiselessly over the dusky fragrant heather.

"Poor chap," he said, "I don't know what to do about him. He's becoming useless."

"Drink?" I asked.

"Yes, drink in a secondary manner. But trouble led to drink, and trouble, I am afraid, is leading him to worse than drink."

"The only thing worse than drink is the devil," I remarked.

"Precisely. That's where he is going. He goes there often."

"What on earth do you mean?" I asked.

"Well, it's rather curious," said Hugh. "You know I dabble a bit in folklore and local superstition, and I believe I am on the track of something odder than odd. Just wait a moment."

We stood there in the gathering dusk till the ponies laboured up the hillside to us, Sandy with his six feet of lithe strength strolling easily beside them up the steep brae, as if his long day's trudging had but served to half awaken his dormant powers of limb.

"Going to see Mistress Macpherson again tonight?" asked Hugh.

"Aye, puir body," said Sandy. "She's auld, and she's lone."

"Very kind of you, Sandy," said Hugh, and we walked on.

"What then?" I asked when the ponies had fallen behind again.

"Why, superstition lingers here," said Hugh, "and it's supposed she's a witch. To be quite candid with you, the thing interests me a good deal. Supposing you asked me, on oath, whether I believed in witches, I should say 'No.' But if you asked me again, on oath, whether I suspected I believed in them, I should, I think, say 'Yes.' And the fifteenth of this month--to-morrow--is Gavon's Eve."

"And what in Heaven's name is that?" I asked. "And who is Gavon? And what's the trouble?"

"Well, Gavon is the person, I suppose, not saint, who is what we should call the eponymous hero of this district. And the trouble is Sandy's trouble. Rather a long story. But there's a long mile in front of us yet, if you care to be told."

During that mile I heard. Sandy had been engaged a year ago to girl of Gavon who was in service at Inverness. In March last he had gone, without giving notice, to see her, and as he walked up the street in which her mistress's house stood, had met her suddenly face to face, in company with a man whose clipped speech betrayed him English, whose manner a kind of gentleman. He had a flourish of his hat for Sandy, pleasure to see him, and scarcely any need of explanation as to how he came to be walking with Catrine. It was the most natural thing possible, for a city like Inverness boasted its innocent urbanities, and a girl could stroll with a man. And for the time, since also Catrine was so frankly pleased to see him, Sandy was satisfied. But after his return to Gavon, suspicion, fungus-like, grew rank in his mind, with the result that a month ago he had, with infinite pains and blottings, written a letter to Catrine, urging her return and immediate marriage. Thereafter it was known that she had left Inverness; it was known that she had arrived by train at Brora. From Brora she had started to walked across the moor by the path leading just above the Picts' Castle, crossing the rapids to Gavon, leaving her box to be sent by the carrier. But at Gavon she had never arrived. Also it was said that, although it was hot afternoon, she wore a big cloak.

By this time we had come to the lodge, the lights of which showed dim and blurred through the thick hill-mists that had streamed sullenly down from the higher ground.

"And the rest," said Hugh, "which is as fantastic as this is sober fact, I will tell you later."

Now, a fruit-bearing determination to go to bed is, to my mind, as difficult to ripen as a fruit-bearing determination to get up, and in spite of our long day, I was glad when Hugh (the rest of the men having yawned themselves out of the smoking-room) came back from the hospitable dispensing of bedroom candlesticks with a briskness that denoted that, as far as he was concerned, the distressing determination was not imminent.

"As regards Sandy," I suggested.

"Ah, I also was thinking of that," he said. "Well, Catrine Gordon left Brora, and never arrived here. That is fact. Now for what remains. Have you any remembrance of a woman always alone walking about the moor by the loch? I think I once called your attention to her."

"Yes, I remember," I said. "Not Catrine, surely; a very old woman, awful to look at.

"Moustache, whiskers, and muttering to herself. Always looking at the ground, too."

"Yes, that is she--not Catrine. Catrine! My word, a May morning! But the other--it is Mrs. Macpherson, reputed witch. Well, Sandy trudges there, a mile and more away, every night to see her. You know Sandy: Adonis of the north. Now, can you account by any natural explanation for that fact? That he goes off after a long day to see an old hag in the hills?"

"It would seem unlikely," said I.

"Unlikely! Well, yes, unlikely."

Hugh got up from his chair and crossed the room to where a bookcase of rather fusty-looking volumes stood between windows. He took a small morocco--backed book from a top shelf.

"Superstitions of Sutherlandshire," he said, as he handed it to me. "Turn to page 128, and read."

"September 15 appears to have been the date of what we may call this devil festival. On the night of that day the powers of darkness held pre-eminent dominion, and over-rode for any who were abroad that night and invoked their aid, the protective Providence of Almighty God.

"Witches, therefore, above all, were peculiarly potent. On this night any witch could entice to herself the heart and the love of any young man who consulted her on matters of philtre or love charm, with the result that on any night in succeeding years of the same date, he, though he was lawfully affianced and wedded, would for that night be hers. If, however, he should call on the name of God through any sudden grace of the Spirit, her charm would be of no avail. On this night, too, all witches had the power by certain dreadful incantations and indescribable profanities, to raise from the dead those who had committed suicide."

"Top of the next page," said Hugh. "Leave out this next paragraph; it does not bear on this last."

"Near a small village in this country," I read, "called Gavon, the moon at midnight is said to shine through a certain gap or fissure in a wall of rock close beside the river on to the ruins of a Pict castle, so that the light of its beams falls on to a large flat stone erected there near the gate, and supposed by some to be an ancient and pagan altar. At that moment, so the superstition still lingers in the countryside, the evil and malignant spirits which hold sway on Gavon's Eve, are at the zenith of their powers, and those who invoke their aid at this moment and in this place, will, though with infinite peril to their immortal souls, get all that they desire of them."

The paragraph on the subject ended here, and I shut the book.

"Well?" I asked.

"Under favourable circumstances two and two make four," said Hugh.

"And four means--"

"This. Sandy is certainly in consultation with a woman who is supposed to be a witch, whose path no crofter will cross after nightfall. He wants to learn, at whatever cost, poor devil, what happened to Catrine. Thus I think it more than possible that to-morrow, at midnight, there will be folk by the Picts' pool. There is another curious thing. I was fishing yesterday, and just opposite the river gate of the castle, someone has set up a great flat stone, which has been dragged (for I noticed the crushed grass) from the debris at the bottom of the slope."

"You mean that the old hag is going to try to raise the body of Catrine, if she is dead?"

"Yes, and I mean to see myself what happens. Come too."

The next day Hugh and I fished down the river from the lodge, taking with us not Sandy, but another gillie, and ate our lunch on the slope of the Picts' Castle after landing a couple of fish there. Even as Hugh had said, a great flat slab of stone had been dragged on to the platform outside the river gate of the castle, where it rested on certain rude supports, which, now that it was in place, seemed certainly designed to receive it. It was also exactly opposite that lancet window in the basaltic rock across the pool, so that if the moon at midnight did shine through it, the light would fall on the stone. This, then, was the almost certain scene of the incantations.

Below the platform, as I have said, the ground fell rapidly away to the level of the pool, which owing to rain on the hills was running very high, and, streaked with lines of greyish bubbles, poured down in amazing and ear-filling volume. But directly underneath the steep escarpment of rock on the far side of the pool it lay foamless and black, a still backwater of great depth. Above the altar-like erection again the ground rose up seven rough-hewn steps to the gate itself, on each side of which, to the height of about four feet, ran the circular wall of the castle. Inside again were the remains of partition walls between the three chambers, and it was in the one nearest to the river gate that we determined to conceal ourselves that night. From there, should the witch and Sandy keep tryst at the altar, any sound of movement would reach us, and through the aperture of the gate itself we could see, concealed in the shadow of the wall, whatever took place at the altar or down below at the pool. The lodge, finally, was but a short ten minutes away, if one went in the direct line, so that by starting at a quarter to twelve that night, we could enter the Picts' Castle by the gate away from the river, thus not betraying our presence to those who might be waiting for the moment when the moon should shine through the lancet window in the wall of rock on to the altar in front of the river gate.

Night fell very still and windless, and when not long before midnight we let ourselves silently out of the lodge, though to the east the sky was clear, a black continent of cloud was creeping up from the west, and had now nearly reached the zenith. Out of the remote fringes of it occasional lightning winked, and the growl of very distant thunder sounded drowsily at long intervals after.

But it seemed to me as if another storm hung over our heads, ready every moment to burst, for the oppression in the air was of a far heavier quality than so distant a disturbance could have accounted for.

To the east, however, the sky was still luminously clear; the curiously hard edges of the western cloud were star-embroidered, and by the dove-coloured light in the east it was evident that the moonrise over the moor was imminent. And though I did not in my heart believe that our expedition would end in anything but yawns, I was conscious of an extreme tension and rawness of nerves, which I set down to the thunder-charged air.

For noiselessness of footstep we had both put on india-rubber-soled shoes, and all the way down to the pool we heard nothing but the distant thunder and our own padded tread. Very silently and cautiously we ascended the steps of the gate away from the river, and keeping close to the wall inside, sidled round to the river gate and peered out. For the first moment I could see nothing, so black lay the shadow of the rock-wall opposite across the pool, but by degrees I made out the lumps and line of the glimmering foam which streaked the water. High as the river was running this morning it was infinitely more voluminous and turbulent now, and the sound of it filled and bewildered the ear with its sonorous roaring. Only under the very base of the rock opposite it ran quite black and unflecked by foam: there lay the deep still surface of the backwater. Then suddenly I saw something black move in the dimness in front of me, and against the grey foam rose up first the head, then the shoulders, and finally the whole figure of a woman coming towards us up the bank. Behind her walked another, a man, and the two came to where the altar of stone had been newly erected and stood there side by side silhouetted against the churned white of the stream. Hugh had seen too, and touched me on the arm to call my attention. So far then he was right: there was no mistaking the stalwart proportions of Sandy.

Suddenly across the gloom shot a tiny spear of light, and momentarily as we watched, it grew larger and longer, till a tall beam, as from some window cut in the rock opposite, was shed on the bank below us. It moved slowly, imperceptibly to the left till it struck full between the two black figures standing there, and shone with a curious bluish gleam on the flat stone in front of them.

Then the roar of the river was suddenly overscored by a dreadful screaming voice, the voice of a woman, and from her side her arms shot up and out as if in invocation of some power.

At first I could catch none of the words, but soon from repetition they began to convey an intelligible message to my brain, and I was listening as in paralytic horror of nightmare to a bellowing of the most hideous and un-nameable profanity. What I heard I cannot bring myself to record; suffice it to say that Satan was invoked by every adoring and reverent name, that cursing and unspeakable malediction was poured forth on Him whom we hold most holy. Then the yelling voice ceased as suddenly as it had began, and for a moment there was silence again, but for the reverberating river.

Then once more that horror of sound was uplifted.

"So, Catrine Gordon," it cried, "I bid ye in the name of my master and yours to rise from where ye lie. Up with ye--up!"

Once more there was silence; then I heard Hugh at my elbow draw a quick sobbing breath, and his finger pointed unsteadily to the dead black water below the rock. And I too looked and saw.

Right under the rock there appeared a pale subaqueous light, which waved and quivered in the stream. At first it was very small and dim, but as we looked it seemed to swim upwards from remote depths and grew larger till I suppose the space of some square yard was illuminated by it.

Then the surface of the water was broken, and a head, the head of a girl, dead-white and with long, flowing hair, appeared above the stream. Her eyes were shut, the corners of her mouth drooped as in sleep, and the moving water stood in a frill round her neck. Higher and higher rose the figure out of the tide, till at last it stood, luminous in itself, so it appeared, up to the middle.

The head was bent down over the breast, and the hands clasped together. As it emerged from the water it seemed to get nearer, and was by now half-way across the pool, moving quietly and steadily against the great flood of the hurrying river.

Then I heard a man's voice crying out in a sort of strangled agony.

"Catrine!" it cried; "Catrine! In God's name; in God's name!"

In two strides Sandy had rushed down the steep bank, and hurled himself out into that mad swirl of waters. For one moment I saw his arms flung up into the sky, the next he had altogether gone. And on the utterance of that name the unholy vision had vanished too, while simultaneously there burst in front of us a light so blinding, followed by a crack of thunder so appalling to the senses, that I know I just hid my face in my hands. At once, as if the flood-gates of the sky had been opened, the deluge was on us, not like rain, but like one sheet of solid water, so that we cowered under it. Any hope or attempt to rescue Sandy was out of the question; to dive into that whirlpool of mad water meant instant death, and even had it been possible for any swimmer to live there, in the blackness of the night there was absolutely no chance of finding him. Besides, even if it had been possible to save him, I doubt whether I was sufficiently master of my flesh and blood as to endure to plunge where that apparition had risen.

Then, as we lay there, another horror filled and possessed my mind. Somewhere close to us in the darkness was that woman whose yelling voice just now had made my blood run ice-cold, while it brought the streaming sweat to my forehead. At that moment I turned to Hugh.

"I cannot stop here," I said. "I must run, run right away. Where is she?"

"Did you not see?" he asked.

"No. What happened?"

"The lightning struck the stone within a few inches of where she was standing. We--we must go and look for her."

I followed him down the slope, shaking as if I had the palsy, and groping with my hands on the ground in front of me, in deadly terror of encountering something human. The thunderclouds had in the last few minutes spread over the moon, so that no ray from the window in the rock guided our search. But up and down the bank from the stone that lay shattered there to the edge of the pool we groped and stumbled, but found nothing. At length we gave it up: it seemed morally certain that she, too, had rolled down the bank after the lightning stroke, and lay somewhere deep in the pool from which she had called the dead.

None fished the pool next day, but men with drag-nets came from Brora. Right under the rock in the backwater lay two bodies, close together, Sandy and the dead girl. Of the other they found nothing.

It would seem, then, that Catrine Gordon, in answer to Sandy's letter, left Inverness in heavy trouble. What happened afterwards can only be conjectured, but it seems likely she took the short cut to Gavon, meaning to cross the river on the boulders above the Picts' pool. But whether she slipped accidentally in her passage, and so was drawn down by the hungry water, or whether unable to face the future, she had thrown herself into the pool, we can only guess. In any case they sleep together now in the bleak, wind-swept graveyard at Brora, in obedience to the inscrutable designs of God.

The Horror-Horn

For the past ten days Alhubel had basked in the radiant midwinter weather proper to its eminence of over 6,000 feet. From rising to setting the sun (so surprising to those who have hitherto associated it with a pale, tepid plate indistinctly shining through the murky air of England) had blazed its way across the sparkling blue, and every night the serene and windless frost had made the stars sparkle like illuminated diamond dust. Sufficient snow had fallen before Christmas to content the skiers, and the big rink, sprinkled every evening, had given the skaters each morning a fresh surface on which to perform their slippery antics. Bridge and dancing served to while away the greater part of the night, and to me, now for the first time tasting the joys of a winter in the Engadine, it seemed that a new heaven and a new earth had been lighted, warmed, and refrigerated for the special benefit of those who like myself had been wise enough to save up their days of holiday for the winter.

But a break came in these ideal conditions: one afternoon the sun grew vapour-veiled and up the valley from the north-west a wind frozen with miles of travel over ice-bound hill-sides began scouting through the calm halls of the heavens. Soon it grew dusted with snow, first in small flakes driven almost horizontally before its congealing breath and then in larger tufts as of swansdown. And though all day for a fortnight before the fate of nations and life and death had seemed to me of far less importance than to get certain tracings of the skate-blades on the ice of proper shape and size, it now seemed that the one paramount consideration was to hurry back to the hotel for shelter: it was wiser to leave rocking-turns alone than to be frozen in their quest.

I had come out here with my cousin, Professor Ingram, the celebrated physiologist and Alpine climber. During the serenity of the last fortnight he had made a couple of notable winter ascents, but this morning his weather-wisdom had mistrusted the signs of the heavens, and instead of attempting the ascent of the Piz Passug he had waited to see whether his misgivings justified themselves. So there he sat now in the hall of the admirable hotel with his feet on the hot-water pipes and the latest delivery of the English post in his hands. This contained a pamphlet concerning the result of the Mount Everest expedition, of which he had just finished the perusal when I entered.

"A very interesting report," he said, passing it to me, "and they certainly deserve to succeed next year. But who can tell, what that final six thousand feet may entail? Six thousand feet more when you have already accomplished twenty-three thousand does not seem much, but at present no one knows whether the human frame can stand exertion at such a height. It may affect not the lungs and heart only, but possibly the brain. Delirious hallucinations may occur. In fact, if I did not know better, I should have said that one such hallucination had occurred to the climbers already."

"And what was that?" I asked.

"You will find that they thought they came across the tracks of some naked human foot at a great altitude. That looks at first sight like an hallucination. What more natural than that a brain excited and exhilarated by the extreme height should have interpreted certain marks in the snow as the footprints of a human being? Every bodily organ at these altitudes is exerting itself to the utmost to do its work, and the brain seizes on those marks in the snow and says 'Yes, I'm all right, I'm doing my job, and I perceive marks in the snow which I affirm are human footprints.' You know, even at this altitude, how restless and eager the brain is, how vividly, as you told me, you dream at night. Multiply that stimulus and that consequent eagerness and restlessness by three, and how natural that the brain should harbour illusions! What after all is the delirium which often accompanies high fever but the effort of the brain to do its work under the pressure of feverish conditions? It is so eager to continue perceiving that it perceives things which have no existence!"

"And yet you don't think that these naked human footprints were illusions," said I. "You told me you would have thought so, if you had not known better."

He shifted in his chair and looked out of the window a moment. The air was thick now with the density of the big snow-flakes that were driven along by the squealing north-west gale.

"Quite so," he said. "In all probability the human footprints were real human footprints. I expect that they were the footprints, anyhow, of a being more nearly a man than anything else.

"My reason for saying so is that I know such beings exist. I have even seen quite near at hand--and I assure you I did not wish to be nearer in spite of my intense curiosity--the creature, shall we say, which would make such footprints. And if the snow was not so dense, I could show you the place where I saw him."

He pointed straight out of the window, where across the valley lies the huge tower of the Ungeheuerhorn with the carved pinnacle of rock at the top like some gigantic rhinoceros-horn.

On one side only, as I knew, was the mountain practicable, and that for none but the finest climbers; on the other three a succession of ledges and precipices rendered it unscalable. Two thousand feet of sheer rock form the tower; below are five hundred feet of fallen boulders, up to the edge of which grow dense woods of larch and pine.

"Upon the Ungeheuerhorn?" I asked.

"Yes. Up till twenty years ago it had never been ascended, and I, like several others, spent a lot of time in trying to find a route up it. My guide and I sometimes spent three nights together at the hut beside the Blumen glacier, prowling round it, and it was by luck really that we found the route, for the mountain looks even more impracticable from the far side than it does from this.

"But one day we found a long, transverse fissure in the side which led to a negotiable ledge; then there came a slanting ice couloir which you could not see till you got to the foot of it. However, I need not go into that."

The big room where we sat was filling up with cheerful groups driven indoors by this sudden gale and snowfall, and the cackle of merry tongues grew loud. The band, too, that invariable appanage of tea-time at Swiss resorts, had begun to tune up for the usual potpourri from the works of Puccini. Next moment the sugary, sentimental melodies began.

"Strange contrast!" said Ingram. "Here are we sitting warm and cosy, our ears pleasantly tickled with these little baby tunes and outside is the great storm growing more violent every moment, and swirling round the austere cliffs of the Ungeheuerhorn: the Horror-Horn, as indeed it was to me."

"I want to hear all about it," I said. "Every detail: make a short story long, if it's short. I want to know why it's your Horror-Horn?"

"Well, Chanton and I (he was my guide) used to spend days prowling about the cliffs, making a little progress on one side and then being stopped, and gaining perhaps five hundred feet on another side and then being confronted by some insuperable obstacle, till the day when by luck we found the route. Chanton never liked the job, for some reason that I could not fathom.

"It was not because of the difficulty or danger of the climbing, for he was the most fearless man I have ever met when dealing with rocks and ice, but he was always insistent that we should get off the mountain and back to the Blumen hut before sunset. He was scarcely easy even when we had got back to shelter and locked and barred the door, and I well remember one night when, as we ate our supper, we heard some animal, a wolf probably, howling somewhere out in the night.

"A positive panic seized him, and I don't think he closed his eyes till morning. It struck me then that there might be some grisly legend about the mountain, connected possibly with its name, and next day I asked him why the peak was called the Horror-Horn. He put the question off at first, and said that, like the Schreckhorn, its name was due to its precipices and falling stones; but when I pressed him further he acknowledged that there was a legend about it, which his father had told him. There were creatures, so it was supposed, that lived in its caves, things human in shape, and covered, except for the face and hands, with long black hair. They were dwarfs in size, four feet high or thereabouts, but of prodigious strength and agility, remnants of some wild primeval race. It seemed that they were still in an upward stage of evolution, or so I guessed, for the story ran that sometimes girls had been carried off by them, not as prey, and not for any such fate as for those captured by cannibals, but to be bred from. Young men also had been raped by them, to be mated with the females of their tribe. All this looked as if the creatures, as I said, were tending towards humanity. But naturally I did not believe a word of it, as applied to the conditions of the present day. Centuries ago, conceivably, there may have been such beings, and, with the extraordinary tenacity of tradition, the news of this had been handed down and was still current round the hearths of the peasants. As for their numbers, Chanton told me that three had been once seen together by a man who owing to his swiftness on skis had escaped to tell the tale.

"This man, he averred, was no other than his grand-father, who had been benighted one winter evening as he passed through the dense woods below the Ungeheuerhorn, and Chanton supposed that they had been driven down to these lower altitudes in search of food during severe winter weather, for otherwise the recorded sights of them had always taken place among the rocks of the peak itself. They had pursued his grandfather, then a young man, at an extraordinarily swift canter, running sometimes upright as men run, sometimes on all-fours in the manner of beasts, and their howls were just such as that we had heard that night in the Blumen hut. Such at any rate was the story Chanton told me, and, like you, I regarded it as the very moonshine of superstition.

"But the very next day I had reason to reconsider my judgment about it.

"It was on that day that after a week of exploration we hit on the only route at present known to the top of our peak. We started as soon as there was light enough to climb by, for, as you may guess, on very difficult rocks it is impossible to climb by lantern or moonlight. We hit on the long fissure I have spoken of, we explored the ledge which from below seemed to end in nothingness, and with an hour's stepcutting ascended the couloir which led upwards from it.

"From there onwards it was a rock-climb, certainly of considerable difficulty, but with no heart-breaking discoveries ahead, and it was about nine in the morning that we stood on the top. We did not wait there long, for that side of the mountain is raked by falling stones loosened, when the sun grows hot, from the ice that holds them, and we made haste to pass the ledge where the falls are most frequent. After that there was the long fissure to descend, a matter of no great difficulty, and we were at the end of our work by midday, both of us, as you may imagine, in the state of the highest elation.

"A long and tiresome scramble among the huge boulders at the foot of the cliff then lay before us. Here the hill-side is very porous and great caves extend far into the mountain. We had unroped at the base of the fissure, and were picking our way as seemed good to either of us among these fallen rocks, many of them bigger than an ordinary house, when, on coming round the corner of one of these, I saw that which made it clear that the stories Chanton had told me were no figment of traditional superstition.

"Not twenty yards in front of me lay one of the beings of which he had spoken. There it sprawled naked and basking on its back with face turned up to the sun, which its narrow eyes regarded unwinking. In form it was completely human, but the growth of hair that covered limbs and trunk alike almost completely hid the sun-tanned skin beneath. But its face, save for the down on its cheeks and chin, was hairless, and I looked on a countenance the sensual and malevolent bestiality of which froze me with horror. Had the creature been an animal, one would have felt scarcely a shudder at the gross animalism of it; the horror lay in the fact that it was a man. There lay by it a couple of gnawed bones, and, its meal finished, it was lazily licking its protuberant lips, from which came a purring murmur of content. With one hand it scratched the thick hair on its belly, in the other it held one of these bones, which presently split in half beneath the pressure of its finger and thumb. But my horror was not based on the information of what happened to those men whom these creatures caught, it was due only to my proximity to a thing so human and so infernal. The peak, of which the ascent had a moment ago filled us with such elated satisfaction, became to me an Ungeheuerhorn indeed, for it was the home of beings more awful than the delirium of nightmare could ever have conceived.

"Chanton was a dozen paces behind me, and with a backward wave of my hand I caused him to halt. Then withdrawing myself with infinite precaution, so as not to attract the gaze of that basking creature, I slipped back round the rock, whispered to him what I had seen, and with blanched faces we made a long detour, peering round every corner, and crouching low, not knowing that at any step we might not come upon another of these beings, or that from the mouth of one of these caves in the mountain-side there might not appear another of those hairless and dreadful faces, with perhaps this time the breasts and insignia of womanhood. That would have been the worst of all.

"Luck favoured us, for we made our way among the boulders and shifting stones, the rattle of which might at any moment have betrayed us, without a repetition of my experience, and once among the trees we ran as if the Furies themselves were in pursuit. Well now did I understand, though I dare say I cannot convey, the qualms of Chanton's mind when he spoke to me of these creatures. Their very humanity was what made them so terrible, the fact that they were of the same race as ourselves, but of a type so abysmally degraded that the most brutal and inhuman of men would have seemed angelic in comparison."

The music of the small band was over before he had finished the narrative, and the chattering groups round the tea-table had dispersed. He paused a moment.

"There was a horror of the spirit," he said, "which I experienced then, from which, I verily believe, I have never entirely recovered. I saw then how terrible a living thing could be, and how terrible, in consequence, was life itself. In us all I suppose lurks some inherited germ of that ineffable bestiality, and who knows whether, sterile as it has apparently become in the course of centuries, it might not fructify again. When I saw that creature sun itself, I looked into the abyss out of which we have crawled. And these creatures are trying to crawl out of it now, if they exist any longer. Certainly for the last twenty years there has been no record of their being seen, until we come to this story of the footprint seen by the climbers on Everest. If that is authentic, if the party did not mistake the footprint of some bear, or what not, for a human tread, it seems as if still this bestranded remnant of mankind is in existence."

Now, Ingram, had told his story well; but sitting in this warm and civilised room, the horror which he had clearly felt had not communicated itself to me in any very vivid manner.

Intellectually, I agreed, I could appreciate his horror, but certainly my spirit felt no shudder of interior comprehension.

"But it is odd," I said, "that your keen interest in physiology did not disperse your qualms.

"You were looking, so I take it, at some form of man more remote probably than the earliest human remains. Did not something inside you say 'This is of absorbing significance'?"

He shook his head.

"No: I only wanted to get away," said he. "It was not, as I have told you, the terror of what according to Chanton's story, might--await us if we were captured; it was sheer horror at the creature itself. I quaked at it."

The snowstorm and the gale increased in violence that night, and I slept uneasily, plucked again and again from slumber by the fierce battling of the wind that shook my windows as if with an imperious demand for admittance. It came in billowy gusts, with strange noises intermingled with it as for a moment it abated, with flutings and moanings that rose to shrieks as the fury of it returned. These noises, no doubt, mingled themselves with my drowsed and sleepy consciousness, and once I tore myself out of nightmare, imagining that the creatures of the Horror-Horn had gained footing on my balcony and were rattling at the window-bolts. But before morning the gale had died away, and I awoke to see the snow falling dense and fast in a windless air. For three days it continued, without intermission, and with its cessation there came a frost such as I have never felt before. Fifty degrees were registered one night, and more the next, and what the cold must have been on the cliffs of the Ungeheuerborn I cannot imagine. Sufficient, so I thought, to have made an end altogether of its secret inhabitants: my cousin, on that day twenty years ago, had missed an opportunity for study which would probably never fall again either to him or another.

I received one morning a letter from a friend saying that he had arrived at the neighbouring winter resort of St. Luigi, and proposing that I should come over for a morning's skating and lunch afterwards. The place was not more than a couple of miles off, if one took the path over the low, pine-clad foot-hills above which lay the steep woods below the first rocky slopes of the Ungeheuerhorn; and accordingly, with a knapsack containing skates on my back, I went on skis over the wooded slopes and down by an easy descent again on to St. Luigi. The day was overcast, clouds entirely obscured the higher peaks though the sun was visible, pale and unluminous, through the mists. But as the morning went on, it gained the upper hand, and I slid down into St. Luigi beneath a sparkling firmament. We skated and lunched, and then, since it looked as if thick weather was coming up again, I set out early about three o'clock for my return journey.

Hardly had I got into the woods when the clouds gathered thick above, and streamers and skeins of them began to descend among the pines through which my path threaded its way. In ten minutes more their opacity had so increased that I could hardly see a couple of yards in front of me. Very soon I became aware that I must have got off the path, for snow-cowled shrubs lay directly in my way, and, casting back to find it again, I got altogether confused as to direction.

But, though progress was difficult, I knew I had only to keep on the ascent, and presently I should come to the brow of these low foot-hills, and descend into the open valley where Alhubel stood. So on I went, stumbling and sliding over obstacles, and unable, owing to the thickness of the snow, to take off my skis, for I should have sunk over the knees at each step. Still the ascent continued, and looking at my watch I saw that I had already been near an hour on my way from St. Luigi, a period more than sufficient to complete my whole journey. But still I stuck to my idea that though I had certainly strayed far from my proper route a few minutes more must surely see me over the top of the upward way, and I should find the ground declining into the next valley. About now, too, I noticed that the mists were growing suffused with rose-colour, and, though the inference was that it must be close on sunset, there was consolation in the fact that they were there and might lift at any moment and disclose to me my whereabouts. But the fact that night would soon be on me made it needful to bar my mind against that despair of loneliness which so eats out the heart of a man who is lost in woods or on mountain-side, that, though still there is plenty of vigour in his limbs, his nervous force is sapped, and he can do no more than lie down and abandon himself to whatever fate may await him...And then I heard that which made the thought of loneliness seem bliss indeed, for there was a worse fate than loneliness. What I heard resembled the howl of a wolf, and it came from not far in front of me where the ridge--was it a ridge?--still rose higher in vestment of pines.

From behind me came a sudden puff of wind, which shook the frozen snow from the drooping pine-branches, and swept away the mists as a broom sweeps the dust from the floor.

Radiant above me were the unclouded skies, already charged with the red of the sunset, and in front I saw that I had come to the very edge of the wood through which I had wandered so long.

But it was no valley into which I had penetrated, for there right ahead of me rose the steep slope of boulders and rocks soaring upwards to the foot of the Ungeheuerhorn. What, then, was that cry of a wolf which had made my heart stand still? I saw.

Not twenty yards from me was a fallen tree, and leaning against the trunk of it was one of the denizens of the Horror-Horn, and it was a woman. She was enveloped in a thick growth of hair grey and tufted, and from her head it streamed down over her shoulders and her bosom, from which hung withered and pendulous breasts. And looking on her face I comprehended not with my mind alone, but with a shudder of my spirit, what Ingram had felt. Never had nightmare fashioned so terrible a countenance; the beauty of sun and stars and of the beasts of the field and the kindly race of men could not atone for so hellish an incarnation of the spirit of life. A fathomless bestiality modelled the slavering mouth and the narrow eyes; I looked into the abyss itself and knew that out of that abyss on the edge of which I leaned the generations of men had climbed. What if that ledge crumbled in front of me and pitched me headlong into its nethermost depths?...

In one hand she held by the horns a chamois that kicked and struggled. A blow from its hindleg caught her withered thigh, and with a grunt of anger she seized the leg in her other hand, and, as a man may pull from its sheath a stem of meadow-grass, she plucked it off the body, leaving the torn skin hanging round the gaping wound. Then putting the red, bleeding member to her mouth she sucked at it as a child sucks a stick of sweetmeat. Through flesh and gristle her short, brown teeth penetrated, and she licked her lips with a sound of purring. Then dropping the leg by her side, she looked again at the body of the prey now quivering in its death-convulsion, and with finger and thumb gouged out one of its eyes. She snapped her teeth on it, and it cracked like a soft-shelled nut.

It must have been but a few seconds that I stood watching her, in some indescribable catalepsy of terror, while through my brain there pealed the panic-command of my mind to my stricken limbs "Begone, begone, while there is time." Then, recovering the power of my joints and muscles, I tried to slip behind a tree and hide myself from this apparition. But the woman--shall I say?--must have caught my stir of movement, for she raised her eyes from her living feast and saw me. She craned forward her neck, she dropped her prey, and half rising began to move towards me. As she did this, she opened her mouth, and gave forth a howl such as I had heard a moment before. It was answered by another, but faintly and distantly.

Sliding and slipping, with the toes of my skis tripping in the obstacles below the snow, I plunged forward down the hill between the pine-trunks. The low sun already sinking behind some rampart of mountain in the west reddened the snow and the pines with its ultimate rays. My knapsack with the skates in it swung to and fro on my back, one ski-stick had already been twitched out of my hand by a fallen branch of pine, but not a second's pause could I allow myself to recover it. I gave no glance behind, and I knew not at what pace my pursuer was on my track, or indeed whether any pursued at all, for my whole mind and energy, now working at full power again under the stress of my panic, was devoted to getting away down the hill and out of the wood as swiftly as my limbs could bear me. For a little while I heard nothing but the hissing snow of my headlong passage, and the rustle of the covered undergrowth beneath my feet, and then, from close at hand behind me, once more the wolf-howl sounded and I heard the plunging of footsteps other than my own.

The strap of my knapsack had shifted, and as my skates swung to and fro on my back it chafed and pressed on my throat, hindering free passage of air, of which, God knew, my labouring lungs were in dire need, and without pausing I slipped it free from my neck, and held it in the hand from which my ski-stick had been jerked. I seemed to go a little more easily for this adjustment, and now, not so far distant, I could see below me the path from which I had strayed.

If only I could reach that, the smoother going would surely enable me to outdistance my pursuer, who even on the rougher ground was but slowly overhauling me, and at the sight of that riband stretching unimpeded downhill, a ray of hope pierced the black panic of my soul. With that came the desire, keen and insistent, to see who or what it was that was on my tracks, and I spared a backward glance. It was she, the hag whom I had seen at her gruesome meal; her long grey hair flew out behind her, her mouth chattered and gibbered, her fingers made grabbing movements, as if already they closed on me.

But the path was now at hand, and the nearness of it I suppose made me incautious. A hump of snow-covered bush lay in my path, and, thinking I could jump over it, I tripped and fell, smothering myself in snow. I heard a maniac noise, half scream, half laugh, from close behind, and before I could recover myself the grabbing fingers were at my neck, as if a steel vice had closed there. But my right hand in which I held my knapsack of skates was free, and with a blind backhanded movement I whirled it behind me at the full length of its strap, and knew that my desperate blow had found its billet somewhere. Even before I could look round I felt the grip on my neck relax, and something subsided into the very bush which had entangled me. I recovered my feet and turned.

There she lay, twitching and quivering. The heel of one of my skates piercing the thin alpaca of the knapsack had hit her full on the temple, from which the blood was pouring, but a hundred yards away I could see another such figure coming downwards on my tracks, leaping and bounding. At that panic rose again within me, and I sped off down the white smooth path that led to the lights of the village already beckoning. Never once did I pause in my headlong going: there was no safety until I was back among the haunts of men. I flung myself against the door of the hotel, and screamed for admittance, though I had but to turn the handle and enter; and once more as when Ingram had told his tale, there was the sound of the band, and the chatter of voices, and there, too, was he himself, who looked up and then rose swiftly to his feet as I made my clattering entrance.

"I have seen them too," I cried. "Look at my knapsack. Is there not blood on it? It is the blood of one of them, a woman, a hag, who tore off the leg of a chamois as I looked, and pursued me through the accursed wood. I--".Whether it was I who spun round, or the room which seemed to spin round me, I knew not, but I heard myself falling, collapsed on the floor, and the next time that I was conscious at all I was in bed. There was Ingram there, who told me that I was quite safe, and another man, a stranger, who pricked my arm with the nozzle of a syringe, and reassured me...

A day or two later I gave a coherent account of my adventure, and three or four men, armed with guns, went over my traces. They found the bush in which I had stumbled, with a pool of blood which had soaked into the snow, and, still following my ski-tracks, they came on the body of a chamois, from which had been torn one of its hindlegs and one eye-socket was empty. That is all the corroboration of my story that I can give the reader, and for myself I imagine that the creature which pursued me was either not killed by my blow or that her fellows removed her body...Anyhow, it is open to the incredulous to prowl about the caves of the Ungeheuerhorn, and see if anything occurs that may convince them.

In the Tube

"It's a convention," said Anthony Carling cheerfully, "and not a very convincing one. Time, indeed! There's no such thing as Time really; it has no actual existence. Time is nothing more than an infinitesimal point in eternity, just as space is an infinitesimal point in infinity. At the most, Time is a sort of tunnel through which we are accustomed to believe that we are travelling.

"There's a roar in our ears and a darkness in our eyes which makes it seem real to us. But before we came into the tunnel we existed for ever in an infinite sunlight, and after we have got through it we shall exist in an infinite sunlight again. So why should we bother ourselves about the confusion and noise and darkness which only encompass us for a moment?"

For a firm-rooted believer in such immeasurable ideas as these, which he punctuated with brisk application of the poker to the brave sparkle and glow of the fire, Anthony has a very pleasant appreciation of the measurable and the finite, and nobody with whom I have acquaintance has so keen a zest for life and its enjoyments as he. He had given us this evening an admirable dinner, had passed round a port beyond praise, and had illuminated the jolly hours with the light of his infectious optimism. Now the small company had melted away, and I was left with him over the fire in his study. Outside the tattoo of wind-driven sleet was audible on the window-panes, over-scoring now and again the flap of the flames on the open hearth, and the thought of the chilly blasts and the snow-covered pavement in Brompton Square, across which, to skidding taxicabs, the last of his other guests had scurried, made my position, resident here till to-morrow morning, the more delicately delightful. Above all there was this stimulating and suggestive companion, who, whether he talked of the great abstractions which were so intensely real and practical to him, or of the very remarkable experiences which he had encountered among these conventions of time and space, was equally fascinating to the listener.

"I adore life," he said. "I find it the most entrancing plaything. It's a delightful game, and, as you know very well, the only conceivable way to play a game is to treat it extremely seriously. If you say to yourself, 'It's only a game,' you cease to take the slightest interest in it. You have to know that it's only a game, and behave as if it was the one object of existence. I should like it to go on for many years yet. But all the time one has to be living on the true plane as well, which is eternity and infinity. If you come to think of it, the one thing which the human mind cannot grasp is the finite, not the infinite, the temporary, not the eternal."

"That sounds rather paradoxical," said I.

"Only because you've made a habit of thinking about things that seem bounded and limited.

"Look it in the face for a minute. Try to imagine finite Time and Space, and you find you can't.

"Go back a million years, and multiply that million of years by another million, and you find that you can't conceive of a beginning. What happened before that beginning? Another beginning and another beginning? And before that? Look at it like that, and you find that the only solution comprehensible to you is the existence of an eternity, something that never began and will never end. It's the same about space. Project yourself to the farthest star, and what comes beyond that?

"Emptiness? Go on through the emptiness, and you can't imagine it being finite and having an end. It must needs go on for ever: that's the only thing you can understand. There's no such thing as before or after, or beginning or end, and what a comfort that is! I should fidget myself to death if there wasn't the huge soft cushion of eternity to lean one's head against. Some people say--I believe I've heard you say it yourself--that the idea of eternity is so tiring; you feel that you want to stop. But that's because you are thinking of eternity in terms of Time, and mumbling in your brain, 'And after that, and after that?' Don't you grasp the idea that in eternity there isn't any 'after,' any more than there is any 'before'? It's all one. Eternity isn't a quantity: it's a quality."

Sometimes, when Anthony talks in this manner, I seem to get a glimpse of that which to his mind is so transparently clear and solidly real, at other times (not having a brain that readily envisages abstractions) I feel as though he was pushing me over a precipice, and my intellectual faculties grasp wildly at anything tangible or comprehensible. This was the case now, and I hastily interrupted.

"But there is a 'before' and 'after,'" I said. "A few hours ago you gave us an admirable dinner, and after that--yes, after--we played bridge. And now you are going to explain things a little more clearly to me, and after that I shall go to bed--"

He laughed.

"You shall do exactly as you like," he said, "and you shan't be a slave to Time either to-night or to-morrow morning. We won't even mention an hour for breakfast, but you shall have it in eternity whenever you awake. And as I see it is not midnight yet, we'll slip the bonds of Time, and talk quite infinitely. I will stop the clock, if that will assist you in getting rid of your illusion, and then I'll tell you a story, which to my mind, shows how unreal so-called realities are; or, at any rate, how fallacious are our senses as judges of what is real and what is not."

"Something occult, something spookish?" I asked, pricking up my ears, for Anthony has the strangest clairvoyances and visions of things unseen by the normal eye.

"I suppose you might call some of it occult," he said, "though there's a certain amount of rather grim reality mixed up in it."

"Go on; excellent mixture," said I.

He threw a fresh log on the fire.

"It's a longish story," he said. "You may stop me as soon as you ye had enough. But there will come a point for which I claim your consideration. You, who cling to your 'before' and 'after,' has it ever occurred to you how difficult it is to say when an incident takes place? Say that a man commits some crime of violence, can we not, with a good deal of truth, say that he really commits that crime when he definitely plans and determines upon it, dwelling on it with gusto? The actual commission of it, I think we can reasonably argue, is the mere material sequel of his resolve: he is guilty of it when he makes that determination. When, therefore, in the term of 'before' and 'after,' does the crime truly take place? There is also in my story a further point for your consideration. For it seems certain that the spirit of a man, after the death of his body, is obliged to re-enact such a crime, with a view, I suppose we may guess, to his remorse and his eventual redemption. Those who have second sight have seen such re-enactments. Perhaps he may have done his deed blindly in this life; but then his spirit re-commits it with its spiritual eyes open, and able to comprehend its enormity. So, shall we view the man's original determination and the material commission of his crime only as preludes to the real commission of it, when with eyes unsealed he does it and repents of it?...That all sounds very obscure when I speak in the abstract, but I think you will see what I mean, if you follow my tale. Comfortable? Got everything you want? Here goes, then."

He leaned back in his chair, concentrating his mind, and then spoke:

"The story that I am about to tell you," he said, "had its beginning a month ago, when you were away in Switzerland. It reached its conclusion, so I imagine, last night. I do not, at any rate expect to experience any more of it. Well, a month ago I was returning late on a very wet night from dining out. There was not a taxi to be had, and I hurried through the pouring rain to the tube-station at Piccadilly Circus, and thought myself very lucky to catch the last train in this direction. The carriage into which I stepped was quite empty except for one other passenger, who sat next the door immediately opposite to me. I had never, to my knowledge, seen him before, but I found my attention vividly fixed on him, as if he somehow concerned me. He was a man of middle age, in dress-clothes, and his face wore an expression of intense thought, as if in his mind he was pondering some very significant matter, and his hand which was resting on his knee clenched and unclenched itself. Suddenly he looked up and stared me in the face, and I saw there suspicion and fear, as if I had surprised him in some secret deed.

"At that moment we stopped at Dover Street, and the conductor threw open the doors, announced the station and added, 'Change here for Hyde Park Corner and Gloucester Road.' That was all right for me since it meant that the train would stop at Brompton Road, which was my destination. It was all right apparently, too, for my companion, for he certainly did not get out, and after a moment's stop, during which no one else got in, we went on. I saw him, I must insist, after the doors were closed and the train had started. But when I looked again, as we rattled on, I saw that there was no one there. I was quite alone in the carriage.

"Now you may think that I had had one of those swift momentary dreams which flash in and out of the mind in the space of a second, but I did not believe it was so myself, for I felt that I had experienced some sort of premonition or clair-voyant vision. A man, the semblance of whom, astral body or whatever you may choose to call it, I had just seen, would sometime sit in that seat opposite to me, pondering and planning."

"But why?" I asked. "Why should it have been the astral body of a living man which you thought you had seen? Why not the ghost of a dead one?"

"Because of my own sensations. The sight of the spirit of someone dead, which has occurred to me two or three times in my life, has always been accompanied by a physical shrinking and fear, and by the sensation of cold and of loneliness. I believed, at any rate, that I had seen a phantom of the living, and that impression was confirmed, I might say proved, the next day. For I met the man himself. And the next night, as you shall hear, I met the phantom again. We will take them in order.

"I was lunching, then, the next day with my neighbour Mrs. Stanley: there was a small party, and when I arrived we waited but for the final guest. He entered while I was talking to some friend, and presently at my elbow I heard Mrs. Stanley's voice--'Let me introduce you to Sir Henry Payle,' she said.

"I turned and saw my vis-à-vis of the night before. It was quite unmistakably he, and as we shook hands he looked at me I thought with vague and puzzled recognition.

"'Haven't we met before, Mr. Carling?' he said. 'I seem to recollect--'

"For the moment I forgot the strange manner of his disappearance from the carriage, and thought that it had been the man himself whom I had seen last night.

"'Surely, and not so long ago,' I said. 'For we sat opposite each other in the last tube-train from Piccadilly Circus yesterday night.'

"He still looked at me, frowning, puzzled, and shook his head.

"'That can hardly be,' he said. 'I only came up from the country this morning.'

"Now this interested me profoundly, for the astral body, we are told, abides in some half-conscious region of the mind or spirit, and has recollections of what has happened to it, which it can convey only very vaguely and dimly to the conscious mind. All lunch-time I could see his eyes again and again directed to me with the same puzzled and perplexed air, and as I was taking my departure he came up to me.

"'I shall recollect some day,' he said, 'where we met before, and I hope we may meet again. Was it not--?'--and he stopped. 'No: it has gone from me,' he added."

The log that Anthony had thrown on the fire was burning bravely now, and its high-flickering flame lit up his face.

"Now, I don't know whether you believe in coincidences as chance things," he said, "but if you do, get rid of the notion. Or if you can't at once, call it a coincidence that that very night I again caught the last train on the tube going westwards. This time, so far from my being a solitary passenger, there was a considerable crowd waiting at Dover Street, where I entered, and just as the noise of the approaching train began to reverberate in the tunnel I caught sight of Sir Henry Payle standing near the opening from which the train would presently emerge, apart from the rest of the crowd. And I thought to myself how odd it was that I should have seen the phantom of him at this very hour last night and the man himself now, and I began walking towards him with the idea of saying, 'Anyhow, it is in the tube that we meet to-night.'...And then a terrible and awful thing happened. Just as the train emerged from the tunnel he jumped down on to the line in front of it, and the train swept along over him up the platform.

"For a moment I was stricken with horror at the sight, and I remember covering my eyes against the dreadful tragedy. But then I perceived that, though it had taken place in full sight of those who were waiting, no one seemed to have seen it except myself. The driver, looking out from his window, had not applied his brakes, there was no jolt from the advancing train, no scream, no cry, and the rest of the passengers began boarding the train with perfect nonchalance.

"I must have staggered, for I felt sick and faint with what I had seen, and some kindly soul put his arm round me and supported me into the train. He was a doctor, he told me, and asked if I was in pain, or what ailed me. I told him what I thought I had seen, and he assured me that no such accident had taken place.

"It was clear then to my own mind that I had seen the second act, so to speak, in this psychical drama, and I pondered next morning over the problem as to what I should do. Already I had glanced at the morning paper, which, as I knew would be the case, contained no mention whatever of what I had seen. The thing had certainly not happened, but I knew in myself that it would happen. The flimsy veil of Time had been withdrawn from my eyes, and I had seen into what you would call the future. In terms of Time of course it was the future, but from my point of view the thing was just as much in the past as it was in the future. It existed, and waited only for its material fulfilment. The more I thought about it, the more I saw that I could do nothing."

I interrupted his narrative.

"You did nothing?" I exclaimed. "Surely you might have taken some step in order to try to avert the tragedy."

He shook his head.

"What step precisely?" he said. "Was I to go to Sir Henry and tell him that once more I had seen him in the tube in the act of committing suicide? Look at it like this. Either what I had seen was pure illusion, pure imagination, in which case it had no existence or significance at all, or it was actual and real, and essentially it had happened. Or take it, though not very logically, somewhere between the two. Say that the idea of suicide, for some cause of which I knew nothing, had occurred to him or would occur. Should I not, if that was the case, be doing a very dangerous thing, by making such a suggestion to him? Might not the fact of my telling him what I had seen put the idea into his mind, or, if it was already there, confirm it and strengthen it? 'It's a ticklish matter to play with souls,' as Browning says."

"But it seems so inhuman not to interfere in any way," said I, "not to make any attempt."

"What interference?" asked he. "What attempt?"

The human instinct in me still seemed to cry aloud at the thought of doing nothing to avert such a tragedy, but it seemed to be beating itself against something austere and inexorable. And cudgel my brain as I would, I could not combat the sense of what he had said. I had no answer for him, and he went on.

"You must recollect, too," he said, "that I believed then and believe now that the thing had happened. The cause of it, whatever that was, had begun to work, and the effect, in this material sphere, was inevitable. That is what I alluded to when, at the beginning of my story, I asked you to consider how difficult it was to say when an action took place. You still hold that this particular action, this suicide of Sir Henry, had not yet taken place, because he had not yet thrown himself under the advancing train. To me that seems a materialistic view. I hold that in all but the endorsement of it, so to speak, it had taken place. I fancy that Sir Henry, for instance, now free from the material dusks, knows that himself."

Exactly as he spoke there swept through the warm lit room a current of ice-cold air, ruffling my hair as it passed me, and making the wood flames on the hearth to dwindle and flare. I looked round to see if the door at my back had opened, but nothing stirred there, and over the closed window the curtains were fully drawn. As it reached Anthony, he sat up quickly in his chair and directed his glance this way and that about the room.

"Did you feel that?" he asked.

"Yes: a sudden draught," I said. "Ice-cold."

"Anything else?" he asked. "Any other sensation?"

I paused before I answered, for at the moment there occurred to me Anthony's differentiation of the effects produced on the beholder by a phantasm of the living and the apparition of the dead. It was the latter which accurately described my sensations now, a certain physical shrinking, a fear, a feeling of desolation. But yet I had seen nothing. "I felt rather creepy," I said.

As I spoke I drew my chair rather closer to the fire, and sent a swift and, I confess, a somewhat apprehensive scrutiny round the walls of the brightly lit room. I noticed at the same time that Anthony was peering across to the chimney-piece, on which, just below a sconce holding two electric lights, stood the clock which at the beginning of our talk he had offered to stop. The hands I noticed pointed to twenty-five minutes to one.

"But you saw nothing?" he asked.

"Nothing whatever," I said. "Why should I? What was there to see? Or did you--"

"I don't think so," he said.

Somehow this answer got on my nerves, for the queer feeling which had accompanied that cold current of air had not left me. If anything it had become more acute.

"But surely you know whether you saw anything or not?" I said.

"One can't always be certain," said he. "I say that I don't think I saw anything. But I'm not sure, either, whether the story I am telling you was quite concluded last night. I think there may be a further incident. If you prefer it, I will leave the rest of it, as far as I know it, unfinished till to-morrow morning, and you can go off to bed now."

His complete calmness and tranquillity reassured me.

"But why should I do that?" I asked.

Again he looked round on the bright walls.

"Well, I think something entered the room just now," he said, "and it may develop. If you don't like the notion, you had better go. Of course there's nothing to be alarmed at; whatever it is, it can't hurt us. But it is close on the hour when on two successive nights I saw what I have already told you, and an apparition usually occurs at the same time. Why that is so, I cannot say, but certainly it looks as if a spirit that is earth-bound is still subject to certain conventions, the conventions of time for instance. I think that personally I shall see something before long, but most likely you won't. You're not such a sufferer as I from these--these delusions--"

I was frightened and knew it, but I was also intensely interested, and some perverse pride wriggled within me at his last words. Why, so I asked myself, shouldn't I see whatever was to be seen?...

"I don't want to go in the least," I said. "I want to hear the rest of your story."

"Where was I, then? Ah, yes: you were wondering why I didn't do something after I saw the train move up to the platform, and I said that there was nothing to be done. If you think it over, I fancy you will agree with me...A couple of days passed, and on the third morning I saw in the paper that there had come fulfilment to my vision. Sir Henry Payle, who had been waiting on the platform of Dover Street Station for the last train to South Kensington, had thrown himself in front of it as it came into the station. The train had been pulled up in a couple of yards, but a wheel had passed over his chest, crushing it in and instantly killing him.

"An inquest was held, and there emerged at it one of those dark stories which, on occasions like these, sometimes fall like a midnight shadow across a life that the world perhaps had thought prosperous. He had long been on bad terms with his wife, from whom he had lived apart, and it appeared that not long before this he had fallen desperately in love with another woman. The night before his suicide he had appeared very late at his wife's house, and had a long and angry scene with her in which he entreated her to divorce him, threatening otherwise to make her life a hell to her. She refused, and in an ungovernable fit of passion he attempted to strangle her. There was a struggle and the noise of it caused her manservant to come up, who succeeded in overmastering him. Lady Payle threatened to proceed against him for assault with the intention to murder her. With this hanging over his head, the next night, as I have already told you, he committed suicide."

He glanced at the clock again, and I saw that the hands now pointed to ten minutes to one.

The fire was beginning to burn low and the room surely was growing strangely cold.

"That's not quite all," said Anthony, again looking round. "Are you sure you wouldn't prefer to hear it to-morrow?"

The mixture of shame and pride and curiosity again prevailed.

"No: tell me the rest of it at once," I said.

Before speaking, he peered suddenly at some point behind my chair, shading his eyes. I followed his glance, and knew what he meant by saying that sometimes one could not be sure whether one saw something or not. But was that an outlined shadow that intervened between me and the wall? It was difficult to focus; I did not know whether it was near the wall or near my chair. It seemed to clear away, anyhow, as I looked more closely at it.

"You see nothing?" asked Anthony.

"No: I don't think so," said I. "And you?"

"I think I do," he said, and his eyes followed something which was invisible to mine. They came to rest between him and the chimney-piece. Looking steadily there, he spoke again.

"All this happened some weeks ago," he said, "when you were out in Switzerland, and since then, up till last night, I saw nothing further. But all the time I was expecting something further. I felt that, as far as I was concerned, it was not all over yet, and last night, with the intention of assisting any communication to come through to me from--from beyond, I went into the Dover Street tube-station at a few minutes before one o'clock, the hour at which both the assault and the suicide had taken place. The platform when I arrived on it was absolutely empty, or appeared to be so, but presently, just as I began to hear the roar of the approaching train, I saw there was the figure of a man standing some twenty yards from me, looking into the tunnel. He had not come down with me in the lift, and the moment before he had not been there. He began moving towards me, and then I saw who it was, and I felt a stir of wind icy-cold coming towards me as he approached. It was not the draught that heralds the approach of a train, for it came from the opposite direction. He came close up to me, and I saw there was recognition in his eyes. He raised his face towards me and I saw his lips move, but, perhaps in the increasing noise from the tunnel, I heard nothing come from them. He put out his hand, as if entreating me to do something, and with a cowardice for which I cannot forgive myself, I shrank from him, for I knew, by the sign that I have told you, that this was one from the dead, and my flesh quaked before him, drowning for the moment all pity and all desire to help him, if that was possible.

"Certainly he had something which he wanted of me, but I recoiled from him. And by now the train was emerging from the tunnel, and next moment, with a dreadful gesture of despair, he threw himself in front of it."

As he finished speaking he got up quickly from his chair, still looking fixedly in front of him.

I saw his pupils dilate, and his mouth worked.

"It is coming," he said. "I am to be given a chance of atoning for my cowardice. There is nothing to be afraid of: I must remember that myself..."

As he spoke there came from the panelling above the chimney-piece one loud shattering crack, and the cold wind again circled about my head. I found myself shrinking back in my chair with my hands held in front of me as instinctively I screened myself against something which I knew was there but which I could not see. Every sense told me that there was a presence in the room other than mine and Anthony's, and the horror of it was that I could not see it. Any vision, however terrible, would, I felt, be more tolerable than this clear certain knowledge that close to me was this invisible thing. And yet what horror might not be disclosed of the face of the dead and the crushed chest...But all I could see, as I shuddered in this cold wind, was the familiar walls of the room, and Anthony standing in front of me stiff and firm, making, as I knew, a call on his courage. His eyes were focused on something quite close to him, and some semblance of a smile quivered on his mouth. And then he spoke again.

"Yes, I know you," he said. "And you want something of me. Tell me, then, what it is."

There was absolute silence, but what was silence to my ears could not have been so to his, for once or twice he nodded, and once he said, "Yes: I see. I will do it." And with the knowledge that, even as there was someone here whom I could not see, so there was speech going on which I could not hear, this terror of the dead and of the unknown rose in me with the sense of powerlessness to move that accompanies nightmare. I could not stir, I could not speak. I could only strain my ears for the inaudible and my eyes for the unseen, while the cold wind from the very valley of the shadow of death streamed over me. It was not that the presence of death itself was terrible; it was that from its tranquillity and serene keeping there had been driven some unquiet soul unable to rest in peace for whatever ultimate awakening rouses the countless generations of those who have passed away, driven, no less, from whatever activities are theirs, back into the material world from which it should have been delivered. Never, until the gulf between the living and the dead was thus bridged, had it seemed so immense and so unnatural. It is possible that the dead may have communication with the living, and it was not that exactly that so terrified me, for such communication, as we know it, comes voluntarily from them. But here was something icy-cold and crime-laden, that was chased back from the peace that would not pacify it.

And then, most horrible of all, there came a change in these unseen conditions. Anthony was silent now, and from looking straight and fixedly in front of him, he began to glance sideways to where I sat and back again, and with that I felt that the unseen presence had turned its attention from him to me. And now, too, gradually and by awful degrees I began to see...

There came an outline of shadow across the chimney-piece and the panels above it. It took shape: it fashioned itself into the outline of a man. Within the shape of the shadow details began to form themselves, and I saw wavering in the air, like something concealed by haze, the semblance of a face, stricken and tragic, and burdened with such a weight of woe as no human face had ever worn. Next, the shoulders outlined themselves, and a stain livid and red spread out below them, and suddenly the vision leaped into clearness. There he stood, the chest crushed in and drowned in the red stain, from which broken ribs, like the bones of a wrecked ship, protruded. The mournful, terrible eyes were fixed on me, and it was from them, so I knew, that the bitter wind proceeded...

Then, quick as the switching off of a lamp, the spectre vanished, and the bitter wind was still, and opposite to me stood Anthony, in a quiet, bright-lit room. There was no sense of an unseen presence any more; he and I were then alone, with an interrupted conversation still dangling between us in the warm air. I came round to that, as one comes round after an anaesthetic. It all swam into sight again, unreal at first, and gradually assuming the texture of actuality.

"You were talking to somebody, not to me," I said. "Who was it? What was it?"

He passed the back of his hand over his forehead, which glistened in the light.

"A soul in hell," he said.

Now it is hard ever to recall mere physical sensations, when they have passed. If you have been cold and are warmed, it is difficult to remember what cold was like: if you have been hot and have got cool, it is difficult to realise what the oppression of heat really meant. Just so, with the passing of that presence, I found myself unable to recapture the sense of the terror with which, a few moments ago only, it had invaded and inspired me.

"A soul in hell?" I said. "What are you talking about?"

He moved about the room for a minute or so, and then came and sat on the arm of my chair.

"I don't know what you saw," he said, "or what you felt, but there has never in all my life happened to me anything more real than what these last few minutes have brought. I have talked to a soul in the hell of remorse, which is the only possible hell. He knew, from what happened last night, that he could perhaps establish communication through me with the world he had quitted, and he sought me and found me. I am charged with a mission to a woman I have never seen, a message from the contrite...You can guess who it is..."

He got up with a sudden briskness.

"Let's verify it anyhow," he said. "He gave me the street and the number. Ah, there's the telephone book! Would it be a coincidence merely if I found that at No. 20 in Chasemore Street, South Kensington, there lived a Lady Payle?"

He turned over the leaves of the bulky volume.

"Yes, that's right," he said.

The Confession of Charles Linkworth

Dr. Teesdale had occasion to attend the condemned man once or twice during the week before his execution, and found him, as is often the case, when his last hope of life has vanished, quiet and perfectly resigned to his fate, and not seeming to look forward with any dread to the morning that each hour that passed brought nearer and nearer. The bitterness of death appeared to be over for him: it was done with when he was told that his appeal was refused. But for those days while hope was not yet quite abandoned, the wretched man had drunk of death daily. In all his experience the doctor had never seen a man so wildly and passionately tenacious of life, nor one so strongly knit to this material world by the sheer animal lust of living. Then the news that hope could no longer be entertained was told him, and his spirit passed out of the grip of that agony of torture and suspense, and accepted the inevitable with indifference. Yet the change was so extraordinary that it seemed to the doctor rather that the news had completely stunned his powers of feeling, and he was below the numbed surface, still knit into material things as strongly as ever. He had fainted when the result was told him, and Dr. Teesdale had been called in to attend him. But the fit was but transient, and he came out of it into full consciousness of what had happened.

The murder had been a deed of peculiar horror, and there was nothing of sympathy in the mind of the public towards the perpetrator. Charles Linkworth, who now lay under capital sentence, was the keeper of a small stationery store in Sheffield, and there lived with him his wife and mother. The latter was the victim of his atrocious crime; the motive of it being to get possession of the sum of five hundred pounds, which was this woman's property. Linkworth, as came out at the trial, was in debt to the extent of a hundred pounds at the time, and during his wife's absence from home on a visit to relations, he strangled his mother, and during the night buried the body in the small back-garden of his house. On his wife's return, he had a sufficiently plausible tale to account for the elder Mrs. Linkworth's disappearance, for there had been constant jarrings and bickerings between him and his mother for the last year or two, and she had more than once threatened to withdraw herself and the eight shillings a week which she contributed to household expenses, and purchase an annuity with her money. It was true, also, that during the younger Mrs. Linkworth's absence from home, mother and son had had a violent quarrel arising originally from some trivial point in household management, and that in consequence of this, she had actually drawn her money out of the bank, intending to leave Sheffield next day and settle in London, where she had friends. That evening she told him this, and during the night he killed her.

His next step, before his wife's return, was logical and sound. He packed up all his mother's possessions and took them to the station, from which he saw them despatched to town by passenger train, and in the evening he asked several friends in to supper, and told them of his mother's departure. He did not (logically also, and in accordance with what they probably already knew) feign regret, but said that he and she had never got on well together, and that the cause of peace and quietness was furthered by her going. He told the same story to his wife on her return, identical in every detail, adding, however, that the quarrel had been a violent one, and that his mother had not even left him her address. This again was wisely thought of: it would prevent his wife from writing to her. She appeared to accept his story completely: indeed there was nothing strange or suspicious about it.

For a while he behaved with the composure and astuteness which most criminals possess up to a certain point, the lack of which, after that, is generally the cause of their detection. He did not, for instance, immediately pay off his debts, but took into his house a young man as lodger, who occupied his mother's room, and he dismissed the assistant in his shop, and did the entire serving himself. This gave the impression of economy, and at the same time he openly spoke of the great improvement in his trade, and not till a month had passed did he cash any of the bank-notes which he had found in a locked drawer in his mother's room. Then he changed two notes of fifty pounds and paid off his creditors.

At that point his astuteness and composure failed him. He opened a deposit account at a local bank with four more fifty-pound notes, instead of being patient, and increasing his balance at the savings bank pound by pound, and he got uneasy about that which he had buried deep enough for security in the back-garden. Thinking to render himself safer in this regard, he ordered a cartload of slag and stone fragments, and with the help of his lodger employed the summer evenings when work was over in building a sort of rockery over the spot. Then came the chance circumstance which really set match to this dangerous train. There was a fire in the lost luggage office at King's Cross Station (from which he ought to have claimed his mother's property) and one of the two boxes was partially burned. The company was liable for compensation, and his mother's name on her linen, and a letter with the Sheffield address on it, led to the arrival of a purely official and formal notice, stating that the company were prepared to consider claims. It was directed to Mrs. Linkworth's and Charles Linkworth's wife received and read it.

It seemed a sufficiently harmless document, but it was endorsed with his death-warrant. For he could give no explanation at all of the fact of the boxes still lying at King's Cross Station, beyond suggesting that some accident had happened to his mother. Clearly he had to put the matter in the hands of the police, with a view to tracing her movements, and if it proved that she was dead, claiming her property, which she had already drawn out of the bank. Such at least was the course urged on him by his wife and lodger, in whose presence the communication from the railway officials was read out, and it was impossible to refuse to take it. Then the silent, uncreaking machinery of justice, characteristic of England, began to move forward. Quiet men lounged about Smith Street, visited banks, observed the supposed increase in trade, and from a house near by looked into the garden where ferns were already flourishing on the rockery. Then came the arrest and the trial, which did not last very long, and on a certain Saturday night the verdict. Smart women in large hats had made the court bright with colour, and in all the crowd there was not one who felt any sympathy with the young athletic-looking man who was condemned. Many of the audience were elderly and respectable mothers, and the crime had been an outrage on motherhood, and they listened to the unfolding of the flawless evidence with strong approval. They thrilled a little when the judge put on the awful and ludicrous little black cap, and spoke the sentence appointed by God.

Linkworth went to pay the penalty for the atrocious deed, which no one who had heard the evidence could possibly doubt that he had done with the same indifference as had marked his entire demeanour since he knew his appeal had failed. The prison chaplain who had attended him had done his utmost to get him to confess, but his efforts had been quite ineffectual, and to the last he asserted, though without protestation, his innocence. On a bright September morning, when the sun shone warm on the terrible little procession that crossed the prison yard to the shed where was erected the apparatus of death, justice was done, and Dr. Teesdale was satisfied that life was immediately extinct. He had been present on the scaffold, had watched the bolt drawn, and the hooded and pinioned figure drop into the pit. He had heard the chunk and creak of the rope as the sudden weight came on to it, and looking down he had seen the queer twitchings of the hanged body. They had lasted but a second for the execution had been perfectly satisfactory.

An hour later he made the post-mortem examination and found that his view had been correct: the vertebrae of the spine had been broken at the neck, and death must have been absolutely instantaneous. It was hardly necessary even to make that little piece of dissection that proved this, but for the sake of form he did so. And at that moment he had a very curious and vivid mental impression that the spirit of the dead man was close beside him, as if it still dwelt in the broken habitation of its body. But there was no question at all that the body was dead: it had been dead an hour. Then followed another little circumstance that at the first seemed insignificant though curious also. One of the warders entered, and asked if the rope which had been used an hour ago, and was the hangman's perquisite, had by mistake been brought into the mortuary with the body. But there was no trace of it, and it seemed to have vanished altogether, though it a singular thing to be lost: it was not here; it was not on the scaffold. And though the disappearance was of no particular moment it was quite inexplicable.

Dr. Teesdale was a bachelor and a man of independent means, and lived in a tall-windowed and commodious house in Bedford Square, where a plain cook of surpassing excellence looked after his food, and her husband his person. There was no need for him to practise a profession at all, and he performed his work at the prison for the sake of the study of the minds of criminals.

Most crime--the transgression, that is, of the rule of conduct which the human race has framed for the sake of its own preservation--he held to be either the result of some abnormality, of the brain or of starvation. Crimes of theft, for instance, he would by no means refer to one head; often it is true they were the result of actual want, but more often dictated by some obscure disease of the brain. In marked cases it was labelled as kleptomania, but he was convinced there were many others which did not fall directly under the dictation of physical need. More especially was this the case where the crime in question involved also some deed of violence, and he mentally placed underneath this heading, as he went home that evening, the criminal at whose last moments he had been present that morning. The crime had been abominable, the need of money not so very pressing, and the very abomination and unnaturalness of the murder inclined him to consider the murderer as lunatic rather than criminal. He had been, as far as was known, a man of quiet and kindly disposition, a good husband, a sociable neighbour. And then he had committed a crime, just one, which put him outside all pales. So monstrous a deed, whether perpetrated by a sane man or a mad one, was intolerable; there was no use for the doer of it on this planet at all. But somehow the doctor felt that he would have been more at one with the execution of justice, if the dead man had confessed. It was morally certain that he was guilty, but he wished that when there was no longer any hope for him he had endorsed the verdict himself.

He dined alone that evening, and after dinner sat in his study which adjoined the dining-room, and feeling disinclined to read, sat in his great red chair opposite the fireplace, and let his mind graze where it would. At once almost, it went back to the curious sensation he had experienced that morning, of feeling that the spirit of Linkworth was present in the mortuary, though life had been extinct for an hour. It was not the first time, especially in cases of sudden death, that he had felt a similar conviction, though perhaps it had never been quite so unmistakable as it had been to-day. Yet the feeling, to his mind, was quite probably formed on a natural and psychical truth.

The spirit--it may be remarked that he was a believer in the doctrine of future life, and the non-extinction of the soul with the death of the body--was very likely unable or unwilling to quit at once and altogether the earthly habitation, very likely it lingered there, earth-bound, for a while.

In his leisure hours Dr. Teesdale was a considerable student of the occult, for like most advanced and proficient physicians, he clearly recognised how narrow was the boundary of separation between soul and body, how tremendous the influence of the intangible was over material things, and it presented no difficulty to his mind that a disembodied spirit should be able to communicate directly with those who still were bounded by the finite and material.

His meditations, which were beginning to group themselves into definite sequence, were interrupted at this moment. On his desk near at hand stood his telephone, and the bell rang, not with its usual metallic insistence, but very faintly, as if the current was weak, or the mechanism impaired. However, it certainly was ringing, and he got up and took the combined ear and mouth-piece off its hook.

"Yes, yes," he said, "who is it?"

There was a whisper in reply almost inaudible, and quite unintelligible.

"I can't hear you," he said.

Again the whisper sounded, but with no greater distinctness. Then it ceased altogether.

He stood there, for some half minute or so, waiting for it to be renewed, but beyond the usual chuckling and croaking, which showed, however, that he was in communication with some other instrument, there was silence. Then he replaced the receiver, rang up the Exchange, and gave his number.

"Can you tell me what number rang me up just now?" he asked.

There was a short pause, then it was given him. It was the number of the prison, where he was doctor.

"Put me on to it, please," he said.

This was done.

"You rang me up just now," he said down the tube. "Yes; I am Doctor Teesdale. What is it? I could not hear what you said."

The voice came back quite clear and intelligible.

"Some mistake, sir," it said. "We haven't rung you up."

"But the Exchange tells me you did, three minutes ago."

"Mistake at the Exchange, sir," said the voice.

"Very odd. Well, good-night. Warder Draycott, isn't it?"

"Yes, sir; good-night, sir."

Dr. Teesdale went back to his big arm-chair, still less inclined to read. He let his thoughts wander on for a while, without giving them definite direction, but ever and again his mind kept coming back to that strange little incident of the telephone. Often and often he had been rung up by some mistake, often and often he had been put on to the wrong number by the Exchange, but there was something in this very subdued ringing of the telephone bell, and the unintelligible whisperings at the other end that suggested a very curious train of reflection to his mind, and soon he found himself pacing up and down his room, with his thoughts eagerly feeding on a most unusual pasture.

"But it's impossible," he said, aloud.

He went down as usual to the prison next morning, and once again he was strangely beset with the feeling that there was some unseen presence there. He had before now had some odd psychical experiences, and knew that he was a "sensitive"--one, that is, who is capable, under certain circumstances, of receiving supernormal impressions, and of having glimpses of the unseen world that lies about us. And this morning the presence of which he was conscious was that of the man who had been executed yesterday morning. It was local, and he felt it most strongly in the little prison yard, and as he passed the door of the condemned cell. So strong was it there that he would not have been surprised if the figure of the man had been visible to him, and as he passed through the door at the end of the passage, he turned round, actually expecting to see it. All the time, too, he was aware of a profound horror at his heart; this unseen presence strangely disturbed him. And the poor soul, he felt, wanted something done for it. Not for a moment did he doubt that this impression of his was objective, it was no imaginative phantom of his own invention that made itself so real. The spirit of Linkworth was there.

He passed into the infirmary, and for a couple of hours busied himself with his work. But all the time he was aware that the same invisible presence was near him, though its force was manifestly less here than in those places which had been more intimately associated with the man. Finally, before he left, in order to test his theory he looked into the execution shed. But next moment with a face suddenly stricken pale, he came out again, closing the door hastily. At the top of the steps stood a figure hooded and pinioned, but hazy of outline and only faintly visible.

But it was visible, there was no mistake about it.

Dr. Teesdale was a man of good nerve, and he recovered himself almost immediately, ashamed of his temporary panic. The terror that had blanched his face was chiefly the effect of startled nerves, not of terrified heart, and yet deeply interested as he was in psychical phenomena, he could not command himself sufficiently to go back there. Or rather he commanded himself, but his muscles refused to act on the message. If this poor earth-bound spirit had any communication to make to him, he certainly much preferred that it should be made at a distance. As far as he could understand, its range was circumscribed. It haunted the prison yard, the condemned cell, the execution shed, it was more faintly felt in the infirmary. Then a further point suggested itself to his mind, and he went back to his room and sent for Warder Draycott, who had answered him on the telephone last night.

"You are quite sure," he asked, "that nobody rang me up last night, just before I rang you up?"

There was a certain hesitation in the man's manner which the doctor noticed.

"I don't see how it could be possible, sir," he said. "I had been sitting close by the telephone for half an hour before, and again before that. I must have seen him, if anyone had been to the instrument."

"And you saw no one?" said the doctor with a slight emphasis.

The man became more markedly ill at ease.

"No, sir, I saw no one," he said, with the same emphasis.

Dr. Teesdale looked away from him.

"But you had perhaps the impression that there was some one there?" he asked, carelessly, as if it was a point of no interest.

Clearly Warder Draycott had something on his mind, which he found it hard to speak of.

"Well, sir, if you put it like that," he began. "But you would tell me I was half asleep, or had eaten something that disagreed with me at my supper."

The doctor dropped his careless manner.

"I should do nothing of the kind," he said, "any more than you would tell me that I had dropped asleep last night, when I heard my telephone bell ring. Mind you, Draycott, it did not ring as usual, I could only just hear it ringing, though it was close to me. And I could only hear a whisper when I put my ear to it. But when you spoke I heard you quite distinctly. Now I believe there was something--somebody--at this end of the telephone. You were here, and though you saw no one, you, too, felt there was someone there."

The man nodded.

"I'm not a nervous man, sir," he said, "and I don't deal in fancies. But there was something there. It was hovering about the instrument, and it wasn't the wind, because there wasn't a breath of wind stirring, and the night was warm. And I shut the window to make certain. But it went about the room, sir, for an hour or more. It rustled the leaves of the telephone book, and it ruffled my hair when it came close to me. And it was bitter cold, sir."

The doctor looked him straight in the face.

"Did it remind you of what had been done yesterday morning?" he asked suddenly.

Again the man hesitated.

"Yes, sir," he said at length. "Convict Charles Linkworth."

Dr. Teesdale nodded reassuringly.

"That's it," he said. "Now, are you on duty to-night?"

"Yes, sir, I wish I wasn't."

"I know how you feel, I have felt exactly the same myself. Now whatever this is, it seems to want to communicate with me. By the way, did you have any disturbance in the prison last night?"

"Yes, sir, there was half a dozen men who had the nightmare. Yelling and screaming they were, and quiet men too, usually. It happens sometimes the night after an execution. I've known it before, though nothing like what it was last night."

"I see. Now, if this--this thing you can't see wants to get at the telephone again to-night, give it every chance. It will probably come about the same time. I can't tell you why, but that usually happens. So unless you must, don't be in this room where the telephone is, just for an hour to give it plenty of time between half-past nine and half-past ten. I will be ready for it at the other end. Supposing I am rung up, I will, when it has finished, ring you up to make sure that I was not being called in--in the usual way."

"And there is nothing to be afraid of, sir!" asked the man.

Dr. Teesdale remembered his own moment of terror this morning, but he spoke quite sincerely.

"I am sure there is nothing to be afraid of," he said, reassuringly.

Dr. Teesdale had a dinner engagement that night, which he broke, and was sitting alone in his study by half past-nine. In the present state of human ignorance as to the law which governs the movements of spirits severed from the body, he could not tell the warder why it was that their visits are so often periodic, timed to punctuality according to our scheme of hours, but in scenes of tabulated instances of the appearance of revenants, especially if the soul was in sore need of help, as might be the case here, he found that they came at the same hour of day or night. As a rule, too, their power of making themselves seen or heard or felt grew greater for some little while after death, subsequently growing weaker as they became less earth-bound, or often after that ceasing altogether, and he was prepared to-night for a less indistinct impression. The spirit apparently for the early hours of its disembodiment is weak, like a moth newly broken out from its chrysalis--and then suddenly the telephone bell rang, not so faintly as the night before, but still not with its ordinary imperative tone.

Dr. Teesdale instantly got up, put the receiver to his ear. And what he heard was heartbroken sobbing, strong spasms that seemed to tear the weeper.

He waited for a little before speaking, himself cold with some nameless fear, and yet profoundly moved to help, if he was able.

"Yes, yes," he said at length, hearing his own voice tremble. "I am Dr. Teesdale. What can I do for you? And who are you?" he added, though he felt that it was a needless question.

Slowly the sobbing died down, the whispers took its place, still broken by crying.

"I want to tell, sir--I want to tell--I must tell."

"Yes, tell me, what is it?" said the doctor.

"No, not you--another gentleman, who used to come to see me. Will you speak to him what I say to you?--I can't make him hear me or see me."

"Who are you?" asked Dr. Teesdale suddenly.

"Charles Linkworth. I thought you knew. I am very miserable. I can't leave the prison--and it is cold. Will you send for the other gentleman?"

"Do you mean the chaplain?" asked Dr. Teesdale.

"Yes, the chaplain. He read the service when I went across the yard yesterday. I shan't be so miserable when I have told."

The doctor hesitated a moment. This was a strange story that he would have to tell Mr. Dawkins, the prison chaplain, that at the other end of the telephone was the spirit of the man executed yesterday. And yet he soberly believed that it was so, that this unhappy spirit was in misery and wanted to "tell." There was no need to ask what he wanted to tell.

"Yes, I will ask him to come here," he said at length.

"Thank you, sir, a thousand times. You will make him come, won't you?"

The voice was growing fainter.

"It must be to-morrow night," it said. "I can't speak longer now. I have to go to see--oh, my God, my God."

The sobs broke out afresh, sounding fainter and fainter. But it was in a frenzy of terrified interest that Dr. Teesdale spoke.

"To see what?" he cried. "Tell me what you are doing, what is happening to you?"

"I can't tell you; I mayn't tell you," said the voice very faint. "That is part--" and it died away altogether.

Dr. Teesdale waited a little, but there was no further sound of any kind, except the chuckling and croaking of the instrument. He put the receiver on to its hook again, and then became aware for the first time that his forehead was streaming with some cold dew of horror. His ears sang; his heart beat very quick and faint, and he sat down to recover himself. Once or twice he asked himself if it was possible that some terrible joke was being played on him, but he knew that could not be so; he felt perfectly sure that he had been speaking with a soul in torment of contrition for the terrible and irremediable act it had committed. It was no delusion of his senses, either; here in this comfortable room of his in Bedford Square, with London cheerfully roaring round him, he had spoken with the spirit of Charles Linkworth.

But he had no time (nor indeed inclination, for somehow his soul sat shuddering within him) to indulge in meditation. First of all he rang up the prison.

"Warder Draycott?" he asked.

There was a perceptible tremor in the man's voice as he answered.

"Yes, sir. Is it Dr. Teesdale?"

"Yes. Has anything happened here with you?"

Twice it seemed that the man tried to speak and could not. At the third attempt the words came "Yes, sir. He has been here. I saw him go into the room where the telephone is."

"Ah! Did you speak to him?"

"No, sir: I sweated and prayed. And there's half a dozen men as have been screaming in their sleep to-night. But it's quiet again now. I think he has gone into the execution shed."

"Yes. Well, I think there will be no more disturbance now. By the way, please give me Mr. Dawkins's home address."

This was given him, and Dr. Teesdale proceeded to write to the chaplain, asking him to dine with him on the following night. But suddenly he found that he could not write at his accustomed desk, with the telephone standing close to him, and he went upstairs to the drawing-room which he seldom used, except when he entertained his friends. There he recaptured the serenity of his nerves, and could control his hand. The note simply asked Mr. Dawkins to dine with him next night, when he wished to tell him a very strange history and ask his help. "Even if you have any other engagement," he concluded, "I seriously request you to give it up. To-night, I did the same.

"I should bitterly have regretted it if I had not."

Next night accordingly, the two sat at their dinner in the doctor's dining-room, and when they were left to their cigarettes and coffee the doctor spoke.

"You must not think me mad, my dear Dawkins," he said, "when you hear what I have got to tell you."

Mr. Dawkins laughed.

"I will certainly promise not to do that," he said.

"Good. Last night and the night before, a little later in the evening than this, I spoke through the telephone with the spirit of the man we saw executed two days ago. Charles Linkworth."

The chaplain did not laugh. He pushed back his chair, looking annoyed.

"Teesdale," he said, "is it to tell me this--I don't want to be rude--but this bogey-tale that you have brought me here this evening?"

"Yes. You have not heard half of it. He asked me last night to get hold of you. He wants to tell you something. We can guess, I think, what it is."

Dawkins got up.

"Please let me hear no more of it," he said. "The dead do not return. In what state or under what condition they exist has not been revealed to us. But they have done with all material things."

"But I must tell you more," said the doctor. "Two nights ago I was rung up, but very faintly, and could only hear whispers. I instantly inquired where the call came from and was told it came from the prison. I rang up the prison, and Warder Draycott told me that nobody had rung me up. He, too, was conscious of a presence."

"I think that man drinks," said Dawkins, sharply.

The doctor paused a moment.

"My dear fellow, you should not say that sort of thing," he said. "He is one of the steadiest men we have got. And if he drinks, why not I also?"

The chaplain sat down again.

"You must forgive me," he said, "but I can't go into this. These are dangerous matters to meddle with. Besides, how do you know it is not a hoax?"

"Played by whom?" asked the doctor. "Hark!"

The telephone bell suddenly rang. It was clearly audible to the doctor.

"Don't you hear it?" he said.

"Hear what?"

"The telephone bell ringing."

"I hear no bell," said the chaplain, rather angrily. "There is no bell ringing."

The doctor did not answer, but went through into his study, and turned on the lights. Then he took the receiver and mouthpiece off its hook.

"Yes?" he said, in a voice that trembled. "Who is it? Yes: Mr. Dawkins is here. I will try and get him to speak to you." He went back into the other room.

"Dawkins," he said, "there is a soul in agony. I pray you to listen. For God's sake come and listen."

The chaplain hesitated a moment.

"As you will," he said.

He took up the receiver and put it to his ear.

"I am Mr. Dawkins," he said.

He waited.

"I can hear nothing whatever," he said at length. "Ah, there was something there. The faintest whisper."

"Ah, try to hear, try to hear!" said the doctor.

Again the chaplain listened. Suddenly he laid the instrument down, frowning.

"Something--somebody said, 'I killed her, I confess it. I want to be forgiven.' It's a hoax, my dear Teesdale. Somebody knowing your spiritualistic leanings is playing a very grim joke on you. I can't believe it."

Dr. Teesdale took up the receiver.

"I am Dr. Teesdale," he said. "Can you give Mr. Dawkins some sign that it is you?"

Then he laid it down again.

"He says he thinks he can," he said. "We must wait."

The evening was again very warm, and the window into the paved yard at the back of the house was open. For five minutes or so the two men stood in silence, waiting, and nothing happened. Then the chaplain spoke.

"I think that is sufficiently conclusive," he said.

Even as he spoke a very cold draught of air suddenly blew into the room, making the papers on the desk rustle. Dr. Teesdale went to the window and closed it.

"Did you feel that?" he asked.

"Yes, a breath of air. Chilly."

Once again in the closed room it stirred again.

"And did you feel that?" asked the doctor.

The chaplain nodded. He felt his heart hammering in his throat suddenly.

"Defend us from all peril and danger of this coming night," he exclaimed.

"Something is coming!" said the doctor.

As he spoke it came. In the centre of the room not three yards away from them stood the figure of a man with his head bent over on to his shoulder, so that the face was not visible. Then he took his head in both his hands and raised it like a weight, and looked them in the face. The eyes and tongue protruded, a livid mark was round the neck. Then there came a sharp rattle on the boards of the floor, and the figure was no longer there. But on the floor there lay a new rope.

For a long while neither spoke. The sweat poured off the doctor's face, and the chaplain's white lips whispered prayers. Then by a huge effort the doctor pulled himself together. He pointed at the rope.

"It has been missing since the execution," he said.

Then again the telephone bell rang. This time the chaplain needed no prompting. He went to it at once and the ringing ceased. For a while he listened in silence.

"Charles Linkworth," he said at length, "in the sight of God, in whose presence you stand, are you truly sorry for your sin?"

Some answer inaudible to the doctor came, and the chaplain closed his eyes. And Dr. Teesdale knelt as he heard the words of the Absolution.

At the close there was silence again.

"I can hear nothing more," said the chaplain, replacing the receiver.

Presently the doctor's man-servant came in with the tray of spirits and syphon. Dr. Teesdale pointed without looking to where the apparition had been.

"Take the rope that is there and burn it, Parker," he said.

There was a moment's silence.
"There is no rope, sir," said Parker.

Negotium Perambulans

The casual tourist in West Cornwall may just possibly have noticed, as he bowled along over the bare high plateau between Penzance and the Land's End, a dilapidated signpost pointing down a steep lane and bearing on its battered finger the faded inscription "Polearn 2 miles," but probably very few have had the curiosity to traverse those two miles in order to see a place to which their guide-books award so cursory a notice. It is described there, in a couple of unattractive lines, as a small fishing village with a church of no particular interest except for certain carved and painted wooden panels (originally belonging to an earlier edifice) which form an altar-rail. But the church at St. Creed (the tourist is reminded) has a similar decoration far superior in point of preservation and interest, and thus even the ecclesiastically disposed are not lured to Polearn. So meagre a bait is scarce worth swallowing, and a glance at the very steep lane which in dry weather presents a carpet of sharp-pointed stones, and after rain a muddy watercourse, will almost certainly decide him not to expose his motor or his bicycle to risks like these in so sparsely populated a district. Hardly a house has met his eye since he left Penzance, and the possible trundling of a punctured bicycle for half a dozen weary miles seems a high price to pay for the sight of a few painted panels.

Polearn, therefore, even in the high noon of the tourist season, is little liable to invasion, and for the rest of the year I do not suppose that a couple of folk a day traverse those two miles (long ones at that) of steep and stony gradient. I am not forgetting the postman in this exiguous estimate, for the days are few when, leaving his pony and cart at the top of the hill, he goes as far as the village, since but a few hundred yards down the lane there stands a large white box, like a sea-trunk, by the side of the road, with a slit for letters and a locked door. Should he have in his wallet a registered letter or be the bearer of a parcel too large for insertion in the square lips of the sea-trunk, he must needs trudge down the hill and deliver the troublesome missive, leaving it in person on the owner, and receiving some small reward of coin or refreshment for his kindness.

But such occasions are rare, and his general routine is to take out of the box such letters as may have been deposited there, and insert in their place such letters as he has brought. These will be called for, perhaps that day or perhaps the next, by an emissary from the Polearn post-office.

As for the fishermen of the place, who, in their export trade, constitute the chief link of movement between Polearn and the outside world, they would not dream of taking their catch up the steep lane and so, with six miles farther of travel, to the market at Penzance. The sea route is shorter and easier, and they deliver their wares to the pier-head. Thus, though the sole industry of Polearn is sea-fishing, you will get no fish there unless you have bespoken your requirements to one of the fishermen. Back come the trawlers as empty as a haunted house, while their spoils are in the fish-train that is speeding to London.

Such isolation of a little community, continued, as it has been, for centuries, produces isolation in the individual as well, and nowhere will you find greater independence of character than among the people of Polearn. But they are linked together, so it has always seemed to me, by some mysterious comprehension: it is as if they had all been initiated into some ancient rite, inspired and framed by forces visible and invisible. The winter storms that batter the coast, the vernal spell of the spring, the hot, still summers, the season of rains and autumnal decay, have made a spell which, line by line, has been communicated to them, concerning the powers, evil and good, that rule the world, and manifest themselves in ways benignant or terrible...

I came to Polearn first at the age of ten, a small boy, weak and sickly, and threatened with pulmonary trouble. My father's business kept him in London, while for me abundance of fresh air and a mild climate were considered essential conditions if I was to grow to manhood. His sister had married the vicar of Polearn, Richard Bolitho, himself native to the place, and so it came about that I spent three years, as a paying guest, with my relations. Richard Bolitho owned a fine house in the place, which he inhabited in preference to the vicarage, which he let to a young artist, John Evans, on whom the spell of Polearn had fallen for from year's beginning to year's end he never left it. There was a solid roofed shelter, open on one side to the air, built for me in the garden, and here I lived and slept, passing scarcely one hour out of the twenty-four behind walls and windows. I was out on the bay with the fisher-folk, or wandering along the gorse-clad cliffs that climbed steeply to right and left of the deep combe where the village lay, or pottering about on the pier-head, or bird's-nesting in the bushes with the boys of the village.

Except on Sunday and for the few daily hours of my lessons, I might do what I pleased so long as I remained in the open air. About the lessons there was nothing formidable; my uncle conducted me through flowering bypaths among the thickets of arithmetic, and made pleasant excursions into the elements of Latin grammar, and above all, he made me daily give him an account, in clear and grammatical sentences, of what had been occupying my mind or my movements. Should I select to tell him about a walk along the cliffs, my speech must be orderly, not vague, slip-shod notes of what I had observed. In this way, too, he trained my observation, for he would bid me tell him what flowers were in bloom, and what birds hovered fishing over the sea or were building in the bushes. For that I owe him a perennial gratitude, for to observe and to express my thoughts in the clear spoken word became my life's profession.

But far more formidable than my weekday tasks was the prescribed routine for Sunday.

Some dark embers compounded of Calvinism and mysticism smouldered in my uncle's soul, and made it a day of terror. His sermon in the morning scorched us with a foretaste of the eternal fires reserved for unrepentant sinners, and he was hardly less terrifying at the children's service in the afternoon. Well do I remember his exposition of the doctrine of guardian angels. A child, he said, might think himself secure in such angelic care, but let him beware of committing any of those numerous offences which would cause his guardian to turn his face from him, for as sure as there were angels to protect us, there were also evil and awful presences which were ready to pounce; and on them he dwelt with peculiar gusto. Well, too, do I remember in the morning sermon his commentary on the carved panels of the altar-rails to which I have already alluded.

There was the angel of the Annunciation there, and the angel of the Resurrection, but not less was there the witch of Endor, and, on the fourth panel, a scene that concerned me most of all.

This fourth panel (he came down from his pulpit to trace its time-worn features) represented the lych-gate of the church-yard at Polearn itself, and indeed the resemblance when thus pointed out was remarkable. In the entry stood the figure of a robed priest holding up a Cross, with which he faced a terrible creature like a gigantic slug, that reared itself up in front of him. That, so ran my uncle's interpretation, was some evil agency, such as he had spoken about to us children, of almost infinite malignity and power, which could alone be combated by firm faith and a pure heart. Below ran the legend "Negotium perambulans in tenebris" from the ninety-first Psalm. We should find it translated there, "the pestilence that walketh in darkness," which but feebly rendered the Latin. It was more deadly to the soul than any pestilence that can only kill the body: it was the Thing, the Creature, the Business that trafficked in the outer Darkness, a minister of God's wrath on the unrighteous...I could see, as he spoke, the looks which the congregation exchanged with each other, and knew that his words were evoking a surmise, a remembrance. Nods and whispers passed between them, they understood to what he alluded, and with the inquisitiveness of boyhood I could not rest till I had wormed the story out of my friends among the fisher-boys, as, next morning, we sat basking and naked in the sun after our bathe. One knew one bit of it, one another, but it pieced together into a truly alarming legend. In bald outline it was as follows:

A church far more ancient than that in which my uncle terrified us every Sunday had once stood not three hundred yards away, on the shelf of level ground below the quarry from which its stones were hewn. The owner of the land had pulled this down, and erected for himself a house on the same site out of these materials, keeping, in a very ecstasy of wickedness, the altar, and on this he dined and played dice afterwards. But as he grew old some black melancholy seized him, and he would have lights burning there all night, for he had deadly fear of the darkness. On one winter evening there sprang up such a gale as was never before known, which broke in the windows of the room where he had supped, and extinguished the lamps. Yells of terror brought in his servants, who found him lying on the floor with the blood streaming from his throat. As they entered some huge black shadow seemed to move away from him, crawled across the floor and up the wall and out of the broken window.

"There he lay a-dying," said the last of my informants, "and him that had been a great burly man was withered to a bag o' skin, for the critter had drained all the blood from him. His last breath was a scream, and he hollered out the same words as passon read off the screen."

"Negotium perambulans in tenebris," I suggested eagerly.

"Thereabouts. Latin anyhow."

"And after that?" I asked.

"Nobody would go near the place, and the old house rotted and fell in ruins till three years ago, when along comes Mr. Dooliss from Penzance, and built the half of it up again. But he don't care much about such critters, nor about Latin neither. He takes his bottle of whisky a day and gets drunk's a lord in the evening. Eh, I'm gwine home to my dinner."

Whatever the authenticity of the legend, I had certainly heard the truth about Mr. Dooliss from Penzance, who from that day became an object of keen curiosity on my part, the more so because the quarry-house adjoined my uncle's garden. The Thing that walked in the dark failed to stir my imagination, and already I was so used to sleeping alone in my shelter that the night had no terrors for me. But it would be intensely exciting to wake at some timeless hour and hear Mr. Dooliss yelling, and conjecture that the Thing had got him.

But by degrees the whole story faded from my mind, overscored by the more vivid interests of the day, and, for the last two years of my out-door life in the vicarage garden, I seldom thought about Mr. Dooliss and the possible fate that might await him for his temerity in living in the place where that Thing of darkness had done business. Occasionally I saw him over the garden fence, a great yellow lump of a man, with slow and staggering gait, but never did I set eyes on him outside his gate, either in the village street or down on the beach. He interfered with none, and no one interfered with him. If he wanted to run the risk of being the prey of the legendary nocturnal monster, or quietly drink himself to death, it was his affair. My uncle, so I gathered, had made several attempts to see him when first he came to live at Polearn, but Mr. Dooliss appeared to have no use for parsons, but said he was not at home and never returned the call.

After three years of sun, wind, and rain, I had completely outgrown my early symptoms and had become a tough, strapping youngster of thirteen. I was sent to Eton and Cambridge, and in due course ate my dinners and became a barrister. In twenty years from that time I was earning a yearly income of five figures, and had already laid by in sound securities a sum that brought me dividends which would, for one of my simple tastes and frugal habits, supply me with all the material comforts I needed on this side of the grave. The great prizes of my profession were already within my reach, but I had no ambition beckoning me on, nor did I want a wife and children, being, I must suppose, a natural celibate. In fact there was only one ambition which through these busy years had held the lure of blue and far-off hills to me, and that was to get back to Polearn, and live once more isolated from the world with the sea and the gorse-clad hills for play-fellows, and the secrets that lurked there for exploration. The spell of it had been woven about my heart, and I can truly say that there had hardly passed a day in all those years in which the thought of it and the desire for it had been wholly absent from my mind. Though I had been in frequent communication with my uncle there during his lifetime, and, after his death, with his widow who still lived there, I had never been back to it since I embarked on my profession, for I knew that if I went there, it would be a wrench beyond my power to tear myself away again. But I had made up my mind that when once I had provided for my own independence, I would go back there not to leave it again. And yet I did leave it again, and now nothing in the world would induce me to turn down the lane from the road that leads from Penzance to the Land's End, and see the sides of the combe rise steep above the roofs of the village and hear the gulls chiding as they fish in the bay. One of the things invisible, of the dark powers, leaped into light, and I saw it with my eyes.

The house where I had spent those three years of boyhood had been left for life to my aunt, and when I made known to her my intention of coming back to Polearn, she suggested that, till I found a suitable house or found her proposal unsuitable, I should come to live with her.

"The house is too big for a lone old woman," she wrote, "and I have often thought of quitting and taking a little cottage sufficient for me and my requirements. But come and share it, my dear, and if you find me troublesome, you or I can go. You may want solitude--most people in Polearn do--and will leave me. Or else I will leave you: one of the main reasons of my stopping here all these years was a feeling that I must not let the old house starve. Houses starve, you know, if they are not lived in. They die a lingering death; the spirit in them grows weaker and weaker, and at last fades out of them. Isn't this nonsense to your London notions?..."

Naturally I accepted with warmth this tentative arrangement, and on an evening in June found myself at the head of the lane leading down to Polearn, and once more I descended into the steep valley between the hills. Time had stood still apparently for the combe, the dilapidated signpost (or its successor) pointed a rickety finger down the lane, and a few hundred yards farther on was the white box for the exchange of letters. Point after remembered point met my eye, and what I saw was not shrunk, as is often the case with the revisited scenes of childhood, into a smaller scale. There stood the post-office, and there the church and close beside it the vicarage, and beyond, the tall shrubberies which separated the house for which I was bound from the road, and beyond that again the grey roofs of the quarry-house damp and shining with the moist evening wind from the sea. All was exactly as I remembered it, and, above all, that sense of seclusion and isolation. Somewhere above the tree-tops climbed the lane which joined the main road to Penzance, but all that had become immeasurably distant. The years that had passed since last I turned in at the well-known gate faded like a frosty breath, and vanished in this warm, soft air. There were law-courts somewhere in memory's dull book which, if I cared to turn the pages, would tell me that I had made a name and a great income there. But the dull book was closed now, for I was back in Polearn, and the spell was woven around me again.

And if Polearn was unchanged, so too was Aunt Hester, who met me at the door. Dainty and china-white she had always been, and the years had not aged but only refined her. As we sat and talked after dinner she spoke of all that had happened in Polearn in that score of years, and yet somehow the changes of which she spoke seemed but to confirm the immutability of it all. As the recollection of names came back to me, I asked her about the quarry-house and Mr. Dooliss, and her face gloomed a little as with the shadow of a cloud on a spring day.

"Yes, Mr. Dooliss," she said, "poor Mr. Dooliss, how well I remember him, though it must be ten years and more since he died. I never wrote to you about it, for it was all very dreadful, my dear, and I did not want to darken your memories of Polearn. Your uncle always thought that something of the sort might happen if he went on in his wicked, drunken ways, and worse than that, and though nobody knew exactly what took place, it was the sort of thing that might have been anticipated."

"But what more or less happened, Aunt Hester?" I asked.

"Well, of course I can't tell you everything, for no one knew it. But he was a very sinful man, and the scandal about him at Newlyn was shocking. And then he lived, too, in the quarry-house...

"I wonder if by any chance you remember a sermon of your uncle's when he got out of the pulpit and explained that panel in the altar-rails, the one, I mean, with the horrible creature rearing itself up outside the lych-gate?"

"Yes, I remember perfectly," said I.

"Ah. It made an impression on you, I suppose, and so it did on all who heard him, and that impression got stamped and branded on us all when the catastrophe occurred. Somehow Mr. Dooliss got to hear about your uncle's sermon, and in some drunken fit he broke into the church and smashed the panel to atoms. He seems to have thought that there was some magic in it, and that if he destroyed that he would get rid of the terrible fate that was threatening him. For I must tell you that before he committed that dreadful sacrilege he had been a haunted man: he hated and feared darkness, for he thought that the creature on the panel was on his track, but that as long as he kept lights burning it could not touch him. But the panel, to his disordered mind, was the root of his terror, and so, as I said, he broke into the church and attempted--you will see why I said 'attempted'--to destroy it. It certainly was found in splinters next morning, when your uncle went into church for matins, and knowing Mr. Dooliss's fear of the panel, he went across to the quarry-house afterwards and taxed him with its destruction. The man never denied it; he boasted of what he had done. There he sat, though it was early morning, drinking his whisky.

"'I've settled your Thing for you,' he said, 'and your sermon too. A fig for such superstitions.'

"Your uncle left him without answering his blasphemy, meaning to go straight into Penzance and give information to the police about this outrage to the church, but on his way back from the quarry-house he went into the church again, in order to be able to give details about the damage, and there in the screen was the panel, untouched and uninjured. And yet he had himself seen it smashed, and Mr. Dooliss had confessed that the destruction of it was his work. But there it was, and whether the power of God had mended it or some other power, who knows?"

This was Polearn indeed, and it was the spirit of Polearn that made me accept all Aunt Hester was telling me as attested fact. It had happened like that. She went on in her quiet voice.

"Your uncle recognised that some power beyond police was at work, and he did not go to Penzance or give informations about the outrage, for the evidence of it had vanished." A sudden spate of scepticism swept over me.

"There must have been some mistake," I said. "It hadn't been broken..."

She smiled.

"Yes, my dear, but you have been in London so long," she said. "Let me, anyhow, tell you the rest of my story. That night, for some reason, I could not sleep. It was very hot and airless; I dare say you will think that the sultry conditions accounted for my wakefulness. Once and again, as I went to the window to see if I could not admit more air, I could see from it the quarry-house, and I noticed the first time that I left my bed that it was blazing with lights. But the second time I saw that it was all in darkness, and as I wondered at that, I heard a terrible scream, and the moment afterwards the steps of someone coming at full speed down the road outside the gate. He yelled as he ran; 'Light, light!' he called out. 'Give me light, or it will catch me!' It was very terrible to hear that, and I went to rouse my husband, who was sleeping in the dressing-room across the passage. He wasted no time, but by now the whole village was aroused by the screams, and when he got down to the pier he found that all was over. The tide was low, and on the rocks at its foot was lying the body of Mr. Dooliss. He must have cut some artery when he fell on those sharp edges of stone, for he had bled to death, they thought, and though he was a big burly man, his corpse was but skin and bones. Yet there was no pool of blood round him, such as you would have expected. Just skin and bones as if every drop of blood in his body had been sucked out of him!"

She leaned forward.

"You and I, my dear, know what happened," she said, "or at least can guess. God has His instruments of vengeance on those who bring wickedness into places that have been holy. Dark and mysterious are His ways."

Now what I should have thought of such a story if it had been told me in London I can easily imagine. There was such an obvious explanation: the man in question had been a drunkard, what wonder if the demons of delirium pursued him? But here in Polearn it was different.

"And who is in the quarry-house now?" I asked. "Years ago the fisher-boys told me the story of the man who first built it and of his horrible end. And now again it has happened. Surely no one has ventured to inhabit it once more?"

I saw in her face, even before I asked that question, that somebody had done so.

"Yes, it is lived in again," said she, "for there is no end to the blindness...I don't know if you remember him. He was tenant of the vicarage many years ago."

"John Evans," said I.

"Yes. Such a nice fellow he was too. Your uncle was pleased to get so good a tenant. And now--" She rose.

"Aunt Hester, you shouldn't leave your sentences unfinished," I said.

She shook her head.

"My dear, that sentence will finish itself," she said. "But what a time of night! I must go to bed, and you too, or they will think we have to keep lights burning here through the dark hours."

Before getting into bed I drew my curtains wide and opened all the windows to the warm tide of the sea air that flowed softly in. Looking out into the garden I could see in the moonlight the roof of the shelter, in which for three years I had lived, gleaming with dew. That, as much as anything, brought back the old days to which I had now returned, and they seemed of one piece with the present, as if no gap of more than twenty years sundered them. The two flowed into one, like globules of mercury uniting into a softly shining globe, of mysterious lights and reflections.

Then, raising my eyes a little, I saw against the black hill-side the windows of the quarry-house still alight.

Morning, as is so often the case, brought no shattering of my illusion. As I began to regain consciousness, I fancied that I was a boy again waking up in the shelter in the garden, and though, as I grew more widely awake, I smiled at the impression, that on which it was based I found to be indeed true. It was sufficient now as then to be here, to wander again on the cliffs, and hear the popping of the ripened seed-pods on the gorse-bushes; to stray along the shore to the bathing-cove, to float and drift and swim in the warm tide, and bask on the sand, and watch the gulls fishing, to lounge on the pier-head with the fisher-folk, to see in their eyes and hear in their quiet speech the evidence of secret things not so much known to them as part of their instincts and their very being. There were powers and presences about me; the white poplars that stood by the stream that babbled down the valley knew of them, and showed a glimpse of their knowledge sometimes, like the gleam of their white underleaves; the very cobbles that paved the street were soaked in it All that I wanted was to lie there and grow soaked in it too; unconsciously, as a boy, I had done that, but now the process must be conscious. I must know what stir of forces, fruitful and mysterious, seethed along the hill-side at noon, and sparkled at night on the sea. They could be known, they could even be controlled by those who were masters of the spell, but never could they be spoken of, for they were dwellers in the innermost, grafted into the eternal life of the world. There were dark secrets as well as these clear, kindly powers, and to these no doubt belonged the negotium perambulans in tenebris which, though of deadly malignity, might be regarded not only as evil, but as the avenger of sacrilegious and impious deeds... All this was part of the spell of Polearn, of which the seeds had long lain dormant in me. But now they were sprouting, and who knew what strange flower would unfold on their stems?

It was not long before I came across John Evans. One morning, as I lay on the beach, there came shambling across the sand a man stout and middle-aged with the face of Silenus. He paused as he drew near and regarded me from narrow eyes.

"Why, you're the little chap that used to live in the parson's garden," he said. "Don't you recognise me?"

I saw who it was when he spoke: his voice, I think, instructed me, and recognising it, I could see the features of the strong, alert young man in this gross caricature.

"Yes, you're John Evans," I said. "You used to be very kind to me: you used to draw pictures for me."

"So I did, and I'll draw you some more. Been bathing? That's a risky performance. You never know what lives in the sea, nor what lives on the land for that matter. Not that I heed them.

"I stick to work and whisky. God! I've learned to paint since I saw you, and drink too for that matter. I live in the quarry-house, you know, and it's a powerful thirsty place. Come and have a look at my things if you're passing. Staying with your aunt, are you? I could do a wonderful portrait of her. Interesting face; she knows a lot. People who live at Polearn get to know a lot, though I don't take much stock in that sort of knowledge myself."

I do not know when I have been at once so repelled and interested. Behind the mere grossness of his face there lurked something which, while it appalled, yet fascinated me. His thick lisping speech had the same quality. And his paintings, what would they be like?...

"I was just going home," I said. "I'll gladly come in, if you'll allow me."

He took me through the untended and overgrown garden into the house which I had never yet entered. A great grey cat was sunning itself in the window, and an old woman was laying lunch in a corner of the cool hall into which the door opened. It was built of stone, and the carved mouldings let into the walls, the fragments of gargoyles and sculptured images, bore testimony to the truth of its having been built out of the demolished church. In one corner was an oblong and carved wooden table littered with a painter's apparatus and stacks of canvases leaned against the walls.

He jerked his thumb towards a head of an angel that was built into the mantelpiece and giggled.

"Quite a sanctified air," he said, "so we tone it down for the purposes of ordinary life by a different sort of art. Have a drink? No? Well, turn over some of my pictures while I put myself to rights."

He was justified in his own estimate of his skill: he could paint (and apparently he could paint anything), but never have I seen pictures so inexplicably hellish. There were exquisite studies of trees, and you knew that something lurked in the flickering shadows. There was a drawing of his cat sunning itself in the window, even as I had just now seen it, and yet it was no cat but some beast of awful malignity. There was a boy stretched naked on the sands, not human, but some evil thing which had come out of the sea. Above all there were pictures of his garden overgrown and jungle-like, and you knew that in the bushes were presences ready to spring out on you...

"Well, do you like my style?" he said as he came up, glass in hand. (The tumbler of spirits that he held had not been diluted.) "I try to paint the essence of what I see, not the mere husk and skin of it, but its nature, where it comes from and what gave it birth. There's much in common between a cat and a fuchsia-bush if you look at them closely enough. Everything came out of the slime of the pit, and it's all going back there. I should like to do a picture of you some day. I'd hold the mirror up to Nature, as that old lunatic said."

After this first meeting I saw him occasionally throughout the months of that wonderful summer. Often he kept to his house and to his painting for days together, and then perhaps some evening I would find him lounging on the pier, always alone, and every time we met thus the repulsion and interest grew, for every time he seemed to have gone farther along a path of secret knowledge towards some evil shrine where complete initiation awaited him...And then suddenly the end came.

I had met him thus one evening on the cliffs while the October sunset still burned in the sky, but over it with amazing rapidity there spread from the west a great blackness of cloud such as I have never seen for denseness. The light was sucked from the sky, the dusk fell in ever thicker layers. He suddenly became conscious of this.

"I must get back as quick as I can," he said. "It will be dark in a few minutes, and my servant is out. The lamps will not be lit."

He stepped out with extraordinary briskness for one who shambled and could scarcely lift his feet, and soon broke out into a stumbling run. In the gathering darkness I could see that his face was moist with the dew of some unspoken terror.

"You must come with me," he panted, "for so we shall get the lights burning the sooner. I cannot do without light."

I had to exert myself to the full to keep up with him, for terror winged him, and even so I fell behind, so that when I came to the garden gate, he was already half-way up the path to the house.

I saw him enter, leaving the door wide, and found him fumbling with matches. But his hand so trembled that he could not transfer the light to the wick of the lamp..."But what's the hurry about?" I asked.

Suddenly his eyes focused themselves on the open door behind me, and he jumped from his seat beside the table which had once been the altar of God, with a gasp and a scream.

"No, no!" he cried. "Keep it off!..."

I turned and saw what he had seen. The Thing had entered and now was swiftly sliding across the floor towards him, like some gigantic caterpillar. A stale phosphorescent light came from it, for though the dusk had grown to blackness outside, I could see it quite distinctly in the awful light of its own presence. From it too there came an odour of corruption and decay, as from slime that has long lain below water. It seemed to have no head, but on the front of it was an orifice of puckered skin which opened and shut and slavered at the edges. It was hairless, and slug-like in shape and in texture. As it advanced its fore-part reared itself from the ground, like a snake about to strike, and it fastened on him...

At that sight, and with the yells of his agony in my ears, the panic which had struck me relaxed into a hopeless courage, and with palsied, impotent hands I tried to lay hold of the Thing.

But I could not: though something material was there, it was impossible to grasp it; my hands sunk in it as in thick mud. It was like wrestling with a nightmare.

I think that but a few seconds elapsed before all was over. The screams of the wretched man sank to moans and mutterings as the Thing fell on him: he panted once or twice and was still. For a moment longer there came gurglings and sucking noises, and then it slid out even as it had entered. I lit the lamp which he had fumbled with, and there on the floor he lay, no more than a rind of skin in loose folds over projecting bones.

The Other Bed

I had gone out to Switzerland just before Christmas, expecting, from experience, a month of divinely renovating weather, of skating all day in brilliant sun, and basking in the hot frost of that windless atmosphere. Occasionally, as I knew, there might be a snowfall, which would last perhaps for forty-eight hours at the outside, and would be succeeded by another ten days of cloudless perfection, cold even to zero at night, but irradiated all day long by the unflecked splendour of the sun.

Instead the climatic conditions were horrible. Day after day a gale screamed through this upland valley that should have been so windless and serene, bringing with it a tornado of sleet that changed to snow by night. For ten days there was no abatement of it, and evening after evening, as I consulted my barometer, feeling sure that the black finger would show that we were coming to the end of these abominations, I found that it had sunk a little lower yet, till it stayed, like a homing pigeon, on the S of storm. I mention these things in depredation of the story that follows, in order that the intelligent reader may say at once, if he wishes, that all that occurred was merely a result of the malaise of nerves and digestion that perhaps arose from those storm-bound and disturbing conditions. And now to go back to the beginning again.

I had written to engage a room at the Hotel Beau Site, and had been agreeably surprised on arrival to find that for the modest sum of twelve francs a day I was allotted a room on the first floor with two beds in it. Otherwise the hotel was quite full. Fearing to be billeted in a twenty-two franc room, by mistake, I instantly confirmed my arrangements at the bureau. There was no mistake: I had ordered a twelve-franc room and had been given one. The very civil clerk hoped that I was satisfied with it, for otherwise there was nothing vacant. I hastened to say that I was more than satisfied, fearing the fate of Esau.

I arrived about three in the afternoon of a cloudless and glorious day, the last of the series. I hurried down to the rink, having had the prudence to put skates in the forefront of my luggage, and spent a divine but struggling hour or two, coming up to the hotel about sunset. I had letters to write, and after ordering tea to be sent up to my gorgeous apartment, No. 23, on the first floor, I went straight up there.

The door was ajar and--I feel certain I should not even remember this now except in the light of what followed--just as I got close to it, I heard some faint movement inside the room and instinctively knew that my servant was there unpacking. Next moment I was in the room myself, and it was empty. The unpacking had been finished, and everything was neat, orderly, and comfortable. My barometer was on the table, and I observed with dismay that it had gone down nearly half an inch. I did not give another thought to the movement I thought I had heard from outside.

Certainly I had a delightful room for my twelve francs a day. There were, as I have said, two beds in it, on one of which were already laid out my dress-clothes, while night-things were disposed on the other. There were two windows, between which stood a large washing-stand, with plenty of room on it; a sofa with its back to the light stood conveniently near the pipes of central heating, there were a couple of good arm-chairs, a writing table, and, rarest of luxuries, another table, so that every time one had breakfast it was not necessary to pile up a drift of books and papers to make room for the tray. My window looked east, and sunset still flamed on the western faces of the virgin snows, while above, in spite of the dejected barometer, the sky was bare of clouds, and a thin slip of pale crescent moon was swung high among the stars that still burned dimly in these first moments of their kindling. Tea came up for me without delay, and, as I ate, I regarded my surroundings with extreme complacency.

Then, quite suddenly and without cause, I saw that the disposition of the beds would never do; I could not possibly sleep in the bed that my servant had chosen for me, and without pause I jumped up, transferred my dress clothes to the other bed, and put my night things where they had been. It was done breathlessly almost, and not till then did I ask myself why I had done it. I found I had not the slightest idea. I had merely felt that I could not sleep in the other bed. But having made the change I felt perfectly content.

My letters took me an hour or so to finish, and I had yawned and blinked considerably over the last one or two, in part from their inherent dullness, in part from quite natural sleepiness. For I had been in the train for twenty-four hours, and was fresh to these bracing airs which so conduce to appetite, activity, and sleep, and as there was still an hour before I need dress, I lay down on my sofa with a book for excuse, but the intention to slumber as reason. And consciousness ceased as if a tap had been turned off.

Then--I dreamed. I dreamed that my servant came very quietly into the room, to tell me no doubt that it was time to dress. I supposed there were a few minutes to spare yet, and that he saw I was dozing, for, instead of rousing me, he moved quietly about the room, setting things in order. The light appeared to me to be very dim, for I could not see him with any distinctness, indeed, I only knew it was he because it could not be any body else. Then he paused by my washing-stand, which had a shelf for brushes and razors above it, and I saw him take a razor from its case and begin stropping it; the light was strongly reflected on the blade of the razor. He tried the edge once or twice on his thumb-nail, and then to my horror I saw him trying it on his throat. Instantaneously one of those deafening dream-crashes awoke me, and I saw the door half open, and my servant in the very act of coming in. No doubt the opening of the door had constituted the crash.

I had joined a previously-arrived party of five, all of us old friends, and accustomed to see each other often; and at dinner, and afterwards in intervals of bridge, the conversation roamed agreeably over a variety of topics, rocking-turns and the prospects of weather (a thing of vast importance in Switzerland, and not a commonplace subject) and the performances at the opera, and under what circumstances as revealed in dummy's hand, is it justifiable for a player to refuse to return his partner's original lead in no trumps. Then over whisky and soda and the repeated "last cigarette," it veered back via the Zantzigs to thought transference and the transference of emotion. Here one of the party, Harry Lambert, put forward the much discussed explanation of haunted houses based on this principle. He put it very concisely.

"Everything that happens," he said, "whether it is a step we take, or a thought that crosses our mind, makes some change in it, immediate material world. Now the most violent and concentrated emotion we can imagine is the emotion that leads a man to take so extreme a step as killing himself or somebody else. I can easily imagine such a deed so eating into the material scene, the room or the haunted heath, where it happens, that its mark lasts an enormous time. The air rings with the cry of the slain and still drips with his blood. It is not everybody who will perceive it, but sensitives will. By the way, I am sure that man who waits on us at dinner is a sensitive."

It was already late, and I rose.

"Let us hurry him to the scene of a crime," I said. "For myself I shall hurry to the scene of sleep."

Outside the threatening promise of the barometer was already finding fulfilment, and a cold ugly wind was complaining among the pines, and hooting round the peaks, and snow had begun to fall. The night was thickly overcast, and it seemed as if uneasy presences were going to and fro in the darkness. But there was no use in ill augury, and certainly if we were to be house-bound for a few days I was lucky in having so commodious a lodging. I had plenty to occupy myself with indoors, though I should vastly have preferred to be engaged outside, and in the immediate present how good it was to lie free in a proper bed after a cramped night in the train.

I was half-undressed when there came a tap at my door, and the waiter who had served us at dinner came in carrying a bottle of whisky. He was a tall young fellow, and though I had not noticed him at dinner, I saw at once now, as he stood in the glare of the electric light, what Harry had meant when he said he was sure he was a sensitive. There is no mistaking that look: it is exhibited in a peculiar "inlooking" of the eye. Those eyes, one knows, see further than the surface...

"The bottle of whisky for monsieur," he said putting it down on the table.

"But I ordered no whisky," said I. He looked puzzled.

"Number twenty-three?" he said. Then he glanced at the other bed.

"Ah, for the other gentleman, without doubt," he said.

"But there is no other gentleman," said I.

"I am alone here."

He took up the bottle again.

"Pardon, monsieur," he said. "There must be a mistake. I am new here; I only came today."

"But I thought--"

"Yes?" said I.

"I thought that number twenty-three had ordered a bottle of whisky," he repeated.

"Goodnight, monsieur, and pardon."

I got into bed, extinguished the light, and feeling very sleepy and heavy with the oppression, no doubt, of the snow that was coming, expected to fall asleep at once. Instead my mind would not quite go to roost, but kept sleepily stumbling about among the little events of the day, as some tired pedestrian in the dark stumbles over stones instead of lifting his feet. And as I got sleepier it seemed to me that my mind kept moving in a tiny little circle. At one moment it drowsily recollected how I had thought I had heard movement inside my room, at the next it remembered my dream of some figure going stealthily about and stropping a razor, at a third it wondered why this Swiss waiter with the eyes of a "sensitive" thought that number twenty-three had ordered a bottle of whisky. But at the time I made no guess as to any coherence between these little isolated facts; I only dwelt on them with drowsy persistence. Then a fourth fact came to join the sleepy circle, and I wondered why I had felt a repugnance against using the other bed.

But there was no explanation of this forthcoming, either, and the outlines of thought grew more blurred and hazy, until I lost consciousness altogether.

Next morning began the series of awful days, sleet and snow falling relentlessly with gusts of chilly wind, making any out-of-door amusement next to impossible. The snow was too soft for tobogganing, it balled on the skis, and as for the rink it was but a series of pools of slushy snow.

This in itself, of course, was quite enough to account for any ordinary depression and heaviness of spirit, but all the time I felt there was something more than that to which I owed the utter blackness that hung over those days. I was beset too by fear that at first was only vague, but which gradually became more definite, until it resolved itself into a fear of number twenty-three and in particular a terror of the other bed. I had no notion why or how I was afraid of it, the thing was perfectly causeless, but the shape and the outline of it grew slowly clearer, as detail after detail of ordinary life, each minute and trivial in itself, carved and moulded this fear, till it became definite. Yet the whole thing was so causeless and childish that I could speak to no one of it; I could but assure myself that it was all a figment of nerves disordered by this unseemly weather.

However, as to the details, there were plenty of them. Once I woke up from strangling nightmare, unable at first to move, but in a panic of terror, believing that I was sleeping in the other bed. More than once, too, awaking before I was called, and getting out of bed to look at the aspect of the morning, I saw with a sense of dreadful misgiving that the bed-clothes on the other bed were strangely disarranged, as if some one had slept there, and smoothed them down afterwards, but not so well as not to give notice of the occupation. So one night I laid a trap, so to speak, for the intruder of which the real object was to calm my own nervousness (for I still told myself that I was frightened of nothing), and tucked in the sheet very carefully, laying the pillow on the top of it. But in the morning it seemed as if my interference had not been to the taste of the occupant, for there was more impatient disorder than usual in the bed-clothes, and on the pillow was an indentation, round and rather deep, such as we may see any morning in our own beds. Yet by day these things did not frighten me, but it was when I went to bed at night that I quaked at the thought of further developments.

It happened also from time to time that I wanted something brought me, or wanted my servant. On three or four of these occasions my bell was answered by the "Sensitive," as we called him, but the Sensitive, I noticed, never came into the room. He would open the door a chink to receive my order and on returning would again open it a chink to say that my boots, or whatever it was, were at the door. Once I made him come in, but I saw him cross himself as, with a face of icy terror, he stepped into the room, and the sight somehow did not reassure me. Twice also he came up in the evening, when I had not rung at all, even as he came up the first night, and opened the door a chink to say that my bottle of whisky was outside. But the poor fellow was in a state of such bewilderment when I went out and told him that I had not ordered whisky, that I did not press for an explanation. He begged my pardon profusely; he thought a bottle of whisky had been ordered for number twenty-three. It was his mistake, entirely--I should not be charged for it; it must have been the other gentleman. Pardon again; he remembered there was no other gentleman, the other bed was unoccupied.

It was on the night when this happened for the second time that I definitely began to wish that I too was quite certain that the other bed was unoccupied. The ten days of snow and sleet were at an end, and to-night the moon once more, grown from a mere slip to a shining shield, swung serenely among the stars. But though at dinner everyone exhibited an extraordinary change of spirit, with the rising of the barometer and the discharge of this huge snow-fall, the intolerable gloom which had been mine so long but deepened and blackened. The fear was to me now like some statue, nearly finished, modelled by the carving hands of these details, and though it still stood below its moistened sheet, any moment, I felt, the sheet might be twitched away, and I be confronted with it. Twice that evening I had started to go to the bureau, to ask to have a bed made up for me, anywhere, in the billiard-room or the smoking-room, since the hotel was full, but the intolerable childishness of the proceeding revolted me. What was I afraid of? A dream of my own, a mere nightmare? Some fortuitous disarrangement of bed linen? The fact that a Swiss waiter made mistakes about bottles of whisky? It was an impossible cowardice.

But equally impossible that night were billiards or bridge, or any form of diversion. My only salvation seemed to lie in downright hard work, and soon after dinner I went to my room (in order to make my first real counter-move against fear) and sat down solidly to several hours of proof-correcting, a menial and monotonous employment, but one which is necessary, and engages the entire attention. But first I looked thoroughly round the room, to reassure myself, and found all modern and solid; a bright paper of daisies on the wall, a floor parquetted, the hot-water pipes chuckling to themselves in the corner, my bed-clothes turned down for the night, the other bed--The electric light was burning brightly, and there seemed to me to be a curious stain, as of a shadow, on the lower part of the pillow and the top of the sheet, definite and suggestive, and for a moment I stood there again throttled by a nameless terror. Then taking my courage in my hands I went closer and looked at it. Then I touched it; the sheet, where the stain or shadow was, seemed damp to the hand, so also was the pillow. And then I remembered; I had thrown some wet clothes on the bed before dinner. No doubt that was the reason. And fortified by this extremely simple dissipation of my fear, I sat down and began on my proofs. But my fear had been this, that the stain had not in that first moment looked like the mere greyness of water-moistened linen.

From below, at first came the sound of music, for they were dancing to-night, but I grew absorbed in my work, and only recorded the fact that after a time there was no more music. Steps went along the passages, and I heard the buzz of conversation on landings, and the closing of doors till by degrees the silence became noticeable. The loneliness of night had come.

It was after the silence had become lonely that I made the first pause in my work, and by the watch on my table saw that it was already past midnight. But I had little more to do; another half-hour would see the end of the business, but there were certain notes I had to make for future reference, and my stock of paper was already exhausted. However, I had bought some in the village that afternoon, and it was in the bureau downstairs, where I had left it, when I came in and had subsequently forgotten to bring it upstairs. It would be the work of a minute only to get it.

The electric light had brightened considerably during the last hour, owing no doubt to many burners being put out in the hotel, and as I left the room I saw again the stain on the pillow and sheet of the other bed. I had really forgotten all about it for the last hour, and its presence there came as an unwelcome surprise. Then I remembered the explanation of it, which had struck me before, and for purposes of self-reassurement I again touched it. It was still damp, but--Had I got chilly with my work? For it was warm to the hand. Warm, and surely rather sticky. It did not seem like the touch of the water-damp. And at the same moment I knew I was not alone in the room. There was something there, something silent as yet, and as yet invisible. But it was there.

Now for the consolation of persons who are inclined to be fearful, I may say at once that I am in no way brave, but that terror which, God knows, was real enough, was yet so interesting, that interest overruled it. I stood for a moment by the other bed, and, half-consciously only, wiped the hand that had felt the stain, for the touch of it, though all the time I told myself that it was but the touch of the melted snow on the coat I had put there, was unpleasant and unclean. More than that I did not feel, because in the presence of the unknown and the perhaps awful, the sense of curiosity, one of the strongest instincts we have, came to the fore. So, rather eager to get back to my room again, I ran downstairs to get the packet of paper. There was still a light in the bureau, and the Sensitive, on night-duty, I suppose, was sitting there dozing. My entrance did not disturb him, for I had on noiseless felt slippers, and seeing at once the package I was in search of, I took it, and left him still unawakened. That was somehow of a fortifying nature. The Sensitive anyhow could sleep in his hard chair; the occupant of the unoccupied bed was not calling to him to-night.

I closed my door quietly, as one does at night when the house is silent, and sat down at once to open my packet of paper and finish my work. It was wrapped up in an old news-sheet, and struggling with the last of the string that bound it, certain words caught my eye. Also the date at the top of the paper caught my eye, a date nearly a year old, or, to be quite accurate, a date fifty-one weeks old. It was an American paper and what it recorded was this:

"The body of Mr. Silas R. Hume, who committed suicide last week at the Hotel Beau Site, Moulin sur Chalons, is to be buried at his house in Boston, Mass. The inquest held in Switzerland showed that he cut his throat with a razor, in an attack of delirium tremens induced by drink. In the cupboard of his room were found three dozen empty bottles of Scotch whisky..."

So far I had read when without warning the electric light went out, and I was left in, what seemed for the moment, absolute darkness. And again I knew I was not alone, and I knew now who it was who was with me in the room.

Then the absolute paralysis of fear seized me. As if a wind had blown over my head, I felt the hair of it stir and rise a little. My eyes also, I suppose, became accustomed to the sudden darkness, for they could now perceive the shape of the furniture in the room from the light of the starlit sky outside. They saw more too than the mere furniture. There was standing by the wash-stand between the two windows a figure, clothed only in night-garments, and its hands moved among the objects on the shelf above the basin. Then with two steps it made a sort of dive for the other bed, which was in shadow. And then the sweat poured on to my forehead.

Though the other bed stood in shadow I could still see dimly, but sufficiently, what was there. The shape of a head lay on the pillow, the shape of an arm lifted its hand to the electric bell that was close by on the wall, and I fancied I could hear it distantly ringing. Then a moment later came hurrying feet up the stairs and along the passage outside, and a quick rapping at my door.

"Monsieur's whisky, monsieur's whisky," said a voice just outside. "Pardon, monsieur, I brought it as quickly as I could."

The impotent paralysis of cold terror was still on me. Once I tried to speak and failed, and still the gentle tapping went on at the door, and the voice telling some one that his whisky was there. Then at a second attempt, I heard a voice which was mine saying hoarsely:

"For God's sake come in; I am alone with it."

There was the click of a turned door-handle, and as suddenly as it had gone out a few seconds before, the electric light came back again, and the room was in full illumination. I saw a face peer round the corner of the door, but it was at another face I looked, the face of a man sallow and shrunken, who lay in the other bed, staring at me with glazed eyes. He lay high in bed, and his throat was cut from ear to ear; and the lower part of the pillow was soaked in blood, and the sheet streamed with it.

Then suddenly that hideous vision vanished, and there was only a sleepy-eyed waiter looking into the room. But below the sleepiness terror was awake, and his voice shook when he spoke.

"Monsieur rang?" he asked.

No, monsieur had not rung. But monsieur made himself a couch in the billiard-room.

Outside the Door

The rest of the small party staying with my friend Geoffrey Aldwych in the charming old house which he had lately bought at a little village north of Sheringham on the Norfolk coast had drifted away soon after dinner to bridge and billiards, and Mrs. Aldwych and myself had for the time been left alone in the drawing-room, seated one on each side of a small round table which we had very patiently and unsuccessfully been trying to turn. But such pressure, psychical or physical, as we had put upon it, though of the friendliest and most encouraging nature, had not overcome in the smallest degree the very slight inertia which so small an object might have been supposed to possess, and it had remained as fixed as the most constant of the stars. No tremor even had passed through its slight and spindle-like legs. In consequence we had, after a really considerable period of patient endeavour, left it to its wooden repose, and proceeded to theorise about psychical matters instead, with no stupid table to contradict in practice all our ideas on the subject.

This I had added with a certain bitterness born of failure, for if we could not move so insignificant an object, we might as well give up all idea of moving anything. But hardly were the words out of my mouth when there came from the abandoned table a single peremptory rap, loud and rather startling.

"What's that?" I asked.

"Only a rap," said she. "I thought something would happen before long."

"And do you really think that is a spirit rapping?" I asked.

"Oh dear no. I don't think it has anything whatever to do with spirits."

"More perhaps with the very dry weather we have been having. Furniture often cracks like that in the summer."

Now this, in point of fact, was not quite the case. Neither in summer nor in winter have I ever heard furniture crack as the table had cracked, for the sound, whatever it was, did not at all resemble the husky creak of contracting wood. It was a loud sharp crack like the smart concussion of one hard object with another.

"No, I don't think it had much to do with dry weather either," said she, smiling. "I think, if you wish to know, that it was the direct result of our attempt to turn the table. Does that sound nonsense?"

"At present, yes," said I, "though I have no doubt that if you tried you could make it sound sense. There is, I notice, a certain plausibility about you and your theories--"

"Now you are being merely personal," she observed.

"For the good motive, to goad you into explanations and enlargements. Please go on."

"Let us stroll outside, then," said she, "and sit in the garden, if you are sure you prefer my plausibilities to bridge. It is deliciously warm, and--"

"And the darkness will be more suitable for the propagation of psychical phenomena. As at séances," said I.

"Oh, there is nothing psychical about my plausibilities," said she. "The phenomena I mean are purely physical, according to my theory."

So we wandered out into the transparent half light of multitudinous stars. The last crimson feather of sunset, which had hovered long in the West, had been blown away with the breath of the night wind, and the moon, which would presently rise, had not yet cut the dim horizon of the sea, which lay very quiet, breathing gently in its sleep with stir of whispering ripples. Across the dark velvet of the close-cropped lawn, which stretched seawards from the house, blew a little breeze full of the savour of salt and the freshness of night, with, every now and then, a hint so subtly conveyed as to be scarcely perceptible of its travel across the sleeping fragrance of drowsy garden-beds, over which the white moths hovered seeking their night-honey. The house itself, with its two battlemented towers of Elizabethan times, gleamed with many windows, and we passed out of sight of it, and into the shadow of a box-hedge, clipped into shapes and monstrous fantasies, and found chairs by the striped tent at the top of the sheltered bowling-alley.

"And this is all very plausible," said I. "Theories, if you please, at length, and, if possible, a full length illustration also."

"By which you mean a ghost-story, or something to that effect?"

"Precisely: and, without presuming to dictate, if possible, firsthand."

"Oddly enough, I can supply that also," said she. "So first I will tell you my general theory, and follow it by a story that seems to bear it out. It happened to me, and it happened here."

"I am sure it will fill the bill," said I.

She paused a moment while I lit a cigarette, and then began in her very clear, pleasant voice.

She has the most lucid voice I know, and to me sitting there in the deep-dyed dusk, the words seemed the very incarnation of clarity, for they dropped into the still quiet of the darkness, undisturbed by impressions conveyed to other senses.

"We are only just beginning to conjecture," she said, "how inextricable is the interweaving between mind, soul, life--call it what you will--and the purely material part of the created world. That such interweaving existed has, of course, been known for centuries; doctors, for instance, knew that a cheerful optimistic spirit on the part of their patients conduced towards recovery; that fear, the mere emotion, had a definite effect on the beat of the heart, that anger produced chemical changes in the blood, that anxiety led to indigestion, that under the influence of strong passion a man can do things which in his normal state he is physically incapable of performing. Here we have mind, in a simple and familiar manner, producing changes and effects in tissue, in that which is purely material. By an extension of this--though, indeed, it is scarcely an extension--we may expect to find that mind can have an effect, not only on what we call living tissue, but on dead things, on pieces of wood or stone. At least it is hard to see why that should not be so."

"Table-turning, for instance?" I asked.

"That is one instance of how some force, out of that innumerable cohort of obscure mysterious forces with which we human beings are garrisoned, can pass, as it is constantly doing, into material things. The laws of its passing we do not know; sometimes we wish it to pass and it does not. Just now, for instance, when you and I tried to turn the table, there was some impediment in the path, though I put down that rap which followed as an effect of our efforts. But nothing seems more natural to my mind than that these forces should be transmissible to inanimate things. Of the manner of its passing we know next to nothing, any more than we know the manner of the actual process by which fear accelerates the beating of the heart, but as surely as a Marconi message leaps along the air by no visible or tangible bridge, so through some subtle gateway of the body these forces can march from the citadel of the spirit into material forms, whether that material is a living part of ourselves or that which we choose to call inanimate nature." She paused a moment.

"Under certain circumstances," she went on, "it seems that the force which has passed from us into inanimate things can manifest its presence there. The force that passes into a table can show itself in movements or in noises coming from the table. The table has been charged with physical energy. Often and often I have seen a table or a chair move apparently of its own accord, but only when some outpouring of force, animal magnetism--call it what you will--has been received by it. A parallel phenomenon to my mind is exhibited in what we know as haunted houses, houses in which, as a rule, some crime or act of extreme emotion or passion has been committed, and in which some echo or re-enactment of the deed is periodically made visible or audible. A murder has been committed, let us say, and the room where it took place is haunted. The figure of the murdered, or less commonly of the murderer, is seen there by sensitives, and cries are heard, or steps run to and fro. The atmosphere has somehow been charged with the scene, and the scene in whole or part repeats itself, though under what laws we do not know, just as a phonograph will repeat, when properly handled, what has been said into it."

"This is all theory," I remarked.

"But it appears to me to cover a curious set of facts, which is all we ask of a theory.

"Otherwise, we must frankly state our disbelief in haunted houses altogether, or suppose that the spirit of the murdered, poor, wretch, is bound under certain circumstances to re-enact the horror of its body's tragedy. It was not enough that its body was killed there, its soul has to be dragged back and live through it all again with such vividness that its anguish becomes visible or audible to the eyes or ears of the sensitive. That to me is unthinkable, whereas my theory is not. Do I make it at all clear?"

"It is clear enough," said I, "but I want support for it, the full-sized illustration."

"I promised you that, a ghost-story of my own experience."

Mrs. Aldwych paused again, and then began the story which was to illustrate her theory.

"It is just a year," she said, "since Jack bought this house from old Mrs. Denison. We had both heard, both he and I, that it was supposed to be haunted, but neither of us knew any particulars of the haunt whatever. A month ago I heard what I believe to have been the ghost, and, when Mrs. Denison was staying with us last week, I asked her exactly what it was, and found it tallied completely with my experience. I will tell you my experience first, and give her account of the haunt afterwards.

"A month ago Jack was away for a few days and I remained here alone. One Sunday evening I, in my usual health and spirits, as far as I am aware, both of which are serenely excellent, went up to bed about eleven. My room is on the first floor, just at the foot of the staircase that leads to the floor above. There are four more rooms on my passage, all of which that night were empty, and at the far end of it a door leads into the landing at the top of the front staircase. On the other side of that, as you know, are more bedrooms, all of which that night were also unoccupied; I, in fact, was the only sleeper on the first floor.

"The head of my bed is close behind my door, and there is an electric light over it. This is controlled by a switch at the bed-head, and another switch there turns on a light in the passage just outside my room. That was Jack's plan: if by chance you want to leave your room when the house is dark, you can light up the passage before you go out, and not grope blindly for a switch outside.

"Usually I sleep solidly: it is very rarely indeed that I wake, when once I have gone to sleep, before I am called. But that night I woke, which was rare; what was rarer was that I woke in a state of shuddering and unaccountable terror; I tried to localise my panic, to run it to earth and reason it away, but without any success. Terror of something I could not guess at stared me in the face, white, shaking terror. So, as there was no use in lying quaking in the dark, I lit my lamp, and, with the view of composing this strange disorder of my fear, began to read again in the book I had brought up with me. The volume happened to be 'The Green Carnation,' a work one would have thought to be full of tonic to twittering nerves. But it failed of success, even as my reasoning had done, and after reading a few pages, and finding that the heart-hammer in my throat grew no quieter, and that the grip of terror was in no way relaxed, I put out my light and lay down again. I looked at my watch, however, before doing this, and remember that the time was ten minutes to two.

"Still matters did not mend: terror, that was slowly becoming a little more definite, terror of some dark and violent deed that was momently drawing nearer to me held me in its vice.

"Something was coming, the advent of which was perceived by the subconscious sense, and was already conveyed to my conscious mind. And then the clock struck two jingling chimes, and the stable-clock outside clanged the hour more sonorously.

"I still lay there, abject and palpitating. Then I heard a sound just outside my room on the stairs that lead, as I have said, to the second story, a sound which was perfectly commonplace and unmistakable. Feet feeling their way in the dark were coming downstairs to my passage: I could hear also the groping hand slip and slide along the bannisters. The footfalls came along the few yards of passage between the bottom of the stairs and my door, and then against my door itself came the brush of drapery, and on the panels the blind groping of fingers. The handle rattled as they passed over it, and my terror nearly rose to screaming point.

"Then a sensible hope struck me. The midnight wanderer might be one of the servants, ill or in want of something, and yet--why the shuffling feet and the groping hand? But on the instant of the dawning of that hope (for I knew that it was of the step and that which was moving in the dark passage of which I was afraid) I turned on both the light at my bed-head, and the light of the passage outside, and, opening the door, looked out. The passage was quite bright from end to end, but it was perfectly empty. Yet as I looked, seeing nothing of the walker, I still heard. Down the bright boards I heard the shuffle growing fainter as it receded, until, judging by the ear, it turned into the gallery at the end and died away. And with it there died also all my sense of terror. It was It of which I had been afraid: now It and my terror had passed. And I went back to bed and slept till morning."

Again Mrs. Aldwych paused, and I was silent. Somehow it was in the extreme simplicity of her experience that the horror lay. She went on almost immediately.

"Now for the sequel," she said, "of what I choose to call the explanation. Mrs. Denison, as I told you, came down to stay with us not long ago, and I mentioned that we had heard, though only vaguely, that the house was supposed to be haunted, and asked for an account of it. This is what she told me:

"'In the year 1610 the heiress to the property was a girl Helen Denison, who was engaged to be married to young Lord Southern. In case therefore of her having children, the property would pass away from Denisons. In case of her death, childless, it would pass to her first cousin. A week before the marriage took place, he and a brother of his entered the house, riding here from thirty miles away, after dark, and made their way to her room on the second story. There they gagged her and attempted to kill her, but she escaped from them, groped her way along this passage, and into the room at the end of the gallery. They followed her there, and killed her. The facts were known by the younger brother turning king's evidence.'

"Now Mrs. Denison told me that the ghost had never been seen, but that it was occasionally heard coming downstairs or going along the passage. She told me that it was never heard except between the hours of two and three in the morning, the hour during which the murder took place."

"And since then have you heard it again?" I asked.

"Yes, more than once. But it has never frightened me again. I feared, as we all do, what was unknown."

"I feel that I should fear the known, if I knew it was that," said I.

"I don't think you would for long. Whatever theory you adopt about it, the sounds of the steps and the groping hand, I cannot see that there is anything to shock or frighten one. My own theory you know--"

"Please apply it to what you heard," I asked.

"Simply enough. The poor girl felt her way along this passage in the despair of her agonised terror, hearing no doubt the soft footsteps of her murderers gaining on her, as she groped along her lost way. The waves of that terrible brainstorm raging within her, impressed themselves in some subtle yet physical manner on the place. It would only be by those people whom we call sensitives that the wrinkles, so to speak, made by those breaking waves on the sands would be perceived, and by them not always. But they are there, even as when a Marconi apparatus is working the waves are there, though they can only be perceived by a receiver that is in tune. If you believe in brain-waves at all, the explanation is not so difficult."

"Then the brain-wave is permanent?"

"Every wave of whatever kind leaves its mark, does it not? If you disbelieve the whole thing, shall I give you a room on the route of that poor murdered harmless walker?"

I got up.

"I am very comfortable, thanks, where I am," I said.

The Room in the Tower

It is probable that everybody who is at all a constant dreamer has had at least one experience of an event or a sequence of circumstances which have come to his mind in sleep being subsequently realized in the material world. But, in my opinion, so far from this being a strange thing, it would be far odder if this fulfilment did not occasionally happen, since our dreams are, as a rule, concerned with people whom we know and places with which we are familiar, such as might very naturally occur in the awake and daylit world. True, these dreams are often broken into by some absurd and fantastic incident, which puts them out of court in regard to their subsequent fulfilment, but on the mere calculation of chances, it does not appear in the least unlikely that a dream imagined by anyone who dreams constantly should occasionally come true. Not long ago, for instance, I experienced such a fulfilment of a dream which seems to me in no way remarkable and to have no kind of psychical significance. The manner of it was as follows.

A certain friend of mine, living abroad, is amiable enough to write to me about once in a fortnight. Thus, when fourteen days or thereabouts have elapsed since I last heard from him, my mind, probably, either consciously or subconsciously, is expectant of a letter from him. One night last week I dreamed that as I was going upstairs to dress for dinner I heard, as I often heard, the sound of the postman's knock on my front door, and diverted my direction downstairs instead. There, among other correspondence, was a letter from him. Thereafter the fantastic entered, for on opening it I found inside the ace of diamonds, and scribbled across it in his well-known handwriting, "I am sending you this for safe custody, as you know it is running an unreasonable risk to keep aces in Italy." The next evening I was just preparing to go upstairs to dress when I heard the postman's knock, and did precisely as I had done in my dream. There, among other letters, was one from my friend. Only it did not contain the ace of diamonds. Had it done so, I should have attached more weight to the matter, which, as it stands, seems to me a perfectly ordinary coincidence. No doubt I consciously or subconsciously expected a letter from him, and this suggested to me my dream. Similarly, the fact that my friend had not written to me for a fortnight suggested to him that he should do so. But occasionally it is not so easy to find such an explanation, and for the following story I can find no explanation at all. It came out of the dark, and into the dark it has gone again.

All my life I have been a habitual dreamer: the nights are few, that is to say, when I do not find on awaking in the morning that some mental experience has been mine, and sometimes, all night long, apparently, a series of the most dazzling adventures befall me. Almost without exception these adventures are pleasant, though often merely trivial. It is of an exception that I am going to speak.

It was when I was about sixteen that a certain dream first came to me, and this is how it befell. It opened with my being set down at the door of a big red-brick house, where, I understood, I was going to stay. The servant who opened the door told me that tea was being served in the garden, and led me through a low dark-panelled hall, with a large open fireplace, on to a cheerful green lawn set round with flower beds. There were grouped about the tea-table a small party of people, but they were all strangers to me except one, who was a schoolfellow called Jack Stone, clearly the son of the house, and he introduced me to his mother and father and a couple of sisters. I was, I remember, somewhat astonished to find myself here, for the boy in question was scarcely known to me, and I rather disliked what I knew of him; moreover, he had left school nearly a year before. The afternoon was very hot, and an intolerable oppression reigned. On the far side of the lawn ran a red-brick wall, with an iron gate in its center, outside which stood a walnut tree. We sat in the shadow of the house opposite a row of long windows, inside which I could see a table with cloth laid, glimmering with glass and silver. This garden front of the house was very long, and at one end of it stood a tower of three stories, which looked to me much older than the rest of the building.

Before long, Mrs. Stone, who, like the rest of the party, had sat in absolute silence, said to me, "Jack will show you your room: I have given you the room in the tower."

Quite inexplicably my heart sank at her words. I felt as if I had known that I should have the room in the tower, and that it contained something dreadful and significant. Jack instantly got up, and I understood that I had to follow him. In silence we passed through the hall, and mounted a great oak staircase with many corners, and arrived at a small landing with two doors set in it. He pushed one of these open for me to enter, and without coming in himself, closed it after me. Then I knew that my conjecture had been right: there was something awful in the room, and with the terror of nightmare growing swiftly and enveloping me, I awoke in a spasm of terror.

Now that dream or variations on it occurred to me intermittently for fifteen years. Most often it came in exactly this form, the arrival, the tea laid out on the lawn, the deadly silence succeeded by that one deadly sentence, the mounting with Jack Stone up to the room in the tower where horror dwelt, and it always came to a close in the nightmare of terror at that which was in the room, though I never saw what it was. At other times I experienced variations on this same theme. Occasionally, for instance, we would be sitting at dinner in the dining-room, into the windows of which I had looked on the first night when the dream of this house visited me, but wherever we were, there was the same silence, the same sense of dreadful oppression and foreboding. And the silence I knew would always be broken by Mrs. Stone saying to me, "Jack will show you your room: I have given you the room in the tower." Upon which (this was invariable) I had to follow him up the oak staircase with many corners, and enter the place that I dreaded more and more each time that I visited it in sleep. Or, again, I would find myself playing cards still in silence in a drawing-room lit with immense chandeliers, that gave a blinding illumination. What the game was I have no idea; what I remember, with a sense of miserable anticipation, was that soon Mrs. Stone would get up and say to me, "Jack will show you your room: I have given you the room in the tower." This drawing-room where we played cards was next to the dining-room, and, as I have said, was always brilliantly illuminated, whereas the rest of the house was full of dusk and shadows. And yet, how often, in spite of those bouquets of lights, have I not pored over the cards that were dealt me, scarcely able for some reason to see them. Their designs, too, were strange: there were no red suits, but all were black, and among them there were certain cards which were black all over. I hated and dreaded those.

As this dream continued to recur, I got to know the greater part of the house. There was a smoking-room beyond the drawing-room, at the end of a passage with a green baize door. It was always very dark there, and as often as I went there I passed somebody whom I could not see in the doorway coming out. Curious developments, too, took place in the characters that peopled the dream as might happen to living persons. Mrs. Stone, for instance, who, when I first saw her, had been black-haired, became gray, and instead of rising briskly, as she had done at first when she said, "Jack will show you your room: I have given you the room in the tower," got up very feebly, as if the strength was leaving her limbs. Jack also grew up, and became a rather ill-looking young man, with a brown moustache, while one of the sisters ceased to appear, and I understood she was married.

Then it so happened that I was not visited by this dream for six months or more, and I began to hope, in such inexplicable dread did I hold it, that it had passed away for good. But one night after this interval I again found myself being shown out onto the lawn for tea, and Mrs. Stone was not there, while the others were all dressed in black. At once I guessed the reason, and my heart leaped at the thought that perhaps this time I should not have to sleep in the room in the tower, and though we usually all sat in silence, on this occasion the sense of relief made me talk and laugh as I had never yet done. But even then matters were not altogether comfortable, for no one else spoke, but they all looked secretly at each other. And soon the foolish stream of my talk ran dry, and gradually an apprehension worse than anything I had previously known gained on me as the light slowly faded.

Suddenly a voice which I knew well broke the stillness, the voice of Mrs. Stone, saying, "Jack will show you your room: I have given you the room in the tower." It seemed to come from near the gate in the red-brick wall that bounded the lawn, and looking up, I saw that the grass outside was sown thick with gravestones. A curious greyish light shone from them, and I could read the lettering on the grave nearest me, and it was, "In evil memory of Julia Stone." And as usual Jack got up, and again I followed him through the hall and up the staircase with many corners. On this occasion it was darker than usual, and when I passed into the room in the tower I could only just see the furniture, the position of which was already familiar to me. Also there was a dreadful odor of decay in the room, and I woke screaming.

The dream, with such variations and developments as I have mentioned, went on at intervals for fifteen years. Sometimes I would dream it two or three nights in succession; once, as I have said, there was an intermission of six months, but taking a reasonable average, I should say that I dreamed it quite as often as once in a month. It had, as is plain, something of nightmare about it, since it always ended in the same appalling terror, which so far from getting less, seemed to me to gather fresh fear every time that I experienced it. There was, too, a strange and dreadful consistency about it. The characters in it, as I have mentioned, got regularly older, death and marriage visited this silent family, and I never in the dream, after Mrs. Stone had died, set eyes on her again. But it was always her voice that told me that the room in the tower was prepared for me, and whether we had tea out on the lawn, or the scene was laid in one of the rooms overlooking it, I could always see her gravestone standing just outside the iron gate. It was the same, too, with the married daughter; usually she was not present, but once or twice she returned again, in company with a man, whom I took to be her husband. He, too, like the rest of them, was always silent. But, owing to the constant repetition of the dream, I had ceased to attach, in my waking hours, any significance to it. I never met Jack Stone again during all those years, nor did I ever see a house that resembled this dark house of my dream. And then something happened.

I had been in London in this year, up till the end of the July, and during the first week in August went down to stay with a friend in a house he had taken for the summer months, in the Ashdown Forest district of Sussex. I left London early, for John Clinton was to meet me at Forest Row Station, and we were going to spend the day golfing, and go to his house in the evening. He had his motor with him, and we set off, about five of the afternoon, after a thoroughly delightful day, for the drive, the distance being some ten miles. As it was still so early we did not have tea at the club house, but waited till we should get home. As we drove, the weather, which up till then had been, though hot, deliciously fresh, seemed to me to alter in quality, and become very stagnant and oppressive, and I felt that indefinable sense of ominous apprehension that I am accustomed to before thunder. John, however, did not share my views, attributing my loss of lightness to the fact that I had lost both my matches. Events proved, however, that I was right, though I do not think that the thunderstorm that broke that night was the sole cause of my depression.

Our way lay through deep high-banked lanes, and before we had gone very far I fell asleep, and was only awakened by the stopping of the motor. And with a sudden thrill, partly of fear but chiefly of curiosity, I found myself standing in the doorway of my house of dream. We went, I half wondering whether or not I was dreaming still, through a low oak-panelled hall, and out onto the lawn, where tea was laid in the shadow of the house. It was set in flower beds, a red-brick wall, with a gate in it, bounded one side, and out beyond that was a space of rough grass with a walnut tree. The facade of the house was very long, and at one end stood a three-storied tower, markedly older than the rest.

Here for the moment all resemblance to the repeated dream ceased. There was no silent and somehow terrible family, but a large assembly of exceedingly cheerful persons, all of whom were known to me. And in spite of the horror with which the dream itself had always filled me, I felt nothing of it now that the scene of it was thus reproduced before me. But I felt intensest curiosity as to what was going to happen.

Tea pursued its cheerful course, and before long Mrs. Clinton got up. And at that moment I think I knew what she was going to say. She spoke to me, and what she said was:

"Jack will show you your room: I have given you the room in the tower."

At that, for half a second, the horror of the dream took hold of me again. But it quickly passed, and again I felt nothing more than the most intense curiosity. It was not very long before it was amply satisfied.

John turned to me.

"Right up at the top of the house," he said, "but I think you'll be comfortable. We're absolutely full up. Would you like to go and see it now? By Jove, I believe that you are right, and that we are going to have a thunderstorm. How dark it has become."

I got up and followed him. We passed through the hall, and up the perfectly familiar staircase. Then he opened the door, and I went in. And at that moment sheer unreasoning terror again possessed me. I did not know what I feared: I simply feared. Then like a sudden recollection, when one remembers a name which has long escaped the memory, I knew what I feared. I feared Mrs. Stone, whose grave with the sinister inscription, "In evil memory," I had so often seen in my dream, just beyond the lawn which lay below my window. And then once more the fear passed so completely that I wondered what there was to fear, and I found myself, sober and quiet and sane, in the room in the tower, the name of which I had so often heard in my dream, and the scene of which was so familiar.

I looked around it with a certain sense of proprietorship, and found that nothing had been changed from the dreaming nights in which I knew it so well. Just to the left of the door was the bed, lengthways along the wall, with the head of it in the angle. In a line with it was the fireplace and a small bookcase; opposite the door the outer wall was pierced by two lattice-paned windows, between which stood the dressing-table, while ranged along the fourth wall was the washing-stand and a big cupboard. My luggage had already been unpacked, for the furniture of dressing and undressing lay orderly on the wash-stand and toilet-table, while my dinner clothes were spread out on the coverlet of the bed. And then, with a sudden start of unexplained dismay, I saw that there were two rather conspicuous objects which I had not seen before in my dreams: one a life-sized oil painting of Mrs. Stone, the other a black-and-white sketch of Jack Stone, representing him as he had appeared to me only a week before in the last of the series of these repeated dreams, a rather secret and evil-looking man of about thirty. His picture hung between the windows, looking straight across the room to the other portrait, which hung at the side of the bed. At that I looked next, and as I looked I felt once more the horror of nightmare seize me.

It represented Mrs. Stone as I had seen her last in my dreams: old and withered and white-haired. But in spite of the evident feebleness of body, a dreadful exuberance and vitality shone through the envelope of flesh, an exuberance wholly malign, a vitality that foamed and frothed with unimaginable evil. Evil beamed from the narrow, leering eyes; it laughed in the demon-like mouth. The whole face was instinct with some secret and appalling mirth; the hands, clasped together on the knee, seemed shaking with suppressed and nameless glee. Then I saw also that it was signed in the left-hand bottom corner, and wondering who the artist could be, I looked more closely, and read the inscription, "Julia Stone by Julia Stone."

There came a tap at the door, and John Clinton entered.

"Got everything you want?" he asked.

"Rather more than I want," said I, pointing to the picture.

He laughed.

"Hard-featured old lady," he said. "By herself, too, I remember. Anyhow she can't have flattered herself much."

"But don't you see?" said I. "It's scarcely a human face at all. It's the face of some witch, of some devil."

He looked at it more closely.

"Yes; it isn't very pleasant," he said. "Scarcely a bedside manner, eh? Yes; I can imagine getting the nightmare if I went to sleep with that close by my bed. I'll have it taken down if you like."

"I really wish you would," I said. He rang the bell, and with the help of a servant we detached the picture and carried it out onto the landing, and put it with its face to the wall.

"By Jove, the old lady is a weight," said John, mopping his forehead. "I wonder if she had something on her mind."

The extraordinary weight of the picture had struck me too. I was about to reply, when I caught sight of my own hand. There was blood on it, in considerable quantities, covering the whole palm.

"I've cut myself somehow," said I.

John gave a little startled exclamation.

"Why, I have too," he said.

Simultaneously the footman took out his handkerchief and wiped his hand with it. I saw that there was blood also on his handkerchief.

John and I went back into the tower room and washed the blood off; but neither on his hand nor on mine was there the slightest trace of a scratch or cut. It seemed to me that, having ascertained this, we both, by a sort of tacit consent, did not allude to it again. Something in my case had dimly occurred to me that I did not wish to think about. It was but a conjecture, but I fancied that I knew the same thing had occurred to him.

The heat and oppression of the air, for the storm we had expected was still undischarged, increased very much after dinner, and for some time most of the party, among whom were John Clinton and myself, sat outside on the path bounding the lawn, where we had had tea. The night was absolutely dark, and no twinkle of star or moon ray could penetrate the pall of cloud that overset the sky. By degrees our assembly thinned, the women went up to bed, men dispersed to the smoking or billiard room, and by eleven o'clock my host and I were the only two left. All the evening I thought that he had something on his mind, and as soon as we were alone he spoke.

"The man who helped us with the picture had blood on his hand, too, did you notice?" he said.

"I asked him just now if he had cut himself, and he said he supposed he had, but that he could find no mark of it. Now where did that blood come from?"

By dint of telling myself that I was not going to think about it, I had succeeded in not doing so, and I did not want, especially just at bedtime, to be reminded of it.

"I don't know," said I, "and I don't really care so long as the picture of Mrs. Stone is not by my bed."

He got up.

"But it's odd," he said. "Ha! Now you'll see another odd thing."

A dog of his, an Irish terrier by breed, had come out of the house as we talked. The door behind us into the hall was open, and a bright oblong of light shone across the lawn to the iron gate which led on to the rough grass outside, where the walnut tree stood. I saw that the dog had all his hackles up, bristling with rage and fright; his lips were curled back from his teeth, as if he was ready to spring at something, and he was growling to himself. He took not the slightest notice of his master or me, but stiffly and tensely walked across the grass to the iron gate. There he stood for a moment, looking through the bars and still growling. Then of a sudden his courage seemed to desert him: he gave one long howl, and scuttled back to the house with a curious crouching sort of movement.

"He does that half-a-dozen times a day." said John. "He sees something which he both hates and fears."

I walked to the gate and looked over it. Something was moving on the grass outside, and soon a sound which I could not instantly identify came to my ears. Then I remembered what it was: it was the purring of a cat. I lit a match, and saw the purrer, a big blue Persian, walking round and round in a little circle just outside the gate, stepping high and ecstatically, with tail carried aloft like a banner. Its eyes were bright and shining, and every now and then it put its head down and sniffed at the grass.

I laughed.

"The end of that mystery, I am afraid." I said. "Here's a large cat having Walpurgis night all alone."

"Yes, that's Darius," said John. "He spends half the day and all night there. But that's not the end of the dog mystery, for Toby and he are the best of friends, but the beginning of the cat mystery. What's the cat doing there? And why is Darius pleased, while Toby is terror-stricken?"

At that moment I remembered the rather horrible detail of my dreams when I saw through the gate, just where the cat was now, the white tombstone with the sinister inscription. But before I could answer the rain began, as suddenly and heavily as if a tap had been turned on, and simultaneously the big cat squeezed through the bars of the gate, and came leaping across the lawn to the house for shelter. Then it sat in the doorway, looking out eagerly into the dark. It spat and struck at John with its paw, as he pushed it in, in order to close the door.

Somehow, with the portrait of Julia Stone in the passage outside, the room in the tower had absolutely no alarm for me, and as I went to bed, feeling very sleepy and heavy, I had nothing more than interest for the curious incident about our bleeding hands, and the conduct of the cat and dog. The last thing I looked at before I put out my light was the square empty space by my bed where the portrait had been. Here the paper was of its original full tint of dark red: over the rest of the walls it had faded. Then I blew out my candle and instantly fell asleep.

My awaking was equally instantaneous, and I sat bolt upright in bed under the impression that some bright light had been flashed in my face, though it was now absolutely pitch dark. I knew exactly where I was, in the room which I had dreaded in dreams, but no horror that I ever felt when asleep approached the fear that now invaded and froze my brain. Immediately after a peal of thunder crackled just above the house, but the probability that it was only a flash of lightning which awoke me gave no reassurance to my galloping heart. Something I knew was in the room with me, and instinctively I put out my right hand, which was nearest the wall, to keep it away. And my hand touched the edge of a picture-frame hanging close to me.

I sprang out of bed, upsetting the small table that stood by it, and I heard my watch, candle, and matches clatter onto the floor. But for the moment there was no need of light, for a blinding flash leaped out of the clouds, and showed me that by my bed again hung the picture of Mrs. Stone. And instantly the room went into blackness again. But in that flash I saw another thing also, namely a figure that leaned over the end of my bed, watching me. It was dressed in some close-clinging white garment, spotted and stained with mold, and the face was that of the portrait.

Overhead the thunder cracked and roared, and when it ceased and the deathly stillness succeeded, I heard the rustle of movement coming nearer me, and, more horrible yet, perceived an odor of corruption and decay. And then a hand was laid on the side of my neck, and close beside my ear I heard quick-taken, eager breathing. Yet I knew that this thing, though it could be perceived by touch, by smell, by eye and by ear, was still not of this earth, but something that had passed out of the body and had power to make itself manifest. Then a voice, already familiar to me, spoke.

"I knew you would come to the room in the tower," it said. "I have been long waiting for you. At last you have come. Tonight I shall feast; before long we will feast together."

And the quick breathing came closer to me; I could feel it on my neck.

At that the terror, which I think had paralyzed me for the moment, gave way to the wild instinct of self-preservation. I hit wildly with both arms, kicking out at the same moment, and heard a little animal-squeal, and something soft dropped with a thud beside me. I took a couple of steps forward, nearly tripping up over whatever it was that lay there, and by the merest good-luck found the handle of the door. In another second I ran out on the landing, and had banged the door behind me. Almost at the same moment I heard a door open somewhere below, and John Clinton, candle in hand, came running upstairs.

"What is it?" he said. "I sleep just below you, and heard a noise as if--Good heavens, there's blood on your shoulder."

I stood there, so he told me afterwards, swaying from side to side, white as a sheet, with the mark on my shoulder as if a hand covered with blood had been laid there.

"It's in there," I said, pointing. "She, you know. The portrait is in there, too, hanging up on the place we took it from."

At that he laughed.

"My dear fellow, this is mere nightmare," he said.

He pushed by me, and opened the door, I standing there simply inert with terror, unable to stop him, unable to move.

"Phew! What an awful smell," he said.

Then there was silence; he had passed out of my sight behind the open door. Next moment he came out again, as white as myself, and instantly shut it.

"Yes, the portrait's there," he said, "and on the floor is a thing--a thing spotted with earth, like what they bury people in. Come away, quick, come away."

How I got downstairs I hardly know. An awful shuddering and nausea of the spirit rather than of the flesh had seized me, and more than once he had to place my feet upon the steps, while every now and then he cast glances of terror and apprehension up the stairs. But in time we came to his dressing-room on the floor below, and there I told him what I have here described.

The sequel can be made short; indeed, some of my readers have perhaps already guessed what it was, if they remember that inexplicable affair of the churchyard at West Fawley, some eight years ago, where an attempt was made three times to bury the body of a certain woman who had committed suicide. On each occasion the coffin was found in the course of a few days again protruding from the ground. After the third attempt, in order that the thing should not be talked about, the body was buried elsewhere in unconsecrated ground. Where it was buried was just outside the iron gate of the garden belonging to the house where this woman had lived. She had committed suicide in a room at the top of the tower in that house. Her name was Julia Stone.

Subsequently the body was again secretly dug up, and the coffin was found to be full of blood.

The Shootings Of Achnaleish

The dining-room windows, both front and back, the one looking into Oakley Street, the other into a small back-yard with three sooty shrubs in it (known as the garden), were all open, so that the table stood in mid-stream of such air as there was. But in spite of this the heat was stifling, since, for once in a way, July had remembered that it was the duty of good little summers to be hot. Hot in consequence it had been: heat reverberated from the house-walls, it rose through the boot from the paving-stones, it poured down from a large superheated sun that walked the sky all day long in a benignant and golden manner. Dinner was over, but the small party of four who had eaten it still lingered.

Mabel Armytage--it was she who had laid down the duty of good little summers--spoke first.

"Oh, Jim, it sounds too heavenly," she said. "It makes me feel cool to think of it. Just fancy, in a fortnight's time we shall all four of us be there, in our own shooting-lodge--"

"Farm-house," said Jim.

"Well, I didn't suppose it was Balmoral, with our own coffee-coloured salmon river roaring down to join the waters of our own loch."

Jim lit a cigarette.

"Mabel, you mustn't think of shooting-lodges and salmon rivers and lochs," he said. "It's a farm-house, rather a big one, though I'm sure we shall find it hard enough to fit in. The salmon river you speak of is a big burn, no more, though it appears that salmon have been caught there."

"But when I saw it, it would have required as much cleverness on the part of a salmon to fit into it as it will require on our parts to fit into our farm-house. And the loch is a tarn."

Mabel snatched the "Guide to Highland Shootings" out of my hand with a rudeness that even a sister should not show her elder brother, and pointed a withering finger at her husband.

"'Achnaleish,'" she declaimed, "'is situated in one of the grandest and most remote parts of Sutherlandshire. To be let from August 12 till the end of October, the lodge with shooting and fishing belonging. Proprietor supplies two keepers, fishing-gillie, boat on loch, and dogs. Tenant should secure about 500 head of grouse, and 500 head of mixed game, including partridge, black-game, woodcock, snipe, roe deer; also rabbits in very large number, especially by ferreting. Large baskets of brown trout can be taken from the loch, and whenever the water is high sea-trout and occasional salmon. Lodge contains'--I can't go on; it's too hot, and you know the rest. Rent only £350!"

Jim listened patiently.

"Well?" he said. "What then?"

Mabel rose with dignity.

"It is a shooting-lodge with a salmon river and a loch, just as I have said. Come, Madge, let's go out. It is too hot to sit in the house."

"You'll be calling Buxton 'the major-domo' next," remarked Jim, as his wife passed him.

I had picked up the "Guide to Highland Shootings" again which my sister had so unceremoniously plucked from me, and idly compared the rent and attractions of Achnaleish with other places that were to let.

"Seems cheap, too," I said. "Why, here's another place, just the same sort of size and bag, for which they ask £500; here's another at £550."

Jim helped himself to coffee.

"Yes, it does seem cheap," he said. "But, of course, it's very remote; it took me a good three hours from Lairg, and I don't suppose I was driving very noticeably below the legal limit. But it's cheap, as you say."

Now, Madge (who is my wife) has her prejudices. One of them--an extremely expensive one--is that anything cheap has always some hidden and subtle drawback, which you discover when it is too late. And the drawback to cheap houses is drains or offices--the presence, so to speak, of the former, and the absence of the latter. So I hazarded these.

"No, the drains are all right," said Jim, "because I got the certificate of the inspector, and as for offices, really I think the servants' parts are better than ours. No--why it's so cheap, I can't imagine."

"Perhaps the bag is overstated," I suggested.

Jim again shook his head.

"No, that's the funny thing about it," he said. "The bag, I am sure, is understated. At least, I walked over the moor for a couple of hours, and the whole place is simply crawling with hares. Why, you could shoot five hundred hares alone on it."

"Hares?" I asked. "That's rather queer, so far up, isn't it?"

Jim laughed.

"So I thought. And the hares are queer, too; big beasts, very dark in colour. Let's join the others outside. Jove! what a hot night!"

Even as Mabel had said, that day fortnight found us all four, the four who had stifled and sweltered in Chelsea, flying through the cool and invigorating winds of the North. The road was in admirable condition, and I should not wonder if for the second time Jim's big Napier went not noticeably below the legal limit. The servants had gone straight up, starting the same day as we, while we had got out at Perth, motored to Inverness, and were now, on the second day, nearing our goal. Never have I seen so depopulated a road. I do not suppose there was a man to a mile of it.

We had left Lairg about five that afternoon expecting to arrive at Achnaleish by eight, but one disaster after another overtook us. Now it was the engine, and now a tyre that delayed us, till finally we stopped some eight miles short of our destination, to light up, for with evening had come a huge wrack of cloud out of the West, so that we were cheated of the clear post-sunset twilight of the North. Then on again, till, with a little dancing of the car over a bridge, Jim said:

"That's the bridge of our salmon river; so look out for the turning up to the lodge. It is to the right, and only a narrow track. You can send her along, Sefton," he called to the chauffeur; "we shan't meet a soul."

I was sitting in front, finding the speed and the darkness extraordinarily exhilarating. A bright circle of light was cast by our lamps, fading into darkness in front, while at the sides, cut off by the casing of the lamps, the transition into blackness was sharp and sudden. Every now and then, across this circle of illumination some wild thing would pass: now a bird, with hurried flutter of wings when it saw the speed of the luminous monster, would just save itself from being knocked over; now a rabbit feeding by the side of the road would dash on to it and then bounce back again; but more frequently it would be a hare that sprang up from its feeding and raced in front of us. They seemed dazed and scared by the light, unable to wheel into the darkness again, until time and again I thought we must run over one, so narrowly, in giving a sort of desperate sideways leap, did it miss our wheels. Then it seemed that one started up almost from under us, and I saw, to my surprise, it was enormous in size, and in colour apparently quite black. For some hundred yards it raced in front of us, fascinated by the bright light pursuing it, then, like the rest, it dashed for the darkness. But it was too late, and with a horrid jolt we ran over it. At once Sefton slowed down and stopped, for Jim's rule is to go back always and make sure that any poor run-over is dead. So, when we stopped, the chauffeur jumped down and ran back.

"What was it?" Jim asked me, as we waited. "A hare."

Sefton came running back.

"Yes, sir, quite dead," he said. "I picked it up, sir."

"What for!"

"Thought you might like to see it, sir. It's the biggest hare I ever see, and it's quite black."

It was immediately after this that we came to the track up to the house, and in a few minutes we were within doors. There we found that if "shooting-lodge" was a term unsuitable, so also was "farm-house," so roomy, excellently proportioned, and well furnished was our dwelling, while the contentment that beamed from Buxton's face was sufficient testimonial for the offices.

In the hall, too, with its big open fireplace, were a couple of big solemn bookcases, full of serious works, such as some educated minister might have left, and, coming down dressed for dinner before the others, I dipped into the shelves. Then--something must long have been vaguely simmering in my brain, for I pounced on the book as soon as I saw it--I came upon Elwes's "Folklore of the North-West Highlands," and looked out "Hare" in the index. Then I read:

"Nor is it only witches that are believed to have the power of changing themselves into animals...Men and women on whom no suspicion of the sort lies are thought to be able to do this, and to don the bodies of certain animals, notably hares...Such, according to local superstition, are easily distinguishable by their size and colour, which approaches jet black."

I was up and out early next morning, prey to the vivid desire that attacks many folk in new places--namely, to look on the fresh country and the new horizons--and, on going out, certainly the surprise was great. For I had imagined an utterly lonely and solitary habitation; instead, scarce half a mile away, down the steep brae-side at the top of which stood our commodious farmhouse, ran a typically Scotch village street, the hamlet no doubt of Achnaleish.

So steep was this hill-side that the village was really remote; if it was half a mile away in crow-flying measurement, it must have been a couple of hundred yards below us. But its existence was the odd thing to me: there were some four dozen houses, at the least, while we had not seen half that number since leaving Lairg. A mile away, perhaps, lay the shining shield of the western sea; to the other side, away from the village, I had no difficulty in recognising the river and the loch.

The house, in fact, was set on a hog's back; from all sides it must needs be climbed to. But, as is the custom of the Scots, no house, however small, should be without its due brightness of flowers, and the walls of this were purple with clematis and orange with tropæolum. It all looked very placid and serene and homelike.

I continued my tour of exploration, and came back rather late for breakfast. A slight check in the day's arrangements had occurred, for the head keeper, Maclaren, had not come up, and the second, Sandie Ross, reported that the reason for this had been the sudden death of his mother the evening before. She was not known to be ill, but just as she was going to bed she had thrown up her arms, screamed suddenly as if with fright, and was found to be dead. Sandie, who repeated this news to me after breakfast, was just a slow, polite Scotchman, rather shy, rather awkward. Just as he finished--we were standing about outside the back-door--there came up from the stables the smart, very English-looking Sefton. In one hand he carried the black hare.

He touched his hat to me as he went in.

"Just to show it to Mr. Armytage, sir," he said. "She's as black as a boot."

He turned into the door, but not before Sandie Ross had seen what he carried, and the slow, polite Scotchman was instantly turned into some furtive, frightened-looking man.

"And where might it be that you found that, sir?" he asked.

Now, the black-hare superstition had already begun to intrigue me.

"Why does that interest you?" I asked.

The slow Scotch look was resumed with an effort.

"It'll no interest me," he said. "I just asked. There are uncommonly many black hares in Achnaleish."

Then his curiosity got the better of him.

"She'd have been nigh to where the road passes by and on to Achnaleish?" he asked.

"The hare? Yes, we found her on the road there."

Sandie turned away.

"She aye sat there," he said.

There were a number of little plantations climbing up the steep hill-side from Achnaleish to the moor above, and we had a pleasant slack sort of morning shooting there, walking through and round them with a nondescript tribe of beaters, among whom the serious Buxton figured. We had fair enough sport, but of the hares which Jim had seen in such profusion none that morning came to the gun, till at last, just before lunch, there came out of the apex of one of these plantations, some thirty yards from where Jim was standing, a very large, dark-coloured hare. For one moment I saw him hesitate--for he holds the correct view about long or doubtful shots at hares--then he put up his gun to fire. Sandie, who had walked round outside, after giving the beaters their instructions, was at this moment close to him, and with incredible quickness rushed upon him and with his stick struck up the barrels of the gun before he could fire.

"Black hare!" he cried. "Ye'd shoot a black hare? There's no shooting of hares at all in Achnaleish, and mark that."

Never have I seen so sudden and extraordinary a change in a man's face: it was as if he had just prevented some blackguard of the street from murdering his wife.

"An' the sickness about an' all," he added indignantly. "When the puir folk escape from their peching fevered bodies an hour or two, to the caller muirs."

Then he seemed to recover himself.

"I ask your pardon, sir," he said to Jim. "I was upset with ane thing an' anither, an' the black hare ye found deid last night--eh, I'm blatherin' again. But there's no a hare shot on Achnaleish, that's sure."

Jim was still looking in mere speechless astonishment at Sandie when I came up. And, though shooting is dear to me, so too is folk-lore.

"But we've taken the shooting of Achnaleish, Sandie," I said. "There was nothing there about not shooting hares."

Sandie suddenly boiled up again for a minute.

"An' mebbe there was nothing there about shooting the bairns and the weemen!" he cried.

I looked round, and saw that by now the beaters had all come through the wood: of them Buxton and Jim's valet, who was also among them, stood apart: all the rest were standing round us two with gleaming eyes and open mouths, hanging on the debate, and forced, so I imagined, from their imperfect knowledge of English to attend closely in order to catch the drift of what went on. Every now and then a murmur of Gaelic passed between them, and this somehow I found peculiarly disconcerting.

"But what have the hares to do with the children or women of Achnaleish?" I asked.

There was no reply to this beyond the reiterated sentence: "There's na shooting of hares in Achnaleish whatever," and then Sandie turned to Jim.

"That's the end of the bit wood, sir," he said. "We've been a'rooound."

Certainly the beat had been very satisfactory. A roe had fallen to Jim (one ought also to have fallen to me, but remained, if not standing, at any rate running away). We had a dozen of black-game, four pigeons, six brace of grouse (these were, of course, but outliers, as we had not gone on to the moor proper at all), some thirty rabbits, and four couple of woodcock. This, it must be understood, was just from the fringe of plantations about the house, but this was all we meant to do to-day, making only a morning of it, since our ladies had expressly desired first lessons in the art of angling in the afternoon, so that they too could be busy. Excellently too had Sandie worked the beat, leaving us now, after going, as he said, all round, a couple of hundred yards only from the house, at a few minutes to two.

So, after a little private signalling from Jim to me, he spoke to Sandie, dropping the hare-question altogether.

"Well, the beat has gone excellently," he said, "and this afternoon we'll be fishing. Please settle with the beaters every evening, and tell me what you have paid out. Good morning to you all."

We walked back to the house, but the moment we had turned a hum of confabulation began behind us, and, looking back, I saw Sandie and all the beaters in close whispering conclave. Then Jim spoke.

"More in your line than mine," he said; "I prefer shooting a hare to routing out some cock-and--bull story as to why I shouldn't. What does it all mean?"

I mentioned what I had found in Elwes last night.

"Then do they think it was we who killed the old lady on the road, and that I was going to kill somebody else this morning?" he asked. "How does one know that they won't say that rabbits are their aunts, and woodcock their uncles, and grouse their children? I never heard such rot, and to-morrow we'll have a hare drive. Blow the grouse! We'll settle this hare-question first."

Jim by this time was in the frame of mind typical of the English when their rights are threatened. He had the shooting of Achnaleish, on which were hares, sir, hares. And if he chose to shoot hares, neither papal bull nor royal charter could stop him.

"Then there'll be a row," said I, and Jim sniffed scornfully.

At lunch Sandie's remark about the "sickness," which I had forgotten till that moment, was explained.

"Fancy that horrible influenza getting here," said Madge. "Mabel and I went down to the village this morning, and, oh, Ted, you can get all sorts of things, from mackintoshes to peppermints, at the most heavenly shop, and there was a child there looking awfully ill and feverish. So we inquired: it was the 'sickness'--that was all they knew. But, from what the woman said, it's clearly influenza. Sudden fever, and all the rest of it."

"Bad type?" I asked.

"Yes; there have been several deaths already among the old people from pneumonia following it."

Now, I hope that as an Englishman I too have a notion of my rights, and attempt anyhow to enforce them, as a general rule, if they are wantonly threatened. But if a mad bull wishes to prevent my going across a certain field, I do not insist on my rights, but go round instead, since I see no reasonable hope of convincing the bull that according to the constitution of my country I may walk in this field unmolested. And that afternoon, as Madge and I drifted about the loch, while I was not employed in disentangling her flies from each other or her hair or my coat, I pondered over our position with regard to the hares and men of Achnaleish, and thought that the question of the bull and the field represented our standpoint pretty accurately. Jim had the shooting of Achnaleish, and that undoubtedly included the right to shoot hares: so too he might have the right to walk over a field in which was a mad bull. But it seemed to me not more futile to argue with the bull than to hope to convince these folk of Achnaleish that the hares were--as was assuredly the case--only hares, and not the embodiments of their friends and relations. For that, beyond all doubt, was their belief, and it would take, not half an hour's talk, but perhaps a couple of generations of education to kill that belief, or even to reduce it to the level of a superstition. At present it was no superstition--the terror and incredulous horror on Sandie's face when Jim raised his gun to fire at the hare told me that--it was a belief as sober and commonplace as our own belief that the hares were not incarnations of living folk in Achnaleish.

Also, virulent influenza was raging in the place, and Jim proposed to have a hare-drive to-morrow! What would happen?

That evening Jim raved about it in the smoking-room.

"But, good gracious, man, what can they do?" he cried. "What's the use of an old gaffer from Achnaleish saying I've shot his grand-daughter and, when he is asked to produce the corpse, telling the jury that we've eaten it, but that he has got the skin as evidence? What skin? A hare-skin! Oh, folklore is all very well in its way, a nice subject for discussion when topics are scarce, but don't tell me it can enter into practical life. What can they do?"

"They can shoot us," I remarked.

"The canny, God-fearing Scotchmen shoot us for shooting hares?" he asked.

"Well, it's a possibility. However, I don't think you'll have much of a hare-drive in any case."

"Why not?"

"Because you won't get a single native beater, and you won't get a keeper to come either."

"You'll have to go with Buxton and your man."

"Then I'll discharge Sandie," snapped Jim.

"That would be a pity: he knows his work."

Jim got up.

"Well, his work to-morrow will be to drive hares for you and me," said Jim. "Or do you funk?"

"I funk," I replied.

The scene next morning was extremely short. Jim and I went out before breakfast, and found Sandie at the back door, silent and respectful. In the yard were a dozen young Highlanders, who had beaten for us the day before.

"Morning, Sandie," said Jim shortly. "We'll drive hares to-day. We ought to get a lot in those narrow gorges up above. Get a dozen beaters more, can you?"

"There will be na hare-drive here," said Sandie quietly.

"I have given you your orders," said Jim.

Sandie turned to the group of beaters outside and spoke half a dozen words in Gaelic. Next moment the yard was empty, and they were all running down the hillside towards Achnaleish.

One stood on the skyline a moment, waving his arms, making some signal, as I supposed, to the village below. Then Sandie turned again.

"An' whaur are your beaters, sir?" he asked.

For the moment I was afraid Jim was going to strike him. But he controlled himself.

"You are discharged," he said.

The hare-drive, therefore, since there were neither beaters nor keeper--Maclaren, the head-keeper, having been given this "day off" to bury his mother--was clearly out of the question, and Jim, still blustering rather, but a good bit taken aback at the sudden disciplined defection of the beaters, was in betting humour that they would all return by to-morrow morning. Meanwhile the post which should have arrived before now had not come, though Mabel from her bedroom window had seen the post-cart on its way up the drive a quarter of an hour ago. At that a sudden idea struck me, and I ran to the edge of the hog's back on which the house was set. It was even as I thought: the post-cart was just striking the high-road below, going away from the house and back to the village, without having left our letters.

I went back to the dining-room. Everything apparently was going wrong this morning: the bread was stale, the milk was not fresh, and the bell was rung for Buxton. Quite so: neither milkman nor baker had called.

From the point of view of folk-lore this was admirable.

"There's another cock-and-bull story called 'taboo,'" I said. "It means that nobody will supply you with anything."

"My dear fellow, a little knowledge is a dangerous thing," said Jim, helping himself to marmalade.

I laughed.

"You are irritated," I said, "because you are beginning to be afraid that there is something in it."

"Yes, that's quite true," he said. "But who could have supposed there was anything in it? Ah, dash it! there can't be. A hare is a hare."

"Except when it is your first cousin," said I.

"Then I shall go out and shoot first cousins by myself," he said. That, I am glad to say, in the light of what followed, we dissuaded him from doing, and instead he went off with Madge down the burn. And I, I may confess, occupied my-myself the whole morning, ensconced in a thick piece of scrub on the edge of the steep brae above Achnaleish, in watching through a field-glass what went on there. One could see as from a balloon almost: the street with its houses was spread like a map below.

First, then, there was a funeral--the funeral, I suppose, of the mother of Maclaren, attended, I should say, by the whole village. But after that there was no dispersal of the folk to their work: it was as if it was the Sabbath; they hung about the street talking. Now one group would break up, but it would only go to swell another, and no one went either to his house or to the fields.

Then, shortly before lunch, another idea occurred to me, and I ran down the hill-side, appearing suddenly in the street, to put it to the test. Sandie was there, but he turned his back square on me, as did everybody else, and as I approached any group talk fell dead. But a certain movement seemed to be going on; where they stood and talked before, they now moved and were silent.

Soon I saw what that meant. None would remain in the street with me: every man was going to his house.

The end house of the street was clearly the "heavenly shop" we had been told of yesterday.

The door was open and a small child was looking round it as I approached, for my plan was to go in, order something, and try to get into conversation. But, while I was still a yard or two off, I saw through the glass of the door a man inside come quickly up and pull the child roughly away, banging the door and locking it. I knocked and rang, but there was no response: only from inside came the crying of the child.

The street which had been so busy and populous was now completely empty; it might have been the street of some long-deserted place, but that thin smoke curled here and there above the houses. It was as silent, too, as the grave, but, for all that, I knew it was watching. From every house, I felt sure, I was being watched by eyes of mistrust and hate, yet no sign of living being could I see. There was to me something rather eerie about this: to know one is watched by invisible eyes is never, I suppose, quite a comfortable sensation; to know that those eyes are all hostile does not increase the sense of security. So I just climbed back up the hillside again, and from my thicket above the brae again I peered down. Once more the street was full.

Now, all this made me uneasy: the taboo had been started, and--since not a soul had been near us since Sandie gave the word, whatever it was, that morning--was in excellent working order. Then what was the purport of these meetings and colloquies? What else threatened? The afternoon told me.

It was about two o'clock when these meetings finally broke up, and at once the whole village left the street for the hill-sides, much as if they were all returning to work. The only odd thing indeed was that no one remained behind: women and children alike went out, all in little parties of two and three. Some of these I watched rather idly, for I had formed the hasty conclusion that they were all going back to their usual employments, and saw that here a woman and girl were cutting dead bracken and heather. That was reasonable enough, and I turned my glass on others.

Group after group I examined; all were doing the same thing, cutting fuel...fuel.

Then vaguely, with a sense of impossibility, a thought flashed across me; again it flashed, more vividly. This time I left my hiding-place with considerable alacrity and went to find Jim down by the burn. I told him exactly what I had seen and what I believed it meant, and I fancy that his belief in the possibility of folk-lore entering the domain of practical life was very considerably quickened. In any case, it was not a quarter of an hour afterwards that the chauffeur and I were going, precisely as fast as the Napier was able, along the road to Lairg. We had not told the women what my conjecture was, because we believed that, making the dispositions we were making, there was no cause for alarm-sounding. One private signal only existed between Jim within the house that night and me outside. If my conjecture proved to be correct, he was to place a light in the window of my room, which I should see returning after dark from Lairg. My ostensible reason for going was to get some local fishing-flies.

As we flowed--there is no other word for the movement of these big cars but that--over the road to Lairg, I ran over everything in my mind. I felt no doubt whatever that all the brushwood and kindling I had seen being gathered in was to be piled after nightfall round our walls and set on fire. This certainly would not be done till after dark; indeed, we both felt sure that it would not be done till it was supposed that we were all abed. It remained to see whether the police at Lairg agreed with my conjecture, and it was to ascertain this that I was now flowing there.

I told my story to the chief constable as soon as I got there, omitting nothing and, I think, exaggerating nothing. His face got graver and graver as I proceeded.

"Yes, sir, you did right to come," he said. "The folk at Achnaleish are the dourest and the most savage in all Scotland. You'll have to give up this hare-hunting, though, whatever," he added.

He rang up his telephone.

"I'll get five men," he said, "and I'll be with you in ten minutes."

Our plan of campaign was simple. We were to leave the car well out of sight of Achnaleish, and--supposing the signal was in my window--steal up from all sides to command the house from every direction. It would not be difficult to make our way unseen through the plantations that ran up close to the house, and hidden at their margins we could see whether the brushwood and heather were piled up round the lodge. There we should wait to see if anybody attempted to fire it. That somebody, whenever he showed his light, would be instantly covered by a rifle and challenged.

It was about ten when we dismounted and stalked our way up to the house. The light burned in my window; all else was quiet. Personally, I was unarmed, and so, when I had planted the men in places of advantageous concealment round the house, my work was over. Then I returned to Sergeant Duncan, the chief constable, at the corner of the hedge by the garden, and waited.

How long we waited I do not know, but it seemed as if æons slipped by over us. Now and then an owl would hoot, now and then a rabbit ran out from cover and nibbled the short sweet grass of the lawn. The night was thickly overcast with clouds, and the house seemed no more than a black dot, with slits of light where windows were lit within. By and by even these slits of illumination were extinguished, and other lights appeared in the top story. After a while they, too, vanished; no sign of life appeared on the quiet house. Then suddenly the end came: I heard a foot grate on the gravel; I saw the gleam of a lantern, and heard Duncan's voice.

"Man," he shouted, "if you move hand or foot I fire. My rifle-bead is dead on you."

Then I blew the whistle; the others ran up, and in less than a minute it was all over. The man we closed in on was Maclaren.

"They killed my mither with that hell-carriage," he said, "as she juist sat on the road, puir body, who had niver hurt them."

And that seemed to him an excellent reason for attempting to burn us all to death.

But it took time to get into the house: their preparations had been singularly workmanlike, for every window and door on the ground floor was wired up.

Now, we had Achnaleish for two months, but we had no wish to be burned or otherwise murdered. What we wanted was not a prosecution of our head-keeper, but peace, the necessaries of life, and beaters. For that we were willing to shoot no hares, and release Maclaren. An hour's conclave next morning settled these things; the ensuing two months were most enjoyable, and relations were the friendliest.

But if anybody wants to test how far what Jim still calls cock-and-bull stories can enter into practical life, I should suggest to him to go a-shooting hares at Achnaleish.

The Terror by Night

The transference of emotion is a phenomenon so common, so constantly witnessed, that mankind in general have long ceased to be conscious of its existence, as a thing worth our wonder or consideration, regarding it as being as natural and commonplace as the transference of things that act by the ascertained laws of matter. Nobody, for instance, is surprised, if when the room is too hot, the opening of a window causes the cold fresh air of outside to be transferred into the room, and in the same way no one is surprised when into the same room, perhaps, which we will imagine as being peopled with dull and gloomy persons, there enters some one of fresh and sunny mind, who instantly brings into the stuffy mental atmosphere a change analogous to that of the opened windows. Exactly how this infection is conveyed we do not know; considering the wireless wonders (that act by material laws) which are already beginning to lose their wonder now that we have our newspaper brought as a matter of course every morning in mid-Atlantic, it would not perhaps be rash to conjecture that in some subtle and occult way the transference of emotion is in reality material too. Certainly (to take another instance) the sight of definitely material things, like writing on a page, conveys emotion apparently direct to our minds, as when our pleasure or pity is stirred by a book, and it is therefore possible that mind may act on mind by means as material as that.

Occasionally, however, we come across phenomena which, though they may easily be as material as any of these things, are rarer, and therefore more astounding. Some people call them ghosts, some conjuring tricks, and some nonsense. It seems simpler to group them under the head of transferred emotions, and they may appeal to any of the senses. Some ghosts are seen, some heard, some felt, and though I know of no instance of a ghost being tasted, yet it will seem in the following pages that these occult phenomena may appeal at any rate to the senses that perceive heat, cold, or smell. For, to take the analogy of wireless telegraphy, we are all of us probably "receivers" to some extent, and catch now and then a message or part of a message that the eternal waves of emotion are ceaselessly shouting aloud to those who have ears to hear, and materialising themselves for those who have eyes to see. Not being, as a rule, perfectly tuned, we grasp but pieces and fragments of such messages, a few coherent words it may be, or a few words which seem to have no sense. The following story, however, to my mind, is interesting, because it shows how different pieces of what no doubt was one message were received and recorded by several different people simultaneously. Ten years have elapsed since the events recorded took place, but they were written down at the time.

Jack Lorimer and I were very old friends before he married, and his marriage to a first cousin of mine did not make, as so often happens, a slackening in our intimacy. Within a few months after, it was found out that his wife had consumption, and, without any loss of time, she was sent off to Davos, with her sister to look after her. The disease had evidently been detected at a very early stage, and there was excellent ground for hoping that with proper care and strict regime she would be cured by the life-giving frosts of that wonderful valley.

The two had gone out in the November of which I am speaking, and Jack and I joined them for a month at Christmas, and found that week after week she was steadily and quickly gaining ground. We had to be back in town by the end of January, but it was settled that Ida should remain out with her sister for a week or two more. They both, I remember, came down to the station to see us off, and I am not likely to forget the last words that passed:

"Oh, don't look so woebegone, Jack," his wife had said; "you'll see me again before long."

Then the fussy little mountain engine squeaked, as a puppy squeaks when its toe is trodden on, and we puffed our way up the pass.

London was in its usual desperate February plight when we got back, full of fogs and still-born frosts that seemed to produce a cold far more bitter than the piercing temperature of those sunny altitudes from which we had come. We both, I think, felt rather lonely, and even before we had got to our journey's end we had settled that for the present it was ridiculous that we should keep open two houses when one would suffice, and would also be far more cheerful for us both.

So, as we both lived in almost identical houses in the same street in Chelsea, we decided to "toss," live in the house which the coin indicated (heads mine, tails his), share expenses, attempt to let the other house, and, if successful, share the proceeds. A French five-franc piece of the Second Empire told us it was "heads."

We had been back some ten days, receiving every day the most excellent accounts from Davos, when, first on him, then on me, there descended, like some tropical storm, a feeling of indefinable fear. Very possibly this sense of apprehension (for there is nothing in the world so virulently infectious) reached me through him: on the other hand both these attacks of vague foreboding may have come from the same source. But it is true that it did not attack me till he spoke of it, so the possibility perhaps inclines to my having caught it from him. He spoke of it first, I remember, one evening when we had met for a good-night talk, after having come back from separate houses where we had dined.

"I have felt most awfully down all day," he said; "and just after receiving this splendid account from Daisy, I can't think what is the matter."

He poured himself out some whisky and soda as he spoke.

"Oh, touch of liver," I said. "I shouldn't drink that if I were you. Give it me instead."

"I was never better in my life," he said.

I was opening letters, as we talked, and came across one from the house agent, which, with trembling eagerness, I read.

"Hurrah," I cried, "offer of five guineas--why can't he write it in proper English--five guineas a week till Easter for number 31. We shall roll in guineas!"

"Oh, but I can't stop here till Easter," he said.

"I don't see why not. Nor by the way does Daisy. I heard from her this morning, and she told me to persuade you to stop. That's to say, if you like. It really is more cheerful for you here. I forgot, you were telling me something."

The glorious news about the weekly guineas did not cheer him up in the least.

"Thanks awfully. Of course I'll stop."

He moved up and down the room once or twice.

"No, it's not me that is wrong," he said, "it's It, whatever It is. The terror by night."

"Which you are commanded not to be afraid of," I remarked.

"I know; it's easy commanding. I'm frightened: something's coming."

"Five guineas a week are coming," I said. "I shan't sit up and be infected by your fears. All that matters, Davos, is going as well as it can. What was the last report? Incredibly better. Take that to bed with you."

The infection--if infection it was--did not take hold of me then, for I remember going to sleep feeling quite cheerful, but I awoke in some dark still house and It, the terror by night, had come while I slept. Fear and misgiving, blind, unreasonable, and paralysing, had taken and gripped me. What was it? Just as by an aneroid we can foretell the approach of storm, so by this sinking of the spirit, unlike anything I had ever felt before, I felt sure that disaster of some sort was presaged.

Jack saw it at once when we met at breakfast next morning, in the brown haggard light of a foggy day, not dark enough for candles, but dismal beyond all telling.

"So it has come to you too," he said.

And I had not even the fighting-power left to tell him that I was merely slightly unwell.

Besides, never in my life had I felt better.

All next day, all the day after that fear lay like a black cloak over my mind; I did not know what I dreaded, but it was something very acute, something that was very near. It was coming nearer every moment, spreading like a pall of clouds over the sky; but on the third day, after miserably cowering under it, I suppose some sort of courage came back to me: either this was pure imagination, some trick of disordered nerves or what not, in which case we were both "disquieting ourselves in vain," or from the immeasurable waves of emotion that beat upon the minds of men, something within both of us had caught a current, a pressure. In either case it was infinitely better to try, however ineffectively, to stand up against it. For these two days I had neither worked nor played; I had only shrunk and shuddered; I planned for myself a busy day, with diversion for us both in the evening.

"We will dine early," I said, "and go to the 'Man from Blankley's.' I have already asked Philip to come, and he is coming, and I have telephoned for tickets. Dinner at seven."

Philip, I may remark, is an old friend of ours, neighbour in this street, and by profession a much-respected doctor.

Jack laid down his paper.

"Yes, I expect you're right," he said. "It's no use doing nothing, it doesn't help things. Did you sleep well?"

"Yes, beautifully," I said rather snappishly, for I was all on edge with the added burden of an almost sleepless night.

"I wish I had," said he.

This would not do at all.

"We have got to play up!" I said. "Here are we two strong and stalwart persons, with as much cause for satisfaction with life as any you can mention, letting ourselves behave like worms. Our fear may be over things imaginary or over things that are real, but it is the fact of being afraid that is so despicable. There is nothing in the world to fear except fear. You know that as well as I do. Now let's read our papers with interest. Which do you back, Mr. Druce, or the Duke of Portland, or the Times Book Club?"

That day, therefore, passed very busily for me; and there were enough events moving in front of that black background, which I was conscious was there all the time, to enable me to keep my eyes away from it, and I was detained rather late at the office, and had to drive back to Chelsea, in order to be in time to dress for dinner instead of walking back as I had intended.

Then the message, which for these three days had been twittering in our minds, the receivers, just making them quiver and rattle, came through.

I found Jack already dressed, since it was within a minute or two of seven when I got in, and sitting in the drawing-room. The day had been warm and muggy, but when I looked in on the way up to my room, it seemed to me to have grown suddenly and bitterly cold, not with the dampness of English frost, but with the clear and stinging exhilaration of such days as we had recently spent in Switzerland. Fire was laid in the grate but not lit, and I went down on my knees on the hearth-rug to light it.

"Why, it's freezing in here," I said. "What donkeys servants are! It never occurs to them that you want fires in cold weather, and no fires in hot weather."

"Oh, for heaven's sake don't light the fire," said he, "it's the warmest muggiest evening I ever remember."

I stared at him in astonishment. My hands were shaking with the cold. He saw this.

"Why, you are shivering!" he said. "Have you caught a chill? But as to the room being cold let us look at the thermometer."

There was one on the writing-table.

"Sixty-five," he said.

There was no disputing that, nor did I want to, for at that moment it suddenly struck us, dimly and distantly, that It was "coming through." I felt it like some curious internal vibration.

"Hot or cold, I must go and dress," I said.

Still shivering, but feeling as if I was breathing some rarefied exhilarating air, I went up to my room. My clothes were already laid out, but, by an oversight, no hot water had been brought up, and I rang for my man. He came up almost at once, but he looked scared, or, to my already-startled senses, he appeared so.

"What's the matter?" I said.

"Nothing, sir," he said, and he could hardly articulate the words. "I thought you rang."

"Yes. Hot water. But what's the matter?"

He shifted from one foot to the other.

"I thought I saw a lady on the stairs," he said, "coming up close behind me. And the front-door bell hadn't rung that I heard."

"Where did you think you saw her?" I asked.

"On the stairs. Then on the landing outside the drawing-room door, sir," he said. "She stood there as if she didn't know whether to go in or not."

"One--one of the servants," I said. But again I felt that It was coming through.

"No, sir. It was none of the servants," he said.

"Who was it then?"

"Couldn't see distinctly, sir, it was dim-like. But I thought it was Mrs. Lorimer."

"Oh, go and get me some hot water," I said.

But he lingered; he was quite clearly frightened.

At this moment the front door bell rang. It was just seven, and already Philip had come with brutal punctuality while I was not yet half dressed.

"That's Dr. Enderly," I said. "Perhaps if he is on the stairs you may be able to pass the place where you saw the lady."

Then quite suddenly there rang through the house a scream, so terrible, so appalling in its agony and supreme terror, that I simply stood still and shuddered, unable to move. Then by an effort so violent that I felt as if something must break, I recalled the power of motion, and ran downstairs, my man at my heels, to meet Philip who was running up from the ground floor. He had heard it too.

"What's the matter?" he said. "What was that?"

Together we went into the drawing-room. Jack was lying in front of the fireplace, with the chair in which he had been sitting a few minutes before overturned. Philip went straight to him and bent over him, tearing open his white shirt.

"Open all the windows," he said, "the place reeks."

We flung open the windows, and there poured in so it seemed to me, a stream of hot air into the bitter cold. Eventually Philip got up.

"He is dead," he said. "Keep the windows open. The place is still thick with chloroform."

Gradually to my sense the room got warmer, to Philip's the drug-laden atmosphere dispersed.

But neither my servant nor I had smelt anything at all.

A couple of hours later there came a telegram from Davos for me. It was to tell me to break the news of Daisy's death to Jack, and was sent by her sister. She supposed he would come out immediately. But he had been gone two hours now.

I left for Davos next day, and learned what had happened. Daisy had been suffering for three days from a little abscess which had to be opened, and, though the operation was of the slightest, she had been so nervous about it that the doctor gave her chloroform. She made a good recovery from the anesthetic, but an hour later had a sudden attack of syncope, and had died that night at a few minutes before eight, by Central European time, corresponding to seven in English time. She had insisted that Jack should be told nothing about this little operation till it was over, since the matter was quite unconnected with her general health, and she did not wish to cause him needless anxiety.

And there the story ends. To my servant there came the sight of a woman outside the drawing-room door, where Jack was, hesitating about her entrance, at the moment when Daisy's soul hovered between the two worlds; to me there came--I do not think it is fanciful to suppose this--the keen exhilarating cold of Davos; to Philip there came the fumes of chloroform. And to Jack, I must suppose, came his wife. So he joined her.

Mr. Tilly's Seance

Mr. Tilly had only the briefest moment for reflection, when, as he slipped and fell on the greasy wood pavement at Hyde Park Corner, which he was crossing at a smart trot, he saw the huge traction-engine with its grooved ponderous wheels towering high above him.

"Oh, dear! oh, dear!" he said petulantly, "it will certainly crush me quite flat, and I shan't be able to be at Mrs. Cumberbatch's séance! Most provoking! A-ow!"

The words were hardly out of his mouth, when the first half of his horrid anticipations was thoroughly fulfilled. The heavy wheels passed over him from head to foot and flattened him completely out. Then the driver (too late) reversed his engine and passed over him again, and finally lost his head, whistled loudly and stopped. The policeman on duty at the corner turned quite faint at the sight of the catastrophe, but presently recovered sufficiently to hold up the traffic, and ran to see what on earth could be done. It was all so much "up" with Mr. Tilly that the only thing possible was to get the hysterical engine-driver to move clear. Then the ambulance from the hospital was sent for, and Mr. Tilly's remains, detached with great difficulty from the road (so firmly had they been pressed into it), were reverently carried away into the mortuary Mr. Tilly during this had experienced one moment's excruciating pain, resembling the severest neuralgia as his head was ground beneath the wheel, but almost before he realised it, the pain was past, and he found himself, still rather dazed, floating or standing (he did no know which) in the middle of the road. There had been no break in his consciousness; he perfectly recollected slipping, and wondered how he had managed to save himself. He saw the arrested traffic, the policeman with white wan face making suggestions to the gibbering engine-driver, and he received the very puzzling impression that the traction engine was all mixed up with him.

He had a sensation of red-hot coals and boiling water and rivets all around him, but yet no feeling of scalding or burning or confinement. He was, on the contrary, extremely comfortable, and had the most pleasant consciousness of buoyancy and freedom. Then the engine puffed and the wheels went round, and immediately, to his immense surprise, he perceived his own crushed remains, flat as a biscuit, lying on the roadway. He identified them for certain by his clothes, which he had put on for the first time that morning, and one patent leather boot which had escaped demolition.

"But what on earth has happened?" he said. "Here am I, and yet that poor pressed flower of arms and legs is me--or rather I--also. And how terribly upset the driver looks. Why, I do believe that I've been run over! It did hurt for a moment, now I come to think of it ...My good man, where are you shoving to? Don't you see me?"

He addressed these two questions to the policeman, who appeared to walk right through him.

But the man took no notice, and calmly came out on the other side: it was quite evident that he did not see him, or apprehend him in any way.

Mr. Tilly was still feeling rather at sea amid these unusual occurrences, and there began to steal into his mind a glimpse of the fact which was so obvious to the crowd which formed an interested but respectful ring round his body. Men stood with bared heads; women screamed and looked away and looked back again.

"I really believe I'm dead," said he. "That's the only hypothesis which will cover the facts."

"But I must feel more certain of it before I do anything. Ah! Here they come with the ambulance to look at me. I must be terribly hurt, and yet I don't feel hurt. I should feel hurt surely if I was hurt. I must be dead."

Certainly it seemed the only thing for him to be, but he was far from realising it yet. A lane had been made through the crowd for the stretcher-bearers, and he found himself wincing when they began to detach him from the road.

"Oh, do take care!" he said. "That's the sciatic nerve protruding there surely, isn't it? A-ow!

"No, it didn't hurt after all. My new clothes, too: I put them on to-day for the first time. What bad luck! Now you're holding my leg upside down. Of course all my money comes out of my trouser pocket. And there's my ticket for the séance; I must have that: I may use it after all."

He tweaked it out of the fingers of the man who had picked it up, and laughed to see the expression of amazement on his face as the card suddenly vanished. That gave him something fresh to think about, and he pondered for a moment over some touch of association set up by it.

"I have it," he thought. "It is clear that the moment I came into connection with that card, it became invisible. I'm invisible myself (of course to the grosser sense), and everything I hold becomes invisible. Most interesting! That accounts for the sudden appearances of small objects at a séance. The spirit has been holding them, and as long as he holds them they are invisible.

"Then he lets go, and there's the flower or the spirit-photograph on the table. It accounts, too, for the sudden disappearances of such objects. The spirit has taken them, though the scoffers say that the medium has secreted them about his person. It is true that when searched he sometimes appears to have done so; but, after all, that may be a joke on the part of the spirit. Now, what am I to do with myself. Let me see, there's the clock. It's just half-past ten. All this has happened in a few minutes, for it was a quarter past when I left my house. Half-past ten now: what does that mean exactly? I used to know what it meant, but now it seems nonsense. Ten what? Hours, is it? What's an hour?"

This was very puzzling. He felt that he used to know what an hour and a minute meant, but the perception of that, naturally enough, had ceased with his emergence from time and space into eternity. The conception of time was like some memory which, refusing to record itself on the consciousness, lies perdu in some dark corner of the brain, laughing at the efforts of the owner to ferret it out. While he still interrogated his mind over this lapsed perception, he found that space as well as time, had similarly grown obsolete for him, for he caught sight of his friend Miss Ida Soulsby, who he knew was to be present at the séance for which he was bound, hurrying with bird-like steps down the pavement opposite. Forgetting for the moment that he was a disembodied spirit, he made the effort of will which in his past human existence would have set his legs in pursuit of her, and found that the effort of will alone was enough to place him at her side.

"My dear Miss Soulsby," he said, "I was on my way to Mrs. Cumberbatch's house when I was knocked down and killed. It was far from unpleasant, a moment's headache--"

So far his natural volubility had carried him before he recollected that he was invisible and inaudible to those still closed in by the muddy vesture of decay, and stopped short. But though it was clear that what he said was inaudible to Miss Soulsby's rather large intelligent-looking ears, it seemed that some consciousness of his presence was conveyed to her finer sense, for she looked suddenly startled, a flush rose to her face, and he heard her murmur, "Very odd. I wonder why I received so vivid an impression of dear Teddy."

That gave Mr. Tilly a pleasant shock. He had long admired the lady, and here she was alluding to him in her supposed privacy as "dear Teddy." That was followed by a momentary regret that he had been killed: he would have liked to have been possessed of this information before, and have pursued the primrose path of dalliance down which it seemed to lead. (His intentions, of course, would, as always, have been strictly honourable: the path of dalliance would have conducted them both, if she consented, to the altar, where the primroses would have been exchanged for orange blossom.) But his regret was quite short-lived; though the altar seemed inaccessible, the primrose path might still be open, for many of the spiritualistic circle in which he lived were on most affectionate terms with their spiritual guides and friends who, like himself, had passed over. From a human point of view these innocent and even elevating flirtations had always seemed to him rather bloodless; but now, looking on them from the far side, he saw how charming they were, for they gave him the sense of still having a place and an identity in the world he had just quitted. He pressed Miss Ida's hand (or rather put himself into the spiritual condition of so doing), and could vaguely feel that it had some hint of warmth and solidity about it. This was gratifying, for it showed that though he had passed out of the material plane, he could still be in touch with it. Still more gratifying was it to observe that a pleased and secret smile overspread Miss Ida's fine features as he gave this token of his presence: perhaps she only smiled at her own thoughts, but in any case it was he who had inspired them.

Encouraged by this, he indulged in a slightly more intimate token of affection, and permitted himself a respectful salute, and saw that he had gone too far, for she said to herself, "Hush, hush!" and quickened her pace, as if to leave these amorous thoughts behind.

He felt that he was beginning to adjust himself to the new conditions in which he would now live or, at any rate, was getting some sort of inkling as to what they were. Time existed no more for him, nor yet did space, since the wish to be at Miss Ida's side had instantly transported him there, and with a view to testing this further he wished himself back in his flat. As swiftly as the change of scene in a cinematograph show he found himself there, and perceived that the news of his death must have reached his servants, for his cook and parlour-maid with excited faces, were talking over the event.

"Poor little gentleman," said his cook. "It seems a shame it does. He never hurt a fly, and to think of one of those great engines laying him out flat. I hope they'll take him to the cemetery from the hospital: I never could bear a corpse in the house."

The great strapping parlour-maid tossed her head.

"Well, I'm not sure that it doesn't serve him right," she observed. "Always messing about with spirits he was, and the knockings and concertinas was awful sometimes when I've been laying out supper in the dining-room. Now perhaps he'll come himself and visit the rest of the loonies. But I'm sorry all the same. A less troublesome little gentleman never stepped. Always pleasant, too, and wages paid to the day."

These regretful comments and encomiums were something of a shock to Mr. Tilly. He had imagined that his excellent servants regarded him with a respectful affection, as befitted some sort of demigod, and the role of the poor little gentleman was not at all to his mind. This revelation of their true estimate of him, although what they thought of him could no longer have the smallest significance irritated him profoundly.

"I never heard such impertinence," he said (so he thought) quite out loud, and still intensely earth-bound, was astonished to see that they had no perception whatever of his presence. He raised his voice, replete with extreme irony, and addressed his cook.

"You may reserve your criticism on my character for your saucepans," he said. "They will no doubt appreciate them. As regards the arrangements for my funeral, I have already provided for them in my will, and do not propose to consult your convenience. At present--"

"Lor'!" said Mrs. Inglis, "I declare I can almost hear his voice, poor little fellow. Husky it was, as if he would do better by clearing his throat. I suppose I'd best be making a black bow to my cap. His lawyers and what not will be here presently."

Mr. Tilly had no sympathy with this suggestion. He was immensely conscious of being quite alive, and the idea of his servants behaving as if he were dead, especially after the way in which they had spoken about him, was very vexing. He wanted to give them some striking evidence of his presence and his activity, and he banged his hand angrily on the dining-room table, from which the breakfast equipage had not yet been cleared. Three tremendous blows he gave it, and was rejoiced to see that his parlour-maid looked startled. Mrs. Inglis's face remained perfectly placid.

"Why, if I didn't hear a sort of rapping sound," said Miss Talton. "Where did it come from?"

"Nonsense! You've the jumps, dear," said Mrs. Inglis, picking up a remaining rasher of bacon on a fork, and putting it into her capacious mouth.

Mr. Tilly was delighted at making any impression at all on either of these impercipient females.

"Talton!" he called at the top of his voice.

"Why, what's that?" said Talton. "Almost hear his voice, do you say, Mrs. Inglis? I declare I did hear his voice then."

"A pack o' nonsense, dear," said Mrs. Inglis placidly. "That's a prime bit of bacon, and there's a good cut of it left. Why, you're all of a tremble! It's your imagination."

Suddenly it struck Mr. Tilly that he might be employing himself much better than, with such extreme exertion, managing to convey so slight a hint of his presence to his parlour-maid, and that the séance at the house of the medium, Mrs. Cumberbatch, would afford him much easier opportunities of getting through to the earth-plane again. He gave a couple more thumps to the table and, wishing himself at Mrs. Cumberbatch's nearly a mile away, scarcely heard the faint scream of Talton at the sound of his blows before he found himself in West Norfolk Street.

He knew the house well, and went straight to the drawing-room, which was the scene of the séances he had so often and so eagerly attended. Mrs. Cumberbatch who had a long spoon-shaped face, had already pulled down the blinds, leaving the room in total darkness except for the glimmer of the night-light which, under a shade of ruby-glass, stood on the chimneypiece in front of the coloured photograph of Cardinal Newman. Round the table were seated Miss Ida Soulsby, Mr. and Mrs. Meriott (who paid their guineas at least twice a week in order to consult their spiritual guide Abibel and received mysterious advice about their indigestion and investments), and Sir John Plaice, who was much interested in learning the details of his previous incarnation as a Chaldean priest, completed the circle. His guide, who resealed to him his sacerdotal career, was playfully called Mespot. Naturally many other spirits visited them, for Miss Soulsby had no less than three guides in her spiritual household, Sapphire, Semiramis, and Sweet William, while Napoleon and Plato were not infrequent guests. Cardinal Newman, too, was a great favourite, and they encouraged his presence by the singing in unison of "Lead, kindly Light": he could hardly ever resist that...

Mr. Tilly observed with pleasure that there was a vacant seat by the table which no doubt had been placed there for him. As he entered, Mrs. Cumberbatch peered at her watch.

"Eleven o'clock already," she said, "and Mr. Tilly is not here yet. I wonder what can have kept him. What shall we do, dear friends? Abibel gets very impatient sometimes if we keep him waiting."

Mr. and Mrs. Meriott were getting impatient too, for he terribly wanted to ask about Mexican oils, and she had a very vexing heartburn.

"And Mespot doesn't like waiting either," said Sir John, jealous for the prestige of his protector, "not to mention Sweet William."

Miss Soulsby gave a little silvery laugh.

"Oh, but my Sweet William's so good and kind," she said; "besides, I have a feeling, quite a psychic feeling, Mrs. Cumberbatch, that Mr. Tilly is very close."

"So I am," said Mr. Tilly.

"Indeed, as I walked here," continued Miss Soulsby, "I felt that Mr. Tilly was somewhere quite close to me. Dear me, what's that?"

Mr. Tilly was so delighted at being sensed, that he could not resist giving a tremendous rap on the table, in a sort of pleased applause. Mrs. Cumberbatch heard it too.

"I'm sure that's Abibel come to tell us that he is ready," she said. "I know Abibel's knock. A little patience, Abibel. Let's give Mr. Tilly three minutes more and then begin. Perhaps, if we put up the blinds, Abibel will understand we haven't begun."

This was done, and Miss Soulsby glided to the window, in order to make known Mr. Tilly's approach, for he always came along the opposite pavement and crossed over by the little island in the river of traffic. There was evidently some lately published news, for the readers of early editions were busy, and she caught sight of one of the advertisement boards bearing in large letters the announcement of a terrible accident at Hyde Park Corner. She drew in her breath with a hissing sound and turned away, unwilling to have her psychic tranquillity upset by the intrusion of painful incidents. But Mr. Tilly, who had followed her to the window and saw what she had seen, could hardly restrain a spiritual whoop of exultation.

"Why, it's all about me!" he said. "Such large letters, too. Very gratifying. Subsequent editions will no doubt contain my name."

He gave another loud rap to call attention to himself, and Mrs. Cumberbatch, sitting down in her antique chair which had once belonged to Madame Blavatsky, again heard.

"Well, if that isn't Abibel again," she said. "Be quiet, naughty. Perhaps we had better begin."

She recited the usual invocation to guides and angels, and leaned back in her chair. Presently she began to twitch and mutter, and shortly afterwards with several loud snorts, relapsed into cataleptic immobility. There she lay, stiff as a poker, a port of call, so to speak, for any voyaging intelligence. With pleased anticipation Mr. Tilly awaited their coming. How gratifying if Napoleon, with whom he had so often talked, recognised him and said, "Pleased to see you, Mr. Tilly. I perceive you have joined us..." The room was dark except for the ruby-shaded lamp in front of Cardinal Newman, but to Mr. Tilly's emancipated perceptions the withdrawal of mere material light made no difference, and he idly wondered why it was generally supposed that disembodied spirits like himself produced their most powerful effects in the dark. He could not imagine the reason for that, and, what puzzled him still more, there was not to his spiritual perception any sign of those colleagues of his (for so he might now call them) who usually attended Mrs. Cumberbatch's séances in such gratifying numbers. Though she had been moaning and muttering a long time now, Mr. Tilly was in no way conscious of the presence of Abibel and Sweet William and Sapphire and Napoleon: "They ought to be here by now," he said to himself.

But while he still wondered at their absence, he saw to his amazed disgust that the medium's hand, now covered with a black glove, and thus invisible to ordinary human vision in the darkness, was groping about the table and clearly searching for the megaphone-trumpet which lay there. He found that he could read her mind with the same ease, though far less satisfaction, as he had read Miss Ida's half an hour ago, and knew that she was intending to apply the trumpet to her own mouth and pretend to be Abibel or Semiramis or somebody, whereas she affirmed that she never touched the trumpet herself. Much shocked at this, he snatched up the trumpet himself, and observed that she was not in trance at all, for she opened her sharp black eyes, which always reminded him of buttons covered with American cloth, and gave a great gasp.

"Why, Mr. Tilly!" she said. "On the spiritual plane too!"

The rest of the circle was now singing "Lead, kindly Light" in order to encourage Cardinal Newman, and this conversation was conducted under cover of the hoarse crooning voices. But Mr. Tilly had the feeling that though Mrs. Cumberbatch saw and heard him as clearly as he saw her, he was quite imperceptible to the others.

"Yes, I've been killed," he said, "and I want to get into touch with the material world. That's why I came here. But I want to get into touch with other spirits too, and surely Abibel or Mespot ought to be here by this time."

He received no answer, and her eyes fell before his like those of a detected charlatan. A terrible suspicion invaded his mind.

"What? Are you a fraud, Mrs. Cumberbatch?" he asked. "Oh, for shame! Think of all the guineas I have paid you."

"You shall have them all back," said Mrs. Cumberbatch. "But don't tell of me."

She began to whimper, and he remembered that she often made that sort of sniffling noise when Abibel was taking possession of her.

"That usually means that Abibel is coming," he said, with withering sarcasm. "Come along, Abibel: we're waiting."

"Give me the trumpet," whispered the miserable medium. "Oh, please give me the trumpet!"

"I shall do nothing of the kind," said Mr. Tilly indignantly. "I would sooner use it myself."

She gave a sob of relief.

"Oh do, Mr. Tilly!" she said. "What a wonderful idea! It will be most interesting to everybody to hear you talk just after you've been killed and before they know. It would be the making of me! And I'm not a fraud, at least not altogether. I do have spiritual perceptions sometimes; spirits do communicate through me. And when they won't come through it's a dreadful temptation to a poor woman to--to supplement them by human agency. And how could I be seeing and hearing you now, and be able to talk to you--so pleasantly, I'm sure--if I hadn't super-normal powers? You've been killed, so you assure me, and yet I can see and hear you quite plainly. Where did it happen, may I ask, if it's not a painful subject?"

"Hyde Park Corner, half an hour ago," said Mr. Tilly. "No, it only hurt for a moment, thanks."

"But about your other suggestion--"

While the third verse of "Lead, kindly Light" was going on, Mr. Tilly applied his mind to this difficult situation. It was quite true that if Mrs. Cumberbatch had no power of communication with the unseen she could not possibly have seen him. But she evidently had, and had heard him too, for their conversation had certainly been conducted on the spirit-plane, with perfect lucidity.

Naturally, now that he was a genuine spirit, he did not want to be mixed up in fraudulent mediumship, for he felt that such a thing would seriously compromise him on the other side, where, probably, it was widely known that Mrs. Cumberbatch was a person to be avoided. But, on the other hand, having so soon found a medium through whom he could communicate with his friends, it was hard to take a high moral view, and say that he would have nothing whatever to do with her.

"I don't know if I trust you," he said. "I shouldn't have a moment's peace if I thought that you would be sending all sorts of bogus messages from me to the circle, which I wasn't responsible for at all. You've done it with Abibel and Mespot. How can I know that when I don't choose to communicate through you, you won't make up all sorts of piffle on your own account?"

She positively squirmed in her chair.

"Oh, I'll turn over a new leaf," she said. "I will leave all that sort of thing behind me. And I am a medium. Look at me! Aren't I more real to you than any of the others? Don't I belong to your plane in a way that none of the others do? I may be occasionally fraudulent, and I can no more get Napoleon here than I can fly, but I'm genuine as well. Oh, Mr. Tilly, be indulgent to us poor human creatures! It isn't so long since you were one of us yourself."

The mention of Napoleon, with the information that Mrs. Cumberbatch had never been controlled by that great creature, wounded Mr. Tilly again. Often in this darkened room he had held long colloquies with him, and Napoleon had given him most interesting details of his life on St. Helena, which, so Mr. Tilly had found, were often borne out by Lord Rosebery's pleasant volume The Last Phase. But now the whole thing wore a more sinister aspect, and suspicion as solid as certainty bumped against his mind.

"Confess!" he said. "Where did you get all that Napoleon talk from? You told us you had never read Lord Rosebery's book, and allowed us to look through your library to see that it wasn't there. Be honest for once, Mrs. Cumberbatch."

She suppressed a sob.

"I will," she said. "The book was there all the time. I put it into an old cover called 'Elegant Extracts...' But I'm not wholly a fraud. We're talking together, you a spirit and I a mortal female. They can't hear us talk. But only look at me, and you'll see...You can talk to them through me, if you'll only be so kind. I don't often get in touch with a genuine spirit like yourself."

Mr. Tilly glanced at the other sitters and then back to the medium, who, to keep the others interested, was making weird gurgling noises like an undervitalised siphon. Certainly she was far clearer to him than were the others, and her argument that she was able to see and hear him had great weight. And then a new and curious perception came to him. Her mind seemed spread out before him like a pool of slightly muddy water, and he figured himself as standing on a header-board above it, perfectly able, if he chose, to immerse himself in it. The objection to so doing was its muddiness, its materiality; the reason for so doing was that he felt that then he would be able to be heard by the others, possibly to be seen by them, certainly to come into touch with them. As it was, the loudest bangs on the table were only faintly perceptible.

"I'm beginning to understand," he said.

"Oh, Mr. Tilly! Just jump in like a kind good spirit," she said. "Make your own test-conditions.

"Put your hand over my mouth to make sure that I'm not speaking, and keep hold of the trumpet."

"And you'll promise not to cheat any more?" he asked.

"Never!"

He made up his mind.

"All right then," he said, and, so to speak, dived into her mind.

He experienced the oddest sensation. It was like passing out of some fine, sunny air into the stuffiest of unventilated rooms. Space and time closed over him again: his head swam, his eyes were heavy. Then, with the trumpet in one hand, he laid the other firmly over her mouth.

Looking round, he saw that the room seemed almost completely dark, but that the outline of the figures sitting round the table had vastly gained in solidity.

"Here I am!" he said briskly.

Miss Soulsby gave a startled exclamation.

"That's Mr. Tilly's voice!" she whispered.

"Why, of course it is," said Mr. Tilly. "I've just passed over at Hyde Park Corner under a traction engine..."

He felt the dead weight of the medium's mind, her conventional conceptions, her mild, unreal piety pressing in on him from all sides, stifling and confusing him. Whatever he said had to pass through muddy water...

"There's a wonderful feeling of joy and lightness," he said. "I can't tell you of the sunshine and happiness. We're all very busy and active, helping others. And it's such a pleasure, dear friends, to be able to get into touch with you all again. Death is not death: it is the gate of life..."

He broke off suddenly.

"Oh, I can't stand this," he said to the medium. "You make me talk such twaddle. Do get your stupid mind out of the way. Can't we do anything in which you won't interfere with me so much?"

"Can you give us some spirit lights round the room?" suggested Mrs. Cumberbatch in a sleepy voice. "You have come through beautifully, Mr. Tilly. It's too dear of you!"

"You're sure you haven't arranged some phosphorescent patches already?" asked Mr. Tilly suspiciously.

"Yes, there are one or two near the chimney-piece," said Mrs. Cumberbatch, "but none anywhere else. Dear Mr. Tilly, I swear there are not. Just give us a nice star with long rays on the ceiling!"

Mr. Tilly was the most good-natured of men, always willing to help an unattractive female in distress, and whispering to her, "I shall require the phosphorescent patches to be given into my hands after the séance," he proceeded, by the mere effort of his imagination, to light a beautiful big star with red and violet rays on the ceiling. Of course it was not nearly as brilliant as his own conception of it, for its light had to pass through the opacity of the medium's mind, but it was still a most striking object, and elicited gasps of applause from the company. To enhance the effect of it he intoned a few very pretty lines about a star by Adelaide Anne Procter, whose poems had always seemed to him to emanate from the topmost peak of Parnassus.

"Oh, thank you, Mr. Tilly!" whispered the medium. "It was lovely! Would a photograph of it be permitted on some future occasion, if you would be so kind as to reproduce it again?"

"Oh, I don't know," said Mr. Tilly irritably. "I want to get out. I'm very hot and uncomfortable. And it's all so cheap."

"Cheap?" ejaculated Mrs. Cumberbatch. "Why, there's not a medium in London whose future wouldn't be made by a real genuine star like that, say, twice a week."

"But I wasn't run over in order that I might make the fortune of mediums," said Mr. Tilly. "I want to go: it's all rather degrading. And I want to see something of my new world. I don't know what it's like yet."

"Oh, but, Mr. Tilly," said she. "You told us lovely things about it, how busy and happy you were."

"No, I didn't. It was you who said that, at least it was you who put it into my head."

Even as he wished, he found himself emerging from the dull waters of Mrs. Cumberbatch's mind.

"There's the whole new world waiting for me," he said. "I must go and see it. I'll come back and tell you, for it must be full of marvellous revelations..."

Suddenly he felt the hopelessness of it. There was that thick fluid of materiality to pierce, and, as it dripped off him again, he began to see that nothing of that fine rare quality of life which he had just begun to experience, could penetrate these opacities. That was why, perhaps, all that thus came across from the spirit-world, was so stupid, so banal. They, of whom he now was one, could tap on furniture, could light stars, could abound with commonplace, could read as in a book the mind of medium or sitters, but nothing more. They had to pass into the region of gross perceptions, in order to be seen of blind eyes and be heard of deaf ears.

Mrs. Cumberbatch stirred.

"The power is failing," she said, in a deep voice, which Mr. Tilly felt was meant to imitate his own. "I must leave you now, dear friends--"

He felt much exasperated.

"The power isn't failing," he shouted. "It wasn't I who said that."

Besides, I have got to see if it's true. Good-bye: don't cheat any more.

He dropped his card of admittance to the seance on the table and heard murmurs of excitement as he floated off.

The news of the wonderful star, and the presence of Mr. Tilly at the séance within half an hour of his death, which at the time was unknown to any of the sitters, spread swiftly through spiritualistic circles. The Psychical Research Society sent investigators to take independent evidence from all those present, but were inclined to attribute the occurrence to a subtle mixture of thought-transference and unconscious visual impression, when they heard that Miss Soulsby had, a few minutes previously, seen a news-board in the street outside recording the accident at Hyde Park Corner. This explanation was rather elaborate, for it postulated that Miss Soulsby, thinking of Mr. Tilly's non-arrival, had combined that with the accident at Hyde Park Corner, and had probably (though unconsciously) seen the name of the victim on another news-board and had transferred the whole by telepathy to the mind of the medium. As for the star on the ceiling, though they could not account for it, they certainly found remains of phosphorescent paint on the panels of the wall above the chimney-piece, and came to the conclusion that the star had been produced by some similar contrivance. So they rejected the whole thing, which was a pity, since, for once, the phenomena were absolutely genuine.

Miss Soulsby continued to be a constant attendant at Mrs. Cumberbatch's séances, but never experienced the presence of Mr. Tilly again. On that the reader may put any interpretation he pleases. It looks to me somewhat as if he had found something else to do.

But he had emerged too far, and perceived that nobody except the medium heard him.

"Oh, don't be vexed, Mr. Tilly," she said. "That's only a formula. But you're leaving us very soon. Not time for just one materialisation? They are more convincing than anything to most inquirers."

"Not one," said he. "You don't understand how stifling it is even to speak through you and make stars. But I'll come back as soon as I find there's anything new that I can get through to you. What's the use of my repeating all that stale stuff about being busy and happy? They've been told that often enough already."

THE END

PAYING GUESTS

CHAPTER I

Bolton Spa, justly famous for the infamous savour of the waters which so magically get rid of painful deposits in the joints and muscles of the lame and the halt, and for the remedial rasp of its saline baths in which the same patients are pickled daily to their great relief, had been crammed all the summer, and the proprietors of its hotels and boarding houses had been proving that for them at least rheumatism and its kindred afflictions had a silver if not a golden lining. Never had Wentworth and Balmoral and Blenheim and Belvoir entertained so continuous a complement of paying guests, and even now, though the year had wheeled into mid-October, and the full season was long past, Mrs. Oxney was still booking rooms for fresh arrivals at Wentworth during the next two months. In fact she did not know when she would get off on her holiday, and as long as this prosperous tide continued to flow, she cared very little whether she got off at all. Though she did not want money, she liked it, and though she liked a holiday, she did not want it.

The existence, or rather the names, of Balmoral, Blenheim and Belvoir was a slight but standing grievance with Mrs. Oxney, the sort of grievance which occasionally kept her awake for half an hour should it perch in her drowsy consciousness as she composed herself to sleep and begin pecking at her mind. 'For naturally,' so she thought to herself in these infrequent vigils, 'if a lady or gentleman was thinking of coming to Bolton Spa, and wanted comfort and, I may say, luxury when they are taking their cure, they would look at the Baths Guide-book, and imagine that Balmoral and Blenheim and Belvoir and Wentworth were all much of a muchness. And then if they chose any of the others they would find themselves in a wretched little gimcrack semi-detached villa down in the hollow, with only one bathroom and that charged extra, and the enamel all off, and cold supper on Sunday and nobody dressing for dinner. Not that it's illegal to call yourself Balmoral, far from it; for there is nothing to prevent you calling your house "Boiled Rabbit" or "Castor Oil," but those who haven't got big houses ought to have enough proper feeling not to mis-call them by big names.'

Mrs. Oxney's grievance was as well founded as most little vexations of the kind, for certainly Wentworth was a very different class of house from Balmoral and Blenheim and Belvoir, which, though it might possibly be libellous to call them gimcrack, could not be described as other than semi-detached. There could not be any divergence of opinion over that point or over the singleness of their bathrooms and the cold supper on Sunday. Wentworth, on the other hand, was so entirely and magnificently detached that nobody would dream of calling it detached at all: you might as well call a ship at sea detached. The nearest house to it was at least a hundred yards away, and on all sides but one more like a quarter of a mile, and the whole of that territory was 'grounds.' It had gardens (kitchen and flower) it had tennis courts (hard and soft) a croquet-lawn (hard or soft according to the state of the weather) and a large field in which Colonel Chase had induced Mrs. Oxney to make five widely sundered putting-greens, one in each corner and one in the middle, like the five of diamonds. The variety of holes therefore was immense, for you could play from any one hole to any other hole, and thus make a round of twenty holes, a total unrivalled by any championship course, which, so the Colonel told Mrs. Oxney, had never more than eighteen. As for bathrooms, Wentworth already had twice as many as any of the semi-detached villas with those magnificent but deceptive names, and Mrs. Oxney was intending to put in a third, while in contrast with their paltry cold supper on Sunday, the guests at Wentworth enjoyed on that day a dinner of peculiar profusion and delicacy, for there was a savoury as well as a sweet, and dessert. All these points of superiority made it a bitter thought that visitors could be so ill-informed as to class Wentworth with establishments of similar title.

But throughout this summer Mrs. Oxney had seldom brooded over this possible misconception, for, as she was saying to her sister as they sat out under the cedar by the croquet-lawn, she asked nothing more than to have Wentworth permanently full. She was a tall grey-haired woman, who, as a girl, with a mop of black hair, a quick beady eye, and a long nose had been remarkably like a crow. But now the black hair had turned a most becoming grey, the beady eye was alive with kindliness, and the long nose was rendered less beak-like by the filling out of her face. From her mouth, when she talked to her guests came a perennial stream of tactful observations, and she presented to the world a very comely and amiable appearance. Her sister, Amy Bertram, who, like herself, was a widow, and ran the house in rather subordinate partnership with her, was still crow-like, but, unlike Mrs. Oxney, had a remarkable capacity for seeing the dark side of every situation, and for suitably croaking over it.

She shook her head over Margaret's contented retrospect.

"Things may not be so bad just for the moment," she said, "and as most of the rooms are engaged up till Christmas, we may get through this year all right. But we must be prepared to be very empty from then onwards, for a good season like this is always followed by a very empty one. How we shall manage to get through the spring is more than I can tell you: don't ask me. And I do hope, Margaret, that you'll think twice before putting in that extra bathroom. It will be a great expense, and you must reckon on spending double the estimate."

"Nonsense, my dear," said Margaret. "They've contracted for a fixed sum--and high enough too--for doing everything down to a hot towel-rail, and they've got to carry it out."

Amy shook her head again.

CHAPTER I

"Then you'll find, if you keep them to the contract there'll be bad workmanship somewhere. I know what plumbers are. The taps will leak, and the towel-rail be cold. Besides I can't think what you want with a third bathroom. It seems to me that it's just to humour Colonel Chase who would like one nearer his bedroom. I'm sure the other bathrooms are hardly used at all as it is. Most of our guests don't want a bath if after breakfast they are going to soak for a quarter of an hour down at the establishment. I shouldn't dream of putting another in. And Miss Howard is sure to make a fuss if there's hammering and workmen going on all day and night next her room."

Mrs. Oxney felt this point was worth considering, for though it was worth while to please Colonel Chase, it was certainly not worth while to displease Miss Howard. These two were not guests who came for a three weeks' cure and were gone again, but practically permanent inmates of Wentworth, who had lived here for more than a year, and when their interests conflicted, it was necessary to be wary.

"I'm sure I don't want to fuss Miss Howard," she said, "though I don't know how I can get out of it now. I've promised the Colonel, that there shall be a new bathroom put in, and I let him choose that white tile-paper--"

Amy gave a short hollow croak.

"That's the most expensive of all the patterns," she said.

"And lasts the longer," said Mrs. Oxney. "But it might be as well to put it off till after Christmas, for Miss Howard is sure to go down to Torquay for a couple of weeks then, and it could be done in her absence."

"As like as not she won't be able to get away," said Mrs. Bertram, "for if the coal-strike goes on, the railways will all have stopped long before that. I saw a leader in the paper about it this morning, which said there wasn't a ray of hope on the whole horizon. Not a ray. And the whole horizon. Indeed I don't know what we shall do as soon as the cold weather begins, as it's bound to do soon, for after a warm autumn there's always a severe winter. How we shall keep a fire going for the kitchen I can't imagine: I could wish there weren't so many rooms booked up till Christmas. And as for hot water for the baths--"

"Oh, that's coke," said Mrs. Oxney. "As soon as we start the central heating, it and the bath water are run by the same furnace. You know that quite well, so where's the use of saying that? There's plenty of coke. You just try to get into the coke-cellar, and shut the door behind you. You couldn't do it."

Amy sighed: there was resignation more than relief in her sigh.

"Anyhow the coal is getting low enough," she said to console herself. "I'm sure I don't see how we shall keep the house open at all, when we have to begin fires in the rooms, unless you mean to burn coke in them. There's Miss Howard: she likes the drawing-room to be nothing else but an oven by after breakfast, and there's the Colonel as grumpy as a bear if the smoking-room isn't fit to roast an ox in after tea. I'm not sure that it wouldn't be better to shut Wentworth up altogether when the frosts begin. There's nothing that makes guests so discontented as a cold house. Once get the reputation for chilliness, and ruin stares at you. People coming here for the cure won't stand it. They'll pack up and go to the Bolton Arms or to Balmoral. Better say that we're closed. Belvoir too: I was walking along the road to the back of it yesterday, and the coal-cellar door was open. Crammed: I shouldn't like to say how many tons. Where they get it from I don't know: some underhand means, I'm sadly afraid."

Mrs. Oxney had not been attending much to her sister's familiar litanies, but the thought of those semi-detached hovels, suggested by the mention of Belvoir, put a bright idea into her head.

"I'll tell you what I shall do," she said. "I shall take a whole page in the Baths Guide-book to Bolton, and advertise Wentworth properly, so that everybody shall know that it isn't an ordinary boarding house in a row with the butcher's opposite. Golf links, twenty holes, two tennis courts, one hard, croquet-lawn, kitchen- and flower-gardens, and a tasteful view of the lounge."

"It will be very expensive," said Mrs. Bertram, who was really enthusiastic about this idea of her sister's, but was compelled by all the dominant instincts of her nature to see the objection to any course of action.

"Not a bit," said Mrs. Oxney. "It will pay for itself ten times over. Let people know they can play lawn-tennis all the winter--"

"Not if it snows," said Mrs. Bertram.

"Amy, let me finish my sentence. Tennis all the winter, and the breakfast lounge as well as the drawing-room and central heating and no extras for baths and three bathrooms, and standing in its own grounds--"

"But they all stand in their own grounds," said Mrs. Bertram.

"Stuff and nonsense, Amy. Grounds mean something spacious, not a gravel path leading round a monkey-puzzle. And no cold supper on Sundays. I shall say that too."

That point was debated: to say that there was no cold supper on Sunday night implied, so Mrs. Bertram sadly surmised, that there was cold supper all the week, and nothing at all on Sundays, and such a misconception would be lamentably alien to the effect that this sumptuous advertisement was designed to produce. Mrs. Oxney therefore agreed to word this differently or omit altogether, and hurried indoors to find the most tasteful view of the lounge for the photographer.

The morning hours between breakfast and lunch were always the least populated time of the day at Wentworth, for the majority of its guests were patients who went down to the baths in the morning to drink the abominable waters or lie pickling in tubs of brine, and returned, some in the motor-bus, and the more stalwart on their feet, in time to have an hour's prescribed rest before lunch. The two permanent inmates of the house, Colonel Chase and Miss Alice Howard were, so far from being patients, in the enjoyment of the rudest health, but they too, were never at home on fine mornings like this, for Miss Howard had left the house by ten o'clock with her satchel of painting apparatus and a small folding stool, which when properly adjusted never pinched her anywhere or collapsed, and sketched from Nature till lunch-time. On her return she put up on the chimney-piece of the lounge the artistic fruit of her labours for the delectation and compliments of her fellow-guests. These water-colour sketches were, for the most part, suave and sentimental, and represented the church tower of St. Giles's, seen over the fields, or trees with reflections in the river, or dim effects of dusk (though painted by broad daylight, since it was impossible to get the colours right otherwise) with scattered lights gleaming from cottage windows, and possibly a crescent moon (body-colour) in the west. Garden-beds, still-life studies of petunias and Mrs. Oxney's cat were rarer subjects, but much admired.

Colonel Chase's occupations in the morning were equally regular and more physically strenuous, for either he bicycled seldom less than thirty miles, or walked not less than eight as recorded by his pedometer. He had two pedometers, one giddily affixed to the hub of his bicycle's hind-wheel, and the other, for pedestrian purposes, incessantly hung by a steel clip into his waistcoat pocket: this one clicked once at each alternate step of his great strong legs, and it was wonderful how far he walked every day. Thus, though his fellow-guests at Wentworth could not, as in Miss Howard's case, feast their eyes on the actual fruit of his energy since this would have implied the visualization of so many miles of road, they could always be (and were) informed of the immense distances he had traversed. This he felt sure, was a source of admiring envy to the crippled and encouraged them to regain their lost activity. Mrs. Holders, for instance, who, a fortnight ago, had only just been able to hobble down to the Bath establishment on two sticks and was always driven up again in the motor-bus, and who now was able, on her good days, to walk both ways, with the assistance of only one stick, had great jokes with him about her increasing mobility. She used to say that when she came back in the spring, she would go out with him for his walk in the morning, and take her treatment in the afternoon when he was resting. She seemed to take the greatest interest in his athletic feats, and used to drink in all he said with an air of reverent and rapt attention. Occasionally, however, when Colonel Chase was least conscious of being humorous (though no one could be more so if he wished) she gave a little mouse-like squeak of laughter and then became intensely serious again. This puzzled him till he thought of what was no doubt the right explanation, namely, that Mrs. Holders had suddenly thought of something amusing, which had nothing to do with him and his conversation. For the rest, she was a middle-aged, round-about little personage, with a plain vivacious face and highly-arched eyebrows, so that she looked in a permanent state of surprise though nobody knew what she was surprised about. Miss Howard thought of her as 'quaint' and Mrs. Holders did not think of Miss Howard at all.

There had lately been a tree felled in the field where the twenty-hole golf links lay, and when her sister went indoors to select a tasteful view of the lounge, Mrs. Bertram walked through the garden and out on to the links to see what it was worth in the way of logs for the fires in this shortage of coal. The tree had been dead for more than a year, and she had repeatedly urged Margaret to have it cut down while it was still sound, and had not degenerated into touchwood. But Mrs. Oxney had been very obstinate about it, weak but obstinate, for a green woodpecker had built in it and she said it would be such a shame to cut it down, and completely upset the poor dickie-bird's domestic arrangements. Then, when the woodpecker had quite finished with it, Colonel Chase said it made a first-rate hazard for the seventeenth and nineteenth holes (the long diagonals across the field) which meant that he was the only player who could loft his ball over it without going round, and it was not till yesterday that Mrs. Oxney had steeled herself to the destruction of this magnificent bunker. Now, of course, as Mrs. Bertram had woefully anticipated, the tree was no more than a great cracknell kept together by bark, and the Colonel might just as well have been left to go on soaring over it or hitting into it as before.

As she walked back to the house from this depressing expedition she heard the hoot of the motor-bus which brought back the patients from the baths, announcing its return. There were the usual three occupants (since Mrs. Holders had taken to walking up) Mr. Kemp and his down-trodden daughter Florence, both habitual guests at Wentworth, and Mr. Bullingdon who was paying his first visit to Bolton Spa. Though he was quite a young man, Mrs. Bertram felt sure that a bath chair would soon be his only mode of locomotion, but in spite of his poor knees, which made him move as if he was performing a cake-walk with his two sticks for a partner, he was full of jokes and gaiety. He laughed at himself in the most engaging manner, and said that he really wasn't sure that he wanted to get better, since he attracted so much flattering attention, wherever he went, by reason of his antics. Apart from these flippant allusions to his own afflictions, he never talked about arthritis at all, which was a great contrast to Mr. Kemp whose idea of pleasant conversation was to pin a listener into a corner from which escape was difficult, and, beginning with the 3rd of March, 1920, which was the date on which he first felt a throbbing in his left hip, recount the progress of his rheumatisms. He had visited Harrogate, Buxton, Bath, Droitwich, Aix and Marienbad, and none of these had really done him any good, but there was still a chance that Bolton in combination with some of the others and Bournemouth for the winter, might benefit him. Just as Mrs. Bertram reached the door, he was balanced on the step of the motor-bus, and warning Mr. Bullingdon about a certain malignant masseur at Aix.

"Don't let him touch your knees with the tips of his fingers," he said, "if you're thinking of going to Aix. I was getting on nicely there, as my daughter will tell you, when my doctor recommended me to have treatment at the hands of this villain. In a week or two he had undone all the good I had derived from Aix, and when I left I wasn't walking much better than you. What was his name, Florence?"

"Jean Cuissot," said Florence in a monotonous voice. She knew her father would ask her that.

"Nonsense: Jean Cuissot was the masseur I went to the year before. No, I believe you're right, it was Jean Cuissot. Judas Iscariot would be a better name for him. Give me your arm, please, unless you want me to stand on this step for the rest of my life. Ah, dear me, I've got a new pain in my ankle this morning. I woke in the night and felt it wasn't comfortable, and expected I should have trouble. Why, there's Mrs. Holders already. She has walked all the way up from the baths. I haven't been able to walk back after my bath since I was at Harrogate two seasons ago, and the hill there is neither so long nor so steep as this. But I used to think nothing of it then. What wouldn't I give to be able to walk up such a hill now!"

Mrs. Bertram who was lending a firm shoulder to Mr. Kemp while his daughter disentangled his sticks which had got muddled up in some inexplicable manner between his legs and the door of the bus, sighed heavily.

"Yes, indeed," she said. "We so seldom appreciate our blessings till they are taken from us, and then we haven't got them to appreciate. But Bolton may set you up yet, Mr. Kemp, you never can tell."

Mr. Bullingdon, now that the doorway of the bus was clear, performed a sort of mystic dance down the steps and on to the ground.

"There we are," he said cheerfully. "You know they ought to engage Mrs. Holders and Mr. Kemp and me for a short turn at a music-hall. It would have an immense success: screams of laughter. There would be a glass of champagne on one side of the stage, and we three toeing the mark on the other. Then at the word 'go', we would start off and see who could grab it first. Mrs. Holders would have to be handicapped though, you and I wouldn't stand a chance against her, Mr. Kemp."

Mr. Kemp was inclined to be offended at the suggestion of his appearing at a music-hall, and his daughter and Mrs. Bertram closed in behind him and propelled him into the house. Besides, as everybody ought to know, champagne was poison to him: you might as well expect him to race for a glass of prussic acid.

With the dispersal of the passengers by the ambulance waggon (as Mr. Bullingdon always flippantly called the bus) to their rooms to rest before lunch, the house was quiet again till the arrival of Miss Howard with her satchel and her camp-stool. The twilight scene on which she had been engaged this sunny morning had been giving her a great deal of trouble, for the dusk, even to her indulgent eye was of a strange soupy quality, as if some dark viscous fluid had been emitted from an unknown source (for she had not intended it) on to the landscape, and the lights from the cottages looked like some curious eruption of orange spots. It was very disappointing, for she had hoped great things from this sketch, but now when she put it up on the chimney-piece of the lounge, the effect was puzzling rather than pleasing. Luckily however, she found that a small flat parcel had arrived for her; this she knew could be nothing else than Evening Bells, which she had sent a week ago to be framed by Mr. Bowen. That, up till now, was certainly her *chef-d'œuvre:* Mrs. Oxney had declared that she could positively hear the bells, and so Miss Howard had caused to be printed on the mount of this masterpiece, 'The mellow lin-lan-lone of evening bells'. There was the tower of St. Giles' church reflected in the river, which had caused that pretty thought to come into Mrs. Oxney's mind, and Miss Howard was sure that everybody would like to see 'Evening Bells' again in its gilt frame. So she replaced the soupy twilight in her satchel, and determined to put it under the tap when she went upstairs to see if a thorough washing-down would not render it more translucent. There was half an hour yet before lunch-time, and she tripped into the drawing-room to get a good practise on the mellow but elderly piano.

Miss Alice Howard was a pathetic person, though she would have been very much surprised if anyone had told her so. She had been an extremely pretty girl, lively and intelligent and facile, but by some backhanded stroke of fate she had never married, and now at the age of forty, though she had parted with her youth, she had relinquished no atom of her girlishness. She hardly ever walked, but tripped, she warbled little snatches of song when she thought that anyone might be within hearing in order to refresh them with her maidenly brightness, and sat on the hearth-rug in front of the fire, even though there was a far more comfortable seat ready. It was not that she felt any profound passion for tripping, warbling and squatting, but from constantly telling herself that she was barely out of her teens she had got to believe in her girlishness and behaved accordingly. Her imagination (here was the root of the matter) was incessantly exercised on herself, and she imagined all sorts of things about herself that had little or no foundation in fact. She could scarcely have told you how or when, for instance, she began to believe that she was closely connected with a noble house, but certainly all Wentworth believed it now. They could have had no other informant but her, and Miss Howard very nearly believed it, too, so constantly had she made rich little allusions which implied it. She had a commodious semi-detached villa of her own, conveniently close to the station at Tunbridge Wells, but it was lonely work to live there by herself, and she had let it furnished for the last year, and hoped to do so again for the next. The occupant was a gentleman on the Stock Exchange called Mr. Gradge, who lived there with his sister, but she always referred to them as "my tenants," and to the semi-detached villa as 'my little place' in Kent. She thus contrived to produce the impression that the villa was a small ancestral manor-house, and sometimes lamented that the monstrously swollen taxes of late years had caused so many country houses to be shut up or let: she thought herself very lucky to be able to let her little place in Kent near (though it really was 'at') Tunbridge Wells. Miss Howard, in fact, though girlish, suffered from the essentially middle-aged disease of fabrication, and whether she looked at her physical image in the tall looking-glass in her bedroom, or contemplated herself in the mirror of her mind, she now saw what she had got to believe about herself.

She was quite alone in the world without near relations or any intimate friend, and, with the little place in Kent let to her tenants, she lived at Wentworth for the greater part of the year, spent a month at a similar boarding house at Torquay which she called her Christmas holidays, and had another holiday in a third boarding-house in South Kensington for a fortnight of the London season. From there she came back to Wentworth quite worn out with gaiety; everyone had been so kind and pleased to see her, and how her cousins had scolded her for insisting on going back to Bolton after so short a visit. But she was much happier at Wentworth than anywhere else, for she had come to be, not only in her own eyes, but in Mrs. Oxney's and those of the other guests a sort of incarnation of all the Muses. She painted, she sang and played, she danced to the strains of the gramophone with any sound pair of legs among the guests, or, if there happened to be none, she was quite willing to execute a *pas seul* in the lounge after dinner, which Mrs. Oxney, who always said the agreeable thing, considered equal to the best Russian dancing. And then there was her lawn-tennis, though she shook her head at the suggestion that she should enter at Wimbledon next year, for that would mean giving up so much of her sketching and her music. And then there was her croquet and her golf . . .

She sat down at the piano after removing her hat (shaped like an inverted waste-paper basket and trimmed with three sorts of grapes, pink, blue and orange) and deftly encouraged her pale brown hair to drop in rebellious disorder over her forehead and nearly conceal the ear that was like a pink shell. She ran her hands over the keys: someone had told her--or had she invented it for herself?--that she had a 'butterfly touch,' and when the butterflies alighted on one or two flowers where the careless things were trespassing, Miss Howard said 'Naughty'! to them, and made them do it again. She was supposed to have an amazing power of improvisation, and these industrious little practices with the soft pedal down, while everyone was resting upstairs, certainly developed her gift. There were some fragments from Chopin which were landmarks for the improvisation when it seemed to be wandering and put it back on the road again. Miss Howard could scarcely tell sometimes whether certain bits belonged to her own butterflies or Chopin's, and if she couldn't tell she felt sure that nobody else at Wentworth could. Presently the gong in the lounge announced that lunch was ready (Miss Howard would have winced at that brazen booming if anyone had been present) but she took no notice of the summons, for she knew that Mrs. Oxney would probably come tiptoeing in, and find her quite lost in her music, sitting there with dreamy eyes fixed on the ceiling, and a smile hovering--just that--on her mouth.

It all happened just as she anticipated: out of the corner of a dreamy eye she saw Mrs. Oxney enter, and sit down with a long elaborate creak beside the door, but she did not officially see her until she stumbled over a chromatic run. She gave a little start and an exclamation of surprise.

"Oh, Mrs. Oxney," she said, "how did you steal in without my noticing? And how wicked of you to creep into the corner and listen to my bunglings! Fingers so naughty and stiff this morning. I could slap the tiresome things for being so stupid. Is it nearly lunch-time? Have you come in to tell me to run upstairs and brush my hair and wash my hands? Must I?"

"Certainly you needn't, for you've given me such a treat," said Mrs. Oxney. "I could listen to you playing for ever, Miss Howard. Tiddle-iddle-iddle-iddle-iddle! I call it wonderful without a note to guide you. I wish my fingers were as naughty as that. As for its being lunch-time, why, the gong rang five minutes ago, but I couldn't punish myself by interrupting you."

Miss Howard was perfectly aware that Mrs. Oxney was a musical imbecile, but in spite of that her appreciation gave her strong satisfaction. She was also aware that the gong had sounded five minutes ago, and so she gave another little exclamation of surprise at the astonishing news.

"Fancy!" she said. "But when I get to the piano I become so stupid and absent-minded. I came in so hungry half an hour ago, hoping it was lunch-time and I declare I've no feeling of hunger left now. Music feeds me, I think: even my feeble little strummings are meat and drink to me. Yes: little bits of Chopin. How lovely to have known Chopin! I wish I had known Chopin."

"Well, why didn't you ever ask your mamma to get him to come down to your place in Kent?" asked Mrs. Oxney. "He'd have liked to hear you play, I'll be bound."

Miss Howard gave her silvery little laugh.

"Dear thing!" she said. "Chopin was a friend of great-grandmamma--let's see, which was it?--yes, great-grandmamma Stanley. She went to see him at Majorca or Minorca."

"I have made a mistake then," said Mrs. Oxney, "but you're so good-natured, Miss Howard. And I've come to trespass on your good nature, too."

"You shan't be prosecuted," said Miss Howard gaily. "Trespass away."

"Well, it's this then," said Mrs. Oxney. "There's to be an entertainment at the Assembly Rooms next week, and the Committee deputed me to ask you if you wouldn't play at it. Such a treat it would be, and I'm sure everybody in Bolton would flock to hear you. It's for a good object too, the Children's Hospital in the town."

"How you all work me!" said Miss Howard, immensely pleased at being asked and beginning to fix on the waste-paper basket. "It's sheer bullying, for you know I couldn't refuse to do anything for the dear mites. How I shall have to practice if I'm to be made to play in public!"

"So much the better for Wentworth," said Mrs. Oxney. "Then I may tell them that you will? I do call that kind. And what bits will you play? They'd like it best, I'll be bound, if you played one of your own beautiful improvisations. That would be a thing people couldn't hear at an ordinary concert, 'Improvisations by Miss Howard'! And then that wouldn't call for any practice at all."

"Dear thing," said Miss Howard again. "If you only knew how it takes it out of me. Such dreaming and yet such concentration. But you shall have your way."

Meals were served with military punctuality at Wentworth and the pianist and her impresario were very late to Colonel Chase's high indignation, for if people were late, the service was delayed, and the punctual suffered for the inconsiderateness of the laggard. At breakfast, which, from habits formed in India he called Chota-hazri, unpunctuality did not matter, but tiffin (lunch) was another affair. He was also soured this morning by the fact that the giddy pedometer on his bicycle had got out of order. He had felt super-normally energetic when he went out for his ride and had pedalled away in the most splendid form for nearly three hours, feeling certain that he was breaking his previous record of thirty-five miles and anticipating many congratulations on this athletic feat, which would give so much pleasure to others as well as himself. . . . But, when, on arrival at Wentworth, he had got off his bicycle with rather trembling knees and completely out of breath, to feast his eyes on the disc which would surely register thirty-six miles at least, he found its idiotic hand pointing to the ridiculous figure of nine miles and a quarter. It was most aggravating; he would have to take the wretched instrument to be repaired this afternoon, instead of resting after lunch, and very likely it would not be ready by tomorrow morning so that once more he would not know how far he had been. That would play the deuce with his aggregate for the month which he sedulously entered in a notebook. At one end of it was the record of the miles he had bicycled, and upside down at the other the miles he had walked, and now it would appear that he had only bicycled nine and a quarter miles on October 17th, and perhaps none at all on October 18th.

These depressing reflections, combined with Miss Howard's unpunctuality, caused him to utter a mere grunt to her salutation as she tripped by his table with all the grapes in her hat wagging, and sat down at her own table in the window where she could see the church tower, and feed the sweet birdies with crumbs when she had fed herself.

"And how many miles did you go this morning, Colonel?" she asked as she unfolded her napkin. Interest in his prowess always pleased him, and of course she did not know how wicked the pedometer had been.

"Most aggravating!" he said. "That wretched instrument of mine got out of order, and after nearly three hours of the hardest riding I've ever done, it registered nine miles and a quarter."

There was a general murmur of sympathy with him and of indignation with the pedometer. Unfortunately Mrs. Holders tried to say something amusing: she could not have done anything more dangerous. Reckless in fact: highly culpable.

"Nine and a quarter miles in under three hours?" she said. "I should call that very good going. I've often been less."

That was like an application of the bellows to Colonel Chase's smouldering wrath. If there was one subject which must be treated with deference and respect it was his bicycling, and he burst into flame.

"Considerably less I should think, ma'am," he said. "Waitress, I said bread and butter pudding half an hour ago, and I don't see why I should be kept waiting till tea-time because others don't come in to lunch."

"He's gone off into one of his tantrums," whispered Mrs. Oxney to her sister. "Run into the kitchen, Amy, and bring it yourself and a nice jug of cream with it."

Miss Howard was grieved at this piece of rudeness. Howards never behaved like that. Such a peppery old thing: as if anybody cared how many miles he went on his bicycle. Sometimes she wished he would ride away for hundreds of miles in a straight line and never come back. And then sometimes she thought that if he had only a clever young wife to look after him, she would soon cure him of his roughnesses. So she put her nose slightly in the air, and ate curried chicken with great elegance in a spoon, which Colonel Chase said was the right way to eat curry.

The nice jug of cream had a mollifying effect, and when Miss Howard came out from her lunch, Colonel Chase was explaining to a sycophantic audience where he had gone, and it was unanimously decided that he must have ridden at least thirty-eight miles, which was indeed joyful. He decided in consequence to forgive Miss Howard for being late for lunch, and to show the plenitude of his magnanimity, he strolled across to the chimney-piece to admire Evening Bells.

"I'll enter it as thirty-eight miles then in my logbook," he said, "if you all insist on it. Why there's another of your sketches, Miss Howard, though I think I've seen it before. Very pretty, I'm sure. What's that written underneath it? The mellow lanoline--"

Miss Howard was also ready to forgive, and gave a laughing peal of bells on her own account.

"How can you be so naughty?" she said. "The mellow lin-lan-lone, Colonel. Tennyson you know. Such a sweet poem. I shall have to find it for you."

"I declare I can hear the bells," said Miss Kemp, shamelessly plagiarising from Mrs. Oxney. "Delicious, Miss Howard. So poetical."

Her father who had been examining the sketch from a purely hygienic point of view, shook his head.

"I shouldn't like to go to evening service in that church," he said. "All among the trees, you know, with the river close by. I should wake up with a bad attack of lumbago next morning, I'm afraid. Churches are draughty places at the best of times, and if you walk there you're liable to get heated and then have to sit for an hour in the cold, while if you drive there, as like as not you've got chilly already and that's even worse. I shan't ever forget the chill I got in church at Harrogate. It was a damp morning, and I should have been wiser not to go. I declare it makes me shiver to look at that church of Miss Howard's so close to the river. I might manage morning service there, but it would be very ill-advised to go in the evening."

Colonel Chase had finished the coffee which Mrs. Oxney had sent him as a propitiation. It had arrived with her compliments, for coffee after lunch was an extra.

"Well, I must get down to the town to have my pedometer looked to," he said, "and then how about a few holes at golf, Miss Howard? I'll be back in twenty minutes. That'll make a pretty good day's exercise for me."

"Marvellous!" said Miss Howard.

"But nothing to what I used to do not so many years back in India," he said. "Military duties, parades and what not in the morning, and a polo-match after tiffin, and perhaps a game of rackets after tea, and a couple of hundred at billiards before I got to my bridge. That's the way to keep fit, and get good news from your liver if the ladies will excuse the expression."

Mrs. Holders was not so forgiving as Miss Howard. She waited till he had passed the window pedalling hard with his chest well out, and then gave her mouse-squeak of laughter.

"And it's early closing," she said. "He'll come tiffining back and serve him right for being rude to me. I can't stand rudeness."

Mrs. Oxney who had joined the group round Evening Bells wrung her hands in dismay.

"Oh, what have you done, Mrs. Holders?" she said. "I am sorry. That beautiful hot coffee which I sent the Colonel, why, I might as well never have sent it at all, so vexed he'll be to find it's early closing. And then, if he's not too much upset to play golf, he'll see that I've had his favourite tree cut down, and it's fallen right across the green in the middle of the field, and that'll be another cause for vexation. I must send the gardeners to see if they can't haul it away before he gets back. Dear me, what a day of misfortunes!"

"And little better than touchwood when all's said and done," moaned Mrs. Bertram.

So the two sisters who usually joined the guests in the lounge after lunch for a friendly chat, cut this short, and the one hurried away to despatch gardeners to the scene of the disaster in hopes of clearing it before the Colonel came back from his futile errand to the town, and the other to order hot scones for tea, of which he was inordinately fond. Though dirty weather might be anticipated, Mrs. Holders was quite impenitent, and kept bursting into little squeals of merriment.

"Serve him right, serve him right," she repeated. "He was rude to me, and that's what he gets for it. If those are army manners, give me the Navy."

This was a revolutionary utterance: the red flag seemed to flutter. Colonel Chase had hitherto been regarded at Wentworth as something cosmic, like a thunderstorm or a fine day. You could dislike or be frightened of the thunderstorm, and hide in a dark place till its fury was past, or you could enjoy the fine day, but you had to accept whichever it might happen to be. He was stuffy on the thunderstorm days and sunny on the others, and you must take the weather as it came.

"Here we all are," continued the rebel, "and we've got to be pleasant to each other, and not fly into passions or behave like kings and emperors, however long we've spent in India, and however many tigers and tiffins we have shot. For my part, I never believed much in his story of the tiger which charged him, and which he shot through the heart when it was two yards away. I'm sure I wish evil to nobody, but I shouldn't have minded if the tiger had given him a good nip first, to teach him manners. And why he should have jugs of cream at lunch and hot scones for tea because he lost his temper I don't know. Skim-milk and a bit of dry bread would have been more suitable."

These awful remarks were addressed to Tim Bullingdon only, for the sisters had gone to avert the wrath to come, Miss Howard had taken the soupy twilight-sketch to the tap, and Florence Kemp had gone out with her father to the chairs under the cedar, where she read aloud to him till he went to sleep.

"I wouldn't have been in his regiment for anything," said Tim, cake-walking about the lounge, for gentle exercise though painful was recommended. "I would sooner have been in hell."

"So would I," said Mrs. Holders cordially, "and thought it very agreeable in comparison. By the way, there's an envelope on the writing-table in the smoking-room addressed to his Excellency the Viceroy. That's meant for us to see. Have you seen it?"

"Good Lord, yes," said Tim. "It's been there since yesterday morning. I put it in the waste-paper basket once, but it's back again and getting quite dusty. If it's there tomorrow morning, I shall address another envelope to King George, Personal."

Mrs. Holders squeaked again.

"That would be a beauty for him," she said. "Mind you do it. Here he is back from the town coming up the drive. What a red face!"

Colonel Chase banged the front door and came puffing in to the lounge.

"Pretty state of things," he said. "It seems a perpetual holiday for the working classes. That's what makes them out of hand. Early closing to-day, and late opening tomorrow, I shouldn't wonder, and then comes Sunday, and I shouldn't be surprised if it was a Bank-holiday on Monday."

"Dear me!" said Mrs Holders. "Then you've had your ride for nothing. What a disappointment. Never mind, get a good game of golf."

Colonel Chase flung himself into a chair, and mopped his face.

"And no sign of Miss Howard," he said. "I told her I should be back in twenty minutes. Women have no idea of time. Qui-hi, Miss Howard."

"I expect that's Hindustanee," said Mrs. Holders. "What a pleasure to talk so many languages. *Parlez-vous Français, monsieur?"*

Colonel Chase had again that horrid sense of uncertainty as to whether Mrs. Holders was not in some obstruse manner poking fun at him, but, as usual, the notion seemed incredible. Then snatches of song were heard from the landing at the top of the stairs, and Miss Howard came tripping along it. The tap-water had done wonders for the viscous fog, and she looked forward to making a success of her sketch after all. It was to be called 'The curfew tolls the knell of parting day'. She carried her bag of golf clubs with her and was quite ready.

The two went out together through the garden to the golf-field. A perfect swarm of gardeners and odd men and chauffeurs and boot-boys were busy hauling the touchwood tree from the middle green.

"Why, what's all this?" said Colonel Chase, stopping short. "My tree, my hazard, my bunker, my favourite hazard. Cut down! Upon my word now! I wonder by whose orders that was done. Ah, there's Mrs. Oxney. What's all this, Mrs. Oxney?"

Mrs. Oxney came forward like Esther before Ahasuerus.

"Oh, dear me, such a sad accident, Colonel," she said, "though it will be all right in a few minutes now. The tree fell right across the green. So clumsy! But they've got it moving. I had to have it cut down: all gone at the root and so dangerous. What should I have felt if it had come crashing down when you were in the middle of one of your beautiful puttings?"

CHAPTER I

This was an improvisation as brilliant as Miss Howard's on the piano, and far less rehearsed. But it gave little satisfaction.

"Well, you've removed the only decent hazard in the place," he said. "I'm sorry it has happened for I've been toiling all the summer to get a few sporting holes for you. I should have thought you might have had it propped up or something of the sort. No matter. Take the honour, Miss Howard, and let's be off, or it will be dark before we've played our twenty holes."

CHAPTER II

This inauspicious afternoon finished better than might have been anticipated. The Colonel's favourite hazard, it is true, was laid low, but the trunk now dragged to the edge of the green, was discovered to be a very well-placed bunker, when Miss Howard put the ball underneath it in an unplayable position, and thus enabled Colonel Chase to win the match. Then it was found that Mrs. Oxney's chauffeur who was an ingenious mechanic could put the pedometer to rights with the greatest ease. (He geared it a shade too high, so that for the future when Colonel Chase had ridden seven-eights of a mile it recorded a full mile, and so ever afterwards when he rode thirty-two miles, as he so often did, he could inform admiring Wentworth with indisputable evidence to back him, that he had ridden thirty-six. A pleasing spell of record-breaking ensued.)

After a quantity of hot scones for tea, he retired to his bedroom according to his usual custom for a couple of hours of solid reading before dinner. He took from a small book-shelf above his bed, which contained for the most part old Army lists, an antique copy of Macaulay's Essays which he had won as a prize for Geography at school, and before settling down to read made himself very comfortable in a large armchair with his pipe and tobacco handy. Then he glanced at the news in the evening paper, which for many months now had put him in a towering passion since it so largely concerned the coal strike. All strikers, according to his firm conviction, were damned lazy skunks, who refused to do a stroke of work, because they preferred to be supported in idle luxury by the dole, while Mr. Cook was a Bolshevist, whom Colonel Chase, so he repeatedly affirmed, would have rejoiced to hang with his own hands, having heartily flogged him first. There would soon have been an end of the strike if the weak-kneed Government had only done what he had recommended from the very beginning. Then, in order to quiet and calm his mind he mused over a cross-word puzzle, jotting down in pencil the solutions which seemed to fit. Half an hour generally sufficed to break the back of it, and then he leaned back in his chair, opened Macaulay's Essays at random, and gave himself up to meditation.

This meditation was always agreeable, for its origin, the cave out of which it so generously gushed was his strong and profound satisfaction with himself, and this gave a pleasant flavour to whatever he thought about. He had had a thoroughly creditable though uneventful career in the army, and on his retirement two years ago, found himself able to contemplate the past and await the future with

British equanimity. Being unmarried and possessed of a comfortable competence, he could live for a couple of months in the year in furnished rooms close to his club in London, and for the other ten at this admirably conducted boarding-establishment, thus escaping all the responsibilities of house-keeping and of friendship. In London armchair acquaintances sufficed for social needs, they afforded him rubbers of bridge in the cardroom and ample opportunity to curse the weather and the Government in company with kindred spirits; for the rest of the day the perusal of the morning and the evening papers and an hour's constitutional tramp round the park, fulfilled the wants of mind and body. At Wentworth similarly, his bicycle rides, his excellent meals, his comfortable bedroom supplied his physical wants and he had the additional mental satisfaction of being undisputed cock of the walk, whereas among the members at his club there was a sad tendency to think themselves as good as he. But here his tastes and his convenience were consulted before those of any other guest, cream was poured forth for the mollification of his tantrums and his wish was of the nature of law to the economies of the establishment. He was convinced that Mrs. Oxney had no greater pleasure in life than to please him, no greater cross to bear than the sense that all had not been as he would have had it; he regarded himself as being looked on with a pleasant mixture of awe and respectful affection. Every now and then, it is true, there appeared here some outsider who did not seem duly reverential, and at the present moment he had occasional doubts about the true state of Mrs. Holders's sentiments with regard to him, but such possible exceptions were negligible and temporary. They came for their few weeks of cure and passed away again. He bore them no real ill will, and hoped they had profited by their stay. He and Miss Howard alone went on for ever; on the whole he was very much pleased with Miss Howard, and when, in his more romantic moments she appeared to unusual advantage as she sat in profile against a dark wall (a rather favourite position of hers) he wondered if he would be more comfortable with an establishment of his own, and a presentable middle-aged woman to look after him, and bear his name. Her occasional allusions to her little place in Kent were interesting. Indeed he really asked very little of life; only that he should be quite well, and ride a great many miles on his bicycle, and that Wentworth should unweariedly admire all he did, and sun itself in his approbation. Given that these modest requirements had been granted when, between half-past ten and eleven at night, he did a few energetic dumb-bell exercises before going to bed, he claimed nothing more of the morrow than that it should be like to-day; sufficient unto the day had been the good thereof. That something should have occurred like the felling of his favourite tree, or the unpunctuality of Miss Howard at lunch, which had caused a tantrum, would not prove to have spoiled the day; he was large-minded enough to take a broader view than that.

Plans and retrospections eddied pleasantly round in his head, the volume of Macaulay's Essays, already upside down, slipped from his hand, and he indulged as usual in half an hour's nap, from which the sound of the dressing-gong and the entry of the maid with his hot water, roused him. Here was a fine opportunity to linger before making his toilet, in order to demonstrate to others what an inconvenient thing it was not to be punctual. But, being very hungry, he scorned so paltry a reprisal. He had not quite finished with his evening paper for there was a leader on the coal strike which a cursory glance had shewn him was written in a vein which he thoroughly approved, and he took it down with him to read it as he dined.

Colonel Chase openly used spectacles for reading when he was alone, and furtively in company, slipping them off if he thought they would be noticed, for they were a little out of keeping with that standard of perfect health and vigour of which he was so striking an example. Still they were useful with small print (print was not what it used to be, or the electric light, probably owing to the coal strike, was not so luminous) and by propping his paper against his cruet he thought they would be unnoticed. Occasionally he glanced over the top of it at the new arrival of the afternoon, who sat at a table close in front of him. She was a good-looking woman of middle age, of healthy and attractive appearance, wearing a fixed bright smile for no particular reason. She was evidently on the best terms with life, and until Colonel Chase saw that at the conclusion of dinner she walked out with a pronounced limp, and leaned heavily on a stick, he had felt sure that she was no patient in search of health. The dining-room had cleared before he finished his glass of port, and when he went out, the guests with Mrs. Oxney and Mrs. Bertram, were sitting in the lounge. This was the usual procedure. They all sat talking there till he joined them and proposed the pastime which he preferred. Usually he liked playing bridge and a table was formed. Sometimes he challenged Mrs. Oxney to a game of chess which always ended in the capture of all her pieces (for he ran no risks,) and a brilliant check-mate. But before that there would generally be two or three guests trying to solve the cross-word puzzle in the evening paper, and though he invariably professed never to glance at a cross-word puzzle, his quiet work at it in his room before dinner often enabled him to help them with some wonderful extempore solutions. To-night, Miss Kemp, Mrs. Oxney and Mrs. Holders formed the cross-word group, and were sadly at loss for nearly everything. In a corner of the lounge, away from any possible draught, Mr. Kemp had successfully cornered the new bright smiling guest and was telling her all about Bath and Buxton and Harrogate and Aix. Mrs. Oxney, with apologies for interrupting Mr. Kemp's conversation introduced Colonel Chase to her as Mrs. Bliss, a name which seemed to suit her excellently, and then claimed his assistance in the puzzle.

"We shall get on better now that the Colonel will help us," she said. "Such a difficult one to-night, Colonel."

Colonel Chase quite forgot that he had pencilled the greater part of this arduous puzzle into his evening paper, and put it carelessly down on the table by the particular armchair that was always reserved for him.

"I'm sure if it's difficult I shan't be of much use to you," he said. "I've no head for these things."

CHAPTER II

"Oh, but you're wonderful," said Mrs. Oxney, "a town in Morocco, six letters. How is one to know that if one's never been there? Perhaps I'd better get an atlas."

"No, no, wait a minute," said Colonel Chase. "Let's do without an atlas if we can. Let me think now. Fez? No, that is too short. Now what is that other place? It's on the tip of my tongue. Six letters, did you say? Ha! Tetuan! How will that suit you?"

A chorus of praise went up and so did Mrs. Holders's eyebrows.

"And it fits unicorn," cried Miss Kemp in ecstasy. "We should never have guessed Tetuan. Then thirteen down, the Latin for south-west wind, eight letters, and if Tetuan's right, which it must be because of unicorn, there's an 'n' for the fifth."

"Latin: come, come! I've forgotten all my Latin," said this fatuous man. "If it was Hindustanee now. . . . But let me try to be a boy again. There's Boreas, but that's north wind I'm afraid, and too short for you. You've stumped me there. Wait a moment though: Ovid; something in Ovid. I've got it. Try 'Favonius'. See if Favonius will help you."

Shrill sounded the chorus of praise, because Favonius fitted 'vampire' and 'alpha'.

"I knew you'd make short work of it, Colonel," said Mrs. Oxney. "You're a positive encyclopædia; that's what I always say of you. And what's a trigonometrical term of six letters with an 's' for the third? You ought to go in for the prizes, indeed you ought, for you'd win every one."

"Upon my word, Mrs. Oxney, you want to know a lot to-night," said he. "I must recollect my mathematics as well as my Latin, and perhaps you'll want Hebrew next. Trigonometry now: there's equation, no, perhaps you'd call that algebra. But there's tangent, only that's got no 's': there's 'sine' . . . oh, put down 'cosine'. Cosine's right."

"Why, I never heard of such a thing," said Mrs. Oxney. "How can I guess what I've never heard of? Cosine! Fancy?"

A diabolical notion, worthy only of a low mind struck Tim Bullingdon. Colonel Chase had got up and was standing commandingly by the fire-place with his back half-turned. So Tim drew his copy of the evening paper from the table, and stealthily turned to the cross-word page, where he found the entire puzzle legibly pencilled in. Then he skilfully replaced the paper again, and pointing to it, winked at Mrs. Holders. That ingenious lady guessed his purport, and gave a little squeal of laughter which she converted into an unconvincing cough . . . So while Colonel Chase now feigned hesitation over 'frieze', 'crampit' and 'piston' Mr. Bullingdon dreamily but fluently supplied them all. These brilliant suggestions finished the puzzle and the Colonel after magnanimously complimenting him on his quickness, invited the three ladies of the group to play bridge with him in the smoking-room. Miss Howard in view of her improvisation at the entertainment next week betook herself to the piano in the drawing-room to fix in her mind a few fragments of extempore melody.

Mr. Kemp meantime had been enjoying a splendid innings. He was accustomed to tell the long and tragic history of his left hip from March 3, 1920, to listeners, over whose eyes, as the sad epic proceeded, there often came a sort of glazed look. That, of course, never deterred him in any way from continuing but he told it much more vividly to-night, for this bright smiling Mrs. Bliss was full of attention and eager interest. She seemed intensely sympathetic, and, at the conclusion, when he had fully recounted the complete stiffening of that once mobile joint, she closed her eyes for a moment as if in prayer, and her mouth grew grave. Then her bright smile returned to it in full radiance, after this short eclipse.

"I can't tell you how sorry I am for you, dear Mr. Kemp," she said. "So sorry, truly sorry."

"Very kind of you, I'm sure," said he. "I feel that you are one of the few who realise what a martyrdom I have to go through. Most people have so little imagination. It has been a real pleasure talking to you, and to go back for a moment to that morning when first I found--"

She leaned forward, smiling more than ever.

"And shall I--may I tell you, why I am so sorry for you?" she asked.

"Please do," said Mr. Kemp. An explanation seemed rather unnecessary for it was clear that her kind and sympathetic nature accounted for that. But he was a little hoarse with talking so much, and he did not mind the interruption.

The radiance of her smile was marvellous.

"It will surprise you," she said. "But the reason I'm so sorry for you is that you think your left hip is stiffened, and that you think you suffer all these agonies. It's a huge mistake: there's nothing whatever the matter with you, and you never have any pain at all. There isn't such a thing as pain. All is harmony and you're perfectly well."

Mr. Kemp could hardly believe his ears. This declaration sounded merely like a coarse and unmerited insult. And yet when he looked at that radiant smile and those sympathetic eyes, it was hard to believe that Mrs. Bliss intended it as such. He curbed the indignant exclamation that rose to his lips.

"What do you mean?" he said. "I've just been telling you how I got worse and worse especially after that miscreant at Aix had been handling the joint."

"I know, and now I tell you that it's all Error. Sin and illness and pain and death are all Error. Omnipotent Mind couldn't have made them and therefore they don't exist. Nothing has any real existence except love, health, harmony and happiness."

"But when I feel a sharp pain like a red-hot knitting-needle being thrust into my hip"--began Mr. Kemp.

"Error. Omnipotent Mind governs all. All is mind, and there can be no sensation in matter."

"But, God bless my soul," said Mr. Kemp.

"He does," said this astonishing lady. "Hold on to that thought and the body will utter no complaints. Dear Mr. Kemp, all belief in pain and sickness comes from Error. Therefore there is neither pain nor sickness: it is unreal and vanishes as soon as we realise its unreality. Hence all healing comes from Mind, and not from *materia medica."*

There was something challenging about so remarkable a statement. Mr. Kemp's head was whirling slightly (but not aching) for Mrs. Bliss seemed to skip about so, but he pulled himself together, and tried, figuratively, to catch hold of her.

"But you yourself," he said. "Aren't you limping very badly, and leaning on a stick? Indeed, I was going to ask you as soon as I had finished telling you about my hip, what form of rheumatism you are suffering from."

Again that radiant smile brightened.

"I'm not suffering from any at all," she said. "Error. It is only a false claim, which I am getting rid of by right thought."

"But why did you come to Bolton then," he asked. "Can't you think rightly at home? Haven't you come here for treatment?"

This question did not disconcert her in the slightest.

"Yes, I'm going to have a course of baths," she said, "but entirely for my dear husband's sake, who is still in blindness. I have, out of love for him, consented to do that--bear ye one another's burdens, you know--but what is curing me, oh, so rapidly, of this false claim of rheumatoid arthritis, as I think they call it, is my own demonstrating over it. All the way down in the train, I treated myself for it, and a friend in London is going to give me absent treatment for it from ten to-night till half-past."

"Absent treatment?" asked Mr. Kemp. "What's that?"

"She will just sit and realise that there is nothing the matter with me, because there can't be anything the matter, since all is health and harmony."

"And will that make it any better?" asked Mr. Kemp.

"It cannot possibly fail to do so. It is the only true healing."

"Then perhaps you won't need your bath to-morrow," said he.

She gave the gayest of laughs.

"Of course I shan't need it, dear Mr. Kemp," she said. "As I told you I am only taking the treatment for my dear husband's sake. That is not really inconsistent. It is only like telling a fairy story to amuse some dear sweet child. Though such a story is not true, it does not mean one is telling lies. What is curing me is the absolute knowledge that Omnipotent Mind never made suffering and never meant us to suffer. Hence, if we think we suffer, it is all a delusion or Error. It can't be real since Mind never made it."

"Dear me, it all sounds most interesting," said Mr. Kemp. "I wonder if it would do me any good."

Mrs. Bliss got up rather too briskly, and the smile completely faded for a moment as a pang of imaginary pain shot through her knee. But almost instantly it reasserted itself.

"There, do you see?" she said. "Surely that will convince you. Just for a moment, I allowed myself to entertain Error, but at once I denied Error, and what I thought was pain has gone. Of course there wasn't any pain really. To-morrow I will lend you my precious, precious book, *The Manual of Mental Science,* which will prove to you that you can't have pain. What a delicious refreshing talk we've had! Now I must be off, for my friend will be giving me absent treatment, and I must be with her in spirit."

Mrs. Bliss limped slowly but smilingly away and clinging on to the banisters which creaked beneath her solid grasp, and leaning heavily on her stick hauled herself upstairs. She paused at the top, panting a little.

"Not a single touch of pain," she said exultantly.

Mr. Kemp was delighted to hear it, for she seemed barely able to get upstairs at all, but she must know best.

Very serious and exciting bridge meantime had been proceeding in the smoking-room. The points could not be ruinous to anybody, for as usual, they were threepence a hundred, and thus anyone who lost as much as a shilling, was heartily condoled with by the resulting capitalist. The game itself, with its subtleties and intricacies, furnished the excitement, and Colonel Chase, of course, was the final authority on all points of play, and instructed partner and adversaries alike with unstinted criticism.

"A golden rule: to draw out trumps is a golden rule," he was asserting. "They always used to say of me at the mess that I never left a trump in my opponent's hands. You lost a trick or two in the last game, partner, by neglecting that, but then our opponents were indulgent to your fault, and let us off. If Mrs. Holders had led a club after you had played your king, she and Mrs. Oxney would have got a couple more tricks, and penalised us soundly."

Mrs. Holders was still feeling Bolshevistic.

"But I hadn't got a club, Colonel," she said. (This was not true, but that made no difference.)

"Ah no: you hadn't," said he. "What I should have said was if Mrs. Oxney had led a club. That's what I meant."

"Yes, to be sure I ought to have," said Mrs. Oxney, who never had a notion what her hand contained the moment she had got rid of it.

"I think so: I think so," said Colonel Chase. "Hammer away at a suit, establish it at all costs. It pays in the end. Now let's have a look. Who dealt this?"

"I did," said Mrs. Holders, "And I pass."

"No bid, then, is what you should say. I must consider: a difficult problem. I shall declare two hearts, partner. Two, mind: let's have no underbidding. You can trust me for having a sound reason when I say two hearts instead of one."

"Fancy! Two hearts straight off," said Mrs. Oxney. "I should never dare to do such a thing. I can do nothing against such a declaration."

"No, I expect you'll find yourselves in the Potarge this time," said Colonel Chase. "No bid then: well, partner?"

Now Miss Kemp had got into terrible trouble last night for taking Colonel Chase out of a major suit into a minor suit, and so though she only held two microscopic hearts, but an immense tiara of diamonds, she also passed, but Mrs. Holders without a moment's hesitation was daring enough to double. This almost amounted to an impertinence, and the Colonel drew himself up as if insulted: he was not accustomed to have his declaration doubled. He stared at her for a withering moment and she saw red.

"Very well, I've nothing more to say," he said. "I pass."

"You should say 'no bid' Colonel," remarked Mrs. Holders.

Colonel Chase was a very fair-minded man, when it was not reasonably possible to be otherwise.

"So I should, so I should," he said. "Peccavi! And I trust I am not too old to learn. No bid, all round is it? And a club led by Mrs. Oxney. So let's have a look at your hand, partner. Ha, six fine diamonds! Potarge indeed. Let's get to work, and discuss our short-comings afterwards. I find it a little difficult to concentrate with so much agreeable conversation going on. A club! I'll play the queen from your hand. Some do, some don't, but I have always maintained it is the correct play."

A perfect whirlwind of disaster descended upon the unfortunate man. The queen of clubs was taken by Mrs. Holders's king, who returned it and Mrs. Oxney took it with her ace. She then pulled out a small diamond by mistake, and pleasantly found that Mrs. Holders had got none. Mrs. Holders trumped it, and led a third club. This established a very jolly cross-ruff, for wicked Mrs. Oxney had opened clubs from an ace and a small one.

"Never saw such luck," said Colonel Chase, as small trumps on each side of him secured tricks with monotonous regularity. "I can't think why you didn't take me out with two diamonds, partner."

"Because she would have required three," said Mrs. Holders.

"Indeed! Well, that would have been cheaper than letting my two hearts stand. Ha! Now we'll make an end of this."

He trumped one of these wretched little clubs with the king: Mrs. Oxney, with many apologies overtrumped with the ace.

"I never saw such bad luck, Colonel," she said. "Everything against you. Too bad! Of course it looked as if Mrs. Holders held the ace."

"I should think so indeed, considering she doubled me," said the Colonel. "I can't think what you doubled me on, Mrs. Holders. The rest I imagine are mine. Let's see. I declared two hearts I believe. Then we're four down. Somewhat expensive, partner, when we should have had the game if you had only declared diamonds. Well, well: we all have to pay for our experience."

"I doubled you on an excellent hand," said Mrs. Holders. "And I can't think why you declared two hearts."

Colonel Chase again stared at her. She had dared to double his declaration, she had dared to justify it, and now she dared to question his declaration. The only thing to do was to answer her quite calmly.

"Two hearts was undoubtedly the right declaration," he said. "I fancy that among experts there would be little difference of opinion about that, nor indeed about my view of what my partner should have done. I wager that if we sent out hands up to Slam or Pons, I should get my verdict."

"Oh, that would be interesting," said Mrs. Oxney. "Let us do that. How exciting to see our game of bridge at Wentworth all printed in the Sunday paper. I'm sure they would say that it was very bad luck on the Colonel and that he played it all quite beautifully."

The suggestion was adopted and Mrs. Holders noted down the reconstructed hands. Colonel Chase did not seem very enthusiastic about it, though he had originated the idea, and thought it very unlikely that Slam would give his opinion on so obvious a question.

This rubber came to an immediate and sensational end, for Colonel Chase naturally anxious to get back on Mrs. Holders's unjustifiable (though justified) double, returned the compliment next hand and thus gave his adversaries the rubber. There was indeed an air of defiance about that lady to-night, she was in a state of rebellion from established authority, and she made this even more painfully apparent by challenging his addition, and incontestably proving that he was wrong. This made Mrs. Oxney, though thereby she gained threepence more, quite uncomfortable; the Colonel's arithmetic and his law-giving had both been called in question, and it was as if Moses, coming down from Sinai with the tables of commandments had been subjected to cross-examination as to their authenticity and the number of them. Moses would not have liked that, nor did Colonel Chase, and it was lucky, in Mrs. Oxney's opinion, that he opened the next rubber with a grand slam, for that smoothed down the frayed edges of his temper, and he explained very carefully the brilliance and difficulty of his achievement.

"An interesting hand," he said, "and it required a bit of playing, if I may say so. That eight of spades, partner: that might have been a nasty card for us. Lucky--at least there wasn't much luck about it, only a little calculation--that I trumped it from my dummy. Some people might have discarded a diamond but I'm too old a bird to go after will-o'-the-wisps like that. The other was the correct game: played like that there wasn't another trick to be made anywhere!"

He was still a little dignified with Mrs. Holders for having dared to double him and to add up the sum right, and turned to her.

"Or can you suggest any plan by which I could have got another trick?" he said.

Mrs. Holders gave a little squeal.

"Not possibly," she said. "You got all the tricks there were."

"Ah, yes. Grand slam, so it was," said he. "Amusing that I should have asked you if any more tricks were to be secured!"

"Very," said Mrs. Holders. "Most."

Play suddenly became slightly hectic. Even Miss Kemp who never bid against no-trumps because, if anybody had got such a good hand as that it was no use fighting against it, developed unusual aggressiveness, and Mrs. Oxney was penalised again and again for supporting her partner's declarations without anything to support them with. The scores above the line went on mounting and mounting and even Colonel Chase got silent and preoccupied as he vainly tried to calculate how many threepences were involved on one side or the other.

CHAPTER II

Every now and then he broke into hectoring instruction, but somehow with the rebellious Mrs. Holders on his right, who gave little acid smiles and elevations of her eyebrows, when he told her what she ought to have played or discarded or declared, and made no reply of any sort, he felt like an autocrat in the presence of some ominously silent mob; while the congratulations of Mrs. Oxney, who just now was his partner, if he fulfilled his contract, and her sympathy with his ill luck if he miserably failed, was only like the assurances of the old *régime,* that all was well with the Czardom. He was not at all sure that all was well; he felt tremors pervading his throne: there was a cold devilish purpose about Mrs. Holders when she outbid him, which was much like the edge of the assassin's knife. There was a patient deadliness about her, when, having failed in her design, she ambushed herself for his further declaration, that really unnerved him. Usually she succeeded in drawing him into an impossible declaration, and when she failed, owing to his surrender, and she was penalised herself, she remained quite unmoved, and instead of finding fault with somebody else, cheerfully entered two or three hundred against her own score.

Bridge generally finished about ten o'clock, for Wentworth with its freight of invalids, was early to bed, but now half-past ten had struck and still this truculent rubber went on.

"Upon my word, most interesting," said Colonel Chase, as, with slightly trembling fingers, he shuffled the cards for the next and fifteenth hand. "You let us off there, Mrs. Holders: if you had led out trumps, as I've often advised you to do, you would have caught my queen--"

"So she would," said Mrs. Oxney admiringly. "You see everything, Colonel."

"--and then you would have cleared your diamonds, and it would have been we who were in the Potarge, instead of you. Funny how a little slip like that sticks to one through the rest of--"

"Five no trumps," said Mrs. Holders, after considering her hand for about two seconds.

Colonel Chase could not command his voice at once. But at the second attempt he mastered it.

"Come, come," he said. "You want to keep me up all night. I've never heard anybody--"

"Five no trumps," said Mrs. Holders with extraordinary distinctness.

Colonel Chase sorted his hand, and found a richness. There was a brilliant array of seven diamonds lacking the king; there were the king and queen of hearts, there was the king of spades by himself, and he thought that with so splendid a hand, this was a wonderful opportunity to give the rebellious woman a good lesson, and establish himself for ever on his rightful throne. He doubled and Mrs. Holders redoubled.

At that, the jovial laugh to the accompaniment of which Colonel Chase was preparing to say to his partner that there was Potarge for two, died in his throat, though he was far from realising that Nemesis, who no doubt had been patiently listening to his lectures on bridge for the last month or two, was licking her hungry lips. He put down his cigarette, and led the ace of diamonds. Miss Kemp displayed her hand. It contained the ace and queen of spades, the king of diamonds with an infinitesimal satellite, three clubs, including the knave, and nothing else of the slightest importance.

Mrs. Holders gave that annoying little squeal of laughter that grated on Colonel Chase's nerves, and discarded a small heart on his noble ace of diamonds. Somehow that made him feel much better. Little he knew that he was destined to be much worse. But at present he felt better.

"That's the danger of declaring no trumps with a suit missing, Mrs. Holders," he said. "I've fallen into that trap before now myself. Let me see: five I think."

He jovially slapped the trick down.

"One more trick, partner," he said, "and then the fun begins."

"That *was* a beautiful double of yours," said Mrs. Oxney. "Wonderful!"

"Not so bad; not so bad," said he. "I'm a highwayman this time, Mrs. Holders, exacting penalties for your rashness in going unguarded."

"Quite," said Mrs. Holders, in a terrible voice.

"Well, I'll just clear that king of diamonds out of the way," said Colonel Chase, "and then we'll settle down and be comfortable."

He cleared the king out of the way, and by way of retaliation Mrs. Holders cleared his king of spades out of the way with dummy's ace and continued with the queen of the same suit. Colonel Chase having no more, and being constitutionally unable to part with one of those winning diamonds threw out a small club. Anything would do.

The Colonel's jaw might have been observed by any careful bystander to drop about half an inch the moment he had done so. He saw that he had left his queen of clubs with only one guard. Perhaps he had settled down to be comfortable, but nobody could possibly have guessed that. Mrs. Holders then led the knave of clubs from her partner's hand, Mrs. Oxney played something of extreme insignificance, and then Mrs. Holders sat and thought. She pulled a card out of her hand, and held it poised. She put it back. She pulled out another card and played the king of clubs. The Colonel played a small one.

Colonel Chase began to perspire.

Mrs. Holders pulled out a card again and put it back. A most annoying habit. Then she pulled it out again and played it. It was the ace of clubs. Colonel Chase put on the queen (it couldn't be helped), and Mrs. Oxney discarded something pathetically unimportant in another suit.

"What? No more clubs?" said Colonel Chase in a voice of intense indignation.

"No, I wish I had," said poor Mrs. Oxney. "Isn't it bad luck? And I've got such a quantity of--oh, I suppose I mustn't say what."

"I don't mind," said Mrs. Holders, who thereupon played out the ace of hearts, and followed it with processions of winning clubs and winning spades.

Colonel Chase said "Pshaw!" Cataracts of diamonds had been spouting from his hand, and rivers of hearts from his partner's.

CHAPTER II

"But don't we get any more?" said Mrs. Oxney. "All my beautiful hearts and all your beautiful diamonds?"

"Fifty for little slam," said Mrs. Holders quite calmly, though her eyebrows had almost disappeared, "and thirty for aces. Then two hundred for my contract, doubled and redoubled, and two hundred more for the extra trick, and below six times two hundred. I think that's all. Dear me!"

This was intolerable.

"Not bridge at all," said Colonel Chase. "With not a single diamond in your hand, and spades headed by the knave. Madness! I would have doubled on my hand every time."

Mrs. Holders knew all that perfectly well. She knew also, (and knew that Colonel Chase knew) that if he had not unguarded his queen of clubs. . . . But then he had, and she went on adding up.

"And two is seven," she said, "and eight is fifteen, and six is twenty-one, and seven is twenty-eight, and seven is thirty-five, and six is forty-one and carry four, and two and three and five is fourteen and four is eighteen--"

"Yes, I make that," said Miss Kemp, licking her pencil, "and oh, just look at the hundreds!"

After they had sufficiently looked at the hundreds, the general reckoning disclosed that Colonel Chase had to pay everybody all round, and he disbursed sums varying from threepence to Mrs. Oxney up to the staggering figure of three and ninepence due to Miss Kemp. All the evenings on which everybody had paid to him were forgotten in general commiseration and nobody dreamed of consoling him with the encouragement he often administered to others, and told him that his game was improving so much that very likely he would soon win it all back again. Mrs. Oxney could scarcely be induced to accept her threepence, and she had to steel herself to the sacrifice by the glad hope that she would lose ten times that sum to him tomorrow. On other nights Colonel Chase usually stood for a long time in front of the fire-place when the rubbers were over, richly rattling coppers in his trousers' pocket, and giving them a few hints about declarations to take up to bed, but now there was no chink of bullion to endorse his wisdom, and he made as short work of his glass of whiskey and water (called 'grog' or 'nightcap') as he had made of the cross-word, and left the victors on the field of battle. Miss Kemp gave him time to get upstairs, in order to avoid the indelicacy of seeing a gentleman open his bedroom door, and perhaps disclose pyjamas warming by the fire, and then followed him in some haste, since her father (there was no indelicacy about that) always expected her to come and talk to him, when he had got to bed, about his evening symptoms, or read to him till he felt sleepy. She knew she was unusually late to-night, and it was possible that he had punished her by already putting out his light. This pathetic proceeding, he was sure, wrung her with agonies of remorse.

No such severity had been inflicted to-night; he was sitting up in bed with a book in front of him; and a fur tippet belonging to Florence round his neck for the protection of the glands of the throat. On the table beside him was the thermos flask filled with hot milk, in case he felt un-nourished during the night, the glass jug of lemonade made with saccharine instead of sugar in case he felt thirsty, and the clock with the luminous hands.

"I am late, Papa, I'm afraid," she said. "We had a most exciting rubber which would not come to an end."

His face wore its most martyred expression: he glanced at the clock which showed the unprecedented hour of eleven.

"Surely my clock is fast," he said.

"No; it is eleven," she said. "Shall I read to you?"

"Far too late: far, far too late. I shall be good for nothing in the morning as it is."

"You would like to go to sleep then?" she asked. "Shall I put out your light?"

"Indeed, I should very much like to go to sleep," he said, "but it is already long past my usual hour for going to sleep, and as you know, if I am not asleep by eleven, I often lie awake half the night. No doubt you were absorbed in your game, and could not spare a thought to me. Very natural. Two hours bridge! I was wrong to expect that perhaps it would occur to you--but no matter."

"Would you like me to talk to you then, if you don't feel you'll go to sleep?" she asked.

"Perhaps a little talk might compose me," said he, "if you can spare me ten minutes. I am very tired to-night, and that makes me wakeful. I have had a great deal to do. My thermos flask was unfilled, and I had to ring. There were no rusks in my little tin and I had to get out the big tin and fill it. My clock was not wound."

Florence sat down by his bed. Her chair grated on the margin of boards as she pulled it forward, and he winced.

"You've got everything now, haven't you?" she asked.

"Yes. I saw to everything myself. Talk to me, please. Yes?"

"I won three and ninepence," said Florence. "Colonel Chase lost to everybody."

"I heard him thumping by just now," said her father. "I supposed he had lost, for he banged his door. I was just beginning to get sleepy. A want of consideration, perhaps. Yes?"

At each interrogative 'yes', as Florence knew, a fresh topic of interest had to be furnished.

"Mrs. Oxney won threepence," she said.

"I am glad. Perhaps she will be able to afford me hot water in my bottle to-morrow. It was tepid tonight. I think you have told me enough about your game of bridge. Yes?"

"Miss Howard is playing at an entertainment in the assembly rooms next week."

"I will not go," said Mr. Kemp with some heat. "I do not see why I should be expected to turn out in the evening. Yes?"

CHAPTER II

Florence felt the swift on-coming of a sneeze. She fumbled in her bag for a handkerchief, and rattled richly among the nine coppers. Several violent explosions followed, and when the spasm subsided, she found her father spraying the air round him with his flask of disinfectant.

"Perhaps it would be wiser if you sat a little further off," he said. "Yes?"

"I don't think anything else has happened," said Florence wheezily. "Oh yes, that new arrival, Mrs. Bliss. I saw you talking to her. How she smiles! I wonder why?"

Mr. Kemp shewed the first sign of withdrawing the blight he had been casting on this commandeered conversation.

"She told me strange things," he said. "I could make little of them, though I must confess they interested me. She said I was perfectly well, and that pain had no real existence. To say that to me of all people appears on the face of it to be the gibbering of a lunatic. Yet as she talked I certainly did begin to feel that there was something behind it. She told me also that she was perfectly well, though I have never seen anybody limp more heavily. I scarcely think that I was as bad as that after my terrible experiences at Aix. I thought she would hardly be able to get upstairs yet she called to me from the landing, though much out of breath, that she had not felt a single twinge. Her theory is that all pain is an illusion or a delusion, I forget which, and if you only deny it, it vanishes. Ever since I came up to bed, which is a long time ago now, I have been denying it and I think--I am not sure, but I think--that I am lying a little more easily to-night than I have done since last Monday. But I must not get too much interested in it at this hour."

Mr. Kemp yawned as he spoke.

"I am beginning to get a little drowsy," he said. "I will not talk any more. Please go out very quietly, and turn off my light from the switch by the door. Don't bang it."

Florence tiptoed away to her room; though it was late, she felt wakeful and exhilarated. She had enjoyed her bridge, but it was not that alone, nor her unusually long remission from her father, nor yet the load of bullion that clinked in her bag which accounted for it. The evening had been adventurous, for Mrs. Holders had fluttered the red flag in the face of that formidable autocrat Colonel Chase: she had called in question the wisdom of his declaration, she had backed her own opinion by doubling, she had invoked the decision of Slam. And no retribution had followed, no thunderbolt had split her: the Colonel had merely paid up all round and gone to bed.

Florence wound up her watch and looked at her plump and rather pleasing image in the glass. Her hair was cropped like a man's, and parted at the side: she wore a stiff linen collar with a small black tie in a bow, and a starched shirt with a sort of Eton jacket; her skirt was about the same length as the jacket. Then crossing her legs in an easy attitude she sat down on her bed, and thought carefully over what had been happening this evening. It was an application of Mrs. Holders's defiance, rather than the defiance itself that claimed her attention. For Wentworth in general dumbly travailed under the domination of the Colonel, and if three hours ago she had been asked what she supposed would happen if anyone questioned his rulings and his bawlings and his tuition, her imagination would have failed to picture so impossible a contingency. Yet the impossible had now occurred and nothing had happened. The application was obvious, and she found herself wondering what would happen if she questioned her father's right to immolate her day and night on the altar of his aches. Daring though such a supposition was, would nothing particular happen?

Florence let the hypochondriac history of the last seven years, from the time when her father had seriously taken up the profession of invalidism instead of having no profession at all, spread itself panoramically out in front of her. Her mother was alive then, and for those first two years of this lean series, the three of them had trodden the uneasy circle of hydropathic establishments. Buxton, Bath, Harrogate, and Bolton (but never Aix again) had grown to be the cardinal points of the year, and these were followed by Torquay, Cromer, Scarborough and Bournemouth for the after-cure of bracing air or sunny climate. At first they had returned to the pleasant little flat in Kensington Square after the quarterly cure to wait for the next cardinal point to come round, but her father who was in his element in boarding houses with all their good opportunities of telling relays of strangers about his ailments, soon discovered that London did not suit him, for it was airless in the summer, treacherous in the autumn and spring and foggy in the winter, and now he and Florence remained at Torquay, Cromer, Scarborough and Bournemouth till the next cure. After two years of this preposterous existence, her mother, who had always been frail and anæmic, simply came to the end of her vitality, and exhausted by her husband's vampirism had stopped living. She had been possessed of a considerable fortune, half of which, with the flat in Kensington Square, she had left to Florence absolutely, the remainder to her husband for life. This appeared to him the most ungrateful return for all the care he had allowed her to take of him, and until his own health had completely driven all other interests from his mind he had sedulously nursed this grievance. Since then, for five years, Florence had been his enslaved companion.

She knew well that her interminable ministries to him were not performed out of the bounty of love, but from her own acquiescence in being crushed, and now it struck her that she thoroughly disliked him. Though she had not definitely stated that to herself before, the emotion must have been habitual, for its discovery did not in the least shock her nor did it shock her to conjecture that he equally disliked her. Probably all these years, he would have been happier with a trained nurse, who was paid for being bullied and bored, and she herself could have lived instead of merely getting older. She might even have married, for women did not become certified spinsters at the age of thirty, as she was when her solitary gyrations with him began, but the idea of marriage had hitherto seemed very embarrassing to her virginal soul. No man alive could justly claim to have raised the beat of her placid blood by a single pulsation; she had no spark of envy for any woman however happily married, compared with one who had her liberty. Miss Howard for instance seemed to her to live an almost ideal existence: she went where she liked, and nobody could claim her time or her energies, she tripped and sang about the passages, so sunlit to her was the normal hour: she devoted herself to her painting and her piano, the pursuits she adored, and had no bond-slave duties to anybody. Happy Miss Howard, gifted and accomplished and free! And how handsome she was: what a charm and vivacity! Though Florence had never experienced any sort of tenderness for a man, she sometimes thought of Miss Howard with a sort of shy, sentimental yearning.

There had been moments, rare and swiftly vanishing, when Florence had seen freedom gleaming on the far horizon, for in the sad hydropathic round, her father sometimes made friends with suitable and sympathetic females, especially those who had sitting-rooms and maids and motors, and once or twice it had really looked as if something was coming of it. He was remarkably handsome with his fine aquiline face, his thick grey hair and tall slim figure, and she was sure that middle-aged spinsters and widows had given him and received from him very promising attention. She knew well the symptoms on his side, for when such friendship was ripening he adopted an attitude of wistful and tender affection towards herself; he would pat her hand (when the lady was by) and ask her what she had been doing, and thank her for being so devoted to her poor old Papa. But nothing had ever come of it, the lady who seemed within an ace of becoming her poor old Mamma, had got some glimpse, Florence supposed, of his unique selfishness, and had shaken off the glamour.

She was ready for bed now, and still under the inspiration of the revolt which Mrs. Holders had made against the authority and omniscience of Colonel Chase, she asked herself what would happen if she refused to be eternally dragged about from Spa to Spa. Naturally she could not throw off so chronic a yoke with one comprehensive gesture of defiance; she would have to begin gently and say, for instance, tomorrow morning, that she was going out for a walk instead of coming down to the baths with him in the bus and, after doing various chemical errands for him, sitting in the waiting-room which faintly smelt of the awful effluvium of the waters, till he was ready to drive up again. Perhaps, if she could summon up nerve, she might ask Miss Howard if she might help her to carry her satchel and stool to the scene of her sketch. As she quenched her light, she heard through the door which communicated with her father's room, a sound so regular and sonorous that, if he had not been sure he was going to lie awake for hours, she would certainly have thought he was fast asleep.

CHAPTER III

The warmth and clemency of October which till now had been so pleasant, and had permitted Miss Howard to make so many notable sketches of noon and evening and night without the risk of catching a chill, completely collapsed during the dark hours, and piercing blasts from the north-east with volleys of half-frozen rain rattled on the windows of Wentworth. Colonel Chase, who often attributed much of his magnificent robustness to the fact that he always slept with his window wide open, top and bottom, had a most alarming dream that Mrs. Holders, with whom he was playing bridge in a restaurant car on a train which was oscillating very much, laid an odd-looking card resembling the ace of hearts, yet somehow different from it, on the table and said, "That card gives me the rubber doubled and redoubled." As she spoke the oscillation increased and the card began to give out sharp reports, and he woke to find his blind blowing out horizontally into the room and cracking like a whip, while the solid walls of Wentworth trembled in the gale. He jumped out of bed, and at the risk of undermining his health by closing the window, shut and bolted it. Mr. Kemp was more fortunate, for knowing that the night air was poison to him, he always slept with his window closed, shuttered and curtained. But even so the driven sleet awoke him, and observing by his luminous clock that it was a quarter past two, took a cup of hot milk and a rusk. Warmed and comforted he turned over in bed without a single twinge from his left hip, which was so surprising that he lay awake a long time and wondered whether it was Mind. Soot poured down Mrs. Holders's chimney, but she could not help that and instantly went to sleep again.

The gale had not abated when the guests began to assemble for breakfast, sleet still rapped at the panes, and the house was bitterly cold, for who, wailed Mrs. Oxney, could have expected so sudden and diabolical a change of weather? As soon as she got down, she ordered wood fires to be lit in lounge and drawing-room and smoking-room, for coal must be husbanded as long as the strike continued, and sent the gardener to kindle the furnace of the central-heating. But the dining-room certainly was like an ice-house at breakfast: Miss Howard's hand shook as she poured the milk over her porridge, Mr. Kemp sent Florence upstairs to get a rug for his knees, and Colonel Chase, in an appalling temper, put on a cap, which he pulled down over his ears, a long woolly muffler and a great coat. He did not really feel cold, but it was only right that Mrs. Oxney should be filled with remorse at not having foreseen the change, and having omitted to have the central-heating put on in anticipation of it. Seeing that she was looking at him, he turned up his coat collar and gave several painful coughs.

The only exception to these suffering breakfasters was Mrs. Bliss. She was limping very badly, and it took her a long time to sidle round the corner of her table, and, leaning heavily on it, to sit down, but throughout the whole of this apparently agonising process she had a bright smile and salutations right and left. She was wearing quite a thin blouse and no jacket, but when Mr. Kemp seeing that there was a reddish tinge on her nose, a bluish tinge round her mouth, and that her hands were deadly white, said that she would surely get double pneumonia, being so lightly clad on such a bitter morning, she protested she had never been so warm and comfortable.

"And what a beautiful day it is going to be!" she said, as the gusts rattled at the window. "Such a refreshing shower! The grey rain-clouds on the hills, driven along by the breeze looked so lovely as I was dressing."

Her teeth chattered slightly as she spoke, but she fixed them in a piece of hot roll.

"But it's a terrible gale," said Mr. Kemp. "I am not sure that I shall go down to the baths at all. I do not know what it is wisest to do. Perhaps if I wore my fur coat, and had a hot water bottle ready for my return I might venture. See to that, please, Florence."

"Ah, then I did hear the sound of wind during the night," said Mrs. Bliss. "That was it! A beautiful rushing noise. But I slept so well I was hardly conscious of it, and awoke so happy and glowing and fresh."

"Either the woman's mad or she's got Esquimaux blood," muttered Colonel Chase, as he listened to these remarkable views. He put his hand on the stack of so-called hot water pipes close to his chair and withdrew it hurriedly.

"Stone-cold," he observed to Miss Howard. "Disgraceful! Pipes as cold as that would keep any room cool in the height of summer."

Mrs. Oxney who had been cheered by Mrs. Bliss's impressions of the morning, overheard this, as she was indeed meant to do, and felt miserable again. She got up, her appetite completely ruined by these scathing observations, and went over to the Colonel's table, with a wretched attempt at cheerfulness.

"Oh, but the pipes will soon be hot, Colonel," she said. "My sister's gone out to see about the furnace herself, and I promise you they shan't spare the coke. That sudden change took us all by surprise. But I've had fires lit everywhere, and we shall soon all be cosy again. . . . Good morning Mrs. Bliss; and you slept well I heard you say?"

Mrs. Bliss beamed on her.

"Beautifully! So comfortable! And so enjoying my breakfast. Delicious! And the rain is clearing. I shall have such a refreshing walk down to the baths, and up again."

Mr. Kemp was thrilled at this astounding programme. Was she sane, he wondered, or was it Mind? Or was she (in another sense) a mental case? Here, anyhow, was this smiling lady, who, in spite of blue lips, said she felt warm in this refrigerating dining-room, and who, making slow sad work about traversing the smooth level of the floor, intended to walk down and up the steep hill between Wentworth and the pickling establishment. It was a good half-mile each way, and he would have considered himself hale and hearty again, if he had been able to accomplish so arduous a feat. He had visions of Mrs. Bliss falling in front of the wheels of a motor as she crossed the road, or dying of exposure as she pursued her way with those minute and halting steps and frequent stoppages through this sleet-sown blizzard. That would have annoyed him, as he wanted to hear more about Mind and its method. He intervened with some agitation.

"Better not, far better not, Mrs. Bliss," he said. "The baths which can be so remedial are very fatiguing; my doctor, and I'm sure yours, recommends the minimum of physical exertion, while the course is going on. I avoid all physical fatigue while I am here."

She laughed merrily.

"Dear Mr. Kemp," she said, "you still think that you are an invalid, whereas I know that I am in perfect health and harmony. Did you demonstrate last night, reminding yourself that all is Mind?"

Mr. Kemp remembered the singular fact of his having turned over without a twinge: all those twinges which he suffered as he dressed had expunged it. He had finished his breakfast, and nodded to Florence to indicate that she might go away, for he wanted to pursue last night's subject, and though he would have welcomed any conviction that he was well, he did not want Florence to get hold of that idea first, or his thermos flask might be left permanently empty, and his smaller tin for rusks unreplenished. But Florence, with the fumes of last night's revolutionary debauch still lingering in her brain, paid no attention to this familiar signal.

"If you've finished your breakfast, Florence," he said, "you will kindly go upstairs and bring down my hat and coat, fur coat I think, so that I shall be ready to start. Goloshes of course. And a hot water bottle when I get back."

Florence waved a minute red flag. This was beginning gently.

"Presently, Papa," she said, "there is plenty of time."

Mr. Kemp was naturally very much shocked at this answer, for never before, to the best of his knowledge, had Florence shown such mutinous independence, and his staring at her, with deep disfavour, which usually had so subduing an effect proved on this occasion to have none. Instead of hurrying away she turned to Mrs. Bliss.

"Do go on telling my father about illness being a delusion," she said. "It would be lovely if you could convince him of it."

Mrs. Bliss was delighted to do so; nothing could possibly be easier than to convince anybody of a self-evident proposition, but owing to the apparently piercing cold of the dining-room, they adjourned to the lounge. The two victims of this tiresome delusion concerning rheumatic joints were for the moment so completely taken in by it, that they took a long while to hobble along the slippery parquet, and Florence certainly saved Mrs. Bliss from the delusion of falling down. When they got there, they found that this gale was causing the chimney to behave as if it was upside-down, and clouds of pungent wood-smoke came pouring out of it. Mr. Kemp then suffered from the further delusion that wood-smoke was very trying to the eyes, and sat with his handkerchief over them, though Mrs. Bliss, with the tears pouring down her cheeks asserted that she felt no inconvenience whatever from it. Her immunity served as an excellent text for her homily, and while Florence and her father as if overcome with emotion, held their pocket-handkerchiefs before their eyes, she told them how wood-smoke could not possibly have any effect on those who realised that all was harmony in Omnipotent Mind.

As if to endorse her words, the chimney began to draw better, and having surreptitiously wiped away her tears, she told them to put down their handkerchiefs and calmly but firmly deny the delusion of that stinging sensation. Sure enough they found they had been the victims of Error.

There was still an apparent lack of harmony in the conditions outside, when the omnibus came round to take the patients to the baths, for it seemed to be pelting with rain, and Mrs. Bliss consented to be driven down though she still said that she would much have enjoyed the walk. But her husband, for whose sake she was undergoing this quite unnecessary cure, would not have liked the thought that she was exposing herself to this odious weather (though the weather whatever it might be, could not hurt anybody) and with this loving thought of him in her mind, she consented to be well wrapped-up, and hoisted into the omnibus. As there was no chance of helping Miss Howard with her sketching things, Florence abandoned the contemplated revolt of refusing to go down to the baths with her father, and Mrs. Bliss lent her the manual of Mental Science, to read while she was waiting. She could give her father absent treatment, while he was being pickled.

The joint exertions of Mrs. Bertram and the gardener had sent rivers of hot water roaring through the central-heating apparatus, and Colonel Chase, sitting in the smoking-room found himself reluctantly compelled to discard his cap, muffler and great coat. Any idea of breaking fresh records on his bicycle was out of the question on so stormy a morning, for the roads, even if the rain stopped, would be a mere muddy liquefaction, and the hours till lunch-time had to be passed indoors. On days like these, he always felt that Nature had fixed her malignant eye on him, and was vomiting from the skies these innumerable gallons of cold water with the sole and express purpose of making the roads impossible for his bicycle. A materialist might hold that she was pursuing the miserable logic of physical laws, but he knew that did not fully account for a wet morning. And then, too, just because it was wet, the paper contained nothing of interest: even the criminal classes seemed to have joined in the conspiracy against him, for there was no news of brutal murders or other interesting crimes which might while away the hours for him. As for the coal strike he was sick of it and despaired of the Government taking the line he had always maintained they should, and sending the miners back to the pits whether they liked it or not.

He threw down the paper in disgust, and moved his chair a little further from the pyramid of logs which was roaring up the chimney, but this brought him closer to the hot water pipes which were now almost as fervent as the fire. But there was positively nowhere else to sit except in the smoking-room, for the lounge was draughty, and Miss Howard was making music--if you could call it music--in the drawing-room. Up and down the piano she went with trills and scales and shakes and roulades: Mrs. Oxney ought really to ask her not to play on a wet morning, when other people were house-bound, for there was no getting away from that irritating tinkle. How could a man read his paper with that going on? It was as distracting as when people insisted on talking while playing bridge. If he ever decided to offer some presentable middle-aged woman the chance of looking after him and sharing his name, it must be distinctly understood that she must not play the piano except in some remote room. He wondered whether there was some such withdrawn boudoir at Miss Howard's little place in Kent near Tunbridge Wells.

The thought of bridge suggested more disagreeable reflections. Last night's game had been very expensive, and it had disclosed, he thought, a very ugly spirit. Several times Mrs. Holders had made a direct frontal attack on his most authoritative manœuvres. She had doubled when he had declared two hearts, openly saying that he had a very good reason for it, she had told him (him!) that he ought to say 'no bid' instead of 'pass': she had redoubled his double of her impossible declaration, and the damned woman had been right (if you could call it right,) every time. Certainly he would not ask her to play with him tonight: he would get Mrs. Bertram to take her place, though Mrs. Bertram had an agonising habit of at once leading out any ace she happened to hold, in order to make sure of it; or, if she was exhorted not to be so insanely prodigal, of refusing to play any ace till it was quite certain to be trumped. But no woman, so he often thought, had any head for cards; the finesse and subtlety of the game was beyond them, and Miss Howard was wise in refusing to play at all. He wished her refusal to play had extended to the use of the piano.

A glint of watery sunlight gleamed on the hot water pipes; the rain had ceased, and though bicycling was impossible Colonel Chase resolved to go out for a good tramp with the pocket pedometer. The morning was a miserable time unless you were out of doors, for without strenuous exercise then, you could not rest properly after lunch, and as for reading in the morning, what was to be done with the hour after tea, if you had read all the morning? Only a bookworm could manage two spells of reading a day, and he thanked God he was not that. Besides that infernal tinkling from the piano was enough to put reading out of the question.

He adjusted his pedometer to zero, and shouldering his mackintosh went briskly down the hill into the town. He turned into the waiting-room at the bath establishment, though he had no right there, since it was provided for patients waiting for their baths, and friends waiting for patients, but there was no chance of Colonel Chase being challenged by the attendants. Far more likely that they would appreciate the honour he did the management by looking at the notice-board which advertised current and coming diversions. Among these was the announcement of the entertainment in aid of the Children's Hospital, and he observed with pain that Miss Howard had 'kindly consented' to give an improvisation on the piano. Miss Kemp was sitting near, waiting for her father and absorbed in some book, but Colonel Chase gave so loud a snort of indignation at this information that she looked up with a start.

"Improvisation indeed!" he scornfully observed. "Why Miss Howard has been practising her improvisation, so as to get it by heart, ever since breakfast! Drove me out of the house! Kindly consented to! I wish she'd kindly consent to leave the piano alone. Humbug!"

Florence put her finger on the line she was reading, and sprang to arms at this monstrous attack on her adored.

"I think it's wonderfully kind of her," she said, "and I look forward to it as the greatest treat. And how on earth do you know that she's going to play at the entertainment what she is practising now? That's a pure invention."

Colonel Chase was considerably startled by this sudden fierceness.

"Well it's the same old tune that she's been hammering at ever since I came to Wentworth," he said.

Florence felt that her indignation was not quite in tune with the spirit of mental science which she had been studying. Poor Colonel Chase had a false claim of malice which should be treated just like a false claim of pain. Neither malice nor pain had any real existence and must be denied. She began to smile like Mrs. Bliss.

"Such lovely tunes," she said. "So sweet and harmonious and refreshing."

But Colonel Chase was clearly out of harmony.

"Make a sort of tinkling noise in my head if you mean that," he said. "Well, I'm off for a tramp. No possibility of bicycling through this mud."

Florence continued to smile.

"How you'll enjoy your walk!" she said. "And the sun is coming out gloriously."

Colonel Chase had not been far wrong in his cynical reflections, for Miss Howard was busy over what might truly be called memorising her improvisation for next week. It would be nice to begin with a few slow minor chords, all her own, (or indeed anybody else's) and an impressive pause, so that the audience would certainly think that something very tragic and funereal was to follow, and so would be pleasantly surprised when instead there came gay chromatic runs up to the very top of the piano and half-way down again, and a long butterfly shake which ushered in a few bars of a waltz by Chopin and a quantity more of her own composition. Never had her fingers been more agile and delicate, there was not a hitch or a stumble anywhere, and Mrs. Oxney, adding up the laundry book in her sitting-room next door felt sure that Miss Howard would get an encore if that was part of her improvisation. Then the waltz-rhythm ceased and something very swoony and mysterious succeeded: it was as if the dancers (so Miss Howard thought to herself) had left the gay and brilliant ball-room and were walking about moonlit glades in miserable and melancholy reverie. She had to play this section of the improvisation several times over, for there came quite unexpected effects in it, which surprised her by their beauty, and she must make sure of these. The pensive mood became more solemn yet, and the dancers seemed to sing a sort of chorale in a minor key which Miss Howard had composed last summer when suffering from toothache. She could not quite remember the last line of it, but she had written it down, and could easily perfect herself in that. A pause again followed during which the final chord of the chorale was struck four times very softly and nobody could tell what would happen next, indeed Miss Howard wished she knew herself. A long shake however must be introduced rather high up on the piano while the left hand played arpeggios up from the very bottom, crossed the shake without disturbing it, and came down again, for that was one of her most remarkable effects. She could go on playing these for ever, but since they were clearly leading up to something, they must come to an end, and make way for what they were introducing. Then she remembered that she had not put in any of those passages of octaves yet, in which the butterfly's place was taken by a powerful hammer, and she began playing octaves with both hands up and down, on black notes and white alike, with increasing speed and crescendo, and still she wondered what would happen next, and so did Mrs. Oxney who sat over the laundry book next door, open-mouthed at this surpassing vigour and brilliancy. Then Miss Howard suddenly saw her way clear and swooped back into the Chopin waltz. Then Bang, Whack, Bump: three enormous chords brought the improvisation to an end. Allowing for the repetition of the swoony section, it had lasted just ten minutes, which would do nicely.

Miss Howard got up, and, hearing in her imagination rounds of enthusiastic applause, smiled and bowed to the delighted audience, just to see what it felt like. It seemed that they quite refused to be content with what she had played them and insisted on an encore. She sat down again, and pressed her fingers to her eyes (a gesture that she must remember) as if wondering what little morsel to give them next. They clearly wanted something more from the same mine, and she ran her hands delicately over the keys, still considering. Perhaps those little variations on 'Tipperary' which she had so often played would be suitable, but there was no need to practise them for she was absolutely note-perfect in this improvisation. She just ran through them for the pleasure of hearing them again.

She went through the main improvisation four or five times more and then, putting on her rings, again went to the window. It was fine, though clearly too cold for sketching, but a short brisk walk would be pleasant after all this concentration, and she went down into the town with the intention of paying for the frame of 'Evening Bells', but with the real object of seeing if the advertisement of the entertainment was displayed yet. As she tripped along she hummed over the more vocal parts of her piece, and visualised her hands performing octaves and arpeggios. She must get them so familiar that she would not have the slightest apprehension of not being able to produce them unerringly.

She paused opposite the bath establishment, and there was the notice prominently exhibited, and 'Pianoforte Solo (improvisation) by Miss Alice Howard' in very gratifying type came fourth on the programme. The church choir of St.

Giles's, was to open with some glees, then Mr. Graves, the amusing *masseur,* was down for 'Stories', then the Revd. H. Banks (vicar) was to sing, and her item followed. After that the choir sang again, and Dr. Dobbs did some conjuring tricks, and the Revd. H. Banks sang again, and Mrs. Banks played a violin solo (Salut d'Amour) and the Revd. H. Banks recited, 'Curfew will not ring to-night', and there was a performing dog and various other rich items followed by a collection and carriages at ten. Miss Howard read this through twice, pausing at the fourth item, and then her eye was caught by another advertisement. This was to say that the Green Salon at the baths, suitable for private parties or picture exhibitions, could be hired at a very reasonable sum by the evening or the week or longer periods.

Miss Howard felt very like all the Muses rolled into one accomplished incarnation that morning, and she thought of the stacks of sketches blushing unseen in her portfolios. Her improvisation still rang in her ears. Just opposite her was the façade of the baths establishment, which she had depicted in her 'Healing Springs', and a textile company in which she had quite a number of shares had that morning announced a bonus distribution of unexpected size: thus she felt rich as well as artistic. Enquiries about the Green Salon she saw were to be made of Town Councillor Bowen, at whose shop 'Evening Bells' had been framed, and she determined, at the least, to make them, and, at the most, to take the Green Salon (suitable for picture exhibitions) for a fortnight. She knew the room: it was close to the office where patients purchased their tickets for the baths, and was thus very conveniently placed, for many of them surely would be tempted to look in while they were waiting for their baths. Moreover, it was not too large: forty or fifty water colours, which she could easily select from her store, would be sufficient, tastefully spaced, to decorate it and to display themselves to the highest advantage. The walls, which might be supposed to be green could equally well be described as grey, and would furnish a suitably neutral background.

Town Councillor Bowen was attending to his municipal duties, and was not at home, but Mrs. Town Councillor was, and she beamed respectfully at Miss Howard as she paid a ten shilling note for the framing of 'Evening Bells' over the counter, and waited for change.

"And I declare I oughtn't to charge you anything at all, Miss Howard," observed this most polite lady, "for it's a pleasure to frame your beautiful pictures. Mr. Bowen was touching up the gilding himself with his own hands, and though he knew his dinner was ready he stood there a-looking and a-looking at the work of art till I called out 'George, come along do, for your chop's getting cold.' 'Evening Bells'! I wish everybody who's fretting and worrying could have a good look at 'Evening Bells', for it would make them all feel peaceful again, I'm sure. And half a crown and a florin make ten."

This little speech seemed to Miss Howard to be nothing less than a 'leading'. She was instantly led, after a modest cough or two.

"I see the Green Salon can be hired by the week, Mrs. Bowen," she said, "and that put it into my head that I might hold a little exhibition of my paintings. A few people, as you're so kind to suggest, might perhaps care to glance at them."

Mrs. Bowen turned up her eyes to the ceiling as if in mute thanksgiving.

"Well, that would be kind of you," she said. "As I was saying to Mr. Bowen only the other day--but never mind that! What a treat for us all! I'm sure I shall be walking round the Green Salon morning, noon and night. And the terms are so moderate and nothing to pay for lighting, as the establishment closes at five, while there's still sufficient daylight to see pictures. Let me see, what did Mr. Bowen say they asked? I declare I forget, but I know you'll find it most moderate. As for the hanging of your works of art, I'll be there with a hammer and nails myself, and think it a privilege. And when would you be meaning your exhibition to commence? Such a treat for everybody."

There was no reason why it should not open as soon as Mr. Bowen could frame the exhibits, and Miss Howard promised to select them at once. The *Bolton Gazette* of which Mr. Bowen was one of the proprietors, would advertise it on most reasonable terms, and unless Miss Howard wanted to put it in the London papers, so that her friends might run down, there would practically be no other expense beyond the wages of an attendant (and no doubt the bath-establishment would let Miss Howard employ one of the uniformed pages) and the charge of a catalogue, which could be typewritten for a song. Mrs. Bowen would see to that, and to the list of prices if Miss Howard was intending to let the public purchase her beautiful works of art. And of course, some small red stars, adhesive stars to affix to those which were sold and prevent disappointment. Such a run there would be on them, Mrs. Bowen opined.

There was no resisting such a rosy statement, and, this agreeable conversation over, Miss Howard hurried back to the baths, in order to catch the omnibus for Wentworth, and begin making her selection without wasting a moment. Another reason for haste was that the clearing of the weather seemed only temporary, and thick fat clouds promising an imminent deluge were blowing up. The omnibus was waiting, and just as Miss Howard arrived, Mrs. Bliss came out of the ladies corridor wreathed in smiles and supported on sticks.

"Such a lovely bath, Miss Howard, so salt and refreshing and exhilarating. And how I look forward to my walk home on this breezy morning! Are you walking too? Mr. Kemp was thinking of it, but he is not quite sure. What a pleasant party we shall be if we all stroll up together."

The door of the waiting-room opened, and Mr. Kemp came out leaning on Florence's arm.

"Yes, my dear, I've been denying it as hard as ever I can," he was saying. "But I know I should never be able to get up the hill. Ah, there's Mrs. Bliss. What do you advise, Mrs. Bliss? Just now every step is agony, or, if it isn't really agony, it is something so like, that nobody could tell the difference. All the same it isn't quite so bad as it was yesterday, I'm sure of that. I walked all the way down the passage from my bath to the waiting-room without holding on to the wall. That's something you know. It's more than I've done for the last week."

Mrs. Bliss staggered towards him.

"Don't force it, dear Mr. Kemp," she said. "If you feel like that, you had better go up in the bus, but keep on telling yourself that you could walk double the distance without a single twinge of pain. Hold on to Mind, and you won't want to hold on to walls."

"Are you going to walk?" he asked.

"Oh yes. I gave myself treatment all the time I was in my bath. It produced such a feeling of buoyancy, I'm sure I should have floated in the water, if my attendant had not put little wooden bars across me to keep me down."

Mr. Kemp became materialistic for a moment.

"Oh, everyone does that," he said. "It's the brine."

Mrs. Bliss of course knew that this buoyancy was the effect of right thought and reliance on Mind, and assured Mr. Kemp that he would very soon get to know that too. Then, as all the others seemed to think they were lame, or were afraid of getting wet, though getting wet could not possibly hurt anybody, she grasped her sticks, and with a loving smile at the black and menacing clouds limped slowly away. The omnibus whizzed up the hill to Wentworth, and just as they arrived, there burst a glacial storm of sleet, and it was decided to send the omnibus back instantly to pick up Mrs. Bliss, who, if she ever got to the top of the hill at all, would be soaked and frozen. But it had hardly started when she drove up in a taxi and came radiantly into the lounge.

"I was having such a lovely walk," she said, "quite free from any false claim of pain, and so much enjoying the freshness, when a taxi drove by. The man stopped and asked if I would not take him, as he had had no fare all the morning. So I popped in just to please him. A sweet little drive: so cosy."

The patients dispersed to their rooms for the prescribed hour's rest after their baths. Though Mrs. Bliss said that she was not going to rest at all, but just lie quiet on her bed and do an hour's strenuous work denying illness and pain, there was a superficial resemblance between her procedure and that of the others, for they all lay on bed or sofa, and kept quiet. . . . Mrs. Holders rather acidly remarked that Mrs. Bliss would soon deny having had a bath at all.

Miss Howard equally scorned the idea of rest. She ran through the improvisation again in order to fix one or two of the more elusive passages in her mind, and then began the work of selection for her exhibition. There were several fat portfolios full of sketches to choose from, and the difficulty at first seemed to be to know what to reject rather than what to choose, for they were all up to the same standard of execution. As she spread them out on her bed and her washing-stand and her table and her chimney-piece and finally, such was their profusion, on her carpet, other difficulties presented themselves, especially when she considered her catalogue. There were for instance nine pictures of St. Giles's Church, of which the famous "Evening Bells" was one: should she group them together under the collective title of "Some aspects of St. Giles's Church?" That was prosaic, but on the other hand if she called them "Evening Bells", and "Lengthening Shadows", and "Morning Sunshine", and "Reflections" (alluding to the river) and "God's Acre" (alluding to the churchyard) people might, in a carping spirit, say that they all represented the same thing. It would be better not to have so many pictures of St. Giles's Church, but it was hard to know which to reject. A similar question arose with regard to the various views of the town. They were chiefly painted from the garden at Wentworth, and in some the mist lay over the town, while the hills beyond were in sunshine, in others the hills were in mist and the town in sunshine, but 'Mist on the Hills', and 'Mist in the Valley' would make pretty titles for the two main types. Then there was 'Healing Springs' which was a representation of the front of the bath-establishment, and 'Bethesda' would be a good title for the same building from the garden at the back. A quantity of country lanes and pools of water and harvest moons must be thinned out, and she weeded diligently among these and then found that those she had rejected had peculiar effects of beauty in them and that some of those she had chosen were practically identical. It was a relief to come to Mrs. Oxney's cat, and the tree on the Colonel's golf links (now prone, which gave a certain historical value to the picture,) and a bed of geraniums, for these were wholly unlike each other, and nobody could say that a cat was another aspect of a geranium. . . . Then there came the question of framing. Miss Howard saw at once that she could not have forty or fifty pictures framed in the style of 'Evening Bells' at five shillings and sixpence, for no bonuses of textile shares would run to that. She must consult the Town Councillor on the subject and obtain definite figures. Something neat, something glazed, was all that was required, without a final touching up of the gilding by his hands. If the public appreciated her pictures they could buy them without that.

Then there came the question of the price she was to put on the exhibits, and instantly Miss Howard felt as if she was dealing with problems quite unknown, for she had not the smallest idea what to ask for them. 'Evening Bells' was undoubtedly the gem of the collection, but when she looked at Mrs. Oxney's cat (which her mistress had often declared she could hear purring) she wondered if she was not positively giving it away, if she charged any smaller sum for it. But what was that sum to be? She knew that pictures had no absolute value, like the price of gold and silver (and even that varied): they were worth neither more nor less than what anybody chose to pay for them. But she had to start the bidding, though she also concluded it, and since 'Evening Bells' was clearly not worth a hundred pounds, and just as clearly worth more than one pound, she started the bidding by putting it in a class by itself at three guineas. 'Puss-cat' and 'Tree on golf links', and perhaps 'Healing Springs' should by this standard be two guineas, and everything else one guinea. . . . Or should she price everything at one guinea, and hope to dispose of a fair number of them, or should she price them all at half a guinea, and hope to dispose of most? So perplexing was the whole question that if at this moment, anybody had offered her five shillings apiece for the whole contents of the portfolios, she would have ecstatically accepted this meagre proposal, and have foregone the Green Salon altogether. Yet the notion of an exhibition was dear to her: it was not everybody who came before the world like that, and, besides, nobody had as yet offered her five shillings for the most accomplished of her efforts. In any case such a sum was a derisory price to ask for the fruit of so much trouble, for each sketch had taken her at least two mornings' work, and many much more, and there was such a thing as a living wage even if you had a little place in Kent. The immediate urgency was to find out from the Town Councillor at what figure he would frame forty or fifty sketches neatly, but on an economical scale. She must also go into the price to be charged for administration. The idea of season tickets at a reduced cost was not practical if the exhibition was to remain open for a fortnight at most, and the idea of having a private view first could not be entertained for a moment, since Miss Howard would have to send complimentary tickets to everyone at Wentworth, who were precisely the people whom the decencies of friendship would compel to pay for admission. She put the selected masterpieces into one of the portfolios, and with rather a haggard face went down to lunch.

The storm which had burst with such violence just as Mrs. Bliss caught the taxi, had caught Colonel Chase a good three miles outside Bolton, on a peculiarly bleak piece of road, and he said damn. Luckily there was a barn standing in a field a few hundred yards away, and finding it locked, he took shelter under its eaves, lit a pipe, and with difficulty reminded himself that he was an old campaigner. Half an hour's waiting in this exiguous protection made him feel very chilly, but the weather, no doubt accepting his challenge of being an old campaigner, showed what it was capable of, and continued to pour forth windy sleet with incredible violence. The eaves began to drip heavily upon him, the wind played about his skirts in a sportive and changeable manner, and after some more damns the old campaigner thought it was better to get wet quickly and then be able to change his clothes and have a hot lunch, rather than get wet slowly and be too late for it. He faced the blast, and with the pedometer ticking briskly in his pocket marched homewards. It should certainly register seven miles before he reached Wentworth which would be a pretty sturdy performance on so vile a day, and the congratulations would be well earned.

Even as that vainglorious thought entered his mind the hook of his pedometer slipped, and it slid unnoticed through a hole in his waistcoat pocket on to the muddy road. His mackintosh flapped, his knees became extremely wet, the rain ran off the back of his cap down his neck, and off its peak on to the end of his nose, and after an hour's odious pilgrimage he came dripping into the lounge where everyone, lunch being over, was sitting comfortably round the fire. Cries of admiration greeted him, but he would sooner have felt less chilly and have foregone this enthusiastic reception.

Mrs. Oxney hurried off to the kitchen to see if there was still any Irish stew in existence, which could be heated up, and be ready for him when he had changed his clothes: the dish was snatched from the very jaws of the parlour-maid, who was about to devour it, and who had to be content with cold mutton instead. Already Colonel Chase had symptoms of a cold coming on: his throat was hot and dry, and a series of prodigious sneezings more than once interrupted his discussion of the Irish stew. What made the malignancy of the weather more marked was that he had no sooner got home than the rain stopped, and there was promise of a bright afternoon, but he thought it would be wiser, with these ominous symptoms, not to go out again, but sit warm in the smoking-room and allow three guests to have a rubber of bridge with him. Of these Mrs. Holders should certainly not be one unless he found it absolutely impossible to get a fourth without her, for it was only right that she should be punished for her revolutionary behaviour last night: even if he was forced to ask her, he would be very cold and polite to her, and not give her any advice at all, nor explain how she might have won ever so many more tricks.

The cheerful group he had left in the lounge had broken up when he came back after his lunch, only Mrs. Bliss with Mr. Kemp and Florence were left. Mrs. Bliss had a book lying open on her lap and all three were seated bolt upright in a row and smiling. Their eyes were shut which looked as if they might be enjoying a sociable nap, but their upright carriage argued against repose. A fresh explosion of sneezing seized him as he approached, at which they all opened their eyes but smiled as before. This was very strange and he could not understand what they were doing with themselves.

"I'm afraid I've caught a fearful cold," he said. "I got wet through in my walk and chilled to the bone."

Mrs. Bliss looked at Mr. Kemp, then at Florence, and finally at Colonel Chase.

"No, Colonel," she said with great sweetness of manner, "you haven't got a cold at all. Error."

"I wish it was," he said, "but there's no error about it. Shiverings, sneezings, sore throat. That spells cold."

"Error!" said Mrs. Bliss again tenderly.

This odd situation was broken in upon by warblings descending the stairs, and Miss Howard tripped lightly down, dressed for walking with a bulky portfolio under her arm and quite unconscious of the presence of other people.

"La donna 'e mobile," sang Miss Howard. "Oh, Colonel Chase! I never saw you! Not coming out again on this beautiful afternoon."

"Not I. I've got a cold coming on and I shall stop in and nurse it. Are you going into the town?"

"Yes. I've got to see about my little pickies being framed. Just fancy! I'm going to hold a little teeny picture-exhibition of some of my rubbishy sketches. So rash! But nobody would give me any peace until I promised to."

This was approximately though not precisely true: Miss Howard had told the group in the lounge that Mrs. Bowen had said that everyone was longing for her to do so, and the group in the lounge had all said "Oh, you must!" again and again and again. She had to yield.

"So frightened about it," said Miss Howard, "I shall certainly leave Bolton the day before it opens, so as not to hear all the unkind things you say about it."

CHAPTER III

"Dear girl," said Mrs. Bliss, "you know how we shall all enjoy it. Such a refreshment!"

Miss Howard kissed her fingers and dropped the portfolio of sketches. The Colonel stooped to pick it up for her, but long before he got down, the sharpest sort of pain shot through the small of his back, and he recovered the erect position with difficulty.

"Attack of lumbago, too, I'm afraid," he said, and Florence, Mr. Kemp and Mrs. Bliss all muttered 'Error'.

"Dear me, I hope not," said Miss Howard, for the social tranquilities of Wentworth were sorely disquieted when the Colonel had lumbago. "Can't I get you something for it in the town?"

"A bottle of quinine if you'd be so good," he said, "and a packet of thermogene. Please tell the chemist to send them up at once."

Miss Howard went gaily off breaking into song again just before she closed the front door. She had every graceful gift, thought Florence, whose eyes followed her as she tripped down the drive.

"And the rest of our party?" asked Colonel Chase.

"In the smoking-room I think," said Mr. Kemp, wishing the Colonel would not stand so close to him with that bad cold coming on. Of course it was Error, but he did not like Error in such immediate proximity. "They talked of playing bridge."

The Colonel took himself and his error off. Of course there was no reason why four people should not play bridge if they felt inclined to, but if there was bridge in the air it was usually round him that it condensed. A sound of laughter came forth from the smoking-room as he opened the door, and he knew the sort of bridge which that meant: chatty, pleasant bridge unworthy of the name. There they were, Mrs. Oxney, Mrs. Bertram and Mrs. Holders and Mr. Bullingdon all very gay, and unconscious for the moment of his entrance.

"Oh, pick it up, Mrs. Oxney," said Tim, "and put it back in your lily-white hand. We don't mind: but if you play any more cards out of turn, I shall trump them as they lie on the table."

"Most kind, I'm sure," said Mrs. Oxney. "I will take it back if no one minds. Such a beautiful card too. Oh there's Colonel Chase. We're just playing a rubber, Colonel, to pass the time till tea. We'll be finished presently, and then you must cut in and show us how."

Colonel Chase pulled up a chair between Tim Bullingdon and Mrs. Oxney. Such a position, at the utmost possible distance from Mrs. Holders compatible with seeing the game, was most marked. But she being a woman of no perception and blandly ignorant that she was in disgrace, greeted him cordially.

"Yes, do, Colonel," she said, "and win back a bit of the fortune you lost last night. Why go to Monte Carlo when we can play bridge at Wentworth?"

Colonel Chase from being able to see two hands, while the third was on the table seemed to have an almost uncanny knowledge of where the other cards were and made useful comments to Mrs. Oxney when she finessed or refused to finesse, or trumped or refrained.

"Yes, you should have taken the finesse then," he said. "Pretty certain that the king was on your right, from the way the cards fell. . . . Ah, you ought to have trumped that: the remaining club was sure to be on your left."

"You always seem to know just where every card is before anything is played at all," said Mrs. Oxney admiringly. "I call it magic."

The magician drew his chair closer to the fire. If only Mrs. Holders had joined Mrs. Oxney in agreeing that he was a magician he might have forgiven her, but she only looked very much surprised and dealt in silence. He felt chilly and cross and grumpy.

"I hear Miss Howard's intending to open a palace of art next week," he observed. "I call it real blackmail, as I suppose we shall all be expected to go and buy something. Blackmail. Bless me, where's my pedometer?"

He felt in pocket after pocket without result.

"Dear me whatever can have happened to it?" said Mrs. Oxney. "That would be your walking pedometer would it?"

"Naturally, as I didn't bicycle this morning," said he. "And I know I took it out with me, for I remember hearing it ticking as I started to come home."

"I warrant it was ticking pretty briskly then," said Mrs. Oxney, pleasantly but absently, for she was sorting her hand and trying to find something above an eight. "I've never seen anyone walk your pace, Colonel."

He got up without acknowledging this compliment.

"I must go and see if I've left it upstairs," he said. "Odd thing if I have, for I usually carry it about with me all day."

Mrs. Holders waited till the door was closed.

"And puts it in his pyjama pocket when he goes to bed," she remarked, "in case he turns over in the night. I pass."

"Two hearts," said Tim Bullingdon, who had heard about the sensational affair yesterday; "and when I say two hearts I've got a reason for it, partner."

"Oh for shame!" said Mrs. Oxney.

"Well, I have a reason for it: it means I've got a lot. I hope he's lost his pedometer: I'm sick and tired of hearing how far he's been. I shall get one I think, and tell you all if I walk more than fifty yards."

"Gracious me, I hope he hasn't lost it," said Mrs. Oxney. "He'll turn the house upside down to find it."

"I stole it," said Mrs. Holders, "and ate it for lunch. I double your two hearts, Tim. Whenever I double two hearts I've got a good reason for it."

The reason must have been that she was tired of this particular rubber, for this ill-advised manœuvre finished it.

"Cut again, quick," she said, "and then we'll begin another before he gets back. It's perfect heaven playing without him."

"Oh, pray wait a minute," said Mrs. Oxney.

"Why? We'll pretend it's the same one. You and me, Tim. Do try to remember when the ace of trumps is played."

CHAPTER III

They had got well on in the next rubber before Colonel Chase came back with an agitated and anxious face.

"Not a sign of it in my bedroom," he said. "But I find there was a hole in the pocket where I carry it, and it may have fallen on the carpet somewhere. I trust everyone will be very careful how they walk about the house till it's found. Valuable instrument, well travelled too, all over India. Do you think you can trust your servants, Mrs. Oxney, not to have--ha--misappropriated it?"

Now if there was one thing on which Mrs. Oxney prided herself even more than on her house-keeping it was the honesty of her staff, and she answered him with unusual sharpness.

"I'd trust them all with a bag of money and never think to count it before or after," she said. "You might as well suspect me or Mrs. Holders."

Colonel Chase could not understand why they all looked at each other and then bent their heads over the cards.

The terrible news went abroad at tea-time that the valuable instrument was missing, and everybody walked about with Agag-delicacy, peering at the places where they proposed to set their feet, for fear of trampling on this pearl. Once Tim Bullingdon's dastardly heart leaped for joy when he planted one of his sticks on a fragment of coal which cracked beneath it, much as the valuable instrument might have done, but his pleasure was short-lived; it wasn't It. Miss Howard had not seen it, she was sure, gleaming on the road between Wentworth and the town. Every spot over which Colonel Chase could have passed since he came in this morning had been systematically searched, and the dreadful surmise that he must have dropped it somewhere on the other side of Bolton was probably only too true. And all the time (what anxiety the knowledge of this would have saved) it was safely reposing on the fender of Mr. Amble's shop, where Miss Howard had ordered quinine and thermogene. His honest lad, bicycling back from an errand along the road where the Colonel had dropped it, saw it gleaming in the miry roadway, and picked it up. A suspicious yellowness below the plating of the valuable instrument had convinced him that it was not silver, and having never seen a pedometer before, it appeared to him to be an unusual type of watch, which was no use for telling the time, and might possibly be traced if he pawned it. So he gave it to Mr. Amble who put it to dry on the parlour fender, and shortly after Miss Howard's departure displayed a notice in his shop window to say a pedometer had been found, apply within. The honest lad then discounted any merit he might have acquired by not retaining a suspicious and useless object, by forgetting to take the quinine and thermogene to Wentworth. Instead he put up the shutters as dark was drawing on, spent the sixpence that Mr. Amble had given him in cigarettes, and Mr. Amble gave the pedometer a brush up.

Tea was always served at Wentworth in the drawing-room. A small dinner-waggon with teapots of Indian and China was wheeled in, solid refreshment was arranged on a convenient table, and usually this was a very pleasant and chatty meal, and one at which Colonel Chase made himself most entertaining. He had a fund of stories, which he lavishly recounted, and often he sat there for nearly an hour before he went upstairs to read, telling them about the Curate's egg and the little boy who took a sip of his father's whiskey and soda, and not liking the taste, put it back in the glass. Then there was the thrilling tale of the man-eating tiger which Mrs. Oxney said she could never hear without trembling, though she knew that it ended all right and the tiger did not eat this man, and the story about the ghost which the Colonel had seen in the dak-bungalow somewhere near Agra, and which was far more terrifying than anything Mr. Kipling had written. Then when he had terrified them so much that Mrs. Oxney said that she, for one, wouldn't be able to sleep a wink that night, he restored confidence and gaiety by the tale of the Dean who gargled with port wine by mistake and told his doctor he thought it would suit him very well taken internally in larger quantities. But to-night Colonel Chase had no such titbits for them; he sneezed and scowled and was silent and made sudden excursions beneath the piano to see whether the pedometer had not secreted itself under the pedals. A great many heads were shaken over his chances of recovering it, and Mrs. Bliss alone was optimistic. She after hearing about it just closed her eyes and then said she was sure that everything would prove to be happy and harmonious. It was very pleasant to know that Mrs. Bliss had no fears about the pedometer, but it did not really help matters.

Colonel Chase roused himself from his melancholy when the parlour-maid came in to clear away tea, to question her sharply as to whether anything had been heard of It, and whether a parcel had arrived for him from the chemist's. The double negative of her answer seemed to intensify the prevailing gloom, and even the drawing of the curtains and the kindling of all the electric lights made but a hollow mockery of cheerful cosiness. Miss Howard, also sharply questioned, was quite sure she had given the order that the packet was to be sent up at once.

"That was all you asked me to do, Colonel Chase," she said with some dignity, "and I did it."

That gave Mrs. Bliss a cue.

"Dear girl," she said, "I'm going to ask you to do something nice, and oh, please do it. Won't you run your hands over the piano? Just one of those sweet little fragments. How dear of you! How you spoil me."

This was better than nothing, for there was a reason for silence if Miss Howard was playing, and she gave them several sweet little fragments, during one of which Colonel Chase left the room and was heard bawling down the telephone in the lounge. Everybody of course had only half an ear for the sweet fragments while this was going on, and Miss Howard very considerately played with the soft pedal down, for she was as interested as anybody. He was heard to give a number to the exchange, which Mrs. Oxney whispered was Mr. Amble's, and presently called out, "Perfectly disgraceful and if your shop's shut up and your boy's gone home, you ought to bring it up yourself now. Shameful!" Mr. Amble, thereupon, so it was easy to make out, must have got a little heated too, and replaced the receiver at his end, for Colonel Chase after saying 'Hullo' eight or nine times in a crescendo of fury, put his receiver back (as anybody could hear) and went upstairs. He walked with a heavy thumping tread, as if he had quite forgotten that every one else was still enjoined to step carefully, for fear of pulverising the pedometer. . . . It was all dramatic enough, but no one knew the full splendour of the situation, for even as Colonel Chase went thumping upstairs, Mr. Amble went back to his parlour and finished polishing up the Colonel's pedometer.

Miss Howard released the soft pedal and trod on the other one: there was nothing now for which to listen elsewhere, so they all concentrated themselves on the long shake with the crossing arpeggios. Florence had stolen to the chair which Colonel Chase had vacated close to the piano and rapturously followed Miss Howard's twinkling fingers. How nimble and slender they were, and those same fingers had been so still and steady when they held the brush which picked out the reflections in the river. Life was becoming exciting for Florence. When the arpeggio passage came to an end, as usual in three crashing chords, everyone felt much better, for Colonel Chase had gone up to his room, and the eclipse for the present was over, and there was Miss Howard at the piano. Mrs. Oxney heaved a sign of relief and rapture.

"I wish the Colonel had heard that," she said. "He is a little worried, isn't he, with the cold and no quinine or pedometer. Most aggravating for him, but please don't get up, Miss Howard. Mayn't we have 'O rest in the Lord', though it isn't Sunday."

Miss Howard let them have it, very slowly and with great feeling, accentuating the melody. She gazed thoughtfully at the ceiling, and all her audience gazed thoughtfully at other inappropriate spots, and Florence gazed at Miss Howard. Mrs. Oxney found herself thinking of the late Mr. Oxney, and Mrs. Bertram thought about coke, and Mrs. Holders thought about the enquiry she had sent to the *Sunday Gazette* about their bridge last night, and Mr. Kemp with closed eyes thought about his left hip, and Mrs. Bliss thought about Mind, and Miss Howard thought about the cost of the frames for her pictures, but all wore precisely the same dreamy and wistful expression. A perfect gale of sighs succeeded the last note and a subdued chorus of 'Thank you, Miss Howard'. Mrs. Bertram had determined to get some more coke in at any cost, Mrs. Holders had calculated that Slam would have plenty of time to answer her enquiry in next Sunday's issue, Mrs. Oxney had regretted that her late husband had sold his shares in the Bolton Electric Company, and Mr. Kemp had lifted his left leg quite high and found that it certainly moved more easily. . . . But something had to be done, for this pious hour could not go on until dinner-time, and Mrs. Holders mercifully put an end to it by staggering towards the door. Tim followed suit, and as the wet and cold of the day had dismally affected them both, she groped her way along the piano and Tim cake-walked more prancingly than ever along the opposite wall. They collided at the door, for each of them tried to open it for the other, and reviled each other's clumsiness. They groped their way across the lounge, and established themselves in the smoking-room.

"That's better," she said. "Now let's be real. Don't let us rest in the Lord: let's--oh Tim, let's contemplate Colonel Chase. I would sooner have twenty colds in the head by the way, and lose a hundred pedometers than ache as I'm aching to-night. You're pretty bad my dear, aren't you? Poke the fire."

Tim poked the fire with one of his sticks. It had an india-rubber ferule which, when he withdrew it, was fizzling and giving off a perfectly sickening smell.

"There!" he said triumphantly. "I made that smell, and all because you told me to poke the fire. You made it, in fact. About aches: don't let us talk about such a boring subject. Nor about the Colonel; what really interests me is Mrs. Bliss. She's holding a sort of healing class. They close their eyes and smile. Did you ever see Kemp smile before? I never did. They close their eyes and smile, I tell you, and assert that they are quite well. I wish his smile didn't make me feel so morose."

"Oh Tim, how thrilling," she said. "I hadn't grasped what they were about. I only thought they looked boiled. I hope she'll leave me and my aches alone, I should consider it great impertinence if she attempted to interfere with them."

This robust view made him laugh.

"I quite agree," he said. "I've got a strong sense of property too. My aches are my own, and they're quite real, and I should resent it very much if anybody denied it. Lord, what bosh! And she has baths too, just like the rest of us. But here we are on the boring topic again. Much better not to think about it and play piquet."

"Come on, then. How I hate my vile body to-day."

"Loathsome, isn't it? But you'll feel better if you rook me."

Mrs. Oxney and her sister meantime had gone back to their sitting-room. Miss Howard (after playing 'O rest in the Lord' again, which Mrs. Bliss sang *sotto voce* in a small buzzing voice like a blue-bottle with a broad smile) went to get on with her catalogue, and the three students of Mental Science were left to their studies. Mr. Kemp refused to be interested in its larger aspects: it existed as far as he was concerned for the purpose of making him better. They all sat with eyes closed realising Omnipotent Mind for a little, and then he stretched out his left leg which was the worst. Encouraged by the absence of pain, he got up and with only one stick hobbled across the room and back again.

"I'm convinced that the joint is moving more freely," he said excitedly. "I don't believe I've walked so easily since that good week I had at Bath in the spring. At Buxton I never stirred a yard without two sticks, did I, Florence?"

"You're walking as well as anybody else can walk, dear Mr. Kemp," said Mrs. Bliss, to whom the most atrocious lies on this subject were beautiful truths.

"If you only chose, you could jump on to that chair like a bird hopping on to a branch."

He looked at this formidable altitude, and even bent his knees as if about to spring.

"I almost believe I could," he said.

"Oh, don't, Papa," exclaimed Florence. "You know that Dr. Dobbs said that any improvement must come slowly. I mean--"

"Dear child!" said Mrs. Bliss. "Naughty! That's the false idea we're working to destroy."

CHAPTER III

"I know. I forgot for a moment," said Florence. "But he'd much better not try to jump, had he?"

Mr. Kemp thought so himself, but he was much encouraged by his long walk across the room.

"Really I'm not sure that I shall have my reclining bath tomorrow," he said. "I shall only have my *masseur.* And yet, I don't know. You mean to go on with your baths, don't you, Mrs. Bliss?"

"Yes, for the sake of my dear husband, as I told you," said she, "and there's no harm in doing it, so long as you're perfectly certain it can't possibly do you any good. All the time I was in my bath this morning, so warm and restful, I fixed all my thoughts on Mind."

Mr. Kemp's walking tour had not ended quite as felicitously as it began, and a few sharp twinges made him glad to get back to his chair.

"And what shall I do next?" he asked. "I've had a good twenty minutes self-treatment, and you and Florence were treating me too."

Mrs. Bliss leaned forward and warmed her hands at the fire. They were not cold, of course.

"We should all spend much of our time in helping others," she said. "We get strength that way. Poor Colonel Chase now: my heart bleeds for him with all his false claims about losing his pedometer and having a bad cold and lumbago. Shall we help him?"

Mr. Kemp did not feel any real spiritual compulsion to help Colonel Chase, whose false claims were such petty little disturbances, but if he could get strength that way which would enable him to treat himself more powerfully, he was quite willing to help him. He would have to rest before dinner and glanced at the clock.

"Well, for ten minutes," he said.

"Dear of you," said Mrs. Bliss. "The poor Colonel is so full of illusions this afternoon, which make him feel worried and ill and anxious. Let us all give him absent treatment."

"Mustn't we send up and tell him?" asked Florence. "I don't think I should like to do that."

"No, dear, it makes no difference whether he knows it or not. Let us deny his worries and chilly feelings. Let us see him healthy and happy and full of sunshine."

This required a good deal of imaginative effort on the part of those who knew Colonel Chase, for it was no use saying that sunshine was one of his characteristic attributes. Mr. Kemp and Florence had to close their eyes very tight on many past memories in their efforts to realise a sunny Colonel. As for seeing him healthy and happy one glance at him when he came down to dinner that evening was enough to make that internal conception very difficult to cling to, for he had a cold of the most violent kind, he incessantly coughed and sneezed, he had a poor appetite, he was bent and stiff with lumbago and looked the picture of misery. Luckily he was extremely hoarse, being hardly able to speak above a whisper, and so the scarifying remarks he addressed to the parlour-maid, who served him, complaining of his food and his drink, and the draught, and his napkin, and the light and the knives and forks could not be made out with any clearness, but the growling noises which accompanied poor Mabel's visits to his table, could not reasonably be interpreted as the utterances of a happy man. There was no news of the pedometer, the infamous Amble had not sent his quinine and thermogene, and when, after sitting almost on the hob of the smoking-room fire for half an hour, he went up to bed without even suggesting a game of bridge, it was felt by those who had tried to see him happy and full of sunshine, that their visions were as yet unfulfilled. Further, Mr. Kemp's hip had suffered a bad relapse and there was no longer any doubt in his mind that he would have his bath as usual next day. He was much disappointed at the general results of the evening's séance, and wondered if his hip had ever been so bad before. Mind, in his view, was of very doubtful value.

But none of these mutinous ideas had the smallest effect on Mrs. Bliss's complete confidence, or diminished the splendour of her smile. She knew, and soon everybody else would know, that all was well with Mr. Kemp's hip and the Colonel's cold and her own arthritis and the missing pedometer.

CHAPTER IV

It has been said that miracles don't happen. This one did. The morning broke warm and sunny again, and Miss Howard who came downstairs, warbling the chorale of her improvisation, a few minutes before the breakfast gong sounded, observed that there was a nice parcel for Colonel Chase on the table of the lounge with perfidious Amble's label. It needed no ingenuity to surmise that this contained quinine and thermogene, and Mrs. Oxney who had been looking at the proofs of her Wentworth advertisement, thought she had better send it up to his room.

"He's sure to stop in bed all morning," she said, "and the best place too for such a nasty cold as he's got, and he can wrap himself up in that wool and dose himself at pleasure. I'll send one of the maids up with it to make sure he'll have his breakfast in bed, and light his fire for him."

At that moment the miracle manifested itself. The words were hardly out of Mrs. Oxney's mouth when a loud cheerful whistle sounded from above and Colonel Chase came tramping downstairs. His face was rosy from the cold bath, which was one of the reasons why Englishmen were stronger than anybody else, and he stronger than any other Englishman, and his whistle betokened his distinguished approval of the dealings of Providence.

"Good morning, ladies," he said standing at the salute. "You observe that Richard is himself again. Most extraordinary thing! When I have a cold like that I had yesterday, I know I shall have two days in hell, if you'll excuse the expression, and three in purgatory. Now I was never worse in my life than I was when I went up to bed last night. Very unwell indeed. I went asleep at once. And I awoke this morning as chirpy as a cricket, and not a trace of my cold left."

"Well, isn't that wonderful!" said Mrs. Oxney. "I know your colds, Colonel, and I always say that nobody I ever saw has such colds as you. Terrific!"

"And I took no remedies at all," said he. "That monstrous chemist--ah, there's the parcel. I shall send it back for I'm no more in need of his muck than I am of prussic acid. It's a miracle, I tell you, a sheer miracle. Such a recovery was never known before. My colds were famous in India. 'Look out for squalls when Colonel Chase has a cold,' was what my officers used to say to the subs when they joined the regiment. Lumbago gone, too: I did my dumb-bell exercises this morning with a boy's suppleness. I declare, if it wasn't for the loss of my pedometer, that I never felt happier in my life."

During that recital of this adorable news Mr. Kemp had negotiated the descent of the stairs, and now stood staring at Colonel Chase as if he had risen from the dead.

"You, Colonel?" he said. "And your cold quite gone? Vanished in the night with no medicines? Miraculous."

"You may well say miraculous, sir," said the Colonel. "Not a spoonful of Amble's rubbish, and here I am, jolly as a sandboy, and hungry as a hunter. Ah, here's Mrs. Bliss. Good morning, Mrs. Bliss. Delightful morning, and me quite well again. Most remarkable thing."

Mrs. Bliss couldn't smile any more, for she always smiled to her full capacity.

"So glad, Colonel," she said. "But I'm not the least surprised. I knew for certain that you would be quite well this morning. Didn't I tell you so, Mr. Kemp?"

"I wish you'd told me too," said Colonel Chase, "and I shouldn't have felt so down and out as I did last night. Ha! Breakfast gong. There's music for a hungry man."

He headed the procession to the dining-room, leaving Mrs. Bliss and Mr. Kemp to limp after him.

"But amazing," said Mr. Kemp. "To think that we did that! There must be something in it."

"Something in it?" said Mrs. Bliss. "There's everything in it, dear Mr. Kemp. And not amazing at all. Omnipotent Mind. It couldn't be otherwise. Error gone."

"But you treated me," said he, "and I'm sure I treated myself half the night, for I slept very poorly. Why am I as bad as ever this morning? Not a sign of improvement."

This was quite easy to explain. Mr. Kemp's erroneous rheumatism was of long standing: Error was deep rooted in him. But Colonel Chase had only been in error for a few hours, and that foolish mistake of his could be annihilated at once. The explanation did not however, fully satisfy Mr. Kemp, for he argued that since rheumatism was *(ex hypothesi)* absolutely non-existent the painful illusion ought to vanish as easily as a cold, when once you turned Mind on to it. But the manifest healing of Colonel Chase had made a great impression on him and he was fully determined to persevere till his rheumatic error followed Colonel Chase's error of catarrh into its native nothingness.

Before the ambulance-waggon from the baths came round, Wentworth was buzzing with excitement and the only person who had not been told that Colonel Chase had been cured by Mind and Mrs. Bliss (and possibly Mr. Kemp and Florence,) was Colonel Chase himself, for Mrs. Oxney and Mrs. Bertram were sadly afraid that if he was informed that his healing was spiritual, he might fly into so savage a tantrum at such an idea, that rage would entirely cancel the spiritual benefit, and perhaps his cold might return again worse than ever. It was indeed a great relief when soon after breakfast he set off on his bicycle to see what could be done in the way of setting up a new record, and so everybody could have a nice gossip about it all before going down to the baths. Mrs. Bliss assured them that the cure was entirely the effect of Mind, and had really nothing to do with her, but naturally nobody believed that.

"To be sure it's most remarkable," said Mrs. Oxney, "and if you can drive a cold away like that I don't see what you can't do. But I shouldn't like to tell the Colonel how it happened, for you can't be certain how he'll take a bit of news like that. At the same time I feel you ought to have the credit of it, for nothing will make me believe that his cold went away of its own accord. And neither quinine nor thermogene did he use--lumbago too--for when he came down this morning with his cold quite gone there was the parcel on the table."

Mrs. Bliss gave a happy little sigh.

"Yes, I'm glad his *materia medica* didn't arrive last night," she said, "or all you dear faithless people would have thought that material remedies had cured him, whereas there is no power in material at all. Indeed, I have no doubt that if he had taken his quinine relying on it, he would have been worse than ever."

"We have had an escape then," said Mrs. Bertram. "But can't medicines help at all? I should have thought a little medicine and some Mind with it, might do wonders. After all, you're taking the baths yourself, and massage as well."

The idea that Mrs. Bliss was taking the baths entirely for her husband's sake, and not for their remedial qualities, somehow seemed difficult for her audience to comprehend, though it was so patently clear and logical to herself. As for massage, that was officially called 'mere manipulation', and even the faithful allowed broken legs to be set and put in splints, for that was 'mere manipulation' too. The power of Mind, she explained would undoubtedly set a broken leg, but a surgeon saved time and trouble. Mind by itself restored everyone to perfect harmony, health and prosperity. All went well in every way with those who relied on Mind.

Miss Howard had been running through her improvisation before this illuminating discussion began. It was most annoying to have again forgotten the passage of octaves which led back into the few bars of Chopin's waltz and she shuddered to think what would happen if a similar lapse of memory occurred when she was on the platform. Would everyone sit there for ever, waiting, eternally waiting for what never came?

"But does that apply to everything?" she asked. "If you rely on Mind, does everything go right?"

Mrs. Bliss was getting worked up now.

"Yes, everything," she said, "for Mind is universal and omnipotent. All is mind and mind is all. The proposition is proved by the rule of inversion. Invert it, and it remains equally true. Hence Evil is nothing and nothing is evil."

"Cats eat mice, therefore mice--" began Mrs. Holders. But the flippancy was cut short by Miss Howard, who, though a little dazed, stuck to her point.

"Quite so, I see," she said. "But what I want to ask is that if there was something one had undertaken to do not for oneself, but for others, would reliance on Mind make you do it beautifully?"

"Yes, dear girl, of course," said Mrs. Bliss. "Mind denies evil, illness, failure. Whatever you want must come to you, if only you rely on Mind."

"Dear me, how comfortable it sounds," said Mrs. Oxney. "If only Colonel Chase relied on Mind, perhaps he would find his pedometer. He's gone along the road where he must have lost it, to look for it and to make it a new record. Couldn't you rely on Mind, Mrs. Bliss, and discover it for him?"

Mrs. Bliss was observed to close her eyes for a few seconds. That was remarked afterwards. Simultaneously a series of hoots from the bus indicated that it had been waiting a long time already, and they all hurried away at their various paces. . . .

Colonel Chase had left the unopened packet from the perfidious Amble to be returned with the withering message that it had arrived too late, and Mrs. Bliss, delighted to purge Wentworth of any fragment of *materia medica,* took charge of it. She found that she had a few minutes to spare before her bath, and since, on the one hand Mind assured her that she was quite well and not at all lame, and her doctor that gentle walking was good for the supposedly affected joints, she limped away to Mr. Amble's shop, to leave the packet there. She was looking, not in scorn, but with indulgent pity at the army of futile bottles and inefficacious drugs that were deployed in his windows, when her attention was attracted to a notice that was affixed there. What met her eye was this:

Found
A plated pedometer.
Apply Within.

She opened the door and a tingling alarm-bell continuously rang in the parlour behind the shop, as if she was a thief intent on pilfering *materia medica.* It ceased as Mr. Amble emerged.

"I have brought back a packet you sent up to Colonel Chase at Wentworth," she said. "It only arrived this morning and as he is now quite well, he would be greatly obliged if you would take your goods back."

Now though Mr. Amble had felt justly incensed at Colonel Chase's very intemperate remarks through the telephone last night, he had been rather sorry that he had rivalled him with tart replies and so sudden a cutting off of his communications, for the Colonel was constantly getting sticking-plaster and soap and bicycle oil and lozenges at his shop, and Mr. Amble would regret losing his valuable patronage. Also the petitioner was a lady of smiling and benevolent address, and she limped heavily, and so was another likely customer.

"Certainly, madam," said he with great suavity. "Anything to oblige Colonel Chase and yourself."

"So good of you," said Mrs. Bliss. "And I saw something about a pedometer in your window. Colonel Chase lost his pedometer yesterday in the road. I wonder if I might take it up to Wentworth, where I am staying, and see if it is his."

Mr. Amble hastened to produce it.

"I'll wager it is the Colonel's," he said, "for if Colonel Chase lost a pedometer on the road yesterday, and my lad found one on the road yesterday, no doubt, they, so to speak, are the ones. Often have I heard it ticking as he's walked about my shop, an old instrument, but I daresay useful still. And is there anything more I can supply you with madam?"

"Nothing thank you. So much obliged--Mr. Amble isn't it?--and how pleased Colonel Chase will be?"

She paused, and a playful innocent idea gleamed in her brain. She made the sweetest face at Mr. Amble, coaxing and child-like, with her head a little on one side, and her chin a little raised, and a really wonderful smile.

"And may the pedometer be a secret between you and me, Mr. Amble?" she said. "I want to make a mysterious surprise about it. Oh, such fun, but nobody else must know."

Mr. Amble thought this was a very pleasant, though an unusual sort of lady and, completely mystified, agreed. The prospect of regaining the Colonel's custom by taking back the goods was reward enough for him, and he did not even dream of suggesting the repayment of his disbursement of sixpence on the honest lad. So Mrs. Bliss went back to the baths with the pedometer ticking jerkily in her bag as she hobbled along.

Miss Howard had not come down by the bus, but had waited up at Wentworth to have a turn at the elusive passage of octaves which had bothered her earlier. While there were so many of those who would listen in a few days to her improvisation, sitting in the lounge, she had been playing very gently with the soft pedal down, for she did not want the extempore to become too familiar before its birth. But now the patients had gone brine-wards and Mrs. Oxney had gone to the chicken-run and Mrs. Bertram to the linen-closet, and there was no reason any more for these surreptitious tinklings. She remembered that Mrs. Bliss had said that any kind deed undertaken for the sake of others would be prosperously performed, if reliance was placed on Mind, and so now, before she began, she told Mind that she was playing in aid of the Children's Hospital, and had complete confidence in its Omnipotence. Then with the freedom of the loud pedal she concentrated on her work, and lo, the stream of octaves flowed along like torrents in spring. Of course it was easier to play when unshackled by the fear of being overheard, but never had she known so flashing an ease of execution, or so perfect a transition into the Chopin waltz. Then she tried the chorale, the last line of which had escaped her at her last attempt and now without the slightest conscious effort on her part it streamed solemnly from her finger tips. 'Most wonderful', thought Miss Howard, as, rather awestruck at her own brilliance, she closed the lid of the piano. "I couldn't remember either of those bits just before and now, relying on Mind, I feel I can never forget them. There must be something in it."

She had to go down to the baths to measure up the Green Salon, and see how many pictures would be needed, to try genteelly to beat Mr. Bower down over the price of framing them and to arrange for the typewriting of the catalogue. She would much have preferred printing but the cost of printing was frankly prohibitive; this seemed to have something to do with the coal strike, but the connection was difficult to understand. She tripped lightly down the hill to the imagined accompaniment of those agile octaves, and arrived at the door of the establishment at the very moment when Mrs. Bliss was entering on her return from Mr. Amble's. She came up behind her without being seen, and noticing that Mrs. Bliss ticked as she moved, wondered if this was a symptom of arthritis. Colonel Chase ticked too, but that was his pedometer, and, alas, it was sadly to be feared that his ticking days were over. Then she said 'Bo!' playfully, and Mrs. Bliss turning briskly round emitted a perfect tattoo of ticks. They seemed to come from her bag or thereabouts rather than her hip, but noises were always hard to localise.

"Sweet girl!" said Mrs. Bliss. "What a mischievous child you are to startle me like that. Have you come to see about your dear exhibition?"

"Yes," said Miss Howard, "and oh, I must tell you . . . I could not recollect, in that passage of my improvisation--I mean I could not remember something I wanted to recollect, when I was practising earlier in the morning, and I just closed my eyes and relied on Mind, because I was going to play in aid of the Children's Hospital next week, and everything I had forgotten came back to me at once. Wasn't that extraordinary?"

Mrs. Bliss laughed her happy laugh, but kept her bag still.

"Not in the least extraordinary," she said. "It would have been extraordinary, impossible in fact, if you hadn't recollected every note of your delicious tunes."

"But it was wonderful, wasn't it?" asked Miss Howard.

"Yes, indeed, little one," said Miss Bliss tenderly. "All is wonderful in Mind: wonderful and loving and perfect. Dear me; it is after eleven I see and I must hurry for my dear husband's sake or I shall have to shorten my bath. Au revoir, dear! In a day or two I shall be climbing step-ladders and helping you arrange your sweet pictures."

The Green Salon looked quite cheerful on this sunny morning, in spite of the uncleaned skylight, the slight odour of rotten eggs which hung about the baths establishment and the bare deal floor, and these slight drawbacks would presently be remedied, for Mr. Bower had promised that the skylight should be resplendent before the day of the opening, Mrs. Oxney had promised a nice piece of carpet for the floor, and Mr. Amble could be trusted to have some sort of aromatic riband in stock which smouldered persistently and would soon overcome the less agreeable aroma. Miss Howard measured up the walls and decided that forty-five sketches properly spaced would be as many as the Green Salon would hold without skying or earthing any of them, and having successfully reduced Mr. Bowen's estimate for framing, tripped into Mr. Amble's to consult him about the fumigatory. It was always pleasant to exchange a few words with that noted conversationalist, and Miss Howard told him that Colonel Chase's cold for which she had ordered remedies yesterday had happily disappeared.

"Yes, I was sorry to have vexed the Colonel last night about the delivery of his order," said Mr. Amble, "but I trust that's put right, Miss, for I've taken the goods back and very glad to do so. A most agreeable and affable lady called here this morning about it, and we soon settled that. Not a lady that I've seen here before, but from Wentworth, as she told me, and walking, you may say dot and go one, as I could see."

CHAPTER IV

"Yes, that must have been Mrs. Bliss," said Miss Howard. "Such a favourite already with us all."

She considered whether she should tell Mr. Amble about the affable lady's treatment of Colonel Chase's cold, but decided that it would be a want of tact to do so. Mental healing was certainly in competition with Mr. Amble's business. Wiser not.

"We were all so glad that the Colonel's cold got better," she said, "for he lost his pedometer yesterday and between the two he was a good deal worried."

Mr. Amble remembered that the affair of the pedometer was a secret between him and the smiling lady, and behaved like a man of honour. He had already removed the notice about it in his window.

"Dear me, he wouldn't like that," he said. "But who knows, Miss, that it mayn't be found one of these days, and that we shall hear it ticking away again?"

There was something reserved and oracular about this sentiment, and Miss Howard received the distinct impression that Mr. Amble knew something about the pedometer. Yet, what could he have known, for surely, he would have thrown any light that he possessed, however small and glimmering, upon the loss, now that he had been told of it? Miss Howard often had these strange sudden impressions, for she was what is called 'very intuitive'. Usually they came to nothing, and she forgot them: occasionally they came to something, and then she remembered them. Descending to business, she told Mr. Amble her errand, and he strongly recommended a fragrant riband called *Souvenir d'Orient,* which he lit and which immediately filled the shop with a swoony Arabian odour of musk, opoponax and incense, against which the rotten eggs would have no chance at all.

The bus had got back to Wentworth and the patients dispersed to their rooms to rest before Miss Howard had finished her jobs. She went out into the garden with her painting apparatus to touch up one of the sketches she had chosen for exhibition, called "Splendid Noon," which seemed to stand in need of a little more splendour, and worked away at the sharpening of the shadows till the first gong told her that lunch was imminent. Colonel Chase had come in from his bicycling in the highest spirits, and she had to guess how many miles he had been since breakfast. Remembering that his record for a morning ride (based upon the conjectural record when *that* pedometer got out of order) was thirty-five miles, and seeing his elation, she guessed thirty-six, and clapped her hands with admiration when she heard he had been thirty-seven.

"Not so bad for a man who thought he would be spending the day in bed," he said, "and I daresay I shall go out again for a short spin this afternoon."

"Oh, you mustn't overdo it," said she. "I think I should be content if I were you. But you haven't found your pedometer?"

His face hardly fell at all, so gratifying to himself and others was the new record.

"No, to break my record and find my pedometer would be too much of a red-letter day," he said. "I'm afraid I shall have to order another."

Mrs. Bliss had joined them in the lounge just as he said this. Mr. Kemp was there, too, and Florence, and Mrs. Oxney, and Mrs. Holders, and all were witnesses of what occurred.

Mrs. Bliss, leaning on her stick, was standing close to the Colonel with her left hand behind her back.

"No, Colonel Chase," she said, "you needn't order another. Guess what I've got in my hand: no peeping!"

"Not my--" began the Colonel. Emotion choked his utterance. Mrs. Bliss held out her left hand to him and said, "Peep-o!" There it lay, bright and clean, for Mr. Amble had polished it up beautifully.

"So glad: such a privilege," she said charmingly.

He grasped the beloved object and shook it. It ticked as brightly as ever.

"My dear lady, I can't thank you enough," he said. "I shall certainly go for a walk this afternoon for the pleasure of using it again. The Bliss-pedometer: may I christen it the Bliss-pedometer? Where did you find it?"

A dreamy absent sort of look came into Mrs. Bliss's eyes.

"Down in the town I think," she said. "Sometimes I lose myself in thought, and this morning, just before my bath, I was meditating deeply and joyfully as I strolled about in the sweet sunshine. And then there it was in my hand! Did I pick it up? Perhaps that was it. Or did someone give it me? Who knows? But somehow I felt sure that I should find it for you. So pleased!"

The effect of this was immense: a sort of awe fell on Wentworth generally, with the exception of Tim Bullingdon, who, when Mrs. Holders told him of the marvellous recovery of the valuable instrument merely said, "Oh, that blasted thing has been found, has it? More pedometer-chat!" But apart from him a very profound impression was made, and the reappearance of the pedometer was generally considered to belong to the same class of manifestations as the disappearance of the Colonel's cold: a notion which Mrs. Bliss certainly did not discourage. A small committee held in Mrs. Oxney's room after lunch inclined to the opinion that Colonel Chase should now be told to whom he owed (in some mysterious manner) both these benefits. The reappearance of the pedometer, taken alone, might be held to be just a lucky chance; so, too, possibly might the miraculous disappearance of his cold; but taken together with Mrs. Bliss as direct agent (under Mind) in both, they clearly outran any reasonable theory of coincidence. He might have got in one tantrum if a spiritual cause had been suggested for his convalescence only, and in another if the same had been assigned to the recovery of his pedometer, but when the two were presented together, it was felt there need be no apprehension about tantrums. Mrs. Bliss took no part in this conference, for they all knew from what source she derived these manifestations of health and harmony, but went out and sat under the cedar, where she pursued her mental work.

Colonel Chase had gone off for a walk, in spite of the morning's record on the wheel, in order to feel the pulse of his pedometer beating again in the region of his liver, and had given some thought to the happy reappearance of the instrument. It was wrapped in mystery: Mrs. Bliss apparently had found it while in a species of trance, and though he would have been naturally inclined to scoff at trances, there seemed to be something to be said for them. He already knew that she was a believer in the power of Mind and such hocus-pocus, but if hocus-pocus could find pedometers, he had no quarrel with it. In consequence, when on his vigorous return from his walk Mrs. Oxney told him that the same lady had given him mental treatment for that tornado of a cold which had fallen on him yesterday, he listened without any symptom of tantrums.

"And you know as well as I do, Colonel, if not better," said Mrs. Oxney in conclusion, "that when you have a cold it *is* a cold, not a matter of two sneezes and a drop of eucalyptus on your handkerchief. Your cold always means a day in bed, and pulls you down dreadfully, and if ever you had a cold in your life yesterday was the day. But here you are now making records in the morning and your pedometer in your pocket in the afternoon, and never looking better, though last night you were in for one of your worst."

Colonel Chase was proud of his fair-mindedness.

"Upon my word, that's all quite true," he said. "I don't wish to deny it. And then, as you say, the whole trouble vanished. Yet it must be stuff and nonsense. The woman's a crank if she thinks she cured me."

"Well, if she's a crank I'm a crank too," said Mrs. Oxney, "and that's a thing I've never been called before. It's not your cold only, there's that pedometer. I said to her, 'Couldn't you rely on Mind, Mrs. Bliss, and discover it for him?' Those were my very words, and no sooner had I said them than she closed her eyes and sat silent. We all noticed it. And then what does she do but find it in her hand?"

This powerful presentment of the case impressed him.

"Yes, I'm bound to say it's most remarkable," said he. "I'm no bigot, I hope: I've got an open mind on every question, and I know there are some things I can't account for. I've seen the mango-trick in India, but really . . . And yet one can hardly believe it. I must look into it. How does Mrs. Bliss explain it?"

"She just says, with that sweet smile of hers, that all is harmony and health, and what she did was to realise it for you."

The Colonel's robust intellect made a final effort to reject all it could not understand, and called his sense of humour to its aid.

"I'm sure it's not all harmony when Miss Howard gets to the piano," he said. "But that's flippant of me. I'm bound to say I can't understand it at all. Amazing! According to all my experience, I should have been in bed all day instead of bicycling thirty-seven miles this morning without fatigue, and going for a walk with my pedometer this afternoon. By all chances, it should have been crushed to bits under some lout's foot."

Colonel Chase, it need hardly be said, would have pooh-poohed the whole affair if it had happened to anybody else, calling it bunkum and piffle, and gammon and spinach, just as he pooh-poohed every ghost story in the world except his own psychical experiences in the dak-bungalow, calling them liver and indigestion, and imagination and nerves. But anything that happened to himself was of another order of phenomena, and that evening he entered into somewhat condescending intercourse with Mrs. Bliss. He shrewdly catechised her about the action of Mind, just as he might have catechised a doctor about the action of quinine, and said, "Ah; so that's your theory, is it?" to her explanations. But the leaven had begun to work, and more than once over bridge that evening, Mrs. Oxney thought she saw him close his eyes and smile like Mr. Kemp and Florence and Mrs. Bliss. And, beyond doubt, his manner to his partner was far less hectoring. He even allowed that on one occasion he might have played a hand better.

The rest of the week passed busily but uneventfully away bringing Wentworth nearer to the momentous days which were coming. The first of the fateful series was Sunday, when there might be expected a reply from Slam to Mrs. Holder's enquiry. Most of the guests at Wentworth took in the *Sunday Telegraph* as a rule, but all those who were interested in bridge, had on this occasion ordered the *Sunday Gazette* instead. Usually it came during breakfast-time, but to-day it was annoyingly late, and most of them were in the lounge, starving for Slam, when it arrived. Every one snatched his copy, and there was a loud rustle of paper as they all simultaneously turned to the page where Slam discussed Bridge and White Knight Chess instead of to the leaf on which the cross-word puzzle for the week was set forth. It was considered certain that Mrs. Holders and Colonel Chase ran a dead heat in the perusal of the judicial paragraph, for just as she gave a little squeal of laughter, Colonel Chase said "Pshaw!" or "Tosh!" (opinion differed as to which), and turned with a very red face to less important items. Then a dead hush followed and everyone but he read the long paragraph through twice. It ran thus, among the "Answers to Correspondents":

> "Wentworth" (Mrs. Holders's pseudonym). "The case you submit is well worth attention, because it is an admirable example of the fatal declarations too often made by ignorant dealers. There was no possible excuse for Z declaring two hearts unless he was burdened with superfluous cash. In so doing he completely ruined his partner's fine hand of diamonds, which would easily have taken Z and Y out and given them the rubber. But, this ludicrous declaration once made, Y was perfectly right to say 'no bid', for he naturally expected an overwhelming strength in hearts from Z, which, when once cleared, gave him six tricks in diamonds. Z's proper call, of course, was 'one heart' (doubtful) or 'No bid', in which case Y would have declared 'two diamonds'. B's 'double' was perfectly sound. In fact, we can only recommend A, B, and Y to disregard any declaration of Z's, if they ever have the misfortune to play with him again, until he has learned the elements of the game. We append the hands with a diagram as a warning to those who make these imbecile declarations."

Among the students of the *Sunday Gazette* was Florence, and she was thrilled to see her hand (Y) just as it had been dealt her with all those beautiful diamonds put in the paper with a diagram, and to be told by the oracle that she was quite right to have said no bid. Altogether forgetting Colonel Chase in the irrepressible joy of this publicity she cried out:

"Oh, look, Papa. Here's the game we had the other night, and I'm Y. That night I was so late, do you remember? Slam says I was quite right to say no bid. Isn't that sweet of him, and aren't my diamonds lovely? And that's where Mrs. Oxney sat and she's A., and Mrs. Holders is B, who doubled. How it all comes back! And Z, why--"

During the painful silence which followed these unfortunate remarks Colonel Chase was seen to close his eyes for a moment and smile, but when he opened them again, he did not seem much better. His hand which held the wretched sheet trembled with fury, and so did his voice which gradually rose to a roar.

"I see Slam comments on the hand you sent up for his decision, Mrs. Holders," he said. "I can only say that I totally disagree with him. Probably he's just a little cock of the walk at Tooting Junior Bridge Club, if all was known. I suppose he likes to play the little tin god. I shall certainly write and put my view of the case, though I expect he's too dense to understand it. I shall sign it, too, instead of cowering under a nickname. 'Slam' indeed! 'Revoke' would be a more suitable name for him, I shouldn't wonder. Impertinent little anonymous jackanapes."

What further ebullition would have followed is unknown, for even as he said jackanapes, Colonel Chase to the awe of the whole assembly was suddenly stopped by an appalling fit of sneezing. Again and again he sneezed, the convulsions seemed interminable.

"God bless me"--(crash), he said. "I believe I've caught another"--(crash)--"cold. Abominable nonsense; enough to make a man--"

He stopped seeing Mrs. Bliss's serene and limpid gaze smilingly fixed on him. She held up her finger as if in tender rebuke of a naughty child.

"Harmony, peace, and health deny inharmony, worry, sickness," she said. "All is Mind: Mind is all. O Colonel Chase!"

If catalepsy or sudden death had fallen on every human being in the lounge, Wentworth could not have been stricken into more rigid immobility. Openly to rebuke Colonel Chase when in a tantrum was not only impossible in fact, but incredible in theory. And yet having done it, Mrs. Bliss smilingly closed her eyes as if she had done nothing at all, and Mr. Kemp and Florence followed her example, calmly demonstrating. Mrs. Oxney tried to do the same, but curiosity as to how the Colonel would take this was too strong, and she had to keep a flickering eyelid open.

Colonel Chase cleared his throat; he sniffed, he sneezed once more and once only, and his catarrh and his fury seemed to vanish like morning mists.

"Dear me, I thought I'd caught cold again," he said, "but it's a false alarm. And . . . I suppose we mustn't harbour unkind thoughts about anyone. And bridge, too, is only a game. Ha! Quite so! Nearly church time, isn't it? I shall walk there on this beautiful morning."

The omnibus which took Wentworth to church on Sunday free of charge was unusually full after this spiritual manifestation, which brought harmony out of tantrums, and Mrs. Oxney was unable to consider it a coincidence that the first hymn was 'O happy band of Pilgrims'. All day harmony, so miraculously restored after that wild outburst, shone on Colonel Chase, he and his pedometer had a wonderful walk that afternoon and throughout the peaceful rubber of bridge in which the criminal Mrs. Holders took part, his hands dripped with trumps and kings and aces and convenient singletons. He adopted an almost reverential attitude towards Mrs. Bliss, and as he performed his dumb-bell exercises that night he beat time to his vigorous movements with denials of anger, malice and colds in the head. He was aware how rightly he had been known in India as a hard-headed fellow, but such a marvellous series of things that had happened to him personally (and therefore could not be bosh and gammon and piffle and spinach) could not be overlooked by a fair-minded man. Their attribution to coincidence must be definitely abandoned: it would not meet the case. Getting into bed he closed his eyes and battened on the conception of himself as completely happy and healthy and prosperous. Under this pleasant treatment he instantly fell fast asleep.

CHAPTER V

Indeed there seemed on the ensuing Monday morning, no conquests which were not within the victorious powers of Mental Science. Wentworth might almost become an establishment in direct competition with the baths and nauseating drinkings and general *materia medica* of Bolton Spa. Mr. Kemp actually refrained from brine that morning, and sat in the lounge reading the Manual, demonstrating over his hip and putting principles to the test by making short walks between window and fire-place. Mrs. Bliss went down to the baths as usual, but Wentworth was now beginning to grant that this violation of right thinking must really be for the sake of her husband, since a woman who could cure colds and tantrums and recover pedometers like that could not be in any need of saline immersion. Before she left, she spoke a few words to a gathering of students in Mrs. Oxney's room, which was really like a regular class of instruction, and was attended by all the guests (except Mrs. Holders and Tim Bullingdon) as well as a couple of parlour-maids with coughs. She told them that Mental Science filled you with health and energy for the harmonious accomplishment of the duties of life which must by no means be neglected, after which Colonel Chase started blithely off on the chief duty of his life, which was riding a bicycle, and Miss Howard wreathed in smiles tripped down to the Green Salon to drive into its faded walls the nails on which to hang the pictures which were to bring joy and refreshment to so many, and, it was hoped, profit to herself, for the labourer, said Mrs. Bliss, was worthy, sweet girl, of her hire. As for the improvisation which was to take place at the entertainment next day, and not only delight the audience, but bring in funds for the Children's Hospital, Miss Howard scarcely gave another thought to it, for she found that a mere closing of the eyes, a smile and a silent lifting of the spirit to Mind was sufficient to make her fingers reel out the most elusive passages, and she now felt she really had them by heart. Mrs. Bliss recommended her to give no further thought at all to the improvisation.

The guests were enjoying a few moments quiet in the lounge after lunch before getting to their jobs again when the Revd. H. Banks, who was responsible for the entertainment tomorrow, and was also himself to sing twice and recite once, came in with 'an unique appeal.' He was known to most of the company and was highly popular, for his ecclesiastical duties performed at St. Giles's amid cottas and banners and maniples and incense and genuflexions were quite a feature at Bolton among visitors, and made you feel, as Miss Howard said, that the Church was a living force. He was a welcome guest also at tennis-parties and teas, and had once said damn, quite out loud in the presence of Colonel Chase, who thought that very broad-minded for a clergyman. In general the Colonel had a low opinion of parsons since they had done nothing to check the abominable selfishness of the lower classes, in striking for a living wage, which had caused taxation to grow to such monstrous proportions. But Banks was an excellent fellow: except in church you would not know he was a padre at all. . . .

"A most calamitous thing has befallen us," said this broad-minded padre, "for Mr. Graves the *masseur* who was to entertain us with his most amusing stories tomorrow night has gone to bed with influenza, and Dr. Dobbs absolutely forbids him to take part in our effort for the Children's Hospital tomorrow, unless he thinks he will enjoy an attack of pneumonia."

The eyes of all the guests which had been fixed on Mr. Banks, wheeled like a flock of plovers and settled on Mrs. Bliss. Would Mind (such was the instinctive though unspoken question) disperse Mr. Graves's influenza as it had dispersed the Colonel's cold? Mr. Banks, of course, could not be expected to understand what these earnest, enquiring glances meant, and though slightly disconcerted by thus suddenly losing everyone's attention, proceeded to make his appeal.

"Jolly rough luck just the day before our entertainment," he said, "but who knows whether there may not be a silver lining to our cloud? Everyone in Bolton has heard that we have among us, present here, a superb *raconteur,* and my Committee unanimously deputed me to find out whether our friend Colonel Chase would not consent to take his place."

All eyes wheeled again to the Colonel. Wonderful though a demonstration of Mind over the *masseur* would have been, there was no need for it now.

"Oh, what a treat that would be," said Mrs. Oxney. "Often and often I've felt quite selfish when Colonel Chase has been telling his wonderful stories to just a handful of listeners, to think how many people longed to hear him and didn't get the chance. Do, Colonel!"

"Oh, do!" said Miss Howard, "I shan't feel nearly so nervous if I'm to follow you, for everyone will be in such a good temper. Padre, you must persuade him."

Florence added her appeal.

"Wouldn't that be lovely, Papa?" she said. "You would have to make an effort to go. Oh, do, Colonel Chase!"

A fugue on the subject of 'Oh, do', followed.

"Upon my word," said Colonel Chase, highly gratified but tremulous, "my little twopenny stories are only fit for a friend's ear, just to pass the time. Really in public, you know, and on a platform it's a very different matter!"

A wail of 'Oh, do' went up in a minor key.

"Think how many more people will come," said Mrs. Oxney, "though to be sure Miss Howard's name alone would fill the hall. There won't be standing room."

"And all the poor little children in hospital."

CHAPTER V

"And helping others," said Mrs. Bliss who had been quite ready to adopt the unspoken suggestion that she would bring Mind to bear upon Mr. Graves's influenza, till this proposition was made.

"And poor Mr. Graves lying there and worrying himself over what will happen if no one can be found to take his place."

"And so much more amusing than Mr. Graves could possibly be."

"And how we shall all shudder if you tell your ghost story, and how we shall laugh if you tell us about the Dean and the port wine."

("And what Slam said about your declaration of two hearts," whispered Tim to Mrs. Holders.).

"And the tiger! What suspense for those who haven't heard it."

It was not in human nature to resist so universal an appeal. Colonel Chase saw himself on the platform before a tense audience.

"Indeed, I hardly like to refuse," he began.

The wailing strains of 'Oh, do' swelled to a joyful chorus. "Well, I yield, I yield," he said. "I am not too proud to fill a gap at the last moment. But my work's cut out for me. I shall have to rehearse my little yarns over and over again to get them ship-shape by tomorrow night. Short notice, you know, padre. Miss Howard's lucky only to be improvising."

"Oh, but you know them all by heart," said Mrs. Oxney. "Tell them all just as you tell them to us after tea. Perfect!"

Mr. Banks warmly shook the Colonel's hand and hurried back to relieve his Committee's suspense with the joyful news, while Colonel Chase abandoning all thought of a walk, retired to the smoking-room to jot down his selection of stories, and trim them into public shape. He was immensely gratified at the strong expressions of entreaty and delighted anticipation which he had heard from those who knew his stories so well, and promised to give his audience something better worth listening to than the yarns with which Mr. Graves entertained the victims of his professional manipulations. (Probably they only laughed at them because Mr. Graves was running his fingers over ticklish places in their anatomy.) So much too lay in the address and appearances of the *raconteur,* and it was pleasant to remember that Mr. Graves was a podgy little bit of a man with no presence at all and a wheezy voice. . . . "We'll begin with a good laugh," he thought: the 'Curate's Egg' would lead off well, and he recited to himself with appropriate gestures of a man wielding an egg-spoon, the story of the Curate breakfasting with his Bishop, and being given an egg which smelt abominable ('something like the waters here,' thought the Colonel) and, on his diocesan making enquiries, how the Curate said that parts of it were excellent. Very likely that yarn had never reached Bolton yet, or, on the other hand, it might have reached Bolton so long ago that the majority of his audience would be too young to recollect its vogue. After that might come the story of the man-eating tiger which he stalked on foot through the jungle and shot as it charged him. Then for relief he would tell them of the Dean who gargled with port wine by mistake, but perhaps two stories making fun of the cloth would be injudicious, with Mr. Banks in the chair, and he decided to tell instead the story of the little boy who took a sip of his father's whisky and soda, and not liking the taste put it back in the glass. That had amused Mr. Banks before now. After that he must make the flesh of his entire audience creep, and the ghost story of the dak-bungalow would be the very thing. It was rather a long story, but he had no reason to suspect that anyone had ever found it so, and if the lights could be turned down during it, and Miss Howard would play a little weird music on the piano during the most thrilling section, the effect would be quite terrific. Then up would go the lights again, and he would make them hold their sides over the member of Parliament who thought he had sat down on his neighbour's hat, and in the middle of his profuse apologies found that it was his own. How his junior officers used to roar when he told them that story at mess. But he must be careful to omit the swear-words tomorrow: that was a pity.

These ought to be enough he thought, and, as an *encore,* he could tell the history of the young grocer who meaning to send a lovely rose to his young lady sent by mistake a piece of strong Gorgonzola, enclosing an amorous note saying 'When I smell it I think of you.' The rose went--he might say--to a peppery old Colonel not a hundred miles from here, as per his esteemed order, and so the young grocer lost his custom and his young lady. . . . He went through them all just as he meant to tell them tomorrow night, and found they had taken twenty-five minutes, which would do very well: but not another yarn should they get out of him, however much they clamoured.

Then he went to look for Miss Howard, to ask her to play the ghost-music, but found she had gone to see about laying the carpet in the Green Salon: he followed her, for it was most important that she should make ghost-music to his recitation, but learned that the carpet had been laid, and Miss Howard had gone to the Assembly Rooms. He just looked into the Green Salon to see how her preparations progressed, but was plunged into so thick a stew of opoponax and musk and incense that it was impossible to breathe, let alone seeing anything. Violently coughing, he proceeded to the Assembly Rooms, and there was Miss Howard seeing what it felt like to improvise on a platform. She readily consented to play weird music to accompany the ghost story, and a couple of workmen, who were arranging chairs for the entertainment tomorrow, sat down in them, so as not to make a 'scraping sound' during this rehearsal of the famous adventures in the dak-bungalow. The climax approached:

"I was just about to light my lamp," said the Colonel in a hollow voice, "when I saw, or seemed to see in the far corner a shadow forming itself into the semblance of a man. . . . No, Miss Howard, I think I should like you to come in with those chords at the word 'far corner'. And the soft pedal, please. I shall be speaking in a very low voice myself, and I fear it would hardly carry. Shall we try that again?"

"I can't play much softer," said Miss Howard, "and the soft pedal has been on the whole time."

"Then perhaps we had better turn the piano away from the audience," said he. "Lend a hand here, one or two of you fellows, will you?"

"But my solo follows very soon after, Colonel," she said. "The piano must be moved back again."

"Oh, that's easily done. The padre and I will see to that. Now, Miss Howard, I'll begin again at 'light my lamp', and your cue is 'far corner'. Now please."

Once more the terrifying tale unfolded itself and when the phantom shrieked, Miss Howard produced so fearful an effect with the loud pedal and both hands violently scampering up the piano that the Colonel nearly jumped out of his skin.

"My word, how you startled me," he said. "Most effective. Just like that tomorrow please. And then dead silence till the beat of the tom-toms is heard, on one note in the bass very slow and measured. . . . Perfect. And now let us take it all through again: we must get it without a hitch. Perhaps at the beginning we might have a line or two of 'On the road to Mandalay', just to give the local colour. Oh, much softer than that. Just a suggestion . . . fading away as I begin."

Now Miss Howard had come here on purpose to have a good practice and get used to the room and the instrument, and here she was tucked away behind the upright piano, and making ghost-music for the Colonel. Already it was growing dark, the chairs were all arranged, and the foreman was jingling his keys, wanting to lock the hall up and get home. He had heard the ghost story three times and now he could not stand it again.

"We're closing the hall for the night, sir, now," he said.

Colonel Chase forgot about Mind for the moment, and was highly indignant.

"Well, upon my soul!" he said. "We're doing our best to give you a good entertainment for your Children's Hospital and we're told we're not wanted. It's enough to make--"

Suddenly he remembered about his cold and his pedometer.

"Just give us two minutes more, there's a good feller," he said. "And perhaps you'd be so kind as to go to the far end of the room, and tell me if you can hear. . . . That's capital of you. . . . Now Miss Howard I'm sure you don't want to keep anybody waiting, any more than I do. So let's practise the rest afterwards, and begin now at 'I was just about to light my lamp'--"

The thrilling section down to the phantom's shriek was rehearsed once more, and Colonel Chase called out to know if he had been heard.

"Not a word, sir," said the foreman cheerfully. "I heard the music though. And now I must really ask you--"

"Yes, yes, at once," said the Colonel. "We can have another practice at home, Miss Howard. Let me see. I must have a table on the centre of the platform with a glass and bottle of water. It would never do if I was to get hoarse, for in the story of the little boy and his father's whisky I mean to use falsetto. And I hope there will be plenty of light; the play of the features counts for so much. The look of tension and terror in the tiger story; that would be quite lost if there was not enough light. But they must be turned down for the ghost story and turned up immediately after it. That must be seen to by some trustworthy man."

The next day was a succession of hectic hours for Wentworth, since Colonel Chase who had so intrepidly faced man-eaters and phantoms found the prospect of facing an audience far more formidable. He recited his stories over and over again to rows of imaginary listeners in the smoking-room, and manifested such want of control if disturbed, that Mrs. Oxney put up a notice on the door of 'Private'. Miss Howard had similarly taken possession of the drawing-room, and in spite of her confidence in Mind, found that the passage of octaves to usher in the re-entry of the Chopin waltz was fading gradually but firmly out of her memory and that constant repetition only served to hasten that distressful process. In order to fix these fugitive beauties in her mind (since Mind seemed so inconsistent an ally) she wrote down some of the most important on music paper, though as her performance was improvised, it would hardly do to play from notes when the time came. Occasionally she closed her eyes and smiled, but the smile grew very wan as its inefficacy manifested itself. Then Colonel Chase wanted to go through the music of the ghost story once or twice more, and it got muddled up with the octaves which now came out like the sun from behind a cloud when she wanted something else, and he forgot the cue he had given her of 'the far corner', and said, 'the other end of the room'. In consequence there were no weird chords at all, for she was waiting for 'far corner'.

"Music, please," rapped out Colonel Chase.

"But my cue is 'far corner'," said Miss Howard in a strangled voice.

"Well, 'the other end of the room' is the same thing," he said. "A little intelligence, Miss Howard. The point is that the ghost is just appearing, and you have to play. I should have thought that was clear. Let us go back to the lighting of the lamp."

Miss Howard moistened her lips with the tip of her tongue. She often did this when determined, under any provocation, to behave like a perfect lady.

"My mistake no doubt," she said. "The lighting of the lamp: yes."

This time she came in with the shriek-motif far too soon, and Colonel Chase, with his nerves worn to fiddle-strings at the prospect of this evening, stamped on the floor with his great feet.

"Good gracious me!" he exclaimed. "It gets worse and worse. We had better have no music at all than this hash."

Miss Howard merely closed the lid of the piano.

"I think that would be far the best course," she said and sat with her hands in her lap looking at the ceiling, till he left the room. Then she opened the piano again and went on with her practice.

Colonel Chase went back to the smoking-room in an ague of passion and nervousness. He told the ghost story again to himself, but now he had got so accustomed to the music that it put him out dreadfully not to have it, and a frenzied effort at reliance on Mind had no calming effect whatever. Though he hated to do it, he felt he must eat humble pie, and beg Miss Howard to forgive him, for he could not get on at all without her. Perhaps Mrs. Oxney would carry his regrets:

that would make the humble pie less hard to swallow. She consented to do her best.

Miss Howard had a sense of dignity, and when the ambassadress with many compliments on the exquisite music, sidled into the drawing-room, she met with a cool reception.

"I am very glad that Colonel Chase feels that he has behaved most rudely," said Miss Howard. "It is his place to tell me so himself. Thank you, Mrs. Oxney."

And she resumed the long shake for the right hand which led towards the Chopin waltz. The octaves went better now, and having given ample time for Colonel Chase to come and apologise, she went out for a stroll in the bright sunshine, strenuously denying malice, nervousness and loss of memory. Naturally she had to be unconscious of his presence at lunch, but that was only proper. He had no existence for Miss Howard: how then could she see him?

Another half-hour's solitary rehearsal in the smoking-room broke Colonel Chase down: he could not manage the ghost story at all without those weird chords. He apologised in person, and they went through it twice more. After tea they sat with Mrs. Bliss in a row and demonstrated over the entertainment. Mr. Kemp and Florence were demonstrating too, he over his left hip, and Florence over her need for Miss Howard as a friend, and they all parted to dress, calm and confident.

Dinner was early that night for the entertainment began at a quarter to eight for eight, whatever that meant. Colonel Chase had pinned a quantity of medals and ribands to his evening coat, among which Mrs. Holders swore she detected an ordinary shilling with a hole in it. The assembly room was packed, all but the front row where seats were reserved for the party from Wentworth, and the four centre ones, so Mr. Banks excitedly told them, for the Dowager Countess of Appledore and her party. She had sent in from the Grange that afternoon to order them, with the intimation that she might be a few minutes late. As she was patroness of the Children's Hospital Mr. Banks was sure that this signified that the entertainment was not to begin without her and her party. He and Town Councillor Bowen had arranged to receive her at the door, and he hoped that Colonel Chase would assist them. So they all three waited for the august arrivals in a strong draught for a quarter of an hour. Then the glad word went about that the motor from the Grange had arrived, and an awed silence settled on the rest of the front row.

The reception committee bowed and smiled and an icy blast swept Lady Appledore and party into the hall. In number and splendour her party was disappointing, for it consisted of two women so wrapped up in cloaks and scarves and capes and woollies that nothing whatever could be seen of them. They were then partially unwound by the reception committee and the bleak and wintry features of Lady Appledore, whose face resembled a frost-bitten pansy with all its marking huddled up together in the middle, were disclosed. 'Party' was her companion, Miss Jobson, whose life was spent in holding skeins of wool for her, reading books to her, and sitting opposite to her in the motor. Lady Appledore then nodded to Mr. Banks to signify that she was ready, and the choir of St. Giles's church sang a lullaby and a drinking song amid indescribable apathy.

Colonel Chase's moment had arrived: Miss Howard slipped into her place behind the piano, and Mr. Banks introduced the gallant Colonel whose stories were so well known to everybody by repute (and, he might have added, to Wentworth by repetition). The gallant Colonel like Horatio of old had thrown himself into the breach caused by the lamented absence of Mr. Graves and so they were going to taste what he might call the choicest of Colonel Chase's anecdotal vintage for themselves.

Wentworth violently led the otherwise tame applause and Colonel Chase's ruddy face had faded to the hue of the cheapest pink blotting paper as he told them about the Curate's egg. Wentworth rocked with laughter but Mrs. Oxney heard Lady Appledore say to her companion, 'I am never amused, Miss Jobson, at jokes about the Church,' and she remembered with dismay that the story of the Dean was coming and that her ladyship was the daughter of one. She whispered her apprehensions to her sister who felt sure that Colonel Chase would substitute the story of the little boy and his father's whisky. That would be far more suitable for Lady Appledore was a savage teetotaller.

The narrator embarked on his story of "My encounter with the Man-eater," which had so often frozen the blood of Wentworth. But the audience, with the curious unanimity of crowds, had made up their minds, after the Curate's egg, that he was a comic, pure and simple, and the crack-jaw Indian names and allusions to tiffin and Chota-hazri and shikari produced little titters of delighted laughter. They became more and more certain of it as he bade them follow him (he was kidding them) into the pathless solitary jungle with the kites whistling overhead (here some dramatic boy at the back whistled piercingly between his fingers) and up the dry nullah-wallah. "All at once," said the Colonel pointing at Mrs. Oxney, "I heard a rustle in the bushes close by me, and turning I saw within a few yards of me the gleaming eyes and flashing teeth of the man-eater." He whisked round, making the movement of putting his rifle to his shoulder, and at that moment, the performing dog which had escaped from its master, leaped on to the stage and sat up and begged. So loud a roar of delighted laughter went up from the entire hall that no one ever knew whether the man killed the man-eater or the man-eater the man. As it slowly subsided amid sporadic cackles, a yelp or two from the performing dog denoted that somebody was "larning" it to be a tiger.

The story of the little boy and the whisky pleased Lady Appledore very much. "A teetotaller for life I expect," she said to Miss Jobson, "I should like some more stories of that sort."

Colonel Chase sat down for a moment after this, and drank a little water out of the glass in which he had pretended as a little boy to put back the whisky. This took the audience's fancy tremendously, and he couldn't conceive why. He was in so strange a mental state that even Mrs. Bliss, the interpreter of Mind, would have found him hard to treat. He was simmering with fury at the story of the man-eater having been received with those ribald gusts of laughter, and felt sure that he would have gripped his audience and made them catch their breath with suspense, had not that wretched mongrel bounded on to the stage at the climax. On the other hand, the roars of laughter and applause which had greeted him went to his head like wine, and he hardly knew whether to be elated or indignant. He rose to tell his ghost story, and little did they think what terrors and goose-flesh were coming: then, as the *encore,* he would restore them with the tale of the grocer.

The little boy with the whisky had rather damped the spirits of his audience, but on the announcement of 'My own ghost' they brightened up again, and cheerfully beat time to the first few bars of 'On the road to Mandalay'.

"In the year 1895," said Colonel Chase, "I was stationed at Futipur-Sekri, and by the order of his Excellency the Viceroy--"

The quicker-witted portion of his audience began to laugh. It was like Mr. George Robey saying 'The last time I had tea with the King'. They knew the sort of thing that was coming. Colonel Chase drew himself up, and fingered his medals. So like George Robey.

"By the order of his Excellency the Viceroy," said Colonel Chase, rather severely, "I was sent into the district of Astmetagaga to make a report on the discontent among the Bizributmas. Bellialonga, the capital of the Bizributma tribe was a three-days journey from Futipur-Sekri, and I had to sleep at two dak-bungalows on the way. Just before sunset on the day of which I am speaking I came in sight of the dak-bungalow of Poona-padra, and sent my khitmagar on with a couple of coolies to cook my dinner, and deal with superfluous cobras."

"Really very good," said Lady Appledore to Miss Jobson, "a perfect parody of Mr. Kipling. I am sure something very comical is coming."

Colonel Chase could not hear what she said, but saw that both she and Miss Jobson had their eyes fixed on him in avid attention.

"The khitmagar was in the cook-house when I arrived," said he, turning slightly towards the piano to show Miss Howard that her cue was imminent, "and night was at hand. My table was laid and I was just about to light the lamp, when I saw at the other end of the room--I mean, in the far corner--"

The piano punctually emitted a moaning wail, and Colonel Chase raised his voice a little.

"--a grey shape forming itself into the semblance of a man. As the lamp burned brighter--"

"You 'aven't lit it yet mister," said some precisian from the back.

"--burned brighter," repeated Colonel Chase, "I saw the dread form with greater distinctness, and my heart stood still. It was clothed in ragged garments, sparse elfin-locks hung over its forehead--forehead," said he, looking wildly round for the man whose duty it was at this particular moment to switch off all the lights in the hall except one close above the platform, by which the audience could see his face of horror surrounded by darkness, "and blood dripped from a jagged wound in its throat. Slowly it detached itself from the wall and advanced on me--"

Every single light went out, including that above the platform, and the man at the switches seeing his mistake, put them all on again. The laughter became general, but, as it were, expectant, holding itself in for the climax.

"--towering ever higher as it approached. Cold sweat broke out on my forehead, my throat was dry as dust--"

"'Ave a drink," said a delighted voice.

"--my knees trembled, and I knew that the powers of Hell were loose. 'Avaunt', I cried, 'In the name of God avaunt' . . . The phantom shrieked--"

Miss Howard, whose hands were poised above the keys, struck a tremendous ascending arpeggio, the end of which was drowned in a roar of laughter. The hall hooted with inextinguishable joy: never was there such a comic as the Colonel.

After this stupendous success Colonel Chase should have stopped: to tell the story of the grocer was to whitewash the lily. But it served to quiet the audience again, though when Mr. Banks in a fruity baritone melodiously bade them come fishing, since tomorrow would be Friday, there were cheerful dissentients who reminded him it would be Thursday. He most obligingly accepted the correction in the second verse, and in the third said it would be Tuesday which gave much satisfaction. He at once sang an *encore,* and then hurried to the 'artists' room', where Dr. Dobbs was arranging top hats and canaries and handkerchiefs, and put it tactfully to the owner of the performing dog that, as that intelligent animal had already scored the success of the evening as the man-eater, and as Lady Appledore had kept them waiting so long, would it be possible to reserve dear little Toby's performance for the next entertainment at Christmas. Toby's master with some asperity, said that it would not only be possible but probable that Toby's next performance would be reserved for ever and ever, and left by the back door in high dudgeon.

Slightly crushed by this severity, Mr. Banks stole back on tiptoe to hear the piano solo. Miss Howard had begun splendidly, and with dreamy eyes fixed on the ceiling and head a little on one side to catch the messages from the harmonious spirits of the air, was improvising that charming fragment from the waltz by Chopin with delicacy and precision. Then she closed her eyes and sank her head over the pensive section by moonlight, and made everybody feel that tomorrow would be Monday, so Sunday-like was the chorale that toothache had inspired. She opened her eyes again, and was wreathed in smiles as the spirits of the air suggested to her that pretty device of the long shake and the crossing arpeggios, but next moment those nearest her might have observed a slightly glazed look coming over her face as the magnificent *fortissimo* passage for octaves in both hands drew near. She tried to calm herself by letting her eyes stray about to shew her complete mastery of her task: now they glanced at Lady Appledore, now at Florence who was leaning forward towards her with a look of yearning ecstasy, rather disconcerting. Now she was among the octaves, but for the life of her once more she could not remember how she rescued herself from this tempestuous sea and slid into the calm waters of the Chopin waltz again, and she projected anxious thoughts into the rapidly approaching future, instead of trusting to Mind, or at least her memory, to prompt her when she came to that point. She wished passionately that she had not improvised this fine passage at all: it would have been so easy to go straight into the Chopin waltz from the chorale. Her agitation increased, and the octaves grew faster and louder: she missed a change of key and found herself with fingers already aching with fatigue apparently committed to thunder forth fortuitous octaves with both hands till she swooned with the exertion. In vain she thought of Mrs. Bliss, in vain she stretched her mouth in an agonised smile and denied octaves and improvisation and forgetfulness and fatigue and anything else that came into her head. Her face was getting crimson, and yet she could not stop and if she could she would now be unable to recollect even the Chopin waltz. Finally, in absolute despair, she took her hands off the notes, hurled them at the piano again in three crashing chords, and rose. The moment she was on her feet she remembered exactly what the transition should have been, but now it was too late. . . . After the tremendous din that had been going on the applause sounded but faint, except for Florence's indefatigable smacks.

Long before the hour for collection and carriages Wentworth collectively had been puzzling over what its demeanour to Colonel Chase should be. He was sitting a little apart from the rest, and sideway glances at him observed that he appeared slightly morose, or as if he was puzzling too. There was no doubt that he had won the success of the evening, but that success had been purchased with strange coin, for his humorous tales had produced depression, and in others the suspense and terror which it had been his firm intention to evoke had roused gales of laughter. Not even the excitement of seeing how much Dowager Countesses gave to collections nor the pained disgust to observe that this one considered sixpence ample, put this difficult problem of demeanour out of Mrs. Oxney's mind, and her sister whom she consulted in whispers was utterly at a loss: Mrs. Bertram merely shook her head sadly, and thought it very awkward. Should they congratulate him on his success, or execrate the odious light-mindedness of the audience, or ignore the whole affair and talk lightly about the weather?

There they all were then in a rather tense group, waiting for Lady Appledore's motor to start and leave the entrance clear for the Wentworth bus. The reception committee including Colonel Chase was bowing its thanks to her for her distinguished patronage and her sixpence, and it was Lady Appledore herself who solved the problem for them.

"I so much enjoyed your very amusing stories, Colonel Chase," she said. "Did I not Miss Jobson? The ghost! Quite killing! How I laughed! And the man-eater! What a clever little dog to come in just when you told it. Beautifully trained! And the comic music for the ghost! Most humorous."

Now two courses were open to Colonel Chase. He might either turn livid with passion and tell Lady Appledore that she was as contemptible as the rest of the yokels who had laughed when they should have shuddered, or he might adopt Lady Appledore's heresy as orthodox, and promulgate it, so to speak, as his own official Bull. The fact that he was a snob to the bottom of his appendix, and soberly considered countesses to be of a clay apart was perhaps the determining factor which settled the puzzling question of his demeanour. He bowed again and all his medals jingled.

"Delighted to have afforded you a little amusement, Lady Appledore," he said in a voice that Wentworth could hear. "We had many a laugh in the mess when I told my ghost story."

That, of course, settled the matter for Wentworth, and when he rejoined his party everybody knew exactly what line to take. That he had told the two thrilling tales of the man-eater and the ghost often and often before, and that they had been received with shudders and gasps and tremblings, and protests from Mrs. Oxney that she wouldn't dare to go to bed to-night, must now be forgotten: from henceforth, world without end, these were comic stories, and Wentworth would scream with laughter at all the points where hitherto it had frozen with horror.

"Oh, Colonel," said Mrs. Oxney, "what a treat you gave us! You made me ache with laughing. How we all enjoyed it! You never told them so wonderfully. Miss Howard, too! Her comic accompaniment: how you must have practised it together. And then your lovely improvisation afterwards, Miss Howard; all coming to you on the spur of the moment like that! At one moment I thought the inspiration was going to fail you, but how foolish of me to have been alarmed. Those grand chords at the end! You two made the whole success of the evening and Mr. and Mrs. Banks of course as well," she hastily added at the approach of these artists. "The violin: such a sweet instrument. And tomorrow will be Tuesday or Wednesday, I declare I don't know what to-day is after that. And 'Curfew shall not ring to-night'! What a heroine! She deserved the Victoria Cross at least. And your dear little choir boys singing so beautifully and of course--good evening, Dr. Dobbs--Dr. Dobbs's wonderful conjuring tricks. I couldn't see how any of them were done, and fancy the Countess of Appledore only giving sixpence!"

The official and orthodox view could not have been more ably stated, and after a pleasant little refection of sandwiches and cake in the lounge, with some hot soup for the artists who must be exhausted with their efforts, Colonel Chase was induced to give them the ghost story again (new style) with piano accompaniment. Mrs. Holders had not been to the entertainment and to her unbounded astonishment she heard the shuddering and gruesome tale received with hoots of merriment. This was quite inexplicable and almost more so was the evident satisfaction of Colonel Chase.

"Well, a good laugh does us no harm now and again," he said, "and I must say that I was pleased with the quickness with which the audience took my points. Nothing so depressing for the entertainer as to find that his humour is not appreciated. Lady Appledore--a charming woman--said she had enjoyed my little stories immensely. Very kind of her, I'm sure. I must bicycle over to the Grange some day soon and leave my card."

"And Miss Howard's playing too, Mrs. Holders," continued Mrs. Oxney, who wanted everyone to feel happy and appreciated. "You did miss something there. Quite a sensation! How I should like to hear it again! You ought to write it down, Miss Howard, you ought indeed, so that your inspiration shouldn't be lost, and that others might play it as well if they had the fingers, though I'm sure only the most superior pianists could do it. What an evening of enjoyment! And the picture exhibition to look forward to next week."

"But fancy the Countess of Appledore only giving sixpence," said Mrs. Bertram, on whom this miserly incident had made the deepest impression. "I thought that was a very paltry sum indeed, and I could hardly believe my eyes. Sixpence, and Miss Jobson nothing at all."

Colonel Chase went up to bed satisfied that he had acted for the best in taking the verdict of the audience (especially when endorsed by a Countess) as final. He had gone through the most poignant emotions that evening, in which rage and disgust were the keenest. His feelings when the house began to laugh at the story of the tiger were indescribable, and when that miserable little terrier came on to the platform and begged, he would willingly have shot it, had the imaginary rifle in his hands, suddenly materialised: and when the house again rocked with merriment at his ghost story, he would, had the rifle undergone a further transmutation into a machine-gun have felt the greatest satisfaction in mowing them down in swathes, beginning with a Countess. Then his comic stories had failed altogether (these rustic audiences had the most perverted sense of humour) and probably no more deeply-chagrined a reciter had ever stepped down from a platform. He really could not see how he could face Wentworth at all: it is true they had not laughed except in the right places, and when others laughed they had worn expressions of pain and sympathy, and throughout the remainder of the entertainment he had been thinking of some very severe things to say about being subjected to the insults of an unmannerly mob. Then, owing to Lady Appledore's comments, he had seized his opportunity, and mounted the throne of the supreme comic artist. It was like a conjuring trick, one of Dr. Dobbs's best.

As he undressed and did his valuable exercises, puffing out his big chest, and bending till he touched his toes, he wondered if a more surprising success had ever come to a man out of ruinous failure. Wentworth, too, had caught on at once, and had laughed at the repetition of the ghost story just now, as if they had never known what it felt like to shudder. . . . And then suddenly the thought of Mrs. Bliss came to him. She had told him that if only he relied on Mind, in his kind and unselfish efforts in aid of the poor children in hospital, they must be crowned with brilliant success. That had certainly happened, though as a matter of fact the poor children in hospital had not even so much as entered his head, since he was first approached by Mr. Banks. And then he remembered also that Mrs. Bliss had said that Mind was often inscrutable in its workings: the aspirations of those who trusted it were always fulfilled, but mortal sense could never accurately predict the manner of it. Certainly he had never expected that Mind would fulfil his aspirations by causing his audience to peal with laughter at what had been designed to make their flesh creep, and when their first giggles broke out he had determined to have nothing to do with Mind. But now that apparent failure wore a different aspect, one that could only be accounted for by the theory of inscrutable dealings, 'Upon my word,' he said to himself, as he got into bed, 'I'll look into it all a bit further. My cold, my pedometer, and now this! It all seems to hang together in the most marvellous fashion.'

Mr. Banks came up to Wentworth again next day to see Colonel Chase, full of congratulations and with a further request to make.

"Stupendous, Colonel," he said, "you were simply stupendous last night. There were some nurses there from the Children's Hospital, and they told me on my visit there this morning that they'd never laughed so much in all their born days. 'Curfew shall not ring to-night' seems to have pleased them too, but that's neither here nor there."

"Remarkably fine, I thought," said Colonel Chase, who could easily afford to commend minor lights.

"Very good of you to say so. I thought I gripped the audience. Well, the matron charged me to ask you if you wouldn't very kindly give the story of the tiger and the ghost in the wards. Poor little mites you know: there've got small cause for laughter in their lives, and it really would be most good of you."

Colonel Chase was highly gratified, and good-naturedly abandoned his walk, and went to the hospital that afternoon. The matron thought she could introduce her cat into the tiger story to take the place of that clever dog, while it was in course of narration, for it was a lethargic cat, usually asleep and good at staying exactly where it was put: she could put it down on one of the beds quite quietly. It was thought better to feed the cat first, for after food sleep was assured, so would the Colonel begin with the ghost story? The children were all agog with pleasure and excitement at the prospect of hearing the funny man.

The nurses, already tittering at what was coming, preceded the funny man into the first ward, and he began his ghost story. But the effect was highly disastrous: child after child broke into shrieks of terror and dismay, nurses hurried from bed to bed to comfort the howling occupants, and assure them they shouldn't be frightened any more, and the matron had to beg the Colonel to leave the ward without delay. So, within ten minutes of his arrival, he was on his way back to Wentworth in a state of complete bewilderment as to whether the ghost story was terrible or comic; its effect seemed to be wholly incalculable. And surely Mind was acting again in the most inscrutable manner.

He stalked into the lounge where Mrs. Bliss was sitting. She hailed him with her widest smile.

"There you are, Colonel!" she said. "How kind and dear of you to have sacrificed your walk. How the poor little mites must have enjoyed it! What brightness you have brought into lives full of Error! I've been demonstrating over the pleasure you have been giving ever since you started. Tell me all about it!"

Colonel Chase's suspicions about Mind deepened to real distrust. But perhaps Mrs. Bliss could explain it.

"I can't make it out," he said. "I meant to give pleasure but when I got to the ghost forming itself in the far corner the children burst into sobs and howls. The matron hurried in and asked me to go away at once. Very disconcerting. What do you make of it?"

CHAPTER V

Mrs. Bliss was not in the least disconcerted.

"Poor little mites!" she said. "You see they are surrounded with thoughts of illness: everything round them suggests illness: doctors, nurses, *materia medica,* and as you know now it is all Error. You came in, radiating Mind, and Error boiled up to the surface, violent for the moment, but dispersing rapidly. It often happens like that. All is Mind. Mind is all. Terror and evil and sickness flee before it. There is no reality in them. There is a wonderful page or two about it in the Manual."

She picked up the Manual and turned quickly over the pages. "Yes, here it is," she said. "Shall I read it? Sweet words and so true! 'Often when Error is brought under the influence of Mind, there takes place a chemicalisation. Error surges to the surface only to be instantly dispersed. An apparent relapse may occur, and this is often the first sign that the healing process is going on.' Quite convincing, is it not? The dear little mites will be so much better in consequence of your visit. I am so glad you went."

CHAPTER VI

For the rest of the week Miss Howard had very little time to attend to Mind, and just about as little inclination. She considered that Mind had shewn the greatest inattention to her improvisation: she had committed herself and it to Mind with the complete trust that a passenger puts in the engine-driver when he makes a journey by train, and there had been an accident. Not only had she quite forgotten the end of the passage for octaves, but there had been no sign whatever of an *encore,* whereas Colonel Chase who had already been cured of a cold, the tantrums and the loss of a pedometer, had been loaded with benefits. It was not fair, and though Mrs. Bliss assured her that those last few chords would linger for ever in her memory like the sound of a great Mental Amen, Miss Howard would far sooner have got back into the Chopin waltz and finished according to plan, than have so agreeably affected Mrs. Bliss. Besides, those chords composing the great Mental Amen, would have come in anyhow.

Mind, too, was doing nothing for Mr. Kemp, and Mrs. Bliss's argument that his baths and massage were a materialistic hindrance to his recovery was met with the deadly parry that she was having baths and massage too, and was improving enormously.

But she only smiled unweariedly, and repeated that she submitted to baths and massage for her husband's sake, and that they did not hinder her progress because she was quite sure that they had no effect whatever on her. But the fact of submitting to them (not the baths and massage themselves) perhaps did her good for this was a sacrifice made to love, and Mind liked that. What did hinder progress was to have faith in *materia medica* and wouldn't dear Mr. Kemp give up his treatment for a week, for he was still believing it might do him good, and see how much better he would be? It was clearly no use arguing with Mrs. Bliss for she only smiled and said it all over again with loving pity (which was so exasperating), but every night as he had a few sips of hot milk or a glass of lemonade without sugar, and a rusk, he argued the position out with Florence. Florence could not make up her mind either, and so after lengthy debate they sat with smiles and closed eyes, and since he was no better in the morning he had his reclining bath as usual. Mr. Kemp in fact served both Mind and Mammon with equal devotion and no reward from either.

But Miss Howard during the few days that remained before the opening of her exhibition of pictures in the Green Salon, worked away, relying entirely on herself and not at all on Mind: she had become, for the time being, a rank a-mentalist. The question of prices was truly difficult, for she wanted to get as much as she could for her pictures, but had not the vaguest idea what anybody would be willing to give. So instead of closing her eyes, and seeking guidance, she looked at her pictures with a critical eye, and eventually made the scale. 'Evening Bells', with a five-and-sixpenny frame positively given away, was two guineas: Mrs. Oxney's cat under the title of 'Pussy-dear' and 'Geraniums' were one guinea, and everything else was half-a-guinea. This price list, to be produced on application, was entrusted to the care of one of the handsomest of the liveried pages at the Baths (who generally spent their days in playing leap-frog with each other) whom Mr. Bowen guaranteed to be the brightest boy in Bolton. He was also given a roll of perforated paper, much like a roll of exceedingly narrow toilet-paper, on each numbered section of which was printed an advertisement of Mr. Bowen, plumber, decorator, picture-framer and carpenter: these rolls were supplied by Mr. Bowen free of charge, for the sake of the publicity. The leap-frog boy, thus made door-keeper, cashier and bureau of information, had merely to tear off one of these sections, and hand it on payment of sixpence to the visitors to the Green Salon: the device seemed fool-proof. But he had to be tactful as well, for if he observed a visitor looking very attentively at the exhibits, he was to touch his cap with an insinuating smile, and ask if he would like to see a price-list. In his left trouser pocket there was a pill box thrown in gratis with *'Souvenir d'Orient'* by Mr. Amble, containing some minute red adhesive stars, and in case a picture was purchased, he had to write down the name and address of the purchaser and with a genteel application of the tip of his tongue to the adhesive star, affix it to the corner of the picture, to indicate that it was sold. For these services he received a shilling a day in addition to the salary he earned from the establishment for playing leap-frog.

The hanging of the pictures was a task no less difficult than their pricing. In some places the walls were so crumbly, (owing probably to the action of the brine) that large flakes came away under the lightest impact of that useful little nail called the 'Small Brad', while in others the walls were so adamantine (owing probably to the action of the rotten-egg water) that the Small Brad curled up and became a minute croquet hoop. In the end a taut copper wire had to be hung from corner to corner of the walls of the Green Salon and the pictures hooked on to it. They had a tendency to sag towards the centre where the wire drooped a little. An advertisement appeared on Friday and Saturday in the *Bolton Gazette,* and Mr. Bowen, who was part-owner of the paper said he was confident that Miss Howard would not regret that little trifle of expense, when all was said and done. This was a dark oracular saying, but Mr. Bowen seemed quite certain about it.

By Saturday afternoon every picture was in its place: Evening Bells, and Pussy-dear, and Geraniums and Reflections and Lengthening Shadows and God's Acre and Bethesda and Healing Springs and Golf Links Wentworth, and Leafy Warwickshire and June's Glory and Suntrap and Frosty Morning and Dewy Eve and Harvest Moon, and Gloaming and Beeches and Hawthorns and St. Giles's

Church and Still Life and Matins and Evensong and 'Oh, to be in England now that April's here', and Campions and Sheep-feeding and Mist in the Valley and Mist on the Hills and Swans and the 'Curfew tolls the knell of parting Day' and many others. Miss Howard then went through the pantomime of being a visitor with the custodian who pretended to tear off a section of toilet-paper quite correctly in return for her imaginary sixpence and looked seraphic as he sidled up to her while she examined 'Pussy-dear' with close attention, and offered to show her the price-list. The light through the scrubbed skylight was admirable and after giving the Green Salon a final whiff of Souvenir d'Orient, Miss Howard, in order to be on the safe side, closed her eyes and smiled, committing the entire undertaking, already terribly expensive, to Mind. The Baths would be shut on Sunday, and she would not look on her handiwork again till it was open to the inspection and the purses of the public. She hoped the purses would be open too.

To say that Miss Howard came down to breakfast on Monday with either appetite or confidence or calm would be highly misleading. She had passed a worried and wakeful night, and her rare snatches of sleep had been chequered by villainous dreams in which she saw with agony that she had hung all her pictures upside down, or that the Green Salon, crowded with Dowager Countesses of forbidding aspect, had no pictures at all on the walls, or that they were entirely occupied with one vast fresco representing Pussy-dear ringing Evening Bells. . . . She was early down after an unrefreshing night, and no one else had yet appeared, but the papers had come in, and there on her table was not only her usual periodical but a copy of the *Bolton Gazette.* She supposed that Mr. Bowen had sent it up as he had done on Friday and Saturday to show that the advertisement for her exhibition had duly appeared, but on the outside leaf he had written in blue pencil underlined 'see page 8', and accordingly she turned there. Big head-lines, that seemed to dance before her enraptured gaze, instantly shewed why she should turn to page 8. A column was entitled 'Exhibition of Water-Colours in the Green Salon at Bolton Baths'. She read:

> "Seldom has a greater treat been afforded to the lover of the beautiful in Bolton (and we know there are many such) than this exhibition of Miss Alice Howard's water-colours which opens to-day. For perfection of technique, for subtle and exquisite observation, for radiant fancy, for that nameless *je ne sais quoi* without which all art is as sounding brass and tinkling cymbal, we doubt whether any modern artist can rival this gifted lady who has at last done justice to and conferred immortality on our lovely countryside. Nor are Miss Howard's truly poetical interpretations of Nature confined to landscape alone: all lovers of the feline species will long to be the happy possessor of 'Pussy-dear', and we could have wished she had given us more animal studies. The Green Salon at the Baths, we are sure, will be thronged all day with eager purchasers. A veritable cabinet of gems."

CHAPTER VI

The artist gave a gasp of delight. She had so lost herself in the perusal of this masterly and sympathetic account of her work, that she had not observed that other guests had entered the dining-room. There they sat at their tables, all silent, and all, oh wonder of wonders, immersed in the *Bolton Gazette.* Admirable Mr. Bowen, whose oracular speech was now explained, must have sent copies of it to everyone at Wentworth.

Mrs. Bliss was the first to finish this eulogy, and catching Miss Howard's eyes, blew her a kiss (which Florence thought a very forward proceeding) and pointed to it.

"Not half what you deserve, dear," she said. "But very nice as far as it goes. I told you how it would be. Mind!"

Murmurs of approval and applause came from other quarters of the dining-room as the breakfasters finished this little appreciation in the *Bolton Gazette,* and Mrs. Oxney said she felt quite upset at the thought that somebody else might purchase "Pussy-dear" before she had time to go down and snap it up. It was so tiresome that on Monday morning household affairs always detained her till lunch-time. The simple expedient of paying Miss Howard a guinea and thus purchasing "Pussy-dear" without more ado did not seem to occur to her, and delicacy naturally prevented the artist from suggesting it. . . . As for Miss Howard, now treading on air, and with her appetite fully restored, she gobbled up her breakfast and hurried warbling away in order to get down to the Baths by the time the Green Salon opened. She meant to go in and out with a busy but diffident air, and everyone who knew who she was would tell those who didn't, and she would be a Public Character. Her one regret at the moment after regarding the Lobgesang in the *Gazette* was that she had not priced all the pictures at double the modest sum that appeared in the list. Such modesty just now seemed almost morbid.

Shortly after she had left the dining-room, Colonel Chase came down to breakfast, extremely late and in a worse temper than he had been in since Mr. Amble had failed to send his quinine and thermogene. He had been drinking his early morning tea and eating his toast when a furtive and adamantine piece of crust caused an important front tooth to part company from its parent plate. In itself that would have been no great inconvenience, for he had a beautiful row of uppers left but he remembered with sad vividness how, only last night, when Mrs. Holders mentioned that she had to pay a visit to the dentist's, he had said in his favourite rôle of the entirely robust and healthy man, 'I never have any bother with my teeth, thank goodness.' In a way that was quite true, because, strictly speaking, he had not got any, but the inference which he had no doubt had been drawn, was that he had got them all. So before he came down to breakfast he spent a long time in front of his looking-glass making the mouth-movements of speech and laughter to see whether the loss would be apparent. He thought that would pass undetected unless he incautiously allowed himself to be very much amused about anything, and he would have to go up to London some day soon. Then, being in a hurry, he cut himself shaving, for he never condescended to the 'safety mowing-machines', as he contemptuously termed the modern type of razor. 'I'm not afraid of the bare blade', he used to say. But he was very angry just now with the bare blade. . . .

These untoward incidents were quite enough thoroughly to ruffle a temper that was never very equable early in the day, and when, on sitting down to his breakfast he demanded a couple of sausages, he was not soothed at being told by the parlour-maid that there were none left; she recommended some 'beautiful' bacon instead. He cast a glance of peculiar annoyance at the unsolicited copy of the *Bolton Gazette* which lay by his plate, and opened it.

"What have they sent me this provincial rag for?" he muttered. "And why page 8? Some local charity, I'll be bound. Children's Hospital probably. I've had enough of the Children's Hospital. Hullo, picture exhibition . . . !"

A sideways glance told him that Miss Howard was not present, and folding the paper back he emitted frequent pshaws and faughs as he read. Then he flung it on the floor.

Mrs. Bliss observed those signs of Error (there was no mistaking them) with tender regret, and put on her brightest smile as she rose from her meal and passed, hardly limping at all, close to his table. Error must not be allowed to poison the sweet morning.

"Such a lovely little notice of Miss Howard's pictures," she said, "So appreciative. Have you seen it?"

"Yes, indeed I have," said he, "and for myself I don't find it lovely. Ludicrous flattery I call it, laid on with a spade. I wonder who wrote it, eh? A little suspicious."

Quite suddenly as he said the word 'suspicious', a loud cheerful whistle sounded through the dining-room. Everybody looked up, wondering where it came from. Colonel Chase himself thought that some rude person had interrupted him (as when the kites whistled in the tiger-story) and angrily resumed.

"Our friend is indeed endowed with all the gifts," he said. "Pianist, artist, and now shall we add, art critic, Mrs. Bliss?"

Once again came that piercing whistle, and Colonel Chase could not doubt, nor indeed could anybody else, that his own unwilling lips had produced it through the gap in the front teeth. He realised at once that he must avoid sibilants (so difficult to do) as the gouty avoided sugar, and go up to London on business without delay, for his speech betrayed him. If he hurried he would be able to catch the ten o'clock train and be back to-night. Most annoying. The only bright spot, and that a small one, was that he could not go at any rate to-day, to Miss Howard's exhibition, and if that eulogy he had just read was really by an unbiassed hand, all the pictures ought to be sold by tomorrow. He gobbled up his bacon and found an urgent call to go to London among his letters.

All that morning and all that afternoon, Miss Howard was diffidently gliding in and out of the Green Salon and welcoming friends who came in to look at her pictures with little deprecating speeches but nobly refraining from accompanying them round, for that would have made it difficult for them to avoid a purchase, and Miss Howard had a pride. But the custodian had his eye on them, and whenever anyone lingered by God's Acre or Bethesda she saw him glide up to them with his insinuating smile and politely tell them of the existence of a catalogue of prices. Unfortunately this information only seemed to have the effect of making them hurry on, and she could not help noticing that as they neared the end of the exhibition, they looked round to see if she was near and glided stealthily from the Green Salon in a way that suggested prisoners escaping. Once the custodian got as far as producing the pill box with the adhesive stars from his trousers pocket, but nothing came of it. It was all a little discouraging, and the rapture inspired by the notice in the *Bolton Gazette* gradually grew dim. Mrs. Bowen, however was a tonic, for she made Miss Howard come all the way round with her, and poured forth a continuous stream of admiring comment.

"And there's St. Giles's Church again," she said. "I should know it anywhere. No. 9--what does the catalogue say about it? Reflections: there they are in the river. Beautiful: so clear! And what an enthusiastic notice wasn't it, in the *Gazette,* though not a word too much. Mr. Bowen was sure you'd like that. It was written by a very clever young man on the staff, whom Mr. Bowen was kind to not so long ago. He's not here himself to-day, and so busy that he was afraid he mayn't be able to pop in before closing time, and I shall get a fine scolding if I can't tell him all about the pictures. I do think he's made a good job of the frames: so quiet and tasteful, and shewing them off, you may say, to the best advantage. Why if that isn't Mrs. Oxney's cat: I could recognise it and pick it out if there were fifty pictures of cats. What does the catalogue say about that? 'Pussy-dear'. Not a doubt about it: so good-natured, and never scratches. And Evening Bells: perhaps that's my favourite, but with so many lovely bits, I hardly know what I like best. How sweet any of them would look above my piano in the parlour! I must have one more look at 'Pussy-dear'"--the custodian glided to her side--"but I mustn't deprive Mrs. Oxney of that, or she would be in a way about it."

The custodian ebbed sadly away.

As dusk fell and closing time for the Green Salon approached, the custodian rendered his financial statement. There had been nineteen visitors, not including a deaf old gentleman who could not for a long time be made to understand that there was an entrance fee, and then retreated in high indignation, entirely declining to pay, but the toilet-roll showed that twenty sections had been detached from it. This was accounted for by the custodian's confession that he had torn one off, not realising that each symbolised sixpence, in order to roll himself a cigarette, for which purpose it was admirably fitted. Miss Howard paid him his shilling out of the takings of the day and enjoined on him to revere the toilet-roll. With the exception of Mrs. Oxney and Colonel Chase, all Wentworth had visited the Green Salon, and Florence had been twice. Colonel Chase, so Miss Howard ascertained on her arrival there at tea-time, had gone up to London after breakfast and had not yet returned.

She was hailed with numerous congratulations, and by Mrs. Oxney with a profusion of valid excuses for her not having visited the Green Salon.

"Such a worry it has been to me all day, Miss Howard, that I haven't been able to get down. First there was the usual Monday morning settling-up, and that took all my morning and half an hour after lunch as well. And then such a fuss in the kitchen for the boot-and-knife boy, so good at his work but peppery, came late to his dinner, and Cook refused to have the cold beef back, but said he must be content with bread and cheese, if he couldn't keep time. So there were words, and Cook came to me to know if it was by my wish that the boot-and-knife boy swore at her. Fancy! As if I had ever wished anything of the sort. And then when that was over, there were the hot-water pipes in the smoking-room leaking, just when I was thinking of putting on my hat and starting, and by the time the plumber had put them to rights, it was getting dark."

"Then, oh, what a pleasure you will have tomorrow," said Mrs. Bliss. "I'm sure I could have spent all day in the Green Salon, going round and round it and seeing fresh beauties every time. Such refreshment! I went quite early, as I knew it would be crowded all day. How many visitors did you have, dear?"

"Nineteen, no twenty," said Miss Howard.

"I call that wonderful for the first day. Just wait a few days till people have had time to tell each other what a treat is in store for them! There'll be quite a *queue* outside of those waiting to get in."

"And I hope my Pussy isn't sold yet," said Mrs. Oxney. "I should be miserable if anybody else got that."

"Let me see!" said Miss Howard, pressing her finger to her forehead. "No, I don't think it is. I can't remember seeing a red star on it."

"My favourite is Evening Bells," said Mrs. Bliss. "Such peace and poetry. How they'll all be snapped up!"

Florence liked Healing Springs best; her father could not understand her preference for that over Bethesda. The discussion grew quite animated, and though it was gratifying to find them all taking such interest and pride in her work (Mrs. Bertram had cut out the notice in the *Bolton Gazette* and was meaning to paste it into her scrap-book as a compliment to Wentworth) Miss Howard could have wished that just one of them had guarded against the certainty of a favourite being snapped up, by snapping first. There seemed to be a lack of prudence in neglecting the opportunities of to-day, which might be gone tomorrow.

Next morning could scarcely rank as a morning at all, so dense and dark were the volleying clouds which swept down from the East, discharged their broadsides of rain on Bolton and hurried on to make room for fresh assailants. Colonel Chase had returned the night before, all smiles and no whistles, and it was evident that his business in town had been satisfactory. But even an old campaigner like himself, as he told Miss Howard at breakfast, could not face the wrath of such weather, and, after the cold that had threatened him last week, he felt it wiser to postpone the pleasure of seeing her delightful pictures. Mrs. Oxney was full of similar lamentations, and though distraught at the notion of Pussy's picture being snapped up by somebody else, it still did not occur to her to telephone to the Baths and bid the custodian affix the adhesive star to the treasure. Even Mr.

CHAPTER VI

Kemp preferred to miss a morning of Bethesda, and see whether Mind would not do something striking for him as he sat close to the log fire in the lounge and the bus went down with only two passengers in it, Mrs. Bliss who for the sake of her husband was willing to brave any erroneous inclemency, particularly as it could not possibly hurt her, and Miss Howard.

The Green Salon was absolutely empty of art lovers, and the skylight was leaking a little on to Mrs. Oxney's nice carpet. Patients from neighbouring hotels and from Belvoir, Blenheim and Balmoral came through the vestibule in dripping mackintoshes, and how much nicer it would be, thought Miss Howard, if it was they who were dripping on to Mrs. Oxney's carpet instead of the skylight. In fact the only focus of cheerfulness about the Green Salon was its custodian who felt certain everyone would come flocking in as soon as the weather cleared: no one in his opinion could 'have the heart to look at pictures, miss', on such a day. Miss Howard paid him his shilling before lunch, not meaning to return if the downpour continued, and inspected the sad integrity of the toilet-roll. But it would never do to present the appearance of a down-hearted exhibitor and after lunch she established herself in the lounge to make an indoor sketch. The perspective of the staircase was a most intricate problem, and no amount of sympathetic colour would make it look other than unscaleable.

Though the old campaigner could not face the weather for the ten minutes walk to the Baths to see the pictures he faced it that afternoon for a solid six miles by his pedometer, leaving and returning to Wentworth by the back door, so that Miss Howard, sketching in the lounge close to the front door should be ignorant of his perfidy. A good deal of diplomacy was needed in these manœuvres, for he had to get his mackintosh from the hall, and take it up to his bedroom for the purpose of sewing a button on, and on his return from his walk, convey it by a roundabout route to the hot-water pipes outside the dining-room in order to dry it. This done, he came thumping down to tea, flushed and rosy with exercise and successful trickery.

"I'm not one to complain of an occasional wet day," he said, "for I've got through some arrears, and had a good spell of reading in my room--wonderful author, Macaulay: he gives you something solid to think about. And if anyone asked if I'd had a snooze as well, I should change the subject."

"Nothing to be ashamed of, Colonel," said Mr. Kemp. "A nap during the afternoon has often been recommended to me. After the wear and tear of the morning nature needs a restorative. I get sounder sleep sometimes in half an hour after lunch, than I do in the whole course of the night. At Buxton it was part of my *régime."*

"Well, it freshens one up," said Colonel Chase, who always interrupted Mr. Kemp's experiences at Spas, "I feel brisk enough for anything now. We might have a rubber perhaps before dinner now the day's work is over. The evenings are drawing in now: we can play with a good conscience, and not feel we're wasting the daylight. Cards and candles, I always say."

Mrs. Oxney had entered as he spoke. She had just come along from the dining-room, where she had been distributing the menu cards for dinner, and had seen Colonel Chase's mackintosh spread over the radiator and sending up clouds of steam.

"Well, that would be very comfortable," she said, "and if you want me to take a hand, I'm ready. But to think of your having gone out on this miserable afternoon, Colonel. I'll be bound you had to make your pedometer tick briskly to keep yourself warm. And your mackintosh, why, you might have thrown it into the river: a button off, too, letting the wet in." Mrs. Holders caught Tim's eye, who, trying to strangle a laugh, swallowed a crumb of cake by an unusual route and violently choked. This happily changed the subject, which Colonel Chase would certainly have had to do for Mr. Kemp who was an authority on false passages of all sorts begged everybody not to pat Tim on the back, for such a well-meant treatment only made matters worse. He ought to sit bolt upright, breathe deeply in through the nose and expel the air vigorously through the mouth. Everyone's attention was therefore diverted to Tim, and they watched him recover by degrees. Mrs. Bliss had clearly been demonstrating during his fit, so it was uncertain whether Mind or Mr. Kemp was responsible.

But though there was then no definite further exposure of Colonel Chase's rank duplicity, everyone was aware of it, for no one could possibly forget that he had told Miss Howard that the weather was too bad for even so old a campaigner to venture out. It was no wonder that she moistened her lips several times and determined that nothing should drag from her the smallest comment on his most deceitful behaviour. What made his falsehoods more revolting to the feelings of a lady was the hearty and rollicking manner in which he said he had been reading in his bedroom and perhaps snoozed. But she scorned to return to the subject and ask how many miles he had walked.

Morning brought a renewal of tranquil and sunny weather, and had it not been for her exhibition, Miss Howard would certainly have returned to lunch at Wentworth with a veritable 'Ode to Autumn' in water-colour to display on the chimney-piece of the lounge. But she could not bear in these critical days to absent herself so long from the Green Salon, and she longed to know whether her custodian's optimism was justified in expecting an influx of visitors now that the improved weather conditions would give them the heart to look at pictures. At present, when she arrived there soon after breakfast, there was only one visitor, a rather odious looking young man, who, so the custodian secretly informed her, had refused to pay for admission on the grounds that he was the press. Instantly she was divided between high hopes and low suspicions. Was he (rapturous thought!) 'our own correspondent' of some influential London paper, sent down to study the contents of the Green Salon, which the *Bolton Gazette* had found so exquisite, or was he some clever thief who intended, when the custodian's small back was turned to cut out from their frames some of the choicest gems and dispose of them to shady dealers? He did not look like her idea of our own correspondent: on the other hand it would have been unlike a clever thief to have called attention to himself by saying that he was the press. In either case, he had better know who she was, for if he was the press he might like to have an interview, while if he was a thief he would know that the artist had taken note of him. So she tripped up to him, and gave him the benefit of the doubt.

"The press, I believe," she said. "I am Miss Howard. These little things of mine--"

The press had not very good manners: it did not remove from the corner of its mouth a cigarette whose fumes mingled strangely with the odour of the waters, perceptible this morning, and that of Souvenir d'Orient.

"Pleased to meet you, miss," he said, "and pleased to have given you a leg up in our organ the *Bolton Gazette*. I laid it on thick, didn't I? Just looked in to see what sort of a show you'd got. Very pretty, I'm sure."

"I thought your article was most sympathetic," she said. "And so pleased you've paid my little exhibition a second visit, after studying it so closely."

He looked much surprised.

"No, I've not been here before," he said. "I just had a look at the catalogue, and wrote my stuff on that."

Poor Miss Howard felt her last support slip from her. Hitherto she had clung to the comforting knowledge that though visitors might be few and purchasers completely non-existent, the trained eye of the professional critic had appreciated and admired. Now that consolation was gone.

"You don't seem to have had any purchasers as yet," went on this dreadful young man, "but I'll give you a tip about that, miss. You tell that young buttons who wanted me to pay sixpence, to fix labels on to half of them to say they're sold, see? You bet other people will begin buying them then, for fear they should be too late. Just make them think that if they're not slippy everything'll be gone, see? I must be off though: wish you luck."

For some time after the departure of this dreadful young man there were no other visitors, and the optimism of the leap-frog boy had to exert its ingenuity, and he supposed that on such a fine morning gents would want to be out of doors. It seemed in fact as if gents required very unusual weather to make them feel drawn to picture exhibitions; neither fine nor wet suited them. Miss Howard had one or two bill-paying errands in the town, and on her return she found that Mrs. Oxney had been in, though there was no token of her visit on the glass of Pussy-dear, but only a message of ardent appreciation. Colonel Chase evidently was one of the gents who wanted to be out of doors, for the custodian had seen him riding by on his bicycle, as if for a wager, and Miss Howard supposed she would be asked to guess at lunch-time what the new record was. Though she had no malice (or very little) in her spiritual outfit, she determined to guess either that he had been eighty miles, which would make his actual accomplishment appear a very paltry feat, or ten miles, which would show that she had a very poor idea of his powers.

Meanwhile the diabolical tip given her by the press, continued to leaven her thoughts. She had rejected the notion at first with scorn as being a dishonest trick, but soon she began to wonder whether there was any harm in it. As long as no one bought her pictures, she might be considered to have bought them herself for they *were* hers, and certainly she had bought and paid for the frames. She did not know what the custodian would think of her if she suddenly told him to put little red stars on half the pictures, but after all, it mattered very little what the custodian thought of her. On the other hand it would be a great chagrin if after having starred 'Oh, to be in England now that April's here' some visitor took a violent fancy to it and found it was sold. She hated deceit, at least she had felt that Colonel Chase had made himself truly contemptible, when he had said yesterday that the inclement weather prevented his going to see her pictures, and was detected in having gone out for a walk instead, but was it deceit to put red stars on pictures? She did not actually state that they were sold, though the custodian, if asked what this decoration meant, would doubtless tell enquirers that such was its significance. But again if nobody further came to see the pictures (a contingency which was beginning to look lamentably likely) nobody would be deceived. Her fingers itched for the pill box, but she could not quite face asking the boy for it. She would wait one day more, and if by that time there were still no purchasers, she would buy five or six herself. . . .

It was getting on for lunch-time: all the morning patients at the Baths had passed and repassed the open door of the Green Salon, but only one of them, an elderly lady like a horse had even paused there. Instantly the custodian, who was beginning to wonder whether a shilling a day compensated him for so much inactivity, sprang to attention with the toilet-roll, but the horse only tossed its head with a sort of neigh, and muttered, 'Only pictures', in a tone of deep disgust. Miss Howard felt she could not stand the kindly and cheerful enquiries that would be put to her, if she drove up with the Wentworth bathers in the bus, and she started to walk. Outside on the wall of the porch was a type-written advertisement of the exhibition which the rain yesterday had partly detached, so that the upper half of it drooped over the lower and the print had run: she had hardly the spirit to fix it up again. She was thoroughly depressed, for apart from the expense, and from the approaching difficulty of knowing what to do with a stack of nearly fifty framed pictures there was the far more bitter loss of prestige. As long as she had not tempted Fate in this manner, she had been the accredited fount of artistic authority at Wentworth: she could shake her head over Sargent's slap-dash methods, and say that of course he was marvellously clever, but she personally admired a more detailed and highly finished technique: careful work was what lived. No doubt if she had the heart to continue putting her sketches on the chimney-piece of the lounge, Wentworth would still say that they were exquisite, but at the back of everybody's mind would be the knowledge that a roomful of such gems had been on view, and had attracted but few visitors and not a single purchaser, even at prices immeasurably below Sargent's. She had piped, but nobody had danced: the Muse felt her insignia slipping from her.

CHAPTER VI

These gloomy reflections so occupied her that she had not seen that she was catching up a woman walking ahead of her up the hill, and it was not till she had got quite close that she saw it was Mrs. Bliss, limping slightly and leaning on her stick, but able to proceed at a very respectable pace. In the ten days that she had been at Bolton she had indeed made the most marvellous progress. "But however much she calls it Mind," thought Miss Howard in a spasm of revolt, "I call it brine."

Mrs. Bliss turned round when she was quite close. It struck Miss Howard that the smile was whisked on when she saw who it was.

"Sweet one!" said Mrs. Bliss. "How fortunate I am to have such a dear companion for the rest of my walk. I'll be bound that your lovely picture-show was crowded with visitors this morning and probably most of them sold. How I demonstrated about it in my bath this morning! How Mind looks after us all! See how I'm flitting along to-day."

That certainly was wonderful, though 'flit' was still slightly on the optimistic side of accuracy. And it wasn't Mind: it was brine.

"No; there wasn't any crowd at all," said the sweet one firmly. "In fact there was no one there at all. And I haven't sold a single picture yet."

A wave of bitter illumination swept over her, calling for her protest.

"In fact I don't think much of Mind," she added.

Mrs. Bliss remained quite unshocked by this blasphemy. That was one of the truly annoying things about her, thought Miss Howard: you couldn't stop her smiling any more than you could stop an express train by defying it, nor could you cool her exasperating certainty that everything was perfect, and that everybody was a skipping lamb in green pastures. She laughed merrily.

"You darling rebel!" she said. "What joy it will be when your dear blind eyes are opened."

"I intend to keep them shut," said Miss Howard in the vain attempt to shake this fearful confidence. "I've got to face the fact that nobody wants to see my pictures or to buy them. So it's no use saying that Mind is looking after my exhibition. I give up Mind."

Even this did not dim Mrs. Bliss's radiance.

"Dear thing!" she said. "But Mind won't give you up. Think of all the wonderful things Mind has done for us quite lately at our pretty Wentworth. Colonel Chase's cold, his pedometer, his success at the entertainment. All Mind! Look at me, too, in spite of the baths and the massage."

"And look at Mr. Kemp," said Miss Howard. "He's no better. If anything, he's worse."

Mrs. Bliss laughed again.

"But, dear, he's well," she said. "He doesn't know it yet but he is. It often happens that Error still blinds people even when they are cured, and they still think they are suffering. But soon that passes. You're just the same about your pictures. Only wait a little: abide patiently."

It was a relief to Miss Howard when they got to Wentworth, and Mrs. Bliss went to lie down on her bed not to rest but to work, for she found such optimism harder to bear than her own pessimism. She felt that after this solitary morning in the Green Salon, a similar afternoon would be intolerable, and determined not to go down again that day. It would be time enough to-morrow morning to learn that not a sixpence had been recorded on the toilet-roll, or a red star appeared on the walls. She occupied herself till lunch-time with the sketch of the lounge.

Now while she was trying to make the staircase appear scaleable, two very important scenes took place in the hollow where the town lay. The first of these began with Mrs. Holders and Tim coming simultaneously out of the ladies' and gentlemen's sections of the establishment after their baths, and meeting in front of the Green Salon. The door was open, and the custodian had gone to eat his dinner and have a little exercise with his friends. They looked in.

"My word, what rubbish, isn't it, Tim?" she said. "She can't paint. I think I shall give a vocal recital, or act Ophelia."

"Do: may I be Hamlet?" said he. "Look at Bethesda falling down, and Healing Springs. I wish they would heal me. And not a picture sold yet, or they would have labels."

"And God's Acre: it's not nearly an acre," said Mrs. Holders. "What a fool the woman is to think they could sell. But rather pathetic: all that trouble, not to mention the frames. I hate middle-aged spinsters being disappointed because they've nothing to look forward to. Tim, I think we shall be obliged to buy some."

"I'm damned if I do," said Tim.

"You'll be damned if you don't, dear, because you'll have been a brute. And I said 'some'. It's no use our buying just one each. We're both rich, thank God. And she hasn't warbled all to-day and all yesterday. Not a note."

"Well, don't set her off again," said Tim.

"And the improvisation wasn't a success. And she's feeling terribly down. Now be a man."

The custodian at this moment returned from dinner and leap-frog, and seeing somebody in the Green Salon rushed gleefully in and pulled out the toilet-roll.

"Sixpence each, please, sir," he said.

"How many people have been in to-day?" asked Tim.

"Only one and he didn't pay. Said he was the press. Sixpence--"

"And yesterday?" asked Mrs. Holders.

"We didn't have any visitors yesterday, ma'am. Catalogue free, and there's a price catalogue, too."

They hobbled round together with it.

"What's that squirrel?" asked Tim.

"Pussy-dear," said she. "One guinea. Oh, it's the Wentworth cat. Mrs. Oxney ought to buy that of course. . . . Tim, I think you and I must have five each. That'll make a start. Half-guinea ones will do. No, we can't do that quite."

"I'm glad," said he.

"I don't mean what you mean. What I mean is that if you and I each buy five, there'll be a sort of indelicacy about it. Compassion you know, which is always objectionable. We must think of another plan. I know. Bring me a chair, you boy, or I shall fall down."

"Two," said Tim.

The conspirators seated themselves.

"Now attend, Tim," she said, "for I'm being very bright. This morning, just now in fact, quite a lot of people came in to the show. You and I, that's two and four more."

"Then they had to pay for admission," said Tim.

"I'm glad you thought of that. Of course they had. Four more tickets, boy. You pay, Tim. I haven't got a sou."

"You're running me into a great deal of expense," said Tim.

"I'm going to run you into more. Give this gentleman four more tickets, boy, and he gives you two shillings. That's right, isn't it? Now go away till we call you again."

Mrs. Holders sat silent a moment, arranging the conspiracy.

"What has happened, Tim, is this," she said at length. "These four people whose tickets you have just so kindly paid for each bought two of Miss Howard's pictures. You must think of two friends of yours and I'll think of two friends of mine, and we'll give their names and addresses and money to the boy, and write to them to say that they will shortly receive two sad little water-colours each. They'll get them, of course, when the exhibition closes. You can tell your friends to send the pictures back to you, if you like. That will be eight pictures, and you and I each buy one on our own account, and that makes ten. Now you've got to think of the names and addresses of two friends: after that all you have to do, is to pay and look just as unpleasant as you choose. I don't mind. I'll give you a cheque for my share."

"Good old thing," said Tim. "Now we'll get the boy and din it into his head."

Leap-frog showed himself very intelligent, and after two minutes coaching, he repeated without flaw the following remarkable occurrences. Mrs. Holders and Mr. Bullingdon (address Wentworth) he rehearsed, had come in, and paid their sixpences, and each had bought a picture (numbers 2 and 11). They hadn't been gone more than a minute, when two ladies came in, and after paying for admittance (toilet-roll as before) called for the price catalogue. They each bought two pictures (numbers 7, 13, 24 and 31) which they paid for, and gave their names and addresses which he duly entered. Just before (or after) they left two gentlemen came in, paid their sixpences and went round. They too called for the price-list--seeming to admire the pictures very much--and bought two each (numbers 20, 35, 39 and 40). They paid their money and gave names and addresses. . . . The custodian then went to the bar to get change, and put into his breast pocket five pound notes and five shillings. A half-crown, the reward of intelligence he put into the pocket where was the pill box. The conspirators waited to see him lick ten adhesive red stars, and fix them to the corners of pictures, 2, 7, 11, 13, 20, 24, 31, 35,

39 and 40. There seemed no possible risk of detection. Then they found they had missed the Wentworth bus, and took a taxi, arriving late for lunch and rather cross with each other.

The other important event was concerned with the spiritual life of Colonel Chase, and was therefore of deeper significance than these mere financial benefits to Miss Howard. He had started that morning meaning to pay a visit to the exhibition at the cost of sixpence, though of course he would not dream of buying one of her faint little daubs. But her pleasure and gratification at his visit would efface from her mind that impression of paltry fibbing which might possibly be rankling there owing to Mrs. Oxney's silly chatter about his mackintosh. Having thus re-established the candour of his character, he would go for a fine ride to make up for having missed one yesterday. . . . But as he went quietly down the hill (it was not worth while getting up speed if he was to dismount so soon) the thought of Miss Howard's exhibition began to arouse acute annoyance in his mind; it was a barefaced levying of blackmail on her friends, they could not in decency refuse to put at least sixpence into Miss Howard's pocket. The thought of this moral compulsion revolted him, and he determined to strike a blow for English freedom, and not go at all. He therefore put on speed and was seen by the custodian pedalling, as if for a wager, past the Baths, feeling that he was a champion of liberty. He did not mind giving Miss Howard sixpence, but he refused to be obliged to . . .

The roads had dried up wonderfully after the deluge of yesterday, he drew in long breaths of the cool fresh air, and his great fat legs revolved as if nothing could ever tire them. It was impossible (and so he did not attempt it) not to reflect with strong satisfaction on his own health and vigour and heartiness. His Indian contemporaries were mostly wizened and yellow little men suffering from liver, or obese waddlers who sat all day in arm-chairs, and perhaps occasionally played a couple of rounds of golf, six or seven miles all told, and were very tired after it, whereas here was he active in mind and body, ready to cover mile after mile on foot or saddle without fatigue, and be fit afterwards for strong brain-work over reading or crossword puzzles or bridge.

These gratifying thoughts put him in a better temper, and forgiving Miss Howard for her exhibition he registered the fact that he had never felt so well as he had done during the last fortnight. His superb vitality had thrown off in a single night the most undoubted symptoms of a crashing cold and his mind shifted to Mrs. Bliss and that extraordinary gospel of hers. Was it perhaps she who had called down on him this amazing access of health and prosperity? There was his cold, there was his pedometer, there was his huge success (though not quite in the manner he had anticipated) at the entertainment, and as for that small distressing incident in the Children's Hospital, she had assured him, though in terms he did not attempt to fathom, that Mind was acting just as beneficently there as in its more obvious manifestations. He had never completely determined whether he seriously ascribed all this benefit to her agency: his cold might possibly have disappeared through natural causes, but the reappearance of the pedometer fairly puzzled him. She had no account to give of it: it had just come to her, like manna, miraculously. But to her it was not miraculous at all: it was a perfectly normal result of relying on Omnipotent Mind, and being full of loving and trusting thoughts. After all he was a thoroughly good-natured fellow: people had only to make themselves pleasant to him, and give him his way on every occasion, and he was as jolly as possible with them. He must keep that up, and with the hope of obtaining further benefits from Mind, he resolved to go to Miss Howard's exhibition. Mind would like that: it would be a good-natured act towards poor Miss Howard who had not got an *encore* at the entertainment nor roused the smallest enthusiasm, and who had not sold a picture. To be sure the whole thing was blackmail but he felt that, in view of Mind, he was big enough to overlook that, and give pleasure to Miss Howard. Her little place in Kent too: he wondered . . .

Though a swift bicyclist, Colonel Chase was not a rapid thinker, and by the time he had arrived at this conclusion, he saw that he had been riding for over an hour. Absorbed in these spiritual problems, he had been paying little attention to the passage of the landscape, and now, looking about him again, he saw that the country was wholly new to him. He had certainly started by the Denton road, and had followed its familiar windings, but here he was at the end of an hour quite beyond his usual beat. Never had an hour or a bicycle sped so swiftly: he could not believe that so much time had passed or so much ground been covered. Behind him lay a long stretch of upward incline, which had flowed under his wheel as if it had been level, and he was neither out of breath nor conscious of any fatigue: he had climbed as if on eagles' wings. "It must be Mind," he said to himself, "it can't possibly be anything else. I shall go to poor Miss Howard's show this very afternoon, and I'm not sure that I shan't buy one of her well-meaning little sketches. I was wrong to think of her as a blackmailer. All is health, kindliness and prosperity!"

A sign post confirmed his immense distance from home, making him exult in the splendour of his powers, and after a round which he had not previously believed was traversible by a leg-driven wheel he found himself back in Bolton again. There had been a slight abrasion on his ankle yesterday and not wanting to bother Mind over so small a matter, he stopped at Mr. Amble's to purchase a phial of New Skin. You painted it on the place and it smarted, but, relying on Mind, very likely he wouldn't feel it. Mr. Amble was delighted to see him in his shop again, for this visit was a token of reconciliation after those choleric speeches on the telephone, and he entirely forgot the existence of the 'little secret' between him and that odd though affable lady. . . .

"New Skin, sir?" he said. "Yes, I can supply you with that. And I was very pleased, Colonel, to have been the means of restoring your pedometer to you. My lad picked it up--"

"Eh, what's that?" said Colonel Chase.

"Your pedometer, Colonel, which you lost last week. My lad picked it up on the Denton road; let me see it would be ten days ago now and I gave it a clean and sent it--Good Lord, why I quite forgot that the lady I gave it to, asked me not to mention it. But there's no harm done, I hope, and anyhow she's not been in here since, nor bought anything then. She saw the notice in my window that a pedometer had been found, and since she looked respectable and said she came from Wentworth, I let her take it to return to you. I hope there's been no--no mistake, and that she did give it you."

Mind's greatest miracle of all had collapsed, as if a flood of corrosive light from some devilish Higher Criticism had been poured on it. Colonel Chase's faith in Mind trembled, tottered and crashed: it was an infidel who stood there holding a bottle of New Skin in his shaking hand. What liars women were! To think that this abandoned wretch distinctly said that she had no notion how she got the pedometer. She said that she was lost in meditation, and, lo, it was in her hand. He felt positively sick.

"No, there was no mistake," he said--the irony of that!--"she gave it me."

He went out of the shop, and pedalled up the hill with a mind reeling with atheism. If this was the true history (and it certainly was) of the most inexplicable of all Mind's miracles it was not any longer possible to credit Mind with his restoration from his cold, or with his success at the entertainment. And if Mind had not showered these benefits upon him, why propitiate it by going to Miss Howard's Green Salon, let alone buying anything therein? Even the joy of having certainly beaten all records this morning almost faded, when he dismounted at Wentworth and when he looked at his pedometer it was completely extinguished, for once more the pedometer had stopped. The hands sarcastically affirmed that he had gone six miles.

Lunch had begun, and he entered the dining-room in the manner of Hyperion "full of wrath." He stopped opposite Mrs. Bliss's table, who, unconscious of what was coming, smiled gaily up at him.

"What a lovely morning you've had for your ride, Colonel," she said. "I expect you've been ever so far away over the blue, blue hills."

He raised his voice. It was right that what he had to say to her should be known to all.

"I have to thank you, Mrs. Bliss," he said, "for restoring to me the pedometer I lost, which Amble the chemist gave you. He tells me that his shop-boy found it."

She did not sink into the earth or behave like Sapphira. She laughed delightedly and clapped her hands.

"That was it!" she said. "I could not recollect how I got it. I only knew I had to give it back to you. But it comes back to me now."

Dead silence had fallen on the lunchers and had it not been for Colonel Chase's heavy tread, as, leaving her without a word, he went to his place, anyone might have heard a pin drop. Then hurried conversation broke out, and Miss Howard so far forgot her malicious design of guessing that he had gone eighty miles as to say to him, "And how far have you been this morning, Colonel?"

"I haven't the slightest idea," he said. "Once more the pedometer on my bicycle (pedometer, he repeated) got out of order and stopped. Odd things happen to my pedometer."

CHAPTER VI

This withering remark had no effect whatever on Mrs. Bliss. She finished her fish and sat gazing out of the window in happy reverie, till the parlour-maid brought her the next dish.

CHAPTER VII

Mr. Banks in his sermon last Sunday had made a very profound observation. It must not be supposed from this statement that profound observations coming from his pulpit were of rare occurrence. They were on the contrary so common that they often passed unnoticed or at any rate not fully appreciated. For instance, when in this same sermon he said, 'If, dear friends, we all invariably acted on our noble rather than our baser impulses, the world would be a very different place,' there was scarcely anyone in his congregation who grasped the whole of the tremendous truth that lurked in these simple words. Shortly afterwards he uttered another truth, which likewise attracted no particular attention at the time but was soon seen to be not only profound but, as regards the affairs of Miss Howard, prophetical.

"People," said this subtle observer, "are like sheep. If one leads, in things great and small, the rest will follow. Let each of us therefore lead in all high thought and selfless deeds, and we shall speedily find that we are not alone as we tread the upward path of Christian endeavour. And now--"

Mrs. Banks had been much struck by this analogy between people and sheep: it seemed to her 'very teaching', and at lunch afterwards she thanked her husband for the enlightenment it had brought her. She was of a quaintly humorous disposition and she knew that a playful application of his words would not displease him, for he often said that what we learn in church we should use in daily life.

"It is true in all sorts of ways, Hildebrand," she said. "For instance at the entertainment the other night, it only needed that one rude boy should laugh at Colonel Chase's ghost story to set the whole room off. I wonder if it was meant to be funny or meant to thrill us."

"Oh, meant to thrill without a doubt," said Hildebrand, "but it just turned out different from what he expected. Like puddings. I only hope Miss Howard's exhibition will turn out different to what I expect, for if it doesn't she won't sell a single picture. But we must both go to it."

"Of course. Poor Miss Howard. But perhaps somebody will buy one, and other people follow as you said."

This duty of going to the Green Salon had escaped their memories (or was inconvenient to fulfil) for the first three days that it was open, and thus, when on Wednesday Mrs. Holders and Tim made their amiable conspiracy, neither the Vicar nor his wife had seen the numerous pictures of his church. But on Thursday morning it so happened that she had to go to the post office, and he to visit a sick parishioner. Their ways lay in the same direction, and they set off together; the sight of the Baths put the forgotten duty into Mrs. Banks's head.

"Let us pop in for a moment and see poor Miss Howard's pictures," said she. "She may not be there yet, which would be a good thing, for if she comes round with us and looks sad, we shall find it difficult not to buy one."

Miss Howard was there, going through some list with the custodian. But so far from looking sad, her face expressed high elation, and she came tripping towards them with the greatest cheerfulness.

"How de-do Mrs. Banks?" she said. "So good of you and the padre to look in. Very little worth seeing, I'm afraid."

"Ah, you mustn't think this is our first visit," said Mrs. Banks, who had a perfect genius for just not telling lies. "And as for there being very little worth seeing, well I can't agree. Oh look, Hildebrand, there's a lovely, lovely picture of St. Giles's. Why it has a little red star on it. Does that mean it is sold Miss Howard? What a disappointment!"

"Yes, I'm afraid that's gone," said Miss Howard. "But you'll find one somewhere from nearly the same point of view, but in the evening. There it is. Ah, that's sold too. I can't keep pace with them."

Somehow this put a very different aspect on poor Miss Howard and her exhibition, and when she went back to the task of verifying the purchased pictures with the custodian, looking the very reverse of sad, and not showing the slightest inclination to go round with them, the two, who had not been near the Green Salon before, began at the very beginning on an attentive and respectful scrutiny. The padre's sermon was assuming the prophetical aspect.

"What a lot she's sold," said Mrs. Banks in discreet tones. "And really they are very charming. Look at No. 7, Hildebrand. 'The curfew tolls the knell of parting Day', with the spire of St. Giles's among the trees. Sweet! But I see that's sold."

"I think I like No. 6 even better," said Mr. Banks. "Number 6, God's Acre. Very feeling. Tombstones. Really I should immensely like to possess that. A truly religious touch about it. God's Acre, too, a beautiful description."

While he stood there with his head on one side, quite lost in admiration, the custodian who had finished the agreeable task with Miss Howard, sidled up to his wife.

"There is a price-list, madam," he softly insinuated.

"Yes, let me look," she whispered, and found it was only ten-and-sixpence.

"I'll take it," she said. "Mrs. Banks, the Vicarage. Put a star on it at once and get me change."

Miss Howard, seeing that business was going on delicately left the Green Salon, and Mrs. Banks joined her husband who was still basking in God's Acre.

"Hildebrand, dear. God's Acre is yours. My Christmas present to you. I had been wondering what to give you."

He gave a start of pleasure and surprise.

"My dear," said he, "what a delicious present. I can't tell you what joy--"

"But you must forget all about it again," she said, "till I give it you on Christmas morning."

After that it was only fair that Mrs. Banks should have her turn to be lost in admiration of another picture, and the one she happened to select for that purpose was Evening Bells. When it was quite clear that she liked this more than any, Hildebrand wandered quietly away to the custodian who was busy at the moment detaching a strip of toilet-paper for Colonel Chase, and asked for the price-list. Two guineas was rather a staggerer, and it was distinctly bad luck that his wife had so firmly set her affections on Evening Bells, when almost anything else might have been had for a quarter of that sum, but he could not be blind to her clear choice. He produced two pound notes, a shilling and two sixpences.

"The Vicar," he said rather sadly. "Put a label on Number 27 as sold."

"Hurroi!" said the custodian, and went out to find Miss Howard and tell her of this huge accession to the treasury.

Colonel Chase was in a rather lofty mood that morning. Kind but lofty.

"Well, padre," he said. "We meet on a charitable errand. Wouldn't do to have nobody coming to our friend's little effort. What? You've been buying one, have you? Well, I call that kind. I'll be bound it's the first that's been sold, and, I shouldn't wonder if it was the last. I suppose I must get a catalogue. What! Is there nothing but that type-written thing? Nothing printed? Oh, they don't charge for it. I dare say it will do very well."

He began reading the catalogue glancing hastily at the pictures to verify the titles.

"Golf links, Wentworth," he said. "Yes, that's right, and a lot of trouble I spent over them too. But that tree has gone now. Quite changed the look of the place, as well as spoiling one of the best holes. Number 5 now. Bethesda. Ah yes, I see, a cat. I suppose Bethesda is the name of the cat. No, no: my mistake. Number 5 is 'Pussy-dear'. That's Mrs. Oxney's cat: I hear enough of it at night without wanting to see a picture of it, and 'Pussy-dear' doesn't quite interpret my feelings about it. Still, the picture has a sort of look of the animal. Good morning, Mrs. Padre: how's the violin? It was a pretty piece you played us the other night. Fully deserved an *encore,* I thought."

"No time for the violin to-day, Colonel Chase," she said. "Every minute that I can spare this morning I shall give to these pictures. Impossible to tear oneself away. And just think, my husband has given me Evening Bells, the loveliest of all, as a Christmas present. Isn't it too dear of him?"

"Very kind I'm sure," said Colonel Chase, "now let's see. Number 6. God's Acre. What are those white things? Ah, tombstones: yes, God's Acre. That's got a little star on it, which I suppose means it's sold. And Number 7 is sold too, and 13. Why, there seems to be a regular run on Miss Howard's pictures. I am surprised."

"I'm sure I'm not," said Mrs. Banks, who being the owner of one picture and the purchaser of another was bound to spur everyone else to buy too. "Such feeling! Such beautiful technique. And the critics think the world of them. There was an article in the *Bolton Gazette,* and the writer couldn't have said more of them if they had been by Mr. Sargent. I think I am indeed fortunate to have Evening Bells before anybody else snapped it up."

All this was beginning to work a subtle change in Colonel Chase: he was looking at these little efforts with quite a different eye. He had come in Baalam's first mood, inclined to curse the expenditure of sixpence as the payment of blackmail, but this public eagerness to secure an example of Miss Howard's skill, made him wonder whether he should not be blessing a blackmail which seemed to offer an opportunity of securing something worth having at a most reasonable outlay. He had hazarded the cynical conjecture that Miss Howard had written that laudatory notice herself, but, however that might be, purchasers were rife, for he saw, looking enquiringly round, that a dozen of the little efforts had already been snapped up, and were twinkling with little red stars. The priced catalogue, into which at this moment the custodian, that fine psychological observer, suggested he might like to glance, told him that almost any of the remaining pearls could be acquired for half-a-guinea, and what if they turned out to be of the true Orient destined to be eagerly sought for by the *cognoscenti?* A bargain always appealed to him if it did not entail much outlay, and the fact that Florence, who had just come in, was looking fixedly at Golf-links, Wentworth made him hate the notion that anyone but he should possess a work which in addition to its artistic merit should surely be owned by the creator of the golf links. 'A pretty sketch,' he could imagine himself saying, 'I laid the links out myself.' He hurriedly produced a ten shilling note and six coppers and entered his name on the lengthening list as its purchaser. Out came the pill box and the custodian's tongue and he shot forward with a red star on the tip of it, and in his eagerness affixed it to the centre of the picture.

"Snapped up, I'm afraid, Miss Kemp," said Colonel Chase jovially. "One has to make up one's mind quickly if one wants one of Miss Howard's sketches. I couldn't let anyone else have that picture of my golf links with the dear old tree still standing by the centre green. Very beautiful effect is it not?"

Colonel Chase had now enrolled himself in the ranks of those who, having bought pictures, were all agog that others should buy as well, thus endorsing their own wisdom and artistic taste, and presently he and the padre and Mrs. Banks were all strongly advising Florence to secure 'Oh, to be in England now that April's here', before it was too late. She had only just put it out of the reach of other aspirants, when there arose a perfect hubbub at the door, and the custodian's voice was heard respectfully but shrilly demanding an entrance fee.

"No, my lady," he said, "the exhibition isn't free to nobody. Admission sixpence each," and there was Lady Appledore and Miss Jobson, the former in a state of dignified resentment.

"Pay it then, Miss Jobson," she said, "though after all I've done for the town, I should have thought my admittance was a matter of course. Let me see: Colonel Chase is it not; who told us those amusing ghost stories. And Mr. Banks. And Mrs. Banks: the violin. Quite a crowd. I cannot understand why I have received no notice of Miss Howard's exhibition before, as it is well known that I make a point of encouraging local industries. An odd omission. It was quite by accident that I saw a small placard outside the Baths as I was driving by. 'Miss Jobson,' I said, 'kindly go and see what that placard is.'"

They all three assailed her with laudatory remarks.

"A lucky accident indeed," said Mrs. Banks. "You will be charmed with Miss Howard's work."

"We all are, Lady Appledore," said Colonel Chase. "The art critic in the *Bolton Gazette* was most enthusiastic."

"My wife has given me God's Acre for a Christmas present, Lady Appledore," said Mr. Banks.

"And I have got 'Oh, to be in England now that April's here'," said Florence, who, not having been introduced, stated the fact to nobody in particular.

"And my husband has given me Evening Bells, which I think you will agree is the gem of them all, Lady Appledore," said Mrs. Banks.

"A catalogue," said Lady Appledore, putting out her hand. Four catalogues were thrust into it.

"I will look round and judge for myself," said she. "Dear me, do all those red stars on the pictures mean that they are sold?"

"Yes," said everybody.

"I am sorry not to have heard about this earlier," said she, "for I have always been a great judge of water-colours. Miss Howard must have made quite a fortune. It was Miss Howard, I think, who played us little pieces of Chopin the other night, but I do not know her, do I, Miss Jobson? I hope I shall like her pictures better than her playing. Number 6 is pretty: a good middle distance. What is Number 6 called, Miss Jobson. Oh, God's Acre, I see to be sure. But it is bought."

"Yes, am I not fortunate? That is mine," said Mr. Banks.

"You have not chosen badly. Full of feeling. Number 9 Miss Jobson."

"'The Curfew tolls the knell of parting day'," said Miss Jobson.

"That is not bad either. It is evening, Miss Jobson. Curfew is invariably in the evening. About eight o'clock. That is not sold, I see. Put a mark against it till I have seen the rest. Somebody will lend you a pencil if you have not got one."

The majestic procession moved slowly on.

"A cat," said Lady Appledore. "I do not like cats. Miss Howard should not have painted a cat. Mist in the Valley represents Bolton Spa, Miss Jobson, but you cannot see it because of the mist. Put a smaller mark opposite Mist in the Valley. Mist on the Hills is Bolton Spa also, but now you can see Bolton Spa because there is no mist in the valley. Put nothing opposite Mist on the Hills. Geraniums: that is better. They are red: I should say that they are decidedly geraniums. Let somebody give me the catalogue of prices. . . . Geraniums, one guinea: that is a great deal of money. Still Life: I should call it Still Death because there is no animation about it."

Mr. Banks who was holding the price catalogue in front of Lady Appledore like the Book of the Gospels gave a sycophantic laugh.

"Excellent!" he said. "How you hit it off, Lady Appledore. Still Death! I must remember that. Did you hear that, Colonel? My lady says that Still Life should be called Still Death. I did not care for the picture myself and now I know the reason. No animation: an admirable criticism."

"Very true, very true indeed," said Colonel Chase. "I hope you like the little picture I have bought Lady Appledore. Golf links, Wentworth. I took a lot of trouble in laying them out."

Lady Appledore kindly retraced her steps to Number 6.

"A matter of taste," she said. "It does not appeal to mine. If I were you I should instantly purchase Geraniums, Colonel Chase. Geraniums is well worth a guinea. I should not let Geraniums slip through my fingers. But I would not buy Still Life. You may trust my judgment, Colonel Chase, and have nothing to do with Still Life, but buy Geraniums before it is snapped up. You will never regret it."

She fixed him with an implacable eye which was not removed till he had told the custodian to put the fatal red star on Geraniums.

"Make a rule, Colonel Chase," she said, "always to buy the best work, and then you will know--well, that you have the best. Geraniums and The Curfew are undoubtedly Miss Howard's masterpieces. (This was agonising for Mr. Banks, who might have bought both masterpieces for less than he had paid for Evening Bells). Of the two I prefer The Curfew which I shall now purchase. Miss Jobson see to a star on Curfew, and say the remittance will follow."

Miss Howard meantime had been hovering about outside the Green Salon, torn between the desire not to appear supplicant for purchase, and the longing to make Lady Appledore's acquaintance, for she had not been introduced to her on the evening of the entertainment. Her curiosity also to see how many more pictures had been bought (for the custodian had been flitting about all this time with the price catalogue) was becoming unbearable. So she tripped in quite unconscious of Lady Appledore's presence, and of the unusual number of visitors in the Green Salon and felt the temperature of the hot-water pipes. She withdrew her fingers with a little exclamation of dismay at their intense fervour and turned off the tap.

"I can't have you all roasted, Mr. Banks," she said. "That would be too bad after your kindness in coming to see my little pictures."

That was sufficient indication of her identity, and Lady Appledore held out her hand.

"I am pleased to have seen your pictures, Miss Howard," she said. "That is not any empty compliment, for I have bought your Curfew. A very creditable effort. Nice tone. Should you ever be in the neighbourhood of the Grange, you will find some fine subjects in the Park. You may tell them at any of the lodges that I have given you leave to paint in the Park. Miss Jobson, kindly tell the motor that I am ready."

Miss Jobson hurried out to inform the intelligent machine, which thereupon ousted the bus for Wentworth that was standing at the entrance, forcing it to drive out of 'Out', and come in again behind it at 'In'. Miss Howard saw Lady Appledore off, leaving Colonel Chase trying to revoke the purchase of Golf links on the grounds of having chosen Geraniums instead. The custodian was contesting the point with great firmness. . . .

It was now so near lunch-time that Mr. Banks who was engaged to take this meal at the Warwickshire Hotel with a button king from Manchester decided to postpone his visit to the sick parishioner till afternoon. As was natural he told his host about the honour Lady Appledore had done to the exquisite exhibition in the Green Salon, and about her purchase of Miss Howard's finest example. The best of the pictures (as well as far the most expensive he was afraid) had already been secured, but there were some very charming pieces left.

"The art critics are wild about them," he said, "it is a great opportunity for any collector."

The button king had most artistic tastes, and owned a gallery of pictures.

"'Oward?" he said. "Never 'eard of 'Oward. Have we got a 'Oward, missus? Don't think we've got a 'Oward. Better 'ave a look at them after lunch before my bath. Glass of champagne for you, Mr. Banks. Wish I could drink champagne, but it's poison to me. And the Countess of Appledore bought one, did she? Pleased to know about them."

This promised well but ended in a fiasco. The button king hobbled into the Green Salon before his bath, but was vexed at being charged sixpence for admission: this was paltry. Paltrier yet was the price-catalogue, for nothing for which you were charged only half-a-guinea could possibly be worth purchase. He had hoped that the least price would be fifty-guineas or a hundred: that might have been worth considering. But who wanted a ten-and-sixpenny picture? Paltry he called it, and went to be pickled instead. Missus, however, took a different view: she thought them sweetly pretty, and bought two for her boudoir.

Colonel Chase mounted his bicycle when he came out having been unable to induce the custodian to refund anything, and went off for his ride. He did not intend to return to Wentworth for lunch, and had taken with him what he called 'a snack', which caused the pockets of his Norfolk jacket to bulge with light refreshment. In one there were some rolls stuffed with ham, and a large lump of cheese, in another a couple of hard-boiled eggs, an apple and a stick of chocolate, in a third a flask of whiskey, a cold sausage and a small thermos flask containing coffee. His regard for Miss Howard had soared since breakfast, and his contemptuous compassion for her unpatronised wares and unpurchased walls had given place to a strong feeling of respect for one whose work was so eminently marketable and had won the admiration of a Dowager Countess. She could go warbling out in the morning with a paint-box and a bit of paper, just for her own amusement, and bring back the best part of half-a-guinea. That was a gift, a solid asset, and as he selected a convenient fallen tree-trunk by the wayside on which he could sit and spread out his little snack, where the sun was warm on his back, and his folded mackintosh kept him safe from damp, he began to consider, as he was periodically wont to do, whether on the whole he would be more comfortable if he was married, and whether he was likely to find anyone more suitable than Miss Howard to make him so. She was not young, she was not, though neat and presentable, pretty any longer, but that was all to the good, for the excited, hysterical element which entered, he believed, into alliance between boys and girls, must have no place in this union. Wentworth, with a few weeks of lodgings in London and meals at his club, was a very easy sort of existence, but the worry and trouble of a house and household would, of course, if he married, be borne by his wife: his part in it would only be to mention if the bath water was not hot, or the food not to his liking, much as he did now. She, in fact, would be a sort of Mrs. Oxney, though honoured with his name. Then there was the question of expense, but since Miss Howard could afford to live at Wentworth, and go off once or twice a year to Torquay, it looked as if she ought to be able to bear half the charge of a small household. Besides, she had her little place in Kent, near Tunbridge Wells; when the lease of her present tenants came to an end, they could live there, rent free. He figured it, on the impression he had got from her allusions to it, as a pleasant manorial house of stone or old brick, with a stable and a garden and 'grounds', too small perhaps to call a Park, but with room no doubt for a miniature golf links, and an air of landed dignity. There was sure to be a club at Tunbridge Wells, frequented by business men, who went up to the City by early trains, and by local gentry, and he could drop into the club for a cup of tea and a rubber of bridge before getting back to his little place and Mrs. Colonel, who would scold him if he was late. The days would pass very pleasantly: he would bicycle as usual all the morning, and she, after seeing to her household duties, would turn sheets of drawing-paper into half-guineas: he would potter about his garden or golf links in the afternoon, and, perhaps he would have a small car. 'Squire Chase' he thought to himself.

The snack had almost completely disappeared during these reflections, and Colonel Chase, nourished now and well-warmed by the sun felt very benevolent towards the whole world. There was just one egg still uneaten, and this he peeled and chipped into small pieces with his pocket-knife generously strewing them on the trunk of the tree where he sat, so that the birds might eat and be filled, and bless him in their pretty twitterings. He mounted his bicycle again and wondered how he could find out more concerning Miss Howard's little place in Kent. She let it, as she had said, because she could not afford to live in it, but with Squire Chase to share expenses, which he would be quite willing to do if the little place was a nice little place, it might be manageable. The more he thought about Miss Howard in connection with her little place the brighter grew Miss Howard's prospect in connection with him. This marriage would be a sensible contract for mutual advantage: she would get a husband who would look after her place for her, and he a wife who would look after his comfort.

Unconscious of these plans for her advantage, Miss Howard meantime had flown rather than walked up to Wentworth for lunch, with all this wonderful news to give of the Green Salon, and positively eager to recant her blasphemy against Mind. Yesterday at this time when no picture had been sold and not a visitor had demanded toilet-paper, she had firmly announced that she gave up Mind, and that fell determination had been confirmed by the subsequent revelation that Colonel Chase's pedometer had not been miraculously wafted into Mrs. Bliss's possession by Mind's mysterious agency but had been placed there in answer to her simple request by an ordinary chemist. But now she thought no more about pedometers: a cataract of purchasers had descended on the Green Salon, and she unhesitatingly accepted the benevolent power which had guided them there and opened their hearts and their purses, as identical with that which had removed the Colonel's cold in a single night. And there was Mrs. Bliss in the lounge smiling and joyful, though as yet she knew nothing of what had occurred.

"Dear one!" she said. "And how have things gone to-day? Have you less of that despondency which keeps you in Error, and of the Error which keeps you in despondency? Sweet one, how lovely! I see it has gone from you. You have been denying it, and Mind has shown you its nothingness. Evil is nothing, nothing is Evil. Love, Mind, Omnipotence deny hate, Error--Tell me all about it. I could jump for joy."

Miss Howard could have jumped too.

"Oh, Mrs. Bliss, it's too wonderful," she said. "It has turned out just as you said it would. I went down to the Green Salon this morning, still in Error, and expecting to find that nobody had been in, or bought anything, and instead there was the most wonderful news. Kind dear Mr. Bullingdon whom I had thought rather unappreciative of my pictures--and oh, how wrong I was--I suppose that was Error too--and dear kind Mrs. Holders, who, I thought, didn't care about them either, each bought a picture yesterday morning, and they had hardly gone when two ladies came in, and would you believe it, each of them bought two pictures, which made six--"

She broke off a moment, as Mrs. Holders hobbled downstairs from her rest.

"Oh, Mrs. Holders," she said, "how good it was of you and Mr. Bullingdon to buy those pictures yesterday! That started everything: I mean Mind began then, I was just telling Mrs. Bliss. Do you know that you and Mr. Bullingdon had scarcely gone when two ladies came in, and each of them bought two more. I can't think who they can have been, for their names were quite unknown to me. I suppose they came from one of the hotels: they were just two ladies, the boy at the door told me, and he couldn't describe them at all. And then they had hardly gone when two gentlemen came in and they each bought two, and I didn't know their names either, and that made ten pictures all in one morning. Wasn't it wonderful? Just when I was beginning to feel so dreadfully low about it, and to wish that I had never thought of having an exhibition at all."

Mrs. Holders looked very much surprised: up went the eyebrows.

"That looks like Mind, doesn't it?" she said, in a rather cold sarcastic tone, and she hobbled off without another word in the direction of the dining-room.

Miss Howard thought it very kind of her to have bought a picture, but her manner was far from sympathetic. She turned to ecstatic Mrs. Bliss again.

"And that wasn't all, not nearly," she resumed, "for soon after I went down this morning, and was hearing about all this, in came the dear padre and Mrs. Banks, and not their first visit either, and though I made myself busy with checking the names and that sort of thing, so as not to look as if I wanted them to buy anything--"

CHAPTER VII

"Quite right, dear one," said Mrs. Bliss, "We have to trust to Mind completely, when we have done our best, and make no interference. Yes?"

"--they asked for the catalogue of prices," said Miss Howard who had held her mouth open during this interruption, so as to go on again at once, "and first she bought God's Acre, and then he bought Evening Bells, which was the highest priced of all. And they had hardly bought theirs, when Colonel Chase came in--dear Colonel Chase, what wrong thoughts I have had about him too, for I thought he was not meaning to come to my exhibition at all, and as for buying anything! But it was all Error. Let me see, where was I? I had gone out, but I kept just peeping in, as I walked about outside. . . . So Colonel Chase came in and he bought Golf Links, Wentworth, and then dear Florence Kemp (I'm getting so much drawn to her) bought 'Oh, to be in England now that April's here', and looked at me so lovingly and sympathetically."

"Mind again!" crowed Mrs. Bliss.

"Yes, and then who do you think? Lady Appledore and Miss Jobson. She thought so highly of them--I was introduced to her afterwards, and she implored me almost to go and sketch in the Park at the Grange--and bought Curfew tolls the knell, and told Colonel Chase, so the boy informed me, that he should certainly buy Geraniums, which was a guinea. I think perhaps he only meant to buy one--"

"But Mind took him by the hand and led him up to Geraniums," said Mrs. Bliss.

"Yes, it really looks like it," said Miss Howard, "or anyhow Lady Appledore did. Oh, Mrs. Bliss, how untrustful I was yesterday, thinking that nobody cared. I shall go down again after lunch, and I shan't be a bit surprised to find that somebody else has come in and bought some more. Sixteen sold already within twenty-four hours: nearly one an hour! Or do you think I ought not to go down this afternoon but leave it all to Mind? Which would Mind like best?"

Mrs. Bliss uttered a peal of musical laughter.

"Sweet one, Mind loves you to do whatever gives you most joy and happiness," she said. "Just deny evil, depression, unhappiness, which don't exist. Didn't I tell you that all would be harmony and prosperity at your lovely exhibition if only you trusted Mind?"

"But I didn't," said Miss Howard, contrite but still joyful. "I gave Mind up yesterday. I remember telling you so."

"No, you only thought you did, and that was Error, as is now proved. I worked away at your Error yesterday, and I knew it would be removed. And the pretty gong--such a beautiful sonorous note--has sounded, and here's Mrs. Oxney come to scold us for not going in to lunch, and to hear your good news."

Mrs. Oxney was seriously alarmed to hear that so many pictures had been sold, and that Miss Howard apparently was not certain whether 'Pussy-dear' was among them. Miss Howard, as a matter of strict fact, was quite sure 'Pussy-dear' was still in the market, but it would be good for Mrs. Oxney to have a little fright owing to her remissness.

"There was such a crowd of purchasers," she said, "and really those little red stars to show that pictures were sold, were being put up here, there and everywhere. I should not wonder if I had to get another supply of them. But 'Pussy-dear' may be unsold still. I don't think Lady Appledore bought it."

"And has the Countess of Appledore been among your visitors?" said the awe-struck Mrs. Oxney. "Dear me, what I've missed by not going down this morning! I must put on my hat directly I've had a bite of lunch. . . . Oh, Mrs. Bliss, but you're walking without a stick, and moving along so that I can scarcely keep up with you! I never saw such an improvement. Dr. Dobbs will be pleased with you. I declare it's like one of his own conjuring tricks. You've got reason to be thankful to Bolton Spa."

Colonel Chase came back with a sound appetite for tea, after the mere snack by the wayside shared with the birds, and heard the new and gratifying intelligence that the button queen staying at the "Warwickshire" had bought two more pictures, and that Mrs. Oxney had secured Pussy-dear, a thing she would never have done had she not seen the button queen regarding it with an admiring eye. Owing to Mrs. Bliss's deceitful conduct with regard to his pedometer he addressed no conversation whatever to her, and had only the shortest and coldest replies for her when she spoke to him, for if there was one thing he disapproved of (and indeed there were many) it was anything that savoured of deception. But his displeasure seemed to have no effect on one who basked in the effulgence of Mind, and, though his attitude was most marked, (for he was full of agreeable conversation for everyone else, including Mrs. Holders) it may be considered doubtful if she ever noticed it. As he had been unable to get out of his purchase of Golflinks, Wentworth, for the leap-frog boy refused to refund a penny of his takings, it was best to be congratulatory to Miss Howard, and console himself with the fact that there were now many financial victims of the Green Salon. Another reason for being pleasant to her was that he wanted to learn more about her little place in Kent.

"My Geraniums!" he said, (grasping the nettle, so to speak, for it was the guinea that smarted most,) "I was delighted to secure Geraniums, and much gratified to find that Lady Appledore, with her fine taste, approved my choice. One of your masterpieces, she said, Miss Howard. Where did you paint that? I cannot remember seeing a bed of geraniums of such wonderful brightness here. Perhaps it was at your little place in Kent."

Miss Howard, secure beneath the aegis of Mind, was rather daring.

"Was it there?" she said, pressing her finger to her forehead in the effort of recollection. "Perhaps it was. Let me see: the herbaceous border and then the little sunk rose-garden. No: I think I painted it here last summer long after my tenants were in possession of my old home. Or did I paint it from memory? Somehow I seem to feel--"

Mrs. Oxney felt she had to claim Geraniums for a product of Wentworth: Pussy-dear and Geraniums and ever so many more were inspired by Wentworth.

CHAPTER VII

"Oh no, Miss Howard," Mrs. Oxney said. "You painted Geraniums from the bed below the dining-room windows. Such a show there was of them. I saw you doing it, and I said to myself, 'Now Miss Howard's got a beautiful subject. That'll be one of her best sketches.' And I was right, for it and Pussy-dear were a guinea each. So here am I with Pussy-dear, and the Colonel with Geraniums, and the Reverend Banks with Evening Bells, which was the choicest of all. How things move about, don't they and what a pleasure they give!"

"And were there no sketches of your old home in the exhibition?" asked Colonel Chase.

Again Miss Howard had to press her finger to her forehead.

"Now did I put Chrysanthemums into it?" she asked. "Or Hearts of Oak? I remember painting Hearts of Oak just before I was obliged to let my little place. Two such wonderful trees, ever so many hundreds of years old, and quite hollow inside. The dear old place! How I long to see it again! Such a lovely view over the valley, and the sweet little old-world town once so fashionable. The Pantiles."

"But a very charming little town still, I believe," said Colonel Chase. "A golf links, isn't there, and a country club?"

"Yes, oh yes," said Miss Howard. "Papa used to like his round of golf and his rubber before dinner. He thought it his duty to take part in the social life of the little town. I have such sweet memories of the Croft--my little place, you know--and it is dreadful to think of it in the hands of strangers. But what was I to do? We're all so hard hit by these monstrous taxes. And my tenants are very good, nice people, and they promised to take great care of my little bits of things."

Miss Howard was enjoying this immensely: without being guilty of downright fabrication, she was building up a most interesting fabric.

"Beautiful furniture, I suppose," said Colonel Chase.

"Just some little family things," said she with a sigh. "But after all what does it matter? If one cannot afford to live in the family place, one has to live somewhere else. It has happened to so many of us."

Miss Howard's chance of matrimony, had she only known it was soaring upwards as on eagle's wings. She had said nothing really definite but a great deal that was truly impressive in a vague and sumptuous manner. Colonel Chase allowed his imagination to run riot and it flowered into a paved courtyard with a sundial, and a gallery-room with Queen Anne furniture and portraits. His regiment, on his retiring had presented him with one of himself, one hand holding a rifle and one foot in a beautifully polished boot on the famous man-eater. It hung at present in the dining room at Wentworth just opposite his table, but Mrs. Oxney could put 'Pussy-dear' there when it was removed to the gallery-room at the Croft. He felt that he might even change his name to Howard-Chase.

Miss Howard was certainly the heroine of the day and to none was she more worshipful than to Florence Kemp. For a couple of weeks now Florence's admiration of her had been ripening into a shy and silent adoration, and this afternoon, as the drawing-room emptied, she felt that it could be stifled in silence no longer, but must be allowed to begin expressing itself. Miss Howard must know in what tender esteem she was held, and how Florence longed to dedicate her affection by open avowal. She aspired to intimate friendship, and if that was out of reach, she wanted definite and indulgent permission to cherish and serve. Miss Howard (who surely would permit herself to be Alice for the future: that would be something) seemed to her the incarnation of brilliant existence. She could improvise, she could paint and sell those beautiful little sketches she dashed off so easily; she was gay and independent and self-reliant. Then again how picturesque was the background she had several times indicated of an ancestral home to which she was evidently so much attached, though she accepted without unavailing regrets the penury which debarred her from living there. But all these gifts and qualities and conditions were but little decorations and fineries fitly adorning the surface; admirable accessories and attributes of the adorable. Florence felt moreover with the infallible certainty of instinct that the other was not one who cared much or indeed at all for the companionship or affection of men, and in this she recognised a secret kinship of nature with herself. Yet at present Miss Howard had no devoted friend or she would not be living at Wentworth in this unattached manner, and Florence longed to take a place that was clearly vacant.

The drawing-room was empty now, but for these two. Mrs. Bliss had been the last to go, smiling herself away, and Florence's virginal heart rose into her throat, as she took the first step, and moved across to an empty chair by Miss Howard, at the thought that a place next and close to her might possibly become hers by right.

"Oh, Miss Howard," she said, "I must tell you how I love your pictures. And I want you to do me a great favour. I want you to let me come down with you tomorrow, and to advise me one to buy. I did get one, such a precious one, this morning, but I must have another, and I should like to have the one you recommend. Is it very bold and forward of me to ask for your advice?"

Miss Howard was by no means surfeited with success: she was quite capable of assimilating more.

"Of course you shall have my advice," she said, "and it's sweet of you to want any of my little daubs."

"Little daubs!" said Florence in a sudden ecstasy of irony. "Aren't they horrid little daubs? How I envy your gift, it must be too lovely to sit down and make beautiful things like you!"

Miss Howard had already observed a little diffident signalling going on from Florence, but this vigorous waving of the flag rather astonished her, for she had looked on Florence as too deeply consecrated to the service of an entirely selfish father to have any vivid emotional interests of her own. But as her 'beautiful things' witnessed, sentimentality was a magnet to her, and now she jumped to it like iron filings.

"Oh, but how dear of you to think of me like that," she said. "And in a way you're right. It is lovely, anyhow, to want to make beautiful things."

The firelight shining encouragingly as the dusk deepened outside made admirable conditions for the growth of intimacy. Florence was naturally reserved, but like most reserved women, when once the cork came out, it made an explosive exit, and a stream of bottled-up effervescence followed.

"And it's not your painting only," she said, "or your music which make you so wonderful, but you, yourself, and your self-reliance and independence. Oh, but I should envy all your gifts if they weren't yours. How I've watched and admired you all this last fortnight since we came here! And this evening I simply could not help myself: I had to tell you. You may laugh at me if you like, but please don't."

Florence gave a gasp of astonishment at her own boldness, wondering whether she had only made the most dreadful fool of herself. If she had, well, there it was, and she would just have to search for the cork which had popped so magnificently, and bottle herself up again. But instead of so lamentable an end to this burst of self-expression, Miss Howard's cork showed signs of popping too: it did not fly forth with the vigour of Florence's explosion, but there was a little fizzing at its edges.

"Indeed I shan't laugh," she said. "I think it's delightful of you to like me, and to tell me so. As for self-reliance and independence, I've got no one to depend on, so I must rely on myself. You've got your father--"

"Would you rely on him if he was yours?" asked Florence.

"But you're so devoted to him. I often have admired the way you give yourself to him."

"I don't," said Florence, with all the candour of devotion. "I don't give, he takes. We thoroughly dislike each other--"

"My dear," began Miss Howard.

"But it's true and it's such a relief to be able to tell anybody that. I don't think anyone was ever so lonely as I am! I long to get away from him: he surrounds me, he cuts me off. He wouldn't miss me: anyone who would read to him, and fill his thermos flask and tuck in his rug would do just as well. I have thought sometimes of trying to get a nurse for him, and having a life of my own. It's you with your lovely independence that put it into my head. I could do something of my own then. It isn't as if he liked me: that would be different. In ten days now I suppose we shall go to Bournemouth, and stop there till we go to Buxton about Easter."

"But he may get better, and then you would settle down. Didn't you say you had a flat in Kensington Square?"

"Yes: but it has been shut up all these years. Besides, he wouldn't know what to do with himself if he got better. And all the time we're at Bournemouth I shall be wishing I was back here."

Something in this touched Miss Howard with a sense of need. Her cork began to fizz a little more.

"So shall I," she said.

"No! But how perfectly wonderful!" said Florence. "Will you really? And will you say 'Florence'?"

"Yes, if you'll say Alice."

"Oh, Alice!" said Florence.

They kissed and then neither of them knew what to say next in a situation which was new to them both. In slight embarrassment Alice, still holding Florence's hand, began out of habit to warble something.

"Oh, sing something or play me something," said Florence. "Sit down at the piano and make something beautiful. Improvise."

It was a relief to do something, and Alice went to the piano.

"Shall I?" she said. "Just anything that comes into my head?"

"Please, and may I sit where I can see you as well as hear you?"

Alice made her light butterfly excursions up and down the keys and from the lounge outside Colonel Chase heard these familiar noises. His mind was now made up to begin his romantic wooing, and the sooner he took it in hand the better. He softly opened the door and stole in: there was Miss Howard with her eyes dreamily fixed on the ceiling, looking really quite attractive, and there was that tiresome Miss Kemp gazing at her as if she was some beautiful vision, and herself, so thought Colonel Chase, as if she was some large swooning frog. He sat himself where he could look at Miss Howard too, and put on the sort of face which concert-goers wear when they listen to slow movements by Beethoven, an expression of remorse and reverie. So there they all sat till the stream of inspiration ran dry, and ended in a minor chord. Miss Howard sighed, they all sighed.

"Beautiful!" said Colonel Chase. "Very fine. Dear me! A great treat."

Miss Howard raised her eyes from the contemplation of the minor chord, and smiled at Florence, quite ignoring the Colonel.

"Did you like it, dear?" she said.

"Don't stop!" said Florence.

So Miss Howard went on again in another key, while her two lovers settled down to see each other out. In the middle of the next improvisation a maid came in to tell Florence that her father wanted her, but she did not move and only whispered 'Hush: presently.' Then the evening paper was brought in for Colonel Chase, and he let it lie unread, and gazed at various points of the ceiling, and strangled a yawn. At the end, which did not come off for a long time, for a perfect flood of half-forgotten fragments poured into Miss Howard's mind, she closed the piano and got up with a gay laugh.

"Florence, darling, you shan't work me and bully me any more," she said, and perched herself airily on the arm of Florence's chair.

"Too lovely, darling," said Florence. "Thank you."

"Thank you indeed," said Colonel Chase with an air of correcting Florence. "Exquisite. What a gift. Never shall I forget your accompaniment to my ghost story."

This was a pretty direct hint that he should be asked for his ghost story, but nobody expressed the slightest desire to hear it.

"What a delicious frock you've got on," said Florence, as if Colonel Chase was non-existent.

"Do you like it, dear? So glad," said Alice. "But gracious me, look at the time! I believe the dressing-bell must have gone, and we never heard it."

CHAPTER VII

"Something better to listen to," said Colonel Chase, very handsomely.

"Dearest, we must fly then," said Florence, and away they flew, arm in arm, leaving the baffled Colonel, alone with his evening paper. He searched his memory in vain for an occasion on which his compliments and attentions had met with so indifferent a reception.

CHAPTER VIII

The tonic of this declared devotion proved itself to be a wonderful stimulant to Florence in her revolt against parental tyranny: it was as if she was taking a course of psychical strychnine, and every hour almost saw some fresh insubordination. She told her father that she had not been able to come to him when he had sent for her just now because Miss Howard was playing to her and that when she had finished, it was time to dress for dinner: and she paid him the briefest of bedside visits that night, leaving him to drink lemonade or eat rusks, or concentrate on the power of Mind, or go to sleep or lie awake just as he pleased, and off she went for a long talk till after midnight with Alice. She flowed into confidences, she babbled and expanded in new found freedom of speech after these sealed up and suppressed years: it was the richest joy to reveal to Alice all the little flutterings of her soul which hitherto had groped in dusk and silence.

Next morning she did not wait to accompany Mr. Kemp in the bus down to the bath, but started off earlier to walk down with Alice to the Green Salon. There a very pleasing tussle took place for Alice, after selecting Dewy Eve for her, as the most creditable Howard that still remained unsold, absolutely refused to be paid for it. She would really be very much hurt if Florence (obstinate Flo!) would not accept it, and so with a squeezing of Alice's hand obstinate Flo did accept it, and instantly bought Gloaming (which made a beautiful 'pair') on her own account. Alice said this was a very shabby trick, but Flo was firm, and so two more red stars were needed. A third was presently required, for Alice determined to give June's Glory to Mrs. Bliss as a slight recognition of the services rendered by Mind. After lunch Florence gave the leap-frog boy the daily wage, and sent him off to amuse himself as he liked, while she enjoyed the office of custodian, sitting on his high stool with the nearly exhausted toilet-roll and the pill box of the few red remaining stars (slightly sticky) in order to be doing something for her new friend. There was not much to do, for visitors were few, but, as compensation, they had the Green Salon almost entirely to themselves.

Mr. Kemp, all that day, naturally felt himself the victim of a series of atrocities, for he had to get in and out of the bus without Florence's aid, in the afternoon he had to read to himself instead of being read to, and fall asleep alone, and personally to ring the bell before doing so, to ask a maid to bring him his second thickest rug. Then again the move to Bournemouth was to take place in only nine short days from now, and it was high time to begin looking up the journey, and settling whether it would be more comfortable to leave Bolton in the morning and lunch in the train, thus arriving at Bournemouth in time to have tea and rest before dinner, or leave Bolton directly after an early lunch and only get into Bournemouth at a quarter to eight at night. Then there was the further alternative of sending Florence on in the morning with the luggage, while he followed later. This would save him waiting about at draughty stations while she got luggage labelled and collected, and she would have time to unpack for him at Bournemouth before he arrived. True, he would be obliged to open and shut windows in the railway carriage for himself, and personally take a taxi for crossing London, but if he provided himself with plenty of small change, he believed he could manage it. These studies in comparative fatigue were very puzzling to pursue alone; it was scandalous of Florence not to be at hand, for she knew so well what sort of thing tired him most.

As he turned over the pages of his Bradshaw, the small print of which, he was sadly afraid, would very likely give him a headache from eye-strain later on, he lit upon a series of stations printed in rather larger type: these were Bolton Spa, Reading, Basingstoke, Southampton, Bournemouth. He gazed at this revelation in astonishment, for there appeared to be trains from here to Bournemouth by these lines and junctions, which would convey him there without a single change. He had for several years now gone at the end of his Bolton-cure to Bournemouth, but Florence looked up the trains, and they had always travelled up to London and changed stations there. At the moment of this dazzling discovery she and Miss Howard came prattling into the lounge, having closed the Green Salon for the day.

"Florence," he said excitedly. "Please verify this for me at once. There seems to be a train which goes from here to Bournemouth without change, and all these years you have taken me up to London. Look: 11.35 a.m. from Bolton."

Florence held out a casual hand for the Bradshaw, and continued speaking to Alice.

"Let's have tea at once, dear," she said, "and then we can have a stroll afterwards: you must have a little more walk, so good for you. What is it, Papa?"

"I beg you will attend," said he shrilly. "At the top of the page there."

Florence, not attending, dropped the Bradshaw and the page of the epoch-making discovery was lost.

"How careless you are," said Mr. Kemp. "Now we shall have to search for it all over again. And I don't know where you've been this afternoon, not near me, anyhow. I've had to forage for myself whenever I wanted anything."

"You've foraged very successfully if you've really found such a wonderful train," she said. "Whereabouts was it?"

Mr. Kemp's excitement was very excusable: even his ill-temper might be pardoned, for it was a long time since so important a railway discovery had been made.

"Pick up the Bradshaw and give it me," he said. "Very stupid of you. And I don't know the page: it wasn't on the ordinary Bolton page."

"Try the index," said Florence, "if you want to look it up yourself. Won't you bring it into the drawing-room? Tea is ready, and we'll find it there."

"Certainly not," said he. "I could not touch my tea, till I've found it again."

"Very well: bring it in when you've got it," she said, "and I'll see if it's right."

She joined Miss Howard in the drawing-room, where others were assembling, while Mr. Kemp in the lounge fruitlessly searched the innumerable pages, and it was not till daylight began to grow dim and tea cold, that his tragic face appeared at the door.

"And here's Mr. Kemp at last," said Mrs. Oxney pleasantly. "Why how late you are, Mr. Kemp, and whatever's happened? You look so worried."

He explained the nature of the catastrophe.

"Most disastrous," he said. "I distinctly saw the train, and I've searched and searched but can't find it again."

"Well, I'm no use," said Mrs. Oxney. "Bradshaw's a sealed book to me, and always has been. How anybody can make it out, I don't know. Send away that tea, Mr. Kemp, and have a cup of fresh."

"I don't really want any," he said. "11.35 a.m. from Bolton. I saw it, and then my daughter dropped the Bradshaw."

"Things do fly out of the hand sometimes," said Mrs. Oxney. "And what's the Colonel been doing?"

The Colonel had been walking, and the record on the pedometer (he glanced darkly at Mrs. Bliss who only smiled in return) was satisfactory. Florence and Miss Howard, seated in a remote window-seat took no notice of anybody, and presently they got up and moved to the door.

"We're going for a little stroll, Papa," she said. "Miss Howard is taking me to the place where she painted Gloaming. Do you want anything done for you in the town?"

"I beg you will not go out till you have found the train," said he. "My eyes are getting very tired: I feel I shall have a headache soon. Go on looking for me, Florence; read every page carefully."

"I'll find it when I come in," said Florence. "Don't fuss, Papa."

He could only gasp in sheer astonishment at the idea that he could be thought fussy.

The two friends went down across the garden and the fields below it, to the site of Gloaming. It was gloaming already: they would see the spot just as it had looked when it inspired Alice, though she had painted it in the morning. There was a nail-paring of a moon in the West, and they duly curtsied to it and sometimes Alice sang staves of song, and sometimes they walked arm-in-arm and then exuberantly *chasséed* for a few steps. This dawn of emotional attraction, rendered and responded to, excited and rejuvenated Florence the repressed and unconsidered: she suddenly found the drab of her dull and monotonous existence shot with colour: she expanded and blossomed with the warm sense of giving herself to someone who wanted her not for service, but for free comradeship. Her virginal heart seemed to sprout with fresh growth under these fruitful showers. She skipped and *chasséed* beneath the sickle moon, rather out of breath but enraptured.

"It's a new life, darling," she panted, as, quite exhausted they dropped to a more sober pace, "and it has gone to my head: I'm tipsy with it. Obstinate, tipsy Flo! And I've got, oh, such a delicious plan in my head, but I shan't tell you a single word about it for fear it shouldn't come off."

"Oh, you must tell me, Flo," said Alice. "I must share it with you. Please!"

"Not if you said please a hundred times."

"Obstinate Flo!" said Alice, pretending to pout. "I don't like you any more. You shall be Miss Kemp again. Good evening, Miss Kemp."

"Good evening, Miss Howard. So pleasant just to have met you before I go away to Bournemouth next week."

"The same to you. . . . But do tell me the plan. Please, please, please, please. . . . Oh, here's the place where I painted the trumpery little sketch you were so obstinate about. Obstinate Flo: O. F."

"Which stands equally well for Old Fool," said Florence.

"Well, it's not my fault if it does. The stream, do you see, and the woods beyond, and just the top of the steeple of St. Giles's. It was just a month ago, at the time of the last new moon. Dear slim girlie of a moon, little did I think that when next you came round, I should be here again, but not alone!"

Florence replied with a hug first.

"But I think your sketch is far more beautiful than the original," she said. "You've left out that ugly siding, with the roof of the station, and filled it with poetry instead!"

Alice put her head a little on one side and half closed her eyes.

"Have I made it poetical?" she said. "How dear of you to think that! I painted it as I *felt* it was. And I didn't feel the station, so I left it out."

"You made a perfect poem of it," said Florence. "You always put yourself into your sketches. Oh, the station. May we pop in for a moment, as we're so close and then I can find out about poor Papa's train. How I hate trains that go away from Bolton while you are here. But perhaps, who knows--"

She broke off.

"Why do you stop?" said Alice. "Oh I guess! What you were going to say concerns the plan. Doesn't it now?"

But Flo was just as obstinate as ever, and Alice again pretended to be cross, and wouldn't let O. F. take her arm, and was very cold and polite. Indeed there was quite a quarrel for exactly two minutes, at the end of which obstinate Flo admitted that she had stopped because what she was going to say did concern the plan in a sort of a way, but that it would be very mean of Alice to try to guess it. So Alice relented, and said she would not bully her any more, and they skipped and sang again. Then, going into the station they found that a portion of the 11.35 train went to Bournemouth every day, without any changing just as it had done for the last ten or twelve years, so that Mr. Kemp need never have gone up to London at all. They tripped back to Wentworth, where Colonel Chase was getting quite anxious about Miss Howard being out so late, but appeared not to care at all how late Miss Kemp was out.

Her father had gone to his room where he was resting after the visit of his *masseur.* He gave her one glance, and then in dead silence continued his search in Bradshaw. The silence, rightly considered, was a chorus of reproaches.

"You need not bother about that train any more," she said. "I went to the station and found out about it. It leaves here at 11.35 and there's a through carriage to Bournemouth."

His sombre face brightened.

"That is good news," he said. "But are you quite certain? Who told you?"

"The station-master."

He handed her the open Bradshaw.

"He ought to be reliable," he said. "But my mind would be easier if I saw it confirmed in Bradshaw."

"But you found it there yourself," said she.

"I certainly thought I did. But it is very mysterious that I could not find it again. Take the book carefully and don't drop it this time, and go on, please from the page at which it is open. My eyes are aching sadly, and I had no tea to speak of. Is it a new train?"

"No; it's been running for years."

"You mean to say that we might have gone by it last year and the year before, and have saved me all the agitation and fatigue of crossing London?"

"Yes," said Florence.

Mr. Kemp felt justly indignant.

"I do not expect much from you, Florence," he said, "and if I did, I shouldn't get it. But considering my condition, my utter helplessness, I do think you might have taken the trouble to find this out before. You would have saved me much. Last year I remember, it was a full week before I recovered from the fatigue of the journey. But I make no complaints. And is there a luncheon car on the train, or shall I have to take my lunch with me?"

"I didn't ask," said Florence. "There is plenty of time to find out. You are not going till the day after tomorrow week."

"A rusk, please," he said. "I had no tea. I am surprised you did not think of ascertaining that. These rusks are not quite fresh. No crispness . . . Florence, I am not sure, but I think my knee is moving a shade more easily. Do you consider that is the effect, if I am right about it, of Mind or massage?"

"Perhaps a little of both," said Florence cautiously. "Mind may be doing it, and massage helping you to believe it, or it may be the other way round. They seem to go together in Mrs. Bliss's case."

Mr. Kemp closed his eyes for a moment. His *masseur* had already been treating him, so now it was Mind's turn.

"Yes, I think they do," he said, "so why shouldn't they go together in my case? Let me see: Mind denies evil, pain: there is no pain in Mind, there is no Mind in pain. Mind is all, all is Mind. Hence there is no pain. . . . Certainly Mrs. Bliss's improvement has been marvellous. I am not sure that I should like to progress quite so quickly as that, for I should be afraid that something else was developing. But I feel sure that I have been on the up-grade this last week, though it would be more satisfactory if I knew exactly what caused it. I could then have more Mind or more massage accordingly. I think that at Bournemouth I shall have no massage at all for a week but work at Mind, and note very carefully if any change takes place."

He thought over this, still muttering incantations, then he shook his head.

"Even then it will be very difficult to be certain," he said. "If there is improvement, it may only be the after effect of Bolton. Or indeed, if I seem to be worse, that may be after effect. The first week after the cure is over is sometimes very discouraging. I do not know what to do."

Florence had been turning over the pages of Bradshaw. At this moment she found the long-sought train.

"I've got it," she said. "And there's an asterisk opposite it which means luncheon car."

Mr. Kemp gave a sigh of relief.

"That's a great weight off my mind," he said. "I was almost beginning to fear I had had a hallucination and that the train did not exist. I ought to have trusted Mrs. Bliss who told us she knew all would be well. You had better go to the station again tomorrow and see about engaging a place in the luncheon car. It would never do to leave that to chance, for if the luncheon car happened to be full when we joined the train, it would be no better than if there was none at all. Get one of those tables for two. They give more room than two places at a table for four. And you never know who may be next you."

Florence turned down the corner of the page, for her father would certainly want to verify this all over again for himself, and, reinforcing her courage with the thought of Alice, divulged the plan.

"I'm going to make a proposal to you, Papa," she said, "which I think may surprise you a good deal."

"Then I beg you will not," said Mr. Kemp nervously. "A surprise always means something unpleasant and agitating."

"It needn't agitate you at all," said Florence, "if you just keep calm, and talk it over quietly. I don't believe you will find it unpleasant."

He clenched his hands tightly.

"Make haste then," he said hoarsely. "Suspense as you ought to know, wears me out more than anything."

"I don't want to come to Bournemouth with you," said Florence. "I want you to take a nurse instead. A nice one who would be a companion to you as well."

Mr. Kemp shut his eyes. Some idea of invoking Mind occurred to him, but he knew he could not manage it.

"Quite impossible," he said.

"No, not at all impossible," said Florence. "She would look after you much more skilfully than I can and she would have nothing else to do."

"But you have nothing else to do," said he.

"We won't argue about that," she said. "But I really believe a good nurse would suit you much better than I do. I think you would soon find yourself much more comfortable."

He opened his eyes again: Florence was speaking in a calm confident voice which impressed him.

"Do you really think I should?" he asked.

"I think it is quite worth trying."

He felt he could now summon Mind to his aid. Naturally, if he would really be more comfortable, Florence's idea was not impossible at all: it was, on the contrary highly likely. And if the nurse did not suit him, Florence could come back at once. But there were other things to be considered too.

"But then there is the expense," he said. "I should have to pay her wages, should I not, and there's her keep as well. That will be a great drain. You have your own money to pay for your keep, as your poor dear mother left you half her fortune. I should be very poor indeed if I had to pay for a nurse: indeed I don't think I could do it. Of course, if you think that I should be more comfortable with a nurse, we must consider it very carefully, but we must not let the idea run away with us, and not consider the expense."

"I will help you with that," said Florence.

"Well, that is very generous of you, though perhaps it is no more than fair, considering how your poor mother left her fortune. By the way, what will you do with yourself?"

"I should stop on here for a little," said she, "and then very likely I should go to live in my flat in Kensington Square. There are a couple of servants there all the time and we've not been there for more than a few weeks during this last year. Let us try my plan. I don't mean to cut myself off from you at all: I will come down to Bournemouth when you are there, and often pay you visits in your hotels. But I want to have some sort of life of my own."

Mr. Kemp suddenly remembered he had not been pathetic, for his brain had been entirely occupied in trying to picture all that this change would mean. Of course a trained nurse would listen to the recital of his symptoms with much more perception and insight than poor Florence: if he felt that tiresome numbness in his right arm she would be able to reassure with real authority that it was not the approach of general paralysis, whereas Florence could only recommend him to think about something else. And she had no true understanding of his endless symptoms: her robust uninteresting health did not realise the many possible significances of a pain in his left side or a throbbing in his throat. But she must not imagine that he was not deeply hurt at her proposed desertion of him. Desertion: that was the keynote.

"You have wounded me," he said. "I had thought that you and I were so happy together, and that you felt it to be a privilege to minister to the needs of your crippled old father. It would not have been for long: I know that my life hangs by a thread. But I was wrong: you want to be quit of me, before my death releases you."

Florence got up. She knew quite well what she was about.

"If you feel like that, Papa," she said, "I give up the idea altogether. We go to Bournemouth together the day after to-morrow week by the luncheon car train. I will see to the seats."

Mr. Kemp saw he had gone too far. The notion of a pleasant nurse, to whose maintenance Florence contributed had begun to assume attractive colours in his mind. He visualised a comprehending woman, who entered into his sufferings and who would bring novelty into Buxton and Bath. Dear Florence often bored him: she listened in a most perfunctory manner to the recital of ailments that were familiar to her, and could not guess from her ignorance of medical knowledge what new complication they might foreshadow. He must push in that bleating *Vox Humana:* it had been too loud.

"I beg you not to be so hasty, dear," he said. "Anything in the nature of hurry always unsettles me. Take the two seats in the luncheon car of course: we shall want two seats for me and another however we settle this. You have told me that you think a trained nurse will be able to look after me better than you can do, and we must not reject your idea in that off-hand manner. We will think it over quietly to-night, and tomorrow morning while I am having my reclining bath, you must talk it over with Dr. Dobbs and get his view. You had better ring him up at once and make an appointment with him for tomorrow. Tell him it is very urgent, for indeed we have not got too much time, if this all has to be settled in nine days: and say you will come at whatever hour suits him. You could slip across after dinner to-night, if he is booked up all morning tomorrow. Indeed that might be the best plan: you had better telephone to him at once. Very urgent. I will try to get a little rest now, but my hour for resting after massage has been sadly encroached on. At dinner you shall tell me what you have arranged."

Florence was at the door when her father called her back.

"My rusks," he said. "They have quite lost their crispness. The tin should be placed open for half an hour in front of a good fire, but not too close."

There was much suppressed excitement and sense of unrest at Wentworth after dinner when it was known on what errand Florence was going to see Dr. Dobbs that very evening: Mrs. Oxney said that the atmosphere reminded her of that of the three days before the beginning of the Great War, for momentous decisions were being made which might alter the whole course of people's lives and nobody could be certain what would happen next. Mr. Kemp felt strongly that Mind should be consulted as well as Dr. Dobbs, and accordingly went into the pros and cons of the scheme very carefully with Mrs. Bliss, and then asked her whether she could obtain any guidance from Mind. It was clear from the way he put the case that so far from thinking it impossible any longer, his personal inclination was all for it: the idea of having a trained listener always at hand whom he could regale with his symptoms, and who was paid (by Florence) to listen to them now strongly attracted him. It was equally clear that Florence was eager to resign these privileges which had been hers for so long. Father and daughter Mrs. Bliss had also observed, were bored to death with each other, and this state of Error no doubt was an impediment to the clear shining forth of Mind. So when she retired to a quiet corner of the lounge, where she closed her eyes and realised that all was harmonious, it took very little time for her to be convinced that Mind was in favour of the scheme. Mr. Kemp was delighted to know that, and by the time Florence came back from her consultation with Dr. Dobbs, it would have needed strong disapproval on his part to have put him off the idea. But as she brought the glad tidings that Dr. Dobbs thought the scheme well worth trying, there was no struggle or antagonism between *materia medica* and Mind. All, as Mrs. Bliss had known, was indeed harmonious.

Mind, in fact, during the last few days had been going strong at Wentworth, and Mrs. Bliss had emerged brilliantly from the slight cloud that hung over her on the discovery of how she had got hold of Colonel Chase's pedometer. For since then, during those black days when from morning till night neither visitor nor purchaser came near the Green Salon, Mrs. Bliss had continued serenely confident that Mind was turning a special smile on the unpopulated exhibition, and was preparing a peculiarly rich harmony with regard to it. That had triumphantly proved to be the case, and now purchasers had come forward in such number that instead of the Green Salon closing at the end of this week, Miss Howard had determined to keep it open for another similar period. Then again, there was Mrs. Bliss's own amazing recovery as a further witness of Mind's beneficent functioning, and so her repeated assurance that Mr. Kemp, though apparently as lame as ever, was quite well, must be received with respect. Truth was nibbling away hard at his Error, and he would very soon find that it was so. This added to the general excitement.

But more thrilling even than the news that Mr. Kemp was quite well, and was therefore going to take a trained nurse with him to Bournemouth and that Florence was to remain here for the present, was the conjectured state of Colonel Chase's heart with reference to Miss Howard. Mrs. Oxney had long felt certain that from time to time he had 'had his eye' on her, and had been 'considering it', but nothing as yet had come of it and indeed a week ago she had almost given up the notion when he called her exhibition a blackmailing project, and had thrown doubt on the *extempore* character of her improvisations.

"I'm afraid he has settled against it, Amy," she had said to her sister on the occasion of his using that unlover-like expression, "for a gentleman doesn't talk like that about the lady of his choice. It would have been a treat to have had a courtship at Wentworth, and perhaps a marriage too."

"We should have lost two of our permanent guests," Amy had said, for she saw the gloomier side of all situations however romantic. "They'd both have gone away."

"Don't be too sure of that," had been Mrs. Oxney's reply. "They might have taken the end of that wing, and made a little flat of it, seeing that Miss Howard's country seat is let, and she couldn't have gone to live in the Colonel's club. That new bath-room would have come in convenient then. But now I'm afraid it's all over. He asked me only just now whether there was no means of stopping Miss Howard chirping all over the house like a canary."

Then suddenly the whole attitude of the Colonel towards the lady had changed. Not only had he paid a visit to the exhibition, in which, as a protest against blackmail, he had sworn he would never set foot, but he had bought two of the blackmailer's pictures, and had asked no end of respectful questions about her little place.

"And if there's as much as a note sounded on the piano," said Mrs. Oxney to-night, as she and her sister had their usual chat when the guests had gone to their rooms, "you'll hear a door opening somewhere, if the Colonel is within hearing, and he'll tiptoe into the drawing-room. Why, this morning I was just dusting the keys, and made a scale up and down with my duster, like one of Miss Howard's commencements, and he came peeping in. What disappointment there was in his face when he saw it was only me, and out he went again in a jiffy! He's after her now and no mistake."

Mrs. Bertram finished her patience: there had been no bridge to-night, for the Colonel had sat the whole evening in the lounge talking to Miss Howard and snubbing Florence.

"You may be right, Margaret," Mrs. Bertram said, "and I'm sure it would be pleasant to let the end of that wing for ever, as you may say, and I should be the last to want you not to put in the new bathroom if that was the way of it. But he can't get a word alone with her these days. There's always Miss Kemp sticking to her like plaster. I call it want of tact not to see that she'd be better away. She won't give him a chance."

"Such faces as he makes at her too," said Mrs. Oxney, "when he finds them together, as they always are now. They would scare me out of the room quick enough, not to mention the snubbings. And now Miss Kemp is settling to leave her Papa to go to Bournemouth with a nurse, and is stopping on here. I can't but be glad she's staying, for a guest is a guest, but I do wish she'd have the sense to let the Colonel have a turn without her. Such friends as she's become lately with Miss Howard, I never saw the like. They go skipping about together like two school-girls and if it isn't 'Alice this' it's 'Flo that'. It would be only friendly if she made herself scarce sometimes. But I wager the Colonel's in earnest now, and 'Love will find out the way' as Mr. Oxney used to whistle when he was after me. Why, if it isn't close on midnight! Just crush the fire down, while I put the burglar alarm on the shutters. You mark my words: Cupid will be busy in Wentworth yet. Such a fine man as the Colonel is too. I wouldn't hesitate long if I was Miss Howard. She's not likely to get such a chance again."

It was not likely that Cupid's elegant flutterings which were so manifest to Mrs. Oxney should have escaped the notice of Miss Howard or obstinate Flo, and to Miss Howard they were both gratifying and embarrassing. Gratifying they could not fail to be (for there was no doubt that Colonel Chase was after her) whether she intended to be caught or not. Obstinate Flo and she made a great joke of the strenuous attentions of her swain, as they sat over their usual midnight cocoa, in the bedroom of one or the other, after Mr. Kemp had summarily been made comfortable with his rusks and milk and hot-water bottle and lemonade, and Flo who had a rough rude gift of mimicry would affix a cotton-wool moustache to her upper lip and reproduce the imaginary wooings of the suitor, and his respectful kiss when accepted and Alice would giggle and slap her and say she was a silly girl, and ask her how she herself *could,* but in her heart of hearts she was not absolutely sure that she couldn't. Herein lay the embarrassment, for Flo took it for granted that their friendship satisfied all Alice's emotional needs for ever, and it was already settled that after Mr. Kemp's departure they were going off together to spend a fortnight alone at the flat in Kensington Square. Alice rightly interpreted this sojourn as being, in Flo's mind, a sort of honeymoon, a symbol of eternal and exclusive friendship, but now, with Colonel Chase so obviously in earnest, she was not sure whether she looked forward to the adventure with quite the rapture of her partner. Flo was a sweet thing, and the Colonel could not possibly be called a sweet thing, and it rather surprised Alice to find that she, who had never seriously felt the need of a man, could be weighing in her mind, as she certainly was doing, the comparative merits of the permanent companionship of a friend and of a husband. Though she found it difficult to imagine herself saying 'yes' to the offer that she felt sure Colonel Chase was ready to make her, whenever obstinate Flo gave him a chance, she found it nearly as difficult to imagine herself saying 'no'.

She put all this to herself as she sat to-night waiting for Florence to come in for cocoa and a chat over her fire. Florence was late, as she thought would most probably be the case, for Mr. Kemp had engaged a sympathetic nurse, and was to leave next morning by the luncheon-car train for Bournemouth: it was therefore certain that a particular suitcase would have to be packed overnight, which must contain all that he could possibly require (with an imaginative margin) on the arduous journey . . . Alice really could not come to any decision, for Florence looked down a much longer perspective than that of this little honeymoon in London, and anticipated that, at the end of it, they would settle to live together in devoted spinsterhood, as so many women did to whom either the desire or the opportunity for matrimony had not come. It was quite an agreeable prospect, and one which, a few weeks ago Alice would have welcomed. But now that the other opportunity was certainly about to offer itself, she saw that though matrimony might not be more permanent, it afforded a certain dignity and completeness which the other lacked. Then too, Colonel Chase seemed really to care for her, he bought her pictures, he listened with a rapt face to her improvisations, and more than once he had preferred to spend the evening talking to her, and trying to get rid of obstinate Flo rather than play bridge. He had even asked her to accompany him on one of his bicycle rides, and what more solid token of esteem could he give? In his judgment they would be very comfortable together, and she could not but respect the opinion of a man who so clearly was an adept in the art of comfort.

CHAPTER VIII

There was another embarrassment entirely private to herself: neither of her suitors had any notion of it and as this topic came into Alice's mind, she drew back a little from the fire feeling a sudden flush of heat invade her. This embarrassment was concerned with the ancestral home at Tunbridge Wells. Of late Colonel Chase, keenly interested in all that pertained to her, had often mentioned her little place, asking her gratifying questions about it, and making gratifying assumptions which were very difficult to contradict. Beyond any doubt the answers she had given to his questions and her own allusions to it, now and previously, had made it dreadfully clear to Alice that the little place as it really was, differed considerably from the little place as he imagined it to be. It was quite true that it was mildly ancestral, since her grandfather, a most respectable auctioneer, had built it (and anyone is at liberty to reckon a grandfather among his ancestors) but it was not quite what Colonel Chase and Mrs. Oxney and anybody who had heard her sigh over the cruel necessity of letting her old home, pictured it. It was quite true also that it had a rose-garden--for who, when all was said and done could deny that a bed of roses was a rose-garden?--and that there were some fine trees just outside the garden, for there were some remarkable old oaks on the common, of which so near a view was visible, and that the dining-room where the family portraits hung, looked out on to the lawn. The family portraits did hang there: there was one of her grandfather, and another of her mother, and, though the artists were not known to fame, these were portraits, for in the English language that word was invariably used for pictures of people. Besides she had distinctly said that there were no Sir Joshua Reynolds' among them . . .

Similarly the little square of plantains, daisies, wormcasts and grass in front of the dining-room, separating 'The Croft' from the Station Road, could not be more accurately described than by calling it the lawn. Alice had not measured it and so could not give the actual dimensions even if anyone had asked for them. In the same way it was perfectly true that, Mr. Gradge (such was his amazing name) who had taken 'The Croft' on a year's lease at a most moderate quarterly rent, and lived there with his sister were 'my tenants'. Alice had every right to call them her tenants: while the gardener (three mornings a week) and the boy who 'did' the knives and coals and boots, and spent the rest of his time in the potato-patch could not, without long and tedious explanations have been alluded to otherwise than as 'my gardeners'. Even the two cucumber frames were in a manner of speaking, a couple of glass houses. All these allusions, casually dropped here and there were strictly founded on fact; indeed they were facts, but it was also a fact, though unknown to Colonel Chase and Mrs. Oxney and all those who had reverentially heard Miss Howard allude to her sober little ancestral splendours, that 'The Croft' was not a Queen Anne house, but a semi-detached villa standing in the Station Road.

It was all rather awkward, and for the life of her, Miss Howard could not imagine how she had got into such a position. She had told no lies, she had hardly been guilty of any infamous exaggeration (except perhaps in the matter of the two cucumber frames), and yet she knew that all Wentworth believed her to have a beautiful little country seat near Tunbridge Wells, the glories of which she had probably dimmed rather than polished. It was like a Saga or the poems of Homer, which by untraceable processes had grown from small oral beginnings into epics. No one could analyse the psychology of such a growth any more than they could analyse the physiological growth of the grain of mustard seed into a bird-haunted tree: it grew and that was all that could be said about it. In the same way she had alluded quite casually and infrequently to the lawn and the fine timber and the rose-garden and her tenants and her gardeners, and she was credited now with a mansion and a park and a pleasaunce and a host of old family retainers. She could no doubt have instantly nipped this sumptuous growth in the bud by stating the plain fact that 'The Croft' was a semi-detached villa, but instead of that she had enjoyed seeing it sprout, and had watered it and tilled the ground. Now, at the thought of Colonel Chase's wooing, the little place had become almost like an angel with a fiery sword preventing her entering that possible Paradise. For if she consented to marry him, it would not be unreasonable in her husband to want to know more of the little place: he might, still not unreasonably, suggest living there on their combined resources, when the lease of 'my tenants', which was only a yearly one, came to an end. Sooner or later, and probably very soon, the truth about the little place must come out, and though she had never told any real lies about it, the aggregate of information amounted to a falsehood that was appalling to contemplate. Obstinate Flo, no doubt, had gleaned the same impression as the Colonel but that was a situation easier to deal with. If the worst came to the worst, and exposure was certain, she could contemplate without intolerable dismay actually telling her that she had got a perfectly wrong idea about 'The Croft' and had oddly exaggerated to herself its splendours, just as she (dear thing!) attributed all sorts of talents and graces to the character of her poor friend. "I think I could tell Flo that," said Miss Howard to herself, "but I feel almost sure that I couldn't tell Colonel Chase."

These disagreeable reflections were interrupted by the arrival of Florence in a blue dressing-gown and slippers.

"Darling, what ages I have been," she said, "and I thought that I would get ready for bed first, so that when I left you I could just hop there, and lie thinking of you and our talk without the interruption of undressing. Dear me! Have you been impatient because I was so long? Do say you have: do tell me that you were furious with me for not coming sooner. But I couldn't help it: Papa has been too tiresome for anything."

"How naughty you are about your father," said Alice. "But tell me about him: I want to be naughty too."

Florence gave her a loud kiss, and assumed her father's voice.

"Mind you put in a pair of old gloves at the top of the suitcase, Florence," she said, "for I shall have to go from my carriage to the luncheon car, and anything I touch on the way will be grimy. And my cachets: the ones I take in water after a meal. You had better pack the bottle of them in my portmanteau and give me a couple of them, done up in a screw of paper, which I can put in my waistcoat pocket. And remember to give me a telegraph form addressed to yourself, for in the bustle of departure you may have forgotten something, so it would be well to have a telegraph form handy. I regret that Nurse Babbit only joins me at the station: it would have been wiser if she had slept at Wentworth to-night. My thermos flask with some hot coffee in it must be seen to in the morning, and do not forget to give me some small change for tips . . . Darling, what a duck he is, and how glad I am that he's going to Bournemouth tomorrow. Now for a happy talk. How sweet of you to have made some cocoa for me! And how weird Colonel Chase-Alice--is not that a good name for him?--was this evening. He can't see that you and I only want to be left to ourselves. You were delicious with him when you said you knew he wanted to go and play bridge: O. F. knew that you meant that you wanted him to. What do you bet he doesn't buy another picture of your's tomorrow? He's crazy about you, and who wouldn't be."

Alice would have let all the Colonels in the British Army go crazy about her and remain unrequited for ever, if she could only have felt towards Florence as Florence felt towards her, for she had the perception to see that the worshipper has a far more exciting time than the image that he worships. She felt no atom of condescension or graciousness towards her worshipper but rather envy at her potentiality for rapture. How amazingly Florence had expanded in the warmth of her own emotion! A fortnight ago, in spite of her sturdy and manly appearance, she had owned a squashed and middle-aged soul; now though she was still essentially the same, all that had been repressed and nipped in her had opened like a flower. Self-expression had vivified her . . .

"I'll bet you any picture in the Green Salon that isn't sold," said Alice, "that Colonel Chase-Alice (how wicked of us!) doesn't buy another. He hasn't got much longer: we close the day after tomorrow."

"Oh, how I love you saying 'we close'," said Florence. "But I shan't love the closing: no more sitting surrounded by your pictures and hoping that no visitors will come in and interrupt."

Alice did not feel that she had ever quite shared this hope, for after all she had not taken the Green Salon only for the purpose of uninterrupted conversation with Florence.

"Dear little Green Salon!" she said. "I have become so much attached to it. Then what a day's work there will be: we shall have to pack up all the pictures that have been sold and send them to the purchasers."

"Miles of string, reams of corrugated paper like Colonel Chase's forehead, oceans of ink, books of labels," said Florence appreciatively. "How I shall enjoy it, simply because we shall be doing it together. Everything that we do together is so lovely, just for that reason. . . . And then we go off alone with no one to bother us for a month in London."

"I thought you said a fortnight," said Alice.

"I shall say a year if you're so tiresome," observed Florence, who had said a week originally and then had lengthened it into a fortnight, and now for the first time mentioned a month. "And then I must go to Bournemouth for Christmas.

Papa insists on that, for he says that he and I have always spent Christmas together, though for that matter we have always spent every other day together. Christmas means as little to Papa as I do: all there is to it, is that he doesn't feel even as well as usual on Boxing Day, because he cannot resist two helpings of rich plum-pudding. But I know that by that time Nurse Babbit will be suiting him so well, that afterwards I shall be free. So you must come back to me in London again, and we will settle what we do next."

Florence's complete confidence that Colonel Chase hadn't a chance still seemed rather premature to Alice, and this complete ignoring of this possibility made his prospects appear brighter. Certainly Alice had not determined she would not marry him. . . . And then she thought of the revelation which must be made to him about the ancestral home, and his prospects grew dark again.

"Yes, we've got to talk about that," she said rather vaguely.

"Oh, and I've got such a delicious plan for us to do one day when we're in London next week," said Florence. "I know you'll love it. I will give you one hint, and then you shall guess. It will mean a day in the country at a place you adore."

A rather sickening sense came over Alice that she could make a pretty good guess, but she hoped she was wrong.

"Darling, how can I guess just from that?" she said. "Is it Epping Forest where I did that picture of the trees reflected in the lake, which you liked?"

"No, but there are trees," said Florence, "and pictures too, and roses, only I suppose they won't be out now. I'll give you another hint: Alice's Wonderland. There! Now you can guess."

This made Florence's plan absolutely certain, and so Alice said she hadn't the slightest idea what it was, while she cudgelled her brains to think of any decent excuse for not going with obstinate Flo to the ancestral home.

"Darling, aren't you a little slow?" asked Florence. "Where else could it be but 'The Croft'? How I long to see the Park ("Has it come to that?" thought Alice) and the lovely rose-garden and the dining-room with the portraits, and your old nursery from which you used to see the sunsets, and learn to love them."

Though Alice had felt that she could perhaps tell Florence the truth about the ancestral home, whereas she could not tell Colonel Chase, the idea of going there with her was a nightmare.

"Oh, that would be fun," she said wretchedly. "But the house is occupied you see; my tenants are there, and I don't even know them. All arrangements between them and me were made by my--my agents."

"Oh, but they will surely love you to come and look round," said Florence. "Or--oh--what a selfish little beast I am: would it be painful to you to see your lovely home in the hands of strangers? I never thought of that."

Alice was delighted that she had thought of it now, for it made an admirable excuse. She had only to admit to Florence this tearing of heart-strings for her to be overwhelmed with compunction at having suggested so cruel an ordeal.

"I'm quite silly about 'The Croft'," she said. "I know how stupid it is of me, but it would hurt just a teeny little bit. But what does that matter. Of course we'll go."

CHAPTER VIII

Florence slid to the ground by her side, and clasped her knees.

"What a pig I am not to have thought of that," she said. "I've got no sensitiveness, no perception: oh, what a lot you've got to teach me! Of course we won't go! But someday I must go alone: you won't mind that, will you darling? I must see your *kinderscenen*--that lovely Reverie by Schumann (or was it Schubert?) you played me--I must see your scenes of childhood--I love everything that tells me more about you."

The prospect opened up by these pretty sentiments was hideous. If obstinate Flo intended to show a touch of her quality in this passion for seeing 'The Croft', what would happen to all those pretty sentiments when some taxi-driver at Tunbridge Wells whom she directed to take her to 'The Croft,' set her down after a career of about fifty yards at the third house on the left in Station Road? That was too ghastly to contemplate: it would be better, thought Alice, if this fell determination persisted, to tell her straight out that 'The Croft' was not what it seemed, and would not repay a sentimental journey. . . . She thought it all over after Florence had said an affectionate good night some half-dozen times, and had come back after each to tell her something she had forgotten about, and resolved to make this odious disclosure when it could no longer be avoided. She had an uneasy dream in which she and Florence and Colonel Chase all went together hand in hand to stay at 'The Croft', and found it to be a cottage in a brickfield with only one bedroom. She woke in agonies of embarrassment.

There was little time next morning, until the 11.35 had irrevocably left Bolton Spa station for embarrassment or anything else except the concerns of Mr. Kemp. Excitement had caused him to pass a night not less troubled than Alice's, and it was not till he had taken his temperature for the second time with encouraging results, that he decided he could undertake the journey. But during these dark watches he had made a further list of memoranda in faint pencillings, and having finished his breakfast by nine, he sat in the lounge and tried to decipher them, with the travelling suitcase open by him on the floor, and Florence ready to perform these last offices.

"Umbrella," he read out. "Yes, as it's fine I want you to take charge of my umbrella, and hand it to me when I am in the train. I will have my two sticks, the pair with crutch handles. Aspirin: I must take ten grains half-an-hour before I start, and then sit quiet till the bus comes. Otherwise all these movings about and going up and down steps into buses and trains will be agony. Really I ought to have insisted that Nurse Babbit should come here: I do not know how we shall get through without her. Ten grains will be two tablets, Florence; you had better make a note of that. Umbrella, Aspirin: I will cross those out. Monkey . . . It can't be Monkey: I should not dream of taking a monkey in my suitcase. What can that be? And it is a very dark morning. I wonder if it will rain before I am safe in the train. Or is it that my eyes are worse this morning?"

In this very natural agitation about monkey, he got up from his chair and walked straight across to the window without using his sticks.

"Ah, I see now," he said. "It is not monkey, it is Mrs. Oxney. I want you, Florence, to get Mrs. Oxney to have my room thoroughly searched after I have gone, to see if you have forgotten to pack anything: last year it was a flannel belt. Now let us get on: we have not too much time."

Mrs. Bliss who was sitting by the fire, suddenly jumped up with a cry of rapture.

"Oh, Mr. Kemp!" she said, "I knew it would come. You have walked to the window and half-way back again to your chair without your sticks. Mind has conquered Error. Didn't I tell you that you were perfectly well? Now you know it."

Mr. Kemp immediately clutched at the back of a sofa, and heavily leaning on it got back to his chair.

"Dear me, I did walk there without my sticks," he said, "and felt no twinge at all. But then why did I begin to hobble again?"

"Error's last effort to deny health and harmony," chanted Mrs. Bliss. "Oh, how pleased I am that you know you are well. But I must say good-bye as I am to have one more bath for my dear husband's sake. When next we meet, I know I shall see you running about like a boy."

Mr. Kemp shook hands.

"Indeed it was most remarkable, most gratifying," he said. "I must have my manual of Mental Science to read in the train, Florence. Please get it out of the green portmanteau, and put it in the suitcase. . . . Now let us get on: Mrs. Oxney, we've done that. Carpet slippers. You can put them in one of the portmanteaux instead of in the suitcase, for I have decided not to change into them in the train. Daily paper: that explains itself. Pencil: ah, yes, I shall partly occupy my time with a cross-word puzzle. If I get through it, I can ink it in at Bournemouth. . . . Florence, do you realise that I walked to the window without a twinge? Shall I trust to Mind and not have my aspirin?"

"I think I should have the aspirin, Papa," said Florence. "You can trust to Mind just the same, and tell yourself that the aspirin can't have any effect. Mrs. Bliss has her baths and massage for her husband's sake."

"True," said Mr. Kemp, much relieved to be excused from this great trial of faith. "So as you wish me to take my aspirin, I will do so for your sake."

"Thank you, Papa," said Florence, and went to get a wine-glass and some newly-decanted water.

The list of agenda and addenda was finished in time to enable Mr. Kemp to sit quiet for a full half-hour before the bus came round, and then once more he walked right across the lounge without assistance.

"It was a mistake to have had any aspirin," he said reproachfully to Florence, "for I am convinced that I am walking so well entirely owing to Mind. But I took it for your sake: remember to tell Mrs. Bliss."

The bus had been ordered in time to give the traveller a full quarter of an hour at the station: this would not be a moment too much to enable Mr. Kemp to confer with Nurse Babbit, to settle finally and irrevocably what baggage was to come into the carriage with him and what to travel in the van, and rest for a little after these decisions. Florence meanwhile would see the heavier pieces labelled, and after a pause make sure that all the labels were duly adhering. Then she had to put a second porter in charge of suitcase, rugs, coats, air-cushions, hot-water bottle, daily paper, and all else that was to be handed in to the travellers after Mr. Kemp had taken his seat. Mrs. Oxney, who had also come to the station, made herself very useful, as soon as the train came in, by ascertaining that the conductor of the luncheon car had reserved a table for two. Though all went off without a hitch, as far as could at present be ascertained, Mr. Kemp's face looked drawn and anxious as Nurse Babbit adjusted the window precisely to his liking, and he shook his head sadly at them through the glass, as the train moved out of the station.

CHAPTER IX

The full and glorious noon of the Green Salon had evidently passed: collectors who were anxious to secure Howards for their galleries must have satisfied themselves, and when, on the morning of the day preceding its closing, neither visitors nor purchasers had entered its pictured walls the friends decided to occupy the remainder of the hours in beginning the packing of the works with little red stars on them. The pill box with these brevets inside was now found to be unaccountably empty, and the custodian when pressed acknowledged that, despairing of employing them for their ordained purpose, he had used them up (so that they should not be wasted) by affixing to the wall behind the door his own initials executed in red stars. There indeed his initials were, and Alice and Florence had to spend a considerable time in soaking them off. That was a matter of difficulty for they proved to be of first rate adhesive quality. But it was done now, and Florence in her homespun Norfolk jacket with no hat had hurried off into the town to purchase strong corrugated cardboard and brown paper.

Alice was feeling on edge: she had spent a sticky hour in detaching the custodian's odious initials, she was disappointed that the last few days of the Green Salon had been fruitless and she was worried over the deception she had been driven to practise on Florence about the ancestral home. That figured itself to her as a black hole in the fabric of life out of which at any moment might pop out something surprisingly unpleasant. So while her friend had gone on her useful errand, she had nagged at the custodian (on the lines of a wage-earning man behaving like a child) for giving them so much trouble and the custodian had grown sulky and sat perched on his stool like a ruffled bird in livery with the pip, instead of the brightest boy in Bolton. Yet after all the exhibition had been a great success, and she thought with fortitude how narrowly she had escaped acting on the diabolical counsel of the young man from the *Bolton Gazette,* who had criticised her pictures without ever seeing them, and had advised her to put a quantity of stars on virgin frames in order to encourage purchasers. She had nearly done so: had it not been for Tim and Mrs. Holders and those mysterious ladies and gentlemen about whom the custodian could remember nothing, she would surely have fallen. Nowadays she knew something of the tangled web of deceit over her fabulous ancestral home, and she was thankful to have been spared further complications over the Green Salon. If she had succumbed, she would now be in the power of the sulky custodian.

CHAPTER IX

This Pharisaical reflection had hardly entered her head when there strolled into the Green Salon just as if he had been the proprietor of the place the odious young man to whom Miss Howard had in effect said 'Get thee behind me, Satan'. But here was Satan in front of her again, and as he looked round at the walls, on which twinkled this red milky way, he broke into a broad grin and quite distinctly winked at the artist in a most familiar manner. The moulting bird slipped off his stool and produced the roll of toilet-paper.

"Sixpence," he said sullenly.

"Press," said the critic.

He turned to Miss Howard.

"Well miss, you've had a rare success," he said, "I see you took that tip I gave you. I remember telling you to make believe to have sold half a dozen pictures and you'd bring the buyers in all right. Very pleased to have been of assistance, for that tip and my little article did the trick for you. I'm not too proud, I may add, to accept any little recognition you might care to make me."

Miss Howard gasped with indignation. It was really no use attempting, as Mrs. Bliss had recommended her to do, to broadcast thoughts of love in every direction, for Mrs. Bliss had clearly no idea how some situations could play the deuce with atmospherics. But though powerless to broadcast loving thoughts, she could still remember she was a Howard, and moistened her lips with the tip of her tongue.

"I do remember your advising me to commit that most dishonourable action," she said, "but I am glad to say that your suggestion only appalled me."

This appeared to nettle Satan.

"Oh, come!" he said. "I gave you a friendly tip which I'm sure you took, and now you call me dishonourable. Nasty of you, miss."

Trembling in every limb with the effort of being a Howard, she turned to the custodian.

"Give me the list of the names and addresses of purchasers," she said. "I want to show it to that (she did not pause at all) gentleman."

A situation of peculiar psychological intensity had arisen. There was Miss Howard in the consciousness of virgin innocence, tempted but unfallen, there was Satan blandly certain that she had fallen, and was a liar too, there was the brightest boy in Bolton sulky from his scolding who knew that there had been some amazing hocus-pocus about the cataract of sales on the first day when purchasers appeared, and had been bribed to silence by half-a-crown. As he produced the list of purchasers he began to think about revenge.

Miss Howard spread this register in front of Satan. All the entries were in order, number of pictures sold, purchasers, addresses, and 'paid'.

Satan sniffed.

"Well, some do it direct, and some by deputy," he jeeringly observed.

At that, as the custodian thought of the two invisible ladies who had bought two pictures each, and the two invisible gentlemen who had done the same, the whole case became clear to his powerful intellect: he no longer entertained the slightest doubt that Miss Howard had bought the pictures herself by deputy.

"Will you kindly tell this gentleman," said Miss Howard, "how you personally sold all these pictures to different ladies and gentlemen and that I made no private arrangements of any sort with you."

He hesitated: vengeance was sweet. It was on the tip of his tongue to say what had actually happened. But some of that half-crown was still in his pocket, for his daily shillings nearly sufficed for his simple needs.

"That's so," he said. "Ladies and gents came in here one after the other and made their buys, and Miss Howard never said a word to me."

At the moment Miss Howard saw through the open door, the approaching figure of Florence carrying the contents of a stationer's shop. She turned her back on Satan, and gave a little silvery laugh.

"Such fun, dear," she said. "This gentleman once advised me to buy some of the pictures myself in order to encourage others, and now he tells me that I took his dishonest advice and wants me to give him something for his suggestion. A little like blackmail."

She turned to Satan again.

"Miss Kemp is one of the purchasers," she said. "You will find her name there. I'm afraid that without notice I cannot produce more of them. So if this is all now quite clear, perhaps you would pay sixpence for admission, if you want to look at my pictures again. Please do not offer me your apologies which no doubt you are anxious to do, because I could not accept them. Good morning."

"Lor, that's a knock-out," said the brightest boy in Bolton, in enthusiastic admiration of this superb effrontery. (Of course Miss Howard had bought her pictures herself.).

"A little off his head poor fellow," said Alice, as soon as Satan had gone back presumably to his own place. "Now let us begin our packing, dearest."

"What a monster," said Florence. "I wish I had been here to tackle him."

"Quite unnecessary, darling," said Alice, still trembling with passion. "Oh, what lovely corrugated cardboard. I always feel it is a shame to use it."

The work of packing so many purchases and making them safe for travel was lengthy, and conduced to meditation except when Alice sat on the scissors or Florence lost the pen for the direction of labels, when it conduced merely to frenzied search. Florence meditated about Alice, and said 'Liebster' to her now and then, when she could not repress her feelings, so that the custodian should not understand. Alice occasionally warbled a phrase of song but the undercurrent of her mind was occupied with the perfidy of men in general as exemplified by her late visitor. Above that ran a stream of thought concerned with the eternal and infernal subject of the ancestral home, which was daily getting more embarrassing. Only last night she had been practically compelled, in answer to a most inquisitive question of Colonel Chase's, to say that the stables were at some little distance from the house, for short of saying there were no stables at all (which would have been incredible in a spacious Queen Anne mansion) there was nothing else to be said. Then too, Mrs. Oxney hoped before long to spend a day or two with a cousin close to Tunbridge Wells, and she wanted to know if the public were admitted to the Park on any particular day of the week, and whether 'The Croft' was visible from the line. Miss Howard had to give a guarded answer to that; she said that her tenants made their own arrangements about admission, and that she did not know what they were. She added (which was absolutely true) that you could see 'The Croft' on the left of the line as you approached Tunbridge Wells, and in answer to a further pestering from the Colonel (how she used to enjoy such pestering once!) that there was no pheasant-shooting. It was really a detestable situation for anyone who was not a professional liar, and it seemed to her thoroughly undeserved. She had just let slip a few hints (all founded on fact) about her little place, and it was her audience, not she, who had distorted them into these monstrous splendours. Colonel Chase was much the worst offender: poor Alice would have been ready to take her oath that she had never mentioned stables at all till he asked about them, or alluded to the shooting, and now her little place had stables at some distance from the house, and though she had flatly denied that there was any pheasant-shooting, she felt that she had given the impression that there was plenty of room for it. All the good that had come out of the growth of her little place was that it had enabled her to make up her mind that, with the Colonel's present conception of it, it was quite impossible to marry him. Below these uncomfortable meditations there continued to flow the undercurrent of thought about the perfidy of men, and suddenly it burst up like a geyser on to the surface of her mind, startling her so much that the ball of string with which she was tying up Lady Appledore's Curfew leapt from her lap and rolled away across the floor. She saw it all . . . this violent interest of the Colonel's in her little place was contemporary with his industrious wooing of her affections. The base wretch wanted to find out what (as well as whom) he would be marrying.

She gave a hoarse cry.

"Oh, the wickedness of him," she exclaimed. "I will never speak to him again."

Florence thought she was speaking of Satan, and laughed as she retrieved the ball of string.

"I ought to have been here to settle him," she said. "But you did it pretty well, liebster."

"No, I don't mean him," said Alice gasping. "I mean that base wicked Colonel. You know how he's been questioning me about my dear little home. I see it all. He wanted to find out about it before asking me to marry him. I couldn't have believed it of him, as I hate thinking evil of anybody, but I feel sure it's true. I am never wrong about the sudden intuitions which sometimes come to me."

Though Florence had repeatedly asserted that Colonel Chase was crazy about Alice for her own sake, she soon began to share this intuition, and the wooing which had been to her up till now a huge joke, assumed a sinister aspect. She had intuitions too, and now she remembered that she had never trusted the Colonel from the first moment that she set eyes on him, and she was never wrong about her first impressions. She would not quite give up her belief that he was crazy about Alice, but he was certainly crazy to live in her lovely house, and shoot over--no there weren't any pheasant-covers--and be the Squire of the countryside. He deserved--what did he not deserve--as punishment for his baseness?

"Punished, punished, he must be punished," said Florence, fiercely folding corrugated cardboard round Geraniums. And look darling, at this very moment I'm packing his picture for him. I do call that a coincidence! You mustn't mind about him: he isn't worth it. Punished."

"But it hurts me," said Alice.

"Only because you're so good, and it hurts you that a man can have been so wicked," said Florence. "They're like that you know, I've often heard of men wanting to marry girls because of their money. Base creatures! But it isn't as if you had ever cared about him: you never dreamed of marrying the fat old bicyclist. What are we to do to punish him? That's the point. For myself I shall simply cut him, though I'm afraid he won't think that much of a punishment. In fact he'll prefer it. We must think of something better than that."

Alice again remembered, but with difficulty, that she was a Howard. She moistened her lips.

"I beg you to drop any such idea altogether," she said. "Because he has behaved like--well, like a cad, that is all the more reason that we should behave like ladies. It will mark the distance between us. If he actually tells me he wants to marry me, I shall permit myself a little scorn in refusing him, but that will be all."

"But you would have done that in any case," said obstinate Flo. "That's not punishment as I mean it, I want something extra. He must be brought to feel that he's not lost you only, for he never would have got you, but all the wonderful things of yours he would have got, if he had got you."

This seemed a very refined and complicated sort of punishment, but as they proceeded with their packings in the gradually fading light of the November day, the shape of it outlined itself to Florence's vindictive imagination. She disliked men, as such, to begin with, she adored her Alice, and what she wanted (as she whittled her idea to a sharp point) was to humble Colonel Chase and exalt her well-beloved by one fell stroke. She had for years suffered dumbly under the yoke of paternal tyranny, and, now, emancipated, she longed in the manner of a suffragette to damage a man. Her emotional awakening had quickened her keenness for the combats of life in which she used mutely to surrender, and the design, yet vague, was that Alice should not only win, but in the hour of victory humiliate her adversary. Florence's chivalry only existed for her own sex, men, as typified by the Colonel, had to be beaten, and then rubbed in the dirt. Simultaneously Alice, though she had told Florence that they must behave like ladies, was following up the same train of thought. Vengeance was surely compatible, if she could only see how, with perfect gentility. But for the life of her she could not see how. She was startled from her gentle vindictive reverie by a hoarse crowing sound from her friend. Only extreme exaltation, she had already learned, made Florence crow like that.

"I've got it," she cried. "Oh, darling, it's too lovely! He wants to know about your little place, so tell him no end of lies about it. Make it bigger and grander and splendider and magnificenter. A lake: a lot of box hedges: a moat. Oh, don't you see? Make it a palace with a family vault and a village of tenants and no entail. And then he'll propose to you, and you'll say no, and he'll be in hell because of what he has lost."

Now it might have been supposed that Miss Howard's own uneasiness about the grandeurs of her ancestral home would have made her recoil in horror from such a suggestion. So for the first moment it did, and she only just checked the exclamation of disdain that rose to her lips. But immediately she saw like the gleam of a lighthouse over stormy seas, a beam that heralded salvation. If she continued, now voluntarily, to ply the mercenary Colonel with visions of splendour and sumptuousness, she could save her face with regard to Florence. All her previous hints about the magnificence of 'The Croft' which had been causing her such serious agitation, would be merged with all future lies as having been punishment for him. Florence no doubt, at this moment, shared Colonel Chase's illusions about her little place, but it would be much easier to muddle her up about them, if now, at her suggestion, Alice deliberately magnified its splendours. "Darling, that would serve him right," she said thoughtfully. "But it wouldn't be truthful. 'The Croft' is really quite a modest little place."

"You *must* do it," said Florence. "He must be punished, and I'm sure there's no better way of degrading him. How lucky he hasn't proposed to you already when he only knows the truth about 'The Croft'!"

Any impulse that Alice ever had to confess to her friend that the truth about 'The Croft' was not known to anyone at Wentworth except herself, vanished. The far better chance was to adopt Florence's suggestion and go on making 'The Croft' more and more manorial, until as might happen, it was necessary to demolish the exquisite old home, and reveal it to her in its true character as a semi-detached villa. Florence would be confused by that time: she would not know what magnificence, lawn or lake or park, ante-dated the Colonel's punishment which she had suggested. But there was Mrs. Oxney to think about as well, for she was one of the greediest imbibers of ancestral grandeur.

"And how about Mrs. Oxney?" she asked. "She will hear it too, and get such a false idea about my little home. And if she goes to Tunbridge Wells as she threatened--I mean, as she thought she might be doing soon--she would be very much perplexed."

"Then wait till you get the Colonel alone," said Florence brilliantly. "You and me and the Colonel I mean, for I'm in the plot, and of course I shan't believe a word you say. I shall egg you on. I shall make you tell lies."

"It will make me very uncomfortable having to exaggerate so," said Alice with a sigh. But she had been very uncomfortable as it was.

Wentworth was emptying, as was usual in late November, but there were fresh paying guests coming in next week, and Mrs. Oxney, though she saw no prospect of getting to Tunbridge Wells yet awhile, observed with strong satisfaction that Balmoral and Blenheim and Belvoir were already closed for the winter. Mrs. Bliss having finished the cure she had undertaken for the love she bore her husband, and miraculously better in spite of it, owing to her persistent denial that anything had ever been wrong with her joints, since all was Harmony, left on the day the Green Salon was closed, in the happy belief that Mind and not Mrs. Holders and Tim had started purchasers. So full of Harmony was she on the morning of her departure that she refused to go to the station in the bus, but set off to walk there (leaving plenty of time in order to enjoy the sweet air) while her luggage was to follow in a hand-cart. It was well that it did so, for Harmony most unaccountably became Discord in the middle of this pedestrian effort, and produced so realistic a similitude of shooting pains in her hip that she was quite unable to proceed, but stood like a statue, though still smiling, by the side of the road waiting for deliverance. The hand-cart overtook her, and she was with difficulty hoisted on to it. Precariously balanced on the edge of it, and holding on to her dress-basket, she was trundled into the station, protesting that she had never enjoyed herself more. A comfortable seat in the train and rest soon brought Harmony back again.

Discussion over her and her gospel raged at Wentworth after she had gone: *pro,* there was the Colonel's cold, the success of his ghost story, her own improvement (or was that brine?) and the miraculous sale of pictures; *contra,* her failure to walk to the station, and the fact that Mr. Kemp had not really improved at all: it was thought that his walking to the window had been a flash in the mental pan. The affair of the pedometer was not mentioned at all, because it always excited Colonel Chase. Tim Bullingdon, supported by Mrs. Holders, said that the whole thing was utter rubbish, and that he would sooner be completely crippled than cured by such charlatanry, and Mrs. Oxney ever pleasant, said, well, what an interesting talk they had all enjoyed.

An even more interesting talk, more stupendous, more imaginative, was held in the lounge that day after tea. Mrs. Holders and Tim had engagements with *masseurs,* Mrs. Oxney and her sister retired to their sitting-room, where their joint efforts over the cross-word puzzle were to compete with the solitary genius of Colonel Chase, who had consented for once to try his hand, and in consequence the three conversationalists were the two devoted friends and he. He had settled down with the paper and a sharp pencil in order to sit Florence out, and proposed to occupy the interval with the defeat of Mrs. Oxney and Mrs. Bertram. 'Small Scotch farmers' (undoubtedly beginning with *c)* was puzzling and Florence's account of the letter she had just received from her father distracted him.

"He's ever so much pleased, darling, with Nurse Babbit," she said to Alice. "Such bright conversation and so much interested in his case. She feels sure that within a week he will get the good effect of Bolton, but she doesn't think anything of Mind, and says that massage is far more reliable. A most comfortable journey, and quite a good lunch. He thinks he has left the small tin that held his night rusks behind, but there are rusks in Bournemouth. . . ."

CHAPTER IX

Colonel Chase made an impatient movement in his chair. Who could concentrate on small Scotch farmers beginning with *c,* with such imbecile drivel going on? She ought to have gone with her father . . .

Florence was silent a moment.

"Now do tell me more about the garden at 'The Croft'," she said. "I'm beginning to picture it."

Colonel Chase rapidly pencilled in the required word.

"Ha, I've got you to thank for that, Miss Kemp," he said, with unusual amiability. "Your saying the word 'croft' put 'crofters' into my mind. A remarkable coincidence."

"Quite extraordinary," said Florence.

"We don't disturb you by our chatter?" asked Alice.

"Indeed no. Charming conversation, I'm sure," said he, laying down his pencil.

"My dear little house!" said Alice. "I insist on your coming down to see it, Flo, when we are in London next week, for indeed I cannot do it justice. The dining-room windows open on to the lawn, or rather on to a raised terrace wall that runs the length of the house. Then you turn round the corner to the right, and there's the shrubbery with the winding walk through it. All beautiful flowering shrubs, some rare, I believe, but I'm so ignorant. It wants thinning out, my gardeners tell me."

"It sounds delicious," said Florence.

"Charming," said Colonel Chase. "Not half enough flowering shrubs in most old English gardens. Pardon for interrupting you, Miss Howard, pray go on."

"Then you come into the bit of the garden which I love most," said Alice. "Another lawn with a little marble fountain and basin in the middle of it. The sweet cool drip of water on a hot day! What a naughty little girl I must have been, for I bathed in it once. Papa only laughed, but Mamma sent me to bed. . . . On each side are the two long borders, very deep you know, as borders ought to be, with hollyhocks and sunflowers at the back. But sad ravage from the hollyhock disease this summer, I hear. I'm afraid it must be replanted. Then at the end the steps leading down into the rose-garden with the box hedges round it. Clumps cut into fantastic shapes, peacocks, and things like that."

"And are there any real peacocks?" asked Florence.

Alice felt she could not manage peacocks.

"Ah, don't talk of them," she said, "for I've no peacocks now. How lovely they used to look sitting on the terrace wall. But they do make such a dreadful screaming, and they used to wake Mamma up in the early summer dawn, and she couldn't go to sleep again. They damage the flowers terribly too, so disappointing for the gardeners. And one day Papa said to me, 'Alice, do you vote for peacocks or gardens?' I felt like a murderer, though we gave them to friends and they got quite happy homes."

Florence cast a reproachful eye on her friend, for not saying that there were flocks of peacocks. But Alice's elaborate explanation almost made amends.

"I'm picturing it all," Florence said. "I am beginning to see it as if I was there. Take me behind the box hedges; isn't the kitchen garden there?"

"Yes: nice, old red-brick walls, and the glasshouses at the end."

"How many?" asked Florence.

Alice sighed.

"Papa was always very particular about the glass," she said. "He liked to eat his own grapes, for then he knew they hadn't been covered with dust in a shop, and picked by goodness knows whom. . . . Let me see. There was the peach-house with the pots of strawberries for forcing; we always had strawberries on Easter Day. Then there was the grape-house, black Hamburgs and Muscats, and a third for flowers. Bougainvillia and plumbago climbing up the walls and regiments of carnations."

Colonel Chase, greedily listening, began to wonder whether all this would not be beyond their joint means. The cross-word puzzle had long lain unregarded on his knee.

"Terribly expensive, was it not?" he asked. "The garden must have cost a fortune to keep up."

Both the conspirators were at once on their guard against discouraging the Colonel: there was really no need for Florence to break in.

"Oh no," she said. "You told me, dearest Alice, that the gardens were self-supporting."

"Papa used always to say so," said Alice, "for after the house was supplied with flowers, the carnations used to be sent up to Covent Garden in great boxes, and they fetched an immense price. Grapes too and peaches. Papa used to say he should have been a fruit and flower merchant."

Colonel Chase was visibly relieved.

"Now take us inside the house," said greedy Florence. "I can't hear enough of it. Oh, it's cruel that you don't live there."

"No use making a fuss," said Alice, "and the same thing has happened to so many of us. Perhaps if I save up for a year, or two more, I might be able to live in a corner of it. But for the present it's let and I don't think about it at all bitterly. Indoors, did you say, Flo? Is there a little summer shower which drives us indoors? Let's come in then at the door opening into the rose-garden from the library. That will be the nearest way."

This voluptuous improvisation was as brilliant as anything that Alice could have executed with a great deal of practice on the piano, but it must be remembered that she had already practised diligently on her little place in Kent. The effect on Colonel Chase was admirable: the evening paper had fallen to the ground, and it was evident that if Miss Howard went on much longer Mrs. Oxney and her sister would easily win the cross-word race, for he had as yet got no further than 'Crofters' and one other word along the top. It had also, as the astute Alice had anticipated a curiously confusing effect on Florence: Florence was already beginning to mix up what she thought was true about 'The Croft' with what she knew was imaginary. Had Alice said there was a rose-garden before to-day, or told her about the shrubbery of flowering rarities? 'Glass' had certainly been mentioned before but without specification: there was only the impression of glass.

"Yes, come indoors quick, darling," said Florence, playing up admirably, "or you'll get wet, and I shall be obstinate and make you change before you show me round."

Colonel Chase said 'pshaw' under his breath: he hated this silly playfulness and wanted to get to work indoors.

"Take care you don't slip on the parquet floor in the library," said Alice, pursuing these pretty fancies. "But just glance at it: cedar-wood parquet, and smells so good. That was Grandpapa Howard's addition: so stravvy of him! But he loved his little library: not large, you see, but such a pleasant room. The chimney-piece looks empty now, but my tenants wouldn't take the responsibility of having the Chelsea figures out. Beauties they were--"

"Quite right of them," said the Colonel. "Fine Chelsea is irreplaceable. I should put them in a cupboard myself. How many, Miss Howard?"

"Only four," said Alice. "Poor little shepherds and shepherdesses all in the dark in the strong room at the Bank! But they've got the Queen Anne silver and a few little odds and ends to keep them company and talk over the dear old times. And then we go out across the hall, a pretty staircase, Flo; there is nothing like it at the Victoria and Albert Museum (this was absolutely true) and into the drawing-room. Rather long, rather narrow, like a gallery."

This was just what Colonel Chase had imagined: telepathic almost.

"And I seem to see Queen Anne furniture again," he interpolated.

"Just a few choice little pieces. But such a ragged carpet, is it not, though it was once a good Aubusson. But Papa would have it used. At the far end is the door into the smoking-room."

Mrs. Oxney and her sister came hurrying out of their room at this rich moment.

"We've finished it all but the top right-hand corner, Colonel," she said. "How far have you got? Don't say you've done it."

Had not four ladies been present, Colonel Chase would certainly have damned two of them for their interruption. He wanted terribly to hear about the smoking-room which would probably be his 'den'.

"What can the small Scotch farmers be?" asked Mrs. Bertram. "That would give us the clue to the difficult corner."

"Aha!" said he. "I'm not going to tell you that. And the time limit for our competition was dinner. I've been lazy, listening to Miss Howard telling us about her charming little place. Now I shall go up to my room, and have a spell at the puzzle."

He picked up Mrs. Oxney's paper which she had carelessly laid down on the table, and saw a word or two which might be useful as starting-points. He put it down again hurriedly.

"God bless me," he said. "I thought that was my paper. Lucky I didn't see any of your words. And may I remind you, Miss Howard, that I put you on your honour not to betray the small Scotch farmers."

It was no use stopping any longer in the lounge, for the ladies would certainly sit chatting and chattering till the dressing-bell sounded, and there would be no chance of getting Miss Howard alone, but he took upstairs with him besides the evening paper, the fixed determination to propose to and be accepted by her, on the first possible opportunity. He had once harboured doubts about the size and quality of the little place in Kent, but it was evident now that instead of its being less imposing than he had cynically supposed, it was far more splendid than he had hitherto allowed himself to imagine. In her talk just now with that podgy masculine friend of hers, it was impossible that Miss Howard should have exaggerated its charms, for she was intending to take her down to see it and, as she had said, she could not do it justice in description; and he was sure it would suit Squire Chase admirably. But he did not care for this friendship which had blazed into such flaming intimacy, and when he was married he would have to make it clear to his wife, firmly and if she was reasonable, kindly, that though 'Kemp' (so he thought of her) had apparently renounced all girlish duties to her father for Alice's sake, there must be no question at all of her living with them or of paying more than brief and occasional visits. A man--the husband's friend--making long visits to the house was a different matter, for men effaced themselves all day on the golf links, and hobnobbed together in the host's 'den' in the evening: besides a man required a little society of his own sex.

About the result of his suit he had no real doubt, for that would imply an absurd lack of self-respect, and, thank God, he had plenty of that. In the early days at Wentworth, before he had contemplated matrimony or had heard about the little place in Kent, he had been obliged several times to take no notice of Miss Howard's hints that she could ride a bicycle too with great speed, for he had not wanted to encourage false hopes. Now he regretted not having encouraged this, for they had ceased to be false, and the great plunge would have been easier to take: he would have slid into the water. Then that matter of the tenants must be looked into: he did not at present know what lease they held: a short one, he hoped, but if not it might be possible to get a clever lawyer to find a hole somewhere in it. Lawyers were all rascals: that was why you paid them so high: the convenient fellows did dirty work for a clean man.

He took a turn at the cross-word puzzle: the glimpse he had got at Mrs. Oxney's paper supplied some useful clues, and before the dressing-bell sounded he had finished with it, and sat down in front of his fire to think over the new life that was soon to open for him. He could not imagine why he had delayed to get married for so long, for, now that he was absolutely face to face with it, matrimony presented great attractions. Comfortable as he was at Wentworth, really remarkably comfortable, a home of his own would suit him better especially such a home as was waiting for him. He had debated at one time whether he should not give Mrs. Oxney the opportunity of providing one for him, but pleasant though that might be, he had never steadily regarded that prospect, and had shied away from matrimony in vague apprehension that it would entail loss of liberty and alarming obligations. But on approaching it now in a businesslike manner, these terrors quite faded: he saw that instead of being bound to take care of a wife, it was her duty to take care of him. The idea of marrying a girl who had romantic notions and expected ecstasies of conjugal tenderness would have been a positive nightmare, but this was quite a different business. He felt himself indeed in luck, and Miss Howard was in luck too. To capture a fine upstanding honourable man like himself, with no blot on his scutcheon but several medals on his coat and a comfortable competence was more than any woman could expect at her age. She need be under no apprehension of frailties and infidelities on his part, which so often wrecked matrimony, nor need he, for they were both well past the skittish age.

With the closing of the Green Salon and the despatch of the purchased pictures to their owners, Miss Howard was now at liberty to paint more, or do anything else that presented itself as an agreeable pastime. She had still to settle what disposition to make of those pieces that remained unsold: of these there were some twenty-five. Christmas presents would absorb some; her bedroom walls would absorb more, or Florence would ecstatically absorb them all. But next morning was warm and tranquil, and instead of tackling the heap of frames that were piled up in her bedroom, she decided to get hand and eye in touch again (for she had not taken up a paint-brush at all for a fortnight) and from the felled tree on the Colonel's golf links, of which a substantial trunk still remained, to make a little picture of Wentworth which, under the title of 'Home, Sweet Home', she would present to Mrs. Oxney as a reward for having bought 'Pussy-dear.' But though this kind scheme was sufficient excuse for her spending the morning in so wonted a manner, it was not the reason for it. The reason she had talked over with Florence, and they had settled that the Colonel was ripe.

They were right about that, for he came down to breakfast, strung up and resolute, and had dreamed he dwelt in marble halls. Alice had moved over to Florence's table after Mr. Kemp's departure and when he appeared they were both demurely eating eggs. He ignored Kemp, but asked Alice what she was going to do on this lovely morning which was quite like spring. She thought she would do a sketch of the house from the links, and he figured her sitting there with Kemp holding her hand or her brushes. For his part, he was going to have a spin on his bicycle: wouldn't she join him? Regretfully she wouldn't: she was going to be very industrious. The girls finished their breakfast first, and as they went out with waists and arms entwined, Alice certainly gave him a little sweet smile. Not a great joyous grimace like Mrs. Bliss; that would have meant nothing, but something secret with a quiver at the corner of her mouth and a quiet glance, which seemed highly propitious. When he had finished his breakfast he found the lounge empty and the smoking-room empty, and the drawing-room empty, and supposed that they had gone out together. He damned Kemp and sat down to look through the illustrated *Morning Standard* which he had been taking in lately. After that he would start for a stupendous pedalling and bring home fresh laurels. Miss Howard reverenced these records. He felt quite up to proposing to her this minute, but he made sure that Kemp was with her. There were advertisements in the paper showing entrancing young ladies in corsets and knickerbockers and of fine stalwart men in plus fours. He thought the plus fours would suit him, and imagined seeing his wife in just such an elegant corset.

Along the landing upstairs came familiar warbling noises and tripping feet. He scarcely looked up from his paper because he felt so certain that he would see the ubiquitous Kemp following Alice with her painting-satchel. Instead there was Alice alone carrying the implements of her craft herself. Alone--was it with a heightened colour that she perceived him?--she went out of the front door, and of Kemp there was no sign. He stole to the window and observed her figure--really a very neat figure for her age--flitting in and out of the shadows of the trees in the garden. She went out of the gate into the golf field, and an obstructing shrub hid her further progress. She had said she was going to sketch there.

Mrs. Oxney, who had been very late that morning came out of the dining-room.

"What a lovely morning you've got for your bicycle ride, Colonel," she said. "Like April, isn't it? I remember your saying that we often got April mornings in November, and November nights in April. So true. Will you be taking your lunch with you? A sandwich or two of that capital cold turkey now."

"No, I shan't be out for lunch," said he. "Just a good spin and home again."

"And a fresh record, please, or I shall be sadly disappointed," said Mrs. Oxney going through to her sitting-room.

The sitting-room looked out the same way as the lounge: they both looked out on to the golf field. Mrs. Oxney was fond of birds and as she stood for a moment in the pale but genial sunshine, that poured in at the window, before ordering the bus that was to take Mr. Bullingdon to the station, she thought she saw a green woodpecker fussing about on the grass near one of the holes. It proved to be only a starling which was less interesting, but the same glance shewed her bits of Miss Howard through the edge of the shrub that had hid her movements from the Colonel in the lounge, seated on the trunk of the felled tree. She was facing the house and was evidently going to sketch.

She heard the front door bang (that would be the Colonel going out) and waited a moment more for the pleasure of seeing him set forth on his bicycle. Such vigour, such legs, such a mastery of the vehicle. There he was, but not on his bicycle whirling down the drive, but crossing it in the direction of the garden and the golf field. But he had not got his golf sticks with him: he was not meaning to play golf instead of going for his ride. Then in a flash the solution struck her. "I believe he's going to do it," she said to herself.

But though a woman, she was still a house-keeper, and she hurried to the bell, and ordered the bus to come round at 10.45 sharp for the London train. When she returned to the window Colonel Chase had vanished behind that tiresome shrub, and she wished she had had it cut down. But specks of him appeared at its edge, and they ranged themselves by those of Miss Howard, and Mrs. Oxney felt certain what his business was. Florence in her bedroom directly overhead knew it too and she had the advantage of being able to see over the tiresome shrub.

Miss Howard seated on her tree-trunk of course saw his approach but quite unaware of it, measured the height of a Wentworth chimney against her pencil. When his advancing presence was too large to disregard, she looked up brightly.

"Not gone for your ride, Colonel?" she asked. "I call that lazy. Not like you."

A suitor's knees, he reflected, ought to tremble. His knees did not: they were as firm as oak-posts.

"No one can accuse you of laziness," said he. "Doing one of your charming sketches I see. A sketch of Wentworth is it? Dear old Wentworth. Ha! Dreams of happiness I've had here."

That was an excellent gambit: an improvisation worthy of Miss Howard.

"Oh, how pleasant," said she. "Tell me about them."

Any suitor would have considered that promising: it sounded like an invitation, like an assured welcome. She appeared quite calm too, though surely she must have known that as he had abandoned his bicycle ride and had come to the golf field, without his clubs, he must have had some special and unusual mission. He thought it would have been more like a lady of true delicacy and refined instincts to have bent her head over her drawing, unable to check the trembling of her fingers, but her hand was as steady as his knees. Or could it be that she had no idea that she was presently to promise to be his wife? Or did she guess his mind more subtly yet, and know that in the approaching alliance, regard and respect were to fill the place of tumultuous passion? In any case she went on drawing the cowl of the chimney with calm precision.

This direct invitation to tell her about his happy dreams encouraged him to sit down on the trunk beside her. Perhaps it was better, in case she was still unaware of her destiny, to make a few more remarks that would lead up to the revelation.

"Somehow I don't seem to have had the opportunity of getting any quiet talk with you of late," he said. "Your friend Miss Kemp--"

"Sweet Florence!" said Miss Howard very unexpectedly. "She never knows when she's not wanted, does she? Such a dear, and such a crashing bore."

That was splendid: he felt they understood each other.

"I've found her so," he said, "I've often wished she was at Bournemouth. Or I should have, if I had not thought she was a friend of yours whose presence always gave you pleasure."

Miss Howard held up her sketch at arm's length and looked at the chimney: she had got it much too large. She looked at Wentworth, and saw the crashing bore at her bedroom window, peeping out from a half-drawn curtain.

"Tell me about your happy dreams, Colonel Chase," she said.

The moment had come. There could not be a better opportunity, nor one more obviously meant for him. He cleared his throat.

"Happy dreams about my future," he said. "I'm getting to be a lonely man, Miss Howard, and though I'm not old yet, the years are passing. I want a companion, a dear companion with whom I can share my joys and my sorrows. One who will make me happy, and whom, I trust I shall make happy. I shall do my best. I've long wanted to tell you this, and ask you, in fact I do so now, to be that companion. Will you marry me, Miss Howard?"

"Certainly not," said Miss Howard.

He jumped to his feet as if he had been pinched, and now he found his knees were trembling. He could hardly believe what he had heard, but there seemed no doubt as to what she had said.

"You don't mean that?" he asked.

"Yes, I do," said Miss Howard.

The little place in Kent seemed to explode into a million fragments with Colonel Chase among them: he fell giddily through the air and found himself again in the golf field at Wentworth, where Miss Howard seated on a tree-trunk was just opening her paint-box. As the incredible truth branded itself on his brain, he found that next to his disappointment, his keenest emotion was the desire that nobody should know of his awful, his astounding humiliation.

"I hope you will regard my proposal of marriage to you," he said, "as absolutely private. I made it out of my regard for you and of affection--"

Miss Howard put down her paint-box in a great hurry: her hand was trembling now as much as Colonel Chase's knees.

"That's the finishing touch," she said. "Are you ashamed of having wanted to marry me? Oh, Colonel Chase, you cut a very poor figure."

Three seconds later, Mrs. Oxney from her sitting-room window to which she had been glued, saw the Colonel reappearing on the left of the tiresome shrub, and her first mental ejaculation was 'Well, he has been quick.' Then, as he completely emerged, she saw he was alone and it looked as if Miss Howard had been quick. "I do believe she's gone and refused him," was her second ejaculation. "Well, I never! What will he be like?"

As he came closer, she fled from the window and busied herself in household affairs, for she had seen enough to know what he would be like. His foot crunched the gravel and she heard the front door bang. Then came the sound of an electric bell ringing, and after a pause in which no parlour-maid, though winged like Mercury, could have answered it, a repeated and a longer summons. At the third peal she reinforced her courage with her curiosity, and went out into the lounge to see what he wanted.

His hand was still on the bell-push.

"My sandwiches, Mrs. Oxney," he roared at her. "It's half-past ten and there's no sign of my sandwiches. Everything is disgracefully late this morning. Wentworth isn't what it used to be."

"But you told me you wouldn't take your lunch out, Colonel," she faltered. "I'll get it ready for you in a jiffy: turkey. But you did tell me--"

"And am I not allowed to change my mind if I choose?" he interrupted. Off she flew to the kitchen, colliding with a parlour-maid who was running to answer the bell, for only Colonel Chase ever rang like that, and when the Colonel rang like that, O Lord!

Mrs. Oxney sliced off the choicest morsels of turkey, the cook cut the most delicate slices of bread, the kitchen-maid tore the heart out of a lettuce, the scullery-maid polished up an apple, and in an incredibly short space of time Mrs. Oxney was hurrying back with a pile of these propitiatory offerings neatly tied up. She could not, being a woman, help glancing at his furious face with eager sympathy as he stored them in his pockets, and the awful conviction came over him that it mattered very little whether Miss Howard behaved like a woman of honour or not, since nothing could be more evident than that Mrs. Oxney, by some infernal feminine instinct, knew all about it. He scowled back at her sympathetic looks, and she saw him from the window recklessly careering down the drive.

"Well, he is taking it like a man," she thought, and went to tell her sister.

It was impossible not to be thrilled, but it was difficult not to be a little anxious about the social atmosphere when Colonel Chase returned. The company of paying guests at Wentworth was now diminished, and out of the four left in the house, one was a rejected swain, the second a rejecting mistress, and the third the mistress's bosom friend. Wentworth prided itself on its harmonious existence for, given that the Colonel was in a good temper, they were all, as Mrs. Oxney often said, more like a happy family party than a collection of promiscuous guests. But it was stretching optimism to breaking point to suppose that he could possibly be in a good temper, and the prospect of a happy family party that evening was indeed small.

Mrs. Bertram (though thrilled) shook her head sadly over the outlook.

"I could almost wish the Colonel would catch one of his worst colds," she said, "such as would keep him in his room till Miss Howard and Miss Kemp leave us, but that's not till the day after to-morrow. Yet I'm afraid there's little chance of that on such a mild day. I can see she's sketching still, and Miss Kemp with her. I didn't see the Colonel after his disappointment. Was he much cut up, Margaret?"

"More as if he'd like to cut somebody else up, and I'm sure I don't wonder," said Mrs. Oxney. "The Colonel refused! It hardly bears thinking of. An awful tantrum I should call it. Such a ringing of bells and such scowls at me when I brought him ever so tasty a lunch."

"More angry than love-sick then?" asked Mrs. Bertram.

"I never thought he was love-sick, Amy," said Mrs. Oxney. "But when he expected a happy future in store for him in that beautiful place of Miss Howard's, it must have been a slap in the face. Enough to make any man in a tantrum, if he'd counted on it. And such a pleasant arrangement for them both! I'm sorry."

"And then at dinner to-night," said Mrs. Bertram. "Very awkward for Miss Howard sitting just opposite the man she's refused. Luckily you can always count on her behaving like a perfect lady. I only hope that she and Miss Kemp won't sit and whisper and giggle in a corner as they do sometimes, for the Colonel's sure to think they're whispering about him, and that'll make him mad. I declare I shall be glad to see the two ladies' backs when they leave us, and never yet have I been glad when a guest has gone from Wentworth."

An after-thought slowly struck her.

"And yet we don't know that the Colonel has proposed to Miss Howard," she said, "or that she's refused him. You only saw him go out into the golf field, and come back quick and alone in a tantrum."

Such a suggestion was not, of course, worth answering.

Meanwhile the bright nickel-plated bicycle had been flashing along up hill and down dale with a speed unequalled in the establishment of any previous record, and its rider's state of mind may be faintly indicated by the fact that he had forgotten to put the pedometer back to zero. Rage and humiliation spurred him on, and it was not till he had left familiar country far behind, and his ankles ached with pedalling, that he dismounted and, sitting on a convenient gate, that he attempted coherently to review the repulsive situation. Love-sick he certainly was not: in a tantrum, yes. He had paid Miss Howard the highest compliment a respectable man can pay a respectable woman, and in refusing to take him, she had not expressed the smallest regret: it was idle to suppose that she felt any. And then there was 'The Croft': in losing Miss Howard he had lost 'The Croft', and all the leisurely dignity of his imagined life there. He had vividly seen himself installed there, looking after his wife's agreeable property and he could scarcely yet believe that there was no more chance of his becoming Squire Chase of 'The Croft', than there was of his being Archbishop of Canterbury. More than that, he had decided that matrimony in the abstract was preferable to bachelor life in the concrete, and now nobody, as far as he knew, was going to marry him at all. More than that, there was the return to Wentworth facing him, and just now he would almost sooner have faced the man-eater again. Wentworth, he unerringly divined, had been expecting him to honour Miss Howard, and in spite of his request to her that she should not mention her disdain of the honour, he already gathered that Mrs. Oxney knew. If Mrs. Oxney knew, Mrs. Bertram would know, and as Miss Howard certainly knew, Kemp would know. He might just as well not have asked her to keep silence on this painful subject, and have been spared the information that he cut a very poor figure. Thinking it over, he was afraid he saw what she meant and, unaccustomed as he was to find fault with himself, it was rather a pity to have said that. . . .

He ate his lunch, and unable to go further, turned his bicycle homewards. Anyhow he would show Wentworth how gallant gentlemen behave in heartbreaking situations.

CHAPTER X

In spite of this manly resolution, Mrs. Bertram's gloomy forebodings were fulfilled, and the evening was ghastly in the extreme. Colonel Chase was rather late for dinner (unlike him) but his soup was being kept warm, and he marched into the dining-room with the evening paper under his arm and a fund of unnaturally cheerful observations. He could not notice Miss Howard, for that would have rendered magnanimity ridiculous, but never had he been otherwise so affable.

"Ha, Mrs. Holders," he said. "I crave your partnership at the bridge table after dinner. Mrs. Oxney and Mrs. Bertram? Yes? How you spoil me! I shall hope to wipe off the memory of the adverse fate--"

From that moment everything went wrong. The news of his 'adverse fate' with Miss Howard that morning instantly occurred to everybody and there was a general exchange of stealthy glances, and a feeling of great unease before the Colonel could indicate that he only alluded to the adverse fate which lost him one and ninepence last night.

"And there looks to be a tough cross-word puzzle this evening," he said to Mrs. Oxney. "I took a glance at it, and I think we shall find a worse crux than crofters."

This time he paused: he felt he must really take care of such pitfalls. Mrs. Oxney gallantly plunged into the silence.

"And you had a good ride I hope, Colonel," she said, skilfully changing the subject. "Where did you go?"

"Out beyond Denton: a considerable way beyond Denton."

"Well, I do call that wonderful! And you starting so much later than usual."

Mrs. Bertram trod heavily on her sister's foot under the table, to remind her what was the cause of the late start, and Mrs. Oxney's voice ceased as if the Telephone Exchange had cut her off. She gave a thin faint cry of dismay at what she had said, and of pain at what her sister had done, and Mrs. Bertram tried her hand at tactful conversation.

"It grows a little chilly," she said, "and we'd better have our game of bridge in the smoking-room. There's a beautiful fire of logs there: that trunk of the tree in the golf field had some sound wood in it--"

So Mrs. Oxney trod on her foot, and again there was silence. It was broken by Florence giving a sudden shriek of laughter for no apparent reason. So Miss

Howard tried to account for that by implying that she had said something very droll.

"I thought that would amuse you, dear," she said loudly. "I saved that up to tell you. I was wondering, do you know, as I sketched this morning . . ."

Everybody joined in to cover up *that.* Mrs. Oxney called across to Mrs. Holders to know if she liked sea-kale cooked like this, and Florence put some eager questions to Mrs. Bertram on the subject of Pekinese dogs. Then it was seen that such pairings of conversationalists would never do, for they left Colonel Chase and Miss Howard sitting as dumb as sphinxes. In this diminished company all the occupied tables had been moved up near the fire for warmth and intimacy and Mrs. Oxney wished she had scattered them to the remotest corners of the room instead. Nervousness gripped them all for it seemed as if every topic of normal conversation had a live bomb entangled in its innocent meshes and no one knew exactly in what trivial subject it might not hide. Even the parlour-maids were becoming jumpy and losing their deft precision, and presently the hapless Mabel who served the Colonel let a perfect avalanche of walnuts fall on to his lap and the table-cloth and his plate and into his finger-bowl. The appalling explosion that followed drowned the rattlings and splashings of the nuts.

Mrs. Oxney hoped that when they settled down to bridge, the awful effort to behave naturally would be less of a strain. But Colonel Chase's resolve to conduct himself like a gallant gentleman produced the most embarrassing effect, for instead of hectoring and instructing and swanking as usual, he was polite and courtly and altogether unreal. Decorous silence reigned since conversation was so dangerous, interspersed with little compliments between partners on each other's sound declarations and skilful play and bad luck. Mrs. Oxney made a few attempts to be natural. She told her sister that she ought to have taken out trumps, and appealed to Colonel Chase to know whether that should not have been the correct course, but instead of lecturing about it, and repeating that he was famous throughout India for the observance of this excellent principle, he only said "I have no doubt you are right," which made Mrs. Holders look more surprised than she had ever been. They all knew that Miss Howard and Miss Kemp were together in the drawing-room, from which there proceeded occasional bursts of laughter, which sounded very merry, and it was impossible not to conjecture what caused them. It could only be one subject, and who could pretend to be interested in bridge, while the exact details of what had occurred that morning were probably being humorously discussed? Certainly Mrs. Oxney could not. At half-past ten precisely, Colonel Chase revoked and, instead of blaming Mrs. Holders for not having asked him if he had any more clubs, had apologised. This finished the rubber: he paid, said good night to the stupefied company and went upstairs.

Tongues were loosed, for the strain was over. All three ladies talked simultaneously, and when the first torrent was spent, they agreed that they had never seen a man so changed.

"Greatly improved," said Mrs. Holders severely. "It would do him good to be refused every day."

"Oh, Mrs. Holders, how unkind!" said Mrs. Oxney. "Just think how affable he'd have been if Miss Howard had accepted him."

"Affable? Intolerable!" said Mrs. Holders. "But I doubt if the improvement's real. Did you hear him when the nuts were spilt?"

"Yes, he seemed more natural then," said Mrs. Bertram. "But what a difficult thing it's been to avoid dangerous ground. I shall go to bed, for it's tired me out."

They were all tired out.

Florence was the first to come down next morning. Papers and letters had arrived, and by her place was the *Morning Standard,* which Colonel Chase also took in, a chatty sheet with many pictures and thrilling stories of how a Marchioness had swallowed a thimble, and a child had rescued a Newfoundland dog from a watery grave, and a golfer had taken a hole of prodigious length in one stroke which was an Eagle or a Dodo, or some picturesque fowl. Alice took in *The Times,* so also did Mrs. Oxney, though she never read it, and Mrs. Holders had no paper at all.

Just as Florence sat down she saw a telegraph boy ride past the window on a red bicycle. She wondered if the telegram was for her, but when a couple of minutes had passed without its being brought her, she came to the very shrewd conclusion that it must be for somebody else. With a pleased anticipation of attractive little tit-bits she opened her paper. And then she opened her eyes and her mouth as well in horrified amazement. Though the letters seemed to dance before her eyes, she read:

FIRE AT TUNBRIDGE WELLS.

> "A fire happily unattended with loss of life broke out about midnight at a semi-detached villa called 'The Croft', in the Station Road at Tunbridge Wells. The house was tenanted by Mr. Algernon Gradge and his sister who with the two servants had a narrow escape. The flames mounted so quickly that they could not descend the only staircase but had to get through a trap door in the roof, and thus made their way into the adjoining house. 'The Croft' itself was entirely burned out with all its contents and a mere shell of the outer walls remains."

For a moment, so wildly dissimilar was 'The Croft' of the paragraph from the ancestral home of the Howards, Florence thought how odd it was that there should be two Crofts at Tunbridge Wells tenanted by four Gradges, but instantly she swept the notion aside as puerile. Then all that was finest and most loyal in her nature rallied from the shock, and thanking God that she was the earliest breakfaster and alone in the dining-room, she scudded across to Colonel Chase's table, plucked from it his copy of the *Morning Standard,* folded it up and sat on it. Hardly had she effected this noble larceny, when the door opened and he came in. Florence felt faint at the thought of what would have happened if he had been half a minute earlier, or if she had not pulled her wits together so quickly. That he should know that 'The Croft' was a semi-detached villa was so appalling a thought that she felt as if her hair had turned grey. Even as it was, she might not have averted the catastrophe, for there might be some mention of the fire in *The Times.* She opened Alice's copy and skimmed the pages: to her unutterable relief there was no record of it.

"Mabel," said Colonel Chase in an awful voice. "The papers have come in, haven't they? Why isn't my *Morning Standard* here?"

Mabel couldn't say. It was not her job to distribute the papers.

"Then get me another copy," said the Colonel.

Florence's heart sank like lead in an unplumbed sea. It rose again like a balloon when Mabel came back to say that the paper boy had gone. All might yet be saved.

"Pshaw!" said Colonel Chase, whose gallantry seemed to have evaporated during the night. "Boiled egg and bacon, not cut in cubes, but in slices."

"Beg your pardon, sir?" said Mabel.

"Thin," said Colonel Chase.

Mabel hurried out and Alice hurried in. She held a telegram in her hand and spread it before Florence.

"The most terrible shock," she began. "All my beautiful--"

"Hush," said Florence in a low voice. "I know all about it. There was a paragraph in the *Morning Standard.* Station Road, semi-detached villa."

She sank her voice lower yet.

"He doesn't know," she said. "I was down first. As soon as I saw it I stole his *Morning Standard.* A narrow squeak. I'm sitting on it."

The immense relief of that took precedence of everything else in Alice's mind.

"You angel!" she said.

"I know. It was smart of me. Now we can't talk here, so finish your breakfast quickly and join me."

By a marvellous piece of legerdemain Florence managed with much rustling to fold the stolen copy of the *Morning Standard* inside Alice's *Times,* and having appointed her own bedroom as a rendezvous where they would be certainly safe from Colonel Chase, she left Alice to follow her. Alice had acknowledged the identity of the ancestral home with a semi-detached villa in the Station Road, and Florence felt rather puzzled.

Alice lingered rather than hurried over her breakfast, for a little quiet meditation would not be amiss before she talked things over with Florence. The more she considered her loss, the less shocking did it appear, for the family seat was an odious little house when shorn of the trailing clouds of glory with which she had decked it, and it was fully insured. She had been anxious also about the disclosure she would have to make to Florence before her projected pilgrimage to visit the shrine; it would have been an unpleasant job, but this convenient conflagration had removed the necessity of telling Florence, for now Florence knew. It was as if she had been dreading the extraction of a tooth, and now awoke (as from an anæsthetic) to find that the agony was over without her having perceived it: the family seat, which had been causing her pangs was gone. Exactly how Florence would take the loss was another question, but she had no very grave apprehensions about that, for Florence had herself suggested that she should tell the Colonel all sorts of lies about the little place, and after that these greater splendours which she knew to be false would eclipse such lesser glories as she might believe to be true. There was therefore not more than a shade of nervousness about her tripping step or her warblings as she went upstairs to Florence's bedroom. The moment she opened the door her friend began to speak: she had been thinking things over too.

"The evening paper is the next danger," she said, "but I daresay there'll be nothing about it. Only a semi-detached villa, you see, and no lives lost, and even if there had been, it would only have been Gradges. Oh, darling, I am so glad that 'The Croft' wasn't what I thought it."

Alice did not much like that last remark: Florence was not as muddled up as she hoped. She pressed her hand to her forehead.

"I feel so confused," she said. "It was only two days ago that you insisted on punishing Colonel Chase--that was what you called it--by making me tell all sorts of fibs about 'The Croft'. But you knew they were fibs."

"Oh, but what I meant was before that," said Florence. "What makes me so glad was that it wasn't a big place as--as I thought it, with rose-garden and a Park and peaches."

"But, I don't understand," said Alice. "I never mentioned a Park or peaches till you insisted on my doing so, in order to encourage Colonel Chase and then make him writhe over what he had lost." Florence did not understand either.

"But the lawn," she said, "and your gardeners, and all those other beautiful things."

"There was a lawn," said Alice, "not large, I never said large, but a lawn."

"And the greenhouses--" said Florence.

"You made me invent the greenhouses," said Alice, "and the box hedge. That was two nights ago."

"But the general sense," said Florence. "Ask Mrs. Oxney what she thought 'The Croft' was like. And you said it would hurt you to go down there with me. A semi-detached villa wouldn't hurt anybody."

There was a dreadful truth in that which it was impossible to combat. But all the wise men in the world in consultation with all the wise women in the world could not have suggested a sounder manœuvre than that which Alice instantly executed. She burst into tears.

"You are very cruel," she sobbed. "To please you I invented a lot of lies, and now you tell me I'm a liar. Whose fault is it that I am?"

"No, but before that, before that," repeated Florence.

"Before or after makes little difference," said Alice, continuing to sob, "if that's what you think of me. If you feel like that, I can't imagine why you took away Colonel Chase's *Morning Standard.* I can't think why you didn't shew it him and laugh over it together. If you believe I've been telling you lies it's your duty to expose me. Tell Mrs. Oxney, tell Mrs. Holders, and particularly tell Colonel Chase."

Reason and affection battled together in Florence's rather male mind. She knew she was right and she knew that Alice knew she was right. It was not just that she should have to give up her point. Meantime the friend of her heart, the brilliant, the accomplished Alice was sobbing.

"Darling, don't suggest such absurd things," she said. "Don't you see that my whole object is to keep this secret? I should hate anybody to know what 'The Croft' was really like. But how--oh, what is there to cry about?--how could I have got the idea that it was an old country-house with lovely gardens except from you? Nobody else ever told me about it or--or I should have known what it really was. And I daresay it was a very nice little house."

Alice took not the smallest notice of this admirable logic. She continued sobbing and sticking to her point. "And now just because you've got a wrong idea about it," she wailed, "owing to what you yourself insisted I should tell Colonel Chase you say I've been deceiving you. First my house is burnt down and all my things, and on the top of that the only person in the world whom I thought trusted and loved me turns against me."

This was heart-breaking.

"But I don't turn against you," said the agonised Florence. "And I do love you."

Alice held out the copy of the *Morning Standard* in the hand that was not engaged with her handkerchief.

"Please take it to Colonel Chase," she said. "I think it's your duty."

"It isn't my duty, and if it was I shouldn't do it," cried Florence.

Alice made a master-stroke. Quite improvised.

"Then I shall," she said. "I shall say my best friend tells me I have been deceiving everybody. I shall not dream of saying that you suggested it. I shall take the whole blame."

"But you can't," said Florence bouncing to the door, and standing in front of it. "Besides I am responsible for all the worst things. Telling anybody is the one thing out of the question. I couldn't bear anybody knowing. You shan't go! Oh, do sit down, darling, and let me think a minute."

Alice sat down again and with tear-dimmed eyes, gazed out of the window over the golf field, while Florence's heart made furious attacks on her brain. She thought over the larger splendours of 'The Croft', the shrubbery of flowering rarities, the sweet rose-garden, the fountain where naughty Alice had bathed, the greenhouses of Muscat grapes, the stables, the pheasant-shooting (no, not the pheasant-shooting; Alice had distinctly stated that there was no pheasant-shooting) and all these, it was true, had been inventions made at her instigation. Indoors there was the library and the cedar-wood parquet, and the gallery-room, and at the bank the Chelsea figures and the Queen Anne silver and all these too, had sprung into being at her behest. She began to wonder on what her earlier impressions (though still distinct) of 'The Croft' were based: she tried to recollect a single definite statement of Alice's made previously, she began to grow confused and vague. Had all the splendours which she knew to be inventions stained her previous memories and rendered them more highly-coloured? She knew that it was not so, but now her heart had got a strangle-hold on her mind, and was forcing it to make admissions under torture, for there was Alice, whom she adored, blowing her nose and wiping her eyes and being miserable. Every now and then reason gasped out to her. 'But Alice *did* lie about 'The Croft.' Ask Mrs. Oxney,' but these rational gaspings were growing fainter as her pain at Alice's distress grew stronger, and the need for her affection more insistent. Florence believed that Alice, too, was fond of her, and it was wretched for her to lose her house and her friend before lunch-time. And she herself could not face the loss of Alice.

"Perhaps I'm altogether wrong," she said. "Perhaps it was only the inventions which I insisted on that made me think you had said the same sort of things before, only less so, about 'The Croft'."

"Far better ask Mrs. Oxney, if you're not sure about it," said Alice, repeating the master-stroke, "or best of all ask Colonel Chase. Tell him all about it."

"How could I do anything of the kind?" asked Florence. "How can you think me so disloyal?"

"It isn't very loyal to think those things of me at all," said Alice.

Florence's heart gave a crow of triumph, for her reason gave one convulsive struggle and expired.

"I must have been entirely mistaken," she said. "Oh, how dreadful of me. And I've hurt you: that's worst of all."

"A little," said Alice huskily. "Not much. It doesn't matter."

"But it does matter. It matters terribly. Oh, do forgive me."

The reconciliation, though now certain, was not fully accomplished. Florence, in contrition, had to abase herself further, and Alice to concede that perhaps, unthinkingly, she had said things about The Croft which might lead imaginative minds to think that it was something of larger scale than a semi-detached villa in the Station Road. She could not think what they were, but there might have been something. . . . Then they turned with kisses and caresses to consider the dangers and exposures that still threatened.

"There's nothing in *The Times*," said Florence, "and I don't think it is likely to have anything tomorrow."

"But there are the evening papers, that *Evening Gazette* which the Colonel takes in," said Alice. "It has columns of little paragraphs."

"That's true. But he's usually out when it comes, and I will lie in wait and glance through it."

"And if there is?" asked Alice.

"Steal it, darling," said Florence, "like his morning paper."

"How brave you are! But won't he think it odd if both his papers go wrong today?"

"I shouldn't wonder if he did," said Florence. "But he would think it odder if he saw about 'The Croft'. And after to-day, there won't really be any risk, and to-morrow we go. Oh, what a lovely time we shall have in London now that we're at one again."

"You dear!" said Alice. "By the way, 'The Croft' is fully insured. And what shall we do now? Shan't we go out?"

"Let's! And may I come and sit with you in the golf field while you finish your sketch? I shall sit just where the Colonel sat and make love to you."

Alice pressed her hand.

"And when my sketch is finished," she said, "it shall be your's. I thought of calling it 'Home Sweet Home', and giving it to Mrs. Oxney. But now it shall be 'Blessings on the falling-out'. No one will understand that but you and I."

They went out together in a stiff gale of renewed tenderness, with linked skippings and gambollings, Florence carrying the satchel with the painting utensils for the falling-out picture, and Alice gaily warbling. Careful though they had been in providing against future perils by the plot of stealing Colonel Chase's evening paper, they forgot, like most criminals, the most obvious precaution of destroying the two copies of the incriminating *Morning Standard.* The consequences might have been dire, for Mabel, hurrying in with duster and slop-pail to 'do' Florence's room, found them there, and bethought herself to take one to the Colonel. Then, luckily, she remembered how odiously disagreeable he had been about the cataracts of walnuts last night, and decided not to gratify him. Instead, she took them away, and tossed them on to the store of paper used for kindling in the kitchen cupboard. There for the present they lay innocuous, but like mines charged with deadly matter, they needed only a touch of blundering circumstance to cause a devastating explosion.

The thieves spent a tuneful, artistic and affectionate morning. Now that the catastrophe had happened, Alice felt greatly relieved, for all anxiety over Florence's discovering the truth about 'The Croft' was over, and so well and pathetically had she herself managed that the crisis had only brought them closer together. The sketch promised to be one of the artist's most successful pieces, and the paint-brush dripped with sentiment, for the window of Florence's room, where the endearing falling out had occurred was visible above the shrub, and Alice attempted to portray her figure standing there. But her face would not look otherwise than like the globe of a lamp, and so she drew a blue curtain over it, and obstinate Flo was now behind the blue curtain just as she had been yesterday morning, when Colonel Chase made his declaration. Then there were plans to be made for the future: the fortnight in London became a firm month, after which Florence must spend Christmas with her father, and Alice would go to Torquay for sea-air and marine material for artistry.

"You must join me there for a bit," said she. "Red sandstone cliffs, the blue, blue sea. Anstey's Cove. Such lovely serpentine rocks."

Florence did not reply for a moment, and Alice having made a blue, blue curtain, nudged her.

"Won't you?" she said.

Florence drew a long breath. She felt her moment had come.

"Yes, of course I will," she said, "but those are only little temporary plans. I want a permanent one. Mayn't we make a permanent plan, darling? I mean, won't you come to live with me altogether in London? The flat is mine, Mamma left it me, and I believe we should be so happy. Don't say 'Certainly not', as you said yesterday to that absurd man. I would do all the housekeeping, or, if it amused you, you should. I think you'd like it better than Wentworth, and as for me, bliss. You shall subscribe to expenses or not just as you like. And Papa won't want me again, for Nurse Babbit exactly suits him. I shall be quite alone otherwise, but that mustn't influence you: I don't appeal to you, though I should be miserable without you."

The sketch, with Florence supposedly behind the blue curtain, slipped unregarded from Alice's hand, for Florence had come out from behind all curtains.

"Oh, Florence, are you sure?" she asked.

"Positive," said Florence.

"So am I, then," said Alice.

The moment had grown quite solemn. They looked at each other in silence, they gravely kissed. Then Alice said:

"I told a heap of lies about that villa, I made it out to be grand and it was a horrible little place, and the shunting at the station used to keep me awake. The rent was fifty pounds a year."

Florence appreciated that at its full value.

"Oh, I am glad you told me," she said hurriedly, "and now it's quite over. Darling, just think; yesterday the Colonel sat just where I'm sitting, when you said 'Certainly not', and now, bless you, you say 'Certainly so'. I long to tell him you're going to live with me instead of him. How he would hate me! Delicious! But then you'll have to tell Mrs. Oxney that you're not coming back here, so it will get round."

The two went off next day on their honeymoon, but as their rooms were to be filled up at once, Mrs. Oxney resigned herself to their departure. She felt, too, that the Colonel would never settle down to his old ways while the constant reminder of his disappointment was there. Indeed the news that Wentworth would never again ring with Miss Howard's bright little snatches of song was compensated for by the consideration that Colonel Chase would very likely have gone away if she had stopped, and of the two she vastly preferred him. A man, and such a fine big man, was a much more valuable social nucleus in the house, for in his robust hectoring way he kept things up to the mark, and told his grim or amusing stories, and laid down the law at bridge, and made it seem an honour to play with him. Of course he lost his temper, and had tantrums, but then he recovered it again and made a fresh record on his bicycle. He was an asset, a distinction, a Colonel was better than a plain Miss to rally round. She quite made up her mind to put in the extra bathroom when he went away for a fortnight at Christmas. It would be ready for his return, and that would be a nice surprise for him.

Colonel Chase made a remarkable recovery after Miss Howard's departure, and in the week or two that remained before his Christmas holiday, so well earned by his busy life at Wentworth, he established himself with the new paying guests, elderly and hobbling ladies, as an athlete and an authority on most subjects. There was some very pleasant bridge the night before he left, but he broke the table up at ten o'clock, as he was off quite early in the morning and had yet his packing to do.

"I never trust anybody to do my packing for me," he said, "and if I had fifty valets I would still do it. In India, whatever the thermometer stood at, I invariably packed for myself. Give me plenty of paper to wrap my kit up in, and there'll be no shaking about or breakages."

"Nobody can pack like you, Colonel," said Mrs. Oxney, "I always used to pride myself on my packing, till once I saw you doing it. Like a mosaic: everything fitting so that there wasn't a chink anywhere. And the amount you get in, astonishing!"

Colonel Chase's bed was piled up high with his clothes and other effects, waiting for his mosaic touch, but he had made very little progress in his astonishing art, when he saw that there was not nearly enough paper. Up came Mabel in answer to his summons, and down went Mabel, and up she came again with a pile of newspapers.

"Thankye," said Colonel Chase, feeling in his pocket for some small change as Christmas was approaching. Three of the larger coins would be a generous tip, but then he remembered the cataract of nuts, and let one of them slip back into his pocket again.

His manual dexterity did not entirely occupy his mind: he could ruminate while he made his mosaic, and as he wrapped up boots and fitted Macaulay's essays among them to keep them tight, he thought over his disappointment. It was still a bitter reflection that owing to a woman's perverseness he could not now look forward to being the master of a fine Queen Anne Manor House with gardens and greenhouses and galleries, for he still felt that he was absolutely cut out to fill that post. Instead the misguided lady had gone off to live in frumpy spinster partnership with one of the most tiresome creatures he had ever come across. Together perhaps, for he understood that Kemp was well off, they would settle into 'The Croft', when Miss Howard's tenants came to the end of their lease, and get cheated by the gardeners and never have a peach or a bunch of grapes for their own table. A woman could manage a house (he had fully intended his wife to manage her's) but with an estate like that a man's grasp and authority were required, or everything ran to seed. The county club, the comfortable little parties, the position of Squire Howard-Chase! Well, it was no use thinking about it, and after all Wentworth was very comfortable, and the newcomers seemed reverential women, and he hoped they would stop on.

He picked up one of the papers that had been brought him by Mabel, and his eye was arrested by a remarkable picture of a baboon on the first page, which was unfamiliar to him. Yet the paper was the *Morning Standard* which he saw every day, and he could not imagine how he had forgotten this grimacing ape. He turned the leaf, and found another picture he was sure he had not seen before, and at that fateful moment he remembered that some few mornings ago his *Standard* had not arrived. Then his eye fell on a headline: "Fire at Tunbridge Wells", and in the ensuing paragraph on the words, "a semi-detached villa called 'The Croft'." He gave one loud raucous exclamation, and next moment, without pausing to put on his coat, which he had shed for his mosaic-work, he was bounding downstairs, with the pedometer clicking madly in his pocket. The smoking-room where they had played bridge, was empty and he hurried to Mrs. Oxney's sitting-room, and entered without knocking. There she was with her skirt turned back over her knees, warming her shins at the fire and eating seed-cake.

"Why, whatever's the matter, Colonel?" she cried, hastily putting down her skirt and her seedcake. "Nothing wrong, I hope?"

"Wrong?" he echoed, brandishing the *Morning Standard.* "Listen to this. Fire at Tunbridge Wells, Mrs. Oxney."

"Gracious me, how dangerous! Not . . . not Miss Howard's beautiful place?" she cried.

"You've guessed! You're right! But there's something you've not guessed. 'The Croft' was burned out, but what do you suppose 'The Croft' was? A semi-detached villa, Mrs. Oxney, a semi-detached villa in the Station Road!"

"It must be another one," said Mrs. Oxney faintly.

"Not a bit of it. Tenants were occupying it: the Gradges. Don't you remember the name? I do. Station Road: semi-detached villa. What a liar the woman is with her manor house and her shrubberies and her rose-gardens, and her gallery-room. Family portraits too: a couple of photographs I expect. I'll tell you what I think: the descendant of the noble house made up all that swaggering nonsense just to entrap me into--"

On second thoughts that wouldn't do, but the Colonel continued with no pause at all.

"--she wanted to make us all think she was of the landed gentry. Swank! Lies! The painful necessity of letting her beautiful place, but no repining, brave girl, because it's happened to so many of her class! But what's the class, I ask you? The semi-detached class. Curates and apothecaries and chimney sweeps! Why my tailor's name is Howard, though I never taxed Miss Howard with that. But to think of the escape I've had! 'The Croft', a semi-detached villa!"

This was a mistake. Mrs. Oxney, horrified as she was (for she had been talking only this evening to some of the new guests, with regret that Miss Howard, who had that lovely place in Kent, had just gone) could not think so ill of the Colonel as to imagine that he had been "after" the exploded and now burned-out 'Croft', instead of its mistress. Yet his words did lend themselves to such an interpretation.

"Why, you speak as if it was The Croft that had enticed you, Colonel," she said. "To be sure, it does look as if Miss Howard had made it out a bit grander than it was, but surely it was she you wanted. I should hate to believe otherwise of you, though to be sure it was disappointing to think that you'd lost all that beautiful property as well as your young lady."

Colonel Chase thought for the moment that he was in a hole. But his excitement had sharpened his wits to an extraordinary acuteness, and he saw a loophole.

"I repeat that I've had an escape," he said weightily. "When I proposed, as I did, to the lady you designate as young, I thought her an accomplished woman within limits, and not without charm, but above all an honourable and truthful woman. This information, which I stumbled on by accident, shows me that her idea of truth is different from mine, and long may it remain so. That's what I mean by an escape. Sooner or later, it would have turned out that she had grossly lied about 'The Croft'. I could never have trusted her again, and misery would have followed on marriage. And when I think of all I have done for her, the pictures I have bought, the offer of a name which though no doubt obscure is yet honourable: then I repeat, as often as you like, that I have had an escape. Ha!"

Mrs. Oxney, pored over the fatal paragraph, sadly clicking her tongue against her teeth.

"It does look as if she had deceived us," she said. "I wouldn't have thought it of her."

"Then I would, Mrs. Oxney," said Colonel Chase. "I never really trusted her. That improvisation at which she had been practising for days! I could have whistled it before she played it at the entertainment. It's all of a piece."

Mrs. Oxney felt that Miss Howard could not be so black as the Colonel was painting her. She had to stand up for her sex.

"But you knew that before you proposed to her," she said. "Besides, where's the harm?"

"I did know it: you are right," said Colonel Chase. "I hoped that these little superficial fibs were no part of her real nature. But now! Instead of the Queen Anne manor house, and the grape-house and the peach-house and the bathing-pool--"

"No! Not bathing-pool?" asked Mrs. Oxney.

"Bathing-pool. She bathed there when a girl--and the shrubberies and ancestralcies, we have a semi-detached villa in the Station Road. Ha, ha, ha! Stupendous I repeat. Enough. Dear me, I am talking to you in my shirt-sleeves. Very remiss of me; I hope I have a better idea of what is due to the other sex than Miss Howard has. The peaches and the Muscat grapes! If a peach or a grape ever found its way into 'The Croft', it came from a barrow in the Station Road. We should have had a banana-grove next. However, I wish Miss Howard well, and I shall certainly send her a sympathetic note, condoling with her on the loss of her semi-detached villa, and hoping that its treasures are amply insured."

So happy a mixture of essential spite and apparent magnanimity could hardly be believed, and, hoarse with rhetoric Colonel Chase ceased foaming at the mouth and straddling in front of the fire-place, and sat down as calm as the centre of a cyclone. Mrs. Oxney he supposed, had got used to the informality of his shirt-sleeves by now, and if she hadn't, she never would.

CHAPTER X

"Well, I'm sure you're very forgiving, Colonel," she said, "after the way Miss Howard has treated you. I've often noticed how large-minded soldiers are. Mr. Oxney was, though, to be sure, he was only in the Militia. And I quite misunderstood you, I see. I thought at first that you meant that you'd had an escape because 'The Croft' wasn't quite what you thought it, now I see you weren't such a mercenary. Poor Miss Howard, what she's lost when you gave her the chance. It all comes of not being quite truthful."

It occurred to Colonel Chase that Miss Howard's painful untruthfulness had been the cause not of her losing him, but of her having the opportunity to win him, if she had been disposed. But to correct Mrs. Oxney (as they were not playing bridge, but having a heart-to-heart talk), would be the act of a pedant, and he let her faulty logic pass. . . . There she sat in her rich evening silk, very sympathetic and very comely, and quite void of deceit. He knew all about her, the solidity of her connexion, the excellence of her table, the admirable housekeeping qualities which made Wentworth so comfortable. After this turmoil of emotion these were peaceful thoughts.

"I have been deceived in Miss Howard," he said, "but I dismiss it from my mind, and will not suffer it to sully the respect in which I have always held her sex. My experience of it has been far otherwise, and I have no doubt that it will continue to be so."

He was astonished at the perfect phrasing of his magnanimous sentiments: Macaulay's Essays could contain nothing more simple and dignified. The clock on the mantel-piece struck, and with scarcely less astonishment he heard it announce midnight.

"God bless my soul," he cried, springing actively up from his low chair. "I had no idea it was so late. My packing still only half-finished, and you--ha, your beauty-sleep. Time for little boys and girls to be in bed, Mrs. Oxney. But this little boy has still to finish his packing. He will be glad when the day comes for him to pack again, and return to charming Wentworth."

Mrs. Oxney was almost daring enough to offer to help in the mosaic-making. But perhaps that was a little too modern, and she contented herself with reciprocating his wish.

"Come back soon, Colonel," she said. "Your room will always be ready for you, and I hope I shall have a little surprise in store for your return. It won't be Wentworth without you."

EPILOGUE

Florence and Alice happened to go to the Zoological Gardens on the afternoon of the day when Colonel Chase's letter of condolence on the loss of the semi-detached villa had arrived. There they visited the monkey-house, and observing the antics of a most indelicate and ill-favoured ape exclaimed simultaneously:

"The Colonel!"

"So like, and just that swaggering manner," said Alice.

"And look at him chattering with rage," said Florence. "Just like his face when there came that avalanche of walnuts. Poor Mabel."

"But this one chatters because there are no nuts," said Alice. "Otherwise there's no difference at all."

"Let's get him some nuts," said Florence, "and we'll see how he behaves when he eats. That'll be a test if he's really the Colonel."

This was done: they burst into shrieks of laughter.

"So it *is* the Colonel," said Alice. "No one else eats like that: no one could. What a sad change for him! No pedometer and bicycle rides. But I daresay that swinging on that rope does as well, and he tells them all how many times he has swung."

They laughed again, and the keeper asked them not to irritate the animals.

The month's honeymoon had gone in a sunny flash, and now after Florence's Christmas visit to Bournemouth they were back in the flat again and had settled down. Alice was terribly busy over the most important picture of her career: Winter Sunset in Kensington Gardens, a very large sketch. She painted chiefly in the morning, because it was warmer then, but often came back towards dark for colour notes. Florence always sat on a camp-stool to her right, in order to keep the admiring connoisseurs of London from encroaching too near her painting-arm.

To-day at breakfast Florence was urging her friend to take a morning off, for she thought she had been working too hard.

"Besides, darling," she said, "the sun's so very bright. You can't paint dusk in very strong sunlight, you've often said so. There'll be plenty of grey days. And you do look a little tired. Stay quiet this morning: you may play the piano."

"Are those Doctor Florence's orders?" asked Alice picking up *The Times.*

"Yes, and she's very firm. This afternoon we'll go to the Zoo again, and see how the Colonel is getting on. We haven't seen him for an age."

Alice's eye had been travelling down the first column of the outside sheet: her answer to Doctor Florence was a shrill scream.

"Flo, darling," she cried. "Talk of the Colonel and he'll appear. Here, the very first thing I saw. Guess!"

"Oh, is he dead?" asked Florence.

"No, guess again."

"Not married?" she asked.

"Yes. Listen! 'On Jan. 4, 1927, at St. Giles's Church, Bolton Spa, by the Reverend Hildebrand Banks, M.A., assisted by the Reverend Eustace Toogood'--yes, it's coming presently--'Colonel Albert Chase late of the Indian Army to Margaret Oxney, widow of the late Septimus Oxney, of Wentworth, Bolton Spa.'"

"My dear, let me look!" cried Florence. "Well, I never! Did you?"

"That settles it," said Alice. "We must go to the Zoo, not this afternoon, but at once, and congratulate him."

They bought a bag of wedding nuts. The Colonel was swinging madly on his rope.

"Probably doing a record," said Alice. "Come, Colonel! Such delicious nuts."

The Colonel paid not the least attention to them, but when he had broken his record, sat and cuddled up to a stout and rather comely lady-ape, who received a few trivial connubialities with marked favour.

"And Mrs. Oxney!" said Alice.

THE END

MRS AMES

CHAPTER I

Certainly the breakfast tongue, which was cut for the first time that morning, was not of the pleasant reddish hue which Mrs. Altham was justified in expecting, considering that the delicacy in question was not an ordinary tinned tongue (you had to take things as you found them, if your false sense of economy led you to order tinned goods) but one that came out of a fine glass receptacle with an eminent label on it. It was more of the colour of cold mutton, unattractive if not absolutely unpleasant to the eye, while to the palate it proved to be singularly lacking in flavour. Altogether it was a great disappointment, and for this reason, when Mr. Altham set out at a quarter-past twelve to stroll along to the local club in Queensgate Street with the ostensible purpose of seeing if there was any fresh telegram about the disturbances in Morocco, his wife accompanied him to the door of that desirable mansion, round which was grouped a variety of chained-up dogs in various states of boredom and irritation, and went on into the High Street in order to make in person a justifiable complaint at her grocer's. She would be sorry to have to take her custom elsewhere, but if Mr. Pritchard did not see his way to sending her another tongue (of course without further charge) she would be obliged . . .

So this morning there was a special and imperative reason why Mrs. Altham should walk out before lunch to the High Street, and why her husband should make a morning visit to the club. But to avoid misconception it may be stated at once that there was, on every day of the week except Sunday, some equally compelling cause to account for these expeditions. If it was very wet, perhaps, Mrs. Altham might not go to the High Street, but wet or fine her husband went to his club. And exactly the same thing happened in the case of most of their friends and acquaintances, so that Mr. Altham was certain of meeting General Fortescue, Mr. Brodie, Major Ames, and others in the smoking-room, while Mrs. Altham encountered their wives and sisters on errands like her own in the High Street. She often professed superior distaste for gossip, but when she met her friends coming in and out of shops, it was but civil and reasonable that she should have a few moments' chat with them. Thus, if any striking events had taken place since the previous afternoon, they all learned about them. Simultaneously there was a similar interchange of thought and tidings going on in the smoking-room at the club, so that when Mr. Altham had drunk his glass of sherry and returned home to lunch at one-thirty, there was probably little of importance and interest which had not reached the ears of himself or his wife. It could then be discussed at that meal.

Queensgate Street ran at right-angles to the High Street, debouching into that thoroughfare at the bottom of its steep slope, while the grocer's shop lay at the top of it. The morning was a hot day of early June, but to a woman of Mrs. Altham's spare frame and active limbs, the ascent was no more than a pleasurable exercise, and the vivid colour of her face (so unlike the discouraging hues of the breakfast tongue) was not the result of her exertions. It was habitually there, and though that and the restlessness of her dark and rather beady eyes might have made a doctor, on a cursory glance (especially if influenza was about), think that she suffered from some slight rise of temperature, he would have been in error. Her symptoms betokened not an unnatural warmth of the blood, but were the visible sign of her eager and slightly impatient mind. Like the inhabitants of ancient Athens, she was always on the alert to hear some new thing (though she disliked gossip), but her mind appreciated the infinitesimal more than the important. The smaller a piece of news was, the more vivid was her perception of it, and the firmer her grip of it: large questions produced but a vague impression on her.

Her husband, a retired solicitor, was singularly well-adapted to be the partner of her life, for his mind was very much akin to hers, and his appetite for news no less rapacious. Indeed, the chief difference between them in this respect was that she snapped at her food like a wolf in winter, whereas he took it quietly, in the manner of a leisurely boa-constrictor. But his capacity was in no way inferior to hers. Similarly, they practised the same harmless hypocrisies on each other, and politely forbore to question each other's sincerity. An instance has already been recorded where such lack of trust might have been manifested, but it never entered Mrs. Altham's head to tell her husband just now that he cared nothing whatever about the disturbances in Morocco, while she would have thought it very odd conduct on his part to suggest that a sharply worded note to Mr. Pritchard would save her the walk uphill on this hot morning. But it was only sensible to go on their quests; had they not ascertained if there was any news, they would have had nothing to talk about at lunch. As it was, conversation never failed them, for this little town of Riseborough was crammed with interest and incident, for all who felt a proper concern in the affairs of other people.

The High Street this morning was very full, for it was market-day, and Mrs. Altham's progress was less swift than usual. Barrows of itinerant vendors were crowded into the road from the edge of the pavements, leaving a straitened channel for a traffic swelled by farmers' carts and occasional droves of dusty and perplexed looking cattle, being driven in from the country round. More than once Mrs. Altham had to step into the doorway of some shop to avoid the random erring of a company of pigs or sheep which made irruption on to the pavement. But it was interesting to observe, in one such enforced pause, the impeded passage of Sir James Westbourne's motor, with the owner, broad-faced and good-humoured, driving himself, and to conjecture as to what business brought him into the town. Then she saw that there was his servant sitting in the body of the car, while there were two portmanteaus on the luggage-rail behind. There was no need for further conjecture: clearly he was coming from the South-Eastern station at the top of the hill, and was driving out to his place four miles distant along the Maidstone road. Then he caught sight of somebody on the pavement whom he knew, and, stopping the car, entered into conversation.

For the moment Mrs. Altham could not see who it was; then, as the car moved on again, there appeared from behind it the tall figure of Dr. Evans. Mrs. Altham was not so foolish as to suppose that their conversation had necessarily anything to do with medical matters; she did not fly to the conclusion that Lady Westbourne or any of the children must certainly be ill. To a person of her mental grasp it was sufficient to remember that Mrs. Evans was Sir James' first cousin. She heard also the baronet's cheerful voice as the two parted, saying, "Saturday the twenty-eighth, then. I'll tell my wife." That, of course, settled it; it required only a moment's employment of her power of inference to make her feel convinced that Saturday the twenty-eighth would be the date for Mrs. Evans' garden-party. There were a good many garden-parties in Riseborough about then, for strawberries might be expected to be reasonably cheap. Probably the date had been settled only this morning; she might look forward to receiving the "At-Home" card (four to seven) by the afternoon post.

The residential quarters of Riseborough lay both at the top of the hill, on which the town stood, clustering round the fine old Norman church, and at the bottom, along Queensgate Street, which passed into the greater spaciousness of St. Barnabas Road. On the whole, that might be taken to be the Park Lane of the place, and commanded the highest rents; every house there, in addition to being completely detached, had a small front garden with a carriage drive long enough to hold three carriages simultaneously, if each horse did not mind putting its nose within rubbing distance of the carriage in front of it, while the foremost projected a little into the road again. But there were good houses also at the top of the hill, where Dr. Evans lived, and those who lived below naturally considered themselves advantageously-placed in being sheltered from the bleak easterly winds which often prevailed in spring, while those at the top wondered among themselves in sultry summer days how it was possible to exist in the airless atmosphere below. The middle section of the town was mercantile, and it was here that the ladies of the place, both from above and below, met each other with such invariable fortuitousness in the hours before lunch. To-day, however, though the street was so full, it was for purposes of news-gathering curiously deserted, and apart from the circumstance of inferentially learning the date of Mrs. Evans' garden-party, Mrs. Altham found nothing to detain her until she had got to the very door of Mr. Pritchard's grocery. But there her prolonged fast was broken; Mrs. Taverner was ready to give and receive, and after the business of the colourless tongue was concluded in a manner that was perfectly creditable to Mr. Pritchard, the two ladies retraced their steps (for Mrs. Taverner was of St. Barnabas Road) down the hill again.

Mrs. Taverner quite agreed about the strong probability of Mrs. Evans' garden-party being on the twenty-eighth; and proceeded to unload herself of far more sensational information. She talked rather slowly, but without ever stopping of her own accord, so that she got as much into a given space of time as most people. Even if she was temporarily stopped by an interruption, she kept her mouth open, so as to be able to proceed at the earliest possible moment.

"Yes, three weeks, as you say, is a long notice, is it not?" she said; "but I'm sure people are wise to give long notice, otherwise they will find all their guests are already engaged, such a quantity of parties as there will be this summer. Mrs. Ames has sent out dinner-cards for exactly the same date, I am told. I daresay they agreed together to have a day full of gaiety. Perhaps you are asked to dine there on the twenty-eighth, Mrs. Altham?"

"No, not at present."

"Well, then, it will be news to you," said Mrs. Taverner, "if what I have heard is true, and it was Mrs. Fortescue's governess who told me; whom I met taking one of the children to the dentist."

"That would be Edward," said Mrs. Altham unerringly. "I have often noticed his teeth are most irregular: one here, another there."

She spoke as if it was more usual for children to have all their teeth on the same spot, but Mrs. Taverner understood.

"Very likely; indeed, I think I have noticed it myself. Well, what I have to tell you seems very irregular, too; Edward's teeth are nothing to it. It was talked about, so Miss--I can never recollect her name, and, from what I hear, I do not think Mrs. Fortescue finds her very satisfactory--it was talked about, so Mrs. Fortescue's governess told me, at breakfast time, and it was agreed that General Fortescue should accept, for if you are asked three weeks ahead it is no use saying you are engaged. No doubt Mrs. Ames gave that long notice for that very reason."

"But what is it that is so irregular?" asked Mrs. Altham, nearly dancing with impatience at these circumlocutions.

"Did I not tell you? Ah, there is Mrs. Evans; I was told she was asked too, without her husband. How slowly she walks; I should not be surprised if her husband had told her never to hurry. She did not see us; otherwise we might have found out more."

"About what?" asked the martyred Mrs. Altham.

"Why, what I am saying. Mrs. Ames has asked General Fortescue to dine that night, without asking Mrs. Fortescue, and has asked Mrs. Evans to dine without asking Dr. Evans. I don't know who the rest of the party are. I must try to find time this afternoon to call on Mrs. Ames, and see if she lets anything drop about it. It seems very odd to ask a husband without his wife, and a wife without her husband. And we do not know yet whether Dr. Evans will allow his wife to go there without him."

Mrs. Altham was suitably astounded.

"But I never heard of such a thing," she said, "and I expect my memory is as" (she nearly said "long," but stopped in time) "clear and retentive as that of most people. It seems very strange: it will look as if General Fortescue and his wife are not on good terms, and, as far as I know, there is no reason to suppose that. However, it is none of my business, and I am thankful to say that I do not concern my-myself with things that do not concern me. Had Mrs. Ames wanted my advice as to the desirability of asking a husband without a wife, or a wife without a husband, I should have been very glad to give it her. But as she has not asked it, I must suppose that she does not want it, and I am sure I am very thankful to keep my opinion to myself. But if she asked me what I thought about it, I should be compelled to tell her the truth. I am very glad to be spared any such unpleasantness. Dear me, here I am at home again. I had no idea we had come all this way."

Mrs. Taverner seemed inclined to linger, but the other had caught sight of her husband's face looking out of the window known as his study, where he was accustomed to read the paper in the morning, and go to sleep in the evening. This again was very irregular, for the watch on her wrist told her that it was not yet a quarter-past one, the hour at which he invariably ordered a glass of sherry at the club, to fortify him for his walk home. Possibly he had heard something about this revolutionary social scheme in the club, and had hastened his return in order to be able to talk it over with her without delay. For a moment it occurred to her to ask Mrs. Taverner to join them at lunch, but, after all, she had heard what that lady had to tell, and one of the smaller bundles of asparagus could not be considered ample for more than two. So she checked the hospitable impulse, and hurried into his study, alert with suppressed information, though she did not propose to let it explode at once, for the method of them both was to let news slip out as if accidentally. And, even as she crossed the hall, an idea for testing the truth of what she had heard, which was both simple and ingenious, came into her head. She despised poor Mrs. Taverner's scheme of calling on Mrs. Ames, in the hope of her letting something drop, for Mrs. Ames never let things drop in that way, though she was an adept at picking them up. Her own plan was far more effective. Also it harmonized well with the system of mutual insincerities.

"I have been thinking, my dear," she said briskly, as she entered his study, "that it is time for us to be asking Major and Mrs. Ames to dinner again. Yes: Pritchard was reasonable, and will send me another tongue, and take back the old one, which I am sure I am quite glad that he should do, though it would have come in for savouries very handily. Still, he is quite within his rights, since he does not charge for it, and I should not think of quarrelling with him because he exercises them."

Mr. Altham was as keen a housekeeper as his wife.

"Its colour would not have signified in a savoury," he said.

"No, but as Pritchard supplies a new tongue without charge, we cannot complain. About Mrs. Ames, now. We dined with them quite a month ago: I do not want her to think we are lacking in the exchange of hospitalities, which I am sure are so pleasant on both sides."

Mr. Altham considered this question, caressing the side of his face. There was no doubt that he had a short pointed beard on his chin, but about half-way up the jawbone the hair got shorter and shorter, and he was quite clean-shaven before it got up to his ear. It was always a question, in fact, among the junior and less respectful members of the club, whether old Altham had whiskers or not. The gen-general opinion was that he had whiskers, but was unaware of that possession.

"It is odd that the idea of asking Mrs. Ames to dinner occurred to you to-day," he said, "for I was wondering also whether we did not owe her some hospitality. And Major Ames, of course," he added.

Mrs. Altham smiled a bright detective smile.

"Next week is impossible, I know," she said, "and so is the week after, as there is a perfect rush of engagements then. But after that, we might find an evening free. How would it suit you, if I asked Mrs. Ames and a few friends to dine on the Saturday of that week? Let me count--seven, fourteen, twenty-one, yes; on the twenty-eighth. I think that probably Mrs. Evans will have her garden-party on that day. It would make a pleasant ending to such an afternoon. And it would be less of an interruption to both of us, if we give up that day. It would be better than disarranging the week by sacrificing another evening."

Mr. Altham rang the bell before replying.

"It is hardly likely that Major and Mrs. Ames would have an engagement so long ahead," he said. "I think we shall be sure to secure them."

The bell was answered.

"A glass of sherry," he said. "I forgot, my dear, to take my glass of sherry at the club. Young Morton was talking to me, though I don't know why I call him young, and I forgot about my sherry. Yes, I should think the twenty-eighth would be very suitable."

Mrs. Altham waited until the parlour-maid had deposited the glass of sherry, and had completely left the room with a shut door behind her.

"I heard a very extraordinary story to-day," she said, "though I don't for a moment believe it is true. If it is, we shall find that Mrs. Ames cannot dine with us on the twenty-eighth, but we shall have asked her with plenty of notice, so that it will count. But one never knows how little truth there may be in what Mrs. Taverner says, for it was Mrs. Taverner who told me. She said that Mrs. Ames has asked General Fortescue to dine with her that night, without asking Mrs. Fortescue, and has invited Mrs. Evans also without her husband. One doesn't for a moment believe it, but if we asked Mrs. Ames for the same night we should very likely hear about it. Was anything said at the club about it?"

Mr. Altham affected a carelessness which he was very far from feeling.

"Young Morton did say something of the sort," he said. "I was not listening particularly, since, as you know, I went there to see if there was anything to be learned about Morocco, and I get tired of his tittle-tattle. But he did mention something of the kind. There is the luncheon-bell, my dear. You might write your note immediately and send it by hand, for James will be back from his dinner by now, and tell him to wait for an answer."

Mrs. Altham adopted this suggestion at once. She knew, of course, perfectly well that the thrilling quality of the news had brought her husband home without waiting to take his glass of sherry at the club, a thing which had not happened since that morning a year ago, when he had learned that Mrs. Fortescue had dismissed her cook without a character, but she did not think of accusing him of du-duplicity. After all, it was the amiable desire to talk these matters over with her without the loss of a moment which was the motive at the base of his action, and so laudable a motive covered all else. So she had her note written with amazing speed and cordiality, and the boot-and-knife boy, who also exercised the function of the gardener, was instructed to wash his hands and go upon his errand.

Criticism of Mrs. Ames' action, based on the hypothesis that the news was true, was sufficient to afford brisk conversation until the return of the messenger, and Mrs. Altham put back on her plate her first stick of asparagus and tore the note open. A glance was sufficient.

"It is all quite true," she said. "Mrs. Ames writes, 'We are so sorry to be obliged to refuse your kind invitation, but General Fortescue and Millicent Evans, with a few other friends, are dining with us this evening.' Well, I am sure! So, after all, Mrs. Taverner was right. I feel I owe her an apology for doubting the truth of it, and I shall slip round after lunch to tell her that she need not call on Mrs. Ames, which she was thinking of doing. I can save her that trouble."

Mr. Altham considered and condemned the wisdom of this slipping round.

"That might land you in an unpleasantness, my dear," he said. "Mrs. Taverner might ask you how you were certain of it. You would not like to say that you asked the Ames' to dinner on the same night in order to find out."

"No, that is true. You see things very quickly, Henry. But, on the other hand, if Mrs. Taverner does go to call, Mrs. Ames might let drop the fact that she had received this invitation from us. I would sooner let Mrs. Taverner know it myself than let it get to her in roundabout ways. I will think over it; I have no doubt I shall be able to devise something. Now about Mrs. Ames' new departure. I must say that it seems to me a very queer piece of work. If she is to ask you without me, and me without you, is the other to sit at home alone for dinner? For it is not to be expected that somebody else will on the very same night always ask the other of us. As likely as not, if there is another invitation for the same night, it will be for both of us, for I do not suppose that we shall all follow Mrs. Ames' example, and model our hospitalities on hers."

Mrs. Altham paused a moment to eat her asparagus, which was getting cold.

"As a matter of fact, my dear, we do usually follow Mrs. Ames' example," he said. "She may be said to be the leader of our society here."

"And if you gave me a hundred guesses why we do follow her example," said Mrs. Altham rather excitedly, picking up a head of asparagus that had fallen on her napkin, "I am sure I could not give you one answer that you would think sensible. There are a dozen of our friends in Riseborough who are just as well born as she is, and as many more much better off; not that I say that money should have anything to do with position, though you know as well as I do that you could buy their house over their heads, Henry, and afford to keep it empty, while, all the time, I, for one, don't believe that they have got three hundred a year between them over and above his pay. And as for breeding, if Mrs. Ames' manners seem to you so worthy of copy, I can't understand what it is you find to admire in them, except that she walks into a room as if it all belonged to her, and looks over everybody's head, which is very ridiculous, as she can't be more than two inches over five feet, and I doubt if she's as much. I never have been able to see, and I do not suppose I ever shall be able to see, why none of us can do anything in Riseborough without asking Mrs. Ames' leave. Perhaps it is my stupidity, though I do not know that I am more stupid than most."

Henry Altham felt himself to blame for this agitated harangue. It was careless of him to have alluded to Mrs. Ames' leadership, for if there was a subject in this world that produced a species of frenzy and a complete absence of full-stops in his wife, it was that. Desperately before now had she attempted to wrest the sceptre from Mrs. Ames' podgy little hands, and to knock the crown off her noticeably small head. She had given parties that were positively Lucullan in their magnificence on her first coming to Riseborough; the regimental band (part of it, at least) had played under the elm-tree in her garden on the occasion of a mere afternoon-party, while at a dance she had given (a thing almost unknown in Riseborough) there had been a cotillion in which the presents cost up to five and sixpence each, to say nothing of the trouble. She had given a party for children at which there was not only a Christmas-tree, but a conjuror, and when a distinguished actor once stayed with her, she had, instead of keeping him to herself, which was Mrs. Ames' plan when persons of eminence were her guests, asked practically the whole of Riseborough to lunch, tea and dinner. To all of these great parties she had bidden Mrs. Ames (with a view to her deposition), and on certainly one occasion--that of the cotillion--she had heard afterwards unimpeachable evidence to show that that lady had remarked that she saw no reason for such display. Therefore to this day she had occasional bursts of volcanic amazement at Mrs. Ames' undoubted supremacy, and made occasional frantic attempts to deprive her of her throne. There was no method of attack which she had not employed; she had flattered and admired Mrs. Ames openly to her face, with a view to be permitted to share the throne; she had abused and vilified her with a view to pulling her off it; she had refrained from asking her to her own house for six months at a time, and for six months at a time she had refused to accept any of Mrs. Ames' invitations. But it was all no use; the vilifications, so she had known for a fact, had been repeated to Mrs. Ames, who had not taken the slightest notice of them, nor abated one jot of her rather condescending cordiality, and in spite of Mrs. Altham's refusing to come to her house, had continued to send her invitations at the usual rate of hospitality. Indeed, for the last year or two Mrs. Altham had really given up all thought of ever deposing her, and her husband, though on this occasion he felt himself to blame for this convulsion, felt also that he might reasonably have supposed the volcano to be extinct. Yet such is the disconcerting habit of these subliminal forces; they break forth with renewed energy exactly when persons of exactly average caution think that there is no longer any life in them.

He hastened to repair his error, and to calm the tempest, by fulsome agreement.

"Well, my dear," he said, "certainly there is a great deal in what you say, for we have no reason to suppose that everybody will ask husband and wife singly, or that two of this new set of invitations will always come for the same night. Then, too, there is the question of carriage-hire, which, though it does not much matter to us, will be an important item to others. For, every time that husband and wife dine out, there will be two carriages needed instead of one. I wonder if Mrs. Ames had thought of that."

"Not she," said Mrs. Altham, whose indignation still oozed and spurted. "Why, as often as not, she comes on foot, with her great goloshes over her evening shoes. Ah, I have it!"

A brilliant idea struck her, which did much to restore her equanimity.

"You may depend upon it," she said, "that Mrs. Ames means to ask just husband or wife, as the case may be, and make that count. That will save her half the cost of her dinners, and now I come to think of it, I am sure I should not be surprised to learn that they have lost money lately. Major Ames may have been speculating, for I saw the *Financial News* on the table last time I was there. I daresay that is it. That would account, too, for the very poor dinner we got. Salmon was in season, I remember, but we only had plaice or something common, and the ordinary winter desert, just oranges and apples. You noticed it, too, Henry. You told me that you had claret that couldn't have cost more than eighteenpence a bottle, and but one glass of port afterwards. And the dinner before that, though there was champagne, I got little but foam. Poor thing! I declare I am sorry for her if that is the reason, and I am convinced it is."

Mrs. Altham felt considerably restored by this explanation, and got briskly up.

"I think I will just run round to Mrs. Taverner's," she said, "to tell her there is no need for her to call on Mrs. Ames, since you have heard the same story at the club, so that we can rest assured that it is true. That will do famously; it will account for everything. And there is Pritchard's cart at the gate. That will be the tongue. I wonder if he has told his man to take away the pale one. If not, as you say, it will serve for savouries."

Summer had certainly come in earnest, and Mr. Altham, when he went out on to the shaded verandah to the east of the house, in order to smoke his cigar before going up to the golf-links, found that the thermometer registered eighty degrees in the shade. Consequently, before enjoying that interval of quiescence which succeeded his meals, and to which he felt he largely owed the serenity of his health, he went upstairs to change his cloth coat for the light alpaca jacket which he always wore when the weather was really hot. Last year, he remembered, he had not put it on at all until the end of July, except that on one occasion he wore it over his ordinary coat (for it was loosely made) taking a drive along an extremely dusty road. But the heat to-day certainly called for the alpaca jacket, and he settled himself in his chair (after tapping the barometer and observing with satisfaction that the concussion produced an upward tremor of the needle, which was at "Set Fair" already) feeling much more cool and comfortable.

Life in general was a very cool and comfortable affair to this contented gentleman. Even in youth he had not been of very exuberant vitality, and he had passed through his early years without giving a moment's anxiety to himself or his parents. Like a good child who eats and digests what is given him, so Mr. Altham, even in his early manhood, had accepted life exactly as he found it, and had seldom wondered what it was all about, or what it was made of. His emotions had been stirred when he met his wife, and he had once tried to write a poem to her--soon desisting, owing to the obvious scarcity of rhymes in the English language, and since then his emotional record had been practically blank. If happiness implies the power to want and to aspire, that quality must be denied him, but his content was so profound that he need not be pitied for the lack of the more effervescent emotions. All that he cared about was abundantly his: there was the *Times* to be read after breakfast, news to be gleaned at the club before lunch, golf to be played in the afternoon, and a little well-earned repose to be enjoyed before dinner, while at odd moments he looked at the thermometer and tapped the aneroid. He was distinctly kindly by nature, and would no doubt have cheerfully put himself to small inconveniences in order to lighten the troubles of others, but he hardly ever found it necessary to practise discomfort, since those with whom he associated were sunk in precisely the same lethargy of content as himself. Being almost completely devoid of imagination, no qualms or questionings as to the meaning of the dramas of life presented themselves to him, and his annual subscriptions to the local hospital and certain parish funds connoted no more to him than did the money he paid at the station for his railway ticket. He was, in fact, completely characteristic of the society of Riseborough, which largely consisted of men who had retired from their professions and spent their days, with unimportant variations, in precisely the same manner as he did. Necessarily they were not aware of the amazing emptiness of their lives, for if they had been, they would probably have found life very dull, and have tried to fill it with some sort of interest. As it was, golf, gardening, and gossip made the days pass so smoothly and quickly that it would really have been hazardous to attempt to infuse any life into them, for it might have produced upset and fermentation. But these chronicles would convey a very false impression if they made it seem as if life at Riseborough appeared dull or empty at Riseborough. The affairs of other people were so perennial a source of interest that it would only be a detached or sluggish mind that was not perpetually stimulated. And this stimulus was not of alcoholic character, nor was it succeeded by reaction and headache after undue indulgence. Mr. Altham woke each morning with a clean palate, so to speak, and an appetite and digestion quite unimpaired. As yet, he had not to seek to fill the hours of the day with gardening, like Major Ames, or with continuous rubbers of bridge in the card-room at the club; his days were full enough without those additional distractions, which he secretly rather despised as signs of senility, and wondered that Major Ames, who was still, he supposed, not much more than forty-five, should so soon have taken to a hobby that was better fitted for ladies and septuagenarians. It was not that he did not like flowers; he thought them pretty enough things in their place, and was pleased when he looked out of the bathroom window in the morning, and saw the neat row of red geraniums which ran along the border by the wall, between calceolarias and lobelias. Very likely when he was older, and other interests had faded, he might take to gardening, too; at present he preferred that the hired man should spend two days a week in superintending the operations of James. Certainly there would be some sense in looking after a vegetable garden, for there was an intelligible end in view there--namely, the production of early peas and giant asparagus for the table, but since the garden at Cambridge House was not of larger capacity than was occupied with a croquet lawn and a couple of flower borders, it was impossible to grow vegetables, and the production of a new red sweet-pea, about which Major Ames had really rendered himself tedious last summer, was quite devoid of interest to him, especially since there were plenty of other red flowers before.

His cigar was already half-smoked before he recalled himself from this pleasant vacancy of mind which had succeeded the summer resumal of his alpaca jacket, and for the ten minutes that still remained to him before the cab from the livery-stables which was to take him up the long hill to the golf-links would be announced, he roused himself to a greater activity of brain. It was natural that his game with Mr. Turner this afternoon should first occupy his thoughts. He felt sure he could beat him if only he paid a very strict attention to the game, and did not let his mind wander. A few days ago, Mr. Turner had won merely because he himself had been rather late in arriving at the club-house, and had started with the sense of hurry about him. But to-day he had ordered the cab at ten minutes to three, instead of at the hour. Thus he could both start from here and arrive there without this feeling of fuss. Their appointed hour was not till a quarter-past three, and it took a bare fifteen minutes to drive up. Also he had on his alpaca jacket; he would not, as on the last occasion of their encounter, be uncomfortably hot. As usual, he would play his adversary for the sum of half-a-crown; that should pay both for cab and caddie.

His thoughts took a wider range. Certainly it was a strange thing that Mrs. Ames should ask husbands without their wives, and wives without their husbands. Of course, to ask Mrs. Evans without the doctor was less remarkable than to ask General Fortescue without his wife, for it sometimes happened that Dr. Evans was sent for in the middle of dinner to attend on a patient, and once, when he was giving a party at his own house, he had received a note which led him to get up at once, and say to the lady on his right, "I am afraid I must go; maternity case," which naturally had caused a very painful feeling of embarrassment, succeeded by a buzz of feverish and haphazard conversation. But to ask General Fortescue without his wife was a very different affair; it was not possible that Mrs. Fortescue should be sent for in the middle of dinner, and cause dislocation in the party. He felt that if any hostess except Mrs. Ames had attempted so startling an innovation, she would, even with her three-weeks' notice, have received chilling refusals coupled with frankly incredible reasons for declining. Thus with growing radius of thought he found himself considering the case of Mrs. Ames' undoubted supremacy in the Riseborough world.

Most of what his wife had said in her excited harangue had been perfectly well-founded. Mrs. Ames was not rich, and a marked parsimony often appeared to have presided over the ordering of her dinners; while, so far as birth was concerned, at least two other residents here were related to baronets just as much as she was; Mrs. Evans, for instance, was first cousin of the present Sir James Westbourne, whereas Mrs. Ames was more distant than that from the same fortunate gentleman by one remove. Her mother, that is to say, had been the eldest sister of the last baronet but one, and older than he, so that beyond any question whatever, if Mrs. Ames' mother had been a boy, and she had been a boy also, she would now have been a baronet herself in place of the cheerful man who had been seen by Mrs. Altham driving his motor-car down the High Street that morning. As for General Fortescue, he was the actual brother of a baronet, and there was the end of the matter. But though Riseborough in general had a very proper appreciation of the deference due to birth, Mr. Altham felt that Mrs. Ames' supremacy was not really based on so wholesale a rearrangement of parents and sexes. Nor, again, were her manners and breeding such as compelled homage; she seemed to take her position for granted, and very seldom thanked her hostess for "a very pleasant evening" when she went away. Nor was she remarkable for her good looks; indeed, she was more nearly remarkable for the absence of them. Yet, somehow, Mr. Altham could not, perhaps owing to his lack of imagination, see anybody else, not even his own wife, occupying Mrs. Ames' position. There was some force about her that put her where she was. You felt her efficiency; you guessed that should situations arise Mrs. Ames could deal with them. She had a larger measure of reality than the majority of Mr. Altham's acquaintances. She did not seem to exert herself in any way, or call attention to what she did, and yet when Mrs. Ames called on some slightly doubtful newcomer to Riseborough, it was certain that everybody else would call too. And one defect she had of the most glaring nature. She appeared to take the most tepid interest only in what every one said about everybody else. Once, not so long ago, Mrs. Altham had shown herself more than ready to question, on the best authority, the birth and upbringing of Mrs. Turner, the election of whose husband to the club had caused so many members to threaten resignation. But all Mrs. Ames had said, when it was clear that the shadiest antecedents were filed, so to speak, for her perusal, was, "I have always found her a very pleasant woman. She is dining with us on Tuesday." Or again, when he himself was full of the praise of Mrs. Taverer, to whom Mrs. Ames was somewhat coldly disposed--(though that lady had called three times, and was perhaps calling again this afternoon, Mrs. Ames had never once asked her to lunch or dine, and was believed to have left cards without even inquiring whether she was in)--Mrs. Ames had only answered his panegyrics by saying, "I am told she is a very good-natured sort of woman."

CHAPTER I

Mr. Altham, hearing the stopping of a cab at his front-door, got up. It was still thirteen minutes to three, but he was ready to start. Indeed, he felt that motion and distraction would be very welcome, for there had stolen into his brain a strangely upsetting idea. It was very likely quite baseless and ill-founded, but it did occur to him that this defect on the part of Mrs. Ames as regards her incuriousness on the subject of the small affairs of other people was somehow connected with her ascendency. He had so often thought of it as a defect that it was quite a shock to find himself wondering whether it was a quality. In any case, it was a quality which he was glad to be without. The possession of it would have robbed him of quite nine points of the laws that governed his nature. He would have been obliged to cultivate a passion for gardening, like Major Ames. Of course, if you married a woman quite ten years your senior, you had to take to something, and it was lucky Major Ames had not taken to drink.

He felt quite cynical, and lost the first four holes. Later, but too late, he pulled himself together. But it was poor consolation to win the bye only.

CHAPTER II

Mrs. Ames put up her black and white sunshade as she stepped into the hot street outside Dr. Evans' house, about half-past six on the evening of the twenty-eighth of June, and proceeded afoot past the half-dozen houses that lay between it and the High Street. In appearance she was like a small, good-looking toad in half-mourning; or, to state the comparison with greater precision, she was small for a woman, but good-looking for a toad. Her face had something of the sulky and satiated expression of that harmless reptile, and her mourning was for her brother, who had mercifully died of delirium tremens some six months before. This scarcely respectable mode of decease did not curtail his sister's observance of the fact, and she was proposing to wear mourning for another three months.

She had not seen him much of late years, and, as a matter of fact, she thought it was much better that his inglorious career, since he was a hopeless drunkard, had been brought to a conclusion, but her mourning, in spite of this, was a faithful symbol of her regret. He had had the good looks and the frailty of her family, while she was possessed of its complementary plainness and strength, but she remembered with remarkable poignancy, even in her fifty-fifth year, birds'-nesting expeditions with him, and the alluring of fish in unpopulous waters. They had shared their pocket-money together, also, as children, and she had not been the gainer by it. Therefore she thought of him with peculiar tenderness.

It would be idle to deny that she was not interested in the Riseborough view of his blackness. It was quite well known that he was a drunkard, but she had stifled inquiry by stating that he had died of "failure." What organ it was that failed could not be inquired into: any one with the slightest proper feeling--and she was well aware that Riseborough had almost an apoplexy of proper feeling--would assume that it was some organ not generally mentioned. She felt that there was no call on her to gratify any curiosity that might happen to be rampant. She also felt that the chief joy in the possession of a sense of humour lies in the fact that others do not suspect it. Riseborough would certainly have thought it very heartless of her to derive any amusement from things however remotely connected with her brother's death; Riseborough also would have been incapable of crediting her with any tenderness of memory, if it had known that he had actually died of delirium tremens.

In this stifling weather she almost envied those who, like Dr. Evans, lived at the top of the town, where, in Castle Street, was situated the charming Georgian house in the garden of which he for a little while only, and his wife for three hours, had been entertaining their friends and detractors at the garden-party. Though the house was in a "Street," and not a "Road," it had a garden which anybody would expect to belong to a "Road," if not a "Place." Streets seemed to imply small backyards looking into the backs of other houses, whereas Dr. Evans' house did not, at its back, look on other houses at all, but extended a full hundred yards, and then looked over the railway cutting of the South-Eastern line, on open fields. Should you feel unkindly disposed, it was easy to ask whether the noise of passing trains was not very disagreeable, and indeed, Mrs. Taverner, in a moment of peevishness arising from the fact that what she thought was champagne cup was only hock cup, had asked that very question of Millicent Evans this afternoon in Mrs. Ames' hearing. But Millicent, in her most confiding and child-like manner, had given what Mrs. Ames considered to be a wholly admirable and suitable answer. "Indeed we do," she had said, "and we often envy you your beautiful big lawn." For everybody, of course, knew that Mrs. Taverner's beautiful big lawn was a small piece of black earth diversified by plantains, and overlooked and made odorous by the new gasworks. Mrs. Taverner had, as was not unnatural, coloured up on receipt of this silken speech, until she looked nearly as red as Mrs. Altham. For herself, Mrs. Ames would not, even under this provocation, have made so ill-natured a reply, though she was rather glad that Millicent had done so, and to account for her involuntary smile, she instantly asked Mrs. Altham to lunch with her next day. Indeed, walking now down the High Street, she smiled again at the thought, and Mr. Pritchard, standing outside his grocery store, thought she smiled at him, and raised his hat. And Mrs. Ames rather hoped he saw how different a sort of smile she kept on tap, so to speak, for grocers.

Mrs. Ames knew very well the manner of speeches that Mrs. Altham had been indulging in during the last three weeks, about the little dinner-party she was giving this evening, for she had been indiscreet enough to give specimens of them to Millicent Evans, who had promptly repeated them to her, and it is impossible adequately to convey how unimportant she thought was anything that Mrs. Altham said. But the fact that she had said so much was indirectly connected with her asking Mrs. Altham ("and your husband, of course," as she had rather pointedly added) to lunch to-morrow, for she knew that Mrs Altham would be bursting with curiosity about the success of the new experiment, and she intended to let her burst. She disliked Mrs. Altham, but that lady's hostility to herself only amused her. Of course, Mrs. Altham could not refuse to accept her invitation, because it was a point of honour in Riseborough that any one bidden to lunch the day after a dinner-party must, even at moderate inconvenience, accept, for otherwise what was to happen to the remains of salmon and of jelly too debilitated to be served in its original shape, even though untouched, but still excellent if eaten out of jelly-glasses? So much malice, then, must be attributed to Mrs. Ames, that she wished to observe the febrile symptoms of Mrs. Altham's curiosity, and not to calm them, but rather excite them further.

Mrs. Ames would not naturally have gone for social purposes to the house of her doctor, had he not married Millicent, whose father was her own first cousin, and would have been baronet himself had he been the eldest instead of the youngest child. As it was, Dr. Evans was on a wholly different footing from that of an ordinary physician, for by marriage he, as she by birth, was connected with "County," which naturally was the crown and cream of Riseborough society. Mrs. Ames was well aware that the profession of a doctor was a noble and self-sacrificing one, but lines had to be drawn somewhere, and it was impossible to contemplate visiting Dr. Holmes. A dentist's profession was self-sacrificing, too, but you did not dine at your dentist's, though his manipulations enabled you to dine with comfort and confident smiles elsewhere. Such lines as these she drew with precision, but automatic firmness, and the apparently strange case of Mr. Turner, whom she had induced her husband to propose for election at the club, whom, with his wife, she herself asked to dinner, was really no exception. For it was not Mr. Turner who had ever been a stationer in Riseborough, but his father, and he himself had been to a public school and a university, and had since then purged all taint of stationery away by twenty years' impartiality as a police magistrate in London. True, he had not changed his name when he came back to live in Riseborough, which would have shown a greater delicacy of mind, and the present inscription above the stationer's shop, "Burrows, late Turner," was obnoxious, but Mrs. Ames was all against the misfortunes of the fathers being visited on the children, and Riseborough, with the exception of Mrs. Altham, had quite accepted Mr. and Mrs. Turner, who gave remarkably good dinners, which were quite equal to the finest efforts of the (Scotch) chef at the club. Mrs. Altham said that the Turners had eaten their way into the heart of Riseborough society, which sounded almost witty, until Mrs. Ames pointed out that it was Riseborough, not the Turners, who had done the eating. On which the wit in Mrs. Altham's *mot* went out like a candle in the wind. It may, perhaps, be open to question whether Mrs. Altham's rooted hostility to the Turners did not predispose Mrs. Ames to accept them before their quiet amiability disposed her to do so, for she was neither disposed nor predisposed to like Mrs. Altham.

Mrs. Ames' way led through Queensgate Street, and she had to hold her black skirt rather high as she crossed the road opposite the club, for the dust was thick. She felt it wiser also to screw her small face up into a tight knot in order to avoid inhaling the fetid blue smoke from an over-lubricated motorcar that very rudely dashed by just in front of her. She did not regard motors with any favour, since there were financial reasons, whose validity was unassailable, why she could not keep one; indeed, partly no doubt owing to her expressed disapproval of them, but chiefly owing to similar financial impediments, Riseborough generally considered that hired flies were a more gentlemanly and certainly more leisurely form of vehicular transport. Mrs. Altham, as usual, raised a dissentient voice, and said that she and her husband could not make up their minds between a Daimler and a Rolls-Royce. This showed a very reasonable hesitancy, since at present they had no data whatever with regard to either.

Mrs. Ames permitted herself one momentary glance at the bow-window of the club, as she regained the pavement after this dusty passage, and then swiftly looked straight in front of her again, since it was not quite *quite* to look in at the window of a man's club. But she had seen several things: her husband was standing there with face contorted by the imminent approach of a sneeze, which showed that his hay-fever was not yet over, as he hoped it might be. There was General Fortescue with a large cigar in his mouth, and a glass, probably of sherry, in his hand; there was also the top of a bald head peering over the geraniums in the window like a pink full moon. That no doubt was Mr. Turner (for no one was quite so bald as he), enjoying the privilege which she had been instrumental in securing for him. Then Mrs. Altham passed her driving, and Mrs. Ames waved and kissed her black-gloved hand to her, thinking how very angular curiosity made people, while Mrs. Altham waved back thinking that it was no use trying to look important if you were only five foot two, so that honours were about divided. Finally, just before she turned into her own gate, she saw coming along the road, walking very fast, as his custom was, the man she respected and even revered more than any one in Riseborough. She would have liked to wave her hand to him too, only the Reverend Thomas Pettit would certainly have thought such a proceeding to be very odd conduct. He was county too--very much county, although a clergyman--being the son of that wealthy and distressing peer, Lord Evesham, who occasionally came into Riseborough on county business. On these occasions he lunched at the club, instead of going to his son's house, but did not eat the club lunch, preferring to devour in the smoking-room, like an ogre with false teeth, sandwiches which seemed to be made of fish in their decline. Mrs. Ames, who could not be called a religious woman, but was certainly very high church, was the most notable of Mr. Pettit's admirers, and, indeed, had set quite a fashion in going to the services at St. Barnabas', which were copiously embellished by banners, vestments and incense. Indeed, she went there in adoration of him as much as for any other reason, for he seemed to her to be a perfect apostle. He was rich, and gave far more than half his goods to feed the poor; he was eloquent, and (she would not have used so common a phrase) let them all "have it" from his pulpit, and she was sure he was rapidly wearing himself out with work. And how thrilling it would be to address her rather frequent notes to him with the title 'The Reverend The Lord Evesham!' . . . She gave a heavy sigh, and decided to flutter her podgy hand in his direction for a greeting as she turned into her gate.

The little dinner which had so agitated Riseborough for the last three weeks gave Mrs. Ames no qualms at all. Whatever happened at her house was right, and she never had any reason to wonder, like minor dinner-givers, if things would go off well, since she and no other was responsible for the feast; it was Mrs. Ames' dinner party. It was summoned for a quarter to eight, and at half-past ten somebody's carriage would be announced, and she would say, "I hope nobody is thinking of going away yet," in consequence of which everybody would go away at twenty minutes to eleven instead. If anybody expected to play cards or smoke in the drawing-room, he would be disappointed, because these diversions did not form part of the curriculum. The gentlemen had one cigarette in the dining-room after their wine and with their coffee: then they followed the ladies and indulged in the pleasures of conversation. Mrs. Ames always sat in a chair by the window, and always as the clock struck ten she re-sorted her conversationalists. That was (without disrespect) a parlour-trick of the most supreme and unfathomable kind. There was always some natural reason why she should get up, and quite as naturally two or three people got up too. Then a sort of involuntary general post took place. Mrs. Ames annexed the seat of the risen woman whose partner she intended to talk to, and instantly said, "Do tell me, because I am so much interested . . ." upon which her new partner sat down again. The ejected female then wandered disconsolately forward till she found herself talking to some man who had also got up. Therefore they sat down again together. But no one in Riseborough could do the trick as Mrs. Ames could do it. Mrs. Altham had often tried, and her efforts always ended in everybody sitting down again exactly where they had been before, after standing for a moment, as if an inaudible grace was being said. But Mrs. Ames, though not socially jealous (for, being the queen of Riseborough society, she had nobody to be jealous of), was a little prone to spoil this parlour-trick when she was dining at other houses, by suddenly developing an earnest conversation with her already existing partner, when she saw that her hostess contemplated a copy of her famous manœuvre. Yet, after all, she was within her rights, for the parlour-trick was her own patent, and it was quite proper to thwart the attempted infringement of it.

Having waggled her hand in the direction of Mr. Pettit, she went straight to the dining-room, where the dinner-table was being laid. There was to be a company of eight to-night, and accordingly she took three little cardboard slips from the top left-hand drawer of her writing-table, on each of which was printed--

PLEASE TAKE IN

....

TO DINNER.

These were presented in the hall to the men before dinner (it was unnecessary to write one for her husband), each folded, with the name of the guest in question being written on the back, while the name of the woman he was to take in filled the second line. Thus there were no separate and hurried communications to be made in the drawing-room, as everything was arranged already. This was not so original as the other parlour-trick, but at present nobody else in Riseborough had attempted it. Then out of the same drawer she took--what she took requires a fresh paragraph.

Printed Menu-cards. There were a dozen packets of them, each packet advertising a different dinner: an astounding device, requiring enlargement of explanation. She discovered them by chance in the Military Stores in London, selected a dozen packets containing fifty copies each, and kept the secret to herself. The parlour-maids had orders to tweak them away as soon as the last course was served, so that no menu-collector, if there was such retrospective glutton in Riseborough, could appropriate them, and thus, perhaps, ultimately get a clue which might lead him to the solution. For by a portent of ill-luck, it might then conceivably happen that a certain guest would find himself bidden for the third or fourth time to eat precisely the same dinner as his odious collection told him that he had eaten six months before. But the tweaking parlour-maids obviated that risk, and if the menu-cards were still absolutely "unsoiled," Mrs. Ames used them again. There was one very sumptuous dinner among the twelve, there were nine dinners good enough for anybody, there were two dinners that might be described as "poor." It was one of these, probably, which Mrs. Altham had in her mind when she was so ruthless in respect to Mrs. Ames' food. But, poor or sumptuous, it appeared to the innocent Riseborough world that Mrs. Ames had her menu-cards printed as required; that, having constructed her dinner, she sent round a copy of it to the printer's to be set up in type. Probably she corrected the proofs also. She never called attention to these menus, and seemed to take them as a matter of course. Mrs. Altham had once directly questioned her about them, asking if they were not a great expense. But Mrs. Ames had only shifted a bracelet on her wrist and said, "I am accustomed to use them."

Mrs. Ames took four copies of one of these dinners which were good enough for anybody, and propped them up, two on each of the long sides of the table. Naturally, she did not want one herself, and her husband, also naturally, sometimes said, "What are you going to give us to-night, Amy?" In which case one of them was passed to him. But he had a good retentive memory with regard to food, and with a little effort he could remember what the rest of the dinner was going to be, when the nature of the soup had given him his cue. Occasionally he criticized, saying in his hearty voice (this would be in the autumn or winter), "What, what? Partridge again? *Perdrix repetita,* isn't it, General, if you haven't forgotten your Latin." And Amy from the other end of the table replied, "Well, Lyndhurst, we must eat the game our friends are so kind as to send us." And yet Mrs. Altham declared that she had seen partridges from the poulterers delivered at Mrs. Ames' house! "But they are getting cheap now," she added to her husband, "particularly the old birds. I got a leg, Henry, and the bird must have roosted on it for years before Mrs. Ames' friends were so kind as to send it her."

So Mrs. Ames propped up the printed menu-cards, and spoke a humorous word to her first parlour-maid.

"I have often told you, Parker, to wear gloves when you are putting out the silver. I am not a detective: I am not wanting to trace you by your finger-prints."

Parker giggled discreetly. Somehow, Mrs. Ames' servants adored their rather exacting mistress, and stopped with her for years. They did not get very high wages, and a great deal was required of them, but Mrs. Ames treated them like human beings and not like machines. It may have been only because they were so far removed from her socially; but it may have been that there was some essential and innate kindliness in her that shut up like a parasol when she had to deal with such foolish and trying folk as Mrs. Altham. Mrs. Altham, indeed, had tried to entice Parker away with a substantial rise in wages, and the prospect of less arduous service. But that admirable serving-maid had declined to be tempted. Also, she had reported the occurrence to her mistress. It only confirmed what Mrs. Ames already thought of the temptress. She did not add any further black mark.

The table at present was devoid of any floral decoration, but that was no part of Mrs. Ames' province. Her husband, that premature gardener, was responsible for flowers and wine when Mrs. Ames gave a party, and always returned home half-an-hour earlier, to pick such of his treasures as looked as if they would begin to go off to-morrow, and make a subterranean excursion with a taper and the wine book to his cellar. In the domestic economy of the house he paid the rent, the rates and taxes, the upkeep of the garden, the wine bills, and the cost of their annual summer holiday, while Mrs. Ames' budget was responsible for coal, electric light, servants' wages, and catering bills. Arising out of this arrangement there occasionally arose clouds (though no bigger than Mrs. Ames' own hand) that flecked the brightness of their domestic serenity. Occasionally--not often--Mrs. Ames would be pungent about the possibility of putting out the electric light on leaving a room, occasionally her husband had sent for his coat at lunch-time, to supplement the heat given out on a too parsimonious hearth. But such clouds were never seen by other eyes than theirs: the presence of guests led Major Ames to speak of the excellence of his wife's cook and say, "'Pon my word, I never taste better cooking than what I get at home," and suggested to his wife to say to Mrs. Fortescue, "My husband so much enjoys having the General to dinner, for he knows a glass of good wine." She might with truth have said that he knew a good many glasses.

Finally, the two shared in equal proportions the upkeep of a rather weird youth who was the only offspring of their marriage, and was mistakenly called Harry, for the name was singularly ill-suited to him. He had lank hair, protuberant eyes, and a tendency to write poetry. Just now he was at home from Cambridge, and had rather agitated his mother that afternoon by approaching her dreamily at the garden-party and saying, "Mother, Mrs. Evans is the most wonderful creature I ever saw!" That seemed to her so wild an exaggeration as to be quite senseless, and to portend poetry. Harry made his father uncomfortable, too, by walking about with some quite common rose in his hand, and pretending that the scent of it was meat and drink to him. Also he had queer notions about vegetarianism, and said that a hunch of brown bread, a plate of beans, and a lump of cheese, contained more nourishment than quantities of mutton chops. But though not much of a hand at victuals, he found inspiration in what he called "yellow wine," and he and a few similarly minded friends belonged to a secret Omar Khayyam Club at Cambridge, the proceedings of which were carried on behind locked doors, not for fear of the Jews, but of the Philistines. A large glass salad-bowl filled with yellow wine and sprinkled with rose-leaves was the inspirer of these mild orgies, and each Omarite had to write and read a short poem during the course of the evening. It was a point of honour among members always to be madly in love with some usually unconscious lady, and paroxysms of passion were punctuated by Byronic cynicism. Just now it seemed likely that Mrs. Evans would soon be the fount of aspiration and despair. That would create quite a sensation at the next meeting of the Omar Club: nobody before had been quite so daring as to fall in love with a married woman. But no doubt that phenomenon has occurred in the history of human passion, so why should it not occur to an Omarite?

The wine at Mrs. Ames' parties was arranged by her husband on a scale that corresponded with the food. At either of the two "poor" dinners, for instance, a glass of Marsala was accorded with the soup, a light (though wholesome) claret moistened the rest of the meal, and a single glass of port was offered at dessert. The course of the nine dinners good enough for anybody was enlivened by the substitution of sherry for Marsala, champagne for claret, and liqueurs presented with coffee, while on the much rarer occasions of the one sumptuous dinner (which always included an ice) liqueur made its first appearance with the ice, and a glass of hock partnered the fish. To-night, therefore, sherry was on offer, and when, the dinner being fairly launched, Mrs. Ames took her first disengaged look round, she observed with some little annoyance, justifiable, even laudable, in a hostess, that Harry was talking in the wrong direction. In fact, he was devoting his attention to Mrs. Evans, who sat between him and his father, instead of entertaining Elsie, her daughter, whom he had taken in, and who now sat isolated and silent, since General Fortescue, who was on her other side, was naturally conversing with his hostess. Certainly it was rubbish to call Mrs. Evans a most wonderful creature; there was nothing wonderful about her. She was fair, with pretty yellow hair (an enthusiast might have called it golden), she had small regular features, and that look of distinction which Mrs. Ames (drawing herself up a little as she thought of it) considered to be inseparable from any in whose veins ran the renowned Westbourne blood. She had also that slim, tall figure which, though characteristic of the same race, was unfortunately not quite inseparable from its members, for no amount of drawing herself up would have conferred it on Mrs. Ames, and Harry took after her in this respect.

Dr. Evans had not long been settled in Riseborough--indeed, it was only last winter that he had bought his practice here, and taken the delightful house in which his wife had given so populous a garden-party that afternoon. Their coming, as advertised by Mrs. Ames, had been looked forward to with a high degree of expectancy, since a fresh tenant for the Red House, especially when he was known to be a man of wealth (though only a doctor), was naturally supposed to connote a new and exclusive entertainer, while his wife's relationship to Sir James Westbourne made a fresh link between the "town" and the "county." Hitherto, Mrs. Ames had been the chief link, and though without doubt she was a genuine one (her mother being a Westbourne), she had been a little disappointing in this regard, as she barely knew the present head of the family, and was apt to talk about old days rather than glorify the present ones by exhibitions of the family to which she belonged. But it was hoped that with the advent of Mrs. Evans a more living intimacy would be established.

Mrs. Evans was the fortunate possessor of that type of looks which wears well, and it was difficult to believe that Elsie, with her eighteen years and elderly manner, was her daughter. She was possessed also of that unemotional temperament which causes the years to leave only the faintest traces of their passage, and they had graven on her face but little record of joys and sorrows. Her mouth still possessed the softness of a girl's, and her eyes, large and blue, had something of the shy, unconscious wonder of childhood in their azure. To judge by appearances (which we shall all continue to do until the end of time, though we have made proverbs to warn us against the fallibility of such conclusions), she must have had the tender and innocent nature of a child, and though Mrs. Ames saw nothing wonderful about her, it was really remarkable that a woman could look so much and mean so little. She did not talk herself with either depth or volume, but she had, so to speak, a deep and voluminous way of listening which was immensely attractive. She made the man who was talking to her feel himself to be interesting (a thing always pleasant to the vainer sex), and in consequence he generally became interested. To fire the word "flirt" at her, point-blank, would have been a brutality that would have astounded her--nor, indeed, was she accustomed to use the somewhat obvious arts which we associate with those practitioners, but it is true that without effort she often established relations of intimacy with other people without any giving of herself in return. Both men and women were accustomed to take her into their confidence; it was so easy to tell her of private affairs, and her eyes, so wide and eager and sympathetic, gave an extraordinary tenderness to her commonplace replies, which accurately, by themselves, reflected her dull and unemotional mind. She possessed, in fact, as unemotional but comely people do, the potentiality of making a great deal of mischief without exactly meaning it, and it would be safe to predict that, the mischief being made, she would quite certainly acquit herself of any intention of having made it. It would be rash, of course, to assert that no breeze would ever stir the pearly sleeping sea of her temperament: all that can be said is that it had not been stirred yet.

Mrs. Ames could not permit Elsie's isolation to continue, and she said firmly to Harry, "Tell Miss Evans all about Cambridge," which straightened conversation out again, and allowed Mrs. Evans to direct all her glances and little sentences to Major Ames. As was usual with men who had the privilege of talking to her, he soon felt himself a vivid conversationalist.

"Yes, gardening was always a hobby of mine," he was saying, "and in the regiment they used to call me Adam. The grand old gardener, you know, as Tennyson says. Not that there was ever anything grand about me."

Mrs. Evans' mouth quivered into a little smile.

"Nor old, either, Major Ames," she said.

Major Ames put down the glass of champagne he had just sipped, in order to give his loud, hearty laugh.

CHAPTER II

"Well, well," he said, "I'm pretty vigorous yet, and can pull the heavy garden roller as well as a couple of gardeners could. I never have a gardener more than a couple of days a week. I do all the work myself. Capital exercise, rolling the lawn, and then I take a rest with a bit of weeding, or picking a bunch of flowers for Amy's table. Weeding, too--

'An hour's weeding a day
Keeps the doctor away.'

I defy you to get lumbago if you do a bit of weeding every morning."

Again a little shy smile quivered on Millie Evans' mouth.

"I shall tell my husband," she said. "I shall say you told me you spend an hour a day in weeding, so that you shouldn't ever set eyes on him. And then you make poetry about it afterwards."

Again he laughed.

"Well, now, I call that downright wicked of you," he said, "twisting my words about in that way. General, I want your opinion about that glass of champagne. It's a '96 wine, and wants drinking."

The General applied his fish-like mouth to his glass.

"Wants drinking, does it?" he said. "Well, it'll get it from me. Delicious! Goo' dry wine."

Major Ames turned to Millie Evans again.

"Beg your pardon, Mrs. Evans," he said, "but General Fortescue likes to know what's before him. Yes, downright wicked of you! I'm sure I wish Amy had asked Dr. Evans to-night, but there--you know what Amy is. She's got a notion that it will make a pleasanter dinner-table not to ask husband and wife always together. She says it's done a great deal in London now. But they can't put on to their tables in London such sweet-peas as I grow here in my bit of a garden. Look at those in front of you. Black Michaels, they are. Look at the size of them. Did you ever see such sweet-peas? I wonder what Amy is going to give us for dinner to-night. Bit of lamb next, is it? and a quail to follow. Hope you'll go Nap, Mrs. Evans; I must say Amy has a famous cook. And what do you think of us all down at Riseborough, now you've had time to settle down and look about you? I daresay you and your husband say some sharp things about us, hey? Find us very stick-in-the-mud after London?"

She gave him one of those shy little deprecating glances that made him involuntarily feel that he was a most agreeable companion.

"Ah, you are being wicked now!" she said. "Every one is delightful. So kind, so hospitable. Now, Major Ames, do tell me more about your flowers. Black Michaels, you said those were. I must go in for gardening, and will you begin to teach me a little? Why is it that your flowers are so much more beautiful than anybody's? At least, I needn't ask: it must be because you understand them better than anybody."

Major Ames felt that this was an uncommonly agreeable woman, and for half a second contrasted her pleasant eagerness to hear about his garden with his wife's complete indifference to it. She liked flowers on the table, but she scarcely knew a hollyhock from a geranium.

"Well, well," he said; "I don't say that my flowers, which you are so polite as to praise, don't owe something to my care. Rain or fine, I don't suppose I spend less than an average of four hours a day among them, year in, year out. And that's better, isn't it, than sitting at the club, listening to all the gossip and tittle-tattle of the place?"

"Ah, you are like me," she said. "I hate gossip. It is so dull. Gardening is so much more interesting."

He laughed again.

"Well, as I tell Amy," he said, "if our friends come here expecting to hear all the tittle-tattle of the place, they will be in for a disappointment. Amy and I like to give our friends a hearty welcome and a good dinner, and pleasant conversation about really interesting things. I know little about the gossip of the town; you would find me strangely ignorant if you wanted to talk about it. But politics now--one of those beastly Radical members of Parliament lunched with us only the week before last, and I assure you that Amy asked him some questions he found it hard to answer. In fact, he didn't answer them: he begged the question, begged the question. There was one, I remember, which just bowled him out. She said, 'What is to happen to the parks of the landed gentry, if you take them away from the owners?' Well, that bowled him out, as they say in cricket. Look at Sir James's place, for instance, your cousin's place, Amy's cousin's place. Will they plant a row of villas along the garden terrace? And who is to live in them if they do? Grant that Lloyd George--she said that--grant that Lloyd George wants a villa there, that will be one villa. But the terrace there will hold a dozen villas. Who will take the rest of them? She asked him that. They take away all our property, and then expect us to build houses on other people's! Don't talk to me!"

The concluding sentence was not intended to put a stop on this pleasant conversation; it was only the natural ejaculation of one connected with landed proprietors. Mrs. Evans understood it in that sense.

"Do tell me all about it," she said. "Of course, I am only a woman, and we are supposed to have no brains, are we not? and to be able to understand nothing about politics. But will they really take my cousin James's place away from him? I think Radicals must be wicked."

"More fools than knaves, I always say," said Major Ames magnanimously. "They are deluded, like the poor Suffragettes. Suffragettes now! A woman's sphere of influence lies in her home. Women are the queens of the earth; I've often said that, and what do queens want with votes? Would Amy have any more influence in Riseborough if she had a vote? Not a bit of it. Well, then, why go about smacking the faces of policemen and chaining yourself to a railing? If I had my way--"

Major Ames became of lower voice and greater confidence.

"Amy doesn't wholly agree with me," he said; "and it's a pleasure to thrash the matter out with somebody like yourself, who has sensible views on the subject.

What use are women in politics? None at all, as you just said. It's for women to rock the cradle, and rule the world. I say, and I have always said, that to give them a vote would be to wreck their influence, God bless them. But Amy doesn't agree with me. I say that I will vote--she's a Conservative, of course, and so am I--I will vote as she wishes me to. But she says it's the principle of the thing, not the practice. But what she calls principle, I call want of principle. Home: that's the woman's sphere."

Mrs. Evans gave a little sigh.

"I never heard it so beautifully expressed," she said. "Major Ames, why don't you go in for politics?"

Major Ames felt himself flattered; he felt also that he deserved the flattery. Hence, to him now, it ceased to be flattery, and became a tribute. He became more confidential, and vastly more vapid.

"My dear lady," he said, "politics is a dirty business now-a-days. We can serve our cause best by living a quiet and dignified life, without ostentation, as you see, but by being gentlemen. It is the silent protest against these socialistic ideas that will tell in the long run. What should I do at Westminster? Upon my soul, if I found myself sitting opposite those Radical louts, it would take me all my time to keep my temper. No, no; let me attend to my garden, and give my friends good dinners,--bless my soul, Amy is letting us have an ice to-night--strawberry ice, I expect; that was why she asked me whether there were plenty of strawberries. *Glace de fraises;* she likes her menu-cards printed in French, though I am sure 'strawberry ice' would tell us all we wanted to know. What's in a name after all?"

Conversation had already shifted, and Major Ames turned swiftly to a dry-skinned Mrs. Brooks who sat on his left. She was a sad high-church widow who embroidered a great deal. Her dress was outlined with her own embroideries, so, too, were many altar-cloths at the church of St. Barnabas. She and Mrs. Ames had a sort of religious rivalry over its decoration; the one arranged the copious white lilies that crowned the cloth made by the other. Their rivalry was not without silent jealousy, and it was already quite well known that Mrs. Brooks had said that lilies of the valley were quite as suitable as Madonna lilies, which shed a nasty yellow pollen on the altar-cloth. But Madonna lilies were larger; a decoration required fewer "blooms." In other moods also she was slightly acid.

Mrs. Evans turned slowly to her right, where Harry was sitting. She might almost be supposed to know that she had a lovely neck, at least it was hard to think that she had lived with it for thirty-seven years in complete unconsciousness of it. If she moved her head very quickly, there was just a suspicion of loose skin about it. But she did not move her head very quickly.

"And now let us go on talking," she said. "Have you told my little girl all about Cambridge? Tell me all about Cambridge too. What fun you must have! A lot of young men together, with no stupid women and girls to bother them. Do you play a great deal of lawn-tennis?"

Harry reconsidered for a moment his verdict concerning the wonderfulness of her. It was hardly happy to talk to a member of the Omar Club about games and the advantages of having no girls about.

"No; I don't play games much," he said. "The set I am in don't care for them."

She tilted her head a little back, as if asking pardon for her ignorance.

"I didn't know," she said. "I thought perhaps you liked games--football, racquets, all that kind of thing. I am sure you could play them beautifully if you chose. Or perhaps you like gardening? I had such a nice talk to your father about flowers. What a lot he knows about them!"

Flowers were better than games, anyhow; Harry put down his spoon without finishing his ice.

"Have you ever noticed what a wonderful colour *La France* roses turn at twilight?" he asked. "All the shadows between the petals become blue, quite blue."

"Do they really? You must show me sometime. Are there some in your garden here?"

"Yes, but father doesn't care about them so much because they are common. I think that is so strange of him. Sunsets are common, too, aren't they? There is a sunset every day. But the fact that a thing is common doesn't make it less beautiful."

She gave a little sigh.

"But what a nice idea," she said. "I am sure you thought of it. Do you talk about these things much at Cambridge?"

Mrs. Ames began to collect ladies' eyes at this moment, and the conversation had to be suspended. Millie Evans, though she was rather taller than Harry, managed, as she passed him on the way to the door, to convey the impression of looking up at him.

"You must tell me all about it," she said. "And show me those delicious roses turning blue at twilight."

Dinner had been at a quarter to eight, and when the men joined the women again in the drawing-room, light still lingered in the midsummer sky. Then Harry, greatly daring, since such a procedure was utterly contrary to all established precedents, persuaded Mrs. Evans to come out into the garden, and observe for herself the chameleonic properties of the roses. Then he had ventured on another violation of rule, since all rights of flower-picking were vested in his father, and had plucked her half-a-dozen of them. But on their return with the booty, and the establishment of the blue theory, his father, so far from resenting this invasion of his privileges, had merely said--

"The rascal might have found you something choicer than that, Mrs. Evans. But we'll see what we can find you to-morrow."

She had again seemed to look up at Harry.

"Nothing can be lovelier than my beautiful roses," she said. "But it is sweet of you to think of sending me some more. Cousin Amy, look at the roses Mr. Harry has given me."

CHAPTER II

Carriages arrived as usual that night at half-past ten, at which hour, too, a gaunt, grenadier-like maid of certain age, rapped loudly on the front door, and demanded Mrs. Brooks, whom she was to protect on her way home, and as usual carriages and the grenadier waited till twenty minutes to eleven. But even at a quarter to, no conveyance, by some mischance, had come for Mrs. Evans, and despite her protests, Major Ames insisted on escorting her and Elsie back to her house. Occasionally, when such mistakes occurred, it had been Harry's duty to see home the uncarriaged, but to-night, when it would have been his pleasure, the privilege was denied him. So, instead, after saying good-night to his mother, he went swiftly to his room, there to write a mysterious letter to a member of the Omar Club, and compose a short poem, which should, however unworthily, commemorate this amorous evening.

There is nothing in the world more rightly sacred than the first dawnings of love in a young man, but, on the other hand, there is nothing more ludicrous if his emotions are inspired, or even tinged, by self-consciousness and the sense of how fine a young spark he is. And our unfortunate Harry was charged with this absurdity; all through the evening it had been present to his mind, how dashing and Byronic a tale this would prove at the next meeting of the Omar Khayyam Club; with what fine frenzy he would throw off, in his hour of inspiration after the yellow wine, the little heart-wail which he was now about to compose, as soon as his letter to Gerald Everett was written. And lest it should seem unwarrantable to intrude in the spirit of ridicule on a young man's rapture and despair, an extract from his letter should give solid justification.

"Of course, I can't give names," he said, "because you know how such things get about; but, my God, Gerald, how wonderful she is. I saw her this afternoon for the first time, and she dined with us tonight. She understands everything--whatever I said, I saw reflected in her eyes, as the sky is reflected in still water. After dinner I took her out into the garden, and showed her how the shadows of the *La France* roses turn blue at dusk. I quoted to her these two lines--

'O, thou art fairer than the evening air,
Clad in the beauty of a thousand stars.'

And I *think* she saw that I quoted *at* her. Of course, she turned it off, and said, 'What pretty lines!' but I think she saw. And she carried my roses home. Lucky roses!

"Gerald, I am miserable! I haven't told you yet. For she is married. She has a great stupid husband, years and years older than herself. She has, too, a great stupid daughter. There's another marvel for you! Honestly and soberly she does not look more than twenty-five. I will write again, and tell you how all goes. But I think she likes me; there is clearly something in common between us. There is no doubt she enjoyed our little walk in the dusk, when the roses turned blue. . . . Have you had any successes lately?"

He finished his letter, and before beginning his poem, lit the candle on his dressing-table, and examined his small, commonplace visage in the glass. It was difficult to arrange his hair satisfactorily. If he brushed it back it revealed an excess of high, vacant-looking forehead; if he let it drop over his forehead, though his resemblance to Keats was distinctly strengthened, its resemblance to seaweed was increased also. The absence of positive eyebrow was regrettable, but was there not fire in his rather pale and far-apart eyes? He rather thought there was. His nose certainly turned up a little, but what, if not that, did tip-tilted imply? A rather long upper-lip was at present only lightly fledged with an adolescent moustache, but there was decided strength in his chin. It stuck out. And having practised a frown which he rather fancied, he went back to the table in the window again, read a few stanzas of *Dolores,* in order to get into tune with passion and bitterness (for this poem was not going to begin or end happily) and wooed the lyric muse.

Major Ames, meantime, had seen Mrs. Evans to her door, and retraced his steps as far as the club, where he was in half-a-mind to go in, and get a game of billiards, which he enjoyed. He played in a loud, hectoring and unskilful manner, and it was noticeable that all the luck (unless, as occasionally happened, he won) was invariably on the side of his opponent. But after an irresolute pause, he went on again, and let himself into his own house. Amy was still sitting in the drawing-room, though usually she went to bed as soon as her guests had gone.

"Very pleasant evening, my dear," he said; "and your plan was a great success. Uncommonly agreeable woman Mrs. Evans is. Pretty woman, too; you would never guess she was the mother of that great girl."

"She was not considered pretty as a girl," said his wife.

"No? Then she must have improved in looks afterwards. Lonely life rather, to be a doctor's wife, with your husband liable to be called away at any hour of the day or night."

"I have no doubt Millie occupies herself very well," said Mrs. Ames. "Good-night, Lyndhurst. Are you coming up to bed?"

"Not just yet. I shall sit up a bit, and smoke another cigar."

He sat in the window, and every now and then found himself saying half aloud, "Uncommonly agreeable woman." Just overhead Harry was tearing passion to shreds in the style (more or less) of Swinburne.

CHAPTER III

Dr. Evans was looking out of the window of his dining-room as he waited the next morning for breakfast to be brought in, jingling a pleasant mixture of money and keys in his trouser pockets and whistling a tune that sounded vague and De Bussy-like until you perceived that it was really an air familiar to streets and barrel-organs, and owed its elusive quality merely to the fact that the present performer was a little uncertain as to the comparative value of tones and semitones. But this slightly discouraging detail was more than compensated for by the evident cheerfulness of the executant; his plump, high-coloured face, his merry eye, the singular content of his whole aspect betokened a personality that was on excellent terms with life.

His surroundings were as well furnished and securely comfortable as himself. The table was invitingly laid; a Sheffield-plate urn (Dr. Evans was an amateur in Georgian decoration and furniture) hissed and steamed with little upliftings of the lid under the pressure within, and a number of hot dishes suggested an English interpretation of breakfast. Fine mezzotints after the great English portrait-painters hung on the walls, and a Chippendale sideboard was spread with fruit dishes and dessert-plates. The morning was very hot, but the high, spacious room, with its thick walls, was cool and fresh, while its potentialities for warmth and cosiness in the winter were sponsored for by the large open fire-place and the stack of hot-water pipes which stood beneath the sideboard. Outside, the windows at which Dr. Evans stood looked out on to the large and secluded lawn, which had been the scene of the garden-party the day before. Red-brick walls ran along the two sides of it at right angles to the house: opposite, a row of espaliered fruit-trees screened off the homeliness of the kitchen-garden beyond, and the railway cutting which formed the boundary of this pleasant place.

Wilfred Evans had whistled the first dozen bars of the "Merry Widow Waltz" some six or seven times through, before, with the retarded consciousness that it was Sunday, he went on to "The Church's One Foundation," and though, with his usual admirable appetite, he felt the allure of the hot dishes, he waited, still whistling, for some other member of his household, wife or daughter, to appear. He was one of the most gregarious and clubbable of men, and no hecatomb of stalled oxen would have given him content, if he had had to eat his beef alone. A firm attachment to his domestic circle, combined with the not very exacting calls of his practice, but truly fervent investigations in the laboratory at the end of the garden, of the habits and economy of phagocytes, comfortably filled up, to the furthest horizon, the scenery of his mental territories.

He had not to wait long for his wife to appear, and he hailed her with his wonted cordiality.

"Morning, little woman," he said. "Slept well, I hope?"

Mrs. Evans did not practise at home all those arts of pleasing with which she was so lavish in other people's houses. Also, this morning she felt rather cross, a thing which, to do her justice, was rare with her.

"Not very," she said. "I kept waking. It was stiflingly hot."

"I'm sorry, my dear," said he.

Mrs. Evans busied herself with tea-making; her long, slender hands moved with extraordinary deftness and silence among clattering things, and her husband whistled the "Merry Widow Waltz" once or twice more.

"Oh, Wilfred, do stop that odious tune," she said, without the slightest hint of impatience in her voice. "It is bad enough on your pianola, which, after all, is in tune!"

"Which is more than can be said for my penny whistle?" asked he, good-humouredly. "Right you are, I'm dumb. Tell me about your party last night."

"My dear, haven't you been to enough Riseborough parties to know that there is nothing to tell about any party?" she asked. "I sat between Major Ames and the son. I talked gardening on one side with the father, and something which I suppose was enlightened Cambridge conversation on the other. Harry Ames is rather a dreadful sort of youth. He took me into the garden afterwards to show me something about roses. And the carriage didn't come. Major Ames saw me home. When did you get in?"

"Not till nearly three. Very difficult maternity case. But we'll pull them both through."

Millie Evans gave a little shudder, which was not quite entirely instinctive. She emphasized it for her husband's benefit. Unfortunately, he did not notice it.

"Will you have your tea now?" she asked.

He looked at her with an air mainly conjugal but tinged with professionalism.

"Bit upset with the heat, little woman?" he asked. "You look a trifle off colour. We can't have you sleeping badly, either. Show me the man who sleeps his seven hours every night, and I'll show you who will live to be ninety."

This prospect did not for the moment allure his wife

"I think I would sooner sleep less and die earlier," she said in her even voice, "though I'm sure Elsie will live to a hundred at that rate. You encourage her to be lazy in the morning, Wilfred. I'm sure any one can manage to be in time for breakfast at a quarter past nine."

He shook his head.

"No, no, little woman," he said. "Let a growing girl sleep just as much as she feels inclined. I would sooner stint a girl's food than her sleep. Give the red corpuscles a chance, eh?"

CHAPTER III

Millie got up from the table, and went to the sideboard to get some fruit. Then suddenly it struck her that all this was hardly worth while. It seemed a stupid business to come down every morning and eat breakfast, to manage the household, to go for a walk, perhaps, or sit in the garden, and after completing the round of these daily futilities, to go to bed again and sleep, just for the recuperation that sleep gave, to enable her to do it all over again. But the strawberries looked cool and moist, and standing by the sideboard she ate a few of them. Just above it hung the oblong Sheraton mirror, which her husband had bought so cheaply at a local sale and had brought home so triumphantly. That, too, seemed to tell her a stale story, and the reflection of her young face, crowned with the shimmer of yellow hair, against the dark oak background of the panelling seemed without purpose or significance. She was doing nothing with her beauty that stayed so long with her. But it would not stay many years longer: this morning even there seemed to be a shadow over it, making it dim. . . . Soon nobody would care if she had ever been pretty or not; indeed, even now Elsie seemed by her height and the maturity of her manner to be reminding everybody of the fact that she herself must be approaching the bar which every woman has to cross when she is forty or thereabouts. . . . And, strange enough it may appear, these doubts and questionings which looked at Millie darkly from the Sheraton glass above the sideboard, selfish and elementary as they were, resembled "thought" far more closely than did the generality of those surface impressions that as a rule mirrored her mind. They were, too, rather actively disagreeable, and generally speaking, nothing disagreeable occurred to her. The experiences of every day might be mildly exhilarating, or mildly tedious. But, whatever they were, she was not accustomed to think closely about them. Now, for the moment, it seemed to her that some shadow, some vague presence confronted her, and menacingly demanded her attention.

Riseborough is notable for the number of its churches, and before long the air was mellow with bells. As a rule, Millie Evans went to church on Sunday morning with the same regularity as she ate hot roast beef for lunch when it was over, but this morning she easily let herself be persuaded to refrain from any act of public worship. It seemed quite within the bounds of possibility that she might feel faint during the psalms and, on her husband's advice, she settled to stop at home, leaving him and Elsie, who was quite unaware what faintness felt like, to attend. But it was not the fear of faintness that prompted her absence: she wanted, almost for the first time in her life, to be alone and to think. Even on the occasion of her marriage, she had not found it necessary to employ herself with original thought: her mother had done the thinking for her, and had advised her, as she felt quite sure, sensibly and well. Nor had she needed to think when she was expecting her only child, for on that occasion she had been perfectly content to do exactly as her husband told her. But now, at the age of thirty-seven, the sight of her own face in the glass had suggested to her certain possibilities, certain limitations.

Ill-health had, on infrequent Sundays, prevented her attendance at church, and now, following merely the dictates of habit, she took out with her to a basket chair below the big mulberry-tree in the garden, a Bible and prayer-book, out of which she supposed that she would read the psalms and lessons for the day. But the Bible remained long untouched, and when she opened it eventually at random, she read but one verse. It was at the end of Ecclesiastes that the leaves parted, and she read, "When desire shall fail, because man goeth to his long home."

That was enough, for it was that, here succinctly expressed, which had been troubling her this morning, though so vaguely, that until she saw her symptoms written down shortly and legibly, she had scarcely known what they were. But certainly this line and a half described them. No doubt it was all very elementary; by degrees one ceased to care, and then one died. But her case was rather different from that, for she felt that with her desire had not failed, simply because she never had had desire. She had waked and slept, she had eaten and walked, she had had a child; but all these things had been of about the same value. Once she had had a tooth out, without gas; that was a slightly more vivid experience. But it was very soon over: she had not really cared.

But though she had not cared for any of those things, she had not been bored with the repetition of them. It had seemed natural that one thing should follow another, that the days should become weeks, and the weeks should become months, insensibly. When the months added themselves into years, she took notice of that fact by having a birthday, and Wilfred, as he gave her some little present in a morocco case, told her that she looked as young as when they first met, which was very nearly true. She had a quantity of these morocco cases now: he never omitted the punctual presentation of each. And the mental vision of all these morocco cases, some round, some square, some oblong, and the thought of their contents--a little pearl brooch, a sapphire brooch, a pair of emerald ear-rings, a jewelled hat-pin--suddenly came upon her with their cumulative effect. A lot of time had gone by; it chiefly lived in her now through the memory of the morocco cases.

By virtue of her unemotional temperament and serene bodily health she looked very young still, and certainly did not feel old. But as the bells for church ceased to jangle and clash in the hot still air, leaving only for the ear the hum of multitudinous bees in the long flower-bed, it dawned on her that whatever she felt, and however she looked, she would soon be on the other side of that barrier which for woman marks the end of their essential and characteristic life. There were a few years left her yet out of the years of which she made so little use, and with a spasm, the keenest perhaps she had ever known, even including the extraction of the tooth without gas, the horror of middle-age fell upon her, making her shiver. All her life she had felt nothing: soon she would be incapable of feeling, except in so far as regret, that pale echo of what might once have been emotion, can be considered an affair of the heart. To feel, she readily perceived, implied the existence of something or somebody to feel about. But she did not know where to look for her participant. Long ago her husband had become as much part of that dead level of life as had her breakfast or her dressing for dinner. Never had he stirred her from her placid passivity, she had never yearned for him, in the sense in which a thirsty man desires water. She had no love of nature: "the primrose by the river's brim" might have been a violet for anything that she cared; charity, in its technical sense, was distasteful to her, because the curious smell in the houses of the poor made her only long to get away. It was hard to know where to turn to find an outlet for that drowsily awakening recognition of life that to-day, so late and as yet so feebly, stirred within her. Yet, though it stirred but feebly, there was movement there: it wanted to be alive for a little, before it was indubitably dead.

Her thoughts went back to the topic concerning which she had told her husband that there was nothing to be told--namely, the dinner-party at the Ames' last night. Certainly there was nothing remarkable about it: she had conducted herself as usual, with the usual result. She was accustomed to deal out her little smiles and deferential glances and flattering speeches to those who sat next her at dinner, because in herself a mild amiability prompted her to make herself pleasant, and because, with so little trouble to herself, she could make a man behave as agreeably as he was capable of behaving. She attracted men very easily, cursorily one might say, without attaching any importance to the interest she aroused, and without looking further than the dinner-table for the fruits of the attraction she exercised. But this morning, this tardy and drowsy recognition of life, beside which, so to speak, lay the shadow of middle-age, gave her pause. Was there some fruition and development of herself, before the withered and barren years came to her, to be found there? It would be quite beyond the mark to say that, sitting here, she definitely proposed to herself to try to make herself emotionally interested in somebody else, in case that might add a zest to life, but she considered the effect which she so easily produced in others, and wondered what it meant to feel like that. Certainly Major Ames had enjoyed escorting her home; certainly Harry had felt a touch of *gauche* romance when he showed her the effect of twilight on the complexion of some rose or other. He had given her a whole bunch of roses, with an attempt at a pretty speech. Yes, that was it--the shadows in them looked pale-blue, and he had said that they were just the colour of her eyes. But the roses were pretty: she hoped that somebody had put them in water.

She was already more than a little interested in her reflections: there was something original and exciting to her in them, and it was annoying to have them broken in upon by the parlour-maid who came towards her from the house. Personally, she thought it absurd not to keep men-servants, but Wilfred always maintained that a couple of good parlour-maids produced greater comfort with less disturbance, and yielding to him, as she always yielded to anybody who expressed a definite opinion, she had acquiesced in female service. But she always called the head parlour-maid Watkins, whereas her husband called her Mary.

"Major Ames wants to know if you will see him, ma'am," said Watkins.

The interest returned.

"Yes, ask him to come out," she said.

Watkins went back to the house and returned with Major Ames in tow, who carried a huge bouquet of sweet-peas. There then followed the difficulty of meeting and greeting gracefully and naturally which is usual when the visitor is visible a long way off. The Major put on a smile far too soon, and had to take it off again, since Mrs. Evans had not yet decided that it was time to see him. Then she began to smile, while he (without his smile) was looking abstractedly at the top of the mulberry-tree, as if he expected to find her there. He looked there a moment too long, for one of the lower branches suddenly knocked his straw hat off his head, and he said, "God bless my soul," and dropped the sweet-peas. However, this was not an unmixed misfortune, for the recognition came quite naturally after that. She hoped he was not hurt, was he *sure* that silly branch had not hit his face? It must be taken off! *What* lovely flowers! And were they for her? They were.

Major Ames replaced his hat rather hastily, after a swift manœuvre with regard to his hair which Mrs. Evans did not accurately follow. The fact was (though he believed the fact not to be generally known) that the top of Major Ames' head was entirely destitute of hair, and that the smooth crop which covered it was the produce of the side of his head--just above the ear--grown long, and brushed across the cranium so as to adorn it with seemingly local wealth and sleekness. The rough and unexpected removal of his hat by the bough of the mulberry-tree had caused a considerable portion of it to fall back nearly to the shoulder of the side on which it actually grew, and his hasty manœuvre with his gathered tresses was designed to replace them. Necessarily he put back his hat again quickly, in the manner of a boy capturing a butterfly.

His mind, and the condition of it, on this Sunday morning, would repay a brief analysis. Briefly, then, a sort of *aurora borealis* of youth had visited him: his heaven was streaked with inexplicable lights. He had told himself that a man of forty-seven was young still, and that when a most attractive woman had manifested an obvious interest in him, it was only reasonable to follow it up. He was not a coxcomb, he was not a loose liver; he was only a very ordinary man, well and healthy, married to a woman considerably older than himself, and living in a town which, in spite of his adored garden, presented but moderate excitements. But indeed, this morning call, paid with this solid tribute of sweet-peas, was something of an adventure, and had not been mentioned by him to his wife. He had seen her start for St. Barnabas, and then had hastily gathered his bouquet and set out, leaving Harry wandering dreamily about the cinder-paths in the kitchen garden, in the full glory of the discovery that the colour of the scarlet runners was like a clarion. Major Ames had plucked almost his rarest varieties, for to pluck the rarest, since he wished to save their first bloom for seed, would have been on the further side of quixotism and have verged on imbecility, but he had brought the best of his second-best. Last night, too, he had hinted at his own remissness in the matter of church attendance on Sunday-morning, and on his way up here had permitted himself to wonder whether Millie would prove (in consequence, perhaps, of that) to have abstained from worship also, expecting, or at least considering possible, a morning call from him. As a matter of fact she had not indulged in any such hopes, since it had been a matter of pure indifference to her whether he went to church on Sunday or not. But when he found on inquiry at the door that she was at home, it was scarcely unreasonable, on the part of a rather vain and gallantly minded man, to connect the fact with the information he had given.

So he hastily readjusted his hat.

"My own stupidity entirely," he said; "do not blame the tree. Yes, I have brought you just a few flowers, and though they are not worthy of your acceptance, they are not the worst bunch of sweet-peas I have ever seen, not the worst. These, Catherine the Great, for instance, are not--well--they do not grow quite in every garden."

Mrs. Evans opened her blue eyes a little wider.

"And are they really for me, Major Ames?" she asked again. "It is good of you. My precious flowers! They must be put in water at once. Watkins, bring me one of the big flower-bowls out here. I will arrange them myself."

"Lucky flowers, lucky flowers," chuckled Major Ames.

"It's I who am lucky," said she, acknowledging this subtle compliment with a little smile. "I stop away from church rather lazily, and am rewarded by a pleasant visit and a beautiful nosegay. And what a charming party we had last night! I could hardly believe it when I came back here and found it was nearly half-past eleven. Such hours!"

Major Ames gave his great loud laugh.

"You are making fun of us, Mrs. Evans," he said; "'pon my word you are making fun of us and our quiet ways down at Riseborough. I'll be bound that when you were in London, half-past eleven was more the sort of time when you began to go out to your dances."

"I used to go out a good deal when I was quite young," she said. "Wilfred used quite to urge me to go out, and certainly people were very kind in asking me. I remember one night in the season, I was asked to two dinner-parties and a ball and an evening party. After all, it is natural to take pleasure in innocent gaiety when one is young."

Major Ames felt very hot after his walk, and, forgetting the adventure of his hair, nearly removed his straw hat. But providentially he remembered it again just in time.

"Upon my word," Mrs. Evans, he said jovially, "you make me feel a hundred years old when you talk like that, as if your days of youth and success were over. Why, some one at your garden-party yesterday afternoon told me for a fact that Miss Elsie was the daughter of your husband's first wife. Wouldn't believe me when I said she was your daughter. Poor Sanders--it was Mr. Sanders who said it--had to pay ten shillings to me for his positiveness. He betted, you know, he insisted on betting. But really, any one who didn't happen to know would be right to make such a bet ninety-nine times out of a hundred."

She gave him a little smile with lowered eyelids.

"Dear Elsie!" she said. "She is such a comfort to me. She quite manages the house for me, and spares me all the trouble. She always knows how much asparagus ought to cost, and what happens to strawberry ice after a party. I never was a good housekeeper. Wilfred always used to say to me, 'Go out and enjoy yourself, my dear, and I'll pay the bills.' Of course, it was all his kindness, I know, but sometimes I wonder if it would not have been truer kindness to have made me think and contrive more. Elsie does it all now, but when my little girl marries it will be my turn again. Tell me, Major Ames, is it you or cousin Amy who makes everything go so beautifully at your house? I think--shall I say it--I think it must be you. When a man manages a house there is always more precision somehow: you feel sure that everything has been foreseen and provided for. Printed menu-cards, for instance--so *chic,* so perfectly *comme-il-faut."*

Watkins had brought out a large dish, rather like a sponging-tin, for the sweet-peas, and Mrs. Evans had begun the really Herculean labour of putting them in water. A grille of wire network fitted over the rim of it: each pea was stuck in separately. She looked up from her task at him.

"Am I right?" she asked.

Major Ames was not really an untruthful man, but many men who are not really untruthful get through a wonderful lot of misrepresentation.

"Oh, you mustn't give me the credit for that," he said (truthfully so far); "it's a dodge we always used to have at mess, so why not at one's own house also? It's better than written cards, which take a lot of time to copy out again and again, and then, you see, my dear Amy is not very strong at French, and doesn't want always to be bothering me to tell her whether there's an accent in one word, or two 's's' in another. Saves time and trouble."

Mrs. Evans applauded softly with pink finger-tips.

"Ah, I knew it was you!" she said.

Now, clearly (though almost without intention) Major Ames had gone too far to retreat: also retreat implied a flat contradiction of what Mrs. Evans said she knew, which would have been a rudeness from which his habitual gallantry naturally revolted. Consequently, being unable to retreat, he had to make himself as safe as possible, to entrench himself.

"Perhaps it's a little extravagance," he said. "Indeed, Amy thinks it is, and I never mention the subject of menu-cards to her. She's apt to turn the subject a bit abruptly on the word menu-card. Dear Amy! After all, it would be a very dull affair, our pleasant life down here, if we all completely agreed with each other."

She gave a little sigh, shaking her head, and smiling at her sweet-peas.

"Ah, how often I think that too," she said. "At least, now you say it, I feel I have often thought it. It is so true. Dear Wilfred is such an angel to me, you see! Whatever I do, he is sure to think right. But sometimes you wonder whether the people who know you best, really understand you. It is like--it is like learning things by heart. If you learn a thing by heart, you so often cease to think what it means."

Mrs. Evans, it must be confessed, did not mean anything very precisely by this: her life, that is to say, was not at all circumstanced in the manner that her speech implied it to be, except in so far that she often wished that more amusing things happened to her, and that she would not so soon be forty years old. But she certainly intended Major Ames to attach to her words their natural implication:

she wanted to seem vaguely unappreciated. At the same time, she desired him to see that she in no way blamed her dear unconscious Wilfred. If Major Ames thought that, it would spoil a most essential feature of the picture she wished to present of herself. Why she wished to present it was also quite easy of comprehension. She wanted to be interesting, and was by nature silly. The fact that she was close on thirty-eight largely conduced to her speech.

Major Ames made a perfectly satisfactory interpretation of it. He saw all the things he was meant to see, and nothing else. And it was deliciously delivered, so affectionately as regarded Wilfred, so shyly as regarded herself. He instantly made the astounding mental discovery that she was somehow not very happy, owing to a failure in domestic affinities. He felt also that it was intuitive of him to have guessed that, since she had not actually said it. And he was tremendously conscious of the seduction of her presence, as she sat there, cool and white on this hot morning, putting in the last of the sweet-peas he had brought her. She looked enchantingly young and fresh, and evidently she found something in him which disposed her to confidences. In justice to him, it may be said that he did not inquire in his own mind as to what that was, but it was easy to see she trusted him.

"I think we all must feel that at times, my dear lady," he said, anxious to haul the circumstance of his own home into the discussion. "I suppose that all of us who are not quite old yet, not quite quite old yet, let us say, in order to include me, feel at times that life is not giving us all that it might give; that people do not really understand us. No doubt many people, and I daresay those, as you said, who know one best, do not understand one. And then we mustn't mind that, but march straight on, march straight on, according to orders."

He sat up very straight in his chair as if about to march, as he made thrillingly noble remarks, and hit himself a couple of sounding blows with his clenched fist on his broad chest. Then a sudden suspicion seized him that he had displayed an almost too Spartan unflinchingness, as if soldiers had no hearts.

"And then perhaps we shall meet some one who does understand us," he added.

The critical observer, the cynic, and that rarest of all products, the entirely sincere and straightforward person, would have found in this conversation nothing that would move anything beyond his raillery or disgust. Here sitting under the mulberry-tree in this pleasant garden, on a Sunday morning, were two people, the man nearly fifty, the woman nearly forty, both trying, with God knows how many little insincerities by the way, to draw near to each other. Both had reached ages that were dangerous to such as had lived (even as they had) extremely respectable and well-conducted lives, without any paramount reason for their morality. About Major Ames' mode of life before he married, which, after all, was at the early age of twenty-five, nothing need be said, because there is really very little to say, and in any case the conduct of a young man not yet in his twenty-fifth year has almost nothing to do with the character of the same man when he is forty-seven. In that very long interval he had conducted himself always as a married man should, and those years, married as he was to a woman much his senior, had not been at all discreditably passed. This chronicle does not in the least intend to impute to him any high principled character, for he had nothing of Galahad in his composition. But he was not a satyr. Consequently, for this is part of the ironical composition of a man--just in the years with which we are dealing, at a time of life when a man might have been condoned for having sown wild oats and seen the huskiness of them, he was in that far more precarious position of not having sown them (except, so to speak, in the smallest of flower-pots), nor of having experienced the jejune quality of such a crop. But it is not implied that he now regretted the respectability of those twenty-two years. He did not do so: he had had a happy and contented life, but he would soon be old. Nor did he now at all contemplate adventure. Merely an Odysseus who had never voyaged wondered what voyaging was like. He was not in love with this seductive long-lashed face that bent over the sweet-peas he had brought her. But if he had the picking of those sweet-peas over again, he would probably have picked the very best, regardless of the fact that he wanted the seeds for next year's sowing. So as regards him the cynic's sneers would have been out of place; he contemplated nothing that the cynic would have called "a conquest." The sincere, straightforward gentleman would have been equally excessive in his disgust. There was nothing, except the slight absurdity of Major Ames' nature, to justify either laughter or tears. He was a moderate man of middle-age, about as well intentioned as most of us.

Mrs. Evans, perhaps, was less laudable, and more deserved laughter and tears. She had consciously tried to produce a false impression without saying false things--a lamentable posture. She had wanted, as was her nature, to attract without being correspondingly attracted. She was prepared for him to go a little further, which is characteristic of the flirt. She succeeded, as the flirt usually does.

His last sentence was received in silence, and he thought well to repeat it with slight variation. The theme was clear.

"We may meet some one who understands us," he said. "Who looks into us, not at us, eh? Who sees not what we wish only, but what we want."

She put the last sweet-pea into the wire-netting.

"Oh, yes, yes," she said; "how beautiful that distinction is."

He was not aware of its being particularly beautiful, until she mentioned it, but then it struck him that it was rather fine. Also the respectability of all his long years tugged at him, as with a chain. He was quite conscious that he was encouraged, and so he was slightly terrified. He had not much power of imagination, but he could picture to himself a very uncomfortable home. . . .

Providence came to his aid--probably Providence. Church time was spent, and two black Aberdeen terriers, followed by Elsie, followed by Dr. Evans, came out of the drawing-room door on to the lawn. They were all in the genial exhilaration that accompanies the sense of duty done. The dogs had been let out from the house, where they were penned on Sunday morning to prevent their unexpected appearance in church; the other two had been let out from church.

Wilfred Evans had most clearly left church behind him: he had also left in the house not only his top hat but his coat, as befitted the heat of the morning, and appeared, stout, and strong, and brisk. Elsie was less vigorous: she sat down on the grass as soon as she reached the shade of the tree. She had the good sense to shake hands with Major Ames first: otherwise her mother would have made remarks to him about her manners. But she was markedly less elderly now than she had been at the formal dinner-party of the night before.

Dr. Evans arrived last at the mulberry-tree.

"Jove! what jolly flowers," he said. "That's you, Major Ames, isn't it? How de'do? Well, little woman, how goes it? You did well not to come to church. Awfully hot it was."

"And a very long sermon, Daddy," said Elsie.

"Twenty-two minutes: I timed it. Very interesting, though. You'll stop to lunch, Major Ames, won't you? We lunch at one always on Sunday."

Now Major Ames knew quite well that there was going to be at his house the lunch that followed parties, the resurrection lunch of what was dead last night. There would be little bits of salmon slightly greyer than on the evening before, peeping out from the fresh salad that covered them. There would be some sort of *chaud-froid;* there would be a pink and viscous fluid which was the debilitated descendant of the strawberry ice which Amy had given them. There would also be several people, including Mrs. Altham, who had not been bidden to the feast last night, but who, since they came according to the authorized Riseborough version of festivities, to the lunch next day, would certainly be bidden to dinner on the next occasion. Also, he knew well, he would have to say to Mrs. Altham, "Amy has given us cold luncheon to-day. Well, I don't mind a cold luncheon on as hot a day as it is. *Chaud-froid* of chicken, Mrs. Altham. I think you'll find that Amy's cook understands *chaud-froid."*

And all the time he knew that *chaud-froid* meant a dinner-party on the night before. So did the viscous fluid in the jelly glasses, so did everything else. And of course Mrs. Altham knew: everybody knew all about the lunch that followed a dinner-party. Even if the dinner-party last night had been as secret as George the Fourth's marriage with Mrs. Fitzherbert, the lunch to-day would have made it as public as any function at St. Peter's, Eaton Square.

He thought over the unimaginable dislocation in all this routine that his absence would entail.

"I wonder if I ought to," he said. "I fancy Amy told me she had a few friends to lunch."

Millie Evans looked up at him. Infinitesimal as was the point as to whether he should lunch here or at home, she knew that she definitely entered herself against his wife at this moment.

"Ah, do stop," she said. "If Cousin Amy has a few friends why shouldn't we have one?"

He got up: he nearly took off his hat again, but again remembered.

"I take it as a command," he said. "Am I ordered to stop?"

"Certainly. Telephone to Mrs. Ames, Wilfred, and say that Major Ames is lunching with us."

"À les ordres de votre Majesté," said he brightly, forgetting for the moment that his wife came to him for help with the elusive language of our neighbours. But the Frenchness of his bearing and sentiment, perhaps, diverted attention from the curious character of his grammar.

CHAPTER IV

It was, of course, as inevitable as the return of day that Mrs. Altham should start half-an-hour earlier than was necessary to go to church that morning, in order to return to Mrs. Brooks, who had been dining last night at the Ames', a couple of books that had been lent her a month or two ago, and that Mrs. Brooks should recount to her the unusual incident of Harry's taking Mrs. Evans into the garden after dinner, and giving her a gradually growing bouquet of roses torn from his father's trees. Indeed, it was difficult to settle satisfactorily which part of Harry's conduct was the most astounding, with such completeness had he revolted against both beneficiaries of the fifth commandment.

"They can't have been out in the garden for less than twenty minutes," said Mrs. Brooks; "and I shouldn't wonder if it was more. For we had scarcely settled ourselves after the gentlemen came in from the dining-room, when they went out, and I'm sure we had hardly got talking again after they came back, before my maid was announced. To be sure the gentlemen sat a long time after dinner before joining us, which I notice is always the case when General Fortescue is at a party, but it can't have been less than half-an-hour that they were in the garden now one comes to add it up."

Mrs. Brooks surveyed for a moment in silence her piece of embroidery. Not for a moment must it be supposed that she would have done embroidery for her own dress on Sunday morning; this was a frontal for the lectern at St. Barnabas, which would make it impossible for Mrs. Ames to decorate the lectern any more with her flowers. There was a cross, and a crown, and some initials, and some rays of light, and a heart, and some passion flowers, and a dove worked on it, with a profusion of gold thread that was positively American in its opulence. Hitherto, the lectern had always been the field of one of Mrs. Ames' most telling embellishments. When this embroidery was finished (which it soon would be) she would be driven from the lectern in disorder and discomfiture.

"A very rich effect," said Mrs. Altham sympathetically. "Half-an-hour! Dear me! And then I think you said she came back with a dozen roses."

Mrs. Brooks closed her eyes, and made a short calculation.

"More than a dozen," she said. "I daresay there were twenty roses. It was very marked, very marked indeed. And if you ask me what I think of Mrs. Ames' plan of asking husband without wife and wife without husband, I must say I do not like it at all. Depend upon it, if Dr. Evans had come too, there would have been no walking about in the garden with our Master Harry. But far be it from me to say there was any harm in it, far! I hope I am not one who condemns other people's actions because I would not commit them myself. All I know is that the first time my late dear husband asked me to walk about the garden after dinner with him, he proposed to me; and the second time he asked me to walk in the garden with him he proposed again, and I accepted him. But then I was not engaged to anybody else at the time, far less married, like Mrs. Evans. But it is none of my business, I am glad to say."

"Indeed, no, it does not concern us," said Mrs. Altham, with avidity; "and as you say, there may be no harm in it at all. But young men are very impressionable, even if most unattractive, and I call it distinct encouragement to a young man to walk about after dinner in the garden with him, and receive a present of roses. And I'm sure Mrs. Evans is old enough to be his mother."

Mrs. Brooks tacked down a length of gold thread which was to form part of the longest ray of all, and made another little calculation. It was not completely satisfactory.

"Anyhow, she is old enough to know better," she said; "but I have noticed that being old enough to know better often makes people behave worse. Mind, I do not blame her: there is nothing I detest so much as this censorious attitude; and I only say that if I gave so much encouragement to any young man I should blame myself."

"And the dinner?" asked Mrs. Altham. "At least, I need not ask that, since I am going to lunch there, and so I shall soon know as well as you what there was."

Mrs. Brooks smiled in a rather superior manner.

"I never know what I am eating," she said. And she looked as if it disagreed with her, too, whatever it was.

This was not particularly thrilling, for though it was generally known that Harry had an emotional temperament and wrote amorous poems, he appeared to Mrs. Altham an improbable Lothario. In any case, the slight interest that this aroused in her was nothing compared to that which awaited her and her husband when they arrived for lunch at Mrs. Ames'.

There had been a long-standing feud between Mrs. Altham and her hostess on the subject of punctuality. About two years ago Mrs. Ames had arrived at Mrs. Altham's at least ten minutes late for dinner, and Mrs. Altham had very properly retorted by arriving a quarter of an hour late when next she was bidden to dinner with Mrs. Ames, though that involved sitting in a dark cab for ten minutes at the corner of the next turning. So, next time that Mrs. Altham "hoped to have the pleasure of seeing you and Major Ames at dinner on Thursday at a quarter to eight," she asked the rest of her guests at eight. With the effect that Mrs. Ames and her husband arrived a few minutes before anybody else, and Riseborough generally considered that Mrs. Altham had scored. Since then there had been but a sort of desultory pea-shooting kept up, such as would harm nobody, and to-day Mrs. Altham and her husband arrived certainly within ten minutes of the hour named. Mr. Pettit, who generally lunched with Mrs. Ames or Mrs. Brooks on

Sunday, was already there with his sister. Harry was morosely fidgeting in a corner, and Mrs. Ames was the only other person present in the small sitting-room where she received her guests, instead of troubling them to go up to the drawing-room and instantly to go down again. She gave Mrs. Altham her fat little hand, and then made this remarkable statement.

"We are not waiting for anybody else, I think."

Upon which they went into lunch, and Harry sat at the head of the table, instead of his father.

Mrs. Ames was in her most conversational mood, and it was not until the *chaud-froid,* consisting mainly of the legs of chickens pasted over with a yellow sauce that concealed the long blue hair-roots with which Nature has adorned their lower extremities, was being handed round, that Mrs. Altham had opportunity to ask the question that had been effervescing like an antiseptic lozenge on the tip of her tongue ever since she remarked the Major's absence.

"And where is Major Ames?" she asked. "I hope he is not ill? I thought he looked far from well at Mrs. Evans' garden-party yesterday."

Mrs. Ames set her mind at rest with regard to the second point, and inflamed it on the first.

"Oh, no!" she said. "Did you think he looked ill? How good of you to ask after him. But Lyndhurst is quite well. Mr. Pettit, a little more chicken? After your sermon."

Mr. Pettit had a shrewd, ugly, delightful face, very lean, very capable. Humanly speaking, he probably abhorred Mrs. Ames. Humanely speaking, he knew there was a great deal of good in her, and a quantity of debatable stuff. He smiled, showing thick white teeth.

"Before and after my sermon," he said. "Also before a children's service and a Bible class. I cannot help thinking that God forgot his poor clergymen when he defined the seventh day as one of rest."

Mrs. Ames hid a small portion of her little face with her little hand. She always said that Mr. Pettit was not like a clergyman at all.

"How naughty of you," she said. "But I must correct you. The seventh day has become the first day now."

Harry gave vent to a designedly audible sigh. The Omar Club were chiefly atheists, and he felt bound to uphold their principles.

"That is the sort of thing that confuses me," he said. "Mr. Pettit says Sunday was called a day of rest, and my mother says that God meant what we call Monday, or Saturday. I have been behaving as if it was Tuesday or Wednesday."

Mr. Pettit gave him a kindly glance.

"Quite right, my dear boy," he said. "Spend your Tuesday or Wednesday properly and God won't mind whether it is Thursday or Friday."

Harry pushed back his lank hair, and became Omar-ish.

"Do you fast on Friday, may I ask?" he said.

Mrs. Ames looked pained, and tried to think of something to say. She failed. But Mrs. Altham thought without difficulty.

"I suppose Major Ames is away, Mr. Harry?" she said.

Even then, though her intentions might easily be supposed to be amiable, she was not allowed the privilege of being replied to, for Mr. Pettit cheerfully answered Harry's question, without a shadow of embarrassment, just as if he did not mind what the Omar Khayyam Club thought.

"Of course I do, my dear fellow," he said, "because our Lord and dearest friend died that day. He allows us to watch and pray with Him an hour or two."

Harry appeared indulgent.

"Curious," he said.

Mr. Pettit looked at him for just the space of time any one looks at the speaker, with cheerful cordiality of face, and then turned to his mother again.

"I want you at church next Sunday," he said, "with a fat purse, to be made thin. I am going to have an offertory to finance a children's treat. I want to send every child in the parish to the sea-side for a day."

Harry interrupted in the critical manner.

"Why the sea-side?" he asked.

Mr. Pettit turned to him with unabated cordiality.

"How right to ask!" he said. "Because the sea is His, and He made it! Also, they will build sand-castles, and pick up shells. You must come too, my dear Harry, and help us to give them a nice day."

Harry felt that this was a Philistine here, who needed to be put in his place. He was not really a very rude youth, but one who felt it incumbent on him to oppose Christianity, which he regarded as superstition. A bright idea came into his head.

"But His hands prepared the dry land," he said, "on the same supposition."

"Certainly; and as the dear mites have always seen the dry land," said Mr. Pettit, with the utmost good-humour, "we want to show them that God thought of something they never thought of. And then there are the sand-castles."

Harry was tired, and did not proceed to crush Mr. Pettit with the atheistical arguments that were but commonplace to the Omar Khayyam Club. He was not worth argument: you could only really argue with the enlightened people who fundamentally agreed with you, and he was sure that Mr. Pettit did not fulfil that requirement. So, indulgently, he turned to Mrs. Altham.

"I saw you at Mrs. Evans' garden-party yesterday," he said. "I think she is the most wonderful person I ever met. She was dining here last night, and I took her into the garden--"

"And showed her the roses," said Mrs. Altham, unable to restrain herself.

Harry became a parody of himself, though that might seem to be a feat of insuperable difficulty.

"I supposed it would get about," he said. "That is the worst of a little place like this. Whatever you do is instantly known."

The slightly viscous remains of the strawberry ice were being handed, and Mr. Pettit was talking to Mrs. Ames and his sister from a pitiably Christian standpoint.

"What did you hear?" asked Harry, in a low voice.

"Merely that she and you went out into the garden after dinner, and that you picked roses for her--"

Harry pushed back his lank hair with his bony hand.

"You have heard all," he said. "There was nothing more than that. I did not see her home. Her carriage did not come: there was some mistake about it, I suppose. But it was my father who saw her home, not I."

He laid down the spoon with which he had been consuming the viscous fluid.

"If you hear that I saw her home, Mrs. Altham," he said, "tell them it is not true. From what you have already told me, I gather there is talk going on. There is no reason for such talk."

He paused a moment, and then a line or two of the intensely Swinburnian effusion which he had written last night fermented in his head, making him infinitely more preposterous.

"I assure you that at present there is no reason for such talk," he said earnestly.

Now Mrs. Altham, with her wide interest in all that concerned anybody else, might be expected to feel the intensest curiosity on such a topic, but somehow she felt very little, since she knew that behind the talk there was really very little topic, and the gallant misgivings of poor, ugly Harry seemed to her destitute of any real thrill. On the other hand, she wanted very much to know where Major Ames was, and being endowed with the persistence of the household cat, which you may turn out of a particular arm-chair a hundred times, without producing the slightest discouragement in its mind, she reverted to her own subject again.

"I am sure there is no reason for such talk, Mr. Harry," she said, with strangely unwelcome conviction, "and I will be sure to contradict it if ever I hear it. I am so glad to hear Major Ames is not ill. I was afraid that his absence from lunch to-day might mean that he was."

Now Harry, as a matter of fact, had no idea where his father was, since the telephone message had been received by Mrs. Ames.

"Father is quite well," he said. "He was picking sweet-peas half the morning. He picked a great bunch."

Mrs. Altham looked round: the table was decorated with the roses of the dinner-party of the evening before.

"Then where are the sweet-peas?" she asked.

But Harry was not in the least interested in the question.

"I don't know," he said. "Perhaps they are in the next room. I showed Mrs. Evans last night how the La France roses looked blue when dusk fell. She had never noticed it, though they turn as blue as her eyes."

"How curious!" said Mrs. Altham. "But I didn't see the sweet-peas in the next room. Surely if there had been a quantity of them I should have noticed them. Or perhaps they are in the drawing-room."

At this moment, Mrs. Ames' voice was heard from the other end of the table.

"Then shall we have our coffee outside?" she said. "Harry, if you will ring the bell--"

There was the pushing back of chairs, and Mrs. Altham passed along the table to the French windows that opened on to the verandah.

"I hear Major Ames has been picking the loveliest sweet-peas all the morning," she said to her hostess. "It would be such a pleasure to see them. I always admire Major Ames' sweet-peas."

Now this was unfortunate, for Mrs. Altham desired information herself, but by her speech she had only succeeded in giving information to Mrs. Ames, who guessed without the slightest difficulty where the sweet-peas had gone, which she had not yet known had been picked. She was already considerably annoyed with her husband for his unceremonious desertion of her luncheon-party, and was aware that Mrs. Altham would cause the fact to be as well known in Riseborough as if it had been inserted in the column of local intelligence in the county paper. But she felt she would sooner put it there herself than let Mrs. Altham know where he and his sweet-peas were. She had no greater objection (or if she had, she studiously concealed it from herself even) to his going to lunch in this improvising manner with Mrs. Evans than if he had gone to lunch with anybody else; what she minded was his non-appearance at an institution so firmly established and so faithfully observed as the lunch that followed the dinner-party. But at the moment her entire mind was set on thwarting Mrs. Altham. She looked interested.

"Indeed, has he been picking sweet-peas?" she said. "I must scold him if it was only that which kept him away from church. I don't know what he has done with them. Very likely they are in his dressing-room: he often likes to have flowers there. But as you admire his sweet-peas so much, pray walk down the garden, and look at them. You will find them in their full beauty."

This, of course, was not in the least what Mrs. Altham wanted, since she did not care two straws for the rest of the sweet-peas. But life was scarcely worth living unless she knew where those particular sweet-peas were. As for their being in his dressing-room, she felt that Mrs. Ames must have a very poor opinion of her intellectual capacities, if she thought that an old wife's tale like that would satisfy it. In this she was partly right: Mrs. Ames had indeed no opinion at all of her mind; on the other hand, she did not for a moment suppose that this suggestion about the dressing-room would content that feeble organ. It was not designed to: the object was to stir it to a wilder and still unsatisfied curiosity. It perfectly succeeded, and from by-ways Mrs. Altham emerged full-speed, like a motor-car, into the high-road of direct question.

"I am sure they are lovely," she said. "And where is Major Ames lunching?"

Mrs. Ames raised the pieces of her face where there might have been eyebrows in other days. She told one of the truths that Bismarck loved.

"He did not tell me before he went out," she said. "Perhaps Harry knows. Harry, where is your father lunching?"

Now this was ludicrous. As if it was possible that any wife in Riseborough did not know where her husband was lunching! Harry apparently did not know either, and Mrs. Ames, tasting the joys of the bull-baiter, goaded Mrs. Altham further by pointedly asking Parker, when she brought the coffee, if she knew where the Major was lunching. Of course Parker did not, and so Parker was told to cut Mrs. Altham a nice bunch of sweet-peas to carry away with her.

This pleasant duty of thwarting undue curiosity being performed, Mrs. Ames turned to Mr. Pettit, though she had not quite done with Mrs. Altham yet. For she had heard on the best authority that Mrs. Altham occasionally indulged in the disgusting and unfeminine habit of cigarette smoking. Mrs. Brooks had several times seen her walking about her garden with a cigarette, and she had told Mrs. Taverner, who had told Mrs. Ames. The evidence was overwhelming.

"Mr. Pettit, I don't think any of us mind the smell of tobacco," she said, "when it is out of doors, so pray have a cigarette. Harry will give you one. Ah! I forgot! Perhaps Mrs. Altham does not like it."

Mrs. Altham hastened to correct that impression. At the same time she had a subtle and not quite comfortable sense that Mrs. Ames knew all about her and her cigarettes, which was exactly the impression which that lady sought to convey.

These tactics were all sound enough in their way, but a profounder knowledge of human nature would have led Mrs. Ames not to press home her victory with so merciless a hand. In her determination to thwart Mrs. Altham's odious curiosity, she had let it be seen that she was thwarting it: she should not, for instance, have asked Parker if she knew of the Major's whereabouts, for it only served to emphasize the undoubted fact that Mrs. Ames knew (that might be taken for granted) and that she knew that Parker did not, for otherwise she would surely not have asked her.

Consequently Mrs. Altham (erroneously, as far as that went) came to the conclusion that the Major was lunching alone where his wife did not wish him to lunch alone. And in the next quarter of an hour, while they all sat on the verandah, she devoted the mind which her hostess so despised, to a rapid review of all houses of this description. Instantly almost, the wrong scent which she was following led her to the right quarry. She argued, erroneously, the existence of a pretty woman, and there was a pretty woman in Riseborough. It is hardly necessary to state that she made up her mind to call on that pretty woman without delay. She would be very much surprised if she did not find there an immense bunch of sweet-peas and perhaps their donor.

Mrs. Ames' guests soon went their ways, Mr. Pettit and his sister to the children's service at three, the Althams on their detective mission, and she was left to herself, except in so far as Harry, asleep in a basket chair in the garden, can be considered companionship. She was not gifted with any very great acuteness of imagination, but this afternoon she found herself capable of conjuring up (indeed, she was incapable of not doing so) a certain amount of vague disquiet. Indeed, she tried to put it away, and refresh her mind with the remembrance of her thwarting Mrs. Altham, but though her disquiet was but vague, and was concerned with things that had at present no real existence at all, whereas her victory over that inquisitive lady was fresh and recent, the disquiet somehow was of more pungent quality, and at last she faced it, instead of attempting any longer to poke it away out of sight.

Millie Evans was undeniably a good-looking woman, undeniably the Major had been considerably attracted last night by her. Undeniably also he had done a very strange thing in stopping to have his lunch there, when he knew perfectly well that there were people lunching with them at home for that important rite of eating up the remains of last night's dinner. Beyond doubt he had taken her this present of sweet-peas, of which Mrs. Altham had so obligingly informed her; beyond doubt, finally, she was herself ten years her husband's senior.

It has been said that Mrs. Ames was not imaginative, but indeed, there seemed to be sufficient here, when it was all brought together, to occupy a very prosaic and literal mind. It was not as if these facts were all new to her: that disparity of age between herself and her husband had long lain dark and ominous, like a distant thunder-cloud on the horizon of her mind. Hitherto, it had been stationary there, not apparently coming any closer, and not giving any hint of the potential tempest which might lurk within it. But now it seemed to have moved a little up the sky, and (though this might be mere fancy on her part), there came from it some drowsy and distant echo of thunder.

It must not be supposed that her disquiet expressed itself in Mrs. Ames' mind in terms of metaphor like this, for she was practically incapable of metaphor. She said to herself merely that she was ten years older than her husband. That she had known ever since they married (indeed, she had known it before), but till now the fact had never seemed likely to be of any significance to her. And yet her grounds for supposing that it might be about to become significant were of the most unsubstantial sort. Certainly if Lyndhurst had not gone out to lunch to-day, she would never have dreamed of finding disquiet in the happenings of the evening before; indeed, apart from Harry's absurd expedition into the garden, the party had been a markedly successful one, and she had determined to give more of those undomestic entertainments. But the principle of them assumed a strangely different aspect when her husband accepted an invitation of the kind instead of lunching at home, and that aspect presented itself in vivid colours when she reflected that he was ten years her junior.

Mrs. Ames was a practical woman, and though her imagination had run unreasonably riot, so she told herself, over these late events, so that she already contemplated a contingency that she had no real reason to anticipate, she considered what should be her practical conduct if this remote state of affairs should cease to be remote. She had altogether passed from being in love with her husband, so much so, indeed, that she could not recall, with any sense of reality, what that unquiet sensation was like. But she had been in love with him years ago, and that still gave her a sense of possession over him. She had not been in the habit of guarding her possession, since there had never been any reason to suppose that anybody wanted to take it away, but she remembered with sufficient distinctness the sense that Lyndhurst's garden was becoming to him the paramount interest in his life. At the time that sense had been composed of mixed feelings: neglect and relief were its constituents. He had ceased to expect from her that indefinable sensitiveness which is one of the prime conditions of love, and the growing atrophy of his demands certainly corresponded with her own inclinations. At the same time, though this cessation on his part of the imperative need of her, was a relief, she resented it. She would have wished him to continue being in love with her on credit, so to speak, without the settlement of the bill being applied for. Years had passed since then, but to-day that secondary discontent assumed a primary importance again. It was more acute now than it had ever been, for her possession was not being quietly absorbed into the culture of impersonal flowers, but, so it seemed possible, was directly threatened.

There was the situation which her imagination presented her with, practically put, and she proceeded to consider it from a practical standpoint. What was she to do?

She had the justice to acknowledge that the first clear signals of coolness in their mutual relations, now fifteen years ago, had been chiefly flown by her: she had essentially welcomed his transference of affection to his garden, though she had secretly resented it. At the least, the cooling had been condoned by her. Probably that had been a mistake on her part, and she determined now to rectify it. She, pathetically enough, felt herself young still, and to confirm herself in her view, she took the trouble to go indoors, and look at herself in the glass that hung in the hall. It was inevitable that she should see there not what she really saw, but what, in the main, she desired to see. Her hair, always slightly faded in tone, was not really grey, and even if there were signs of greyness in it there was nothing easier, if you could trust the daily advertisements in the papers, than to restore the colour, not by dyes, but by "purely natural means." There had been an advertisement of one such desirable lotion, she remembered, in the paper to-day, which she had noticed was supplied by any chemist. Certainly there was a little grey in her hair: that would be easy to remedy. That act of mental frankness led on to another. There were certain premonitory symptoms of stringiness about her throat and of loose skin round her mouth and eyes. But who could keep abreast of the times at all, and not know that there were skin-foods which were magical in their effect? There was one which had impressed itself on her not long before: an actress had written in its praise, affirming that her wrinkles had vanished with three nights' treatment. Then there was a little, just a little, sallowness of complexion, but after all, she had always been rather sallow. It was a fortunate circumstance: when she got hot she never got crimson in the face like poor Mrs. Taverner. . . . She was going to town next week for a night, in order to see her dentist, a yearly precaution, unproductive of pain, for her teeth were really excellent, regular in shape, white, undecayed. Lyndhurst, in his early days, had told her they were like pearls, and she had told him he talked nonsense. They were just as much like pearls still, only he did not tell her so. He, poor fellow, had had great trouble in this regard, but it might be supposed his trouble was over now, since artifice had done its utmost for him. She was much younger than him there, though his last set fitted beautifully. But probably Millie had seen they were not real. And then he was distinctly gouty, which she was not. Often had she heard his optimistic assertion that an hour's employment with the garden-roller rendered all things of rheumatic tendency an impossibility. But she, though publicly she let these random statements pass, and even endorsed them, knew the array of bottles that beleaguered the washing-stand in his dressing-room, where the sweet-peas were not.

The silent colloquy with the mirror in the hall occupied her some ten minutes, but the ten minutes sufficed for the arrival of one conclusion--namely, that she did not intend to be an old woman yet. Subtle art, the art of the hair-restorer (which was not a dye), the art of the skin-feeder must be invoked. She no longer felt at all old, now that there was a possibility of her husband's feeling young. And lip-salve: perhaps lip-salve, yet that seemed hardly necessary: a few little bitings and mumblings of her lips between her excellent teeth seemed to restore to them a very vivid colour.

She went back to the verandah, where her little luncheon-party had had their coffee, and pondered the practical manœuvres of her campaign of invasion into the territory of youth which had once been hers. The lotion for the hair, as she verified by a consultation with the Sunday paper, took but a fortnight's application to complete its work. The wrinkle treatment was easily comprised in that, for it took, according to the eminent actress, no more than three days. It might therefore be wiser not to let the work of rejuvenation take place under Lyndhurst's eye, for there might be critical passages in it. But she could go away for a fortnight (a fortnight was the utmost time necessary for the wonderful lotion to restore faded colour) and return again after correspondence that indicated that she felt much better and younger. Several times before she had gone to stay alone with a friend of hers on the coast of Norfolk: there would be nothing in the least remarkable in her doing it again.

An objection loomed in sight. If there was any reality in the supposition that prompted her desire to seem young again--namely, a possible attraction of her husband towards Millie Evans, she would but be giving facility and encouragement to that by her absence. But then, immediately the wisdom of the course, stronger than the objection to it, presented itself. Infinitely the wiser plan for her was to act as if unconscious of any such danger, to disarm him by her obvious rejection of any armour of her own. She must either watch him minutely or not at all. Mr. Pettit had alluded in his sermon that morning to the finer of the two attitudes when he reminded them that love thought no evil. It seemed to poor Mrs. Ames that if by her conduct she appeared to think no evil, it came to the same thing.

Her behaviour towards Lyndhurst, when he should come back from Millie's house, followed as a corollary. She would be completely genial: she would hope he had had a pleasant lunch, and, if he made any apology for his absence, assure him that it was quite unnecessary. Her charity would carry her even further than that: she would say that his absence had been deplored by her guests, but that she had been so glad that he had done as he felt inclined. She would hope that Millie was not tired with her party, and that she and her husband would come to dine with them again soon. It must be while Harry was at home, for he was immensely attracted by Millie. So good for a boy to think about a nice woman like that.

CHAPTER IV

Mrs. Ames carried out her programme with pathetic fidelity. Her husband did not get home till nearly tea-time, and she welcomed him with a cordiality that would have been unusual even if he had not gone out to lunch at all. And to do him justice, it must be confessed that his wife's scheme, as already recounted, was framed to meet a situation which at present had no real existence, except in the mind of a wife wedded to a younger husband. There were data for the situation, so to speak, rather than there was danger of it. He, on his side, was well aware of the irregularity of his conduct, and was prepared to accept, without retaliation, a modicum of blame for it. But no blame at all awaited him; instead of that a cordiality so genuine that, in spite of the fact that a particularly good dinner was provided him, the possible parallel of the prodigal son did not so much as suggest itself to his mind.

Harry had retired to his bedroom soon after dinner with a certain wildness of eye which portended poetry rather than repose, and after he had gone his father commented in the humorous spirit about this.

"Poor old Harry!" he said. "Case of lovely woman, eh, Amy? I was just the same at his age, until I met you, my dear."

This topic of Harry's admiration for Mrs. Evans, which his mother had intended to allude to, had not yet been touched on, and she responded cordially.

"You think Harry is very much attracted by Millie, do you mean?" she said.

He chuckled.

"Well, that's not very difficult to see," he said. "Why, the rascal tore off a dozen of my best roses for her last night, though I hadn't the heart to scold him for it. Not a bad thing for a young fellow to burn a bit of incense before a charming woman like that. Keeps him out of mischief, makes him see what a nice woman is like. As I said, I used to do just the same myself."

"Tell me about it," said she.

"Well, there was the Colonel's wife. God bless me, how I adored her. I must have been just about Harry's age, for I had only lately joined, and she was a woman getting on for forty. Good thing, too, for me, as I say, for it kept me out of mischief. They used to say she encouraged me, but I don't believe it. Every woman likes to know that she's admired, eh? She doesn't snub a boy who takes her out in the garden, and picks his father's roses for her. But we mustn't have Harry boring her with his attentions. That'll never do."

It seemed to Mrs. Ames of singularly little consequence whether Harry bored Millie Evans or not. She would much have preferred to be assured that her husband did. But the subsequent conversation did not reassure her as to that.

"Nice little woman, she is," he said. "Thoroughly nice little woman, and naturally enough, my dear, since she is your cousin, she likes being treated in neighbourly fashion. We had a great talk after lunch to-day, and I'm sorry for her, sorry for her. I think we ought to do all we can to make life pleasant for her. Drop in to tea, or drop in to lunch, as I did to-day. A doctor's wife, you know. She told me that some days she scarcely set eyes on her husband, and when she did, he could think of nothing but microbes. And there's really nobody in Riseborough, except you and me, with whom she feels--dear me, what's that French word--yes, with whom she feels in her proper *milieu.* I should like us to be on such terms with her--you being her cousin--that we could always telephone to say we were dropping in, and that she would feel equally free to drop in. Dropping in, you know: that's the real thing; not to be obliged to wait till you are asked, or to accept weeks ahead, as one has got to do for some formal dinner-party. I should like to feel that we mightn't be surprised to find her picking sweet-peas in the garden, and that she wouldn't be surprised to find you or me sitting under her mulberry-tree, waiting for her to come in. After all, intimacy only begins when formality ceases. Shall I give you some soda water?"

Mrs. Ames did not want soda-water: she wanted to think. Her husband had completely expressed the attitude she meant to adopt, but her own adoption of it had presupposed a certain contrition on his part with regard to his unusual behaviour. But he gave her no time for thought, and proceeded to propose just the same sort of thing as she (in her magnanimity) had thought of suggesting.

"Dinner, now," he said. "Up till last night we have always been a bit formal about dinner here in Riseborough. If you asked General Snookes, you asked Mrs. Snookes; if you asked Admiral Jones, you asked Lady Jones. You led the way, my dear, about that, and what could have been pleasanter than our little party last night? Let us repeat it: let us be less formal. If you want to see Mr. Altham, ask him to come. Mrs. Altham, let us say, wants to ask me: let her ask me. Or if you meet Dr. Evans in the street, and he says it is lunch time, go and have lunch with him, without bothering about me. I shall do very well at home. I'm told that in London it is quite a constant practice to invite like that. And it seems to me very sensible."

All this had seemed very sensible to Mrs. Ames, when she had thought of it herself. It seemed a little more hazardous now. She was well aware that this plan had caused a vast amount of talk in Riseborough, the knowledge of which she had much enjoyed, since it was of the nature of subjects commenting on the movements of their queen, without any danger to her of dethronement. But she was not so sure that she enjoyed her husband's cordial endorsement of her innovation. Also, in his endorsement there was some little insincerity. He had taken as instance the chance of his wishing to dine without his wife at Mrs. Altham's, and they both knew how preposterous such a contingency would be. But did this only prepare the way for a further solitary excursion to Mrs. Evans'? Had Mrs. Evans asked him to dine there? She was immediately enlightened.

"Of course, we talked over your delightful dinner-party of last night," he said, "and agreed in the agreeableness of it. And she asked me to dine there, *en garçon,* on Tuesday next. Of course, I said I must consult you first; you might have asked other people here, or we might be dining out together. I should not dream of upsetting any existing arrangement. I told her so: she quite understood. But if there was nothing going on, I promised to dine there *en garçon."*

CHAPTER IV

That phrase had evidently taken Major Ames' fancy; there was a ring of youth about it, and he repeated it with gusto. His wife, too, perfectly understood the secret smack of the lips with which he said it: she knew precisely how he felt. But she was wise enough to keep the consciousness of it completely out of her reply.

"By all means," she said; "we have no engagement for that night. And I am thinking of proposing myself for a little visit to Mrs. Bertram next week, Lyndhurst. I know she is at Overstrand now, and I think ten days on the east coast would do me good."

He assented with a cordiality that equalled hers.

"Very wise, I am sure, my dear," he said. "I have thought this last day or two that you looked a little run down."

A sudden misgiving seized her at this, for she knew quite well she neither looked nor felt the least run down.

"I thought perhaps you and Harry would take some little trip together while I was away," she said.

"Oh, never mind us, never mind us," said he. "We'll rub along, *en garçon,* you know. I daresay some of our friends will take pity on us, and ask us to drop in."

This was not reassuring: nor would Mrs. Ames have been reassured if she could have penetrated at that moment unseen into Mrs. Altham's drawing-room. She and her husband had gone straight from Mrs. Ames' house that afternoon to call on Mrs. Evans, and had been told she was not at home. But Mrs. Altham of the eagle-eye had seen through the opened front door an immense bowl of sweet-peas on the hall table, and by it a straw hat with a riband of regimental colours round it. Circumstantial evidence could go no further, and now this indefatigable lady was looking out Major Ames in an old army list.

"Ames, Lyndhurst Percy," she triumphantly read out. "Born 1860, and I daresay he is older than that, because if ever there was a man who wanted to be thought younger than his years, that's the one. So in any case, Henry, he is over forty-seven. And there's the front-door bell. It will be Mrs. Brooks. She said she would drop in for a chat after dinner."

There was plenty to chat about that evening.

CHAPTER V

Mrs. Ames might or might not have been run down when she left Riseborough the following week, but nothing can be more certain than that she was considerably braced up seven days after that. The delicious freshness of winds off the North Sea, tempering the heat of brilliant summer suns, may have had something to do with it, and she certainly had more colour in her face than was usual with her, which was the legitimate effect of the felicitous weather. There was more colour in her hair also, and though that, no doubt, was a perfectly legitimate effect too, being produced by purely natural means, as the label on the bottle stated, the sun and wind were not accountable for this embellishment.

She had spent an afternoon in London--chiefly in Bond Street--on her way here, and had gone to a couple of addresses which she had secretly snipped out of the daily press. The expenditure of a couple of pounds, which was already yielding her immense dividends in encouragement and hope, had put her into possession of a bottle with a brush, a machine that, when you turned a handle, quivered violently like a motor-car that is prepared to start, and a small jar of opaque glass, which contained the miraculous skin-food. With these was being wrought the desired marvels; with these, as with a magician's rod, she was conjuring, so she believed, the remote enchantments of youth back to her.

After quite a few days change became evident, and daily that change grew greater. As regards her hair, the cost, both of time and material, in this miracle-working, was of the smallest possible account. Morning and evening, after brushing it, she rubbed in a mere teaspoonful of a thin yellow liquid, which, as the advertisement stated, was quite free from grease or obnoxious smell, and did not stain the pillow. This was so simple that it really required faith to embark upon the treatment, for from the time of Hebrew prophets, mankind have found it easier to do "some great thing" than merely to wash in the Jordan. But Mrs. Ames, luckily, had shown her faith, and by the end of a week the marvellous lotion had shown its works. Till now, though her hair could not be described as grey, there was a considerable quantity of grey in it: now she examined it with an eye that sought for instead of shutting itself to such blemish, and the reward of its search was of the most meagre sort. There was really no grey left in it: it might have been, as far as colour could be taken as a test of age, the hair of a young woman. It was not very abundant in quantity, but the lotion had held out no promises on that score; quality, not quantity, was the sum of its beckoning. The application of the skin-food was more expensive: she had to use more and it took longer. Nightly she poured a can of very hot water into her basin, and with a towel over her head to concentrate the vapour, she steamed her face over it for some twenty minutes. Emerging red and hot and stifled, she wiped off the streams of moisture, and with finger-tips dipped in this marvellous cream, tapped and dabbed at the less happy regions between her eyebrows, outside her eyes, across her forehead, at the corners of her mouth, and up and down her neck. Then came the use of the palpitating machine; it whirred and buzzed over her, tickling very much. For half-an-hour she would make a patient piano of her face, then gently remove such of the skin-food as still stayed on the surface, and had not gone within to do its nurturing work. Certainly this was a somewhat laborious affair, but the results were highly prosperous. There was no doubt that to a perfectly candid and even sceptical eye, a week's treatment had produced a change. The wrinkles were beginning to be softly erased: there was a perceptible plumpness observable in the leaner places. Between the bouts of tapping and dabbing she sipped the glass of milk which she brought up to bed with her, as the deviser of the skin-food recommended. She drank another such glass in the middle of the morning, and digested them both perfectly.

As these external signs appeared and grew there went on within her an accompanying and corresponding rejuvenation of spirit. She felt very well, owing, no doubt, to the brisk air, the milk, the many hours spent out-of-doors, and in consequence she began to feel much younger. An unwonted activity and lightness pervaded her limbs: she took daily a walk of a couple of hours without fatigue, and was the life and soul of the dinner-table, whose other occupants were her hosts, Mrs. Bertram, a cold, grim woman with a moustache, and her husband, milder, with whiskers. Their only passion was for gardening, and they seldom left their grounds; thus Mrs. Ames took her walks unaccompanied.

Miles of firm sands, when the tide was low, subtended the cliffs on which Mr. Bertram's house stood, and often Mrs. Ames preferred to walk along the margin of the sea rather than pursue more inland routes, and to-day, after her large and wholesome lunch (the physical stimulus of the east coast, combined with this mental stimulus of her object in coming here, gave her an appetite of dimensions unknown at Riseborough) she took a maritime way. The tide was far out, and the lower sands, still shining and firm from the retained moisture of its retreat, made uncommonly pleasant walking. She had abandoned heeled footgear, and had bought at a shop in the village, where everything inexpensive, from wooden spades to stamps and sticking plaster, was sold, a pair of canvas coverings technically known as sandshoes. They laced up with a piece of white tape, and were juvenile, light, and easily removable. They, and the great sea, and the jetsam of stranded seaweed, and the general sense of youth and freshness, made most agreeable companions, and she felt, though neither Mr. nor Mrs. Bertram was with her, charmingly accompanied. Her small, toadlike face expressed a large degree of contentment, and piercing her pleasant surroundings as the smell of syringa pierces through the odour of all other flowers, was the sense of her brown hair and fast-fading wrinkles. That gave her an inward happiness which flushed with pleasure and interest all she saw. In the lines of pebbles left by the retreating tide was an orange-coloured cornelian, which she picked up, and put in her pocket. She could have bought the same, ready polished, for a shilling at the cheap and comprehensive shop, but to find it herself gave her a pleasure not to be estimated at all in terms of silver coinage. Further on there was an attractive-looking shell, which she also picked up, and was about to give as a companion to the cornelian, when a sudden scurry of claw-like legs about its aperture showed her that a hermit-crab was domiciled within, and she dropped it with a little scream and a sense of danger escaped both by her and the hermit-crab. There were attractive pieces of seaweed, which reminded her of years when she collected the finer sorts, and set them, with the aid of a pin, on cartridge-paper, spreading out their delicate fronds and fern-like foliage. There were creamy ripples of the quiet sea, long-winged gulls that hovered fishing; above all there was the sense of her brown hair and smoothed face. She felt years younger, and she felt she looked years younger, which was scarcely less solid a satisfaction.

It pleased her, but not acutely or viciously, to think of Mrs. Altham's feelings when she made her rejuvenated appearance in Riseborough. It was quite certain that Mrs. Altham would suspect that she had been "doing something to herself," and that Mrs. Altham would burst with envy and curiosity to know what it was she had done. Although she felt very kindly towards all the world, she did not deceive herself to such an extent as to imagine that she would tell Mrs. Altham what she had done. Mrs. Altham was ingenious and would like guessing. But that lady occupied her mind but little. The main point was that in a week from now she would go home again, and that Lyndhurst would find her young. She might or might not have been right in fearing that Lyndhurst was becoming sentimentally interested in Millie Evans, and she was quite willing to grant that her grounds for that fear were of the slenderest. But all that might be dismissed now. She herself, in a week from now, would have recaptured that more youthful aspect which had been hers while he was still of loverlike inclination towards her. What might be called regular good looks had always been denied her, but she had once had her share of youth. To-day she felt youthful still, and once again, she believed, looked as if she belonged to the enchanted epoch. She had no intention of using this recapture promiscuously: she scarcely desired general admiration: she only desired that her husband should find her attractive.

For a little while, as she took her quick, short steps along these shining sands, she felt herself grow bitter towards Millie Evans. A sort of superior pity was mixed with the bitterness, for she told herself that poor Millie, if she had tried to flirt with Lyndhurst, would speedily find herself flirting all alone. Very likely Millie was guiltless in intention; she had only let her pretty face produce an unchecked effect. Men were attracted by a pretty face, but the owners of such faces ought to keep a curb on them, so to speak. Their faces were not their faults, but rather their misfortunes. A woman with a pretty face would be wise to make herself rather reserved, so that her manner would chill anybody who was inclined. . .

. But the whole subject now was obsolete. If there had been any danger, there would not be any more, and she did not blame Millie. She must ask Millie to dine with them *en famille,* which was much nicer than *en garçon,* as soon as she got back.

It might be gathered from this account of Mrs. Ames' self-communings that deep down in her nature there lay a strain of almost farcical fatuousness. But she was not really fatuous, unless it is fatuous to have preserved far out into the plains of middle-age some vision of the blue mountains of youth. It is true that for years she had been satisfied to dwell on these plains; now, her fear that her husband, so much younger than herself, was turning his eyes to blue mountains that did not belong to him, made her desire to get out of the plains and ascend her own blue mountains again and wave to him from there, and encourage his advance. She felt exceedingly well, and in consequence told herself that in mind, as well as physical constitution, she was young still, while the effect of the bottles which she used with such regularity made her believe that the outward signs of age were erasible. She seemed to have been granted a new lease of life in a tenement that it was easy to repair. Her whole nature felt itself to be quickened and vivified.

She had gone far along the sands, and the tide was beginning to flow again. All round her were great empty spaces, a shipless sea, a cloudless sky, a beach with no living being in sight. A sudden unpremeditated impulse seized her, and without delay she sat down on the shore, and took off her shoes and stockings. Then, pulling up her skirts, she hastily ran down to the edge of the water, across a little belt of pebbles that tickled and hurt her soft-soled feet, and waded out into the liquid rims of the sea. She was astonished and amazed at herself that the idea of paddling had ever come into her head, and more amazed that she had had the temerity to put it into execution. For the first minute or two the cold touch of the water on her unaccustomed ankles and calves made her gasp a little, but for all the strangeness of these sensations she felt that paddling, playing like a child in the shallow waters, expressed the tone of her mind, just as the melody of a song expresses the words to which it is set. If she had had a spade, she would certainly have built a sand-castle and dug moats about it, and a smile lit up her small face at the thought of purchasing one at the universal shop, and furtively conveying it to these unfrequented beaches. And the smile almost ended in a blush when she tried to imagine what Riseborough society would say if it became known that their queen not only paddled in the sea, but seriously contemplated buying a wooden spade in order to conduct building operations on lonely shores.

The paddling, though quite pleasant, was not so joyous as the impulse to paddle had been, and it was not long before she sat down again on the beach and tried to get the sand out of the small, tight places between her toes, and to dry her feet and plump little legs with a most exiguous handkerchief. But even in the midst of these troublesome operations, her mind still ran riot, and she planned to secrete about her person one of her smaller bedroom towels when she went for her walk next day. And she felt as if this act of paddling must have aided in the elimination of wrinkles. For who except the really young could want to paddle? To find that she had the impulse of the really young was even better than to cultivate, though with success, the appropriate appearance. All the way home this effervescence of spirit was hers, which, though it definitely sprang from the effects of the lotion, the skin-food and the tonic air, produced in her an illusion that was complete. She was certainly ascending her remote blue mountains again, and through a clarified air she could look over the plains, and see how very flat they had been. That must all be changed: there must be more variety and gaiety introduced into her days. For years, as she saw now, her life had been spent in small, joyless hospitalities, in keeping her place as accredited leader of Riseborough's socialities, in paying her share towards the expenses of the house. They did not laugh much at home: there had seemed nothing particular to laugh about, and certainly they did not paddle. She was forming no plan for paddling there now, irrespective of the fact that a muddy canal, which was the only water in the neighbourhood, did not encourage the scheme, but there must be introduced into her life and Lyndhurst's more of the spirit that had to-day prompted her paddling. Exactly what form it should take she did not clearly foresee, but when she had recaptured the spirit as well as the appearance of youth, there was no fear that it would find any difficulty in expressing itself suitably. All aglow, especially as to her feet, which tingled pleasantly, she arrived at her host's house again. They were both at work in the garden: Mrs. Bertram was killing slugs in the garden beds, Mr. Bertram worms on the lawn.

Major Ames proved himself during the next week to be a good correspondent, if virtue in correspondents is to be measured by the frequency of their communications. His letters were not long, but they were cheerful, since the garden was coming on well in this delightful weather, which he hoped embraced Cromer also, and since he had on two separate occasions made a grand slam when playing Bridge at the club. He and Harry were jogging along quite pleasantly, but there had been no gaieties to take them out, except a tea-party with ices at Mrs. Brooks'. Unfortunately, some disaster had befallen the ices: personally, he thought it was salt instead of sugar, but Harry had been unwell afterwards, which suggested sour cream. But his indisposition had been but short, though violent. He himself had dropped in to dine *en garçon* with the Evans', and the doctor was very busy. Finally (this came at the end of every letter), as the place was doing her so much good, why not stop for another week? He was sure the Bertrams (poor things!) would be delighted if she would.

But that suggestion did not commend itself to Mrs. Ames. She had come here for a definite purpose, and when on the morning before her departure she looked very critically at herself in the glass, she felt that her purpose had been accomplished. Her skin had not, so much she admitted, the unruffled smoothness of a young woman's, but she had not been a young woman when she married. But search where she might in her hair, there was no sign of greyness in it all, while the contents of the bottle were not yet half used. But she would take back the more than moiety with her, since an occasional application when the hair had resumed its usual colour was recommended. It appeared to her that it undoubtedly had resumed its original colour: the change, though slight (for the grey had never been conspicuous), was complete; she felt equipped for youth again. And psychologically she felt equipped: every day since the first secret paddling she had pad-paddled again in secret, and from a crevice in a tumble of fallen rock she daily extracted a small wooden spade, by aid of which, with many glancings around for fear of possible observers, she dug in the sand, making moats and ramparts. The "first fine careless rapture" of this, it must be admitted, had evaporated: after one architectural afternoon she had dug not because this elementary pursuit expressed what she felt, so much as because it expressed what she desired to feel. After all, she did not propose to rejuvenate herself to the extent of being nine or ten years old again. . . .

The manner of her return to Riseborough demanded consideration: it was not sufficient merely to look up in a railway guide the swiftest mode of transit and adopt it, for this was not quite an ordinary entry, and it would never do to take the edge off it by making a travel-soiled and dusty first appearance. So she laid down a plan.

The bare facts about the trains were these. A train starting at a convenient hour would bring her to London a short half-hour before another convenient train from another and distant terminus started for Riseborough. It was impossible to make certain of catching this, so she wrote to her husband saying that she would in all probability get to Riseborough by a later train that arrived there at eight. She begged him not to meet her at the station, but to order dinner for half-past eight. It would be nice to be at home again. Then came the plan. Clearly it would never do to burst on him like that, to sit down opposite him at the dinner-table beneath the somewhat searching electric light there, handicapped by the fatigues of a hot journey only imperfectly repaired by a hasty toilet. She must arrive by the early train, though not expected till the later. Thus she would secure a quiet two hours for bathing, resting and dressing. If Lyndhurst did not expect her to arrive till eight it was a practical certainty that he would be at the club till that hour, and walk home in time to welcome her arrival. He would then learn that she had already come and was dressing. She would be careful to let him go downstairs first, and a minute later she would follow. He should see. . . .

So in order to catch this earlier train from town she left Cromer while morning was yet dewy, and had the peculiar pleasure, on her arrival at Riseborough, of seeing her husband, from the windows of her cab, passing along the street to the club. She had a moment's qualm that he would see her initialled boxes on the top, but by grace of a punctual providence Mrs. Brooks came out of her house at the moment, and the Major raised a gallant hat and spoke a cheerful word to her. Certainly he looked very handsome and distinguished, and Mrs. Ames felt a little tremor of anticipation in thinking of the chapters of life that were to be re-read by them. She felt confident also; it never entered her head to have any misgivings as to what the last fortnight, which had contained so much for her, might have contained for him.

Harry had gone back to Cambridge for the July term the day before, and she found on her arrival that she had the house to herself. The afternoon had turned a little chilly, and she enjoyed the invigoration of a hot bath, and a subsequent hour's rest on her sofa. Then it was time to dress, and though the dinner was of the simplest conjugal character, she put on a dress she had worn but some half-dozen of times before, but which on this one occasion it was meet should descend from the pompous existence that was its destiny for a year or two to come. It was of daring rose-colour, the most resplendent possible, and never failed to create an impression. Indeed, she had, on one of its infrequent appearances, heard Lyndhurst say to his neighbour in an undertone, "Upon my soul, Amy looks very well to-night." And Amy meant to look very well again.

All happened as she had planned. Shortly after eight Lyndhurst tapped at her door on his return from the club, but could not be admitted, and at half-past, having heard him go downstairs, she followed him. He had not dressed, according to their custom when they were alone.

Major Ames was writing a note when she entered, and only turned round in his chair, not getting up.

"Glad to see you home, my dear," he said. "Excuse me one moment. I must just direct this."

She kissed him and waited while he scrawled an address. Then he got up and rang the bell.

"Just in time to catch the post," he said. "By Jove! Amy, you've put on the famous pink gown. I would have dressed if I had known. You're tired with your journey, I expect. It was a very hot day here, until a couple of hours ago."

He gave the note to the servant.

"And dinner's ready, I think," he said.

They sat down opposite each other at ends of the rather long table. There were no flowers on it, for it had not occurred to him to get the garden to welcome her home-coming, and the whole of her resplendency was visible to him. He began eating his soup vigorously.

"Capital plan in summer to have dinner at half-past eight," he said. "Gives one most of the daylight and not so long an evening afterwards. Excellent pea-soup, this. Fresh peas from my garden. The Evans' dine at eight-thirty. And how have you been, Amy?"

Some indefinable chill of misgiving, against which she struggled, had laid cold fingers on her. Things were not going any longer as she had planned them. He had noticed her gown, but he had noticed nothing else. But then he had scarcely looked up since they had come into the dining-room. But now he finished his soup, and she challenged his attention.

"I have been very well indeed," she said. "Don't I look it?"

He looked her straight in the face, saw all that had seemed almost a miracle to her--the softened wrinkles, the recovered colour of her hair.

"Yes, I think you do," he said. "You've got a bit tanned too, haven't you, with the sun?"

CHAPTER V

The cold fingers closed a little more tightly on her.

"Have I?" she said. "That is very likely. I was out-of-doors all day. I used to take quite long walks every afternoon."

He glanced at the menu-card.

"I hope you'll like the dinner I ordered you," he said. "Your cook and I had a great talk over it this morning. 'She'll have been in the train all day,' I said, 'and will feel a little tired. Appetite will want a bit of tempting, eh?' So we settled on a grilled sole, and a chicken and a macédoine of fruit. Hope that suits you, Amy. So you used to take long walks, did you? Is the country pretty round about? Bathing, too. Is it a good coast for bathing?"

Again he looked at her as he spoke, and for the moment her heart-beat quickened, for it seemed that he could not but see the change in her. Then his sole required dissection, and he looked at his plate again.

"I believe it is a good coast," she said. "There were a quantity of bathing-machines. I did not bathe."

"No. Very wise, I am sure. One has to be careful about chills as one gets on. I should have been anxious about you, Amy, if I had thought you would be so rash as to bathe."

Some instinct of protest prompted her.

"There would have been nothing to be anxious about," she said. "I seldom catch a chill. And I often paddled."

He laid down his knife and fork and laughed.

"You paddled!" he asked. "Nonsense, nonsense!"

She had not meant to tell him, for her reasonable mind had informed her all the time that this was a secret expression of the rejuvenation she was conscious of. But it had slipped out, a thoughtless assertion of the youthfulness she felt.

"I did indeed," she said, "and I found it very bracing and invigorating."

Then for a moment a certain bitterness welled up within her, born from disappointment at his imperceptiveness.

"You see I never suffer from gout or rheumatism like you, Lyndhurst," she said. "I hope you have been quite free from them since I have been away."

But his amusement, though it had produced this spirit of rancour in her, had not been in the least unkindly. It was legitimate to find entertainment in the thought of a middle-aged woman gravely paddling, so long as he had no idea that there was a most pathetic side to it. Of that he had no inkling: he was unaware that this paddling was expressive of her feeling of recaptured youth, just as he was unaware that she believed it to be expressed in her face and hair. But this remark was distinctly of the nature of an attack: she was retaliating for his laughter. He could not resist one further answer which might both soothe and smart (like a patent ointment) before he changed the subject.

"Well, my dear, I'm sure you are a wonderful woman for your years," he said. "By Jove! I shall be proud if I'm as active and healthy as you in ten years' time."

Dinner was soon over after this, and she left him, as usual, to have his cigarette and glass of port, and went into the drawing-room, and stood looking on the last fading splendour of the sunset in the west. The momentary bitterness in her mind had quite died down again: there was nothing left but a vague, dull ache of flatness and disappointment. He had noticed nothing of all that had caused her such tremulous and secret joy. He had looked on her smoothed and softened face, and seen no difference there, on her brown unfaded hair and found it unaltered. He had only seen that she had put her best gown on, and she almost wished that he had not noticed that, since then she might have had the consolation of thinking that he was ill. It was not, it must be premised, that she meant she would find pleasure in his indisposition, only that an indisposition would have explained his imperceptiveness, which she regretted more than she would have regretted a slight headache for him.

For a few minutes she was incapable of more than blank and empty contemplation of the utter failure of that from which she had expected so much. Then, like the stars that even now were beginning to be lit in the empty spaces of the sky, fresh points in the dreary situation claimed her attention. Was he preoccupied with other matters, that he was blind to her? His letters, it is true, had been uniformly cheerful and chatty, but a preoccupied man can easily write a letter without betraying the preoccupation that is only too evident in personal intercourse. If this was so, what was the nature of his preoccupation? That was not a cheerful star: there was a green light in it. . . . Another star claimed her attention. Was it Lyndhurst who was blind, or herself who saw too much? She had no idea, till she came to look into the matter closely, how much grey hair was mingled with the brown. Perhaps he had no idea either: its restoration, therefore, would not be an affair of surprise and admiration. But the wrinkles. . . .

She faced round from the window as he entered, and made another call on her courage and conviction. Though he saw so little, she, quickened perhaps by the light of the green star, saw how good-looking he was. For years she had scarcely noticed it. She put up her small face to him in a way that suggested, though it did not exactly invite a kiss.

"It is so nice to be home again," she said.

The suggestion that she meant to convey occurred to him, but, very reasonably, he dismissed it as improbable. A promiscuous caress was a thing long obsolete between them. Morning and evening he brushed her cheek with the end of his moustaches.

"Well, then, we're all pleased," he said good-humouredly. "Shall I ring for coffee, Amy?"

She was not discouraged.

"Do," she said, "and when we have had coffee, will you fetch a shawl for me, and we will stroll in the garden. You shall show me what new flowers have come out."

CHAPTER V

The intention of that was admirable, the actual proposal not so happy, since a glimmering starlight through the fallen dusk would not conduce to a perception of colour.

"We'll stroll in the garden by all means," he said, "if you think it will not be risky for you. But as to flowers, my dear, it will be easier to appreciate them when it is not dark."

Again she put up her face towards him. This time he might, perhaps, have taken the suggestion, but at the moment Parker entered with the coffee.

"How foolish of me," she said. "I forgot it was dark. But let us go out anyhow, unless you were thinking of going round to the club."

"Oh, time for that, time for that," said he. "I expect you will be going to bed early after your long journey. I may step round then, and see what's going on."

Without conscious encouragement or welcome on her part, a suspicion darted into her mind. She felt by some process, as inexplicable as that by which certain people are aware of the presence of a cat in the room, that he was going round to see Mrs. Evans.

"I suppose you have often gone round to the club in the evening since I have been away," she said.

"Yes, I have looked in now and again," he said. "On other evenings I have dropped in to see our friends. Lonely old bachelor, you know, and Harry was not always very lively company. It's a good thing that boy has gone back to Cambridge, Amy. He was always mooning round after Mrs. Evans."

That was a fact: it had often been a slightly inconvenient one. Several times the Major had "dropped in" to see Millie, and found his son already there.

"But I thought you were rather pleased at that, Lyndhurst," she said. "You told me you considered it not a bad thing: that it would keep Harry out of mischief."

He finished his coffee rather hastily.

"Yes, within reason, within reason," he said. "Well, if we are to stroll in the garden, we had better go out. You wanted a shawl, didn't you? Very wise: where shall I find one?"

That diverted her again to her own personal efforts.

"There are several in the second tray of my wardrobe," she said. "Choose a nice one, Lyndhurst, something that won't look hideous with my pink silk."

The smile, as you might almost say, of coquetry, which accompanied this speech, faded completely as soon as he left the room, and her face assumed that business-like aspect, which the softest and youngest faces wear, when the object is to attract, instead of letting a mutual attraction exercise its inevitable power. Even though Mrs. Ames' object was the legitimate and laudable desire to attract her own husband, it was strange how common her respectable little countenance appeared. She had adorned herself to attract admiration: coquetry and anxiety were pitifully mingled, even as you may see them in haunts far less respectable than this detached villa, and on faces from which Mrs. Ames would instantly have averted her own. She hoped he would bring a certain white silk shawl: two nights ago she had worn it on the verandah after dinner at Overstrand, and the reflected light from it, she had noticed, as she stood beneath a light opposite a mirror in the hall, had made her throat look especially soft and plump. She stood underneath the light now waiting for his return.

Fortune was favourable: it was that shawl that he brought, and she turned round for him to put it on her shoulders. Then she faced him again in the remembered position, underneath the light, smiling.

"Now, I am ready, Lyndhurst," she said.

He opened the French window for her, and stood to let her pass out. Again she smiled at him, and waited for him to join her on the rather narrow gravel path. There was actually room for two abreast on it, for, on the evening of her dinner-party, Harry had walked here side by side with Mrs. Evans. But there was only just room.

"You go first, Amy," he said, "or shall I? We can scarcely walk abreast here."

But she took his arm.

"Nonsense, my dear," she said. "There: is there not heaps of room?"

He felt vaguely uncomfortable. It was not only the necessity of putting his feet down one strictly in front of the other that made him so.

"Anything the matter, my dear?" he asked.

The question was not cruel: it was scarcely even careless. He could hardly be expected to guess, for his perceptions were not fine. Also he was thinking about somebody else, and wondering how late it was. But even if he had had complete knowledge of the situation about which he was completely ignorant, he could not have dealt with it in a more peremptory way. The dreary flatness to which she had been so impassive a prey directly after dinner, the sense of complete failure enveloped her like impenetrable fog. Out of that fog, she hooted, so to speak, like an undervitalized siren.

"I am only so glad to get back," she said, pressing his arm a little. "I hoped you were glad, too, that I was back. Tell me what you have been doing all the time I have been away."

This, like banns, was for the third time of asking. He recalled for her the days one by one, leaving out certain parts of them. Even at the moment, he was astonished to find how vivid his recollection of them was. On Thursday, when he had played golf in the morning, he had lunched with the Evans' (this he stated, for Harry had lunched there too) and he had culled probably the last dish of asparagus in the afternoon. He had dined alone with Harry that night, and Harry had toothache. Next day, consequently, Harry went to the dentist in the morning, and he himself had played golf in the afternoon. That he remembered because he had gone to tea with Mrs. Evans afterwards, but that he did not mention, for he had been alone with her, and they had talked about being misunderstood and about affinities. On Saturday Harry had gone back to Cambridge, but, having missed his train, he had made a second start after lunch. He had met Dr. Evans in the street that day, going up to the golf links, and since he would otherwise be quite alone in the evening, he had dined with them, "*en garçon.*"

CHAPTER V

This catalogue of trivial happenings took quite a long time in the recitation. But below the trivialities there was a lurking significance. He was not really in love with Millie Evans, and his assurance to himself on that point was perfectly honest. But (this he did not put so distinctly to himself) he thought that she was tremendously attracted by him. Here was an appeal to a sort of deplorable sense of gallantry--so terrible a word only can describe his terrible mind--and mentally he called her "poor little lady." She was pretty, too, and not very happy. It seemed to be incumbent on him to interest and amuse her. His "droppings in" amused her: when he got ready to drop out again, she always asked when he would come to see her next. These "droppings in" were clearly bright spots to her in a drab day. They were also bright spots to him, for he was more interested in them than in all his sweet-peas. There was a "situation" come into his life, something clandestine. It would never do, for instance, to let Amy or the estimable doctor get a hint of it. Probably they would misunderstand it, and imagine there was something to conceal. He had the secret joys of a bloodless intrigue. But, considering its absolute bloodlessness, he was amazingly wrapped up in it. It was no wonder that he did not notice the restored colour of Amy's hair.

He, or rather Mrs. Evans, had made a conditional appointment for to-night. If possible, the possibility depending upon Amy's fatigue, he was going to drop in for a chat. Primarily the chat was to be concerned with the lighting of the garden by means of Chinese lanterns, for a nocturnal fête that Mrs. Evans meant to give on her birthday. The whole garden was to be lit, and since the entertainment of an illuminated garden, with hot soup, quails and ices, under the mulberry-tree was obviously new to Riseborough, it would be sufficiently amusing to the guests to walk about the garden till supper-time. But there would be supererogatory diversions beyond that, bridge-tables in the verandah, a small band at the end of the garden to intervene its strains between the guests and the shrieks of South-Eastern expresses, and already there was an idea of fancy dress. Major Ames favoured the idea of fancy dress, for he had a red velvet garment, sartorially known as a Venetian cloak, locked away upstairs, which was a dazzling affair if white tights peeped out from below it. He knew he had a leg, and only lamented the scanty opportunities of convincing others of the fact. But the lighting of the garden had to be planned first: there was no use in having a leg in a garden, if the garden was not properly lit. But the whole affair was as yet a pledged secret: he could not, as a man of honour, tell Amy about it. Short notice for a fête of this sort was of no consequence, for it was to be a post-prandial entertainment, and the only post-prandial entertainment at present existent in Riseborough was going to bed. Thus everybody would be able to be happy to accept.

A rapid *résumé* of this made an undercurrent in his mind, as he went through, in speaking voice, the history of the last days. Up and down the narrow path they passed, she still with her hand in his arm, questioning, showing an inconceivable interest in the passage of the days from which he had left out all real points of interest. His patience came to an end before hers.

"Upon my word, my dear," he said, "it's getting a little chilly. Shall we go in, do you think? I'm sure you are tired with your journey."

There was nothing more coming: she knew that. But even in the midst of her disappointment, she found consolation. Daylight would show the re-establishment of her youthfulness more clearly than electric light had done. Every one looked about the same by electric light. And though, in some secret manner, she distrusted his visit to the club, she knew how impolitic it would be to hint, however remotely, at such distrust. It was much better this evening to acquiesce in the imputation of fatigue. Nor was the imputation groundless; for failure fatigues any one when under the same conditions success would only stimulate. And in the consciousness of that, her bitterness rose once more to her lips.

"You mustn't catch cold," she said. "Let us go in."

It was still only half-past ten: all this flatness and failure had lasted but a couple of hours, and Major Ames, as soon as his wife had gone upstairs, let himself out of the house. His way lay past the doors of the club, but he did not enter, merely observing through its lit windows that there were a good many men in the smoking-room. On arrival at the Doctor's he found that Elsie and her father were playing chess in the drawing-room, and that Mrs. Evans was out in the garden. He chose to go straight into the garden, and found her sitting under the mulberry, dressed in white, and looking rather like the Milky Way. She did not get up, but held out her hand to him.

"That is nice of you," she said. "How is Cousin Amy?"

"Amy is very well," said he. "But she's gone to bed early, a little tired with the journey. And how is Cousin Amy's cousin?"

He sat down on the basket chair close beside her which creaked with his weight.

"I must have a special chair made for you," she said. "You are so big and strong. Have you seen Cousin Amy's cousin's husband?"

"No: I heard you were out here. So I came straight out."

She got up.

"I think it will be better, then, if we go in, and tell him you are here," she said. "He might think it strange."

Major Ames jumped up with alacrity: with his alacrity was mingled a pleasing sense of adventure.

"By all means," he said. "Then we can come out again."

She smiled at him.

"Surely. He is playing chess with Elsie. I do not suppose he will interrupt his game."

Apparently Dr. Evans did not think anything in the least strange. On the whole, this was not to be wondered at, since he knew quite well that Major Ames was coming to talk over garden illumination with his wife.

CHAPTER V

"Good evening, Major," he said; "kind of you to come. You and my little woman are going to make a pauper of me, I'm told. There, Elsie, what do you say to my putting my knight there? Check."

"Pig!" said Elsie.

"Then shall we go out, Major Ames?" said Millie. "Are you coming out, Wilfred?"

"No, little woman. I'm going to defeat your daughter indoors. Come and have a glass of whisky and soda with me before you go, Major."

They went out again accordingly into the cool starlight.

"Wilfred is so fond of chess," she said. "He plays every night with Elsie, when he is at home. Of course, he is often out."

This produced exactly the effect that she meant. She did not comment or complain: she merely made a statement which arose naturally from what was going on in the drawing-room.

But Major Ames drew the inference that he was expected to draw.

"Glad I could come round," he said. "Now for the lanterns. We must have them all down the garden wall, and not too far apart, either. Six feet apart, eh? Now I'll step the wall and we can calculate how many we shall want there. I think I step a full yard still. Not cramped in the joints yet."

It took some half hour to settle the whole scheme of lighting, which, since Major Ames was not going to pay for it, he recommended being done in a somewhat lavish manner. With so large a number of lanterns, it would be easily possible to see his leg, and he was strong on the subject of fancy dress.

"There'll be some queer turn-outs, I shouldn't wonder," he said; "but I expect there will be some creditable costumes too. By Jove! it will be quite the event of the year. Amy and I, with our little dinners, will have to take a back seat, as they say."

"I hope Cousin Amy won't think it forward of me," said Millie.

Major Ames said that which is written "Pshaw." "Forward?" he cried. "Why, you are bringing a bit of life among us. Upon my word, we wanted rousing up a bit. Why, you are a public benefactor."

They had sat down to rest again after their labour of stepping out the brick walls under the mulberry-tree, where the grass was dry, and only a faint shimmer of starlight came through the leaves. At the bottom of the garden a train shrieked by, and the noise died away in decrescent thunder. She leaned forward a little towards him, putting up her face much as Amy had done.

"Ah, if only I thought I was making things a little pleasant," she said.

Suddenly it struck Major Ames that he was expected to kiss her. He leaned forward, too.

"I think you know that," he said. "I wish I could thank you for it."

She did not move, but in the dusk he could see she was smiling at him. It looked as if she was waiting. He made an awkward forward movement and kissed her.

There was silence a moment: she neither responded to him nor repelled him.

"I suppose people would say I ought not to have let you," she said. "But there is no harm, is there? After all, you are a--a sort of cousin. And you have been so kind about the lanterns."

Major Ames was thinking almost entirely about himself, hardly at all about her. An adventure, an intrigue had begun. He had kissed somebody else's wife and felt the devil of a fellow. But with the wine of this emotion was mingled a touch of alarm. It would be wise to call a halt, take his whisky and soda with her husband, and get home to Amy.

CHAPTER VI

Mrs. Altham waited with considerable impatience next day for the return of her husband from the club, where he went on most afternoons, to sit in an arm-chair from tea-time to dinner and casually to learn what had happened while he had been playing golf. She had been to call on Mrs. Ames in the afternoon, and in consequence had matter of considerable importance to communicate. She could have supported that retarded spate of information, though she wanted to burst as soon as possible, but she had also a question to ask Henry on which a tremendous deal depended. At length she heard the rattle of his deposited hat and stick in the hall, and she went out to meet him.

"How late you are, Henry," she said; "but you needn't dress. Mrs. Brooks, if she does come in afterwards, will excuse you. Dinner is ready: let us come in at once. Now, you were at the club last night, after dinner. You told me who was there; but I want to be quite sure."

Mr. Altham closed his eyes for a moment as he sat down. It looked as if he was saying a silent grace, but appearances were deceptive. He was only thinking, for he knew his wife would not ask such a question unless something depended on it, and he desired to be accurate.

Then he opened them again, and helped the soup with a name to each spoonful.

"General Fortescue," he said. "Young Morton. Mr. Taverner, Turner, Young Turner."

That was five spoonfuls--three for his wife, two for himself. He was not very fond of soup.

"And you were there all the time between ten and eleven?" asked his wife.

"Till half-past eleven."

"And there was no one else?"

Mr. Altham looked up brightly.

"The club waiter," he said, "and the page. The page has been dismissed for stealing sugar. The sugar bill was preposterous. That was how we found out. Did you mean to ask about that?"

"No, my dear. Nor do I want to know."

At the moment the parlour-maid left the room, and she spoke in an eager undertone.

"Mrs. Ames told me that Major Ames went up to the club last night, when she went to bed at half-past ten," she said. "You told me at breakfast whom you found there, but I wanted to be sure. Call them Mr. and Mrs. Smith and then we can go on talking."

The parlour-maid came back into the room.

"Yes, Mr. Smith apparently went up to the club at half-past ten," she said. "But he can't have gone to the club, for in that case you would have seen him. It has occurred to me that he didn't feel well, and went to the doctor's."

"It seems possible," said Mr. Altham, not without enthusiasm, understanding that "doctor" meant "doctor," and which doctor.

"We have all noticed how many visits he has been paying to--to Dr. Jones," said Mrs. Altham, "during the time Mrs. Smith was away. But to pay another one on the very evening of her return looks as if--as if something serious was the matter."

"My dear, there's nothing whatever to show that Major Ames went to the doctor's last night," he said.

Mrs. Altham gave him an awful glance, for the parlour-maid was in the room, and this thoughtless remark rendered all the diplomatic substitution of another nomenclature entirely void and useless.

"Mrs. Smith, I should say," added Mr. Altham in some confusion, proceeding to make it all quite clear to Jane, in case she had any doubts about it.

"Suggest to me any other reasonable theory as to where he was, then," said Mrs. Altham.

"I can't suggest where he was, my dear," said Mr. Altham, finding his legal training supported him, "considering that there is no evidence of any kind that bears upon the matter. But to know that a man was not in one given place does not show with any positiveness that he was at any other given place."

"No doubt, then, he went shopping at half-past ten last night," said Mrs. Altham, with deep sarcasm. "There are so many shops open then. The High Street is a perfect blaze of light."

Mr. Altham could be sarcastic, too, though he seldom exercised this gift.

"It quite dazzles one," he observed.

Mrs. Altham no doubt was vexed at her husband's sceptical attitude, and she punished him by refraining from discussing the point any further, and from giving him the rest of her news. But this severity punished herself also, for she was bursting to tell him. When Jane had finally withdrawn, the internal pressure became irresistible.

"Mrs. Ames has done something to her hair, Henry," she said; "and she has done something to her face. I had a good mind to ask her what she had used. I assure you there was not a grey hair left anywhere, and a fortnight ago she was as grey as a coot!"

"Coots are bald, not grey," remarked her husband.

"That is mere carping, Henry. She is brown now. Is this another fashion she is going to set us at Riseborough? What does it all mean? Shall we all have to plaster our faces with cold cream, and dye our hair blue?"

Mr. Altham was in a painfully literal mood this evening and could not disentangle information from rhetoric.

"Has she dyed her hair blue?" he asked in a slightly awestricken voice.

"No, my dear: how can you be so stupid? And I told you just now she was brown. But at her age! As if anybody cared what colour her hair was. Her face, too! I don't deny that the wrinkles are less marked, but who cares whether she is wrinkled or not?"

These pleasant considerations were discontinued by the sound of the postman's tap on the front door, and since the postman took precedence of everybody and everything, Mr. Altham hurried out to see what excitements he had piloted into port. Unfortunately, there was nothing for him, but there was a large, promising-looking envelope for his wife. It was stiff, too, and looked like the receptacle of an invitation card.

"One for you, my dear," he said.

Mrs. Altham tore it open, and gave a great gasp.

"You would not guess in a hundred tries," she said.

"Then be so kind as to tell me," remarked her husband.

Mrs. Altham read it out all in one breath without stops.

"Mrs. Evans at home Thursday July 20 10 p.m. Shakespeare Fancy Dress well I never!"

For a little while the silence of stupefaction reigned. Then Mr. Altham gave a great sigh.

"I have never been to a fancy dress ball," he said. "I think I should feel very queer and uncomfortable. What are we meant to do when we get there, Julia? Just stand about and look at each other. It will seem very strange. What would you recommend me to be? I suppose we ought to be a pair."

Mrs. Altham, to do her justice, had not thought seriously about her personal appearance for years. But, as she got up from the table, and consciously faced the looking-glass over the chimney-piece, it is idle to deny that she considered it now. She was not within ten years of Mrs. Ames' age, and it struck her, as she carefully regarded herself in a perfectly honest glass, that even taking into full consideration all that Mrs. Ames had been doing to her hair and her face, she herself still kept the proper measure of their difference of years between them. But it was yet too early to consider the question of her impersonation. There were other things suggested by the contemplation of a fancy-dress ball to be considered first. There was so much, in fact, that she hardly knew where to begin. So she whisked everything up together, in the manner of a sea-pie, in which all that is possibly edible is put in the oven and baked.

"There will be time enough to talk over that, my dear," she said, "for if Mrs. Evans thinks we are all going to lash out into no end of expense in getting dresses for her party, she is wrong as far as I, for one, am concerned. For that matter you can put on your oldest clothes, and I can borrow Jane's apron and cap, and we can go as Darby and Joan. Indeed, I do not know if I shall go at all--though, of course, one wouldn't like to hurt Mrs. Evans' feelings by refusing. Do you know, Henry, I shouldn't in the least wonder if we have seen the last of Mrs. Ames and all her airs of superiority and leadership. You may depend upon it that Mrs. Evans did not consult her before she settled to give a fancy dress party. It is far more likely that she and Major Ames contrived it all between them, while Mrs. Ames was away, and settled what they should go as, and I daresay it will be Romeo and Juliet. I should not be in the least surprised if Mrs. Ames did not go to the party at all, but tried to get something up on her own account that very night. It would be like her, I am sure. But whether she goes or not, it seems to me that we have seen the last of her queening it over us all. If she does not go, I should think she would be the only absentee, and if she does, she goes as Mrs. Evans' guest. All these years she has never thought of a fancy dress party--"

Mrs. Altham broke off in the middle of her address, stung by the splendour of a sudden thought.

"Or does all this staying away on her part," she said, "and dyeing her hair, and painting her face, mean that she knew about it all along, and was going to be the show-figure of it all? I should not wonder if that was it. As likely as not, she and Major Ames will come as Hamlet and Ophelia, or something equally ridiculous, though I am sure as far as the 'too too solid flesh' goes, Major Ames would make an admirable Hamlet, for I never saw a man put on weight in the manner he does, in spite of all the garden rolling, which I expect the gardener does for him really. But whatever is the truth of it all, and I'm sure every one is so secretive here in Riseborough nowadays, that you never know how many dined at such a place on such a night unless you actually go to the poulterer's and find out whether one chicken or two was sent,--what was I saying?"

She had been saying a good deal. Mr. Altham correctly guessed the train of thought which she desired to recall.

"In spite of the secretiveness--" he suggested.

That served the purpose.

"No, my dear Henry," said his wife rapidly, "I accuse no one of secretiveness: if I did, you misunderstood me. All I meant was that when we have settled what we are to go as, we will tell nobody. There is very little sense in a fancy dress entertainment if you know exactly what you may expect, and as soon as you see a Romeo can say for certain that it is Major Ames, for instance; and I'm sure if he is to go as Romeo, it would be vastly suitable if Mrs. Ames went as Juliet's nurse."

"I am not sure that I shall like so much finery," said Mr. Altham, who was thinking entirely about his own dress, and did not care two straws about Major or Mrs. Ames. "It will seem very strange."

"Nonsense, my dear; we will dine in our fancy dresses for an evening or two before, and you will get quite used to it, whatever it is. Henry, do you remember my white satin gown, which I scarcely wore a dozen times, because it seemed too grand for Riseborough? It was too, I am sure: you were quite right. It has been in camphor ever since. I used to wear my Roman pearls with it. There are three rows, and the clasp is of real pearls. The very thing for Cleopatra."

"I recollect perfectly," said Mr. Altham. His mind instantly darted off again to the undoubted fact that whereas Major Ames was stout, he himself was very thin. If he had been obliged to describe his figure at that moment, he would have said it was boyish. The expense of a wig seemed of no account.

"Well, my dear, white dress and pearls," said his wife. "You are not very encouraging. With that book of Egyptian antiquities, I can easily remodel the dress. And I remember reading in a Roman history that Cleopatra was well over thirty when Julius Cæsar was so devoted to her. And by the busts he must have been much balder than you!"

It is no use denying that this was a rather heavy blow. Ever since the mention of the word Cleopatra, he had seen himself complete, with a wig, in another character.

"But Julius Cæsar was sixty," he observed, with pardonable asperity. "I do not see how I could make up as a man of sixty. And for that matter, my dear, though I am sure no one would think you were within five years of your actual age, I do not see how you could make up as a mere girl of thirty. Why should we not go as 'Antony and Cleopatra, ten years later'? It would be better than to go as Julius Cæsar arid Cleopatra ten years before!"

Mrs. Altham considered this. It was true that she would find it difficult to look thirty, however many Roman pearls she wore.

"I do not know that it is such a bad idea of yours, Henry," she said. "Certainly there is no one in the world who cares about her age, or wants to conceal it, less than I. And there is something original about your suggestion--Antony and Cleopatra ten years later--Ah, there is the bell, that will be Mrs. Brooks coming in. And there is the telephone also. Upon my word, we never have a moment to ourselves. I should not wonder if half Riseborough came to see us to-night. Will you go to the telephone and tell it we are at home? And not a word to anybody, Henry, as to what we are thinking of going as. There will be our surprise, at any rate, however much other people go talking about their dresses. If you are being rung up to ask about your costume, say that you haven't given it a thought yet."

For the next week Mrs. Altham was thoroughly in her element. She had something to conceal, and was in a delicious state of tension with the superficial desire to disclose her own impersonation, and the deep-rooted satisfaction of not doing so. To complete her happiness, the famous white satin still fitted her, and she was nearly insane with curiosity to know what Major and Mrs. Ames "were going to be," and what the whole history of the projected festivity was. In various other respects her natural interest in the affairs of other people was satiated. Mrs. Turner was to be Mistress Page, which was very suitable, as she was elderly and stout, and did not really in the least resemble Miss Ellen Terry. Mr. Turner had selected Falstaff, and could be recognized anywhere. Young Morton, with unwonted modesty, had chosen the part of the Apothecary in Romeo and Juliet. Mrs.

Taverner was to be Queen Catherine, and--almost more joyous than all--she had persuaded Mrs. Brooks not to attempt to impersonate Cleopatra. What Mrs. Brooks' feelings would be when it dawned on her, as it not inconceivably might, that Mrs. Altham had seen in her a striking likeness to her conception of Hermione, because she did not want there to be two Cleopatras, did not particularly concern her. She had asked Mrs. Brooks to dinner the day after the entertainment, and her acceptance would bury the hatchet, if indeed there was such a thing as a hatchet about. Finally, she had called on Mrs. Evans, who had vaguely talked about Midsummer Night's Dream. Mrs. Altham had taken that to be equivalent to the fact that she would appear as Titania, and Mrs. Evans had distinctly intended that she should so take it. Indeed, the idea had occurred to her, but not very vividly. Her husband was going to be Timon of Athens. That, again, was quite satisfactory: nobody knew at all distinctly who Timon of Athens was, and nobody knew much about Dr. Evans, except that he was usually sent for in the middle of something. Probably the same thing happened to Timon of Athens.

Indeed, within a couple of hours of the reception of Mrs. Evans' invitations, which all arrived simultaneously by the local evening post, a spirit of demoniacal gaiety, not less fierce than that which inspired Mrs. Altham, possessed the whole of those invited. Though it was gay, it was certainly demoniacal, for a quite prodigious amount of ill-feeling was mingled with it which from time to time threatened to wreck the proceedings altogether. For instance, only two days after all the invitations had been accepted, Mrs. Evans had issued a further intimation that there was to be dancing, and that the evening would open at a quarter past ten precisely with a quadrille in which it was requested that everybody would take part. It is easy to picture the private consternation that presided over that evening; how in one house, Mrs. Brooks having pushed her central drawing-room table to one side, all alone and humming to herself, stepped in perplexed and forgotten measures, and how next door Mrs. and Mr. Altham violently wrangled over the order of the figures, and hummed different tunes, to show each other, or pranced in different directions. For here was the bitter affair: these pains had to be suffered in loneliness, for it was clearly impossible to confess that the practice of quadrilles was so long past that the memory of them had vanished altogether. But luckily (though at the moment the suggestion caused a great deal of asperity in Mrs. Altham's mind) Mrs. Ames came to the rescue with the suggestion that as many of them, no doubt, had forgotten the precise manner of quadrilles, she proposed to hold a class at half-past four to-morrow afternoon, when they would all run through a quadrille together.

"There! I thought as much!" said Mrs. Altham. "That means that neither Major nor Mrs. Ames can remember how the quadrille goes, and we, forsooth, must go and teach them. And she puts it that she is going to teach us! I am sure she will never teach me: I shall not go near the house. I do not require to be taught quadrilles by anybody, still less by Mrs. Ames. There is no answer," she added to Jane.

Mr. Altham fidgeted in his chair. Last night he had been quite sure he was right, in points where he and his wife differed, and that the particular "setting partners" which they had shown each other so often did not come in the quadrille at all, but occurred in lancers, just before the ladies' chain. But she had insisted that both the setting to partners and ladies' chain came in quadrilles. This morning, however, he did not feel quite so certain about it.

"You might send a note to Mrs. Ames," he observed, "and tell her you are not coming."

"No answer was asked for," said his wife excitedly. "She just said there was to be a quadrille practice at half-past four. Let there be. I am sure I have no objection, though I do think you might have thought of doing it first, Henry."

"But she will like to know how many to expect," said Henry. "If it is to be at half-past four, she must be prepared for tea. It is equivalent to a tea-party, unless you suppose that the class will be over before five."

During the night Mrs. Altham had pondered her view about the ladies' chain. It would be an awful thing if Henry happened to be right, and if, on the evening of the dance itself, she presented her hand for the ladies' chain, and no chain of any sort followed. She decided on a magnanimous course.

"Upon my word, I am not sure that I shall not go," she said, "just to see what Mrs. Ames' idea of a quadrille is. I should not wonder if she mixed it up with something quite different, which would be laughable. And after all, we ought not to be so unkind, and if poor Mrs. Ames feels she will get into difficulties over the quadrille, I am sure I shall be happy to help her out. No doubt she has summoned us like this, so that she need not show that she feels she wants to be helped. We will go, Henry, and I daresay I shall get out of her what she means to dress up as! But pray remember to say that we, at any rate, have not given a thought to our costumes yet. And on our way, we may as well call in at Mr. Roland's, for if I am to wear my three rows of pearls, he must get me a few more, since I find there is a good deal of string showing. I daresay that ordinary pearl beads would answer the purpose perfectly. I have no intention of buying more of the real Roman pearls. They belonged to my mother, and I should not like to add to them. And if you will insist on having some red stone in your cap, to make a buckle for the feather, I am sure you could not do better than get a piece of what he called German ruby that is in his shop now. I do not suppose anybody in Riseborough could tell it from real, and after all this is over, I would wear it as a pendant for my pearls. If you wish, I will pay half of it, and it is but a couple of pounds altogether."

It did not seem a really handsome offer, but Henry had the sense to accept it. He wanted a stone to buckle the feather in a rather coquettish cap that they had decided to be suitable for Mark Antony, and did not really care what happened to it after he had worn it on this occasion, since it was unlikely that another similar occasion would arise. Deep in his mind had been an idea of turning it into a solitaire, but he knew he would not have the practical courage of this daring conception. It would want another setting, also.

In other houses there were no fewer anticipatory triumphs and present perplexities. There was also, in some cases, wild and secret intrigue. For instance, a few evenings after, Mrs. Brooks next door, sorting out garments in her wardrobe from which she might devise a costume that should remind the beholder of Hermione, looked from her bedroom window, where her quest was in progress, and saw a strange sight in the next garden. There was a lady in white satin with pearls; there was a gentleman in Roman toga with a feathered cap. The Roman gentleman was a dubious figure; the lady indubitable. If ever there was an elderly Cleopatra, this was she.

Mrs. Brooks sat heavily down, after observing this sight. It certainly was Cleopatra in the next garden: as certainly it was a snake in the grass. In a moment her mind was made up. She saw why she had been discouraged from being Cleopatra; the false Mrs. Altham had wanted to be Cleopatra herself, without rival. But she would be Cleopatra too. Riseborough should judge between the effectiveness of the two representations. Of course, every one knew that Mrs. Altham had three rows of Roman pearls, which were nothing but some sort of vitreous enamel. But Mrs. Brooks, as Riseborough also knew, had five or six rows of real seed-pearls. It was impossible to *denigrer* seed-pearls: they were pearls, though small, and did not pretend to be anything different to what they were. But the Roman prefix, to any fair-minded person, invalidated the word "pearls." Besides, even as Cleopatra without pearls, she would have been willing to back herself against Mrs. Altham. Cleopatra ought to be tall, which she was. Also Cleopatra ought to be beautiful, which neither was. And Mrs. Altham had urged her to go as Hermione! Of course, she had to revise her toilet, but luckily it had progressed no further than the sewing of white rosettes on to a pair of slightly worn satin shoes, which were equally suitable for any of Shakespeare's heroines.

The week which had passed for Mr. and Mrs. Altham in a succession of so pleasing excitements and anxieties, had not been without incident to Mrs. Ames. When (by the same post that bore their invitations to the other guests) the announcement of the fancy dress ball reached her, and she read it out to her husband (even as Mrs. Altham had done) towards the end of dinner, he expressed his feelings with a good deal of pooh-ing and the opinion that he, at any rate, was past the years of dressing-up. This attitude (for it had been settled that the invitation was to come as a surprise to him) he somewhat overdid, and found to his dismay that his wife quite agreed with him, and was prepared as soon as dinner was over to write regrets. The reason was not far to seek.

"I hope I am not what--what the servants call 'touchy,'" she said (and indeed, it was difficult to see what else the servants could call it), "but I must say that, considering the length of time we have been in Riseborough, and the number of entertainments we have provided for the people here, I think dear Millie might have consulted me--or you, of course, Lyndhurst, in my absence--as to any such novelty as a fancy dress ball. I have no wish to interfere in any way with any little party that dear Millie may choose to give, but I suppose since she can plan it without me, she can also enjoy it without me. I am aware I am by no means necessary to the success of any party. And since you think that you are a little beyond the age of dressing up, Lyndhurst--though I do not say I agree with you--I think we shall be happier at home that night. I will write quite kindly to dear Millie, and say we are engaged. No doubt the Althams would dine with us, as I do not imagine that she would care to get up in fancy dress."

Major Ames was not a quick thinker, but he saw several things without a pause. One was that he, at any rate, must certainly go, but that he did not much care whether Amy went or not. A second was that, having expressed surprise at the announcement of the party, it was too late now to say that he knew about it from the first, and was going to impersonate Antony, while Mrs. Evans was to be Cleopatra. A third was that something had to be done, a fourth that he did not know what.

"I will leave you to your cigarette, Lyndhurst," said his wife, rising, "and will write to dear Millie. Let us stroll in the garden again to-night."

She passed out of the dining-room, he closed the door behind her, and she went straight to her writing-table in the drawing-room. Above it hung a looking-glass, and (still not in the frame of mind which servants call "touchy") she sat down to write the kind note. A considerable degree of sunset still lingered in the western sky, and there would be no need to light a candle to write by. There was light enough also for her to see a rosy-tinted image of herself in the glass, and she paused. She saw there, what she was aware Mrs. Altham had seen this afternoon--namely, the absence of grey in her hair, and the softened and liquated wrinkles of her face. True, not even yet had her husband observed, or at any rate commented on those refurbished signals of her youth, but Mrs. Ames had by no means yet despaired, and daily (as directed) tapped in the emollient cream. This rosy light of sunset gave her face a flush of delicate colour, and she unconsciously claimed for her own the borrowed enchantment of the light. . . . Then that which was not touchiness underwent a similar softening to that of her wrinkles. She knew she had been guilty of sarcastic intention when she said she was aware that her presence was not necessary to the success of any party. It would be unkind to dear Millie if she refused to go, for a dinner-party at home was no excuse at all; she could perfectly well go on there when carriages came at twenty minutes to eleven. Also it was absurd for Lyndhurst to say that he was past the age when "dressing up" is seemly. In spite of his hair, which he managed very well, he was still young enough in face to excuse the yielding to the temptation of embellishing himself, and a Venetian mantle would naturally conceal his tendency to corpulence. No doubt dear Millie had not meant to put herself forward in any way; no doubt she had not yet really grasped the fact that Mrs. Ames was acknowledged autocrat in all that concerned festivity.

All this train of thought needed but a few seconds for passage, and, as she still regarded herself, the name of the heroines of enchantment sounded delicately in her brain. Juliet and Ophelia she passed over without a pang, for she was not so unfocussed of imagination as to see her reflection capable of recapturing the budding spring of those, or the slim youthfulness of Rosalind. She wanted no girlish role, nor did she read into herself the precocious dignity of Portia. But was there not one who came down the green Nile to the sound of flutes in a gilded barge--no girl, but a woman in the charm of her full maturity?

The idea detailed itself in plan and manœuvre. She wanted to burst on Lyndhurst like that, to let him see in a flash of revelation how bravely she could support the rôle of that sorceress. . . . At the moment the drawing-room door opened, and simultaneously they both began a sentence in identical words.

"Do you know, my dear, I've been thinking . . ."

They both stopped, and he gave his genial laugh.

"Upon my soul, my dear Amy," he said, "I believe we always have the same thoughts. I'll tell you what you were going to say. You were going to say, 'I've been thinking it wouldn't be very kind to dear Millie'--that is what *you* would say, of course--not very kind to Mrs. Evans if we declined. And I agree with you, my dear. No doubt she should have consulted you first, or if you were away she might even, as you suggested, have mentioned it to me. But you can afford to be indulgent, my dear--after all, she is your cousin--and you wouldn't like to spoil her party, poor thing, by refusing to go. And if you go, why, of course, I shall put on one side my natural feelings about an old fogey like myself making a guy of himself, and I shall dress up somehow. I think I have an old costume with a Venetian cloak laid aside somewhere, though I daresay it's moth-eaten and rusty now, and I'll dress myself up somehow and come with you. I suppose there are some old stagers in Shakespeare--I must have a look at the fellow's plays again--which even a retired old soldier can impersonate. Falstaff, for instance--some stout old man of that sort."

Some of this speech, to say the least of it, was not, it is to be feared, quite absolutely ingenuous. But then, Major Ames was not naturally quite ingenuous. He had already satisfied himself that the old costume in question had been perfectly preserved by the naphthaline balls which he was careful to renew from time to time, and was not in the least moth-eaten or rusty. Again, since he had settled to go as Antony, it was not perfectly straightforward to make allusion to Falstaff. But after all, the speech expressed all he meant to say, and it is only our most fortunate utterances that can do as much. Indeed, perhaps it leaned over a little to the further side of expression, for it struck Mrs. Ames at that moment (struck her as violently and inexplicably as a cocoa-nut falling on her head) that the question of the Venetian cloak had not come into her husband's mind for the first time that evening. She felt, without being able to explain her feeling, that the idea of the fancy dress ball was not new to him. But it was impossible to tax him with so profound a duplicity; indeed, when she gave a moment's consideration to the question, she dismissed her suspicion. But the suspicion had been there.

She met him quite half-way.

"You have guessed quite right, Lyndhurst," she said; "I think it would be unkind to dear Millie if you and I did not go. I dare say she will have difficulty enough as it is to make a gathering. I will write at once."

This was soon done, and even as she wrote, poor Mrs. Ames' vision of herself grew more roseate in her mind. But she must burst upon her husband, she must burst upon him. Supposing her preposterous suspicion of a moment before was true, there was all the more need for bursting upon him, for Cleopatraizing herself. . . . He, meantime, was wondering how on earth to keep the secret of his costume and his hostess's, should Amy proceed to discuss costumes, or suggest the King and Queen of Denmark as suitable for themselves. It might even be better to accept the situation as such, and tell Mrs. Evans that his wife wanted to go as "a pair" (so Mrs. Altham expressed it) and that it was more prudent to abandon the idea of a stray Antony and a stray Cleopatra meeting on the evening itself unpremeditatedly. But her next words caused all these difficulties to disappear; they vanished as completely as a watch or a rabbit under the wave of the conjurer's wand.

Mrs. Ames never licked envelopes; she applied water on a camel's-hair brush, from a little receptacle like a tear-bottle.

"What nonsense, my dear Lyndhurst," she said. "Fancy you going as Falstaff! You must think of something better than that! Dear me, it is a very bold idea of Millie's, but really it seems to me that we might have great fun. I do hope that all Riseborough will not talk their costumes over together, so that we shall know exactly what to expect. There is little point in a fancy dress ball unless there are some surprises. I must think over my costume too. I am not so fortunate as to have one ready."

She got up from the table, still with the roseate image of herself in her mind.

"I think I shall not tell you who I am going to be," she said, "even when I have thought of something suitable. I shall keep myself as a surprise for you. And keep yourself as a surprise for me, Lyndhurst. Let us meet for the first time in our costumes when the carriage is at the door ready to take us to the party. Do you not think that would be fun? But you must promise me, my dear, that you will not make yourself up as Falstaff, or any old guy. Else I shall be quite ashamed of you."

He rang the bell effusively (the heartiness of the action was typical of the welcome he gave to his wife's suggestion), and ordered the note to be sent.

"By Jove! Amy," he said, "what a one you always are for thinking of things. And if you wish it, I'll try to make a presentable figure of myself, though I'm sure I should be more in place at home waiting for your return to hear all about it. But I'll do my best, I'll do my best, and I dare say the Venetian cloak isn't so shabby after all. I have always been careful to keep a bit of naphthaline in the box with it."

Flirtation may not be incorrectly defined as making the pretence of being in love, and yet it is almost too solid a word to apply to Major Ames' relations with Mrs. Evans during the week or two before the ball, and it would be more accurate to say that he was making the pretence of having a flirtation. Even as when he kissed her on that daring evening already described, he was thinking entirely about himself and the dashingness of this proceeding, so in the days that succeeded, this same inept futility and self-satisfaction possessed him. He made many secret visits to the house, entering like a burglar, in the middle of the afternoon, by an unfrequented passage from the railway cutting, at hours when she had told him that her husband and daughter would certainly be out, and the secrecy of those meetings added spice to them. He felt--so deplorable a frame of mind almost defies description--he felt a pleasing sense of wickedness which was en-endorsed, so to speak, by the certificate which attested to his complete innocence. As far as he was concerned, it was a mere farce of a flirtation. But the farce filled him with a kind of childish glee; he persuaded himself that his share in it was real, and that by a tragic fate he and the woman who were made for each other were forbidden to find the fruition of their affinity. It was an adventure without danger, a mine without gunpowder. For even on two occasions when he was paying one of these clandestine visits, Dr. Evans had unexpectedly returned and found them together. The poor blind man, it seemed, suspected nothing; indeed, his welcome had been extremely cordial.

"Good of you to come and help my wife over her party," he said. "What you'd do without Major Ames, little woman, I don't know. Won't you stop for dinner, Major?"

Then, after a suitable reply, and a digression to other matters, the Major's foolish eye would steal a look at Millie, and for a moment her eyes would meet his, and flutter and fall. And considering that there was not in all the world probably a worse judge of human nature than Major Ames, it is a strange thing that his mental comment was approximately true.

"Dear little woman," he said to himself; "she's deuced fond of me!"

CHAPTER VII

Jupiter Pluvius, or Mr. J. Pluvius, by which name Major Ames was facetiously wont to allude to the weather, seemed amiably inclined to co-operate with Mrs. Evans' scheme, for the evening of her party promised to be ideal for the purpose. The few days previous had been very hot, and no particle of moisture lurked in the baked lawns, so that her guests would be able to wander at will without risk of contracting catarrh, or stains on such shoes as should prove to be white satin. Moreover, by a special kindness of Providence, there was no moon, so that the illumination of fairy-lights and Chinese lanterns would suffer no dispiriting comparison with a more potent brightness. Over a large portion of the lawn Mrs. Evans, at Major Ames' suggestion (not having to pay for these paraphernalia he was singularly fruitful in suggestions), had caused a planked floor to be laid; here the opening procession and quadrille and the subsequent dances would take place, while conveniently adjacent was the mulberry-tree under shade of which were spread the more material hospitalities. Tree and dancing-floor were copiously outlined with lanterns, and straight rows of fairy-lights led to them from the garden door of the house. Similarly outlined was the garden wall and the hedge by the railway-cutting, while the band (piano, two strings and a cornet of amazingly piercing quality) was to be concealed in the small *cul-de-sac* which led to the potting shed and garden roller. The shrubbery was less vividly lit; here Hamlets and Rosalinds could stray in sequestered couples, unharassed by too searching an illumination. Major Ames had paid his last clandestine visit this afternoon, and had expressed himself as perfectly pleased with the arrangements. Both Elsie and the doctor had been there.

The party had been announced to begin at half-past ten, and it was scarcely that hour when Mrs. Ames came downstairs from her bedroom where she had so long been busy since the end of the early dinner. Her arms were bare from fingertip to her little round shoulders, over which were clasped, with handsome cairngorm brooches, the straps of her long tunic. But there was no effect of an excessive display of human flesh, since her arms were very short, and in addition they were plentifully bedecked. On one arm a metallic snake writhed from wrist to elbow, on the other there was clasped above the elbow a plain circlet of some very bright and shining metal. A net of blue beads altogether too magnificent to be turquoises, was pinned over her unfaded hair, and from the front of it there depended on her forehead a large pear-shaped pearl, suggestive of the one which the extravagant queen subsequently dissolved in vinegar. Any pearl, so scientists tell us, which is capable of solution in vinegar must be a curious pearl; that which Mrs. Ames wore in the middle of her forehead was curious also. Art had been specially invoked, over and above the normal skin-food to-night, in the matter of Mrs. Ames' face, and a formal Egyptian eyebrow, as indicated in the illustration to "Rameses" in the *Encyclopœdia,* decorated in charcoal the place where her own eyebrow once was. Below her eye a touch of the same charcoal added brilliancy to the eye itself; several touches of rouge contributed their appropriate splendour to her cheeks.

The long tunic which was held up over her shoulders by the cairngorm brooches, reached to her knee. It was a little tight, perhaps, but when you have only one Arab shawl, shot with copious gold thread, you have to make it go as far as it can, and after all, it went to her knees. A small fold of it was looped up, and fell over her yellow girdle, it was parted at the sides below the hips, and disclosed a skirt made of two Arab shawls shot with silver, which, stitched together, descended to her ankle. She did not mean to dance anything except the opening quadrille. Below this silver-streaked skirt appeared, as was natural, her pretty plump little feet. On them she wore sandals which exhibited their plumpness and prettiness and smallness to the fullest extent. A correct strap lay between the great toe and the next, and the straps were covered with silver paper. For years Riseborough had known how small were her shoes; to-night Riseborough should see that those shoes had been amply large enough for what they contained. Round her neck, finally, were four rows of magnificent pearl beads; no wonder Cleopatra thought nothing of dissolving one pearl, when its dissolution would leave intact so populous a company of similar treasures.

As she came downstairs she heard a sudden noise in the drawing-room, as if a heavy man had suddenly stumbled. It required no more ingenuity than was normally hers to conjecture that Lyndhurst was already there, and had tripped himself up in some novel accoutrement. And at that, a sudden flush of excitement and anticipation invaded her, and she wondered what he would be like. As regards herself she felt the profoundest confidence in the success of her garniture. He could scarcely help being amazed, delighted. And an emotion never keenly felt by her, but as such long outworn, shook her and made her knees tremulous. She felt so young, so daring. She wished that at this moment he would come out, for as she descended the stairs he could not but see how small and soft were her feet. . . .

Almost before her wish was formed, it was granted.

A well-smothered oath succeeded the stumbling noise, and Major Ames, in white Roman toga and tights came out into the hall. There was no vestige of Venetian cloak about him; he was altogether different from what she had expected. A profuse wig covered his head, the toga completely masked what the exercise with the garden roller had not completely removed, and below, his big calves rose majestic over his classical laced shoes. If ever there was a Mark Antony with a military moustache, he was not in Egypt nor in Rome, but here; by a divine chance, without consultation, he had chosen for himself the character complementary to hers. He looked up and saw her, she looked down and saw him.

"Bless my soul," he said. "Amy! Cleopatra!"

She gave him a happy little smile.

"Bless my soul," she said. "Lyndhurst! Mark Antony!"

There was a long and an awful pause. It was quite clear to her that something had occurred totally unexpected. She had wanted to be unexpected, but there was something wrong about the quality of his surprise. Then such manliness as there was in him came to his aid.

"Upon my word," he said, "you have got yourself up splendidly, Amy. Cleopatra now, pearls and all, and sandals! Why, you'll take the shine out of them all! Here we go, eh? Antony and Cleopatra! Who would have thought of it! The cab's round, dear. We had better be starting, if we're to take part in the procession. Not want a cloak or anything? Antony and Cleopatra; God bless my soul!"

That was sufficient to allay the immediate embarrassment. True, he had not been knocked over by this apparition of her in the way she had meant, and the astonished pause, she was afraid, was not one of surrendering admiration. And yet, perhaps, he was feeling shy, even as she was; standing here in all this splendour of shining pantomime he might well feel her to be as strange to him, as she felt him to be to her. Moreover, she had not only to look Cleopatra, but to be Cleopatra, to behave herself with the gaiety and youth which her appearance gave him the right to expect. In the meantime he also had earned her compliments, for no man who thinks it worth while to assume a fancy dress has a soul so unhuman as to be unappreciative of applause.

She fell back a step or two to regard him comprehensively.

"My dear," she said, "you are splendid; that toga suits you to admiration. And your arms look so well coming out of the folds of it. What great strong arms, Lyndhurst! You could pick up your little Cleopatra and carry her back--back to Egypt so easily."

Something of their irresponsibility which, as by a special Providence, broods over the audacity of assuming strange guises, descended on her. She could no more have made such a speech to him in her ordinary morning-clothes, nor yet in the famous rose-coloured silk, than she could have flown. But now her costume unloosed her tongue. And despite the dreadful embarrassment that he knew would await him when they got to the party, and a second Cleopatra welcomed them, this intoxication of costume (liable, unfortunately, to manifest itself not only in *vin gai)* mounted to his head also.

"*Ma reine!"* he said, feeling that French brought them somehow closer to the appropriate Oriental atmosphere.

She held up her skirt with one hand, and gave him the other.

"We must be off, my Antony," she said.

They got into the cab; a somewhat jaded-looking horse was lashed into a slow and mournful trot, and they rattled away down the hard, dry road.

A queue of carriages was already waiting to disembark its cargoes when they drew near the house, and leaning furtively and feverishly from the window, Mrs. Ames saw a Hamlet or two and some Titanias swiftly and shyly cross the pavement between two rows of the astonished proletariat. Beside her in the cab her husband grunted and fidgeted; she guessed that to him this entrance was of the nature of bathing on a cold day; however invigorating might be the subsequent swim, the plunge was chilly. But she little knew the true cause of his embarrassment and apprehension; had his military career ever entailed (which it had not) the facing of fire, it was probable, though his courage was of no conspicuous a kind, that he would have met the guns with greater blitheness than he awaited the moment that now inevitably faced him. Then came their turn; there was a pause, and then their carriage door was flung open, and they descended from the innocent vehicle that to him was as portentous as a tumbril. In a moment Cleopatra would meet Cleopatra, and he could form no idea how either Cleopatra would take it. The Cleopatra-hostess, as he knew, was going to wear sandals also; snakes were to writhe up her long white arms. . . .

Mrs. Ames adjusted the pear-shaped pearl on her forehead.

"I think if we say half-past one it will be late enough, Lyndhurst," she said. "If we are not ready he can wait."

It seemed to Lyndhurst that half-past one would probably be quite late enough.

The assemblage of guests took place in the drawing-room which opened into the garden; a waiter from the "Crown" inn, with a chin beard and dressed in a sort of white surplice and carrying a lantern in his hand, who might with equal reasonableness be supposed to be the Man in the Moon out of the *Midsummer Night's Dream,* or a grave-digger out of *Hamlet,* said "Character names, please, ma'am," and preceded them to the door of this chamber. He bawled out "Cleopatra and Mark Antony."

Another Cleopatra, a "different conception of this part," as the *Kent Chronicle* said in its next issue, a Cleopatra dim and white and willowy, advanced to them. She looked vexed, but as she ran her eyes up and down Mrs. Ames' figure, like a practised pianist playing a chromatic scale, her vexation seemed completely to clear.

"Dear Cousin Amy," she said, "how perfectly lovely! I never saw--Wilfred, make your bow to Cleopatra. And Antony! Oh, Major Ames!"

Again she made the chromatic scale, starting at the top, so to speak (his face), with a long note, and dwelling there again when she returned to it.

Other arrivals followed, and this particular Antony and Cleopatra mingled with such guests as were already assembled. The greater part had gathered, and Mrs. Ames' habitual manner and bearing suited excellently with her regal role. The Turner family, at any rate, who were standing a little apart from the others, not being quite completely "in" Riseborough society, and, feeling rather hot and feverish in the thick brocaded stuffs suitable to Falstaff, Mistress Page and King Theseus, felt neither more nor less uncomfortable when she made a few complimentary remarks to them than they did when, with her fat prayer-book in her hand, she spoke to them after church on Sunday. Elsewhere young Morton, with a white face and a red nose, was the traditional Apothecary, and Mrs. Taverner was so copiously apparalled as Queen Catherine that she was looking forward very much indeed to the moment when the procession should go forth into the greater coolness of the night air. Then a stentorian announcement from the waiter at the Crown made every one turn again to the door.

"Antony and Cleopatra ten years later," he shouted.

There was a slight pause. Then entered Mr. and Mrs. Altham with high-held hands clasped at fingertips. They both stepped rather high, she holding her skirt away from her feet, and both pointing their toes as if performing a *pavanne.* This entry had been much rehearsed, and it was arresting to the point of producing a sort of stupefaction.

Mrs. Evans ran her eye up and down the pair, and was apparently satisfied.

"Dear Mrs. Altham," she said, "how perfectly lovely! *And* Mr. Altham. But ten years later! You must not ask us to believe that."

She turned to her husband and spoke quickly, with a look on her face less amiable than she usually wore in public.

"Wilfred," she said, "tell the band to begin the opening march at once for the procession, in case there are any more--"

But he interrupted--

"Here's another, Millie," he said cheerfully. "Yes, we'd better begin."

His speech was drowned by the voice of the brazen-lunged waiter.

"Cleopatra!" he shouted.

Mrs. Brooks entered with all the rows of seed-pearls.

Riseborough, if the census papers were consulted, might perhaps not prove to have an abnormally large percentage of inhabitants who had reached middle-age, but certainly in the festivities of its upper circles, maturity held an overwhelming majority over youth. It was so to-night, and of the half-hundred folk who thus masqueraded, there were few who were not, numerically speaking, of thoroughly discreet years. The diffused knowledge of this undoubtedly gave confidence to their gaiety, for there was no unconscious standard of sterling youth by which their slightly mature exhilaration could be judged and found deficient in genuine and natural effervescence. Thus, despite the somewhat untoward conjunction of four matronly Cleopatras, a spirit of extraordinary gaiety soon possessed the entire party. Odious comparisons might conceivably spring up mushroom-like tomorrow, and (unmushroom-like) continue to wax and flourish through many days and dinners, but to-night so large an environment of elderly people gave to every one of those elderly people a pleasant sense of not suffering but rather shining in comparison with the others. Even the Cleopatras themselves were content; Mrs. Ames, for instance, saw how sensible it was that Mrs. Altham should announce herself as a Cleopatra of ten years later, while Mrs. Altham, observing Mrs. Ames, saw how supererogatory her titular modesty had been, and wondered that Mrs. Ames cared to show her feet like that, while Mrs. Brooks knew that everybody was mentally contrasting her queenliness of height with Mrs. Ames' paucity of inches, and her abundance of beautiful hair with Mrs. Altham's obvious wig. While, all the time, Mrs. Evans, whom the appearance of a fourth Cleopatra had considerably upset for the moment, felt that at this rate she could easily continue being Cleopatra for more years than "the ten after," so properly assumed by Mrs. Altham. In the same way Major Ames, with his six feet of solid English bone and muscle, and his fifth decade of years still but half-consumed, felt that Mr. Altham had but provided a scale of comparison uncommonly flattering to himself. Simultaneously, Mr. Altham, with a laurel-wreath round his head, reflected how uncomfortable he would have felt if his laurel-wreath was anchored on no sounder a foundation than a wig, and wondered if gardening (on the principle that all flesh is grass) invariably resulted in so great a growth of tissue. But all these pleasant self-communings were, indeed, but a minor tributary to the real river of enjoyment that danced and chattered through the starlit hours of this July night. Somehow the whole assembly seemed to have shifted off themselves the natural and inevitable burden of their years; they danced and mildly flirted, they sat out in the dim shrubbery, and played on the sea-shore of life again, finding the sand-castles had become real once more. Mrs. Ames, for instance, had intended to dance nothing but the opening quadrille, but before the second dance, which was a waltz, had come to a close, she had accepted Mr. Altham's offer, and was slowly capering round with him. A little care was necessary in order not to put too unjust a strain on the sandal straps, but she exercised this precaution, and was sorry, though hot, when the dance came to an end. Then Major Ames, who had been piloting Mrs. Altham, joined them at the moselle-cup table.

"'Pon my word, Altham," he said, "I don't know what to say to you. You've taken my Cleopatra, but then I've taken yours. Exchange no robbery, hey?"

His wife tapped him on the arm with her palmette fan.

"Lyndhurst, go along with you!" she said, employing an expression, the mental equivalent of which she did not know ever existed in her mind.

"I'll go along," he said. "But which is my Cleopatra?"

At the moment, Mrs. Evans approached.

"My two Cleopatras must excuse me," said this amazing man. "I am engaged for this next dance to the Cleopatra of us all. Ha! Ha!"

He offered his arm to Mrs. Evans, and they went out of the cave of the mulberry-tree again.

The band had not yet struck up for the next dance, the majority of the guests were flocking under the mulberry-tree at the conclusion of the last, and for the moment they had the cool starlit dusk to themselves. And then, all at once, the Major's sense of boisterous enjoyment deserted him; he felt embarrassed with a secret knowledge that he was expected to say something in tune with this privacy. How that expectation was conveyed he hardly knew; the slight pressure on his arm seemed to announce it unmistakably. It reminded him that he was a man, and yet with all that gaiety and gallantry that were so conspicuous a feature in his behaviour to women in public, he felt awkward and ill at ease. He embarked on a course of desperate and fulsome eulogy, longing in his private soul for the band to begin.

"'Pon my soul, you are an enchantress, Millie!" he said. "You come to our staid, respectable old Riseborough, and before you have been here six months you take us all into fairyland. Positively fairyland. And--and I've never seen you looking so lovely as to-night."

"Let us stroll all round the garden," she said. "I want you to see it all now it is lit up. And the shrubbery is pretty, too, with--with the filter of starlight coming through the trees. Do tell me truthfully, like a friend, is it going all right? Are they enjoying themselves?"

"Kicking up their heels like two-year-olds," said Major Ames.

"How wicked of you to say that! But really I had one bad moment, when--when the last Cleopatra came in."

She paused a moment. Then in her clear, silky voice--

"Dear old things!" she said.

Now Mrs. Evans was not in any way a clever woman, but had she had the brains and the wit of Cleopatra herself, she could not have spoken three more consummately chosen words. All the cool, instinctive confidence of a younger woman, and a pretty woman speaking of the more elderly and plain was there; there, too, was the deliberate challenge of the coquette. And Major Ames was quite helpless against the simplicity of such art. Mere manners, the ordinary code of politeness, demanded that he should agree with his hostess. Besides, though he was not in any way in love with her, he could not resist the assumption that her words implied, and, after all, she was a pretty woman, whom he had kissed, and he was alone in the star-hung dusk with her.

"Poor dear Amy!" he said.

Millie Evans gave a soft little sigh, as of a contented child. He had expressed with the most ruthless accuracy exactly what she wished him to feel. Then, in the manner of a woman whose nature is warped throughout by a slight but ingrained falsity, she spoke as if it was not she who had prompted the three words which she had almost made him say.

"She is enjoying herself so," she said. "I have never seen Cousin Amy look so thoroughly pleased and contented. I thought she looked so charming, too, and what dear, plump little feet she has. But, my dear, it was rather a surprise when you and she were announced. It looked as if this poor Cleopatra was going to be Antony-less! Dear me, what a word."

Here was a more direct appeal, and again Major Ames was powerless in her soft clutch. Hers was not exactly an iron hand in a velvet glove, but a hand made of fly-catching paper. She had taken her glove off now. And he was beginning to stick to her.

"Pshaw!" he said.

That, again, had a perfectly satisfactory sound to her ears. The very abruptness and bluffness of it pleased her more than any protestation could have done. He was so direct, so shy, so manly.

She laughed softly.

"Hush, you mustn't say those things," she said. "Ah, there is the band beginning, and it is our dance. But let us just walk through the shrubbery before we go back. The dusk and quiet are such a relief after the glare. Lyndhurst--ah, dear me. Cousin Lyndhurst I ought to say--you really must not go home till my little dance is quite finished. You make things go so well. Dear Wilfred is quite useless to me. Does he not look an old darling as Timon of Athens? A sort of mixture between George the Fourth in tights and a lion-tamer."

Mrs. Evans was feeling more actively alive to-night than she had felt for years. Her tongue, which was generally a rather halting adjutant to her glances and little sinuous movements, was almost vivified to wit. Certainly her description of her husband had acuteness and a sense of the ludicrous to inspire it. Through the boughs of laburnums in the shrubbery they could see him now, escorting the tallest and oldest Cleopatra, who was Mrs. Brooks, to the end of the garden. Dimly, through the curtain of intervening gloom, they saw the populous wooden floor that had been laid down on the grass; Mrs. Ames--the dance was a polka--was frankly pirouetting in the arms of a redoubtable Falstaff. Mrs. Altham was wrestling with the Apothecary, and Elsie Evans, one of the few young people present, was vainly trying to galvanize General Fortescue, thinly disguised as Henry VII, into some semblance of activity.

Mrs. Evans gave another sigh, a sigh of curious calibre.

"It all seems so distant," she said. "All the lights and dancing are less real than the shadows and the stillness."

That was not quite extemporaneous; she had thought over something of the sort. It had the effect of making Major Ames feel suddenly hot with an anxious kind of heat. He was beginning to perceive the truth of that which he had foppishly imagined in his own self-communings, namely, that this "poor little lady" was very, very much attached to him. He had often dwelt on the thought before with odious self-centred satisfaction; now the thought was less satisfactory; it was disquieting and mildly alarming. Like the fly on the fly-paper, with one leg already englued, he put down a second to get leverage with which to free the first, and found that it was adhering also.

Mrs. Evans spoke again.

"I took such pleasure in all the preparations." she said. "You were so much interested in it all. Tell me, Cousin Lyndhurst, that you are not disappointed."

It was hardly possible for him to do less than what he did. What he did was little enough. He pressed the arm that lay in his rather close to his white toga, and an unwonted romanticism of speech rose to his lips.

"You have enchanted me," he said. "Me, us, all of us."

She gave a little laugh; in the dusk it sounded no louder than a breeze stirring.

"You needn't have added that," she said.

CHAPTER VII

Where she stood a diaper of light and shadow played over her. A little spray of laburnum between her face and the lights on the lawn outside, swaying gently in a breeze that had gone astray in this calm night, cast wavering shadows over her. Now her arms shone white under freckles of shadow, now it was her face that was a moon to him. Or again, both would be in shade and a diamond star on her bright yellow hair concentrated all the light into itself. All the elusive mysterious charm of her womanhood was there, made more real by the fantastic setting. He was kindled to a greater warmth than he had yet known, but, all the time, some dreadful creature in his semi-puritanical semi-immoral brain, told him that this was all "devilish naughty." He was as unused to such scruples as he was unused to such temptations, and in some curious fashion he felt as ashamed of the one as he felt afraid of the other. At length he summed up the whole of these despicable conclusions.

"Will you give me just one kiss, Millie!" he said; "just one cousin-kiss, before we go and dance?"

Such early worms next morning in Major Ames' garden as had escaped the early bird, must certainly have all been caught and laid out flat by the garden roller, so swift and incessant were its journeyings. For though the dawn had overspread the sky with the hueless tints of approaching day when Antony and Cleopatra were charioteered home again by a somnolent cabman; though Major Ames' repose had been of the most fragmentary kind, and though breakfast, in anticipation of late hours, had been ordered the night before at an unusual half-past nine, he found his bed an intolerable abode by seven o'clock, and had hoped to expatriate somewhat disquieting thoughts from his mind by the application of his limbs to severe bodily exertion.

He and his wife had been the last guests to leave; indeed, after the others had gone they lingered a little, smoking a final cigarette. Even Mrs. Ames had been persuaded to light one, but a convulsive paroxysm of coughing, which made the pear-shaped pearl to quiver and shake like an aspen-leaf, led her to throw it away, saying she enjoyed it very much. He had danced with Mrs. Evans three or four times; three or four times they had sat in the cool darkness of the shrubbery, and he had said to her several things which at the moment it seemed imperative to say, but which he did not really mean. But as the evening went on he had meant them more; she had a helpless, childlike charm about her that began to stir his senses. And yet below that childlike confiding manner he was dimly aware that there was an eager woman's soul that sought him. Her charm was a weapon; a very efficient will wielded it. All the same, he reflected as the honest dews of toil poured from his forehead this morning in the hot early sunlight, he had not said very much . . . he had said that Riseborough was a different place since she--or had he said "they"? had come there; that her eyes looked black in the starlight, that--honestly, he could not remember anything more intimate than this. But that which had made his bed intolerable was the sense that the situation had not terminated last night, that his boat, so to speak, had not been drawn up safely ashore, but was still in the midst of accelerating waters. And yet it was in his own power to draw the boat ashore at any moment; he had but to take a decisive stroke to land, to step out and beach it, to return--surely it was not difficult--to his normal thoughts and activities. For years his garden, his club, his domestic concerns, his daily paper, had provided him with a sufficiency of pursuits; he had but to step back into their safe if monotonous circle, and look upon these disturbances as episodic. But already he had ceased to think of Mrs. Evans as "dear little woman" or "poor little woman"; somehow it seemed as if she had got her finger--to use a prosaic metaphor--into his works. She was prodding about among the internal wheels and springs of his mechanism. Yet that was stating his case too strongly; it was that of contingency that he was afraid. But with the curious irresponsibility of a rather selfish and unimaginative man, the fact that he had allowed himself to prod about in her internal mechanism represented itself to him as an unimportant and negligible detail. It was only when she began prodding about in him, producing, as it were, extraordinary little whirrings and racings of wheels that had long gone slow and steady, that he began to think that anything significant was occurring. But, after all, there was nothing like a pull at the garden roller for giving a fellow an appetite for breakfast and for squashing worms and unprofitable reflections.

Though half-past nine had seemed "late enough for anybody," as Mrs. Ames had said the evening before, it was not till nearly ten that she put an extra spoonful of tea into her silver teapot, for she felt that she needed a more than usually fortifying beverage, to nullify her disinclination for the day's routine. The sight of her Cleopatra costume also, laid upon the sofa in her bedroom, and shone upon by a cheerful and uncompromising summer sun, had awakened in her mind a certain discontent, a certain sense of disappointment, of age, of grievance. The gilt paper had moulted off one of the sandal-straps, a spilt dropping of strawberry-ice made a disfiguring spot on the tunic of Arab shawl, and she herself felt vaguely ungilded and disfigured.

The cigarette, too--she had so often said in the most liberal manner that she did not think it wicked of women to smoke, but only horrid. Certainly she did not feel wicked this morning, but as certainly she felt disposed to consider anybody else horrid, and--and possibly wicked. Decidedly a cup of strong tea was indicated.

Major Ames had gone upstairs again to have his bath, and to dress after his exercise in the garden, and came down a few minutes later, smelling of soap, with a jovial boisterousness of demeanour that smelt of unreality.

"Good-morning, my dear Amy," he said. "And how do you feel after the party? I've been up a couple of hours; nothing like a spell of exercise to buck one up after late hours."

"Will you have your tea now, Lyndhurst?" she asked.

"Have it now, or wait till I get it, eh? I'll have it now. Delicious! I always say that nobody makes tea like you."

Now boisterous spirits at breakfast were not usual with Major Ames, and, as has been said, his wife easily detected a false air about them. Her vague sense of disappointment and grievance began to take more solid outlines.

CHAPTER VII

"It is delightful to see you in such good spirits, Lyndhurst," she observed, with a faint undertone of acidity. "Sitting up late does not usually agree with you."

There was enough here to provoke repartee. Also his superficial boisterousness was rapidly disappearing before his wife's acidity, like stains at the touch of ammonia.

"It does not, in this instance, seem to have agreed with you, my dear," he said. "I hope you have not got a headache. It was unwise of you to stop so late. However, no doubt we shall feel better after breakfast. Shall I give you some bacon? Or will you try something that appears to be fish?"

"A little kedjeree, please," said Mrs. Ames, pointedly ignoring this innuendo on her cook.

"Kedjeree, is it? Well, well, live and learn."

"If you have any complaint to make about Jephson," said she, "pray do so."

"No, not at all. One does not expect, a *cordon bleu.* But I dare say Mrs. Evans pays no more for her cook than we do, and look at the supper last night."

"I thought the quails were peculiarly tasteless," said Mrs. Ames; "and if you are to be grand and have *péches à la Melba,* I should prefer to offer my guests real peaches and proper ice-cream, instead of tinned peaches and custard. I say nothing about the champagne, because I scarcely tasted it."

"Well then, my dear, I'm sure you are quite right not to criticize it. All I can say is that I never want to eat a better supper."

Suddenly Mrs. Ames became aware that another piece of solid outline had appeared round her vague discontent and reaction.

"No doubt you think that all Millie's arrangements are perfect in every way," she observed.

"I don't know what you mean by that," said he, rather hotly; "but I do know that when a woman has been putting herself to all that trouble and expense to entertain her friends, her friends would show a nicer spirit if they refrained from carping and depreciating her."

"No amount of appreciation would make tinned peaches fresh, or turn custard into ice-cream," said Mrs. Ames, laying down the fork with which she had dallied with the kedjeree, which indeed was but a sordid sort of creation. "It is foolish to pretend that a thing is perfect when it is not. Nor do I consider her manners as a hostess by any means perfect. She looked as cross as two sticks when poor Mrs. Brooks appeared. I suppose she thought that nobody had a right to be Cleopatra besides herself. To be sure poor Mrs. Brooks looked very silly, but if everybody who looked silly last night should have stayed away, there would not have been much dancing done."

She took several more sips of the strong tea, while he unfolded and appeared engrossed in the morning paper, and under their stimulating influence saw suddenly and distinctly how ill-advised was her attack. She had yielded to temporary ill-temper, which is always a mistake. It was true that in her mind she was feeling that Lyndhurst last night had spent far too much time with his hostess; in a word, she felt jealous. It was, therefore, abominably stupid, from a merely worldly point of view, to criticize and belittle Millie to him. If there was absolutely no ground for her jealousy--which at present was but a humble little green bud--such an attack was uncalled for; if there was ground it was most foolish, at this stage, at any rate, to give him the least cause for suspecting that it existed. But she was wise enough now, not to hasten to repair her mistake, but to repair it slowly and deliberately, as if no repair was going on at all.

"But I must say the garden looked charming," she said after a pause. "Did she tell you, Lyndhurst, whether it was she or her husband who saw to the lighting? The scheme was so comprehensive; it took in the whole of the lawn; there was nothing patchy about it. I suspect Dr. Evans planned it; it looked somehow more like a man's work."

A look of furtive guilt passed over the Major's face; luckily it was concealed by the *Daily Mail.*

"No; Evans told me himself that he had nothing to do with it," he said. "It was pretty, I thought; very pretty."

"If the nights continue hot," said she, "it would be nice to have the garden illuminated one night, if dear Millie did not think we were appropriating her ideas. I do not think she would; she is above that sort of thing. Well, dear, I must go and order dinner. Have you any wishes?"

Clearly it was wiser, from the Major's point of view, to accept this bouquet of olive branches. After all, Amy was far too sensible to imagine that there could be anything to rouse the conjugal watch-dog. Nor was there; hastily he told himself that. A cousinly kiss, which at the moment he would willingly have foregone.

Certainly last night he had been a little super-stimulated. There was the irresponsibility of fancy dress, there was the knowledge that Millie was not insensitive to him; there was the sense of his own big, shapely legs in tights, there was dancing and lanterns, and all had been potent intoxicants to Riseborough, which for so long had practised teetotalism with regard to such excitements. Amy herself had been so far carried away by this effervescence of gaiety as to smoke a cigarette, and Heaven knew how far removed from her ordinary code of conduct was such an adventure. Generously, he had forborne to brandish that cigarette as a weapon against her during this acrimonious episode at breakfast, and he had no conscious intention of hanging it, like Damocles' sword over her head, in case she pursued her critical and carping course against Millie. But whatever he had said last night, she had done that. Without meaning to make use of his knowledge, he knew it was in his power to do so. What would not Mrs. Altham, for instance, give to be informed by an eye-witness that Mrs. Ames had blown--it was no more than that--on the abhorred weed? So, conscious of a position that he could make offensive at will, he accepted the olive branch, and suggested a cold curry for lunch.

Breakfast at Mrs. Altham's reflected less complicated conditions of mind. Both she and her husband were extremely pleased with themselves, and in a state of passion with regard to everybody else. Since their attitude was typical of the view that Riseborough generally took of last night's festivity, it may be given compendiously in a rhetorical flight of Mrs. Altham's, with which her husband was in complete accord.

In palliation, it may be mentioned that they had both partaken of large quantities of food at an unusual hour. It is through the body that the entry is made by the subtle gateways of the soul, and vitriolic comments in the morning are often the precise equivalent of unusual indulgence the night before.

"Well, I'm sure if I had known," said Mrs. Altham, "I should not have taken the trouble I did. Of course, everybody said 'How lovely your dress is,' simply to make one say the same to them. And I never want to hear the word Cleopatra again, Henry, so pray don't repeat it. Fancy Mrs. Ames appearing as Cleopatra, and us taking the trouble to say we were Antony and Cleopatra ten years later! Twenty years before would have been more the date if we had known. Perhaps I am wrong, but when a woman arrives at Mrs. Ames' time of life, whether she dyes her hair or not, she is wiser to keep her feet concealed, not to mention what she must have looked like in the face of half the tradesmen of Riseborough who were lining the pavements when she stepped out of her cab. I thought I heard a great roar of laughter as we were driving up the High Street; I should not wonder if it was the noise of them all laughing as she got out of her carriage. Of course, it was all very prettily done, as far as poor Mrs. Evans was concerned, but I wonder that Dr. Evans likes her to spend money like that, for, however unsuitable the supper was, I feel sure it was very expensive, for it was all truffles and aspic. There must have been a sirloin of beef in the cup of soup I took between two of the dances, and strong soup like that at dead of night fills one up dreadfully. And Mrs. Brooks appearing as another Cleopatra, after all I had said about Hermione! Well, I'm sure if she chooses to make a silly of herself like that, it is nobody's concern but hers. She looked like nothing so much as a great white mare with the staggers. If you are going up to the club, Henry, I should not wonder if I came out with you. It seems to me a very stuffy morning, and a little fresh air would do me good. As for the big German ruby in your cap, I don't believe a soul noticed it. They were all looking at Mrs. Evans' long white arms. Poor thing, she is probably very anæmic; I never saw such pallor. I saw little of her the whole evening. She seemed to be popping in and out of the shrubbery like a rabbit all the time with Major Ames. I should not wonder if Mrs. Ames was giving him a good talking-to at this moment."

Then, like all the rest of Riseborough, and unlike the scorpion, there was a blessing instead of a sting in her tail.

"But certainly it was all very pretty," she said; "though it all seemed very strange at the time. I can hardly believe this morning that we were all dressed up like that, hopping about out of doors. Fancy dress balls are very interesting; you see so much of human nature, and though I looked the procession up and down, Henry, I saw nobody so well dressed as you. But I suppose there is a lot of jealousy everywhere. And anyhow, Mrs. Evans has quite ousted Mrs. Ames now. Nobody will talk about anything but last night for the next fortnight, and I'm sure that when Mrs. Ames had the conjurer who turned the omelette into the watch, we had all forgotten about it three days afterwards. And after all, Mrs. Evans is a very pleasant and hospitable woman, and I wouldn't have missed that party for anything. If you hear anything at the club about her wanting to sell her Chinese lanterns and fairy-lights second-hand, Henry, or if you find any reason to believe that she had hired them out for the night from the Mercantile Stores, you might ask the price, and if it is reasonable get a couple of dozen. If the weather continues as hot as this we might illuminate the garden when we give our August dinner-party. At least, I suppose Mrs. Evans does not consider that she has a monopoly of lighting up gardens!"

Henry found himself quite in accord with the spirit of this address.

"I will remember, my dear," he said; "if I hear anything said at the club. I shall go up there soon, for I should not be surprised if most of the members spent their morning there. I think I will have another cup of tea."

"You have had two already," said his wife.

He was feeling a little irritable.

"Then this will make three," he observed.

Mrs. Evans, finally, had breakfast in her room. When she came downstairs, she found that her husband had already left the house on his visits, which was a relief. She felt that if she had seen his cheerful smiling face this morning, she would almost have hated it.

She ordered dinner, and then went out into the garden. Workmen were already there, removing the dancing-floor, and her gardener was collecting the fairy-lights in trays, and carrying them indoors. Here and there were charred, burnt places on the grass, and below the mulberry-tree the *débris* of supper had not yet been removed. But the shrubbery, as last night, was sequestered and cool, and she sat for an hour there on the garden bench overlooking the lawn. Little flakes of golden sunlight filtered down through the foliage, and a laburnum, delicate-sprayed, oscillated in the light breeze. She scarcely knew whether she was happy or not, and she gave no thought to that. But she felt more consciously alive than ever before.

CHAPTER VIII

Discussion about the fancy dress ball, as Mrs Altham had said, was paramount over all other topics for at least a fortnight after the event, and the great question which annually became of such absorbing interest during July--namely, as to where to spend August, was dwarfed and never attained to its ordinary proportions till quite late on in the month. These discussions did not, as a rule, bear fruit of any kind, since, almost without exception, everybody spent August exactly where August had been spent by him for the last dozen years or so, but it was clearly wise to consider the problem afresh every year, and be prepared, in case some fresh resort suggested itself, to change the habit of years, or at least to consider doing so. The lists of hotels at the end of Bradshaw, and little handbooks published by the South-Eastern Railway were, as a rule, almost the only form of literature indulged in during these evenings of July, and Mr. Altham, whose imagination was always fired by pictures of ships, often studied the sailings of River Plate steamers, and considered that the fares were very reasonable, especially steerage. The fact that he was an appalling bad sailor in no way diminished the zest with which he studied their sailings and the prices thereof. Subsequently he and Mrs. Altham always spent August at Littlestone-on-Sea, in a completely detached villa called Blenheim, where a capable Scotchwoman, who, to add colour to the illusion, maintained that her name really was Churchill, boarded and lodged them on solid food and feather beds. During July, it may be remarked, Mrs. Altham usually contrived to quarrel with her cook, who gave notice. Thus there was one mouth less to feed while they were away, and yearly, on their return, they had the excitement of new and surprising confections from the kitchen.

Mrs. Ames, it may be remembered, had already enjoyed a fortnight's holiday at Overstrand this year, and the last week of July saw her still disinclined to make holiday plans. They had taken a sort of bungalow near Deal for the last year or two, which, among other advantages, was built in such a manner that any remark made in any part of the house could be heard in any other part of the house. It was enough almost for her to say, as she finished dressing, "We are ready for breakfast," to hear Parker replying from the kitchen, "The kettle's just on the boil, ma'am." This year, however, she had been late in inquiring whether it was vacant for August, and she found, when her belated letter was answered, that it was already engaged.

This fact she broke to her husband and Harry, who had returned from Cambridge with hair unusually wild and lank, with tempered indignation.

"Considering how many years we have taken it," she said, "I must say that I think they should have told us before letting it over our heads like this. But I always thought that Mrs. Mackenzie was a most grasping sort of person who would be likely to take the first offer that turned up, and I'm sure the house was never very comfortable. I have no doubt we can easily find a better without much bother!"

"My bedroom ceiling always leaked," said Harry; "and there was nowhere to write at!"

Mrs. Ames had finished her breakfast and got up. She felt faintly in her mind that after the fancy dress ball it was time for her to do something original. Yet the whole idea was so novel. . . . Riseborough would be sure to say that they had not been able to afford a holiday. But, after all, that mattered very little.

"I really don't know why we always take the trouble to go away to an uncomfortable lodging during August," she said, "and leave our own comfortable house standing vacant."

Major Ames, had he been a horse, would have pricked up his ears at this. But the human ear being unadapted to such movements, he contented himself with listening avidly. He had seen little of Millie this last fortnight, and was beginning to realize how much he missed her presence. Between them, it is true, they had come near to an intimacy which had its dangers, which he really feared more than he desired, but he felt, with that self-deception that comes so easily to those who know nothing about themselves, that he was on his guard now. Meantime, he missed her, and guessed quite truly that she missed him. And, poor prig, he told himself that he had no right to cut off that which gave her pleasure. He could be Spartan over his own affairs, if so minded, but he must not play Lycurgus to others. And an idea that had privately occurred to him, which at the time seemed incapable of realization, suddenly leaped into the possible horizons.

"And you always complain of the dampness of strange houses, Lyndhurst," she added; "and as Harry says, he has no place for writing and study. Why should we go away at all? I am sure, after the excitement of the last month, it would be a complete rest to remain here when everybody else is gone. I have not had a moment to myself this last month, and I should not be at all sorry to stop quietly here."

Major Ames knew with sufficient accuracy the influence he had over his wife. He realized, that is to say, as far as regarded the present instance, that slight opposition on his part usually produced a corresponding firmness on hers. Accentuated opposition produced various results; sometimes he won, sometimes she. But mild remonstrance always confirmed her views in opposition to his. He had a plan of his own on this occasion, and her determination to remain in Riseborough would prove to be in alliance with it. Therefore he mildly remonstrated.

"You would regret it before the month was out," he said. "For me, I'm an old campaigner, and I hope I can make myself comfortable anywhere. But you would get bored before the end of August, Amy, and when you get bored your digestion is invariably affected."

"I should like to stop in Riseborough," said Harry. "I hate the sea."

"You will go wherever your mother settles to go, my boy," said Major Ames, still pursuing his plan. "If she wishes to go to Sheffield for August, you and I will go too, and--and no doubt learn something useful about cutlery. But don't try stopping in Riseborough, my dear Amy. At least, if you take my advice, you won't."

Major Ames was not very intelligent, but the highest intelligence could not have done better. He had learned the trick of slight opposition, just as a stupid dog with a Conservative master can learn to growl for Asquith by incessant repetition. When it has learned it, it does it right. The Major had done it right on this occasion.

"I do not see why Harry should not have a voice in the question of where we spend his vacation," she said. "Certainly your room at the bungalow, Lyndhurst, was comfortable enough, but that was the only decent room in the house. In any case we cannot get the bungalow for this August. Have you any other plans as to where we should go?"

There was room for a little more of his policy of opposition.

"Well, now, Brighton," he said. "Why not Brighton? There's a club there; I dare say I should get a little Bridge in the evening, and no doubt you would pick up some acquaintances, Amy. I think the Westbournes went there last year."

This remarkable reason for going to Brighton made Mrs. Ames almost epigrammatic.

"And then we could go on to Margate," she remarked, "and curry favour there."

"By all means, my dear," said he. "I dare say the curry would be quite inexpensive."

Mrs. Ames opened the door on to the verandah.

"Pray let me know, Lyndhurst," she said, "if you have any serious proposition to make."

It was Major Ames' custom to start work in the garden immediately after breakfast, but this morning he got out one of his large-sized cheroots instead (these conduced to meditation), and established himself in a chair on the verandah. His mental development was not, in most regards, of a very high or complex order, but he possessed that rather rare attainment of being able to sit down and think about one thing to the exclusion of others. With most of us to sit down and think about one thing soon resolves itself into a confused survey of most other things; Major Ames could do better than that, for he could, and on this occasion did exclude all other topics from his mind, and at the end return, so to speak, "bringing his sheaves with him." He had made a definite and reasonable plan.

Harry had communicated the interesting fact of his passion for Mrs. Evans to the Omar Khayyam Club, and was, of course, bound to prosecute his nefarious intrigue. He had already written several galloping lyrics, a little loose in grammar and rhyme, to his enchantress, which he had copied into a small green morocco note-book, the title-page of which he had inscribed as "Dedicated to M. E." This looked a Narcissus-like proceeding to any one who did not remember what Mrs. Evans' initials were. This afternoon, feeling the poetic afflatus blowing a gale within him, but having nothing definite to say, he decided to call on the inspirer of his muse, in order to gather fresh fuel for his fire. Arrayed in a very low collar, which showed the full extent of his rather scraggy neck, and adorned with a red tie, for socialism was no less an orthodoxy in the club than atheistic principles and illicit love, he set secretly out, and had the good fortune to find the goddess alone, and was welcomed with that rather timid, childlike deference that he had found so adorable before.

"But how good of you to come and see me," she said, "when I'm sure you must have so many friends wanting you. I think it is so kind."

Clearly she was timid; she did not know her power. Her eyes were bluer than ever; her hair was of palest gold, "As I remembered her of old," he thought to himself, referring to the evening at the end of June. Indeed, there was a poem dated June 28, rather a daring one.

"The kindness is entirely on your side," he said, "in letting me come, and"--he longed to say--"worship," but did not quite dare--"and have tea with you."

"Dear me, that is a selfish sort of kindness," she said. "Let us go into the garden. I think it was very unkind of you, Mr. Harry, not to come to my dance last week. But of course you Cambridge men have more serious things to think about than little country parties."

"I thought about nothing else but your dance for days," said he; "but my tutor simply refused to let me come down for it. A narrow, pedantic fellow, who I don't suppose ever danced. Tell me about your dress; I like to picture you in a fancy dress."

She could not help appearing to wish to attract. It was as much the fault of the way her head was set on to her neck, of the colour of her eyes, as of her mind.

"Oh, quite a simple white frock," she said; "and a few pearls. They--they wanted me to go as Cleopatra. So silly--me with a grown-up daughter. But my husband insisted."

The fancy dress ball had not been talked about at Mrs. Ames' lately, and he had heard nothing about it in the two days he had been at home. Both his parents had reason for letting it pass into the region of things that are done with.

"Did mother and father go?" he asked. "I suppose they felt too old to dress up?"

"Oh, no. They came as Antony and Cleopatra. Have they not told you? Cousin Amy looked so--so interesting. And your father was splendid as Mark Antony."

"Then was Dr. Evans Mark Antony too?" asked Harry.

"No; he was Timon of Athens."

"Then who was your Mark Antony?" he asked.

CHAPTER VIII

Mrs. Evans felt herself flushing, and her annoyance at herself made her awkward in the pouring out of tea.

She felt that Harry's narrow, gimlet-like eyes were fixed on her.

"See how stupid I am," she said. "I have spilled your tea in the saucer. Dear Mr. Harry, we had heaps of Cleopatras: Mrs. Altham was one, Mrs. Brooks was another. We danced with Hamlets, and--and anybody."

But this crude, ridiculous youth, she felt, had some idea in his head.

"And did father and mother dance together all the evening?" he asked.

She felt herself growing impatient.

"Of course not. Everybody danced with everybody. We had quadrilles; all sorts of things."

Then, with the mistaken instinct that makes us cautious in the wrong place, she determined to say a little more.

"But your father was so kind to me," she said. "He helped me with all the arrangements. I could never have managed it except for him. We had tremendous days of talking and planning about it. Now tell me all about Cambridge."

But Harry was scenting a sonnet of the most remarkable character. It might be called The Rivals, and would deal with a situation which the Omar Khayyam Club would certainly feel to be immensely "parful."

"I suppose mother helped you, too?" he said.

This was Byronic, lacerating. She had to suffer as well as he . . . there was a pungent line already complete. "But who had suffered as much as me?" was the refrain. There were thrills in store for the Omar Khayyam Club. After a sufficiency of yellow wine.

"Cousin Amy was away," said Mrs. Evans. "She was staying at Cromer till just before my little dance. That is not far from Cambridge, is it? I suppose she came over to see you."

Harry spared her, and did not press these questions. But enough had been said to show that she had broken faith with him. "Rivals" could suitably become quite incoherent towards the close. Incoherency was sometimes a great convenience, for exclamatory rhymes were not rare.

He smoothed the lank hair off his forehead, and tactfully changed the subject.

"And I suppose you are soon going away now," he said. "I am lucky to have seen you at all. We are going to stop here all August, I think. My mother does not want to go away. Nor do I; not that they either of them care about that."

Mrs. Evans' slight annoyance with him was suddenly merged in interest.

"How wise!" she said. "It is so absurd to go to stay somewhere uncomfortably instead of remaining comfortably. I wish we were doing the same. But my husband always has to go to Harrogate for a few weeks. And he likes me to be with him. I shall think of you all and envy you stopping here in this charming Riseborough."

"You like it?" asked Harry.

"How should I not with so many delightful people being friendly to me? Relations too; Cousin Amy, for instance, and Major Ames, and, let me see, if Mrs. Ames is my cousin, surely you are cousin Harry?"

Harry became peculiarly fascinating, and craned his long neck forward.

"Oh, leave out the 'cousin,'" he said.

"How sweet of you--Harry," she said.

That, so to speak, extracted the poison-fangs from the projected "Rivals," and six mysterious postcards were placed by the author's hand in the pillar-box that evening. Each consisted of one mystic sentence. "She calls me by my Christian name." By a most convenient circumstance, too apt to be considered accidental, there had here come to birth an octosyllabic line, of honeyed sweetness and simplicity. He was not slow to take advantage of it, and the moon setting not long before daybreak saw another completed gem of the M. E. series.

Mrs. Evans that afternoon, like Major Ames that morning, "sat and thought," after Harry had left her. Independently of the fact that all admirers, even the weirdest, always found welcome in her pale blue eyes, she felt really grateful to Harry, for he had given her the information on which she based a plan which was quite as sound and simple as Major Ames', and was designed to secure the same object. Since the night of the fancy dress ball she had only seen him once or twice, and never privately, and the greater vitality which, by the wondrous processes of affinity, he had stirred in her, hungered for its sustenance. It cannot be said that she was even now really conscious in herself of disloyalty to her husband, or that she actually contemplated any breach of faith. She had not at present sufficient force of feeling to imagine a decisive situation; but she could at most lash her helm, so to speak, so that the action of the wind would take her boat in the direction in which she wished to go, and then sit idly on deck, saying that she was not responsible for the course she was pursuing. The wind, the tide, the currents were irresistibly impelling her; she had nothing to do with the rudder, having tied it, she did not touch it. Like the majority in this world of miserable sinners, she did not actively court the danger she desired, but she hung about expectant of it. At the same time she kept an anxious eye on the shore towards which she was driving. Was it really coming closer? If so, why did she seem to have made no way lately?

To-day her plan betokened a more active hand in what she thought of as fate, but unfortunately, though it was as sound in itself as Major Ames', it was made independently and ignorantly of that which had prompted his slight opposition this morning, so that, while each plan was admirable enough in itself, the two, taken in conjunction, would, if successful, result in a fiasco almost sublime in its completeness. The manner of which was as follows.

Elsie, it so happened, was not at home that evening, and she and her husband dined alone, and strolled out in the garden afterwards.

"You will miss your chess this evening, dear," she said. "Or would it amuse you to give me a queen and a few bishops and knights, and see how long it takes you to defeat me? Or shall we spend a little cosy chatty evening together? I hope no horrid people will be taken ill, and send for you."

"So do I, little woman," he said (she was getting to detest the appellation). "And as if I shouldn't enjoy a quiet evening of talk with you more than fifty games of chess! But, dear me, I shall be glad to get away to Harrogate this year! I need a month of it badly. I shall positively enjoy the foul old rotten-egg smell."

She gave a little shudder.

"Oh, don't talk of it," she said. "It is bad enough without thinking of it beforehand."

"Poor little woman! Almost a pity you are not gouty too. Then we should both look forward to it."

She sat down on one of the shrubbery seats, and drew aside her skirts, making room for him to sit beside her.

"Yes, but as I am not gouty, Wilfred," she said. "It is no use wishing I was. And I do hate Harrogate so. I wonder--"

She gave a little sigh and put her arm within his.

"Well, what's the little woman wondering now?" he asked.

"I hardly like to tell you. You are always so kind to me that I don't know why I am afraid. Wilfred, would you think it dreadful of me, if I suggested not going with you this year? I'm sure it makes me ill to be there. You will have Elsie; you will play chess as usual with her all evening. You see all morning you are at your baths, and you usually are out bicycling all afternoon with her. I don't think you know how I hate it."

She had begun in her shy, tentative manner. But her voice grew more cold and decided. She put forward her arguments like a woman who has thought it all carefully over, as indeed she had.

"But what will you do with yourself, my dear?" he said. "It seems a funny plan. You can't stop here alone."

She sat up, taking her hand from his arm.

"Indeed, I should not be as lonely here as I am at Harrogate," she said. "We don't know anybody there, and if you think of it, I am really alone most of the time. It is different for you, because it is doing you good, and, as I say, you are bicycling with Elsie all the afternoon, and you play chess together in the evening."

A shade of trouble and perplexity came over the doctor's face; the indictment, for it was hardly less than that, was as well-ordered and digested as if it had been prepared for a forensic argument. And the calm, passionless voice went on.

"Think of my day there," she said, going into orderly detail. "After breakfast you go off to your baths, and I have to sit in that dreadful sitting-room while they clear the things away. Even a hotel would be more amusing than those furnished lodgings; one could look at the people going in and out. Or if I go for a stroll in the morning, I get tired, and must rest in the afternoon. You come in to lunch, and go off with Elsie afterwards. That is quite right; the exercise is good for you, but what is the use of my being there? There is nobody for me to go to see, nobody comes to see me. Then we have dinner, and I have the excitement of learning where you and Elsie have been bicycling. You two play chess after dinner, and I have the excitement of being told who has won. Here, at any rate, I can sit in a room that doesn't smell of dinner, or I can sit in the garden. I have my own books and things about me, and there are people I know whom I can see and talk to."

He got up, and began walking up and down the path in front of the bench where they had been sitting, his kindly soul in some perplexity.

"Nothing wrong, little woman?" he asked.

"Certainly not. Why should you think that? I imagine there is reason enough in what I have told you. I do get so bored there, Wilfred. And I hate being bored. I am sure it is not good for me, either. Try to picture my life there, and see how utterly different it is from yours. Besides, as I say, it is doing you good all the time, and as you yourself said, you welcome the thought of that horrible smelling water."

He still shuffled up and down in the dusk. That, too, got on her nerves.

"Pray sit down, Wilfred," she said. "Your walking about like that confuses me. And surely you can say 'Yes' or 'No' to me. If you insist on my going with you, I shall go. But I shall think it very unreasonable of you."

"But I can't say 'Yes' or 'No' like that, little woman," he said. "I don't imagine you have thought how dull Riseborough will be during August. Everybody goes away, I believe."

For a moment she thought of telling him that the Ames' were going to stop here: then, with entirely misplaced caution, she thought wiser to keep that to herself. She, guilty in the real reason for wishing to remain here, though coherent and logical enough in the account she had given him of her reason, thought, grossly wronging him, that some seed of suspicion might hereby enter her husband's mind.

"There is sure to be some one here," she said. "The Althams, for instance, do not go away till the middle of August."

"You do not particularly care for them," said he.

"No, but they are better than nobody. All day at Harrogate I have nobody. It is not companionship to sit in the room with you and Elsie playing chess. Besides, the Westbournes will be at home. I shall go over there a great deal, I dare say. Also I shall be in my own house, which is comfortable, and which I am fond of. Our lodgings at Harrogate disgust me. They are all oilcloth and plush; there is nowhere to sit when they are clearing away."

His face was still clouded.

"But it is so odd for a married woman to stop alone like that," he said.

"I think it is far odder for her husband to want her to spend a month of loneliness and boredom in lodgings," she said. "Because I have never complained, Wilfred, you think I haven't detested it. But on thinking it over it seems to me more sensible to tell you how I detest it, and ask you that I shouldn't go."

He was silent a moment.

"Very well, little woman," he said at length. "You shall do as you please."

CHAPTER VIII

Instantly the cold precision of her speech changed. She gave that little sigh of conscious content with which she often woke in the morning, and linked her arm into his again.

"Ah, that is dear of you," she said. "You are always such a darling to me."

He was not a man to give grudging consents, or spoil a gift by offering it except with the utmost cordiality.

"I only hope you'll make a great success of it, little woman," he said. "And it must be dull for you at Harrogate. So that's settled, and we're all satisfied. Let us see if Elsie has come in yet."

She laughed softly.

"You are a dear," she said again.

Wilfred Evans was neither analytical regarding himself nor curious about analysis that might account for the action of others. Just as in his professional work he was rather old-fashioned, but eminently safe and sensible, so in the ordinary conduct of his life he did not seek for abstruse causes and subtle motives. It was quite enough for him that his wife felt that she would be excruciatingly bored at Harrogate, and less acutely desolate here. On the other hand, it implied violation of one of the simplest customs of life that a wife should be in one place and her husband in another. That was vaguely disquieting to him. Disquieting also was the cold, precise manner with which she had conducted her case. A dozen times only, perhaps, in all their married life had she assumed this frozen rigidity of demeanour; each time he had succumbed before it. In the ordinary way, if their inclinations were at variance, she would coax and wheedle him into yielding or, though quietly adhering to her own opinion, she would let him have his way. But with her calm rigidity, rarely assumed, he had never successfully combated; there was a steeliness about it that he knew to be stronger than any opposition he could bring to it. Nothing seemed to affect it, neither argument nor conjugal command. She would go on saying "I do not agree with you," in the manner of cool water dripping on a stone. Or with the same inexorable quietness she would repeat, "I feel very strongly about it: I think it very unkind of you." And a sufficiency of that always had rendered his opposition impotent: her will, when once really aroused, seemed to paralyse his. Once or twice her line had turned out conspicuously ill. That seemed to make no difference: the cold, precise manner was on higher plane than the material failure which had resulted therefrom. She would merely repeat, "But it was the best thing to do under the circumstances."

In this instance he wondered a little that she had used this manner over a matter that seemed so little vital as the question of Harrogate, but by next morning he had ceased to concern himself further with it. She was completely her usual self again, and soon after breakfast set off to accomplish some little errands in the town, looking in on him in his laboratory to know if there were any commissions she could do for him. His eye at the moment was glued to his microscope: a culture of staphylococcus absorbed him, and without looking up, he said--

"Nothing, thanks, little woman."

He heard her pause: then she came across the room to him, and laid her cool hand on his shoulder.

"Wilfred, you are such a dear to me," she said. "You're not vexed with me?"

He interrupted his observations, and put his arm round her.

"Vexed?" he said. "I'll tell you when I'm vexed."

She smiled at him, dewily, timidly.

"That's all right, then," she said.

So her plan was accomplished.

The affair of the staphylococcus did not long detain the doctor, and presently after Major Ames was announced. He had come to consult Dr. Evans with regard to certain gouty symptoms into which the doctor inquired and examined.

"There's nothing whatever to worry about," he said, after a very short investigation. "I should recommend you to cut off alcohol entirely, and not eat meat more than once a day. A fortnight's dieting will probably cure you. And take plenty of exercise. I won't give you any medicine. There is no use in taking drugs when you can produce the same effect by not taking other things."

Major Ames fidgeted and frowned a little.

"I was thinking," he said at length, "of taking myself more thoroughly in hand than that. I've never approved of half-measures, and I can't begin now. If a tooth aches have it out, and be done with it. No fiddling about for me. Now my wife does not want to go away this August, and it seemed to me that it would be a very good opportunity for me to go, as you do, I think, and take a course of waters. Get rid of the tendency, don't you know, eradicate it. What do you say to that? Harrogate now; I was thinking of Harrogate, if you approved. Harrogate does wonders for gout, does it not?"

The doctor laughed.

"I am certainly hoping that Harrogate will do wonders for me," he said. "I go there every year. And no doubt many of us who are getting on in years would be benefited by it. But your symptoms are very slight. I think you will soon get rid of them if you follow the course I suggest."

But Major Ames showed a strange desire for Harrogate.

"Well, I like to do things thoroughly," he said. "I like getting rid of a thing root and branch, you know. You see I may not get another opportunity. Amy likes me to go with her on her holiday in August, but there is no reason why I should stop in Riseborough. I haven't spoken to her yet, but if I could say that you recommended Harrogate, I'm sure she would wish me to go. Indeed, she would insist on my going. She is often anxious about my gouty tendencies, more anxious, as I often tell her, than she has any need to be. But an aunt of hers had an attack which went to her heart quite unexpectedly, and killed her, poor thing. I think, indeed, it would be a weight off Amy's mind if she knew I was going to take myself thoroughly in hand, not tinker and peddle about with diet only. So would you be able to recommend me to go to Harrogate?"

"A course of Harrogate wouldn't be bad for any of us who eat a good dinner every night," said Dr. Evans. "But I think that if you tried--"

CHAPTER VIII

Major Ames got up, waving all further discussion aside.

"That's enough, doctor," he said. "If it would do me good, I know Amy would wish me to go; you know what wives are. Now I'm pressed for time this morning, and so I am sure are you. By the way, you needn't mention my plan till I've talked it over with Amy. But about lodgings, now. Do you recommend lodgings or an hotel?"

Dr. Evans did not mention that his wife was not going to be with him this year, for, having obtained permission to say that Harrogate would do him good, Major Ames had developed a prodigious hurry, and a few moments after was going jauntily home, with the address of Dr. Evans' lodgings in his pocket. He trusted to his own powers of exaggeration to remove all possible opposition on his wife's part, and felt himself the devil of a diplomatist.

So his plan was arranged.

The third factor in this network of misconceived plots occurred the same morning. Mrs. Ames, visiting the High Street on account of an advanced melon, met Cousin Millie on some similar errand to the butcher's on account of advanced cutlets, for the weather was trying. It was natural that she announced her intention of remaining in Riseborough with her family during August: it was natural also that Cousin Millie signified the remission from Harrogate. Cousin Amy was cordial on the subject, and returned home. Probably she would have mentioned this fact to her husband, if he had given her time to do it. But he was bursting with a more immediate communication.

"I didn't like to tell you before, Amy," he said, "because I didn't want to make you unnecessarily anxious. And there's no need for anxiety now."

Mrs. Ames was not very imaginative, but it occurred to her that the newly-planted magnolia had not been prospering.

"No real cause for anxiety," he said. "But the fact is that I went to see Dr. Evans this morning--don't be frightened, my dear--and got thoroughly overhauled by him, thoroughly overhauled. He said there was no reason for anxiety, assured me of it. But I'm gouty, my dear, there's no doubt of it, and of course you remember about your poor Aunt Harriet. Well, there it is. And he says Harrogate. A bore, of course, but Harrogate. But no cause for anxiety: he told me so twice."

Mrs. Ames gave one moment to calm, clear, oysterlike reflection, unhurried, unalarmed. There was no shadow of reason why she should tell him what Mrs. Evans' plans were. But it was odd that she should suddenly decide to stop in Riseborough, instead of going to Harrogate, having heard from Harry that the Ames' were to remain at home, and Lyndhurst as suddenly be impelled to go to Harrogate, instead of stopping in Riseborough. A curious coincidence. Everybody seemed to be making plans. At any rate she would not add to their number, but only acquiesce in those which were made.

"My dear Lyndhurst, what an upset!" she said. "Of course, if you tell me there is no cause for anxiety, I will not be anxious. Does Dr. Evans recommend you to go to Harrogate now? You must tell me all he said. They always go in August, do they not? That will be pleasant for you. But I am afraid you will find the waters far from palatable."

Major Ames felt that he had not made a sufficiently important impression.

"Of course, I told Dr. Evans I could decide nothing till I had consulted you," he said. "It seems a great break-up to leave you and Harry here and go away like this. It was that I was thinking of, not whether waters are palatable or not. I have more than half a mind not to go. I daresay I shall worry through all right without."

Again Mrs. Ames made a little pause.

"You must do as Dr. Evans tells you to do," she said. "I am sure he is not faddy or fussy."

Major Ames' experience of him this morning fully endorsed this. Certainly he had been neither, whatever the difference between the two might be.

"Well, my dear, if both you and Dr. Evans are agreed," he said, "I mustn't set myself up against you."

"Now did he tell you where to go?"

"He gave me the address of his own lodgings."

"What a convenient arrangement! Now, my dear, I beg you to waste no time. Send off a telegram, and pay the reply, and we'll pack you off to-morrow. I am sure it is the right thing to do."

A sudden conviction, painfully real, that he was behaving currishly, descended on Major Ames. The feeling was so entirely new to him that he would have liked to put it down to an obsession of gout in a new place--the conscience, for instance, for he could hardly believe that he should be self-accused of paltry conduct. He felt as if there must be some mistake about it. He almost wished that Amy had made difficulties; then there would have been the compensatory idea that she was behaving badly too. But she could not have conducted herself in a more guilelessly sympathetic manner; she seemed to find no inherent improbability in Dr. Evans having counselled Harrogate, no question as to the advisability of following his advice. It was almost unpleasant to him to have things made so pleasant.

But then this salutary impression was effaced, for anything that savoured of self-reproach could not long find harbourage in his mind. Instead, he pictured himself at Harrogate station, welcoming the Evans'. She would probably be looking rather tired and fragile after the journey, but he would have a cab ready for her, and tea would be awaiting them when they reached the lodgings. . . .

CHAPTER IX

A week later Mrs. Ames was sitting at breakfast, with Harry opposite her, expecting the early post, and among the gifts of the early post a letter from her husband. He had written one very soon after his arrival at Harrogate, saying that he felt better already. The waters, as Amy had conjectured, could not be described as agreeable, since their composition chiefly consisted of those particular ingredients which gave to rotten eggs their characteristic savour, but what, so said the valiant, did a bad taste in the mouth matter, if you knew it was doing you good? An excellent band encouraged the swallowing of this disagreeable fluid, and by lunch-time baths and drinking were over for the day. He was looking forward to the Evans' arrival; it would be pleasant to see somebody he knew. He would write again before many days.

The post arrived; there was a letter for her in the Major's large sprawling handwriting, and she opened it. But it was scarcely a letter: a blister of expletives covered the smoking pages . . . and the Evans'--two of them--had arrived.

Mrs. Ames' little toadlike face seldom expressed much more than a ladylike composure, but had Harry been watching his mother he might have thought that a shade of amusement hovered there.

"A letter from your father," she said. "Rather a worried letter. The cure is lowering, I believe, and makes you feel out of sorts."

Harry was looking rather yellow and dishevelled. He had sat up very late the night before, and the chase for rhymes had been peculiarly fatiguing and ineffectual.

"I don't feel at all well, either," he said. "And I don't think Cousin Millie is well."

"Why?" asked Mrs. Ames composedly.

"I went to see her yesterday and she didn't attend. She seemed frightfully surprised to hear that father had gone to Harrogate."

"I suppose Dr. Evans had not told her," remarked Mrs. Ames. "Please telephone to her after breakfast, Harry, and ask her to dine with us this evening."

"Yes. How curious women are! One day they seem so glad to see you, another you are no more to them than foam on a broken wave."

This was one of the fragments of last night.

"On a broken what?" asked Mrs. Ames. The rustling of the turning leaf of the *Morning Post* had caused her not to hear. There was no sarcastic intention in her inquiry.

"It does not matter," said Harry.

His mother looked up at him.

"I should take a little dose, dear," she said, "if you feel like that. The heat upsets us all at times. Will you please telephone now, Harry? Then I shall know what to order for dinner."

Mrs. Ames' nature was undeniably a simple one; she had no misty profundities or curious dim-lit clefts on the round, smooth surface of her life, but on occasion simple natures are capable of curious complexities of feeling, the more elusive because they themselves are unable to register exactly what they do feel. Certainly she saw a connection between the non-arrival of dear Millie at Harrogate and the inflamed letter from her husband. She had suspected also a connection between dear Millie's decision to spend August at Riseborough and her belief that Major Ames was going to do so too. But the completeness of the fiasco sucked the sting out of the resentment she might otherwise have felt: it was impossible to be angry with such sorry conspirators. At the same time, with regard to her husband, she felt the liveliest internal satisfaction at his blistering communication, and read it through again. The thought of her own slighted or rather unperceived rejuvenescence added point to this; she felt that he had been "served out." Not for a moment did she suspect him of anything but the most innocent of flirtations, and she was disposed to credit dear Millie with having provoked such flirtation as there was. By this time also it must have been quite clear to both the thwarted parties that she was in full cognizance of their futile designs; clearly, therefore, her own *beau rôle* was to appear utterly unconscious of it all, and, unconsciously, to administer nasty little jabs to each of them with a smiling face. "They have been making sillies of themselves," expressed her indulgent verdict on the whole affair. Then in some strange feminine way she felt a sort of secret pride in her husband for having had the manhood to flirt, however mildly, with somebody else's wife; but immediately there followed the resentment that he had not shown any tendency to flirt with his own, when she had encouraged him. But, anyhow, he had chosen the prettiest woman in Riseborough, and he was the handsomest man.

But her mood changed; the thought at any rate of administering some nasty little jabs presented itself in a growingly attractive light. The two sillies had been wanting to dance to their own tune; they should dance to hers instead, and by way of striking up her own tune at once she wrote as follows, to her husband.

> "MY DEAREST LYNDHURST,"I can't tell you how glad I was to get your two letters, and to know how much good Harrogate is doing you. What an excellent thing that you went to Dr. Evans (please remember me to him), and that he insisted so strongly on your taking yourself thoroughly in hand."

CHAPTER IX

She paused a moment, wondering exactly how strong this insistence had been. It was possible that it was not very strong. So much the more reason for letting the sentence stand. She now underlined the words "so strongly."

> "Of course the waters are disgusting to take, and I declare I can almost smell them when I read your vivid description, but, as you said in your first letter, what is a bad taste in the mouth when you know it is doing you good? And your second letter convinces me how right you were to go, and when things like gout begin to come out, it naturally makes you feel a little low and worried. I want you to stop there the whole of August, and get thoroughly rid of it. "Here we are getting along very happily, and I am so glad I did not go to the sea. Millie is here, as you will know, and we see a great deal of her. She is constantly dropping in, *en fille,* I suppose you would call it, and is in excellent spirits and looks so pretty. But I am not quite at ease about Harry (this is private). He is very much attracted by her, and she seems to me not very wise in the way she deals with him, for she seems to be encouraging him in his silliness. Perhaps I will speak to her about it, and yet I hardly like to."

Again Mrs. Ames paused: she had no idea she had such a brilliant touch in the administration of these jabs. What she said might not be strictly accurate, but it was full of point.

> "I remember, too, what you said, that it was so good for a boy to be taken up with a thoroughly nice woman, and that it prevented his getting into mischief, I am sure Harry is writing all sorts of poems to her, because he sighs a great deal, and has a most inky forefinger, for which I give him pumice-stone. But if she were not so nice a woman, and so far from anything like flirtatiousness, I should feel myself obliged to speak to Harry and warn him. She seems very happy and cheerful. I daresay she feels like me, and is rejoiced to think that Harrogate is doing her husband good. "Write to me soon again, my dear, and give me another excellent account of yourself. Was it not queer that you settled to go to Harrogate just when Millie settled not to? If you were not such good friends, one would think you wanted to avoid each other! Well, I must stop. Millie is dining with us, and I must order dinner."

She read through what she had written with considerable content. "That will be nastier than the Harrogate waters," she thought to herself, "and quite as good for him." And then, with a certain largeness which lurked behind all her littlenesses, she practically dismissed the whole silly business from her mind. But she continued the use of the purely natural means for restoring the colour of the hair, and tapped and dabbed the corners of her eyes with the miraculous skin-food. That was a prophylactic measure; she did not want to appear "a fright" when Lyndhurst came back from Harrogate.

Mrs. Ames was well aware that the famous fancy dress ball had caused her a certain loss of prestige in her capacity of queen of society in Riseborough. It had followed close on the heels of her innovation of asking husbands and wives separately to dinner, and had somewhat taken the shine out of her achievement, and indeed this latter had not been as epoch-making as she had expected. For the last week or two she had felt that something new was required of her, but as is often the case, she found that the recognition of such a truth does not necessarily lead to the discovery of the novelty. Perhaps the paltriness of Lyndhurst's conduct, leading to reflections on her own superior wisdom, put her on the path, for about this time she began to take a renewed interest in the Suffragette movement which, from what she saw in the papers, was productive of such adventurous alarums in London. For herself, she was essentially law-abiding by nature, and though, in opposition to Lyndhurst, sympathetically inclined to women who wanted the vote, she had once said that to throw stones at Prime Ministers was unladylike in itself, and only drew on the perpetrators the attention of the police to themselves, rather than the attention of the public to the problem. But a recrudescence of similar acts during the last summer had caused her to wonder whether she had said quite the last word on the subject, or thought the last thought. Certainly the sensational interest in such violent acts had led her to marvel at the strength of feeling that prompted them. Ladies, apparently, whose breeding--always a word of potency with Mrs. Ames--she could not question, were behaving like hooligans. The matter interested her in itself apart from its possible value as a novelty for the autumn. Also an election was probably to take place in November. Hitherto that section of Riseborough in which she lived had not suffered its tranquillity to be interrupted by political excitements, but like a man in his sleep, drowsily approved a Conservative member. But what if she took the lead in some political agitation, and what if she introduced a Suffragette element into the election? That was a solider affair than that a quantity of Cleopatras should skip about in a back garden.

She had always felt a certain interest in the movement, but it was the desire to make a novelty for the autumn, peppered, so to speak, by an impatience at the futile treachery of her husband's Harrogate plans, and an ambition to take a line of her own in opposition to him, that presented their crusade in a serious light to her. The militant crusaders she had hitherto regarded as affected by a strange lunacy, and her husband's masculine comment, "They ought to be well smacked, by Jove!" had had the ring of common-sense, especially since he added, for the benefit of such crusaders as were of higher social rank, "They're probably mad, poor things."

But during this tranquil month of August her more serious interest was aroused, and she bought, though furtively, such literature in the form of little tracts and addresses as was accessible on the subject. And slowly, though still the desire for an autumn novelty that would eclipse the memory of the congregations of Cleopatras was a moving force in her mind, something of the real ferment began to be yeasty within her, and she learned by private inquiry what the Suffragette colours were. Naturally the introduction of an abstract idea into her mind was a laborious process, since her life had for years consisted of an endless chain of small concrete events, and had been lived among people who had never seen an abstract idea wild, any more than they had seen an elephant in a real jungle. It was always tamed and eating buns, as in the Zoo, just as other ideas reached them peptonized by the columns of daily papers. But a wild thing lurked behind the obedient trunk; a wild thing lurked behind the reports of ludicrous performances in the Palace Yard at Westminster.

August was still sultry, and Major Ames was still at Harrogate, when one evening she and Harry dined with Millie. Since nothing of any description happened in Riseborough during this deserted month, the introductory discussion of what events had occurred since they last met in the High Street that morning was not possible of great expansion. None of them had seen the aeroplane which was believed to have passed over the town in the afternoon, and nobody had heard from Mrs. Altham. Then Mrs. Ames fired the shot which was destined to involve Riseborough in smoke and brimstone.

"Lyndhurst and I," she said, "have never agreed about the Suffragettes, and now that I know something about them, I disagree more than ever."

Millie looked slightly shocked: she thought of Suffragettes as she thought of the persons who figure in police news. Indeed, they often did. She knew they wanted to vote about something, but that was practically all she knew except that they expressed their desire to vote by hitting people.

"I know nothing about them," she said. "But are they not very unladylike?"

"They are a disgrace to their sex," said Harry. "We soon made them get out of Cambridge! They tried to hold a meeting in the backs, but I and a few others went down there, and--well, there wasn't much more heard of them. I don't call them women at all. I call them females."

Mrs. Ames had excellent reasons for suspecting romance in her son's account of his exploits.

"Tell me exactly what happened in the backs at Cambridge, Harry," she said.

Harry slightly retracted.

"There is nothing much to tell," he said. "Our club felt bound to make a protest, and we went down there, as I said. It seemed to cow them a bit!"

"And then did the proctors come and cow you?" asked his inexorable mother.

"I believe a proctor did come; I did not wait for that. They made a perfect fiasco, anyhow. They told me it was all a dead failure, and we heard no more about it."

"So that was all?" said Mrs. Ames.

"And quite enough. I agree with father. They disgrace their sex!"

"My dear, you know as little about it as your father," she said.

"But surely a man's judgment--" said Millie, making weak eyes at Harry.

"Dear Millie, a man's judgment is not of any value, if he does not know anything about what he is judging. We have all read accounts in the papers, and heard that they are very violent and chain themselves up to inconvenient places like railings, and are taken away by policemen. Sometimes they slap the policemen, but surely there must be something behind that makes them like that. I am finding out what it is. It is all most interesting. They say that they have to pay their rates and taxes, but get no privileges. If a man pays rates and taxes he gets a vote, and why shouldn't a woman? It is all very well expressed. They seem to me to reason just as well as a man. I mean to find out much more about it all. Personally I don't pay rates and taxes, because that is Lyndhurst's affair, but if we had arranged differently and I paid for the house and the rates and taxes, why shouldn't I have a vote instead of him? And from what I can learn the gardener has a vote, just the same as Lyndhurst, although Lyndhurst does all the garden-rolling, and won't let Parkins touch the flowers."

Mrs. Evans sighed.

"It all seems very confused and upside down," she said. "Do smoke, Harry, if you feel inclined. Will you have a cigarette, Cousin Amy? I am afraid I have none. I never smoke."

Harry was a little sore from his mother's handling, and was not unwilling to hit back.

"I never knew mother smoked," he said. "Do you smoke, mother? How delightful! How Eastern! I never knew you were Eastern. I always thought you said it was not wicked for women to smoke, but only horrid. Do be horrid. I am sure Suffragettes smoke."

Mrs. Ames turned a swift appealing eye on Millie, entreating confidence. Then she lied.

"Dear Millie, what are you thinking of?" she said. "Of course I never smoke, Harry."

But the appeal of the eyes had not taken effect.

"But on the night of my little dance, Cousin Amy," she said, "surely you had a cigarette. It made you cough, and you said how nice it was!"

Mrs. Ames wished she had not been so ruthless about the Suffragettes at Cambridge.

"There is a great difference between doing a thing once," she said, "and making a habit of it. I think I did want to see what it was like, but I never said it was nice, and as for its being Eastern, I am sure I am glad to belong to the West. I always thought it unfeminine, and then I knew it. I did not feel myself again till I had brushed my teeth and rinsed my mouth. Now, dear Millie, I am really interested in the Suffragettes. Their demands are reasonable, and if we are unreasonable about granting them, they must be unreasonable too. For years they have been reasonable and nobody has paid any attention to them. What are they to do but be violent, and call attention to themselves? It is all so well expressed; you cannot fail to be interested."

CHAPTER IX

"Wilfred would never let me hit a policeman," said Millie. "And I don't think I could do it, even if he wanted me to."

"But it is not the aim of the movement to hit policemen," said Mrs. Ames. "They are very sorry to have to--"

"They are sorrier afterwards," said Harry.

Mrs. Ames turned a small, withering eye upon her offspring.

"If you had waited to hear what they had to say instead of running away before the proctor came," she said, "you might have learnt a little about them, dear. They are not at all sorry afterwards; they go to prison quite cheerfully, in the second division, too, which is terribly uncomfortable. And many of them have been brought up as luxuriously as any of us."

"I could not go to prison," said Mrs. Evans faintly, but firmly. "And even if I could, it would be very wrong of me, for I am sure it would injure Wilfred's practice. People would not like to go to a doctor whose wife had been in prison. She might have caught something. And Elsie would be so ashamed of me."

Mrs. Ames gave the suppressed kind of sigh which was habitual with her when Lyndhurst complained that the water for his bath was not hot, although aware that the kitchen boiler was being cleaned.

"But you need not go to prison in order to be a Suffragette, dear Millie," she said. "Prison life is not one of the objects of the movement."

Mrs. Evans looked timidly apologetic.

"I didn't know," she said. "It is so interesting to be told. I thought all the brave sort went to prison, and had breakfast together when they were let out. I am sure I have read about their having breakfast together."

A faint smile quivered on her mouth. She was aware that Cousin Amy thought her very stupid, and there was a delicate pleasure in appearing quite idiotic like this. It made Cousin Amy dance with irritation in her inside, and explain more carefully yet.

"Yes, dear Millie," she said, "but their having breakfast together has not much to do with their objects--"

"I don't know about that," said Harry; "there is a club at Cambridge to which I belong, whose object is to dine together."

"Then it is very greedy of you, dear," said Mrs. Ames, "and the Suffragettes are not like that. They go to prison and do all sorts of unladylike things for the sake of their convictions. They want to be treated justly. For years they have asked for justice, and nobody has paid the least attention to them; now they are making people attend. I assure you that until I began reading about them, I had very little sympathy with them. But now I feel that all women ought to know about them. Certainly what I have read has opened my eyes very much, and there are a quantity of women of very good family indeed who belong to them."

Harry pulled his handkerchief out of the sleeve of his dress-coat; he habitually kept it there. Just now the Omar Khayyam Club was rather great on class distinctions.

"I do not see what that matters," he said. "Because a man's great-grandmother was created a duchess for being a king's mistress--"

Mrs. Evans and Mrs. Ames got up simultaneously; if anything Mrs. Ames got up a shade first.

"I do not think we need go into that, Harry," said Mrs. Ames.

Millie tempered the wind.

"Will you join us soon, Harry?" she said. "If you are too long I shall come and fetch you. We have been political to-night! Will it be too cold for you in the garden, Cousin Amy?"

Left to himself, Harry devoted several minutes' pitiful reflection to his mother's state of mind. In spite of her awakened interest in the Suffragette movement, she seemed to him deplorably old-fashioned. But with his second glass of port his thoughts assumed a rosier tone, and he determined to wait till Cousin Millie came to fetch him. Surely she meant him to do that: no doubt she wanted to have just one private word with him. She had often caught his eye during dinner, with a deprecating look, as if to say this tiresome rigmarole about Suffragettes was not her fault. He felt they understood each other. . . .

There was a large Chippendale looking-glass above the sideboard, and he got up from the table and observed the upper part of his person which was reflected in it. A wisp of hair fell over his forehead; it might more rightly be called a plume. He appeared to himself to have a most interesting face, uncommon, arresting. He was interestingly and characteristically dressed, too, with a collar Byronically low, a soft frilled shirt, and in place of a waistcoat a black cummerbund. Then hastily he mounted on a chair in order to see the whole of his lean figure that seemed so slender. It was annoying that at this moment of critical appreciation a parlour-maid should look in to see if she could clear away. . . .

There is nothing that so confirms individualism in any character as periods of comparative solitude. In men such confirmation is liable to be checked by the boredom to which their sex is subject, but women, less frequently the prey of this paralysing emotion, when the demands made upon them by household duties and domestic companionship are removed, enter very swiftly into the kingdoms of themselves. This process was very strongly at work just now with Millie Evans; superficially, her composure and meaningless smoothness were unaltered, so that Mrs. Ames, at any rate, almost wondered whether she had been right in crediting her with any hand in the Harrogate plans, so unruffled was her insipid and deferential cordiality, but down below she was exploring herself and discovering a capacity for feeling that astonished her by its intensity. All her life she had been content to arouse emotion without sharing it, liking to see men attentive to her, liking to see them attracted by her and disposed towards tenderness. They were more interesting like that, and she gently basked in the warmth of their glow, like a lizard on the wall. She had not wanted more than that; she was lizard, not vampire, and to sun herself on the wall, and then glide gently into a crevice again, seemed quite sufficient exercise for her emotions. Luckily or unluckily (those who hold that calm and complete respectability is the aim of existence would prefer the former adverb, those who think that development of individuality is worth the risk of a little scorching, the latter) she had married a man who required little or nothing more than she was disposed to give. He had not expected unquiet rapture, but a comfortable home with a "little woman" always there, good-tempered, as Millie was, and cheerful and pliable as, with a dozen exceptions when the calm precision came into play, she had always been. Temperamentally, he was nearly as undeveloped as she, and the marriage had been what is called a very sensible one. But such sensible marriages ignore the fact that human beings, like the shores of the bay of Naples, are periodically volcanic, and the settlers there assume that their little property, because no sulphurous signs have appeared on the surface, is essentially quiescent, neglecting the fact that at one time or another emotional disturbances are to be expected. But because many quiet years have passed undisturbed, they get to believe that the human and natural fires have ceased to smoulder, and are no longer alive down below the roots of their pleasant vines and olive trees. All her life up till now, Millie Evans had been like one of these quiescent estates; now, when middle-age was upon her, she began to feel the stir of vital forces. The surface of her life was still undisturbed, she went about the diminished business of the household with her usual care, and in the weeks of this solitary August knitted a couple of ties for her husband, and read a couple of novels from the circulating library, with an interest not more markedly tepid than usual. But subterranean stir was going on, though no fire-breathing clefts appeared on the surface. Subconsciously she wove images and dreams, scarcely yet knowing that it is out of such dreams that the events and deeds of life inevitably spring. She had scarcely admitted even to herself that her projects for August had gone crookedly: the conviction that Lyndhurst Ames had found himself gouty and in need of Harrogate punctually at the date when he knew that she might be expected there, sufficiently straightened them. The intention more than compensated the miscarriage of events.

To-night, when her two guests had gone, the inevitable step happened: her unchecked impulses grew stronger and more definite, and out of the misty subconsciousness of her mind the disturbance flared upwards into the light of her everyday consciousness. With genuine flame it mounted; it was no solitary imagining of her own that had kindled it; he, she knew, was a conscious partner, and she had as sign the memory that he had kissed her. Somehow, deep in her awakening heart, that meant something stupendous to her. It had been unrealized at the time, but it had been like the touch of some corrosive, sweet and acid, burrowing down, eating her and yet feeding her. Up till now, it seemed to have signified little, now it invested itself with a tremendous significance. Probably to him it meant little; men did such things easily, but it was that which had burrowed within her, making so insignificant an entry, but penetrating so far. It was not a proof that he loved her, but it had become a token that she loved him. Otherwise, it could not have happened. There was something final in the beginning of it all. Then he had kissed her a second time on the night of the fancy dress ball. He had called that a cousinly kiss, and she smiled at the thought of that, for it showed that it required to be accounted for, excused. She felt a sort of tenderness for that fluttering, broken-winged subterfuge, so transparent, so undeceptive. If cousins kissed, they did not recollect their relationship afterwards, especially if there was no relationship. He had not kissed her because she was some sort of cousin to his wife.

Yet it was hardly stating the case correctly to say that he had kissed her. Doubtless, on that first occasion below the mulberry-tree it was his head that had bent down to hers, while she but remained passive, waiting. But it was she who had made him do it, and she gloried in the soft compulsion she had put on him. Even as she thought of it this evening, her eye sparkled. "He could not help it," she said to herself. "He could not help it."

Out of the sequestered cloistral twilight of her soul there had stepped something that had slumbered there all her life, something pagan, something incapable of scruples or regrets, as void of morals as a nymph or Bacchanal on a Greek frieze. It did not trouble, so it seemed, to challenge or defy the traditions and principles in which she had lived all these years; it appeared to be ignorant of their existence, or, at the most, they were but shadows that lay in unsubstantial bars across a sunlit pavement. At present, it stood there trembling and quiescent, like a moth lately broken out from its sheathed chrysalis, but momently, now that it had come forth, it would grow stronger, and its crumpled wings expand into pinions feathered with silver and gold.

But she made no plans, she scarcely even turned her eyes towards the future, for the future would surely be as inevitable as the past had been. One by one the hot August days dropped off like the petals of peach blossom, which must fall before the fruit begins to swell. She neither wanted to delay or hurry their withering. There were but few days left, few petals left to fall, for within a week, so her husband had written, he would be back, vastly better for his cure, and Major Ames was coming with him. "I shall be so glad to see my little woman again," he had said. "Elsie and I have missed her."

Occasionally she tried to think about her husband, but she could not concentrate her mind on him. She was too much accustomed to him to be able to fix her thoughts on him emotionally. She was equally well accustomed to Elsie, or rather equally well accustomed to her complete ignorance about Elsie. She could no more have drawn a chart of the girl's mind than she could have drawn a picture of the branches of the mulberry-tree under which she so often sat, beholding the interlacement of its boughs but never really seeing them. Never had she known the psychical bond of motherhood; even the physical had meant little to her. She was Elsie's mother by accident, so to speak; and she was but as a tree from which a gardener has made a cutting, planting it near, so that sapling and parent stem grow up in sight of each other, but quite independently, without sense of their original unity. Even when her baby had lain at her breast, helpless, and still deriving all from her, the sweet intimate mystery of the life that was common to them both had been but a whispered riddle to her; and that was long ago, its memory had become a faded photograph that might really have represented not herself and her baby, but any mother and child. It was very possible that before long Elsie would be transplanted by marriage, and she herself would have to learn a little more about chess in order to play with her husband in the evening.

Such, hitherto, had been her emotional life: this summary of it and its meagre total is all that can justly be put to her credit. She liked her husband, she knew he was kind to her, and so, in its inanimate manner, was the food which she ate kind to her, in that it nourished and supported her. But her gratitude to it was untinged with emotion; she was not sentimental over her breakfast, for it was the mission of food to give support, and the mission of her husband had not been to her much more than that. Neither wifehood nor motherhood had awakened her womanhood. Yet, in that she was a woman, she was that most dangerous of all created or manufactured things, an unexploded shell, liable to blow to bits both itself and any who handled her. The shell was alive still, its case uncorroded, and its contents still potentially violent. That violence at present lay dark and quiet within it; its sheath was smooth and faintly bright. It seemed but a plaything, a parlour-ornament; it could stand on any table in any drawing-room. But the heart of it had never been penetrated by the love that could transform its violence into strength: now its cap was screwed and its fuse fixed. Until the damp and decay of age robbed it of its power, it would always be liable to wreck itself and its surroundings.

These same days that for her were kindling dangerous stuff, passed for Mrs. Ames in a *crescendo* of awakening interest. All her life she had been wrapped round like the kernel of a nut, in the hard, dry husk of conventionalities, her life had been encased in a succession of minute happenings, and, literally speaking, she had never breathed the outer air of ideas. As has been noticed, she gave regular patronage to St. Barnabas' Church, and spent a solid hour or two every week in decorating it with the produce of her husband's garden, from earliest spring, when the faint, shy snowdrops were available, to late autumn, when October and November frosts finally blackened the salvias and chrysanthemums. But all that had been of the nature of routine: a certain admiration for the vicar, a passionless appreciation of his nobly ascetic life, his strong, lean face, and the fire of his utterances had made her attendance regular, and her contributions to his charities quite creditably profuse in proportion to her not very ample means. But she had never denied herself anything in order to increase them, while the time she spent over the flowers was amply compensated for when she saw the eclipse they made of Mrs. Brooks' embroideries, or when the lilies dropped their orange-staining pollen on to the altar-cloth. Stranger, perhaps, from the emotional point of view, had been her recently attempted rejuvenescence, but even that had been a calculated and materialistic effort. It had not been a manifestation of her love for her husband, or of a desire to awaken his love for her. It was merely a decorative effort to attract his attention, and prevent it wandering elsewhere.

But now, with her kindled sympathy for the Suffragette movement, there was springing up in her the consciousness of a kinship with her sex whom, hitherto, she had regarded as a set of people to whom, in the matter of dinner-giving and entirely correct social behaviour, she must be an example and a law, while even her hospitalities had not been dictated by the spirit of hospitality but rather by a sort of pompous and genteel competition. Now she was beginning to see that behind the mere events of life, if they were to be worth anything, must lie an idea, and here behind this woman's crusade, with all its hooliganism, its hysteria, its apish fanaticism, lay an idea of justice and sisterhood. They seemed simple words, and she would have said off-hand that she knew what they meant. But, as she began faintly to understand them, she knew that she had been as ignorant of them as of what Australia really was. To her, as it was a geographical expression only, so justice was an abstract expression. But the meaning of justice was known to those who gave up the comforts and amenities of life for its sake, and for its sake cheerfully suffered ridicule and prison life and misunderstanding. And the fumes of an idea, to one who had practically never tasted one, intoxicated her as new wine mounts to the head of a teetotaler.

Ideas are dangerous things, and should be kept behind a fireguard, for fear that the children, of whom this world largely consists, should burn their fingers, thinking that these bright, sparkling toys are to be played with. Mrs Ames, in spite of her unfamiliarity with them, did not fall into this error. She realized that if she was to warm herself, to get the glow of the fire in her cramped and frozen limbs, she must treat it with respect, and learn to handle it. That, at any rate, was her intention, and she had a certain capacity for thoroughness.

It was in the last week of August that Major Ames was expected back, after three weeks of treatment. At first, as reflected in his letters, his experiences had been horrifying; the waters nauseated him, and the irritating miscarriage of the plan which was the real reason for his going to Harrogate, caused him fits of feeble rage which were the more maddening because they had to be borne secretly and silently. Also the lodgings he had procured seemed to him needlessly expensive, and all this efflux of bullion was being poured out on treatment which Dr. Evans had told him was really quite unnecessary. Regular and sparkling letters from his wife, in praise of August spent at Riseborough, continued to arrive and filled him with impotent envy. He, too, might be spending August at Riseborough if he had not been quite so precipitate. As it was, his mornings were spent in absorbing horrible draughts and gently stewing in the fetid waters of the Starbeck spring: his meals were plain to the point of grotesqueness, his evenings were spent in playing inane games of patience, while Elsie and the doctor pored silently over their chessboard, saying "Check" to each other at intervals. But through the days and their tedious uniformity there ran a certain unquietness and desire. It was clear that Millie, no less than he, had planned that they should be together in August, but his desire did not absorb him, rather it made him restless and anxious about the future. He did not even know if he was really in love with her; he did not even know if he wanted to be. The thought of her kindled his imagination, and he could picture himself in love with her: at the same time he was not certain whether, if the last two months could be lived over again, he would let himself drift into the position where he now found himself. There was neither ardour nor anything imperative in his heart; something, it is true, was heated, but it only smouldered and smoked. It was of the nature of such fire as bursts out in haystacks: it was born of stuffiness and packed confinement, and was as different as two things of the same nature can be, from the swift lambency and laudable flame of sun-kindled and breeze-fed flame. It disquieted and upset him; he could not soberly believe in the pictures his imagination drew of his being irresistibly in love with her: their colour quickly faded, their outlines were wavering and uncertain. And the background was even more difficult to fill in . . . how was the composition to be arranged? Where would Amy stand? What aspect would Riseborough wear? And then, after a long silence, Elsie said "Check."

Major Ames was due to arrive at Riseborough soon after four in the afternoon, and Mrs. Ames was at pains to be at home by that hour to welcome him and give him tea, and had persuaded Harry to go up to the station to meet him. She had gathered a charming decoration of flowers to make the room bright, and had put a couple more vases of them in his dressing-room. Before long a cab arrived from the station bearing his luggage, but neither he nor Harry occupied it. So it was natural to conclude that they were walking down, and she made tea, since they would not be many minutes behind the leisurely four-wheeler. She wanted very particularly to give him an auspicious and comfortable return: he must not think that, because this Suffragette movement occupied her thoughts so much, she was going to become remiss in care for him. But still the minutes went on, and she took a cup of tea herself, and found it already growing astringent. What could have detained him she could not guess, but certainly he should have another brew of tea made for him, for he hated what in moments of irritation he called tincture of tannin. Five o'clock struck, and the two quarters that duly followed it. Before that a conjecture had formed itself in her mind.

Then came the rattle of his deposited hat and stick in the hall, and the rattle of the door-handle for his entry.

"Well, Amy," he said, "and here's your returned prodigal. Train late as usual, and I walked down. How are you?"

She got up and kissed him.

"Very well indeed, Lyndhurst," she said; "and there is no need to ask you how you are."

She paused a moment.

"Your luggage arrived nearly an hour ago," she said.

He had forgotten that detail.

"An hour ago? Surely not," he said.

She gave him one more pause in which he could say more, but nothing came.

"You have had tea, I suppose," she said.

"Yes; Evans insisted on my dropping in to his house, and taking a cup there. That rogue Harry has stopped on. Well, well: we were all young once! You remember the old story I told you about the Colonel's wife when I was a lad."

She remembered it perfectly. She felt sure also that he had not meant to tell her where he had been since his arrival at the station.

CHAPTER X

The day was of early October, and Dr. Evans, who was driving his swift, steady cob, harnessed to the light dogcart, along the flat road towards Norton, had leisure to observe the beauty of the flaming season. He had but a couple of visits to make, and neither of the cases caused him any professional anxiety. But it was with conscious effort that he commanded his obedient mind to cease worrying, and drink in the beneficent influence of this genial morning that followed on a night that had given them the first frost of the year. The road, after leaving Riseborough, ran through a couple of level miles of delectable woodland; ditches filled and choked with the full-grown grass and herbage of the summer bordered it on each side. On the left, the sun had turned the frozen night-dews into a liquid heraldry, on the right where the roadside foliage was still in shadow, the faceted jewels of the frost that hinted of the coming winter still stiffened the herbage, and was white on the grey beards of the sprawling clematis in the hedges. But high above these low-growing tangles of vegetation, an ample glory flamed, and the great beech forest was all ablaze with orange and red flame tremulous in the breeze. Here and there a yew-tree, tawny-trunked and green-velveted with undeciduous leaf, seemed like a black spot of unconsumed fuel in the fire of the autumn; here a company of sturdy oaks seemed like a group of square-shouldered young men amid the maidens of the woodland. It had its fairies too, the sylph-like birches, whose little leaves seemed shed about their white shapeliness like a shower of confetti. Then, in the more open glades, short and rabbit-cropped turf sparkled emerald-like amid the sober greys and browns of the withering heather and the russet antlers of the bracken. Now and then a rabbit with white scutt, giving a dot-and-dash signal of danger to his family, would scamper into shelter at the rattle of the approaching dogcart. Now and then a pheasant, whose plumage seemed to reproduce in metal the tints of the golden autumn, strode with lowered head and tail away from the dangerous vicinity of man. Below the beeches the ground was uncarpeted by any vegetation, but already the "fallen glories" of the leaf were beginning to lie there, and occasionally a squirrel ran rustling across them, and having gained the security of his lofty ways among the trees, scolded Puck-like at the interruption that had made him leave his breakfast of the burst beech-nuts. To the right, below the high-swung level road, the ground declined sharply, and gave glimpses of the distant sun-burnished sea; above, small companies of feathery clouds, assembled together as if migrating for the winter, fluttered against the summer azure of the sky.

Dr. Evans' alert and merry eye dwelt on those delectable things, and in obedience to his brain, noted and appreciated the manifold festivity of the morning, but it did so not as ordinarily, by instinct and eager impulses, but because he consciously bade it. It needed the spur; its alertness and its merriness were pressed on it, and by degrees the spur failed to stimulate it, and he fell to regarding the well-groomed quarters of his long-stepping cob, which usually afforded him so pleasant a contemplation of strong and harmonious muscularity. But this morning even they failed to delight him, and the rhythm of its firm trot made no music in his mind. There came a crease which deepened into a decided frown between his eyes, and he communed with the trouble in his mind.

There were various lesser worries, not of sufficient importance to disturb seriously the equanimity of a busy and well-balanced man, and though each was trivial enough in itself, and distinctly had a humorous side to a mind otherwise content, the cumulative effect of them was not amusing. In the first place, there was the affair of Harry Ames, who, in a manner sufficiently ludicrous and calfish, had been making love to his wife. As any other sensible man would have done, Wilfred Evans had seen almost immediately on his return to Riseborough that Harry was disposed to make himself ridiculous, and had given a word of kindly warning to his wife.

"Snub him a bit, little woman," he had said. "We're having a little too much of him. It's fairer on the boy, too. You're too kind to him. A woman like you so easily turns a boy's head. And you've often said he is rather a dreadful sort of youth."

But for some reason she took the words in ill part, becoming rather precise.

"I don't know what you mean," she said. "Will you explain, please?"

"Easy enough, my dear. He's here too much; he's dangling after you. Laugh at him a little, or yawn a little."

"You mean that he's in love with me?"

"Well, that's too big a word, little woman, though I'm sure you see what I mean."

"I think I do. I think your suggestion is rather coarse, Wilfred, and quite ill-founded. Is every one who is polite and attentive supposed to be in love with me? I only ask for information."

"I think your own good sense will supply you with all necessary information," he said.

But her good sense apparently had done nothing of the kind, and eventually Dr. Evans had spoken to Harry's father on the subject. The visits had ceased with amazing abruptness after that, and Dr. Evans had found himself treated to a stare of blank unrecognition when he passed Harry in the street, and a curl of the lip which he felt must have been practised in private. But the Omar Khayyam Club would be the gainers, for they owed to it those stricken and embittered stanzas called "Parted."

CHAPTER X

Here comedy verged on farce, but the farce did not amuse him. He knew that his own interpretation of Harry's assiduous presence was correct, so why should his wife have so precisely denied that those absurd attentions meant nothing? There was nothing to resent in the sensible warning that a man was greatly attracted by her. Nor was there warrant for Colonel Ames' horror and dismay at the suggestion, when the doctor spoke to him about it. "Infamous young libertine" was surely a hyperbolical expression.

Dr. Evans unconsciously flicked the cob rather sharply with his whip-lash, to that excellent animal's surprise, for he was covering his miles in five minutes apiece, and the doctor conveyed his apologies for his unintentional hint with a soothing remark. Then his thoughts drifted back again. That was not all the trouble with the Ames' family, for his wife had had a quarrel with Mrs. Ames. This kindly man hated to quarrel with anybody, and, for his part, successfully refused to do so, and that his wife should find herself in such a predicament was equally distressing to him. No doubt it was all a storm in a tea-cup, but if you happen to be living in the tea-cup too, a storm there is just as upsetting as a gale on the high seas. It is worse, indeed, for on the high seas a ship can run into fairer weather, but there is no escape from these tea-cup disturbances. The entire tea-cup was involved: all Riseborough, which a year ago had seemed to him so suitable a place in which to pursue an unexacting practice, to conduct mild original work, in the peace and quiet of a small society and domestic comfort, was become a tempest of conflicting winds. "And all arising from such a pack of nonsense," as the doctor thought impatiently to himself, only just checking the whip-lash from falling again on the industrious cob.

The interest of Mrs. Ames in the Suffragette movement had given rise to all this. She had announced a drawing-room meeting to be held in her house, now a fortnight ago, and the drawing-room meeting had exploded in mid-career, like a squib, scattering sparks and combustible material over all Riseborough. It appeared that Mrs. Ames, finding that the comprehension of Suffragette aims extended to the middle-class circles in Riseborough, had asked the wives and daughters of tradesmen to take part in it. It wanted but little after that to make Mrs. Altham remark quite audibly that she had not known that she was to have the privilege of meeting so many ladies with whom she was not previously acquainted, and the sarcastic intention of her words was not lost upon her new friends. Tea seemed but to increase the initial inflammation, and the interest Mrs. Ames had intended to awake on the subject of votes for women was changed into an interest in ascertaining who could be most offensively polite, a very pretty game. It is not to be wondered at that, before twenty-four hours had passed, Mrs. Altham had started an anti-Suffragette league, and Millie, still strong in the conviction that under no circumstances could she go to prison, had allowed herself to be drawn into it. Next night at dinner she softly made a terrible announcement.

"I passed Cousin Amy in the street just now," she said; "she did not seem to see me."

"Perhaps she didn't see you, little woman," said her husband.

"So I did not seem to see her," added Millie, who had not finished her sentence. "But if she cares to come to see me and explain, I shall behave quite as usual to her."

"Come, come, little woman!" said Dr. Evans in a conciliating spirit.

"And I do not see what is the good of saying 'Come, come,'" she said, with considerable precision.

All this was sufficient to cause very sensible disquiet to a man who attached so proper an importance to peaceful and harmonious conditions of life, yet it was but a small thing compared to a far deeper anxiety that brooded over him. Till now he had not let himself directly contemplate it, but to-day, as he returned from his two visits, he made himself face this last secret trouble. He felt it was necessary for him to ascertain, for the sake of others no less than himself, what part, if any, of his disquiet was grounded on certainty, what part, if any, might be the figment of an over-anxious imagination. But he knew he was not anxious by temperament, nor given to imagine troubles. If anything, he was more prone, in his desire for a pleasant and studious life, to shut his eyes to the apparent approach of storm, trusting that it would blow by. He was anxious about Millie, not without cause; a hundred symptoms justified his anxiety. She who for so long had been of such imperturbable serenity of temper that a man who did not feel her charm might have called her jelly-fish was the prey of fifty moods a day. She had strange little fits of tenderness to him, with squalls of peevishness quite as strange. She was restless and filled with an energy that flamed and flickered and vanished, leaving her indolent and inert. She would settle herself for a morning of letter writing, and after tearing up a couple of notes, put on her gardening gloves and get as far as the herbaceous bed. Then she would find an imperative reason for going into the town, and so sit down at her piano to practise. Her appetite, usually of the steady reliable order, failed her, and she passed broken and tossing nights. Had she been a girl, he would have said those symptoms all pointed one way; and it would probably not have been difficult to guess who was the young man in question. Yet he could scarcely face the conclusion applied to his wife. It was a hideous thing that a husband should harbour such a suspicion, more hideous that the husband should be himself. And perhaps more hideous of all, that he should guess--again without difficulty--who was the man in question.

He had no conception what to do, or whether to do nothing; it seemed that action and inaction might alike end in disaster. And, again, the whole of his explanation of Millie's symptoms might be erroneous. There might be other explanations--indeed, there were others possible. As to that, time would show; at present the best course, perhaps the only right course, was to be watchful, yet not suspicious, observant, not prying. Rather than pry or be suspicious he would go to Millie herself, and without reservation tell her all that had been in his mind. He was well aware what the heroic attitude, the attitude of the virile, impetuous Englishman, dear to melodrama, would have been. It was quite easy for him to "tax" Major Ames with baseness, to grind his teeth at his wife, and then burst into manly tears, each sob of which seemed to rend him. But to his quiet, sensible nature, it seemed difficult to see what was supposed to happen next. In melodrama the curtain went down, and you started ten years later in Queensland with regenerated natures distributed broadcast. But in actual life it was impossible to start again ten years later, or ten minutes later. You had to go on all the time. Willingly would he, on this divine October morning, have started again, indefinitely later. The difficulty was how to go on now.

His cases had not long detained him, and it was still not long after noon when the cob, still pleased and alert with motion, but with smoking flanks, drew up at his door. The clear chill of the morning had altogether passed, and the air in the basin or tea-cup of a town was still and sultry. There was a familiar hat on the table in the hall, a bunch of long-stemmed tawny chrysanthemums lay by it. And at that sight some distant echo of barbaric and simple man, deplorable to the smoothness of civilization and altogether obsolete, was resonant in him. He pitched the chrysanthemums into the street, where they flew like a shooting star close by the head of General Fortescue, who was tottering down to the club, and slammed the door. It was melodramatic and foolish enough, but the desire that prompted it was quite sincere and irresistible, and if at the moment Major Ames had been in that cool oak-panelled hall, there is little doubt that Dr. Evans would have done his best to pitch him out after his flowers.

The doctor gave himself a moment to recover from his superficial violence, and then went out into the garden. They were sitting together on the bench under the mulberry-tree, and Major Ames got up with his usual briskness as he approached. Somehow Dr. Evans felt as if he was being welcomed and made to feel at home.

"Good morning," said Major Ames. "Glorious day, isn't it? I just stepped over with a handful of flowers, and we've been having a bit of a chat, a bit of a chat."

"Cousin Lyndhurst has very kindly come to talk over all these little disturbances," said Millie.

She looked at him.

"Shall I explain?" she asked.

Dr. Evans took the seat that Major Ames had vacated, leaving him free to sit down in a garden chair opposite, or to stand, just as he pleased.

"It is like this, Wilfred," she said. "Cousin Amy did not like my joining the anti-Suffragette league which Mrs. Altham started, and I have told Lyndhurst that I did not care a straw one way or the other, except that I could not go to prison to please Cousin Amy or any one else. But it looked like taking sides, she thought. So Lyndhurst thought it would make everything easy if I didn't join any league at all. I think it very clever and tactful of him to think of that, and I will certainly tell Mrs. Altham I find I am too busy. Of course, there is no quarrel between Cousin Amy and me, and Lyndhurst wants to assure us that he isn't mixed up in it, though there isn't any--and, of course, if Cousin Amy didn't see me the other day when I thought she pretended not to, it makes a difference."

Millie delivered herself of these lucid statements with her usual deferential air.

"I think it is very kind of Cousin Lyndhurst to take so much trouble," she added. "He is stopping to lunch."

Major Ames made a noble little gesture that disclaimed any credit.

"It's nothing, a mere nothing," he said, quite truly. "But I'm sure you hate little domestic jars as much as I do. As Amy once said, my profession was to be a man of war, but my instinct was to be a man of peace. Ha! Ha! I'm only delighted my little olive branch has--has met with success," he added rather feebly, being unable to think of any botanical metaphor.

The doctor got up. It is to be feared that, in his present state of mind, he felt not the smallest admiration or gratitude for the work of Lyndhurst the Peacemaker, but only saw in it a purely personal desire to secure an uninterrupted *va et vient* between the two houses.

"I'm sure I haven't the slightest intention of quarrelling with anybody," he said. "It seems to me the most deplorable waste of time and energy, besides being very uncomfortable. Let us go in to lunch, Millie; I have to go out again at two o'clock."

Millie wrote an amiable and insincere little note to Mrs. Altham, which Major Ames undertook to deliver on his way home, explaining how, since Elsie had gone to Dresden to perfect herself in the German language, she herself had become so busy that she did not know which way to turn, besides missing Elsie very much. She felt, therefore, that since she would not be able to give as much time as she wished to this very interesting anti-Suffragette movement, it would be better not to give to it any time at all. This she wrote directly after her husband had gone out again, and brought to Major Ames, who was waiting for it. He, too, had said he would have to be off at once. She gave him the note.

"There it is," she said; "and so many thanks for leaving it. But you are not hurrying away at once, are you?"

"Am I not keeping you in?" he asked.

She pulled down the lace blinds over the window that looked into the street; the October sun, it is true, beat rather hotly into the room, but the instinct that dictated her action was rather a desire for privacy.

"As if I would not sooner sit and talk to you," she said, "than go out. I have no one to go out with. I am rather lonely since Elsie has gone, and I daresay I shall not see Wilfred again till dinner-time. It is rather amusing that I have just written to Mrs. Altham to say how busy I am."

He came and sat a little closer to her.

"Upon my word," he said, "I am in the same boat as you. I haven't set eyes on Amy all morning, and this afternoon I know she has a couple of meetings. It's extraordinary how this idea of votes for women has taken hold of her. Not a bad thing, though, as long as she doesn't go making a fool of herself in public, and as long as she doesn't have any more quarrels with you."

"What would you have done if she had really wished to quarrel with me over Mrs. Altham's league?" she asked.

CHAPTER X

"Just what I told her. I said I would be no partner to it, and as long as you would receive me here *en garçon* I should always come."

"That was dear of you," she said softly.

She paused a moment.

"Sometimes I think we made a mistake in coming to settle here," she said; "but you know how obstinate Wilfred is, and how little influence I have with him. But then, again, I think of our friendship. I have not had many friends. I think, perhaps, I am too shy and timid with people. When I like them very much I find it difficult to express myself. It is rather sad not to be able to show what you feel quite frankly. It prevents your being understood by the people whom you most want to understand you."

But beneath this profession of incompetence, it seemed to Major Ames that there lurked a very efficient strength. He felt himself being gradually overpowered by a superior force, a force that did not strike and disable and overbear, but cramped and paralysed the power of its adversary, enfolding him, clinging to him. There was still something in him, some part of his will which was hostile and opposed to her: it was just that which she assailed. And in alliance with that paralysing force was her attraction and charm--soft, yielding, feminine; the two advanced side by side, terrible twins.

He did not answer for a moment, and it flashed across his mind that this cool room, shaded from the street glare by the lace curtains, and suffused with the greenish glow of the sunlight reflected from the lawn outside, was like a trap. . . . She gave a little laugh.

"See how badly I express myself," she said. "You are puzzling, frowning. Don't frown, you look best when you are laughing. I get so tired of frowning faces. Wilfred so often frowns all dinner-time when he is thinking over something connected with microbes. And he frowns over his chess, when he cannot make up his mind whether to exchange bishops. We play chess every evening."

Instinctively she had drawn back a little, when she saw he did not advance to meet her, and spoke as if chess and the pathos of her dumbness to express friendship were things of equal moment. There was no calculation about it: it was the expression of one type, the eternal feminine attracted and wishing to attract. Her descent to these commonplaces restored his confidence; the room was a trap no longer, but the pleasant drawing-room he knew so well, with its charming mistress seated by him. It was almost inevitable that he should contrast the hot plushes and saddle-bag cushions of his own, its angular chairs and Axminster carpets with the cool chintzes here, the lace-shrouded windows, the Persian rugs. More marked was the contrast between the mistresses of the two houses. Amy had been writing at her davenport a good deal lately, and her short, stiff back had been the current picture of her. Here was a woman, dim in the half light, wanting to talk to him, to make timid confidences, to make him realize how much his friendship meant to her. His confidence returned with disarming completeness.

"Well, I'm sure I should find it dismal enough at home," he said, "if I hadn't somewhere to go to, knowing I should find a welcome. Mind you, I don't blame

Amy. For years now, when we've been alone in the evening, she has done her work, and I have read the paper, and I daresay we haven't said a dozen words till Parker brought in the bedroom candles, or sometimes we play picquet--for love. But now evenings spent like that seem to me very prosy and dismal. Perhaps it's Harrogate that has made me a bit more supple and youthful, though I'm sure it's ridiculous enough that a tough old campaigner like me should feel such things--"

Mrs. Evans put forward her chin, raising her face towards him.

"But why ridiculous?" she asked. "You must be so much younger than dear Cousin Amy. I wonder--I wonder if she feels that too?"

There was there a very devilish suggestion, the more so because, in proportion to the suggestion, so very little was stated. It succeeded admirably.

"Poor dear Amy!" said he.

He had said that once before, when Cleopatra-Amy was contrasted with Cleopatra-Millie. But there was a significance in the repetition of it. Once the assumed identity of character had suggested the comment, now there was no assumed character. It concerned Millie and Amy themselves.

Mrs. Evans put back her chin.

"I am sure Cousin Amy ought to be very happy," she said softly. "You are so devoted to her, and all. I almost think you spoil her, Lyndhurst. It is all so romantic. Fancy being a woman, and as old as Cousin Amy, and yet having a young man so devoted. Harry, too!"

Again a billow of confidence tinged with self-appreciation surged over Major Ames. After all, his wife was much older than him, for he was still a young man, and his youth was being expanded on sweet-peas and the garden roller. And he was stirred into a high flight of philosophical conjecture.

"My God, what a puzzle life is!" he observed.

She rose to this high-water mark.

"And it might be so simple," she said. "It should be so easy to be happy."

Then Major Ames knew where he was. In one sense he was worthy of the occasion, in another he did not feel up to all that it implied. He rose hastily.

"I had better go," he said rather hoarsely.

But he had smoked five cigarettes since lunch. The hoarseness might easily have been the result of this indulgence.

She did not attempt to keep him, nor did she make it incumbent on him to give her a kiss, however cousinly. She did not even rise, but only looked up at him from her low chair as she gave him her hand, smiling a little secretly, as Mona Lisa smiles. But she felt quite satisfied with their talk; he would think over it, and find fresh signals and private beckonings in it.

"Come and see me again," she said. There was a touch of imperativeness in her tone.

She looked through the lace curtain and saw him go out into the street. There was something in the gutter of the roadway which he inquired into with the end of his stick. It looked like a withered bunch of dusty chrysanthemums.

CHAPTER X

Mrs. Ames, meantime, had lunched at home, and gone off immediately afterwards, as her husband had conjectured, to a meeting. In the last month the membership of her league had largely increased, and it was no longer possible to convene its meetings in her own drawing-room, for it numbered some fifty persons, including a dozen men of enlightened principles. Even at first, as has been seen, she had welcomed (thereby incurring Mrs. Altham's disapproval) several ladies with whom she did not usually associate, and now the gathering was entirely independent of all class distinctions. The wife of the station-master, for instance, was one of the most active members and walked up and down the platform with a large rosette of Suffragette colours selling current copies of the *Clarion.* And no less remarkable than this growth of the league was the growth of Mrs. Ames. She was neither pompous nor condescending to those persons whom, a couple of months ago, she would have looked upon as being barely existent, except if they were all in church, when she would very probably have shared a hymn-book with any of them, the "Idea" for which they had assembled galvanizing them, though strictly temporarily, into the class of existent people. Now, the idea which brought them together in the commodious warehouse, kindly lent and sufficiently furnished by Mr. Turner, had given them a permanent existence, and they were not automatically blotted out of her book of life the moment these meetings were over, as they would have been so short a time ago in church, when the last "Amen" was said. The bonds of her barren and barbaric conventionality were bursting; indeed, it was not so much that others, not even those of "her class," were becoming women to her, as that she was becoming a woman herself. She had scarcely been one hitherto; she had been a piece of perfect propriety. And how far she had travelled from her original conception of the Suffragette movement as suitable to supply a novelty for the autumn that would eclipse the memory of the Shakespearean ball, may be gathered from the fact that she no longer took the chair at these meetings, but was an ordinary member. Mr. Turner had far more experience in the duties of a chairman: she had herself proposed him and would have seconded him as well, had such a step been in order.

To-day the meeting was assembled to discuss the part which the league should take in the forthcoming elections. The Tory Government was at present in power, and likely to remain in office, while Riseborough itself was a fairly safe seat for the Tory member, who was Sir James Westbourne. Before polemical or obstructive measures could be decided on, it had clearly been necessary to ascertain Sir James' views on the subject of votes for women, and to-day his answer had been received and was read to the meeting. It was as unsatisfactory as it was brief, and their "obedient servant" had no sympathy with, and so declined to promise any support to, their cause. Mr. Turner read this out, and laid it down on his desk.

"Will ladies or gentlemen give us their views on the course we are to adopt?" he said.

A dozen simultaneously rose, and simultaneously sat down again. The chairman asked Mrs. Brooks to address the meeting. Another and another succeeded her, and there was complete unanimity of purpose in their suggestions. Sir James' meetings and his speeches to his constituents must not be allowed to proceed without interruption. If he had no sympathy with the cause, the cause would show a marked lack of sympathy with him. Thereafter the league resolved itself into a committee of ways and means. The President of the Board of Trade was coming to support Sir James' candidature at a meeting the date of which was already fixed for a fortnight hence, and it was decided to make a demonstration in force. And as the discussion went on, and real practical plans were made, that strange fascination and excitement at the thought of shouting and interrupting at a public meeting, of becoming for the first time of some consequence, began to seethe and ferment. Most of the members were women, whose lives had been passed in continuous self-repression, who had been frozen over by the narcotic ice of a completely conventional and humdrum existence. Many of them were unmarried and already of middle-age; their natural human instincts had never known the blossoming and honey which the fulfilment of their natures would have brought. To the eagerness and sincerity with which they welcomed a work that demanded justice for their sex, there was added this excitement of doing something at last. There was an opportunity of expansion, of stepping out, under the stimulus of an idea, into an experience that was real. In kind, this was akin to martyrs, who rejoiced and sang when the prospects of persecution came near; as martyrs for the sake of their faith thought almost with glee of the rack and the burning, so, minutely, the very prospect of discomfort and rough handling seemed attractive, if, by such means, the cause was infinitesimally advanced. To this, a sincere and wholly laudable desire, was added the more personal stimulus. They would be doing something, instead of suffering the tedium of passivity, acting instead of being acted on. For it is only through centuries of custom that the woman, physically weak and liable to be knocked down, has become the servant of the other sex. She is fiercer at heart, more courageous, more scornful of consequences than he; it is only muscular inferiority of strength that has subdued her into the place that she occupies, that, and the periods when, for the continuance of the race, she must submit to months of tender and strong inaction. There she finds fruition of her nature, and there awakes in her a sweet indulgence for the strange, childish lust of being master, of parading, in making of laws and conventions, his adventitious power, of the semblance of sovereignty that has been claimed by man. At heart she knows that he has but put a tinsel crown on his head, and robed himself in spangles that but parody real gold. She lays a woman's hand on his child-head, and to please him says, "How wise you are, how strong, how clever." And the child is pleased, and loves her for it. And there is her weakness, for the most dominant thing in her nature is the need of being loved. From the beginning it must have been so. When Adam's rib was taken from him in sleep, he lost more than was left him, and woke to find all his finer self gone from him. He was left a blundering bumble-bee: to the rib that was taken from him clung the courage of the lioness, the wisdom of the serpent, the gentleness of the dove, the cunning of the spider, and the mysterious charm of the firefly that dances in the dusk. But to that rib also clung the desire to be loved. Otherwise, in the human race, the male would be slain yearly like the drone of the hive. But the strange thing that grew from the rib, like flowers from buried carrion, desired love. There was its strength and its weakness.

It desired love, and in its desire it suffered all degradation to obtain it. And no leanness of soul entered into the gratification of its desire. Only when its desire was pinched and rationed, or when, by the operation of civilized law, all fruit of desire was denied it, so that the blossom of sex was made into one unfruitful bud, did revolt come. Long generations produced the germ, long generations made it active. At length it swam up to sight, from subaqueous dimnesses, feeble and violent, conscious of the justice of its cause and demanding justice. But what helped to make the desire for justice so attractive was the violence, the escape from self-repression that the demand gave opportunity for, to many who, all their lives, had been corked or wired down in comfort, which no woman cares about, or sealed up in spinster-hood and decorous emptiness of days. There was justice in the demand, and hysterical excitement in demanding.

To others, and in this little league of Riseborough there were many such, the prospect of making those demands was primarily appalling, and to none more than to poor Mrs. Ames, when the plan of campaign was discussed, decided on, and entrusted to the members of the league. It required almost more courage than the idea was capable of inspiring to face, even in anticipation, the thought of shouting "Votes for Women" when good-humoured Cousin James rose and said "Ladies and gentlemen!" Very possibly, as had often happened in Cousin James' previous candidatures, Lyndhurst would wish his wife to ask him and the President of the Board of Trade to dinner before the meeting, an occasion which would warrant the materialization of the most sumptuous of all the dinners tabulated on the printed menu-cards, while sherry would be given with soup, hock with fish, and a constant flow of champagne be kept up afterwards, until port time. In that case Cousin James would certainly ask them to sit on the platform, and they would roll richly to the town hall in his motor, all blazing with Conservative colours, while she, in a small bag, would be surreptitiously conveying there her great Suffragette rosette, and a small steel chain with a padlock. She would be sitting probably next the Mayor, who would introduce the speakers, and no doubt refer to "the presence of the fair sex" who graced the platform. During this she would have to pin her colours on her dress, chain herself up like Andromeda, snap the patent spring-lock of the padlock, and when Sir James rose . . . her imagination could not grapple with the picture: it turned sickly away, refusing to contemplate. And this to a cousin and a guest, who had just eaten the best salt, so to speak, of her table, from one who all her life had been so perfect a piece of propriety! She felt far too old a bottle for such new wine. Sitting surrounded by fellow-crusaders, and infected by the proximity of their undiluted enthusiasm, it would be difficult enough, but that she should chain herself, perhaps, to the very leg of the table which Cousin James would soon thump in the fervour of his oratory, as he announced all those Tory platitudes in which she so firmly believed, and which she must so shrilly interrupt, while sitting solitary in the desert of his sleek and staid supporters, was not only an impossible but an unthinkable achievement. Whatever horrors fate, that gruesome weaver of nightmares, might have in store for her, she felt that here was something that transcended imagination. She could not sit on the platform with Lyndhurst and Cousin James and the Mayor and Lady Westbourne, and do what was required of her, for the sake of any crusade. Curfew, so to speak, would have to ring that night.

She and Lyndhurst were dining alone the evening after this meeting of "ways and means," he in that state of mind which she not inaptly described as "worried" when she felt kind, and "cross" when she felt otherwise. He had come home hot from his walk, and, having sat in his room where there was no fire, when evening fell chilly, had had a smart touch of lumbago. Thus there were clearly two causes for complaint against Amy, and a third disturbing topic, for there was no shadow of doubt that it was his bouquet of chrysanthemums that he had found in the road outside Dr. Evans' house, and even before the lumbago had produced its characteristic pessimism, he had been unable to find any encouraging explanation of this floral castaway.

"I'm sure I don't know what was the good of my spending all August," he said, "in that filthy hole of a Harrogate, at no end of expense, too, if I'm to be crippled all winter. But you urged me to so strongly: should never have thought of going there otherwise."

"My dear, you have only been crippled for half-an-hour at present," she observed. "It is a great bore, but if only you will take a good hot bath to-night, and have a very light dinner, I expect you will be much better in the morning. Parker, tell them to see that there is plenty of hot water in the kitchen boiler."

"It'll be the only warm thing in the house, if there is," said he. "My room was like an ice-house when I came in. Positively like an ice-house. Enough to give a man pneumonia, let alone lumbago. Soup cold, too."

"My dear, you should take more care of yourself," said Mrs. Ames placidly. "Why did you not light the fire instead of being cold? I'm sure it was laid."

"And have it just burning up at dinner-time," said he, "when I no longer wanted it."

It was still early in the course of dinner.

"Light the fire in the drawing-room, Parker," said Mrs. Ames. "Let there be a good fire when we come out of dinner."

"Get roasted alive," said Major Ames, half to himself, but intending to be heard.

But Mrs. Ames' mind had been feasting for weeks past on things which had a solider existence than her husband's unreasonable strictures. Since this new diet had been hers, his snaps and growls had produced no effect: they often annoyed her into repartee, and as likely as not, a few months ago, she would have said that his claret seemed a very poor kind of beverage. But to-night she felt not the smallest desire to retort. She was very sorry for his lumbago, but felt no inclination to carry the war into his territories, or to tell him that if people, perspiring freely, and of gouty habit, choose to sit down without changing, and get chilly, they must expect reprisal for their imprudence.

"Then we will open the window, dear," she said, "if we find we are frizzling. But I don't think it will be too hot. Evenings are chilly in October. Did you have a pleasant lunch, Lyndhurst? Indeed, I don't know where you lunched. I ordered curry for you. I sat down at a quarter to two as you did not come in."

It was all so infinitesimal . . . yet it was the mental diet which had supported her for years. Perhaps after dinner they would play picquet. The garden, the kitchen, for years, except for gossip infinitely less real, these had been the topics. There had been no joy for him in the beauty of the garden, only a pleased sense of proprietorship, if a rare plant flowered, or if there were more roses than usual. For her, she had been vaguely pleased if Lyndhurst had taken two helpings of a dish, and both of them had been vaguely disquieted if Harry quoted Swinburne.

"I lunched with the Evans'," he said. "By the way, I met your cousin James Westbourne this afternoon, when I was on my walk. Extraordinarily cordial he gets when there's business ahead that brings him into Riseborough, and he wants to cadge a dinner or two. It's little notice he takes of us the rest of the year, and I'm sure it's a couple of years since he so much as sent you a brace of pheasants, and more than that since he asked me to shoot there. But as I say, when he wants to pick up a dinner or two in Riseborough, he's all heartiness, and saying he doesn't see half enough of us. He doesn't seem to strain himself in trying to see more, and there's seldom a week-end when he and that great guy of a wife of his don't have the house packed with people. I suppose we're not smart enough for them, except when it's convenient to dine in Riseborough. Then he's not above drinking a bottle of my champagne."

Mrs. Ames was eager in support of her husband.

"I'm sure there's no call for you to open any more bottles for him, my dear," she said. "If Cousin James wants to see us, he can take his turn in asking us. And Harriet is a great guy, as you say, with her big fiddle-head."

Major Ames shrugged his shoulders rather magnificently.

"I'm sure I don't grudge him his dinner," he said, "and, in point of fact, I told him he could come and dine with us before his first meeting. He's got some Cabinet Minister with him, and I said he could bring him too. You might get up a little party, that's to say if I'm not in bed with this infernal lumbago. And Cousin James will return our hospitality by giving us seats on the platform to hear him stamp and stammer and rant. An infernal bad speaker. Never heard a worse. Wretched delivery, nothing to say, and says it all fifty times over. Enough to make a man turn Radical. However, he'll have made himself at home with my Mumm, and perhaps he'll go to sleep himself before he sends us off."

This, of course, represented the lumbago-view. Major Ames had been fulsomely cordial to Cousin James, and had himself urged the dinner that he represented now as being forced on him.

"Have you actually asked him, Lyndhurst?" said Mrs. Ames rather faintly. "Did he say he would come?"

"Did you ever know your Cousin James refuse a decent dinner?" asked Lyndhurst. "And he was kind enough to say he would like it at a quarter past seven. Cool, upon my word! I wish I had asked him if he'd have thick soup or clear, and if he preferred a wing to a leg. That's the sort of thing one never thinks of till afterwards."

Mrs. Ames was not attending closely: there was that below the surface which claimed all her mind. Consequently she missed the pungency of this irony, hearing only the words.

"Cousin James never takes soup at all," she said. "He told me it always disagreed."

Major Ames sighed; his lumbago felt less acute, his ill-temper had found relief in words, and he had long ago discovered that women had no sense of humour. On the whole, it was gratifying to find the truth of this so amply endorsed. For the moment it put him into quite a good temper.

"I'm afraid I've been grumbling all dinner," he said. "Shall we go into the other room? There's little sense in my looking at the decanters, if I mayn't take my glass of port. Eh! That was a twinge!"

CHAPTER XI

"It is no use, Henry," said Mrs. Altham on that same evening, "telling me it is all stuff and nonsense, when I've seen with my own eyes the parcel of Suffragette riband being actually directed to Mrs. Brooks; for pen and ink is pen and ink, when all is said and done. Tapworth measured off six yards of it on the counter-measure that gives two feet, for he gave nine lengths of it and put it in paper and directed it. Of course, if nine lengths of two feet doesn't make eighteen feet, which is six yards, I am wrong and you are right, and twice two no longer makes four. And there were two other parcels already done up of exactly the same shape. You will see if I am not right. Or do you suppose that Mrs. Brooks is ordering it just to trim her nightgown with it?"

"I never said anything about Mrs. Brooks' nightgown," said Henry, who, to do him justice, had been goaded into slightly Rabelaisian mood: "I never thought about Mrs. Brooks' nightgown. I didn't know she wore one--I mean--"

Mrs. Altham made what children would call "a face." Her eyes grew suddenly fixed and boiled, and her mouth assumed an acidulated expression as if with a plethora of lemon-juice. The "face" was due to the entry of the parlour-maid with the pudding. It was jelly, and was served in silence. Mrs. Altham waited till the door was quietly closed again.

"It is not a question of Mrs. Brooks' nightgown," she said, "since we both agree that she would not order six yards of Suffragette riband to trim it. I spoke sarcastically, Henry, and you interpreted me literally, as you often do. It was the same at Littlestone in August, when the bacon was so salt one day that I said to Mrs. Churchill that a little bacon in the bath would be equivalent to sea-bathing. Upon which you must needs tell her next morning to send your bacon to the bath-room, which she did, and there was a plate of bacon on the sponge-tray, so extraordinary. But all that is beside the point, though what she can have thought of you I can't imagine. After all, your gift of being literal may help you now. Why does Mrs. Brooks want six yards of Suffragette riband, and why are there two similar parcels on Tapworth's counter? If I had had a moment alone I would certainly have looked at the other addresses, and seen where they were being sent. But young Tapworth was there all the time--that one with the pince-nez, and the ridiculous chin--and he put them into the errand-boy's basket, and told him to be sharp about it. So I had no chance of seeing."

"You might have strolled along behind the boy to see where he went," suggested Mr. Altham.

"He went on a bicycle," said Mrs. Altham, "and it is impossible to stroll behind a boy on a bicycle and hope to get there in time. But he went up the High Street. I should not in the least wonder if Mrs. Evans had turned Suffragette, after that note to me about her not having time to attend the anti-Suffragette meetings."

"Especially since there was only one," said Henry, in the literal mood that had been forced on him, "and nobody came to that. It would not have sacrificed very much of her time. Not that I ever heard it was valuable."

"What she can do with her day I can't imagine," said Mrs. Altham, her mind completely diverted by this new topic. "Her cook told Griffiths that as often as not she doesn't go down to the kitchen at all in the morning, and she's hardly ever to be seen shopping in the High Street before lunch, and what with Elsie gone to Dresden, and her husband away on his rounds all day, she must be glad when it's bedtime. And she's a small sleeper, too, for she told me herself that she considers six hours a good night, though I expect she sleeps more than she knows, and I daresay has a nap after lunch as well. Dear me, what were we talking about? Ah, yes, I was saying I should not wonder if she had turned Suffragette, though I can't recall what made me think so."

"Because Tapworth's boy went up the High Street on a bicycle," said Mr. Altham, who had a great gift of picking out single threads from the tangle of his wife's conversation; "though, after all, the High Street leads to other houses besides Mrs. Evans'. The station, for instance."

"You seem to want to find fault with everything I say, to-night, Henry. I don't know what makes you so contrary. But there it is: I saw eighteen yards of Suffragette riband being sent out when I happened to be in Tapworth's this morning, and I daresay that's but a tithe of what has been ordered, though I can't say as to that, unless you expect me to stand in the High Street all day and watch. And as to what it all means, I'll let you conjecture for yourself, since if I told you what I thought, you would probably contradict me again."

It was no wonder that Mrs. Altham was annoyed. She had been thrilled to the marrow by the parcels of Suffragette riband, and when she communicated her discovery, Henry, who usually was so sympathetic, had seen nothing to be thrilled about. But he had not meant to be unsympathetic, and repaired his error.

"I'm sure, my dear, that you will have formed a very good guess as to what it means," he said. "Tell me what you think."

"Well, if you care to know," said she, "I think it all points to there being some demonstration planned, and I for one should not be surprised if I looked out of the window some morning, and saw Mrs. Ames and Mrs. Brooks and the rest of them marching down the High Street with ribands and banners. They've been keeping very quiet about it all, at least not a word of what they've been doing has come to my ears, and I consider that's a proof that something is going on and that they want to keep it secret."

CHAPTER XI

Mr. Altham's legal mind cried out to him to put in the plea that a complete absence of news does not necessarily constitute a proof that exciting events are occurring, but he rightly considered that such logic might be taken to be a sign of continued "contrariness." So he gave an illogical assent to his wife's theory.

"Certainly it is odd that nothing more has been heard of it all," he said. "I wonder what they are planning. The election coming on so soon, too! Can they be planning anything in connection with that?"

Mrs. Altham got up, letting her napkin fall on the floor.

"Henry, I believe you have hit it," she said. "Now what can it be? Let us go into the drawing-room, and thresh it out."

But the best threshing-machines in the world cannot successfully fulfil their function unless there is some material to work upon; they can but show by their whirling wheels and rattling gear that they are capable of threshing should anything be provided for them. The poor Althams were somewhat in this position, for their rations of gossip were sadly reduced, their two chief sources being cut off from them. For ever since the mendacious Mrs. Brooks had appeared as Cleopatra, when she had as good as promised to be Hermione, chill politeness had taken the place of intimacy between the two houses, since there was no telling what trick she might not play next, while the very decided line which Mrs. Altham had taken when she found she was expected to meet people like tradesmen's wives had caused a complete rupture in relations with the Ames'. That Suffragette meetings were going on was certain, else what sane mind could account for the fact that only to-day a perfect stream of people, some of them not even known by sight to Mrs. Altham, and therefore probably of the very lowest origin, with Mrs. Ames and the wife of the station-master among them, had been seen coming out of Mr. Turner's warehouse. It was ridiculous "to tell me" that they had been all making purchases (nobody had told her), and such a supposition was thoroughly negatived by the subsequent discovery that the warehouse in question contained only a quantity of chairs. All this, however, had been threshed out at tea-time, and the fly-wheels buzzed emptily. Against the probability of an election-demonstration was the fact that the Unionist member, to whom these attentions would naturally be directed, was Mrs. Ames' cousin, though "cousin" was a vague word, and Mrs. Altham would not wonder if he was a very distant sort of cousin indeed. Still, it would be worth while to get tickets anyhow for the first of Sir James' meetings, when the President of the Board of Trade was going to speak, so as to be certain of a good place. *He* was not Mrs. Ames' cousin, so far as Mrs. Altham knew, though she did not pretend to follow the ramifications of Mrs. Ames' family.

The fly-wheels were allowed to run on in silence for some little while after this meagre material had been thoroughly sifted, in case anything further offered itself; then Mr. Altham proposed another topic.

"You were saying that you wondered how Mrs. Evans got through her time," he began.

But there was no need for him to say another word, nor any opportunity.

Mrs. Altham stooped like a hawk on the quarry.

"You mean Major Ames," she said. "I'm sure I never pass the house but what he's either going in or coming out, and he does a good deal more of the going in than of the other, in my opinion."

Henry penetrated into the meaning of what sounded a rather curious achievement and corroborated.

"He was there this morning," he said, "on the doorstep at eleven o'clock, or it might have been a quarter-past, with a bouquet of chrysanthemums big enough to do all Mrs. Ames' decorations at St. Barnabas. What is the matter, my dear?"

For Mrs. Altham had literally bounced out of her chair, and was pointing at him a forefinger that trembled with a nameless emotion.

"At a quarter-past one, or a few minutes later," she said, "that bouquet was lying in the middle of the road. Let us say twenty minutes past one, because I came straight home, took off my hat, and was ready for lunch. It was more like a haystack than a bouquet: I'm sure if I hadn't stepped over it, I should have tripped and fallen. And to think that I never mentioned it to you, Henry! How things piece themselves together, if you give them a chance! Now did you actually see Major Ames carry it into the house?"

"The door was opened to him, just as I came opposite," said Henry firmly, "and in he went, bouquet and all."

"Then somebody *must* have thrown it out again," said Mrs. Altham.

She held up one hand, and ticked off names on its fingers.

"Who was then in the house?" she said. "Mrs. Evans, Dr. Evans, Major Ames. Otherwise the servants--how they can find work for six servants in that house I can't understand--and servants would never have thrown chrysanthemums into the street. So we needn't count the servants. Now can you imagine Mrs. Evans throwing away a bouquet that Major Ames had brought her? If so, I envy you your power of imagination. Or--"

She paused a moment.

"Or can there have been a quarrel, and did she tell him she had too much of him and his bouquets? Or--"

"Dr. Evans," said Henry.

She nodded portentously.

"Turned out of the house, he and his bouquet," she said. "Dr. Evans is a powerful man, and Major Ames, for all his size, is mostly fat. I should not wonder if Dr. Evans knocked him down. Henry, I have a good mind to treat Mrs. Ames as if she had not been so insulting to me that day (and after all that is only Christian conduct) and to take round to her after lunch to-morrow the book she said she wanted to see last July. I am sure I have forgotten what it was, but any book will do, since she only wants it to be thought that she reads. After all, I should be sorry to let Mrs. Ames suppose that anything she can do should have the power of putting me out, and I should like to see if she still dyes her hair. After the chrysanthemums in the road I should not be the least surprised to be told that Major Ames is ill. Then we shall know all. Dear me, it is eleven o'clock already, and I never felt less inclined to sleep."

Henry stepped downstairs to drink a mild whisky and soda after all this conversation and excitement, but while it was still half drunk, he felt compelled to run upstairs and tap at his wife's door.

"I am not coming in, dear," he said, in answer to her impassioned negative. "But if you find Major Ames is not ill?"

"No one will be more rejoiced than myself, Henry," said she, in a disappointed voice.

Henry went gently downstairs again.

Mrs. Ames was at home when the forgiving Mrs. Altham arrived on the following afternoon, bearing a copy of a book of which there were already two examples in the house. But she clearly remembered having wanted to see some book of which they had spoken together, last July, and it was very kind of Mrs. Altham to have attempted to supply her with it. Beyond doubt she had ceased to dye her hair, for the usual grey streaks were apparent in it, a proof (if Mrs. Altham wanted a proof, which she did not) that artificial means had been resorted to. And even as Mrs. Altham, with her powerful observation, noticed the difference in Mrs. Ames' hair, so also she noticed a difference in Mrs. Ames. She no longer seemed pompous: there was a kindliness about her which was utterly unlike her usual condescension, though it manifested itself only in the trivial happenings of an afternoon call, such as putting a cushion in her chair, and asking if she found the room, with its prospering fire, too hot. This also led to interesting information.

"It is scarcely cold enough for a fire to-day," she said, "but my husband is laid up with a little attack of lumbago."

"I am so sorry to hear that," said Mrs. Altham feverishly. "When did he catch it?"

"He felt it first last night before dinner. It is disappointing, for he expected Harrogate to cure him of such tendencies. But it is not very severe: I have no doubt he will be in here presently for tea."

Mrs. Altham felt quite convinced he would not, and hastened to glean further enlightenment.

"You must be very busy thinking of the election," she said. "I suppose Sir James is safe to get in. I got tickets for the first of his meetings this morning."

"That will be the one at which the President of the Board of Trade speaks," said Mrs. Ames. "My cousin and he dine with us first."

Mrs. Altham determined on more direct questions.

"Really, it must require courage to be a politician nowadays," she said, "especially if you are in the Cabinet. Mr. Chilcot has been hardly able to open his mouth lately without being interrupted by some Suffragette. Dear me, I hope I have not said the wrong thing! I quite forgot your sympathies."

"It is certainly a subject that interests me," said Mrs. Ames, "though as for saying the wrong thing, dear Mrs. Altham, why, the world would be a very dull place if we all agreed with each other. But I think it requires just as much courage for a woman to get up at a meeting and interrupt. I cannot imagine myself being bold enough. I feel I should be unable to get on my feet, or utter a word. They must be very much in earnest, and have a great deal of conviction to nerve them."

This was not very satisfactory; if anything was to be learned from it, it was that Mrs. Ames was but a tepid supporter of the cause. But what followed was still more vexing, for the parlour-maid announced Mrs. Evans.

"So sorry to hear about Major Ames, dear cousin Amy," she said. "Wilfred told me he had been to see him."

Mrs. Ames made a kissing-pad, so to speak, of her small toad's face, and Millie dabbed her cheek on it.

"Dear Millie, how nice of you to call! Parker, tell the Major that tea is ready, and that Mrs. Evans and Mrs. Altham are here."

But by the time Major Ames arrived Mrs. Altham was there no longer. She was thoroughly disgusted with the transformation into chaff of all the beautiful grain that they had taken the trouble to thresh out the night before. She summed it up succinctly to her husband when he came back from his golf.

"I don't believe the Suffragettes are going to do anything at all, Henry," she said, "and I shouldn't wonder if these chrysanthemums had nothing to do with anybody. The only thing is that her hair is dyed, because it was all speckled with grey again as thickly as yours, and I declare I left *The Safety of the Race* behind me, instead of bringing it back again, as I meant to do."

Henry, who had won his match at golf, was naturally optimistic.

"Then you didn't actually see Major Ames?" he asked.

"No, but there was no longer any doubt about it all," she said. "I do not think I am unduly credulous, but it was clear there was nothing the matter with him except a touch of lumbago. And all this Suffragette business means nothing at all, in spite of the yards of riband. You may take my word for it."

"Then there will be no point in going to Sir James' meeting," said Henry, "though the President of the Board of Trade is going to speak."

"Not unless you want to hear the biggest windbag in the country buttering up the greatest prig in the county. I should be sorry to waste my time over it; and he is dining with the Ames', and so I suppose all there will be to look at will be the row of them on the platform, all swollen with one of Mrs. Ames' biggest dinners. We might have gone to bed at our usual time last night, for all the use that there has been in our talk. And it was you saw the chrysanthemums, from which you expected so much and thought it worth while to tell me about them."

And Henry felt too much depressed at the utter flatness of all that had made so fair a promise, to enter any protest against the palpable injustice of these conclusions.

Major Ames' lumbago was of the Laodicean sort, neither hot nor cold. It hung about, occasionally stabbing him shrewdly, at times retreating in the Parthian mode, so that he was encouraged to drink a glass of port, upon which it shot at him again, and he had to get back to his stew of sloppy diet and depressing reflections. Most of all, the relations into which he had allowed himself to drift with regard to Millie filled him with a timorous yet exultant agitation, but he almost, if not quite, exaggerated his indisposition, in order to escape from the responsibility of deciding what should come of it. Damp and boisterous weather made it prudent for him to keep to the house, and she came to see him daily. Behind her demure quietness he divined a mind that was expectant and sure: there was no doubt as to her view of the situation that had arisen between them. She had played with the emotions of others once too often, and was caught in the agitation which she had so often excited without sharing in it. Mrs. Ames was generally present at these visits, but when it was quite certain that she was not looking, Millie often raised her eyes to his, and this disconcerting conviction lurked behind them. Her speech was equally disconcerting, for she would say, "It will be nice when you are well again," in a manner that quite belied the commonplace words. And this force that lay behind strangely controlled him. Involuntarily, almost, he answered her signals, gave himself the lover-like privilege of seeming to understand all that was not said. All the time, too, he perfectly appreciated the bad taste of the affair--namely, that a woman who was in love with him, and to whom he had given indications of the most unmistakable kind that he was on her plane of emotion, should play these unacted scenes in his wife's house, coming there to make pass his invalid hours, and that he should take his part in them. It was common, and he could not but contrast that commonness with the unconsciousness of his wife. Occasionally he was inclined to think, "Poor Amy, how little she sees," but as often it occurred to him that she was too big to be aware of such smallnesses as he and Millie were guilty of. And, in reality, the truth lay between these extreme views. She was not too big to be aware of it; she was quite aware of it, but she was big enough to appear too big to be aware of it. She watched, and scorned herself for her watching. She fed herself with suspicions, but was robust enough to spew them forth again. Also, and this allowed the robuster attitude to flourish, she was concerned with a nightmare of her own which daily grew more vivid and unescapable.

A decade of streaming October days passed in this trying atmosphere of suspicion and uncertainty and apprehension. Of the three of them it was Major Ames who was most thoroughly ill at ease, for he had no inspiration which enabled him to bear this sordid martyrdom. He divined that Millie was evolving some situation in which he would be expected to play a very prominent part, and such ardour as was his he felt not to be of the adequate temperature, and he looked back over the peaceful days when his garden supplied him not only with flowers, but with the most poignant emotions known to his nature, almost with regret. It had all been so peaceful and pleasant in that land-locked harbour, and now she, like a steam-tug, was slowly towing him out past the pier-head into a waste of breakers. Strictly speaking, it was possible for him at any moment to cast the towing-rope off and return to his quiet anchorage, but he was afraid he lacked the moral power to do so. He had let her throw the rope aboard him, he had helped to attach it to the bollard, thinking, so to speak, that he was the tug and she the frail little craft. But that frail little craft had developed into an engined apparatus, and it was his turn to be towed, helpless and at least unwilling, and wholly uninspired. The others, at any rate, had inspiration to warm their discomfort: Mrs. Ames the sense of justice and sisterhood which was leavening her dumpy existence, Mrs. Evans the fire which, however strange and illicit are its burnings, however common and trivial the material from which it springs, must still be called love.

It was the evening of Sir James' first meeting, and Mrs. Ames at six o'clock was satisfying herself that nothing had been omitted in the preparations for dinner. The printed menu-cards were in place, announcing all that was most sumptuous; the requisite relays of knives, spoons and forks were on the sideboard; the plates of opalescent glass for ice were to hand, and there was no longer anything connected with this terrible feast, that to her had the horror of a murderer's breakfast on the last morning of his life, which could serve to distract her mind any more. Millie was to dine with them and with them come to the meeting, but just now it did not seem to matter in the slightest what Millie did. All day Mrs. Ames had been catching at problematic straws that might save her: it was possible that Mr. Chilcot would be seized with sudden indisposition, and the meeting be postponed. But she herself had seen him drive by in Cousin James' motor, looking particularly hearty. Or Cousin James might catch influenza: Lady Westbourne already had it, and it was pleasantly infectious. Or Lyndhurst might get an attack of really acute lumbago, but instead he felt absolutely well again to-day, and had even done a little garden-rolling. One by one these bright possibilities had been extinguished--now no reasonable anchor remained except that dinner would acutely disagree with her (and that was hardly likely, since she felt incapable of eating anything) or that the motor which was to take them to the town hall would break down.

At half-past six she went upstairs to dress; she would thus secure a quarter of an hour before the actual operation of decking herself began, in which to be alone and really face what was going to happen. It was no use trying to face it in one piece: taken all together the coming evening had the horror and unreality of nightmare brooding over it. She had to take it moment by moment from the time when she would welcome her guests, whom, so it seemed to her, she was then going to betray, till the time when, perhaps four hours from now, she would be back again here in her room, and everything that had happened had woven itself into the woolly texture of the past, in place of being in the steely, imminent future. There was dinner to be gone through; that was only tolerable to think of because of what was to follow: in itself it would please her to entertain her cousin and so notable a man as a Cabinet Minister. Clearly, then, she must separate dinner from the rest, and enjoy it independently. But when she went down to dinner she must have left here in readiness the little black velvet bag . . . that was not so pleasant to think of. Yet the little black velvet bag had nothing to do yet. Then there would follow the drive to the town hall: that would not be unpleasant: in itself she would rather enjoy the stir and pomp of their arrival. Sir James would doubtless say to the scrutinizing doorkeeper, "These ladies are with me," and they would pass on amid demonstrations of deference. Probably there would be a little procession on to the platform . . . the Mayor would very likely lead the way with her, her and her little black velvet bag . . .

And then poor Mrs. Ames suddenly felt that if she thought about it any more she would have a nervous collapse. And at that thought her inspiration, so to speak, reached out a cool, firm hand to her. At any cost she was going through with this nightmare for the sake of that which inspired it. It was no use saying it was pleasant, nor was it pleasant to have a tooth out. But any woman with the slightest self-respect, when once convinced that it was better to have the tooth out, went to the dentist at the appointed hour, declined gas (Mrs. Ames had very decided opinions about those who made a fuss over a little pain), opened her mouth, and held the arms of the chair very firmly. One wanted something to hold on to at these moments. She wondered what she would find to hold on to this evening. Perhaps the holding on would be done by somebody else--a policeman, for instance.

There was one more detail to attend to before dressing, and she opened the little black velvet bag. In it were two chains--light, but of steel: they had been sold her with the gratifying recommendation that either of them alone would hold a mastiff, which was more than was required. One was of such length as to go tightly round her waist: a spring lock with hasp passing through the last link of it, closing with an internal snap, obviated the necessity of a key. This she proposed to put on below the light cloak she wore before they started. The second chain was rather longer but otherwise similar. It was to be passed through the one already in place on her waist, and round the object to which she desired to attach herself. Another snap lock made the necessary connection.

She saw that all was in order and, putting the big Suffragette rosette on top of the other apparatus, closed the bag: it was useless to try to accustom herself to it by looking; she might as well inspect the dentist's forceps, hoping thus to mollify their grip. Cloak and little velvet bag she would leave here and come up for them after dinner. And already the quarter of an hour was over, and it was time to dress.

The daring rose-coloured silk was to be worn on this occasion, and she hoped that it would not experience any rough treatment. Yet it hardly mattered: after tonight she would very likely never care to set eyes on it again, and emphatically Lyndhurst would find it full of disagreeable associations. And then she felt suddenly and acutely sorry for him and for the amazement and chagrin that he was about to feel. He could not fail to be burningly ashamed of her, to choke with rage and mortification. Perhaps it would bring on another attack of lumbago, which she would intensely regret. But she did not anticipate feeling in the least degree ashamed of herself. But she intensely wished it had not got to be.

And now she was ready: the rose-coloured silk glowed softly in the electric light, the pink satin shoes which "went with it" were on her plump, pretty little feet, the row of garnets was clasped round her neck. There was a good deal of colour in her face, and she was pleased to see she looked so well. The last time she had worn all these fine feathers was on the evening she returned home with brown hair and softened wrinkles from Overstrand. That was not a successful evening: it seemed that the rose-coloured silk was destined to shine on inauspicious scenes. But now she was ready: this was her last moment alone. And she plumped down on her knees by the bedside, in a sudden of despair at what lay before her, and found her lips involuntarily repeating the words that were used in the hugest and most holy agony that man's spirit has ever known, when for one moment He felt that even He could not face the sacrifice of Himself or to drink of the cup. But next moment she sprang from her knees again, her face all aflame with shame at her paltriness. "You wretched little coward!" she said to herself. "How dare you?"

Dinner, that long expensive dinner, brought with it trouble unanticipated by Mrs. Ames. Mr. Chilcot, it appeared, was a teetotaler at all times, and never ate anything but a couple of poached eggs before he made a speech. He was also, owing to recent experiences, a little nervous about Suffragettes, and required reiterated assurances that unaccountable females had not been seen about.

"It's true that a week or two ago I received a letter asking me my views," said Sir James, "but I wrote a fairly curt reply, and have heard nothing more about it. My agent's pretty wide awake. He would have known if there was likely to be any disturbance. No thanks, Major, one glass of champagne is all I allow myself before making a speech. Capital wine, I know; I always say you give one the best glass of wine to be had in Kent. How's time, by the way? Ah, we've got plenty of time yet."

"I like to have five minutes' quiet before going on to the platform," said Mr. Chilcot.

"Yes, that will be all right. Perhaps we might have the motor five minutes earlier, Cousin Amy. No, no sweetbread thanks. Dear me, what a great dinner you are giving us."

An awful and dismal atmosphere descended. Mr. Chilcot, thinking of his speech, frowned at his poached eggs, and, when they were finished, at the tablecloth. Cousin James refused dish after dish, Mrs. Ames felt herself incapable of eating, and Major Ames and Mrs. Evans, who was practically a vegetarian, were left to do the carousing. Wines went round untouched, silences grew longer, and an interminable succession of dishes failed to tempt anybody except Major Ames. At this rate, not one, but a whole series of luncheon-parties would be necessary to finish up the untouched dainties of this ill-starred dinner. Outside, a brisk tattoo of rain beat on the windows, and the wind having got up, the fire began to smoke, and Mr. Chilcot to cough. A readjustment of door and window mended this matter, but sluiced Cousin James in a chilly draught. Mr. Chilcot brightened up a little as coffee came round, but the coffee was the only weak spot in an admirable repast, being but moderately warm. He put it down. Mrs. Ames tried to repair this error.

CHAPTER XI

"I'm afraid it is not hot enough," she said. "Parker, tell them to heat it up at once."

Cousin James looked at his watch.

"Really, I think we ought to be off," he said. "I'm sure they can get a cup of coffee for Mr. Chilcot from the hotel. We might all go together unless you have ordered something, Cousin Amy. The motor holds five easily."

A smart, chill October rain was falling, and they drove through blurred and disconsolate streets. A few figures under umbrellas went swiftly along the cheerless pavements, a crowd of the very smallest dimensions, scarce two deep across the pavement opposite the town hall, watched the arrival of those who were attending the meeting. There was an insignificant queue of half-a-dozen carriages awaiting their disembarkments, but as the hands of the town hall clock indicated that the meeting was not timed to begin for twenty minutes yet, even Mr. Chilcot could not get agitated about the possibility of a cup of coffee before his effort. Through the rain-streaked windows Mrs. Ames could see how meagre, owing no doubt to the inclement night, was the assembly of the ticket-holders. It was possible, of course, that crowds might soon begin to arrive, but Riseborough generally made a point of being in its place in plenty of time, and she anticipated a sparsely attended room. Mrs. Brooks hurried by in mackintosh and goloshes, the cheerful Turner family, who were just behind them in a cab, dived into the wet night, and emerged again under the awning. Mrs. Currie (wife of the station-master), with her Suffragette rosette in a paper parcel, had a friendly word with a policeman at the door, and at these sights, since they indicated a forcible assemblage of the league, she felt a little encouraged. Then the car moved on and stopped again opposite the awning, and their party dismounted.

A bustling official demanded their tickets, and was summarily thrust aside by another, just as bustling but more enlightened, who had recognized Sir James, and conducted them all to the Mayor's parlour, where that dignitary received them. There was coffee already provided, and all anxiety on that score was removed. Mr. Chilcot effaced himself in a corner with his cup and his notes, while the others, notably Sir James, behaved with that mixture of social condescension and official deference which appears to be the right attitude in dealing with mayors. Then the Mayoress said, "George, dear, it has gone the half-hour; will you escort Mrs. Ames?"

George asked Mrs. Ames if he might have the honour, and observed--

"We shall have but a thin meeting, I am afraid. Most inclement for October."

Mrs Ames pulled her cloak a little closer round her, in order to hide a chain that was more significant than the Mayor's, and felt the little black velvet bag beating time to her steps against her knee.

They walked through the stark bare passages, with stone floors that exuded cold moisture in sympathy with the wetness of the evening, and came out into a sudden blaze of light.

A faint applause from nearly empty benches heralded their appearance, and they disposed themselves on a row of plush arm-chairs behind a long oak table. The Mayor sat in the centre, to right and left of him Sir James and Mr. Chilcot. Just opposite Mrs. Ames was a large table-leg, which had for her the significance of the execution-shed.

She put her bag conveniently on her knees, and quietly unloosed the latch that fastened it. There were no more preparations to be made just yet, since the chain was quite ready, and in a curious irresponsible calm she took further note of her surroundings. Scarcely a hundred people were there, all told, and face after face, as she passed her eyes down the seats, was friendly and familiar. Mrs. Currie bowed, and the Turner family, in a state of the pleasantest excitement, beamed; Mrs. Brooks gave her an excited hand-wave. They were all sitting in encouraging vicinity to each other, but she was alone, as on the inexorable seas, while they were on the pier . . . Then the Mayor cleared his throat.

It had been arranged that the Mayor was to be given an uninterrupted hearing, for he was the local grocer, and it had, perhaps, been tacitly felt that he might adopt retaliatory measures in the inferior quality of the subsequent supplies of sugar. He involved himself in sentences that had no end, and would probably have gone on for ever, had he not, with commendable valour, chopped off their tails when their coils threatened to strangle him, and begun again. The point of it all was that they had the honour to welcome the President of the Board of Trade and Sir James Westbourne. Luckily, the posters, with which the town had been placarded for the last fortnight, corroborated the information, and no reasonable person could any longer doubt it.

He was rejoiced to see so crowded an assembly met together--this was not very happy, but the sentence had been carefully thought out, and it was a pity not to reproduce it--and was convinced that they would all spend a most interesting and enjoyable evening, which would certainly prove to be epoch-making. Politics were taken seriously in Riseborough, and it was pleasant to see the gathering graced by so many members of the fair sex. He felt he had detained them all quite long enough (no) and he would detain them no longer (yes), but call on the Right Honourable Mr. Chilcot (cheers).

As Mr. Chilcot rose, Mr. Turner rose also, and said in a clear, cheerful voice, "Votes for Women." He had a rosette, pinned a little crookedly, depending from his shoulder. Immediately his wife and daughter rose too, and in a sort of Gregorian chant said, "Women's rights," and a rattle of chains made a pleasant light accompaniment. From beneath her seat Mrs. Currie produced a banner trimmed with the appropriate colours, on which was embroidered "Votes for Women." But the folds clung dispiritingly together: there was never a more dejected banner. Two stalwart porters whom she had brought with her also got up, wiped their mouths with the backs of their hands, and said in low, hoarse tones, "Votes for Women."

CHAPTER XI

This lasted but a few seconds, and there was silence again. It was impossible to imagine a less impressive demonstration: it seemed the incarnation of ineffectiveness. Mr. Chilcot had instantly sat down when it began, and, though he had cause to be shy of Suffragettes, seemed quite undisturbed; he was smiling good-naturedly, and for a moment consulted his notes again. And then, suddenly, Mrs. Ames realized that she had taken no share in it; it had begun so quickly, and so quickly ended, that for the time she had merely watched. But then her blood and her courage came back to her: it should not be her fault, in any case, if the proceedings lacked fire. The Idea, all that had meant so much to her during these last months, seemed to stand by her, asking her aid. She opened the little black velvet bag, pinned on her rosette, passed the second chain (strong enough to hold a mastiff) through the first, and round the leg of the table in front of her, heard the spring lock click, and rose to her feet, waving her hand.

"Votes for Women!" she cried. "Votes for Women. Hurrah!"

Instantly every one on the platform turned to her: she saw Lyndhurst's inflamed and astonished face, with mouth fallen open in incredulous surprise, like a fish in an aquarium: she saw Cousin James' frown of distinguished horror. Mrs. Evans looked as if about to laugh, and the Mayoress said, "Lor'!" Mr. Chilcot turned round in his seat, and his good-humoured smile faded, leaving an angry fighting face. But all this hostility and amazement, so far from cowing or silencing her, seemed like a draught of wine. "Votes for Women!" she cried again.

At that the cry was taken up in earnest: by a desperate effort Mrs. Currie unfurled her banner, so that it floated free, her porters roared out their message with the conviction they put into their announcements to a stopping train that this was Riseborough, the Turner family gleefully shouted together: Mrs. Brooks, unable to adjust her rosette, madly waved it, and a solid group of enthusiasts just below the platform emitted loud and militant cries. All that had been flat and lifeless a moment before was inspired and vital. And Mrs. Ames had done it. For a moment she had nothing but glory in her heart.

Mr. Chilcot leaned over the table to her.

"I had no idea," he said, "when I had the honour of dining with you that you proposed immediately afterwards to treat me with such gross discourtesy."

"Votes for Women!" shouted Mrs. Ames again.

This time the cry was less vehemently taken up, for there was nothing to interrupt. Mr. Chilcot conferred a moment quietly with Sir James, and Mrs. Ames saw that Lyndhurst and Mrs. Evans were talking together: the former was spluttering with rage, and Mrs. Evans had laid her slim, white-gloved hand on his knee, in the attempt, it appeared, to soothe him. At present the endeavour did not seem to be meeting with any notable measure of success. Even in the midst of her excitement, Mrs, Ames thought how ludicrous Lyndhurst's face was; she also felt sorry for him. As well, she had the sense of this being tremendous fun: never in her life had she been so effective, never had she even for a moment paralysed the plans of other people. But she was doing that now; Mr. Chilcot had come here to speak, and she was not permitting him to. And again she cried "Votes for Women!"

An inspector of police had come on to the platform, and after a few words with Sir James, he vaulted down into the body of the hall. Next moment, some dozen policemen tramped in from outside, and immediately afterwards the Turner family, still beaming, were being trundled down the gangway, and firmly ejected. Sundry high notes and muffled shoutings came from outside, but after a few seconds they were dumb, as if a tap had been turned off. There was a little more trouble with Mrs. Currie, but a few smart tugs brought away the somewhat flimsy wooden rail to which she had attached herself, and she was taken along in a sort of tripping step, like a cheerful dancing bear, with her chains jingling round her, after the Turners, and quietly put out into the night. Then Sir James came across to Mrs. Ames.

"Cousin Amy," he said, "you must please give us your word to cause no more disturbance, or I shall tell a couple of men to take you away."

"Votes for Women!" shouted Mrs. Ames again. But the excitement which possessed her was rapidly dying, and from the hall there came no response except very audible laughter.

"I am very sorry," said Cousin James

And then, with a sudden overwhelming wave, the futility of the whole thing struck her. What had she done? She had merely been extremely rude to her two guests, had seriously annoyed her husband, and had aroused perfectly justifiable laughter. General Fortescue was sitting a few rows off: he was looking at her through his pince-nez, and his red, good-humoured face was all a-chink with smiles. Then two policemen, one of whom had his beat in St. Barnabas Road, vaulted up on to the platform, and several people left their places to look on from a more advantageous position.

"Beg your pardon, ma'am," said the St. Barnabas policeman, touching his helmet with imperturbable politeness. "She's chained up too, Bill."

Bill was a slow, large, fatherly-looking man, and examined Mrs. Ames' fetters. Then a broad grin broke out over his amiable face.

"It's only just passed around the table-leg," he said. "Hitch up the table-leg, mate, and slip it off."

It was too true . . . patent lock and mastiff-holding chain were slipped down the table-leg, and Mrs. Ames, with the fatherly-looking policeman politely carrying her chains and the little velvet bag, was gently and inevitably propelled through the door which, a quarter of an hour ago, she had entered escorted by the Mayor, and down the stone passage and out into the dripping street. The rain fell heavily on to the rose-coloured silk dress, and the fatherly policeman put her cloak, which had half fallen off, more shelteringly round her.

"Better have a cab, ma'am, and go home quietly," he said. "You'll catch cold if you stay here, and we can't let you in again, begging your pardon, ma'am."

Mrs. Ames looked round: Mrs. Currie was just crossing the road, apparently on her way home, and a carriage drove off containing the Turner family. A sense of utter failure and futility possessed her: it was cold and wet, and a chilly wind flapped the awning, blowing a shower of dripping raindrops on to her. The excitement and courage that had possessed her just now had all oozed away: nothing had been effected, unless to make herself ridiculous could be counted as an achievement.

"Call a cab for the lady, Bill," said her policeman soothingly.

This was soon summoned, and Bill touched his helmet as she got in, and before closing the door pulled up the window for her. The cabman also knew her, and there was no need to give him her address. The rain pattered on the windows and on the roof, and the horse splashed briskly along through the puddles in the roadway.

Parker opened the door to her, surprised at the speediness of her return.

"Why, ma'am!" she exclaimed, "has anything happened?"

"No, nothing, Parker," said she, feeling that a dreadful truth underlay her words. "Tell the Major, when he comes in, that I have gone to bed."

She looked for a moment into the dining-room. So short a time had passed that the table was not yet cleared: the printed menu-cards had been collected, but the coffee, which had not been hot enough, still stood untasted in the cups, and the slices of pineapple, cut, but not eaten, were ruinously piled together. The thought of all the luncheons that would be necessary to consume all this expensive food made her feel sick. . . . These little things had assumed a ridiculous size to her mind; that which had seemed so big was pitifully dwindled. She felt desperately tired, and cold and lonely.

CHAPTER XII

"And what's to be done now?" said Major Ames, chipping his bacon high into the air above his plate. "If you didn't hear me, I said, 'What's to be done now?' I don't know how you can look Riseborough in the face again, and, upon my word, I don't see how I can. They'll point at me in the street, and say, 'That's Major Ames, whose wife made a fool of herself.' That's what you did, Amy. You made a fool of yourself. And what was the good of it all? Are you any nearer getting the vote than before, because you've screamed 'Votes for Women' a dozen times? You've only given a proof the more of how utterly unfit you are to have anything at all of your own, let alone a vote. I passed a sleepless night with thinking of your folly, and I feel infernally unwell this morning."

This clearly constituted a climax, and Mrs. Ames took advantage of the rhetorical pause that followed.

"Nonsense, Lyndhurst," she said; "I heard you snoring."

"It's enough to make a man snore," he said. "Snore, indeed! Why couldn't you even have told me that you were going to behave like a silly lunatic, and if I couldn't have persuaded you to behave sanely, I could have stopped away, instead of looking on at such an exhibition? Every one will suppose I must have known about it, and have countenanced you. I've a good mind to write to the *Kent Chronicle* and say that I was absolutely ignorant of what you were going to do. You've disgraced us; that's what you've done."

He took a gulp of tea, imprudently, for it was much hotter than he anticipated.

"And now I've burned my mouth!" he said.

Mrs. Ames put down her napkin, left her seat, and came and stood by him.

"I am sorry you are so much vexed," she said, "but I can't and I won't discuss anything with you if you talk like that. You are thinking about nothing but yourself, whether you are disgraced, and whether you have had a bad night."

"Certainly you don't seem to have thought about me," he said.

"As a matter of fact I did," she said. "I knew you would not like it, and I was sorry. But do you suppose I liked it? But I thought most about the reason for which I did it."

"You did it for notoriety," said Major Ames, with conviction. "You wanted to see your name in the papers, as having interrupted a Cabinet Minister's speech. You won't even have that satisfaction, I am glad to say. Your cousin James, who is a decent sort of fellow after all, spoke to the reporters last night and asked them to leave out all account of the disturbance. They consented; they are decent fellows too; they didn't want to give publicity to your folly. They were sorry for you, Amy; and how do you like half-a-dozen reporters at a pound a week being sorry for you? Your cousin James was equally generous. He bore no malice to me, and shook hands with me, and said he saw you were unwell when he sat down to dinner. But when a man of the world, as your Cousin James is, says he thinks that a woman is unwell, I know what he means. He thought you were intoxicated. Drunk, in fact. That's what he thought. He thought you were drunk. My wife drunk. And it was the kindest interpretation he could have put upon it. Mad or drunk. He chose drunk. And he hoped I should be able to come over some day next week and help him to thin out the pheasants. Very friendly, considering all that had happened."

Mrs. Ames moved slightly away from him.

"Do you mean to go?" she asked.

"Of course I mean to go. He shows a very generous spirit, and I think I can account for the highest of his rocketters. He wants to smooth things over and be generous, and all that--hold out the olive branch. He recognizes that I've got to live down your folly, and if it's known that I've been shooting with him, it will help us. Forgive and forget, hey? I shall just go over there, *en garçon,* and will patch matters up. I dare say he'll ask you over again some time. He doesn't want to be hard on you. Nor do I, I am sure. But there are things no man can stand. A man's got to put his foot down sometimes, even if he puts it down on his wife. And if I was a bit rough with you just now, you must realize, Amy, you must realize that I felt strongly, strongly and rightly. We've got to live down what you have done. Well, I'm by you. We'll live it down together. I'll make your peace with your cousin. You can trust me."

These magnificent assurances failed to dazzle Mrs. Ames, and she made no acknowledgment of them. Instead, she went back rather abruptly and inconveniently to a previous topic.

"You tell me that Cousin James believed I was drunk," she said. "Now you knew I was not. But you seem to have let it pass."

Major Ames felt that more magnanimous assurances might be in place.

"There are some things best passed over," he said. "Let sleeping dogs lie. I think the less we talk about last night the better. I hope I am generous enough not to want to rub it in, Amy, not to make you more uncomfortable than you are."

Mrs. Ames sat down in a chair by the fireplace. A huge fire burned there, altogether disproportionate to the day, and she screened her face from the blaze with the morning paper. Also she made a mental note to speak to Parker about it.

"You are making me very uncomfortable indeed, Lyndhurst," she said; "by not telling me what I ask you. Did you let it pass, when you saw James thought I was drunk?"

"Yes; he didn't say so in so many words. If he had said so, well, I dare say I should have--have made some sort of answer. And, mind you, it was no accusation he made against you; he made an excuse for you!"

Mrs. Ames' small, insignificant face grew suddenly very firm and fixed.

"We do not need to go into that," she said. "You saw he thought I was drunk, and said nothing. And after that you mean to go over and shoot his pheasants. Is that so?"

"Certainly it is. You are making a mountain out of--"

"I am making no mountain out of anything. Personally, I don't believe Cousin James thought anything of the kind. What matters is that you let it pass. What matters is that I should have to tell you that you must apologize to me, instead of your seeing it for yourself."

Major Ames got up, pushing his chair violently back.

"Well, here's a pretty state of things," he cried; "that you should be telling me to apologize for last night's degrading exhibition! I wonder what you'll be asking next? A vote of thanks from the Mayor, I shouldn't wonder, and an illuminated address. You teaching me what I ought to do! I should have thought a woman would have been only too glad to trust to her husband, if he was so kind, as I have been, as to want to get her out of the consequences of her folly. And now it's you who must sit there, opposite a fire fit to roast an ox, and tell me I must apologize. Apologies be damned! There! It's not my habit to swear, as you well know, but there are occasions--Apologies be damned!"

And a moment later the house shook with the thunder of the slammed front door.

Mrs. Ames sat for a couple of minutes exactly where she was, still shielding her face from the fire. She felt all the chilling effects of the reaction that follows on excitement, whether the excitement is rapturous or as sickening as last night's had been, but not for a moment did she regret her share either in the events of the evening before or in the sequel of this morning. Last night had ended in utter fiasco, but she had done her best; this morning's talk had ended in a pretty sharp quarrel, but again she found it impossible to reconsider her share in it. Humanly she felt beaten and ridiculed and sick at heart, but not ashamed. She had passed a sleepless night, and was horribly tired, with that tiredness that seems to sap all pluck and power of resistance, and gradually her eyes grew dim, and the difficult meagre tears of middle age, which are so bitter, began to roll down her cheeks, and the hard inelastic sobs to rise in her throat. . . . Yet it was no use sitting here crying, lunch and dinner had to be ordered whether she felt unhappy or not; she had to see how extensive was the damage done to her pink satin shoes by the wet pavements last night; she had to speak about this ox-roasting fire. Also there was appointed a Suffragette meeting at Mr. Turner's house for eleven o'clock, at which past achievements and future plans would be discussed. She had barely time to wash her face, for it was unthinkable that Parker or the cook should see she had been crying, and get through her household duties, before it was time to start.

She dried her eyes and went to the window, through which streamed the pale saffron-coloured October sunshine. All the stormy trouble of the night had passed, and the air sparkled with "the clear shining after rain." But the frost of a few nights before had blackened the autumn flowers, and the chill rain had beaten down the glory of her husband's chrysanthemums, so that the garden-beds looked withered and dishevelled, like those whose interest in life is finished, and who no longer care what appearance they present. The interest of others in them seemed to be finished also; it was not the gardener's day here, for he only came twice in the week, and Major Ames, who should have been assiduous in binding up the broken-stemmed, encouraging the invalids, and clearing away the havoc wrought by the storm, had left the house. Perhaps he had gone to the club, perhaps even now he was trying to make light of it all. She could almost hear him say, "Women get queer notions into their heads, and the notions run away with them, bless them. You'll take a glass of sherry with me, General, won't you? Are you by any chance going to Sir James' shoot next week? I'm shooting there one day." Or was he talking it over somewhere else, perhaps not making light of it? She did not know; all she knew was that she was alone, and wanted somebody who understood, even if he disagreed. It did not seem to matter that Lyndhurst utterly disagreed with her, what mattered was that he had misunderstood her motives so entirely, that the monstrous implication that she had been intoxicated seemed to him an excuse. And he was not sorry. What could she do since he was not sorry? It was as difficult to answer that as it was easy to know what to do the moment he was sorry. Indeed, then it would be unnecessary to do anything; the reconciliation would be automatic, and would bring with it something she yearned after, an opportunity of making him see that she cared, that the woman in her reached out towards him, in some different fashion now from that in which she had tried to recapture the semblance of youth and his awakened admiration. To-day, she looked back on that episode shamefacedly. She had taken so much trouble with so paltry a purpose. And yet that innocent and natural coquetry was not quite dead in her; no woman's heart need be so old that it no longer cares whether she is pleasing in her husband's eyes. Only to-day, it seemed to Mrs. Ames that her pains had been as disproportionate to her purpose as they had been to its result; now she longed to take pains for a purpose that was somewhat deeper than that for which she softened her wrinkles and refreshed the colour of her hair.

She turned from the window and the empty garden, wishing that the rain would be renewed, so that there would be an excuse for her to go to Mr. Turner's in a shut cab. As it was, there was no such excuse, and she felt that it would require an effort to walk past the club window, and to traverse the length of the High Street. Female Riseborough, on this warm sunny morning, she knew would be there in force, popping in and out of shops, and holding little conversations on the pavement. There would be but one topic to-day, and for many days yet; it would be long before the autumn novelty lost anything of its freshness. She wondered how her appearance in the town would be greeted; would people smile and turn aside as she approached, and whisper or giggle after she had gone by? What of the Mayor who, like an honest tradesman, was often to be seen at the door of his shop, or looking at the "dressing" of his windows? A policeman always stood at the bottom of the street, controlling the cross-traffic from St. Barnabas Road.

Would he be that one who had helped to further her movements last night? . . . She almost felt she ought to thank him. . . . And then quite suddenly her pluck returned again, or it was that she realized that she did not, comparatively speaking, care two straws for any individual comment or by-play that might take place in the High Street, or for its accumulated weight. There were other things to care about. For them she cared immensely.

The High Street proved to be paved with incident. Turning quickly round the corner, she nearly ran into Bill, the policeman, off duty at this hour, and obviously giving a humorous recital of some sort to a small amused circle outside the public-house. It was abruptly discontinued when she appeared, and she felt that the interest that his audience developed in the sunny October sky, which they contemplated with faint grins, would be succeeded by stifled laughter after she had passed. A few paces further on, controlling the traffic of market-day, was her other policeman Bill, who smiled in a pleasant and familiar manner to her, as if there was some capital joke private to them. Twenty yards further along the street was standing the Mayor, contemplating his shop-window; he saw her, and urgent business appeared to demand his presence inside. After that there came General Fortescue tottering to the club; he crossed the street to meet her, and took off his hat and shook hands.

"By Jove! Mrs. Ames," he said, "I never enjoyed a meeting so much, and my wife's wild that she didn't go. What a lark! Made me feel quite young again. I wanted to shout too, and tell them to give the ladies a vote. Monstrously amusing! Just going to the club to have a chat about it all."

And he went on his way, with his fat old body shaking with laughter. Then, feeling rather ill from this encounter, she heard rapid steps in pursuit of her, and Mrs. Altham joined her.

"Oh, Mrs. Ames," she said. "I could die of vexation that I was not there. Is it really true that you threw a glass of water at Mr. Chilcot and hit the policeman? Fancy, that it should have been such a terribly wet night, and Henry and I just sat at home, never thinking that five minutes in a cab would make such a difference. We sat and played patience; I should have been most impatient if I had known. And what is to happen next? It was so stupid of me not to join your league; I wonder if it is too late."

This was quite dreadful; Mrs. Ames had been prepared for her husband's anger, and for pride and aversion from people like Mrs. Altham. What was totally unexpected and unwelcome was that she was supposed to have scored a sort of popular success, that Riseborough considered the dreadful fiasco of last night as an achievement, something not only to talk about, but a kind of new game, more exciting than croquet or criticism. She had begun by thinking of the Suffragette movement as an autumn novelty, but leanness came very near her soul when she found that it now appeared to others as she had first thought of it herself. She had travelled since then; she had seen the *hinterland* of it; the idea that rose up behind it, austere and beautiful and wise. All that these others saw was just the hysterical jungle that bounded the coast. To her this morning, after her experience of it, the hysterical jungle seemed--an hysterical jungle. If it was only by that route that the heights could be attained, then that route must be followed. She was willing to try it again. But was there not somewhere and somehow a better road?

It was not necessary to be particularly cordial to Mrs. Altham, and she held out no certain prospect of an immediate repetition of last night's scenes, nor of a desire for additional recruits. But further trials awaited her in this short walk. Dr. Evans, driving the high-stepping cob, wheeled round, and dismounted, throwing the reins to the groom.

"I must just congratulate you," he said, "for Millie told me about last night. I've been telling her that if she had half your pluck, she would be the better for it. I hope you didn't catch cold; beastly night, wasn't it? Do let me know when it will come on again. I hate your principles, you know, but I love your practise. I shall come and shout, too!"

This was perfectly awful. Nobody understood; they all sympathized with her, but cared not two straws for that which had prompted her to do these sensational things. . . . They liked the sensational things . . . it was fun to them. But it was no fun to those who believed in the principles which prompted them. They thought of her as a clown at a pantomime; they wanted to see Dan Leno. . . .

She was some minutes late when she reached Mr. Turner's house, depressed and not encouraged by this uncomprehending applause that took as an excellent joke all the manifestations which had been directed by so serious a purpose. What to her was tragic and necessary, was to them a farce of entertaining quality. But now she would meet her coreligionists again, those who knew, those whose convictions, of the same quality as hers, were of such weight as to make her feel that even her quarrel with Lyndhurst was light in comparison.

The jovial Turner family, father, mother, daughter, were in the drawing-room, and they hailed her as a heroine. If it had not been for her, there would have been no "scene" at all. Did the policemen hurt? Mr. Turner had got a small bruise on his knee, but it was quite doubtful whether he got it when he was taken out. Mrs. Turner had lost a small pearl ornament, but she was not sure whether she had put it on before going to the meeting. Miss Turner had a cold to-day, but it was certain that she had felt it coming on before they were all put out into the rain. None of them had seen the end; it was supposed that Mrs. Ames had thrown a glass of water at a policeman, and had hit Mr. Chilcot. They were all quite ready for Sir James' next meeting; or would he be a coward, and cause scrutiny to be held on those who desired admittance?

Mrs. Brooks arrived; she had not been turned out last night, but she had caught cold, and did not think that much had been achieved. Mr. Chilcot had made his speech, apparently a very clever one, about Tariff Reform, and Sir James had followed, without interruption, telling the half empty but sympathetic benches about the House of Lords. There had been no allusion made to the disturbance, or to the motives that prompted it. Also she had lost her Suffragette rosette. It must have been torn off her, though she did not feel it go.

Mrs. Currie brought more life into the proceedings. She could get four porters to come to the next meeting, and could make another banner, as well as ensuring the proper unfurling of the first, which had stuck so unaccountably. It had waved quite properly when she had tried it an hour before, and it had waved quite properly (for it had been returned to her after she had been ejected) when she tried it again an hour later at home. Two banners expanding properly would be a vastly different affair from one that did not expand at all. Her husband had laughed fit to do himself a damage over her account of the proceedings.

A dozen more only of the league made an appearance, for clearly there was a reaction and a cooling after last night's conflagration, but all paid their meed of appreciation to Mrs. Ames. Their little rockets had but fizzed and spluttered until she "showed them the way," as Mrs. Currie expressed it. But to them even it was the ritual, so to speak, the disturbance, the shouting, the sense of doing something, rather than the belief that lay behind the ritual, which stirred their imaginations. Could the cause be better served by the endurance of an hour's solitary toothache, than by waving banners in the town hall, and being humanely ejected by benevolent policemen, there would have been less eagerness to suffer. And Mrs. Ames would so willingly have passed many hours of physical pain rather than suffer the heartache which troubled her this morning. And nobody seemed to understand; Mrs. Currie with her four porters and two banners, Mrs. Brooks with her cold in the head and odour of eucalyptus, the cheerful Turners who thought it would be such a good idea to throw squibs on to the platform, were all as far from the point as General Fortescue, chatting at the club, or even as Lyndhurst with the high-chipped bacon and the slammed front door. It was a game to them, as it had originally presented itself to her, an autumn novelty for, say, Thursday afternoon from five till seven. If only the opposite effects had been produced; if they all had taken it as poignantly as Lyndhurst, and he as cheerily as they!

He, meantime, after slamming the front door, had stormed up St. Barnabas Road, in so sincere a passion that he had nearly reached the club before he remembered that he had hardly touched his breakfast or glanced at the paper. So, as there was no sense in starving himself (the starvation consisting in only having half his breakfast), he turned in at those hospitable doors, and ordered himself an omelette. Never in his life had he been so angry, never in the amazing chronicle of matrimony, so it seemed to him, had a man received such provocation from his wife. She had insulted the guests who had dined with her, she made a public and stupendous ass of herself, and when, next morning, he, after making such expostulations as he was morally bound to make, had been so nobly magnanimous as to assure her that he would patch it all up for her, and live it down with her, he had been told that it was for him to apologize! No wonder he had sworn; Moses would have sworn; it would have been absolutely wrong of him not to swear. There were situations in which it was cowardly for a man not to say what he thought. Even now, as he waited for his omelette, he emitted little squeaks and explosive exclamations, almost incredulous of his wrongs.

He ate his omelette, which seemed but to add fuel to his rage, and went into the smoking-room, where, over a club cigar, for he had actually forgotten to bring his own case with him, he turned to the consideration of practical details. It was not clear how to re-enter his house again. He had gone out with a bang that made the windows rattle, but it was hardly possible to go on banging the door each time he went in and out, for no joinery would stand these reiterated shocks. And what was to be done, even if he could devise an effective re-entry? Unless Amy put herself into his hands, and unreservedly took back all that she had said, it was impossible for him to speak to her. Somehow he felt that there were few things less likely to happen than this. Certainly it would be no good to resume storming operations, for he had no guns greater than those he had already fired, and if they were not of sufficient calibre, he must just beleaguer her with silence--dignified, displeased silence.

He looked up and saw that Mr. Altham was regarding him through the glass door; upon which Mr. Altham rapidly withdrew. Not long afterwards young Morton occupied and retired from the same observatory. A moment's reflection enabled Major Ames to construe this singular behaviour. They had heard of his wife's conduct, and were gluttonously feeding on so unusual a spectacle as himself in the club at this hour, and reconstructing in their monkey-minds his domestic disturbances. They would probably ascertain that he had breakfasted here. It was all exceedingly unpleasant; there was no sympathy in their covert glances, only curiosity.

No one who is not a brute, and Major Ames was not that, enjoys a quarrel with his wife, and no one who is not utterly self-centred, and he was not quite that either, fails to desire sympathy when such a quarrel has occurred. He wanted sympathy now; he wanted to pour out into friendly ears the tale of Amy's misdeeds, of his own magnanimity, to hear his own estimation of his conduct confirmed, fairly confirmed, by a woman who would see the woman's point of view as well as his. The smoking-room with these peeping Toms was untenable, but he thought he knew where he could get sympathy.

Millie was in and would see him; from habit, as he crossed the hall he looked to the peg where Dr. Evans hung his hat and coat, and, seeing they were not there, inferred that the doctor was out. That suited him; he wanted to confide and be sympathized with, and felt that Evans' breezy optimism and out-of-door habit of mind would not supply the kind of comfort he felt in need of. He wanted to be told he was a martyr and a very fine fellow, and that Amy was unworthy of him. . . .

Millie was in the green, cool drawing-room, where they had sat one day after lunch. She rose as he entered and came towards him with a tremulous smile on her lips, and both hands outstretched.

"Dear Lyndhurst," she said. "I am so glad you have come. Sit down. I think if you had not come I should have telephoned to ask if you would not see me. I should have suggested our taking a little walk, perhaps, for I do not think I could have risked seeing Cousin Amy. I know how you feel, oh, so well. It was abominable, disgraceful."

Certainly he had come to the right place. Millie understood him: he had guessed she would. She sat down close beside him, and for a moment held her hand over her eyes.

"Ah, I have been so angry this morning," she said; "and it has given me a headache. Wilfred laughed about it all; he said also that what Amy did showed a tremendous lot of pluck. It was utterly heartless. I knew how you must be suffering, and I was so angry with him. He did not understand. Oh no, my headache is nothing; it will soon be gone--now."

She faintly emphasized the last word, stroked it, so to speak, as if calling attention to it.

"I'm broken-hearted about it," said Major Ames, which sounded better than to say, "I'm in a purple rage about it." "I'm broken-hearted. She's disgraced herself and me--"

"No, not you."

"Yes; a woman can't do that sort of thing without the world believing that her husband knew about it. And that's not all. Upon my word I'm not sure whether what she did this morning isn't worse than what you saw last night."

Millie leaned forward.

"Tell me," she said, "if it doesn't hurt you too much."

He decided it did not hurt him too much.

"Well, I came down this morning," he said, "willing and eager to make the best of a bad job. So were we all: James Westbourne last night was just as generous, and asked the reporters to say nothing about it, and invited me to a day's shooting next week. Very decent of him. As I say, I came down this morning, willing to make it as easy as I could. Of course, I knew I had to give Amy a good talking to: I should utterly have failed in my duty to her as a husband if I did not do that. I gave her a blowing-up, though not half of what she deserved, but a blowing up. Even then, when I had said my say I told her we would live it down together, which was sufficiently generous, I think. But, for her good, I told her that James Westbourne said he saw she was unwell, and that when a man says that he means that she is drunk. Perhaps Westbourne didn't mean that, but that's what it sounded like. And would you believe it, just because I hadn't knocked him down and stamped on his face, she tells me I ought to apologize to her for letting such a suggestion pass. Well, I flared up at that: what man of spirit wouldn't have flared up? I left the house at once, and went and finished my breakfast at the club. I should have choked--upon my word, I should have choked if I had stopped there, or got an apoplexy. As it is, I feel devilish unwell."

Millie got up, and stood for a moment in silence, looking out of the window, white and willowy.

CHAPTER XII

"I can never forgive Cousin Amy," she said at length. "Never!"

"Well, it is hard," said Major Ames. "And after all these years! It isn't exactly the return one might expect, perhaps."

"It is infamous," said Millie.

She came and sat down by him again.

"What are you going to do?" she asked.

"I don't know. If she apologizes, I shall forgive her, and I shall try to forget. But I didn't think it of her. And if she doesn't apologize--I don't know. I can't be expected to eat my words: that would be countenancing what she has done. I couldn't do it: it would not be sincere. I'm straight, I hope: if I say a thing it may be taken for granted that I mean it."

She looked up at him with her chin raised.

"I think you are wonderful," she said, "to be able even to think of forgiving her. If I had behaved like that, I should not expect Wilfred to forgive me. But then you are so big, so big. She does not understand you: she can't understand one thing about you. She doesn't know--oh, how blind some women are!"

It was little wonder that by this time Major Ames was beginning to feel an extraordinarily fine fellow, nor was it more wonderful that he basked in the warm sense of being understood. But from the first Millie had understood him. He felt that particularly now, at this moment, when Amy had so hideously flouted and wronged him. All through this last summer, the situation of to-day had been foreshadowed; it had always been in this house rather than in his own that he had been welcomed and appreciated. He had been the architect and adviser in the Shakespeare ball, while at home Amy dealt out her absurd printed menu-cards without consulting him. And the garden which he loved--who had so often said, "These sweet flowers, are they really for me?" Who, on the other hand, had so often said, "The sweet-peas are not doing very well, are they?" And then he looked at Millie's soft, youthful face, her eyes, that sought his in timid, sensitive appeal, her dim golden hair, her mouth, childish and mysterious. For contrast there was the small, strong, toad's face, the rather beady eyes, the hair--grey or brown, which was it? Also, Millie understood; she saw him as he was--generous, perhaps, to a fault, but big, big, as she had so properly said. She always made him feel so comfortable, so contented with himself. That was the true substance of a woman's mission, to make her husband happy, to make him devoted to her, instead of raising hell in the town hall, and insisting on apologies afterwards.

"You've cheered me up, Millie," he said; "you've made me feel that I've got a friend, after all, a friend who feels with me. I'm grateful; I'm--I'm more than grateful. I'm a tough old fellow, but I've got a heart still, I believe. What's to happen to us all?"

It was emotion, real and genuine emotion, that made Millie clever at that moment. Her mind was of no high order; she might, if she thought about a thing, be trusted to exhibit nothing more subtle than a fair grasp of the obvious. But now she did not think: she was prompted by an instinct that utterly transcended any achievement of which her brain was capable.

"Go back to your house," she said, "and be ready for Cousin Amy to say she is sorry. Very likely she is waiting for you there now. Oh, Lyndhurst--"

He got up at once: those few words made him feel completely noble; they made her feel noble likewise. The atmosphere of nobility was almost suffocating. . . .

"You are right," he said; "you are always all that is right and good and delicious? Ha!"

There was no question about the cousinly relations between them. So natural and spontaneous a caress needed no explanation.

The house was apparently empty when he got back, but he made sufficiently noisy an entry to advise the drawing-room, in any case, that he was returned, and personally ready, since he did not enter "full of wrath," like Hyperion, to accept apologies. Eventually he went in there, as if to look for a paper, in case of its being occupied, and, with the same pretext, strolled into his wife's sitting-room. Then, still casually, he went into his dressing-room, where he had slept last night, and satisfied himself that she was not in her bedroom. Her penitence, therefore, which would naturally be manifested by her waiting, dim-eyed, for his return, had not been of any peremptory quality.

He went out into the garden, and surveyed the damage of last night's rain. There was no need to punish the plants because Amy had been guilty of behaviour which her own cousin said was infamous: he also wanted something to employ himself with till lunch-time. As his hands worked mechanically, tying up some clumps of chrysanthemums which had a few days more of flame in their golden hearts, removing a débris of dead leaves and fallen twigs, his mind was busy also, working not mechanically but eagerly and excitedly. How different was the sympathy with which he was welcomed and comforted by Millie from the misunderstandings and quarrels which made him feel that he had wasted his years with one who was utterly unappreciative of him. Yet, if Amy was sorry, he was ready to do his best. But he wondered whether he wanted her to be sorry or not.

At half-past one the bell for lunch sounded, and, going into the drawing-room, he found that she had returned and was writing a note at her table. She did not look up, but said to him, just as if nothing had happened--

"Will you go in and begin, Lyndhurst? I want to finish my note."

He did not answer, but passed into the dining-room. In a little while she joined him.

"There seems to have been a good deal of rain in the night," she said. "I am afraid your flowers have suffered."

Certainly this did not look like penitence, and he had no reply for her. In some strange way this seemed to him the dignified and proper course.

Then Mrs. Ames spoke for the third time.

"I think, Lyndhurst, if we are not going to talk," she said, "I shall see what news there is. Parker, please fetch me the morning paper."

At that moment he hated her.

CHAPTER XII

CHAPTER XIII

Three days later Major Ames was walking back home in the middle of the afternoon, returning from the house in which he had lately spent so considerable a portion of his time. But this was the last day on which he would go there, nor would he, except for this one time more, cross the threshold of his own house. The climax had come, and within an hour or two he and Millie were going to leave Riseborough together.

Now that their decision had been made, it seemed to him that it had been inevitable from the first. Ever since the summer, when, from some mixture of genuine liking and false gallantry, he had allowed himself to drift into relations with her, the force that drew and held him had steadily increased in strength, and to-day it had proved itself irresistible. The determining factor no doubt had been his quarrel with his wife; that gave the impulse that had been still lacking, the final push which upset the equilibrium of that which was tottering and ready to fall over.

The scene this afternoon had been both short and quiet, as such scenes are. Dr. Evans had been called up to town on business yesterday morning, returning possibly this evening but more probably to-morrow, and they had lunched alone. Afterwards Major Ames had again spoken of his wife.

"The situation is intolerable," he had said. "I can't stand it. If it wasn't for you, Millie, I should go away."

She had come close to him.

"I'm not very happy, either," she said. "If it wasn't for you, I don't think I could stand it."

And then it was already inevitable.

"It's too strong for us," she said. "We can't help it. I will face anything with you. We will go right away, Lyndhurst, and live, instead of being starved like this."

She took both his hands in hers, completely carried away for the first time in her life by something outside herself. Treacherous and mean as was that course on which she was determined, she was, perhaps, a finer woman at this moment of supreme disloyalty than in all the years of her blameless married life.

"I've never loved before, Lyndhurst," she said quietly, "nor have I ever known what it meant. Now I can't consider anything else; it doesn't matter what happens to Wilfred and Elsie. Nothing matters except you."

CHAPTER XIII

This time it was not he who kissed her; it was she who pressed her mouth to his.

There was but little to settle, their plans were perfectly simple and ruthless. They would cross over to Boulogne that night, and, as soon as the law set them free, marry each other. A train to Folkestone left Riseborough in a little over an hour's time, running in connection with the boat. They could easily catch it. But it was wiser not to go to the station together: they would meet there.

As he walked home through the gleaming October afternoon, Major Ames was conscious neither of struggle nor regret. The power which Millie had had over him all these months, so that it was she always who really took the lead, and urged him one step forward and then another, gripped him and led him on here to the last step of all. He still obeyed and followed that slender, fragile woman who so soon would be his; it was as necessary to do her bidding here as it had been to kiss her, when first, under the mulberry-tree, she had put up her face towards his. These last days seemed to have killed all sense of loyalty and manhood within him; he gave no thought at all to his wife, and thought of Harry only as Amy's son. Besides, he was not responsible: man though he was, he was completely in the hands of this woman. All his life he had had no real principles to direct him, he had lived a decent life only because no temptation to live otherwise had ever really come near him, and even now it was in no way the wickedness of what he purposed that at all dragged him back; it was mere timidity at taking an irrevocable step.

Amy, he knew, was out: at breakfast she had announced to him that she did not expect to be in till dinner-time, and he had told her that he would be out for dinner. Such sentences dealing with household arrangements had been the sum of their discourse for the last days, and they were spoken not so much to each other as to the air, heard by, rather than addressed to any one in particular.

And yet the prospect of the life that should open for him, when once this irrevocable step had been taken, did not fill him with the resistless longing which, though it cannot excuse, at any rate accounts for the step itself. Millie, though throughout she had led him on until the climax was reached, had at least the authentic goad to drive her: life with him seemed to her to be real life: it was passionately that she desired it. But with him, apart from the force with which she dominated him, it was the escape from the very uncomfortable circumstances of home that chiefly attracted him. In a way, he loved her; he felt for her a warmth and a tenderness of stronger quality than he could remember having ever experienced before, and since it is not given to all men to love violently, it may be granted that he was feeling the utmost fire of which his nature was capable. But it was of sufficient ardour to burn up in his mind the rubbish of minor considerations and material exigencies.

Cabs were of infrequent occurrence at this far end of St. Barnabas Road, and meeting one by hazard just outside his house, he told the driver to wait. Then, letting himself in, he went straight up to his dressing-room. There was not time for him to pack his whole wardrobe, and a moderate portmanteau would be all he really needed. And here the trivialities began to wax huge and engrossing: though the afternoon was warm, it would no doubt be fresh, if not chilly on the boat, and it would certainly be advisable to take his thick overcoat, which at present had not left its summer quarters. Those were in a big cupboard in the passage outside, overlooking the garden, where it was packed away with prophylactic little balls of naphthaline. These had impregnated it somewhat powerfully, but it was better to be odorously than insufficiently clad. Passing the window he saw that the chrysanthemums had responded bravely to his comforting a few mornings ago: if there was no more frost they would be gay for another fortnight yet. Should he take a bouquet of them with him? He did not see why he should not have the enjoyment of them. Yet there was scarcely time to pick them: he must hurry on with the packing of his small portmanteau, which presented endless problems.

A panama hat should certainly be included; also a pair of white tennis shoes, in which he saw himself promenading on the parade: a white flannel suit, though it was October, seemed to complete the costume. He need not cumber himself with a dress coat: a dinner jacket was all that would be necessary. She had told him she had six hundred a year of her own: he had another three. It was annoying that his sponge was rather ragged; he had meant to buy a new one this morning. Perhaps Parker could draw it together with a bit of thread. An untidy sponge always vexed him: it was unsoldierly and slovenly. "Show me a man's washhand-stand," he had once said, "and I'll tell you about the owner." His own did not invite inspection, with its straggly sponge.

Then for a moment all these trivialities stood away from him, and for an interval he saw where he stood and what he was doing--the vileness, the sordidness, the vulgarity of it. High principles, nobility of life were not subjects with which hitherto he had much concerned himself, and it would be useless to expect that they should come to his rescue now, but for this moment his kindliness, such as it was, his affection for his wife, such as it was, but above all the continuous, unbroken smug respectability of his days read him a formidable indictment. What could he plead against such an accusation? No irresistible or imperative necessity of soul that claimed Millie as his by right of love. He knew that his desire for her was not of that fiery order, for he could see, undazzled and unburned, the qualities which attracted him. He admired her frail beauty, the youth that still encompassed her, he fed with the finest appetite on the devotion and admiration which she brought him. He loved being the god and the hero of this attractive woman, and it was this, far more than the devotion he brought her, that dominated him.

Respectability cried out against him and his foolishness. There would be no more strutting and swelling about the club among the mild and honourable men who frequented it, and looked up to him as an authority on India and gardening, nor any more of those pompous and satisfactory evenings when General Fortescue assured him that there was not such a good glass of port in Kent as that with which the Major supplied his guests. To be known as Major Ames, late of the Indian Army, had been to command respect; now, the less that he was known as Major Ames, late of Riseborough, the better would be the chance of being held in esteem. And to what sort of life would he condemn the woman, who for his sake was leaving a respectability no less solid than his own? To the companionship of such as herself, to the soiled doves of a French watering-place. That, of course, would be but a temporary habitation, but after that, what? Where was the society which would receive them, by which there would be any satisfaction in being received? Neither of them had the faintest touch of Bohemianism in their natures: both were of the school that is accustomed to silver teapots and life in houses with a garden behind. For a moment he hesitated as he folded back the sleeves of his dinner-jacket: then the tide of trivialities swept over him again, and he noticed that there was a spot of spilled wax on the cuff.

Among other engagements that Saturday afternoon, Mrs. Ames was occupied with the decoration of St. Barnabas' Church for the Sunday service next day, and she had gone there after lunch with an adornment of foliage tinted red by October, for she had not felt disposed to ask Lyndhurst if she might pick the remnant of his chrysanthemums. She, too, like him, felt the impossibility of the present situation, and, as she worked, she asked herself if it was in any way in her power to end this parody of domestic life. Every day she had made the attempt to begin the breaking of this ridiculous and most uncomfortable silence which lay between them, by the introduction of ordinary topics, hoping by degrees to build up again the breach that yawned between them, but at present she had got no sense of the slightest answering effort on his side. Psychically no less than conversationally he had nothing whatever to say to her. If in the common courtesies of daily life he had nothing for her, it seemed idle to hope to find further receptiveness if she opened discussion of their quarrel. Besides, a certain very natural pride blocked her way: he owed her an apology, and when she indicated that, he had sworn at her. It did not seem unreasonable (even when decorating a church) to expect the initiatory step to be taken by him. But what if he did not do so?

Mrs. Ames gave a little sigh, and her mouth and throat worked uncomfortably. The quarrel was so childish, yet it was serious, for it was not a light thing, whatever her provocation might have been, to pass days like these. Half-a-dozen times she went over the circumstances, and half-a-dozen times she felt that it was only just that he should make the advance to her, or at any rate behave with ordinary courtesy in answer to her ordinary civilities. It was true that the original dissension was due to her, but she believed with her whole heart in the cause for which she provoked it. All these last months she had felt her nature expand under the influence of this idea: she knew herself to be a better and a bigger woman than she had been. She believed in the rights of her sex, but had they not their duties too? It was nearly twenty-five years since she had voluntarily undertaken a certain duty. What if that came first, before any rights or privileges? What if that which she had undertaken then as a duty was in itself a right?

Yet even then, what could she do? In itself, she was very far from being ashamed of the part she had taken, yet was it possible to weigh this independently, without considering the points at which it conflicted with duties which certainly concerned her no less? She could not hope to convince her husband of the justice of the cause, nor of the expediency of promoting it in ways like these. For herself, she knew the justice of it, and saw no other expedient for promoting it. Those who had worked for the cause for years said that all else had been tried, that there remained only this violent crusading. But was not she personally, considering what her husband felt about it, debarred from taking part in the crusade? She had deeply offended and vexed him. Could anything but the stringency of moral law justify that? Nothing that he had done, nothing that he could do, short of the violation of the essential principles of married life, could absolve her from the accomplishment of one tittle of her duty towards him.

For a moment, in spite of her perplexity and the difficulty of her decision, Mrs. Ames smiled at herself for the mental use of all these great words like duty and privilege, over so small an incident. For what had happened? She had been a militant Suffragette on one occasion only, and at breakfast next morning he had, in matters arising therefrom, allowed himself to swear at her. Yet it seemed to her that, with all the pettiness and insignificance of it, great laws were concerned. For the law of kindness is broken by the most trumpery exhibition of inconsiderateness, the law of generosity by the most minute word of spite or backbiting. Indeed, it is chiefly in little things, since most of us are not concerned with great matters, that these violations occur, and in cups of cold water that they are fulfilled. And for once Mrs. Ames did not finish her decoration with tidiness and precision, a fact clearly noted by Mrs. Altham next day.

There was a Suffragette meeting at four, but she was prepared to be late for that, or, if necessary, to fail in attendance altogether. In any case, she would call in at home on her way there, on the chance that her husband might be in. She made no definite plan: it was impossible to forecast her share in the interview. But she had determined to try to suffer long, to be kind . . . to keep the promise of twenty-five years ago. There was a cab drawn up at the entrance, and it vaguely occurred to her that Millie might be here, for she had not seen her for some days, and it was possible she might have called. Yet it was hardly likely that she would have waited, since the servants would have told her that she herself was not expected home till dinner-time. Or was Lyndhurst giving her tea? And Mrs. Ames grew suddenly alert again about matters to which she had scarcely given a thought during these last months.

She let herself in, and went to the drawing-room: there was no one there, nor in the little room next it where they assembled before dinner on nights when they gave a party. But directly overhead she heard steps moving: that was in Lyndhurst's dressing-room.

She went up there, knocked, and in answer to his assent went in. The portmanteau was nearly packed, he stood in shirt-sleeves by it. In his hand was his sponge-bag--he had anticipated the entry of Parker with the stitched sponge.

She looked from the portmanteau to him, and back and back again.

"You are going away, Lyndhurst?" she asked.

CHAPTER XIII

He made a ghastly attempt to devise a reasonable answer, and thought he succeeded.

"Yes, I'm going--going to your cousin's to shoot. I told you he had asked me. You objected to my going, but I'm going all the same. I should have left you a note. Back to-morrow night."

Then she felt she knew all, as certainly as if he had told her.

"Since when has Cousin James been giving shooting parties on Sunday?" she asked. "Please don't lie to me, Lyndhurst. It makes it much worse. You are not going to Cousin James, and--you are not going alone. Shall I tell you any more?"

She was not guessing: all the events of the last month, the Shakespeare ball, Harrogate, their own quarrel, and on the top this foolish lie about a shooting party made a series of data which proclaimed the conclusion. And the suddenness of the discovery, the magnitude of the issues involved, but served to steady her. There was an authentic valour in her nature; even as she had stood up to interrupt the political meeting, without so much as dreaming of shirking her part, so now her pause was not timorous, but rather the rallying of all her forces, that came eager and undismayed to her summons.

Apparently Lyndhurst did not want to be told any more: he did not, at any rate, ask for it. Just then Parker came in with the mended sponge. She gave it him, and he stood with sponge-bag in one hand, sponge in the other.

"Shall I bring up tea, ma'am?" she said to Mrs. Ames.

"Yes, take it to the drawing-room now. And send the cab away. The Major won't want it."

Lyndhurst crammed the sponge into its bag.

"I shall want the cab, Parker," he said. "Don't send it away."

Mrs. Ames whisked round on Parker with amazing rapidity.

"Do as I tell you, Parker," she said, "and be quick!"

It was a mere conflict of will that, for the next five seconds, silently raged between them, but as definite and as hard-hitting as any affair of the prize ring. And it was impossible that there should be any but the one end to it, for Mrs. Ames devoted her whole strength and will to it, while from the first her husband's heart was not in the battle. But she was fighting for her all, and not only her all, but his, and not only his, but Millie's. Three existences were at stake, and the ruin of two homes was being hazarded. And when he spoke, she knew she was winning.

"I must go," he said. "She will be waiting at the station."

"She will wait to no purpose," said Mrs. Ames.

"She will be"--no word seemed adequate--"be furious," he said. "A man cannot treat a woman like that."

Any blow would do: he had no defence: she could strike him as she pleased.

"Elsie comes home next week," she said. "A pleasant home-coming. And Harry will have to leave Cambridge!"

"But I love her!" he said.

"Nonsense, my dear," she said. "Men don't ruin the women they love. Men, I mean!"

That stung; she meant that it should.

"But men keep their word," he said. "Let me pass."

"Keep your word to me," said she, "and try to help poor Millie to keep hers to her husband. It is not a fine thing to steal a man's wife, Lyndhurst. It is much finer to be respectable."

"Respectable!" he said. "And to what has respectability brought us? You and me, I mean?"

"Not to disgrace, anyhow," she said.

"It's too late," said he.

"Never quite too late, thank God," she said.

Mrs. Ames gave a little sigh. She knew she had won, and quite suddenly all her strength seemed to leave her. Her little trembling legs refused to uphold her, a curious buzzing was in her ears, and a crinkled mist swam before her eyes.

"Lyndhurst, I'm afraid I am going to make a goose of myself and faint," she said. "Just help me to my room, and get Parker--"

She swayed and tottered, and he only just caught her before she fell. He laid her down on the floor and opened the door and window wide. There was a flask of brandy in his portmanteau, laid on the top, designed to be easily accessible in case of an inclement crossing of the Channel. He mixed a tablespoonful of this with a little water, and as she moved, and opened her eyes again, he knelt down on the floor by her, supporting her.

"Take a sip of this, Amy," he said.

She obeyed him.

"Thank you, my dear," she said. "I am better. So silly of me."

"Another sip, then."

"You want to make me drunk, Lyndhurst," she said.

Then she smiled: it would be a pity to lose the opportunity for a humorous allusion to what at the time had been so far from humour.

"Really drunk, this time," she said. "And then you can tell Cousin James he was right."

She let herself rest longer than was physically necessary in the encircling crook of his arm, and let herself keep her eyes closed, though, if she had been alone, she would most decidedly have opened them. But those first few minutes had somehow to be traversed, and she felt that silence bridged them over better than speech. It was appropriate, too, that his arm should be round her.

"There, I am better," she said at length. "Let me get up, Lyndhurst. Thank you for looking after me."

She got on to her feet, but then sat down again in his easy-chair.

"Not quite steady yet?" he said.

"Very nearly. I shall be quite ready to come downstairs and give you your tea by the time you have unpacked your little portmanteau."

She did not even look at him, but sat turned away from him and the little portmanteau. But she heard the rustle of paper, the opening and shutting of drawers, the sound of metallic articles of toilet being deposited on dressing-table and washing-stand. After that came the click of a hasp. Then she got up.

"Now let us have tea," she said.

"And if Millie comes?" he asked.

She had been determined that he should mention her name first. But when once he had mentioned it she was more than ready to discuss the questions that naturally arose.

"You mean she may come back here to see what has happened to you?" she asked. "That is well thought of, dear. Let us see. But we will go downstairs."

She thought intently as they descended the staircase, and busied herself with tea-making before she got to her conclusion.

"She will ask for you," she said, "if she comes, and it would not be very wise for you to see her. On the other hand, she must be told what has happened. I will see her, then. It would be best that way."

Major Ames got up.

"No, I can't have that," he said. "I can't have that!"

"My dear, you have got to have it. You are in a dreadful mess. I, as your wife, am the only person who can get you out of it. I will do my best, anyhow."

She rang the bell.

"I am going to tell Parker to tell Millie that you are at home if she asks for you, and to show her in here," she said. "There is no other way that I can see. I do not intend to have nothing more to do with her. At least I want to avoid that, if possible, for that is a weak way out of difficulties. I shall certainly have to see her some time, and there is no use in putting it off. I am afraid, Lyndhurst, that you had better finish your tea at once, or take it upstairs. Take another cup upstairs; you have had but one, and drink it in your dressing-room, in the comfortable chair."

There was an extraordinary wisdom in this minute attention to detail, and it was by this that she was able to rise to a big occasion. It was necessary that he should feel that her full intention was to forgive him, and make the best of the days that lay before them. She had no great words and noble sentiment with which to convey this impression, but, in a measure, she could show him her mind by minute arrangements for his comfort. But he lingered, irresolute.

"You have got to trust me," she said. "Do as I tell you, my dear."

She had not long to wait after he had gone upstairs. She heard the ring at the bell, and next moment Millie came into the room. Her face was flushed, her breathing hurried, her eyes alight with trouble, suspense, and resentment.

"Lyndhurst," she began. "I waited--"

Then she saw Mrs. Ames, and turned confusedly about, as if to leave the room again. But Amy got up quickly.

"Come and sit down at once, Millie," she said. "We have got to talk. So let us make it as easy as we can for each other."

Millie was holding her muff up to her face, and peered at her from above it, wild-eyed, terrified.

"It isn't you I want," she said. "Where is Lyndhurst? I--I had an appointment with him. He was late--we--we were going a drive together. What do you know, Cousin Amy?" she almost shrieked; "and where is he?"

"Sit down, Millie, as I tell you," said Mrs. Ames very quietly. "There is nothing to be frightened at. I know everything."

"We were going a drive," began Millie again, still looking wildly about. "He did not come, and I was frightened. I came to see where he was. I asked you if you knew--if you knew anything about him, did I not? Why do you say you know everything?"

Suddenly Mrs. Ames saw that there was something here infinitely more worthy of pity than she had suspected. There was no question as to the agonized earnestness that underlay this futile, childish repetition of nonsense. And with that there came into her mind a greater measure of understanding with regard to her husband. It was not so wonderful that he had been unable to resist the face that had drawn him.

"Let us behave like sensible women, Millie," she said. "You have come down from the station. Lyndhurst was not there. Do you want me to tell you anything more?"

Millie wavered where she stood, then she stumbled into a chair.

"Has he given me up?" she said.

"Yes, if you care to put it like that. It would be truer to say that he has saved you and himself. But he is not coming with you."

"You made him?" she asked.

"I helped to make him," said Mrs. Ames.

Millie got up again.

"I want to see him," she said. "You don't understand, Cousin Amy. He has got to come. I don't care whether it is wicked or not. I love him. You don't understand him either. You don't know how splendid he is. He is unhappy at home; he has often told me so."

Mrs. Ames took hold of the wretched woman by both hands.

"You are raving, Millie," she said. "You must stop being hysterical. You hardly know whom you are talking to. If you do not pull yourself together, I shall send for your husband, and say you have been taken ill."

Millie gave a sudden gasp of laughter.

"Oh, I am not so stupid as you think!" she said. "Wilfred is away. Where is Lyndhurst?"

Mrs. Ames did not let go of her.

"Millie," she said, "if you are not sensible at once, I will tell you what I shall do. I shall call Parker, and together we will put you into your cab, and you shall be driven straight home. I am perfectly serious. I hope you will not oblige me to do that. You will be much wiser to pull yourself together, and let us have a talk. But understand one thing quite clearly. You are not going to see Lyndhurst."

The tension of those wide, childish eyes slowly relaxed, and her head sank forward, and there came the terrible and blessed tears, in wild cataract and streaming storm. And Mrs. Ames, looking at her, felt all her righteousness relax; she had only pity for this poor destitute soul, who was blind to all else by force of that mysterious longing which, in itself, is so divine that, though it desires the disgraceful and the impossible, it cannot wholly make itself abominable, nor discrown itself of its royalty. Something of the truth of that, though no more than mere fragments and moulted feather, came to Mrs. Ames now, as she sat waiting till the tempest of tears should have abated. The royal eagle had passed over her; as sign of his passage there was this feather that had fallen, and she understood its significance.

Slowly the tears ceased and the sobs were still, and Millie raised her dim, swollen eyes.

"I had better go home," she said. "I wonder if you would let me wash my face, Cousin Amy. I must be a perfect fright."

"Yes, dear Millie," said she; "but there is no hurry. See, shall I send your cab back to your house? It has your luggage on it; yes? Then Parker shall go with it, and tell them to take it back to your room and unpack it, and put everything back in place. Afterwards, when we have talked a little, I will walk back with you."

Again the comfort of having little things attended to reached Millie, that and the sense that she was not quite alone. She was like a child that has been naughty and has been punished, and she did not much care whether she had been naughty or not. What she wanted primarily was to be comforted, to be assured that everybody was not going to be angry with her for ever. Then, returning, Mrs. Ames made her some fresh tea, and that comforted her too.

"But I don't see how I can ever be happy again," she said.

There was something childlike about this, as well as childish.

"No, Millie," said the other. "None of us three see that exactly. We shall all have to be very patient. Very patient and ordinary."

There was a long silence.

"I must tell you one thing," said Millie, "though I daresay that will make you hate me more. But it was my fault from the first. I led him on--I--I didn't let him kiss me, I made him kiss me. It was like that all through!"

She felt that Mrs. Ames was waiting for something more, and she knew exactly what it was. But it required a greater effort to speak of that than she could at once command. At last she raised her eyes to those of Mrs. Ames.

"No, never," she said.

Mrs. Ames nodded.

"I see," she said baldly. "Now, as I said, we have got to be patient and ordinary. We have got, you and I, to begin again. You have your husband, so have I. Men are so easily pleased and made happy. It would be a shame if we failed."

Again the helpless, puzzled look came over Millie's face.

"But I don't see how to begin," she said. "Tomorrow, for instance, what am I to do all to-morrow? I shall only be thinking of what might have happened."

Mrs. Ames took up her soft, unresisting, unresponsive hand.

"Yes, by all means, think what might have happened," she said. "Utter ruin, utter misery, and--and all your fault. You led him on, as you said. He didn't care as you did. He wouldn't have thought of going away with you, if he hadn't been so furious with me. Think of all that."

Some straggler from that host of sobs shook Millie for a moment.

"Perhaps Wilfred would take me away instead," she said. "I will ask him if he cannot. Do you think I should feel better if I went away for a fortnight, Cousin Amy?"

Mrs. Ames' twisted little smile played about her mouth.

"Yes," she said. "I think that is an excellent plan. I am quite sure you will feel better in a fortnight, if you can look forward like that, and want to be better. And now would you like to wash your face? After that, I will walk home with you."

CHAPTER XIV

It was a brisk morning in November, and Mr. and Mrs. Altham, who breakfasted at half-past eight in the summer, and nine in the winter, were seated at breakfast, and Mr. Altham was thinking how excellent was the savour of grilled kidneys. But he was not sure if they were really wholesome, and he was playing an important match at golf this afternoon. Perhaps two kidneys approached the limits of wisdom. Besides, his wife was speaking of really absorbing things; he ought to be able to distract his mind from the kidneys he was proposing to deny himself, under the sting of so powerful a counter-interest.

"And to think that Mrs. Ames isn't going to be a Suffragette any more!" she said. "I met Mrs. Turner when I took my walk just now, and she told me all about it."

A word of explanation is necessary. The fact was that Swedish exercises, and a short walk on an empty stomach, were producing wonderful results in Riseborough at the moment, especially among its female inhabitants. They now, instead of meeting in the High Street before lunch, to stand about on the pavement and exchange news, met there before breakfast, when on these brisk autumn mornings it was wiser not to stand about. They therefore skimmed rapidly up and down the street together, in short skirts and walking boots. Rain and sunny weather, in this first glow of enthusiasm, were alike to them, and they had their baths afterwards. These exercises gave a considerable appetite for breakfast, and produced a very pleasant and comfortable feeling of fatigue. But this fatigue was a legitimate, indeed, a desirable effect, for their systems naturally demanded repose after exertion, and an hour's rest after breakfast was recommended. Thus this getting up earlier did not really result in any actual saving of time, though it made everybody feel very busy, and they all went to bed a little earlier.

Mr. Altham found he got on very nicely without these gymnastics, but then he played golf after lunch. It was no use playing tricks with your health if it was already excellent: you might as well poke about in the works of a punctual watch. He had already had a pretty sharp lesson on this score, over the consumption of sour milk. It had made him exceedingly unwell, and he had sliced his drive for a fortnight afterwards. Just now he weaned his mind from the thoughts of kidneys, and gave it in equitable halves to marmalade and his wife's conversation. To enjoy either, required silence on his part.

"She went to a meeting yesterday," said Mrs. Altham, "so Mrs. Turner told me, and said that though she had the success of the cause so deeply at heart as ever, she would not be able to take any active part in it. That is a very common form of sympathy. I suppose, from what one knows of Mrs. Ames, we might have expected something of the sort. Do you remember her foolish scheme of asking wives without husbands, and husbands without wives? I warned you at the time, Henry, not to take any notice of it, because I was sure it would come to nothing, and I think I may say I am justified. I don't know what *you* think."

Mr. Altham, by a happy coincidence, had finished masticating his last piece of toast at this moment, and was at liberty to reply.

"I do not think anything about it at present," said he. "I daresay you are quite right, but why?"

Mrs. Altham gave a little shrill laugh. The sprightliness at breakfast produced by this early walk and the exercises was very marked.

"I declare," she said, "that I had forgotten to tell you. Mrs. Ames wrote to ask us both to dine on Saturday. I had quite forgotten! There is something in the air before breakfast that makes one forgetful of trifles. It says so in the pamphlet. Worries and household cares vanish, and it becomes a joy to be alive. I don't think we have any engagement. Pray do not have a third cup of tea, Henry. Tannin combines the effects of stimulants and narcotics. A cup of hot water, now--you will never regret it. Let me see! Yes, dinner at the Ames' on Saturday, and she isn't a Suffragette any longer. As I said, one might have guessed. I daresay her husband gave her a good talking-to, after the night when she threw the water at the policeman. I should not wonder if there was madness in the family. I think I heard that Sir James' mother was very queer before she died!"

"She lived till ninety," remarked Mr. Altham.

"That is often the case with deranged people," said Mrs. Altham. "Lunatics are notoriously long-lived. There is no strain on the brain."

"And she wasn't any relation of Mrs. Ames," continued Henry. "Mrs. Ames is related to the Westbournes. She has no more to do with Sir James' mother than I have to do with yours. I will take tea, my dear, not hot water."

"You want to catch me up, Henry," said she, "and prove I am wrong somehow. I was only saying that very likely there is madness in Mrs. Ames' family, and I was going to add that I hoped it would not come out in her. But you must allow that she has been very flighty. You would have thought that an elderly woman like that could make up her mind once and for all about things, before she made an exhibition of herself. She thinks she is like some royal person who goes and opens a bazaar, and then has nothing more to do with it, but hurries away to Leeds or somewhere to unveil a memorial. She thinks it is sufficient for her to help at the beginning, and get all the advertisement, and then drop it all like cold potatoes."

"Hot," said Henry.

CHAPTER XIV

"Hot or cold: that is just like her. She plays hot and cold. One day she is a Suffragette and the next day she isn't. As likely as not she will be a vegetarian on Saturday, and we shall be served with cabbages."

"Major Ames went over to Sir James' to shoot,--she wasn't asked," said Henry, reverting to a previous topic.

"There you are!" exclaimed Mrs. Altham. "That will account for her abandoning this husband and wife theory. I am sure she did not like that, she being Sir James' relative and not being asked. But I never could quite understand what the relationship is, though I daresay Mrs. Ames can make it out. There are people who say they are cousins, because a grandmother's niece married the other grandmother's nephew. We can all be descendants of Queen Elizabeth or of Charles the Second at that rate."

"It would be easier to be a descendant of Charles the Second than of Queen Elizabeth, my dear," remarked Henry.

Mrs. Altham pursed her lips up for a moment.

"I do not think we need enter into that," she said. "I was asking you if you wished to accept Mrs. Ames' invitation for Saturday. She says she expects Sir James and his wife, so perhaps we shall hear some more about this wonderful relationship, and Dr. Evans and his wife and one or two others. To my mind that looks rather as if the husband and wife plan was not quite what she expected it would be. And giving up all active part in the Suffragette movement, too! But I daresay she feels her age, though goodness only knows what it is. However, it is clearly going to be a grand party on Saturday, and the waiter from the Crown will be there to help Parker, going round and pouring a little foam into everybody's glass. I do not know where Major Ames gets his champagne from, but I never get anything but foam. But I am sure I do not wish to be unkind, and certainly poor Major Ames does not look well. I daresay he has worries we do not know of, and, of course, there is no reason why he should speak of them to us. The Evans', too! I never satisfied myself as to why they went away in October. They must have been away nearly three weeks, for it was only yesterday that I saw them driving down from the station, with so much luggage on the top of the cab I wonder it did not fall over."

"It can't have been yesterday, my dear," said Mr. Altham, "because you spoke of it to me two days ago."

"You shall have it your own way, Henry," said she. "I am quite willing that you should think it was a twelvemonth ago, if you choose. But I suppose you will not dispute that they went away in October, which is a very odd time to take for a holiday. Of course, Mrs. Evans stopped here all August, or so she says, and she might answer that she wanted a little change of air. But for my part, I think there must have been something more, though, as I say, I cannot guess what it is. Luckily, it is no concern of mine, and I need not worry my head about it. But I have always thought Mrs. Evans looked far from strong, and it seems odd that a doctor's wife should not be more robust, when she has all his laboratory to choose from."

Henry lit his cigarette, and strolled to the window. The lawn was still white with the unmelted hoar-frost, and the gardener was busy in the beds, putting things tidy for the winter. This consisted in plucking up anything of vegetable origin and carrying it off in a wheelbarrow. Thus the beds were ready to receive the first bedded-out plants next May.

"I remember, my dear," said Henry, "that you once thought that there had been some--some understanding between Mrs. Evans and Major Ames, and some misunderstanding between Major Ames and Dr. Evans."

Mrs. Altham brought her eyebrows together and put her finger on her forehead.

"I seem to remember some ridiculous story of yours, Henry, about a bunch of chrysanthemums in the road outside Dr. Evans' house, how you had seen Major Ames take them in, and there they were afterwards in the road. I seem to remember your being so much excited about it that I made a point of going round to Mrs. Ames' next day with--with a book. I think that at the time--correct me if I am wrong--I convinced you that there was nothing whatever in it. . . . Or have you seen or heard anything since that makes you think differently?" she added rather more briskly.

"No, my dear, nothing whatever," said he.

Mrs. Altham got up.

"I am glad, very glad," she said. "At any rate, we know in Riseborough that we are safe from that sort of thing. I declare when I went to London last week, I hardly slept with thinking of the dreadful things that might be going on round me. Dear me, it is nearly ten o'clock. I do not know whether the hours or the days go quickest! It is always half-an-hour later than I expect it to be, and here we are in November already. I shall rest for an hour, Henry, and I will write to Mrs. Ames before lunch saying we shall be delighted to come on Saturday. November the twelfth, too! Nearly half November will be gone by then, and that leaves us but six weeks to Christmas, and it will be as much as we shall be able to manage to get through all that has to be done before that. But with these Swedish exercises, I declare I feel younger every day, and more able to cope with everything. You should take to them, Henry; by eleven o'clock they are finished and you have had your rest. With a little management you would find time for everything."

Henry sat over the dining-room fire, considering this. As has been mentioned, he did not want to make any change in his excellent health, but, on the other hand, a little rest after breakfast would be pleasant, and when that was over it would be almost time to go to the club.

But it was impossible to settle a question like that offhand. After he had read the paper he would think about it.

Mrs. Altham came hurrying back into the room.

"Henry, you would never guess what I have seen!" she said. "I glanced out of the window in the hall on the way to my room, and there was Mrs. Ames wobbling about the road on a bicycle. Major Ames was holding it upright with both hands, and it looked to be as much as he could manage. Yet she has no time for

Suffragettes! I should be sorry if I thought I should ever make such a hollow excuse as that. And at her age, too! I had no time to call you, but I dare say she will be back soon if you care to watch. The window-seat in the hall is quite comfortable."

Henry took his paper there.

THE END

SPOOK STORIES

I RECONCILIATION

Garth Place lies low in a dip of the hills which, north, east, and west, enclose its sequestered valley, as in the palm of a hollowed hand. To the south the valley broadens out and the encompassing hills merge themselves into the wide strip of flat country once reclaimed from the sea, and now, with intersections of drainage dykes, forming the fat pasture of the scattered farms. Thick woods of beech and oak, which climb the hillsides above the house up to the top of the ridge, give it further shelter, and it dozes in a soft and sundered climate of its own when the bleak uplands above it are swept by the east winds of spring or the northerly blasts of winter; and, sitting in its terraced garden in the mild sunshine of a clear December day, you may hear the gale roaring through the tree-tops on the upper slopes, and see the clouds scudding high above you, yet never feel a breath of the wind that shreds them seawards. The clearings in these woods are thick with anemones and full-blown clumps of primroses a month before the tiniest bud has appeared in the copses of the upland, and its gardens are still bright with the red blossoms of the autumn long after the flower-borders in the village that huddles on the hill-top to the west have been blackened by the frosts. Only when the south wind blows is its tranquillity disturbed, and then the sound of the waves is heard, and the wind is salt with the sea.

The house itself dates from the beginning of the seventeenth century, and has miraculously escaped the destructive hand of the restorer. Its three low storeys are built of the grey stone of the district, the roof is made of thin slabs of the same, between which the blown seeds have found anchorage, and the broad mullioned windows are many-paned. Never a creak comes from its oaken floors, solid and broad are its staircases, its panelling is as firm as the walls in which it is laid. A faint odour of wood smoke from the centuries of fires that have burned on its open hearths pervades it, that and an extraordinary silence. A man who lay awake all night in one of its chambers would hear no whisper of cracking wood-work, or rattling pane, and all night long there would come to his listening ears no sound from outside but the hoot of the tawny owl, or in June the music of the nightingale. At the back a strip of garden has been anciently levelled out of the hillside, in front the slope has been built up to form a couple of terraces. Below, a spring feeds a small sheet of water, bordered by marshy ground set with tufts of rushes, and out of it a stream much stifled in herbage wanders exiguously past the kitchen garden, and joins the slow-flowing little river which, after a couple of miles of lazy travel, debouches through broadening mud-flats into the English Channel.

Along the further margin of the stream a footpath with right-of-way leads from the village of Garth on the hill above to the main road across the plain. Just below the house a small stone bridge with a gate crosses the stream and gives access to this footpath.

I first saw the house to which now for so many years I have been a constant visitor when I was an undergraduate at Cambridge. Hugh Verrall, the only son of its widowed owner, was a friend of mine, and he proposed to me one August that we should have a month there together. His father, he explained, was spending the next six weeks at a foreign health resort. Mine, so he understood, was tied in London, and this really seemed a more agreeable way of getting through August than that he should inhabit his house in melancholy solitude, and that I should stew in town. So if the notion at all appealed to me, I had but to get the parental permission; it had already received his father's sanction. Hugh, in fact, produced Mr. Verrall's letter in which he stated his views as to his son's disposal of his time with great lucidity.

"I won't have you hanging about at Marienbad all August," he said, "for you'll only get into mischief, and spend the rest of your allowance for the year. Besides, there's your work to think of; you didn't do a stroke, so your tutor informed me, all last term, so you'd better make up for it now. Go down to Garth, and get some pleasant, idle scamp like yourself to stay with you, and then you'll have to work, for you won't find anything else to do! Besides, nobody wants to do anything at Garth."

"All right, the idle scamp will come," said I. I knew my father didn't want me to be in London, either.

"Mark you, the idle scamp has to be pleasant," said Hugh. "Well, you'll come anyhow; that's ripping. You'll see what my father means by not wanting to do anything. That's Garth."

The end of the next week saw us installed there, and never in all the first sights of the various splendours of the world that have since then been accorded to me, have I felt so magical and potent a spell as that which caught the breath in my throat when on the evening of that hot August day I first saw Garth. For a mile before the road had lain through the woods that clothe the slope above it; from there my cab emerged as from a tunnel, and there in the clear twilight, with sunset flaming overhead, was the long grey façade, with the green lawns about it, and its air of antique and native tranquillity. It seemed an incarnation of the very soul and spirit of England: there in the south was the line of sea, and all round it the immemorial woods. Like its oaks, like the velvet of its lawns, the house had grown from the very soil, and the life of the soil still richly nurtured it. Venice was not more authentically born from the sea, nor Egypt from the mystery of the Nile, than Garth was born from the woods of England.

There was time for a stroll round before dinner, and Hugh casually recounted the history of it. His forebears had owned it since the time of Queen Anne.

"But we're interlopers," he said, "and not very creditable ones. Before that, my people had been tenants of the farm you passed at the top of the hill, and the

Garths were in possession. It was a Garth who built the house in the reign of Elizabeth."

"Ah, then you've got a ghost," I said. "That makes it quite complete. Don't tell me that there isn't a Garth who haunts the house?"

"Anything to oblige," said he, "but that I am afraid I can't manage for you. You're too late: a hundred years ago it certainly was supposed to be haunted by a Garth."

"And then?" I asked.

"Well, I know nothing about spooks, but it looks as if the haunt wore itself out. It must be tiresome, you know, for a spirit to be chained to a place, and have to walk about the garden in the evening, and patrol the passages and bedrooms at night, if nobody pays any attention to it. My forebears didn't care the least, it appears, whether the ghost haunted the place or not. In consequence, it evaporated."

"And whose ghost was it supposed to be?" I asked.

"The ghost of the last Garth, who lived here in the time of Queen Anne. What happened was this. A younger son of my family, Hugh Verrall—same name as me—went up to London to seek his fortune. He made a lot of money in a very short time, and when he was a middle-aged man he retired, and took it into his head that he would like to be a country gentleman with an estate of his own. He was always fond of this country, and came to live at a house in the village up there, while he looked about, and no doubt he had ulterior purposes. For Garth Place was at that time in the hands of a wild fellow called Francis Garth, a drunkard and a great gambler, and Hugh Verrall used to come down here night after night and thoroughly fleece him. Francis had one daughter, who of course was heiress to the place; and at first Hugh made up to her with the idea of marrying her, but when that was no use, he took to the other way of getting hold of it. Eventually, in the fine traditional manner, Francis Garth, who by that time owed my ancestor something like thirty thousand pounds, staked the Garth property against his debt and lost. There was a tremendous excitement over it, with stories of loaded dice and marked cards, but nothing could be proved, and Hugh evicted Francis and took possession. Francis lived for some years yet, in a labourer's cottage in the village, and every evening he used to walk down the path there, and standing opposite the house, curse the inhabitants. At his death, the haunt began, and then, simply it died out."

"Perhaps it's storing force," I suggested. "Perhaps it's intending to come out strong again. You ought to have a ghost here, you know."

"Not a trace of one, I'm afraid," said Hugh; "or I wonder if you'll think there is still a trace of it. But it's such a silly trace that I'm almost ashamed to tell you about it."

"Go on quickly," said I.

He pointed up to the gable above the front door. Underneath it, in an angle formed by the roof, there was a big square stone, evidently of later date than the wall. The surface of it was in contrast to the rest of the wall, much crumbled, but it had evidently been carved, and the shape of a heraldic shield could be seen on it, though of the arms it carried there was nothing left.

"It's too silly," said Hugh, "but it is a fact that my father remembers that stone being placed there. His father put it up, and it bore our coat of arms: you can just see the shape of the shield. But, though it was of the stone of the district, exactly like the rest of the house, it had hardly been put up when the surface began to decay, and in ten years our arms were absolutely obliterated. Odd, that just that one stone should have perished so quickly, when all the rest really seems to have defied time."

I laughed.

"That's Francis Garth's work beyond a doubt," I said. "There's life in the old dog yet."

"Sometimes I think there is," he said. "Mind you, I've never seen or heard anything here which is in the smallest way suggestive of spooks, but constantly I feel that there is something here that waits and watches. It never manifests itself, but it's there."

As he spoke, I caught some faint psychical glimpse of what he meant. There was something there, something sinister and malevolent. But the impression was of the most momentary sort; hardly had it conveyed itself to me when it vanished again, and the amazing beauty and friendliness of the house overwhelmingly reasserted itself. If ever there was an abode of ancient peace, it was here.

We settled down at once into a delightful existence. Being very great friends, we were completely at ease with each other; we talked as we felt disposed but if a silence fell there was no constraint about it, and it would continue, perfectly happily, till one of us was moved to speak again. In the morning for three hours or so we applied ourselves very studiously to our books, but by lunch-time they were closed for the day, and we would walk across the marsh for a swim in the sea or stray through the woods, or play bowls on the lawn behind the house. The weather, blazing hot, predisposed to laziness, and in that cupped hollow of the hills, where the house stood, it was almost impossible to remember what it felt like to be energetic. But, as Hugh's father had indicated, that was the proper state of body and mind to be in when you resided at Garth. You must be sleepy and hungry and well, but without desires or energies; life moved along there as on some lotus-eater's shore, very softly and quietly without disturbance. To be lazy without scruple or compunction but with a purring content was to act in accordance with the spirit of Garth. But, as the days went on, I knew that below this content there was something in us both that grew ever more alert and watchful for that which was watching us.

We had been there about a week when on an afternoon of still and sultry heat, we went down to the sea for a dip before dinner. There was clearly a storm coming up, but it seemed possible to get a bathe and return before it broke. It came up, however, more quickly than we had thought, and we were still a mile from home when the rain began, heavy and windless. The clouds, which had spread right across the sky, made a darkness as of late twilight, and when we struck the little public footpath on the far side of the stream in front of the house, we were both drenched to the skin. Just as we got to the bridge I saw the figure of a man standing there, and it struck me at once as odd that he should wait out in this deluge and not seek shelter. He stood quite still looking towards the house, and as I passed him I had one good stare at his face and instantly knew that I had seen a face very like it before, though I could not localise my memory. He was of middle-age, clean-shaven, and there was something curiously sinister about that lean, dark-skinned profile.

However, it was no business of mine if a stranger chose to stand out in the rain and look at Garth Place, and I went on a dozen steps, and then spoke to Hugh in a low voice.

"I wonder what that man's doing there," I said.

"Man? What man?" said Hugh.

"The man by the bridge whom we passed just now," I said.

He turned round to look.

"There's no one there," he said.

Now it seemed quite impossible that this stranger who had certainly been there so few seconds ago, could have vanished into the darkness, thick as it was, and at that moment for the first time it occurred to me that this was no creature of flesh and blood into whose face I had looked. But Hugh had hardly spoken when he pointed to the path up which we had come.

"Yes, there is someone there," he said. "Odd that I didn't see him as we passed. But if he likes to stand about in the rain, I suppose he can."

We went on quickly up to the house, and as I changed I cudgelled my brain to think when and where I had seen that face before. I knew it was quite lately, and I knew I had looked with interest at it. And then suddenly the solution came to me. I had never seen the man before, but only a picture of him, and that picture hung in the long gallery at the front of the house, into which Hugh had taken me the first day that I was here, but I had not been there since. Portraits of Verralls and Garths hung on the walls, and the portrait in question was that of Francis Garth. Before going downstairs I verified this, and there was no doubt whatever about it. The man whom I had passed on the bridge was the living image of him who, in the time of Anne, had forfeited the house to Hugh's ancestral namesake.

I said nothing about this identification to Hugh, for I did not want to put any suggestion into his mind. For his part, he made no further allusion to our encounter; it had evidently made no particular impression on him, and we spent the evening as usual. Next morning, we sat at our books in the parlour overlooking the bowling-green. After an hour's work, Hugh got up for a few minutes' relaxation, and strolled whistling, to the window. I was not following his movements with any attention, but I noticed that his whistling stopped in the middle of a phrase. Presently he spoke in rather a queer voice.

"Come here a minute," he said.

I joined him, and he pointed out of the window.

"Is that the man you saw yesterday by the bridge?" he said. There he was at the far end of the bowling-green looking straight at us.

"Yes, that's he," I said.

"I shall go and ask him what he's doing here," said Hugh. "Come with me!"

We went together out of the room and down the short passage to the garden door. The quiet sunlight slept on the grass, but there was no one there.

"That's queer," said Hugh. "That's very queer. Come up to the picture gallery a minute."

"There's no need," said I.

"So you've seen the likeness, too," he said. "I say—is it a likeness only, or is it Francis Garth? Whatever it is, it's that which is watching us."

The apparition which, from that time, we both thought and spoke of as Francis Garth, had now been seen twice. During the next week it seemed to be drawing nearer to the house that had once been its haunt, for Hugh saw it just outside the porch by the front door, and a day or two afterwards, as I sat at twilight in the room overlooking the bowling-alley waiting for him to come down to dinner, I saw it close outside the window looking narrowly into the room with malevolent scrutiny. Finally, a few days only before my visit here came to an end, as we returned one evening from a ramble in the woods, we saw it together, standing by the big open fireplace in the hall. This time its appearance was not momentary, for on our entry it remained where it was, taking no notice of us for perhaps ten seconds, and then moved away towards the far doorway. There it stopped and turned, looking directly at Hugh. At that he spoke to it, and without answer it passed out through the door. It had now definitely come inside; and from that time onwards was seen only within the house. Francis Garth had taken possession again.

Now I do not pretend that the sight of this apparition did not affect my nerves. It affected them very unpleasantly; fright, perhaps, is too superficial a word with which to describe the effect it had on me. It was rather some still, dark horror of the spirit that closed over me, not (to be precise) at the moment when I actually saw it, but some few seconds before, so that I knew by this dire terror that invaded me that the apparition was about to manifest itself. But mingled with that was an intense interest and curiosity as to the nature of this strange visitant, who, though long dead, still wore the semblance of the living, and clothed itself in the body which had long crumbled to dust. Hugh, however, felt nothing of this; the spectre alarmed him as little now on its second inhabiting of the house, as it had alarmed those who lived here when first it appeared.

"And it's so interesting," he said, as he saw me off on the conclusion of my visit. "It's got some business here, but what can that business be? I'll let you know if there's any further development."

From that time onwards the ghost was constantly seen. It alarmed some people, it interested others, but it harmed none. Often during the next five years or so, I stayed there, and I do not think that any visit passed without my seeing it once or twice. But always to me its appearance was heralded by that terror of which I have spoken, in which neither Hugh nor his father shared. And then quite suddenly Hugh's father died. After the funeral, Hugh came up to London for interviews with lawyers and for the settlement of affairs connected with the will, and told me that his father was not nearly so well-off as had been supposed, and that he hardly knew if he could afford to live at Garth Place at all. He intended, however, to shut up part of the house, and with a greatly reduced household to attempt to continue there.

"I don't want to let it," he said; "in fact, I should hate to let it. And I don't really believe that there's much chance of my being able to do so. The story of its being haunted is widely known now, and I don't fancy it would be very easy to get a tenant for it. However, I hope it won't be necessary."

But six months later he found that in spite of all economies it was no longer possible to live there, and one June I went down for a final visit, after which, unless he succeeded in getting a tenant, the house would be shut up.

"I can't tell you how I dislike having to go," he said, "but there's no help for it. And what are the ethics of letting a haunted house, do you think? Ought one to tell an intending tenant? I advertised the house last week in *Country Life*, and there's been an enquirer already. In fact, he's coming down with his daughter to see the house to-morrow morning. Name of Francis Jameson."

"I hope he'll hit it off with the other Francis," I said. "Have you seen him much lately?"

Hugh jumped up.

"Yes, fairly often," he said. "But there's an odd thing I want to show you. Come out of doors a minute."

He took me out to the front of the house, and pointed to the gable below which was the shield containing his obliterated arms.

"I'll give you no hint," he said. "But look at it and make any comment."

"There's something appearing there," said I. "I can see two bends crossing the shield, and some device between them."

"And you're sure you didn't see them there before?" he asked.

"I certainly thought the surface had quite perished," I said. "Of course, it can't have. Or have you had it restored?"

He laughed.

"I certainly haven't," he said. "In fact, what you see there isn't part of my arms at all, but the Garth arms."

"Nonsense. It's some chance cracks and weatherings that have come on the stone, rather regular, certainly, but accidental."

He laughed again.

"You don't really believe that," he said. "Nor do I, for that matter. It's Francis: Francis is busy."

I had gone up to the village next morning, over some small business, and as I came back down the footpath opposite the house saw a motor drive up to the door, and concluded that this was Mr. Jameson who had just arrived. I went indoors, and into the hall, and next moment was standing there with staring eyes and open mouth. For just inside were three people talking together: there was Hugh, there was a very charming-looking girl, obviously Miss Jameson, and the third, so my eyes told me, was Francis Garth. As surely as I had recognised the spectre as him whose portrait hung in the gallery, so surely was this man the living and human incarnation of the spectre itself. You could not say it was a likeness: it was an identity.

Hugh introduced me to his two visitors, and I saw in his glance that he had been through much the same experience as I. The interview and the inquiries had evidently only just begun, for after this little ceremony Mr. Jameson turned to Hugh again.

"But before we see the house or garden," he said, "there is one most important question I have to ask, and if your answer to that is unsatisfactory, I shall but waste your time in asking you to show me over."

I thought that some inquiry about the ghost was sure to follow, but was quite wrong. This paramount consideration was climate, and Mr. Jameson began explaining to Hugh with all the ardour of the invalid, his requirements. A warm, soft air, with an absence of easterly and northerly winds in winter, was what he was seeking for, a sheltered and sunny situation.

The replies to these questions were sufficiently satisfactory to warrant an inspection of the house, and presently all four of us were starting on our tour.

"Go on first, my dear Peggy, with Mr. Verrall," said Mr. Jameson to his daughter, "and leave me to follow a little more leisurely with this gentleman, if he will kindly give me his escort. We will receive our impressions independently, too, in that way."

It occurred to me once again that he wanted to make some inquiry about the house, and preferred to get his information not from the owner, but from someone who knew the place, but was in no way connected with the business of letting it. And again I waited to hear some questions about the ghost. But what came surprised me much more.

He waited, evidently with purpose, till the other two had passed some distance on, and then turned to me.

"Now a most extraordinary thing has happened," he said. "I have never set eyes on this house before, and yet I know it intimately. As soon as we came to the front door I knew what this room would be like, and I can tell you what we shall see when we follow the others. At the end of the passage up which they have gone there are two rooms, of which the one looks out on to a bowling-green behind the house, the other on to a path close below the windows, from which you can look into the room. A broad staircase ascends from there in two short flights to the first floor, there are bedrooms at the back, along the front runs a long panelled room with pictures. Beyond that again are two bedrooms with a bathroom in between. A smaller staircase, rather dark, ascends from there to the second floor. Is that correct?"

"Absolutely," said I.

"Now you mustn't think I've dreamed these things," he said. "They are in my consciousness, not as a dream at all, but as actual things I knew in my own life. And they are accompanied by a feeling of hostility in my mind. I can tell you this also, that about two hundred years ago my ancestor in the direct line married a daughter of Francis Garth and assumed her arms. This is Garth Place. Was a family of Garth ever here, or is the house simply named after the village?"

"Francis Garth was the last of the Garths who lived here," said I. "He gambled the place away, losing it to the direct ancestor of the present owner; his name also was Hugh Verrall."

He looked at me a moment with a puzzled air, that gave his face a curiously sharp and malevolent expression.

"What does it all mean?" he said. "Are we dreaming or awake? And there's another thing I wanted to ask you. I have heard—it may be mere gossip—that the house is haunted. Can you tell me anything about that? Have you ever seen anything of the sort here? Let us call it a ghost, though I don't believe in the existence of such a thing. But have you ever seen any inexplicable appearance?"

"Yes, frequently," I said.

"And may I ask what it was?"

"Certainly. It was the apparition of the man of whom we have been speaking. At least, the first time I saw it I at once recognised it as the ghost—if I may use the word—of Francis Garth, whose portrait hangs in the gallery you have correctly described."

I hesitated a moment, wondering if I had better tell him that not only had I recognised the apparition from the portrait, but that I had recognised him from the apparition. He saw my hesitation.

"There is something more," he said.

I made up my mind.

"There is something more," I said, "but I think it would be better if you saw the portrait for yourself. Possibly it will tell you more directly and convincingly what that is."

We went up the stairs which he had described without first visiting the other rooms on the ground floor, from which I heard the voice of Hugh and his companion. There was no need for me to point out to Mr. Jameson the portrait of Francis Garth, for he went straight to it, and looked at it for a long while in silence. Then he turned to me.

"So it's I who ought to be able to tell you about the ghost," he said, "instead of your telling me."

The others joined us at this moment, and Miss Jameson came up to her father.

"Oh, Daddy, it's the most delicious home-like house," she said. "If you won't take it, I shall."

"Have a look at my portrait, Peggy," said he.

We changed partners after that, and presently Miss Peggy and I were strolling round the outside of the house while the others lingered within. Opposite the front door she stopped and looked up at the gable.

"Those arms," she said. "It's hard to make them out, and I suppose they're Mr. Verrall's? But they're wonderfully like my father's."

After we had lunched, Hugh and his proposed tenant had a private talk together, and soon after his visitors left.

"It's practically settled," he said as we turned back into the hall again after seeing them off. "Mr. Jameson wants a year's lease with option to renew. And now what do you make of it all?"

We talked it out lengthways and sideways and right way up, and upside down, and theory after theory was tried and found wanting, for some pieces seemed to fit together, but we could not dovetail them in with others. Eventually, after hours of talk, we reasoned it out, granting that it was all inexplicable, in a manner that may or may not commend itself to the reader, but seems to cover the facts and to present what I may perhaps call a uniform surface of inexplicability.

To start then at the beginning, shortly summing up the facts, Francis Garth, dispossessed, possibly with fraud, of his estate, had cursed the incomers and apparently haunted it after his death. Then came a long intermission from any ghostly visitant, and once more the haunt began again at the time when I first stayed here with Hugh. Then to-day there had come to the house a direct descendant of Francis Garth, who was the living image of the apparition we had both so constantly seen, which, by the portrait, was also identified with Francis Garth himself. And already, before Mr. Jameson had entered the house, he was familiar with it and knew what was within, its staircases and rooms and corridors, and remembered that he had often been here with hostility in his soul, even as we had seen hostility on the face of the apparition. What, then (here is the theory that slowly emerged), if we see in Francis Jameson some reincarnation of Francis Garth, purged, so to speak, of his ancient hostility, and coming back to the house which two hundred years ago was his home, and finding a home there once more? Certainly from that day no apparition, hostile and malevolent, has looked in through its windows, or walked in its bowling-alley.

In the sequel, too, I cannot help seeing some correspondence between what happened now and what happened when in the time of Anne Hugh Verrall took possession: here was what we may think of as the reverse of the coin that was hot-minted then. For now another Hugh Verrall, unwilling, for reasons that soon became very manifest, to leave the place altogether, established himself in a house in the village, even as his ancestor had done, and amazingly frequent were his visits to the home of his fathers, which was for the present the house of those whose family had owned it before the first of his forefathers came there. I see, too, a correspondence, which Hugh certainly would be the last to pass lightly over, in the fact that Francis Jameson, like Francis Garth, had a daughter. At that point, however, I am bound to say that strict correspondence is rudely broken, for whereas Hugh Verrall the first had no luck when he went a-wooing the daughter of Francis Garth, a much better fortune attended the venture of Hugh Verrall the second. In fact, I have just returned from their marriage.

I RECONCILIATION

II THE FACE

Hester Ward, sitting by the open window on this hot afternoon in June, began seriously to argue with herself about the cloud of foreboding and depression which had encompassed her all day, and, very sensibly, she enumerated to herself the manifold causes for happiness in the fortunate circumstances of her life. She was young, she was extremely good-looking, she was well-off, she enjoyed excellent health, and above all, she had an adorable husband and two small, adorable children. There was no break, indeed, anywhere in the circle of prosperity which surrounded her, and had the wishing-cap been handed to her that moment by some beneficent fairy, she would have hesitated to put it on her head, for there was positively nothing that she could think of which would have been worthy of such solemnity. Moreover, she could not accuse herself of a want of appreciation of her blessings; she appreciated enormously, she enjoyed enormously, and she thoroughly wanted all those who so munificently contributed to her happiness to share in it.

She made a very deliberate review of these things, for she was really anxious, more anxious, indeed, than she admitted to herself, to find anything tangible which could possibly warrant this ominous feeling of approaching disaster. Then there was the weather to consider; for the last week London had been stiflingly hot, but if that was the cause, why had she not felt it before? Perhaps the effect of these broiling, airless days had been cumulative. That was an idea, but, frankly, it did not seem a very good one, for, as a matter of fact, she loved the heat; Dick, who hated it, said that it was odd he should have fallen in love with a salamander.

She shifted her position, sitting up straight in this low window-seat, for she was intending to make a call on her courage. She had known from the moment she awoke this morning what it was that lay so heavy on her, and now, having done her best to shift the reason of her depression on to anything else, and having completely failed, she meant to look the thing in the face. She was ashamed of doing so, for the cause of this leaden mood of fear which held her in its grip, was so trivial, so fantastic, so excessively silly.

"Yes, there never was anything so silly," she said to herself. "I must look at it straight, and convince myself how silly it is." She paused a moment, clenching her hands.

"Now for it," she said.

She had had a dream the previous night, which, years ago, used to be familiar to her, for again and again when she was a child she had dreamed it. In itself the dream was nothing, but in those childish days, whenever she had this dream which had visited her last night, it was followed on the next night by another, which contained the source and the core of the horror, and she would awake screaming and struggling in the grip of overwhelming nightmare. For some ten years now she had not experienced it, and would have said that, though she remembered it, it had become dim and distant to her. But last night she had had that warning dream, which used to herald the visitation of the nightmare, and now that whole store-house of memory crammed as it was with bright things and beautiful contained nothing so vivid.

The warning dream, the curtain that was drawn up on the succeeding night, and disclosed the vision she dreaded, was simple and harmless enough in itself. She seemed to be walking on a high sandy cliff covered with short down-grass; twenty yards to the left came the edge of this cliff, which sloped steeply down to the sea that lay at its foot. The path she followed led through fields bounded by low hedges, and mounted gradually upwards. She went through some half-dozen of these, climbing over the wooden stiles that gave communication; sheep grazed there, but she never saw another human being, and always it was dusk, as if evening was falling, and she had to hurry on, because someone (she knew not whom) was waiting for her, and had been waiting not a few minutes only, but for many years. Presently, as she mounted this slope, she saw in front of her a copse of stunted trees, growing crookedly under the continual pressure of the wind that blew from the sea, and when she saw those she knew her journey was nearly done, and that the nameless one, who had been waiting for her so long was somewhere close at hand. The path she followed was cut through this wood, and the slanting boughs of the trees on the sea-ward side almost roofed it in; it was like walking through a tunnel. Soon the trees in front began to grow thin, and she saw through them the grey tower of a lonely church. It stood in a graveyard, apparently long disused, and the body of the church, which lay between the tower and the edge of the cliff, was in ruins, roofless, and with gaping windows, round which ivy grew thickly.

At that point this prefatory dream always stopped. It was a troubled, uneasy dream, for there was over it the sense of dusk and of the man who had been waiting for her so long, but it was not of the order of nightmare. Many times in childhood had she experienced it, and perhaps it was the subconscious knowledge of the night that so surely followed it, which gave it its disquiet. And now last night it had come again, identical in every particular but one. For last night it seemed to her that in the course of these ten years which had intervened since last it had visited her, the glimpse of the church and churchyard was changed. The edge of the cliff had come nearer to the tower, so that it now was within a yard or two of it, and the ruined body of the church, but for one broken arch that remained, had vanished. The sea had encroached, and for ten years had been busily eating at the cliff.

Hester knew well that it was this dream and this alone which had darkened the day for her, by reason of the nightmares that used to follow it, and, like a sensible woman, having looked it once in the face, she refused to admit into her mind any conscious calling-up of the sequel. If she let herself contemplate that, as likely or not the very thinking about it would be sufficient to ensure its return, and of one thing she was very certain, namely, that she didn't at all want it to do so. It was not like the confused jumble and jangle of ordinary nightmare, it was very simple, and she felt it concerned the nameless one who waited for her.... But she must not think of it; her whole will and intention was set on not thinking of it, and to aid her resolution, there was the rattle of Dick's latch-key in the front-door, and his voice calling her.

She went out into the little square front hall; there he was, strong and large, and wonderfully undreamlike.

"This heat's a scandal, it's an outrage, it's an abomination of desolation," he cried, vigorously mopping. "What have we done that Providence should place us in this frying-pan? Let us thwart him, Hester! Let us drive out of this inferno and have our dinner at—I'll whisper it so that he shan't overhear—at Hampton Court!"

She laughed: this plan suited her excellently. They would return late, after the distraction of a fresh scene; and dining out at night was both delicious and stupefying.

"The very thing," she said, "and I'm sure Providence didn't hear. Let's start now!"

"Rather. Any letters for me?"

He walked to the table where there were a few rather uninteresting-looking envelopes with half penny stamps.

"Ah, receipted bill," he said. "Just a reminder of one's folly in paying it. Circular ... unasked advice to invest in German marks.... Circular begging letter, beginning 'Dear Sir or Madam.' Such impertinence to ask one to subscribe to something without ascertaining one's sex.... Private view, portraits at the Walton Gallery.... Can't go: business meetings all day. You might like to have a look in, Hester. Some one told me there were some fine Vandycks. That's all: let's be off."

Hester spent a thoroughly reassuring evening, and though she thought of telling Dick about the dream that had so deeply imprinted itself on her consciousness all day, in order to hear the great laugh he would have given her for being such a goose, she refrained from doing so, since nothing that he could say would be so tonic to these fantastic fears as his general robustness. Besides, she would have to account for its disturbing effect, tell him that it was once familiar to her, and recount the sequel of the nightmares that followed. She would neither think of them, nor mention them: it was wiser by far just to soak herself in his extraordinary sanity, and wrap herself in his affection.... They dined out-of-doors at a river-side restaurant and strolled about afterwards, and it was very nearly midnight when, soothed with coolness and fresh air, and the vigour of his strong companionship, she let herself into the house, while he took the car back to the garage. And now she marvelled at the mood which had beset her all day, so distant and unreal had it become. She felt as if she had dreamed of shipwreck, and had awoke to find herself in some secure and sheltered garden where no tempest raged nor waves beat.

But was there, ever so remotely, ever so dimly, the noise of far-off breakers somewhere?

He slept in the dressing-room which communicated with her bedroom, the door of which was left open for the sake of air and coolness, and she fell asleep almost as soon as her light was out, and while his was still burning. And immediately she began to dream.

She was standing on the sea-shore; the tide was out, for level sands strewn with stranded jetsam glimmered in a dusk that was deepening into night. Though she had never seen the place it was awfully familiar to her. At the head of the beach there was a steep cliff of sand, and perched on the edge of it was a grey church tower. The sea must have encroached and undermined the body of the church, for tumbled blocks of masonry lay close to her at the bottom of the cliff, and there were gravestones there, while others still in place were silhouetted whitely against the sky. To the right of the church tower there was a wood of stunted trees, combed sideways by the prevalent sea-wind, and she knew that along the top of the cliff a few yards inland there lay a path through fields, with wooden stiles to climb, which led through a tunnel of trees and so out into the churchyard. All this she saw in a glance, and waited, looking at the sand-cliff crowned by the church tower, for the terror that was going to reveal itself. Already she knew what it was, and, as so many times before, she tried to run away. But the catalepsy of nightmare was already on her; frantically she strove to move, but her utmost endeavour could not raise a foot from the sand. Frantically she tried to look away from the sand-cliffs close in front of her, where in a moment now the horror would be manifested....

It came. There formed a pale oval light, the size of a man's face, dimly luminous in front of her and a few inches above the level of her eyes. It outlined itself, short reddish hair grew low on the forehead, below were two grey eyes, set very close together, which steadily and fixedly regarded her. On each side the ears stood noticeably away from the head, and the lines of the jaw met in a short pointed chin. The nose was straight and rather long, below it came a hairless lip, and last of all the mouth took shape and colour, and there lay the crowning terror. One side of it, soft-curved and beautiful, trembled into a smile, the other side, thick and gathered together as by some physical deformity, sneered and lusted.

The whole face, dim at first, gradually focused itself into clear outline: it was pale and rather lean, the face of a young man. And then the lower lip dropped a little, showing the glint of teeth, and there was the sound of speech. "I shall soon come for you now," it said, and on the words it drew a little nearer to her, and the smile broadened. At that the full hot blast of nightmare poured in upon her. Again she tried to run, again she tried to scream, and now she could feel the breath of that terrible mouth upon her. Then with a crash and a rending like the tearing asunder of soul and body she broke the spell, and heard her own voice yelling, and felt with her fingers for the switch of her light. And then she saw that the room was not dark, for Dick's door was open, and the next moment, not yet undressed, he was with her.

"My darling, what is it?" he said. "What's the matter?"

She clung desperately to him, still distraught with terror.

"Ah, he has been here again," she cried. "He says he will soon come to me. Keep him away, Dick."

For one moment her fear infected him, and he found himself glancing round the room.

"But what do you mean?" he said. "No one has been here."

She raised her head from his shoulder.

"No, it was just a dream," she said. "But it was the old dream, and I was terrified. Why, you've not undressed yet. What time is it?"

"You haven't been in bed ten minutes, dear," he said. "You had hardly put out your light when I heard you screaming."

She shuddered.

"Ah, it's awful," she said. "And he will come again...."

He sat down by her.

"Now tell me all about it," he said.

She shook her head.

"No, it will never do to talk about it," she said, "it will only make it more real. I suppose the children are all right, are they?"

"Of course they are. I looked in on my way upstairs."

"That's good. But I'm better now, Dick. A dream hasn't anything real about it, has it? It doesn't mean anything?"

He was quite reassuring on this point, and soon she quieted down. Before he went to bed he looked in again on her, and she was asleep.

Hester had a stern interview with herself when Dick had gone down to his office next morning. She told herself that what she was afraid of was nothing more than her own fear. How many times had that ill-omened face come to her in dreams, and what significance had it ever proved to possess? Absolutely none at all, except to make her afraid. She was afraid where no fear was: she was guarded, sheltered, prosperous, and what if a nightmare of childhood returned? It had no more meaning now than it had then, and all those visitations of her childhood had passed away without trace.... And then, despite herself, she began thinking over that vision again. It was grimly identical with all its previous occurrences, except.... And then, with a sudden shrinking of the heart, she remembered that in earlier years those terrible lips had said: "I shall come for you when you are older," and last night they had said: "I shall soon come for you now." She remembered, too, that in the warning dream the sea had encroached, and it had now demolished the body of the church. There was an awful consistency about these two changes in the otherwise identical visions. The years had brought their change to them, for in the one the encroaching sea had brought down the body of the church, in the other the time was now near....

It was no use to scold or reprimand herself, for to bring her mind to the contemplation of the vision meant merely that the grip of terror closed on her again; it was far wiser to occupy herself, and starve her fear out by refusing to bring it the sustenance of thought. So she went about her household duties, she took the children out for their airing in the park, and then, determined to leave no moment unoccupied, set off with the card of invitation to see the pictures in the private view at the Walton Gallery. After that her day was full enough, she was lunching out, and going on to a matinée, and by the time she got home Dick would have returned, and they would drive down to his little house at Rye for the week-end. All Saturday and Sunday she would be playing golf, and she felt that fresh air and physical fatigue would exorcise the dread of these dreaming fantasies.

The gallery was crowded when she got there; there were friends among the sightseers, and the inspection of the pictures was diversified by cheerful conversation. There were two or three fine Raeburns, a couple of Sir Joshuas, but the gems, so she gathered, were three Vandycks that hung in a small room by themselves. Presently she strolled in there, looking at her catalogue. The first of them, she saw, was a portrait of Sir Roger Wyburn. Still chatting to her friend she raised her eye and saw it....

Her heart hammered in her throat, and then seemed to stand still altogether. A qualm, as of some mental sickness of the soul overcame her, for there in front of her was he who would soon come for her. There was the reddish hair, the projecting ears, the greedy eyes set close together, and the mouth smiling on one side, and on the other gathered up into the sneering menace that she knew so well. It might have been her own nightmare rather than a living model which had sat to the painter for that face.

"Ah, what a portrait, and what a brute!" said her companion. "Look, Hester, isn't that marvellous?"

She recovered herself with an effort. To give way to this ever-mastering dread would have been to allow nightmare to invade her waking life, and there, for sure, madness lay. She forced herself to look at it again, but there were the steady and eager eyes regarding her; she could almost fancy the mouth began to move. All round her the crowd bustled and chattered, but to her own sense she was alone there with Roger Wyburn.

And yet, so she reasoned with herself, this picture of him—for it was he and no other—should have reassured her. Roger Wyburn, to have been painted by Vandyck, must have been dead near on two hundred years; how could he be a menace to her? Had she seen that portrait by some chance as a child; had it made some dreadful impression on her, since overscored by other memories, but still alive in the mysterious subconsciousness, which flows eternally, like some dark underground river, beneath the surface of human life? Psychologists taught that these early impressions fester or poison the mind like some hidden abscess. That might account for this dread of one, nameless no longer, who waited for her.

That night down at Rye there came again to her the prefatory dream, followed by the nightmare, and clinging to her husband as the terror began to subside, she told him what she had resolved to keep to herself. Just to tell it brought a measure of comfort, for it was so outrageously fantastic, and his robust common sense upheld her. But when on their return to London there was a recurrence of these visions, he made short work of her demur and took her straight to her doctor.

"Tell him all, darling," he said. "Unless you promise to do that, I will. I can't have you worried like this. It's all nonsense, you know, and doctors are wonderful people for curing nonsense."

She turned to him.

"Dick, you're frightened," she said quietly.

He laughed.

"I'm nothing of the kind," he said, "but I don't like being awakened by your screaming. Not my idea of a peaceful night. Here we are."

The medical report was decisive and peremptory. There was nothing whatever to be alarmed about; in brain and body she was perfectly healthy, but she was run down. These disturbing dreams were, as likely as not, an effect, a symptom of her condition, rather than the cause of it, and Dr. Baring unhesitatingly recommended a complete change to some bracing place. The wise thing would be to send her out of this stuffy furnace to some quiet place to where she had never been. Complete change; quite so. For the same reason her husband had better not go with her; he must pack her off to, let us say, the East coast. Sea-air and coolness and complete idleness. No long walks; no long bathings; a dip, and a deck-chair on the sands. A lazy, soporific life. How about Rushton? He had no doubt that Rushton would set her up again. After a week or so, perhaps, her husband might go down and see her. Plenty of sleep—never mind the nightmares—plenty of fresh air.

Hester, rather to her husband's surprise, fell in with this suggestion at once, and the following evening saw her installed in solitude and tranquillity. The little hotel was still almost empty, for the rush of summer tourists had not yet begun, and all day she sat out on the beach with the sense of a struggle over. She need not fight the terror any more; dimly it seemed to her that its malignancy had been relaxed. Had she in some way yielded to it and done its secret bidding? At any rate no return of its nightly visitations had occurred, and she slept long and dreamlessly, and woke to another day of quiet. Every morning there was a line for her from Dick, with good news of himself and the children, but he and they alike seemed somehow remote, like memories of a very distant time. Something had driven in between her and them, and she saw them as if through glass. But equally did the memory of the face of Roger Wyburn, as seen on the master's canvas or hanging close in front of her against the crumbling sand-cliff, become blurred and indistinct, and no return of her nightly terrors visited her. This truce from all emotion reacted not on her mind alone, lulling her with a sense of soothed security, but on her body also, and she began to weary of this day-long inactivity.

The village lay on the lip of a stretch of land reclaimed from the sea. To the north the level marsh, now beginning to glow with the pale bloom of the sea-lavender, stretched away featureless till it lost itself in distance, but to the south a spur of hill came down to the shore ending in a wooded promontory. Gradually, as her physical health increased, she began to wonder what lay beyond this ridge which cut short the view, and one afternoon she walked across the intervening level and strolled up its wooded slopes. The day was close and windless, the invigorating sea-breeze which till now had spiced the heat with freshness had died, and she looked forward to finding a current of air stirring when she had topped the hill. To the south a mass of dark cloud lay along the horizon, but there was no imminent threat of storm. The slope was easily surmounted, and presently she stood at the top and found herself on the edge of a tableland of wooded pasture, and following the path, which ran not far from the edge of the cliff, she came out into more open country. Empty fields, where a few sheep were grazing, mounted gradually upwards. Wooden stiles made a communication in the hedges that bounded them. And there, not a mile in front of her, she saw a wood, with trees growing slantingly away from the push of the prevalent sea winds, crowning the upward slope, and over the top of it peered a grey church tower.

For the moment, as the awful and familiar scene identified itself, Hester's heart stood still: the next a wave of courage and resolution poured in upon her. Here, at last was the scene of that prefatory dream, and here was she presented with the opportunity of fathoming and dispelling it. Instantly her mind was made up, and under the strange twilight of the shrouded sky, she walked swiftly on through the fields she had so often traversed in sleep, and up to the wood, beyond which he was waiting for her. She closed her ears against the clanging bell of terror, which now she could silence for ever, and unfalteringly entered that dark tunnel of wood. Soon in front of her the trees began to thin, and through them, now close at hand, she saw the church tower. In a few yards farther she came out of the belt of trees, and round her were the monuments of a graveyard long disused. The cliff was broken off close to the church tower: between it and the edge there was no more of the body of the church than a broken arch, thick hung with ivy. Round this she passed and saw below the ruin of fallen masonry, and the level sands strewn with headstones and disjected rubble, and at the edge of the cliff were graves already cracked and toppling. But there was no one here, none waited for her, and the churchyard where she had so often pictured him was as empty as the fields she had just traversed.

A huge elation filled her; her courage had been rewarded, and all the terrors of the past became to her meaningless phantoms. But there was no time to linger, for now the storm threatened, and on the horizon a blink of lightning was followed by a crackling peal. Just as she turned to go her eye fell on a tombstone that was balanced on the very edge of the cliff, and she read on it that here lay the body of Roger Wyburn.

Fear, the catalepsy of nightmare, rooted her for the moment to the spot; she stared in stricken amazement at the moss-grown letters; almost she expected to see that fell terror of a face rise and hover over his resting-place. Then the fear which had frozen her lent her wings, and with hurrying feet she sped through the arched pathway in the wood and out into the fields. Not one backward glance did she give till she had come to the edge of the ridge above the village, and, turning, saw the pastures she had traversed empty of any living presence. None had followed; but the sheep, apprehensive of the coming storm, had ceased to feed, and were huddling under shelter of the stunted hedges.

Her first idea, in the panic of her mind, was to leave the place at once, but the last train for London had left an hour before, and besides, where was the use of flight if it was the spirit of a man long dead from which she fled? The distance from the place where his bones lay did not afford her safety; that must be sought for within. But she longed for Dick's sheltering and confident presence; he was arriving in any case to-morrow, but there were long dark hours before to-morrow, and who could say what the perils and dangers of the coming night might be? If he started this evening instead of to-morrow morning, he could motor down here in four hours, and would be with her by ten o'clock or eleven. She wrote an urgent telegram: "Come at once," she said. "Don't delay."

The storm which had flickered on the south now came quickly up, and soon after it burst in appalling violence. For preface there were but a few large drops that splashed and dried on the roadway as she came back from the post-office, and just as she reached the hotel again the roar of the approaching rain sounded, and the sluices of heaven were opened. Through the deluge flared the fire of the lightning, the thunder crashed and echoed overhead, and presently the street of the village was a torrent of sandy turbulent water, and sitting there in the dark one picture leapt floating before her eyes, that of the tombstone of Roger Wyburn, already tottering to its fall at the edge of the cliff of the church tower. In such rains as these, acres of the cliffs were loosened; she seemed to hear the whisper of the sliding sand that would precipitate those perished sepulchres and what lay within to the beach below.

By eight o'clock the storm was subsiding, and as she dined she was handed a telegram from Dick, saying that he had already started and sent this off *en route*. By half-past ten, therefore, if all was well, he would be here, and somehow he would stand between her and her fear. Strange how a few days ago both it and the thought of him had become distant and dim to her; now the one was as vivid as the other, and she counted the minutes to his arrival. Soon the rain ceased altogether, and looking out of the curtained window of her sitting-room where she sat watching the slow circle of the hands of the clock, she saw a tawny moon rising over the sea. Before it had climbed to the zenith, before her clock had twice told the hour again, Dick would be with her.

It had just struck ten when there came a knock at her door, and the page-boy entered with the message that a gentleman had come for her. Her heart leaped at the news; she had not expected Dick for half an hour yet, and now the lonely vigil was over. She ran downstairs, and there was the figure standing on the step outside. His face was turned away from her; no doubt he was giving some order to his chauffeur. He was outlined against the white moonlight, and in contrast with that, the gas-jet in the entrance just above his head gave his hair a warm, reddish tinge.

She ran across the hall to him.

"Ah, my darling, you've come," she said. "It was good of you. How quick you've been!" Just as she laid her hand on his shoulder he turned. His arm was thrown out round her, and she looked into a face with eyes close set, and a mouth smiling on one side, the other, thick and gathered together as by some physical deformity, sneered and lusted.

The nightmare was on her; she could neither run nor scream, and supporting her dragging steps, he went forth with her into the night.

Half an hour later Dick arrived. To his amazement he heard that a man had called for his wife not long before, and that she had gone out with him. He seemed to be a stranger here, for the boy who had taken his message to her had never seen him before, and presently surprise began to deepen into alarm; enquiries were made outside the hotel, and it appeared that a witness or two had seen the lady whom they knew to be staying there walking, hatless, along the top of the beach with a man whose arm was linked in hers. Neither of them knew him, but one had seen his face and could describe it.

The direction of the search thus became narrowed down, and though with a lantern to supplement the moonlight they came upon footprints which might have been hers, there were no marks of any who walked beside her. But they followed these until they came to an end, a mile away, in a great landslide of sand, which had fallen from the old churchyard on the cliff, and had brought down with it half the tower and a gravestone, with the body that had lain below.

The gravestone was that of Roger Wyburn, and his body lay by it, untouched by corruption or decay, though two hundred years had elapsed since it was interred there. For a week afterwards the work of searching the landslide went on, assisted by the high tides that gradually washed it away. But no further discovery was made.

III SPINACH

Ludovic Byron and his sister Sylvia had adopted these pretty, though quite incredible names because those for which their injudicious parents and god-parents were responsible were not so suitable, though quite as incredible. They rightly felt that there was a lack of spiritual suggestiveness in Thomas and Caroline Carrot which would be a decided handicap in their psychical careers, and would cool rather than kindle the faith of those inquirers who were so eager to have séances with the Byrons.

The change, however, had not been made without earnest thought on their parts, for they were two very scrupulous young people, and wondered whether it would be "acting a lie" thus to profess to be what they were not, and whether, in consequence, the clearness of their psychical sight would be dimmed. But they found to their great joy that their spiritual guides or controls, Asteria and Violetta, communicated quite as freely with the Byrons as with the Carrots, and by now they called each other by their assumed names quite naturally, and had almost themselves forgotten that they had ever been other than what they were styled on their neat professional engagement cards.

While it would be tedious to trace Ludovic's progress from the time when it was first revealed to him that he had rare mediumistic gifts down to the present day, when he was quite at the head of his interesting profession, it is necessary to explain the manner in which his powers were manifested. When the circle was assembled (fees payable in advance), he composed himself in his chair, and seemed to sink into a sort of trance, in which Asteria took possession of him and communicated through his mouth with the devotees. Asteria, when living on the material plane, had been a Greek maiden of ancient Athens, who had become a Christian and suffered martyrdom in Rome about the same time as St. Peter. She had wonderful things to tell them all about her experiences on this earth, a little vague, perhaps, as was only natural after so long a lapse of time, but she spoke dreamily yet convincingly about the Parthenon and the Forum and the Ægean sea (so blue) and the catacombs (so black), and the beautiful Italian and Greek sunsets, and this was all the more remarkable because Ludovic had never been outside the country of his birth.

But far more interesting to the circle, any of whom could take a ticket for Rome or Athens and see the sunsets and the catacombs for themselves, were the encouraging things she said about her present existence. Everyone was wonderfully happy and busy helping those who had lately passed over to the other side, and they all lived in an industrious ecstasy of spiritual progress. There were refreshments and relaxations as well, quantities of the most beautiful flowers and exquisite fruits and crystal rivers and azure mountains, and flowing robes and delightful habitations. None of these things was precisely material; you "thought" a flower or a robe, and there it was!

Asteria knew many of the friends and relatives, who had passed over, of Ludovic's circle, and they sent through her loving messages and sweet thoughts. There was George, for instance, did any of the sitters know George? Very often somebody did know George. George was the late husband of one of the sitters, or the father of another, or the little son, who had passed over, of a third, and so George would say how happy he was, and how much love he sent. Then Asteria would tell them that Jane wanted to talk to her dear one, and if nobody knew Jane, it was Mary. And Asteria explained quite satisfactorily how it was that, among all the thousands who were continually passing over, just those who had friends and relations among the ladies and gentlemen who sat with Ludovic Byron were clever enough to "spot" Asteria as being his spiritual guide, who would put them into communication with their loved ones. This was due to currents of sympathy which immediately drew them to her.

Then, when the séance had gone on for some time, Asteria would say that the power was getting weak, and she would bid them good-bye and fade into silence. Presently Ludovic came out of his trance, and they would all tell him how wonderful it had been. At other séances he would not go into trance at all, but Asteria used his hand and his pencil, and wrote pages of automatic script in quaint, slightly foreign English, with here and there a word in strange and undecipherable characters, which was probably Greek. George and Jane and Mary were then dictating to Asteria, who caused Ludovic to write down what she said, and sometimes they were very playful, and did not like their wife's hat or their husband's tie, just by way of showing that they were really there. And then any member of the circle could ask Asteria questions, and she gave them beautiful answers.

Sylvia and her guide, Violetta, were not in so advanced a stage of development as Ludovic and Asteria; indeed, it was only lately that Sylvia had discovered that she had psychical gifts and had got into touch with her guide. Violetta had been a Florentine lady of noble birth, and was born (on the material plane) in the year 1452, which was a very interesting date, as it made her an exact contemporary of Savonarola and Leonardo da Vinci. She had often heard Savonarola preach, and had seen Leonardo at his easel, and it was splendid to know that Savonarola often preached now to enraptured audiences, and that Leonardo was producing pictures vastly superior to anything he had done on earth. They were not material pictures exactly, but thought-pictures. He thought them, and there the pictures were. This corresponded precisely with what Asteria had said about the flowers, and was, therefore, corroborative evidence.

This winter and spring had been a very busy time for Ludovic, and Mrs. Sapson, one of the most regular attendants at his séances, had been trying to persuade him to go for a short holiday. He was very unwilling to do so, for he was giving five full séances every day (which naturally "mounted up,") and he was loth to abandon, even for a short time, the work that so many people found so enlightening. But then Mrs. Sapson had been very clever, and had asked Asteria at one of the séances whether he ought not to take a rest, and Asteria distinctly said: "Wisdom counsels prudence; be it so." After the séance was over, therefore, Mrs. Sapson, strong in spiritual support, renewed her arguments with redoubled force. She was a large, emphatic widow, who received no end of messages from her husband, William. He had been a choleric stockbroker on this plane, but his character had marvellously mellowed and improved, and now he knew what a waste of time it had been to make so much money and lose so much temper.

"Dear Mr. Ludovic," she said, "you must have a rest. You can't fly in the face of sweet Asteria. Besides, I have just got a lovely plan for you. I own a charming little cottage near Rye, which is vacant. My tenant has—has suddenly quitted it. It is a dear little place, everything quite ready for you. No expense at all, except what you eat and drink, and sea-bathing and golf at your door. Such a place for quiet and meditation, and—who knows—some wonderful visitor (not earthly, of course, for there are no bothering neighbours) might come to you there."

Of course, this charming offer made a great difference. Ludovic felt that he could give up his spiritual work for a fortnight with less of a wrench than was possible when he thought that he would have to pay for lodgings. He expressed his gratitude in suitable terms, and promised to consult Sylvia, who at the moment was engaged with Violetta. She leaped at the idea when it was referred to her, and the matter was instantly settled.

The two were chatting together on the eve of their departure.

"Wonderfully kind of Mrs. Sapson," said Ludovic. "But it's odd that she didn't offer us the cottage before. She was wanting me to take a holiday a month ago."

"Perhaps the tenant has only just left," said Sylvia.

"That may be so. Dear me, the country and sea-breezes! How nice. But I don't mean to be idle."

"Golf?" suggested Sylvia. "Isn't it very difficult?"

He walked across to the table and took up a square parcel, which had just been delivered.

"No, not golf," he said. "But I am going to take up spirit photography. It pays very—I mean it's very helpful. So I've bought a camera and some rolls of films, and the developing and fixing solutions. I shall do it all myself. I used to photograph when I was a boy."

"That must have cost a good deal of money," said Sylvia, who had a great gift for economy.

"Ten pounds, but don't look pained; I think it's worth it. Besides, we get our lodging free. And if I have the power of spirit-photography, it will repay us over and over again."

"Explain the process to me," said Sylvia.

"Well, it's very mysterious, but there's no doubt that if a medium who has got the gift takes a photograph, there sometimes appears on the negative what is called an 'extra.' In other words, if I took a photograph of you, there might appear on the film not only your photograph, but that of some spirit, connected with you or the place, standing by you, or perhaps its face floating in the air near you. It would make another branch of our work, it would bring in fresh clients. The old ones too; I think they want something new. Mrs. Sapson would love a photograph of herself with her William leaning over her shoulder. Anyhow, it's worth trying. I shall practise down at the cottage."

He put the parcel containing the photographic apparatus with other property for packing, and made himself comfortable in his chair.

"I want you to work, too," he said. "I want you to develop your *rapport* with Violetta. There's nothing like practice. Mediumistic power is just as much a gift as music. But you must practice on the piano to be able to play."

The two were alone, and the utmost confidence existed between them. They talked to each other with a frankness which would have appalled their sitters.

"Sometimes I wonder whether I have any mediumistic power at all," she said. "I get in a dreamy sort of state when I am writing automatic script, but is Violetta really communicating, or am I only putting down the thoughts of my sub-conscious self? Or when Asteria speaks through you is she really an independent intelligence, or is she part of your own?"

Ludovic was in a very candid mood.

"I don't know, and I don't care," he said. "But my conscious self certainly can't invent all the things Asteria says, so they come from outside my normal perceptions. And then, after all, Asteria tells things about George and Jane, and so on, concerning their life on earth, which I never knew at all."

"But their relations who are sitting with you know them," said Sylvia. "Isn't it possible that you may get at those facts through telepathy?"

"Yes, but then that's extremely clever of me if I do," said Ludovic. "And it's just as reasonable to say that it's Asteria. Besides, if it's all me, how do you account for it that Asteria sometimes says something which goes against all my intentions and inclinations? For instance, when she said 'Wisdom counsels prudence: be it so,' in answer to Mrs. Sapson's asking if I was not overworked and wanted a holiday, that quite contradicted my own wishes. I didn't want to go for a holiday at all. Therefore it looks as if Asteria was an external intelligence controlling me."

"Sub-consciously you might have known you wanted a holiday," said the ingenious Sylvia.

"That's far-fetched. Better stick to Asteria. Besides, I sincerely believe that sometimes things come to me from outside my consciousness. And I don't know—not always, that's to say—what Asteria has been telling them while I'm in trance. Sometimes it really astonishes me."

He poured out a moderate whisky-and-soda.

"I'm looking forward to a holiday from séances," he said, "now that it's settled, for, frankly, Asteria has been a little thin and feeble lately. And I'm not sure that Mrs. Sapson doesn't think so, too. I think she feels that she's heard about all that Asteria has got to say, and it would never do to lose her as a sitter. That's why I should very much like to find that I can produce spirit photographs. It—it would vary the menu."

They took with them a grim and capable general servant called Gramsby, and arrived next afternoon at Mrs. Sapson's cottage. It was romantically situated near a range of great sand-dunes which ran along the coast, and was only a few minutes' walk from the sea. The place was very remote; a minute village with a shop or two and a cluster of fishermen's huts stood half a mile away, and inland there stretched the empty levels of the Romney marsh away to Rye, which smouldered distantly in the afternoon sunlight. The cottage itself was an enchanting abode, built of timber and rough-cast, with a broad verandah facing south, and a gay little garden in front. Inside, on the ground floor, there were kitchen and dining-room, and a large living-room with access to the verandah. This was well and plainly furnished and had an open fireplace with a wide hearth for a wood fire and an immense chimney. Logs were ready laid there and, indeed, the whole house had the aspect of having been lately tenanted. Upstairs there were sunny bedrooms facing south, which, overlooking the sand-dunes, gave a restful view of the sea beyond; it was impossible to conceive a more tranquil haven for an overworked medium.

They had a hasty cup of tea, and hurried out to enjoy the last hours of daylight in exploration among the sand-dunes and along the beach, and came back soon after sunset. Though the day had been warm, the evening air had a nip in it, and Sylvia gave a little shiver as they stepped in from the verandah to the sitting-room.

"It's rather cold," she said. "I think I'll light the fire."

Ludovic shared her sensations.

"An excellent idea," he said. "And we'll draw the curtains and be cosy. What a charming room! I shall take some interiors to-morrow. Time exposure, I think they told me, for an interior."

Their supper was soon ready, and presently they came back to the sitting-room and laid out a hectic Patience. But they were both strangely absent-minded, neglecting the most glaring opportunities for getting spaces and putting up kings.

"I can't concentrate on it to-night," said Ludovic. "I feel as if someone was trying to attract my attention.... I wonder if Asteria wants to communicate."

Sylvia looked up at him.

"Now it's very odd that you should say that," she observed. "I feel exactly as if Violetta was wanting to come through, and yet it doesn't seem quite like Violetta."

He gave an uneasy glance round the room.

"A curious sensation," he said. "I have the consciousness of some presence here, which isn't quite Asteria. But it may be she. Tiresome of her, if it is, for she ought to know I came down here for a holiday, considering that she recommended it herself. I think I'll get a pencil and paper, and see if she wants to say anything."

He composed himself in a chair, with the stationery for Asteria on his knee.

"Ask her a question or two, Sylvia," he said, "when I go off."

Sylvia waited till her brother's eyelids fluttered and fell.

"Is that you, Asteria?" she asked.

His hand twitched and quivered. Then the pencil scribbled "Certainly not" in large, firm letters, quite unlike Asteria's pretty writing.

Sylvia asked if it was Violetta, but got an emphatic denial.

"Who is it, then?" she said.

And then a very absurd thing happened. The pencil spelt out "Thomas Spinach."

Sylvia was puzzled for a moment. Then the explanation occurred to her, and she laughed.

"Wake up, dear," she said to Ludovic. "It says it is Thomas Spinach. Of course, that's your sub-conscious self trying to remember Carrot."

But Ludovic did not stir, and to her surprise the pencil began writing again.

"I don't know who you are," wrote the unknown control. "But I'm Spinach, young Spinach. And"—there was a long pause—"I want you to help me. I can't remember … I'm very unhappy."

As she followed the words, there suddenly came a very loud rap on the wall just above her, which considerably startled her, for why, if "Spinach" was an attempt on the part of Ludovic's sub-consciousness to write "Carrot," should he announce his presence? She sprang up, and shook Ludovic by the shoulder.

"Wake up," she said. "There's a strange spirit here, and I don't like it. Wake up, Ludovic."

He came drowsily to himself.

"Hullo!" he said. "Anything been happening? was it Asteria?"

His eye fell on the paper.

"What's all this?" he said. "Thomas Spinach? That's only me. My subconsciousness said it was Asparagus once."

"But look what it has been writing," said Sylvia.

He read it.

"That's queer," he said. "That can't be me. I'm not very unhappy. I don't want my own help. I know who I am."

He jumped up.

"Most interesting," he said. "It looks like a new control. Young Spinach must be powerful, too; he came through the first time he tried. We'll investigate this, Sylvia. It would be fine to get a new control for our séances."

"But not to-night, Ludovic," said she. "I really shouldn't sleep if you went on now. And he's violent. He made the loudest rap I ever heard."

"Did he, indeed?" said Ludovic. "I must have been in deep trance then, for I never heard it. We'll certainly try to snap him with the camera to-morrow."

The morning was bright and sunny, and directly after breakfast Ludovic set to work with his photography. The first three or four films showed nothing but impenetrable blackness, and a consultation of his handbook convinced him that they must have been over-exposed. He corrected this, and after a few errors on the other side, produced a negative which quite clearly showed Sylvia sitting by the long window into the verandah. This, though it revealed no "extra," was an encouraging achievement, and he took half a dozen more exposures with which he hurried away into the small dark cupboard under the stairs, where he had installed his developing and fixing baths. Shortly afterwards Sylvia heard her name called in crowing, exultant tones, and ran to see what had happened.

"Don't open the door," he called, "or you'll spoil it. But I've got a picture of you with a magnificent extra—a face hanging in the air by your shoulder."

"How lovely!" shouted Sylvia. "Do be quick and fix it."

There was no sort of doubt about it. There she sat by the window, and close by her was a strange, inexplicable face. So much could be seen from the negative, and when a print was taken of it, the details were wonderfully clear. It was the face of a young man; his handsome features wore an expression of agonized entreaty.

"Poor boy!" said Sylvia, sympathetically. "So good looking, too, but somehow I don't like him."

Then a brilliant idea struck her.

"Oh, Ludovic!" she said. "Is it young Spinach?"

He snatched the print from her.

"I must fix it," he said, "or it will be ruined. Of course it's young Spinach. Who else could it be, I should like to know? We'll find out more about him this evening. Fancy obtaining that the very first morning!"

They spent the afternoon on the beach, in order to get in an elevated frame of mind by contemplating the beauties of nature, and after a light supper, prepared for a double séance. Two hooks, so to speak, were baited for Spinach, for in one chair sat Sylvia, with pencil and paper, ready to take down his slightest word, and in another Ludovic, similarly equipped. They both let themselves sink into that drowsy and vacant condition which they knew to be favourable to communications from the unseen, but for a long time they neither of them got a bite. Then Ludovic heard the dash and clatter of his sister's pencil, suddenly beginning to write very rapidly, and this aroused in him disturbing feelings of envy and jealousy, for something was coming through to Sylvia and not to him.

This inharmonious emotion quite dissipated the tranquillity which was a *sine qua non* of the receptive state, and he got up to see what was coming through to her. Probably some mawkish rubbish from Violetta about Savonarola's sermons. But the moment he saw her paper he was thrilled to the marrow.

"Yes, I'm Thomas Spinach," he read, "and I'm very unhappy. I came and stood by you this morning when the man was photographing. I want you to help me. Oh, do help me! It's something I've forgotten, though it is so important. I want you to look everywhere and see if you can't find something very unusual, and tell them. It is somewhere here. It must be, because I put it there, and I hardly like to tell you what it is, because it's terrible...."

The pencil stopped. Ludovic was wildly excited, and his jealousy of Sylvia was almost forgotten. After all, it was he who had taken Spinach's photograph....

Sylvia's hand continued idle so long that Ludovic, in order to stir it into activity again, began to ask questions.

"Have you passed over, Spinach?" he said.

Her hand began to write in a swift and irritated manner. "Of course I have," it scribbled. "Otherwise I should know where it was."

"Used you to live here?" asked Ludovic. "And when did you pass over?"

"Yes, I lived here," came the answer. "I passed over a week ago. Very suddenly. There was a thunderstorm that night, and I had just finished it all, and was in the garden cooling down, when lightning struck me, and when I came to—on this side, you understand—I couldn't remember where it was."

"Where what was?" asked Ludovic. "Do you mean the thing you had finished? What was it you had finished?"

The pencil seemed to give a loud squeak, as if it was a slate pencil.

"Oh, here it is again," it wrote in trembling characters. "I can't go on now. It's terrible. I'm so frightened. Please, please find it."

Just as on the previous evening, there came an appalling rap somewhere on the wall close to him, and, seriously startled, Ludovic sprang up, and shook Sylvia into consciousness. Whoever this spirit was, it was not a good, kind, mild one like Asteria, who, whenever she rapped, did so very softly and pleasantly.

Sylvia yawned and stretched herself.

"Spinach?" she said, drowsily. "Any Spinach?"

"Yes, dear, quantities," said Ludovic.

"And what did he say? Oh, I went off deep then, Ludovic. I don't know what's been happening. Violetta isn't nearly so powerful. Such an odd feeling! Did I write all that?"

"Yes, in answer to some pretty good questions of mine," he said. "It's really wonderful. We're on the track of young Spinach, or, rather, he's on ours."

Sylvia was reading her manuscript.

"'I passed over a week ago,'" she said. "'Very suddenly—there was a thunderstorm that night——' Why, Ludovic, there was! That's quite true. You slept through it, but I didn't, and I remember reading in the paper that it had been very violent in the Rye district. How strange!"

Ludovic clicked his fingers.

"I know what I'll do," he said. "I shall send a telegram to Mrs. Sapson. Give me a piece of paper. She said that wonderful visitors might perhaps come to me here."

Sylvia grasped his thoughts.

"I see!" she cried. "You mean to tell her that her late tenant, young Thomas Spinach, who was killed by lightning last week, has communicated with us. That will impress her tremendously, if you think she's had enough of Asteria. Indeed, I shouldn't wonder if she lent us this cottage just in order to test us, and see if we really received messages from the other side. What a score!"

She hastily scribbled on a leaf of her writing-block, counting up the words on her fingers. Her economical mind exerted itself to contrive the message in exactly twelve words.

"There!" she read out triumphantly. "Listen! 'Sapson, 29, Brompton Avenue, London. Tenant Spinach killed last week, thunderstorm, communicated.' Just twelve. You needn't sign it, as it will have the Rye postmark."

"My dear," said he, "it's no time for such petty economies. Better spend a few pence more and make it impressive and rather more intelligible. Give me some paper; I asked you before. And we must make it clear that it's not a chance word of local gossip that has inspired it. I shall tell her about the photograph, too."

Before they went to bed, Ludovic composed a more explicit telegram, and in the course of the next morning he received an enthusiastic reply from Mrs. Sapson.

"All quite correct and most wonderful," she wrote. "Delighted you have got into communication. Find out more, and ask him about his uncle. Wire again if fresh revelations occur."

In order to secure themselves from the possibility of interruption, Sylvia gave Gramsby an afternoon out, which she proposed to spend in the excitements of Rye, and as soon as she was gone the mediums prepared for a séance. As Spinach seemed to fancy Sylvia, she composed herself for the trance-condition, with pencil and paper handy, and Ludovic sat by to ask questions. Very soon Sylvia's eyes closed, her head fell forward, and the pencil she held began to tremble violently, like a motor-car ready to start.

"Are you Spinach?" asked Ludovic, observing these signs of possession. Instantly the pencil began to write.

"Yes; have you found it?"

"We don't know what it is," said Ludovic. Then he remembered Mrs. Sapson's telegram. "Has it anything to do with your uncle?" he asked.

There was a long pause. Then the pencil began to move again.

"Please find him," it wrote.

"But how are we to find your uncle?" asked Ludovic. "We don't know where to look or what he's like. Tell us where to look."

The pencil moved in a most agitated fashion.

"I don't know," it wrote. "If I knew I would tell you. But it's somewhere about. I had just put it somewhere, when the lightning came and killed me, and I can't remember. My memory's gone like—like after concussion of the brain."

An uneasy thought struck Ludovic. Why did young Spinach allude to his uncle as "it"?

"Is your uncle dead?" he asked. "Is it his body that you mean by 'it'?"

Sylvia's fingers writhed as if in mortal agony. Then the pencil jerked out, "Yes."

Ludovic, accustomed as he was to spirits, felt an icy shudder run through him. But he waited in silence, for the pencil looked as if it had something more to write. Then, great heavens! it came.

"I will tell you all," it wrote. "I killed him, and I can't remember where I put him."

A spasm of moral indignation seized Ludovic.

"That was very wrong of you," he justly observed. "But we'll try to help you if you will tell us all about it. Come; you're dead. Nobody can hang you."

Shocked as Ludovic was, and extremely uneasy also at the thought of the proximity not only of the spirit of a murderer, but the corpse of young Spinach's uncle, it was only natural that he should feel an overwhelming professional interest in the revelations that appeared to be imminent. It would be a glorious thing for his career to receive from a departed spirit the first-hand account of this undetected crime, and to be able to corroborate it by the discovery of the corpse. Though he had come down here for a holiday, the chance of such a unique piece of work made him feel quite rested already, for it was impossible to conceive a more magnificent advertisement. What a wonderful confirmation it would be also to Mrs. Sapson's wavering faith in his psychical powers. She would publish the news of it far and wide, and the séances would be more popular than ever. Moreover, there was the chance of learning all sorts of fresh information about the conditions that prevailed on the other side, of a far more sensational and exciting quality than the method of the production of thought-flowers and flowing robes and general love and helpfulness.... He waited with the intensest expectation for anything that Spinach might vouchsafe.

At last it began, and now there was no need for further questions, for the pencil streamed across the page. Sheet after sheet of the writing-block was filled, and twice Ludovic had to sharpen Sylvia's pencil, for the point was quite worn down with these remarkable disclosures, and only made illegible scratches on the paper. For half an hour it careered over the sheets; then finally it made a great scrawl, and Sylvia's hand dropped inert. She stretched and yawned, and came to herself.

The next hour was the most absorbing that Ludovic had ever spent in his professional work. Together they read the account of the crime. Alexander Spinach, the uncle, was the most wicked of elderly gentlemen, who made his nephew's life an intolerable burden to him. He had found out that the orphan boy had committed a petty forgery with regard to a cheque which he had signed with his uncle's name, and, holding exposure and arrest over his head, had made him work for him day and night, fishing and farming and doing the work of the house without a penny-piece of wages, while he himself boozed his days away in the chimney-corner.

Long brooding over his wrongs and the misery of his life made young Spinach (very properly, as he still thought) determine to kill the odious old wretch, and he adroitly poisoned his whisky with weed-killer. He went out to his work next morning as usual, leaving the corpse in the locked-up house, and casually mentioned to the folk he came across that his uncle had gone up to London and would probably not be back for some time. When he returned in the evening he hid the body somewhere, meaning to dig a handsome excavation in the garden, and having buried it, plant some useful vegetables above it. But hardly had he made this temporary disposition of the corpse, than he was struck by lightning in the terrific storm that visited the district a week ago, and killed. When he came to himself on the spiritual plane, he could not remember what he had done with the body.

So far the story was ordinary enough, apart from the interest in the manner of its communication, but now came that part of the confession which these ardent young psychicists saw would be a veritable gold mine to them. For on emerging on the other side, young Spinach found himself terrifyingly haunted not by the spirit, but by the body of his uncle. Just as on the material plane, so he explained, murderers are sometimes haunted by the spirit of their victim, so on the spiritual plane, quite logically, they may be haunted by the body of their victim. His uncle's bodily and palpable presence grimly pursued him wherever he went; even as he gathered sweet thought-flowers or thought-fruits, the terrible body appeared. If he woke at night he found it watching by his bed, if he bathed in the crystal rivers it swam beside him, and he had learned that he could never find peace till it was given proper burial. No doubt, he said, Ludovic had heard of the skeletons of murdered folk being walled up in secret chambers, and how their spirits haunted the place till their bones were discovered and interred. The converse was true on the other side, and while murdered corpses lay about unburied in the material world, their bodies haunted the perpetrator of the crime.

It was here that poor young Spinach's difficulty came in. The sudden lightning-stroke had bereft him of all memory of what he was doing just before, and, puzzle as he might, he could not recollect where he had put the corpse.... Then he broke out into passionate entreaties: "Help me, help me, kind mediums," he wrote. "I know it is somewhere about, so search for it and get it buried. He was an awful old man and I can't describe the agony of being haunted by his beastly body. Find it and have it buried, and then I shall be free from its dreadful presence."

They read this unique document together by the fading light, strung up to the highest pitch of professional interest, and yet peering awfully round from time to time in vague apprehension of what might happen next. During the séance the wind had got up, and now it was moaning round the corners of the house, and dusk was falling rapidly, with prospects of a wild night to follow. The curtains bulged and bellied in the draught, hollow voices sounded in the chimney, and Sylvia clung to her brother.

"I don't like it," she wailed. "I don't like this spirit of Spinach; Violetta and Asteria are far preferable. And then there's 'It.' It is somewhere about, and it may be anywhere."

Ludovic made an attempt at gaiety.

"It may be anywhere, as you say," he remarked, "but it actually is somewhere. And we've got to find it, dear. Better find it before it gets dark. And think of the sensation there will be when we publish the account of how, in answer to the entreaty of a remorseful spirit——"

"But he isn't remorseful," said Sylvia. "There's not a word of remorse, but only terror at being haunted. There's not only a corpse about, but the spirit of an unrepentant murderer. It isn't pleasant. I would sooner be in expensive lodgings than here."

"Oh, nonsense," said Ludovic. "Besides, young Spinach is friendly enough to us. We're his one hope. And if we find it, he will certainly be very grateful. I shouldn't wonder if he sent us many more revelations. Even as it is, how deeply interesting. Nobody ever guessed that there were material ghosts in the spiritual world. But now we must get busy and search for Alexander. Fix your mind on what a tremendously paying experience this will be. Now, where shall we begin? There's the house and the garden——"

"Oh, I hope it will be in the garden," said Sylvia. "But there's no chance of that, for he meant to bury it in the garden afterwards."

"True. We'll begin with the house, then. Now most murderers bury the body under the floor of the kitchen, cover it with quicklime, and fill in with cement."

"But he wouldn't have had time for that," said Sylvia. "Besides, this was to be only a temporary resting-place."

"Perhaps he cut it up," said Ludovic, "and we shall find a piece here and a piece there."

The search began. In the growing dusk, with the wild wind increasing to a gale, they annealed themselves for the gruesome business. They investigated the coal cellar, they peered into housemaids' cupboards, and with quaking hearts examined the woodshed. Here there were signs that its contents had been disturbed, and the sight of an old boot peeping out from behind some logs nearly caused Sylvia to collapse. Then Ludovic got a ladder, and, climbing up to the roof, interrogated the water-tank, from the contents of which they had already drunk. But all their explorations were in vain; there was no sign of the corpse. For a nerve-racking hour they persevered, and a dismal idea occurred to Ludovic.

"It can't be a practical joke on the part of Spinach, can it?" he said "That would be in the worst possible taste. Good gracious, what's that?"

There came a loud tapping at the front door, and Sylvia hid her face on his shoulder.

"That's Spinach," she whispered. "That terrible Spinach!"

They tottered to the door and opened it. On the threshold was a man, who told them he was the carrier from Rye, and brought a note for Miss Byron.

"I'm going back in half an hour, miss," he said, "if there's any answer. A box, I understood."

The note was from Gramsby, who, though unwilling to "upset" them, declined to come back to the cottage. She had heard things, and she didn't like it, and she would be obliged if they would pack her box and send it in.

"The coward!" said Sylvia, trembling violently. "She shan't have her box unless she comes to fetch it."

They went back into the sitting-room, lit the fire, and made it as cheerful as they could with many candles. Their flames wagged ominously in the eddying draughts, and the two drew their chairs close to the hearth. By now the full fury of the gale was unloosed, the whole house shuddered at the blasts, doors creaked, curtains whispered, flurries of rain were flung against the windows, and strange noises and stirrings muttered in the chimney.

"I shall just get warm," said Ludovic, "and then go on with the search. I shan't know a moment's peace till I find it."

"I shan't know a moment's peace when you do!" wailed Sylvia.

They were sitting in the fire almost, and suddenly something up the chimney caught Ludovic's eye.

"What's that?" he said.

He got a candle and held it up the chimney.

"It's a rope," he said, "tied round a staple in the wall."

His look met hers, and read the answering horror there.

"I'm going to undo it," he said. "Step back, Sylvia."

There was no need to say that, for she had already retreated to the farthest corner of the room. He pulled the rope off the staple and let it go.

There was a scrambling, shuffling noise from high up in the chimney, and in a cloud of soot It fell, with a heavy thud, sprawling across the hearth.

They fled into the night; the carrier had only just got to the garden gate.

"Take us into Rye," cried Ludovic. "Take us to the police-station. Murder has been done——"

The account of these amazing events duly appeared in all the psychical papers and many others. Long queues of would-be sitters formed up for the Byron séances, in the hopes of getting fresh revelations from young Spinach. But from association with Asteria and Violetta he gradually became quite commonplace, and only told them about thought-flowers and white robes.

IV BAGNELL TERRACE

I had been for ten years an inhabitant of Bagnell Terrace, and, like all those who have been so fortunate as to secure a footing there, was convinced that for amenity, convenience, and tranquillity it is unrivalled in the length and breadth of London. The houses are small; we could, none of us, give an evening party or a dance, but we who live in Bagnell Terrace do not desire to do anything of the kind. We do not go in for sounds of revelry at night, nor, indeed, is there much revelry during the day, for we have gone to Bagnell Terrace in order to be anchored in a quiet little backwater. There is no traffic through it, for the terrace is a cul-de-sac, closed at the far end by a high brick wall, along which, on summer nights, cats trip lightly on visits to their friends. Even the cats of Bagnell Terrace have caught something of its discretion and tranquillity, for they do not hail each other with long-drawn yells of mortal agony like their cousins in less well-conducted places, but sit and have quiet little parties like the owners of the houses in which they condescend to be lodged and boarded.

But, though I was more content to be in Bagnell Terrace than anywhere else, I had not got, and was beginning to be afraid I never should get, the particular house which I coveted above all others. This was at the top end of the terrace adjoining the wall that closed it, and in one respect it was unlike the other houses, which so much resemble each other. The others have little square gardens in front of them, where we have our bulbs abloom in the spring, when they present a very gay appearance, but the gardens are too small, and London too sunless to allow of any very effective horticulture. The house, however, to which I had so long turned envious eyes, had no garden in front of it; instead, the space had been used for the erection of a big, square room (for a small garden will make a very well-sized room) connected with the house by a covered passage. Rooms in Bagnell Terrace, though sunny and cheerful, are not large, and just one big room, so it occurred to me, would give the final touch of perfection to those delightful little residences.

Now, the inhabitants of this desirable abode were something of a mystery to our neighbourly little circle, though we knew that a man lived there (for he was occasionally seen leaving or entering his house), he was personally unknown to us. A curious point was that though we had all (though rarely) encountered him on the pavements, there was a considerable discrepancy in the impression he had made on us. He certainly walked briskly, as if the vigour of life was still his, but while I believed that he was a young man, Hugh Abbot, who lived in the house next his, was convinced that, in spite of his briskness, he was not only old, but very old. Hugh and I, life-long bachelor friends, often discussed him in the ramble of conversation when he had dropped in for an after-dinner pipe, or I had gone across for a game of chess. His name was not known to us, so, by reason of my desire for his house, we called him Naboth. We both agreed that there was something odd about him, something baffling and elusive.

I had been away for a couple of months one winter in Egypt; the night after my return Hugh dined with me, and after dinner I produced those trophies which the strongest-minded are unable to refrain from purchasing, when they are offered by an engaging burnoused ruffian in the Valley of the Tombs of the Kings. There were some beads (not quite so blue as they had appeared there), a scarab or two, and for the last I kept the piece of which I was really proud, namely, a small lapis-lazuli statuette, a few inches high, of a cat. It sat square and stiff on its haunches, with upright forelegs, and, in spite of the small scale, so good were the proportions and so accurate the observation of the artist, that it gave the impression of being much bigger. As it stood on Hugh's palm, it was certainly small, but if, without the sight of it, I pictured it to myself, it represented itself as far larger than it really was.

"And the odd thing is," I said, "that though it is far and away the best thing I picked up, I cannot for the life of me remember where I bought it. Somehow I feel that I've always had it."

He had been looking very intently at it. Then he jumped up from his chair and put it down on the chimney-piece.

"I don't think I quite like it," he said, "and I can't tell you why. Oh, a jolly bit of workmanship: I don't mean that. And you can't remember where you got it, did you say? That's odd.... Well, what about a game of chess."

We played a couple of games, without much concentration or fervour, and more than once I saw him glance with a puzzled look at my little image on the chimney-piece. But he said nothing more about it, and when our games were over, he gave me the discursive news of the terrace. A house had fallen vacant and been instantly snapped up.

"Not Naboth's?" I asked.

"No, not Naboth's. Naboth is in possession still. Very much in possession; going strong."

"Anything new?" I asked.

"Oh, just bits of things. I've seen him a good many times lately, and yet I can't get any clear idea of him. I met him three days ago, as I was coming out of my gate, and had a good look at him, and for a moment I agreed with you and thought he was a young man. Then he turned and stared me in the face for a second, and I thought I had never seen anyone so old. Frightfully alive, but more than old, antique, primeval."

"And then?" I asked.

"He passed on, and I found myself, as has so often happened before, quite unable to remember what his face was like. Was he old or young? I didn't know.

What was his mouth like, or his nose? But it was the question of his age which was the most baffling."

Hugh stretched his feet out towards the blaze, and sank back in his chair, with one more frowning look at my lapis lazuli cat.

"Though after all, what is age?" he said. "We measure age by time, we say 'so many years,' and forget that we're in eternity here and now, just as we say we're in a room or in Bagnell Terrace, though we're much more truly in infinity."

"What has that got to do with Naboth?" I asked.

Hugh beat his pipe out against the bars of the grate before he answered.

"Well, it will probably sound quite cracked to you," he said, "unless Egypt, the land of ancient mystery, has softened your rind of materialism, but it struck me then that Naboth belonged to eternity much more obviously than we do. We belong to it, of course, we can't help that, but he's less involved in this error or illusion of time than we are. Dear me, it sounds amazing nonsense when I put it into words."

I laughed.

"I'm afraid my rind of materialism isn't soft enough yet," I said. "What you say implies that you think Naboth is a sort of apparition, a ghost, a spirit of the dead that manifests itself as a human being, though it isn't one!"

He drew his legs up to him again.

"Yes; it must be nonsense," he said. "Besides he has been so much in evidence lately, and we can't all be seeing a ghost. It doesn't happen. And there have been noises coming from his house, loud and cheerful noises which I've never heard before. Somebody plays an instrument like a flute in that big, square room you envy so much, and somebody beats an accompaniment as if with drums. Odd sort of music; it goes on often now at night.... Well, it's time to go to bed."

Again he glanced up at the chimney-piece.

"Why, it's quite a little cat," he said.

This rather interested me, for I had said nothing to him about the impression left on my mind that it was bigger than its actual dimensions.

"Just the same size as ever," I said.

"Naturally. But I had been thinking of it as life-size for some reason," said he.

I went with him to the door, and strolled out with him into the darkness of an overcast night. As we neared his house, I saw that big patches of light shone into the road from the windows of the square room next door. Suddenly Hugh laid his hand on my arm.

"There!" he said. "The flutes and drums are at it to-night."

The night was very still, but, listen as I would, I could hear nothing but the rumble of traffic in the street beyond the terrace.

"I can't hear it," I said.

Even as I spoke, I heard it, and the wailing noise whisked me back to Egypt again. The boom of the traffic became for me the beat of the drum, and upon it floated just that squeal and wail of the little reed pipes which accompany the Arab dances, tuneless and rhythmless, and as old as the temples of the Nile.

"It's like the Arab music that you hear in Egypt," I said.

As we stood listening it ceased to his ears as well as mine, as suddenly as it had begun, and simultaneously the lights in the windows of the square room were extinguished.

We waited a moment in the roadway opposite Hugh's house, but from next door came no sound at all, nor glimmer of illumination from any of its windows....

I turned; it was rather chilly to one lately arrived from the South.

"Good night," I said, "we'll meet to-morrow sometime."

I went straight to bed, slept at once, and woke with the impress of a very vivid dream on my mind. There was music in it, familiar Arab music, and there was an immense cat somewhere. Even as I tried to recall it, it faded, and I had but time to recognise it as a hash-up of the happenings of the evening before I went to sleep again.

The normal habits of life quickly reasserted themselves. I had work to do, and there were friends to see; all the minute events of each day stitched themselves into the tapestry of life. But somehow a new thread began to be woven into it, though at the time I did not recognise it as such. It seemed trivial and extraneous that I should so often hear a few staves of that odd music from Naboth's house, or that as often as it fixed my attention it was silent again, as if I had imagined, rather than actually heard it. It was trivial, too, that I should so often see Naboth entering or leaving his house. And then one day I had a sight of him, which was unlike any previous experience of mine.

I was standing one morning in the window of my front room. I had idly picked up my lapis lazuli cat, and was holding it in the splash of sunlight that poured in, admiring the soft texture of its surface which, though it was of hard stone, somehow suggested fur. Then, quite casually, I looked up, and there a few yards in front of me, leaning on the railings of my garden, and intently observing not me, but what I held, was Naboth. His eyes, fixed on it, blinked in the April sunshine with some purring sensuous content, and Hugh was right on the question of his age; he was neither old nor young, but timeless.

The moment of perception passed; it flashed on and off my mind like the revolving beam of some distant lighthouse. It was just a ray of illumination, and was instantly shut off again, so that it appeared to my conscious mind like some hallucination. He suddenly seemed aware of me, and turning, walked briskly off down the pavement.

I remember being rather startled, but the effect soon faded, and the incident became to me one of those trivial little things that make a momentary impression and vanish. It was odd, too, but in no way remarkable, that more than once I saw one of those discreet cats of which I have spoken sitting on the little balcony outside my front room, and gravely regarding the interior. I am devoted to cats, and several times I got up in order to open the window and invite it to enter, but each time on my movement it jumped down and slunk away. And April passed into May.

I came back after dining out one night in this month; and found a telephone message from Hugh that I should ring him up on my return. A rather excited voice answered me.

"I thought you would like to know at once," he said. "An hour ago a board was put up on Naboth's house to say that the freehold was for sale. Martin and Smith are the agents. Good night; I'm in bed already."

"You're a true friend," I said.

Early next morning, of course, I presented myself at the house-agent's. The price asked was very moderate, the title perfectly satisfactory. He could give me the keys at once, for the house was empty, and he promised that I could have a couple of days to make up my mind, during which time I was to have the prior right of purchase if I was disposed to pay the full price asked. If, however, I only made an offer, he could not guarantee that the trustees would accept it.... Hot-foot, with the keys in my pocket, I sped back up the terrace again.

I found the house completely empty, not of inhabitants only, but of all else. There was not a blind, not a strip of drugget, not a curtain-rod in it from garret to cellar. So much the better, thought I, for there would be no tenants' fixtures to take on. Nor was there any débris of removal, of straw and waste paper; the house looked as if it was prepared for an occupant instead of just rid of one. All was in apple-pie order, the windows clean, the floors swept, the paint and woodwork bright; it was a clean and polished shell ready for its occupier. My first inspection, of course, was of the big built-out room, which was its chief attraction, and my heart leaped at the sight of its plain spaciousness. On one side was an open fire-place, on the other a coil of pipes for central heating, and at the end, between the windows, a niche let into the wall, as if a statue had once stood there; it might have been designed expressly for my bronze Perseus. The rest of the house presented no particular features; it was on the same plan as my own, and my builder, who inspected it that afternoon, pronounced it to be in excellent condition.

"It looks as if it had been newly done up, and never lived in," he said, "and at the price you mention is a decided bargain."

The same thing struck Hugh when, on his return from his office, I dragged him over to see it.

"Why, it all looks new," he said, "and yet we know that Naboth has been here for years, and was certainly here a week ago. And then there's another thing. When did he remove his furniture? There have been no vans at the house that I have seen."

I was much too pleased at getting my heart's desire to consider anything except that I had got it.

"Oh, I can't bother about little things like that," I said. "Look at my beautiful big room. Piano there, bookcases all along the wall, sofa in front of the fire, Perseus in the niche. Why, it was made for me."

Within the specified two days the house was mine, and within a month papering and distempering, electric fittings, and blinds and curtain rods were finished, and my move began. Two days were sufficient for the transport of my goods, and at the close of the second my old house was dismantled, except for my bedroom, the contents of which would be moved next day. My servants were installed in the new abode, and that night, after a hurried dinner with Hugh, I went back for a couple more hours' work of hauling and tugging and arranging books in the large room, which it was my purpose to finish first. It was a chilly night for May, and I had had a log-fire lit on the hearth, which from time to time I replenished, in intervals of dusting and arranging. Eventually, when the two hours had lengthened themselves into three, I determined to give over for the present, and, much tired, sat down for a recuperative pause on the edge of my sofa and contemplated with satisfaction the result of my labours. At that moment I was conscious that there was a stale, but aromatic, smell in the room that reminded me of the curious odour that hangs about an Egyptian temple. But I put it down to the dust from my books and the smouldering logs.

The move was completed next day, and after another week I was installed as firmly as if I had been there for years. May slipped by, and June, and my new house never ceased to give me a vivid pleasure: it was always a treat to return to it. Then came a certain afternoon when a strange thing happened.

The day had been wet, but towards evening it cleared up: the pavements soon dried, but the road remained moist and miry. I was close to my house on my way home, when I saw form itself on the paving-stones a few yards in front of me the mark of a wet shoe, as if someone invisible to the eye had just stepped off the road. Another and yet another briskly imprinted themselves going up towards my house. For the moment I stood stock still, and then, with a thumping heart I followed. The marks of these strange footsteps preceded me right up to my door: there was one on the very threshold faintly visible.

I let myself in, closing the door, I confess, very quickly behind me. As I stood there I heard a resounding crash from my room, which, so to speak, startled my fright from me, and I ran down the little passage, and burst in. There, at the far end of the room was my bronze Perseus fallen from its niche and lying on the floor. And I knew, by what sixth sense I cannot tell, that I was not alone in the room and that the presence there was no human presence.

Now fear is a very odd thing: unless it is overmastering and overwhelming, it always produces its own reaction. Whatever courage we have rises to meet it, and with courage comes anger that we have given entrance to this unnerving intruder. That, at any rate, was my case now, and I made an effective emotional resistance. My servant came running in to see what the noise was, and we set Perseus on his feet again and examined into the cause of his fall. It was clear enough: a big piece of plaster had broken away from the niche, and that must be repaired and strengthened before we reinstated him. Simultaneously my fear and the sense of an unaccountable presence in the room slipped from me. The footsteps outside were still unexplained and I told myself that if I was to shudder at everything I did not understand, there would be an end to tranquil existence for ever.

I was dining with Hugh that night: he had been away for the last week, only returning to-day, and he had come in before these slightly agitating events happened to announce his arrival and suggest dinner. I noticed that as he stood chatting for a few minutes, he had once or twice sniffed the air but he had made no comment, nor had I asked him if he perceived the strange faint odour that every now and then manifested itself to me. I knew it was a great relief to some secretly-quaking piece of my mind that he was back, for I was convinced that there was some psychic disturbance going on, either subjectively in my mind, or a real invasion from without. In either case his presence was comforting, not because he is of that stalwart breed which believes in nothing beyond the material facts of life, and pooh-poohs these mysterious forces which surround and so strangely interpenetrate existence, but because, while thoroughly believing in them, he has the firm confidence that the deadly and evil powers which occasionally break through into the seeming security of existence are not really to be feared, since they are held in check by forces stronger yet, ready to assist all who realise their protective care. Whether I meant to tell him what had occurred to-day I had not fully determined.

It was not till after dinner that such subjects came up at all, but I had seen there was something on his mind of which he had not spoken yet.

"And your new house," he said at length, "does it still remain as all your fancy painted?"

"I wonder why you ask that," I said.

He gave me a quick glance.

"Mayn't I take any interest in your well-being?" he said.

I knew that something was coming, if I chose to let it.

"I don't think you've ever liked my house from the first," I said. "I believe you think there's something queer about it. I allow that the manner in which I found it empty was odd."

"It was rather," he said. "But so long as it remains empty, except for what you've put in it, it is all right."

I wanted now to press him further.

"What was it you smelt this afternoon in the big room?" I said. "I saw you nosing and sniffing. I have smelt something, too. Let's see if we smelt the same thing."

"An odd smell," he said. "Something dusty and stale, but aromatic."

"And what else have you noticed?" I asked.

He paused a moment.

"I think I'll tell you," he said. "This evening from my window I saw you coming up the pavement, and simultaneously I saw, or thought I saw, Naboth cross the road and walk on in front of you. I wondered if you saw him, too, for you paused as he stepped on to the pavement in front of you, and then you followed him."

I felt my hands grow suddenly cold, as if the warm current of my blood had been chilled.

"No, I didn't see him," I said, "but I saw his step."

"What do you mean?"

"Just what I say. I saw footprints in front of me, which continued on to my threshold."

"And then?"

"I went in, and a terrific crash startled me. My bronze Perseus had fallen from his niche. And there was something in the room."

There was a scratching noise at the window. Without answering, Hugh jumped up and drew aside the curtain. On the sill was seated a large grey cat, blinking in the light. He advanced to the window, and on his approach the cat jumped down into the garden. The light shone out into the road, and we both saw, standing on the pavement just outside, the figure of a man. He turned and looked at me, and then moved away towards my house, next door.

"It's he," said Hugh.

He opened the window and leaned out to see what had become of him. There was no sign of him anywhere, but I saw that light shone from behind the blinds of my room.

"Come on," I said. "Let's see what is happening. Why is my room lit?"

I opened the door of my house with my latch-key, and followed by Hugh went down the short passage to the room. It was perfectly dark, and when I turned the switch, we saw that it was empty. I rang the bell, but no answer came, for it was already late, and doubtless my servants had gone to bed.

"But I saw a strong light from the windows two minutes ago," I said, "and there has been no one here since."

Hugh was standing by me in the middle of the room. Suddenly he threw out his arm as if striking at something. That thoroughly alarmed me.

"What's the matter?" I asked. "What are you hitting at?"

He shook his head.

"I don't know," he said. "I thought I saw——But I'm not sure. But we're in for something if we stop here. Something is coming, though I don't know what."

The light seemed to me to be burning dim; shadows began to collect in the corner of the room, and though outside the night had been clear, the air here was growing thick with a foggy vapour, which smelt dusty and stale and aromatic. Faintly, but getting louder as we waited there in silence, I heard the throb of drums and the wail of flutes. As yet I had no feeling that there were other presences in the place beyond ours, but in the growing dimness I knew that something was coming nearer. Just in front of me was the empty niche from which my bronze had fallen, and looking at it, I saw that something was astir. The shadow within it began to shape itself into a form, and out of it there gleamed two points of greenish light. A moment more and I saw that they were eyes of antique and infinite malignity.

I heard Hugh's voice in a sort of hoarse whisper.

"Look there!" he said. "It's coming! Oh, my God, it's coming!"

Sudden as the lightning that leaps from the heart of the night it came. But it came not with blaze and flash of light, but, as it were, with a stroke of blinding darkness, that fell not on the eye, or on any material sense, but on the spirit, so that I cowered under it in some abandonment of terror. It came from those eyes which gleamed in the niche, and which now I saw to be set in the face of the figure that stood there. The form of it, naked, but for a loin-cloth, was that of a man, the head seemed now human, now to be that of some monstrous cat. And as I looked, I knew that if I continued looking there I should be submerged and drowned in that flood of evil that poured from it. As in some catalepsy of nightmare I struggled to tear my eyes from it, but still they were riveted there, gazing on incarnate hate.

Again I heard Hugh's whisper.

"Defy it," he said. "Don't yield an inch."

A swarm of disordered and hellish images were buzzing in my brain, and now I knew as surely as if actual words had been spoken to us that the presence there told me to come to it.

"I've got to go to it," I said. "It's making me go."

I felt his hand tighten on my arm.

"Not a step," he said. "I'm stronger than it is. It will know that soon. Just pray—pray."

Suddenly his arm shot out in front of me, pointing at the presence.

"By the power of God," he shouted. "By the power of God."

There was dead silence. The light of those eyes faded, and then came dawn on the darkness of the room. It was quiet and orderly, the niche was empty, and there on the sofa by me was Hugh, his face white and streaming with sweat.

"It's over," he said, and without pause fell fast asleep.

Now we have often talked over together what happened that evening. Of what seemed to happen, I have already given the account, which anyone may believe or not, precisely as they please. He, as I, was conscious of a presence wholly evil, and he tells me that all the time that those eyes gleamed from the niche, he was trying to realise what he believed, namely, that only one power in the world is Omnipotent, and that the moment he gained that realisation the presence collapsed. What exactly that presence was it is impossible to say. It looks as if it was the essence or spirit of one of those mysterious Egyptian cults, of which the force survived, and was seen and felt in this quiet terrace. That it was embodied in Naboth seems (among all these incredibilities) possible, and Naboth certainly has never been seen again. Whether or not it was connected with the worship and cult of cats might occur to the mythological mind, and it is perhaps worthy of record that I found next morning my little lapis lazuli image, which stood on the chimneypiece, broken into fragments. It was too badly damaged to mend, and I am not sure that, in any case, I should have attempted to have it restored.

Finally, there is no more tranquil and pleasant room in London than the one built out in front of my house in Bagnell Terrace.

V A TALE OF AN EMPTY HOUSE

It had been a disastrous afternoon: rain had streamed incessantly from a low grey sky, and the road was of the vilest description. There were sections consisting of sharp flints, newly laid down and not yet rolled into amenity, and the stretches in between were worn into deep ruts and bouncing holes, so that it was impossible anywhere to travel at even a moderate speed. Twice we had punctured, and now, as the stormy dusk began to fall, something went wrong with the engine, and after crawling on for a hundred yards or so we stopped. My driver, after a short investigation, told me that there was a half-hour's tinkering to be done, and after that we might, with luck, trundle along in a leisurely manner, and hope eventually to arrive at Crowthorpe which was the proposed destination.

We had come, when this stoppage occurred, to a crossroad. Through the driving rain I could see on the right a great church, and in front a huddle of houses. A consultation of the map seemed to indicate that this was the village of Riddington. The guide-book added the information that Riddington possessed an hotel, and the sign-post at the corner endorsed them both. To the right along the main road, into which we had just struck, was Crowthorpe, fifteen miles away and straight in front of us, half a mile distant, was the hotel.

The decision was not difficult. There was no reason why I should get to Crowthorpe to-night instead of to-morrow, for the friend whom I was to meet there would not arrive until next afternoon and it was surely better to limp half a mile with a spasmodic engine than to attempt fifteen on this inclement evening.

"We'll spend the night here," I said to my chauffeur. "The road dips down hill, and it's only half a mile to the hotel. I daresay we shall get there without using the engine at all. Let's try, anyhow."

We hooted and crossed the main road, and began to slide very slowly down a narrow street. It was impossible to see much, but on either side there were little houses with lights gleaming through blinds, or with blinds still undrawn, revealing cosy interiors. Then the incline grew steeper, and close in front of us I saw masts against a sheet of water that appeared to stretch unbroken into the rain-shrouded gloom of the gathering night.

Riddington then must be on the open sea, though how it came about that boats should be tied up to an open quay-wall was a puzzle, but perhaps there was some jetty, invisible in the darkness, which protected them. I heard the chauffeur switch on his engine, as we made a sharp turn to the left, and we passed below a long row of lighted windows, shining out on to a rather narrow road, on the right edge of which the water lapped. Again he turned sharply to the left, described a half-circle on crunching gravel, and drew up at the door of the hotel. There was a room for me, there was a garage, there was a room for him, and dinner had not long begun.

Among the little excitements and surprises of travel there is none more delightful than that of waking in a new place at which one has arrived after nightfall on the previous evening. The mind has received a few hints and dusky impressions, and probably during sleep it has juggled with these, constructing them into some sort of coherent whole and next morning its anticipations are put to the proof. Usually the eye has seen more than it has consciously registered, and the brain has fitted together as in the manner of a jig-saw puzzle a very fair presentment of its immediate surroundings. When I woke next morning a brilliantly sunny sky looked in at my windows; there was no sound of wind or of breaking waves, and before getting up and verifying my impressions of the night before I lay and washed-in my imagined picture. In front of my windows there would be a narrow roadway bordered by a quay-wall: there would be a breakwater, forming a harbour for the boats that lay at anchor there, and away, away to the horizon would stretch an expanse of still and glittering sea. I ran over these points in my mind; they seemed an inevitable inference from the glimpses of the night before and then, assured of my correctness, I got out of bed and went to the window.

I have never experienced so complete a surprise. There was no harbour, there was no breakwater, and there was no sea. A very narrow channel, three-quarters choked with sand-banks on which now rested the boats whose masts I had seen the previous evening, ran parallel to the road, and then turned at right angles and went off into the distance. Otherwise no water of any sort was visible; right and left and in front stretched a limitless expanse of shining grasses with tufts of shrubby growth, and great patches of purple sea-lavender. Beyond were tawny sand-banks, and further yet a line of shingle and scrub and sand-dunes. But the sea which I had expected to fill the whole circle of the visible world till it met the sky on the horizon, had totally disappeared.

After the first surprise at this colossal conjuring trick was over, I dressed quickly, in order to ascertain from local authorities how it was done. Unless some hallucination had poisoned my perceptive faculties, there must be an explanation of this total disappearance, alternately, of sea and land, and the key, when supplied, was simple enough. That line of shingle and scrub and sand dunes on the horizon was a peninsula running for four or five miles parallel with the land, forming the true beach, and it enclosed this vast basin of sand-banks and mud-banks and level lavender-covered marsh, which was submerged at high tide, and made an estuary. At low tide it was altogether empty but for the stream that struggled out through various channels to the mouth of it two miles away to the left, and there was easy passage across it for a man who carried his shoes and stockings, to the far sand dunes and beaches which terminated at Riddington Point, while at high tide you could sail out from the quay just in front of the hotel and be landed there.

The tide would be out of the estuary for five or six hours yet; I could spend the morning on the beach, or, taking my lunch, walk out to the Point, and be back before the returning waters rendered the channel impassable. There was good bathing on the beach, and there was a colony of terns who nested there.

Already, as I ate my breakfast at a table in the window overlooking the marsh, the spell and attraction of it had begun to work. It was so immense and so empty; it had the allure of the desert about it, with none of the desert's intolerable monotony, for companies of chiding gulls hovered over it, and I could hear the pipe of redshank and the babble of curlews. I was due to meet Jack Granger in Crowthorpe that evening, but if I went I knew that I should persuade him to come back to Riddington, and from my knowledge of him, I was aware that he would feel the spell of the place not less potent than I. So, having ascertained that there was a room for him here, I wrote him a note saying that I had found the most amazing place in the world, and told my chauffeur to take the car into Crowthorpe to meet the train that afternoon and bring him here. And with a perfectly clear conscience, I set off with a towel and a packet of lunch in my pocket to explore vaguely and goallessly that beckoning immensity of lavender-covered, bird-haunted expanse.

My way, as pointed out to me, led first along a sea-bank which defended the drained pastureland on the right of it from the high tides, and at the corner of that I struck into the basin of the estuary. A contour line of jetsam, withered grass, strands of seaweed, and the bleached shells of little crabs showed where the last tide had reached its height, and inside it the marsh growth was still wet. Then came a stretch of mud and pebbles, and presently I was wading through the stream that flowed down to the sea. Beyond that were banks of ribbed sand swept by the incoming tides, and soon I regained the wide green marshes on the further side, beyond which was the bar of shingle that fringed the sea.

I paused as I re-shod myself. There was not a sign of any living human being within sight, but never have I found myself in so exhilarating a solitude. Right and left were spread the lawns of sea-lavender, starred with pink tufts of thrift and thickets of suæda bushes. Here and there were pools left in depressions of the ground by the retreated tide, and here were patches of smooth black mud, out of which grew, like little spikes of milky-green asparagus, a crop of glass-wort, and all these happy vegetables flourished in sunshine or rain or the salt of the flooding tides with impartial amphibiousness. Overhead was the immense arc of the sky, across which flew now a flight of duck, hurrying with necks outstretched, and now a lonely black-backed gull, flapping his ponderous way seawards. Curlews were bubbling, and redshank and ringed plover fluting, and now as I trudged up the shingle bank, at the bottom of which the marsh came to an end, the sea, blue and waveless, lay stretched and sleeping, bordered by a strip of sand, on which far off a mirage hovered. But from end to end of it, as far as eye could see, there was no sign of human presence.

I bathed and basked on the hot beach, walked along for half a mile, and then struck back across the shingle into the marsh. And then with a pang of disappointment I saw the first evidence of the intrusion of man into this paradise of solitude, for on a stony spit of ground that ran like some great rib into the amphibious meadows, there stood a small square house built of brick, with a tall flagstaff set up in front of it. It had not caught my eye before, and it seemed an unwarrantable invasion of the emptiness. But perhaps it was not so gross an infringement of it as it appeared, for it wore an indefinable look of desertion, as if man had attempted to domesticate himself here and had failed. As I approached it this impression increased, for the chimney was smokeless, and the closed windows were dim with the film of salt air and the threshold of the closed door was patched with lichen and strewn with débris of withered grasses. I walked twice round it, decided that it was certainly uninhabited, and finally, leaning against the sun-baked wall, ate my lunch.

The glitter and heat of the day were at their height. Warmed and exercised, and invigorated by my bathe, I felt strung to the supreme pitch of physical well-being, and my mind, quite vacant except for these felicitous impressions, followed the example of my body, and basked in an unclouded content. And, I suppose by a sense of the Lucretian luxury of contrast, it began to picture to itself, in order to accentuate these blissful conditions, what this sunlit solitude would be like when some November night began to close in underneath a low, grey sky and a driving storm of sleet. Its solitariness would be turned into an abominable desolation: if from some unconjecturable cause one was forced to spend the night here, how the mind would long for any companionship, how sinister would become the calling of the birds, how weird the whistle of the wind round the cavern of this abandoned habitation. Or would it be just the other way about, and would one only be longing to be assured that the seeming solitude was real, and that no invisible but encroaching presence, soon to be made manifest, was creeping nearer under cover of the dusk, and be shuddering to think that the wail of the wind was not only the wind, but the cry of some discarnate being, and that it was not the curlews who made that melancholy piping? By degrees the edge of thought grew blunt, and melted into inconsequent imaginings, and I fell asleep.

I woke with a start from the trouble of a dream that faded with waking, but felt sure that some noise close at hand had aroused me. And then it came again: it was the footfall of someone moving about inside the deserted house, against the wall of which my back was propped. Up and down it went, then paused and began again; it was like that of a man who waited with impatience for some expected arrival. I noticed also that the footfall had an irregular beat, as if the walker went with a limp. Then in a minute or two the sound ceased altogether.

An odd uneasiness came over me, for I had been so certain that the house was uninhabited. Then turning my head I noticed that in the wall just above me was a window, and the notion, wholly irrational and unfounded, entered my mind that the man inside who tramped was watching me from it. When once that idea got hold of me, it became impossible to sit there in peace any more, and I got up and shovelled into my knapsack my towel and the remains of my meal. I walked a little further down the spit of land which ran out into the marsh, and turning looked at the house again, and again to my eyes it seemed absolutely deserted. But after all, it was no concern of mine and I proceeded on my walk, determining to inquire casually on my return to the hotel who it was that lived in so hermetical a place, and for the present dismissed the matter from my mind.

It was some three hours later that I found myself opposite the house again, after a long wandering walk. I saw that, by making an only slightly longer detour, I could pass close to the house again, and I knew that the sound of those footsteps within it had raised in me a curiosity that I wanted to satisfy. And then, even as I paused, I saw that a man was standing by the door: how he came there I had no idea, for the moment before he had not been there, and he must have come out of the house. He was looking down the path that led through the marsh, shielding his eyes against the sun, and presently he took a step or two forward and he dragged his left leg as he walked, limping heavily. It was his step then which I had heard within, and any mystery about the matter was of my own making. I therefore took the shorter path, and got back to the hotel to find that Jack Granger had just arrived.

We went out again in the gleam of the sunset, and watched the tide sweeping in and pouring up the dykes, until again the great conjuring trick was accomplished, and the stretch of marsh with its fields of sea-lavender was a sheet of shining water. Far away across it stood the house by which I had lunched, and just as we turned Jack pointed to it.

"That's a queer place for a house," he said. "I suppose no one lives there."

"Yes, a lame man," said I, "I saw him to-day. I'm going to ask the hotel porter who he is."

The result of this inquiry was unexpected.

"No; the house has been uninhabited several years," he said. "It used to be a watch-house from which the coastguards signalled if there was a ship in distress, and the lifeboat went out from here. But now the lifeboat and the coastguards are at the end of the Point."

"Then who is the lame man I saw walking about there, and heard inside the house?" I asked.

He looked at me, I thought, queerly.

"I don't know who that could be," he said. "There's no lame man about here to my knowledge."

The effect on Jack of the marshes and their gorgeous emptiness, of the sun and the sea, was precisely what I had anticipated. He vowed that any day spent anywhere than on these beaches and fields of sea-lavender was a day wasted, and proposed that the tour, of which the main object had originally been the golf links of Norfolk, should for the present be cancelled. In particular, it was the birds of this long solitary headland that enchanted him.

"After all, we can play golf anywhere," he said. "There's an oyster-catcher scolding, do you hear?—and how silly to whack a little white ball—ringed plover, but what's that calling as well?—when you can spend the day like this! Oh! don't let us go and bathe yet: I want to wander along that edge of the marsh—ha! there's a company of turnstones, they make a noise like the drawing of a cork—there they are, those little chaps with chestnut-coloured patches! Let's go along the near edge of the marsh, and come out by the house where your lame man lives."

We took, therefore, the path with the longer detour, which I had abandoned last night. I had said nothing to him of what the hotel porter had told me that the house was unlived in, and all he knew was that I had seen a lame man, apparently in occupation there. My reason for not doing so (to make the confession at once) was that I already half believed that the steps I had heard inside, and the lame man I had seen watching outside, did not imply in the porter's sense of the word that the house was occupied, and I wanted to see whether Jack as well as myself would be conscious of any such tokens of a presence there. And then the oddest thing happened.

All the way up to the house his attention was alert on the birds, and in especial on a piping note which was unfamiliar to him. In vain he tried to catch sight of the bird that uttered it, and in vain I tried to hear it. "It doesn't sound like any bird I know," he said, "in fact it doesn't sound like a bird at all, but like some human being whistling. There it is again! Is it possible you don't hear it?"

We were now quite close to the house.

"There must be someone there who is whistling," he said, "it must be your lame man.... Lord! yes, it comes from inside the house. So that's explained, and I hoped it was some new bird. But why can't you hear it?"

"Some people can't hear a bat's squeak," said I.

Jack, satisfied with the explanation, took no more interest in the matter, and we struck across the shingle, bathed and lunched, and tramped on to the tumble of sand dunes in which the Point ended. For a couple of hours we strolled and lazed there in the liquid and sunny air, and reluctantly returned in order to cross the ford before the tide came in. As we retraced our way, I saw coming up from the west a huge continent of cloud: and just as we reached the spit of land on which the house stood, a jagged sword of lightning flickered down to the low-lying hills across the estuary, and a few big raindrops plopped on the shingle.

"We're in for a drenching," he said. "Ha! Let's ask for shelter at your lame man's house. Better run for it!" Already the big drops were falling thickly, and we scuttled across the hundred yards that lay between us and the house, and came to the door just as the sluices of heaven were pulled wide. He rapped on it, but there came no answer; he tried the handle of it, but the door did not yield, and then, by a sudden inspiration, he felt along the top of the lintel and found a key. It fitted into the wards and next moment we stood within.

We found ourselves in a slip of a passage, at the end of which went up the staircase to the floor above. On each side of it was a room, one a kitchen, the other a living-room, but in neither was there any stick of furniture. Discoloured paper was peeling off the walls, the windows were thick with spidery weavings, the air heavy with unventilated damp.

"Your lame man dispenses with the necessities as well as the luxuries of life," said Jack. "A Spartan fellow."

We were standing in the kitchen: outside the hiss of the rain had grown to a roar, and the bleared window was suddenly lit up with a flare of lightning. A crack of thunder answered it, and in the silence that followed there came from just outside, audible now to me, the sound of a piping whistle. Immediately afterwards I heard the door by which we had just entered violently banged, and I remembered that I had left it open.

His eyes met mine.

"But there's no breath of wind," I said. "What made it bang like that?"

"And that was no bird that whistled," said he.

There was the shuffle in the passage outside of a limping step: I could hear the drag of a man's lame foot along the boards.

"He has come in," said Jack.

Yes, he had come in, and who had come in? At that moment not fright, but fear, which is a very different matter, closed in on me. Fright, as I understand it, is an emotion, startling, but not unnerving; you may under the finger of fright spring aside, you may scream, you may shout, you have the command of your muscles. But as that limping step moved down the passage I felt fear, the hand of the nightmare that, as it clutches, paralyses and inhibits not action only, but thought. I waited frozen and speechless for what should happen next.

Exactly opposite the open door of the kitchen in which we stood the step stopped. And then, soundlessly and invisibly, the presence that had made itself manifest to the outward ear, entered. Suddenly I heard Jack's breath rattle in his throat.

"O my God!" he cried in a voice hoarse and strangled, and he threw his left arm across his face as if defending himself, and his right arm shooting out, seemed to hit at something which I could not see, and his fingers crooked themselves as if clutching at that which had evaded his blow. His body was bent back as if resisting some invisible pressure, then lunged forward again, and I heard the noise of a resisting joint, and saw on his throat the shadow (or so it seemed) of a clutching hand. At that some power of movement came back to me, and I remember hurling myself at the empty space between him and me, and felt under my grip the shape of a shoulder and heard on the boards of the floor the slip and scoop of a foot. Something invisible, now a shoulder, now an arm, struggled in my grasp, and I heard a panting respiration that was not Jack's, nor mine, and now and then in my face I felt a hot breath that stank of corruption and decay. And all the time this physical contention was symbolical only: what he and I wrestled with was not a thing of flesh and blood, but some awful spiritual presence. And then....

There was nothing. The ghostly invasion ceased as suddenly as it had begun, and there was Jack's face gleaming with sweat close to mine, as we stood with dropped arms opposite each other in an empty room, with the rain beating on the roof and the gutters chuckling. No word passed between us, but next moment we were out in the pelting rain, running for the ford. The deluge was sweet to my soul, it seemed to wash away that horror of great darkness and that odour of corruption in which we had been plunged.

Now I have no certain explanation to give of the experience which has here been shortly recounted, and the reader may or may not connect with it a story that I heard a week or two later on my return to London.

A friend of mine and I had been dining at my house one evening, and we had discussed a murder trial then going on of which the papers were full.

"It isn't only the atrocity that attracts," he said, "I think it is the place where the murder occurs that is the cause of the interest in it. A murder at Brighton or Margate or Ramsgate, any place which the public associates with pleasure trips, attracts them because they know the place and can visualise the scene. But when there is a murder at some small unknown spot, which they have never heard of, there is no appeal to their imagination. Last spring, for instance, there was the murder at that small village on the coast of Norfolk. I've forgotten the name of the place, though I was in Norwich at the time of the trial and was present in court. It was one of the most awful stories I ever heard, as ghastly and sensational as this last affair, but it didn't attract the smallest attention. Odd that I can't remember the name of the place when all the rest is so vivid to me!"

"Tell me about it," I said; "I never heard of it."

"Well, there was this little village, and just outside it was a farm, owned by a man called John Beardsley. He lived there with his only daughter, an unmarried woman of about thirty, a good-looking, sensible creature apparently, the last in the world you would have thought to do anything unexpected. There worked at the farm as a day labourer a young fellow called Alfred Maldon, who, in the trial of which I am speaking, was the prisoner. He had one of the most dreadful faces I ever saw, a cat-like receding forehead, a broad, short nose, and a great red sensual mouth, always on the grin. He seemed positively to enjoy being the central figure round whom all the interest of those ghoulish women who thronged the court was concentrated, and when he shambled into the witness-box——"

"Shambled?" I asked.

"Yes, he was lame, his left foot dragged along the floor as he walked. As he shambled into the witness-box he nodded and smiled to the judge, and clapped his counsel on the shoulder, and leered at the gallery.... He worked on the farm, as I was saying, doing jobs that were within his capacity, among which was certain housework, carrying coals and what-not, for John Beardsley, though very well-off, kept no servant, and this daughter Alice—that was her name—ran the house. And what must she do but fall in love, it was no less than that, with this monstrous and misshapen fellow. One afternoon her father came home unexpectedly and caught them together in the parlour, kissing and cuddling. He turned the man out of the house, neck and crop, gave him his week's wages, and dismissed him, threatening him with a fine thrashing if he ever caught him hanging about the place. He forbade his daughter ever to speak to him again, and in order to keep watch over her, got in a woman from the village who would be there all day while he was out on the farm.

"Young Maldon, deprived of his job, tried to get work in the village, but none would employ him, for he was a black-tempered fellow ready to pick a quarrel with anyone, and an unpleasant opponent, for, with all his lameness, he was of immense muscular strength. For some weeks he idled about in the village getting a chance job occasionally and no doubt, as you will see, Alice Beardsley managed to meet him. The village—its name still escapes me—lay on the edge of a big tidal estuary, full at high water, but on the ebb of a broad stretch of marsh and sand and mud-banks, beyond which ran a long belt of shingle that formed the seaward side of the estuary. On it stood a disused coastguard house, a couple of miles away from the village, and in as lonely a place as you would find anywhere in England. At low tide there was a shallow ford across to it, and in the sand-banks round about it some beds of cockle. Maldon, unable to get regular work, took to cockle-digging, and during the summer when the tide was low, Alice (it was no new thing with her) used to go over the ford to the beach beyond and bathe. She would go across the sand-banks where the cockle-diggers, Maldon among them, were at work, and if he whistled as she passed that was the signal between them that he would slip away presently and join her at the disused coastguard house, and there throughout the summer they used to meet.

"As the weeks went on her father saw the change that was coming in her, and suspecting the cause, often left his work and, hidden behind some sea-bank, used to watch her. One day he saw her cross the ford, and soon after she had passed he saw Maldon, recognisable from a long way off by his dragging leg, follow her. He went up the path to the coastguard house, and entered. At that John Beardsley crossed the ford, and hiding in the bushes near the house, saw Alice coming back from her bathe. The house was off the direct path to the ford, but she went round that way, and the door was opened to her, and closed behind her. He found them together, and mad with rage attacked the man. They fought and Maldon got him down and then and there in front of his daughter strangled him.

"The girl went off her head, and is in the asylum at Norwich now. She sits all day by the window whistling. The man was hanged."

"Was Riddington the name of the village?" I asked.

"Yes. Riddington, of course," he said. "I can't think how I forgot it."

VI NABOTH'S VINEYARD

Ralph Hatchard had for the last twenty years been making a very good income at the Bar; no one could marshal facts so tellingly as he, no one could present a case to a jury in so persuasive and convincing a way, nor make them see the situation he pictured to them with so sympathetic an eye. He disdained to awaken sentiment by moving appeals to humanity, for he had not, either in his private or his public life, any use for mercy, but demanded mere justice for his client. Many were the cases in which, not by distorting facts, but merely by focusing them for the twelve intelligent men whom he addressed, he had succeeded in making them look through the telescope of his mind, and see at the end of it precisely what he wished them to see. But if he had been asked of which out of all his advocacies he was most intellectually proud, he would probably have mentioned one in which that advocacy had not been successful. This was in the famous Wraxton case of seven years ago, in which he had defended a certain solicitor, Thomas Wraxton, on a charge of embezzlement and conversion to his own use of the money of a client.

As the case was presented by the prosecution, it seemed as if any defence would merely waste the time of the court, but when the speech for the defence was concluded, most of them who heard it, not the public alone, but the audience of trained legal minds, would probably have betted (had betting been permitted in a court of justice) that Thomas Wraxton would be acquitted. But the twelve intelligent men were among the minority, and after being absent from court for three hours had brought in a verdict of guilty. A sentence of seven years was passed on Thomas Wraxton, and his counsel, thoroughly disgusted that so much ingenuity should have been thrown away, felt, ever afterward, a sort of contemptuous irritation with him. The irritation was rendered more acute by an interview he had with Wraxton after sentence had been passed. His client raged and stormed at him for the stupidity and lack of skill he had shown in his defence.

Hatchard was a bachelor; he had little opinion of women as companions, and it was enough for him in town when his day's work was over to take his dinner at the club, and after a stern rubber or two at bridge, to retire to his flat, and more often than not work at some case in which he was engaged till the small hours. Apart from the dinner-table and the card-table, the only companion he wanted was an opponent at golf for Saturday and Sunday, when he went down for his week-end to the seaside links at Scarling. There was a pleasant dormy-house in the town, at which he put up, and in the summer he was accustomed to spend the greater part of the long vacation here, renting a house in the neighbourhood. His only near relation was a brother who had a Civil Service appointment at Bareilly, in the North-West province of India, whom he had not seen for some years, for he spent the hot season in the hills and but seldom came to England.

Hatchard got from acquaintances all the friendship that he needed, and though he was a solitary man, he was by no means to be described as a lonely one. For loneliness implies the knowledge that a man is alone, and his wish that it were otherwise. Hatchard knew he was alone, but preferred it. His golf and his bridge of an evening gave him all the companionship he needed; a further recreation of his was botany. "Plants are good to look at, they're interesting to study, and they don't bore you by unwished-for conversation" would have been his manner of accounting for so unexpected a hobby. He intended, when he retired from practice, to buy a house with a good garden in some country town, where he could enjoy at leisure this trinity of innocuous amusements. Till then, there was no use in having a garden from which his work would sever him for the greater part of the year.

He always took the same house at Scarling when he came to spend his long vacation there. It suited him admirably, for it was within a few doors of the local club, where he could get a rubber in the evening, and find a match at golf for next day, and the motor omnibuses that plied along the seaside road to the links passed his door. He had long ago settled in his mind that Scarling was to be the home of his late and leisured years, and of all the houses in that compact mediæval little town the one which he most coveted lay close to that which he was now accustomed to take for the summer months. Opposite his windows ran the long red-brick wall of its garden, and from his bedroom above he could look over this and see the amenities which in its present proprietorship seemed so sadly undervalued.

An acre of lawn with a gnarled and sprawling mulberry tree lay there, a pergola of rambler-roses separated this from the kitchen garden, and all round in the shelter of the walls which defended them from the chill northerly and easterly blasts lay deep flower beds. A paved terrace faced the garden side of Telford House, but weeds were sprouting there, the grass of the lawn had been suffered to grow long and rank, and the flower beds were an untended jungle. The house, too, seemed exactly what would suit him, it was of Queen Anne date, and he could conjecture the square panelled rooms within. He had been to the house-agent's in Scarling to ask if there was any chance of obtaining it, and had directed him to make inquiries of the occupying tenant or proprietor as to whether he had any thoughts of getting rid of it to a purchaser who was prepared to negotiate at once for it. But it appeared that it had only been bought some six years ago by the present owner, Mrs. Pringle, when she came to live at Scarling, and she had no idea of parting with it.

Ralph Hatchard, when he was at Scarling, took no part whatever in the local life and society of the place except in so far as he encountered it among the men whom he met in the card-room of the club and out at the links, and it appeared that Mrs. Pringle was as recluse as he. Once or twice in casual conversation mention had been made by one or another of her house or its owner, but nothing was forthcoming about her. He learned that when she had come there first, the usual country-town civilities had been paid her, but she either did not return the call or soon suffered the acquaintanceship to drop, and at the present time she appeared to see nobody except occasionally the vicar of the church or his wife. Hatchard made no particular note of all this, and did not construct any such hypothesis as might be supposed to divert the vagrant thoughts of a legal mind by picturing her as a woman hiding from justice or from the exposure that justice had already subjected her to. As far as he was aware he had never set eyes on her, nor had he any object in wishing to do so, as long as she was not willing to part with her house; it was sufficient for a man who was not in the least inquisitive (except when conducting a cross-examination) to suppose that she liked her own company well enough to dispense with that of others. Plenty of sensible folk did that, and he thought no worse of them for it.

More than six years had now elapsed since the Wraxton trial, and Hatchard was spending the last days of the long vacation at the house that overlooked that Naboth's vineyard of a garden. The day was one of squealing wind and driving rain, and even he, who usually defied the elements to stop his couple of rounds of golf, had not gone out to the links to-day. Towards evening, however, it cleared, and he set out to get a mouthful of fresh air and a little exercise, and returned just about sunset past the house he coveted. There were two women standing on the threshold as he approached, one of them hatless, and it came into his mind that here, no doubt, was the retiring Mrs. Pringle. She stood side-face to him for that moment, and at once he knew that he had seen her before; her face and her carriage were perfectly but remotely familiar to him. Then she turned and saw him; she gave him but one glance, and without pause went back into the house and shut the door. The sight he had of her was but instantaneous, but sufficient to convince him not only that he had seen her before, but that she was in no way desirous of seeing him again.

Mrs. Grampound, the vicar's wife, had been talking to her, and Hatchard raised his hat, for he had been introduced to her one day when he had been playing golf with her husband. He alluded to the malignity of the weather, which, after being wet all day, was clearly going to be uselessly fine all night.

"And that lady, I suppose," he said, "with whom you were speaking, was Mrs. Pringle? A widow, perhaps? One does not meet her husband at the club."

"No; she is not a widow," said Mrs. Grampound. "Indeed, she told me just now that she expected her husband home before long. He has been out in India for some years."

"Indeed! I heard only to-day from my brother, who is also in India. I expect him home in the spring for six months' leave. Perhaps I shall find that he knows Mr. Pringle."

They had come to his house, and he turned in. Somehow, Mrs. Pringle had ceased to be merely the owner of the house he so much desired. She was somebody else, and good though his memory was, he could not recall where he had met her before. He could not in the least remember the sound of her voice, perhaps he had never heard it. But he knew her face.

During the winter he was often down at Scarling again for his week-ends, and now he was definitely intending to retire from practice before the summer. He had made sufficient money to live with all possible comfort, and he was certainly beginning to feel the strain of his work. His memory was not quite what it had been, and he who had been robust as a piece of ironwork all his life, had several times been in the doctor's hands. It was clearly time, if he was going to enjoy the long evening of life, to begin doing so while the capacity for enjoyment was still unimpaired, and not linger on at work till his health suffered. He could not concentrate as he had been used; even when he was most occupied in his own argument the train of his thought would grow dim, and through it, as if through a mist, vague images of thought would fleetingly appear, images not fully tangible to his mind, and evade him before he could grasp them.

That logical constructive brain of his was certainly getting tired with its years of incessant work, and knowing that, he longed more than ever to have done with business, and more vividly than ever he saw himself established in that particular house and garden at Scarling. The thought of it bid fair to become an obsession with him; he began to look upon Mrs. Pringle as an enemy standing in the way of the fulfilment of his dream, and still he cudgelled his brain to think when and where and how he had seen her before. Sometimes he seemed close to the solution of that conundrum, but just as he pounced on it, it slipped away again, like some object in the dusk.

He was down there one week-end in March and instead of playing golf, spent his Saturday morning in looking over a couple of houses which were for sale. His brother, whom he now expected back in a week or two, and who, like himself, was a bachelor, would be living with him all the summer, and now at last despairing of getting the house he wanted, he must resign himself to the inevitable, and get some other permanent home. One of these two houses, he thought, would do for him fairly well, and after viewing it he went to the house agent's and secured the first refusal of it, with a week in which to make up his mind.

"I shall almost certainly purchase it," he said, "for I suppose there is still no chance of my getting Telford House."

The agent shook his head.

"I'm afraid not, sir," he said. "Mr. Pringle, you may have heard, has come home, and lives there now."

As he left the office an idea occurred to him. Though Mrs. Pringle might not, when living there alone, have felt disposed to face the inconvenience of moving, it was possible that a firm and adequate offer made to her husband might effect something. He had only just come there, it was not to be supposed that he had any very strong attachment to the house, and a definite offer of so many thousand pounds down might perhaps induce him to give it up. Hatchard determined, before definitely purchasing another house, to make a final effort to get that on which his heart was set.

He went straight to Telford House and rang. He gave the maid his card, asking if he could see Mr. Pringle, and at that moment a man came into the little hall from the door into the garden, and seeing someone there paused as he entered. He was a tall fellow, but bent; and walked limpingly with the aid of a stick. He wore a short grey beard and moustache, his eyes were sunk deep below the overhanging brows.

Hatchard gave one glance at him, and a curious thing happened. Instantly there sprang into his mind not, first of all, the knowledge of who this man was, but the knowledge which had so long evaded him. He remembered everything: Mrs. Pringle's white, drawn face as she looked at the jury filing into the box again at the end of their consultation, in which they had decided the guilt or the innocence of Thomas Wraxton. No wonder she was all suspense and anxiety, for it was her husband's fate that was being decided. And then, a moment afterwards, he could trace in the face of the man who stood at the garden door the shattered identity of him who had stood in the dock. But had it not been for his wife, he thought he would not have recognised him, so terribly had suffering changed him. He looked very ill, and the high colour in his face clearly pointed to a weakness of the heart rather than a vigorous circulation.

Hatchard turned to him. He did not intend to use his deadliest weapon unless it was necessary. But at that moment he told himself that Telford House would be his.

"You will excuse me, Mr. Pringle," he said, "for calling on you so unceremoniously. My name is Hatchard, Ralph Hatchard, and I should be most grateful if you would let me have a few minutes' conversation with you."

Pringle took a step forward. He told himself that he had not been recognised; that was no wonder. But the shock of the encounter had left him trembling.

"Certainly," he said; "shall we go into my room here?"

The two went into a little sitting-room close by the front door.

"My business is quite short," said Hatchard. "I am on the look-out for a house here, and of all the houses in Scarling yours is the one which I have long wanted. I am willing to pay you £6,000 pounds for it. I may add that there is an extremely pleasant house, which I have the option to purchase, which you can obtain for half that sum."

Pringle shook his head.

"I am not thinking of parting with my house," he said.

"If it is a matter of price," said Hatchard, "I am willing to make it £6,500."

"It is not a matter of price," said Pringle. "The house suits my wife and me, and it is not for sale."

Hatchard paused a moment. The man had been his client, but a guilty and a very ungrateful one.

"I am quite determined to get this house, Mr. Pringle," he said. "You will make, I feel sure, a very handsome profit by accepting the price I offer, and if you are attached to Scarling you will be able to purchase a very convenient residence!"

"The house is not for sale," said Pringle.

Hatchard looked at him closely.

"You will be more comfortable in the other house," he said. "You will live there, I assure you, in peace and security, and I hope you will spend many pleasant years there as Mr. Pringle from India. That will be better than being known as Mr. Thomas Wraxton, of His Majesty's prison."

The wretched man shrunk into a mere nerveless heap in his chair, and wiped his forehead.

"You know me, then?" he said.

"Intimately, I may say," retorted Hatchard.

Five minutes later, Hatchard left the house. He had in his pocket Mr. Pringle's acceptance of his offer of £6,500 for Telford House with possession in a month's time. That night the doctor was hurriedly sent for to Telford House, but his skill was of no avail against the heart attack which proved fatal to his patient.

Ralph Hatchard was sitting on the flagged terrace on the garden side of his newly-acquired house one warm evening in May. He had spent his morning on the links with his brother Francis, his afternoon in the garden, weeding and planting, and now he was glad enough to sprawl in his low easy basket-chair and glance at the paper which he had not yet read. He had been a month here, and looking back through his happy and busy life, he could not recollect having ever been busier and happier. It was said, how falsely he now knew, that if a man gave up his work, he often went downhill both in mind and body, growing stout and lazy and losing that interest in life which keeps old-age in the background, but the very opposite had been his own experience. He played his golf and his bridge with just as much zest as when they had been the recreation from his work, and he found time now for serious reading. He gardened, too, you might say with gluttony; awaking in the morning found him refreshed and eager for the pleasurable toil and exercise of the day, and every evening found him ready for bed and long dreamless sleep.

He sat, alone for the time being, content to take his ease and glance at the news. Even now he gave but a cursory attention to it and his eye wandered over the lawn, and the long-neglected flower-beds, which the joint labours of the gardener and himself were quickly bringing back into orderly cultivation. The lawn must be cut to-morrow, and there were some late-flowering roses to be planted.... Then perhaps he dozed a little, for though he had heard no one approach, there was the sound of steps somewhere at his back quite close to him, and the tapping of a stick on the paving-stones of the terrace. He did not look round, for of course it must be Francis returned from his shopping; he had occasional twinges of rheumatism which made him a little lame, but Ralph had not noticed till to-day that he limped like that.

"Is your rheumatism bothering you, Francis?" he said, still not looking round. There was no answer and he turned his head. The terrace was quite empty: neither his brother nor anyone else was there.

For the moment he was startled: then he was aware that he certainly had been dozing, for his paper had slipped off his knee without his noticing it. No doubt this impression was the fag-end of some dream. Confirmation of that immediately came, for there in the street outside was the noise of a tapping footfall; it was that no doubt that had mingled itself with some only half-waking impression. He had dreamed, too, now that he came to think about it; he had dreamed something about poor Wraxton. What it was he could not recollect, beyond that Wraxton was angry with him and railed at him just as he had done after that long sentence had been passed on him.

The sun had set, and there was a slight chill in the air which caused him a moment's goose-flesh. So getting out of his basket-chair he took a turn along the gravel path which bordered the lawn, his eye dwelling with satisfaction on the labours of the day. The bed had been smothered in weeds a week ago; now there was not a weed to be seen on it.... Ah! just one; that small piece of chickweed had evaded notice, and he bent down to root it up. At that moment he heard the limping step again, not in the street at all, but close to him on the terrace, and the basket-chair creaked, as if someone had sat down in it. But again the terrace was void of occupants, and his chair empty.

It would have been strange indeed if a man so hard-headed and practical as Hatchard had allowed himself to be disturbed by an echoing stone and a creaking chair, and it was with no effort that he dismissed them. He had plenty to occupy him without that, but once or twice in the next week he received impressions which he definitely chucked into the lumber-room of his mind as among the things for which he had no use. One morning, for instance, after the gardener had gone to his dinner, he thought he saw him standing on the far side of the mulberry tree, half screened by the foliage. He took the trouble to walk round the tree on this occasion, but found no one there, neither his gardener nor any other, and coming back to the place where he had received this impression, he saw (and was secretly relieved to see) that a splash of light on the wall beyond might have tricked him into constructing a human figure there. But though his waking moments were still untroubled he began to sleep badly, and when he slept to be the prey of vivid and terrible dreams, from which he would awake in disordered panic.

The recollection of these was vague, but always he had been pursued by something invisible and angry that had come in from the garden, and was limping swiftly after him upstairs and along the passage at the end of which his room lay. Invariably, too, he just escaped into his room before the pursuer clutched him, and banged his door, the crash of which (in his dream) awoke him. Then he would turn on the light, and, despite himself, cast a glance at the door, and the oblong of glass above it which gave light to this dark end of the passage, as if to be sure that nothing was looking through it; and once, upbraiding himself for his cowardice, he had gone to the door and opened it, and turned on the light in the passage outside. But it was empty.

By day he was master of himself, though he knew that his self-control was becoming a matter that demanded effort. Often and often, though still nothing was visible, he heard the limping steps on the terrace and along the weeded gravel-path; but instead of becoming used to so harmless an hallucination, which seemed to usher in nothing further, he grew to fear it. But until a certain day, it was only in the garden that he heard that step....

July was now half way through, when a broiling morning was succeeded by a storm that raced up from the south. Thunder had been remotely muttering for an hour or two, and now as he worked on the garden beds, the first large tepid drops of rain warned him that the downpour was imminent, and he had scarcely reached the door into the hall when it descended. The sluices of heaven were opened, and thick as a tropical tempest the rain splashed and steamed on the terrace. As he stood in the doorway, he heard the limping step come slowly and unhurried through the deluge, and up to the door where he stood. But it did not pause there; he felt something invisible push by him, he heard the steps limp across the hall within, and the door of the sitting-room, where he had sat one morning in March and watched Wraxton's tremulous signature traced on the paper, swing open and close again.

Ralph Hatchard stood steady as a rock, holding himself firmly in hand. "So it's come into the house," he said to himself. "So it's come in—ha!—out of the rain," he added. But he knew, when that unseen presence had pushed by him to the door, that at that moment terror real and authentic had touched some inmost fibre of him. That touch had quitted him now; he could reassert his dominion over himself, and be steady, but as surely as that unseen presence had entered the house, so surely had fear found entry into his soul.

All the afternoon the rain continued; golf and gardening were alike out of the question, and presently he went round to the club to find a rubber of bridge. He was wise to be occupied, occupation was always good, especially for one who now had in his mind a prohibited area where it was better not to graze. For something invisible and angry had come into the house, and he must starve it into quitting it again, not by facing it and defying it, but by the subtler and the safe process of denying and disregarding it. A man's soul was his own enclosed garden, nothing could obtain admittance there without his invitation and permission. He must forget it till he could afford to laugh at the fantastic motive of its existence.... Besides, the perception of it was purely subjective, so he argued to himself: it had no real existence outside himself; his brother, for instance, and the servants were quite unaware of the limping steps that so constantly were heard by him. The invisible phantom was the product of some derangement of his own senses, some misfunction of the nerves. To convince himself of that, as he passed through the hall on his way to the club, he went into the room into which the limping steps had passed. Of course there was nothing there, it was just the small quiet, unoccupied sitting-room that he knew.

There was some brisk bridge, which he enjoyed in his usual grim and magisterial manner, and dusk, hastened on by the thick pall of cloud which still overset the sky, was falling when he got back home again. He went into the panelled sitting-room looking out on the garden, and found Francis there, cheery and robust. The lamps were lit, but the blinds and curtains not yet drawn, and outside an illuminated oblong of light lay across the terrace.

"Well, pleasant rubbers?" asked Francis.

"Very decent," said Ralph. "You've not been out?"

"No, why go out in the rain, when there's a house to keep you dry? By the way, have you seen your visitor?"

Ralph knew that his heart checked and missed a beat. Had that which was invisible to him become visible to another?... Then he pulled himself together; why shouldn't there have been a visitor to see him?

"No," he said, "who was it?"

Francis beat out his pipe against the bars of the grate.

"I'm sure I don't know," he said. "But ten minutes ago, I passed through the hall, and there was a man sitting on a chair there. I asked him what he wanted, and he said he was waiting to see you. I supposed it was somebody who had called by appointment, and I said you would no doubt be in presently, and suggested that he would be more comfortable in that little sitting-room than waiting in the hall. So I showed him in there, and shut the door on him."

Ralph rang the bell.

"Who is it who has called to see me?" he asked the parlourmaid.

"Nobody, sir, that I know of," she said; "I haven't let anyone in!"

"Well, somebody has called," he said, "and he's in the little sitting-room near the front door. Just see who it is; and ask him his name and his business."

He paused a moment, making a call on his courage.

"No; I'll go myself," he said.

He came back in a few seconds.

"Whoever it was, he has gone," he said. "I suppose he got tired of waiting. What was he like, Francis?"

"I couldn't see him very distinctly, for it was pretty dark in the hall. He had a grey beard, I saw that, and he walked with a limp."

Ralph turned to the window to pull down the blind. At that moment he heard a step on the terrace outside, and there stepped into the illuminated oblong the figure of a man. He leaned heavily on a stick as he walked, and came close up to the window, his eyes blazing with some devilish fury, his mouth mumbling and working in his beard.... Then down came the blind, and the rattle of the curtain-rings along the pole followed.

The evening passed quietly enough: the two brothers dined together, and played a few hands at piquet afterwards, and before going up to bed looked out into the garden to see what promise the weather gave. But the rain still dripped, and the air was sultry with storm. Lightning quivered now and again in the west, and in one of these blinks Francis suddenly pointed towards the mulberry-tree.

"Who is that?" he said.

"I saw no one," said Ralph.

Once more the lightning made things visible, and Francis laughed.

"Ah! I see," he said. "It's only the trunk of the tree and that grey patch of sky through the leaves. I could have sworn there was somebody there. That's a good example of how ghost stories arise. If it had not been for that second flash, we should have searched the garden, and, finding nobody, I should have been convinced I had seen a ghost!"

"Very sound," said Ralph.

He lay long awake that night, listening to the hiss of the rain on the shrubs outside his window, and to a footfall that moved about the house....

The next few days passed without the renewal of any direct manifestations of the presence that had entered the house. But the cessation of it brought no relief to the pressure of some force that seemed combing in over Ralph Hatchard's mind. When he was out on the links or at the club it relaxed its hold on him, but the moment he entered his door it gripped him again. It mattered not that he neither saw nor heard anything for which there was no normal and material explanation; the power, whatever it was, was about his path and about his bed, driving terror into him. He confessed to strange lassitude and depression, and eventually yielded to his brother's advice, and made an appointment with his doctor in town for next day.

"Much the wisest course," said Francis. "Doctors are a splendid institution. Whenever I feel down I go and see one, and he always tells me there's nothing the matter. In consequence I feel better at once. Going up to bed? I shall follow in half an hour. There's an amusing tale I'm in the middle of."

"Put out the light then," said Ralph, "and I'll tell the servants they can go to bed."

The half-hour lengthened into an hour, and it was not much before midnight that Francis finished his tale. There was a switch in the hall to be turned off, and another half-way up the stairs. As his finger was on this, he looked up to see that the passage above was still lit, and saw, leaning on the banister at the top of the stairs the figure of a man. He had already put out the light on the stairs, and this figure was silhouetted in black against the bright background of the lit passage. For a moment he supposed that it must be his brother, and then the man turned, and he saw that he was grey-bearded, and limped as he walked.

"Who the devil are you?" cried Francis.

He got no reply, but the figure moved away up the passage, at the end of which was Ralph's room. He was now in full pursuit after it, but before he had traversed one half of the passage it was already at the end of it, and had gone into his brother's room. Strangely bewildered and alarmed, he followed, knocked on Ralph's door, calling him loudly by name, and turned the handle to enter. But the door did not yield for all his pushing, and again "Ralph! Ralph!" he called aloud, but there was no answer.

Above the door was a glass pane that gave light to the passage, and looking up he saw that this was black, showing that the room was in darkness within. But even as he looked, it started into light, and simultaneously from inside there rose a cry of mortal agony.

"Oh, my God, my God!" rang out his brother's voice, and again that cry of agony resounded.

Then there was another voice, speaking low and angry....

"No, no!" yelled Ralph again, and again in a panic of fear Francis put his shoulder to the door and strove quite in vain to open it, for it seemed as if the door had become a part of the solid wall.

Once more that cry of terror burst out, and then, whatever was taking place within, was all over, for there was dead silence. The door which had resisted his most frenzied efforts now yielded to him, and he entered.

His brother was in bed, his legs drawn up close under him, and his hands, resting on his knees, seemed to be attempting to beat off some terrible intruder. His body was pressed against the wall at the head of the bed, and the face was a mask of agonised horror and fruitless entreaty. But the eyes were already glazed in death, and before Francis could reach the bed the body had toppled over and lay inert and lifeless. Even as he looked, he heard a limping step go down the passage outside.

VII EXPIATION

Philip Stuart and I, unattached and middle-aged persons, had for the last four or five years been accustomed to spend a month or six weeks together in the summer, taking a furnished house in some part of the country, which, by an absence of attractive pursuits, was not likely to be over-run by gregarious holiday-makers. When, as the season for getting out of London draws near, and we scan the advertisement columns which set forth the charms and the cheapness of residences to be let for August, and see the mention of tennis-clubs and esplanades and admirable golf-links within a stone's throw of the proposed front door, our offended and disgusted eyes instantly wander to the next item.

For the point of a holiday, according to our private heresy, is not to be entertained and occupied and jostled by glad crowds, but to have nothing to do, and no temptation which might lead to any unseasonable activity. London has held employments and diversion enough; we want to be without both. But vicinity to the sea is desirable, because it is easier to do nothing by the sea than anywhere else, and because bathing and basking on the shore cannot be considered an employment but only an apotheosis of loafing. A garden also is a requisite, for that tranquillises any fidgety notion of going for a walk.

In pursuance of this sensible policy we had this year taken a house on the south coast of Cornwall, for a relaxing climate conduces to laziness. It was too far off for us to make any personal inspection of it, but a perusal of the modestly-worded advertisement carried conviction. It was close to the sea; the village Polwithy, outside which it was situated, was remote and, as far as we knew, unknown; it had a garden, and there was attached to it a cook-housekeeper who made for simplification. No mention of golf-links or attractive resorts in the neighbourhood defiled the bald and terse specification, and though there was a tennis-court in the garden, there was no clause that bound the tenants to use it. The owner was a Mrs. Hearne, who had been living abroad, and our business was transacted with a house-agent in Falmouth.

To make our household complete, Philip sent down a parlourmaid, and I a housemaid, and after leaving them a day in which to settle in, we followed. There was a six-mile drive from the station across high uplands, and at the end a long steady descent into a narrow valley, cloven between the hills, that grew ever more luxuriant in verdure as we descended. Great trees of fuchsia spread up to the eaves of the thatched cottages which stood by the wayside, and a stream, embowered in green thickets, ran babbling through the centre of it. Presently we came to the village, no more than a dozen houses, built of the grey stone of the district, and on a shelf just above it a tiny church with parsonage adjoining. High above us now flamed the gorse-clad slopes of the hills on each side, and now the valley opened out at its lower end, and the still warm air was spiced and renovated by the breeze that drew up it from the sea. Then round a sharp angle of the road we came alongside a stretch of brick wall, and stopped at an iron gate above which flowed a riot of rambler rose.

It seemed hardly credible that it was this of which that terse and laconic advertisement had spoken. I had pictured something of villa-ish kind, yellow bricked perhaps, with a roof of purplish slate, a sitting-room one side of the entrance, a dining-room the other; with a tiled hall and a pitch-pine staircase, and instead, here was this little gem of an early Georgian manor house, mellow and gracious, with mullioned windows and a roof of stone slabs. In front of it was a paved terrace, below which blossomed a herbaceous border, tangled and tropical, with no inch of earth visible through its luxuriance. Inside, too, was fulfilment of this fair exterior: a broad-balustered staircase led up from the odiously-entitled "lounge hall," which I had pictured as a medley of Benares ware and saddle-bagged sofas, but which proved to be cool, broad and panelled, with a door opposite that through which we entered, leading on to the further area of garden at the back. There was the advertised but innocuous tennis court, bordered on the length of its far side by a steep grass bank, along which was planted a row of limes, once pollarded, but now allowed to develop at will. Thick boughs, some fourteen or fifteen feet from the ground, interlaced with each other, forming an arcaded row; above them, where Nature had been permitted to go her own way, the trees broke into feathered and honey-scented branches. Beyond lay a small orchard climbing upwards, above that the hillside rose more steeply, in broad spaces of short-cropped turf and ablaze with gorse, the Cornish gorze that flowers all the year round, and spreads its sunshine from January to December.

There was time for a stroll through this perfect little domain before dinner, and for a short interview with the housekeeper, a quiet capable-looking woman, slightly aloof, as is the habit of her race, from strangers and foreigners, for so the Cornish account the English, but who proved herself at the repast that followed to be as capable as she appeared. The evening closed in hot and still, and after dinner we took chairs out on to the terrace in front of the house.

"Far the best place we've struck yet," observed Philip. "Why did no one say Polwithy before?"

"Because nobody had ever heard of it, luckily," said I.

"Well, I'm a Polwithian. At least I am in spirit. But how aware Mrs.—Mrs. Criddle made me feel that I wasn't really."

Philip's profession, a doctor of obscure nervous diseases, has made him preternaturally acute in the diagnosis of what other people feel, and for some reason, quite undefined, I wanted to know what exactly he meant by this. I was in sympathy with his feeling, but I could not analyse it.

"Describe your symptoms," I said.

"I have. When she came up and talked to us, and hoped we should be comfortable, and told us that she would do her best, she was just gossiping. Probably it was perfectly true gossip. But it wasn't she. However, as that's all that matters, there's no reason why we should probe further."

"Which means that you have," I said.

"No; it means that I tried to and couldn't. She gave me an extraordinary sense of her being aware of something, which we knew nothing of; of being on a plane which we couldn't imagine. I constantly meet such people; they aren't very rare. I don't mean that there's anything the least uncanny about them, or that they know things that are uncanny. They are simply aloof, as hard to understand as your dog or your cat. She would find us equally aloof if she succeeded in analysing her sensations about us, but like a sensible woman she probably feels not the smallest interest in us. She is there to bake and to boil, and we are there to eat her bakings and appreciate her boilings."

The subject dropped, and we sat on in the dusk that was rapidly deepening into night. The door into the hall was open at our backs, and a panel of light from the lamps within was cast out on to the terrace. Wandering moths, invisible in the darkness, suddenly became manifest as they fluttered into this illumination, and vanished again as they passed out of it. One moment they were there, living things with life and motion of their own, the next they had quite disappeared. How inexplicable that would be, I thought, if one did not know from long familiarity, that light of the appropriate sort and strength is needed to make material objects visible.

Philip must have been following precisely the same train of thought, for his voice broke in, carrying it a little further.

"Look at that moth," he said, "and even while you look it has gone like a ghost, even as like a ghost it appeared. Light made it visible. And there are other sorts of light, interior psychical light which similarly makes visible the beings which people the darkness of our blindness."

Just as he spoke I thought for the moment that I heard the tingle of a telephone bell. It sounded very faintly, and I could not have sworn that I had actually heard it. At the most it gave one staccato little summons and was silent again.

"Is there a telephone in the house?" I asked "I haven't noticed one."

"Yes, by the door into the back garden," said he. "Do you want to telephone?"

"No, but I thought I heard it ring. Didn't you?"

He shook his head; then smiled.

"Ah, that was it," he said.

Certainly now there was the clink of glass, rather bell-like, as the parlourmaid came out of the dining-room with a tray of syphon and decanter, and my reasonable mind was quite content to accept this very probable explanation. But behind that, quite unreasonably, some little obstinate denizen of my consciousness rejected it. It told me that what I had heard was like the moth that came out of darkness and went on into darkness again....

My room was at the back of the house, overlooking the lawn tennis-court, and presently I went up to bed. The moon had risen, and the lawn lay in bright illumination bordered by a strip of dark shadow below the pollarded limes. Somewhere along the hillside an owl was foraging, softly hooting, and presently it swept whitely across the lawn. No sound is so intensely rural, yet none, to my mind, so suggests a signal. But it seemed to signal nothing, and, tired with the long hot journey, and soothed by the deep tranquillity of the place, I was soon asleep. But often during the night I woke, though never to more than a dozing dreamy consciousness of where I was, and each time I had the notion that some slight noise had roused me, and each time I found myself listening to hear whether the tingle of a telephone bell was the cause of my disturbance. There came no repetition of it, and again I slept, and again I woke with drowsy attention for the sound which I felt I expected, but never heard.

Daylight banished these imaginations, but though I must have slept many hours all told, for these wakings had been only brief and partial, I was aware of a certain weariness, as if though my bodily senses had been rested, some part of me had been wakeful and watching all night. This was fanciful enough to disregard, and certainly during the day I forgot it altogether. Soon after breakfast we went down to the sea, and a short ramble along a shingly shore brought us to a sandy cove framed in promontories of rock that went down into deep water. The most fastidious connoisseur in bathing could have pictured no more ideal scene for his operations, for with hot sand to bask on and rocks to plunge from, and a limpid ocean and a cloudless sky, there was indeed no lacuna in perfection. All morning we loafed here, swimming and sunning ourselves, and for the afternoon there was the shade of the garden, and a stroll later on up through the orchard and to the gorse-clad hillside. We came back through the churchyard, looked into the church, and coming out, Philip pointed to a tombstone which from its newness among its dusky and moss-grown companions, easily struck the eye. It recorded without pious or scriptural reflection the date of the birth and death of George Hearne; the latter event had taken place close on two years ago, and we were within a week of the exact anniversary. Other tombstones near were monuments to those of the same name, and dated back for a couple of centuries and more.

"Local family," said I, and strolling on we came to our own gate in the long brick wall. It was opened from inside just as we arrived at it, and there came out a brisk middle-aged man in clergyman's dress, obviously our vicar.

He very civilly introduced himself.

"I heard that Mrs. Hearne's house had been taken, and that the tenants had come," he said, "and I ventured to leave my card."

We performed our part of the ceremony, and in answer to his inquiry professed our satisfaction with our quarters and our neighbourhood.

"That is good news," said Mr. Stephens, "I hope you will continue to enjoy your holiday. I am Cornish myself, and like all natives think there is no place like Cornwall!"

Philip pointed with his stick towards the churchyard. "We noticed that the Hearnes are people of the place," he said. Quite suddenly I found myself understanding what he had meant by the aloofness of the race. Something between reserve and suspicion came into Mr. Stephens's face.

"Yes, yes, an old family here," he said, "and large landowners. But now some remote cousin——The house, however, belongs to Mrs. Hearne for life."

He stopped, and by that reticence confirmed the impression he had made. In consequence, for there is something in the breast of the most incurious, which, when treated with reserve becomes inquisitive, Philip proceeded to ask a direct question.

"Then I take it that the George Hearne who, as I have just seen, died two years ago, was the husband of Mrs. Hearne, from whom we took the house?"

"Yes, he was buried in the churchyard," said Mr. Stephens quickly. Then, for no reason at all, he added:

"Naturally he was buried in the churchyard here."

Now my impression at that moment was that Mr. Stephens had said something he did not mean to say, and had corrected it by saying the same thing again. He went on his way, back to the vicarage, with an amiably expressed desire to do anything that was in his power for us, in the way of local information, and we went in through the gate. The post had just arrived; there was the London morning paper and a letter for Philip which cost him two perusals before he folded it up and put it into his pocket. But he made no comment, and presently, as dinner-time was near, I went up to my room. Here in this deep valley with the great westerly hill towering above us, it was already dark, and the lawn lay beneath a twilight as of deep clear water. Quite idly as I brushed my hair in front of the glass on the table in the window, of which the blinds were not yet drawn, I looked out, and saw that on the bank along which grew the pollarded limes, there was lying a ladder. It was just a shade odd that it should be there, but the oddity of it was quite accounted for by the supposition that the gardener had had business among the trees in the orchard, and had left it there, for the completion of his labours to-morrow. It was just as odd as that, and no odder, just worth a twitch of the imagination to account for it, but now completely accounted for.

I went downstairs, and passing Philip's door heard the swish of ablutions which implied he was not quite ready, and in the most loafer-like manner I strolled round the corner of the house. The kitchen window which looked on to the tennis-court was open, and there was a good smell, I remember, coming from it. And still without thought of the ladder I had just seen, I mounted the slope of grass on to the tennis-court. Just across it was the bank where the pollarded limes grew, but there was no ladder lying there. Of course, the gardener must have remembered he had left it, and had returned to remove it exactly as I came downstairs. There was nothing singular about that, and I could not imagine why the thing interested me at all. But for some inexplicable reason I found myself saying: "But I did see the ladder just now."

A bell—no telephone bell, but a welcome harbinger to a hungry man—sounded from inside the house, and I went back on to the terrace, just as Philip got downstairs. At dinner our speech rambled pleasantly over the accomplishments of to-day, and the prospects of to-morrow, and in due course we came to the consideration of Mr. Stephens. We settled that he was an aloof fellow, and then Philip said:

"I wonder why he hastened to tell us that George Hearne was buried in the churchyard, and then added that naturally he was!"

"It's the natural place to be buried in," said I.

"Quite. That's just why it was hardly worth mentioning."

I felt then, just momentarily, just vaguely, as if my mind was regarding stray pieces of a jig-saw puzzle. The fancied ringing of the telephone bell last night was one of them, this burial of George Hearne in the churchyard was another, and, even more inexplicably, the ladder I had seen under the trees was a third. Consciously I made nothing whatever out of them, and did not feel the least inclination to devote any ingenuity to so fortuitous a collection of pieces. Why shouldn't I add, for that matter, our morning's bathe, or the gorse on the hillside? But I had the sensation that, though my conscious brain was presently occupied with piquet, and was rapidly growing sleepy with the day of sun and sea, some sort of mole inside it was digging passages and connecting corridors below the soil.

Five eventless days succeeded, there were no more ladders, no more phantom telephone bells, and emphatically no more Mr. Stephens. Once or twice we met him in the village street and got from him the curtest salutation possible short of a direct cut. And yet somehow he seemed charged with information, so we lazily concluded, and he made for us a field of imaginative speculation. I remember that I constructed a highly fanciful romance, which postulated that George Hearne was not dead at all, but that Mr. Stephens had murdered some inconvenient blackmailer, whom he had buried with the rites of the church. Or—these romances always broke down under cross-examination from Philip—Mr. Stephens himself was George Hearne, who had fled from justice, and was supposed to have died. Or Mrs. Hearne was really George Hearne, and our admirable housekeeper was the real Mrs. Hearne. From such indications you may judge how the intoxication of the sun and the sea had overpowered us.

But there was one explanation of why Mr. Stephens had so hastily assured us that George Hearne was buried in the churchyard which never passed our lips. It was just because both Philip and I really believed it to be the true one, that we did not mention it. But just as if it was some fever or plague, we both knew that we were sickening with it. And then these fanciful romances stopped because we knew that the Real Thing was approaching. There had been faint glimpses of it before, like distant sheet-lightning; now the noise of it, authentic and audible, began to rumble.

There came a day of hot overclouded weather. We had bathed in the morning, and loafed in the afternoon, but Philip, after tea, had refused to come for our usual ramble, and I set out alone. That morning Mrs. Criddle had rather peremptorily told me that a room in the front of the house would prove much cooler for me, for it caught the sea-breeze, and though I objected that it would also catch the southerly sun, she had clearly made up her mind that I was to move from the bedroom overlooking the tennis-court and the pollarded limes, and there was no resisting so polite and yet determined a woman.

When I set out for my ramble after tea, the change had already been effected, and my brain nosed slowly about as I strolled sniffing for her reason, for no self-respecting brain could accept the one she gave. But in this hot drowsy air I entirely lacked nimbleness, and when I came back, the question had become a mere silly unanswerable riddle. I returned through the churchyard, and saw that in a couple of days we should arrive at the anniversary of George Hearne's death.

Philip was not on the terrace in front of the house, and I went in at the door of the hall, expecting to find him there or in the back garden. Exactly as I entered my eye told me that there he was, a black silhouette against the glass door, at the end of the hall, which was open, and led through into the back garden. He did not turn round at the sound of my entry, but took a step or two in the direction of the far door, still framed in the oblong of it. I glanced at the table, where the post lay, found letters both for me and him, and looked up again. There was no one there.

He had hastened his steps, I supposed, but simultaneously I thought how odd it was that he had not taken his letters, if he was in the hall, and that he had not turned when I entered. However, I should find him just round the corner, and with his post and mine in my hand, I went towards the far door. As I approached it I felt a sudden cold stir of air, rather unaccountable, for the day was notably sultry, and went out. He was sitting at the far end of the tennis-court.

I went up to him with his letters.

"I thought I saw you just now in the hall," I said. But I knew already that I had not seen him in the hall.

He looked up quickly.

"And have you only just come in?" he said.

"Yes; this moment. Why?"

"Because half an hour ago I went in to see if the post had come, and thought I saw you in the hall."

"And what did I do?" I asked.

"You went out on to the terrace. But I didn't find you there."

There was a short pause as he opened his letters.

"Damned interesting," he observed. "Because there's someone here who isn't you or me."

"Anything else?" I asked.

He laughed, pointing at the row of trees.

"Yes, something too silly for words," he said. "Just now I saw a piece of rope dangling from the big branch of that pollarded lime. I saw it quite distinctly. And then there wasn't any rope there at all any more than there is now."

Philosophers have argued about the strongest emotion known to man. Some say "love," others "hate," others "fear." I am disposed to put "curiosity" on a level, at least, with these august sensations, just mere simple inquisitiveness. Certainly at the moment it rivalled fear in my mind, and there was a hint of that.

As he spoke the parlourmaid came out into the garden with a telegram in her hand. She gave it to Philip, who without a word scribbled a line on the reply-paid form inside it, and handed it back to her.

"Dreadful nuisance," he said, "but there's no help for it. A few days ago I got a letter which made me think I might have to go up to town, and this telegram makes it certain. There's an operation possible on a patient of mine, which I hoped might have been avoided, but my locum tenens won't take the responsibility of deciding whether it is necessary or not."

He looked at his watch.

"I can catch the night train," he said, "and I ought to be able to catch the night train back from town to-morrow. I shall be back, that is to say, the day after to-morrow in the morning. There's no help for it. Ha! That telephone of yours will come in useful. I can get a taxi from Falmouth, and needn't start till after dinner."

He went into the house, and I heard him rattling and tapping at the telephone. Soon he called for Mrs. Criddle, and presently came out again.

"We're not on the telephone service," he said. "It was cut off a year ago, only they haven't removed the apparatus. But I can get a trap in the village, Mrs. Criddle says, and she's sent for it. If I start at once I shall easily be in time. Spicer's packing a bag for me, and I'll take a sandwich."

He looked sharply towards the pollarded trees.

"Yes, just there," he said. "I saw it plainly, and equally plainly I saw it not. And then there's that telephone of yours."

I told him now about the ladder I had seen below the tree where he saw the dangling rope.

"Interesting," he said, "because it's so silly and unexpected. It is really tragic that I should be called away just now, for it looks as if the—well, the matter were coming out of the darkness into a shaft of light. But I'll be back, I hope, in thirty-six hours. Meantime do observe very carefully, and whatever you do, don't make a theory. Darwin says somewhere that you can't observe without a theory, but to make a theory is a great danger to an observer. It can't help influencing your imagination; you tend to see or hear what falls in with your hypothesis. So just observe; be as mechanical as a phonograph and a photographic lens."

Presently the dog-cart arrived and I went down to the gate with him. "Whatever it is that is coming through, is coming through in bits," he said. "You heard a telephone; I saw a rope. We both saw a figure, but not simultaneously nor in the same place. I wish I didn't have to go."

I found myself sympathising strongly with this wish, when after dinner I found myself with a solitary evening in front of me, and the pledge to "observe" binding me. It was not mainly a scientific ardour that prompted this sympathy, and the desire for independent combination, but, quite emphatically, fear of what might be coming out of the huge darkness which lies on all sides of human experience. I could no longer fail to connect together the fancied telephone bell, the rope, and the ladder, for what made the chain between them was the figure that both Philip and I had seen. Already my mind was seething with conjectural theory, but I would not let the ferment of it ascend to my surface consciousness; my business was not to aid but rather stifle my imagination.

I occupied myself, therefore, with the ordinary devices of a solitary man, sitting on the terrace, and subsequently coming into the house, for a few spots of rain began to fall. But though nothing disturbed the outward tranquillity of the evening, the quietness administered no opiate to that seething mixture of fear and curiosity that obsessed me. I heard the servants creep bedwards up the back stairs and presently I followed them. Then, forgetting for the moment that my room had been changed, I tried the handle of the door of that which I had previously occupied. It was locked.

Now here, beyond doubt, was the sign of a human agency, and at once I was determined to get into the room. The key, I could see, was not in the door, which must therefore have been locked from outside. I therefore searched the usual cache for keys along the top of the door-frame, found it, and entered.

The room was quite empty, the blinds not drawn, and after looking round it, I walked across to the window. The moon was up, and though obscured behind clouds, gave sufficient light to enable me to see objects outside with tolerable distinctness. There was the row of pollarded limes, and then with a sudden intake of my breath I saw that a foot or two below one of the boughs there was suspended something whitish and oval which oscillated as it hung there. In the dimness I could see nothing more than that, but now conjecture crashed into my conscious brain. But even as I looked it was gone again; there was nothing there but deep shadow, the trees steadfast in the windless air. Simultaneously I knew that I was not alone in the room.

I turned swiftly about, but my eyes gave no endorsement of that conviction, and yet their evidence that there was no one here except myself failed to shake it. The presence, somewhere close to me, needed no such evidence; it was self-evident though invisible, and my forehead was streaming with the abject sweat of terror. Somehow I knew that the presence was that of the figure both Philip and I had seen that evening in the hall, and, credit it or not as you will, the fact that it was invisible made it infinitely the more terrible. I knew, too, that though my eyes were blind to it, it had got into closer touch with me; I knew more of its nature now, it had had tragic and awful commerce with evil and despair. Some sort of catalepsy was on me, while it thus obsessed me; presently, minutes afterwards or perhaps mere seconds, the grip and clutch of its power was relaxed, and with shaking knees I crossed the room and went out, and again locked the door. Even as I turned the key I smiled at the futility of that. With my emergence the terror completely passed; I went across the passage leading to my room, got into bed, and was soon asleep. But I had no more need to question myself as to why Mrs.

Criddle made the change. Another guest, she knew, would come to occupy it as the season arrived when George Hearne died and was buried in the churchyard.

The night passed quietly and then succeeded a day hot and still and sultry beyond belief. The very sea had lost its coolness and vitality, and I came in from my swim tired and enervated instead of refreshed. No breeze stirred; the trees stood motionless as if cast in iron, and from horizon to horizon the sky was overlaid by an ever-thickening pall of cloud. The cohorts of storm and thunder were gathering in the stillness, and all day I felt that power, other than that of these natural forces, was being stored for some imminent manifestation.

As I came near to the house the horror deepened, and after dinner I had a mind to drop into the vicarage, according to Mr. Stephens's general invitation, and get through an hour or two with other company than my own. But I delayed till it was past any reasonable time for such an informal visit, and ten o'clock still saw me on the terrace in front of the house. My nerves were all on edge, a stir or step in the house was sufficient to make me turn round in apprehension of seeing I knew not what, but presently it grew still. One lamp burned in the hall behind me; by it stood the candle which would light me to bed.

I went indoors soon after, meaning to go up to bed, then suddenly ashamed of this craven imbecility of mind, took the fancy to walk round the house for the purpose of convincing myself that all was tranquil and normal, and that my fear, that nameless indefinable load on my spirit, was but a product of this close and thundery night. The tension of the weather could not last much longer; soon the storm must break and the relief come, but it would be something to know that there was nothing more than that. Accordingly I went out again on to the terrace, traversed it and turned the corner of the house where lay the tennis lawn.

To-night the moon had not yet risen, and the darkness was such that I could barely distinguish the outline of the house, and that of the pollarded limes, but through the glass door that led from this side of the house into the hall, there shone the light of the lamp that stood there. All was absolutely quiet, and half reassured I traversed the lawn, and turned to go back. Just as I came opposite the lit door, I heard a sound very close at hand from under the deep shadow of the pollarded limes. It was as if some heavy object had fallen with a thump and rebound on the grass, and with it there came the noise of a creaking bough suddenly strained by some weight. Then interpretation came upon me with the unreasoning force of conviction, though in the blackness I could see nothing. But at the sound a horror such as I have never felt laid hold on me. It was scarcely physical at all, it came from some deep-seated region of the soul.

The heavens were rent, a stream of blinding light shot forth, and straight in front of my eyes a few yards from where I stood, I saw. The noise had been of a ladder thrown down on the grass, and from the bough of the pollarded lime, there was the figure of a man, white-faced against the blackness, oscillating and twisting on the rope that strangled him. Just that I saw before the stillness was torn to atoms by the roar of thunder, and as from a hose the rain descended. Once again, even before that first appalling riot had died, the clouds were shredded again by the lightning, and my eyes which had not moved from the place saw only the framed shadow of the trees, and their upper branches bowed by the pelting rain. All night the storm raged and bellowed making sleep impossible, and for an hour at least, between the peals of thunder, I heard the ringing of the telephone bell.

Next morning Philip returned, to whom I told exactly what is written here, but watch and observe as we might, neither of us, in the three further weeks which we spent at Polwithy, heard or saw anything that could interest the student of the occult. Pleasant lazy days succeeded each other, we bathed and rambled and played piquet of an evening, and incidentally we made friends with the vicar. He was an interesting man, full of curious lore concerning local legends and superstitions, and one night, when in our ripened acquaintanceship he had dined with us, he asked Philip directly whether either of us had experienced anything unusual during our tenancy.

Philip nodded towards me.

"My friend saw most," he said.

"May I hear it?" asked the vicar.

When I had finished, he was silent awhile.

"I think the—shall we call it explanation?—is yours by right," he said. "I will give it you if you care to hear it."

Our silence, I suppose, answered him.

"I remember meeting you two on the day after your arrival here," he said, "and you inquired about the tombstone in the churchyard erected to the memory of George Hearne. I did not want to say more of him then, for a reason that you will presently know. I told you, I recollect, perhaps rather hurriedly, that it was Mrs. Hearne's husband who was buried there. Already, I imagine, you guess that I concealed something. You may even have guessed it at the time."

He did not wait for any confirmation or repudiation of this. Sitting out on the terrace in the deep dusk, his communication was very impersonal. It was just a narrating voice, without identity, an anonymous chronicle.

"George Hearne succeeded to the property here, which is considerable, only two years before his death. He was married shortly after he succeeded. According to any decent standard, his life both before and after his marriage was vile. I think—God forgive me if I wrong him—he made evil his good; he liked evil for its own sake. But out of the middle of the mire of his own soul there sprang a flower: he was devoted to his wife. And he was capable of shame.

"A fortnight before his—his death, she got to know what his life was like, and what he was in himself. I need not tell you what was the particular disclosure that came to her knowledge; it is sufficient to say that it was revolting. She was here at the time; he was coming down from London that night. When he arrived he found a note from her saying that she had left him and could never come back. She told him that he must give her opportunity for her to divorce him, and threatened him with exposure if he did not.

"He and I had been friends, and that night he came to me with her letter, acknowledged the justice of it, but asked me to intervene. He said that the only thing that could save him from utter damnation was she, and I believe that there he spoke sincerely. But, speaking as a clergyman, I should not have called him penitent. He did not hate his sin, but only the consequences of it. But it seemed to me that if she came back to him, he might have a chance, and next day I went to her. Nothing that I could say moved her one atom, and after a fruitless day I came back, and told him of the uselessness of my mission.

"Now, according to my view, no man who deliberately prefers evil to good, just for the sake of wickedness, is sane, and this refusal of hers to have anything more to do with him, I fully believe upset the unstable balance of his soul altogether. There was just his devotion to her which might conceivably have restored it, but she refused—and I can quite understand her refusal—to come near him. If you knew what I know, you could not blame her. But the effect of it on him was portentous and disastrous, and three days afterwards I wrote to her again, saying quite simply that the damnation of his soul would be on her head unless, leaving her personal feelings altogether out of the question, she came back. She got that letter the next evening, and already it was too late.

"That afternoon, two years ago, on the 15th of August, there was washed up in the harbour here a dead body, and that night George Hearne took a ladder from the fruit-wall in the kitchen garden and hanged himself. He climbed into one of the pollarded limes, tied the rope to a bough, and made a slip-knot at the other end of it. Then he kicked the ladder away.

"Mrs. Hearne meantime had received my letter. For a couple of hours she wrestled with her own repugnance and then decided to come to him. She rang him up on the telephone, but the housekeeper here, Mrs. Criddle, could only tell her that he had gone out after dinner. She continued ringing him up for a couple of hours, but there was always the same reply.

"Eventually she decided to waste no more time, and motored over from her mother's house where she was staying at the north end of the county. By then the moon had risen, and looking out from his bedroom window she saw him."

He paused.

"There was an inquest," he said, "and I could truthfully testify that I believed him to be insane. The verdict of suicide during temporary insanity was brought in, and he was buried in the churchyard. The rope was burned, and the ladder was burned."

The parlourmaid brought out drinks, and we sat in silence till she had gone again.

"And what about the telephone my friend heard?" asked Philip.

He thought a moment.

"Don't you think that great emotion like that of Mrs. Hearne's may make some sort of record," he asked, "so that if the needle of a sensitive temperament comes in contact with it, a reproduction takes place? And it is the same perhaps about that poor fellow who hanged himself. One can hardly believe that his spirit is bound to visit and revisit the scene of his follies and his crimes year by year."

"Year by year?" I asked.

"Apparently. I saw him myself last year, Mrs. Criddle did also."

He got up.

"How can one tell?" he said. "Expiation, perhaps. Who knows?"

VIII HOME, SWEET HOME

It was pleasant to get out of the baked train into an atmosphere that tingled with the subtle vitality of the sea, and though nothing could be duller than the general prospect of flat fields and dusty hedgerows, and the long white road that lay straight as a ruled line between them, I surmised that when it had climbed that long upward slope, there would be a new horizon altogether, grey and liquid. Eyethorpe Junction was the name of the station, and though that appeared a strange misnomer, for nothing seemed to join anything, I presently perceived a weedy, derelict branch line, and a loquacious porter explained that the line to Eyethorpe had long been untraversed by railway traffic. There had once been high hopes that it would develop into a popular watering-place. But the public had preferred its established favourites.

The affairs that led to my disembarkation on this broiling August day at a jointless junction had been conducted in my sister Margery's most characteristic style. Her husband, Walter Mostyn, the eminent nerve specialist, had been threatened during July with a breakdown owing to overstrain in his work, and, in obedience to the ironical ordinance of "Physician, heal thyself," had prescribed for himself a complete rest. His idea of resting his mind was not, as is the usual practice of those on holiday, to overtire his body, but to get away to some place where there was no temptation to do anything of the kind. There must be no golf-links, or he would want to play golf, and he would prefer his retreat to be by the sea, because the very fact of being in a boat at all made him feel seasick, and he hated bathing. A rest-cure in a nursing-home would be horrible to him, and he thought that if Margery could find some deadly seaside resort, where there was nothing that could tempt him into activity of mind or body, that would do just as well. He wanted to be a beast of the field, and recover his nervous force by sheer vegetation.

Margery, with these instructions to guide her, had thereupon set off, and scoured the coasts of Kent and Sussex, discovering on the second day of her wild career this amazing and unique Eyethorpe. There was a house there to let, which she at once saw was just what she was looking for, and with that most unfeminine instinct of hers of knowing that she had got what she wanted, and not making any further search, she went straight to the house-agent at Hastings and took "The Firs" for a month as from to-morrow. She drove back to London that evening, informed Walter what she had done, sent down her servants next morning, and took down her husband the same evening. A fortnight later she wrote to me that the cure was progressing splendidly, and that he, emerging from his languor, was getting rather cross and argumentative, which she took to be the sign of returning vitality. He was excessively bored with her, and wanted some man in the house, and had grudgingly said that I would "do." So would I come soon for a couple of weeks? In fact, I must, and she would expect me on Thursday. It was Thursday now, and, in consequence, I was driving up the straight, white road from Eyethorpe Junction.

We topped the rise, and there, as I had expected, was a new horizon. The sea sprang up to eye-level, the ground declined steeply over a stretch of open downland dotted with furze bushes to a line of low cliffs that fringed the shore. Along the edge of these was a huddle of red-roofed cottages, among which rose a conspicuous church-tower, and presently we jolted over the level-crossing of the line from Eyethorpe Junction, which the public had scorned. On the left was a small abandoned station with weed-grown platform, and a board, much defaced by the weather, bearing the inscription "Eyethorpe and Coltham." The name Coltham stirred some remote vibration in my mind; I felt that I had heard the name before, but could not recall the reason for its faint familiarity. The road forked, the left-hand branch of it leading up the village street; the other, which we took, had a signpost with the information that Coltham was one mile distant. We traversed, I should have guessed, two or three furlongs, and there, close at hand, separated from the highway by a field, through which led a grass-grown drive, stood a big mellow-walled farmhouse. A clump of rather fine Scotch firs at one end of it was sufficient indication of its identity.

I was taken into and through a broad passage (you might call it a hall) which intersected the house, and from which a dignified staircase led to the upper storey. At its further end a glass-paned door opened into the garden. But there was no one here, and the servant supposed that they had gone strolling, perhaps down to the beach. The afternoon was still very hot, and, deciding to wait for them rather than vaguely pursue, I admired the luck that had attended Margery's search for a tranquil sanatorium. Not a house was visible; the clean emptiness of the downland was laid like a broad green riband east and west, and in front, through a V-shaped gap, gleamed the sea. A one-storied wing, evidently a later addition, sprouted from the west end of the house; this cast just now a very welcome shade over the square space, laid with old paving-stones, where long, low chairs and the tea-table stood. The added wing, it is scarcely necessary to mention, was of far more antique design than the house, and, looking in through its open door which gave on to this flagged space, I found a very big, pleasant room, with rafters in the ceiling, and small diamond-shaped panes in the mullioned windows. The oak floor was bare but for a few rugs, and at the far end, near an open fireplace, stood a grand piano. The lid was open, and I read there, to my great surprise, the world-famous name of Barenstein. That, too, was just like Margery, to take a remote farmhouse and find a Barenstein grand waiting for her very gifted fingers, and this fine spacious room. How cool it was in here, too—more than cool, it was positively cold;

and at that moment, hearing familiar voices outside, I stepped out again on to the paved space from which I had entered.

Certainly Walter did not look as if a fortnight ago he had been on the edge of nervous breakdown. His face was bronzed and ruddy, he strode along with a firm step, and was talking in that loud, confident voice that had so often brought comfort to sufferers.

"But I tell you, darling," he was saying, "that it isn't that our senses occasionally deceive us, they habitually deceive us. Ah! there he is. Welcome, my dear Ted. You have come to a place beyond the limits of the civilised world, and it has done me a world of good already. Distractions, things that interest us are what starves the nerves. Boredom, there's the panacea for nerves. I've never been so bored in my life, and I'm a new man."

Margery laughed.

"I wonder how often you've told your patients exactly the opposite," she said. "(Ted, there's a magnificent Barenstein here; did you ever know such luck?) But isn't it so, Walter? You always say that there's hope even for people who take an interest in postage-stamps. Never mind. You hate being consistent, and I won't press it. What about the senses habitually deceiving us?"

"Obvious. Your eyes, for instance. If you see a house half a mile off, your eyes tell you it is about a quarter of an inch in height. If another train passes you as yours is standing in a station, they will tell you that you are moving in the opposite direction. Smell and taste are the same; if you shut your eyes you have no idea whether your cigarette is alight. Your sense of warmth and cold too; if you put your hand on a piece of very cold metal, it gives you the sensation of burning. I'm just as bad as you, perhaps worse, for my senses tell me that that room in there is bitterly cold to-day, but the thermometer says it is 65 degrees. I was suffering from some subjective disturbance, that was all, and my imbecile senses told me it was cold. There was the thermometer saying it was warm. The senses, as I tell you, are habitually deceptive. Liars!"

There was all his usual vehemence in this, and, so I thought, a little more. He was clearly upset at this divergence of view between his senses and the thermometer.

"But I'm on the side of your senses," I said. "I went in there just now, and I swear it was more than chilly."

He threw a quick glance over to Margery before he answered.

"More liars then!" he said. "Another instance of the deceptiveness of the senses."

He said this with the air of bringing the discussion to an end; our talk became desultory and trivial, and before long Margery closed it by saying that, whatever anybody else did, she intended to have a dip in the sea before dinner. Presently she appeared again, with sandals and a dressing-gown over her bathing-suit, for there was but this strip of empty downland between the garden and the steep short descent on the beach. She insisted on my accompanying her as far as that V-shaped gap, and her very casual manner made me sure that she had some communication to make. It came as soon as we were out of earshot.

"Walter's ever so much better, as you can see for yourself," she said, "and till to-day he has been lying fallow with the most excellent results. But now that awful activity of his mind has begun to work again, and twenty times since lunch he has alluded to that strange feeling of chill in the big room in the wing. He keeps on saying that it's subjective, but you and I know him, and that means he thinks there's something queer about it. And you felt it, too, apparently."

"I thought I did, but then I had just come into it from the broiling air outside. But hadn't he felt it before?"

"No, for the simple reason that he hadn't been into the room before," said she. "When we came here, and, indeed, till this morning, it was locked and shuttered. The gardener, who has been caretaker here, told me that the owner had stored things in it, and that it was to be left closed. Till this morning Walter did not seem to mind whether it was shut or open, but to-day he told the gardener that it was all nonsense to keep the biggest room in the house shut up, and demanded the key. Denton, that's his name, talked about disobeying his owner, but Walter insisted, and he produced the key. There was nothing stored there, and I drove over to the house-agent's at Hastings this morning to ask if there was any such order. None at all. What does it mean?"

"Nothing," said I, "except that Denton was a lazy brute, and didn't want the bother of airing and dusting the room before you came, and of putting it to rights again after you'd gone. Perhaps also the owner didn't want to prohibit your playing the great Barenstein, but hoped you wouldn't. Also this accounts for the fact that Walter and I found the room very chilly after it had been shut up for so long. When was the house last occupied, by the way?"

"I don't know. It had been unlet for some time, so the agent told me, and I didn't care in the least about its history provided I got it for Walter now."

Her jolly brown eyes made a complete circuit round my head, instead of looking at me straight when she answered.

"Don't be so foolish, Margery," I said, "but look straight at me. You told me just now that Walter thought there was something queer about the room. What do you think?"

Her eyes rested on mine.

"I think there's something queer about the house," she said. "I find myself looking up suddenly from a book or a paper to see who is in the room. And I think Walter does the same. But he—he thinks he hears something, and then finds he hasn't, just as I think I see something, and find I haven't. I cock an eye, he cocks an ear. But don't say a word to him. He hates the idea of anything you can't account for by the ordinary functions of the senses, which, he says, habitually deceive you. But since that room was opened, he's been arguing with himself."

"Oh, put the stopper in," said I. "Do you remember the gurgle of the hot-water pipes in the nursery thirty years ago, and how you knew it was the groan of a murdered woman? You frightened me out of my wits then, but I'm too old to be frightened now. You haven't seen anything, and he hasn't heard anything; eye hath not seen nor ear heard. Don't imagine things; half the trouble in the world comes from imagining. Have a nice bathe, and wash it all off."

For a moment, as she looked at me, I saw somewhere behind her eyes a sense of uneasiness, but it vanished.

"I shan't wash off my gladness that you've joined us," she said, and ran off down the steep little path to the beach.

I strolled back through the garden thinking how unlike Margery it was to be within the grip of vague apprehension like this, or to imagine that there was anything "queer" about the house, for in spite of the famous episode of the gurgling pipes, she was singularly free from imagined alarms. Even more unusual, if she was right about him, was it that Walter should be affected in the same sort of way. Margery certainly showed her good sense in demanding that her odd apprehensions should be kept apart from his, and not be given the meeting-ground of discussion. But she had noticed, or imagined, his, and I was soon to learn that he was not blind to hers.

Walter had gone up to his room when I got back, and I went into the lately opened sitting-room, where I found that my books and papers had been disposed on a big table, which was thus clearly consecrated to my use. I was engaged on a memoir which it interested me to write, though I had grave doubts about its interesting anybody else to read. The piano stood a little beyond my table, with the keyboard towards me; between it and me, on my left, was the open window looking on to the garden. The room still seemed chilly, but I speedily forgot that and, indeed, everything else but my delightful task.

How long I had been at work I had no idea, when suddenly—even as I turned a page to carry on the note I had begun—I became vividly aware of my surroundings again and knew with absolute conviction that I was not alone. I glanced up and saw that there was a man outside the window looking at the piano. For a second or two he gazed fixedly at it, and then, turning his head, perceived me at my table. He had not, I imagined, observed that there was anyone here, for he touched his hat, and would have gone away, but I called to him.

"Do you want anything?" I asked. "Denton, is it?"

"Yes, sir. I—I was only just looking to see if the room was all right," and immediately he withdrew. But, oddly enough, I felt that it was not Denton's presence at the window that gave me the sense that there was someone here; it had nothing to do with Denton. And why, I asked myself, as the man walked briskly off, why on earth should Denton look in to see if the room was all right? It was the piano that riveted him; did he want to be sure that all was well with the piano?

I tried to attach myself to my work again, but the connection would no longer hold. There was still that sense of some presence in the room, which came between me and my page. Time and again I held my mind down to its task, but it slipped away, and presently at its bidding my eyes left the paper and scrutinised the room. Certainly there was nothing behind me, nor at my side, but I found myself—was it Denton's example which had infected me?—looking at the piano, as if what I sought was invisibly there. Its japanned case, darkly, like black glass, reflected my table, the white keys gleamed in their ebony setting. And then I saw that some of them were moving—a group, three or four at a time, and now a succession of single notes sank and recovered as if under the pressure of fingers.

I cannot hope to describe the curiosity and the dismay with which this filled my mind. I gazed fascinated at this inexplicable movement, but at the same time my mind cried out in horror at the invisible cause of it. Then, as suddenly as it had begun, this fantastic spectacle ceased, but the presence was still there. Then from outside there came the sound of steps. Walter entered.

"Margery here?" he asked. "No? Was it you playing, then?"

"Deceptive senses," I said. "I haven't touched the piano."

He looked at me a moment, puzzled.

"But I would swear I heard the piano," he said.

Instantly I made up my mind not to tell Walter what I had seen, and already, so fantastic was it, I was beginning to doubt if I had seen anything. Yet deep in my mind remained that intense curiosity, and deeper yet some unreasoning terror.

The evening passed quite normally; Walter bewailed the hideous necessity of going in to Hastings next day to have his hair cut, and the even darker fate of having the Vicar of Eyethorpe to dinner.

It was still early when we went up to bed and, conscious of an overwhelming somnolence, I instantly fell asleep. I woke, staring wide awake, with the answer to the question which had slightly worried me yesterday, as to why the name of the neighbouring Coltham was remotely familiar to me, clear in my mind. There had occurred there, about a year before, a very brutal murder, which still remained among the unsolved mysteries of criminal history. An elderly spinster lady, living with her spinster sister at some house there, had been found strangled on the floor of her sitting-room. It was supposed that robbery was the motive for the crime, but the murderer seemed to have heard some stir in the house, and left a cashbox containing thirty or forty pounds in the drawer he had just opened. I could remember no further details, but I thought I would stroll over to Coltham next morning and, with that appetite for the horrible which lurks in us all, find out which the house was.

The two went off to Hastings next morning and, in pursuance of my plan, I strolled up the road to Coltham. It was a melancholy little bunch of cottages perched on the edge of the downs, and I had just decided that a rather stricken-looking house, with a board up to say it was to let, was a suitable site for the murder, when I saw Denton coming down the little street.

"Which was the house where that murder took place last year, Denton?" I asked him.

He stared at me a moment, and I saw his throat-apple jerk up and down. Then he pointed to the house I had picked out.

"That was the one, sir," he said.

"And what was the name of the old lady?" I asked.

"Miss Ellershaw," said he, and rather abruptly, much in the manner in which he had retreated from the window last night, he turned and left me. Rather pleased with myself for my perspicacity I strolled homewards again.

Margery and Walter, he shorn and self-respecting again, came back about one o'clock, and Margery announced her determination of writing overdue letters till the really intolerable heat of the day had declined.

"Hopeless arrears," she said, "bills and bills, and the rent of the house for the next fortnight, which ought to have been paid two days ago. But I'll send it straight to our landlord—or is it landlady?—instead of the agent; that will save a day."

The clear burning of the sun had given place to an extreme sultriness; the sky was overcast with clouds which all afternoon thickened to a still density portending thunder. Margery retired to the piano-room to perform her overdues, Walter fell asleep and, leaving him on the paved space, I joined Margery for coolness. She jumped up as I entered.

"I was dying to be interrupted," she said, "because I long to see what's in that cupboard by the piano. I've muddled up your papers, Ted, I'm afraid. Unmuddle them again while I have an interval."

She had, indeed, muddled my papers up. Half-finished letters, and addressed envelopes, and bills were mixed up with my notes. As I disentangled them, I came across a cheque she had drawn. It was made out to Miss Ellershaw. There was also a half-sheet on which Mrs. Mostyn "much regretted not having sent cheque for a fortnight's rent sooner."... So Miss Ellershaw was owner of "The Firs," and two Miss Ellershaws, one of whom had been murdered, lived together. Had they lived in that house at Coltham, where Denton had told me the murder was committed, or had they...?

Margery interrupted these rather disquieting thoughts.

"What a disappointment!" she said. "Empty cupboard, all but one leaf of a book of English songs, and that's 'Home, Sweet Home!' You may laugh at it, but it's a wonderful melody. I must just play it, and then I shall get on with my jobs."

The window close to which I sat commanded a view of the garden. Out of it, I could see Denton plucking sweet peas. As the notes of the old-fashioned tune streamed out through the open window, I saw him drop his basket and stop his ears. Simultaneously, I knew that there was some presence, here in the room, not Margery's nor mine.

She played two lines and stopped. She turned round and faced me.

"What is there here?" she said. "And what——?"

Walter, whom I had left asleep, looked in at the door.

"Ah, it's you playing," he said. "That's all right."

By strange interweavings of emotion, that common consciousness between us all of the presence of something that came not from among the humming wheels of life but from the grey mists that encompassed it, grew thicker in texture. There was some presence in the room—not mine, nor Margery's, nor Walter's—here now, though invisible, and somehow gathering strength from our recognition of its existence. In our different ways we all contributed to it in that moment of absolute and appalling silence.

Some sort of babble broke it. I babbled of the disorder of my papers, Margery babbled apology and promised to put them straight, if she might be allowed to deal with them. Some sort of crisis passed. I can explain it no better than that.

As evening drew on the clouds gathered even more thickly. The sea was leaden, the air dead, and when, about half-past ten that night, Mr. Bird, who had proved himself a charming guest, said good night, and I went with him to the door, we looked out on to a pit of impenetrable darkness. I saw the opportunity I wanted, and assuring him that I should really like a stroll to get such air as there was, insisted on fetching a lantern and lighting him back as far as the village. I then went straight to the point.

"There was a fearful tragedy in Coltham last year," I said. "Denton pointed me out the house where the murder was committed."

Mr. Bird stopped dead.

"Denton pointed you out the house?" he asked.

"Yes, but perhaps he was wrong," said I. "In fact, Mr. Bird, I should be very much obliged to you if you would tell me whether I am not right in thinking that the scene of the tragedy was 'The Firs.' My sister and brother-in-law know nothing about it, and I hope they won't. But I learned accidentally to-day that she pays the rent to Miss Ellershaw, which I think is the name. And I hazard the guess that the precise scene was the room outside which we sat to-night."

He did not reply for a moment.

"I can't deny what you suggest," he said, "and my mere refusal to reply would do no good. You are quite right. Denton's telling you, by the way, that the scene was in the village, itself, is quite intelligible, for Miss Ellershaw, who does not intend to live in the house again, wants to let it, and if it was known that the murder took place there, it would be prejudicial, Denton knows that. And in turn I want to ask you something. Why do you guess that particular room?"

I hesitated as to whether I should tell him about the crop of strange impressions which were growing up round it, but decided not to.

"There are queer things," I said. "My sister was told, for instance, that there were orders that the room should not be used. Denton told her that."

"I can understand that, too," he said. "The room has terrible memories for those who were in the house at the time. Any more queer things?"

"None that I can think of at present," I said. "But I will wish you good night here, as the rest of your way is clear."

I retraced my steps, and found that Walter and Margery had both gone upstairs. There was a lamp still burning on the paved space where we had sat after dinner, and I went out there, disinclined to go to bed, with my nerves all strung up by the stimulus of the approaching storm. All feeling of fear about what was creeping out into the light concerning this room, and what might, I felt, suddenly burst forth with some blaze of revelation, was gone, and I was conscious only of intense curiosity, as I summed up in my mind what I believed, owing to these strange hints and signals out of the mists, had actually taken place. I figured Miss Ellershaw as having been sitting at the piano when the strangling cord was slipped round her neck; I figured her as having been playing "Home, Sweet Home"; I figured Denton as having heard her. Then there would have been silence, but for some few gasps, some quivering convulsions, like the shaking of leaves in a tree, and then the discovery, perhaps by Denton, of the crime which was still unexplained. Certainly that afternoon, the fragment of the tune which Margery had played, gave him a sudden shock of horror....

The night was absolutely still; neither from inside the house nor from outside came the slightest stir of life, and the silence rang in my ears. And then from the room close at hand I heard, faint but distinct, the tinkle of the piano. A couple of bars of the familiar tune were played, and some voice, thin and quavering, began to sing the air. Curiosity, violent and irresistible, drowned all other feeling in my mind, and taking up the lamp, I opened the door of the room and entered. It burned brightly, and by its light, which gleamed on the keys of the piano, I could see that the room was empty. But the tune went on, softly played and faintly sung, and looking more closely at the piano, I saw that once more the keys were moving. At that the sense of fear which till then had lain coiled and quiet in my mind, began to stir. But I felt absolutely powerless to go; fear, now in swift invasion of my mind, held me where I was.

Something began to form in the air by the piano, a mist, a greyness. Then in a second it solidified, and there sat with her back to me the figure of a little white-haired woman. Then the singing stopped, her arms shot up with quivering, clutching fingers; she struggled, she turned, and I saw her face, swollen and purple, with gasping mouth and protruding eyes. Her head lolled and nodded; her body swayed backwards and forwards, and she slid off the music-stool to the ground. At that moment a blaze of light poured through the unsheltered windows, and I saw pressed against the pane, and seemingly quite unaware of my presence, Denton's white and staring countenance. His eyes were fixed on the piano. Simultaneously with the light came an appalling crack of thunder. The storm had burst.

For that moment Denton and I faced each other; the next he had gone, and I heard his feet running down the garden path. I had seen enough, too, and with my mind submerged in terror I stumbled from the room. As I paused for a moment outside, another flash flooded the gross darkness, and I saw him scudding across the down to the white edge of the cliffs. Then down came the rain, solid and hissing, my lamp was extinguished, and by the flare of the lightning, standing still between the flashes, I groped my way up to bed.

All night the prodigious storm streamed and rattled, but about dawn, as I lay still sleepless, and quaking with the prodigy of horror I had looked upon, it passed away, and I dozed and then slept deeply, and woke to find the morning tranquil and fresh and sunny. All the intolerable depression of the day before, not physical alone, seemed to me to have vanished, the house was wholesome as the breeze from the sea, and so, too, when, not without making a strong call on my courage, I entered it, I found the room where last night I had witnessed that ghastly pageant-ry. In no way could I account for that inward conviction, even less could I question it; all I knew was that some tragic stain had passed from it.

I was down before either of the others, and strolling through the garden as I waited for them, I saw advancing along the paved walk the figure of the Vicar.

"A very dreadful thing has happened," he said. "Denton's body was found half an hour ago by some fishermen at the foot of the cliff down there. His head was smashed in; he must have fallen sheer on to the rocks."

Now the reader may put any interpretation he pleases on the events which I have here briefly recorded, and on certain facts which may or may not seem to him to be connected with them, namely, that Miss Ellershaw, the elder of the two sisters who lived together at "The Firs," was found strangled on the floor by the piano in the room which juts out into the garden; that her sister not many minutes before her body was found had heard her singing "Home, Sweet Home" to her own accompaniment, and that the author of the murder had never been found. It is a fact also that late on the night of which I have been speaking, I saw Denton looking in through the window of that room, and shortly afterwards running across the strip of downland towards the cliff, at the bottom of which next morning his body was found.

But beyond that point we deal not with material facts, but with impressions. Three separate people fancied that there was something strange about the room; one of them found herself expecting to see some unaccountable appearance; one of them thought there was a peculiar chill in the room, and also that he heard the piano being played when nobody had touched it; the third, as I have related, believed that he both saw and heard things in that room which he cannot explain. Whether Denton shared that experience we cannot tell, nor can we tell for certain whether it was a pure accident that he fell over the cliff, or whether he had seen and heard something which drove him to make an end of himself.

It remains only to add that Walter and Margery agreed that some strange sense, which they had both felt as of an unexplained presence in that room, had passed away from it during the night on which Denton met his death. Walter was inclined to attribute our original impressions to some purely subjective disturbance of the nerves caused by the approach of that great storm. Not then, but later when thoroughly restored, he had gone back to his work I told him and Margery what I had seen that night and what, perhaps, Denton had seen.

IX "AND NO BIRD SINGS"

The red chimneys of the house for which I was bound were visible from just outside the station at which I had alighted, and, so the chauffeur told me, the distance was not more than a mile's walk if I took the path across the fields. It ran straight till it came to the edge of that wood yonder, which belonged to my host, and above which his chimneys were visible. I should find a gate in the paling of this wood, and a track traversing it, which debouched close to his garden. So, in this adorable afternoon of early May, it seemed a waste of time to do other than walk through meadows and woods, and I set off on foot, while the motor carried my traps.

It was one of those golden days which every now and again leak out of Paradise and drip to earth. Spring had been late in coming, but now it was here with a burst, and the whole world was boiling with the sap of life. Never have I seen such a wealth of spring flowers, or such vividness of green, or heard such melodious business among the birds in the hedgerows; this walk through the meadows was a jubilee of festal ecstasy. And best of all, so I promised myself, would be the passage through the wood newly fledged with milky green that lay just ahead. There was the gate, just facing me, and I passed through it into the dappled lights and shadows of the grass-grown track.

Coming out of the brilliant sunshine was like entering a dim tunnel; one had the sense of being suddenly withdrawn from the brightness of the spring into some subaqueous cavern. The tree-tops formed a green roof overhead, excluding the light to a remarkable degree; I moved in a world of shifting obscurity. Presently, as the trees grew more scattered, their place was taken by a thick growth of hazels, which met over the path, and then, the ground sloping downwards, I came upon an open clearing, covered with bracken and heather, and studded with birches. But though now I walked once more beneath the luminous sky, with the sunlight pouring down, it seemed to have lost its effulgence. The brightness—was it some odd optical illusion?—was veiled as if it came through crêpe. Yet there was the sun still well above the tree-tops in an unclouded heaven, but for all that the light was that of a stormy winter's day, without warmth or brilliance. It was oddly silent, too; I had thought that the bushes and trees would be ringing with the song of mating-birds, but listening, I could hear no note of any sort, neither the fluting of thrush or blackbird, nor the cheerful whirr of the chaffinch, nor the cooing wood-pigeon, nor the strident clamour of the jay. I paused to verify this odd silence; there was no doubt about it. It was rather eerie, rather uncanny, but I supposed the birds knew their own business best, and if they were too busy to sing it was their affair.

As I went on it struck me also that since entering the wood I had not seen a bird of any kind; and now, as I crossed the clearing, I kept my eyes alert for them, but fruitlessly, and soon I entered the further belt of thick trees which surrounded it. Most of them I noticed were beeches, growing very close to each other, and the ground beneath them was bare but for the carpet of fallen leaves, and a few thin bramble-bushes. In this curious dimness and thickness of the trees, it was impossible to see far to right or left of the path, and now, for the first time since I had left the open, I heard some sound of life. There came the rustle of leaves from not far away, and I thought to myself that a rabbit, anyhow, was moving. But somehow it lacked the staccato patter of a small animal; there was a certain stealthy heaviness about it, as if something much larger were stealing along and desirous of not being heard. I paused again to see what might emerge, but instantly the sound ceased. Simultaneously I was conscious of some faint but very foul odour reaching me, a smell choking and corrupt, yet somehow pungent, more like the odour of something alive rather than rotting. It was peculiarly sickening, and not wanting to get any closer to its source I went on my way.

Before long I came to the edge of the wood; straight in front of me was a strip of meadow-land, and beyond an iron gate between two brick walls, through which I had a glimpse of lawn and flower-beds. To the left stood the house, and over house and garden there poured the amazing brightness of the declining afternoon.

Hugh Granger and his wife were sitting out on the lawn, with the usual pack of assorted dogs: a Welsh collie, a yellow retriever, a fox-terrier, and a Pekinese. Their protest at my intrusion gave way to the welcome of recognition, and I was admitted into the circle. There was much to say, for I had been out of England for the last three months, during which time Hugh had settled into this little estate left him by a recluse uncle, and he and Daisy had been busy during the Easter vacation with getting into the house. Certainly it was a most attractive legacy; the house, through which I was presently taken, was a delightful little Queen Anne manor, and its situation on the edge of this heather-clad Surrey ridge quite superb. We had tea in a small panelled parlour overlooking the garden, and soon the wider topics narrowed down to those of the day and the hour. I had walked, had I, asked Daisy, from the station: did I go through the wood, or follow the path outside it?

The question she thus put to me was given trivially enough; there was no hint in her voice that it mattered a straw to her which way I had come. But it was quite clearly borne in upon me that not only she but Hugh also listened intently for my reply. He had just lit a match for his cigarette, but held it unapplied till he heard my answer. Yes, I had gone through the wood; but now, though I had received some odd impressions in the wood, it seemed quite ridiculous to mention what they were. I could not soberly say that the sunshine there was of very poor quality, and that at one point in my traverse I had smelt a most iniquitous odour. I had walked through the wood; that was all I had to tell them.

I had known both my host and hostess for a tale of many years, and now, when I felt that there was nothing except purely fanciful stuff that I could volunteer about my experiences there, I noticed that they exchanged a swift glance, and could easily interpret it. Each of them signalled to the other an expression of relief; they told each other (so I construed their glance) that I, at any rate, had found nothing unusual in the wood, and they were pleased at that. But then, before any real pause had succeeded to my answer that I had gone through the wood, I remembered that strange absence of bird-song and birds, and as that seemed an innocuous observation in natural history, I thought I might as well mention it.

"One odd thing struck me," I began (and instantly I saw the attention of both riveted again), "I didn't see a single bird or hear one from the time I entered the wood to when I left it."

Hugh lit his cigarette.

"I've noticed that too," he said, "and it's rather puzzling. The wood is certainly a bit of primeval forest, and one would have thought that hosts of birds would have nested in it from time immemorial. But, like you, I've never heard or seen one in it. And I've never seen a rabbit there either."

"I thought I heard one this afternoon," said I. "Something was moving in the fallen beech leaves."

"Did you see it?" he asked.

I recollected that I had decided that the noise was not quite the patter of a rabbit.

"No, I didn't see it," I said, "and perhaps it wasn't one. It sounded, I remember, more like something larger."

Once again and unmistakably a glance passed between Hugh and his wife, and she rose.

"I must be off," she said. "Post goes out at seven, and I lazed all morning. What are you two going to do?"

"Something out of doors, please," said I. "I want to see the domain."

Hugh and I accordingly strolled out again with the cohort of dogs. The domain was certainly very charming; a small lake lay beyond the garden, with a reed bed vocal with warblers, and a tufted margin into which coots and moorhens scudded at our approach. Rising from the end of that was a high heathery knoll full of rabbit holes, which the dogs nosed at with joyful expectations, and there we sat for a while overlooking the wood which covered the rest of the estate. Even now in the blaze of the sun near to its setting, it seemed to be in shadow, though like the rest of the view it should have basked in brilliance, for not a cloud flecked the sky and the level rays enveloped the world in a crimson splendour. But the wood was grey and darkling. Hugh, also, I was aware, had been looking at it, and now, with an air of breaking into a disagreeable topic, he turned to me.

"Tell me," he said, "does anything strike you about that wood?"

"Yes: it seems to lie in shadow."

He frowned.

"But it can't, you know," he said. "Where does the shadow come from? Not from outside, for sky and land are on fire."

"From inside, then?" I asked

He was silent a moment.

"There's something queer about it," he said at length. "There's something there, and I don't know what it is. Daisy feels it too; she won't ever go into the wood, and it appears that birds won't either. Is it just the fact that, for some unexplained reason, there are no birds in it that has set all our imaginations at work?"

I jumped up.

"Oh, it's all rubbish," I said. "Let's go through it now and find a bird. I bet you I find a bird."

"Sixpence for every bird you see," said Hugh.

We went down the hillside and walked round the wood till we came to the gate where I had entered that afternoon. I held it open after I had gone in for the dogs to follow. But there they stood, a yard or so away, and none of them moved.

"Come on, dogs," I said, and Fifi, the fox-terrier, came a step nearer and then with a little whine retreated again.

"They always do that," said Hugh, "not one of them will set foot inside the wood. Look!"

He whistled and called, he cajoled and scolded, but it was no use. There the dogs remained, with little apologetic grins and signallings of tails, but quite determined not to come.

"But why?" I asked.

"Same reason as the birds, I suppose, whatever that happens to be. There's Fifi, for instance, the sweetest-tempered little lady; once I tried to pick her up and carry her in, and she snapped at me. They'll have nothing to do with the wood; they'll trot round outside it and go home."

We left them there, and in the sunset light which was now beginning to fade began the passage. Usually the sense of eeriness disappears if one has a companion, but now to me, even with Hugh walking by my side, the place seemed even more uncanny than it had done that afternoon, and a sense of intolerable uneasiness, that grew into a sort of waking nightmare, obsessed me. I had thought before that the silence and loneliness of it had played tricks with my nerves; but with Hugh here it could not be that, and indeed I felt that it was not any such notion that lay at the root of this fear, but rather the conviction that there was some presence lurking there, invisible as yet, but permeating the gathered gloom. I could not form the slighted idea of what it might be, or whether it was material or ghostly; all I could diagnose of it from my own sensations was that it was evil and antique.

As we came to the open ground in the middle of the wood, Hugh stopped, and though the evening was cool I noticed that he mopped his forehead.

"Pretty nasty," he said. "No wonder the dogs don't like it. How do you feel about it?"

Before I could answer, he shot out his hand, pointing to the belt of trees that lay beyond.

"What's that?" he said in a whisper.

I followed his finger, and for one half-second thought I saw against the black of the wood some vague flicker, grey or faintly luminous. It waved as if it had been the head and forepart of some huge snake rearing itself, but it instantly disappeared, and my glimpse had been so momentary that I could not trust my impression.

"It's gone," said Hugh, still looking in the direction he had pointed; and as we stood there, I heard again what I had heard that afternoon, a rustle among the fallen beech-leaves. But there was no wind nor breath of breeze astir.

He turned to me.

"What on earth was it?" he said. "It looked like some enormous slug standing up. Did you see it?"

"I'm not sure whether I did or not," I said. "I think I just caught sight of what you saw."

"But what was it?" he said again. "Was it a real material creature, or was it——"

"Something ghostly, do you mean?" I asked.

"Something half-way between the two," he said. "I'll tell you what I mean afterwards, when we've got out of this place."

The thing, whatever it was, had vanished among the trees to the left of where our path lay, and in silence we walked across the open till we came to where it entered tunnel-like among the trees. Frankly I hated and feared the thought of plunging into that darkness with the knowledge that not so far off there was something the nature of which I could not ever so faintly conjecture, but which, I now made no doubt, was that which filled the wood with some nameless terror. Was it material, was it ghostly, or was it (and now some inkling of what Hugh meant began to form itself into my mind) some being that lay on the borderland between the two? Of all the sinister possibilities that appeared the most terrifying.

As we entered the trees again I perceived that reek, alive and yet corrupt, which I had smelt before, but now it was far more potent, and we hurried on, choking with the odour that I now guessed to be not the putrescence of decay, but the living substance of that which crawled and reared itself in the darkness of the wood where no bird would shelter. Somewhere among those trees lurked the reptilian thing that defied and yet compelled credence.

It was a blessed relief to get out of that dim tunnel into the wholesome air of the open and the clear light of evening. Within doors, when we returned, windows were curtained and lamps lit. There was a hint of frost, and Hugh put a match to the fire in his room, where the dogs, still a little apologetic, hailed us with thumpings of drowsy tails.

"And now we've got to talk," said he, "and lay our plans, for whatever it is that is in the wood, we've got to make an end of it. And, if you want to know what I think it is, I'll tell you."

"Go ahead," said I.

"You may laugh at me, if you like," he said, "but I believe it's an elemental. That's what I meant when I said it was a being half-way between the material and the ghostly. I never caught a glimpse of it till this afternoon; I only felt there was something horrible there. But now I've seen it, and it's like what spiritualists and that sort of folk describe as an elemental. A huge phosphorescent slug is what they tell us of it, which at will can surround itself with darkness."

Somehow, now safe within doors, in the cheerful light and warmth of the room, the suggestion appeared merely grotesque. Out there in the darkness of that uncomfortable wood something within me had quaked, and I was prepared to believe any horror, but now commonsense revolted.

"But you don't mean to tell me you believe in such rubbish?" I said. "You might as well say it was a unicorn. What is an elemental, anyway? Who has ever seen one except the people who listen to raps in the darkness and say they are made by their aunts?"

"What is it then?" he asked.

"I should think it is chiefly our own nerves," I said. "I frankly acknowledge I got the creeps when I went through the wood first, and I got them much worse when I went through it with you. But it was just nerves; we are frightening ourselves and each other."

"And are the dogs frightening themselves and each other?" he asked. "And the birds?"

That was rather harder to answer; in fact I gave it up.

Hugh continued.

"Well, just for the moment we'll suppose that something else, not ourselves, frightened us and the dogs and the birds," he said, "and that we did see something like a huge phosphorescent slug. I won't call it an elemental, if you object to that; I'll call it It. There's another thing, too, which the existence of It would explain."

"What's that?" I asked.

"Well, it is supposed to be some incarnation of evil, it is a corporeal form of the devil. It is not only spiritual, it is material to this extent that it can be seen bodily in form, and heard, and, as you noticed, smelt, and, God forbid, handled. It has to be kept alive by nourishment. And that explains perhaps why, every day since I have been here, I've found on that knoll we went up some half-dozen dead rabbits."

"Stoats and weasels," said I.

"No, not stoats and weasels. Stoats kill their prey and eat it. These rabbits have not been eaten; they've been drunk."

"What on earth do you mean?" I asked.

"I examined several of them. There was just a small hole in their throats, and they were drained of blood. Just skin and bones, and a sort of grey mash of fibre, like, like the fibre of an orange which has been sucked. Also there was a horrible smell lingering on them. And was the thing you had a glimpse of like a stoat or a weasel?"

There came a rattle at the handle of the door.

"Not a word to Daisy," said Hugh as she entered.

"I heard you come in," she said. "Where did you go?"

"All round the place," said I, "and came back through the wood. It is odd; not a bird did we see, but that is partly accounted for because it was dark."

I saw her eyes search Hugh's, but she found no communication there. I guessed that he was planning some attack on It next day, and he did not wish her to know that anything was afoot.

"The wood's unpopular," he said. "Birds won't go there, dogs won't go there, and Daisy won't go there. I'm bound to say I share the feeling too, but having braved its terrors in the dark I've broken the spell."

"All quiet, was it?" asked she.

"Quiet wasn't the word for it. The smallest pin could have been heard dropping half a mile off."

We talked over our plans that night after she had gone up to bed. Hugh's story about the sucked rabbits was rather horrible, and though there was no certain connection between those empty rinds of animals and what we had seen, there seemed a certain reasonableness about it. But anything, as he pointed out, which could feed like that was clearly not without its material side—ghosts did not have dinner, and if it was material it was vulnerable.

Our plans, therefore, were very simple; we were going to tramp through the wood, as one walks up partridges in a field of turnips, each with a shot-gun and a supply of cartridges. I cannot say that I looked forward to the expedition, for I hated the thought of getting into closer quarters with that mysterious denizen of the woods; but there was a certain excitement about it, sufficient to keep me awake a long time, and when I got to sleep to cause very vivid and awful dreams.

The morning failed to fulfil the promise of the clear sunset; the sky was lowering and cloudy and a fine rain was falling. Daisy had shopping-errands which took her into the little town, and as soon as she had set off we started on our business. The yellow retriever, mad with joy at the sight of guns, came bounding with us across the garden, but on our entering the wood he slunk back home again.

The wood was roughly circular in shape, with a diameter perhaps of half a mile. In the centre, as I have said, there was an open clearing about a quarter of a mile across, which was thus surrounded by a belt of thick trees and copse a couple of hundred yards in breadth. Our plan was first to walk together up the path which led through the wood, with all possible stealth, hoping to hear some movement on the part of what we had come to seek. Failing that, we had settled to tramp through the wood at the distance of some fifty yards from each other in a circular track; two or three of these circuits would cover the whole ground pretty thoroughly. Of the nature of our quarry, whether it would try to steal away from us, or possibly attack, we had no idea; it seemed, however, yesterday to have avoided us.

Rain had been falling steadily for an hour when we entered the wood; it hissed a little in the tree-tops overhead; but so thick was the cover that the ground below was still not more than damp. It was a dark morning outside; here you would say that the sun had already set and that night was falling. Very quietly we moved up the grassy path, where our footfalls were noiseless, and once we caught a whiff of that odour of live corruption; but though we stayed and listened not a sound of anything stirred except the sibilant rain over our heads. We went across the clearing and through to the far gate, and still there was no sign.

"We'll be getting into the trees then," said Hugh. "We had better start where we got that whiff of it."

We went back to the place, which was towards the middle of the encompassing trees. The odour still lingered on the windless air.

"Go on about fifty yards," he said, "and then we'll go in. If either of us comes on the track of it we'll shout to each other."

I walked on down the path till I had gone the right distance, signalled to him, and we stepped in among the trees.

I have never known the sensation of such utter loneliness. I knew that Hugh was walking parallel with me, only fifty yards away, and if I hung on my step I could faintly hear his tread among the beech leaves. But I felt as if I was quite sundered in this dim place from all companionship of man; the only live thing that lurked here was that monstrous mysterious creature of evil. So thick were the trees that I could not see more than a dozen yards in any direction; all places outside the wood seemed infinitely remote, and infinitely remote also everything that had occurred to me in normal human life. I had been whisked out of all wholesome experiences into this antique and evil place. The rain had ceased, it whispered no longer in the tree-tops, testifying that there did exist a world and a sky outside, and only a few drops from above pattered on the beech leaves.

Suddenly I heard the report of Hugh's gun, followed by his shouting voice.

"I've missed it," he shouted; "it's coming in your direction."

I heard him running towards me, the beech-leaves rustling, and no doubt his footsteps drowned a stealthier noise that was close to me. All that happened now, until once more I heard the report of Hugh's gun, happened, I suppose, in less than a minute. If it had taken much longer I do not imagine I should be telling it today.

I stood there then, having heard Hugh's shout, with my gun cocked, and ready to put to my shoulder, and I listened to his running footsteps. But still I saw nothing to shoot at and heard nothing. Then between two beech trees, quite close to me, I saw what I can only describe as a ball of darkness. It rolled very swiftly towards me over the few yards that separated me from it, and then, too late, I heard the dead beech-leaves rustling below it. Just before it reached me, my brain realised what it was, or what it might be, but before I could raise my gun to shoot at that nothingness, it was upon me. My gun was twitched out of my hand, and I was enveloped in this blackness, which was the very essence of corruption. It knocked me off my feet, and I sprawled flat on my back, and upon me, as I lay there, I felt the weight of this invisible assailant.

I groped wildly with my hands and they clutched something cold and slimy and hairy. They slipped off it, and next moment there was laid across my shoulder and neck something which felt like an india-rubber tube. The end of it fastened on to my neck like a snake, and I felt the skin rise beneath it. Again, with clutching hands, I tried to tear that obscene strength away from me, and as I struggled with it, I heard Hugh's footsteps close to me through this layer of darkness that hid everything.

My mouth was free, and I shouted at him.

"Here, here!" I yelled "Close to you, where it is darkest."

I felt his hands on mine, and that added strength detached from my neck that sucker that pulled at it. The coil that lay heavy on my legs and chest writhed and struggled and relaxed. Whatever it was that our four hands held, slipped out of them, and I saw Hugh standing close to me. A yard or two off, vanishing among the beech trunks, was that blackness which had poured over me. Hugh put up his gun, and with his second barrel fired at it.

The blackness dispersed, and there, wriggling and twisting like a huge worm lay what we had come to find. It was alive still, and I picked up my gun which lay by my side and fired two more barrels into it. The writhings dwindled into mere shudderings and shakings, and then it lay still.

With Hugh's help I got to my feet, and we both reloaded before going nearer. On the ground there lay a monstrous thing, half-slug, half worm. There was no head to it; it ended in a blunt point with an orifice. In colour it was grey covered with sparse black hairs; its length I suppose was some four feet, its thickness at the broadest part was that of a man's thigh, tapering towards each end. It was shattered by shot at its middle. There were stray pellets which had hit it elsewhere, and from the holes they had made there oozed not blood, but some grey viscous matter.

As we stood there some swift process of disintegration and decay began. It lost outline, it melted, it liquified, and in a minute more we were looking at a mass of stained and coagulated beech leaves. Again and quickly that liquor of corruption faded, and there lay at our feet no trace of what had been there. The overpowering odour passed away, and there came from the ground just the sweet savour of wet earth in springtime, and from above the glint of a sunbeam piercing the clouds. Then a sudden pattering among the dead leaves sent my heart into my mouth again, and I cocked my gun. But it was only Hugh's yellow retriever who had joined us.

We looked at each other.

"You're not hurt?" he said.

I held my chin up.

"Not a bit," I said. "The skin's not broken, is it?"

"No; only a round red mark. My God, what was it? What happened?"

"Your turn first," said I. "Begin at the beginning."

"I came upon it quite suddenly," he said. "It was lying coiled like a sleeping dog behind a big beech. Before I could fire, it slithered off in the direction where I knew you were. I got a snap shot at it among the trees, but I must have missed, for I heard it rustling away. I shouted to you and ran after it. There was a circle of absolute darkness on the ground, and your voice came from the middle of it. I couldn't see you at all, but I clutched at the blackness and my hands met yours. They met something else, too."

We got back to the house and had put the guns away before Daisy came home from her shopping. We had also scrubbed and brushed and washed. She came into the smoking-room.

"You lazy folk," she said. "It has cleared up, and why are you still indoors? Let's go out at once."

I got up.

"Hugh has told me you've got a dislike of the wood," I said, "and it's a lovely wood. Come and see; he and I will walk on each side of you and hold your hands. The dogs shall protect you as well."

"But not one of them will go a yard into the wood," said she.

"Oh yes, they will. At least we'll try them. You must promise to come if they do."

Hugh whistled them up, and down we went to the gate. They sat panting for it to be opened, and scuttled into the thickets in pursuit of interesting smells.

"And who says there are no birds in it?" said Daisy. "Look at that robin! Why, there are two of them. Evidently house-hunting."

X THE CORNER HOUSE

Firham-by-sea had long been known to Jim Purley and myself, though we had been careful not to talk about it, and for years we had been accustomed to skulk quietly away from London, either alone or together, for a day or two of holiday at that delightful and unheard-of little village. It was not, I may safely say, any secretive or dog-in-the-manger instinct of keeping a good thing to ourselves that was the cause of this reticence, but it was because if Firham had become known at all the whole charm of it would have vanished. A popular Firham, in fact, would cease to be Firham, and while we should lose it nobody else would gain it. Its remoteness, its isolation, its emptiness were its most essential qualities; it would have been impossible, so we both of us felt, to have gone to Firham with a party of friends, and the idea of its little inn being peopled with strangers, or its odd little nine-hole golf-course with the small corrugated-iron shed for its club-house becoming full of serious golfers would certainly have been sufficient to make us desire never to play there again. Nor, indeed, were we guilty of any selfishness in keeping the knowledge of that golf-course to ourselves, for the holes were short and dull and the fairway badly kept. It was only because we were at Firham that we so often strolled round it, losing balls in furse bushes and marshy ground, and considering it quite decent putting if we took no more than three putts on a green. It was bad golf in fact, and no one in his senses would think of going to Firham to play bad golf, when good golf was so vastly more accessible. Indeed, the only reason why I have spoken of the golf-links is because in an indirect and distant manner they were connected with the early incidents of the story which strung itself together there, and which, to me at any rate, has destroyed the secure tranquillity of our remote little hermitage.

To get to Firham at all from London, except by a motor drive of some hundred and twenty miles, is a slow progress, and after two changes the leisurely railway eventually lands you no nearer than five miles from your destination. After that a switch-back road terminating in a long decline brings you off the inland Norfolk hills, and into the broad expanse of lowland, once reclaimed from the sea, and now protected from marine invasion by big banks and dykes. From the top of the last hill you get your first sight of the village, its brick-built houses with their tiled roofs smouldering redly in the sunset, like some small, glowing island anchored in that huge expanse of green, and, a mile beyond it, the dim blue of the sea. There are but few trees to be seen on that wide landscape, and those stunted and slanted in their growth by the prevailing wind off the coast, and the great sweep of the country is composed of featureless fields intersected with drainage dykes, and dotted with sparse cattle. A sluggish stream, fringed with reed-beds and loose-strife, where moor-hens chuckle, passes just outside the village, and a few hundred yards below it is spanned by a bridge and a sluice-gate. From there it broadens out into an estuary, full of shining water at high tide, and of grey mud-banks at the ebb, and passes between rows of tussocked sand-dunes out to sea.

The road, descending from the higher inlands, strikes across these reclaimed marshes, and after a mile of solitary travel enters the village of Firham. To right and left stand a few outlying cottages, whitewashed and thatched, each with a strip of gay garden in front and perhaps a fisherman's net spread out to dry on the wall, but before they form anything that could be called a street the road takes a sudden sharp-angled turn, and at once you are in the square which, indeed, forms the entire village. On each side of the broad cobbled space is a line of houses, on one side a post office and police-station with a dozen small shops where may be bought the more rudimentary needs of existence, a baker's, a butcher's, a tobacconist's. Opposite is a row of little residences midway between villa and cottage, while at the far end stands the dumpy grey church with the vicarage, behind green and rather dilapidated palings, beside it. At the near end is the "Fisherman's Arms," the modest hostelry at which we always put up, flanked by two or three more small red-brick houses, of which the farthest, where the road leaves the square again, is the Corner House of which this story treats.

The Corner House was an object of mild curiosity to Jim and me, for while the rest of the houses in the square, shops and residences alike, had a tidy and well-cared-for appearance, with an air of prosperity on a small contented scale, the Corner House presented a marked and curious contrast. The faded paint on the door was blistered and patchy, the step of the threshold always unwhitened and partly overgrown with an encroachment of moss, as if there was little traffic across it. Over the windows inside were stretched dingy casement curtains, and the Virginia creeper which straggled untended up the discoloured front of the house drooped over the dull panes like the hair over a terrier's eyes. Sometimes in one or other of these windows, between the curtains and the glass, there sat a mournful grey cat, but all day long no further sign of life within gave evidence of occupation. Behind the house was a spacious square of garden enclosed by a low brick wall, and from the upper windows of "The Fisherman's Arms" it was possible to look into it. There was a gravel path running round it, entirely overgrown, and a flower-bed underneath the wall was a jungle of rank weeds among which, in summer, two or three neglected rose trees put out a few meagre flowers. A broken water-butt stood at the end of it, and in the middle a rusty iron seat, but never at morning or at noon or at evening did I see any human figure in it; it seemed entirely derelict and unvisited.

At dusk shabby curtains were drawn across the windows that looked into the square, and then between chinks you could see that one room was lit within. The house, it was evident, had once been a very dignified little residence; it was built of red brick and was early Georgian in date, square and comfortable with its enclosed plot behind; one wondered, as I have said, with mild curiosity what blight had fallen on it, what manner of folk moved silent and unseen behind the dingy casement curtains all day and sat in that front room when night had fallen.

It was not only to us but also to the Firhamites generally that the inhabitants of the Corner House were veiled in some sort of mystery. The landlord of our inn, for instance, in answer to casual questions, could tell us very little of their life nowadays, but what he knew of them indicated that something rather grim lurked behind the drawn curtains. It was a married couple who lived there, and he could remember the arrival of Mr. and Mrs. Labson some ten years before.

"She was a big, handsome woman," he said, "and her age might have been thirty. He was a good deal younger; at that time he looked hardly out of his teens, a slim little slip of a fellow, half a head shorter than his wife. I daresay you've seen him on the golf-links, knocking a ball about by himself, for he goes out there every afternoon."

I had more than once noticed a man playing alone, and carrying a couple of clubs. If he was on a green, and saw us coming up, he always went hurriedly on or stood aside at a little distance, with back turned, and waited for us to pass. But neither of us had paid any particular attention to him.

"She doesn't go out with him?" I asked.

"She never leaves the house at all to my knowledge," said the landlord, "though to be sure it wasn't always like that. When first they came here they were always out together, playing golf or boating or fishing, and in the evening there would be the sound of singing or piano-playing from that front room of theirs. They didn't live here entirely, but came down from London, where they had a house, for two or three months in the summer and perhaps a month at Christmas and another month at Easter. There would be friends staying with them much of the time, and merriment and games always going on, and dancing, too, with a gramophone to play their tunes for them till midnight and later. And then, all of a sudden, five years ago now or perhaps a little more, something happened and everything was changed. Yes, that was a queer thing, and sudden, as I say, like a clap of thunder."

"Interesting," said Jim. "What was it that happened?"

"Well, as we saw it, it was like this," said he, "Mr. and Mrs. Labson were down here together in the summer, and one morning as I passed their door I heard her voice inside scolding and swearing at him or at some one. Him it must have been, as we knew later. All that day she went on at him; it was a wonder to think that a woman had so much breath in her body or so much rage in her mind. Next day all their servants, five or six they kept then, butler and lady's maid and valet and housemaid and cook, were all dismissed and off they went. The gardener got his month's wages, too, and was told he'd be wanted no more, and so there were Mr. and Mrs. Labson alone in the house. But half that day, too, she went on shouting and yelling, so it must have been him she was scolding and swearing at. Like a mad woman she was, and never a word from him. Then there would be silence a bit, and she'd break out again, and day after day it was like that, silence and then that screaming voice of hers. As the weeks went on, silence shut down on them; now and then she'd break out again, even as she does to this day, but a month and more will pass now, and you'll never hear a sound from within the house."

"And what had been the cause of it all?" I asked.

"That came out in the papers," said he, "when Mr. Labson was made a bankrupt. He had been speculating on the Stock Exchange, not with his own money alone, but with hers, and had lost nigh every penny. His house in London was sold, and all they had left was this house which belonged to her, and a bit of money he hadn't got at, which brings them in a pound or two a week. They keep no servants, and every morning Mr. Labson goes out early with his basket on his arm and brings provisions for their dinner with the shilling or two she gives him. They say he does the cooking as well, and the housework too, though there's not too much of that, if you can judge from what you see from outside, while she sits with her hands in her lap doing nothing from morning till night. Sitting there and hating him, you may say."

It was a weird, grim sort of story, and from that moment the house, to my mind, took on, as with a deeper dye of forbiddingness, something of its quality. Its desolate and untended aspect was fully earned, the uncleaned windows and discoloured door seemed a fit expression of the spirit that dwelt there: the house was the faithful expression of those who lived in it, of the man whose folly or knavery had brought them to a penury that was near ruin, and of the woman who was never seen, but sat behind the dirty curtained windows hating him, and making him her drudge. He was her slave; those hours when she screamed and raved at him must surely have broken his spirit utterly, or, whatever his fault had been, he must have rebelled against so servile and dismal an existence. Just that hour or two of remission she gave him in the afternoon that he might get air and exercise to keep his health, and continue his life of bondage, and then back again he went to the seclusion and the simmering hostility.

As sometimes happens when a subject has got started, the round of trivial, everyday experiences begins to bristle with allusions and hints that bear on it, so now when this matter of the Corner House had been set going, Jim and I began to be constantly aware of its ticking. It was just that: it was as if a clock had been wound up and started off, and now we were aware in a way we had not been before that it was steadily ticking on, and the hands silently moving towards some unconjecturable hour. Fancifully, and fantastically enough I wondered what the hour would be towards which the silent pointers were creeping. Would there be some sort of jarring whirr that gave warning that the hour was imminent, or should we miss that, and be suddenly startled by some reverberating shock? Such an idea was, of course, purely an invention of the imagination, but somehow it had got hold of me, and I used to pass the Corner House with an uneasy glance at its dingy windows, as if they were the dial that interpreted the progress of the sombre mechanism within.

The reader must understand that all this formed no continuous series of impressions. Jim and I were at Firham only on short visits, with intervals of weeks or even of months in between. But certainly after the subject had been started we had more frequent glimpses of Mr. Labson. Day after day we saw his flitting figure on the links, keeping its distance, and retreating before us, but once we approached close up to him before he was aware of our presence. It was an afternoon that threatened rain, and in order to be nearer shelter if the storm burst suddenly we had cut two holes and walked across an intervening tract of rough ground to a hole which took us in a homeward direction. He was just addressing his ball on this teeing-ground when, looking up, he saw that we were beside him; he gave a little squeal as of terror, picked up his ball, and scuttled away, at a shuffling run, with abject terror written on his lean white face. Not a word did he give us in answer to Jim's begging him to precede us, not once did he look round.

"But the man's quaking with fear," said I, as he disappeared. "He could hardly pick up his ball."

"Poor devil!" said Jim. "There's something formidable at the Corner House."

He had hardly spoken when the rain began in torrents, and we trotted with the best speed of middle-aged gentlemen towards the corrugated-iron shed of the club-house. But Mr. Labson did not join us there for shelter; for we saw him plodding homewards through the downpour rather than face his fellow-creatures.

That close glimpse of Mr. Labson had made the affair of the Corner House much more real. Behind the curtains where the light was lit in the evening there sat a man in whose soul terror was enthroned. Was it terror of his companion who sat there with him that reigned so supreme that even when he was away out on the links it still was master of him? Had it also so drained from him all dregs of manhood and of courage that he could not even run away, but must return to the grim house for fear of his fear, as a rabbit on whose track is a weasel has not the courage to gallop off and easily save itself from the sharp white teeth? Or were there ties of affection between him and the woman whom his folly had brought to penury, so that as a willing penance he cooked and drudged for her? And then I thought of the voice that had yelled at him all day; it was more likely that, as Jim had said, there was something formidable at the Corner House, before which he cowered and from which he had not the strength to fly.

There were other glimpses of him as, with his basket on his arm in the early morning, he brought home bread and milk and some cheap cut from the butcher's. Once I saw him enter his house on his return from his marketing. He must have locked the door before going out, for now he unlocked it again, slipped in, and I heard the key click in the wards again. Once, too, though only in featureless outline, I saw her who shared his solitude, for passing by the Corner House in the dusk, the lamp had been lit within, and I had a glimpse through the thin casement blinds of a carpetless room, a blackened ceiling and one big armchair drawn up to the fire. And at that moment the form of a woman silhouetted itself between me and the light. She was very tall, and immensely broad and stout, and her hands, large as a man's, grasped the curtain. Next moment, with a jingle of running rings, she had drawn it, and shut up herself and the man for the long winter evening and the night that followed.

The same evening, I remember, Jim had occasion to go to the post office and came back to our snug little sitting-room with something of horror in his eyes.

"You've seen her to-day," he said, "and I've heard her."

"Who? Oh! at the Corner House?" I asked.

"Yes. I was just passing it, when she began. I tell you it scared me. It was scarcely like a human voice at all, or at any rate not like a sane voice. A shrill, swearing gabble all on one note, and going on without a pause. Maniac."

The conjectured picture of the two grew more grim. It was an awful thought that behind those dingy curtains in the bare room there were the pair of them, the little terrified man, and that greater monster of a woman, yelling and bawling at him. Yet what could we do? It seemed impossible to interfere in any way. It was not the business of a couple of visitors from London to intrude on the domestic differences of total strangers. And yet the sequel showed that any interference would have been justified.

The day following was wet from morning till night. A gale of rain mingled with sleet roared in from the north-east, and neither of us stirred abroad, but kept close by the fire listening to the wind bugling in the chimney, and the gale flinging the sheets of water solidly against the window-pane. But after nightfall the wind abated and the sky cleared, and when I went up to bed, sleepy with the day indoors, I saw the shadows of the window bars black against a brightness outside, and pulling up the blind looked on to a blaze of moonlight. Below, a little to the left, was the neglected garden of the Corner House, and there, standing on the grass-grown path, was the figure of the woman I had seen in black silhouette against the lamplight in her room. Now the moonlight shone full on her face and my breath caught in my throat as I looked on that appalling countenance. It was fat and bloated beyond belief, the eyes were but slits above her cheeks, and the lines of her mouth were invisible in their shadows. But even the whiteness of the moonlight gave no pallor to her face, for it was flushed with some purplish hue that seemed nearly black. One glimpse only I had for perhaps she had heard the rattle of my blind, and she looked up and next minute had stepped back into the house again. But that moment was enough; I felt that I had looked on something hellish, something almost outside the wide range of humanity. It was not only the appalling physical ugliness of that monstrous face that was so shocking; it was the expression in the eyes and mouth, visible in that second when she raised her face to look upwards to my window. An inhuman hatred and cruelty were there that made the heart quake; the featureless outline was filled in with details more awful than I had ever conjectured.

We were out on the links again next afternoon on a day of liquid sunshine and brisk air, but some nameless oppression of the spirits held me sundered from the genial and bracing warmth. The idea of that frightened little man being imprisoned all day and night, but for his brief outing, with her who at any moment might break into that screaming torrent of speech, was like a nightmare that came between me and the sun. It would have been something to have seen him out to-day, and know that he was having a respite from that terrible presence; but we caught no sight of him, and when we returned and passed the Corner House the curtains were already drawn, and, as usual, there was silence within.

Jim touched me on the arm as we walked by the windows.

"But there's no light inside this evening," he said.

This was quite true; the curtains were torn, as I knew, in half a dozen places, but neither through these holes nor from the chinks at their edges was there any light showing. Somehow this gave an added horror, which set my nerves jangling.

"Well, we can't knock and tell them they've forgotten to light the lamp," I said.

We had halted for a moment, and even as I spoke I saw coming across the square towards us in the gathering dusk the figure of the man whom we had missed on the links that afternoon. Though I had not seen him approach, nor heard the noise of his footfall on the cobbles, he was now within a few yards of us.

"Here *he* is anyhow," I said.

Jim turned.

"Where?" he asked.

We were standing perhaps two yards apart, and as he asked that the man stepped between us and advanced to the door of the Corner House. And then, instantaneously, I saw that Jim and I were alone. The door of the Corner House had not opened, but there was no one there.

Jim gave a startled exclamation.

"What was that?" he said. "Something brushed by me."

"Didn't you see anything?" I asked.

"No, but I felt something. I don't know what it was."

"I saw him," said I.

My jangled nerves seemed to have infected Jim.

"Nonsense!" he said. "How could you have seen him? Where has he gone if you saw him? And I don't know what we're standing here for."

Before I could answer I heard from within the Corner House the sound of heavy and shuffling steps; a key grated in the lock, and the door was flung open. Out of it, panting and heaving with some strange agitation, came the woman I had seen last night in her garden.

She had shut the door and locked it before she saw us. She was hatless and shod in great carpet slippers the heels of which tapped on the pavement as she moved, and on her face was the vacancy of some nameless terror. Her mouth, a cavern in that mountain of flesh, was wide, and now there came from it something between a gasp and a rattle. Then, seeing us, quick as a lizard, she whisked round again, fumbled for a moment with the key which she still held in her hand, and there once more was the shut door and the empty pavement. The whole scene passed like a blink of strong light seen in the dusk and vanishing again. She had come out, driven by some terror of her own; she had gone back in terror, it would seem, of us.

It was without a word passing between us that we went back to the inn. Just then there was nothing to be said; for myself, at least. I knew that there was, covering my brain, so to speak, some frozen surface of abject fear which must be thawed. I knew that I had seen, I knew that Jim had felt, something which had no tangible existence in the material world. He had felt what I had seen, and I had seen the form and bodily semblance of the man who lived at the Corner House. But what his wife had seen that drove her from the house, and why, seeing us, she had whisked back into it again I had no notion. Perhaps when a certain physical horror in my brain was uncongealed I should know.

Presently we were sitting in the small, cosy room, with our tea ready for us, and the fire burning bright on the hearth. We talked, odd as it may appear, of anything else but *that*. But the silences between the abandonment of our topic and the introduction of another grew longer, and at last Jim spoke.

"Something has happened," he said. "You saw what wasn't there, and I felt what wasn't there. What did we see or feel? And what did *she* see or feel?"

He had hardly spoken when there came a rap at the door, and our landlord entered. For the moment, during which the door was open, I heard from the bar of the inn a shrill, gabbling voice, which I had never heard before, but which I knew Jim had heard.

"There's Mrs. Labson come into the bar, gentlemen," he said, "and she wants to know if it was you who were standing outside her house ten minutes ago. She's got a notion——"

He paused.

"It's hard to make out what she's after," he said. "Her husband has not been at home all day, and he's not home yet, and she thinks you may have seen him on the golf-links. And then she says she's thinking of letting her house for a month, and wonders if you would care to take it, but she runs on so——"

The door opened again, and there she stood, filling the doorway. She had on her head a great feathered hat, and over her shoulders a red satin evening cloak, now moth-eaten and ragged, while on her feet were still those carpet slippers.

"So odd it must seem to you for a lady to intrude like this," she said, "but you are the gentlemen, are you not, whom I saw admiring my house just now?"

Her eyes, now utterly vacant, now suddenly keen and searching, fell on the window. The curtains were not drawn and outside the last of the daylight was fading. She shuffled quickly across the floor and rattled the blind down, first peering out into the dusk.

"I'm sure I don't wonder at that," she gabbled on, "for my house is much admired by visitors here. I was thinking of letting it for a few weeks, though I am not sure that it would be convenient to do so just yet, and even if I did, I should have to put some of my treasures away in a little attic at the top of the house, and lock that up. Some heirlooms, you understand. But that's all by the way. I came in, a very odd intrusion I know, to ask if either of you had seen my husband, Mr. Labson—I am Mrs. Labson, as I should have told you—if you'd seen him on the golf-links this afternoon. He went out about two o'clock, and he's not been back. Most unusual, for there's his tea ready for him always at half-past four."

She paused and seemed to listen intently, then went across to the window again and drew the blind aside.

"I thought I heard a step in my garden just out there," she said, "and I wondered if it was Mr. Labson. Such a pleasant little garden, a bit over-grown maybe; I think I saw one of you gentlemen looking down into it last night, when I was taking a breath of air. Or even if you didn't care to take the whole of my house, perhaps you would like a couple of rooms there. I could make everything most comfortable for you, for Mr. Labson always said I was a wonderful cook and manager, and not a word of complaint have I ever had from him all these years. Still, if he's taken it into his head to go off suddenly like this, I should be pleased to have a lodger in the house, for I'm not accustomed to be alone. Being alone in a house was a thing I never could bear."

She turned to our landlord:

"I'll take a room here for to-night," she said, "if Mr. Labson doesn't come back. Perhaps you would send across for a bag into which I have put what I shall want. No; that would never do; I'll go and get it myself, if you would be so good as to come with me as far as the door. One never knows who is about at this time of night. And if Mr. Labson should come here to look for me, don't let him in whatever you do. Say I'm not here; say I've left home for a day or two and have given no address. You don't want Mr. Labson here, for he's not got a penny of his own, and couldn't pay for his board and lodging, and I won't support him in idleness any longer. He ruined me and I'll be even with him yet. I told him——"

The stream of insane babble suddenly ceased; her eyes, fixing themselves on a dusky corner of the room behind where I stood, grew wide with terror, and her mouth gaped. Simultaneously I heard a gasp of startled amazement from Jim, and turned quickly to see what he and Mrs. Labson were looking at.

There he stood, he whom I had seen half an hour ago appearing suddenly in the square, and as suddenly disappearing as he came to the Corner House. Next minute she had flung the door wide and bolted out. Jim and I followed and saw her rush down the passage outside, and through the open door of the bar into the square. Terror winged her feet, and that great misshapen bulk sped away and was lost in the darkness of the fallen night.

We went straight to the police office, and the country was scoured for the mad woman who, I felt sure, was also a murderess. The river was dragged, and about midnight two fishermen found the body below the sluice-gate at the head of the estuary. Search meantime had been made in the Corner House, and her husband's corpse was discovered, strangled with a silk handkerchief, behind the water-butt in the corner of the garden. Close by was a half-dug excavation, where no doubt she had intended to bury him.

XI CORSTOPHINE

Fred Bennett had proposed himself for a visit of a couple of nights, and had said in his letter that he had a curious story to tell me. The date he suggested was perfectly convenient, and he arrived just before dinner. We were alone, but when I hinted that I was more than ready to hear his curious story he said that would come later.

"I want to clear the ground first," he said, "for it is always better to agree or disagree on a principle before you advance your illustration."

"Spook?" I asked, knowing that the occult side of life is far more real to him than the happenings of normal existence.

"I really don't know whether you'll think it is spooky or not," he said. "You may think it is only a coincidence. But, you see, I don't believe in coincidences. There isn't such a thing as blind chance, to my mind: what we call chance is only the working out of a law which we are ignorant of."

"Explain," said I.

"Well, take the rising of the sun. If we were ignorant of the movement of the earth, we should think it a coincidence that the sun will rise to-morrow very nearly at the same time as it rose to-day. But we don't call it a coincidence because we know, more or less, the law that makes it do so. That's clear, isn't it?"

"That will do for the present," I said. "I won't argue yet."

"Right. Now since we know about the movement of the earth, we can safely prophesy that the sun will rise to-morrow. Our knowledge of what is past makes us able to see into the future, and, in fact, we shouldn't call it prophecy at all if we were told the sun would rise to-morrow. In just the same way, if a man had known the exact movement of a certain iceberg, and the exact course of the 'Titanic,' he would have been able to prophesy that the 'Titanic' would founder on that iceberg at a certain moment. Our knowledge of the future, in a word, depends entirely on our knowledge of the past, and if we knew absolutely all about the past, we should know absolutely all about the future."

"Not quite," said I. "A fresh factor might come in."

"But that factor would be dependent on the past, too," he said.

"Is the story going to be as difficult as the preliminaries?" I asked.

He laughed.

"Much more difficult," he said. "At least the explanation is much more difficult, if you don't accept these very simple facts. To my mind the idea that the past and present and future are all really one is the only possible way of accounting for it."

He pushed back his plate, and leaned his elbows on the table, looking fixedly at me. He has the most extraordinary eyes I have ever seen: they seem sometimes to look quite through what they are regarding, and then to come back as from some remote focus to your face again.

"Of course time, the whole sum of time, cannot be more than an infinitesimal point in eternity," he said, "even if it is as much as that. When we get out of time, when we die, in fact, we shall regard time as just a point, visible all round, so to speak. Some people, even now, get glimpses of it in its entirety. We call them clairvoyants: they have visions of the future which are actually and literally fulfilled. Or, perhaps, they have, when they see such things, some revelation of the past which enables them, like the man prophesying about the sinking of the 'Titanic,' to foretell the future. If he had found people to believe him a disaster like that might have been averted. Take it which way you like."

Now Fred, as I already knew, had more than once in his life experienced this mysterious enlightenment, and I guessed now the nature of the curious story of which he had spoken.

"You've seen something," I said, rising. "I long to hear all about it."

The night was very hot, and instead of adjourning to another room, we went out into the garden, where there was some coolness of breeze and dew. The sun was set, but light still lingered in the sky, screeching companies of swifts wheeled overhead, and the warmth drew out in subtle distillation the fragrance from the rose-beds. My servant had already put out a little encampment of basket-chairs and a table with cards, if we felt so disposed, on the lawn, and here we settled ourselves.

"And above all things," I said, "tell me your story fully and at length. Otherwise I shall only be asking questions as to details, and that will interrupt you."

With his permission I give the story very much as he told it me. As he spoke the night darkened round us, the swifts ceased their shrill foraging, and bats took their place with shriller and barely audible squeakings. Occasionally there was the flare of a lit match, and the creak of a basket-chair, but there was no other interruption.

"One evening about three weeks ago," he said, "I was dining with Arthur Temple. His wife and his sister-in-law were there, but about half-past ten they went out to a ball. He hates dancing as much as I do, and proposed that we should have a game of chess. I adore chess, and play it quite atrociously, but when I am playing chess I can think of nothing whatever else. That night, however, things went strangely well, and with trembling excitement I saw that after some twenty moves the unwonted prospect of winning my game was opening out in front of me. I mention this to show that I was very wide-awake and concentrated on what I was doing.

"As I meditated the move which was soon to prove fatal to my adversary, a vision such as I have had once or twice before leaped into being before my eyes. My hand was raised to take hold of my queen, when the chess-board at which I was looking and my actual surroundings entirely vanished, and I was standing on the platform of a railway station. There was a train drawn up by it, out of which I was aware I had just stepped, and I knew I had an hour to wait for the one that was to take me on to my unknown destination. Just opposite me was the board on which was painted the name of the station; this I shall not tell you at present, because you might guess what my story is going to be. But though it seemed perfectly natural that I should be there, I had never at that time, to the best of my knowledge, heard of the name of the station before. There was my luggage on the platform, and I gave it in charge of a porter who was exactly like Arthur Temple, told him that I was going for a walk, and would be back before my train was due.

"It was a very dark afternoon—somehow I knew it was afternoon—and the air oppressively close and sultry, as if a storm was coming up. I walked through the booking office of the station and out into a big yard. To the right were some allotment gardens, beyond which the ground rose rapidly up to a distant line of moors, to the left were rows upon rows of sheds, with tall chimneys vomiting smoke, and in front a long street with huddled houses stretching right and left. They were built of grey discoloured stone, with slate roofs, mean and dismal dwellings, and neither in the station-yard nor in the long perspective of the street in front of me was there a sign of any human being. Probably, I thought, the men and women of the place were engaged in those manufacturing buildings, but there were no children playing on the pavements. The place seemed absolutely deserted, and somehow disquieting and appalling.

"I stood there a moment, hesitating as to whether I should start on a walk among such charmless surroundings or stop in the station and while away the hour with my book. Then I became aware that there was waiting for me something which very closely concerned me, and that whatever it was it lay beyond that long untenanted street. I had to go, though I had no idea where I was going or what I should find. I crossed the yard and started to walk up the street.

"As soon as I got on the move that sense of being obliged to go completely vanished; it had given me the required push, I suppose, and I realised that I was just waiting for my train and filling in the time. The street stretched endlessly in front of me, up a steepish hill, and on each side were these low, two-storied houses. Their doors and windows, in spite of the stifling heat, were all shut, and never a face showed from within, nor was there a single footstep but my own to break the silence. No sparrow fluttered in the eaves or foraged in the gutters; no cat slunk along the house-walls or blinked on the doorsteps; there was nothing visible nor audible of the evidence of life.

"On and on I walked, and presently the street began to show signs of coming to an end. The houses on one side ceased, and I looked over long stretches of grimy fields, tenantless of any grazing beasts. At that, like a blink of distant lightning, there flashed on my mind the notion that I did not see any living things because I no longer had anything to do with the living. All about me probably were children and men and women, and cats and sparrows, but I did not belong to them. I was there in some other capacity, and whatever it was that was of significance for me in this desolate place it was not concerned with life. I can't express it more definitely than that, because the notion itself was indefinite, and it flashed upon me but for a moment and was gone again. Then the houses on the other side of the street came to an end also, and I was walking along a black country road, with stunted hedges on each side. Meantime the dusk was coming rapidly on, a thick and murky dusk, hot and windless. The road made a sharp right-angled turn, and while it was open to the fields on one side the other was bounded by a high stone wall that rose above my head. I was beginning to wonder what this enclosure was when I came to a big iron gate in it, and I saw through the bars that it was a graveyard. Row upon row the tombstones glimmered faintly in the dusk, and at the far end of it only just visible in the gathering darkness were the roofs and small spire of a cemetery chapel. The gate was open, and feeling that there was something here which concerned me, I entered and began walking up an unweeded gravel path in the direction of the chapel. As I did this, I looked at my watch and saw that half of my hour of waiting was nearly spent, and that I must soon be retracing my steps. But I knew I had business here which must be performed.

"The tombstones came to an end, and there was a broad space of open grass between me and the chapel. Then I saw that there was one grave standing alone there, and with that odd curiosity that prompts us to read the names on tombstones I left the path and went to it.

"Though it appeared rather new, glimmering whitely in the dusk, I saw that already moss and lichen had covered the face of it, and I wondered whether it was the grave of some stranger who had died a lonely death here, and had no one, friend or relation, who looked after it. The name, whatever it was, was quite overgrown, and with some impulse of pity for him who lay below, and had so soon been forgotten, I began scraping it with the ferule of my stick. The moss peeled off quite easily, coming away in long shreds and fibres, and presently I saw that the name was visible. But as I worked the darkness had so gathered that I could not read it, and I lit a match and held it to the surface of the stone. And the name I read there was my own.

"I heard myself give some exclamation of surprise and horror, and immediately afterwards I heard Arthur Temple's laugh, and then again I was in his room, staring at the chess-board, and looking with dismay at the move he had made. I had not anticipated that, and my wonderful plan was ruined.

"'For half a minute,' he said, 'I thought you had got me.' A few moves were sufficient to bring the game to a most undesired conclusion, and after a short chat I went home. The vision apparently had lasted just the space of his own move, for mine was already being made when it began."

He paused, and I supposed the story was over.

"What an odd affair," I said, "it's just one of those meaningless but interesting intrusions into everyday life, coming from God knows where, which doesn't lead to anything. What was the name of the station, by the way? Did you take the trouble to find out whether your vision resembled the actual place? Was that the coincidence?"

I was, I confess, rather disappointed, though indeed, he had been telling his story very well. But like so many of these strange glimpses which clairvoyants and mediums seem genuinely to get into the world of powers and unseen agencies, which we know lies so closely round us, and sometimes manifests itself to the senses of those who are still on the material plane, it seemed so pointless. Even if it turned out that eventually he was buried in the cemetery of this twilit, untenanted town, what good would it have done him to have known of that before it happened? What is the use of communications between this world and some other world inaccessible to the ordinary perceptions of mankind if these communications contain nothing that is of value or interest?

He looked at me with that distant penetrating glance, which seemed to be focused on some inconceivable remoteness, and laughed.

"No, that wasn't the coincidence," he said, "at least that coincidence, if you call it so, is not the point of the story. As for the name of the station, that will come very soon now."

"Oh, there is more then, is there?" I asked.

"Certainly, you told me to tell it you at length. That's only the prologue, or the first act. Shall I go on?"

"Yes, of course. Sorry."

"Well there I was again in Arthur's room, the whole vision had lasted perhaps a minute, and he was quite unaware that I had done anything but stare at the chess-board, and when he made that move which upset my plans, give a cry of surprise and dismay.... And then as I told you, we talked for a little, and he mentioned that he and his wife were possibly going up to Yorkshire for Whitsuntide, to a place called Helyat, which she had lately inherited on the death of an uncle. It was up on the moors, he said, with a little shooting in the autumn, and just now some rather good trout fishing. If they went, they would be there for a fortnight or so; perhaps I would come up for a week, if I was doing nothing particular. I said I should be delighted to, but this was contingent, of course, on their going, and the matter was left vague. I saw neither of them again, nor did I hear any more till, ten days afterwards, I got a telegram from him—he always sends a telegram in preference to a letter, because he says it receives more attention—asking me to come up as soon as ever I liked. If I would let him know the day and the time of my train, they would meet me: their station was Helyat. Helyat, I may say, was not the name of the station in the vision I have told you."

"There was an ABC time-table in the house, I looked out Helyat, found a train that started and arrived at convenient hours, and I telegraphed to Arthur that I would travel by it next day. So that was settled.

"The weather in London that week had been extremely oppressive, and I welcomed the idea of getting up on to the Yorkshire moors. Moreover, since the day when I had experienced that odd vision I had gone about with a strong sense of some impending disaster. I told myself in the way one does, that the heat and sultriness of town were responsible for my depressed spirits, but I knew very well that it was the vision that lay at the root of them. I never shook off the consciousness of it, it lay like some leaden weight upon me, it got between the normal sunlight of life and myself like some menacing thunder-cloud. And now, the moment that I had sent off that telegram, the exhilaration at the thought of getting into a high and bracing air completely passed, and the dread of some imminent peril took such possession of me that I very nearly sent a second telegram on the heels of the first to say that I could not manage to come after all. But why I connected these forebodings with my journey or my stay at Helyat I had no idea, and search my mind as I might there was no conceivable reason for doing so. I told myself that this was one of those causeless fears which sometimes obsess people of the steadiest nerves, and that to yield to it was to take a definite step in the direction of mental unbalance. It would never do to let oneself become the prey of such unreasonable terrors.

"I made up my mind therefore to go through it with, not only for the sake of not losing a pleasant week in the country, but even more for the sake of proving to myself the unreasonableness of my fears. I arrived accordingly at the terminus next morning, with a quarter of an hour to spare, found a corner seat, engaged a place in the restaurant-car for lunch, and settled down. Just before the train started the ticket-inspector came round, and as he clipped my ticket, looked at the name of my destination.

"'Change at Corstophine, sir,' he said, and now you know the name of the station at which I alighted in that vision.

"I felt panic invading my very bones, but I asked one question.

"'Do I wait there long?' I said.

"He consulted a time-table which he pulled out of his pocket.

"'Just an hour, sir,' he said. 'A branch line takes you on to Helyat.'"

I broke my determination not to interrupt him.

"Corstophine?" I said, "I've seen that name lately in the paper."

"So have I. We're just coming to that," said he. "And then the panic grew beyond my control. I could not resist it any longer, and I got out of the train. With some difficulty I managed to obtain my luggage from the van, and I sent a telegram to Arthur Temple saying I was detained. A minute later the train started, and there I was on the platform, already terribly ashamed of myself, but knowing in some interior cell of my brain that I was right in doing what I had done. In some manner, as yet inscrutable to me, I had obeyed the warning which I had received ten days ago.

"I dined that evening at my club, and after dinner read in an evening paper about a terrible railway accident that had occurred during the afternoon at Corstophine. The fast train from London, by which I should have travelled, stopped there at 2.53 p.m.; the train taking the branch line which goes up into the moors and stops at Helyat was due to start at 3.54; it starts, so said the account, from the down platform, crosses on to the up line along which it runs for some hundred yards, and then branches off to the right. About the same time an up-express is due to pass through Corstophine without stopping. Usually the local train to Helyat waits on the down-line for it to pass; this afternoon, however, the express was late, and the Helyat train was signalled to start. Whether owing to a mistake of the signalman, who had not put up the signal against the express, or whether the driver of the express had not seen it, was not yet clear, but what had happened was that while the Helyat train was on the section of the up-line, the express, running at full speed to make up time, dashed into it. The engine and front carriage of the express was wrecked, and the other train reduced simply to matchwood: the express had gone through it like a bullet."

Again he paused; this time I did not interrupt.

"So, there was my vision," he said, "and there was the interpretation of the warning it sent me. But there remains a little more to tell you, which, to my mind, is as curious from the point of view of the scientific investigator of such phenomena as anything yet. It is this:

"I instantly made up my mind to start for Helyat next day. Vision and fulfilment alike, as far as I was concerned, had done their work, and I had an immense curiosity to ascertain whether all the imagery and scenery of the vision had an actual existence here on earth, or whether it was an impulse, so to speak, from the immaterial world, clothing itself in forms of time and space. I must confess that I hoped it was the former, that I should find at Corstophine what I imagined I had seen there, for that would show me how closely the two worlds are interlinked or dovetailed together, so that the one can use for our mortal sense the scenery of the other.... So I telegraphed again to Arthur Temple, saying that I should arrive at the same hour next day.

"Again, therefore, I went to the London terminus, and again the ticket inspector told me I must change at Corstophine. The papers that morning were full of this terrible accident, but he assured me that the line was already clear, and that I should get through. An hour before we were due there we passed into the black country of collieries and manufacture, the sun was hidden in the murk of the smoke-belching chimneys, and when we stopped at the station where I was to change, the earth was shrouded under that gross and unnatural twilight in which I had seen it before. And exactly as before, I gave my luggage in charge of the porter, and set out to explore a place I had never seen but knew with a vividness which no normal exercise of memory can give. There, on the right of the station yard, were the allotment gardens, behind which rose the line of moors, among which, no doubt, Helyat lay, and there, to the left, were the roofs of sheds, with tall chimneys vomiting smoke, and there in front of me was the mean steep street stretching into an endless perspective. But to-day, instead of finding a dead and uninhabited town, it was full of busy crowds hurrying about. Children were playing in the gutters; cats sat and made their toilets on doorsteps; the sparrows pecked at the refuse heaps that strewed the road. That seemed natural; when my spirit, or my astral body or whatever you care to call it, visited Corstophine before I belonged, potentially, to the dead, and the living were outside my ken. Now, potentially, I belonged to the living, and they swarmed about me.

"I went quickly up the street, for from my previous experience I knew that there was not more than time to go to the place which I must visit, and return to catch my train. It was swelteringly hot, and curiously dark: the darkness increased every moment as I hurried along. Then the houses on the left came to an end, and I looked over grimy fields, and then the houses on the right ceased also, and the road made a sharp turn. Presently I was walking below the stone wall, too high to look over, and there was the iron gate ajar, and the rows of tombstones within, and against the blackened sky the roofs and spire of the cemetery chapel. Once more I passed up the grass-grown gravel, and there was an empty space in front of the chapel, with just one gravestone standing apart from the rest.

"I crossed the grass to it and saw that it was overgrown with moss and lichen. I scraped with my stick the surface of the stone on which was cut the name of the man who lay below it—or woman, maybe—and then, lighting a match, for it was impossible to read the letters in the darkness, I saw that it was my own name and none other that was chiselled there. There was no date, there was no text; there was just my name and nothing else."

He paused again. Sometime during the course of his story, my servant must have brought out a tray of syphons and whisky, and put on the table a lamp that now burned there unwaveringly in the still air. But I had not been aware of his coming or going; I had known no more of it than Fred had known of his opponent's move at chess while the vision filled the field of his conscious perceptions. He helped himself to something, I did the same, and he spoke again.

"It is arguable," he said, "that at some time in my life I had been to Corstophine, and had done exactly what I did in my vision. I can't prove that I haven't, because I can't account for every day that I have spent since I was born. I can only say that I have absolutely no recollection of having done so, or of ever having heard of such a place as Corstophine. But if I had, it is on the cards that my vision was only a recollection, and that its preventing my going to Corstophine on a particular day when, if I had gone there, I should certainly have been killed in a railway accident was only a coincidence. If that had happened, and if my body had been identified, my remains would certainly have been buried in that cemetery, because my executor would have found in my will the wish that, unless there were strong reasons for the contrary, I should be buried in the graveyard nearest to the place in which I had died. Naturally I don't care what happens to my body when I have done with it, and I don't want it to be a sentimental nuisance to other people."

He sat up, stretched himself, and laughed.

"That would have been a very elaborate coincidence," he said, "and the coincidence would have had a longer arm than ever, if they had observed that close to my grave there was buried another Fred Bennett. I must say that the simpler explanation appeals to me more."

"And what is the simpler explanation?" I asked.

"The one that you really believe in, though your reason revolts against it because it has not the faintest idea of the law that lies behind it. It's a law all the same, though it doesn't manifest itself so often as that which governs the rising of the sun. Let's say, then, that it's a law loosely analogous to that which regulates the appearance of comets, though of course it is far more frequent in its manifestations. Perhaps it requires for its manifestation a certain psychical perception given to some people and not to others, just in the same way as it requires a certain physical perception to hear the squeal of those bats which are flitting overhead. I can't hear them personally, but I think you told me before that you can. I perfectly accept your word for it, though the noise doesn't reach my senses."

"And the law?" I asked.

"The law is that in the real world, in the true existence beyond the 'muddy vesture of decay,' the past and the present and the future are one. They are a point in eternity which can be perceived and handled all round. Difficult to express, but that's the kind of thing. Occasionally, and in the case of some people the muddy vesture can be stripped off, though only intermittently and for a moment, and then they perceive and know. It's very simple really, and, as a matter of fact, you believe it all the time."

"I know I do," said I, "but just because it is so rare, and because it is so abnormal, I want to try to account for everything of the sort which I hear by an extension of the physical senses. Thought reading, telepathy, suggestion: all these are natural phenomena. We know a little about them, and we've got to exclude them first before we accept anything so strange as a vision of the future."

"Exclude them, then," he said. "I'm quite with you. But you mustn't think that I put clairvoyance or knowledge of the future on a different plane to any of those. It's only an extension of a natural law, a branch line, so to speak, that led to Helyat, off the main line. It's part of the system."

There was something to think about there, and we were both silent. I could hear the squeak of the bats, and Fred couldn't, but I should have thought it very materialistic of him to deny that I heard them just because his ears were deaf to them. I thought over the story, point by point; and, as he had said, I knew I really agreed with him on the principle that from somewhere out of what we think of as the great void, merely because we do not rightly know what is there, there did come, and had come, and would come these wireless messages to the receivers that were in tune with them. There was the dead town of his vision, uninhabited, because potentially he was of the dead, and then it became a live town, because, having taken the warning, he was of the living. And then a bright and brilliant and go-to-bed notion struck me.

"Ha! I've picked a hole," I said. "When you saw the vision, Corstophine was without inhabitants, because you were dead. Wasn't it so?"

He laughed again.

"I know exactly what you are going to ask," he said. "You're going to ask about the porter at the station to whom I gave my luggage. I can't explain that. Perhaps his appearance was like the last conscious view of the anæsthetist, who stands by you when you are having gas, and is the final link with the material world. He was like Arthur Temple, you will remember."

XII THE TEMPLE

Frank Ingleton and I had left London early in July with the intention of spending a couple of months at least in Cornwall. This sojourn was not by any means to be a complete holiday, for he was a student of those remains of prehistoric civilisation which are found in such mysterious abundance in the ancient county, and I was employed on a book which should have already been approaching completion, but which was still lamentably far from its consummation. Naturally there was to be a little golf and a little sea-bathing for relaxation, but we were both keen on our work and meant to have gathered in a respectable harvest of industry before we returned.

The village of St. Caradoc, from all accounts, seemed likely to be favourable to our projects, for there were remains in the neighbourhood which had never been thoroughly investigated by any archæologist, and its position on the map, remote from any of the more celebrated holiday centres, promised a reasonable tranquillity. It supplied also the desirable relaxations; the club-house of a pleasantly hazardous golf-course stood at the bottom of the hotel garden, and five minutes' walk across the sand-dunes among which the holes were placed, led to the beach. The hotel was comfortable, and at present half-empty, and fortune seemed to smile on our undertakings. We settled down, therefore, without further plans. Frank meant, before he left, to visit other parts of the county, but here, within a mile of the hotel, was that curious circle of monoliths, like some Stonehenge in miniature, known as the "Council of Penruth." It had always been supposed, so Frank told me, that it was some place of Druidical worship, but he distrusted the conclusion and wanted to study it minutely on the spot.

I went there with him by way of an evening saunter on the second day after our arrival. The shortest way was along the sand-dunes, and thence up a steep, grassy slope on to the ploughed stretches of the uplands. In that warm, soft climate the wheat was in full ear, and beginning already to turn ripe and tawny. A very narrow path led across these cornfields to our destination, and from far off one could see the circle of stones, four to five feet high, standing there, black and austere, against the yellowing grain. Though all the country round was in cultivation no plough had furrowed the interior of the circle, and inside was the ancient turf of the downs, short and velvety, with patches of thyme and hare-bells. It seemed odd; a plough could have passed backwards and forwards between the monoliths and a half-acre of land have been made fruitful.

"But why isn't it ploughed?" I asked.

"Oh, you're in the land of superstitions and ancient sorceries," he said. "These circles are never touched or made use of. And do you see, the path across the fields by which we have come passes round it; it doesn't run across it. There it goes again on the far side, pursuing the same line, after making the detour."

He laughed.

"The farmer of the land was up here this morning when I was making some measurements," he said. "He went round it, I noticed, and when his dog came inside after some interesting smell, he called it back, and cuffed it, and rapped out: 'Come out of that there; and never do you go within again.'"

"But what's the idea?" I asked.

"Something clings to it, some curse, some abomination. They think no doubt, just as the archæologists do, that the place has been a Druidical temple, where dreadful rites were performed and human sacrifices made. But they are all wrong; this was never a temple at all, it was a Council Chamber, and the very name of it, the 'Council of Penruth,' confirms that. No doubt there was a temple somewhere about; dearly should I like to find it."

It had been hot work climbing up that steep, slippery hillside from the village, and we sat down within the circle, leaning our backs against two adjacent stones, and as we sat and rested Frank explained to me the grounds of his belief.

"If you care to count them," he said, "you'll find there are twenty-one of these monoliths, against two of which you and I are leaning, and if you care to measure the distances between them you will find that they are all equal. Each stone, in fact, represents the seat of a member of the council of twenty-one. But if the place had been a temple there would have been a larger gap between two of the stones towards the east, where the gate of the temple was, facing the rising sun, and somewhere within the circle, probably exactly in the middle, there would have been a large, flat stone, which was the stone of sacrifice, where no doubt human victims were offered. Or, if the stone had disappeared, there would have been a depression where it once was. Those are the distinguishing marks of a temple, and this place lacks them. It has always been assumed that it was a temple, and it has been described as such. But I am sure I am right about it."

"But there is a temple somewhere about?" I asked.

"Certain to be. If any of these prehistoric settlements was large enough to have a council hall, it would certainly have had a temple, though the remains of it have very likely disappeared. When the country was Christianised, the old religion—if you can call it a religion—was reckoned an abomination, and the places of worship were destroyed, just as the Israelites destroyed the groves of Baal. But I mean to explore very thoroughly here: there may be remains in some of those woods down there. This is just the sort of remote place where the temple might have escaped destruction."

"And what was the ancient religion?" I asked.

"Very little is known about it. It certainly was a religion not of love but fear. The gods were the blind powers of nature, manifesting themselves in storms and destruction and plague, and had to be propitiated with human sacrifices. And the priests, of course, dealt in magic and sorcery. They were the governing class, and kept their power alive by terror. If you offended them, as likely as not you would be sent for and told that the gods required your eldest son as a blood-offering next mid-summer day at sunrise when the first beams of morning shone through the eastern gate of the temple. It was wise to be a good churchman in those days."

"It looks a kindly country nowadays," I said. "The temples of the old gods are empty."

"Yes, but it's extraordinary how old superstitions linger. It isn't a year ago that there was a witch-craft trial in Penzance. The cattle belonging to some farmer near here began to pine and die, and he went to an old woman who said that a spell had been cast on them, and that if he paid her she could remove it. He went on paying and paying, and at last got tired of that and prosecuted her instead."

He looked at his watch.

"Let's take a stroll before dinner," he said. "Instead of going back the way we came, we might make a ramble down the hillside in front and through the woods. They look rather attractive."

"And may conceal a pagan temple," said I, getting up.

We skirted the harvest fields, and found a path leading through a big fir-wood that climbed up the hillside. The trees were of no great growth as regards height, and the prevalent wind from the south-west, to which they stood exposed, had combed and pressed their branches landwards. But the foliage of the tree-tops was very dense, making a curious sombre twilight as we penetrated deeper into the wood. There was no undergrowth whatever below them, the ground was spread thick and smooth with fallen pine needles, and with the tree trunks rising straight and column-like and that thick roof of branches above, the place looked like some great hall of nature's building. No whisper of wind moved overhead, and so dark and still was it that you might easily have conceived yourself to be walking up the aisle of some walled-in place. The smell of the firs was thick in the air like incense, and the foot went noiselessly as over spread carpets. No birds flitted between the tree trunks or called to each other, the only noise was the murmurous buzz of flies, which sounded like some long-held organ note.

It had been hot enough outside in the fresh draught off the sea, but here where no breeze winnowed the air it was stiflingly close, and as we plunged deeper into the dimness I was conscious of some gathering oppression of the spirit. It was an uncomfortable place, it seemed thick with unseen presences. And the same notion must have struck Frank as well.

"I feel as if we were being watched," he said. "There are eyes peeping at us from behind the trunks, and they don't like us. Now what makes so silly an idea enter my head?"

"A grove of Baal is it?" I suggested. "One that has escaped destruction and is full of the spirits of murderous priests."

"I wish it was," he said. "Then we could inquire the way to the temple."

Suddenly he pointed ahead.

"Hullo, what's that?" he said.

I followed the direction of his finger, and for one half-second thought I saw the glimmer of something white moving among the trees. But before I could focus it it was gone. Somehow, the heat and the oppression had got on my nerves.

"Well, it's not our wood," I said. "I suppose other people have just as much right to walk here. But I've had enough of tree-trunks, I should like to have done with the wood."

Even as I spoke, I saw it was getting lighter in front of us; glimmers of day began to show between the thick-set trunks, and presently we found ourselves threading the last row of the trees. The light of day poured in again and the stir of the sea breeze; it was like coming out of some crowded and airless building into the open air.

We emerged into a delectable place; a broad stretch of downland turf was spread in front of us, smooth and ancient turf like that in the circle, jewelled with thyme and centaury and bugloss. The path we had been following lay straight across this, and dipping down over the edge of it we came suddenly on the most enchanting little house, low and two-storied, standing in a small enclosure of lawn and garden beds. The hill behind it had evidently once been quarried, but long ago, for now the sheer sides of it were overgrown with a tangle of ivy and briony, and at their base lay a pool of water. Beyond and bordering the lawn was a copse of birches and hornbeams, which half encircled the clearing in which stood house and garden. The house itself, smothered in honeysuckle and climbing fuchsia, seemed unoccupied, for the chimneys were smokeless and the blinds drawn down over the windows. As we turned the corner of its low fence and came on to the front of it, the impression was verified, for there by the gate was a notice proclaiming that it was to be let furnished, and directing that application should be made to a house agent in St. Caradoc's.

"But it's a pocket Paradise," said I. "Why shouldn't we——"

Frank interrupted me.

"Of course there's no reason why we shouldn't," he said. "In fact, there's every reason why we should. The manager at the hotel told me they were filling up next week and wanted to know for how long we should stop. We'll make inquiries tomorrow morning, and find the agent and the keys."

The keys next morning revealed a charm within that came up to the promise of what we had seen without, and, what was as wonderful, the agent could provide our staff as well. This consisted of a rotund and capable Cornishwoman who, with her daughter to help her, would arrive early every morning, and remain till she had served our dinner, and then go back to her cottage in St. Caradoc's. If that would suffice us, she was ready to be in charge as soon as we settled to take the little house; it must be understood, however, that she would not sleep there. Without making any further inquiries, the assurance that she was a clean and capable cook and competent in every way was enough, and two days afterwards we entered into possession. The rent asked was extraordinarily low, and my suspicious mind, as we went through the house, visualised an absence of water-supply or a kitchen range that, while getting red hot, left its ovens as in the chill of an Arctic night. But no such dispiriting discoveries awaited us; Mrs. Fennell turned taps and manipulated dampers, and, scouring capably through the house, pronounced on her solemn guarantee that we should be very comfortable. "But I go back to my own house at night, gentlemen," she said, "and I promise you the water will be hot and your breakfast ready for you by eight in the morning."

We entered that afternoon; our luggage had been sent up an hour before, and when we arrived the portmanteaux were already unpacked and clothes bestowed in their drawers, and tea ready in the sitting-room. It and its adjoining dining-room with a small parqueted hall, formed the ground floor accommodation. Beyond the dining-room was the kitchen, the convenience of which had already satisfied Mrs. Fennell. Upstairs there were two good bedrooms, and above the kitchen two smaller servants' rooms, which, by our arrangement, would be unoccupied. There was a bathroom between the two bedrooms with a door into it from each; for two friends occupying the house nothing could have been more exactly what was wanted with nothing to spare. Mrs. Fennell gave us an admirable plain dinner, and by nine o'clock she had locked the outer kitchen door and left us.

Before going to bed we wandered out into the garden, marvelling at our luck. The hotel, as the manager had told us, was already beginning to fill up, the dining-room to-night would have been a cackle of voices, the sitting-room crowded, and surely it was a wonderfully good exchange to be housed in this commodious little tranquillity of a place, with our own unobtrusive establishment that came at dawn and left at night. It remained only to see if this paragon who was so proficient in her kitchen would be as punctual in the morning.

"But I wonder why she and her daughter would not establish themselves here," said Frank. "They live alone down in the village. You'd have thought that they would have shut their cottage up, and saved themselves a morning and evening tramp."

"Gregariousness," said I. "They like to know that there are people, just people, close at hand and to right and left. I like to know that there are not. I like——"

As I spoke we turned at the garden gate, where the notice that the house was to let had been, and my eyes, quite idly, travelled across the space of open downland to the black fringe of the wood that stood above it, and for a moment, bright, and then quenched again like the line of fire made by a match that has been struck and has not flared, I saw a light there. It was only for a second that it was visible, but it must have been somewhere inside the wood, for against that luminous streak I saw the shape of the fir trunks.

"Did you see that?" I said to Frank.

"A light in the wood?" he asked. "Yes, it has appeared there several times. Just for a moment and then disappearing again. Some farmer, perhaps, finding his way home."

That was a very sensible conclusion, and, for some reason that I did not trouble to probe, my mind hastened to adopt it. After all, who was more likely to be passing through the wood than men from the upland farms going home at closing time from the Red Lion at St. Caradoc's?

XII THE TEMPLE

I was roused next morning out of very deep sleep by the entry of Mrs. Fennell with hot water; it was a struggle to join myself up with the waking world again. I had the impression of having dreamed very vividly of things dark and dim, and of perilous places, and though I had certainly slept for something like eight hours at a stretch I felt curiously unrefreshed. At breakfast Frank was more silent than his wont, but presently we were making plans for the day. He proposed to explore the wood again, while I was busy with my work; in the afternoon a round of golf would bring us to teatime. Before he started and I settled down, we strolled about the garden that dozed tranquilly in the hot morning sun, and again congratulated ourselves on our exchange from the hotel. We went down to the pool below the quarried cliff, and there I left him to return to the house, while he, in order to start exploring at once, followed an overgrown path that led into the copse of birch and hornbeam of which I have spoken. But I had not crossed the lawn before I heard myself called.

"Come here a minute," he shouted, "I've found something interesting." I retraced my steps, and pushing through the trees found him standing by a tall, black granite stone that pushed its moss-green head above the undergrowth.

"It's a monolith," he said excitedly. "It's like one of those stones in the circle. Perhaps there has been another circle here, or, perhaps, it's a stone of the temple. It's deep in the earth, it looks as if it was in place. Let's see if we can find another in this copse."

He pushed on into the thick growing trees to the right of the path, and I, infected with his enthusiasm, made an exploration to the left. Before long I came upon another stone of the same character as the first, and my shout of discovery was echoed by his. Yet another rewarded his hunting, and as I emerged from the copse on the edge of the quarry pool I found a fifth, standing but fallen forward in a bed of rushes that fringed the water.

In the excitement of this find, my planned studiousness was, of course, abandoned; so, too, when we had eaten a hearty lunch, was the projected game of golf, and before evening we had arrived at a rough scheme of the entire place. Most of the stones were in the belt of copse that half-encircled the house, and with a tape-measure we found that these were set at uniform intervals from each other except that exactly twice that interval separated the two stones that lay due east of the circle. In the bank that lay to the south of the house several were missing, but in each case, by digging at the proper intervals, we found fragments of granite grassed over in the soil, which indicated that these stones had been broken up and used, probably, for building materials, and this conjecture of Frank's was confirmed by the discovery of pieces of granite built into the walls of the house we occupied.

He had jotted down the approximate position of the stones, and passed over to me the paper on which he had drawn his plan.

"Without doubt it's a temple," he said, "there's the double interval at the east, which I told you about, and which was the gate into it."

I looked at what he had drawn.

"Then our house stands just in the centre of it," I said.

"Yes; what vandals they were to build it just there," said he. "Probably the stone of sacrifice lies somewhere below it. Good Lord, dinner ready, Mrs. Fennell? I had no idea it was so late."

The sky had clouded over during the afternoon, and while we sat at dinner, a windless and heavy rain began to fall and thunder to mutter over the sea. Mrs. Fennell came in to enquire into our tastes for to-morrow, and as there was every appearance of a violent storm approaching, I asked her whether she and her girl would not stop here for the night and save themselves a wetting.

"No, I'll be off now, sir, thank you," she said. "We don't mind a wetting in Cornwall."

"But not very good for your rheumatism," I said. She had mentioned that she was a sufferer in this respect.

A blink of lightning flashed rather vividly across the uncurtained windows, and the rain hissed more heavily.

"No, I'll be off now," she said, "for it's late already. Good night, gentlemen."

We heard her turn the key in the kitchen door, and presently the figures of herself and her girl passed the window.

"Not even umbrellas," said Frank. "They'll be drenched before they get down."

"I wonder why they wouldn't stop," said I.

Frank was soon employed on preparations for a plan to scale that he was meaning to make to-morrow, and he began putting in the house, which he had ascertained stood just in the centre of the temple. The size of the ground plan of it was all he required on the scale he intended for the complete plan, and after measuring the sitting-room, passage, and dining-room, he went through into the kitchen. Meanwhile, I had settled down to the work I had intended to do this morning, and proposed to get a couple of solid hours at it before I went to bed. It was rather hard to get the thread of it again, and for some time I floundered with false starts and erased sentences, but before long I got into better form, and was already happily absorbed in it when he called me from the kitchen.

"Oh, I can't come," I said, "I'm busy."

"Just a moment, please," he shouted.

I laid down my pen and went to him. He had moved the kitchen table aside and turned up the drugget that covered the floor.

"Look there!" he said.

The floor was paved with stone of the district, very likely from the quarry just outside. But in the centre was an oblong slab of granite, some six feet by four in dimensions.

"That's a whacking big stone," I said. "Odd of them to have been at the trouble of putting that there."

"They didn't," said he. "I'll bet it was there when they laid the floor!"

Then I understood.

"The stone of sacrifice?" I asked.

"Rather. Granite and just in the centre of the temple. It can't be anything else."

Some sudden thrill of horror seized me. It was on that stone that young boys and maidens, torn from their mother's arms and bound hand and foot, were laid, while the priest, with one hand over the victim's eyes, plunged the flint knife into the smooth, white throat, sawing through the tissue till the blood spurted from the severed artery.... In the flickering light of the candle Frank carried the stone seemed wet and darkly glistening, and was that noise only the rain volleying on the roof, or the beating of drums to drown the cries of the victim?...

"It's terrible," I said. "I wish you hadn't found it."

Frank was on his knees by it, examining the surface of it. "I can't say I agree with you," he said. "It just puts the final touch of certainty on my discovery. Besides, whether I had found it or not, it would have been there just the same."

"Well, I'm going on with my work," I said. "It's more cheerful than stones of sacrifice."

He laughed.

"I hope it's as interesting," he said.

It appeared, when I went back to it, that it was not, and try as I would I could not recapture the interest which is necessary to production of any kind. Even my eye wandered from the words I wrote; as for my mind, it would give only the most cursory glance at that for which I demanded its fixed attention. It was busy elsewhere. I found myself, at its bidding, scrutinizing the shadowy corners of the room, but there was nothing there, and all the time some strange darkness, blacker than that which pressed in upon the house, began to grow upon my spirit. There was fear mingled with it, though I did not know what I was afraid of, but chiefly it was some sort of despair and depression, distant as yet and undefined, but quietly closing in upon me.... As I sat with my pen still in my hand, trying to analyse these perturbed and troubled sensations, I heard Frank call out sharply from the kitchen, the door of which, on my return, I had left open.

"Hullo!" he cried. "What's that? Is anyone there?"

I jumped from my seat and went to join him. He was standing close to the stove, holding his candle above his head, and looking at the door into the garden, which Mrs. Fennell had locked on her departure.

"What's the matter?" I asked.

He looked round at me, startled by the sound of my voice.

"Curious," he said, "I was just measuring the stone, when out of the corner of my eye I thought I saw that door open. But it's locked, isn't it?"

He tried the handle, but sure enough it was locked.

"Optical delusion," he said. "Well, I've finished here for the present. But what a night! Frightfully oppressive, isn't it? And not a breath of air stirring."

We went back to the sitting-room. I put away my laboured manuscript and we got out the cards for a game of piquet. But after one *partie*, he rose with a yawn.

"I really don't think I could keep awake for another," he said, "I'm heavy with sleep. Let's have a breath of air, the rain seems to have stopped, and go to bed. Or are you going to sit up and work?"

I had not meant to do so, but his suggestion made me determine to have another try. There was certainly some mysterious pall of depression on me, and the wisest thing to do was to fight it.

"I shall try for half an hour," I said, "and see how it goes," and I followed him to the front door of the house. The rain, as he said, had ceased, but the darkness was impenetrable, and shuffling with our feet, we took a few steps along the gravel path to the corner of the house. There the light from the sitting-room windows cast a circle of illumination, and one could see the flower-beds glistening with the wet. Though it was night, the air was still so hot that the gravel path was steaming. Beyond that nothing was visible of the lawn or the hill that sloped up to the fir-wood. But, as we stood there, I saw, as last night, a light moving up there. Now, however, it seemed to be outside the wood, for its progress was not interrupted by the tree-trunks.

Frank saw it too, and pointed at it.

"It's too wet to-night," he said, "but to-morrow evening, I vote we go up there, and see who these nightly wanderers are. It's coming closer, and there's another of them."

Even as we looked a third light sprang up, and in another moment all had vanished again.

I carried out my intention of trying to work, but I could make nothing of it, and presently I found myself nodding over a page that contained nothing but erasures. With head bent forward, I drifted into a doze and from dozing into sleep, and when I woke I found the lamp burning low and the wick smouldering. I seemed to have come back from some very distant place, and, only half awake, I lit a candle and quenched the lamp and went to the windows to bolt them. And then my heart stood still, for I thought I saw someone standing outside and looking in through the intervening glass. But it must have been a sleepy fancy, for now, broad awake again, I was staring at my own reflection cast by the candle on the window. I told myself that what I had seen was no more than that, but as I creaked my way upstairs I found myself asking if I really believed that....

As I dressed next morning, after another long but unrefreshing night, I began puzzling over a lost memory to which I had tried to find the clue yesterday. There was a bookcase in the sitting-room with some two or three dozen volumes in it, and opening one or two of these I had found the name Samuel Townwick inscribed in them. I knew I had seen that name not so many months ago in the daily Press, but I could not recapture the connection in which I had read it; but from the recurrence of it in these books it was reasonable to conjecture that he was the owner of the house we occupied. In taking it, his name had not come up; the house agent had plenary powers, and our deposit of a fortnight's rent clinched the contract. But this morning the name still haunted me, and since I had other small businesses in St. Caradoc's, I settled to walk down there and make some definite inquiry at the agent's. Frank was too busy with his plan to accompany me, and I set out alone.

The feeling of depression and vague foreboding was more leaden than ever this morning, and I was aware by that sixth sense, which needs no speech or language, that he was a prey to the same causeless weight. But I had not gone fifty yards from the house when the burden of it was lifted from me, and I knew again the exhilaration proper to such a morning. The rain of last evening had cleared the air, the sea breeze drew lightly landwards and, as if I had come out of some tunnel, I rejoiced in the morning splendour. The village hummed with holiday: Mr. Cranston received me with polite enquiries as to our comfort and Mrs. Fennell's capability, and having assured him on that score, I approached my point.

"Mr. Samuel Townwick is the owner, is he not?" I asked.

The agent's smile faded a little.

"He was, sir," he said. "I act for the executors."

Suddenly, in a flash, some of what I had been groping for came back to me. "I begin to remember," I said. "He died suddenly; there was an inquest. I want to know the rest. Hadn't you better tell me?"

He shifted his glance and came back to me again.

"It was a painful affair," he said. "The executors naturally do not want it talked about."

Another glimpse of what I had forgotten blinked on my memory.

"Suicide," I said. "The usual verdict of unsound mind was brought in. And—and is that why Mrs. Fennell won't sleep in the house? She left last night in a deluge of rain."

I readily gave him my promise of secrecy, for I had not the slightest desire to tell Frank, and he told me the rest. Mr. Townwick had been for some days in a very depressed state of mind, and one morning the servants coming down had found him lying underneath the kitchen table with his throat cut. Beside him was a sharp, curiously-shaped fragment of flint covered with blood. The jagged nature of the wound had confirmed the idea that he had sawn at his throat till he had severed the jugular vein. Murder was ruled out, for he was a strong man, and there were no marks on his body or about the room of there having been any struggle, nor any sign of an assailant having entered. Both kitchen doors were locked on the inside, his valuables were untouched, and from the position of the body the only reasonable inference was that he had laid down under the table, and there deliberately done himself to death.... I repeated my assurance of silence and went out.

I knew now what the source of my nameless horror and depression had been. It was no haunting spectre of Townwick that I feared; it was the power, whatever that was, which had driven him to kill himself on the stone of sacrifice.

I went back up the hill: there was the garden blazing in the July noon, and the sweet tranquillity of the place was spread abroad in the air. But I had no sooner passed the copse and come within the circle than the dead weight of something unseen began to lay its burden on me again. There *was* something here, horrible and menacing and potent.

I found Frank in the sitting-room. His head was bent over his plan, and he started as I entered.

"Hullo!" he said. "I've made all my measurements and I want to sit tight and finish my plan to-day. I don't know why, but I feel I must hurry about it and get it done. And I've got the most awful fit of the blues. I can't account for it, but anyhow, occupation is the best thing. Go in to lunch, will you, I don't want any."

I looked at him and saw some indefinable change had come over his face. There was terror in his eyes that came from within: I can express it in no other way than that.

"Anything wrong?" I asked.

"No; just blues. I want to go on working. This evening, you know, we have to see where those lights come from."

All afternoon he sat close over his work, and it was not till the day was fading that he got up.

"That's done," he said. "Good Lord, we have found a temple and a half! And I'm horribly tired. I shall have a snooze till dinner."

The invasion of fear beleaguered me, it seemed to pour in through the open windows in the gathering dusk, it gathered its reinforcements outside, ready to support the onrush of it. And yet how childish it was to yield to it. By now we were alone in the house, for we had told Mrs. Fennell that a cold meal would serve us in this heat, and while Frank slept I had heard the lock of the outside kitchen door turn and she and the girl went by the window.

Presently he stirred and awoke. I had lit the lamp, and I saw his hand feel in his waistcoat pocket, and he drew out a small object which he held out to me.

"A flint knife," he said. "I picked it up in the garden this morning. It's got a fine edge to it."

At that I felt a prickle of terror run through the hair of my head, and I jumped up.

"Look here," I said, "you've had no walk to-day, and that always gives you the blues. Let's go down and dine at the hotel."

His head was outside the illumination of the lamp, and from the dimness there came a curious cackle of laughter.

"But I can't," he said. "How strange that you don't know that I can't. They've surrounded the place, and there's no way out. Listen! Can't you hear the drums and the squeal of their pipes? And their hands are about me. Christ! It's terrible to die."

He got up and began to move with curious little shuffling steps towards the kitchen. I had laid the flint knife down on the table and he snatched it up. The horror of presences unseen and multitudinous closed in round me, but I knew they were concentrated not on me, but on him. They poured in, not through the window alone but through the solid walls of the house; outside on the lawn there were lights moving, slow and orderly.

I had still control of my mind, the awfulness and the imminence of what so closely beset us gave me the courage and clearness of despair. I darted from my chair and stood with my back to the kitchen door.

"You're not to go in there," I said. "You must come away with me out of this. Pull yourself together, Frank. We'll get through yet; once outside the garden we're safe."

He paid no attention to what I said; it was as if he did not hear me. He laid his hand on my shoulder, and I felt his fingers press through the muscles and grind like points of steel on the underlying bone. Some maniac force possessed them, and he pulled me aside as if I had been a feather.

There was one thing only to be done. With my disengaged arm I hit him full on the chin, and he fell like a log across the floor. Without pausing for a second I gripped him round the knees and began dragging him senseless and inert towards the door.

It is difficult to state in words what those next few minutes held. I saw nothing. I heard nothing. I felt no touch of invisible hands upon me, but I can imagine no grinding agony of pain that wrenches body and soul asunder to equal that war of the evil and the unseen that raged about me. I struggled against no visible adversary, and there was the horror of it, for I am sure that no phantom of the dead that die not could have evoked so unnerving a terror.

Before those intangible hosts had fully closed in round me and my unconscious burden, I had got him on to the lawn, and it was then that the full stress of their beleaguering might poured in upon me. Strange fugitive lights wavered round me and muttered voices filled the air, and as I dragged Frank over the grass his weight seemed to grow till it was not a man's body that I was pulling along, but something well-nigh immovable, so that I had to tug and pant for breath and tug again.

"God help us both," I heard myself muttering. "Deliver us from our ghostly enemies ..." and again I tugged and panted for breath. Close at hand now was the ring of enclosing copse, where the stones of the circle stood, and I made one final effort of concentration, for I knew that my spirit was spent, and soon there would be no power of fight left in me at all.

"In the name of the Holiest, and by the power of the Highest," I cried aloud, and waited for a moment, gathering what dregs of strength were still left in me. And then I leaned forward, and the strained sinews of my legs were slackened as the weight of Frank's body moved after me, and I made another step, and yet another, and we had passed beyond the copse, and out of the accursed precinct.

I knew no more after that. I had fallen forwards half across him, and when I regained my senses he was stirring, and the dew of the grass was on my face. There stood the house, with the lamp still burning in the window of the sitting-room, and the quiet night was around us, with a clear and starry heaven.

THE END

Make Way for Lucia - The Complete Mapp & Lucia - Queen Lucia, Miss Mapp including 'The Male Impersonator', Lucia in London, Mapp and Lucia, Lucia's Progress (also known as The Worshipful Lucia), & Trouble for Lucia
E F Benson
Benediction Classics, 2012
1052 pages
ISBN: 978-1-78139-148-8

Available from www.amazon.com, www.amazon.co.uk

Make way for Lucia is a series of novels written by E.F Benson. They feature hilarious incidents in the lives of upper-middle class people in the 1920s and '30s. The characters vie for social standing in an extremely snobby world. In the series the two main characters - sophisticated Lucia and frumpy Miss Mapp compete with each other and have to extricate themselves from a series of social disasters in comical style. The novels are: Queen Lucia (1920) Miss Mapp (1922) The Male Impersonator (a short story) Lucia in London (1927) Mapp and Lucia (1931) Lucia's Progress (1935) (published in the U.S. as The Worshipful Lucia) Trouble for Lucia (1939)

Eve's Diary, Complete with original cover design and over 50 illustrations
Mark Twain
Benediction Classics, 2011
116 pages
ISBN 978-1-84902-286-6

Available from www.amazon.com, www.amazon.co.uk

Eve's Diary, by Mark Twain, is a beautiful book with pictures of Eve exploring the delights of Eden on every other page, with the text on the adjacent page. The book is written in Eve's voice and gives her description of the events in Eden and her relationship with Adam, as if she wrote a diary. Shelley Fisher Fishkin, a Twain scholar at Stanford University, said the book was "infused with his appreciation for the women he was close to." This is perhaps because Twain wrote it shortly after his wife, Olivia, died. This book comes fully illustrated with over fifty delightful illustrations and the original cover design.

Good-bye, Mr. Chips & To You, Mr. Chips
James Hilton
Oxford City Press, 2012
158 pages
ISBN: 978-1-78139-161-7

Available from www.amazon.com, www.amazon.co.uk

Goodbye, Mr. Chips was published in both the United States and the United Kingdom 1934. Such is its popularity that it has been adapted into two films and two television series. Mr Chips is a much loved schoolteacher at Brookfield, a fictional boys' English public (private in US English) boarding school. It is a sentimental book showing how he overcomes his own mediocre academic record and his profound shyness to become a tremendous educator. It also depicts the sweeping social changes that Mr Chips experiences. He begins his tenure at Brookfield in 1870, at the beginning of the Franco-Prussion War and covers Victoria's death and along with her the social order, and the devastating impact of war on British society, with countless old masters and schoolboys dying on the battlefield in World War I. Mr Chips dies just as Adolf Hilter rises to power. This version also includes the book "To you, Mr Chips" which includes an autobiographical chapter and several additional Mr Chips stories.

Famous Novels -(unabridged) Lost Horizon, Knight Without Armour, Goodbye, Mr. Chips, Random Harvest, The Story of Dr Wassell, & So Well Remembered
James Hilton
Oxford City Press, 2012
830 pages
ISBN: 978-1-78139-202-7

Available from www.amazon.com, www.amazon.co.uk

James Hilton was an eminent novelist, many of his stories critiquing English culture. His first novel was published when he was just 20, and several of his books were international best sellers and successfully adapted for film. This is a compilation brings together Hilton's most famous novels, all unabridged: Lost Horizon, Knight Without Armour , Goodbye, Mr. Chips, Random Harvest, The Story of Dr Wassell and So Well Remembered.

Also from Benediction Books ...

Wandering Between Two Worlds: Essays on Faith and Art
Anita Mathias
Benediction Books, 2007
152 pages
ISBN: 0955373700

Available from www.amazon.com, www.amazon.co.uk

In these wide-ranging lyrical essays, Anita Mathias writes, in lush, lovely prose, of her naughty Catholic childhood in Jamshedpur, India; her large, eccentric family in Mangalore, a sea-coast town converted by the Portuguese in the sixteenth century; her rebellion and atheism as a teenager in her Himalayan boarding school, run by German missionary nuns, St. Mary's Convent, Nainital; and her abrupt religious conversion after which she entered Mother Teresa's convent in Calcutta as a novice. Later rich, elegant essays explore the dualities of her life as a writer, mother, and Christian in the United States-- Domesticity and Art, Writing and Prayer, and the experience of being "an alien and stranger" as an immigrant in America, sensing the need for roots.

About the Author

Anita Mathias is the author of *Wandering Between Two Worlds: Essays on Faith and Art*. She has a B.A. and M.A. in English from Somerville College, Oxford University, and an M.A. in Creative Writing from the Ohio State University, USA. Anita won a National Endowment of the Arts fellowship in Creative Nonfiction in 1997. She lives in Oxford, England with her husband, Roy, and her daughters, Zoe and Irene.

Anita's website:
http://www.anitamathias.com, and
Anita's blog Dreaming Beneath the Spires:
http://dreamingbeneaththespires.blogspot.com

The Church That Had Too Much
Anita Mathias
Benediction Books, 2010
52 pages
ISBN: 9781849026567

Available from www.amazon.com, www.amazon.co.uk

The Church That Had Too Much was very well-intentioned. She wanted to love God, she wanted to love people, but she was both hampered by her muchness and the abundance of her possessions, and beset by ambition, power struggles and snobbery. Read about the surprising way The Church That Had Too Much began to resolve her problems in this deceptively simple and enchanting fable.

About the Author

Anita Mathias is the author of *Wandering Between Two Worlds: Essays on Faith and Art*. She has a B.A. and M.A. in English from Somerville College, Oxford University, and an M.A. in Creative Writing from the Ohio State University, USA. Anita won a National Endowment of the Arts fellowship in Creative Non-fiction in 1997. She lives in Oxford, England with her husband, Roy, and her daughters, Zoe and Irene.

Anita's website:
http://www.anitamathias.com, and
Anita's blog Dreaming Beneath the Spires:
http://dreamingbeneaththespires.blogspot.com

www.ingramcontent.com/pod-product-compliance
Lightning Source LLC
Chambersburg PA
CBHW081129300726
48982CB00005B/896

* 9 7 8 1 7 8 1 3 9 2 9 0 4 *